Dedicated to
Robert Marks

Writer, teacher, scholar, philosopher, friend and inspiration.

CONTENTS

The Shadow shall rise across the world, and darken every land, even to the smallest corner, and there shall be neither Light nor safety. And he who shall be born of the Dawn, born of the Maiden, according to Prophecy, he shall stretch forth his hands to catch the Shadow, and the world shall scream in the pain of salvation. All Glory be to the Creator, and to the Light, and to he who shall be born again. May the Light save us from him.

—from *Commentaries on the Karaethon Cycle*
Sereine dar Shamelle Motara
Counsel-Sister to Comaelle, High Queen of Jaramide
(circa 325 AB, the Third Age)

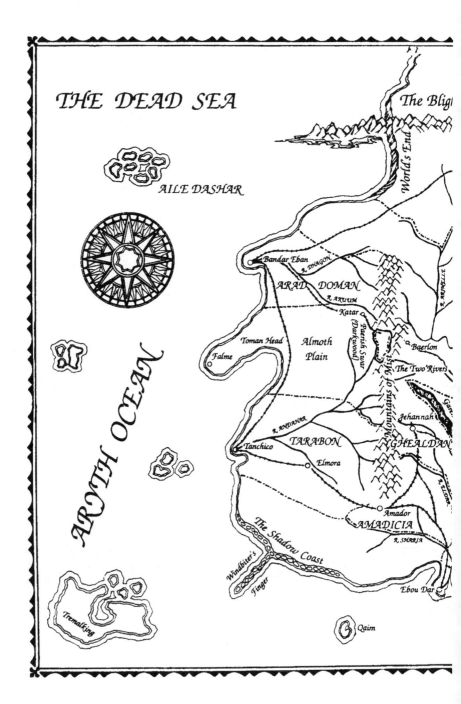

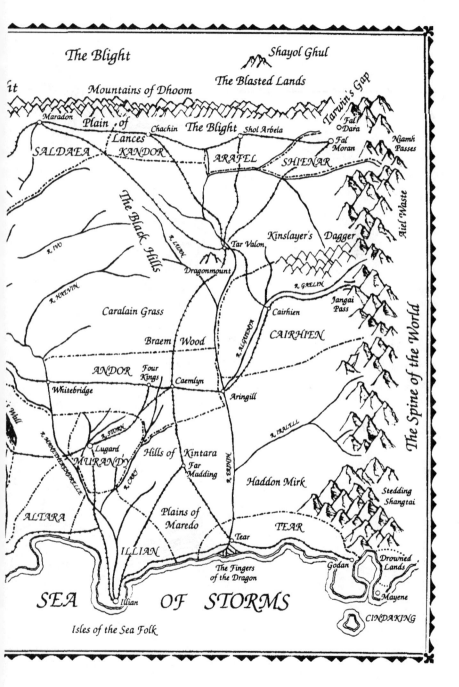

CHAPTER
1

Seeds of Shadow

The Wheel of Time turns, and Ages come and pass, leaving memories that become legend. Legend fades to myth, and even myth is long forgotten when the Age that gave it birth comes again. In one Age, called the Third Age by some, an Age yet to come, an Age long past, a wind rose on the great plain called the Caralain Grass. The wind was not the beginning. There are neither beginnings nor endings to the turning of the Wheel of Time. But it was *a* beginning.

North and west the wind blew beneath early morning sun, over endless miles of rolling grass and far-scattered thickets, across the swift-flowing River Luan, past the broken-topped fang of Dragonmount, mountain of legend towering above the slow swells of the rolling plain, looming so high that clouds wreathed it less than halfway to the smoking peak. Dragonmount, where the Dragon had died—and with him, some said, the Age of Legends—where prophecy said he would be born again. Or had been. North and west, across the villages of Jualdhe and Darein and Alindaer, where bridges like stone lacework arched out to the Shining Walls, the great white walls of what many called the greatest city in the world. Tar Valon. A city just touched by the reaching shadow of Dragonmount each evening.

Within those walls Ogier-made buildings well over two thousand years old seemed to grow out of the ground rather than having been built, or to be the work of wind and water rather than that of even the fabled hands of Ogier stone-masons. Some suggested birds taking flight, or huge shells from distant seas. Soaring towers, flared or fluted or spiraled, stood connected by bridges hundreds of feet in the air, often without rails. Only those long in Tar Valon could avoid gaping like country folk who had never been off the farm.

Greatest of those towers, the White Tower dominated the city, gleaming like polished bone in the sun. *The Wheel of Time turns around Tar Valon,* so people said in the city, *and Tar Valon turns around the Tower.* The first sight travelers had of Tar Valon, before their horses came in view of the bridges, before their river boat captains sighted the island, was the Tower reflecting the sun like a beacon. Small wonder then that the great square surrounding the walled Tower grounds seemed smaller than it was under the massive Tower's gaze, the people in it dwindling to insects. Yet the White Tower could have been the smallest in Tar Valon, the fact that it was the heart of Aes Sedai power would still have overawed the island city.

Despite their numbers, the crowd did not come close to filling the square. Along the edges people jostled each other in a milling mass, all going about their day's business, but closer to the Tower grounds there were ever fewer people, until a band of bare paving stones at least fifty paces wide bordered the tall white walls. Aes Sedai were respected and more in Tar Valon, of course, and the Amyrlin Seat ruled the city as she ruled the Aes Sedai, but few wanted to be closer to Aes Sedai power than they had to. There was a difference between being proud of a grand fireplace in your hall and walking into the flames.

A very few did go closer, to the broad stairs that led up to the Tower itself, to the intricately carved doors wide enough for a dozen people abreast. Those doors stood open, welcoming. There were always some people in need of aid or an answer they thought only Aes Sedai could give, and they came from far as often as near, from Arafel and Ghealdan, from Saldaea and Illian. Many would find help or guidance inside, though often not what they had expected or hoped for.

Min kept the wide hood of her cloak pulled up, shadowing her face in its depths. In spite of the warmth of the day, the garment was light enough not to attract comment, not on a woman so obviously shy. And a good many people were shy when they went to the Tower. There was nothing about her to attract notice. Her dark hair was longer than when she was last in the Tower, though still not quite to her shoulders, and her dress, plain blue except for narrow bands of white Jaerecuz lace at neck and wrists, would have suited the daughter of a well-to-do farmer, wearing her feastday best to the Tower just like the other women approaching the wide stairs. Min hoped she looked the same, at least. She had to stop herself from staring at them to see if they walked or held themselves differently. *I can do it,* she told herself.

She had certainly not come all this way to turn back now. The dress was a good disguise. Those who remembered her in the Tower remembered a young woman with close-cropped hair, always in a boy's coat and breeches, never in a dress. It had to be a good disguise. She had no choice about what she was doing. Not really.

Her stomach fluttered the closer she came to the Tower, and she tightened her grip on the bundle clutched to her breast. Her usual clothes were in there, and her good boots, and all her possessions except the horse she had left at an inn not far from the square. With luck, she would be back on the gelding in a few hours, riding for the Ostrein Bridge and the road south.

She was not really looking forward to climbing onto a horse again so soon, not after weeks in the saddle with never a day's pause, but she longed to leave this place. She had never seen the White Tower as hospitable, and right now it seemed nearly as awful as the Dark One's prison at Shayol Ghul. Shivering, she wished she had not thought of the Dark One. *I wonder if Moiraine thinks I came just because she asked me? The Light help me, acting like a fool girl. Doing fool things because of a fool man!*

She mounted the stairs uneasily—each was deep enough to take two strides for her to reach the next—and unlike most of the others, she did not pause for an awed stare up the pale height of the Tower. She wanted this over.

Inside, archways almost surrounded the large, round entry hall, but the petitioners huddled in the middle of the chamber, shuffling together beneath a flat-domed ceiling. The pale stone floor had been worn and polished by countless nervous feet over the centuries. No one thought of anything except where they were, and why. A farmer and his wife in rough woolens, clutching each other's callused hands, rubbed shoulders with a merchant in velvet-slashed silks, a maid at her heels clutching a small worked-silver casket, no doubt her mistress's gift for the Tower. Elsewhere, the merchant would have stared down her nose at farm folk who brushed so close, and they might well have knuckled their foreheads and backed away apologizing. Not now. Not here.

There were few men among the petitioners, which was no surprise to Min. Most men were nervous around Aes Sedai. Everyone knew it had been male Aes Sedai, when there still had been male Aes Sedai, who were responsible for the Breaking of the World. Three thousand years had not dimmed that memory, even if time had altered many of the details. Children were still frightened by tales of men who could channel the One Power, men doomed to go mad from the Dark One's taint on *saidin,* the male half of the True Source. Worst was the story of Lews Therin Telamon, the Dragon, Lews Therin Kinslayer, who had begun the Breaking. For that matter, the stories frightened adults, too. Prophecy said the Dragon would be born again in mankind's greatest hour of need, to fight the Dark One in Tarmon Gai'don, the Last Battle, but that made little difference in how most people looked at any connection between men and the Power. Any Aes Sedai would hunt down a man who could channel, now; of the seven Ajahs, the Red did little else.

Of course, none of that had anything to do with seeking help from Aes Sedai, yet few men felt easy about being linked in any way to Aes Sedai and the Power. Few, that is, except Warders, but each Warder was bonded to an Aes Sedai; Warders could hardly be taken for the general run of men. There was a saying: "A man will cut off his own hand to get rid of a splinter before asking help from Aes Sedai." Women meant it as a comment on men's stubborn foolishness, but Min had heard some men say the loss of a hand might be the better decision.

She wondered what these people would do if they knew what she knew. Run screaming, perhaps. And if they knew her reason for being here, she might not survive to be taken up by the Tower guards and thrown into a cell. She did have friends in the Tower, but none with power or influence. If her purpose was discovered, it was much less likely that they could help her than that she would pull them to the gallows or the headsman behind her. That was saying she lived to be tried, of course; more likely her mouth would be stopped permanently long before a trial.

She told herself to stop thinking like that. *I'll make it in, and I'll make it out. The Light burn Rand al'Thor for getting me into this!*

Three or four Accepted, women Min's age or perhaps a little older, were circulating through the round room, speaking softly to the petitioners. Their white dresses had no decoration except for seven bands of color at the hem, one band for each Ajah. Now and again a novice, a still younger woman or girl all in white, came to lead someone deeper into the Tower. The petitioners always followed the novices with an odd mix of excited eagerness and foot-dragging reluctance.

Min's grip tightened on her bundle as one of the Accepted stopped in front of her. "The Light illumine you," the curly-haired woman said perfunctorily. "I am called Faolain. How may the Tower help you?"

Faolain's dark, round face held the patience of someone doing a tedious job when she would rather be doing something else. Studying, probably, from what Min knew of the Accepted. Learning to be Aes Sedai. Most important, however, was the lack of recognition in the Accepted's eyes; the two of them had met when Min was in the Tower before, though only briefly.

Just the same, Min lowered her face in assumed diffidence. It was not unnatural; a good many country folk did not really understand the great step up from Accepted to full Aes Sedai. Shielding her features behind the edge of her cloak, she looked away from Faolain.

"I have a question I must ask the Amyrlin Seat," she began, then cut off abruptly as three Aes Sedai stopped to look into the entry hall, two from one archway and one from another.

Accepted and novices curtsied when their rounds took them close to one of the Aes Sedai, but otherwise went on about their tasks, perhaps a trifle more briskly. That was all. Not so for the petitioners. They seemed to catch their breaths all together. Away from the White Tower, away from Tar Valon, they might simply have thought the Aes Sedai three women whose ages they could not guess, three women in the flush of their prime, yet with more maturity than their smooth cheeks suggested. In the Tower, though, there was no question. A woman who had worked very long with the One Power was not touched by time in the same way as other women. In the Tower, no one needed to see a golden Great Serpent ring to know an Aes Sedai.

A ripple of curtsies spread through the huddle, and jerky bows from the few men. Two or three people even fell to their knees. The rich merchant looked frightened; the farm couple at her side stared at legends come to life. How to deal with Aes Sedai was a matter of hearsay for most; it was unlikely that any here, except those who actually lived in Tar Valon, had seen an Aes Sedai before, and probably not even the Tar Valoners had been this close.

But it was not the Aes Sedai themselves that halted Min's tongue. Sometimes, not often, she saw things when she looked at people, images and auras that usually flared and were gone in moments. Occasionally she knew what they meant. It happened rarely, the knowing—much more rarely than the seeing, even—but when she knew, she was always right.

Unlike most others, Aes Sedai—and their Warders—always had images and auras, sometimes so many dancing and shifting that they made Min dizzy. The numbers made no difference in interpreting them, though; she knew what they meant for Aes Sedai as seldom as for anyone else. But this time she knew more than she wanted to, and it made her shiver.

A slender woman with black hair falling to her waist, the only one of the three she recognized—her name was Ananda; she was Yellow Ajah —wore a sickly brown halo, shriveled and split by rotting fissures that fell in and widened as they decayed. The small, fair-haired Aes Sedai beside Ananda was Green Ajah, by her green-fringed shawl. The White Flame of Tar Valon on it showed for a moment when she turned her back. And on her shoulder, as if nestled among the grape vines and flowering apple branches worked on her shawl, sat a human skull. A small woman's skull, picked clean and sun-bleached. The third, a plumply pretty woman halfway around the room, wore no shawl; most Aes Sedai did not except for ceremony. The lift of her chin and the set of her shoulders spoke of strength and pride. She seemed to be casting cool blue eyes on the petitioners through a tattered curtain of blood, crimson streamers running down her face.

Blood and skull and halo faded away in the dance of images around the three, came and faded again. The petitioners stared in awe, seeing only three women who could touch the True Source and channel the One Power. No one but Min saw the rest. No one but Min knew those three women were going to die. All on the same day.

"The Amyrlin cannot see everyone," Faolain said with poorly hidden impatience. "Her next public audience is not for ten days. Tell me what you want, and I will arrange for you to see the sister who can best help you."

Min's eye flew to the bundle in her arms and stayed there, partly so she would not have to see again what she had already seen. *All* three *of them! Light!* What chance was there that three Aes Sedai would die on the same day? But she knew. She knew.

"I have the right to speak to the Amyrlin Seat. In person." It was a right seldom demanded—who would dare?—but it existed. "Any woman has that right, and I ask it."

"Do you think the Amyrlin Seat herself can see everyone who comes to the White Tower? Surely another Aes Sedai can help you." Faolain gave heavy weight to the titles as if to overpower Min. "Now tell me what your question is about. And give me your name, so the novice will know who to come for."

"My name is . . . Elmindreda." Min winced in spite of herself. She had always hated the name, but the Amyrlin was one of the few people living who had ever heard it. If only she remembered. "I have the right to speak to the Amyrlin. And my question is for her alone. I have the right."

The Accepted arched an eyebrow. "Elmindreda?" Her mouth twitched toward an amused smile. "And you claim your rights. Very well. I will send word to the Keeper of the Chronicles that you wish to see the Amyrlin Seat personally, Elmindreda."

Min wanted to slap the woman for the way she emphasized "Elmindreda," but instead she forced out a murmured "Thank you."

"Do not thank me yet. No doubt it will be hours before the Keeper finds time to reply, and it will certainly be that you can ask your question at the Mother's next public audience. Wait with patience, Elmindreda." She gave Min a tight smile, almost a smirk, as she turned away.

Grinding her teeth, Min took her bundle to stand against the wall between two of the archways, where she tried to blend into the pale stonework. *Trust no one, and avoid notice until you reach the Amyrlin,* Moiraine had told her. Moiraine was one Aes Sedai she did trust. Most of the time. It was good advice in any case. All she had to do was reach the Amyrlin, and it would be over. She could don her own clothes again, see her friends, and leave. No more need for hiding.

She was relieved to see that the Aes Sedai had gone. Three Aes Sedai dying on one day. It was impossible; that was the only word. Yet it was going to happen. Nothing she said or did could change it—when she knew what an image meant, it happened—but she had to tell the Amyrlin about this. It might even be as important as the news she brought from Moiraine, though that was hard to believe.

Another Accepted came to replace one already there, and to Min's eyes bars floated in front of her apple-cheeked face, like a cage. Sheriam, the Mistress of Novices, looked into the hall—after one glance, Min kept her gaze on the stone under her feet; Sheriam knew her all too well—and the red-haired Aes Sedai's face seemed battered and bruised. It was only the viewing, of course, but Min still had to bite her lip to stifle a gasp. Sheriam, with her calm authority and sureness, was as indestructible as the Tower. Surely nothing could harm Sheriam. But something was going to.

An Aes Sedai unknown to Min, wearing the shawl of the Brown Ajah, accompanied a stout woman in finely woven red wool to the doors. The stout woman walked as lightly as a girl, face shining, almost laughing with pleasure. The Brown sister was smiling, too, but her aura faded like a guttering candle flame.

Death. Wounds, captivity, and death. To Min it might as well have been printed on a page.

She set her eyes on her feet. She did not want to see any more. *Let her remember,* she thought. She had not felt desperation at any time on her long ride from the Mountains of Mist, not even on the two occasions when someone tried to steal her horse, but she felt it now. *Light, let her remember that bloody name.*

"Mistress Elmindreda?"

Min gave a start. The black-haired novice who stood before her was barely old enough to be away from home, perhaps fifteen or sixteen, though she made a great effort at dignity. "Yes? I am. . . . That is my name."

"I am Sahra. If you will come with me—" Sahra's piping voice took on a note of wonder—"the Amyrlin Seat will see you in her study now."

Min gave a sigh of relief and followed eagerly.

Her cloak's deep hood still hid her face, but it did not stop her seeing, and the more she saw, the more she grew eager to reach the Amyrlin. Few people walked the broad corridors that spiraled upward with their brightly colored floor tiles, and their wall hangings and golden lampstands—the Tower had been built to hold far greater numbers than it did now—but nearly everyone she saw as she climbed higher wore an image or aura that spoke to her of violence and danger.

Warders hurried by with barely a glance for the two women, men who moved like hunting wolves, their swords only an afterthought to their deadliness, but they seemed to have bloody faces, or gaping wounds. Swords and spears danced about their heads, threatening. Their auras flashed wildly, flickered on the knife edge of death. She saw dead men walking, knew they would die on the same day as the Aes Sedai in the entry hall, or at most a day later. Even some of the servants, men and women with the Flame of Tar Valon on their breasts, hurrying about their work, bore signs of violence. An Aes Sedai glimpsed down a side hallway appeared to have chains in the air around her, and another, crossing the corridor ahead of Min and her guide, seemed for most of those few strides to wear a silver collar around her neck. Min's breath caught at that; she wanted to scream.

"It can all be overwhelming to someone who's never seen it before," Sahra said, trying and failing to sound as if the Tower were as ordinary to her now as her home village. "But you are safe here. The Amyrlin Seat will make things right." Her voice squeaked when she mentioned the Amyrlin.

"Light, let her do just that," Min muttered. The novice gave her a smile that was meant to be soothing.

By the time they reached the hall outside the Amyrlin's study, Min's stomach was churning and she was treading almost on Sahra's heels. Only the need to pretend that she was a stranger had kept her from running ahead long since.

One of the doors to the Amyrlin's chambers opened, and a young man with red-gold hair came stalking out, nearly striding into Min and her escort. Tall and straight and strong in his blue coat thickly embroidered with gold on sleeves and collar, Gawyn of House Trakand, eldest son of Queen Morgase of Andor, looked every inch the proud young lord. A furious young lord. There was no time to drop her head; he was staring down into her hood, right into her face.

His eyes widened in surprise, then narrowed to slits of blue ice. "So you are back. Do you know where my sister and Egwene have gone?"

"They are not here?" Min forgot everything in a rising flood of panic. Before she knew what she was doing she had seized his sleeves, peering up at him urgently, and forced him back a step. "Gawyn, they started for the Tower months ago! Elayne and Egwene, and Nynaeve, too. With Verin Sedai and. . . . Gawyn, I . . . I. . . ."

"Calm yourself," he said, gently undoing her grip on his coat. "Light! I didn't mean to frighten you so. They arrived safely. And would not say a word of where they had been, or why. Not to me. I suppose there's scant hope you will?" She thought she kept her face straight, but he took one look and said, "I thought not. This place has more secrets than. . . . They've vanished again. And Nynaeve, too." Nynaeve was almost an offhand addition; she might be one of Min's friends, but she meant nothing to him. His voice began to roughen once more, growing tighter by the second. "Again without a word. Not a word! Supposedly they're on a farm somewhere as penance for running away, but I cannot find out where. The Amyrlin won't give me a straight answer."

Min flinched; for a moment, streaks of dried blood had made his face a grim mask. It was like a double hammer blow. Her friends were gone—it had eased her coming to the Tower, knowing they were here —and Gawyn was going to be wounded on the day the Aes Sedai died.

Despite all she had seen since entering the Tower, despite her fear, none of it had really touched her personally until now. Disaster striking the Tower would spread far from Tar Valon, yet she was not of the Tower and never could be. But Gawyn was someone she knew, someone she liked, and he was going to be hurt more than the blood told, hurt somehow deeper than wounds to his flesh. It hit her that if catastrophe seized the Tower, not only distant Aes Sedai would be harmed, women she could never feel close to, but her friends as well. They *were* of the Tower.

In a way she was glad Egwene and the others were not there, glad she could not look at them and perhaps see signs of death. Yet she wanted to look, to be sure, to look at her friends and see nothing, or see that they would live. Where in the Light were they? Why had they gone? Knowing those three, she thought it possible that if Gawyn did not know where they were, it was because they did not want him to know. It could be that.

Suddenly she remembered where she was and why, and that she was not alone with Gawyn. Sahra seemed to have forgotten she was taking Min to the Amyrlin; she seemed to have forgotten everything but the young lord, making calf-eyes that he was not noticing. Even so, there was no use pretending any longer to be a stranger to the Tower. She was at the Amyrlin's door; nothing could stop her now.

"Gawyn, I don't know where they are, but if they are doing penance on a farm, they're probably all sweat, and mud to their hips, and you are the last one they will want to see them." She was not much easier about their absence than Gawyn was, in truth. Too much had happened, too much was happening, too much with ties to them, and to her. But it was not impossible they had been sent off for punishment. "You won't help them by making the Amyrlin angry."

"I don't know that they *are* on a farm. Or even alive. Why all this hiding and sidestepping if they're just pulling weeds? If anything happens to my sister. . . . Or to Egwene." He frowned at the toes of his boots. "I am supposed to look after Elayne. How can I protect her when I don't know where she is?"

Min sighed. "Do you think she needs looking after? Either of them?" But if the Amyrlin had sent them somewhere, maybe they did. The Amyrlin was capable of sending a woman into a bear's den with nothing but a switch if it suited her purposes. And she would expect the woman to come back with a bearskin, or the bear on a leash, as instructed. But telling Gawyn that would only inflame his temper and his worries. "Gawyn, they have pledged to the Tower. They won't thank you for meddling."

"I know Elayne isn't a child," he said patiently, "even if she does bounce back and forth between running off like one and playing at being Aes Sedai. But she *is* my sister, and beyond that, she is Daughter-

Heir of Andor. She'll be queen, after Mother. Andor needs her whole and safe to take the throne, not another Succession."

Playing at being Aes Sedai? Apparently he did not realize the extent of his sister's talent. The Daughter-Heirs of Andor had been sent to the Tower to train for as long as there had been an Andor, but Elayne was the first to have enough talent to be raised to Aes Sedai, and a powerful Aes Sedai at that. Very likely he also did not know Egwene was just as strong.

"So you will protect her whether she wants it or not?" She said it in a flat voice meant to let him know he was making a mistake, but he missed the warning and nodded agreement.

"That has been my duty since the day she was born. My blood shed before hers; my life given before hers. I took that oath when I could barely see over the side of her cradle; Gareth Bryne had to explain to me what it meant. I won't break it now. Andor needs her more than it needs me."

He spoke with a calm certainty, an acceptance of something natural and right, that sent chills through her. She had always thought of him as boyish, laughing and teasing, but now he was something alien. She thought the Creator must have been tired when it came time to make men; sometimes they hardly seemed human. "And Egwene? What oath did you take about her?"

His face did not change, but he shifted his feet warily. "I'm concerned about Egwene, of course. And Nynaeve. What happens to Elayne's companions might happen to Elayne. I assume they're still together; when they *were* here, I seldom saw one without the others."

"My mother always told me to marry a poor liar, and you qualify. Except that I think someone else has first claim."

"Some things are meant to be," he said quietly, "and some never can. Galad is heartsick because Egwene is gone." Galad was his half-brother, the pair of them sent to Tar Valon to train under the Warders. That was another Andoran tradition. Galadedrid Damodred was a man who took doing the right thing to the point of a fault, as Min saw it, but Gawyn could see no wrong in him. And he would not speak his feelings for a woman Galad had set his heart on.

She wanted to shake him, shake some sense into him, but there was no time now. Not with the Amyrlin waiting, not with what she had to tell the Amyrlin waiting. Certainly not with Sahra standing there, calf-eyes or no calf-eyes. "Gawyn, I am summoned to the Amyrlin. Where can I find you, when she is done with me?"

"I will be in the practice yard. The only time I can stop worrying is when I am working the sword with Hammar." Hammar was a blademaster, and the Warder who taught the sword. "Most days I'm there until the sun sets."

"Good, then. I will come as soon as I can. And try to watch what you say. If you make the Amyrlin angry with you, Elayne and Egwene might share in it."

"That I cannot promise," he said firmly. "Something is wrong in the world. Civil war in Cairhien. The same and worse in Tarabon and Arad Doman. False Dragons. Troubles and rumors of troubles everywhere. I don't say the Tower is behind it, but even here things are not what they should be. Or what they seem. Elayne and Egwene vanishing isn't the whole of it. Still, they are the part that concerns me. I *will* find out where they are. And if they have been hurt. . . . If they are dead. . . ."

He scowled, and for an instant his face was that bloody mask again. More: a sword floated above his head, and a banner waved behind it. The long-hilted sword, like those most Warders used, had a heron engraved on its slightly curved blade, symbol of a blademaster, and Min could not say whether it belonged to Gawyn or threatened him. The banner bore Gawyn's sigil of the charging White Boar, but on a field of green rather than the red of Andor. Both sword and banner faded with the blood.

"Be careful, Gawyn." She meant it two ways. Careful of what he said, and careful in a way she could not explain, even to herself. "You must be very careful."

His eyes searched her face as if he had heard some of her deeper meaning. "I . . . will try," he said finally. He put on a grin, almost the grin she remembered, but the effort was plain. "I suppose I had better get myself back to the practice yard if I expect to keep up with Galad. I managed two out of five against Hammar this morning, but Galad actually won three, the last time he bothered to come to the yard." Suddenly he appeared to really see her for the first time, and his grin became genuine. "You ought to wear dresses more often. It's pretty on you. Remember, I will be there till sunset."

As he strode away with something very close to the dangerous grace of a Warder, Min realized she was smoothing the dress over her hip and stopped immediately. *The Light burn all men!*

Sahra exhaled as if she had been holding her breath. "He is very good-looking, isn't he?" she said dreamily. "Not as good-looking as Lord Galad, of course. And you really know him." It was half a question, but only half.

Min echoed the novice's sigh. The girl would talk with her friends in the novices' quarters. The son of a queen was a natural topic, especially when he was handsome and had an air about him like the hero in a gleeman's tale. A strange woman only made for more interesting speculation. Still, there was nothing to be done about it. At any rate, it could hardly cause any harm now.

"The Amyrlin Seat must be wondering why we haven't come," she said.

Sahra came to herself with a wide-eyed start and a loud gulp. Seizing Min's sleeve with one hand, she jumped to open one of the doors, pulling Min behind her. The moment they were inside, the novice curtsied hastily and burst out in panic, "I've brought her, Leane Sedai. Mistress Elmindreda? The Amyrlin Seat wants to see her?"

The tall, coppery-skinned woman in the anteroom wore the hand-wide stole of the Keeper of the Chronicles, blue to show she had been raised from the Blue Ajah. Fists on hips, she waited for the girl to finish, then dismissed her with a clipped "Took you long enough, child. Back to your chores, now." Sahra bobbed another curtsy and scurried out as quickly as she had entered.

Min stood with her eyes on the floor, her hood still pulled up around her face. Blundering in front of Sahra had been bad enough—though at least the novice did not know her name—but Leane knew her better than anyone in the Tower except the Amyrlin. Min was sure it could make no difference now, but after what had happened in the hallway, she meant to hold to Moiraine's instructions until she was alone with the Amyrlin.

This time her precautions did no good. Leane took two steps, pushed back the hood, and grunted as if she had been poked in the stomach. Min raised her head and stared back defiantly, trying to pretend she had not been attempting to sneak past. Straight, dark hair only a little longer than her own framed the Keeper's face; the Aes Sedai's expression was a blend of surprise and displeasure at being surprised.

"So you are Elmindreda, are you?" Leane said briskly. She was always brisk. "I must say you look it more in that dress than in your usual . . . garb."

"Just Min, Leane Sedai, if you please." Min managed to keep her face straight, but it was difficult not to glare. The Keeper's voice had held too much amusement. If her mother had had to name her after someone in a story, why did it have to be a woman who seemed to spend most of her time sighing at men, when she was not inspiring them to compose songs about her eyes, or her smile?

"Very well. Min. I'll not ask where you've been, nor why you've come back in a dress, apparently wanting to ask a question of the Amyrlin. Not now, at least." Her face said she meant to ask later, though, and get answers. "I suppose the Mother knows who Elmindreda is? Of course. I should have known that when she said to send you straight in, and alone. The Light alone knows why she puts up with you." She broke off with a concerned frown. "What is the matter, girl? Are you ill?"

Min carefully blanked her face. "No. No, I am all right." For a moment the Keeper had been looking through a transparent mask of her own face, a screaming mask. "May I go in now, Leane Sedai?"

Leane studied her a moment longer, then jerked her head toward the inner chamber. "In with you." Min's leap to obey would have satisfied the hardest taskmistress.

The Amyrlin Seat's study had been occupied by many grand and powerful women over the centuries, and reminders of the fact filled the room, from the tall fireplace all of golden marble from Kandor, cold now, to the paneled walls of pale, oddly striped wood, iron hard yet carved in wondrous beasts and wildly feathered birds. Those panels had been brought from the mysterious lands beyond the Aiel Waste well over a thousand years ago, and the fireplace was more than twice as old. The polished redstone of the floor had come from the Mountains of Mist. High arched windows let onto a balcony. The iridescent stone framing the windows shone like pearls, and had been salvaged from the remains of a city sunk into the Sea of Storms by the Breaking of the World; no one had ever seen its like.

The current occupant, Siuan Sanche, had been born a fisherman's daughter in Tear, though, and the furnishings she had chosen were simple, if well made and well polished. She sat in a stout chair behind a large table plain enough to have served a farmhouse. The only other chair in the room, just as plain and usually set off to one side, now stood in front of the table atop a small Tairen rug, simple in blue and brown and gold. Half a dozen books rested open on tall reading stands about the floor. That was all of it. A drawing hung above the fireplace: tiny fishing boats working among reeds in the Fingers of the Dragon, just as her father's boat had.

At first glance, despite her smooth Aes Sedai features, Siuan Sanche herself looked as simple as her furnishings. She herself was sturdy, and handsome rather than beautiful, and the only bit of ostentation in her clothing was the broad stole of the Amyrlin Seat she wore, with one colored stripe for each of the seven Ajahs. Her age was indeterminate, as with any Aes Sedai; not even a hint of gray showed in her dark hair. But her sharp blue eyes brooked no nonsense, and her firm jaw spoke of the determination of the youngest woman ever to be chosen Amyrlin Seat. For over ten years Siuan Sanche had been able to summon rulers, and the powerful, and they had come, even if they hated the White Tower and feared Aes Sedai.

As the Amyrlin strode around in front of the table, Min set down her bundle and began an awkward curtsy, muttering irritably under her breath at having to do so. Not that she wanted to be disrespectful—that did not even occur to one facing a woman like Siuan Sanche—but the bow she usually would have made seemed foolish in a dress, and she had only a rough idea of how to curtsy.

Halfway down, with her skirts already spread, she froze like a crouching toad. Siuan Sanche was standing there as regal as any queen, and for a moment she was also lying on the floor, naked. Aside from her being in only her skin, there was something odd about the image, but it vanished before Min could say what. It was as strong a viewing as she had ever seen, and she had no idea what it meant.

"Seeing things again, are you?" the Amyrlin said. "Well, I can certainly make use of that ability of yours. I could have used it all the months you were gone. But we'll not talk of that. What's done is done. The Wheel weaves as the Wheel wills." She smiled a tight smile. "But if you do it again, I'll have your hide for gloves. Stand up, girl. Leane forces enough ceremony on me in a month to last any sensible woman a year. I don't have time for it. Not these days. Now, what did you just see?"

Min straightened slowly. It was a relief to be back with someone who knew of her talent, even if it was the Amyrlin Seat herself. She did not have to hide what she saw from the Amyrlin. Far from it. "You were. . . . You weren't wearing any clothes. I . . . I don't know what it means, Mother."

Siuan barked a short, mirthless laugh. "No doubt that I'll take a lover. But I have no time for that, either. There's no time for winking at the men when you're busy bailing the boat."

"Maybe," Min said slowly. It could have meant that, though she doubted it. "I just do not know. But, Mother, I've been seeing things ever since I walked into the Tower. Something bad is going to happen, something terrible."

She started with the Aes Sedai in the entry hall and told everything she had seen, as well as what everything meant, when she was sure. She held back what Gawyn had said, though, or most of it; it was no use telling him not to anger the Amyrlin if she did it for him. The rest she laid out as starkly as she had seen it. Some of her fear came out as she dredged it all up, seeing it all again; her voice shook before she was done.

The Amyrlin's expression never changed. "So you spoke with young Gawyn," she said when Min finished. "Well, I think I can convince him to keep quiet. And if I remember Sahra correctly, the girl could do with some time working in the country. She'll spread no gossip hoeing a vegetable patch."

"I don't understand," Min said. "Why should Gawyn keep quiet? About what? I told him nothing. And Sahra . . . ? Mother, perhaps I didn't make myself clear. Aes Sedai and Warders are going to die. It has to mean a battle. And unless you send a lot of Aes Sedai and Warders off somewhere—and servants, too; I saw servants dead and injured, too—unless you do that, that battle will be here! In Tar Valon!"

"Did you see that?" The Amyrlin demanded. "A battle? Do you know, with your . . . your talent, or are you guessing?"

"What else could it be? At least four Aes Sedai are as good as dead. Mother, I've only laid eyes on nine of you since coming back, and four are going to die! And the Warders. . . . What else could it be?"

"More things than I like to think of," Siuan said grimly. "When? How long before this . . . *thing* . . . occurs?"

Min shook her head. "I do not know. Most of it will happen in the space of a day, maybe two, but that could be tomorrow or a year from now. Or ten."

"Let us pray for ten. If it comes tomorrow, there isn't much I can do to stop it."

Min grimaced. Only two Aes Sedai besides Siuan Sanche knew of what she could do: Moiraine, and Verin Mathwin, who had tried to study her talent. None of them knew how it worked any more than she did, except that it had nothing to do with the Power. Perhaps that was why only Moiraine seemed able to accept the fact that when she knew what a viewing meant, it happened.

"Maybe it's the Whitecloaks, Mother. They were everywhere in Alindaer when I crossed the bridge." She did not believe the Children of the Light had anything to do with what was coming, but she was reluctant to say what she believed. Believed, not knew; yet that was bad enough.

But the Amyrlin had begun shaking her head before she finished. "They would try something if they could, I've no doubt—they would love to strike at the Tower—but Eamon Valda won't move openly without orders from the Lord Captain Commander, and Pedron Niall will not strike unless he thinks we're injured. He knows our strength too well to be foolish. For a thousand years the Whitecloaks have been like that. Silverpike in the reeds, waiting for a hint of Aes Sedai blood in the water. But we've showed them none yet, nor will we, if I can help it."

"Yet if Valda did try something on his own—"

Siuan cut her off. "He has no more than five hundred men close to Tar Valon, girl. He sent the rest away weeks ago, to cause trouble elsewhere. The Shining Walls held off the Aiel. And Artur Hawkwing, too. Valda will never break into Tar Valon unless the city is already falling apart from the inside." Her voice did not change as she went on. "You very much want me to believe the trouble will come from the Whitecloaks. Why?" There was no gentleness in her eyes.

"Because *I* want to believe it," Min muttered. She licked her lips and spoke the words she did not want to say. "The silver collar I saw on that one Aes Sedai. Mother, it looked. . . . It looked like one of the collars the . . . the Seanchan use to . . . to control women who can channel." Her voice dwindled as Siuan's mouth twisted with distaste.

"Filthy things," the Amyrlin growled. "As well most people don't believe a quarter of what they hear about the Seanchan. But there's more chance of it being the Whitecloaks. If the Seanchan land again, anywhere, I will know it in days by pigeon, and it is a long way from the sea to Tar Valon. If they do reappear, I will have plenty of warning. No, I fear what you see is something far worse than the Seanchan. I fear it can only be the Black Ajah. Only a handful of us know about them, and I don't relish what will happen when the knowledge becomes common, but they are the greatest immediate threat to the Tower."

Min realized she was clutching her skirt so hard that her hands hurt; her mouth was dry as dust. The White Tower had always coldly denied the existence of a hidden Ajah, dedicated to the Dark One. The surest way to anger an Aes Sedai was merely to mention such a thing. For the Amyrlin Seat herself to give the Black Ajah reality so casually made Min's spine turn to ice.

As if she had said nothing out of the ordinary, the Amyrlin went on. "But you didn't come all this way just to do your viewings. What word from Moiraine? I know everything from Arad Doman to Tarabon is in chaos, to say the least." That was saying the least, indeed; men supporting the Dragon Reborn were fighting those opposing him, and had turned both countries to civil war while they still fought each other for control of Almoth Plain. Siuan's tone dismissed all that as a detail. "But I've heard nothing of Rand al'Thor for months. He is the focus of everything. Where is he? What does Moiraine have him doing? Sit, girl. Sit." She gestured to the chair in front of the table.

Min approached the chair on wobbly legs and half fell into it. *The Black Ajah! Oh, Light!* Aes Sedai were supposed to stand for the Light. Even if she did not really trust them, there was always that. Aes Sedai, and all the power of the Aes Sedai, stood for the Light and against the Shadow. Only now it was not true any longer. She hardly heard herself say, "He's on his way to Tear."

"Tear! It's *Callandor,* then. Moiraine means him to take the Sword That Cannot Be Touched out of the Stone of Tear. I swear I'll hang her in the sun to dry! I will make her wish she were a novice again! He cannot be ready for that yet!"

"It was not. . . ." Min stopped to clear her throat. "It was not Moiraine's doing. Rand left in the middle of the night, by himself. The others followed, and Moiraine sent me to tell you. They could be in Tear by now. For all I know, he could have *Callandor* by now."

"Burn him!" Siuan barked. "By now, he could be dead! I wish he had never heard a word of the Prophecies of the Dragon. If I could keep him from hearing another, I would."

"But doesn't he have to fulfill the Prophecies? I don't understand."

The Amyrlin leaned back against her table wearily. "As though anyone even understands most of them! The Prophecies aren't what makes him the Dragon Reborn; all that takes is for him to admit it, and he must have if he is going for *Callandor.* The Prophecies are meant to announce to the world who he is, to prepare him for what is coming, to prepare the world for it. If Moiraine can keep some control over him, she will guide him to the Prophecies we can be sure of—when he is ready to face them!—and for the rest, we trust that what he does is enough. We hope. For all I know, he has already fulfilled Prophecies none of us understands. The Light send it's enough."

"So you do mean to control him. He said you'd try to use him, but this is the first I've heard you admit it." Min felt cold inside. Angry, she added, "You haven't done such a good job of it so far, you and Moiraine."

Siuan's tiredness seemed to slide from her shoulders. She straightened and stood looking down at Min. "You had best hope we can. Did you think we could just let him run about loose? Headstrong and stubborn, untrained, unprepared, maybe going mad already. Do you think we could trust to the Pattern, to his *destiny,* to keep him alive, like some story? This isn't a story, he isn't some invincible hero, and if his thread is snipped out of the Pattern, the Wheel of Time won't notice his going, and the Creator will produce no miracles to save us. If Moiraine cannot reef his sails, he very well may get himself killed, and where are we then? Where is the world? The Dark One's prison is failing. He *will* touch the world again; it is only a matter of time. If Rand al'Thor is not there to face him in the Last Battle, if the headstrong young fool gets himself killed first, the world is doomed. The War of the Power all over again, with no Lews Therin and his Hundred Companions. Then fire and shadow, forever." She stopped suddenly, peering at Min's face. "So that's the way the wind sets, is it? You and Rand. I did not expect this."

Min shook her head vigorously, felt her cheeks coloring. "Of course not! I was. . . . It's the Last Battle. And the Dark One. Light, just thinking about the Dark One loose ought to be enough to freeze a Warder's marrow. And the Black Ajah—"

"Don't try to dissemble," the Amyrlin said sharply. "Do you think this is the first time I ever saw a woman afraid for her man's life? You might as well admit it."

Min squirmed on her chair. Siuan's eyes dug at her, knowing and impatient. "All right," she muttered finally, "I'll tell you all of it, and much good it does either of us. The first time I ever saw Rand, I saw three women's faces, and one of them was mine. I've never seen anything about myself before or since, but I knew what it meant. I was going to fall in love with him. All three of us were."

"Three. The other two. Who are they?"

Min gave her a bitter smile. "The faces were blurred; I don't know who they are."

"Nothing to say that he would love you in return?"

"Nothing! He has never looked at me twice. I think he sees me as . . . as a *sister*. So don't think you can use me as leash on him, because it will not work!"

"Yet you do love him."

"I don't have any choice." Min tried to make her voice less sullen. "I tried treating it as a joke, but I can't laugh anymore. You may not believe me, but when I know what it means, it happens."

The Amyrlin tapped a finger against her lips and looked at Min consideringly.

That look worried Min. She had not meant to make such a show of herself, nor to tell as much as she had. She had not told everything, but she knew she should have learned by now not to give an Aes Sedai a lever, even if she did not see how it could be used. Aes Sedai were skilled at finding ways. "Mother, I've delivered Moiraine's message, and I've told everything I know of what my viewings meant. There's no reason now I can't put on my own clothes and go."

"Go where?"

"Tear." After talking with Gawyn, trying to make sure he did not do something foolish. She wished she dared ask where Egwene and the other two were, but if the Amyrlin would not tell Elayne's brother, there was small chance she would tell Min. And Siuan Sanche still had that weighing look in her eyes. "Or wherever Rand is. I may be a fool, but I'm not the first woman to be a fool over a man."

"The first to be a fool over the Dragon Reborn. It will be dangerous, being close to Rand al'Thor once the world finds out who he is, what he is. And if he now wields *Callandor,* the world will learn soon enough. Half will want to kill him anyway, as if by killing him they can stop the Last Battle, stop the Dark One from breaking free. A good many will die, close to him. It might be better for you to stay here."

The Amyrlin sounded sympathetic, but Min did not believe it. She did not believe Siuan Sanche was capable of sympathy. "I'll take the risk; maybe I can help him. With what I see. It isn't even as if the Tower would be that much safer, not so long as there is one Red sister here. They'll see a man who can channel and forget the Last Battle, and the Prophecies of the Dragon."

"So will many others," Siuan broke in calmly. "Old ways of thinking are hard to shed, for Aes Sedai as for anyone else."

Min gave her a puzzled look. She seemed to be taking Min's side of the thing now. "It is no secret I am friends with Egwene and Nynaeve, and no secret they're from the same village as Rand. For the Red Ajah, that will be connection enough. When the Tower finds out what he is, I would probably be arrested before the day is out. So will Egwene and Nynaeve, if you don't have them hidden away somewhere."

"Then you mustn't be recognized. You catch no fish if they see the net. I suggest you forget your coat and breeches for a time." The Amyrlin smiled like a cat smiling at a mouse.

"What fish do you expect to catch with me?" Min asked in a faint voice. She thought she knew, and hoped desperately she was wrong.

Her hope did not stop the Amyrlin from saying, "The Black Ajah. Thirteen of them fled, but I fear some remain. I cannot be sure who I can trust; for a while I was afraid to trust anyone. You are no Dark-friend, I know, and your particular talent may just be some help. At the very least, you'll be another trustworthy pair of eyes."

"You've been planning this since I walked in, haven't you? That's why you want to keep Gawyn and Sahra quiet." Anger built up inside Min like steam in a kettle. The woman said frog and expected people to jump. That they usually did just made it worse. She was no frog, no dancing puppet. "Is this what you did to Egwene and Elayne and Nynaeve? Send them off after the Black Ajah? I wouldn't put it past you!"

"You tend your own nets, child, and let those girls tend theirs. As far as you are concerned, they are working penance on a farm. Do I make myself plain?"

That unwavering stare made Min shift on her chair. It was easy to defy the Amyrlin—until she started staring at you with those sharp, cold blue eyes. "Yes, Mother." The meekness of her reply rankled, but a glance at the Amyrlin convinced her to let it lie. She plucked at the fine wool of her dress. "I suppose it won't kill me to wear this a little longer." Suddenly Siuan looked amused; Min felt her hackles rising.

"I fear that won't be enough. Min in a dress is still Min in a dress to anyone who looks close. You cannot always wear a cloak with the hood up. No, you must change everything that can be changed. For one thing, you will continue to go by Elmindreda. It is your name, after all." Min winced. "Your hair is almost as long as Leane's, long enough to put in curls. For the rest. . . . I never had any use for rouge and powder and paints, but Leane remembers the use of them."

Min's eyes had grown wider by the word since the mention of curls. "Oh, no," she gasped.

"No one will take you for Min who wears breeches once Leane makes you into a perfect Elmindreda."

"Oh, NO!"

"As to why you are staying in the Tower—a reason suitable for a fluttery young woman who looks and acts nothing at all like Min." The Amyrlin frowned thoughtfully, ignoring Min's efforts to break in. "Yes. I will let it be put about that Mistress Elmindreda managed to encourage two suitors to the point that she has to take shelter from them in the Tower until she can decide between them. A few women still claim sanctuary each year, and sometimes for reasons as silly." Her face hardened, and her eyes sharpened. "If you're still thinking of Tear, think again. Consider whether you can be of more help to Rand there, or here. If the Black Ajah brings the Tower down, or worse, gains control, he loses even the little help I can give. So. Are you a woman, or a lovesick girl?"

Trapped. Min could see it as plainly as a shackle on her leg. "Do you always get your way with people, Mother?"

The Amyrlin's smile was even colder this time. "Usually, child. Usually."

Shifting her red-fringed shawl, Elaida stared thoughtfully at the door to the Amyrlin's study, through which the two young women had just vanished. The novice came back out almost immediately, took one look at Elaida's face, and bleated like a frightened sheep. Elaida thought she recognized her, though she could not bring the girl's name to mind. She had more important uses for her time than teaching wretched children.

"Your name?"

"Sahra, Elaida Sedai." The girl's reply was a breathless squeak. Elaida might have no interest in novices, but the novices knew her, and her reputation.

She remembered the girl now. A daydreamer with moderate ability who would never be of any real power. It was doubtful she knew anything more than Elaida had already seen and heard—or remembered much more than Gawyn's smile, for that matter. A fool. Elaida flicked a dismissive hand.

The girl dropped a curtsy so deep her face almost touched the floor tiles, then fled at a dead run.

Elaida did not see her go. The Red sister had turned away, already forgetting the novice. As she swept down the corridor, not a line marred her smooth features, but her thoughts boiled furiously. She did not even notice the servants, the novices and Accepted, who scrambled out of her way, curtsying as she passed. Once she almost walked over a Brown sister with her nose in a sheaf of notes. The plump Brown jumped back with a startled squawk that Elaida did not hear.

Dress or no dress, she knew the young woman who had gone in to see the Amyrlin. Min, who had spent so much time with the Amyrlin on her first visit to the Tower, though for no reason anyone knew. Min, who was such close friends with Elayne, Egwene, and Nynaeve. The Amyrlin was hiding the whereabouts of those three. Elaida was sure of it. All reports that they were serving penance on a farm had come at third or fourth hand from Siuan Sanche, more than enough distance to hide any twisting of words to avoid an outright lie. Not to mention the fact that all Elaida's considerable efforts to find this farm had yielded nothing.

"The Light burn her!" For a moment open anger painted her face. She was not sure whether she meant Siuan Sanche or the Daughter-Heir. Either would serve. A slender Accepted heard her, glanced at her face, and went as white as her own dress; Elaida strode by without seeing her.

Apart from everything else, it infuriated her that she could not find Elayne. Elaida had the Foretelling sometimes, the ability to foresee future events. If it came seldom and faintly, that was still more than any Aes Sedai had had since Gitara Moroso, dead now twenty years. The very first thing Elaida had ever Foretold, while still an Accepted—and had known enough even then to keep to herself—was that the Royal line of Andor would be the key to defeating the Dark One in the Last Battle. She had attached herself to Morgase as soon as it was clear Morgase would succeed to the throne, had built her influence year by patient year. And now all her effort, all her sacrifice—she might have been Amyrlin herself had she not concentrated all her energies on Andor—might be for naught because Elayne had disappeared.

With an effort she forced her thoughts back to what was important now. Egwene and Nynaeve came from the same village as that strange young man, Rand al'Thor. And Min knew him as well, however much she had tried to hide the fact. Rand al'Thor lay at the heart of it.

Elaida had only seen him once, supposedly a shepherd from the Two Rivers, in Andor, but looking every inch the Aielman. The Foretelling had come to her at the sight of him. He was *ta'veren,* one of those rare individuals who, instead of being woven into the Pattern as the Wheel of Time chose, forced the Pattern to shape itself around them, for a time at least. And Elaida had seen chaos swirling around him, division and strife for Andor, perhaps for even more of the world. But Andor must be kept whole, whatever else happened; that first Foretelling had convinced her of that.

There were more threads, enough to snare Siuan in her own web. If the rumors were to be believed, there were three *ta'veren,* not just one. All three from the same village, this Emond's Field, and all three near the same age, odd enough to occasion a good deal of talk in the Tower. And on Siuan's journey to Shienar, near a year ago now, she had seen them, even talked with them. Rand al'Thor. Perrin Aybara. Matrim Cauthon. It was said to be mere happenstance. Just fortuitous chance. So it was said. Those who said it did not know what Elaida knew.

When Elaida saw the young al'Thor man, it had been Moiraine who spirited him away. Moiraine who had accompanied him, and the other two *ta'veren,* in Shienar. Moiraine Damodred, who had been Siuan

Sanche's closest friend when they were novices together. Had Elaida
been one to make wagers, she would have wagered that no one else in
the Tower remembered that friendship. On the day they were raised
Aes Sedai, at the end of the Aiel War, Siuan and Moiraine had walked
away from one another and afterward behaved almost like strangers.
But Elaida had been one of the Accepted over those two novices, had
taught their lessons and chastised them for slacking at chores, and she
remembered. She could hardly believe that their plot could stretch
back so far—al'Thor could not have been born much before that—yet
it was the last link to tie them all together. For her, it was enough.

Whatever Siuan was up to, she had to be stopped. Turmoil and chaos
multiplied on every side. The Dark One was sure to break free—the
very thought made Elaida shiver and wrap her shawl around her more
tightly—and the Tower had to be aloof from mundane struggles to face
that. The Tower had to be free to pull the strings to make the nations
stand together, free of the troubles Rand al'Thor would bring. Somehow, he had to be stopped from destroying Andor.

She had told no one what she knew of al'Thor. She meant to deal
with him quietly, if possible. The Hall of the Tower already spoke of
watching, even guiding, these *ta'veren*; they would never agree to dispose of them, of the one in particular, as he must be disposed of. For
the good of the Tower. For the good of the world.

She made a sound in her throat, close to a growl. Siuan had always
been headstrong, even as a novice, had always thought much of herself
for a poor fisherman's daughter, but how could she be fool enough to
mix the Tower in this without telling the Hall? She knew what was
coming as well as anyone. The only way it could be worse was
if. . . .

Abruptly Elaida stopped, staring at nothing. Could it be that this
al'Thor could channel? Or one of the others? Most likely it would be
al'Thor. No. Surely not. Not even Siuan would touch one of those. She
could not. "Who knows what that woman could do?" she muttered.
"She was never fit to be the Amyrlin Seat."

"Talking to yourself, Elaida? I know you Reds never have friends
outside your own Ajah, but surely you have friends to talk to inside it."

Elaida turned her head to regard Alviarin. The swan-necked Aes
Sedai stared back with the insufferable coolness that was a hallmark of
the White Ajah. There was no love lost between Red and White; they
had stood on opposite sides in the Hall of the Tower for a thousand
years. White stood with Blue, and Siuan had been a Blue. But Whites
prided themselves on dispassionate logic.

"Walk with me," Elaida said. Alviarin hesitated before falling in beside her.

At first the White sister arched a disparaging eyebrow at what Elaida had to say concerning Siuan, but before the end she was frowning in concentration. "You have no proof of anything . . . improper," she said when Elaida finally fell silent.

"Not yet," Elaida said firmly. She permitted herself a tight smile when Alviarin nodded. It was a beginning. One way or another, Siuan would be stopped before she could destroy the Tower.

Well hidden in a stand of tall leatherleaf above the north bank of the River Taren, Dain Bornhald tossed back his white cloak, with its flaring golden sun on the breast, and raised the stiff leather tube of a looking glass to his eye. A cloud of tiny bitemes buzzed around his face, but he ignored them. In the village of Taren Ferry, across the river, tall stone houses stood on high foundations against the floods that came every spring. Villagers hung out of windows or waited on stoops to stare at the thirty white-cloaked riders sitting their horses in burnished plate-and-mail. A delegation of village men and women were meeting with the horsemen. Rather, they were listening to Jaret Byar, from what Bornhald could see, which was much the best.

Bornhald could almost hear his father's voice. *Let them think there is a chance, and some fool will try to take it. Then there's killing to do, and another fool will try to avenge the first, so there's more killing. Put the fear of the Light into them from the first, let them know no one will be harmed if they do as they're told, and you'll have no trouble.*

His jaw tightened at the thought of his father, dead now. He was going to do something about that, and soon. He was sure only Byar knew why he had leaped to accept this command, aimed at an all-but-forgotten district in the hinterlands of Andor, and Byar would hold his tongue. Byar had been as dedicated to Dain's father as a hound, and he had transferred all that loyalty to Dain. Bornhald had had no hesitation in naming Byar second under him when Eamon Valda gave him the command.

Byar turned his horse and rode back onto the ferry. Immediately the ferrymen cast off and began hauling the barge across by means of a heavy rope slung over the swiftly flowing water. Byar glanced at the men at the rope; they eyed him nervously as they tramped the length of the barge, then trotted back to take up the cable again. It all looked good.

"Lord Bornhald?"

Bornhald lowered the looking glass and turned his head. The hard-faced man who had appeared at his shoulder stood rigid, staring straight ahead from under a conical helmet. Even after the hard journey from Tar Valon—and Bornhald had pressed every mile—his armor shone as brightly as his snowy cloak with its golden sunburst.

"Yes, Child Ivon?"

"Hundredman Farran sent me, my Lord. It's the Tinkers. Ordeith was talking to three of them, my Lord, and now none of the three can be found."

"Blood and ashes!" Bornhald spun on his bootheel and strode back into the trees, Ivon at his heels.

Out of sight of the river, white-cloaked horsemen clogged the spaces between leatherleafs and pines, lances held with casual familiarity or bows laid across their pommels. The horses stamped their hooves impatiently and flicked their tails. The riders waited more stolidly; this would not be their first river crossing into strange territory, and this time no one would be trying to stop them.

In a large clearing beyond the mounted men stood a caravan of the Tuatha'an, the Traveling People. Tinkers. Nearly a hundred horse-drawn wagons, like small, boxy houses on wheels, made an eye-jarring blend of colors, red and green and yellow and every hue imaginable in combinations only a Tinker's eye could like. The people themselves wore clothes that made their wagons look dull. They sat on the ground in a large cluster, eyeing the mounted men with an oddly calm unease; the thin crying of a child was swiftly comforted by its mother. Nearby, dead mastiffs made a mound already buzzing with flies. Tinkers would not raise a hand even to defend themselves, and the dogs had been mostly show, but Bornhald had not been willing to take a chance.

Six men were all he had thought necessary to watch Tinkers. Even with stiff faces, they looked embarrassed. None glanced at the seventh man sitting a horse near the wagons, a bony little man with a big nose, in a dark gray coat that looked too big for him despite the fineness of its cut. Farran, a bearded boulder of a man yet light on his feet for all his height and width, stood glaring at all seven equally. The hundredman pressed a gauntleted hand to his heart in salute but left all talking to Bornhald.

"A word with you, Master Ordeith," Bornhald said quietly. The bony man cocked his head, looking at Bornhald for a long moment before dismounting. Farran growled, but Bornhald kept his voice low. "Three of the Tinkers cannot be found, Master Ordeith. Did you perhaps put your own suggestion into practice?" The first words out of Ordeith's mouth when he saw the Tinkers had been "Kill them. They're of no use." Bornhald had killed his share of men, but he had never matched the casualness with which the little man had spoken.

Ordeith rubbed a finger along the side of his large nose. "Now, why would I be killing them? And after you ripped me so for just suggesting it." His Lugarder accent was heavy today; it came and went without him seeming to notice, another thing about the man that disturbed Bornhald.

"Then you allowed them to escape, yes?"

"Well, as to that, I did take a few of them off where I could see what they knew. Undisturbed, you see."

"What they knew? What under the Light could Tinkers know of use to us?"

"There's no way of telling until you ask, now is there?" Ordeith said. "I didn't hurt any of them much, and I told them to get themselves back to the wagons. Who would be thinking they'd have the nerve to run away with so many of your men about?"

Bornhald realized he was grinding his teeth. His orders had been to make the best time possible to meet this odd fellow, who would have more orders for him. Bornhald liked none of it, though both sets of orders bore the seal and signature of Pedron Niall, Lord Captain Commander of the Children of the Light.

Too much had been left unsaid, including Ordeith's exact status. The little man was there to advise Bornhald, and Bornhald was to cooperate with Ordeith. Whether Ordeith was under his command had been left vague, and he did not like the strong implication that he should heed the fellow's advice. Even the reason for sending so many of the Children into this backwater had been vague. To root out Darkfriends, of course, and spread the Light; that went without saying. But close to half a legion on Andoran soil without permission—the order risked much if word of it reached the Queen in Caemlyn. Too much to be balanced by the few answers Bornhald had been given.

It all came back to Ordeith. Bornhald did not understand how the Lord Captain Commander could trust this man, with his sly grins and his black moods and his haughty stares so you could never be sure what kind of man you were talking to. Not to mention his accent changing in the middle of a sentence. The fifty Children who had accompanied Ordeith were as sullen and frowning a lot as Bornhald had ever seen. He thought Ordeith must have picked them himself to have so many sour scowls, and it said something of the man that he would choose that sort. Even his name, Ordeith, meant "wormwood" in the Old Tongue. Still, Bornhald had his own reasons for wanting to be where he was. He would cooperate with the man, since he had to. But only as much as he had to.

"Master Ordeith," he said in a carefully level tone, "this ferry is the only way in or out of the Two Rivers district." That was not quite the truth. According to the map he had, there was no way across the Taren except here, and the upper reaches of the Manetherendrelle, bordering the region on the south, had no fords. To the east lay bogs and swamps. Even so, there must be a way out westward, across the Mountains of Mist, though his map stopped at the edge of the range. At best, however, it would be a hard crossing that many of his men might not survive, and he did not intend to let Ordeith know of even that small chance. "When it is time to leave, if I find Andoran soldiers holding this bank, you will ride with the first to cross. You will find it interesting to see at close hand the difficulty of forcing a way across a river this wide, yes?"

"This is your first command, is it not?" Ordeith's voice held a hint of mockery. "This may be part of Andor on the map, but Caemlyn has not sent a tax collector this far west in generations. Even if those three talk, who will believe three Tinkers? If you think the danger is too great, remember whose seal is on your orders."

Farran glanced at Bornhald, half reached for his sword. Bornhald shook his head slightly, and Farran let his hand fall. "I mean to cross the river, Master Ordeith. I will cross if the next word I hear is that Gareth Bryne and the Queen's Guards will be here by sundown."

"Of course," Ordeith said, suddenly soothing. "There will be as much glory here as at Tar Valon, I assure you." His deep, dark eyes took a glazed look, stared at something in the distance. "There are things in Tar Valon I want, too."

Bornhald shook his head. *And I must cooperate with him.*

Jaret Byar drew up and swung down from his saddle beside Farran. As tall as the hundredman, Byar was a long-faced man with dark, deep-set eyes. He looked as if every ounce of fat had been boiled off of him. "The village is secured, my Lord. Lucellin is making certain no one slips off. They nearly soiled themselves when I mentioned Darkfriends. None in their village, they say. The folk further south are the Dark-friend kind, though, they say."

"Further south, is it?" Bornhald said briskly. "We shall see. Put three hundreds across the river, Byar. Farran's first. The rest to follow after the Tinkers cross. And make sure no more of them get away, yes?"

"We will scour the Two Rivers," Ordeith broke in. His narrow face was twisted; saliva bubbled at his lips. "We will flog them, and flay them, and sear their souls! I promised him! He'll come to me, now! He will come!"

Bornhald nodded for Byar and Farran to carry out his commands. *A madman,* he thought. *The Lord Captain Commander has tied me to a madman. But at least I will find my path to Perrin of the Two Rivers. Whatever it takes, I will* avenge *my father!*

From a colonnaded terrace on a hilltop, the High Lady Suroth looked across the wide, lopsided bowl of Cantorin Harbor. The shaven sides of her scalp left a wide crest of black hair that fell down her back. Her hands rested lightly on a smooth stone balustrade as white as her pristine gown with its hundreds of pleats. There was a faint rhythmic clicking as she unconsciously drummed her fingers with their inch-long nails, the first two on each hand lacquered blue.

A slight breeze blew off of the Aryth Ocean, carrying more than a hint of salt in its coolness. Two young women kneeling against the wall behind the High Lady held white-plumed fans ready if the breeze should fail. Two more women and four young men completed the line of crouching figures waiting to serve. Barefoot, all eight wore sheer robes, to please the High Lady's aesthetic senses with the clean lines of their limbs and the grace of their motions. At the moment Suroth truly did not see the servants, no more than one saw furniture.

She saw the six Deathwatch Guards at either end of the colonnade, though, stiff as statues with their black-tasseled spears and black-lacquered shields. They symbolized her triumph, and her danger. The Deathwatch Guard served only the Empress and her chosen representatives, and they would kill or die with equal fervor, whichever was necessary. There was a saying: "On the heights, the paths are paved with daggers."

Her fingernails clicked on the stone balustrade. How thin was the razor's edge she walked.

Vessels of the Atha'an Miere, the Sea Folk, filled the inner harbor behind the seawall, even the largest looking too narrow for their length. Cut rigging made their yards and booms slant at crazy angles. Their decks were empty, their crews ashore and under guard, as were any in these islands who had the skill to sail the open sea. Great, bluff-bowed Seanchan ships by the score lay in the outer harbor, and anchored off the harbor mouth. One, its ribbed sails bellied with wind, escorted a swarm of small fishing boats back toward the island port. If the smaller craft scattered, some of them might escape, but the Seanchan ship carried a *damane,* and one demonstration of a *damane's* power had quelled any such thoughts. The charred, shattered hulk of the Sea Folk ship still lay on a mudflat near the harbor mouth.

How long she would manage to keep Sea Folk elsewhere—and the accursed mainlanders—from learning that she held these islands, Suroth did not know. *It will be long enough,* she told herself. *It must be long enough.*

She had worked something of a miracle in rallying most of the Seanchan forces after the debacle the High Lord Turak had led them to. All but a handful of the vessels that had escaped from Falme lay under her control, and no one questioned her right to command the *Hailene,* the Forerunners. If her miracle held, no one on the mainland suspected they were here. Waiting to take back the lands the Empress had sent them to reclaim, waiting to achieve the *Corenne,* the Return. Her agents already scouted the way. There would be no need to return to the Court of the Nine Moons and apologize to the Empress for a failure not even hers.

The thought of having to apologize to the Empress sent a tremor through her. Such an apology was always humiliating, and usually painful, but what made her shiver was the chance of being denied death at the end, of being forced to continue as if nothing had occurred while everyone, common as well as the Blood, knew her degradation. A handsome young serving man sprang to her side, bearing a pale green robe worked in brilliantly plumaged birds-of-delight. She held her arms out for the garment and noticed him no more than a clod of dirt beside her velvet slipper.

To escape that apology, she must retake what had been lost a thousand years ago. And to do that, she must deal with this man who, her mainland agents told her, claimed to be the Dragon Reborn. *If I cannot find a way to deal with him, the displeasure of the Empress will be the least of my worries.*

Turning smoothly, she entered the long room fronting the terrace, its outer wall all doors and tall windows to catch the breezes. The pale wood of the walls, smooth and glistening like satin, pleased Suroth, but she had removed the furnishings of the old owner, the former Atha'an Miere governor of Cantorin, and replaced them with a few tall screens, most painted with birds or flowers. Two were different. One showed a great spotted cat of the Sen T'jore, as large as a pony, the other a black mountain eagle, crest erect like a pale crown and snowy-tipped wings spread to their full seven feet. Such screens were considered vulgar, but Suroth liked animals. Unable to bring her menagerie with her across the Aryth Ocean, she had had the screens made to depict her two favorites. She had never taken kindly to being balked in anything.

Three women awaited her as she had left them, two kneeling, one lying prostrate on the bare, polished floor, patterned in inlays of light and dark wood. The kneeling women wore the dark blue dresses of *sul'dam*, red panels embroidered with forked silver lightning on the breast and on the sides of their skirts. One of the two, Alwhin, a sharp-faced, blue-eyed woman with a perpetual glower, had the left side of her head shaved. The rest of her hair hung to her shoulder in a light brown braid.

Suroth's mouth tightened momentarily at the sight of Alwhin. No *sul'dam* had ever before been raised to the *so'jhin*, the hereditary upper servants of the Blood, much less to a Voice of the Blood. Yet there had been reasons in Alwhin's case. Alwhin knew too much.

Still, it was to the woman lying facedown, all in plain dark gray, that Suroth directed her attention. A wide collar of silvery metal encircled the woman's neck, connected by a shining leash to a bracelet of the same material on the wrist of the second *sul'dam*, Taisa. By means of leash and collar, the *a'dam*, Taisa could control the gray-clad woman. And she had to be controlled. She was *damane*, a woman who could channel, and thus too dangerous to be allowed to run loose. Memories of the Armies of the Night were still strong in Seanchan a thousand years after their destruction.

Suroth's eyes flickered uneasily to the two *sul'dam*. She no longer trusted any *sul'dam*, and yet she had no choice but to trust them. No one else could control the *damane*, and without the *damane*. . . . The very concept was unthinkable. The power of Seanchan, the very power of the Crystal Throne, was built on controlled *damane*. There were too many things about which Suroth had no choice to suit her. Such as Alwhin, who watched as if she had been *so'jhin* all of her life. No. As if she were of the Blood itself, and knelt because she chose to.

"Pura." The *damane* had had another name when she was one of the hated Aes Sedai, before falling into Seanchan hands, but Suroth neither knew what it had been nor cared. The gray-clad woman tensed, but did not raise her head; her training had been particularly harsh. "I will ask again, Pura. How does the White Tower control this man who calls himself the Dragon Reborn?"

The *damane* moved her head a fraction, enough to shoot a frightened look at Taisa. If her answer was displeasing, the *sul'dam* could make her feel pain without raising a finger, by means of the *a'dam*. "The Tower would not try to control a false Dragon, High Lady," Pura said breathily. "They would capture him, and gentle him."

Taisa looked an indignant question at the High Lady. The answer had avoided Suroth's query, had perhaps even implied that one of the Blood had spoken untruth. Suroth gave a slight shake of her head, the merest sideways motion—she had no wish to wait while the *damane* recovered from punishment—and Taisa bowed her head in acquiescence.

"Once again, Pura, what do you know of Aes Sedai . . ." Suroth's mouth twisted at being defiled with that name; Alwhin gave a grunt of distaste ". . . Aes Sedai aiding this man? I warn you. Our soldiers fought women of the Tower, women channeling the Power, at Falme, so do not attempt to deny it."

"Pura. . . . Pura does not know, High Lady." There was urgency in the *damane*'s voice, and uncertainty; she darted another wide-eyed glance at Taisa. It was clear that she wanted desperately to be believed. "Perhaps. . . . Perhaps the Amyrlin, or the Hall of the Tower. . . . No, they would not. Pura does not know, High Lady."

"The man can channel," Suroth said curtly. The woman on the floor moaned, though she had heard the same words from Suroth before. Saying it again made Suroth's stomach knot, but she allowed nothing to show on her face. Little of what had happened at Falme had been the work of women channeling; *damane* could sense that, and the *sul'dam* wearing the bracelet always knew what her *damane* felt. That meant it had to have been the work of the man. It also meant he was incredibly powerful. So powerful that Suroth had once or twice found herself wondering, growing queasy, whether he might really be the Dragon Reborn. *That cannot be,* she told herself firmly. In any case, it made no difference to her plans. "It is impossible to believe that even the White Tower would allow such a man to walk free. How do they control him?"

The *damane* lay there silently, face to the floor, shoulders shaking, weeping.

"Answer the High Lady!" Taisa said sharply. Taisa did not move, but Pura gasped, flinching as if struck across the hips. A blow delivered through the *a'dam*.

"P-Pura does not kn-know." The *damane* stretched out a hesitant hand as though to touch Suroth's foot. "Please. Pura has learned to obey. Pura speaks only the truth. Please do not punish Pura."

Suroth stepped back smoothly, letting none of her irritation show. That she should be forced to move by a *damane*. That she could almost be touched by one who could channel. She felt a need to bathe, as if the touch had actually landed.

Taisa's dark eyes bulged in outrage at the *damane*'s effrontery; her cheeks were scarlet with shame that this should happen while she wore the woman's bracelet. She seemed torn between prostrating herself beside the *damane* to beg forgiveness and punishing the woman then and there. Alwhin stared a thin-lipped contempt, every line of her face saying that such things did not happen when she wore a bracelet.

Suroth raised one finger a fraction, making a small gesture every *so'jhin* knew from childhood, a simple dismissal.

Alwhin hesitated before interpreting it, then tried to cover her slip by rounding harshly on Taisa. "Take this . . . creature from the presence of the High Lady Suroth. And when you have punished her, go to Surela and tell her that you control your charges as if you had never worn the bracelet before. Tell her that you are to be—"

Suroth shut Alwhin's voice from her mind. None of that had been her command except the dismissal, but quarrels between *sul'dam* were beneath her notice. She wished she knew whether Pura was managing to hide something. Her agents reported claims that the women of the White Tower could not lie. It had not been possible to force Pura to tell even a simple lie, to say that a white scarf was black, yet that was not enough to be conclusive. Some might accept the tears of the *damane*, her protests of inability whatever the *sul'dam* did, but none who did would have risen to lead the Return. Pura might have some reservoir of will left, might be clever enough to try using the belief that she was incapable of lying. None of the women collared on the mainland were fully obedient, trustworthy, not like the *damane* brought from Seanchan. None of them truly accepted what they were, as Seanchan *damane* did. Who could say what secrets might hide in one who had called herself Aes Sedai?

Not for the first time Suroth wished she had the other Aes Sedai who had been captured on Toman Head. With two to question, there would have been a better chance to catch lies and evasions. It was a useless wish. The other could be dead, drowned at sea, or on display at the Court of the Nine Moons. Some of the ships Suroth had failed to gather in must have managed the journey back across the ocean, and one might well have carried the woman.

She herself had sent a ship carrying carefully crafted reports, nearly half a year ago now, as soon as she had solidified her control of the Forerunners, with a captain and crew from families that had served hers since Luthair Paendrag had proclaimed himself Emperor, nearly a thousand years ago. Dispatching the ship had been a gamble, for the Empress might send back someone to take Suroth's place. Not sending the vessel would have been a greater, though; only utter and crushing victory could have saved her then. Perhaps not even that. So the Empress knew of Falme, knew of Turak's disaster and Suroth's intention to go on. But what did she think of that knowledge, and what was she doing about it? That was a greater concern than any *damane,* whatever she had been before collaring.

Yet the Empress did not know everything. The worst could not be entrusted to any messenger, no matter how loyal. It would only be passed from Suroth's lips directly to the ear of the Empress, and Suroth had taken pains to keep it so. Only four still lived who knew the secret, and two of those would never speak of it to anyone, not of their own volition. *Only three deaths can hold it more tightly.*

Suroth did not realize she had murmured the last aloud until Alwhin said, "And yet the High Lady needs all three alive." The woman had a properly humble suppleness to her stance, even to the trick of downcast eyes that still managed to watch for any sign from Suroth. Her voice was humble, too. "Who can say, High Lady, what the Empress—may she live forever!—might do if she learned of an attempt to keep such knowledge from her?"

Instead of answering, Suroth made the tiny dismissing gesture once more. Again Alwhin hesitated—this time it had to be simple reluctance to leave; the woman rose above herself!—before bowing deeply and backing out of Suroth's presence.

With an effort Suroth found calmness. The *sul'dam* and the other two were a problem she could not solve now, but patience was a necessity for the Blood. Those who lacked it were likely to end in the Tower of Ravens.

On the terrace, kneeling servants leaned forward a hair in readiness as she appeared again. The soldiers maintained their watch to see she was undisturbed. Suroth took up her place before the balustrade, this time staring out to sea, toward the mainland hundreds of miles to the east.

To be the one who successfully led the Forerunners, who began the Return, would bring much honor. Perhaps even adoption into the family of the Empress, though that was an honor not without complications. To also be the one who captured this Dragon, whether false or real, along with the means of controlling his incredible power. . . .

But if—when I take him, do I give him to the Empress? That is the question.

Her long nails began to click again on the wide stone rail.

CHAPTER
2

Whirlpools in the Pattern

Inland the hot night wind blew, north across the vast delta called the Fingers of the Dragon, a winding maze of waterways broad and narrow, some choked with knifegrass. Vast plains of reeds separated clusters of low islands forested with spider-rooted trees seen nowhere else. Eventually the delta gave way to its source, the River Erinin, the river's great width spotted with the lights of small boats lantern-fishing. Boats and lights bobbed wildly, sudden and unexpected, and some older men muttered of evil things passing in the night. Young men laughed, but they hauled the nets more vigorously, too, eager to be home and out of the dark. The stories said evil could not cross your threshold unless you invited it in. That was what the stories said. But out in the darkness. . . .

The last tang of salt had vanished by the time the wind reached the great city of Tear, hard by the river, where tile-roofed inns and shops shouldered against tall, towered palaces gleaming in the moonlight. Yet no palace was half so tall as the massive bulk, almost a mountain, that stretched from city's heart to water's edge. The Stone of Tear, fortress of legend, the oldest stronghold of mankind, erected in the last days of the Breaking of the World. While nations and empires rose and fell, were replaced and fell anew, the Stone stood. It was the rock on which armies had broken spears and swords and hearts for three thousand years. And in all that time it had never fallen to invading arms. Until now.

The streets of the city, the taverns and inns, were all but empty in the muggy darkness, people keeping cautiously within their own walls. Who held the Stone was lord of Tear, city and nation. That was the way it had always been, and the people of Tear accepted it always. By daylight they would cheer their new lord with enthusiasm as they had cheered the old; by night they huddled together, shivering despite the heat when the wind howled across their rooftops like a thousand keening mourners. Strange new hopes danced in their heads, hopes none in Tear had dared for a hundred generations, hopes mixed with fears as old as the Breaking.

The wind lashed the long, white banner catching the moon above the Stone as if trying to rip it away. Along its length marched a sinuous figure like a legged serpent, golden-maned like a lion, scaled in scarlet and gold, seeming to ride the wind. Banner of prophecy, hoped for and dreaded. Banner of the Dragon. The Dragon Reborn. Harbinger of the world's salvation, and herald of a new Breaking to come. As if outraged at such defiance, the wind dashed itself against the hard walls of the Stone. The Dragon banner floated, unheeding in the night, awaiting greater storms.

In a room more than halfway up the Stone's southern face, Perrin sat on the chest at the foot of his canopied bed and watched the dark-haired young woman pacing up and down. There was a trace of wariness in his golden eyes. Usually Faile bantered with him, maybe poked a little gentle fun at his deliberate ways; tonight she had not said ten words since coming through the door. He could smell the rose petals that had been folded into her clothes after cleaning, and the scent that was just her. And in the hint of clean perspiration, he smelled nervousness. Faile almost never showed nerves. Wondering why she did now set an itch between his shoulders that had nothing to do with the night's heat. Her narrow, divided skirts made a soft *whisk-whisk-whisk* with her strides.

He scratched his two-week growth of beard irritably. It was even curlier than the hair on his head. It was also hot. For the hundredth time he thought of shaving.

"It suits you," Faile said suddenly, stopping in her tracks.

Uncomfortably, he shrugged shoulders heavy from long hours working at a forge. She did that sometimes, seemed to know what he was thinking. "It itches," he muttered, and wished he had spoken more forcefully. It was his beard; he could shave it off any time he wanted.

She studied him, her head tilted to one side. Her bold nose and high cheekbones made it seem a fierce study, a contrast to the soft voice in which she said, "It looks right on you."

Perrin sighed, and shrugged again. She had not asked him to keep the beard, and she would not. Yet he knew he was going to put off shaving again. He wondered how his friend Mat would handle this situation. Probably with a pinch and a kiss and some remark that made her laugh until he brought her around to his way of thinking. But Perrin knew he did not have Mat's way with the girls. Mat would never find himself sweating behind a beard just because a woman thought he should have hair on his face. Unless, maybe, the woman was Faile. Perrin suspected that her father must deeply regret her leaving home, and not just because she was his daughter. He was the biggest fur trader in Saldaea, so she claimed, and Perrin could see her getting the price she wanted every time.

"Something is troubling you, Faile, and it isn't my beard. What is it?"

Her expression became guarded. She looked everywhere but at him, making a contemptuous survey of the room's furnishings.

Carvings of leopards and lions, stooping hawks and hunting scenes decorated everything from the tall wardrobe and bedposts as thick as his leg to the padded bench in front of the cold marble fireplace. Some of the animals had garnet eyes.

He had tried to convince the majhere that he wanted a simple room, but she did not seem to understand. Not that she was stupid or slow. The majhere commanded an army of servants greater in numbers than the Defenders of the Stone; whoever commanded the Stone, whoever held its walls, she saw to the day-to-day matters that let everything function. But she looked at the world through Tairen eyes. Despite his clothes, he must be more than the young countryman he seemed, because commoners were never housed in the Stone—save for Defenders and servants, of course. Beyond that, he was one of Rand's party, a friend or a follower or in any case close to the Dragon Reborn in some way. To the majhere, that set him on a level with a Lord of the Land at the very least, if not a High Lord. She had been scandalized enough at putting him in here, without even a sitting room; he thought she might have fainted if he had insisted on an even plainer chamber. If there were such things short of the servants' quarters, or the Defenders'. At least nothing here was gilded except the candlesticks.

Faile's opinions, though, were not his. "You should have better than this. You deserve it. You can wager your last copper that Mat has better."

"Mat likes gaudy things," he said simply.

"You do not stand up for yourself."

He did not comment. It was not his rooms that made her smell of unease, any more than his beard.

After a moment, she said, "The Lord Dragon seems to have lost interest in you. All his time is taken by the High Lords, now."

The itch between his shoulders worsened; he knew what was troubling her now. He tried to make his voice light. "The Lord Dragon? You sound like a Tairen. His name is Rand."

"He's your friend, Perrin Aybara, not mine. If a man like that has friends." She drew a deep breath and went on in a more moderate tone. "I have been thinking about leaving the Stone. Leaving Tear. I don't think Moiraine would try to stop me. News of . . . of Rand has been leaving the city for two weeks, now. She can't think to keep him secret any longer."

He only just stopped another sigh. "I don't think she will, either. If anything, I think she considers you a complication. She will probably give you money to see you on your way."

Planting fists on hips, she moved to stare down at him. "Is that all you have to say?"

"What do you want me to say? That I want you to stay?" The anger in his own voice startled him. He was angry with himself, not her. Angry because he had not seen this coming, angry because he could not see how to deal with it. He liked being able to think things through. It was easy to hurt people without meaning to when you were hasty. He'd done that now. Her dark eyes were large with shock. He tried to smooth his words. "I do want you to stay, Faile, but maybe you should leave. I know you're no coward, but the Dragon Reborn, the Forsaken. . . ." Not that anywhere was really safe—not for long, not now —yet there were safer places than the Stone. For a while, anyway. Not that he was stupid enough to put it to her that way.

But she did not appear to care how he put it. "Stay? The Light illumine me! Anything is better than sitting here like a boulder, but. . . ." She knelt gracefully in front of him, resting her hands on his knees. "Perrin. I do not like wondering when one of the Forsaken is going to walk around the corner in front of me, and I do not like wondering when the Dragon Reborn is going to kill us all. He did it back in the Breaking, after all. Killed everyone close to him."

"Rand isn't Lews Therin Kinslayer," Perrin protested. "I mean, he *is* the Dragon Reborn, but he isn't . . . he wouldn't. . . ." He trailed off, not knowing how to finish. Rand was Lews Therin Telamon reborn;

that was what being the Dragon Reborn meant. But did it mean Rand was doomed to Lews Therin's fate? Not just going mad—any man who channeled had that fate in front of him, and then a rotting death—but killing everyone who cared for him?

"I have been talking to Bain and Chiad, Perrin."

That was no surprise. She spent considerable time with the Aiel women. The friendship made some trouble for her, but she seemed to like the Aiel women as much as she despised the Stone's Tairen noblewomen. But he saw no connection to what they were talking about, and he said so.

"They say Moiraine sometimes asks where you are. Or Mat. Don't you see? She would not have to do that if she could watch you with the Power."

"Watch me with the Power?" he said faintly. He had never even considered that.

"She cannot. Come with me, Perrin. We can be twenty miles across the river before she misses us."

"I can't," he said miserably. He tried diverting her with a kiss, but she leaped to her feet and backed away so fast he nearly fell on his face. There was no point going after her. She had her arms crossed beneath her breasts like a barrier.

"Don't tell me you are that afraid of her. I know she is Aes Sedai, and she has all of you dancing when she twitches the strings. Perhaps she has the . . . Rand . . . so tied he cannot get loose, and the Light knows Egwene and Elayne, and even Nynaeve, don't want to, but you can break her cords if you try."

"It has nothing to do with Moiraine. It's what I have to do. I—"

She cut him short. "Don't you dare hand me any of that hairy-chested drivel about a man having to do his duty. I know duty as well as you, and you have no duty here. You may be *ta'veren*, even if I don't see it, but he is the Dragon Reborn, not you."

"Will you listen?" he shouted, glaring, and she jumped. He had never shouted at her before, not like that. She raised her chin and shifted her shoulders, but she did not say anything. He went on. "I think I am part of Rand's destiny, somehow. Mat, too. I think he can't do what he has to unless we do our part, as well. That is the duty. How can I walk away if it might mean Rand will fail?"

"Might?" There was a hint of demand in her voice, but only a hint. He wondered if he could make himself shout at her more often. "Did Moiraine tell you this, Perrin? You should know by now to listen closely to what an Aes Sedai says."

"I worked it out for myself. I think *ta'veren* are pulled toward each other. Or maybe Rand pulls us, Mat and me both. He's supposed to be the strongest *ta'veren* since Artur Hawkwing, maybe since the Breaking. Mat won't even admit he's *ta'veren*, but however he tries to get away, he always ends up drawn back to Rand. Loial says he has never heard of three *ta'veren*, all the same age and all from the same place."

Faile sniffed loudly. "Loial does not know everything. He isn't very old for an Ogier."

"He's past ninety," Perrin said defensively, and she gave him a tight smile. For an Ogier, ninety years was not much older than Perrin. Or maybe younger. He did not know much about Ogier. In any case, Loial had read more books than Perrin had ever seen or even heard of; sometimes he thought Loial had read every book ever printed. "And he knows more than you or I do. He believes maybe I have the right of it. And so does Moiraine. No, I haven't asked her, but why else does she keep a watch on me? Did you think she wanted me to make her a kitchen knife?"

She was silent for a moment, and when she spoke it was in sympathetic tones. "Poor Perrin. I left Saldaea to find adventure, and now that I'm in the heart of one, the greatest since the Breaking, all I want is to go somewhere else. You just want to be a blacksmith, and you're going to end up in the stories whether you want it or not."

He looked away, though the scent of her still filled his head. He did not think he was likely to have any stories told about him, not unless his secret spread a long way beyond the few who knew already. Faile thought she knew everything about him, but she was wrong.

An axe and a hammer leaned against the wall opposite him, each plain and functional, with a haft as long as his forearm. The axe was a wicked half-moon blade balanced by a thick spike, meant for violence. With the hammer he could make things, had made things, at a forge. The hammerhead weighed more than twice as much as the axe blade, but it was the axe that felt heavier by far every time he picked it up. With the axe, he had. . . . He scowled, not wanting to think about that. She was right. All he wanted was to be a blacksmith, to go home, and see his family again, and work at the smithy. But it was not to be; he knew that.

He got to his feet long enough to pick up the hammer, then sat back down. There was something comforting in holding it. "Master Luhhan always says you can't walk away from what has to be done." He hurried on, realizing that was a little too close to what she had called hairy-chested drivel. "He's the blacksmith back home, the man I was apprenticed to. I've told you about him."

To his surprise, she did not take the opportunity to point out his near echo. In fact, she said nothing, only looked at him, waiting for something. After a moment it came to him.

"Are you leaving, then?" he asked.

She stood up, brushing her skirt. For a long moment she kept silent, as if deciding on her answer. "I do not know," she said finally. "This is a fine mess you've put me in."

"Me? What did I do?"

"Well, if you don't know, I am certainly not going to tell you."

Scratching his beard again, he stared at the hammer in his other hand. Mat would probably know exactly what she meant. Or even old Thom Merrilin. The white-haired gleeman claimed no one understood women, but when he came out of his tiny room in the belly of the Stone he soon had half a dozen girls young enough to be his granddaughters sighing and listening to him play the harp and tell of grand adventure and romance. Faile was the only woman Perrin wanted, but sometimes he felt like a fish trying to understand a bird.

He knew she wanted him to ask. He knew that much. She might or might not tell him, but he was supposed to ask. Stubbornly he kept his mouth shut. This time he meant to wait her out.

Outside in the darkness, a cock crowed.

Faile shivered and hugged herself. "My nurse used to say that meant a death coming. Not that I believe it, of course."

He opened his mouth to agree it was foolishness, though he shivered, too, but his head whipped around at a grating sound and a thump. The axe had toppled to the floor. He only had time to frown, wondering what could have made it fall, when it shifted again, untouched, then leaped straight for him.

He swung the hammer without thought. Metal ringing on metal drowned Faile's scream; the axe flew across the room, bounced off the far wall, and darted back at him, blade first. He thought every hair on his body was trying to stand on end.

As the axe sped by her, Faile lunged forward and grabbed the haft with both hands. It twisted in her grip, slashing toward her wide-eyed face. Barely in time Perrin leaped up, dropping the hammer to seize the axe, just keeping the half-moon blade from her flesh. He thought he would die if the axe—his axe—harmed her. He jerked it away from her so hard that the heavy spike nearly stabbed him in the chest. It would have been a fair trade, to stop the axe from hurting her, but with a sinking feeling he began to think it might not be possible.

The weapon thrashed like a thing alive, a thing with a malevolent will. It wanted Perrin—he knew that as if it had shouted at him—but it fought with cunning. When he pulled the axe away from Faile, it used his own movement to hack at him; when he forced it from himself, it tried to reach her, as if it knew that would make him stop pushing. No matter how hard he held the haft, it spun in his hands, threatening with spike or curved blade. Already his hands ached from the effort, and his thick arms strained, muscles tight. Sweat rolled down his face. He was not sure how much longer it would be before the axe fought free of his grip. This was all madness, pure madness, with no time to think.

"Get out," he muttered through gritted teeth. "Get out of the room, Faile!"

Her face was bloodless pale, but she shook her head and wrestled with the axe. "No! I will not leave you!"

"It will kill both of us!"

She shook her head again.

Growling in his throat, he let go of the axe with one hand—his arm quivered with holding the thing one-handed; the twisting haft burned his palm—and thrust Faile away. She yelped as he wrestled her to the door. Ignoring her shouts and her fists pounding at him, he held her against the wall with a shoulder until he could pull the door open and shove her into the hallway.

Slamming the door behind her, he put his back against it, sliding the latch home with his hip as he seized the axe with both hands again. The heavy blade, gleaming and sharp, trembled within inches of his face. Laboriously, he pushed it out to arm's length. Faile's muted shouts penetrated the thick door, and he could feel her beating on it, but he was barely conscious of her. His yellow eyes seemed to shine, as if they reflected every scrap of light in the room.

"Just you and me, now," he snarled at the axe. "Blood and ashes, how I hate you!" Inside, a part of him came close to hysterical laughter. *Rand is the one who's supposed to go mad, and here I am, talking to an axe! Rand! Burn him!*

Teeth bared with effort, he forced the axe back a full step from the door. The weapon vibrated, fighting to reach flesh; he could almost taste its thirst for his blood. With a roar he suddenly pulled the curved blade toward him, threw himself back. Had the axe truly been alive, he was sure he would have heard a cry of triumph as it flashed toward his head. At the last instant, he twisted, driving the axe past himself. With a heavy *thunk* the blade buried itself in the door.

He felt the life—he could not think what else to call it—go out of the imprisoned weapon. Slowly, he took his hands away. The axe stayed where it was, only steel and wood again. The door seemed a good place to leave it for now, though. He wiped sweat from his face with a shaking hand. *Madness. Madness walks wherever Rand is.*

Abruptly he realized he could no longer hear Faile's shouts, or her pounding. Throwing back the latch, he hastily pulled the door open. A gleaming arc of steel stuck through the thick wood on the outside, shining in the light of wide-spaced lamps along the tapestry-hung hallway.

Faile stood there, hands raised, frozen in the act of beating on the door. Eyes wide and wondering, she touched the tip of her nose. "Another inch," she said faintly, and. . . ."

With a sudden start, she flung herself on him, hugging him fiercely, raining kisses on his neck and beard between incoherent murmurs. Just as quickly, she pushed back, running anxious hands over his chest and arms. "Are you hurt? Are you injured? Did it . . . ?"

"I'm all right," he told her. "But are you? I did not mean to frighten you."

She peered up at him. "Truly? You are not hurt in any way?"

"Completely unhurt. I—" Her full-armed slap made his head ring like hammer on anvil.

"You great hairy lummox! I thought you were dead! I was afraid it had killed you! I thought—!" She cut off as he caught her second slap in midswing.

"Please don't do that again," he said quietly. The smarting imprint of her hand burned on his cheek, and he thought his jaw would ache the rest of the night.

He gripped her wrist as gently as he would have a bird, but though she struggled to pull free, his hand did not budge an inch. Compared to swinging a hammer all day at the forge, holding her was no effort at all, even after his fight against the axe. Abruptly she seemed to decide to ignore his grip and stared him in the eye; neither dark nor golden eyes blinked. "I could have helped you. You had no right—"

"I had every right," he said firmly. "You could not have helped. If you had stayed, we'd both be dead. I couldn't have fought—not the way I had to—and kept you safe, too." She opened her mouth, but he raised his voice and went on. "I know you hate the word. I'll try my best not to treat you like porcelain, but if you ask me to watch you die, I will tie you like a lamb for market and send you off to Mistress Luhhan. She won't stand for any such nonsense."

Tonguing a tooth and wondering if it was loose, he almost wished he could see Faile trying to ride roughshod over Alsbet Luhhan. The blacksmith's wife kept her husband in line with scarcely more effort than she needed for her house. Even Nynaeve had been careful of her sharp tongue around Mistress Luhhan. The tooth still held tight, he decided.

Faile laughed suddenly, a low, throaty laugh. "You would, too, wouldn't you? Don't think you would not dance with the Dark One if you tried, though."

Perrin was so startled he let go of her. He could not see any real difference between what he had just said and what he had said before, but the one had made her blaze up, while this she took . . . fondly. Not that he was certain the threat to kill him was entirely a joke. Faile carried knives hidden about her person, and she knew how to use them.

She rubbed her wrist ostentatiously and muttered something under her breath. He caught the words "hairy ox," and promised himself he would shave every last whisker of that fool beard. He would.

Aloud, she said, "The axe. That was him, wasn't it? The Dragon Reborn, trying to kill us."

"It must have been Rand." He emphasized the name. He did not like thinking of Rand the other way. He preferred remembering the Rand he had grown up with in Emond's Field. "Not trying to kill us, though. Not him."

She gave him a wry smile, more a grimace. "If he was not trying, I hope he never does."

"I don't know what he was doing. But I mean to tell him to stop it, and right now."

"I don't know why I care for a man who worries so about his own safety," she murmured.

He frowned at her quizzically, wondering what she meant, but she only tucked her arm through his. He was still wondering as they started off through the Stone. The axe he left where it was; stuck in the door, it would not harm anyone.

Teeth clamped on a long-stemmed pipe, Mat opened his coat a bit more and tried to concentrate on the cards lying facedown in front of him, and on the coins spilled in the middle of the table. He had had the bright red coat made to an Andoran pattern, of the best wool, with golden embroidery scrolling around the cuffs and long collar, but day by day he was reminded how much farther south Tear lay than Andor. Sweat ran down his face, and plastered the shirt to his back.

None of his companions around the table appeared to notice the heat at all, despite coats that looked even heavier than his, with fat, swollen sleeves, all padded silks and brocades and satin stripes. Two men in red-and-gold livery kept the gamblers' silver cups full of wine and proffered shining silver trays of olives and cheeses and nuts. The heat did not seem to affect the servants, either, though now and again one of them yawned behind his hand when he thought no one was looking. The night was not young.

Mat refrained from lifting his cards to check them again. They would not have changed. Three rulers, the highest cards in three of the five suits, were already good enough to win most hands.

He would have been more comfortable dicing; there was seldom a deck of cards to be found in the places he usually gambled, where silver changed hands in fifty different dice games, but these young Tairen lordlings would rather wear rags than play at dice. Peasants tossed dice, though they were careful not to say so in his hearing. It was not his temper they feared, but who they thought his friends were. This game called chop was what they played, hour after hour, night after night, using cards hand-painted and lacquered by a man in the city who had been made well-to-do by these fellows and others like them. Only women or horses could draw them away, but neither for long.

Still, he had picked up the game quickly enough, and if his luck was not as good as it was with dice, it would do. A fat purse lay beside his cards, and another even fatter rested in his pocket. A fortune, he would have thought once, back in Emond's Field, enough to live the rest of his life in luxury. His ideas of luxury had changed since leaving the Two Rivers. The young lords kept their coin in careless, shining piles, but some old habits he had no intention of changing. In the taverns and inns it was sometimes necessary to depart quickly. Especially if his luck was really with him.

When he had enough to keep himself as he wanted, he would leave the Stone just as quickly. Before Moiraine knew what he was thinking. He would have been days gone by now, if he had had his way. It was just that there was gold to be had here. One night at this table could earn him more than a week of dicing in taverns. If only his luck would catch.

He put on a small frown and puffed worriedly at his pipe, to look unsure whether his cards were good enough to go on with. Two of the young lords had pipes in their teeth, too, but silver-worked, with amber bits. In the hot, still air, their perfumed tabac smelled like a fire in a lady's dressing chamber. Not that Mat had ever been in a lady's dressing chamber. An illness that nearly killed him had left his memory as full of holes as the best lace, yet he was sure he would have remembered that. *Not even the Dark One would be mean enough to make me forget that.*

"Sea Folk ship docked today," Reimon muttered around his pipe. The broad-shouldered young lord's beard was oiled and trimmed to a neat point. That was the latest fashion among the younger lords, and Reimon chased the latest fashions as assiduously as he chased women. Which was only a little less diligently than he gambled. He tossed a silver crown onto the pile in the middle of the table for another card. "A raker. Fastest ships there are, rakers, so they say. Outrun the wind, they say. I would like to see that. Burn my soul, but I would." He did not bother to look at the card he was dealt; he never did until he had a full five.

The plump, pink-cheeked man between Reimon and Mat gave an amused chuckle. "You want to see the ship, Reimon? You mean the girls, do you not? The women. Exotic Sea Folk beauties, with their rings and baubles and swaying walks, eh?" He put in a crown and took his card, grimacing when he peeked at it. That meant nothing; going by his face, Edorion's cards were always low and mismatched. He won more than he lost, though. "Well, perhaps my luck will be better with the Sea Folk girls."

The dealer, tall and slender on Mat's other side, with a pointed beard even more darkly luxuriant than Reimon's, laid a finger alongside his nose. "You think to be lucky with those, Edorion? The way they keep to themselves, you'll be lucky to catch a whiff of their perfume." He made a wafting gesture, inhaling deeply with a sigh, and the other lordlings laughed, even Edorion.

A plain-faced youth named Estean laughed loudest of all, scrubbing a hand through lank hair that kept falling over his forehead. Replace his fine yellow coat with drab wool, and he could have passed for a farmer, instead of the son of a High Lord with the richest estates in Tear and in his own right the wealthiest man at the table. He had also drunk much more wine than any of the others.

Swaying across the man next to him, a foppish fellow named Baran who always seemed to be looking down his sharp nose, Estean poked the dealer with a none too steady finger. Baran leaned back, twisting his mouth around his pipestem as if he feared Estean might throw up.

"That's good, Carlomin," Estean gurgled. "You think so too, don't you, Baran? Edorion won't get a sniff. If he wants to try his luck . . . take a gamble . . . he ought to go after the Aiel wenches, like Mat, here. All those spears and knives. Burn my soul. Like asking a lion to dance." Dead silence dropped around the table. Estean laughed on alone, then blinked and scrubbed fingers through his hair again. "What's the matter? Did I say something? Oh! Oh, yes. Them."

Mat barely stopped a scowl. The fool had to bring up the Aiel. The only worse subject would have been Aes Sedai; they would almost rather have Aiel walking the corridors, staring down any Tairen who got in their way, than even one Aes Sedai, and these men thought they had four, at least. He fingered an Andoran silver crown from his purse on the table and pushed it into the pot. Carlomin dealt out the card slowly.

Mat lifted it carefully with a thumbnail, and did not let himself so much as blink. The Ruler of Cups, a High Lord of Tear. The rulers in a deck varied according to the land where the cards were made, with the nation's own ruler always as Ruler of Cups, the highest suit. These cards were old. He had already seen new decks with Rand's face or something like it on the Ruler of Cups, complete with the Dragon banner. Rand the ruler of Tear; that still seemed ludicrous enough to make him want to pinch himself. Rand was a shepherd, a good fellow to have fun with when he was not going all over-serious and responsible. Rand the Dragon Reborn, now; that told him he was a stone fool to be sitting there, where Moiraine could put her hand on him whenever she wanted, waiting to see what Rand would do next. Maybe Thom Merrilin would go with him. Or Perrin. Only, Thom seemed to be settling into the Stone as if he never meant to leave, and Perrin was not going anywhere unless Faile crooked a finger. Well, Mat was ready to travel alone, if need be.

Yet there was silver in the middle of the table and gold in front of the lordlings, and if he was dealt the fifth ruler, there was no hand in chop could beat him. Not that he really needed it. Suddenly he could feel luck tickling his mind. Not tingling as it did with the dice, of course, but he was already certain no one was going to beat four rulers. The Tairens had been betting wildly all night, the price of ten farms crossing the table on the quickest hands.

But Carlomin was staring at the deck of cards in his hand instead of buying his fourth, and Baran was puffing his pipe furiously and stacking the coins in front of him as if ready to stuff them into his pockets. Reimon wore a scowl behind his beard, and Edorion was frowning at his nails. Only Estean appeared unaffected; he grinned uncertainly around the table, perhaps already forgetting what he had said. They usually managed to put some sort of good face on the situation if the Aiel came up, but the hour was late, and the wine had flowed freely.

Mat scoured his mind for a way to keep them and their gold from walking away from his cards. One glance at their faces was enough to tell him that simply changing the subject would not be enough. But there was another way. If he made them laugh at the Aiel. . . . *Is it worth making them laugh at me, too?* Chewing his pipestem, he tried to think of something else.

Baran picked up a stack of gold in each hand and moved to stick them in his pockets.

"I might just try these Sea Folk women," Mat said quickly, taking his pipe to gesture with. "Odd things happen when you chase Aiel girls. Very odd. Like the game they call Maidens' Kiss." He had their attention, but Baran had not put down the coins, and Carlomin still showed no sign of buying a card.

Estean gave a drunken guffaw. "Kiss you with steel in your ribs, I suppose. Maidens of the Spear, you see. Steel. Spear in your ribs. Burn my soul." No one else laughed. But they were listening.

"Not quite." Mat managed a grin. *Burn me, I've told this much. I might as well tell the rest.* "Rhuarc said if I wanted to get along with the Maidens, I should ask them how to play Maidens' Kiss. He said that was the best way to get to know them." It still sounded like one of the kissing games back home, like Kiss the Daisies. He had never considered the Aiel clan chief a man to play tricks. He would be warier the next time. He made an effort to improve the grin. "So I went along to Bain and . . ." Reimon frowned impatiently. None of them knew any Aiel's name but Rhuarc, and none of them wanted to. Mat dropped the names and hurried on ". . . went along dumb as a bull-goose fool, and asked them to show me." He should have suspected something from the wide smiles that had bloomed on their faces. Like cats who had been asked to dance by a mouse. "Before I knew what was happening, I had a fistful of spears around my neck like a collar. I could have shaved myself with one sneeze."

The others around the table exploded in laughter, from Reimon's wheezing to Estean's wine-soaked bray.

Mat left them to it. He could almost feel the spearpoints again, pricking if he so much as twitched a finger. Bain, laughing all the while, had told him she had never heard of a man actually asking to play Maidens' Kiss.

Carlomin stroked his beard and spoke into Mat's hesitation. "You cannot stop there. Go on. When was this? Two nights ago, I'll wager. When you didn't come for the game, and no one knew where you were."

"I was playing stones with Thom Merrilin that night," Mat said quickly. "This was days ago." He was glad he could lie with a straight face. "They each took a kiss. That's all. If she thought it was a good kiss, they eased up with the spears. If not, they pushed a little harder; to encourage, you might say. That was all. I'll tell you this; I got nicked less than I do shaving."

He stuck his pipe back between his teeth. If they wanted to know more, they could go ask to play the game themselves. He almost hoped some of them were fool enough. *Bloody Aiel women and their bloody spears.* He had not made it to his own bed until daybreak.

"It would be more than enough for me," Carlomin said dryly. "The Light burn my soul if it would not." He tossed a silver crown into the center of the table and dealt himself another card. "Maidens' Kiss." He shook with mirth, and another ripple of laughter ran around the table.

Baran bought his fifth card, and Estean fumbled a coin from the heap scattered in front of him, peering at it to see what it was. They would not stop now.

"Savages," Baran muttered around his pipe. "Ignorant savages. That is all they are, burn my soul. Live in caves, out in the Waste. In caves! No one but a savage could live in the Waste."

Reimon nodded. "At least they serve the Lord Dragon. I would take a hundred Defenders and clean them out of the Stone, if not for that." Baran and Carlomin growled fierce agreement.

It was no effort for Mat to keep his face straight. He had heard much the same before. Boasting was easy when no one expected you to carry through. A hundred Defenders? Even if Rand stood aside for some reason, the few hundred Aiel holding the Stone could probably keep it against any army Tear could raise. Not that they seemed to want the Stone, really. Mat suspected they were only there because Rand was. He did not think any of these lordlings had figured that out—they tried to ignore the Aiel as much as possible—but he doubted it would make them feel any better.

"Mat." Estean fanned his cards out in one hand, rearranging them as if he could not decide what order they were meant to go in. "Mat, you will speak to the Lord Dragon, won't you?"

"About what?" Mat asked cautiously. Too many of these Tairens knew he and Rand had grown up together to suit him, and they seemed to think he was arm in arm with Rand whenever he was out of their sight. None of them would have gone near his own brother if he could channel. He did not know why they thought him a bigger fool.

"Didn't I say?" The plain-faced man squinted at his cards and scratched his head, then brightened. "Oh, yes. His proclamation, Mat. The Lord Dragon's. His last one. Where he said commoners had the right to call lords before a magistrate. Who ever heard of a lord being summoned to a magistrate? And for peasants!"

Mat's hand tightened on his purse until the coins inside grated together. "It would be a shame," he said quietly, "if you were tried and judged just for having your way with a fisherman's daughter whatever she wanted, or for having some farmer beaten for splashing mud on your cloak."

The others shifted uneasily, catching his mood, but Estean nodded, head bobbing so it seemed about to fall off. "Exactly. Though it wouldn't come to that, of course. A lord being tried before a magistrate? Of course not. Not really." He laughed drunkenly at his cards. "No fishermen's daughters. Smell of fish, you see, however you have them washed. A plump farm girl is best."

Mat told himself he was there to gamble. He told himself to ignore the fool's blather, reminded himself of how much gold he could take out of Estean's purse. His tongue did not listen, though. "Who knows what it might come to? Hangings, maybe."

Edorion gave him a sidelong look, guarded and uneasy. "Do we have to talk about . . . about commoners, Estean? What about old Astoril's daughters? Have you decided which you'll marry yet?"

"What? Oh. Oh, I'll flip a coin, I suppose." Estean frowned at his cards, shifted one, and frowned again. "Medore has two or three pretty maids. Perhaps Medore."

Mat took a long drink from his silver winecup to keep from hitting the man in his farmer's face. He was still on his first cup; the two servants had given up trying to add more. If he hit Estean, none of them would lift a hand to stop him. Not even Estean. Because he was the Lord Dragon's friend. He wished he was in a tavern somewhere out in the city, where some dockman might question his luck and only a quick tongue, or quick feet, or quick hands would see him leave with a whole skin. Now that *was* a fool thought.

Edorion glanced at Mat again, measuring his mood. "I heard a rumor today. I hear the Lord Dragon is taking us to war with Illian."

Mat gagged on his wine. "War?" he spluttered.

"War," Reimon agreed happily around his pipestem.

"Are you certain?" Carlomin said, and Baran added, "I've heard no rumors."

"I heard it just today, from three or four tongues." Edorion seemed to be absorbed in his cards. "Who can say how true it is?"

"It must be true," Reimon said. "With the Lord Dragon to lead us, holding *Callandor,* we'll not even have to fight. He will scatter their armies, and we will march straight into Illian. Too bad, in a way. Burn my soul if it isn't. I would like a chance to match swords with the Illianers."

"You'll get no chance with the Lord Dragon leading," Baran said. "They will fall on their knees as soon as they see the Dragon banner."

"And if they do not," Carlomin added with a laugh, "the Lord Dragon will blast them with lightning where they stand."

"Illian first," Reimon said. "And then. . . . Then we'll conquer the world for the Lord Dragon. You tell him I said so, Mat. The whole world."

Mat shook his head. A month gone, they would have been horrified by even the idea of a man who could channel, a man doomed to go mad and die horribly. Now they were ready to follow Rand into battle, and trust his power to win for them. Trust the Power, though it was not likely they would put it that way. Yet he supposed they had to find something to hang on to. The invincible Stone was in the hands of the Aiel. The Dragon Reborn was in his chambers a hundred feet above their heads, and *Callandor* was with him. Three thousand years of Tairen belief and history lay in ruins, and the world had been turned on its head. He wondered whether he had handled it any better; his own world had gone all askew in little more than a year. He rolled a gold Tairen crown across the backs of his fingers. However well he had done, he would not go back.

"When will we march, Mat?" Baran asked.

"I don't know," he said slowly. "I don't think Rand would start a war." Unless he had gone mad already. That hardly bore thinking about.

The others looked as if he had assured them the sun would not come up tomorrow.

"We are all loyal to the Lord Dragon, of course." Edorion frowned at his cards. "Out in the countryside, though. . . . I hear that some of the High Lords, a few, have been trying to raise an army to take back the Stone." Suddenly no one was looking at Mat, though Estean still seemed to be trying to make out his cards. "When the Lord Dragon takes us to war, of course, it will all melt away. In any case, we are loyal, here in the Stone. The High Lords, too, I am certain. It is only the few out in the countryside."

Their loyalty would not outlast their fear of the Dragon Reborn. For a moment Mat felt as though he were planning to abandon Rand in a pit of vipers. Then he remembered what Rand was. It was more like abandoning a weasel in a henyard. Rand had been a friend. The Dragon Reborn, though. . . . Who could be a friend to the Dragon Reborn? *I'm not abandoning anybody. He could probably pull the Stone down on their heads, if he wanted to. On my head, too.* He told himself again that it was time to be gone.

"No fishermen's daughters," Estean mumbled. "You will speak to the Lord Dragon?"

"It is your turn, Mat," Carlomin said anxiously. He looked half afraid, though what he feared—that Estean would anger Mat again, or that the talk might go back to loyalty—was impossible to say. "Will you buy the fifth card, or stack?"

Mat realized he had not been paying attention. Everyone but himself and Carlomin had five cards, though Reimon had neatly stacked his facedown beside the pot to show that he was out. Mat hesitated, pretending to think, then sighed and tossed another coin toward the pile.

As the silver crown bounced end over end, he suddenly felt luck grow from trickles to a flood. Every ping of silver against wooden tabletop rang clear in his head; he could have called face or sigil and known how the coin would land on any bounce. Just as he knew what his next card would be before Carlomin laid it in front of him.

Sliding his cards together on the table, he fanned them in one hand. The Ruler of Flames stared at him alongside the other four, the Amyrlin Seat balancing a flame on her palm, though she looked nothing like Siuan Sanche. However the Tairens felt about Aes Sedai, they acknowledged the power of Tar Valon, even if Flames was the lowest suit.

What were the odds of being dealt all five? His luck was best with random things, like dice, but perhaps a little more was beginning to rub off on cards. "The Light burn my bones to ash if it is not so," he muttered. Or that was what he meant to say.

"There," Estean all but shouted. "You cannot deny it this time. That was the Old Tongue. Something about burning, and bones." He grinned around the table. "My tutor would be proud. I ought to send him a gift. If I can find out where he went."

Nobles were supposed to be able to speak the Old Tongue, though in reality few knew more than Estean seemed to. The young lords set to arguing over exactly what Mat had said. They seemed to think it had been a comment on the heat.

Goose bumps pebbled Mat's skin as he tried to recall the words that had just come out of his mouth. A string of gibberish, yet it almost seemed he should understand. *Burn Moiraine! If she'd left me alone, I wouldn't have holes in my memory big enough for a wagon and team, and I wouldn't be spouting . . . whatever it bloody is!* He would also be milking his father's cows instead of walking the world with a pocketful of gold, but he managed to ignore that part of it.

"Are you here to gamble," he said harshly, "or babble like old women over their knitting!"

"To gamble," Baran said curtly. "Three crowns, gold!" He tossed the coins onto the pot.

"And three more besides." Estean hiccoughed and added six golden crowns to the pile.

Suppressing a grin, Mat forgot about the Old Tongue. It was easy enough; he did not want to think about it. Besides, if they were starting this strongly, he might win enough on this hand to leave in the morning. *And if he's crazy enough to start a war, I'll leave if I have to walk.*

Outside in the darkness, a cock crowed. Mat shifted uneasily and told himself not to be foolish. No one was going to die.

His eyes dropped to his cards—and blinked. The Amyrlin's flame had been replaced by a knife. While he was telling himself he was tired and seeing things, she plunged the tiny blade into the back of his hand.

With a hoarse yell, he flung the cards away and hurled himself backward, overturning his chair, kicking the table with both feet as he fell. The air seemed to thicken like honey. Everything moved as if time had slowed, but at the same time everything seemed to happen at once. Other cries echoed his, hollow shouts reverberating inside a cavern. He and the chair drifted back and down; the table floated upward.

The Ruler of Flames hung in the air, growing larger, staring at him with a cruel smile. Now close to life-size, she started to step out of the card; she was still a painted shape, with no depth, but she reached for him with her blade, red with his blood as if it had already been driven into his heart. Beside her the Ruler of Cups began to grow, the Tairen High Lord drawing his sword.

Mat floated, yet somehow he managed to reach the dagger in his left sleeve and hurl it in the same motion, straight for the Amyrlin's heart. If this thing had a heart. The second knife came into his left hand smoothly and left more smoothly. The two blades drifted through the air like thistledown. He wanted to scream, but that first yell of shock and outrage still filled his mouth. The Ruler of Rods was expanding beside the first two cards, the Queen of Andor gripping the rod like a bludgeon, her red-gold hair framing a madwoman's snarl.

He was still falling, still yelling that drawn-out yell. The Amyrlin was free of her card, the High Lord striding out with his sword. The flat shapes moved almost as slowly as he. Almost. He had proof the steel in their hands could cut, and no doubt the rod could crack a skull. His skull.

His thrown daggers moved as if sinking in jelly. He was sure the cock had crowed for him. Whatever his father said, the omen had been real. But he would not give up and die. Somehow he had two more daggers out from under his coat, one in either hand. Struggling to twist in midair, to get his feet under him, he threw one knife at the golden-haired figure with the bludgeon. The other he held on to as he tried to turn himself, to land ready to face. . . .

The world lurched back into normal motion, and he landed awkwardly on his side, hard enough to drive the wind out of him. Desperately he struggled to his feet, drawing another knife from under his coat. You could not carry too many, Thom claimed. Neither was needed.

For a moment he thought cards and figures had vanished. Or maybe he had imagined it all. Maybe he was the one going mad. Then he saw the cards, back to ordinary size, pinned to one of the dark wood panels by his still quivering knives. He took a deep, ragged breath.

The table lay on its side, coins still spinning across the floor where lordlings and servants crouched among scattered cards. They gaped at Mat and his knives, those in his hands and those in the wall, with equally wide eyes. Estean snatched a silver pitcher that had somehow escaped being overturned and began pouring wine down his throat, the excess spilling over his chin and down his chest.

"Just because you do not have the cards to win," Edorion said hoarsely, "there is no need to—" He cut off with a shudder.

"You saw it, too." Mat slipped the knives back into their sheaths. A thin trickle of blood ran down the back of his hand from the tiny wound. "Don't pretend you went blind!"

"I saw nothing," Reimon said woodenly. "Nothing!" He began crawling across the floor, gathering up gold and silver, concentrating on the coins as if they were the most important thing in the world. The others were doing the same, except Estean, who scrambled about checking the fallen pitchers for any that still held wine. One of the servants had his face hidden in his hands; the other, eyes closed, was apparently praying in a low, breathless whine.

With a muttered oath, Mat strode to where his knives pinned the three cards to the panel. They were only playing cards again, just stiff paper with the clear lacquer cracked. But the figure of the Amyrlin still held a dagger instead of a flame. He tasted blood and realized he was sucking the cut in the back of his hand.

Hastily he wrenched his knives free, tearing each card in half before tucking the blade away. After a moment, he hunted through the cards littering the floor until he found the rulers of Coins and Winds, and tore them across, too. He felt a little foolish—it was over and done with; the cards were just cards again—but he could not help it.

None of the young lords crawling about on hands and knees tried to stop him. They scrambled out of his way, not even glancing at him. There would be no more gambling tonight, and maybe not for some nights to come. At least, not with him. Whatever had happened, it had been aimed at him, clearly. Even more clearly, it had to have been done with the One Power. They wanted no part of that.

"Burn you, Rand!" he muttered under his breath. "If you have to go mad, leave me out of it!" His pipe lay in two pieces, the stem bitten through cleanly. Angrily he grabbed his purse from the floor and stalked out of the room.

In his darkened bedchamber Rand tossed uneasily on a bed wide enough for five people. He was dreaming.

Through a shadowy forest Moiraine was prodding him with a sharp stick toward where the Amyrlin Seat waited, sitting on a stump with a rope halter for his neck in her hands. Dim shapes moved half-seen through the trees, stalking, hunting him; here a dagger blade flashed in the failing light, over there he caught a glimpse of ropes ready for binding. Slender and not as tall as his shoulder, Moiraine wore an expression he had never seen on her face. Fear. Sweating, she prodded harder, trying to hurry him to the Amyrlin's halter. Darkfriends and the Forsaken in the shadows, the White Tower's leash ahead and Moiraine behind. Dodging Moiraine's stick, he fled.

"It is too late for that," she called after him, but he had to get back. Back.

Muttering, he thrashed on the bed, then was still, breathing more easily for a moment.

He was in the Waterwood back home, sunlight slanting through the trees to sparkle on the pond in front of him. There was green moss on the rocks at this end of the pond, and thirty paces away at the other end a small arc of wildflowers. This was where, as a child, he had learned to swim.

"You should have a swim now."

He spun around with a start. Min stood there, grinning at him in her boy's coat and breeches, and next to her, Elayne, with her red-golden curls, in a green silk gown fit for her mother's palace.

It was Min who had spoken, but Elayne added, "The water looks inviting, Rand. No one will bother us here."

"I don't know," he began slowly. Min cut him off by twining her fingers behind his neck and pulling herself up on tiptoe to kiss him.

She repeated Elayne's words in a soft murmur. "No one will bother us here." She stepped back and doffed her coat, then attacked the laces of her shirt.

Rand stared, the more so when he realized Elayne's gown was lying on the mossy ground. The Daughter-Heir was bending, arms crossed, gathering up the hem of her shift.

"What are you doing?" he demanded in a strangled voice.

"Getting ready to go swimming with you," Min replied.

Elayne flashed him a smile, and hoisted the shift over her head.

He turned his back hastily, though half wanting not to. And found himself staring at Egwene, her big, dark eyes looking back at him sadly. Without a word she turned and vanished into the trees.

"Wait!" he shouted after her. "I can explain."

He began to run; he had to find her. But as he reached the edge of trees, Min's voice stopped him.

"Don't go, Rand."

She and Elayne were in the water already, only their heads showing as they swam lazily in the middle of the pond.

"Come back," Elayne called, lifting a slim arm to beckon. "Do you not deserve what you want for a change?"

He shifted his feet, wanting to move but unable to decide which way. What he wanted. The words sounded strange. What did he want? He raised a hand to his face, to wipe away what felt like sweat. Festering flesh almost obliterated the heron branded on his palm; white bone showed through red-edged gaps.

With a jerk, he came awake, lying there shivering in the dark heat. Sweat soaked his smallclothes, and the linen sheets beneath his back. His side burned, where an old wound had never healed properly. He traced the rough scar, a circle nearly an inch across, still tender after all this time. Even Moiraine's Aes Sedai Healing could not mend it completely. *But I'm not rotting yet. And I'm not mad, either. Not yet.* Not yet. That said it all. He wanted to laugh, and wondered if that meant he was a little mad already.

Dreaming about Min and Elayne, dreaming of them like that. . . . Well, it was not madness, but it was surely foolishness. Neither one of them had ever looked at him in that way when he was awake. Egwene he had been all but promised to since they were both children. The betrothal words had never been spoken in front of the Women's Circle, but everyone in and around Emond's Field knew they would marry one day.

That one day would never come, of course; not now, not with the fate that lay ahead of a man who channeled. Egwene must have realized that, too. She must have. She was all wrapped up in becoming Aes Sedai. Still, women were odd; she might think she could be an Aes Sedai and marry him anyway, channeling or no channeling. How could he tell her that he did not want to marry her anymore, that he loved her like a sister? But there would not be any need to tell her, he was sure. He could hide behind what he was. She had to understand that. What man could ask a woman to marry him when he knew he had only a few years, if he was lucky, before he went insane, before he began to rot alive? He shivered despite the heat.

I need sleep. The High Lords would be back in the morning, maneuvering for his favor. For the Dragon Reborn's favor. *Maybe I won't dream, this time.* He started to roll over, searching for a dry place on the sheets—and froze, listening to small rustlings in the darkness. He was not alone.

The Sword That Is Not a Sword lay across the room, beyond his reach, on a thronelike stand the High Lords had given him, no doubt in the hopes he would keep *Callandor* out of their sight. *Someone wanting to steal* Callandor. A second thought came. *Or to kill the Dragon Reborn.* He did not need Thom's whispered warnings to know that the High Lords' professions of undying loyalty were only words of necessity.

He emptied himself of thought and emotions, assuming the Void; that much came without effort. Floating in the cold emptiness within himself, thought and emotion outside, he reached for the True Source. This time he touched it easily, which was not always the case.

Saidin filled him like a torrent of white heat and light, exalting him with life, sickening him with the foulness of the Dark One's taint, like a

skim of sewage floating on pure, sweet water. The torrent threatened
to wash him away, burn him up, engulf him.

Fighting the flood, he mastered it by bare effort of will and rolled
from the bed, channeling the Power as he landed on his feet in the
stance to begin the sword-form called Apple Blossoms in the Wind. His
enemies could not be many or they would have made more noise; the
gently named form was meant for use against more than one opponent.

As his feet hit the carpet, a sword was in his hands, with a long hilt
and a slightly curved blade sharp on only one edge. It looked to have
been wrought from flame yet it did not feel even warm. The figure of a
heron stood black against the yellow-red of the blade. In the same
instant every candle and gilded lamp burst alight, small mirrors behind
them swelling the illumination. Larger mirrors on the walls and two
stand-mirrors reflected it further, until he could have read comfortably
anywhere in the large room.

Callandor sat undisturbed, a sword seemingly of glass, hilt and blade,
on a stand as tall as a man and just as wide, the wood ornately carved
and gilded and set with precious stones. The furnishings, too, were all
gilded and begemmed, bed and chairs and benches, wardrobes and
chests and washstand. The pitcher and bowl were golden Sea Folk
porcelain, as thin as leaves. The broad Tarabon carpet, in scrolls of
scarlet and gold and blue, could have fed an entire village for months.
Almost every flat surface held more delicate Sea Folk porcelain, or else
goblets and bowls and ornaments of gold worked with silver, and silver
chased with gold. On the broad marble mantel over the fireplace, two
silver wolves with ruby eyes tried to pull down a golden stag a good
three feet tall. Draperies of scarlet silk embroidered with eagles in
thread-of-gold hung at the narrow windows, stirring slightly in a failing
wind. Books lay wherever there was room, leather-bound, wood-bound,
some tattered and still dusty from the deepest shelves of the Stone's
library.

Now, where he had thought to see assassins, or thieves, one beautiful
young woman stood hesitant and surprised in the middle of the carpet,
black hair falling in shining waves to her shoulders. Her thin, white silk
robe emphasized more than it hid. Berelain, ruler of the city-state of
Mayene, was the last person he had expected.

After one wide-eyed start, she made a deep, graceful curtsy that
drew her garments tight. "I am unarmed, my Lord Dragon. I submit
myself to your search, if you doubt me." Her smile suddenly made him
uncomfortably aware that he wore nothing but his smallclothes.

I'll be burned if she makes me scramble around trying to cover myself.

The thought floated beyond the Void. *I didn't ask her to walk in on me. To sneak in!* Anger and embarrassment drifted along the borders of emptiness too, but his face reddened all the same; dimly he was aware of it, aware of the knowledge deepening the flush in his cheeks. So coldly calm within the Void; outside. . . . He could feel each individual droplet of sweat sliding down his chest and back. It took a real effort of stubborn will to stand there under her eyes. *Search her? The Light help me!*

Relaxing his stance, he let the sword vanish but held the narrow flow connecting him to *saidin*. It was like drinking from a hole in a dike when the whole long mound of earth wanted to give way, the water sweet as honeyed wine and sickening as a rivulet through a midden.

He did not know much of this woman, except that she walked through the Stone as if it were her palace in Mayene. Thom said the First of Mayene asked questions constantly, of everyone. Questions about Rand. Which might have been natural, given what he was, but they made him no easier in his mind. And she had not returned to Mayene. That was not natural. She had been held captive in all but name for months, until his arrival, cut off from her throne and the ruling of her small nation. Most people would have taken the first opportunity to get away from a man who could channel.

"What are you doing here?" He knew he sounded harsh, and did not care. "There were Aiel guarding that door when I went to sleep. How did you come past them?"

Berelain's lips curved up a trifle more; to Rand it seemed the room had gotten suddenly even hotter. "They passed me through immediately, when I said I had been summoned by the Lord Dragon."

"Summoned? I didn't summon anybody." *Stop this,* he told himself. *She's a queen, or the next thing to it. You know as much about the ways of queens as you do about flying.* He tried to make himself be civil, only he did not know what to call the First of Mayene. "My Lady . . ." That would have to do. ". . . why would I summon you at this time of night?"

She gave a low, rich laugh, deep in her throat; even wrapped in emotionless emptiness it seemed to tickle his skin, make the hairs stir on his arms and legs. Suddenly he took in her clinging garb as if for the first time, and felt himself go red all over again. *She can't mean. . . . Can she? Light, I've never said two words to her before.*

"Perhaps I wish to talk, my Lord Dragon." She let the pale robe fall to the floor, revealing an even thinner white silk garment he could only call a nightgown. It left her smooth shoulders completely bare, and exposed a considerable expanse of pale bosom. He found himself wondering distantly what held it up. It was difficult not to stare. "You are a long way from your home, like me. The nights especially seem lonely."

"Tomorrow, I will be happy to talk with you."

"But during the day, people surround you. Petitioners. High Lords. Aiel." She gave a shiver; he told himself he really ought to look away, but he could as easily have stopped breathing. He had never before been so aware of his own reactions when wrapped in the Void. "The Aiel frighten me, and I do not like Tairen lords of any sort."

About the Tairens he could believe her, but he did not think anything frightened this woman. *Burn me, she's in a strange man's bedchamber in the middle of the night, only half-dressed, and I'm the one who's jumpy as a cat in a dog run, Void or no.* It was time to put an end to things before they went too far.

"It would be better if you return to your own bedchamber, my Lady." Part of him wanted to tell her to put on a cloak, too. A thick cloak. Part of him did. "It. . . . It is really too late for talking. Tomorrow. In daylight."

She gave him a slanted, quizzical look. "Have you absorbed stuffy Tairen ways already, my Lord Dragon? Or is this reticence something from your Two Rivers? We are not so . . . formal . . . in Mayene."

"My Lady. . . ." He tried to sound formal; if she did not like formality, that was what he wanted. "I am promised to Egwene al'Vere, my Lady."

"You mean the Aes Sedai, my Lord Dragon? If she really is Aes Sedai. She is quite young—perhaps too young—to wear the ring and the shawl." Berelain spoke as if Egwene were a child, though she herself could not be more than a year older than Rand, if that, and he had only a little over two years on Egwene. "My Lord Dragon, I do not mean to come between you. Marry her, if she is Green Ajah. I would never aspire to wed the Dragon Reborn himself. Forgive me if I overstep myself, but I told you we are not so . . . formal in Mayene. May I call you Rand?"

Rand surprised himself by sighing regretfully. There had been a glint in her eye, a slight shift of expression, gone quickly, when she mentioned marrying the Dragon Reborn. If she had not considered it before, she had now. The Dragon Reborn, not Rand al'Thor; the man of prophecy, not the shepherd from the Two Rivers. He was not shocked, exactly; some girls back home mooned over whoever proved himself fastest or strongest in the games at Bel Tine and Sunday, and now and again a woman set her eyes on the man with the richest fields or the largest flocks. It would have been good to think she wanted Rand al'Thor. "It is time for you to go, my Lady," he said quietly.

She stepped closer. "I can feel your eyes on me, Rand." Her voice was smoky heat. "I am no village girl tied to her mother's apron, and I know you want—"

"Do you think I'm made of stone, woman?" She jumped at his roar, but the next instant she was crossing the carpet, reaching for him, her eyes dark pools that could pull a man into their depths.

"Your arms look as strong as stone. If you think you must be harsh with me, then be harsh, so long as you hold me." Her hands touched his face; sparks seemed to leap from her fingers.

Without thinking he channeled the flows still linked to him, and suddenly she was staggering back, eyes wide with startlement, as if a wall of air pushed her. It was air, he realized; he did things without knowing what he was doing more often than he did know. At least, once done, he could usually remember how to do them again.

The unseen, moving wall scraped ripples along the carpet, sweeping along Berelain's discarded robe, a boot he had tossed aside undressing, and a red leather footstool supporting an open volume of Eban Vandes's *The History of the Stone of Tear,* pushing them along as it forced her almost to the wall, fenced her in. Safely away from him. He tied off the flow—that was all he could think to call what he did—and no longer needed to maintain the shield himself. For a moment he studied what he had done, until he was sure he could repeat it. It looked useful, especially the tying off.

Dark eyes still wide, Berelain felt along the confines of her invisible prison with trembling hands. Her face was almost as white as her skimpy silk shift. Footstool, boot and book lay at her feet, jumbled with the robe.

"Much as I regret it," he told her, "we will not speak again, except in public, my Lady." He really did regret it. Whatever her motives, she was beautiful. *Burn me, I* am *a fool!* He was not sure how he meant that —for thinking of her beauty, or for sending her away. "In fact, it is best you arrange your journey back to Mayene as soon as possible. I prom-ise you that Tear will not trouble Mayene again. You have my word." It was a promise good only for his lifetime, perhaps only as long as he stood in the Stone, but he had to offer her something. A bandage for wounded pride, a gift to take her mind off being afraid.

But her fear was already under control, on the outside, at least. Honesty and openness filled her face, all efforts at allure gone. "For-give me. I have handled this badly. I did not mean to offend. In my country, a woman may speak her mind to a man freely, or he to her. Rand, you must know that you are a handsome man, tall and strong. I would be the one made of stone, if I did not see it, and admire. Please do not send me away from you. I will beg it, if you wish." She knelt smoothly, like a dance. Her expression still said she was being open, confessing everything, but on the other hand, in kneeling she had managed to tug her already precarious gown down until it looked in real danger of falling off. "Please, Rand?"

Even sheltered in emptiness as he was, he gaped at her, and it had nothing to do with her beauty or her near undress. Well, only partly. If the Defenders of the Stone had been half as determined as this woman, half as steadfast in purpose, ten thousand Aiel could never have taken the Stone.

"I am flattered, my Lady," he said diplomatically. "Believe me, I am. But it would not be fair to you. I cannot give you what you deserve." *And let her make of that what she will.*

Outside in the darkness, a cock crowed.

To Rand's surprise, Berelain suddenly stared past him, eyes as big as teacups. Her mouth dropped open, and her slim throat corded with a scream that would not come. He spun, the yellow-red sword flashing back into his hands.

Across the room, one of the stand-mirrors threw his reflection back at him, a tall young man with reddish hair and gray eyes, wearing only white linen smallclothes and holding a sword carved from fire. The reflection stepped out onto the carpet, raising its sword.

I have gone mad. Thought drifted on the borders of the Void. *No! She saw it. It's real!*

Movement to his left caught the corner of his eye. He twisted before he could think, sword sweeping up in The Moon Rises Over Water. The blade slashed through the shape—his shape—climbing out of a mirror on the wall. The form wavered, broke up like dust motes floating on air, vanished. Rand's reflection appeared in the mirror again, but even as it did, it put hands on the mirror frame. He was aware of movement in mirrors all around the room.

Desperately, he stabbed at the mirror. Silvered glass shattered, yet it seemed that the image shattered first. He thought he heard a distant scream inside his head, his own voice screaming, fading. Even as shards of mirror fell, he lashed out with the One Power. Every mirror in the room exploded silently, fountaining glass across the carpet. The dying scream in his head echoed again and again, sending shivers down his back. It was his voice; he could hardly believe it was not himself who made the sounds.

He spun back to face the one that had gotten out, just in time to meet its attack, Unfolding the Fan to counter Stones Falling Down the Mountain. The figure leaped back, and suddenly Rand realized it was not alone. As quickly as he had smashed the mirrors, two more reflections had escaped. Now they stood facing him, three duplicates of himself down to the puckered round scar on his side, all staring at him, faces twisted with hatred and contempt, with a strange hunger. Only their eyes seemed empty, lifeless. Before he could take a breath, they rushed at him.

Rand stepped sideways, pieces of broken mirror slicing his feet, ever sideways, from stance to stance and form to form, trying to face only one at a time. He used everything Lan, Moiraine's Warder, had taught him of the sword in their daily practice.

Had the three fought together, had they supported one another, he would have died in the first minute, but each fought him alone, as if the others did not exist. Even so, he could not stop their blades entirely; in minutes blood ran down the side of his face, his chest, his arms. The old wound tore open, adding its flow to stain his smallclothes with red. They had his skill as well as his face, and they were three to his one. Chairs and tables toppled; priceless Sea Folk porcelain shattered on the carpet.

He felt his strength ebbing. None of his cuts was major by itself, except the old wound, but all together. . . . He never thought of calling for help from the Aiel outside his door. The thick walls would stifle even a death scream. Whatever was done, he must do alone. He fought wrapped in the cold emotionlessness of the Void, but fear scraped at its boundaries like wind-lashed branches scratching a window in the night.

His blade slipped past its opponent to slash across a face just below the eyes—he could not help wincing; it was his face—its owner sliding back just far enough to avoid a killing cut. Blood welled from the gash, veiling mouth and chin in dark crimson, but the ruined face did not change expression, and its empty eyes never flickered. It wanted him dead the way a starving man wanted food.

Can anything kill them? All three bled from the wounds he had managed to inflict, but bleeding did not seem to slow them as he knew it was slowing him. They tried to avoid his sword, but did not appear to realize they had been hurt. *If they have been,* he thought grimly. *Light, if they bleed, they can be hurt! They must!*

He needed a respite, a moment to catch his breath, to gather himself. Suddenly he leaped away from them, onto the bed, rolling across its width. He sensed rather than saw blades slashing the sheets, barely missing his flesh. Staggering, he landed on his feet, caught at a small table to steady himself. The shining, gold-worked silver bowl on the table wobbled. One of his doubles had climbed onto the torn bed, kicking goose feathers as it padded across warily, sword at the ready. The other two came slowly around, still ignoring each other, intent only on him. Their eyes glistened like glass.

Rand shuddered as pain stabbed his hand on the table. An image of himself, no more than six inches tall, drew back its small sword. Instinctively, he grabbed the figure before it could stab again. It writhed in his grip, baring teeth at him. He became aware of small movements all around the room, of small reflections by the score stepping out of polished silver. His hand began to numb, to grow cold, as if the thing were sucking the warmth out of his flesh. The heat of *saidin* swelled inside him; a rushing filled his head, and the heat flowed into his icy hand.

Suddenly the small figure burst like a bubble, and he felt something flow into him—from the bursting—some little portion of his lost strength. He jerked as tiny jolts of vitality seemed to pelt him.

When he raised his head—wondering why he was not dead—the small reflections he had half-glimpsed were gone. The three larger stood wavering, as if his gain in strength had been their loss. Yet as he looked up, they steadied on their feet and came on, if more cautiously.

He backed away, thinking furiously, sword threatening first one and then another. If he continued to fight them as he had been, they would kill him sooner or later. He knew that as surely as he knew he was bleeding. But something linked the reflections. Absorbing the small one—the far-off thought made him queasy, but that was what it had been—had not only brought the others with it, it had also affected the bigger, for a moment at least. If he could do the same to one of them, it might destroy all three.

Even thinking of absorbing them made him vaguely aware of wanting to empty his stomach, but he did not know another way. *I don't know this way. How did I do it? Light, what did I do?* He had to grapple with one of them, to touch it at least; he was somehow sure of that. But if he tried to get that close, he would have three blades through him in as many heartbeats. *Reflections. How much are they still reflections?*

Hoping he was not being a fool—if he was, he might well be a dead one—he let his sword vanish. He was ready to bring it back on the instant, but when his carved-fire blade winked out of existence, the others' did, too. For a moment, confusion painted three copies of his face, one a bloody ruin. But before he could seize one of them, they leaped for him, all four crashing to the floor in a tangle of grappling limbs, rolling across the glass-littered carpet.

Cold soaked into Rand. Numbness crept along his limbs, through his bones, until he barely felt the shards of mirror, the slivers of porcelain grinding into his flesh. Something close to panic flickered across the emptiness surrounding him. He might have made a fatal mistake. They were larger than the one he had absorbed, and they were drawing more heat from him. And not only heat. As he grew colder, the glassy gray eyes staring into his took on life. With chill certainty he knew that if he died, that would not end the struggle. The three would turn on one another until only one remained, and that one would have his life, his memories, would *be* him.

Stubbornly he fought, struggling harder the weaker he became. He pulled on *saidin,* trying to fill himself with its heat. Even the stomach-turning taint was welcome, for the more of it he felt, the more *saidin* suffused him. If his stomach could rebel, then he was still alive, and if he lived, he could fight. *But how? How? What did I do before? Saidin* raged through him till it seemed that if he survived his attackers, he would only be consumed by the Power. *How did I do it?* All he could do was pull at *saidin,* and try . . . reach . . . strain. . . .

One of the three vanished—Rand felt it slide into him; it was as if he had fallen from a height, flat onto stony ground—and then the other two together. The impact flung him onto his back, where he lay staring up at the worked plaster ceiling with its gilded bosses, lay luxuriating in the fact that he was still breathing.

The Power still swelled in every crevice of his being. He wanted to spew up every meal he had ever eaten. He felt so alive that, by comparison, life not soaked in *saidin* was living a shadow. He could smell the beeswax of the candles, and the oil in the lamps. He could feel every fiber of the carpet against his back. He could feel every gash in his flesh, every cut, every nick, every bruise. But he held on to *saidin.*

One of the Forsaken had tried to kill him. Or all of them had. It must have been that, unless the Dark One was free already, in which case he did not think he would have faced anything as easy or as simple as this. So he held his link to the True Source. *Unless I did it myself. Can I hate what I am enough to try to kill myself? Without even knowing it? Light, I have to learn to control it. I have to!*

Painfully, he pushed himself up. Leaving bloody footprints on the carpet, he limped to the stand where *Callandor* rested. Blood from hundreds of cuts covered him. He lifted the sword, and its glassy length glowed with the Power flowing into it. The Sword That Is Not a Sword. That blade, apparently glass, would cut as well as the finest steel, yet *Callandor* truly was not a sword, but instead a remnant of the Age of Legends, a *sa'angreal*. With the aid of one of the relatively few *angreal* known to have survived the War of the Shadow and Breaking of the World, it was possible to channel flows of the One Power that would have burned the channeler to ash without it. With one of the even rarer *sa'angreal*, the flows could be increased as much over those possible with an *angreal* as an *angreal* increased them over channeling naked. And *Callandor*, usable only by a man, linked to the Dragon Reborn through three thousand years of legend and prophecy, was one of the most powerful *sa'angreal* ever made. Holding *Callandor* in his hands, he could level a city's walls at a blow. Holding *Callandor* in his hands, he could face even one of the Forsaken. *It* was *them. It must have been.*

Abruptly he realized he had not heard a sound from Berelain. Half fearing to see her dead, he turned.

Still kneeling, she flinched. She had donned her robe again, and hugged it around her like steel armor, or stone walls. Face as white as snow, she licked her lips. "Which one are . . . ?" She swallowed and began again. "Which one . . . ?" She could not finish it.

"I am the only one there is," he said gently. "The one you were treating as if we were betrothed." He meant it to soothe her, perhaps make her smile—surely a woman as strong as she had shown herself to be could smile, even facing a blood-drenched man—but she bent forward, pressing her face to the floor.

"I apologize humbly for having most grievously offended you, Lord Dragon." Her breathy voice did sound humble, and frightened. Completely unlike herself. "I beg you to forget my offense, and forgive. I will not bother you again. I swear it, my Lord Dragon. On my mother's name and under the Light, I swear it."

He loosed the knotted flow; the invisible wall confining her became a momentary stir that ruffled her robe. "There is nothing to forgive," he said wearily. He felt very tired. "Go as you wish."

She straightened hesitantly, stretched out a hand, and gave a relieved gasp when it encountered nothing. Gathering the skirts of her robe, she began to pick her way across the glass-littered carpet, shards grating under her velvet slippers. Short of the door, she stopped, facing him with an obvious effort. Her eyes could not quite meet his. "I will send the Aiel in to you, if you wish. I could send for one of the Aes Sedai to tend your wounds."

She would as soon be in a room with a Myrddraal, now, or the Dark One himself, but she's no milksop. "Thank you," he said quietly, "but no. I would appreciate it if you told no one what happened here. Not yet. I will do what needs to be done." *It* had *to be the Forsaken.*

"As my Lord Dragon commands." She gave him a tight curtsy and hurried out, perhaps afraid he might change his mind about letting her go.

"As soon the Dark One himself," he murmured as the door closed behind her.

Limping to the foot of the bed, he lowered himself into the chest there and laid *Callandor* across his knees, bloody hands resting on the glowing blade. With that in his hands, even one of the Forsaken would fear him. In a moment he would send for Moiraine to Heal his wounds. In a moment he would speak to the Aiel outside, and become the Dragon Reborn again. But for now, he only wanted to sit, and remember a shepherd named Rand al'Thor.

CHAPTER
3

Reflection

Despite the hour, a good many people were hurrying through the Stone's wide corridors, a steady trickle of men and women in the black and gold of Stone servants or the livery of one High Lord or another. Now and again a Defender or two appeared, bareheaded and unarmed, some with their coats undone. The servants bowed or curtsied to Perrin and Faile if they came close, then hurried on with hardly a pause. Most of the soldiers gave a start on seeing them. Some bowed stiffly, hand to heart, but one and all quickened their steps as if eager to be away.

Only one lamp in three or four was lit. In the dim stretches between their tall stands, shadows blurred the hanging tapestries and obscured the occasional chest against the wall. For any eyes but Perrin's, they did. His eyes glowed like burnished gold in those murky lengths of hall. He walked quickly from lamp to lamp and kept his gaze down unless he was in full light. Most people in the Stone knew about his strangely colored eyes, one way or another. None of them mentioned it, of course. Even Faile seemed to assume the color was part of his association with an Aes Sedai, something that simply was, to be accepted but never explained. Even so, a prickling always ran across his back whenever he realized that a stranger had seen his eyes shining in the dark.

When they held their tongues, the silence only emphasized his apart-
ness.

"I wish they wouldn't look at me like that," he muttered as a grizzled
Defender twice his age came close to running once he had passed. "As
though they are afraid of me. They haven't before; not this way. Why
aren't all these people in bed?" A woman carrying a mop and a bucket
bobbed a curtsy and scurried by with her head down.

Her arm twined through his, Faile glanced at him. "I would say the
guards are not supposed to be in this part of the Stone unless they are
on duty. A good time to cuddle a maid on a lord's chair, and maybe
pretend they are the lord and lady, while lord and lady are asleep. They
are probably worried that you might report them. And servants do
most of their work at night. Who would want them underfoot, sweeping and dusting and polishing, in daylight?"

Perrin nodded doubtfully. He supposed she would know about such
things from her father's house. A successful merchant likely had servants, and guards for his wagons. At least these folk were not out of
their beds because what had happened to him had happened to them,
too. If that were the case, they would be out of the Stone altogether,
and likely still running. But why had he been a target, singled out, as it
seemed? He was not looking forward to confronting Rand, but he had
to know. Faile had to stretch her stride to keep up with him.

For all its splendor, all the gold and fine carving and inlays, the
interior of the Stone had been designed for war as much as its exterior
had been. Murderholes dotted the ceiling wherever corridors crossed.
Never-used arrowslits peeked into the halls at places where they might
cover an entire hallway. He and Faile climbed narrow, curving staircase
after narrow, curving staircase, all built into the walls or else enclosed,
with more arrowslits looking down on the corridor below. None of this
design had hampered the Aiel, of course, the first enemy ever to get
beyond the outer wall.

As they trotted up one of the winding stairs—Perrin did not realize
they were trotting, though he would have been moving faster if not for
Faile on his arm—he caught a whiff of old sweat and a hint of sickly-
sweet perfume, but they registered only in the back of his brain. He was
caught up in what he was going to say to Rand. *Why did you try to kill
me? Are you going mad already?* There was no easy way to ask, and he
did not expect easy answers.

Stepping out into a shadowed corridor nearly at the top of the Stone,
he found himself staring at the backs of a High Lord and two of the
nobleman's personal guards. Only the Defenders were allowed to wear

armor inside the Stone, but these three had swords at their hips. That was not unusual, of course, but their presence here, on this floor, in the shadows, staring intently at the bright light at the far end of the hall, that was not usual at all. That light came from the anteroom in front of the chambers Rand had been given. Or taken. Or maybe been pushed into by Moiraine.

Perrin and Faile had made no effort to be quiet in climbing the stairs, but the three men were so intent in their watching that none of them noticed the new arrivals at first. Then one of the blue-coated bodyguards twisted his head as if working a cramp in his neck; his mouth dropped open when he saw them. Biting off an oath, the fellow whirled to face Perrin, baring a good hand of his swordblade. The other was only a heartbeat slower. Both stood tensed, ready, but their eyes shifted uneasily, sliding off Perrin's. They gave off a sour smell of fear. So did the High Lord, though he had his fear tightly reined.

The High Lord Torean, white streaking his dark, pointed beard, moved languidly, as if at a ball. Pulling a too sweetly scented handkerchief from his sleeve, he dabbed at a knobby nose that appeared not at all large when compared with his ears. A fine silk coat with red satin cuffs only exaggerated the plainness of his face. He eyed Perrin's shirt-sleeves and dabbed his nose again before inclining his head slightly. "The Light illumine you," he said politely. His glance touched Perrin's yellow stare and flinched away, though his expression did not change. "You are well, I trust?" Perhaps too politely.

Perrin did not really care for the man's tone, but the way Torean looked Faile up and down, with a sort of casual interest, clenched his fists. He managed to keep his voice level, though. "The Light illumine you, High Lord Torean. I am glad to see you helping keep watch over the Lord Dragon. Some men in your place might resent him being here."

Torean's thin eyebrows twitched. "Prophecy has been fulfilled, and Tear has fulfilled its place in that prophecy. Perhaps the Dragon Reborn will lead Tear to a still greater destiny. What man could resent that? But it is late. A good night to you." He eyed Faile again, pursing his lips, and walked off down the hall just a bit too briskly, away from the anteroom's lights. His bodyguards heeled him like well-trained dogs.

"There was no need for you to be uncivil," Faile said in a tight voice when the High Lord was out of hearing. "You sounded as if your tongue were frozen iron. If you do intend to remain here, you had better learn to get on with the lords."

"He was looking at you as if he wanted to dandle you on his knee. And I do not mean like a father."

She sniffed dismissively. "He is not the first man ever to look at me. If he found the nerve to try more, I could put him in his place with a frown and a glance. I do not need you to speak for me, Perrin Aybara." Still, she did not sound entirely displeased.

Scratching his beard, he peered after Torean, watching the High Lord and his guards vanish around a distant corner. He wondered how the Tairen lords managed without sweating to death. "Did you notice, Faile? His heel-hounds did not take their hands off their swords until he was ten paces clear of us."

She frowned at him, then down the hall after the three, and nodded slowly. "You're right. But I do not understand. They do not bow and scrape the way they do for *him,* but everyone walks as warily around you and Mat as they do around the Aes Sedai."

"Maybe being a friend of the Dragon Reborn isn't as much protection as it used to be."

She did not suggest leaving again, not in words, but her eyes were full of it. He was more successful in ignoring the unspoken suggestion than he had been with the spoken.

Before they reached the end of the hallway, Berelain came hurrying out of the bright lights of the anteroom, clutching a thin white robe tightly around her with both arms. If the First of Mayene had been walking any faster, she would have been running.

To show Faile he could be as civil as she could possibly wish, Perrin swept a bow that he wagered even Mat could not have bettered. By contrast, Faile's curtsy was the barest nod of her head, the merest bending of a knee. He hardly noticed. As Berelain rushed past them without a glance, the smell of fear, rank and raw as a festering wound, made his nostrils twitch. Beside this, Torean's fear was nothing. This was mad panic tied with a frayed rope. He straightened slowly, staring after her.

"Filling your eyes?" Faile asked softly.

Intent on Berelain, wondering what had driven her so near the brink, he spoke without thinking. "She smelled of—"

Far down the corridor, Torean suddenly stepped out of a side hallway to seize Berelain's arm. He was talking a torrent, but Perrin could not make out more than a handful of scattered words, something about her overstepping herself in her pride, and something else that seemed to be Torean offering her his protection. Her reply was short, sharp, and even more inaudible, delivered with lifted chin. Pulling herself free roughly, the First of Mayene walked away, back straight and seemingly more in command of herself. On the point of following, Torean saw Perrin watching. Dabbing at his nose with his handkerchief, the High Lord vanished back into the crossing corridor.

"I do not care if she smelled of the Essence of Dawn," Faile said darkly. "That one is not interested in hunting a bear, however fine his hide would look stretched on a wall. She hunts the sun."

He frowned at her. "The sun? A bear? What are you talking about?"

"You go on by yourself. I think I will go to my bed after all."

"If that's what you want," he said slowly, "but I thought you were as eager to find out what happened as I am."

"I think not. I'll not pretend I am eager to meet the . . . Rand . . . not after avoiding it until now. And now I am especially not eager. No doubt the two of you will have a fine talk without me. Especially if there's wine."

"You don't make any sense," he muttered, scrubbing a hand through his hair. "If you want to go to bed, then fine, but I wish you would say something I understand."

For a long moment she studied his face, then suddenly bit her lip. He thought she was trying not to laugh. "Oh, Perrin, sometimes I believe it is your innocence I enjoy most of all." Sure enough, traces of laughter silvered her voice. "You go on to . . . to your friend and tell me of it in the morning. As much as you want to." She pulled his head down to brush his lips with a kiss and, as quick as the kiss, ran back down the hallway.

Shaking his head, he watched until she turned in to the stairs with no sign of Torean. Sometimes it was as if she spoke another language. He headed toward the lights.

The anteroom was a round chamber fifty paces or more across. A hundred gilded lamps hung on golden chains from its high ceiling. Polished redstone columns made an inner ring, and the floor appeared to be one huge slab of black marble, streaked with gold. It had been the anteroom of the king's chambers, in the days when Tear had kings, before Artur Hawkwing put everything from the Spine of the World to the Aryth Ocean under one king. The Tairen kings had not returned when Hawkwing's empire collapsed, and for a thousand years the only inhabitants of these apartments had been mice tracking through dust. No High Lord had ever had enough power to dare claim them for his own.

A ring of fifty Defenders stood rigidly in the middle of the room, breastplates and rimmed helmets gleaming, spears all slanted at exactly the same angle. Facing every direction as they did, they were supposed to keep all intruders from the current lord of the Stone. Their commander, a captain distinguished by two short white plumes on his helmet, held himself only a trifle less stiffly. He posed with one hand on his sword hilt and the other on his hip, self-important with his duty. They all smelled of fear and uncertainty, like men who lived under a crumbling cliff and had almost managed to convince themselves it would never fall. Or at least not tonight. Not in the next hour.

Perrin walked on by them, his bootheels making echoes. The officer started toward him, then hesitated when Perrin did not stop to be challenged. He knew who Perrin was, of course; at least, he knew as much as any Tairen knew. Traveling companion of Aes Sedai, friend of the Lord Dragon. Not a man to be interfered with by a mere officer of the Defenders of the Stone. There was his apparent task of guarding the Lord Dragon's rest, of course, but though he probably did not admit it even to himself, the officer had to know that he and his brave show of polished armor were simply that. The real guards were those Perrin met when he strode beyond the columns and approached the doors to Rand's chambers.

They had been sitting so still behind the columns that they seemed to fade into the stone, though their coats and breeches—in shades of gray and brown, made to hide them in the Waste—stood out here as soon as they moved. Six Maidens of the Spear, Aiel women who had chosen a warrior's life over the hearth, flowed between him and the doors on soft, laced boots that reached their knees. They were tall for women, the tallest barely a hand shorter than he, sun-darkened, with short-cropped hair, yellow or red or something in between. Two held curved horn bows with arrows nocked, if not drawn. The others carried small hide bucklers and three or four short spears each—short, but with spearheads long enough to stick through a man's body with inches to spare.

"I do not think I can let you go in," a woman with flame-colored hair said, smiling slightly to take the sting out of the words. Aiel did not go about grinning as much as other folk, or show a great deal of any outward emotion for that matter. "I think he does not want to see anyone tonight."

"I am going in, Bain." Ignoring her spears, he took her by the upper arms. That was when it became impossible to ignore the spears, since she had managed to get a spearpoint hard against the side of his throat. For that matter, a somewhat blonder woman named Chiad suddenly had one of her spears at the other side, as if the two were intended to meet somewhere in the middle of his neck. The other women only watched, confident that Bain and Chiad could handle whatever had to be done. Still, he did his best. "I don't have time to argue with you. Not that you listen to people who argue with you, as I remember. I am going in." As gently as he could, he picked Bain up and set her out of his way.

Chiad's spear only needed her to breathe on it to draw blood, but after one startled widening of dark blue eyes, Bain abruptly took hers away and grinned. "Would you like to learn a game called Maidens' Kiss, Perrin? You might play well, I think. At the very least you would learn something." One of the others laughed aloud. Chiad's spearpoint left his neck.

He took a deep breath, hoping they would not notice it was his first since the spears touched him. They had not veiled their faces—their *shoufa* lay coiled around their necks like dark scarves—but he did not know if Aiel had to do so before they killed, only that veiling meant they were ready to.

"Another time, perhaps," he said politely. They were all grinning as if Bain had said something amusing, and his not understanding was part of the humor. Thom was right. A man could go crazy trying to understand women, of any nation and any station in life; that was what Thom said.

As he reached for a door handle in the shape of a rearing golden lion, Bain added, "On your head be it. He has already chased out what most men would consider better company by far than you."

Of course, he thought, pulling open the door, *Berelain. She was coming from here. Tonight, everything is revolving around—*

The First of Mayene vanished from his thoughts as he got a look into the room. Broken mirrors hung on the walls and broken glass covered the floor, along with shards of shattered porcelain and feathers from the slashed mattress. Open books lay tumbled among overturned chairs and benches. And Rand was sitting at the foot of his bed, slumped against one of the bedposts with eyes closed and hands limp atop *Callandor,* which lay across his knees. He looked as if he had taken a bath in blood.

"Get Moiraine!" Perrin snapped at the Aiel women. Was Rand still alive? If he was, he needed Aes Sedai Healing to stay that way. "Tell her to hurry!" He heard a gasp behind him, then soft boots running.

Rand lifted his head. His face was a smeared mask. "Shut the door."

"Moiraine will be here soon, Rand. Rest easy. She will—"

"Shut the door, Perrin."

Murmuring among themselves, the Aiel women frowned, but moved back. Perrin pulled the door to, cutting off a questioning shout from the white-plumed officer.

Glass crunched under his boots as he crossed the carpet to Rand. Tearing a strip from a wildly sliced linen sheet, he wadded it against the wound in Rand's side. Rand's hands tightened on the transparent sword at the pressure, then relaxed. Blood soaked through almost immediately. Cuts and gashes covered him from the soles of his feet to his head; slivers of glass glittered in many of them. Perrin rolled his shoulders helplessly. He did not know what more to do, other than wait for Moiraine.

"What under the Light did you try to do, Rand? You look as though you tried to skin yourself. And you nearly killed me, as well." For a moment he thought Rand was not going to answer.

"Not me," Rand said finally, in a near whisper. "One of the Forsaken."

Perrin tried to relax muscles he did not remember tensing. The effort was only partly successful. He had mentioned the Forsaken to Faile, not exactly casually, but by and large he had been trying not to think of what the Forsaken might do when they found out where Rand was. If one of them could bring down the Dragon Reborn, he or she would stand high above the others when the Dark One broke free. The Dark One free, and the Last Battle lost before it was fought.

"Are you sure?" he said, just as quietly.

"It had to be, Perrin. It had to be."

"If one of them came after me as well as you . . . ? Where's Mat, Rand? If he was alive, and went through what I did, he'd be thinking what I did. That it was you. He'd be here by now to bless you out."

"Or on a horse and halfway to the city gates." Rand struggled to sit erect. Drying blood smears cracked, and fresh trickles started on his chest and shoulders. "If he is dead, Perrin, you had best get as far from me as you can. I think you and Loial are right about that." He paused, studying Perrin. "You and Mat must wish I had never been born. Or at least that you'd never seen me."

There was no point in going to check; if anything had happened to Mat, it was over and done now. And he had a feeling that his makeshift bandage pressed against Rand's side might be what would keep him alive long enough for Moiraine to get there. "You don't seem to care if he *has* gone off. Burn me, he's important, too. What are you going to do if he's gone? Or dead, the Light send it not so."

"What they least expect." Rand's eyes looked like morning mist covering the dawn, blue-gray with a feverish glow seeping through. His voice had a knife edge. "That is what I have to do in any case. What *everyone* least expects."

Perrin took a slow breath. Rand had a right to taut nerves. It was not a sign of incipient madness. He had to stop watching for signs of madness. Those signs would come soon enough, and watching would do nothing but keep his stomach tied in knots. "What's that?" he asked quietly.

Rand closed his eyes. "I only know I have to catch them by surprise. Catch everyone by surprise," he muttered fiercely.

One of the doors opened to admit a tall Aielman, his dark red hair touched with gray. Behind him the Tairen officer's plumes bobbed as he argued with the Maidens; he was still arguing when Bain pushed the door shut.

Rhuarc surveyed the room with sharp blue eyes, as if he suspected enemies hiding behind a drape or an overturned chair. The clan chief of the Taardad Aiel had no visible weapon except the heavy-bladed knife at his waist, but he carried authority and confidence like weapons, quietly, yet as surely as if they were sheathed alongside the knife. And his *shoufa* hung about his shoulders; no one who knew the slightest about Aiel took one for less than dangerous when he wore the means to veil his face.

"That Tairen fool outside sent word to his commander that something had happened in here," Rhuarc said, "and rumors are already sprouting like corpse moss in a deep cave. Everything from the White Tower trying to kill you to the Last Battle fought here in this room." Perrin opened his mouth; Rhuarc raised a forestalling hand. "I happened to meet Berelain, looking as if she had been told the day she would die, and she told me the truth of it. And it does look to be the truth, though I doubted her."

"I sent for Moiraine," Perrin said. Rhuarc nodded. Of course, the Maidens would have told him everything they knew.

Rand gave a painful bark of a laugh. "I told her to keep quiet. It seems the Lord Dragon doesn't rule Mayene." He sounded more wryly amused than anything else.

"I have daughters older than that young woman," Rhuarc said. "I do not believe she will tell anyone else. I think she would like to forget everything that happened tonight."

"And I would like to know what happened," Moiraine said, gliding into the room. Slight and slender as she was, Rhuarc towered over her as much as the man who followed her in—Lan, her Warder—but it was the Aes Sedai who dominated the room. She must have run to come so fast, but she was calm as a frozen lake now. It took a great deal to ruffle Moiraine's serenity. Her blue silk gown had a high lace neck and sleeves slashed with darker velvet, but the heat and humidity did not appear to touch her. A small blue stone, suspended on her forehead from a fine golden chain in her dark hair, flashed in the light, emphasizing the absence of the slightest sheen of sweat.

As always when they met, Lan's and Rhuarc's icy blue stares nearly struck sparks. A braided leather cord held Lan's dark hair, gray-streaked at the temples. His face looked to have been carved from rock, all hard planes and angles, and his sword rode his hip like part of his body. Perrin was not sure which of the two men was more deadly, but he thought a mouse could starve on the difference.

The Warder's eyes swung to Rand. "I thought you were old enough to shave without someone to guide your hand."

Rhuarc smiled, a slight smile but the first Perrin had ever seen from him in Lan's presence. "He is young yet. He will learn."

Lan glanced back at the Aielman, then returned the smile, just as slightly.

Moiraine gave the two men a brief, withering look. She did not seem to pick her way as she crossed the carpet, but she stepped so lightly, holding her skirts up, that not one shard of glass crunched under her slippers. Her eyes swept around the room; taking in the smallest details, Perrin was sure. For a moment she studied him—he did not meet her gaze; she knew too much about him for comfort—but she bore down on Rand like a silent, silken avalanche, icy and inexorable.

Perrin dropped his hand and moved out of her way. The wadded cloth stayed against Rand's side, held by congealing blood. From head to foot the blood was beginning to dry in black streaks and smears. The slivers of glass in his skin glittered in the lamplight. Moiraine touched the blood-caked cloth with her fingertips, then took her hand back as though changing her mind about looking underneath. Perrin wondered how the Aes Sedai could look at Rand without wincing, but her smooth face did not change. She smelled faintly of rose-scented soap.

"At least you are alive." Her voice was musical, a chill, angry music at the moment. "What happened can wait. Try to touch the True Source."

"Why?" Rand asked in a wary voice. "I cannot Heal myself, even if I knew how to Heal. No one can. I know that much."

For the space of a breath Moiraine seemed on the point of an outburst, strange as that would have been, but in another breath she was once again layered in calm so deep that surely nothing could crack it. "Only some of the strength for Healing comes from the Healer. The Power can replace what comes from the Healed. Without it, you will spend tomorrow flat on your back and perhaps the next day as well. Now, draw on the Power, if you can, but do nothing with it. Simply hold it. Use this, if you must." She did not have to bend far to touch *Callandor*.

Rand moved the sword from under her hand. "Simply hold it, you say." He sounded about to laugh out loud. "Very well."

Nothing happened that Perrin could see, not that he expected to. Rand sat there like the survivor of a lost battle, looking at Moiraine. She hardly blinked. Twice she scrubbed her fingers against her palms as if unaware.

After a time Rand sighed. "I cannot even reach the Void. I can't seem to concentrate." A quick grin cracked the blood drying on his face. "I do not understand why." A thick red thread snaked its way down past his left eye.

"Then I will do it as I always have," Moiraine said, and took Rand's head in her hands, careless of the blood that ran over her fingers.

Rand lurched to his feet with a roaring gasp, as if all the breath were being squeezed from his lungs, back arching so his head nearly tore free of her grasp. One arm flung wide, fingers spread and bending back so far it seemed they must break; the other hand clamped down on *Callandor*'s hilt, the muscles of that arm knotting visibly into cramps. He shook like cloth caught in a windstorm. Dark flakes of dried blood fell, and bits of glass tinkled onto the chest and floor, forced out of cuts closing up and knitting themselves together.

Perrin shivered as if that windstorm roared around him. He had seen Healing done before, that and more, greater and worse, but he could never be complacent about seeing the Power used, about knowing it was being used, not even for this. Tales of Aes Sedai, told by merchants' guards and drivers, had embedded themselves in his mind long years before he met Moiraine. Rhuarc smelled sharply uneasy. Only Lan took it as a matter of course. Lan and Moiraine.

Almost as soon as it began, it was done. Moiraine took her hands away, and Rand slumped, catching the bedpost to hold himself on his feet. It was difficult to say whether he clutched the bedpost or *Callandor* more tenaciously. When Moiraine tried to take the sword to replace it on the ornate stand against the wall, he drew it away from her firmly, even roughly.

Her mouth tightened momentarily, but she contented herself with pulling the wad of cloth from his side, using it to scrub away some of the surrounding smears. The old wound was a tender scar again. The other injuries were simply gone. The mostly dried blood that still covered him could have come from someone else.

Moiraine frowned. "It still does not respond," she murmured, half to herself. "It will not heal completely."

"That is the one that will kill me, isn't it?" he asked her softly, then quoted, " 'His blood on the rocks of Shayol Ghul, washing away the Shadow, sacrifice for man's salvation.' "

"You read too much," she said sharply, "and understand too little."

"Do you understand more? If you do, then tell me."

"He is only trying to find his way," Lan said suddenly. "No man likes to run forward blindly when he knows there is a cliff somewhere ahead."

Perrin gave a twitch of surprise. Lan almost never disagreed with Moiraine, or at least not where anyone could overhear. He and Rand had been spending a good deal of time together, though, practicing the sword.

Moiraine's dark eyes flashed, but what she said was "He needs to be in bed. Will you ask that washwater be brought, and another bedchamber prepared? This one needs a thorough cleaning and a new mattress." Lan nodded and put his head into the anteroom for a moment, speaking quietly.

"I will sleep here, Moiraine." Letting go of the bedpost, Rand pushed himself erect, grounding *Callandor*'s point on the littered carpet and resting both hands on the hilt. If he leaned a little on the sword, it did not show much. "I won't be chased any more. Not even out of a bed."

"Tai' shar Manetheren," Lan murmured.

This time even Rhuarc looked startled, but if Moiraine heard the Warder compliment Rand, she gave no sign of it. She was staring at Rand, her face smooth but thunderheads in her eyes. Rand wore a quizzical little smile, as if wondering what she would try next.

Perrin edged toward the doors. If Rand and the Aes Sedai were going to match wills, he would just as soon be elsewhere. Lan did not appear to care; it was hard to tell with that stance of his, somehow standing with his back straight and slouching at the same time. He could have been bored enough to sleep where he stood or ready to draw his sword; his manner suggested either, or both. Rhuarc stood much the same, but he was eyeing the doors, too.

"Stay where you are!" Moiraine did not look away from Rand, and her outflung finger pointed halfway between Perrin and Rhuarc, but Perrin's feet stopped just the same. Rhuarc shrugged and folded his arms.

"Stubborn," Moiraine muttered. This time the word was for Rand. "Very well. If you mean to stand there until you drop, you can use the time before you fall on your face to tell me what occurred here. I cannot teach you, but if you tell me perhaps I can see what you did wrong. A small chance, but perhaps I can." Her voice sharpened. "You must learn to control it, and I do not mean just because of things like this. If you do not learn to control the Power, it will kill you. You know that. I have told you often enough. You must teach yourself. You must find it within yourself."

"I did nothing except survive," he said in a dry voice. She opened her mouth, but he went on. "Do you think I could channel and not know it? I didn't do it in my sleep. This happened awake." He wavered, and caught himself on the sword.

"Even you could not channel anything but Spirit asleep," Moiraine said coolly, "and this was never done with Spirit. I was about to ask what *did* happen."

Perrin felt his hackles rising as Rand told his story. The axe had been bad enough, but at least the axe was something solid, something real. To have your own reflection jump out of mirrors at you. . . . Unconsciously he shifted his feet, trying not to stand on any fragments of glass.

Soon after he began speaking, Rand glanced behind him at the chest, a quick look, as if he did not want it observed. After a moment the slivers of silvered glass that were scattered across the lid of the chest stirred and slid off onto the carpet as though pushed by an unseen broom. Rand exchanged looks with Moiraine, then sat down slowly and went on. Perrin was not sure which of them had cleared the chest top. There was no mention of Berelain in the tale.

"It must have been one of the Forsaken," Rand finished at last. "Maybe Sammael. You said he's in Illian. Unless one of them is here in Tear. Could Sammael reach the Stone from Illian?"

"Not even if *he* held *Callandor*," Moiraine told him. "There are limits. Sammael is only a man, not the Dark One."

Only a man? Not a very good description, Perrin thought. A man who could channel, but who somehow had not gone mad; at least, not yet, not that anyone knew. A man perhaps as strong as Rand, but where Rand was trying to learn, Sammael knew every trick of his talents already. A man who had spent three thousand years trapped in the

Dark One's prison, a man who had gone over to the Shadow of his own choice. No. "Only a man" did not begin to describe Sammael, or any of the Forsaken, male or female.

"Then one of them is here. In the city." Rand put his head down on his wrists, but jerked himself erect immediately, glaring at those in the room. "I'll not be chased again. I'll be the hound, first. I will find him—or her—and I will—"

"Not one of the Forsaken," Moiraine cut in. "I think not. This was too simple. And too complex."

Rand spoke calmly. "No riddles, Moiraine. If not the Forsaken, who? Or what?"

The Aes Sedai's face could have done for an anvil, yet she hesitated, feeling her way. There was no telling whether she was unsure of the answer or deciding how much to reveal.

"As the seals holding the Dark One's prison weaken," she said after a time, "it may be inevitable that a . . . miasma . . . will escape even while he is still held. Like bubbles rising from the things rotting on the bottom of a pond. But these bubbles will drift through the Pattern until they attach to a thread and burst."

"Light!" It slipped out before Perrin could stop it. Moiraine's eyes turned to him. "You mean what happened to . . . to Rand is going to start happening to everybody?"

"Not to everyone. Not yet, at least. In the beginning I think there will only be a few bubbles, slipping through cracks the Dark One can reach through. Later, who can say? And just as *ta'veren* bend the other threads in the Pattern around them, I think perhaps *ta'veren* will tend to attract these bubbles more powerfully than others do." Her eyes said she knew Rand was not the only one to have had a waking nightmare. A brief touch of a smile, there and gone almost before he saw it, said he could keep silent if he wished to hold it secret from others. But she knew. "Yet in the months to come—the years, should we be lucky enough to have that long—I fear a good many people will see things to give them white hairs, if they survive."

"Mat," Rand said. "Do you know if he . . . ? Is he . . . ?"

"I will know soon enough," Moiraine replied calmly. "What is done cannot be undone, but we can hope." Whatever her tone, though, she smelled ill at ease until Rhuarc spoke.

"He is well. Or was. I saw him on my way here."

"Going where?" Moiraine said with an edge in her voice.

"He looked to be heading for the servants' quarters," the Aielman told her. He knew that the three were *ta'veren,* if not as much else as he thought he did, and he knew Mat well enough to add, "Not the stables, Aes Sedai. The other way, toward the river. And there are no boats at the Stone's docks." He did not stumble over words like "boat" and "dock" the way most of the Aiel did, although in the Waste such things existed only in stories.

She nodded as if she had expected nothing else. Perrin shook his head; she was so used to hiding her real thoughts, she seemed to veil them out of habit.

Suddenly one of the doors opened and Bain and Chiad slipped in, without their spears. Bain was carrying a large white bowl and a fat pitcher with steam rising from the top. Chiad had towels folded under her arm.

"Why are *you* bringing this?" Moiraine demanded.

Chiad shrugged. "She would not come in."

Rand barked a laugh. "Even the servants know enough to stay clear of me. Put it anywhere."

"Your time is running out, Rand," Moiraine said. "The Tairens are becoming used to you, after a fashion, and no one fears what is familiar as much as what is strange. How many weeks, or days, before someone tries to put an arrow in your back or poison in your food? How long before one of the Forsaken strikes, or another bubble comes sliding along the Pattern?"

"Don't try to harry me, Moiraine." He was blood filthy, half naked, more than half leaning on *Callandor* to stay sitting up, but he managed to fill those words with quiet command. "I will not run for you, either."

"Choose your way soon," she said. "And this time, inform me what you mean to do. My knowledge cannot aid you if you refuse to accept my help."

"Your help?" Rand said wearily. "I'll take your help. But I will decide, not you." He looked at Perrin as if trying to tell him something without words, something he did not want the others to hear. Perrin had not a clue what it was. After a moment Rand sighed; his head sank a little. "I want to sleep. All of you, go away. Please. We will talk tomorrow." His eyes flickered to Perrin again, underscoring the words for him.

Moiraine crossed the room to Bain and Chiad, and the two Aiel women leaned close so she could speak for their ears alone. Perrin heard only a buzz, and wondered if she was using the Power to stop him eavesdropping. She knew the keenness of his hearing. He was sure of it when Bain whispered back and he still could not make out anything. The Aes Sedai had done nothing about his sense of smell, though. The Aiel women looked at Rand as they listened, and they smelled wary. Not afraid, but as if Rand were a large animal that would be dangerous if they misstepped.

The Aes Sedai turned back to Rand. "We *will* talk tomorrow. You cannot sit like a partridge waiting for a hunter's net." She was moving for the door before Rand could reply. Lan looked at Rand as if about to say something, but followed her without speaking.

"Rand?" Perrin said.

"We do what we have to." Rand did not look up from the clear hilt between his hands. "We all do what we have to." He smelled afraid.

Perrin nodded and followed Rhuarc out of the room. Moiraine and Lan were nowhere in sight. The Tairen officer was staring at the doors from ten paces off, trying to pretend the distance was his choice and had nothing to do with the four Aiel women watching him. The other two Maidens were still in the bedchamber, Perrin realized. He heard voices from the room.

"Go away," Rand said tiredly. "Just put that down and go away."

"If you can stand up," Chiad said cheerfully, "we will. Only stand."

There was the sound of water splashing into a bowl. "We have tended to wounded before," Bain said in soothing tones. "And I used to wash my brothers when they were little."

Rhuarc pushed the door shut, cutting off the rest.

"You do not treat him the way the Tairens do," Perrin said quietly. "No bowing and scraping. I don't think I have heard one of you call him Lord Dragon."

"The Dragon Reborn is a wetlander prophecy," Rhuarc said. "Ours is He Who Comes With the Dawn."

"I thought they were the same. Else why did you come to the Stone? Burn me, Rhuarc, you Aiel are the People of the Dragon, just as the Prophecies say. You've as good as admitted it, even if you won't say it out loud."

Rhuarc ignored the last part. "In your Prophecies of the Dragon, the fall of the Stone and the taking of *Callandor* proclaim that the Dragon has been Reborn. Our prophecy says only that the Stone must fall before He Who Comes With the Dawn appears to take us back to what was ours. They may be one man, but I doubt even the Wise Ones could say for sure. If Rand is the one, there are things he must do yet to prove it."

"What?" Perrin demanded.

"If he is the one, he will know, and do them. If he does not, then our search still goes on."

Something unreadable in the Aielman's voice pricked Perrin's ears. "And if he isn't the one you search for? What then, Rhuarc?"

"Sleep well and safely, Perrin." Rhuarc's soft boots made no sound on the black marble as he walked away.

The Tairen officer was still staring past the Maidens, smelling of fear, failing to mask the anger and hatred on his face. If the Aiel decided Rand was not He Who Comes With the Dawn. . . . Perrin studied the Tairen officer's face and thought of the Maidens not being there, of the Stone empty of Aiel, and he shivered. He had to make sure Faile decided to leave. That was all there was for it. She had to decide to go, and without him.

CHAPTER
4

Strings

Thom Merrilin sprinkled sand across what he had written to blot the ink, then carefully poured the sand back into its jar and flipped the lid shut. Riffling through the papers scattered in rough piles across the table—six tallow candles made fire a real danger, but he needed the light—he selected a crumpled sheet marred by an inkblot. Carefully he compared it with what he had written, then stroked a long white mustache with a thumb in satisfaction and permitted himself a leathery-faced smile. The High Lord Carleon himself would have thought it was his own hand.

Be wary. Your husband suspects.

Only those words, and no signature. Now if he could arrange for the High Lord Tedosian to find it where his wife, the Lady Alteima, might carelessly have left it. . . .

A knock sounded at the door, and he jumped. No one came to see him at this time of the night.

"A moment," he called, hastily stuffing pens and inkpots and selected papers into a battered writing chest. "A moment while I put on a shirt."

Locking the chest, he shoved it under the table where it might escape

casual notice and ran an eye over his small, windowless room to see if
he had left anything out that should not be seen. Hoops and balls for
juggling littered his narrow, unmade bed, and lay among his shaving
things on a single shelf with fire wands and small items for sleight of
hand. His gleeman's cloak, covered with loose patches in a hundred
colors, hung from a peg on the wall along with his spare clothes and the
hard leather cases holding his harp and flute. A woman's diaphanous
red silk scarf was tied around the strap of the harp case, but it could
have belonged to anyone.

He was not sure he remembered who had tied it there; he tried to
pay no more attention to one woman than any other, and all of it
lighthearted and laughing. Make them laugh, even make them sigh, but
avoid entanglements, that was his motto; he had no time for those.
That was what he told himself.

"I'm coming." He limped to the door irritably. Once he had drawn
oohs and *aahs* from people who could hardly believe, even while they
watched, that a rawboned, white-haired old man could do backsprings
and handstands and flips, limber and quick as a boy. The limp had put
an end to that, and he hated it. The leg ached worse when he was tired.
He jerked open the door, and blinked in surprise. "Well. Come in, Mat.
I thought you would be hard at work lightening lordlings' purses."

"They didn't want to gamble any more tonight," Mat said sourly,
dropping onto the three-legged stool that served as a second chair. His
coat was undone and his hair disheveled. His brown eyes darted
around, never resting on one spot long, but their usual twinkle, suggesting that the lad saw something funny where no one else did, was
missing tonight.

Thom frowned at him, considering. Mat never stepped across this
threshold without a quip about the shabby room. He accepted Thom's
explanation that his sleeping beside the servants' quarters would help
people forget that he had arrived in the shadow of Aes Sedai, but Mat
seldom let a chance for a joke pass. If he realized that the room also
assured that no one could think of Thom having any connection to the
Dragon Reborn, Mat, being Mat, probably thought that a reasonable
wish. It had taken Thom all of two sentences, delivered in haste during
a rare moment when no one was looking, to make Rand see the real
point. Everyone listened to a gleeman, everyone watched him, but no
one really saw him or remembered who he talked to, as long as he was
only a gleeman, with his hedgerow entertainments fit for country folk
and servants, and perhaps to amuse the ladies. That was how Tairens
saw it. It was not as if he were a bard, after all.

What was bothering the boy to bring him down here at this hour? Probably one or another of the young women, and some old enough to know better, who had let themselves be caught by Mat's mischievous grin. Still, he would pretend it was one of Mat's usual visits until the lad said otherwise.

"I'll get the stones board. It is late, but we have time for one game." He could not resist adding, "Would you care for a wager on it?" He would not have tossed dice with Mat for a copper, but stones was another matter; he thought there was too much order and pattern in stones for Mat's strange luck.

"What? Oh. No. It's too late for games. Thom, did . . . ? Did anything . . . happen down here?"

Leaning the stones board against a table leg, Thom dug his tabac pouch and long-stemmed pipe out of the litter remaining on the table. "Such as what?" he asked, thumbing the bowl full. He had time to stick a twist of paper in the flame of one of the candles, puff the pipe alight and blow out the spill before Mat answered.

"Such as Rand going insane, that's what. No, you'd not have had to ask if it had."

A prickling made Thom shift his shoulders, but he blew a blue-gray streamer of smoke as calmly as he could and took his chair, stretching his gimpy leg out in front of him. "What happened?"

Mat drew a deep breath, then let everything out in a rush. "The playing cards tried to kill me. The Amyrlin, and the High Lord, and. . . . I didn't dream it, Thom. That's why those puffed-up jackdaws don't want to gamble anymore. They're afraid it will happen again. Thom, I'm thinking of leaving Tear."

The prickling felt as if he had blackwasp nettles stuffed down his back. Why had he not left Tear himself long since? Much the wisest thing. Hundreds of villages lay out there, waiting for a gleeman to entertain and amaze them. And each with an inn or two full of wine to drown memories. But if he did, Rand would have no one except Moiraine to keep the High Lords from maneuvering him into corners, and maybe cutting his throat. She could do it, of course. Using different methods than his. He thought she could. She was Cairhienin, which meant she had probably taken in the Game of Houses with her mother's milk. And she would tie another string to Rand for the White Tower while she was about it. Mesh him in an Aes Sedai net so strong he would never escape. But if the boy was going mad already. . . .

Fool, Thom called himself. A pure fool to stay mixed in this because of something fifteen years in the past. Staying would not change that;

what was done was done. He had to see Rand face-to-face, no matter what he had told him about keeping clear. Perhaps no one would think it too odd if a gleeman asked to perform a song for the Lord Dragon, a song especially composed. He knew a deservedly obscure Kandori tune, praising some unnamed lord for his greatness and courage in grandiose terms that never quite managed to name deeds or places. It had probably been bought by some lord who had no deeds worth naming. Well, it would serve him now. Unless Moiraine decided it was strange. That would be as bad as the High Lords taking notice. *I am a fool! I should be out of here tonight!*

He was roiling inside, his stomach churning acid, but he had spent long years learning to keep his face straight before ever he put on a gleeman's cloak. He puffed three smoke rings, one inside the other, and said, "You have been thinking of leaving Tear since the day you walked into the Stone."

Perched on the edge of the stool, Mat shot him an angry look. "And I mean to. I do. Why not come with me, Thom? There are towns where they think the Dragon Reborn hasn't drawn a breath yet, where nobody's given a thought to the bloody Prophecies of the bloody Dragon in years, if ever. Places where they think the Dark One is a grandmother's tale, and Trollocs are travelers' wild stories, and Myrddraal ride shadows to scare children. You could play your harp and tell your stories, and I could find a game of dice. We could live like lords, traveling as we want, staying where we want, with no one trying to kill us."

That hit too close for comfort. Well, he was a fool and there it was; he just had to make the best of it. "If you really mean to go, why haven't you?"

"Moiraine watches me," Mat said bitterly. "And when she isn't, she has somebody else doing it."

"I know. Aes Sedai don't like to let someone go once they lay hands on them." It was more than that, he was sure, more than what was openly known, certainly, but Mat denied any such thing, and no one else who knew was talking either, if anyone besides Moiraine did know. It hardly mattered. He liked Mat—he even owed him, in a fashion—but Mat and his troubles were a street-corner raree compared to Rand. "But I cannot believe she really has someone watching you all the time."

"As good as. She's always asking people where I am, what I'm doing. It gets back to me. Do you know anybody who won't tell an Aes Sedai what she wants to know? I don't. As good as being watched."

"You could avoid eyes if you put your mind to it. I've never seen anyone as good at sneaking about as you. I mean that as a compliment."

"Something always comes up," Mat muttered. "There's so much gold to be had here. And there's a big-eyed girl in the kitchens who likes a little kiss and tickle, and one of the maids has hair like silk, to her waist, and the roundest. . . ." He trailed off as if he had suddenly realized how foolish he sounded.

"Have you considered that maybe it's because—"

"If you mention *ta'veren*, Thom, I'm leaving."

Thom changed what he had been going to say. "—that maybe it's because Rand is your friend and you don't want to desert him?"

"Desert him!" The boy jumped up, kicking over the stool. "Thom, he is the bloody Dragon Reborn! At least, that's what he and Moiraine say. Maybe he is. He can channel, and he has that bloody sword that looks like glass. Prophecies! I don't know. But I know I would have to be as crazy as these Tairens to stay." He paused. "You don't think. . . . You don't think Moiraine is keeping me here, do you? With the Power?"

"I do not believe she can," Thom said slowly. He knew a good bit about Aes Sedai, enough to have some idea how much he did not know, and he thought he was right on this.

Mat raked his fingers through his hair. "Thom, I think about leaving all the time, but. . . . I get these strange feelings. Almost as if something was going to happen. Something. . . . Momentous; that's the word. It's like knowing there'll be fireworks for Sunday, only I don't know what it is I'm expecting. Whenever I think too much about leaving, it happens. And suddenly I've found some reason to stay another day. Always just one more bloody day. Doesn't that sound like Aes Sedai work to you?"

Thom swallowed the word *ta'veren* and took his pipe from between his teeth to peer into the smoldering tabac. He did not know much about *ta'veren*, but then no one did except the Aes Sedai, or maybe some of the Ogier. "I was never much good at helping people with their problems." *And worse with my own,* he thought. "With an Aes Sedai close to hand, I'd advise most people to ask her for help." *Advice I'd not take myself.*

"Ask Moiraine!"

"I suppose that is out of the question in this case. But Nynaeve was your Wisdom back in Emond's Field. Village Wisdoms are used to answering people's questions, helping with their problems."

Mat gave a raucous snort of laughter. "And put up with one of her lectures about drinking and gambling and . . . ? Thom, she acts like I'm ten years old. Sometimes I think she believes I'll marry a nice girl and settle down on my father's farm."

"Some men would not find it an objectionable life," Thom said quietly.

"Well, I would. I want more than cows and sheep and tabac for the rest of my life. I want—" Mat shook his head. "All these holes in memory. Sometimes I think if I could just fill them in, I'd know. . . . Burn me, I don't know what I'd know, but I know I want to know it. That's a twisty riddle, isn't it?"

"I'm not certain even an Aes Sedai can help with that. A gleeman surely can't."

"I said no Aes Sedai!"

Thom sighed. "Calm yourself, boy. I was not suggesting it."

"I *am* leaving. As soon as I can fetch my things and find a horse. Not a minute longer."

"In the middle of the night? The morning will do." He refrained from adding, *If you really do leave.* "Sit down. Relax. We'll play a game of stones. I have a jar of wine here, somewhere."

Mat hesitated, glancing at the door. Finally he jerked his coat straight. "The morning will do." He sounded uncertain, but he picked up the overturned stool and set it beside the table. "But no wine for me," he added as he sat down. "Strange enough things happen when my head is clear. I want to know the difference."

Thom was thoughtful as he put the board and the bags of stones on the table. Just that easily the lad was diverted. Pulled along by an even stronger *ta'veren* named Rand al'Thor, was how Thom saw it. It occurred to him to wonder if he was caught in the same way. His life had certainly not been headed toward the Stone of Tear and this room when he first met Rand, but since then it had been twitched about like a kite string. If he decided to leave, say if Rand really had gone mad, would he find reasons to keep putting it off?

"What is this, Thom?" Mat's boot had encountered the writing case under the table. "Is it all right if I move it out of my way?"

"Of course. Go right ahead." He winced inside as Mat shoved the case aside roughly with his foot. He hoped he had corked all the ink bottles tightly. "Choose," he said, holding out his fists.

Mat tapped the left, and Thom opened it to reveal a smooth black stone, flat and round. The boy chortled at having the first go and placed the stone on the crosshatched board. No one seeing the eagerness in his eyes would have suspected that only moments before he had been twice as eager to go. A greatness he refused to recognize clinging to his back, and an Aes Sedai intent on keeping him for one of her pets. The lad was well and truly caught.

If he was caught, too, Thom decided, it would be worth it to help one man, at least, keep free of Aes Sedai. Worth it, to make a payment on that fifteen-year-old debt.

Suddenly and strangely content, he set a white stone. "Did I ever tell you," he said around his pipestem, "about the wager I once made with a Domani woman? She had eyes that could drink a man's soul, and an odd-looking red bird she had bought off a Sea Folk ship. She claimed it could tell the future. This bird had a fat yellow beak nearly as long as its body, and it. . . ."

CHAPTER
5

Questioners

T hey should be back by now." Egwene fluttered the painted silk
    fan vigorously, glad the nights were at least a little cooler than
    the days. Tairen women carried the fans all the time—the
nobles, at least, and the wealthy—but as far as she could see they did
no good at all except when the sun was down, and not much then. Even
the lamps, great golden, mirrored things on silvered wall brackets,
seemed to add to the heat. "What can be keeping them?" An hour,
Moiraine had promised them, for the first time in days, and then she
had left without explanation after a bare five minutes. "Did she give
any hint of why they wanted her, Aviendha? Or who wanted her, for
that matter?"

Seated cross-legged on the floor beside the door, large green eyes
startling in her dark tanned face, the Aiel woman shrugged. In coat and
breeches and soft boots, *shoufa* looped about her neck, she appeared
unarmed. "Careen whispered her message to Moiraine Sedai. I would
not have been proper to listen. I am sorry, Aes Sedai."

Guiltily, Egwene fingered the Great Serpent ring on her right hand,
the golden serpent biting its own tail. As an Accepted, she should have
been wearing it on the third finger of her left hand, but letting the High
Lords believe that they had four full Aes Sedai inside the Stone kept
them on their best manners, or what passed for manners among Tairen

nobles. Moiraine did not lie, of course; she never said they were more than Accepted. But she never said they *were* Accepted, either, and let everyone think what they wanted to think, believe what they thought they saw. Moiraine could not lie, but she could make truth dance a fine jig.

It was not the first time Egwene and the others had pretended to full sisterhood since leaving the Tower, but more and more she felt uncomfortable deceiving Aviendha. She liked the Aiel woman, thought they could be friends if they could ever come to know one another; but that hardly seemed possible as long as Aviendha thought Egwene was Aes Sedai. The Aiel woman was there only at Moiraine's order, issued for unspoken purposes of her own. Egwene suspected it was to give them an Aiel bodyguard, as if they had not learned to protect themselves. Still, even if she and Aviendha did become friends, she could not tell her the truth. The best way to keep a secret was to make sure no one knew who did not absolutely have to know. Another point Moiraine had made. Sometimes Egwene found herself wishing the Aes Sedai could be wrong, glaringly wrong, just once. In a way that would not mean disaster, of course. That was the rub.

"Tanchico," Nynaeve muttered. Her dark, wrist-thick braid hung down her back to her waist as she stared out of one of the narrow windows, casements swung out in the hope of catching a night breeze. On the broad River Erinin below bobbed the lanterns of a few fishing boats that had not ventured downriver, but Egwene doubted she saw them. "There is nothing for it but to go to Tanchico, it seems." Nynaeve gave an unconscious hitch to her green dress, with its wide neck that bared her shoulders; she did that a good deal. She would have denied wearing the dress for Lan, Moiraine's Warder—she would have if Egwene had dared make the suggestion—but green, blue and white seemed to be Lan's favorite colors on women, and every dress that was not green, blue or white had vanished from Nynaeve's wardrobe. "Nothing for it." She did not sound happy.

Egwene caught herself giving an upward tug to her own dress. They felt odd, these dresses that just clung to the shoulders. On the other hand, she did not believe she could bear to be more covered. Light as it was, the pale red linen felt like wool. She wished she could bring herself to wear the filmy gowns Berelain wore. Not that they were suitable for public eyes, but they certainly did appear to be cool.

Stop fretting over comfort, she told herself sternly. *Keep your mind on the business at hand.* "Perhaps," she said aloud. "Myself, I am not convinced."

A long, narrow table, polished till it glistened, ran down the middle of the room. A tall chair stood at the end near Egwene, lightly carved and touched here and there with gilt, quite plain for Tear, while the sidechairs had progressively lower backs, until those at the far end seemed little more than benches. Egwene had no idea what purpose the Tairens had put the room to. She and the others used it for questioning two prisoners taken when the Stone fell.

She could not force herself to go into the dungeons, though Rand had ordered all of the implements that had decorated the guardroom walls melted or burned. Neither Nynaeve nor Elayne had been eager to return, either. Besides, this brightly lit room, with its clean-swept green tile floor and its wall panels carved with the Three Crescents of Tear, was a sharp contrast to the grim, gray stone of the cells, all dim and dank and dirty. That had to have some softening effect on the two women in prisoners' rough-woven woolens.

Only that drab brown dress, however, would have told most people that Joiya Byir, standing beyond the table with her back turned, was a prisoner at all. She had been White Ajah, and had lost none of the Whites' cool arrogance on shifting her allegiance to the Black. Every line of her proclaimed that she stared rigidly at the far wall of her own choice, and for no other reason. Only a woman who could channel would have seen the thumb-thick flows of Air that held Joiya's arms to her sides and lashed her ankles together. A cage woven of Air kept her eyes straight ahead. Even her ears were stopped up, so she could not hear what anyone said until they wanted her to.

Once again Egwene checked the shield woven from Spirit that blocked Joiya from touching the True Source. It held, as she knew it must. She herself had woven all the flows around Joiya and tied them to maintain themselves, but she could not be easy in the same room with a Darkfriend who had the ability to channel, even if it was blocked. Worse than just a Darkfriend. Black Ajah. Murder was the least of Joiya's crimes. She should have been bowed down under her weight of broken oaths, blasted lives and blighted souls.

Joiya's fellow prisoner, her sister in the Black Ajah, lacked her strength. Standing stoop-shouldered at the far end of the table, head down, Amico Nagoyin seemed to sink in on herself under Egwene's gaze. There was no need to shield her. Amico had been stilled during her capture. Still able to sense the True Source, she would never again touch it, never again channel. The desire to, the need to, would remain, as sharp as the need to breathe, and her loss would be there for as long as she lived, *saidar* forever out of reach. Egwene wished she could find in herself even a shred of pity. But she did not wish for it very hard.

Amico murmured something at the tabletop.

"What?" Nynaeve demanded. "Speak up."

Amico raised her face humbly on its slender neck. She was still a beautiful woman, with large, dark eyes, but there was something different about her that Egwene could not quite put her finger on. Not the fear that made her clutch her coarse prisoner's dress with both hands. Something else.

Swallowing, Amico said, "You should go to Tanchico."

"You've told us that twenty times," Nynaeve said roughly. "Fifty times. Tell us something new. Name names we do not already know. Who still in the White Tower is Black Ajah?"

"I do not know. You must believe me." Amico sounded tired, utterly beaten. Not at all the way she had sounded when they were the prisoners and she the gaoler. "Before we left the Tower, I knew only Liandrin, Chesmal and Rianna. No one knew more than two or three others, I think. Except Liandrin. I have told you everything I know."

"Then you are remarkably ignorant for a woman who expected to rule part of the world when the Dark One breaks free," Egwene said dryly, snapping her fan shut for emphasis. It still stunned her, how easily she could say that now. Her stomach still clenched, and icy fingers still crawled her spine, but she no longer wanted to scream, or run weeping. It was possible to become used to anything.

"I overheard Liandrin that once, talking to Temaile," Amico said wearily, starting a tale she had told them many times. In the first days of her captivity she had tried to improve her story, but the more she elaborated the more she had tangled herself in her own lies. Now she almost always told it the same way, word for word. "If you could have seen Liandrin's face when she saw me. . . . She would have murdered me on the spot had she thought I had heard anything. And Temaile likes to hurt people. She enjoys it. I only heard a little before they saw me. Liandrin said there was something in Tanchico, something dangerous to . . . to him." She meant Rand. She could not say his name, and a mention of the Dragon Reborn was enough to send her into tears. "Liandrin said it was dangerous to whoever used it, too. Almost as dangerous as to . . . him. That is why she had not already gone after it. And she said being able to channel would not protect him. She said, 'When we find it, his filthy ability will bind him for us.' " Sweat ran down her face, but she shivered almost uncontrollably.

Not a word had changed.

Egwene opened her mouth, but Nynaeve spoke first. "I've heard enough of this. Let us see if the other has anything new to say."

Egwene glared at her, and Nynaeve stared back just as hard, neither blinking. *Sometimes she thinks she's still the Wisdom,* Egwene thought grimly, *and I'm still the village girl to teach about herbs. She had better realize things are different now.* Nynaeve was strong in the Power, stronger than Egwene, but only when she could actually manage to channel; unless angry, Nynaeve could not channel at all.

Elayne usually smoothed things over when it came to this, as it did more often than it should. By the time Egwene thought of smoothing matters herself, she had almost always dug in her heels and flared back, and trying to be soothing then would only be backing down. That was how Nynaeve would see it, she was sure. She could not remember Nynaeve ever making any move to back down, so why should she? This time Elayne was not there; Moiraine had summoned the Daughter-Heir with a word and a gesture to follow the Maiden who had come for the Aes Sedai. Without her, the tension stretched, each of the Accepted waiting for the other to blink first. Aviendha barely breathed; she kept herself strictly out of their confrontations. No doubt she considered it simple wisdom to stand clear.

Strangely, it was Amico who broke the impasse this time, though likely all she meant to do was demonstrate her cooperation. She turned to face the far wall, waiting patiently to be bound.

The foolishness of it struck Egwene suddenly. She was the only woman in the room who could channel—unless Nynaeve grew angry, or Joiya's shield failed; she tested the weave of Spirit again without thinking—and she indulged in a staring match while Amico waited to accept her bonds. At another time she might have laughed at herself aloud. Instead, she opened herself to *saidar,* that never-seen, ever-felt glowing warmth that seemed always to be just beyond the corner of her eye. The One Power filled her, like joyous life itself redoubled, and she wove the flows around Amico.

Nynaeve merely grunted; it was doubtful she was mad enough to sense what Egwene was doing—she could not, without her temper up —yet she could see Amico stiffen as the flows of Air touched her, then slump, half supported by the flows, as if to show how little she was resisting.

Aviendha shuddered, the way she had taken to doing whenever she knew the Power was being channeled near her.

Egwene wove blocks for Amico's ears—questioning them one at a time did little good if they could hear each other's stories—and turned to Joiya. She shifted her fan from hand to hand so she could wipe them on her dress, and stopped with a grimace of distaste. Her sweaty palms had nothing to do with the temperature.

"Her face," Aviendha said abruptly. And surprisingly; she almost never spoke unless addressed by Moiraine or one of the others. "Amico's face. She does not have the look she did, as if the years had passed her by. Not as much as she did. Is that because she was . . . because she was stilled?" she finished in a breathless rush. She had picked up a few habits being so much around them. No woman of the Tower could speak of stilling without a chill.

Egwene moved down the table, to where she could see Amico's face from the side and yet stay out of Joiya's vision. Joiya's eyes always turned her stomach to a lump of ice.

Aviendha was right; that was the difference she herself had noticed and not understood. Amico looked young, perhaps younger than her years, but it was not quite the agelessness of Aes Sedai who had worked years with the One Power. "You have sharp eyes, Aviendha, but I don't know if this has anything to do with stilling. It must, though, I suppose. I don't know what else could cause it."

She realized that did not sound very much like an Aes Sedai, who generally spoke as if they knew everything; when an Aes Sedai said she did not know, she usually managed to make her denial appear to cloak volumes of knowledge. While she was racking her brain for something properly portentous, Nynaeve came to her rescue.

"Relatively few Aes Sedai have ever been burned out, Aviendha, and far fewer stilled."

"Burned out" was what it was called when it happened by accident; officially, stilling resulted from trial and sentence. Egwene could not see the point of it, really; it was like having two words for falling down the stairs, depending on whether you tripped or were pushed. For that, most Aes Sedai seemed to see it the same, except when teaching novices or Accepted. Three words, actually. Men were "gentled," must be gentled, before they went mad. Only now there was Rand, and the Tower did not dare gentle him.

Nynaeve had put on a lecturing tone, no doubt trying to sound Aes Sedai. She was doing an imitation of Sheriam before a class, Egwene realized, hands clasped at her waist, smiling slightly as if it were all so simple when you applied yourself.

"Stilling is not a thing anyone would choose to study, you understand," Nynaeve continued. "It is generally accepted to be irreversible. What makes a woman able to channel cannot be replaced once it is removed, any more than a hand that has been cut off can be Healed back into existence." At least, no one had ever been able to Heal stilling. There had been attempts. What Nynaeve said was generally true, yet some sisters of the Brown Ajah would study almost anything if given the chance, and some Yellow sisters, the best Healers, would try to learn to Heal anything. But even a hint of success at Healing a woman who had been stilled was nonexistent. "Aside from that one hard fact, little is known. Women who are stilled seldom live more than a few years. They seem to stop wanting to live; they give up. As I said, it is an unpleasant subject."

Aviendha shifted uncomfortably. "I only thought that might be it," she said in a low voice.

Egwene thought it might be, too. She resolved to ask Moiraine. If she ever saw her without Aviendha there as well. It seemed to her that their deceit got in the way almost as much as it helped.

"Let us see if Joiya still tells the same tale, too." Even so, she had to take herself in hand before she could unravel the flows of Air woven around the Darkfriend.

Joiya must have been stiff from standing so still for so long, but she turned smoothly to face them. The sweat beading her forehead could not diminish her dignity and presence, any more than her drab, rough dress lessened the sense of her being there by choice. She was a handsome woman with something motherly about her face despite its ageless smoothness, something comforting. But the dark eyes set in that face made a hawk's look kind. She smiled at them, a smile that never reached those eyes. "The Light illumine you. May the hand of the Creator shelter you."

"I will not hear that out of you." Nynaeve's voice was quiet and calm, but she tossed her braid over her shoulder and gripped the end in her fist, the way she did when angry or uneasy. Egwene did not think she was uneasy; Joiya did not seem to make Nynaeve's skin crawl as she did Egwene's.

"I have repented my sins," Joiya said smoothly. "The Dragon is Reborn, and he holds *Callandor*. The Prophecies are fulfilled. The Dark One must fail. I can see that, now. My repentance is real. No one can walk so long in the Shadow that she cannot come again to the Light."

Nynaeve's face had grown darker by the word. Egwene was sure she was furious enough to channel now, but if she did it would probably be to strangle Joiya. Egwene did not believe Joiya's repentance any more than Nynaeve, of course, but the woman's information might be real.

Joiya was quite capable of a cold decision to go over to what she believed would be the winning side. Or she might only be buying time, lying in hope of rescue.

Lies should not have been possible for an Aes Sedai, even one who had lost all right to the name, not outright lies. The very first of the Three Oaths, taken with the Oath Rod in hand, should have seen to that. But whatever oaths to the Dark One were sworn on joining the Black Ajah, they seemed to sever all Three Oaths.

Well. The Amyrlin had sent them out to hunt the Black Ajah, to hunt Liandrin and the other twelve who had done murder and fled the Tower. And all they had to go on now was what these two could, or would, tell them.

"Give us your tale again," Egwene commanded. "Use different words, this time. I am tired of listening to memorized stories." If she was lying, there was more chance she would trip herself up telling it differently. "We will hear you out." That was for Nynaeve's benefit; she gave a loud sniff, then a curt nod.

Joiya shrugged. "As you wish. Let me see. Different words. The false Dragon, Mazrim Taim, who was captured in Saldaea, can channel with incredible strength. Perhaps as much as Rand al'Thor, or nearly so, if the reports can be believed. Before he can be brought to Tar Valon and gentled, Liandrin means to break him free. He will be proclaimed as the Dragon Reborn, his name given as Rand al'Thor, and then he will be set to destruction on such a scale as the world has not seen since the War of the Hundred Years."

"That is impossible," Nynaeve broke in. "The Pattern will not accept a false Dragon, not now that Rand has proclaimed himself."

Egwene sighed. They had had this out before, but Nynaeve always argued the point. She was not sure Nynaeve really believed that Rand was the Dragon Reborn, no matter what she said, no matter the Prophecies and *Callandor* and the fall of the Stone. Nynaeve was just enough older than he to have looked after him when he was a child, just as she had after Egwene. He was an Emond's Fielder, and Nynaeve still saw her first duty as protecting the people of Emond's Field.

"Is that what Moiraine told you?" Joiya asked with a touch of contempt. "Moiraine has spent little time in the Tower since she was raised, and not much more with her sisters anywhere. I suppose she knows the workings of village life, perhaps even something of the politics between nations, but she does claim certainty about matters learned only through study and discussion with those who know. Still, she might be correct. Mazrim Taim might well find it impossible to proclaim himself. But if others do it for him, is there a difference that matters?"

Egwene wished Moiraine would come back. The woman would not speak so confidently if Moiraine were there. Joiya knew very well that she and Nynaeve were only Accepted. It made a difference.

"Go on," Egwene said, almost as harshly as Nynaeve. "And remember, different words."

"Of course," Joiya replied, as though responding to a gracious invitation, but her eyes glittered like chips of black glass. "You can see the obvious result. Rand al'Thor will be blamed for the depredations of . . . Rand al'Thor. Even proof that they are not the same man may well be dismissed. After all, who can say what tricks the Dragon Reborn can play? Perhaps put himself in two places at once. Even the sort who have always rallied to a false Dragon will hesitate in the face of the indiscriminate slaughter and worse laid at his feet. Those who do not shrink at such butchery will seek out the Rand al'Thor who seems to revel in blood. The nations will unite as they did in the Aiel War . . ." She gave Aviendha an apologetic smile, incongruous beneath those merciless eyes. ". . . but no doubt much more quickly. Even the Dragon Reborn cannot stand against that, not forever. He will be crushed before the Last Battle even begins, by the very ones he was meant to save. The Dark One will break free, the day of Tarmon Gai'don will come, and the Shadow will cover the earth and remake the Pattern for all time. That is Liandrin's plan." There was not a hint of satisfaction in her voice, but no horror, either.

It was a plausible story, more plausible than Amico's tale of a few eavesdropped sentences, but Egwene believed Amico and not Joiya. Perhaps because she wanted to. A vague threat in Tanchico was easier to face than this fully fleshed plan to turn every hand against Rand. *No, she thought. Joiya is lying. I am sure she is.* Yet they could not afford to ignore either story. But they could not chase after both, not with any hope of success.

The door banged open, and Moiraine strode in, with Elayne following. The Daughter-Heir was frowning at the floor in front of her toes, lost in dark thoughts, but Moiraine. . . . For once the Aes Sedai's serenity had vanished; fury painted her face.

CHAPTER
6

Doorways

R and al'Thor," Moiraine told the air in a low, tight voice, "is a mule-headed, stone-willed fool of a . . . a . . . a man!"

Elayne lifted her chin angrily. Her childhood nurse, Lini, used to say you could weave silk from pig bristles before you could make a man anything but a man. But that was no excuse for Rand.

"We breed them that way in the Two Rivers." Nynaeve was suddenly all half-suppressed smiles and satisfaction. She seldom hid her dislike of the Aes Sedai half as well as she thought she did. "Two Rivers women never have any trouble with them." From the startled look Egwene gave her, that was a lie big enough to warrant having her mouth washed out.

Moiraine's brows drew down as if she were about to reply to Nynaeve in harder kind. Elayne stirred, but she could not find anything to say that would head off argument. Rand kept dancing through her head. He had no right! But what right did she have?

Egwene spoke instead. "What did he do, Moiraine?"

The Aes Sedai's eyes swung to Egwene, a stare so hard that the younger woman stepped back and snapped her fan open, nervously fluttering it at her face. But Moiraine's gaze settled on Joiya and Amico, the one watching her warily, the other bound and unaware of anything but the far wall.

Elayne gave a small start at realizing Joiya was not bound. Hastily she checked the shield blocking the woman from the True Source. She hoped none of the others had noticed her jump; Joiya frightened her nearly to death, but Egwene and Nynaeve were no more scared of the woman than Moiraine was. Sometimes it was difficult being as brave as the Daughter-Heir of Andor should be; she often found herself wishing she could manage as well as those two.

"The guards," Moiraine muttered as if to herself. "I saw them in the corridor still, and never thought." She smoothed her dress, composing herself with an obvious effort. Elayne did not believe she had ever seen Moiraine so out of herself as tonight. But then, the Aes Sedai had cause. *No more than I do. Or do I?* She found herself trying not to meet Egwene's eyes.

Had it been Egwene or Nynaeve or Elayne who was off balance, Joiya would surely have said something, subtle and of two meanings, calculated to upset them a little more. If they had been alone, at least. With Moiraine, she only watched uneasily, silently.

Moiraine walked the length of the table, her calm restored. Joiya was nearly a head the taller, but had she also been dressed in silks, there would have been no doubt which was in command of the situation. Joiya did not quite draw back, but her hands tightened on her skirts for a moment before she could master them.

"I have made arrangements," Moiraine said quietly. "In four days you will be taken upriver by ship, to Tar Valon and the Tower. There they are not so gentle as we have been. If you have not found the truth so far, find it before you reach Southharbor, or you will assuredly go to the gallows in the Traitors' Court. I will not speak to you again unless you send word that you have something new to tell. And I do not want to hear a word from you—not one word—unless it *is* new. Believe me, it will save you pain in Tar Valon. Aviendha, will you tell the captain to bring in two of his men?" Elayne blinked as the Aiel woman unfolded herself and vanished through the doorway; sometimes Aviendha could be so still she seemed not to be there.

Joiya's face worked as if she wanted to speak, but Moiraine stared up at her, and finally the Darkfriend turned her eyes away. They glittered like a raven's, full of black murder, but she held her tongue.

To Elayne's eyes a golden-white glow suddenly surrounded Moiraine, the glow of a woman embracing *saidar*. Only another woman trained to channel could have seen it. The flows holding Amico unraveled more quickly than Elayne could have managed. She was stronger than Moiraine, potentially, at least. In the Tower, the women teaching her had been almost unbelieving at her potential, and at Egwene's and Nynaeve's. Nynaeve was the strongest of them all—when she could manage to channel. But Moiraine had the experience. What they were still learning to do, Moiraine could do half asleep. Yet there were some things Elayne could do, and the other two, that the Aes Sedai could not. It was a small satisfaction in the face of how easily Moiraine cowed Joiya.

Freed, able to hear, Amico turned and became aware of Moiraine for the first time. With a squeak, she dropped a curtsy as deep as any new novice. Joiya was glaring at the door, avoiding anyone's gaze. Nynaeve, arms crossed and knuckles white from gripping her braid, was giving Moiraine a stare almost as murderous as Joiya's. Egwene fingered her skirt and glowered at Joiya; Elayne frowned, wishing she were as brave as Egwene, wishing she did not feel she was betraying her friend. Into that walked the captain with two more Defenders in black and gold on his heels. Aviendha was not with them; it seemed she had taken her opportunity to escape Aes Sedai.

The grizzled officer, two short white plumes on his rimmed helmet, shied as his eyes met Joiya's, though she did not even seem to see him. His gaze skittered from woman to woman uncertainly. The mood of the room was trouble, and a wise man did not want any part of trouble among this sort of women. The two soldiers clutched their tall spears to their sides almost as if they feared they might have to defend themselves. Perhaps they did fear it.

"You will take these two back to their cells," Moiraine told the officer curtly. "Repeat your instructions. I want no mistakes."

"Yes, Ae—" The captain's throat seemed to seize. He gulped a breath. "Yes, my Lady," he said, watching her anxiously to see if that would do. When she only continued to look at him, waiting, he gave an audible sigh of relief. "The prisoners are to talk to no one except myself, not even each other. Twenty men in the guardroom and two outside each cell at all times, four if a cell door has to be opened for any reason. I myself will watch their food prepared and take it to them. All as you have commanded, my Lady." A hint of question tinged his voice. A hundred rumors floated through the Stone concerning the prisoners, and why two women needed to be guarded so heavily. And there were whispered stories about the Aes Sedai, each darker than the last.

"Very good," Moiraine said. "Take them."

It was not clear who was more eager to leave the room, the prisoners or the guards. Even Joiya stepped quickly, as if she could not bear keeping silent near Moiraine for another moment.

Elayne was certain she had kept her face calm since entering the room, but Egwene came to her, put an arm around her. "What is the matter, Elayne? You look about to cry."

The concern in her voice made Elayne feel like bursting into tears. *Light!* she thought. *I will not be that silly. I will not! "A weeping woman is a bucket with no bottom."* Lini had been full of sayings like that.

"Three times—" Nynaeve burst out at Moiraine, "only three!—you have consented to help us question them. This time you vanish before we begin, and now you calmly announce you are sending them off to Tar Valon! If you will not help, at least do not interfere!"

"Do not presume on the Amyrlin's authority too far," Moiraine said coolly. "She may have set you to chase Liandrin, but you are still only Accepted, and woefully ignorant, whatever letters you carry. Or did you mean to keep questioning them forever before reaching a decision? You Two Rivers people seem to work at avoiding decisions that must be made." Nynaeve opened and closed her mouth, eyes bulging, as if wondering which accusation to answer first, but Moiraine turned to Egwene and Elayne. "Pull yourself together, Elayne. How you can carry out the Amyrlin's orders if you think every land has the customs you were born to, I do not know. And I do not know why you are so upset. Do not let your feelings hurt others."

"What do you mean?" Egwene said. "What customs? What are you talking about?"

"Berelain was in Rand's chambers," Elayne said in a small voice before she could stop herself. Her eyes flickered guiltily toward Egwene. Surely she had kept her own feelings hidden.

Moiraine gave her a reproachful look and sighed. "I would have spared you this if I could, Egwene. If Elayne had not let her disgust with Berelain overcome her sense. The customs of Mayene are not those either of you were born to. Egwene, I know what you feel for Rand, but you must realize by now that nothing can come of it. He belongs to the Pattern, and to history."

Seemingly ignoring the Aes Sedai, Egwene peered into Elayne's eyes. Elayne wanted to look away, and could not. Suddenly Egwene leaned closer, whispering behind a cupped hand. "I love him. Like a brother. And you like a sister. I wish you well of him."

Elayne's eyes widened, a smile spreading slowly across her face. She answered Egwene's hug with a fierce hug of her own. "Thank you," she murmured softly. "I love you too, sister. Oh, thank you."

"She got it wrong," Egwene said half to herself, a delighted grin blooming on her face. "Have you ever been in love, Moiraine?"

What a startling question. Elayne could not imagine the Aes Sedai in love. Moiraine was Blue Ajah, and it was said Blue sisters gave all their passions to causes.

The slender woman was not at all taken aback. For a long moment she looked levelly at the pair of them, each with an arm around the other. Finally she said, "I could wager I know the face of the man I will marry better than either of you knows that of your future husband."

Egwene gaped in surprise.

"Who?" Elayne gasped.

The Aes Sedai appeared regretful of having spoken. "Perhaps I only meant we share an ignorance. Do not read too much into a few words." She looked at Nynaeve consideringly. "Should I ever choose a man—should, I say—it will not be Lan. That much I will say."

That was a sop to Nynaeve, but Nynaeve did not seem to like hearing it. Nynaeve had what Lini would have called "a hard patch to hoe," loving not just a Warder but a man who tried to deny returning her love. Fool man that he was, he talked of the war against the Shadow he could not stop fighting and could never win, of refusing to dress Nynaeve in widow's clothes for her wedding feast. Silly things of that sort. Elayne did not see how Nynaeve put up with it. She was not a very patient woman.

"If you are finished chatting about men," Nynaeve said acidly, as though to prove just that, "perhaps we can go back to what is important?" Gripping her braid hard, she picked up speed and force as she went along, like a waterwheel with the gears disengaged. "How are we to decide whether Joiya is lying, or Amico, if you send them away? Or whether they both are? Or neither? I don't relish dithering here, Moiraine, no matter what you think, but I have walked into too many traps to want to walk into another. And I don't want to run after Jak-o'-the-Wisps, either. I . . . we . . . are the ones the Amyrlin sent after Liandrin and her cronies. Since you don't seem to think they are important enough to spare more than a moment to help us, the least you can do is not crack our ankles with a broom!"

She seemed about to rip that braid free and try to strangle the Aes Sedai with it, and Moiraine wore a dangerously cool crystalline calm that suggested she might be ready to teach again the lesson on holding her tongue that she had taught Joiya. It was, Elayne decided, time for her to stop moping. She did not know how she had fallen into the role of peacemaker among these women—sometimes she wanted to take them all by the scruff of the neck and shake them—but her mother always said no good decision was ever made in anger. "You might add to your list of what you want to know," she said, "why were we summoned to Rand? That is where Careen took us. He is all right, now, of course. Moiraine Healed him." She could not repress a shudder, thinking of her brief glimpse inside his chamber, but the diversion worked a charm.

"Healed!" Nynaeve gasped. "What happened to him?"

"He almost died," the Aes Sedai said, as calmly as if she were saying he had a pot of tea.

Elayne felt Egwene tremble as they listened to Moiraine's dispassionate report, but perhaps some of the trembling was her own. Bubbles of evil drifting through the Pattern. Reflections leaping out of mirrors. Rand a mass of blood and wounds. Almost as an afterthought, Moiraine added that she was sure Perrin and Mat had experienced something of the same, but escaped unharmed. The woman must have ice instead of blood. *No, she was heated enough about Rand's stubbornness. And she wasn't cold when she spoke of marrying, however much she pretended to be.* But now she could have been discussing whether a bolt of silk was the right color for a dress.

"And these . . . these *things* will keep on?" Egwene said when Moiraine finished. "Is there nothing you can do to stop it? Or that Rand can do?"

The small blue stone dangling from Moiraine's hair swung as she shook her head. "Not until he learns to control his abilities. Perhaps not then. I do not know if even he will be strong enough to push the miasma away from himself. At the least, though, he will be better able to defend himself."

"Can't you do something to help him?" Nynaeve demanded. "You are the one of us who is supposed to know everything, or pretends to. Can't you teach him? Some part of it, anyway? And don't quote proverbs about birds teaching fish to fly."

"You would know better," Moiraine replied, "if you had taken the advantage of your studies that you should have. You should know better. You want to know how to use the Power, Nynaeve, but you do not care to learn *about* the Power. *Saidin* is not *saidar*. The flows are different, the ways of weaving are different. The bird has a better chance."

This time Egwene took a turn at diffusing tension. "What is Rand being stubborn about, now?" Nynaeve opened her mouth, and she added, "He can be stubborn as a stone, sometimes." Nynaeve shut her mouth with a snap; they all knew how true that was.

Moiraine eyed them, considering. At times, Elayne was not sure how much the Aes Sedai trusted them. Or anyone. "He must move," the Aes Sedai said at last. "Instead, he sits here, and the Tairens already begin to lose their fear of him. He sits here, and the longer he sits, doing nothing, the more the Forsaken will see his inaction as a sign of weakness. The Pattern moves and flows; only the dead are still. He must act, or he will die. From a crossbow bolt in his back, or poison in his food, or the Forsaken banding together to rip his soul from his body. He must act or die." Elayne winced at each danger on her list; that they were real only made it worse.

"And you know what he must do, don't you?" Nynaeve said tightly. "You have this action planned."

Moiraine nodded. "Would you rather he go haring off alone once more? I dare not risk it. This time he might be dead, or worse, before I find him."

That was true enough. Rand hardly knew what he was doing. And Elayne was sure Moiraine had no wish to lose the little guidance she still gave him. The little he allowed her to give.

"Will you share your plan for him with us?" Egwene demanded. She was certainly not helping soothe the air now.

"Yes, do," Elayne said, surprising herself with a cool echo of Egwene's tone. Confrontation was not her way when it could be avoided; her mother always said it was better to guide people than try to hammer them into line.

If their manner irritated Moiraine, she gave no sign of it. "As long as you understand that you must keep it to yourselves. A plan revealed is a plan doomed to fail. Yes, I see you do understand."

Elayne certainly did; the plan was dangerous, and Moiraine was not sure it would work.

"Sammael is in Illian," the Aes Sedai went on. "The Tairens are always as ripe for war with Illian as the other way around. They have been killing each other off and on for a thousand years, and they speak of their chance for it as other men speak of the next feastday. I doubt even knowing of Sammael's presence would change that, not with the Dragon Reborn to lead them. Tear will follow Rand eagerly enough in that enterprise, and if he brings Sammael down, he—"

"Light!" Nynaeve exclaimed. "You not only want him to start a war, you want him to seek out one of the Forsaken! No wonder he is being stubborn. He is not a fool, for a man."

"He must face the Dark One in the end," Moiraine said calmly. "Do you truly think he can avoid the Forsaken now? As for war, there are wars enough without him, and every one worse than useless."

"Any war is useless," Elayne began, then faltered as comprehension suddenly filled her. Sadness and regret had to show on her face, too, but certainly comprehension. Her mother had lectured her often on how a nation was led as well as how it was governed, two very different things, but both necessary. And sometimes things had to be done for both that were worse than unpleasant, although the price of not doing them was worse still.

Moiraine gave her sympathetic look. "It is not always pleasant, is it? Your mother began when you were just old enough to understand, I suppose, teaching you what you will need to rule after her." Moiraine had grown up in the Royal Palace in Cairhien, not destined to reign, but related to the ruling family and no doubt overhearing the same lectures. "Yet sometimes it seems ignorance would be better, to be a farm woman knowing nothing beyond the boundaries of her fields."

"More riddles?" Nynaeve said contemptuously. "War used to be something I heard about from peddlers, something far away that I didn't really understand. I know what it is, now. Men killing men. Men behaving like animals, reduced to animals. Villages burned, farms and fields burned. Hunger, disease and death, for the innocent as the guilty. What makes this war of yours better, Moiraine? What makes it cleaner?"

"Elayne?" Moiraine said quietly.

She shook her head—she did not want to be the one to explain this —but she was not sure even her mother sitting on the Lion Throne could have kept silent under Moiraine's compelling, dark-eyed stare. "War will come whether Rand begins it or not," she said reluctantly. Egwene stepped back a pace, staring at her in disbelief no sharper than that on Nynaeve's face; the incredulity faded from both women as she continued. "The Forsaken will not stand idly and wait. Sammael cannot be the only one to have seized a nation's reins, just the lone one we know. They will come after Rand eventually, in their own persons per- haps, but certainly with whatever armies they command. And the na- tions that are free of the Forsaken? How many will cry glory to the Dragon banner and follow him to Tarmon Gai'don, and how many will convince themselves the fall of the Stone is a lie and Rand only another false Dragon who must be put down, a false Dragon perhaps strong enough to threaten them if they do not move against him first? One way or another, war *will* come." She cut off sharply. There was more to it, but she could not, would not, tell them that part.

Moiraine was not so reticent. "Very good," she said, nodding, "yet incomplete." The look she gave Elayne said she knew Elayne had left out what she had on purpose. Hands folded calmly at her waist, she addressed Nynaeve and Egwene. "Nothing makes this war better, or cleaner. Except that it will cement the Tairens to him, and the Illianers will end up following him just as the Tairens do now. How could they not, once the Dragon banner flies over Illian? Just the news of his victory might decide the wars in Tarabon and Arad Doman in his favor; there are wars *ended* for you.

"In one stroke he will make himself so strong in terms of men and swords that only a coalition of every remaining nation from here to the Blight can defeat him, and with the same blow he shows the Forsaken that he is not a plump partridge on a limb for the netting. That will make them wary, and buy him time to learn to use his strength. He must move first, be the hammer, not the nail." The Aes Sedai grimaced slightly, a hint of her earlier anger marring her calm. "He *must* move first. And what does he do? He reads. Reads himself into deeper trouble."

Nynaeve looked shaken, as if she could see all the battles and death; Egwene's dark eyes were large with horrified understanding. Their faces made Elayne shiver. One had watched Rand grow up, the other had grown up with him. And now they saw him starting wars. Not the Dragon Reborn, but Rand al'Thor.

Egwene struggled visibly, latching onto the smallest part, the most inconsequential, of what Moiraine had said. "How can reading put him in trouble?"

"He has decided to find out for himself what the Prophecies of the Dragon say." Moiraine's face remained cool and smooth, but suddenly she sounded almost as tired as Elayne felt. "They may have been proscribed in Tear, but the Chief Librarian had nine different translations in a locked chest. Rand has them all, now. I pointed out the verse that applies here, and he quoted it to me, from an old Kandori translation.

> " *'Power of the Shadow made human flesh,*
> *wakened to turmoil, strife and ruin.*
> *The Reborn One, marked and bleeding,*
> *dances the sword in dreams and mist,*
> *chains the Shadowsworn to his will,*
> *from the city, lost and forsaken,*
> *leads the spears to war once more,*

breaks the spears and makes them see,
truth long hidden in the ancient dream.' "

She grimaced. "It applies to this as well as it does to anything. Illian under Sammael is surely a forsaken city. Lead the Tairen spears to war, chain Sammael, and he has fulfilled the verse. The ancient dream of the Dragon Reborn. But he will not see it. He even has a copy in the Old Tongue, as if he understood two words. He runs after shadows, and Sammael, or Rahvin, or Lanfear may have him by the throat before I can convince him of his mistake."

"He is desperate." Nynaeve's gentle tone was not for Moiraine, Elayne was sure, but for Rand. "Desperate and trying to find his way."

"So am I desperate," Moiraine said firmly. "I have dedicated my life to finding him, and I will not let him fail if I can prevent it. I am almost desperate enough to—" She broke off, pursing her lips. "Let it be enough that I will do what I must."

"But it isn't enough," Egwene said sharply. "What is it you'll do?"

"You have other matters to concern you," the Aes Sedai said. "The Black Ajah—"

"No!" Elayne's voice was knife-edged and commanding, her knuckles a hard white where she gripped her soft blue skirts. "You keep many secrets, Moiraine, but tell us this. What do you mean to do to him?" An image flashed in her mind of seizing Moiraine and shaking the truth out of her if need be.

"Do to him? Nothing. Oh, very well. There is no reason you should not know. You have seen what the Tairens call the Great Holding?"

Oddly for a people that feared the Power so, the Tairens held in the Stone a collection of objects connected to the Power second only to that in the White Tower. Elayne, for one, thought it was because they had been forced to guard *Callandor* so long, whether they wanted or not. Even the Sword That Is Not a Sword might seem less than what it was when it was one among many. But the Tairens had never been able to make themselves display their prizes. The Great Holding was kept in a filthy series of crowded rooms buried even deeper than the dungeons. When Elayne had first seen them the locks on the doors had long since rusted shut, where the doors had not simply collapsed from dry rot.

"We spent an entire day down there," Nynaeve said. "To see if Liandrin and her *friends* took anything. I don't think they did. Everything was buried in dust and mold. It will take ten riverboats to transport all of it to the Tower. Perhaps they can make some sense of it there; I surely could not." The temptation to prod Moiraine was apparently too great to avoid, for she added, "You would know all this if you had given us a little more of your time."

Moiraine took no notice. She seemed to be looking inward, examining her own thoughts, and she spoke almost to herself. "There is one particular *ter'angreal* in the Holding, a thing like a redstone doorframe, subtly twisted to the eye. If I cannot make him reach *some* decision, I may have to step through." The small blue stone on her forehead trembled, sparkling. Apparently she was not eager to take that step.

At the mention of *ter'angreal*, Egwene instinctively touched the bodice of her dress. She had sewn a small pocket there herself, to hide the stone ring it now held. That ring was a *ter'angreal*, powerful in its way if small, and Elayne was one of only three women who knew she had it. Moiraine was not one of the three.

They were strange things, *ter'angreal*, fragments of the Age of Legends like *angreal* and *sa'angreal*, if more numerous. *Ter'angreal* used the One Power instead of magnifying it. Each had apparently been made to do one thing and one thing alone, but though some were used now, no one was sure if those uses were anything like what they had been made for. The Oath Rod, on which a woman took the Three Oaths on being raised Aes Sedai, was a *ter'angreal* that made those oaths a part of her flesh and bone. The last test a novice took on being raised to Accepted was inside another *ter'angreal* that ferreted out her most heartfelt fears and made them seem real—or perhaps took her to a place where they *were* real. Odd things could happen with *ter'angreal*. Aes Sedai had been burned out or killed, or had simply vanished, in studying them. And in using them.

"I saw that doorway," Elayne said. "In the last room at the end of the hall. My lamp went out, and I fell three times before I made it to the door." A slight flush of embarrassment reddened her cheeks. "I was afraid to channel in there, even to relight the lamp. Much of it looks rubbish, to me—I think the Tairens simply grabbed anything that anyone hinted might be connected to the Power—but I thought if I channeled, I might accidentally empower something that wasn't rubbish, and who knows what it might do."

"And if you had stumbled in the dark and fallen through the twisted doorway?" Moiraine said wryly. "That needs no channeling, only to step through."

"To what purpose?" Nynaeve asked.

"To gain answers. Three answers, each true, about past, present or future."

Elayne's first thought was for the children's tale, *Bili Under the Hill,* but only because of the three answers. A second thought came on its heels, and not to her alone. She spoke while Nynaeve and Egwene were still opening their mouths. "Moiraine, this solves our problem. We can ask whether Joiya or Amico is telling the truth. We can ask where Liandrin and the others are. The names of the Black Ajah still in the Tower—"

"We can ask what this thing is that is dangerous to Rand," Egwene put in, and Nynaeve added, "Why haven't you told us of this before? Why have you let us go on listening to the same tales day after day when we could have settled it all by now?"

The Aes Sedai winced and threw up her hands. "You three rush in blindly where Lan and a hundred Warders would tread warily. Why do you think I have not stepped through? Days ago I could have asked what Rand must do to survive and triumph, how he can defeat the Forsaken and the Dark One, how he can learn to control the Power and hold off madness long enough to do what he must." She waited, hands on hips, while it sank in. None of them spoke. "There are rules," she went on, "and dangers. No one may step through more than once. Only once. You may ask three questions, but you must ask all three and hear the answers before you may leave. Frivolous questions are punished, it seems, but it also seems what may be serious for one can be frivolous coming from another. Most importantly, questions touching the Shadow have dire consequences.

"If you asked about the Black Ajah, you might be returned dead, or come out a gibbering madwoman, if you came out at all. As for Rand. . . . I am not certain it is possible to ask a question about the Dragon Reborn that does not touch the Shadow in some way. You see? Sometimes there are reasons for caution."

"How do you know all this?" Nynaeve demanded. Planting fists on hips she confronted the Aes Sedai. "The High Lords surely never let Aes Sedai study anything in the Holding. From the filth down there, none of it has seen sunlight in a hundred years or more."

"More, I should think," Moiraine told her calmly. "They ceased their collecting nearly three hundred years gone. It was just before they stopped completely that they acquired this *ter'angreal.* Up until then it was the possession of the Firsts of Mayene, who used its answers to help keep Mayene out of Tear's grasp. And they allowed Aes Sedai to study it. In secret, of course; Mayene has never dared anger Tear too openly."

"If it was so important to Mayene," Nynaeve said suspiciously, "why is it here, in the Stone?"

"Because Firsts have made bad decisions as well as good in trying to keep Mayene free of Tear. Three hundred years ago the High Lords were planning to build a fleet to follow Mayener ships and find the oilfish shoals. Halvar, the then First, raised the price of Mayener lamp oil well above that of oil from Tear's olives, and to further convince the High Lords that Mayene would always put its own interests behind those of Tear, made them a gift of the *ter'angreal.* He had already used it, so it was no further good to him, and he was almost as young as Berelain is now, apparently with a long reign ahead of him and many years of needing Tairen goodwill."

"He was a fool," Elayne muttered. "My mother would never make such a mistake."

"Perhaps not," Moiraine said. "But then, Andor is not a small nation cornered by a much larger and stronger. Halvar *was* a fool as it turned out—the High Lords had him assassinated the very next year—but his foolishness does present me with an opportunity, if I need it. A dangerous one, yet better than none."

Nynaeve muttered to herself, perhaps disappointed that the Aes Sedai had not tripped herself up.

"It leaves the rest of us right where we were." Egwene sighed. "Not knowing who is lying, or whether they both are."

"Question them again, if you wish," Moiraine said. "You have until they are put on the ship, though I very much doubt either will change her tale now. My advice is to concentrate on Tanchico. If Joiya speaks truly, it will take Aes Sedai and Warders to guard Mazrim Taim, not just the three of you. I sent a warning to the Amyrlin by pigeon when I first heard Joiya's story. In fact, I sent three pigeons, to make sure one reaches the Tower."

"So kind of you to keep us informed," Elayne murmured coolly. The woman did go her own way. Just because they were only pretending to be full Aes Sedai was no reason for Moiraine to keep them in the dark. The Amyrlin had sent *them* out to hunt the Black Ajah.

Moiraine inclined her head briefly, as if accepting the thanks for real. "You are welcome. Remember that you are the hounds the Amyrlin set after the Black Ajah." Her slight smile at Elayne's start said she knew exactly what Elayne had been thinking. "The decision on where to course must be yours. You have pointed that out to me, as well," she added drily. "I trust it will prove an easier decision than mine. And I trust you will sleep well, what sleep is left before daybreak. A good night to you."

"That woman . . ." Elayne muttered when the door had closed behind the Aes Sedai. "Sometimes I could almost strangle her." She dropped into one of the chairs at the table and sat frowning at her hands in her lap.

Nynaeve gave a grunt that might have been agreement as she went to a narrow table against the wall where silver goblets and spice jars stood next to two pitchers. One pitcher, full of wine, rested in a gleaming bowl of now mostly melted ice, brought all the way from the Spine of the World packed in chests of sawdust. Ice in the summer to chill a High Lord's drink; Elayne could barely imagine such a thing.

"A cool drink before bed will do us all good," Nynaeve said, busying herself with wine and water and spices.

Elayne lifted her head as Egwene took a seat next to her. "Did you mean what you said, Egwene? About Rand?" Egwene nodded, and Elayne sighed. "Do you remember what Min used to say, all her jokes about sharing him? I sometimes wondered if that was a viewing she did not tell us about. I thought she meant we both loved him, and she knew it. But you had the right to him, and I didn't know what to do. I still don't. Egwene, he loves you."

"He will just have to be put straight," Egwene said firmly. "When I marry, it will be because I want to, not just because a man expects me to love him. I will be gentle with him, Elayne, but before I am done, he will know he is free. Whether he wants to be or not. My mother says men are different from us. She says we want to be in love, but only with the one we want; a man needs to be in love, but he will love the first woman to tie a string to his heart."

"That is all very well," Elayne said in a tight voice, "but Berelain was in his chambers."

Egwene sniffed. "Whatever she intends, Berelain won't keep her mind on one man long enough to make him love her. Two days ago she was casting eyes at Rhuarc. In two more, she'll be smiling at someone else. She is like Else Grinwell. You remember her? The novice who spent all her time out at the practice yards fluttering her eyelashes at the Warders?"

"She was not just fluttering her eyelashes, in his bedchamber at this hour. She was wearing even less than usual, if that is possible!"

"Do you mean to let her have him, then?"

"No!" Elayne said it very fiercely, and she meant it, but in the next breath she was full of despair. "Oh, Egwene, I do not know what to do. I love him. I want to marry him. Light! What will mother say? I would rather spend a night in Joiya's cell than listen to the lectures mother will give me." Andoran nobles, even in royal families, married commoners often enough that it hardly occasioned comment—in Andor, at least—but Rand was not exactly the usual run of commoner. Her mother was quite capable of actually sending Lini to drag her home by her ear.

"Morgase can hardly say much if Mat is to be believed," Egwene said comfortingly. "Or even half believed. This Lord Gaebril your mother is mooning after hardly sounds the choice of a woman thinking with her head."

"I am sure Mat exaggerated," Elayne replied primly. Her mother was too shrewd to make herself a fool over any man. If Lord Gaebril— she had never even heard of him before Mat spoke his name—if this fellow dreamed he could gain power through Morgase, she would give him a rude awakening.

Nynaeve brought three goblets of spiced wine to the table, beads of condensation running down their shining sides, and small green-and-gold woven straw mats to put them on so the damp would not mar the table's polish. "So," she said, taking a chair, "you've discovered you are in love with Rand, Elayne, and Egwene has discovered she isn't."

The two younger women gaped at her, one dark, the other fair, yet a near mirror image of astonishment.

"I have eyes," Nynaeve said complacently. "And ears, when you don't take the trouble to whisper." She sipped at her wine, and her voice grew cold when she continued. "What do you mean to do about it? If that chit Berelain has her claws into him, it will not be easy to pry them loose. Are you sure you want to go to the effort? You know what he is. You know what lies ahead of him, even setting the Prophecies aside. Madness. Death. How long does he have? A year? Two? Or will it begin before summer's end? He is a man who can channel." She bit off each word in tones of iron. "Remember what you were taught. Remember what he is."

Elayne held her head high and met Nynaeve stare for stare. "It does not matter. Perhaps it should, but it doesn't. Perhaps I am being foolish. I do not care. I cannot change my heart to order, Nynaeve."

Suddenly Nynaeve smiled. "I had to be sure," she said warmly. "You must be sure. It isn't easy loving any man, but loving this man will be harder yet." Her smile faded as she went on. "My first question still has to be answered. What do you mean to do about it? Berelain may look soft—she certainly makes men see her so!—but I do not think she is. She will fight for what she wants. And she's the kind to hold hard to something she doesn't particularly want, just because someone else does want it."

"I would like to stuff her in a barrel," Egwene said, gripping her goblet as if it were the First's throat, "and ship her back to Mayene. In the bottom of the hold."

Nynaeve's braid swung as she shook her head. "All very well, but try to offer advice that helps. If you cannot, keep silent and let her decide what she must do." Egwene stared at her, and she added, "Rand is Elayne's to deal with, now, not yours. You have stepped aside, remember."

The remark should have made Elayne smile, but it did not. "This was all supposed to be different." She sighed. "I thought I would meet a man, learn to know him over months or years, and slowly I would come to realize I loved him. That is the way I always thought it would be. I hardly know Rand. I've talked with him no more than half a dozen times in the space of a year. But I knew I loved him five minutes after I first set eyes on him." Now that *was* foolish. Only, it was true, and she did not care if it was foolish. She would tell her mother the same to her face, and Lini. Well, perhaps not Lini. Lini had drastic ways of dealing with foolishness, and she seemed to think Elayne had not aged beyond ten. "As matters stand, though, I don't even have the right to be angry with him. Or Berelain." But she was. *I would like to slap his face till his ears ring for a year! I'd like to switch her all the way to the ship that takes her back to Mayene!* Only, she did *not* have the right, and that made it all the worse. Infuriatingly, a plaintive tone touched her voice. "What can I do? He has never looked at me twice."

"In the Two Rivers," Egwene said slowly, "if a woman wants a man to know she is interested in him, she puts flowers in his hair at Bel Time or Sunday. Or she might embroider a feastday shirt for him any time. Or make a point of asking him to dance and no one else." Elayne gave her an incredulous look, and she hastened to add, "I am not suggesting you embroider a shirt, but there are ways to let him know how you feel."

"Mayeners believe in speaking out." Elayne's voice held a brittle edge. "Perhaps that is the best way. Just tell him right out. At least he'll know how I feel, then. At least I'll have some right to—"

She snatched her spiced wine and tilted her head back, drinking. Speak out? Like some *Mayener* hussy! Setting the empty goblet back on the small mat, she drew a deep breath and murmured, "What *will* Mother say?"

"What's more important," Nynaeve said gently, "is what you will do when we have to leave here. Whether it's Tanchico, or the Tower, or somewhere else, we will have to go. What will you do when you've just told him you love him, and you must leave him behind? If he asks you to stay with him? If you want to?"

"I will go." There was no hesitation in Elayne's reply, but a touch of asperity. The other woman should not have had to ask. "If I must accept him being the Dragon Reborn, he must accept that I am what I am, that I have duties. I want to be Aes Sedai, Nynaeve. It isn't some idle amusement. Neither is the work we three have to do. Could you really think I would abandon you and Egwene?"

Egwene hurried to assure her that the thought had never crossed her mind; Nynaeve did the same, but slowly enough to give herself the lie.

Elayne looked from one to the other of them. "In truth, I feared you might tell me I was foolish, fretting over a thing like this when we have the Black Ajah to worry about."

A slight flicker of Egwene's eyes said the thought had occurred to her, but Nynaeve said, "Rand is not the only one who might die next year, or next month. We might, too. Times are not what they were, and we cannot be, either. If you sit and wish for what you want, you may not see it this side of the grave."

It was a chilling sort of reassurance, but Elayne nodded. She was *not* being silly. If only the Black Ajah could be settled so easily. She pressed her empty silver goblet to her forehead for the coolness. What were they to do?

CHAPTER
7

Playing With Fire

With the sun barely above the horizon the next morning, Egwene presented herself at the doors to Rand's chambers, followed by a foot-dragging Elayne. The Daughter-Heir wore a long-sleeved dress of pale blue silk, cut in the Tairen fashion, and pulled low after some little discussion. A necklace of sapphires like a deep morning sky, and another strand woven into her red-gold curls, showed up the blue of her eyes. Despite the damp warmth, Egwene wore a plain, deep red scarf, as large as a shawl, around her shoulders. Aviendha had supplied the scarf, and the sapphires too. Surprisingly, the Aiel woman had a tidy store of such things somehow.

For all she had known they were there, Egwene gave a start when the Aiel guards glided to their feet with startling suddenness. Elayne let out a small gasp, but quickly eyed them with that regal bearing she managed so well. It seemed to have no effect on these sun-dark men. The six were *Shae'en M'taal*, Stone Dogs, and appeared relaxed for Aiel, meaning they seemed to be looking everywhere, seemed ready to move in any direction.

Egwene drew herself up in imitation of Elayne—she did wish she could do that as well as the Daughter-Heir—and announced, "I . . . we . . . want to see how the Lord Dragon's wounds are."

Her remark was plainly foolish, if they knew much about Healing, but that likelihood was small; few people did, and Aiel probably less than most. She had not intended to give any reason for being there—it was enough that they thought her Aes Sedai—but when the Aiel appeared almost to spring out of the black marble floor, it suddenly seemed a good idea. Not that they were making any move to stop Elayne and her, of course. But these men were all so tall, so stone-faced, and they carried those short spears and horn bows as if using them would be as natural as breathing, and as easy. With those light-colored eyes regarding her so intently, it was all too easy to remember stories of black-veiled Aiel, without mercy or pity, of the Aiel War and the men like these who had destroyed every army sent against them until the last, who had only turned back to the Waste after fighting the allied nations to a standstill during three blood-soaked days and nights before Tar Valon itself. She very nearly embraced *saidar*.

Gaul, the Stone Dogs' leader, nodded, looking down at Elayne and her with a touch of respect. He was a handsome man, in a rugged way, a little older than Nynaeve, with eyes as green and clear as polished gems and long eyelashes so dark they seemed to outline his eyes in black. "They may be troubling him. He is in a foul mood this morning." Gaul grinned, just a quick flash of white teeth, in understanding of a temper when wounded. "He has chased off a group of these High Lords already, and threw one of them out himself. What was his name?"

"Torean," another, even taller man replied. He had an arrow nocked, the short, curved bow held almost casually. His gray eyes rested on the two women for an instant, then went back to searching among the anteroom's columns.

"Torean," Gaul agreed. "I thought he would slide as far as those pretty carvings . . ." He pointed a spear to the ring of stiff-standing Defenders. ". . . but he came short by three paces. I lost a good Tairen hanging, all hawks in gold thread, to Mangin." The taller man gave a brief, contented smile.

Egwene blinked at the image of Rand physically pitching a High Lord across the floor. He had never been violent; far from it. How much had he changed? She had been too busy with Joiya and Amico, and he too busy with Moiraine or Lan or the High Lords, to do more than speak in passing, a few words about home here and there, about how the Bel Tine festival might have gone this year and what Sunday would be like. It had all been so brief. How much had he changed?

"We have to see him," Elayne said, a slight tremor in her voice.

Gaul made a bow, grounding the point of one spear on the black marble. "Of course, Aes Sedai."

It was with some trepidation that Egwene entered Rand's chambers, and Elayne's face spoke volumes of the effort those few steps took.

No evidence of last night's horror remained, unless it was the absence of mirrors; lighter patches marked the wall panels where those hanging there had been taken away. Not that the room came anywhere near neatness; books lay everywhere, on everything, some lying open as if abandoned in the middle of a page, and the bed was still unmade. The crimson draperies were pulled open on all the windows, facing westward toward the river that was Tear's heartvein, and *Callandor* sparkled like polished crystal on a huge gilded stand of surpassing gaudiness. Egwene thought the stand the ugliest thing she had ever seen decorating a room—until she glimpsed the silver wolves savaging a golden stag on the mantel above the fireplace. Scant breezes off the river kept the room surprisingly cool compared to the rest of the Stone.

Rand sat in his shirtsleeves, sprawled in a chair with one leg over the arm and a leather-bound book propped against his knee. At the sound of their footsteps, he snapped the book shut and dropped it among the others on the scroll-worked carpet, bounding to his feet ready to fight. The scowl on his face faded as he took in who they were.

For the first time in the Stone, Egwene looked for changes in him and found them. How many months before then since she had seen him last? Enough for his face to have grown harder, for the openness that had once been there to fade. He moved differently, too, a little like Lan, a little like the Aiel. With his height and his reddish hair, and eyes that seemed now blue, now gray, as the light took them, he looked all too much like an Aielman, too much for comfort. But had he changed inside?

"I thought you were . . . someone else," he mumbled, sharing out embarrassed glances between them. That was the Rand she knew, even to the flush that rose in his cheeks every time he looked at her or Elayne, either one. "Some . . . people want things I can't give. Things I *will* not give." Suspicion grew on his face with shocking suddenness, and his tone hardened. "What do *you* want? Did Moiraine send you? Are you supposed to convince me to do what she wants?"

"Don't be a goose," Egwene said sharply before she thought. "I do not want you to start a war!"

Elayne added in pleading tones, "We came to . . . to help you, if we can." That was one of their reasons, and the easiest to bring up, they had decided over breakfast.

"You know about her plans for . . ." he began roughly, then made a sudden shift. "Help me? How? That is what Moiraine says."

Egwene sternly folded her arms beneath her breasts, holding the scarf tight, in the way Nynaeve used to address the Village Council when she meant to have her way no matter how stubborn they were. It was too late to start over; the only thing was to go on as she had begun. "I told you not to be a fool, Rand al'Thor. You may have Tairens bowing to your boots, but I remember when Nynaeve switched your bottom for letting Mat talk you into stealing a jar of apple brandy." Elayne kept her face carefully composed. Too carefully; it was plain to Egwene that she wanted to laugh out loud.

Rand did not notice, of course. Men never did. He grinned at Egwene, close to laughing himself. "We had just turned thirteen. She found us asleep behind your father's stable, and our heads hurt so much we didn't even feel her switch." That was not at all the way Egwene recalled it. "Not like when you threw that bowl at her head. Remember? She'd dosed you with dogweed tea because you had been moping about for a week, and as soon as you tasted it, you hit her with her best bowl. Light, did you squeal! When was that? Two years ago come this—"

"We are not here to talk over old times," Egwene said, shifting the scarf irritably. It was thin wool, but still far too hot. Really, he did have the habit of remembering the most unfortunate things.

He grinned as if he knew what she was thinking, and went on in better humor. "You are here to help me, you say. With what? I don't suppose you know how to make a High Lord keep his word when I'm not staring over his shoulder. Or how to stop unwanted dreams? I could surely use help with—" Eyes darting to Elayne and back to her, he made another abrupt shift. "What about the Old Tongue? Did you learn any of that in the White Tower?" Without waiting for an answer he began rooting through the volumes scattered across the carpet. There were more on the chairs, among the tumbled bedclothes. "I have a copy here . . . somewhere . . . of. . . ."

"Rand." Egwene raised her voice. "Rand, I cannot read the Old Tongue." She shot a look at Elayne, warning her not to admit to any such knowledge. They had not come to translate the Prophecies of the Dragon for him. The sapphires in the Daughter-Heir's hair swayed as she nodded agreement. "We had other things to learn."

He straightened from the books with a sigh. "It was too much to hope." For a moment he seemed on the point of saying more, but stared at his boots. Egwene wondered how he managed to deal with the High Lords in all their arrogance if she and Elayne put him so out of countenance.

"We came to help you with channeling," she told him. "With the Power." What Moiraine claimed was supposed to be true; a woman could not teach a man to channel any more than she could teach him how to bear a child. Egwene was not so sure. She had felt something woven from *saidin,* once. Or rather, she had felt nothing, something blocking her own flows as surely as stone dammed water. But she had learned as much outside the Tower as within; surely in her knowledge there was something she could teach him, some guidance she could offer.

"If we can," Elayne added.

Suspicion flashed across his face again. It was unnerving how his mood changed so quickly. "I have more chance of reading the Old Tongue than you do of. . . . Are you sure this isn't Moiraine's doing? Did she send you here? Thinks she can convince me by some round-about way, does she? Some twisty Aes Sedai plot I'll not see the point of until I am mired in it?" He grunted sourly and pulled a dark green coat from the floor behind one of the chairs, shrugging into it hastily. "I agreed to meet some more of the High Lords this morning. If I don't keep an eye on them, they just find ways to get around what I want. They'll learn sooner or later. I rule Tear, now. Me. The Dragon Reborn. I will teach them. You will have to excuse me."

Egwene wanted to shake him. He ruled Tear? Well, perhaps he did, if it came to that, but she remembered a boy with a lamb nestled inside his coat, proud as a rooster because he had driven off the wolf that tried to take it. He was a shepherd, not a king, and even if he had call to give himself airs, it was no good to him that he did.

She was about to tell him as much, but before she could Elayne spoke up fiercely. "No one sent us. No one. We came because . . . because we care for you. Perhaps it will not work, but you can try. If I . . . if we care enough to try, you can try, too. Is it so unimportant to you that you cannot spare us an hour? For your life?"

He stopped buttoning up his coat, staring at the Daughter-Heir so intently that for a moment Egwene thought he had forgotten she was there. With a shiver he pulled his eyes away. Glancing at Egwene, he shifted his feet and frowned at the floor. "I will try," he muttered. "It'll do no good, but I will. . . . What do you want me to do?"

Egwene drew a deep breath. She had not thought convincing him would be this easy; he had always been like a boulder buried in mud when he decided to dig his heels in, which he did far too often.

"Look at me," she said, embracing *saidar*. She let the Power fill her as completely as it ever had, more completely, accepting every drop she could hold; it was as if light suffused every particle of her, as if the Light itself filled every cranny. Life seemed to burst inside her like fireworks. She had never before let this much in. It was a shock to realize she was not quivering; surely she could not bear this glorious sweetness. She wanted to revel in it, to dance and sing, to simply lie back and let it roll through her, over her. She made herself speak. "What do you see? What do you feel? Look at me, Rand!"

He lifted his head slowly, still frowning. "I see you. What am I supposed to see? Are you touching the Source? Egwene, Moiraine has channeled around me a hundred times, and I never saw anything. Except what she did. It doesn't work that way. Even I know that much."

"I am stronger than Moiraine," she told him firmly. "She would be whimpering on the floor, or insensible, if she tried to hold as much as I hold now." It was true, though she had never before rated the Aes Sedai's ability so closely.

It cried out to be used, this Power pulsing through her stronger than heartblood. With this much, she could do things Moiraine could not dream of doing. The wound in Rand's side that Moiraine could never Heal completely. She did not know Healing—it was considerably more complex than anything she had ever done—but she had watched Nynaeve Heal, and perhaps, with this great pool of the Power filling her, she could see something of how that could be Healed. Not to do it, of course; only to see.

Carefully she spun out hair-fine flows of Air and Water and Spirit, the Powers used for Healing, and felt for his old injury. One touch, and she recoiled, shivering, snatching back her weaving; her stomach churned as if every meal she had ever eaten wanted to come up. It seemed that all the darkness in the world rested there in Rand's side, all the world's evil in a festering sore only lightly covered by tender scar tissue. A thing like that would soak up Healing flows like drops of water on dry sand. How could he bear the pain? Why was he not weeping?

From first thought to action had taken only a moment. Shaken, and desperately hiding it, she went on without a pause. "You are as strong as I. I know it; you must be. Feel, Rand. What do you feel?" *Light, what can Heal that? Can anything?*

"I don't feel anything," he muttered, shifting his feet. "Goose bumps. And no wonder. It's not that I don't trust you, Egwene, but I cannot help being nervous when a woman is channeling around me. I am sorry."

She did not bother explaining to him the difference between channeling and merely embracing the True Source. There was so much he did not know, even compared to her own scant knowledge. He was a blind man trying to work a loom by touch, with no idea of colors or what the threads, or even the loom, looked like.

With an effort she released *saidar,* and it was an effort. Part of her wanted to cry at the loss. "I am not touching the Source now, Rand." She stepped closer and peered up at him. "Do you still feel goose bumps?"

"No. But that's just because you told me." He gave an abrupt shrug of his shoulders. "You see? I started thinking about it, and I have them again."

Egwene smiled triumphantly. She did not need to look around at Elayne to confirm what she had already sensed, what they had agreed upon earlier for this point. "You can sense a woman embracing the Source, Rand. Elayne is doing just that right now." He squinted at the Daughter-Heir. "It doesn't matter what you see or don't see. You felt it. We have that much. Let's see what else we can find. Rand, embrace the Source. Embrace *saidin.*" The words came out hoarsely. They had agreed on this, too, she and Elayne. He was Rand, not a monster from the stories, and they had agreed on it, but still, asking a man to. . . . The wonder was that she had gotten the words out at all. "Do you see anything?" she asked Elayne. "Or feel anything?"

Rand still doled out glances between them, in between staring at the floor and sometimes blushing. Why *was* he so out of countenance? Studying him fixedly, the Daughter-Heir shook her head. "He could just be standing there for all I can tell. Are you sure he is doing anything?"

"He can be stubborn, but he isn't foolish. At least, he isn't foolish most of the time."

"Well, stubborn or foolish or something else, I feel nothing at all."

Egwene frowned at him. "You said you would do as we asked, Rand. Are you? If you felt something, so should I, and I do not—" She broke off with a stifled yelp. *Something* had pinched her bottom. Rand's lips twitched, clearly fighting a grin. "That," she told him crisply, "was not nice."

He tried to keep his face innocent, but the grin slipped. "You said you wanted to feel something, and I just thought—" His sudden roar made Egwene jump. Clapping a hand to his left buttock, he hobbled in a pained circle. "Blood and ashes, Egwene! There was no need to—" He fell off into deeper, inaudible mutters Egwene was just as glad she did not understand.

She took the opportunity to flap the scarf for a little air, and shared a small smile with Elayne. The glow faded around the Daughter-Heir. They both came close to giggling as they rubbed themselves surreptitiously. That should show him. About a hundred for one, Egwene estimated.

Turning back to Rand, she put on her sternest face. "I would have expected something like that from Mat. I thought you, at least, had grown up. We came here to help you, if we can. Try to cooperate. Do something with the Power, something that isn't childish. Perhaps we will be able to sense that."

Hunched, he glared at them. "Do something," he muttered. "You had no call to— I'll limp for— You want me to do something?"

Suddenly she lifted into the air, and Elayne, too; they stared at each other, wide-eyed, as they floated a pace above the carpet. There was nothing holding them, no flows Egwene could feel or see. Nothing. Her mouth tightened. He had no right to do this. No right at all, and it was time he learned it. The same sort of shield of Spirit that cut Joiya off from the Source would stop him, too; Aes Sedai used it on the rare men they found who could channel.

She opened herself to *saidar*—and her stomach sank. *Saidar* was there—she could feel its warmth and light—but between her and the True Source stood something, nothing, an absence that shut her away from the Source like a stone wall. She felt hollow inside, until panic welled up to fill her. A man was channeling, and she was caught in it. He was Rand, of course, but dangling there like a basket, helpless, all she could think of was a man channeling, and the taint on *saidin*. She tried to shout at him, but all that came out was a croak.

"You want me to do something?" Rand growled. A pair of small tables flexed their legs awkwardly, the wood creaking, and began to stumble about in a stiff parody of dance, gilt flaking off and falling. "Do you like this?" Fire flared up in the fireplace, filling the hearth from side to side, burning on stone bare of ashes. "Or this?" The tall stag and wolves above the fireplace began to soften and slump. Thin streams of gold and silver flowed out from the mass, fining down to shining threads, snaking, weaving themselves into a narrow sheet of metallic cloth; the length of glittering fabric hung in the air as it grew, its far end still linked to the slowly melting statuette on the stone mantel. "Do something," Rand said. "Do something! Do you have any idea what it is like to touch *saidin,* to hold it? Do you? I can feel the madness waiting. Seeping into me!"

Abruptly the capering tables burst into flame like torches, dancing still; books spun into the air, pages fluttering; the mattress on the bed erupted, showering feathers across the room like snow. Feathers falling onto the burning tables filled the room with their sharp, sooty stink.

For a moment Rand stared wildly at the blazing tables. Then whatever was holding Egwene and Elayne vanished, along with the shield; their heels thumped onto the carpet in the same instant the flames went out as if sucked into the wood they had been consuming. The blaze in the fireplace winked out, as well, and the books fell to the floor in a worse jumble than before. The length of gold-and-silver cloth dropped, too, along with strands of rough-melted metal, no longer liquid or even hot. Only three largish lumps, two silver and one gold, remained on the mantel, cold and unrecognizable.

Egwene had staggered into Elayne as they landed. They clutched each other for support, but Egwene felt the other woman doing exactly what she was doing, embracing *saidar* as quickly as she could. In moments she had a shield ready to throw around Rand if he even appeared to be channeling, but he stood stunned, staring at the charred tables with feathers still drifting down around him, flecking his coat.

He did not seem to be a danger, now, but the room was certainly a mess. She wove tiny flows of Air to pull all the floating feathers together, and those already on the carpet, as well. As an afterthought, she added those on his coat. The rest of it he could have the majhere straighten, or see to himself.

Rand flinched as the feathers floated past him to alight on the tattered ruins of the mattress. It did nothing for the smell, burned feathers and burned wood, but at least the room was neater, and the open windows and faint breezes were already lessening the stench.

"The majhere may not want to give me another," he said with a strained laugh. "A mattress a day is probably more than she is willing to. . . ." He avoided looking at her or Elayne. "I'm sorry. I did not mean to . . . Sometimes it runs wild. Sometimes there's nothing there when I reach for it, and sometimes it does things I don't. . . . I'm sorry. Perhaps you had better go. I seem to say that a lot." He blushed again and cleared his throat. "I am not touching the Source, but maybe you had best go."

"We are not done yet," Egwene said gently. More gently than she felt—she wanted to box his ears; the idea of picking her up like that, shielding her—and Elayne—but he was on the ragged edge. Of what, she did not know, and she did not want to find out, not now, not here. With so many exclaiming over their strength—everyone said she and Elayne would be among the strongest Aes Sedai, if not the strongest, in a thousand years or more—she had assumed they were as strong as he. Near to it, at least. She had just been rudely disabused. Perhaps Nynaeve could come close, if she was angry enough, but Egwene knew she herself could never have done what he just had, split her flows that many ways, worked that many things at once. Working two flows at once was far more than twice as hard as working one of the same magnitude, and working three much more than twice again working two. He had to have been weaving a dozen. He did not even look tired, yet exertion with the Power took energy. She very much feared he could handle her and Elayne both like kittens. Kittens he might decide to drown, if he went mad.

But she would not, could not, just walk away. That would be the same as quitting, and she was not made that way. She meant to do what she had come there for—all of it—and he was not going to chase her off short of it. Not him or anything else.

Elayne's blue eyes were filled with determination, and the moment Egwene fell silent she added in a much firmer voice, "And we will not go until we are. You said you would try. You must try."

"I did say that, didn't I?" he murmured after a time. "At least we can sit down."

Not looking at the blackened tables or the band of metallic cloth lying crumpled on the carpet, he led them, limping slightly, to high-backed chairs near the windows. They had to move books from the red silk cushions in order to sit; Egwene's chair held Volume Twelve of *The Treasures of the Stone of Tear,* a dusty, wood-bound book entitled *Travels in the Aiel Waste, with Various Observations on the Savage Inhabitants,* and a thick, tattered leather volume called *Dealings with the Territory of Mayene, 500 to 750 of the New Era.* Elayne had a bigger stack to move, but Rand hurriedly took them from her along with those from his chair and put them all on the floor, where the pile promptly fell over. Egwene laid hers neatly beside them.

"What do you want me to do now?" He sat on the edge of his seat, hands on his knees. "I promise I won't do anything but what you ask this time."

Egwene bit her tongue to keep from telling him that promise came a bit late. Perhaps she had been a little vague in what she had asked for, but that was no excuse. Still, that was something to be dealt with another time. She realized she was thinking of him as just Rand again, but he looked as if he had just splashed mud on her best dress and was worried she would not believe it an accident. Yet she had not let go of *saidar*, and neither had Elayne. There was no need to be foolish. "This time," she said, "we just want you to talk. How do you embrace the Source? Just tell us. Take it step by step, slowly."

"More like wrestling than embracing." He grunted. "Step by step? Well, first I imagine a flame, and then I push everything into it. Hate, fear, nervousness. Everything. When they're all consumed, there's an emptiness, a void, inside my head. I am in the middle of it, but I'm a part of whatever I am concentrating on, too."

"That sounds familiar," Egwene said. "I've heard your father talk about a trick of concentration he uses to win the archery competitions. What he calls the Flame and the Void."

Rand nodded; sadly, it seemed. She thought he must be missing home, and his father. "Tam taught it to me first. And Lan uses it, too, with the sword. Selene—someone I met once—called it the Oneness. A good many people seem to know about it, whatever they call it. But I found out for myself that when I was inside the void, I could feel *saidin*, like a light just beyond the corner of my eye in the emptiness. There's nothing but me and that light. Emotion, even thought, is outside. I used to have to take it bit by bit, but it all comes at once, now. Most of it does, anyway. Most of the time."

"Emptiness," Elayne said with a shiver. "No emotion. That doesn't sound very much like what we do."

"Yes, it does," Egwene insisted eagerly. "Rand, we just do it a little differently, that's all. I imagine myself to be a flower, a rosebud, imagine it until I *am* the rosebud. That is like your void, in a way. The rosebud's petals open out to the light of *saidar*, and I let it fill me, all light and warmth and life and wonder. I surrender to it, and by surrendering, I control it. That was the hardest part to learn, really; how to master *saidar* by submitting, but it seems so natural now that I do not even think about it. That is the key to it, Rand. I am sure. You must learn to surrender—" He was shaking his head vigorously.

"That's nothing like what I do," he protested. "Let it fill me? I have to reach out and take hold of *saidin*. Sometimes there's still nothing there when I do, nothing I can touch, but if I didn't reach for it, I could stand there forever and nothing would happen. It fills me all right, once I take hold, but surrender to it?" He raked his fingers through his hair. "Egwene, if I surrendered—even for a minute—*saidin* would consume me. It's like a river of molten metal, an ocean of fire, all the light of the sun gathered in one spot. I must fight it to make it do what I want, fight it to keep from being eaten up."

He sighed. "I know what you mean about life filling you, though, even with the taint turning my stomach. Colors are sharper, smells clearer. Everything is more real, somehow. I don't want to let go, once I have it, even while it's trying to swallow me. But the rest. . . . Face the facts, Egwene. The Tower is right about this. Accept it for the truth, because it is."

She shook her head. "I will accept it when it is proved to me." She did not sound as sure as she wanted to, not as sure she had been. What he told sounded like some twisted half-reflection of what she did, similarities only emphasizing differences. Yet there were similarities. She would not give up. "Can you tell the flows apart? Air, Water, Spirit, Earth, Fire?"

"Sometimes," he said slowly. "Not usually. I just take what I need to do what I want. Fumble for it, mostly. It's very strange. Sometimes I need to do a thing, and I do it, but only afterward do I know what it was I did, or how. It's almost like remembering something I've forgotten. But I can remember how to do it again. Most of the time."

"Yet you do remember how," she insisted. "How did you set fire to those tables?" She wanted to ask him how he had made them dance— she thought she saw a way, with Air and Water—but she wanted to start with something simple; lighting a candle and putting it out were things a novice could do.

Rand's face took on a pained expression. "I don't know." He sounded embarrassed. "When I want fire, for a lamp or a fireplace, I just make it, but I do not know *how*. I don't really need to think to do things with fire."

That almost stood to reason. Of the Five Powers, Fire and Earth had been strongest in men in the Age of Legends, and Air and Water in women; Spirit had been shared equally. Egwene hardly had to think to use Air or Water, once she had learned to do a thing in the first place. But the thought did not further their purpose.

This time it was Elayne who pressed him. "Do you know how you extinguished them? You seemed to think before they went out."

"That I do remember, because I don't believe I have ever done it before. I took in the heat from the tables and spread it into the stone of the fireplace; a fireplace wouldn't even notice that much heat."

Elayne gasped, unconsciously cradling her left arm for a moment, and Egwene winced in sympathy. She remembered when that arm had been a mass of blisters because the Daughter-Heir had done what

Rand had just described, and with just the lamp in her room. Sheriam had threatened to let the blisters heal by themselves; she had not done it, but she had threatened. It was one of the warnings novices were given; never draw heat in. A flame could be extinguished using Air or Water, but using Fire to pull the heat away meant disaster with a flame of any size. It was not a matter of strength, so Sheriam had said; heat once taken in could not be gotten rid of, not by the strongest woman ever to come out of the White Tower. Women had actually burst into flame themselves that way. Women had burst into flame. Egwene drew a ragged breath.

"What's the matter?" Rand asked.

"I think you just proved the difference to me." She sighed.

"Oh. Does that mean you're ready to give up?"

"No!" She tried to make her voice softer. She was not angry with him. Exactly. She was not sure who she was angry with. "Maybe my teachers were right, but there has to be a way. Some way. Only I cannot think of one, right now."

"You tried," he said simply. "I thank you for that. It is not your fault it did not work."

"There must be a way," Egwene muttered, and Elayne murmured, "We will find it. We will."

"Of course you will," he said with a forced cheerfulness. "But not today." He hesitated. "I suppose you'll be going, then." He sounded half-regretful, half-glad. "I do need to tell the High Lords a few things about taxes this morning. They seem to think they can take as much from a farmer in a poor year as a good without beggaring him. And I suppose you have to get back to questioning those Darkfriends." He frowned.

He had not said anything, but Egwene was sure he would like to keep them as far from the Black Ajah as possible. She was a little surprised he had not already tried to make them return to the Tower. Perhaps he knew that she and Nynaeve would put a flea in his ear the size of a horse if he tried.

"We do," she said firmly. "But not right away. Rand . . ." The time had come to bring up her second reason for being there, but it was even more difficult than she had expected. This was going to hurt him; those sad, wary eyes convinced her it would. But it had to be done. She snugged the scarf around her; it enveloped her from shoulders to waist. "Rand, I cannot marry you."

"I know," he said.

She blinked. He was not taking it as hard as she expected. She told herself that was good. "I do not mean to hurt you—really, I don't—but I do not want to marry you."

"I understand, Egwene. I know what I am. No woman could—"

"You wool-brained idiot!" she snapped. "This had nothing to do with you channeling. I do not love you! At least, not in the way to want to marry you."

Rand's jaw dropped. "You don't . . . love me?" He sounded as surprised as he looked. And hurt, too.

"Please try to understand," she said in a gentler voice. "People change, Rand. Feelings change. When people are apart, sometimes they grow apart. I love you as I would a brother, perhaps more than a brother, but not to marry. Can you understand that?"

He managed a rueful grin. "I really am a fool. I didn't really believe you might change, too. Egwene, I do not want to marry you, either. I did not want to change, I didn't try to, but it happened. If you knew how much this means to me. Not having to pretend. Not being afraid I'll hurt you. I never wanted to do that, Egwene. Never to hurt you."

She very nearly smiled. He was putting on such a brave face; he was actually quite close to convincing. "I am glad you are taking it so well," she told him in a soft voice. "I did not want to hurt you, either. And now I really must go." Rising from her chair, she bent to brush a kiss across his cheek. "You will find someone else."

"Of course," he said, getting to his feet, the lie loud in his voice. "You will."

She slipped out with a sense of satisfaction and hurried across the anteroom, letting *saidar* go as she took the scarf from her shoulders. The thing was abominably hot.

He was ready for Elayne to pick up like a lost puppy if she handled him the way they had discussed. She thought Elayne would manage him nicely, now and later. For as much later as they had. Something had to be done about his control. She was willing to admit that what she had been told was right—no woman could teach him; fish and birds —but that was not the same as giving up. Something had to be done, so a way had to be found. That horrible wound and the madness were problems for later, but they would be dealt with eventually. Somehow. Everyone said Two Rivers men were stubborn, but they could not match Two Rivers women.

CHAPTER
8

Hard Heads

E layne was not certain Rand realized she was still in the room, the way he stared after Egwene with a half-bewildered expression. Now and again he shook his head as if arguing with himself, or trying to straighten his mind. She was content to wait him out. Anything that put off the moment a while longer. She concentrated on maintaining an outward composure, back straight and head high, hands folded in her lap, a calmness on her face that could have rivaled Moiraine's best. Butterflies the size of hedgehogs frolicked in her stomach.

It was not fear of him channeling. She had let go of *saidin* as soon as Egwene stood to leave. She wanted to trust him, and she had to. It was what she wanted to happen that had her trembling inside. She had to concentrate not to finger her necklace or fiddle with the strand of sapphires in her hair. Was her perfume too heavy? No. Egwene said he liked the smell of roses. The dress. She wanted to tug it up, but . . .

He turned—the slight limp in his step tightened her lips thoughtfully —saw her sitting in her chair, and gave a start, eyes widening with what seemed very close to panic. She was glad to see it; the effort of keeping her own face serene had leaped tenfold as soon as his eyes touched her. Those eyes were blue now, like a misty morning sky.

He recovered on the instant and made a quite unnecessary bow, wiping his hands once nervously on his coat. "I did not realize you were still—" Flushing, he cut off; forgetting her presence might be taken as an insult. "I mean . . . I didn't . . . that is, I. . . ." He took a deep breath and began again. "I am not as much of a fool as I sound, my Lady. It isn't every day someone tells you they don't love you, my Lady."

She put on a tone of mock severity. "If you call me that again, I shall call you my Lord Dragon. And curtsy. Even the Queen of Andor might curtsy to you, and I am only Daughter-Heir."

"Light! Don't do that." He seemed uneasy out of all proportion to the threat.

"I will not, Rand," she said in a more serious voice, "if you call me by my name. Elayne. Say it."

"Elayne." He spoke awkwardly, yet, delightfully, as if he were savoring the name, too.

"Good." It was absurd to be so pleased; all he had done was say her name, after all. There was something she had to know before she could go on. "Did it hurt you very much?" That could be taken two ways, she realized. "What Egwene told you, I mean."

"No. Yes. Some. I don't know. Fair is fair, after all." His small grin took some of the edge off of his wariness. "I sound a fool again, don't I?"

"No. Not to me."

"I told her the pure truth, but I don't think she believed me. I suppose I did not want to believe it of her, either. Not really. If that isn't foolish, I don't know what is."

"If you tell me one more time that you are a fool, I may begin to believe it." *He won't try to hold on to her; I won't have to deal with that.* Her voice was calm, with a light enough tone to let him know she did not really mean what she said. "I saw a Cairhienin lord's fool, once, a man in a funny striped coat, too big for him and sewn with bells. You would look silly wearing bells."

"I suppose I would," he said ruefully. "I will remember that." His slow grin was wider this time, warming his whole face.

The butterflies' wings flogged her for haste, but she occupied herself with straightening her skirts. She had to go slowly, carefully. *If I don't, he'll think I am just a foolish girl. And he will be right.* The butterflies in her belly were beating kettle drums, now.

"Would you like a flower?" he asked suddenly, and she blinked in confusion.

"A flower?"

"Yes." Striding to the bed, he scooped up a double handful of feathers from the tattered mattress and held them out to her. "I made one for the majhere last night. You'd have thought I had given her the Stone. But yours will be much prettier," he added hastily. "Much prettier. I promise."

"Rand, I—"

"I will be careful. It takes only a trickle of the Power. Just a thread, and I will be very careful."

Trust. She had to trust him. It was a small surprise to realize that she did. "I would like that, Rand."

For long moments he stared at the fluffy mound in his hands, a slow frown on his face. Abruptly he let the feathers fall, dusting his hands. "Flowers," he said. "That's no fit gift for you." Her heart went out to him; clearly he had tried to embrace *saidin* and failed. Masking disappointment in action, he limped hurriedly to the metallic cloth and began gathering it over his arm. "Now this is a proper gift for the Daughter-Heir of Andor. You could have a seamstress make. . . ." He floundered over what a seamstress might make from a four-pace length of gold-and-silver cloth, less than two feet wide.

"I am sure a seamstress will have many ideas," she told him diplomatically. Pulling a handkerchief from her sleeve, she knelt for a moment to collect the feathers he had dropped into the square of pale blue silk.

"The maids will take care of that," he said as she tucked the small bundle securely into her belt pouch.

"Well, this bit is done." How could he understand that she would keep the feathers because he had wanted them to be a flower? He shifted his feet, holding the glittering folds as if he did not know what to do with them. "The majhere must have seamstresses," she told him. "I will give that to one of them." He brightened, smiling; she saw no reason to tell him she meant it as a gift. Those thundering butterflies would not let her hold back any longer. "Rand, do you . . . like me?"

"Like you?" he frowned. "Of course, I like you. I like you very much."

Did he have to look as if he did not understand at all? "I am fond of you, Rand." She was startled that she said it so calmly; her stomach seemed to be trying to writhe up into her throat, and her hands and feet felt like ice. "More than fond." That was enough; she was not going to make a fool of herself. *He has to say more than "like," first.* She almost giggled hysterically. *I will keep control of myself. I will not let him see me behave like a moon-eyed girl. I will not.*

"I am fond of you," he said slowly.

"I am not usually so forward." No; that might make him think of
Berelain. There was red in his cheeks; he *was* thinking of Berelain.
Burn him! Her voice came as smooth as silk. "Soon I will have to go,
Rand. To leave Tear. I may not see you again for months." *Or ever,* a
tiny voice cried in her head. She refused to listen. "I could not go
without letting you know how I feel. And I am . . . very fond of you."

"Elayne, I *am* fond of you. I feel. . . . I want. . . ." The scarlet
spots on his cheeks grew. "Elayne, I don't know what to say, how
to . . ."

Suddenly it was her face that was flaming. He must think she was
trying to force him into saying more. *Aren't you?* the small voice
mocked, which only made her cheeks hotter. "Rand, I am not asking
for. . . ." Light! How to say it? "I only wanted you to know how I feel.
That is all." Berelain would not have let it go at that. Berelain would
have been wrapped around him by now. Telling herself she would not
let that half-dressed snip better her, she moved closer to him, took the
glittering cloth from his arm, and dropped it on the carpet. For some
reason he seemed taller than he ever had before. "Rand. . . . Rand, I
want you to kiss me." There. It was out.

"Kiss you?" he said as if he had never heard of kissing before.
"Elayne, I don't want to promise more than. . . . I mean, it isn't as if
we were betrothed. Not that I am suggesting we should be. It's just
that. . . . I *am* fond of you, Elayne. More than fond. I just do not want
you to think I. . . ."

She had to laugh at him, with all his confused earnestness. "I do not
know how things are done in the Two Rivers, but in Caemlyn you don't
wait until you are betrothed before kissing a girl. And it does not mean
you must become betrothed, either. But perhaps you do not know
how—" His arms went around her almost roughly, and his lips came
down on hers. Her head spun; her toes tried to curl up in her slippers.
Some time later—she was not certain how long—she realized she was
leaning against his chest, knees trembling, trying to gulp air.

"Forgive me for interrupting you," he said. She was glad to hear a
touch of breathlessness in his voice. "I am just a backward shepherd
from the Two Rivers."

"You are uncouth," she murmured against his shirt, "and you did not
shave this morning, but I would not say you are backward."

"Elayne, I—"

She put a hand over his mouth. "I do not want to hear anything from you that you do not mean with your whole heart," she said firmly. "Not now, or ever."

He nodded, not as if he understood why, but at least as if he understood that she meant what she said. Straightening her hair—the strand of sapphires was tangled beyond mending without a mirror—she stepped out of his encircling arms, not without reluctance; it would be all too easy to remain there, and she had already been more forward than she had ever dreamed of before. Speaking up like that; asking for a kiss. Asking! She was not Berelain.

Berelain. Perhaps Min had had a viewing. What Min saw, happened, but she would not share him with Berelain. Perhaps she needed to do a bit more plain speaking. Obliquely plain, at least. "I expect you will not lack for company after I go. Just remember that some women see a man with their hearts, while others see no more than a bauble to wear, no different than a necklace or a bracelet. Remember that I will come back, and I am one who sees with her heart." He looked confused, at first, then a little alarmed. She had said too much, too fast. She had to divert him. "Do you know what you have not said to me? You have not tried to frighten me away by telling me how dangerous you are. Don't try now. It is too late."

"I did not think of it." Another thought came to him, though, and his eyes crinkled with suspicion. "Did you and Egwene scheme this up between you?"

She managed to combine wide-eyed innocence with mild outrage. "How could you even consider such a thing? Do you imagine we would hand you around between us like a package? You think a good deal of yourself. There is such a thing as being overproud." He did look confused, now. Quite satisfactory. "Are you sorry for what you did to us, Rand?"

"I did not mean to frighten you," he said hesitantly. "Egwene made me angry; she's always been able to without half trying. That's no excuse, I know. I said I was sorry, and I am. Look what it got me. Burned tables and another mattress ruined."

"And for . . . the pinch?"

His face reddened again, but he faced her firmly even so. "No. No, I am not sorry for that. The two of you, talking over my head, as if I were a lump of wood with no ears. You deserved as much, both of you, and I won't say different."

For a moment she considered him. He rubbed his arms through his coat sleeves as she momentarily embraced *saidar*. She did not know Healing to any degree, but she had learned bits and pieces on the edge of it. Channeling, she soothed away the hurt she had given him for the pinch. His eyes widened in surprise, and he shifted on his feet as if testing the absence of pain. "For being honest," she told him simply.

There was a rap at the door, and Gaul looked in. At first the Aielman had his head down, but after a quick glance at them he raised it. Color flooded Elayne's face as she realized he had suspected that he might be interrupting something he should not see. She very nearly embraced *saidar* again and taught him a lesson.

"The Tairens are here," Gaul said. "The High Lords you were expecting."

"I will go, then," she told Rand. "You must tell them about—taxes, was it not? Think on what I have said." She did not say "think of me," but she was sure the effect would be the same.

He reached out as if to stop her, but she slipped away from him. She had no intention of putting on a display in front of Gaul. The man was Aiel, but what must he think of her, wearing perfume and sapphires at that hour of the morning? It required real effort not to pull the neckline of her dress up higher.

The High Lords entered as she reached the door, a cluster of graying men in pointed beards and colorful, ornate coats with puffy sleeves. They crowded out of her way with reluctant bows, their bland faces and polite murmurs not hiding their relief that she was leaving.

She glanced back once from the doorway. A tall, broad-shouldered young man in a plain green coat among the High Lords in their silks and satin stripes, Rand looked like a stork among peacocks, yet there was something about him, a presence that said he commanded there by right. The Tairens recognized it, bending their stiff necks reluctantly. He thought probably they bowed just because he was the Dragon Reborn, and perhaps they thought so, too. But she had seen men, like Gareth Bryne, the Captain-Commander of her mother's Guards, who could have dominated a room in rags, with no title and no one knowing their name. Rand might not know it, but he was such a man. He had not been when she first saw him, but he was now. She pulled the door shut behind her.

The Aiel around the entrance glanced at her, and the captain commanding the ring of Defenders in the middle of the anteroom stared uneasily, but she barely noticed them. It was done. Or at least it was begun. Four days she had before Joiya and Amico were put on that ship, four days at most to twine herself so firmly into Rand's thoughts that he had no room for Berelain. Or if not that, firmly enough that she stayed inside his head until she had the chance to do more. She had never thought she might do a thing like this, stalk a man like a huntress stalking a wild boar. The butterflies were still gamboling in her stomach. At least she had not let him see how nervous she was. And it occurred to her that she had not once thought of what her mother would say. With that, the flutterings vanished. She did not care what her mother said. Morgase had to accept her daughter as a woman; that was all there was to it.

The Aiel bowed as she moved away, and she acknowledged them with a gracious nod that would have done Morgase proud. Even the Tairen captain looked at her as if he could see her new serenity. She did not think she would be troubled by butterflies again. For the Black Ajah perhaps, but not for Rand.

Ignoring the High Lords in their anxious semicircle, Rand watched the door close behind Elayne with wonder in his eyes. Dreams coming true, even only this much, made him uneasy. A swim in the Waterwood was one thing, but he would never have believed a dream where she came to him like this. She had been so cool and collected, while he was tripping over his own tongue. And Egwene, giving his own thoughts back to him and only concerned she might hurt him. Why was it women could go to pieces or fly into a rage at the smallest thing, yet never flicker an eyelash at what left you gaping?

"My Lord Dragon?" Sunamon murmured even more diffidently than usual. Word of this morning must have spread through the Stone already; that first lot had nearly run on their way out, and it was doubtful Torean would show his face, or his filthy suggestions, anywhere Rand was.

Sunamon essayed an ingratiating smile, then smothered it, drywashing his plump hands, when Rand only looked at him. The rest pretended they did not see the burned tables, or the shattered mattress and scattered books, or the half-melted lumps over the fireplace that had been the stag and wolves. High Lords were good at seeing only what they wanted to see. Carleon and Tedosian, false self-effacement in every line of their thick bodies, surely never realized there was anything suspicious in never looking at one another. But then, Rand might never have noticed if not for Thom's note, found in the pocket of a coat just back from being brushed.

"The Lord Dragon wished to see us?" Sunamon managed.

Could Egwene and Elayne have worked it up between them? Of course not. Women did not do things like that any more than men. Did they? It had to be coincidence. Elayne heard that he was free and decided to speak. That was it. "Taxes," he barked. The Tairens did not move, but they gave the impression of stepping back. How he hated dealing with these men; he wanted to dive back into the books.

"It is a bad precedent, my Lord Dragon, lowering taxes," a lean, gray-haired man said in an oily voice. Meilan was tall for a Tairen, only a hand shorter than Rand, and hard as any Defender. He held himself in a stoop in Rand's presence; his dark eyes showed how he hated it. But he had hated it when Rand told them to stop crouching around him, too. None of them straightened, but Meilan especially had not liked being reminded of what he did. "The peasants have always paid easily, but if we lower their taxes, when the day comes that we raise them back to where they now are, the fools will complain as bitterly as if we had doubled the present levy. There might well be riots when that day comes, my Lord Dragon."

Rand strode across the room to stand before *Callandor;* the crystal sword glittered, outshining the gilt and gemstones surrounding it. A reminder of who he was, of the power he could wield. Egwene. It was foolish to feel hurt because she said she no longer loved him. Why should he expect her to have feelings for him that he did not have for her? Yet it did hurt. A relief, but not a pleasant one. "You will have riots if you drive men off their farms." Three books stood in a stack almost by Meilan's feet. *The Treasures of the Stone of Tear, Travels in the Waste,* and *Dealings with the Territory of Mayene.* The keys lay in those, and in the various translations of *The Karaethon Cycle,* if he could only find them and fit them to the proper locks. He pushed his mind back to the High Lords. "Do you think they will watch their families starve and do nothing?"

"The Defenders of the Stone have put down riots before, my Lord Dragon," Sunamon said soothingly. "Our own guards can keep peace in the countryside. The peasants will not disturb you, I give you my assurance."

"There are too many farmers as it is." Carleon flinched at Rand's glare. "It is the civil war in Cairhien, my Lord Dragon," he explained hurriedly. "The Cairhienin can buy no grain, and the granaries are bursting. This year's harvest will go to waste as it is. And next year . . . ? Burn my soul, my Lord Dragon, but what we need is for some of those peasants to stop their eternal digging and planting." He seemed to realize he had said too much, though he clearly did not understand why. Rand wondered whether he had any idea how food got to his table. Did he see anything but gold, and power?

"What will you do when Cairhien is buying grain again?" Rand said coolly. "For that matter, is Cairhien the only land that needs grain?" Why *had* Elayne spoken up like that? What *did* she expect of him? Fond, she said. Women could play games with words like Aes Sedai. Did she mean she loved him? No, that was plain foolishness. Overproud to a degree.

"My Lord Dragon," Meilan said, half subservient, half as if explaining something to a child, "if the civil wars stopped today, Cairhien still could not buy more than a few bargeloads for two, even three years. We have always sold our grain to Cairhien."

Always—for the twenty years since the Aiel War. They were so bound up in what they had *always* done that they could not see what was so simple. Or would not see it. When the cabbages sprouted like weeds around Emond's Field, it was a near certainty that bad rain or whiteworm had struck Deven Ride or Watch Hill. When Watch Hill had too many turnips, Emond's Field would have a shortage, or Deven Ride.

"Offer it in Illian," he told them. What did Elayne expect? "Or Altara." He did like her, but he liked Min as much. Or thought he did. It was impossible to sort out his feelings for either of them. "You have ships for the sea as well as riverboats and barges, and if you don't have enough, hire them from Mayene." He liked both women, but beyond that. . . . He had spent very nearly his whole life mooning after Egwene; he was not about to dive into that again until he was sure. Sure of something. Sure. If *Dealings with the Territory of Mayene* was to be believed. . . . *Stop this,* he told himself. *Keep your mind on these weasels, or they'll find cracks to slip through, and bite you on the way.* "Pay with grain; I'm sure the First will be amenable, for a good price. And maybe a signed agreement, a treaty. . . ." That was a good word; the sort they used. ". . . pledging to leave Mayene alone in return for ships." He owed her that.

"We trade little with Illian, my Lord Dragon. They are vultures, and scum." Tedosian sounded scandalized, and so did Meilan when he said, "We have always dealt with Mayene from strength, my Lord Dragon. Never with bent knee."

Rand took a deep breath. The High Lords tensed. It always came to this. He always tried to reason with them, and it always failed. Thom said the High Lords had heads as hard as the Stone, and he was right. *What do I feel for her? Dreaming about her. She's certainly pretty.* He was not sure if he meant Elayne or Min. *Stop this! A kiss means no more than a kiss. Stop it!* Putting women firmly out of his head, he set himself to telling these stone-brained fools what they were going to do. "First, you will cut taxes on farmers by three-quarters, and on everyone else by half. Don't argue! Just do it! Second, you go to Berelain and ask—ask! —her price for hiring. . . ."

The High Lords listened with false smiles and grinding teeth, but they listened.

Egwene was considering Joiya and Amico when Mat fell in beside her, just walking down the hallway as if he merely happened to be going the same way. He was frowning to himself, and his hair needed brushing, as if he had been scrubbing his fingers through it. Once or twice he glanced at her but did not speak. The servants they passed bowed or curtsied, and so did the occasional High Lords and Ladies, if with markedly less enthusiasm. Mat's lip-curling stares at the nobles would have brought trouble if she had not been there, friend of the Lord Dragon or not.

This silence was not like him, not like the Mat she knew. Except for his fine red coat—wrinkled as if he had slept in it—he seemed no different than the old Mat, yet they were surely all different now. His quiet was unsettling. "Is last night troubling you?" she asked at last.

He missed a step. "You know about that? Well, you would, wouldn't you. Doesn't bother me. Wasn't much to it. Over and done with now, anyway."

She pretended to believe him. "Nynaeve and I do not see much of you." That was a rank understatement.

"I have been busy," he muttered with an uncomfortable shrug, looking everywhere but at her again.

"Dicing?" she asked dismissively.

"Cards." A plump maid, curtsying with her arms full of folded towels, glanced at Egwene and, apparently thinking she was not looking, winked at Mat. He grinned at her. "I've been busy playing cards."

Egwene's eyebrows rose sharply. That woman had to be ten years older than Nynaeve. "I see. It must use up a great deal of time. Playing cards. Too much to spare a few moments for old friends."

"The last time I spared you a moment, you and Nynaeve tied me up with the Power like a pig for market so you could rummage through my room. Friends don't steal from friends." He grimaced. "Besides, you're always with that Elayne, with her nose in the air. Or Moiraine. I do not like—" Clearing his throat, he shot her a sideways glance. "I don't like taking up your time. You are busy, from what I hear. Questioning

Darkfriends. Doing all sorts of important things, I should imagine. You know these Tairens think you are Aes Sedai, don't you?"

She shook her head ruefully. It was Aes Sedai he did not like. However much of the world Mat saw, nothing would ever change him. "It is not stealing to take back what was supposed to be a loan," she told him.

"I don't remember you saying anything about a loan. Aaah, what use do I have for a letter from the Amyrlin? Just get me in trouble. You could have asked, though."

She refrained from pointing out that they had asked. She wanted neither an argument nor a sulky departure. He would not call it that, of course. This time she would let him get away with his version. "Well, I am glad you are still willing to talk to me. Was there a special reason for it today?"

He shoved his fingers through his hair and muttered to himself. What he needed was his mother to haul him off by his ear for a long talking to. Egwene counseled herself to patience. She could be patient when she wanted to. She would not say a word before he did, if she burst for it.

The corridor opened into a railed colonnade of white marble, looking down on one of the Stone's few gardens. Large white blossoms covered a few small, waxy-leafed trees and gave a scent even sweeter than the banks of red and yellow roses. A sullen breeze failed to stir the hangings on the inner wall, but it did cut the morning's growing damp warmth. Mat took a seat on the wide balustrade with his back against a column and one foot up in front of him. Peering down into the garden, he finally said, "I . . . need some advice."

He wanted advice from *her?* She goggled at him. "Whatever I can do to help," she said faintly. He turned his head to her, and she did her best to assume something like Aes Sedai calm. "What do you want advice about?"

"I don't know."

It was a ten-pace drop to the garden. Besides, there were men down there weeding among the roses. If she pushed him over, he might land on one. A gardener, not a rosebush. "How am I supposed to advise you, then?" she asked in a thin voice.

"I am . . . trying to decide what to do." He looked embarrassed; he had a right to, in her opinion.

"I hope you are not thinking of trying to leave. You know how important you are. You cannot run away from it, Mat."

"You think I don't know that? I don't think I could leave if Moiraine told me I could. Believe me, Egwene, I am not going anywhere. I just want to know what's going to happen." He gave a rough shake of his head, and his voice grew tighter. "What comes next? What's in these holes in my memory? There are chunks of my life that aren't even there; they don't exist, as if they never happened! Why do I find myself spouting gibberish? People say it's the Old Tongue, but it's goose gabble to me. I want to know, Egwene. I have to know, before I go as crazy as Rand."

"Rand is not crazy," she said automatically. So Mat was not trying to run away. That was a pleasant surprise; he had not seemed to believe in responsibility. But there was pain and worry in his voice. Mat never worried, or never let anyone see it if he did. "I do not know the answers, Mat," she said gently. "Perhaps Moiraine—"

"No!" He was on his feet in a bound. "No Aes Sedai! I mean. . . . You're different. I know you, and you aren't. . . . Didn't they teach you anything in the Tower, some trick or other, something that would serve?"

"Oh, Mat, I am sorry. I am so sorry."

His laugh reminded her of their childhood. Just so he had always laughed when his grandest expectations went astray. "Ah, well, I guess it does not matter. It'd still be the Tower, if at second hand. No offense to you." Just so he had moaned over a splinter in his finger and treated a broken leg as if it were nothing at all.

"There might be a way," she said slowly. "If Moiraine says it is all right. She might."

"Moiraine! Haven't you heard a word I said? The last thing I want is Moiraine meddling. What way?"

Mat had always been rash. But he wanted no more than she did, to know. If only he showed a little sense and caution for once. A passing Tairen noblewoman with dark braids coiled about her head, shoulders bare above yellow linen, bent her knee slightly, looking at them with no expression; she walked on quickly, with a stiff back. Egwene watched her until she was well beyond earshot, and they were alone. Unless the gardeners, thirty feet below, counted. Mat was staring at her expectantly.

In the end, she told him of the *ter'angreal,* the twisted doorway that held answers on its other side. It was the dangers she emphasized, the consequences of foolish questions, or those touching the Shadow, the dangers even Aes Sedai might not know. She was more than flattered that he had come to her, but he had to show a little sense. "You must remember this, Mat. Frivolous questions can get you killed, so if you do use it, you will have to be serious for a change. And you mustn't ask any questions that touch the Shadow."

He had listened with greater and greater incredulity. When she was done, he exclaimed, "Three questions? You go in like Bili, I suppose, spend a night and come out ten years later with a purse that's always full of gold and a—"

"For once in your life, Matrim Cauthon," she snapped, "do not talk like a fool. You know very well *ter'angreal* are not stories. It's the dangers you have to be aware of. Maybe the answers you seek are inside this one, but you must not try it before Moiraine says you can. You must promise me that, or I promise you I will take you to her like a trout on a string. You know I can."

He gave a loud snort. "I'd be a fool if I did try it, no matter what Moiraine says. Walk into a bloody *ter'angreal*? It's less I want to do with the bloody Power, not more. You can blot it right out of your mind."

"It is the only chance I know, Mat."

"Not for me, it isn't," he said firmly. "No chance at all is better than that."

Despite his tone, she wanted to put an arm around him. Only he would likely make some joke at her expense, and try to goose her. He had been incorrigible from the day he was born. But he had come to her for help. "I'm sorry, Mat. What will you do?"

"Oh, play cards, I suppose. If anyone will play with me. Play stones with Thom. Dice in the taverns. I can still go as far as the city, at least." His gaze strayed toward a passing maidservant, a slender, dark-eyed girl, near his own age. "I'll find something to take up time."

Her hand itched to slap him, but instead she said cautiously, "Mat, you really aren't thinking of leaving, are you?"

"Would you tell Moiraine, if I was?" He put up his hands to forestall her. "Well, there's no need. I told you I wouldn't. I'll not pretend I'd not like to, but I won't. Is that good enough for you?" A pensive frown crept onto his face. "Egwene, do you ever wish you were back home? That none of this had ever happened?"

It was a startling question, coming from him, but she knew her answer. "No. Even with everything, no. Do you?"

"I would be a fool then, wouldn't I?" he laughed. "It's cities I like, and this one will do for now. This one will do. Egwene, you won't tell Moiraine about this, will you? About me asking for advice and all?"

"Why shouldn't I?" she asked suspiciously. He was Mat, after all.

He gave an embarrassed hitch of his shoulders. "I've been keeping wider of her than I have of. . . . Anyway, I've been staying clear, especially when she wants to root around in my head. She might think I'm weakening. You won't tell her, will you?"

"I won't," she said, "if you promise me you will not go near that *ter'angreal* without asking her permission. I shouldn't even have told you about it."

"I promise." He grinned. "I won't go near that thing unless my life depends on it. I swear." He finished with mock solemnity.

Egwene shook her head. However much everything else changed, Mat just never would.

CHAPTER
9

Decisions

Three days passed with heat and damp that seemed to sap even the Tairens' strength. The city slowed to a lethargic walk, the Stone to a crawl. Servants worked nearly in their sleep; the majhere tore her coiled braids in frustration, but even she could not find the energy to rap knuckles or flick ears with a hard finger. Defenders of the Stone slumped at their posts like half-melted candles, and the officers showed more interest in chilled wine than in making their rounds. The High Lords kept largely to their apartments, sleeping through the hottest part of the day, and a few left the Stone entirely for the relative cool of estates far to the east, on the slopes of the Spine of the World. Oddly, only the outlanders, who felt the heat worst of all, pushed on with their lives as hard as ever, if not harder. For them, the heavy heat did not weigh nearly as much as did the hours rushing by.

Mat quickly discovered that he had been right about the young lords who saw the playing cards try to kill him. Not only did they avoid him, they spread the word among their friends, often garbled; no one in the Stone who had two pieces of silver in hand would say more than hasty excuses while backing away. The rumors spread beyond the lordlings. More than one serving woman who had enjoyed a cuddle now declined, too, and two said uneasily that they had heard it was dangerous to be alone with him. Perrin appeared all wrapped up in his own worries, and

Thom seemed to vanish by sleight of hand; Mat had no idea what
occupied the gleeman, but he was seldom to be found, day or night.
Moiraine, the one person Mat wished would ignore him, instead
seemed to be there whenever he turned around; she was just passing
by, or crossing the corridor in the distance, but her eyes met his every
last time, looking as if she knew what he was thinking and what he
wanted, knew how she was going to make him do exactly what she
wanted instead. None of it made any difference in one respect; he still
managed to find excuses to put off leaving for another day. As he saw
it, he had not *promised* Egwene he would stay. But he did.

Once, he carried a lamp down into the belly of the Stone, to the so-
called Great Holding, as far as the dry-rotted door at the far end of the
narrow hallway. A few minutes of peering into the shadowy interior at
dim shapes covered with dusty canvas, roughly stacked crates and barrels, their flat ends used as shelves for jumbles of figurines and carvings
and peculiar things of crystal and glass and metal—a few minutes of
that, and he hurried away, muttering, "I'd have to be the biggest bloody
fool in the whole bloody world!"

Nothing kept him from going into the city, though, and there was no
chance at all of meeting Moiraine in the dockside taverns of the Maule,
the port district, or the inns in the Chalm, where the warehouses were,
dimly lit, cramped, often dirty places of cheap wine, bad ale, occasional
fights and unending dice games. The stakes in the dice games were
small, compared to what he had grown used to, but that was not why he
always found himself back in the Stone after a few hours. He tried not
to think about what always drew him back, near to Rand.

Perrin sometimes saw Mat in the waterfront taverns, drinking too
much cheap wine, dicing as if he did not care whether he won or lost,
once flashing a knife when a burly shipman pressed him on how often
he did win. It was not like Mat to be so irritable, but Perrin avoided
him instead of trying to find out what was troubling him. Perrin was not
there for wine or dice, and the men who thought of fighting changed
their minds after a good look at his shoulders—and his eyes. He
bought bad ale, though, for sailors in wide leather trousers and for
undermerchants with thin silver chains across their coat fronts, for any
man who looked to be from a distant land. It was rumor he hunted,
word of something that might draw Faile away from Tear. Away from
him.

He was sure if he found an adventure for her, something that
smacked of a chance at putting her name in the stories, she would go.
She pretended to understand why he had to stay, but occasionally she

still hinted that she wanted to leave and hoped he would go with her. He was certain the right bait would pull her, without him.

Most rumors she would know for outdated twistings of the truth, just as he did. The war that burned along the Aryth Ocean was said to be the work of a people no one had ever heard of before called the Sawchin, or something like it—he heard many variations from many tellers—a strange folk who might be Artur Hawkwing's armies come back after a thousand years. One fellow, a Taraboner in a round, red hat and a mustache as thick as a bull's horns, solemnly informed him that Hawkwing himself led these people, his legendary sword Justice in hand. There were rumors that the fabled Horn of Valere, meant to call dead heroes from the grave to fight in the Last Battle, had been found. In Ghealdan, riots had broken out all over the country; Illian was suffering from outbreaks of mass madness; in Cairhien, famine was slowing the killing; someplace in the Borderlands, Trolloc raids were on the increase. Perrin could not send Faile into any of that, not even to get her away from Tear.

Reports of trouble in Saldaea seemed promising—her own home must be attractive to her, and he had heard that Mazrim Taim, the false Dragon, was safely in Aes Sedai hands—but no one knew what sort of trouble. Making something up would do no good; whatever he found, she would surely ask her own questions before chasing after it. Besides, any turmoil in Saldaea might easily be as bad as the other things he heard.

He could not tell her where he was spending his time, either, because she would inevitably ask why. She knew he was not Mat, to enjoy lolling about taverns. He had never been good at lying, so he put her off as best he could, and she began to give him long, silent, slanted looks. All he could do was redouble his efforts to find a tale to lure her away. He had to send her away from him before he got her killed. He had to.

Egwene and Nynaeve spent more hours with Joiya and Amico, to no avail. Their stories never wavered. Over Nynaeve's protests, Egwene even tried telling each of them what the other had said, to see if anything joggled loose. Amico stared at them, whining that she had never heard any such plan. But it might be true, she added. It might. She sweated with eagerness to please. Joiya coolly told them to go to Tanchico if they wished. "It is an uncomfortable city now, I hear," she said smoothly, raven eyes glittering. "The King holds little more than the city itself, and I understand the Panarch has ceased keeping civil order. Strong arms and quick knives rule Tanchico. But go, if it pleases you."

No word came from Tar Valon, nothing to say if the Amyrlin was dealing with the possible threat to free Mazrim Taim. There had been plenty of time for a message to come, by quick riverboat or a man changing horses, since Moiraine had sent the pigeons—provided she had sent them. Egwene and Nynaeve argued about that; Nynaeve admitted the Aes Sedai could not lie, but she tried to find some twist in Moiraine's words. Moiraine did not seem to fret over the lack of response from the Amyrlin, though it was hard to tell through her crystal calm.

Egwene did fret over it, and over whether Tanchico was a false trail, or a real one, or a trap. The Stone's library held books about Tarabon and Tanchico, but though she read until her eyes ached she found no clue to anything dangerous to Rand. Heat and worry did nothing for her temper; she was sometimes as snappish as Nynaeve.

Some things were going well, of course. Mat was still in the Stone; obviously he really was growing up and learning about responsibility. She regretted failing him, but she was not certain any woman in the Tower could have done more. She understood his thirst to know, because she thirsted, too, although for other knowledge, for the things she could only learn in the Tower, the things she might discover that no one else had known how to do before, the lost things she might relearn.

Aviendha began to visit with Egwene, apparently of her own choice. If the woman was wary at first, well, she was Aiel, after all, and she did think Egwene was full Aes Sedai. Still, her company was enjoyable, although Egwene sometimes thought she saw unasked questions in her eyes. If Aviendha kept her reserve, it soon became apparent that she had a quick wit, and a sense of humor akin to Egwene's; they sometimes ended up giggling together like girls. Aiel ways were nothing Egwene was used to, though, such as Aviendha's discomfort at sitting in a chair, and her shock at finding Egwene in her bath, a silver-plated tub the majhere had had brought up. Not shock at walking in on her naked—in fact, when she saw that Egwene was uncomfortable, she peeled off her own clothes and sat down on the floor to talk—but at seeing Egwene sitting chest-deep in water. It was dirtying so much water that made her eyes pop. For another thing, Aviendha refused to understand why she and Elayne had not done something drastic to Berelain, since they wanted her out of the way. It was all but forbidden for a warrior to kill a woman not wed to the spear, but since neither Elayne nor Berelain were Maidens of the Spear, it was apparently quite all right in Aviendha's view for Elayne to challenge the First of Mayene to fight with knives, or failing that with fists and feet. Knives were best, as she saw it. Berelain looked the sort of woman who could be beaten several times without giving up. Best simply to challenge and kill her. Or Egwene could do it for her, as friend and near-sister.

Even with that, it was a pleasure to have someone to talk and laugh with. Elayne was occupied most of the time, of course, and Nynaeve, seeming to feel the rush of time as keenly as Egwene, gave her free moments over to moonlit walks on the battlements with Lan and to preparing foods the Warder liked with her own hands, not to mention curses that sometimes drove the cooks from the kitchen; Nynaeve did not know very much about cooking. If not for Aviendha, Egwene was not sure what she would have done in the muggy hours between questionings of the Darkfriends: sweated, undoubtedly, and worried that she might have to do something that gave her nightmares thinking of it.

By agreement, Elayne was never present at those questionings; one more set of ears listening would make no difference. Instead, whenever Rand had a moment to spare, the Daughter-Heir just happened to be close by, to talk, or simply walk holding his arm, even if it was only from a meeting with some High Lords to a room where others waited, or to a lightning inspection of the Defenders' quarters. She became quite good at finding secluded corners where the two of them could pause, alone. Of course, he always had Aiel trailing after him, but she soon cared as little for what they thought as for what her mother would. She even entered a sort of conspiracy with the Maidens of the Spear; they seemed to know every hidden nook in the Stone, and they let her know whenever Rand was alone. They seemed to think the game great sport.

The surprise was that he asked her about the governing of nations and listened to what she said. That, she wished her mother could see. More than once Morgase had laughed, half-despairingly, and told her she had to learn to concentrate. Which crafts to protect and how, and which not and why, might be dry decisions, but as important as how to care for the sick. It might be fun to guide a stubborn lord or merchant into doing what he did not want to while thinking it was his own idea, it might be warming to feed the hungry, but if the hungry were to be fed it was necessary to decide how many clerks and drivers and wagons were needed. Others might arrange it, but then you would never know until it was too late whether they had made a mistake. He listened to her, and often took her advice. She thought she could have loved him for those two things alone. Berelain was not setting foot outside her chambers; Rand had begun smiling as soon as he saw her; nothing could be finer about the world. Unless the days could stop passing.

Three short days, slipping away like water through her fingers. Joiya and Amico would be sent north and the reason for staying in Tear would vanish; it would be time for her and Egwene and Nynaeve to leave, too. She would go, when that time came; she had never considered not. Knowing that made her proud of behaving like a woman, not a girl; knowing it made her want to cry.

And Rand? He met with High Lords in his chambers and issued orders. He startled them by appearing at secret gatherings of three or four that Thom had ferreted out, just to reiterate some point from his last commands. They smiled and bowed and sweated and wondered how much he knew. A use had to be found for their energy before one of them decided that if Rand could not be manipulated, he must be killed. Whatever it took to divert them, he would not start a war. If he had to confront Sammael, so be it; but he would not start a war.

Forming his plan of action occupied most of his time not given over to hounding the High Lords. Bits and pieces came from the books he had the librarians bring to his rooms by armloads, and from his talks with Elayne. Her advice was certainly useful with the High Lords; he could see them hastily reassessing him when he displayed knowledge of things they themselves only half-knew. She stopped him when he wanted to give her the credit.

"A wise ruler takes advice," she told him, smiling, "but should never be seen to take it. Let them think you know more than you do. It will not harm them, and it will help you." She seemed pleased he had suggested it, though.

He was not entirely sure that he was not still putting off some decision, at least, because of her. Three days of planning, of trying to puzzle out what was still missing. Something was. He could not react to the Forsaken; he had to make them react to him. Three days, and on the fourth she would go—back to Tar Valon, he hoped—but once he moved, he suspected even their brief moments together would end. Three days of stolen kisses, when he could forget he was anything but a man with his arms around a woman. He knew it for a foolish reason, if true. He was relieved she did not seem to want more than his company, but in those moments alone he could forget decisions, forget the fate awaiting the Dragon Reborn. More than once he considered asking her to stay, but it would not be fair to raise her expectations when he had no idea what he wanted from her beyond her presence. If she had any expectations, of course. Much better just to think of them as a man and a young woman walking out together of a feastday evening. That became easier; sometimes he forgot she was the Daughter-Heir, and he a shepherd. But he wished she were not going. Three days. He had to decide. He had to move. In a direction no one expected.

The sun slid slowly toward the horizon on the evening of the third day. The half-drawn draperies of Rand's bedchamber lessened the reddish yellow glare. *Callandor* glittered on its ornate stand like the purest crystal.

Rand stared at Meilan and Sunamon, then tossed the thick bundle of large vellum sheets at them. A treaty, all neatly scribed, lacking only signatures and seals. It hit Meilan in the chest, and he caught it by reflex; he bowed as if honored, but his tight smile revealed clenched teeth.

Sunamon shifted from foot to foot, dry-washing his hands. "All is as you said, my Lord Dragon," he said anxiously. "Grain for ships—"

"And two thousand Tairen levies," Rand cut him off. " 'To see to proper distribution of the grain and protect Tairen interests.' " His voice was like ice, but his stomach seemed to be boiling; he nearly shook with the desire to pound at these fools with his fists. "Two thousand men. Under the command of Torean!"

"The High Lord Torean has an interest in affairs with Mayene, my Lord Dragon," Meilan said smoothly.

"He has an interest in forcing his attentions on a woman who won't look at him!" Rand shouted. "Grain for ships, I said! No soldiers. And certainly no bloody Torean! Have you even spoken to Berelain?"

They blinked at him as if they did not understand the words. It was too much. He snatched at *saidin;* the vellum in Meilan's arms erupted into flame. With a yell, Meilan hurled the fiery bundle into the bare fireplace and hurriedly brushed at sparks and scorch marks on his red silk coat. Sunamon stared at the burning sheets, which were crackling and turning black, with his mouth hanging open.

"You will go to Berelain," he told them, surprised at how calm his voice was. "By tomorrow midday you will have offered her the treaty I want, or by sunset tomorrow I'll hang both of you. If I have to hang High Lords every day, two by two, I will. I will send every last one of you to the gallows if you won't obey me. Now, get out of my sight."

The quiet tone seemed to affect them more than his shouting had. Even Meilan looked uneasy as they backed away, bowing at every other step, murmuring protestations of undying loyalty and everlasting obedience. They sickened him.

"Get out!" he roared, and they abandoned dignity, almost fighting with one another to pull the doors open. They ran. One of the Aiel guards put his head in for a moment, to see that Rand was all right, before drawing the door shut.

Rand trembled openly. They disgusted him almost as much as he disgusted himself. Threatening to hang men because they did not do as he told them. Worse, meaning it. He could remember when he did not have a temper, or, at least, when he rarely had, and had managed to keep it on a short rein.

He crossed the room to where *Callandor* sparkled with the light streaming in between the draperies. The blade looked like the finest glass, absolutely clear; it felt like steel to his fingers, sharp as a razor. He had come close to reaching for it, to deal with Meilan and Sunamon. Whether to use it as a sword or for its real purpose, he did not know. Either possibility horrified him. *I am not mad yet. Only angry. Light, so angry!*

Tomorrow. The Darkfriends would be put on a ship, tomorrow. Elayne would be leaving. And Egwene and Nynaeve, of course. Back to Tar Valon, he prayed; Black Ajah or no Black Ajah, the White Tower had to be as safe a place as there was now. Tomorrow. No more excuses to put off what he had to do. Not after tomorrow.

He turned his hands over, looking at the heron branded into each palm. He had examined them so often that he could have sketched every line perfectly from memory. The Prophecies foretold them.

> *Twice and twice shall he be marked,*
> *twice to live, and twice to die.*
> *Once the heron to set his path.*
> *Twice the heron, to name him true.*
> *Once the Dragon, for remembrance lost.*
> *Twice the Dragon, for the price he must pay.*

But if the herons "named him true," what need for Dragons? For that matter, what was a Dragon? The only Dragon he had ever heard of was Lews Therin Telamon. Lews Therin Kinslayer had been the Dragon; the Dragon was the Kinslayer. Except now there was himself. But he could not be marked with himself. Perhaps the figure on the banner was a Dragon; not even Aes Sedai seemed to know what that creature was.

"You are changed from when I last saw you. Stronger. Harder."

He spun, gaping at the young woman standing by the door, fair of skin and dark of hair and eye. Tall, dressed all in white and silver, she arched an eyebrow at the half-melted lumps of gold and silver over the fireplace. He had left them there to remind him what could happen when he acted without thinking, when he lost control. Much good it had done.

"Selene," he gasped, hurrying to her. "Where did you come from? How did you get here? I thought you must still be in Cairhien, or. . . ." Looking down at her, he did not want to say he feared she might be dead, or a starving refugee.

A woven silver belt glittered around her narrow waist; silver combs worked with stars and crescent moons shone in hair that fell to her shoulders like waterfalls of night. She was still the most beautiful woman he had ever seen. Elayne and Egwene were only pretty beside her. For some reason, though, she did not affect him the way she had; perhaps it was the long months since he had last seen her, in a Cairhien not yet racked by civil war.

"I go where I wish to be." She frowned at his face. "You have been marked, but no matter. You were mine, and you are mine. Any other is no more than a caretaker whose time has passed. I will lay claim to what is mine openly, now."

He stared at her. Marked? Did she mean his hands? And what did she mean, he was hers? "Selene," he said gently, "we had pleasant days together—and hard days; I'll never forget your courage, or your help— but there was never more between us than companionship. We traveled together, but that was the end of it. You will stay here in the Stone, in the best apartments, and when peace returns to Cairhien, I will see that your estates there are returned to you, if I can."

"You *have* been marked." She smiled wryly. "Estates in Cairhien? I may have had estates in those lands, once. The land has changed so much that nothing is as it was. Selene is only a name I sometimes use, Lews Therin. The name I made my own is Lanfear."

Rand barked a shallow laugh. "A poor joke, Selene. I'd as soon make jests about the Dark One as one of the Forsaken. And my name is Rand."

"We call ourselves the Chosen," she said calmly. "Chosen to rule the world forever. We *will* live forever. You can, also."

He frowned at her worriedly. She actually thought she was. Her travails in reaching Tear must have unhinged her. But she did not look mad. She was calm, cool, certain. Without thinking, he found himself reaching for *saidin*. He reached for it—and struck a wall he could not see or feel, except that it kept him from the Source. "You can't be." She smiled. "Light," he breathed. "You *are* one of them."

Slowly, he backed away. If he reached *Callandor,* at least he would have a weapon. Perhaps it could not work as an *angreal,* but it would do for a sword. Could he use a sword against a woman, against Selene? No, against Lanfear, against one of the Forsaken.

His back came up hard against something, and he looked around to see what it was. There was nothing there. A wall of nothing, with his back pressed against it. *Callandor* glittered not three paces away—on the other side. He thumped a fist against the barrier in frustration; it was as unyielding as rock.

"I cannot trust you fully, Lews Therin. Not yet." She came closer, and he considered simply seizing her. He was bigger and stronger by far—and blocked as he was, she could wrap him up with the Power like a kitten tangled in a ball of string. "Not with that, certainly," she added, grimacing at *Callandor.* "There are only two more powerful that a man can use. One at least, I know, still exists. No, Lews Therin. I will not trust you yet with that."

"Stop calling me that," he growled. "My name is Rand. Rand al'Thor."

"You are Lews Therin Telamon. Oh, physically, nothing is the same except your height, but I would know who is behind those eyes even if I'd found you in your cradle." She laughed suddenly. "How much easier everything would be if I had found you then. If I had been free to. . . ." Laughter faded into an angry stare. "Do you wish to see my true appearance? You can't remember that, either, can you?"

He tried to say no, but his tongue would not work. Once he had seen two of the Forsaken together, Aginor and Balthamel, the first two loosed, after three thousand years trapped just beneath the seal on the Dark One's prison. The one had been more withered than anything could be and still live; the other hid his face behind a mask, hid every bit of his flesh as though he could not bear to see it or have it seen.

The air rippled around Lanfear, and she changed. She was—older than he, certainly, but older was not the right word. More mature. Riper. Even more beautiful, if that was possible. A lush blossom in full flower compared to a bud. Even knowing what she was, she made his mouth go dry, his throat tighten.

Her dark eyes examined his face, full of confidence yet with a hint of questioning, as if wondering what he saw. Whatever she perceived seemed to satisfy her. She smiled again. "I was buried deeply, in a dreamless sleep where time did not flow. The turnings of the Wheel passed me by. Now you see me as I am, and I have you in my hands."

She drew a fingernail along his jaw hard enough to make him flinch. "The time for games and subterfuge is past, Lews Therin. Long past."

His stomach lurched. "Do you mean to kill me, then? The Light burn you, I—"

"Kill you?" she spat incredulously. "Kill you! I mean to have you, forever. You were mine long before that pale-haired milksop stole you. Before she ever saw you. You loved me!"

"And you loved power!" For a moment he felt dazed. The words sounded true—he knew they were true—but where had they come from?

Selene—Lanfear—seemed as startled as he, but she recovered quickly. "You've learned much—you have done much I'd not have believed you could, unaided—but you are still fumbling your way through a maze in the dark, and your ignorance may kill you. Some of the others fear you too much to wait. Sammael, Rahvin, Moghedien. Others, perhaps, but those of a certainty. They will come after you. They will not try to turn your heart. They will come at you by stealth, destroy you while you sleep. Because of their fear. But there are those who could teach you, show you what you once knew. None would dare oppose you then."

"Teach me? You want me to let one of the Forsaken teach me?" One of the Forsaken. A male Forsaken. A man who had been Aes Sedai in the Age of Legends, who knew the ways of channeling, knew how to avoid the pitfalls, knew—As much had been offered him before. "No! Even if it was offered, I'd refuse, and why should it be? I oppose them —and you! I hate everything you've done, everything you stand for." *Fool!* he thought. *Trapped here, and I spout defiance like some idiot in a story who never suspects he might make his captor angry enough to do something about it.* But he could not force himself to take the words back. Stubbornly, he plowed ahead and made it worse. "I'll destroy you, if I can. You, and the Dark One, and every last Forsaken!"

A dangerous gleam flashed in her eyes and was gone. "Do you know why some of us fear you? Do you have any idea? Because they are afraid the Great Lord of the Dark will give you a place above them."

Rand surprised himself by managing a laugh. "Great Lord of the Dark? Can't you say his true name, either? Surely you don't fear to attract his attention, as decent people do. Or do you?"

"It would be blasphemy," she said simply. "They are right to be afraid, Sammael and the rest. The Great Lord does want you. He wants to exalt you above all other men. He told me."

"That's ridiculous! The Dark One is still bound in Shayol Ghul, or I would be fighting Tarmon Gai'don right now. And if he knows I exist, he'd want me dead. I mean to fight him."

"Oh, he knows. The Great Lord knows more than you would suspect. It *is* possible to talk with him. Go to Shayol Ghul, into the Pit of Doom, and you can . . . hear him. You can . . . bathe in his presence." A different light shone on her face, now. Ecstasy. She breathed through parted lips, and for a moment seemed to stare at something distant and wondrous. "Words cannot even begin to describe it. You must experience it to know. You must." She was seeing his face again, with eyes large and dark and insistent. "Kneel to the Great Lord, and he will set you above all others. He will leave you free to reign as you will, so long as you bend knee to him only once. To acknowledge him. No more than that. He told me this. Asmodean will teach you to wield the Power without it killing you, teach what you can do with it. Let me help you. We can destroy the others. The Great Lord will not care. We can destroy all of them, even Asmodean, once he has taught you all you need to know. You and I can rule the world together under the Great Lord, forever." Her voice dropped to a whisper, equal parts eagerness and fear. "Two great *sa'angreal* were made just before the end, one that you can use, one that I can. Far greater than that sword. Their power is beyond imagining. With those, we could challenge even . . . the Great Lord himself. Even the Creator!"

"You are mad," he said raggedly. "The Father of Lies says he will leave me free? I was born to fight him. That is why I am here, to fulfill the Prophecies. I'll fight him, and all of you, until the Last Battle! Until my last breath!"

"You do not have to. Prophecy is no more than the sign of what people hope for. Fulfilling the Prophecies will only bind you to a path leading to Tarmon Gai'don and your death. Moghedien or Sammael can destroy your body. The Great Lord of the Dark can destroy your soul. An end utter and complete. You will never be born again no matter how long the Wheel of time turns!"

"No!"

For what seemed a long time she studied him; he could almost see the scales weighing alternatives. "I could take you with me," she said finally. "I could have you turned to the Great Lord whatever you want or believe. There are ways."

She paused, perhaps to see if her words had had any effect. Sweat rolled down his back, but he kept his face straight. He would have to do something, whether he had a chance or not. A second attempt to reach *saidin* battered vainly against that invisible barrier. He let his eyes wander as if he were thinking. *Callandor* was behind him, as far out of reach as the other side of the Aryth Ocean. His belt knife lay on a table by the bed, together with a half-made fox he had been carving. The shapeless lumps of metal mocking him from above the fireplace, a drably clad man slipping in at the doors with a knife in his hand, the books lying everywhere. He turned back to Lanfear, tensing.

"You were always stubborn," she muttered. "I won't take you, this time. I want you to come to me of your own will. And I will have it. What is the matter? You're frowning."

A man slipping in at the doors with a knife; his eyes had slid past the fellow almost without seeing. Instinctively he pushed Lanfear out of the way and reached for the True Source; the shield blocking him vanished as he touched it, and his sword was in his hands like a red-gold flame. The man rushed at him, knife held low and point up for a killing stroke. Even then it was difficult to keep his eyes on the fellow, but Rand pivoted smoothly, and The Wind Blows Over the Wall took off the hand holding the knife and finished by driving through his assailant's heart. For an instant he stared into dull eyes—lifeless while that heart still pumped—then pulled his blade free.

"A Gray Man." Rand took what felt like his first breath in hours. The corpse at his feet was messy, bleeding onto the scroll-worked carpet, but there was no difficulty in fixing an eye on him now. It was always that way with the Shadow's assassins; when they were noticed, it was usually too late. "This makes no sense. You could have killed me easily. Why distract me for a Gray Man to sneak up on me?"

Lanfear was watching him warily. "I make no use of the Soulless. I told you there are . . . differences among the Chosen. It seems I was a day late in my judgment, but there is still time for you to come with me. To learn. To live. That sword," she all but sneered. "You do not do the tenth part of what you can. Come with me, and learn. Or do you mean to try to kill me, now? I loosed you to defend yourself."

Her voice, her stance, said she expected an attack, or at the very least was ready to counter it, but that was not what stopped him, any more than her loosing the bonds in the first place. She was one of the Forsaken; she had served evil so long she made a Black sister look like a newborn babe. Yet he saw a woman. He called himself nine kinds of fool, but he could not do it. Maybe if she tried to kill him. Maybe. But all she did was stand there, watching, waiting. No doubt ready to do things with the Power he did not even know were possible, if he attempted to hold her. He had managed to block Elayne and Egwene, but that had been one of those things he did without thinking, the way of it buried somewhere in his head. He could only remember that he had done it, not how. At least he had a firm grip on *saidin;* she would not surprise him that way again. The stomach-wrenching taint was nothing; *saidin* was life, perhaps in more ways than one.

A sudden thought boiled up in his head like a hot spring. The Aiel. Even a Gray Man should have found it impossible to sneak through doors watched by half a dozen Aiel.

"What did you do to them?" His voice grated as he backed toward the doors, keeping his eyes on her. If she used the Power, maybe he would have some warning. "What did you do to the Aiel outside?"

"Nothing," she replied coolly. "Do not go out there. This may be only a testing to see how vulnerable you are, but even a testing may kill you if you are a fool."

He flung open the left-hand door onto a scene of madness.

CHAPTER
10

The Stone Stands

D
ead Aielmen lay at Rand's feet, tangled with the bodies of
three very ordinary men in very ordinary coats and breeches.
Ordinary-looking men, except that six Aiel, the entire guard,
had been slain, some obviously before they knew what was happening,
and each of those ordinary men had at least two Aiel spears through
him.

That was not the half of it, though. As soon as he pulled the door
open, a roar of battle had washed over him: shouting, howling, steel
clashing on steel among the redstone columns. The Defenders in the
anteroom were fighting for their lives beneath the gilded lamps, against
bulky, black-mailed shapes head-and-shoulders taller than they, shapes
like huge men, but with heads and faces distorted by horns or feathers,
by muzzle or beak where mouth and nose should be. Trollocs. They
strode on paws or hooves as often as on booted feet, cutting men down
with oddly spiked axes and hooked spears and scythelike swords that
curved the wrong way. And with them, a Myrddraal, like a sleek-mov-
ing man with maggot-white skin in black armor, like death made bloodless flesh.

Somewhere in the Stone an alarm gong sounded, then stopped with
lethal suddenness. Another took it up, and another, in brazen tolls.

The Defenders fought, and they still outnumbered the Trollocs, but there were more men down than Trollocs. Even as Rand's eyes found them, the Myrddraal tore off half the Tairen captain's face with one bare hand while the other drove a dead black blade through a Defender's throat, slipping Defenders' spear thrusts like a snake. The Defenders faced what they had thought were only travelers' tales to frighten children; their nerve was frayed to snapping. One man who had lost his rimmed helmet threw down his spear and tried to flee, only to have his head split like a melon by a Trolloc's massive axe. Yet another man looked at the Myrddraal and fled screaming. The Myrddraal darted sinuously to intercept. In a moment the humans would all be running.

"Fade!" Rand shouted. "Try me, Fade!" The Myrddraal stopped as if it had never moved, its pale, eyeless face turning to him. Fear rippled through Rand at that stare, sliding over the bubble of cold calm that encased him when he held *saidin;* in the Borderlands they said, "The look of the Eyeless is fear." Once he had believed Fades rode shadows like horses and disappeared when they turned sideways. Those old beliefs were not so very far wrong.

The Myrddraal flowed toward him, and Rand leaped the dead men in front of the doorway to meet it, his boots skidding on bloody black marble as he landed. "Rally to the Stone!" he shouted as he leaped. "The Stone stands!" Those were the battle cries he had heard on the night the Stone had not stood.

He thought he heard a vexed shout of "Fool!" from the room he had left, but he had no time for Lanfear or what she might do. That skid very nearly cost him his life; his red-gold blade barely turned the Myrddraal's black one as he fought for balance. "Rally to the Stone! The Stone stands!" He had to keep the Defenders together, or face the Myrddraal and twenty Trollocs alone. "The Stone stands!"

"The Stone stands!" he heard someone echo him, then another. "The Stone stands!"

The Fade moved as fluidly as a serpent, the snakelike illusion heightened by the overlapping plates of black armor down its chest. Yet not even a blacklance ever struck so quickly. For a time it was all Rand could do to keep its blade from his own unarmored flesh. That black metal could make wounds that festered, almost as hard to Heal as the one that ached in his side now. Each time dark steel forged in Thakandar, below the slopes of Shayol Ghul, met red-gold Power-wrought blade, light flashed like sheet lightning in the room, a sharp bluish white that hurt the eyes. "You will die this time," the Myrddraal rasped at him in a voice like the crumbling of dead leaves. "I will give your flesh to the Trollocs and take your women for my own."

Rand fought as coldly as he ever had, and as desperately. The Fade knew the use of a sword. Then an instant came when he could strike a blow squarely at the sword itself, not merely divert it. With a hiss as of ice falling on molten metal the red-gold blade sheared through the black. His next blow took that eyeless head from its shoulders; the shock of hacking through bone shivered up his arms. Inky blood fountained from the stump of its neck. The thing did not fall, though. Thrashing blindly with its broken sword, the headless figure stumbled about, striking randomly at the air.

As the Fade's head fell to roll across the floor, the remaining Trollocs fell, too, shrieking, kicking, tearing at their heads with coarse-haired hands. It was a weakness of Myrddraal and Trollocs. Even Myrddraal did not trust Trollocs, so they often linked with them in some way Rand did not understand; it apparently ensured the Trollocs' loyalty, but those linked to a Myrddraal did not survive its death long.

The Defenders still standing, fewer than two dozen, did not wait. In twos and threes they stabbed each Trolloc repeatedly with their spears until it stopped moving. Some of them had the Myrddraal down, but it flailed wildly no matter how much they stabbed. As the Trollocs fell silent, a few surviving human wounded could be heard moaning, weeping. There were still more men littering the floor than Shadowspawn. The black marble was slick with blood, almost invisible against the dark stone.

"Leave it," Rand told the Defenders trying to finish the Myrddraal. "It's dead already. Fades just don't want to admit they're dead." Lan had told him that, what seemed a long time ago; he had had proof of it before this. "See to the injured."

Peering at the headless, thrashing shape, its torso a tatter of gaping wounds, they shivered and moved back, muttering about Lurks. That was what they called Fades in Tear, in tales meant for children. Some began to hunt among the downed humans for any still alive, pulling aside those who could not stand, helping those who could to their feet. All too many were left where they lay. Hasty bandages ripped from a man's own bloody shirt were the only comfort that could be offered now.

They did not look so pretty as they had, these Tairens. Their no longer gleaming breast- and backplates bore dents and scuffs; blood-soaked slashes marred once fine black-and-gold coats and breeches. Some had no helmets, and more than one leaned on his spear as if it were the only thing holding him on his feet. Perhaps it was. They breathed heavily, wild expressions on their faces, that blend of stark terror and blind numbness that afflicts men in battle. They stared at Rand uncertainly—fleeting, fearful stares—as if he might have called these creatures out of the Blight himself.

"Wipe those spearpoints," he told them. "A Fade's blood will etch steel like acid if it's left on long enough." Most moved slowly to obey, hesitantly using what was available, the coatsleeves of their own dead.

The sounds of more fighting drifted through the corridors, distant shouts, the muted clash of metal. They had obeyed him twice; it was time to see if they would do more. Turning his back on them, he started across the anteroom, toward the sounds of battle. "Follow me," he ordered. He raised his fire-wrought blade to remind them of who he was, hoping the reminder did not bring a spear in his back. It had to be risked. "The Stone stands! For the Stone!"

For a moment his own hollow footsteps were the only sound in the columned chamber; then boots began to follow. "For the Stone!" a man shouted, and another, "For the Stone and the Lord Dragon!" Others took it up. "For the Stone and the Lord Dragon!" Quickening to a trot, Rand led his bloodied army of twenty-three deeper into the Stone.

Where was Lanfear, and what part had she played in this? He had little time for wondering. Dead men spotted the halls of the Stone in pools of their own blood, one here and farther on two or three more, Defenders, servants, Aiel. Women, too, linen-gowned noble and wool-clad servant alike struck down as they fled. Trollocs did not care whom they killed; they took pleasure in it. Myrddraal were worse; Halfmen gloried in pain and death.

A little deeper in, the Stone of Tear boiled. Knots of Trollocs rampaged through the halls, sometimes with a Myrddraal leading, sometimes alone, battling Aiel or Defenders, cutting down the unarmed, hunting for more to kill. Rand led his small force at any Shadowspawn they found, his sword slicing coarse flesh and black mail with equal ease. Only the Aiel faced a Fade without flinching. The Aiel and Rand. He passed up Trollocs to reach Fades; sometimes the Myrddraal took a dozen or two Trollocs with it in dying, sometimes none.

Some of his Defenders fell and did not rise, but Aiel joined them, nearly doubling their number. Groups of men broke off in furious battles that drifted away in shouts and clatter like a forge gone mad. Other men fell in behind Rand, broke away, were replaced, till none of those who had started with him remained. Sometimes he fought alone, or ran down a hallway, empty save for himself and the dead, following the sounds of distant combat.

Once, with two Defenders, in a colonnade looking down into a long chamber with many doorways, he saw Moiraine and Lan, surrounded by Trollocs. The Aes Sedai stood, head high like some storied queen of battles, and bestial shapes burst into flame around her—but only to be replaced by more, dashing in through this door or that, six or eight at a time. Lan's sword accounted for those who escaped Moiraine's fire. The Warder had blood on both sides of his face, yet he flowed through the forms as coolly as if practicing before a mirror. Then a wolf-snouted Trolloc thrust a Tairen spear toward Moiraine's back. Lan whirled as though he had eyes in the back of his head, taking off the Trolloc's leg at the knee. The Trolloc fell, howling, yet still managed to thrust spearpoint at Lan just as another clubbed the Warder awkwardly with the flat of its axe, buckling his knees.

Rand could do nothing, for at that moment five Trollocs fell upon him and his two companions, all snouts and boars' tusks and rams' horns, pushing the humans out of the colonnade by the sheer weight of their rush. Five Trollocs should have been able to kill three men without much difficulty, except that one of the men was Rand, with a sword that treated their mail like cloth. One of the Defenders died, and the other vanished chasing after a wounded Trolloc, the lone survivor of the five. When Rand hurried back to the colonnade, there was a smell of burned meat from the chamber below, and great burned bodies on its floor, but no sign of Moiraine or Lan.

That was the way of the contest for the Stone. Or the contest for Rand's life. Battles sprang up and drifted away from where they began, or died when one side fell. Not only did men fight Trollocs and Myrddraal. Men fought men; there were Darkfriends siding the Shadowspawn, roughly dressed fellows who looked like former soldiers and tavern brawlers. They seemed as fearful of the Trollocs as the Tairens did, but they killed as indiscriminately, where they could. Twice Rand actually saw Trollocs battling Trollocs. He could only assume the Myrddraal had lost control of them and their bloodlust had taken over. If they wanted to slay each other, he left them to it.

Then, alone once more and seeking, he trotted 'round a corner and right into three Trollocs, each twice as wide as he and nearly half again as tall. One of them, with an eagle's hooked beak thrusting out of an otherwise human face, was hacking an arm from the corpse of a Tairen noblewoman while the other two watched eagerly, licking their snouts. Trollocs ate anything, so long as it was meat. It was an even chance whether he was more surprised or they were, but he was the first to recover.

The one with the eagle's beak went down, mail and belly alike opened across. The sword-form called Lizard in the Thornbush should have done for the other two, but that first fallen Trolloc, thrashing still, half-kicked his foot out from under him, and he staggered, his blade only scoring a slice along his target's mail, right into the path of the second Trolloc as it fell, wolf's muzzle snapping at nothing. It crushed him to the stone tiles beneath its bulk, trapping sword arm and sword alike. The one still standing raised its spiked axe, coming as close to a smile as a boar's snout and tusks would allow. Rand struggled to move, to breathe.

A scythe-curved sword split the boar's snout to the neck.

Wrenching its blade free, a fourth Trolloc bared goat teeth at him in a snarl, ears twitching beside its horns. Then it darted away, sharp hooves clicking on the floor tiles.

Rand heaved himself out from under the dead weight of the Trolloc, half-stunned. *A Trolloc saved me. A Trolloc?* Trolloc blood was all over him, thick and dark. Far down the hallway, in the opposite direction from where the goat-horned Trolloc had fled, blue-white flashed as two Myrddraal moved into view. Fighting each other, in an almost boneless blur of continuous motion. One forced the other into a crossing corridor, and the flashing light faded from sight. *I'm mad. That's what it is. I am mad, and this is all some crazed dream.*

"You risk everything, rushing about wildly with that . . . that sword."

Rand turned to face Lanfear. She had put on the appearance of a girl again, no older than he, perhaps younger. She lifted her white skirts to step over the Tairen lady's torn body; for all the emotion on her face, it might as well have been a log.

"You build a hut of twigs," she went on, "when you could have marble palaces for the snap of your fingers. You could have had their lives and such souls as Trollocs possess with little effort, and instead they nearly killed you. You must learn. Join with me."

"Was this your doing?" he demanded. "That Trolloc, saving me? Those Myrddraal? Was it?"

She considered him a moment before giving a slight, regretful shake of her head. "If I take credit, you will expect it again, and that could be deadly. None of the others is really certain where I stand, and I like it that way. You can expect no open aid from me."

"Expect your aid?" he growled. "You want me to turn to the

Shadow. You can't make me forget what you are with soft words." He channeled, and she slammed against a wall hanging hard enough to make her grunt. He held her there, spread-eagled over a woven hunting scene, feet off the floor and snowy gown spread out and flattened. How had he blocked Egwene and Elayne? He had to remember.

Suddenly he flew across the hallway to crash into the wall opposite Lanfear, pressed there like an insect by *something* that barely allowed him to breathe.

Lanfear appeared to have no trouble breathing. "Whatever you can do, Lews Therin, I can do. And better." Pinned against the wall as she was, she seemed unperturbed. The din of fighting surged up somewhere nearby, then faded as the battle moved away. "You half-use the smallest fraction of what you are capable of, and walk away from what would allow you to crush all who come against you. Where is *Callandor,* Lews Therin? Still up in your bedchamber like some useless ornament? Do you think yours is the only hand that can wield it, now that you have drawn it free? If Sammael is here, he will take it, and use it against you. Even Moghedien would take it to deny you its use; she could gain much by trading it to any male Chosen."

He struggled against whatever held him; nothing moved but his head, flung from side to side. *Callandor* in the hands of a male Forsaken. The thought drove him half-mad with fear and frustration. He channeled, tried to pry at what held him, but there might as well have been nothing to pry. And then abruptly it was gone; he lurched away from the wall, still fighting, before he realized he was free. And from nothing he had done.

He looked at Lanfear. She still hung there, as complacently as if taking the air on a streamside. She was trying to lull him, to gull him into softening toward her. He hesitated over the flows holding her. If he tied them off and left her, she might tear half the Stone down trying to get free—if a passing Trolloc did not kill her, thinking she was one of the Stone's folk. That should not have troubled him—not the death of a Forsaken—but the thought of leaving a woman, or anyone, helpless for Trollocs repelled him. A glance at her unruffled composure rid him of that thought. No one, nothing, in the Stone would harm her as long as she could channel. If he could find Moiraine to block her. . . .

Once more Lanfear took the decision from him. The impact of severed flows jolted him, and she dropped lightly to the floor. He stared as she stepped away from the wall, calmly brushing her skirts. "You can't do that," he gasped foolishly, and she smiled.

"I do not have to see a flow to unravel it, if I know what it is and where. You see, you have much to learn. I like you like this. You were always too stiff-necked and sure of yourself for comfort. It was always better when you were a bit uncertain of your footing. Are you forgetting *Callandor,* then?"

Still he hesitated. One of the Forsaken stood there. And there was absolutely nothing he could do. Turning, he ran for *Callandor.* Her laughter seemed to follow him.

This time he did not turn aside to fight Trollocs or Myrddraal, did not slow his wild climb through the Stone unless they got in his way. Then his sword carved of fire sliced a way through for him. He saw Perrin and Faile, he with axe in hand, she guarding his back with her knives; the Trollocs seemed as reluctant to face Perrin's yellow-eyed stare as his axe blade. Rand left them behind without a second look. If one of the Forsaken took *Callandor,* none of them would live to see the sun rise.

Breathless, he scrambled through the columned anteroom, leaping the dead still lying there, Defenders and Trollocs alike, in his haste to reach *Callandor.* He flung open both doors. The Sword That Is Not a Sword sat on its gilded and gem-set stand, shining with the light of the setting sun. Waiting for him.

Now that he had it in sight, safe, he was almost loath to touch it. Once, he had used *Callandor* as it was truly meant to be used. Only once. He knew what awaited him when he took it up again, used it to draw on the True Source far beyond what any human could hold unaided. Letting go the red-gold blade seemed more than he could do; when it vanished, he almost called it back.

Feet dragging, he skirted the corpse of the Gray Man and put his hands slowly on *Callandor*'s hilt. It was cold, like crystal long in the dark, but it did not feel so smooth that it would slip in the hand.

Something made him look up. A Fade stood in the doorway, hesitating, its pale-faced, eyeless gaze on *Callandor.*

Rand pulled at *saidin.* Through *Callandor.* The Sword That Is Not a Sword blazed in his hands, as if he held noonday. The Power filled him, hammering down like solid thunder. The taint rushed through him in a flood of blackness. Molten rock pulsed along his veins; the cold inside him could have frozen the sun. He had to use it, or burst like a rotted melon.

The Myrddraal turned to flee, and suddenly black clothes and armor crumpled to the floor, leaving oily motes floating in the air.

Rand was not even aware he had channeled until it was done; he could not have said what he had done if his life had depended upon it.

But nothing could threaten his life while he held *Callandor*. The Power throbbed in him like the heartbeat of the world. With *Callandor* in his hands, he could do anything. The Power hammered at him, a hammer to crack mountains. A channeled thread whisked the Myrddraal's drifting remains out into the anteroom, and its clothes and armor, too; a trickled flow incinerated both. He strode out to hunt those who had come hunting him.

Some of them had come as far as the anteroom. Another Fade and a huddle of cowering Trollocs stood before the columns at the far side staring at ash that sifted out of the air, the last fragments of the Myrddraal and all its garb. At the sight of Rand with *Callandor* flaring in his hands, the Trollocs howled like beasts. The Fade stood paralyzed with shock. Rand gave them no chance to run. Maintaining his deliberate pace toward them, he channeled, and flames roared from the bare, black marble beneath the Shadowspawn, so hot that he flung up a hand against it. By the time he reached them, the flames were gone; nothing remained but dull circles on the marble.

Back down into the Stone he went, and every Trolloc, every Myrddraal he saw died wreathed in fire. He burned them fighting Aiel or Tairens, and killing servants trying to defend themselves with spears or swords snatched from the dead. He burned them as they ran, whether stalking more victims or fleeing him. He began to move faster, trotting, then running, past the wounded, often lying untended, past the dead. It was not enough; he could not move fast enough. While he killed Trollocs in handfuls, others still slew, if only to escape.

Suddenly he stopped, surrounded by the dead, in a wide hallway. He had to do something—something more. The Power slid along his bones, pure essence of fire. Something more. The Power froze his marrow. Something to kill them all; all of them at once. The taint on *saidin* rolled over him, a mountain of rotting filth threatening to bury his soul. Raising *Callandor,* he drew on the Source, drew on it till it seemed he must scream screams of frozen flame. He had to kill them all.

Just beneath the ceiling, right above his head, air slowly began to revolve, spinning faster, milling in streaks of red and black and silver. It roiled and collapsed inward, boiling harder, whining as it whirled and grew smaller still.

Sweat rolled down Rand's face as he stared up at it. He had no idea what it was, only that racing flows he could not begin to count connected him to the mass. It had mass; a weight growing greater while the *thing* fell inward on itself. *Callandor* flared brighter and brighter, too brilliant to look at; he closed his eyes, and the light seemed to burn through his eyelids. The Power raced through him, a raging torrent that threatened to carry all that was him into the spinning. He had to let go. He had to. He forced his eyes open, and it was like looking at all the thunderstorms in the world compressed to the size of a Trolloc's head. He had to . . . had to . . . had to. . . .

Now. The thought floated like cackling laughter on the rim of his awareness. He severed the flows rushing out of him, leaving the thing still whirling, whining like a drill on bone. *Now.*

And the lightnings came, flashing out along the ceiling left and right like silver streams. A Myrddraal stepped out of a side corridor, and before it could take a second step half a dozen flaring streaks stabbed down, blasting it apart. The other streams flowed on, fanning down every branching of the corridor, replaced by more and more erupting every second.

Rand had not a clue to what he had made, or how it worked. He could only stand there, quivering with the Power that filled him with the need to use it. Even if it destroyed him. He could feel Trollocs and Myrddraal dying, feel the lightnings strike and kill. He could kill them everywhere, everywhere in the world. He knew it. With *Callandor* he could do anything. And he knew trying would kill him just as surely.

The lightnings faded and died with the last Shadowspawn; the spinning mass imploded with a loud clap of inrushing air. But *Callandor* still shone like the sun; he shook with the Power.

Moiraine was there, a dozen paces away, staring at him. Her dress was neat, every fold of blue silk in place, but wisps of her hair were disarrayed. She looked tired—and shocked. "How . . . ? What you have done, I would not have believed possible." Lan appeared, half-trotting up the hall, sword in hand, face bloodied, coat torn. Without taking her eyes from Rand, Moiraine flung out a hand, halting the Warder short of her. Well short of Rand. As if he were too dangerous for even Lan to approach. "Are you . . . well, Rand?"

Rand pulled his gaze away from her, and it fell on the body of a dark-haired girl, little more than a child. She lay sprawled on her back, eyes wide and fixed on the ceiling, blood blackening the bosom of her dress. Sadly, he bent to brush strands of hair from her face. *Light, she is only a child. I was too late. Why didn't I do it sooner? A child!*

"I will see that someone takes care of her, Rand," Moiraine said gently. "You cannot help her now."

His hand shook so hard on *Callandor* that he could barely hold on. "With this, I can do anything." His voice was harsh in his own ears. "Anything!"

"Rand!" Moiraine said urgently.

He would not listen. The Power was in him. *Callandor* blazed, and he *was* the Power. He channeled, directing flows into the child's body, searching, trying, fumbling; she lurched to her feet, arms and legs unnaturally rigid and jerky.

"Rand, you cannot do this. Not this!"

Breathe. She has to breathe. The girl's chest rose and fell. *Heart. Has to beat.* Blood already thick and dark oozed from the wound in her chest. *Live. Live, burn you! I didn't mean to be too late.* Her eyes stared at him, filmed. Lifeless. Tears trickled unheeded down his cheeks. "She has to live! Heal her, Moiraine. I don't know how. Heal her!"

"Death cannot be Healed, Rand. You are not the Creator."

Staring into those dead eyes, Rand slowly withdrew the flows. The body fell stiffly. The body. He threw back his head and howled, as wild as any Trolloc. Braided fire sizzled into walls and ceiling as he lashed out in frustration and pain.

Sagging, he released *saidin,* pushed it away; it was like pushing away a boulder, like pushing away life. Strength drained out of him with the Power. The taint remained, though, a stain weighing him down with darkness. He had to ground *Callandor* on the floor tiles and lean on it to stay on his feet.

"The others." It was hard to speak; his throat hurt. "Elayne, Perrin, the rest? Was I too late for them, too?"

"You were not too late," Moiraine said calmly. But she had come no closer, and Lan looked ready to dart between her and Rand. "You must not—"

"Are they still alive?" Rand shouted.

"They are," she assured him.

He nodded in weary relief. He tried not to look at the girl's body. Three days waiting, so he could enjoy a few stolen kisses. If he had moved three days ago. . . . But he had learned things in those three days, things he might be able to use if he could put them together. If. Not too late for his friends, at least. Not too late for them. "How did the Trollocs get in? I don't think they climbed the walls like Aiel, not with the sun still up. Is it still up?" He shook his head to dispel some of the fog. "No matter. The Trollocs. How?"

Lan was the one who answered. "Eight large grain barges tied up at the Stone's docks late this afternoon. Apparently no one thought to question why laden grain barges would be coming *down*river"—his voice was heavy with contempt—"or why they'd dock at the Stone, or why the crews left the hatches shut until nearly sunfall. Also, a train of wagons arrived—about two hours ago, now—thirty of them, supposedly bringing some lord or other's things from the country for his return to the Stone. When the canvas was thrown back, they were packed with Halfmen and Trollocs, too. If they came in any other way, I don't know of it, yet."

Rand nodded again, and the effort buckled his knees. Suddenly Lan was there, pulling Rand's arm over his shoulder to hold him up. Moiraine took his face in her hands. A chill rippled through him, not the blasting cold of full Healing, but a chill that pushed weariness out as it passed. Most of the weariness. A seed remained, as if he had worked a day hoeing tabac. He moved away from the support he no longer needed. Lan watched him warily, to see if he could really stand alone, or perhaps because the Warder was not certain how dangerous he was, how sane.

"I left some apurpose," Moiraine told him. "You need to sleep tonight."

Sleep. There was too much to do to sleep. But he gave another nod. He did not want her shadowing him. Yet what he said was "Lanfear was here. This was not her doing. She said so, and I believe her. You don't seem surprised, Moiraine." Would Lanfear's offer surprise her? Would anything? "Lanfear was here, and I talked with her. She didn't try to kill me, and I didn't try to kill her. And you are not surprised."

"I doubt you could kill her. Yet." Her glance at *Callandor* was the merest flicker of dark eyes. "Not unaided. And I doubt she will try to kill you. Yet. We know little of any of the Forsaken, and least of all Lanfear, but we do know she loved Lews Therin Telamon. To say you are safe from her is certainly too strong—there is a good deal she can do to harm you short of murder—but I do not think she will try to kill as long as she thinks she might win Lews Therin back again."

Lanfear wanted him. The Daughter of the Night, used by mothers who only half-believed in her to frighten children. She certainly frightened him. It was nearly enough to make him laugh. He had always felt guilty for looking at any woman besides Egwene, and Egwene did not want him, but the Daughter-Heir of Andor wanted to kiss him, at least, and one of the Forsaken claimed to love him. Nearly enough for laughter, but not quite. Lanfear seemed jealous of Elayne; that pale-haired milksop, she had called her. Madness. All madness.

"Tomorrow." He started away from them.

"Tomorrow?" Moiraine said.

"Tomorrow, I will tell you what I am going to do." Some of it, he would. The thought of Moiraine's face if he told her everything made him want to laugh. If he knew everything himself, yet. Lanfear had given him almost the last piece, without knowing it. One more step, tonight. The hand holding *Callandor* by his side trembled. With that, he could do anything. *I am not mad yet. Not mad enough for that.* "Tomorrow. A good night to us all, the Light willing." Tomorrow he would begin to unleash another kind of lightning. Another lightning that might save him. Or kill him. He was not mad yet.

CHAPTER
11

What Lies Hidden

C lad in her shift, Egwene drew a deep breath and left the stone ring lying beside an open book on her bedside table. All flecked and striped in brown and red and blue, it was slightly too large for a finger ring, and shaped wrong, flattened and twisted so that a fingertip run along the edge would circle both inside and out before coming back to where it had started. There *was* only one edge, impossible though that seemed. She was not leaving the ring there because she might fail without it, because she wanted to fail. She had to try without the ring sooner or later, or she could never do more than dabble her toes where she dreamed of swimming. It might as well be now. That was the reason. It was.

The thick leather-bound book was *A Journey to Tarabon,* written by Eurian Romavni, from Kandor—fifty-three years ago, according to the date the author gave in the first line, but little of any consequence would have changed in Tanchico in that short a time. Besides, it was the only volume she had found with useful drawings. Most of the books only had portraits of kings, or fanciful renderings of battles by men who had not seen them.

Darkness filled both windows, but the lamps gave more than adequate light. One tall beeswax candle burned in a gilded candlestick on the bedside table. She had gone to fetch that herself; this was no night to be sending a maid for a candle. Most of the servants were tending the wounded or weeping over loved ones, or being tended themselves. There had been too many for Healing any but those who would have died without it.

Elayne and Nynaeve waited with high-backed chairs pulled to either side of the wide bed with its tall, swallow-carved posts; they tried to hide their anxiety with differing degrees of success. Elayne managed a passably stately calm, and only spoiled it by frowning and chewing her underlip when she thought Egwene was not looking. Nynaeve was all brisk confidence, the sort that made you feel comforted when she tucked you into a sickbed, but Egwene recognized the set of her eyes; they said Nynaeve was afraid.

Aviendha sat cross-legged beside the door, her browns and grays standing out sharply against the deep blue of the carpet. This time the Aiel woman had her long-bladed knife at one side of her belt, a bristling quiver at the other, and four short spears across her knees. Her round, hide buckler lay close at hand, atop a horn bow in a worked leather case with straps that could hold it on her back. After tonight, Egwene could not fault her for going armed. She still wanted to hold a lightning bolt ready to fling herself.

Light, what was that Rand did? Burn him, he frightened me almost as badly as the Fades did. Maybe worse. It isn't fair he can do something like that and I can't even see the flows.

She climbed onto the bed and took the leatherbound book on her knees, frowning at an engraved map of Tanchico. Little of any use was marked, really. A dozen fortresses, surrounding the harbor, guarding the city on its three hilly peninsulas, the Verana to the east, the Maseta in the center, and the Calpene nearest the sea. Useless. Several large squares, some open areas that seemed to be parks, and a number of monuments to rulers long since dust. All useless. A few palaces, and things that seemed strange. The Great Circle, for instance, on the Calpene. On the map it was just a ring, but Master Romavni described it as a huge gathering place that could hold thousands to watch horse races or displays of fireworks by the Illuminators. There was also a King's Circle, on the Maseta and larger than the Great Circle, and a Panarch's Circle, on the Verana, just a little smaller. The Chapter House of the Guild of Illuminators was marked as well. They were all useless. The text certainly had nothing of use.

"Are you certain you want to try this without the ring?" Nynaeve asked quietly.

"Certain," Egwene replied as calmly as she could. Her stomach was leaping as badly as it had when she saw that first Trolloc tonight, holding that poor woman by the hair and slitting her throat like a rabbit's. The woman had screamed like a rabbit, too. Killing the Trolloc had done her no good; the woman was as dead as the Trolloc. Only her shrill scream would not go away. "If it doesn't work, I can always try again with the ring." She leaned over to mark the candle with a thumbnail. "Wake me when it burns down to there. Light, but I wish we had a clock."

Elayne laughed at her, a lighthearted trill, and it very nearly sounded unforced. "A clock in a bedchamber? My mother has a dozen clocks, but I never heard of a clock in a bedchamber."

"Well, my father has one clock," Egwene grumbled, "the only one in the whole village, and I wish I had it here. Do you think it will burn that far in an hour? I don't want to sleep longer than that. You must wake me as soon as the flame reaches that mark. As soon as!"

"We will," Elayne said soothingly. "I promise it."

"The stone ring," Aviendha said suddenly. "Since you are not using it, Egwene, could not someone—one of us—use it to go with you?"

"No," Egwene muttered. *Light, I wish they would all come with me.* "Thank you for the thought, though."

"Can only you use it, Egwene?" the Aiel woman asked.

"Any of us might," Nynaeve replied, "even you, Aviendha. A woman needn't be able to channel, only sleep with it touching her skin. A man might be able to, for all we know. But we do not know *Tel'aran'rhiod* as well as Egwene, or the rules of it."

Aviendha nodded. "I see. A woman can make mistakes where she does not know the ways, and her mistakes can kill others as well as herself."

"Exactly," Nynaeve said. "The World of Dreams is a dangerous place. That much we do know."

"But Egwene will be careful," Elayne added, speaking to Aviendha but obviously meaning it for Egwene's ears. "She promised. She will look around—carefully!—and no more."

Egwene concentrated on the map. Careful. If she had not guarded her twisted stone ring so jealously—she thought of it as hers; the Hall of the Tower might not agree, but they did not know she had it—if she had been willing to let Elayne or Nynaeve use it more than once or twice, they might know enough to come with her now. Yet it was not regret that made her avoid looking at the other women. She did not want them to see the fear in her eyes.

Tel'aran'rhiod. The Unseen World. The World of Dreams. Not the dreams of ordinary people, though sometimes they touched *Tel'aran'rhiod* briefly, in dreams that seemed as true as life. Because they were. In the Unseen World, what happened was real, in a strange way. Nothing that happened there affected what was—a door opened in the World of Dreams would still be shut in the real world; a tree cut down there still stood here—yet a woman could be killed there, or stilled. "Strange" barely began to describe it. In the Unseen World the whole world lay open, and maybe other worlds, too; any place was attainable. Or at least, its reflection in the World of Dreams was. The weave of the Pattern could be read there—past, present and future—by one who knew how. By a Dreamer. There had not been a Dreamer in the White Tower since Corianin Nedeal, nearly five hundred years earlier.

Four hundred and seventy-three years, to be exact, Egwene thought. *Or is it four hundred seventy-four now? When did Corianin die?* If Egwene had had a chance to finish novice training in the Tower, to study there as an Accepted, perhaps she would know. There was so much she might have known, then.

A list lay in Egwene's pouch of the *ter'angreal,* most small enough to slip into a pocket, that had been stolen by the Black Ajah when they fled the Tower. They all three had a copy. Thirteen of those stolen *ter'angreal* had "no known use" written alongside, and "last studied by Corianin Nedeal." But if Corianin Sedai had truly not discovered their uses, Egwene was sure of one of them. They gave entrance to *Tel'aran'rhiod;* not as easily as the stone ring, perhaps, and perhaps not without channeling, but they did it.

Two they had recovered from Joiya and Amico: an iron disc, three inches across, scribed on both sides with a tight spiral, and a plaque no longer than her hand, apparently clear amber yet hard enough to scratch steel, with a sleeping woman somehow carved into the middle of it. Amico had spoken freely of them, and so had Joiya, after a session alone in her cell with Moiraine that had left the Darkfriend pale-faced and almost civil. Channel a flow of Spirit into either *ter'angreal,* and it would take you into sleep and then into *Tel'aran'rhiod.* Elayne had tried both of them briefly, and they worked, though all she saw was the inside of the Stone, and Morgase's Royal Palace in Caemlyn.

Egwene had not wanted her to try, however fleeting the visit, but not from jealousy. She had not been able to argue very effectively, though, for she had been afraid Elayne and Nynaeve would hear what was in her voice.

Two recovered meant eleven still with the Black Ajah. That was the point Egwene had tried to make. Eleven *ter'angreal* that could take a woman to *Tel'aran'rhiod,* all in the hands of Black sisters. When Elayne made her short journeys into the Unseen World, she could have found the Black Ajah waiting for her, or walked into them before she knew they were there. The thought made Egwene's stomach writhe. They could be waiting for her now. Not likely; not on purpose—how would they know she was coming?—but they could be there when she stepped through. One she could face, unless she was caught by surprise, and she did not mean to allow that. But if they did surprise her? Two or three of them together? Liandrin and Rianna, Chesmal Emry and Jeane Caide and all the rest at once?

Frowning at the map, she made her hands loosen their white-knuck-led grip. Tonight had given everything urgency. If Shadowspawn could attack the Stone, if one of the Forsaken could suddenly appear in their midst, she could not give in to fear. They had to know what to do. They had to have something besides Amico's vague tale. Something. If only she could learn where Mazrim Taim was in his caged journey to Tar Valon, or if she could somehow slip into the Amyrlin's dreams and speak to her. Perhaps those things were possible for a Dreamer. If they were, she did not know how. Tanchico was what she had to work with.

"I must go alone, Aviendha. I must." She thought her voice was calm and steady, but Elayne patted her shoulder.

Egwene did not know why she was scrutinizing the map. She already had it fixed in her head, everything in relation to everything else. What-ever existed in this world existed in the World of Dreams, and some-times more besides, of course. She had her destination chosen. She thumbed through the book to the only engraving showing the inside of a building named on the map, the Panarch's Palace. It would do no good to find herself in a chamber if she had no idea where it was in the city. None of it might do any good in any case. She put that out of her mind. She had to believe there was some chance.

The engraving showed a large room with a high ceiling. A rope strung along waist-high posts would keep anyone from going too close to the things displayed on stands and in open-fronted cabinets along the walls. Most of those displays were indistinct, but not what stood at the far end of the room. The artist had taken pains to show the massive skeleton standing there as if the rest of the creature had that moment disappeared. It had four thick-boned legs, but otherwise resembled no animal Egwene had ever seen. For one thing, it had to stand at least two spans high, well over twice her height. The rounded skull, set low on the shoulders like a bull's, looked big enough for a child to climb inside, and in the picture it seemed to have four eye sockets. The skeleton marked the room off from any other; there was no mistaking it for anything but itself. Whatever it was. If Eurian Romavni had known, he had not named it in these pages.

"What is a panarch, anyway?" she asked, laying the book aside. She had studied the picture a dozen times. "All of these writers seem to think you know already."

"The Panarch of Tanchico is the equal of the king in authority," Elayne recited. "She is responsible for collecting taxes, customs and duties; he for spending them properly. She controls the Civil Watch and the courts, except for the High Court, which is the king's. The army is his, of course, except for the Panarch's Legion. She—"

"I didn't really want to know." Egwene sighed. It had only been something to say, another few moments to delay what she was going to do. The candle was burning down; she was wasting precious minutes. She knew how to step out of the dream when she wanted, how to wake herself, but time passed differently in the World of Dreams, and it was easy to lose track. "As soon as it reaches the mark," she said, and Elayne and Nynaeve murmured reassurances.

Settling back on her feather pillows, at first she only stared at the ceiling, painted with blue sky and clouds and swooping swallows. She did not see them.

Her dreams had been bad enough lately, most of them. Rand was in them, of course. Rand as tall as a mountain, walking through cities, crushing buildings beneath his feet, with screaming people like ants fleeing from him. Rand in chains, and it was he who was screaming. Rand building a wall with him on one side and her on the other, her and Elayne and others she could not make out. "It has to be done," he was saying as he piled up stones. "I'll not let you stop me now." His were not the only nightmares. She had dreamed of Aiel fighting each other, killing each other, even throwing away their weapons and running as if they had gone mad. Mat wrestling with a Seanchan woman who tied an invisible leash to him. A wolf—she was sure it was Perrin, though—fighting a man whose face kept changing. Galad wrapping himself in white as though putting on his own shroud, and Gawyn with his eyes full of pain and hatred. Her mother weeping. They were the sharp dreams, the ones she knew meant something. They were hideous, and she did not know what any of them meant. How could she presume to think she could find any meanings or clues in *Tel'aran'rhiod*? But there was no other choice. No other choice but ignorance, and she could not choose that.

Despite her anxiety, going to sleep was no problem; she was exhausted. It was just a matter of closing her eyes and taking deep, regular breaths. She fixed in her thoughts the room in the Panarch's Palace and the huge skeleton. Deep, regular breaths. She could remember how using the stone ring felt, the step into *Tel'aran'rhiod*. Deep—regular—breaths.

Egwene stepped back with a gasp, one hand to her throat. This close, the skeleton seemed even larger than she had thought, the bones bleached dull and dry. She stood right in front of it, inside the rope. A white rope, as thick as her wrist and apparently silk. She had no doubt this was *Tel'aran'rhiod*. The detail was as fine as reality, even for things half-seen from the corner of her eye. That she could even be aware of the differences between this and an ordinary dream told her where she was. Besides, it felt . . . right.

She opened herself to *saidar*. A nick on the finger in the World of Dreams would still be there on waking; there would be no waking from a killing stroke with the Power, or even from a sword, or a club. She did not intend to be vulnerable for an instant.

Instead of her shift, she wore something very much like Aviendha's Aiel garb, but in red brocaded silk; even her soft boots, laced to the knee, were supple red leather, suitable for gloves, with gold stitching and laces. She laughed softly to herself. Clothes in *Tel'aran'rhiod* were what you wanted them to be. Apparently part of her mind wanted to be ready to move quickly, while another part wanted to be ready for a ball. It would not do. The red faded to grays and browns; the coat and breeches and boots became exact copies of the Maidens'. No better, really, not in a city. Abruptly she was in a copy of the dresses Faile always wore, dark, with narrow divided skirts, long sleeves and a high snug bodice. *Foolish to worry about it. No one is going to see me except in their dreams, and few ordinary dreams reach here. It would make no difference if I were naked.*

For a moment she *was* naked. Her face colored with embarrassment; there was no one there to see her bare as in her bath, before she hastily brought the dark dress back, but she should have remembered how stray thoughts could affect things here, especially when you had embraced the Power. Elayne and Nynaeve thought she was so knowledgeable. She knew a few of the rules of the Unseen World, and knew there were a hundred, a thousand more of which she was ignorant. Somehow, she had to learn them, if she was to be the Tower's first Dreamer since Corianin.

She took a closer look at the huge skull. She had grown up in a country village, and she knew what animal bones looked like. Not four eye sockets after all. Two seemed to be for tusks of some kind instead, on either side of where its nose had been. Some sort of monstrous boar, perhaps, though it looked like no pig skull she had ever seen. It had a feel of age, though; great age.

With the Power in her, she could sense things like that, here. The usual enhancement of senses was with her, of course. She could feel tiny cracks in the gilded plaster bosses covering the ceiling fifty feet up, and the smooth polish of the white stone floor. Infinitesimal cracks, invisible to the eye, spread across the floorstones as well.

The chamber was huge, perhaps two hundred paces long and nearly half as wide, with rows of thin white columns, and that white rope running all the way around except where there were doorways, with double-pointed arches. More ropes encircled polished wooden stands and cabinets holding other exhibits out in the floor. Up under the ceiling, an elaborate pattern of tiny carvings pierced the walls, letting in plenty of light. Apparently she had dreamed herself into a Tanchico where it was day.

"A grand display of artifacts of Ages long past, of the Age of Legends and Ages before, open to all, even the common folk, three days in the month and on feastdays," Eurian Romavni had written. He had spoken in glowing terms of the priceless display of *cuendillar* figures, six of them, in a glass-sided case in the center of the hall, always watched by four of the Panarch's personal guards when people were allowed in, and had gone on for two pages about the bones of fabulous beasts "never seen alive by the eyes of man." Egwene could see some of those. On one side of the room was the skeleton of something that looked a little like a bear, if a bear had two front teeth as long as her forearm, and opposite it on the other side were the bones of some slender, four-footed beast with a neck so long the skull was half as high as the ceiling. There were more, spaced down the chamber's walls, just as fantastic. All of them felt old enough to make the Stone of Tear seem new-built. Ducking under the rope barrier, she walked down the chamber slowly, staring.

A weathered stone figurine of a woman, seemingly unclothed but wrapped in hair that fell to her ankles, was outwardly no different from the others sharing its case, each not much bigger than her hand. But it gave an impression of soft warmth that she recognized. It was an *angreal*, she was sure; she wondered why the Tower had not managed to get it away from the Panarch. A finely jointed collar and two bracelets of dull black metal, on a stand by themselves, made her shiver; she felt darkness and pain associated with them—old, old pain, and sharp. A silvery thing in another cabinet, like a three-pointed star inside a circle, was made of no substance she knew; it was softer than metal, scratched and gouged, yet even older than any of the ancient bones. From ten paces she could sense pride and vanity.

One thing actually seemed familiar, though she could not say why. Tucked into a corner of one of the cabinets, as if whoever put it there had been uncertain that it was worthy of display, lay the upper half of a broken figure carved from some shiny white stone, a woman holding a crystal sphere in one upraised hand, her face calm and dignified and full of wise authority. Whole, she would have been perhaps a foot tall. But why did she appear so familiar? She almost seemed to call to Egwene to pick her up.

Not until Egwene's fingers closed on the broken statuette did she realize she had climbed over the rope. *Foolish, when I don't know what it is,* she thought, but it was already too late.

As her hand grasped it, the Power surged within her, into the half-figure then back into her, into the figure and back, in and back. The crystal sphere flickered in fitful, lurid flashes, and needles stabbed her brain with each flash. With a sob of agony, she loosed her hold and clasped both hands to her head.

The crystal sphere shattered as the figure hit the floor and broke into pieces, and the needles vanished, leaving only dull memories of the pain and a queasiness that wobbled her knees. She squeezed her eyes shut so she could not see the room heaving. The figure had to be a *ter'angreal*, but why had it hurt her like that when she only touched it? Perhaps because it was broken; perhaps, broken, it could not do what it was meant for. She did not even want to think of what it might have been made for; testing *ter'angreal* was dangerous. At least it must be broken beyond danger now. Here, at least. *Why did it seem to call me?*

Nausea faded, and she opened her eyes. The figure was back on the shelf, as whole as it had been when she first saw it. Strange things happened in *Tel'aran'rhiod*, but that was stranger than she wanted to see. And this was not what she had come for. First she had to find her way out of the Panarch's Palace. Climbing back over the rope, she hurried out of the chamber, trying not to run.

The palace was empty of life, of course. Human life, at least. Colorful fish swam in large fountains that splashed merrily in the courtyards surrounded by delicately columned walks and balconies screened by stonework like intricately carved lace. Lily pads floated on the waters, and white flowers as big as dinner plates. In the World of Dreams, a place was as it was in the so-called real world. Except for people. Elaborate golden lamps stood in the hallways, wicks uncharred, but she could smell the perfumed oil in them. Her feet raised no hint of dust from the bright carpets that surely could never have been beaten, not here.

Once she did see another person walking ahead of her, a man in gilded, ornately worked plate-and-mail armor, a pointed golden helmet crested with white egret plumes under his arm. "Aeldra?" he called, smiling. "Aeldra, come look at me. I am named the Lord Captain of the Panarch's Legion. Aeldra?" He walked on another pace, still calling, and suddenly was not there. Not a Dreamer. Not even someone using a *ter'angreal* like her stone ring or Amico's iron disc. Only a man whose dream had touched a place he was not aware of, with dangers he did not know. People who died unexpectedly in their sleep had often dreamed their way into *Tel'aran'rhiod* and in truth had died there. He was well out of it, back into an ordinary dream.

The candle was burning down beside that bed back in Tear. Her time in *Tel'aran'rhiod* was burning away.

Hastening her steps, she came to tall, carved doors leading outside, to wide white stairs and a huge empty square. Tanchico spread out in every direction across steep hills, white buildings upon white buildings shining in the sun, hundreds of thin towers and almost as many pointed domes, some gilded. The Panarch's Circle, a tall round wall of white stone, stood in plain sight not half a mile away and a little lower than the palace. The Panarch's Palace rose atop one of the loftiest hills. At the top of the deep stairs, she was high enough to see water glinting to the west, inlets separating her from more hilly fingers where the rest of the city lay. Tanchico was larger than Tear, perhaps larger than Caemlyn.

So much to search, and she did not even know for what. For something that signified the presence of the Black Ajah, or something that indicated some sort of danger to Rand, if either existed here. Had she been a real Dreamer, trained in the use of her talent, she would surely have known what to look for, how to interpret what she saw. But no one remained who could teach her. Aiel Wise Ones supposedly knew how to decipher dreams. Aviendha had been so reluctant to talk about the Wise Ones that Egwene had not asked any of the other Aiel. Perhaps a Wise One could teach her. If she could find one.

She took a step toward the square, and suddenly she was somewhere else.

Great stone spires rose around her in a heat that sucked the moisture out of her breath. The sun seemed to bake right through her dress, and the breeze blowing in her face seemed to come from a stove. Stunted trees dotted a landscape almost bare of other growth, except for a few patches of tough grass and some prickly plants she did not recognize. She recognized the lion, however, even if she had never seen one in the flesh. It lay in a crevice in the rocks not twenty paces away, black-tufted tail switching idly, looking not at her but at something another hundred strides on. The large boar covered in coarse hair was rooting and snuffling at the base of a thorny bush, never noticing the Aiel woman creeping up on it with a spear ready to thrust. Garbed like the Aiel in the Stone, she had her *shoufa* around her head but her face uncovered.

The Waste, Egwene thought incredulously. *I've jumped into the Aiel Waste! When will I learn to watch what I think here?*

The Aiel woman froze. Her eyes were on Egwene now, not the boar. If it was a boar; it did not seem to be shaped exactly right.

Egwene was sure the woman was not a Wise One. Not dressed like a Maiden, from what Egwene had been told, a Maiden of the Spear who wanted to become a Wise One had to "give up the spear." This had to be just an Aiel woman who had dreamed herself into *Tel'aran'rhiod,* like that fellow in the palace. He would have seen her, too, if he had ever turned around. Egwene closed her eyes and concentrated on her one clear image of Tanchico, that huge skeleton in the great hall.

When she opened them again, she was staring at the massive bones. They had been wired together, she noticed this time. Quite cleverly, so that the wires hardly showed at all. The half-figurine with its crystal sphere was still on its shelf. She did not go near it, any more than the black collar and bracelets that felt of so much pain and suffering. The *angreal,* the stone woman, was a temptation. *What are you going to do with it? Light, you're here to look, to search! Nothing more than that. Get on with it, woman!*

This time she quickly found her way back to the square. Time passed differently here; Elayne and Nynaeve could be waking her up any moment, and she still had not even begun. There might be no more minutes to waste. She had to be careful of what she thought from here on. No more thinking about the Wise Ones. Even the admonition made everything lurch around her. *Keep your mind on what you are doing,* she told herself firmly.

She set out through the empty city, walking fast, sometimes trotting. Winding, stone-paved streets slanted up and down, curving every which way, all empty, except for green-backed pigeons and pale gray gulls that rose in thunderclaps of wings when she came close. Why birds and not people? Flies buzzed by, and she could see roaches and beetles scurrying along in the shadows. A pack of lean dogs, all different colors, loped across the street far ahead of her. Why dogs?

She pulled herself back to why she was there. What would be a sign of the Black Ajah? Or of this danger to Rand, if it existed? Most of the white buildings were plastered, the plaster chipped and cracked, often showing weathered wood or pale brown brick beneath. Only the towers and the larger structures—palaces, she supposed—were stone, if still white. Even the stone had tiny fissures, though, most of it; cracks too minute for the eye to catch, but she could feel them with the Power in her, spiderwebbing domes and towers. Perhaps that meant something. Perhaps it meant Tanchico was a city not looked after by its inhabitants. As likely that as anything else.

She jumped as a shrieking man suddenly plummeted out of the sky in front of her. She only had time to register baggy white trousers and thick mustaches covered by a transparent veil before he vanished, only a pace above the pavement. Had he struck, here in *Tel'aran'rhiod,* he would have been found dead in his bed.

He probably has as much to do with anything as the roaches, she told herself.

Perhaps something inside the buildings. It was a small chance, a wild hope, but she was desperate enough to try anything. Almost anything. Time. How much time did she have left? She began running from doorway to doorway, putting her head into shops and inns and houses.

Tables and benches stood in common rooms awaiting customers, as neatly arranged as the dully gleaming pewter mugs and plates on their shelves. The shops were as tidy as if the shopkeeper had just opened for the morning, yet while a tailor's tables held bolts of cloth, and a cutler's knives and scissors, the ceiling hooks hung empty in a butcher's shop and the shelves stood bare. A finger run along anywhere picked up no dust at all; everything was clean enough to suit her mother.

In the narrower streets there were homes, small simple white-plastered buildings with flat roofs and no windows onto the street, ready for families to walk in and sit on benches before cold fireplaces or around narrow tables with carved legs where a goodwife's best bowl or

platter was given pride of place. Clothes hung on pegs, pots hung from
ceilings, handtools lay on benches, waiting.

On a hunch she retraced her steps once, just to see, back a dozen
doors, and peered a second time into what was some woman's home in
the real world. It was almost the way it had been. Almost. The red-
striped bowl that had been on the table was now a narrow blue vase;
one of the benches, on it a broken harness and the tools for mending it,
that had been near the fireplace now sat by the door holding a darning
basket and a child's embroidered dress.

Why did it change? she wondered. *But for that matter, why should it
stay the same? Light, I don't know anything!*

There was a stable across the street, the white plaster showing large
patches of brick. She trotted to it and pulled open one of the big doors.
Straw covered the dirt floor, just as in every stable she had ever seen,
but the stalls stood empty. No horses. Why? Something rustled in the
straw, and she realized the stalls were not empty after all. Rats. Dozens
of them, staring at her boldly, noses testing the air for her scent. None
of the rats ran, or even shied away; they behaved as if they had more
right there than she. In spite of herself she stepped back. *Pigeons and
gulls and dogs, flies and rats. Maybe a Wise One would know why.*

As suddenly as that she was back in the Waste.

With a scream she fell flat on her back as the hairy boarlike creature
darted straight for her, looking as large as a small pony. Not a pig, she
saw as it leaped nimbly over her; the snout was too sharp and full of
keen teeth, and it had four toes on each foot. The thought was calm,
but she shuddered as the beast scampered away through the rocks. It
was big enough to have trampled her, breaking bones and worse; those
teeth could have ripped and torn as well as any wolf's. She would have
awakened with the wounds. If she had waked at all.

The gritty rock under her back was a blistering stovetop. She scrambled to her feet, angry with herself. If she could not keep her mind on
what she was doing, she would accomplish nothing. Tanchico was
where she was supposed to be; she had to concentrate on that. Nothing
else.

She stopped brushing at her skirts when she saw the Aiel woman
watching her with sharp blue eyes from ten paces off. The woman was
Aviendha's age, no older than herself, but the wisps of hair that stuck
out from under her *shoufa* were so pale as to be almost white. The
spear in her hands was ready to be cast, and at that distance she was
not likely to miss.

The Aiel were said to be more than rough with those who entered the Waste without permission. Egwene knew she could wrap woman and spear in Air, hold them safely, but would the flows keep long enough when she began to fade? Or would they just anger the woman enough to make her cast her spear the moment she was able, perhaps before Egwene was truly gone? Much good it would do to take herself back to Tanchico with an Aiel spear through her. If she tied the flows, that would leave the woman trapped in *Tel'aran'rhiod* until they were unraveled, helpless if that lion or the boarlike creature returned.

No. She simply needed the woman to lower her spear, just long enough to feel safe closing her eyes, to take herself back to Tanchico. Back to what she was supposed to be doing. She had no more time for these flights of fancy. She was not entirely sure someone who had only dreamed themselves into *Tel'aran'rhiod* could harm her the way other things there could, but she was not going to risk finding out with an Aiel spearpoint. The Aiel woman should vanish in a few moments. Something to put her off balance until then.

Changing her clothes was easy; as soon as the thought came, Egwene was wearing the same browns and grays as the woman. "I mean you no harm," she said, outwardly calm.

The woman did not lower her weapon. Instead, she frowned and said, "You have no right to wear *cadin'sor*, girl." And Egwene found herself standing there in her skin, the sun burning her from overhead, the ground searing her bare feet.

For a moment she gaped in disbelief, dancing from foot to foot. She had not thought it possible to change things about someone else. So many possibilities, so many rules, that she did not know. Hurriedly she thought herself back into stout shoes and the dark dress with its divided skirts and at the same time made the Aiel woman's garments vanish. She had to draw on *saidar* to do it; the woman must have been concentrating on keeping Egwene naked. She had a flow ready to seize the spear if the other woman made to throw it.

It was the Aiel woman's turn to look shocked. She let the spear fall to her side, too, and Egwene seized the moment to shut her eyes and take herself back to Tanchico, back to the skeleton of that huge boar. Or whatever it was. She barely gave it a second glance this time. She was growing tired of things that looked like boars and were not. *How did she do that? No! It's wondering about how and why that keeps pulling me off the path. This time I'll stick to it.*

She did hesitate, though. Just as she had closed her eyes it had seemed she saw another woman, beyond the Aiel woman, watching them both. A golden-haired woman holding a silver bow. *You are letting*

*wild fancies take you, now. You've been listening to too many of Thom
Merrilin's stories.* Birgitte was long dead; she could not come again until
the Horn of Valere called her back from the grave. Dead women, even
heroes of legend, surely could not dream themselves into
Tel'aran'rhiod.

It was only a moment's pause, though. Shutting off futile speculation,
she ran back to the square. How much time did she have left? The
whole city to search, and time slipping away, and she as ignorant as
when she started. If only she had some idea of what to look for. Or
where. Running did not seem to tire her here in the World of Dreams,
but run as hard as she might, she would never cover the entire city
before Elayne and Nynaeve woke her. She did not want to have to
come back.

A woman appeared suddenly among the flock of pigeons that had
gathered in the square. Her gown was pale green, thin and draped
closely enough to have satisfied Berelain, her dark hair was in dozens
of narrow braids, and her face was covered to the eyes by a transparent
veil like the one the falling man had worn. The pigeons soared up, and
so did the woman gliding over the nearest rooftops with them before
abruptly winking out of existence.

Egwene smiled. She dreamed of flying like a bird all the time, and
this was a dream, after all. She leaped into the air, and kept going up,
toward the roofs. She wobbled as she thought how ridiculous this was—
Flying? People did not fly!—then steadied again as she forced herself
to be confident. She was doing it, and that was all there was to it. This
was a dream, and she was flying. The wind rushed in her face, and she
wanted to laugh giddily.

She skimmed across the Panarch's Circle, where rows of stone
benches slanted down from the high wall to a broad field of packed dirt
in the center. Imagine so many people gathered, and to watch a fireworks display by the Guild of Illuminators themselves. Back home fireworks were a rare treat. She could remember the handful of times in
her life Emond's Field had had them, with the grown-ups as excited as
the children.

She sailed over rooftops like a falcon, over palaces and mansions,
humble dwellings and shops, warehouses and stables. She slid by
domes topped with golden spires and bronze weathervanes, by towers
ringed with lacy stone balconies. Carts and wagons dotted wagonyards,
waiting. Ships crowded the great harbor and the fingers of water between the city's peninsulas; they lined the docks. Everything seemed in

a poor state of repair, from the carts to the ships, but nothing she saw pointed to the Black Ajah. As far as she knew.

She considered trying to envision Liandrin—she knew that doll's face all too well, with its multitude of blond braids, its self-satisfied brown eyes, and its smirking rosebud mouth—picture her in the hopes she might be drawn to where the Black sister was. But if it worked, she might find Liandrin in *Tel'aran'rhiod*, too, and maybe others of them. She was not ready for that.

It suddenly occurred to her that if any of the Black Ajah were in Tanchico, in the Tanchico of *Tel'aran'rhiod*, she was flaunting herself for them. Any eye looking at the sky would notice a woman flying, one who did not vanish after a few moments. Her smooth flight staggered, and she swooped down below roof level, floating along the streets more slowly than before but still faster than a horse could run. She might be rushing toward them, but she could not make herself stop and wait for them.

Fool! she called herself furiously. *Fool! They could know I'm here now. They could be laying a trap already.* She considered stepping out of the dream, back to her bed in Tear, but she had found nothing. If there was anything to find.

A tall woman was suddenly standing in the street ahead of her, slim in a bulky brown skirt and loose white blouse, with a brown shawl around her shoulders and a folded scarf around her forehead to hold white hair that spilled to her waist. Despite her plain clothes she wore a great many necklaces and bracelets of gold or ivory or both. Fists planted on her hips, she stared straight at Egwene, frowning.

Another fool woman who's dreamed herself where she has no right to be and doesn't believe what she's seeing, Egwene thought. She had the description of every woman who had gone with Liandrin, and this woman certainly matched none of them. But the woman did not vanish again; she stood there as Egwene approached swiftly. *Why doesn't she go? Why . . . ? Oh, Light! She's really . . . !* She snatched for the flows to weave lightning, to tangle the woman in Air, fumbling in startled haste.

"Put your feet on the ground, girl," the woman barked. "I had enough trouble finding you again without you flying off like some bird when I do."

Abruptly Egwene stopped flying. Her feet thumped hard on the pavement, and she staggered. It was the Aiel woman's voice, but this was an older woman. Not as old as Egwene had thought at first—in fact, she looked much younger than her white hair suggested—but with the voice, and those sharp blue eyes, she was sure it was the same woman. "You're . . . different," she said.

"You can be what you wish to be, here." The woman sounded embarrassed, but only a little. "At times I like to remember. . . . That is not important. You are from the White Tower? It has been long since they had a dreamwalker. Very long. I am Amys, of the Nine Valleys sept of the Taardad Aiel."

"You are a Wise One? You are! And you know dreams, you know *Tel'aran'rhiod!* You can. . . . My name is Egwene. Egwene al'Vere. I. . . ." She took a deep breath; Amys did not look a woman to lie to. "I am Aes Sedai. Of the Green Ajah."

Amys's expression did not change, really. A slight crinkling of her eyes, perhaps in skepticism. Egwene hardly looked old enough to be full Aes Sedai. What she said, though, was "I meant to leave you standing in your skin until you asked for some proper clothes. Putting on *cadin'sor* that way, as though you were. . . . You surprised me, pulling free as you did, turning my own spear on me. But you are still untaught, are you not, however strong. Else you would not have popped into the middle of my hunt that way, where you obviously did not wish to be. And this flying about? Did you come to *Tel'aran'rhiod—Tel'aran'rhiod!*—to stare at this city, wherever it is?"

"It's Tanchico," Egwene said faintly. *She didn't know.* But then how had Amys followed her, or found her? It was obvious she knew more of the World of Dreams than Egwene did, by far. "You can help me. I am trying to find women of the Black Ajah, Darkfriends. I think they are here, and I have to find them if they are."

"It truly exists, then." Amys almost whispered it. "An Ajah of Shadowrunners in the White Tower." She shook her head. "You are like a girl just wedded to the spear who thinks now she can wrestle men and leap mountains. For her it means a few bruises and a valuable lesson in humility. For you, here, it could mean death." Amys eyed the white buildings around them and grimaced. "Tanchico? In . . . Tarabon? This city is dying, eating itself. There is a darkness here, an evil. Worse than men can make. Or women." She looked at Egwene pointedly. "You cannot see it, or feel it, can you? And you want to hunt Shadowrunners in *Tel'aran'rhiod.*"

"Evil?" Egwene said quickly. "That could be them. Are you sure? If I told you what they look like, could you be certain it was them? I can describe them. I can describe one to her last braid."

"A child," Amys muttered, "demanding a silver bracelet from her father this minute when she knows nothing of trading or the making of bracelets. You have much to learn. Far more than I can begin to teach you, now. Come to the Three-fold Land. I will have the word spread through the clans that an Aes Sedai called Egwene al'Vere is to be brought to me at Cold Rocks Hold. Give your name and show your Great Serpent ring, and you will have safe running. I am not there now, but I will return from Rhuidean before you can arrive."

"Please, you must help me. I need to know if they are here. I have to know."

"But I cannot tell you. I do not know them, or this place, this Tanchico. You must come to me. What you do is dangerous, far more dangerous than you know. You must— Where are you going? Stay!"

Something seemed to snatch at Egwene, pulling her into darkness.

Amys's voice followed her, hollow and dwindling. "You must come to me and learn. You must. . . ."

CHAPTER 12

Tanchico or the Tower

Elayne drew a ragged, relieved breath as Egwene finally stirred and opened her eyes. At the foot of the bed, Aviendha's features lost their tinge of frustration and anxiety, and she flashed a quick smile that Egwene returned. The candle had burned past the mark minutes ago; it seemed an hour.

"You would not wake up," Elayne said unsteadily. "I shook you and shook you, but you would not wake." She gave a small laugh. "Oh, Egwene, you even frightened Aviendha."

Egwene put a hand on her arm and squeezed reassuringly. "I am back, now." She sounded tired, and she had sweated her shift through. "I suppose I had reason to stay a little longer than we planned. I will be more careful next time. I promise."

Nynaeve returned the pitcher of water to the washstand vigorously, sloshing some out. She had been on the point of throwing it in Egwene's sleeping face. Her features were composed, but the pitcher rattled the washbowl, and she let the spilled water drip to the carpet. "Was it something you found? Or was it . . . ? Egwene, if the World of Dreams can hold on to you in some way, maybe it is too dangerous until you learn more. Maybe the more often you go, the harder it is to come back. Maybe. . . . I don't know. But I do know we cannot risk letting you become lost." She crossed her arms under her breasts, ready for an argument.

"I know," Egwene said, very close to meekly. Elayne's eyebrows shot up; Egwene was never meek with Nynaeve. Anything but.

Egwene struggled off the bed, refusing Elayne's help, and made her way to the washstand to bathe her face and arms in the relatively cool water. Elayne found a dry shift in the wardrobe while Egwene pulled off her sodden one.

"I met a Wise One, a woman named Amys." Egwene's voice was muffled until her head popped out of the top of the new shift. "She said I should come to her, to learn about *Tel'aran'rhiod.* At some place in the Waste called Cold Rocks Hold."

Elayne had caught a flicker of Aviendha's eye at the mention of the Wise One's name. "Do you know her? Amys?"

The Aiel woman's nod could only be described as reluctant. "A Wise One. A dreamwalker. Amys was *Far Dareis Mai* until she gave up the spear to go to Rhuidean."

"A Maiden!" Egwene exclaimed. "So that's why she. . . . No matter. She said she is at Rhuidean, now. Do you know where this Cold Rocks Hold is, Aviendha?"

"Of course. Cold Rocks is Rhuarc's hold. Rhuarc is Amys's husband. I visit there, sometimes. I used to. My sister-mother, Lian, is sister-wife to Amys."

Elayne exchanged confused glances with Egwene and Nynaeve. Once Elayne had thought she knew a good bit about Aiel, all learned from her teachers in Caemlyn, but she had discovered since meeting Aviendha how little she did know. Customs and relationships all were a maze. First-sisters meant having the same mother; except that it was possible for friends to *become* first-sisters by making a pledge before Wise Ones. Second-sisters meant your mothers were sisters; if your fathers were brothers, you were father-sisters, and not considered as closely related as second-sisters. After that, it truly grew bewildering.

"What does 'sister-wife' mean?" she asked hesitantly.

"That you have the same husband." Aviendha frowned at the way Egwene gasped and Nynaeve's eyes opened as wide as they would go. Elayne had been half-expecting the answer, but she still found herself fussing with skirts that were perfectly straight. "This is not your custom?" the Aiel woman asked.

"No," Egwene said faintly. "No, it is not."

"But you and Elayne care for one another as first-sisters. What would you have done had one of you been unwilling to step aside for

Rand al'Thor? Fight over him? Let a man damage the ties between you? Would it not have been better if you both had married him, then?"

Elayne looked at Egwene. The thought of. . . . Could she have done such a thing? Even with Egwene? She knew her cheeks were red. Egwene merely looked startled.

"But I wanted to step aside," Egwene said.

Elayne knew the remark was as much for her as for Aviendha, but the thought would not go away. Had Min had a viewing? What would she do if Min had? *If it's Berelain, I will strangle her, and him too! If it has to be someone, why couldn't it be Egwene? Light, what am I thinking?* She knew she was becoming flustered, and to cover it, she made her voice light. "You sound as if the man has no choice in the matter."

"He can say no," Aviendha said as if it were obvious, "but if he wishes to marry one, he must marry both when they ask. Please take no offense, but I was shocked when I learned that in your lands a man can ask a woman to marry him. A man should make his interest known, then wait for the woman to speak. Of course, some women lead a man to see where his interest lies, but the right of the question is hers. I do not really know very much of these things. I have wanted to be *Far Dareis Mai* since I was a child. All I want in life is the spear and my spear-sisters," she finished quite fiercely.

"No one is going to try to make you marry," Egwene said soothingly. Aviendha gave her a startled look.

Nynaeve cleared her throat loudly. Elayne wondered if she had been thinking about Lan; there were certainly hard spots of color in her cheeks. "I suppose, Egwene," Nynaeve said in a slightly too energetic voice, "that you did not find what you were looking for, or you would have said something by now."

"I found nothing," Egwene replied regretfully. "But Amys said. . . . Aviendha, what sort of woman is Amys?"

The Aiel woman had taken up a study of the carpet. "Amys is hard as the mountains and pitiless as the sun," she said without looking up. "She is a dreamwalker. She can teach you. Once she lays her hands on you, she will drag you by the hair toward what she wants. Rhuarc is the only one who can stand up to her. Even the other Wise Ones step carefully when Amys speaks. But she can teach you."

Egwene shook her head. "I meant would being in a strange place unsettle her, make her nervous? Being in a city? Would she see things that weren't there?"

Aviendha's laugh was a short, sharp sound. "Nervous? Waking to find a lion in her bed would not make Amys nervous. She was a Maiden, Egwene, and she has grown no softer, you can be sure of it."

"What did this woman see?" Nynaeve asked.

"It wasn't something she saw, exactly," Egwene said slowly. "I *think* not seeing. She said Tanchico had an evil in it. Worse than men could make, she said. That could be the Black Ajah. Don't argue with me, Nynaeve," she added in a firmer voice. "Dreams have to be interpreted. It very well could be."

Nynaeve had begun frowning as soon as Egwene mentioned evil in Tanchico, and her frown turned to a heated glare when Egwene told her not to argue. Sometimes Elayne wanted to shake both women. She stepped in quickly, before the older woman could erupt. "It very well could be, Egwene. You did find something. More than Nynaeve or I thought you could. Didn't she, Nynaeve? Don't you think so?"

"It could be," Nynaeve said grudgingly.

"It could be." Egwene did not sound happy about it. She took a deep breath. "Nynaeve is right. I have to learn what I'm doing. If I knew what I should, I would not have had to be told about the evil. If I knew what I should, I could have found the very room Liandrin is staying in, wherever she is. Amys can teach me. That is why. . . . That is why I have to go to her."

"Go to her?" Nynaeve sounded appalled. "Into the Waste?"

"Aviendha can take me right to this Cold Rocks Hold." Egwene's look, half-defiant, half-anxious, darted between Elayne and Nynaeve. "If I was certain they were in Tanchico, I wouldn't let you go alone. If you decide to. But with Amys to help me, maybe I can find out where they are. Maybe I can. . . . That is just it; I do not even know what I'll be able to do, only that I am certain it will be far more than I can now. It isn't as if I will be abandoning you. You can take the ring with you. You know the Stone well enough to come back here in *Tel'aran'rhiod*. I can come to you in Tanchico. Whatever I learn from Amys, I can teach you. Please say you understand. I can learn so much from Amys, and then I can use it to help you. It will be as if all three of us had been trained by her. A dreamwalker; a woman who *knows!* Liandrin and the rest of them will be like children; they won't know a quarter of what we do." She chewed her lip, one pensive bite. "You don't believe I am running out on you, do you? If you do, I won't go."

"Of course you must go," Elayne told her. "I will miss you, but no one promised us we could stay together until this was done."

"But the two of you . . . going alone . . . I should go with you. If they really are in Tanchico, I should be with you."

"Nonsense," Nynaeve said briskly. "Training is what you need. That will do us far more good in the long run than your company to Tanchico. It isn't even as if we know any of them are in Tanchico. If they are, Elayne and I will do very well together, but we could arrive and find that this evil is no more than the war after all. The Light knows, war should be evil enough for anyone. We may be back in the Tower before you are. You must be careful in the Waste," she added in a practical tone. "It is a dangerous place. Aviendha, you will look after her?"

Before the Aiel woman could open her mouth, there was a knock at the door, followed immediately by Moiraine. The Aes Sedai took them in with one sweeping look that weighed, measured and considered them and what they had been doing, all without the twitch of an eyelid to suggest her conclusions. "Joiya and Amico are dead," she announced.

"Was that the reason for the attack, then?" Nynaeve said. "All that to kill them? Or perhaps to kill them if they could not be freed. I've been sure Joiya was so confident because she expected rescue. She must have been lying after all. I never trusted her repentance."

"Not the main purpose, perhaps," Moiraine replied. "The captain very wisely kept his men to their posts in the dungeons during the attack. They never saw a single Trolloc or Myrddraal. But they found the pair dead, after. Each with her throat rather messily cut. After her tongue had been nailed to her cell door." She might as well have been speaking of having a dress mended.

Elayne's stomach heaved leadenly at the detached description. "I would not have wanted that for them. Not like that. The Light illumine their souls."

"They sold their souls to the Shadow long ago," Egwene said roughly. She had both hands pressed to her stomach, though. "How. . . . How was it done? Gray Men?"

"I doubt even Gray Men could have managed that," Moiraine said dryly. "The Shadow has resources beyond what we know, it seems."

"Yes." Egwene smoothed her dress, and her voice. "If there was no attempt at rescue, it must mean they were both telling the truth. They were killed because they talked."

"Or to stop them from it," Nynaeve added grimly. "We can hope they do not know that those two told us anything. Perhaps Joiya did repent, but I'll not believe it."

Elayne swallowed, thinking of being in a cell, having your face pressed to the door so your tongue could be pulled out and. . . . She shivered, but made herself say, "They might have been killed simply to punish them for being captured." She left out her thought that the killing might have been to make them believe whatever Joiya and Amico had said; they had enough doubts about what to do as it was. "Three possibilities, and only one says the Black Ajah knows they revealed a word. Since all three are equal, the chances are that they do not know."

Egwene and Nynaeve looked shocked. "To *punish* them?" Nynaeve said incredulously.

They were both tougher than she in many ways—she admired them for it—but they had not grown up watching the maneuverings at court in Caemlyn, hearing tales of the cruel way Cairhienin and Tairens played the Game of Houses.

"I think the Black Ajah might be less than gentle with failure of any kind," she told them. "I can imagine Liandrin ordering it. Joiya surely could have done it easily." Moiraine eyed her briefly, a reassessing look.

"Liandrin," Egwene said, her tone absolutely flat. "Yes, I can imagine Liandrin or Joiya giving that command."

"You did not have much longer to question them in any case," Moiraine said. "They would have been shipbound by midday tomorrow." A hint of anger touched her voice; Elayne realized Moiraine must see the Black sisters' deaths as an escape from justice. "I hope you reach some decision soon. Tanchico or the Tower."

Elayne met Nynaeve's eyes and gave a slight nod.

Nynaeve nodded back, more assertively, before turning to the Aes Sedai. "Elayne and I will be going to Tanchico as soon as we can find a ship. A fast ship, I hope. Egwene and Aviendha will be going to Cold Rocks Hold, in the Aiel Waste." She gave no reasons, and Moiraine's eyebrows rose.

"Jolien can take her," Aviendha said into the momentary silence. She avoided looking at Egwene. "Or Sefela, or Bain and Chiad. I. . . . I have a thought to go with Elayne and Nynaeve. If there is war in this Tanchico, they have need of a sister to watch their backs."

"If that is what you want, Aviendha," Egwene said slowly.

She looked surprised and hurt, but no more surprised than Elayne. She had thought the two of them were becoming friends. "I am glad you want to help us, Aviendha, but you should be the one to take Egwene to Cold Rocks Hold."

"She is going neither to Tanchico nor Cold Rocks Hold," Moiraine said, taking a letter from her pouch and unfolding the pages. "This was placed in my hand an hour gone. The young Aielman who brought it told me it was given to him a month ago, before any of us reached Tear, yet it is addressed to me by name, at the Stone of Tear." She glanced at the last sheet. "Aviendha, do you know Amys, of the Nine Valleys sept of the Taardad Aiel; Bair, of the Haido sept of the Shaarad Aiel; Melaine, of the Jhirad sept of the Goshien Aiel; and Seana, of the Black Cliff sept of the Nakai Aiel? They signed it."

"They are all Wise Ones, Aes Sedai. All dreamwalkers." Aviendha's stance had shifted to wariness, though she did not seem aware of it. She looked ready to fight or flee.

"Dreamwalkers," Moiraine mused. "Perhaps that explains it. I have heard of dreamwalkers." She turned to the second page of the letter. "Here is what they say about you. What they said perhaps before you had even decided to come to Tear. 'There is among the Maidens of the Spear in the Stone of Tear a willful girl called Aviendha, of the Nine Valleys sept of the Taardad Aiel. She must now come to us. There can be no more waiting or excuses. We will await her on the slopes of Chaendaer, above Rhuidean.' There is more about you, but mainly telling me that I must see you come to them without delay. They issue commands like the Amyrlin, these Wise Ones of yours." She made a vexed sound, which brought Elayne to wonder if the Wise Ones had tried issuing commands to the Aes Sedai, too. Not very likely. And unlikely to be successful if tried. Still, something about that letter irritated the Aes Sedai.

"I am *Far Dareis Mai*," Aviendha said angrily. "I do not go running like a child when someone calls my name. I will go to Tanchico if I wish."

Elayne pursed her lips thoughtfully. This was something new from the Aiel woman. Not the anger—she had seen Aviendha angry before, if not quite to this degree—but the undertone. She could call it nothing but sulkiness. That seemed as unlikely as Lan being sulky, but there it was.

Egwene heard it, too. She patted Aviendha's arm. "It's all right. If you want to go to Tanchico, I'll be pleased that you are protecting Elayne and Nynaeve." Aviendha gave her a truly miserable look.

Moiraine shook her head, only slightly, but still deliberate. "I showed this to Rhuarc." Aviendha opened her mouth, her face irate, but the Aes Sedai raised her voice and went on smoothly. "As the letter asks me to. Only the part concerning you, of course. He seems quite determined that you will do as the letter asks. As it orders. I think it wisest to do as Rhuarc and the Wise Ones wish, Aviendha. Do you not agree?"

Aviendha stared around the room wildly, as at a trap. "I am *Far Dareis Mai,"* she muttered, and strode for the door without another word.

Egwene took a step, half-raising a hand to stop her, then let it fall as the door banged shut. "What do they want with her?" she demanded of Moiraine. "You always know more than you let on. What are you holding back this time?"

"Whatever the Wise Ones' reason," Moiraine said coolly, "it is surely a matter between Aviendha and them. If she wished you to know, she would have told you."

"You cannot stop trying to maneuver people," Nynaeve said bitterly. "You're maneuvering Aviendha into something now, aren't you?"

"Not I. The Wise Ones. And Rhuarc." Moiraine folded the letter, returning it to her belt pouch with a touch of acerbity in her manner. "She can always say no to him. A clan chief is not the same as a king, as I understand Aiel ways."

"Can she?" Elayne asked. Rhuarc reminded her of Gareth Bryne. The Captain-General of her mother's Royal Guards had seldom put his foot down, but when he did, not even Morgase could bring him around, short of a royal command. There would be no command from the throne this time—not that Morgase had ever issued one to Gareth Bryne when he had decided he was right, now that Elayne thought of it —and without one, she expected that Aviendha was going to the slopes of Chaendaer, above Rhuidean. "At least she can journey with you, Egwene. Amys can hardly meet you at Cold Rocks Hold if she plans to wait for Aviendha at Rhuidean. You can go to Amys together."

"But I do not want her to," Egwene said sadly. "Not if she doesn't want to."

"Whatever anyone wants," Nynaeve said, "we have work to do. You will need many things for a trip into the Waste, Egwene. Lan will tell me what. And Elayne and I must make preparations to sail for Tanchico. I suppose we can find a ship tomorrow, but that means deciding what to pack tonight."

"There is a ship of the Atha'an Miere at the docks in the Maule," Moiraine told them. "A raker. There are no ships faster. You did want a fast ship." Nynaeve gave a grudging nod.

"Moiraine," Elayne said, "what is Rand going to do now? After this attack. . . . Will he start the war you want?"

"I do not want a war," the Aes Sedai replied. "I want what will see him alive to fight Tarmon Gai'don. He says he will tell us all what he means to do tomorrow." The smallest frown creased her smooth forehead. "Tomorrow, we will all know more than we do tonight." Her departure was abrupt.

Tomorrow, Elayne thought. *What will he do when I tell him? What will he say? He has to understand.* Determinedly, she joined the other two to discuss their preparations.

CHAPTER
13

Rumors

The tavern's business rocked along like any in the Maule, a wagonload of geese and crockery careering downhill through the night. The babble of voices fought with the musicians' offerings on three assorted drums, two hammered dulcimers, and a bulbous semseer that produced whining trills. The serving maids in dark, ankle-length dresses with necks up to the chin and short white aprons hustled between crowded tables, holding clusters of pottery mugs overhead so they could squeeze through. Barefoot leather-vested dockmen mixed with fellows in coats tight to the waist and bare-chested men with broad, colorful sashes to hold up their baggy breeches. So close to the docks, vestments of outlanders were everywhere among the crowd; high collars from the north and long collars from the west, silver chains on coats and bells on vests, knee-high boots and thigh-high boots, necklaces or earrings on men, lace on coats or shirts. One man with wide shoulders and a big belly had a forked yellow beard, and another had smeared something on his mustaches to make them glisten in the lamplight and curl up on either side of his narrow face. Dice rolled and tumbled in three corners of the room and on a number of tabletops, silver changing hands briskly to shouts and laughter.

Mat sat alone with his back to the wall where he could see all the doors, though mostly he peered into a still untouched mug of dark wine. He did not go near the dice games, and he never glanced at the serving girls' ankles. With the tavern so crowded, men occasionally thought to share his table, but a good look at his face made them sheer away and crowd onto a bench elsewhere.

Dipping a finger in his wine, he sketched aimlessly on the tabletop. These fools had no idea what had happened in the Stone tonight. He had heard a few Tairens mention some kind of trouble, quick words that trailed off into nervous laughter. They did not know and did not want to. He almost wished he did not know himself. No, he wished he had a better idea of what had happened. The images kept flashing in his head, flashing through the holes in his memory, making no real sense.

The din of fighting somewhere in the distance echoed down the corridor, dulled by the wall hangings. He retrieved his knife from the Gray Man's corpse with a shaking hand. A Gray Man, and hunting him. It had to have been after him. Gray Men did not wander about killing at random; they had targets as surely as an arrow. He turned to run, and there was a Myrddraal striding toward him like a black snake on legs, its pasty-faced, eyeless stare sending shivers into his bones. At thirty paces he hurled the knife straight at where an eye should have been; at that distance he could hit a knothole no larger than an eye four times in five.

The Fade's black sword blurred as it knocked the dagger away, almost casually; it did not even break stride. "Time to die, Hornsounder." Its voice was a red adder's dry hiss, warning of death.

Mat backed away. He had a knife in either hand, now, though he did not remember drawing them. Not that knives would be much good against a sword, but running meant that black blade in his back as sure as five sixes beat four threes. He wished he had a good quarterstaff. Or a bow; he would like to see this thing try to deflect a shaft from a Two Rivers long-bow. He wished he were somewhere else. He was going to die, here.

Suddenly a dozen Trollocs roared out of a side hallway, piling onto the Fade in a frenzy of chopping axes and stabbing swords. Mat stared in amazed disbelief. The Halfman fought like a black-armored whirlwind. More than half the Trollocs were dead or dying before the Fade lay in a twitching heap; one arm flexed and thrashed like a dying snake three paces away from the body, still with that black sword in its fist.

A ram-horned Trolloc peered toward Mat, snout lifted to sniff the air. It snarled at him, then whined and began licking a long gash that had laid open mail and hairy forearm. The others finished cutting the throats of their wounded, and one barked a few harsh, guttural words. Without an-

other glance at Mat, they turned and trotted away, hooves and boots mak-
ing hollow sounds on the stone floor.

Away from him. Mat shivered. Trollocs to the rescue. What had
Rand gotten him into now? He saw what he had drawn with the wine—
an open door—and scrubbed it out angrily. He had to get away from
here. He had to. And he could also feel that urge in the back of his
head, that it was time to go back to the Stone. He pushed it away
angrily, but it kept buzzing at him.

He caught a snatch of talk from the table to his right, where the lean-
faced fellow with the curling mustaches was holding forth in a heavy
Lugarder accent. "Now this Dragon of yours is a great man no doubt,
I'll not be denying it, but he's not a patch on Logain. Why, Logain had
all of Ghealdan at war, and half of Amadicia and Altara, as well. He
made the earth swallow whole towns that resisted him, he did. Buildings, people and all entire. And the one up in Saldaea, Maseem? Why,
they say he made the sun stand still till he defeated the Lord of
Bashere's army. 'Tis a fact, they do say."

Mat shook his head. The Stone fallen and *Callandor* in Rand's hand,
and this idiot still thought he was another false Dragon. He had
sketched that doorway again. Rubbing a hand through it, he grabbed
up the mug of wine, then stopped with it halfway to his mouth.
Through the commotion his ear had picked out a familiar name spoken
at a nearby table. Scraping back his bench, he made his way to that
table, mug in hand.

The people around it were the sort of odd mixture made in taverns
in the Maule. Two barefoot sailors wearing oiled coats over bare chests,
one with a thick gold chain close around his neck. A once fat man with
sagging jowls, in a dark Cairhienin coat with slashes of red and gold
and green across his chest which might have indicated that he was a
noble, though one sleeve was torn at the shoulder; a good many
Cairhienin refugees had come down far in the world. A gray-haired
woman all in subdued dark blue, with a hard face and a sharp eye and
heavy gold rings on her fingers. And the speaker, the fork-bearded
fellow, with a ruby the size of a pigeon's egg in his ear. The three silver
chains looped across the straining chest of his dark, reddish coat
named him a Kandori master merchant. They had a guild for merchants in Kandor.

The talk ceased and all eyes swung to Mat when he stopped at their
table. "I heard you mention the Two Rivers."

Forkbeard ran a quick eye over him, the unbrushed hair, the tight
expression on his face and the wine in his fist, the gleaming black boots,

the green coat with its gold scrollwork, open to the waist to reveal a snowy linen shirt, but both coat and shirt heavily wrinkled. In short, the very image of a young noble sporting himself among the commoners. "I did, my Lord," he said heartily. "I was saying there'll be no tabac out of there this year, I'll wager. I have twenty casks of the finest Two Rivers leaf, though, than which there is none finer. Fetch an excellent price later in the year. If my Lord wishes a cask for his own stock . . ." He tugged one point of his yellow beard and laid a finger alongside his nose. ". . . I am certain I could manage to—"

"You'll wager that, will you?" Mat said softly, cutting him short. "Why would there be no tabac out of the Two Rivers?"

"Why, the Whitecloaks, my Lord. The Children of the Light."

"What about Whitecloaks?"

The master merchant peered around the table for help; there was a dangerous note in that quiet tone. The sailors looked as if they would leave if they dared. The Cairhienin was glaring at Mat, sitting up too straight and smoothing his worn coat as he swayed; the empty mug in front of him was obviously not his first. The gray-haired woman had her mug to her mouth, her sharp eyes watching Mat over the rim in a calculating way.

Managing a seated bow, the merchant put on an ingratiating tone. "The rumor is, my Lord, that the Whitecloaks have gone into the Two Rivers. Hunting the Dragon Reborn, it's said. Though of course, that cannot be, since the Lord Dragon is here in Tear." He eyed Mat to see how that had been taken; Mat's face did not change. "These rumors can run very wild, my Lord. Perhaps it's only wind in a bucket. The same rumor claims the Whitecloaks are after some Darkfriend with yellow eyes, too. Did you ever hear of a man with yellow eyes, my Lord? No more have I. Wind in a bucket."

Mat set his mug on the table and leaned closer to the man. "Who else are they hunting? According to this rumor. The Dragon Reborn. A man with yellow eyes. Who else?"

Beads of sweat formed on the merchant's face. "No one, my Lord. No one that I heard. Only rumor, my Lord. Straws in the wind; no more. A puff of smoke, soon vanished. If I might have the honor of presenting my Lord a cask of Two Rivers tabac? A gesture of appreciation . . . the honor of . . . to express my. . . ."

Mat tossed an Andoran gold crown onto the table. "Buy your drink on me till that runs out."

As he turned away he heard mutters from the table. "I thought he'd cut my throat. You know these lordlings when they're full of wine."

That from the fork-bearded merchant. "An odd young man," the woman said. "Dangerous. Do not try your ploys on that kind, Paetram." "I do not think he is a lord at all," another man said petulantly. The Cairhienin, Mat supposed. His lip curled. A lord? He would not be a lord if it was offered to him. *Whitecloaks in the Two Rivers. Light! Light help us!*

Plowing his way to the door, he pulled a pair of wooden clogs from the pile against the wall. He had no idea whether they were the ones he had worn in—they all looked alike—and did not care. They fit his boots.

It had started raining outside, a light fall that made the darkness that much deeper. Turning up his collar, he splashed along the muddy streets of the Maule in an awkward trot, past blaring taverns and well-lit inns and dark-windowed houses. When mud gave way to paving stones at the wall marking the inner city, he kicked the clogs off and left them lying as he ran on. The Defenders guarding the nearest gate into the Stone let him pass without a word; they knew who he was. He ran all the way to Perrin's room and flung open the door, barely noticing the splintered split in the wood. Perrin's saddlebags lay on the bed, and Perrin was stuffing shirts and stockings into them. There was only one candle lit, but he did not seem to notice the gloom.

"You've heard, then," Mat said.

Perrin went on with what he was doing. "About home? Yes. I went down to sniff out a rumor for Faile. After tonight, more than ever, I have to get her. . . ." The growl, deep in his throat, made Mat's hackles rise; it sounded like an angry wolf. "No matter. I heard. Maybe this will do as well."

As well as what? Mat wondered. "You believe it?"

For a moment Perrin looked up; his eyes gathered the light of the candle, shining a burnished golden yellow. "There doesn't seem to be much doubt, to me. It's all too close to the truth."

Mat shifted uncomfortably. "Does Rand know?" Perrin only nodded and went back to his packing. "Well, what does he say?"

Perrin paused, staring at the folded cloak in his hands. "He started muttering to himself. 'He said he'd do it. He said he would. I should have believed him.' Like that. It made no sense. Then he grabbed me by the collar and said he had to do 'what they don't expect.' He wanted me to understand, but I'm not certain he does himself. He didn't seem to care whether I leave or stay. No, I take that back. I think he was relieved I'm leaving."

"Boil it down, and he's not going to do anything," Mat said. "Light,

with *Callandor* he could blast a thousand Whitecloaks! You saw what
he did to those bloody Trollocs. You're going, are you? Back to the Two
Rivers? Alone?"

"Unless you are coming, too." Perrin stuffed the cloak into the saddlebags. "Are you?"

Instead of answering, Mat paced back and forth, his face in half-light
and shadow by turns. His mother and father were in Emond's Field,
and his sisters. Whitecloaks had no reason to hurt them. If he went
home, he had the feeling he would never leave again, that his mother
would marry him off before he could sit down. But if he did not go, if
the Whitecloaks harmed them. . . . All it took was rumor, for
Whitecloaks, so he had heard. But why should there be any rumor
about them? Even the Coplins, liars and troublemakers to a man, liked
his father. Everyone liked Abell Cauthon.

"You don't have to," Perrin said quietly. "Nothing I heard mentioned you. Only Rand, and me."

"Burn me, I will g—" He could not say it. Thinking of going was easy
enough, but saying he would? His throat tightened up to strangle the
words. "Is it easy for you, Perrin? Going, I mean? Don't you . . . feel
anything? Trying to hold you back? Telling you reasons you shouldn't
go?"

"A hundred of them, Mat, but I know it comes down to Rand, and
ta'veren. You won't admit that, will you? A hundred reasons to stay, but
the one reason to go outweighs them. The Whitecloaks are in the Two
Rivers, and they'll hurt people trying to find me. I can stop it, if I go."

"Why should the Whitecloaks want you enough to hurt anybody?
Light, if they go asking for somebody with yellow eyes, nobody in
Emond's Field will know who they're talking about! And how can you
stop anything? One more pair of hands won't do much good. Aaah!
The Whitecloaks have bitten a mouthful of leather if they think they
can push Two Rivers folk around."

"They know my name," Perrin said softly. His gaze swung to where
his axe hung on the wall, the belt tied around the haft and the wall
hook. Or maybe it was his hammer he was staring at, standing propped
against the wall beneath the axe; Mat could not be sure. "They can find
my family. As for why, they have their reasons, Mat. Just as I have
mine. Who can say who has the better?"

"Burn me, Perrin. Burn me! I want to g-g— See? I can't even say it,
now. Like my head knows I'll do it if I say it. I can't even get it out in
my mind!"

"Different paths. We've been sent down different paths before."

"Different paths be bloodied," Mat grunted. "I've had all I want of Rand, and Aes Sedai, shoving me down their bloody paths. I want to go where I want for a change, do what I want!" He turned for the door, but Perrin's voice halted him.

"I hope your path is a happy one, Mat. The Light send you pretty girls and fools who want to gamble."

"Oh, burn me, Perrin. The Light send you what you want, too."

"I expect it will." He did not sound happy at the prospect.

"Will you tell my da I'm all right? And my mother? She always did worry. And look after my sisters. They used to spy on me and tell Mother everything, but I wouldn't want anything to happen to them."

"I promise, Mat."

Closing the door behind him, Mat wandered down the hallways aimlessly. His sisters. Eldrin and Bodewhin had always been ready to run shouting "Mama, Mat's in trouble again, Mat's doing what he shouldn't, Mama." Especially Bode. They would be sixteen and seventeen, now. Probably thinking of marriage before too much longer, already with some dull farmer picked out whether the fellow knew it or not. Had he really been gone so long? It did not seem so, sometimes. Sometimes he felt as if he had left Emond's Field just a week or two past. Other times it seemed years gone, only dimly remembered at all. He could remember Eldrin and Bode smirking when he had been switched, but their faces were no longer sharp. His own sisters' faces. These bloody holes in his memory, like holes in his life.

He saw Berelain coming toward him and grinned in spite of himself. For all her airs, she was a fine figure of a woman. That clinging white silk was thin enough for a handkerchief, not to mention being scooped low enough at the top to expose a considerable amount of excellent pale bosom.

He swept her his best bow, elegant and formal. "A good evening to you, my Lady." She started to sweep by without a glance, and he straightened angrily. "Are you deaf as well as blind, woman? I'm not a carpet to walk over, and I distinctly heard myself speak. If I pinch your bottom, you can slap my face, but until I do, I expect a civil word for a civil word!"

The First stopped dead, eyeing him in that way women had. She could have sewn him a shirt and told his weight, not to mention when he had his last bath, from that look. Then she turned away, murmuring something to herself. All he caught was "too much like me."

He stared after her in amazement. Not a word to him! That face, that walk, and her nose so far in the air it was a wonder her feet touched the ground. That was what he got, speaking to the likes of Berelain and Elayne. Nobles who thought you were dirt unless you had a palace and bloodlines back to Artur Hawkwing. Well, he knew a plump cook's helper—just plump enough—who did not think he was dirt. Dara had a way of nibbling his ears that. . . .

His thoughts stopped dead in their tracks. He had been considering seeing whether Dara was awake and up for a cuddle. He had even considered flirting with Berelain. Berelain! And the last words he had said to Perrin. *Look after my sisters.* As if he had already decided, already knew what to do. Only he had not. He would not, not so easily, just sliding into it. There was a way, perhaps.

Digging a gold coin from his pocket, he flipped it into the air and snatched it onto the back of his other hand. A Tar Valon mark, he saw for the first time, and he was staring at the Flame of Tar Valon, stylized like a teardrop. "Burn all Aes Sedai!" he announced loudly. "And burn Rand al'Thor for getting me into this!"

A black-and-gold liveried servant stopped in midstride, staring at him worriedly. The man's silver tray was piled high with rolled bandages and jars of ointment. As soon as he realized Mat had seen him, he gave a jump.

Mat tossed the gold mark onto the man's tray. "From the biggest fool in the world. Mind you spend it well, on women and wine."

"T-thank you, my Lord," the man stammered as if stunned.

Mat left him standing there. *The biggest fool in the world. Aren't I just!*

CHAPTER
14

Customs of Mayene

P errin shook his head as the door closed behind Mat. Mat would as soon hit himself on the head with a hammer as go back to the Two Rivers. Not unless he must. Perrin wished there was some way he could avoid going home, too. But there was no way; it was a fact as hard as iron and less forgiving. The difference between Mat and himself was that he was willing to accept that, even when he did not want to.

Easing his shirt off made him grunt, careful as he could be. A large bruise, already faded to browns and yellows, stained his entire left shoulder. A Trolloc had slipped past his axe, and only Faile's quick work with a knife had kept it from being more than it was. The shoulder made washing painful, but at least there was no worry about cold water in Tear.

He was packed and ready, only a change of clothes for the morning remaining out of his saddlebags. As soon as the sun rose, he would go find Loial. No point in bothering the Ogier tonight. He was probably already abed, where Perrin meant to be shortly. Faile was the only problem he had not figured out how to deal with. Even staying in Tear would be better for her than going with him.

The door opened, surprising him. Perfume wafted in to him as soon as the door cracked; it made him think of climbing flowers on a hot summer night. A tantalizing scent, not heavy, not to anyone but him, but nothing Faile would wear. Still, he was even more surprised when Berelain stepped into his room.

Holding the edge of the door, she blinked, making him realize how dim the light must be for her. "You are going somewhere?" she said hesitantly. With the light of the hallway's lamps behind her, it was difficult not to stare.

"Yes, my Lady." He bowed; not smoothly, but as well as he could. Faile could give all the sharp sniffs she wanted, but he saw no reason not to be polite. "In the morning."

"So am I." She closed the door and crossed her arms beneath her breasts. He looked away, watching her from the corner of his eye, so she would not think he was goggling. She went on without noticing his reaction. The single candle flame was reflected in her dark eyes. "After tonight. . . . Tomorrow I will leave by carriage for Godan, and from there take ship for Mayene. I should have gone days ago, but I thought there must be some way to work matters out. Only, there wasn't, of course. I should have seen that sooner. Tonight convinced me. The way he. . . . All that lightning, flowing down the halls. I will leave tomorrow."

"My Lady," Perrin said in confusion, "why are you telling me?"

The way she tossed her head reminded him of a mare he had sometimes shoed in Emond's Field; that mare would try to take a bite out of you. "So you can tell the Lord Dragon, of course."

That made no more sense to him. "You can tell him yourself," he said with more than a little exasperation. "I've no time for carrying messages before I go."

"I . . . do not think he would wish to see me."

Any man would want to see her, and she was beautiful to look at; she knew both things. He thought she had started to say something else. Could she have been that frightened by what had happened that night in Rand's bedchamber? Or the attack and the way Rand had ended it? Perhaps, but this was not a woman to frighten easily, not from the cool way she was eyeing him. "Give your message to a servant. I doubt I'll see Rand again. Not before I leave. Any servant will take a note to him."

"It would come better from you, a friend of the Lord—"

"Give it to a servant. Or one of the Aiel."

"You will not do as I ask?" she asked incredulously.

"No. Haven't you been listening to me?"

She tossed her head again, but there was a difference this time, though he could not have said what. Studying him thoughtfully, she murmured half to herself, "Such striking eyes."

"What?" Suddenly he realized he was standing there naked to the waist. Her intense scrutiny abruptly seemed like the study of a horse before purchase. Next thing, she would be feeling his ankles and inspecting his teeth. He snatched the shirt meant for morning from the bed and pulled it over his head. "Give your message to a servant. I want to go to bed now. I mean to be up early. Before sunrise."

"Where are you going tomorrow?"

"Home. The Two Rivers. It is late. If you are leaving tomorrow, too, I suppose you want to get some sleep. I know I'm tired." He yawned as widely as he could.

She still made no move toward the door. "You are a blacksmith? I have need of a blacksmith in Mayene. Making ornamental ironwork. A short stay before returning to the Two Rivers? You would find Mayene . . . entertaining."

"I am going home," he told her firmly, "and you are going back to your own rooms."

Her small shrug made him look away again hastily. "Perhaps another day. I always get what I want in the end. And I think I want . . ." She paused, eyeing him up and down. ". . . ornamental ironwork. For the windows of my bedchamber." She smiled so innocently that he felt alarm gongs sounding in his head.

The door opened again, and Faile came in. "Perrin, I went into the city looking for you, and I heard a rumor—" She stopped stock still, her eyes hard on Berelain.

The First ignored her. Stepping close to Perrin, she ran a hand up his arm, across his shoulder. For an instant he thought she meant to try pulling his head down for a kiss—she certainly lifted her face as if for one—but she only trailed her hand along the side of his neck in a quick caress and stepped back. It was over and done before he could move to stop her. "Remember," she said softly, as if they were alone, "I always get what I want." And she swept past Faile and out of the room.

He waited for an explosion from Faile, but she glanced at his stuffed saddlebags on the bed and said, "I see you've heard the rumor already. It *is* only a rumor, Perrin."

"Yellow eyes make it more than that." She should have been erupting like a bundle of dry twigs tossed on a fire. Why was she so cool? "Very well. Moiraine is the next problem, then. Will she try to stop you?"

"Not if she doesn't know. If she tries, I will go anyway. I have family and friends, Faile; I won't leave them to Whitecloaks. But I hope to keep it from her until I am well out of the city." Even her eyes were calm, like dark pools in the forest. It made his hackles rise.

"But it had to take weeks for that rumor to reach Tear, and it will take weeks more to ride to the Two Rivers. The Whitecloaks could be gone by then. Well, I have been wanting you to leave here. I should not complain. I just want you to know what to expect."

"It won't take weeks by the Ways," he told her. "Two days, maybe three." Two days. He supposed there was no means to make it faster.

"You are as mad as Rand al'Thor," she said disbelievingly. Dropping on the foot of his bed, she folded her legs crosswise and addressed him in a voice suitable for lecturing children. "Go into the Ways, and you come out hopelessly mad. If you come out at all, which it is most likely you will not. The Ways are tainted, Perrin. They have been dark for—what?—three hundred years? Four hundred? Ask Loial. He could tell you. It was Ogiers built the Ways, or grew them, or whatever it was. Not even they use the Ways. Why, even if you managed to make it through them unscathed, the Light alone knows where you would come out."

"I have traveled them, Faile." And a frightening trip it had been, too. "Loial can guide me. He can read the guideposts; that's how we went before. He will do it for me again when he knows how important it is." Loial was eager to be away from Tear, too; he seemed to be afraid that his mother knew where he was. Perrin was sure he would help.

"Well," she said, rubbing her hands together briskly. "Well. I wanted adventure, and this is certainly it. Leaving the Stone of Tear and the Dragon Reborn, traveling the Ways to fight Whitecloaks. I wonder whether we can persuade Thom Merrilin to come along. If we cannot have a bard, a gleeman will do. He could compose the story, and you and I the heart of it. No Dragon Reborn or Aes Sedai about to swallow up the tale. When do we leave? In the morning?"

He took a deep breath to steady his voice. "I will be going alone, Faile. Just Loial and me."

"We will need a packhorse," she said as if he had not spoken. "Two, I think. The Ways are dark. We will need lanterns, and plenty of oil. Your Two Rivers people. Farmers? Will they fight Whitecloaks?"

"Faile, I said—"

"I heard what you said," she snapped. Shadows gave her a dangerous look, with her tilted eyes and high cheekbones. "I heard, and it makes no sense. What if these farmers won't fight? Or don't know how? Who is going to teach them? You? Alone?"

"I will do what has to be done," he said patiently. "Without you."

She bounced to her feet so fast he thought she was coming for his throat. "Do you think Berelain will go with you? Will she guard your back? Or perhaps you prefer her to sit on your lap and squeal? Tuck your shirt in, you hairy oaf! Does it have to be so dark in here? Berelain likes dim light, does she? Much good she will do you against the Children of the Light!"

Perrin opened his mouth to protest, and changed what he had been going to say. "She looks a pleasant armful, Berelain. What man wouldn't want her on his lap?" The hurt on her face banded his chest with iron, but he made himself go on. "When I am done at home, I may go to Mayene. She asked me to come, and I might."

Faile said not a word. She stared at him with a face like stone, then whirled and ran out, slamming the door behind her with a crash.

In spite of himself he started to follow, then stopped with his hands gripping the doorframe till his fingers hurt. Staring at the splintered gash his axe had made in the door, he found himself telling it what he could not tell her. "I killed Whitecloaks. They would have killed me if I hadn't, but they still call it murder. I'm going home to die, Faile. That's the only way I can stop them hurting my people. Let them hang me. I cannot let you see that. I can't. You might even try to stop it, and then they'd. . . ."

His head dropped against the door. She would not be sorry to see the last of him now; that was what was important. She would go find her adventure somewhere else, safe from Whitecloaks and *ta'veren* and bubbles of evil. That was all that was important. He wished he did not want to howl with grief.

Faile strode through the halls at a near run, oblivious of who she passed or who had to scramble out of her way. Perrin. Berelain. Perrin. Berelain. *He wants a milk-faced vixen who runs about half-naked, does he? He doesn't know what he wants. Hairy lummox! Wooden-headed buffoon! Blacksmith! And that sneaking sow, Berelain. That prancing she-goat!*

She did not realize where she was going until she saw Berelain ahead of her, gliding along in that dress that left nothing to the imagination, swaying along as if that walk of hers was not deliberately calculated to make male eyes pop. Before Faile knew what she was doing, she had darted ahead of Berelain and turned to face her where two corridors met.

"Perrin Aybara belongs to me," she snapped. "You keep your hands and your smiles away from him!" She flushed to her hairline when she heard what she had said. She had promised herself she would never do this, never fight over a man like a farmgirl rolling in the dirt at harvest.

Berelain arched a cool eyebrow. "Belongs to you? Strange, I saw no collar on him. You serving girls—or are you a farmer's daughter?—you have the most peculiar ideas."

"Serving girl? Serving girl! I am—" Faile bit her tongue to stop the furious words. The First of Mayene, indeed. There were estates in Saldaea larger than Mayene. She would not last a week in the courts of Saldaea. Could she recite poetry while hawking? Could she ride in the hunt all day, then play the bittern at night while discussing how to counter Trolloc raids? She thought she knew men, did she? Did she know the language of fans? Could she tell a man to come or go or stay, and a hundred things more, all with the twist of a wrist and the placement of a lace fan? *Light shine on me, what am I thinking? I swore I would never even hold a fan again!* But there were other Saldaean customs. She was surprised to see the knife in her hand; she had been taught not to draw a knife unless she meant to use it. "Farm girls in Saldaea have a way of dealing with women who poach others' men. If you do not swear to forget Perrin Aybara, I will shave your head as bald as an egg. Perhaps the boys who tend the chickens will pant after you, then!"

She was not sure exactly how Berelain gripped her wrist, but suddenly she was flying through the air. The floor crashing into her back drove all the air from her lungs.

Berelain stood smiling, tapping the blade of Faile's knife on her palm. "A custom of Mayene. The Tairens do like to use assassins, and the guards cannot always be close at hand. I despise being attacked, farmgirl, so this is what I will do. I will take the blacksmith away from you and keep him as a pet for as long as he amuses me. Ogier's oath on it, farmgirl. He is quite ravishing, really—those shoulders, those arms; not to mention those eyes of his—and if he is a bit uncultured, I can have that remedied. My courtiers can teach him how to dress, and rid him of that awful beard. Wherever he goes, I will find him and make him mine. You can have him when I am finished. If he still wants you, of course."

Finally managing to draw a breath, Faile struggled to her feet, pulling a second knife. "I will drag you to him, after I cut off those clothes you are almost wearing, and make you tell him you are nothing but a sow!" *Light help me, I* am *behaving like a farmgirl, and talking like one!* The worst part was that she meant it.

Berelain set herself warily. She meant to use her hands, obviously, not the knife. She held it like a fan. Faile advanced on the balls of her feet.

Suddenly Rhuarc was there between them, towering over them, snatching the knives away before either woman was really aware of him. "Have you not seen enough blood already tonight?" he said coldly. "Of all those I thought I might find breaking the peace, the two of you would be the last named."

Faile gaped at him. With no warning, she pivoted, driving her fist toward Rhuarc's short ribs. The toughest man would feel it there.

He seemed to move without looking at her, caught her hand, forced her arm straight to her side, twisted. Abruptly she was standing very straight and hoping he did not push her arm right up out of her shoulder.

As if nothing had happened, he addressed Berelain. "You will go to your room, and you will not come out until the sun is above the horizon. I will see that no breakfast is brought to you. A little hunger will remind you that there is a time and place for fighting."

Berelain drew herself up indignantly. "I am the First of Mayene. I will not be ordered about like—"

"You will go to your rooms. Now," Rhuarc told her flatly. Faile wondered if she could kick him; she must have tensed, because as soon as she thought of it, he increased the pressure on her wrist, and she was up on her tiptoes. "If you do not," he went on to Berelain, "we will repeat our first talk together, you and I. Right here."

Berelain's face went white and red by turns. "Very well," she said stiffly. "If you insist, I will perhaps—"

"I did not propose a discussion. If I can still see you when I have counted three. . . . One."

With a gasp, Berelain hiked her skirts and ran. She even managed to sway doing that.

Faile stared after her in amazement. It was almost worth having her arm nearly disjointed. Rhuarc was watching Berelain go, too, a small appreciative smile on his lips.

"Do you mean to hold me all night?" she demanded. He released her—and tucked her knives into his belt. "Those are mine!"

"Forfeit," he said. "Berelain's punishment for fighting was to have you see her sent to bed like a willful child. Yours is to lose these knives you prize. I know you have others. If you argue, I might take those, too. I will not have the peace broken."

She glared at him, but she suspected he meant just what he said.

Those knives had been made for her by a man who knew what he was doing; the balance was just right. "What 'first talk' did you have with her? Why did she run like that?"

"That is between her and me. You will not go near her again, Faile. I do not believe she started this; that one's weapons are not knives. If either of you makes trouble again, I will put both of you to carrying offal. Some of the Tairens thought they could keep on fighting their duels after I had declared peace on this place, but the smell of the refuse carts soon taught them their mistake. Be sure you do not have to learn it the same way."

She waited until he had gone before nursing her shoulder. He reminded her of her father. Not that her father had ever twisted her arm, but he had small patience with those who made trouble, whatever their position, and no one ever caught him by surprise. She wondered if she could bait Berelain into something, just to see the First of Mayene sweating among the refuse carts. But Rhuarc had said both of them. Her father meant what he said, too. Berelain. Something Berelain had said was tickling the back of her mind. Ogier's oath. That was it. An Ogier never broke an oath. To say "Ogier oathbreaker" was like saying "brave coward," or "wise fool."

She could not help laughing aloud. "You will take him from me, you silly peahen? By the time you see him again, if you ever do, he'll be mine once more." Chuckling to herself, and occasionally rubbing her shoulder, she walked on with a light heart.

CHAPTER
15

Into the Doorway

Holding the glass-mantled lamp high, Mat peered down the narrow corridor, deep in the belly of the Stone. *Not unless my life depended on it. That's what I promised. Well, burn me if it doesn't!*

Before doubt could seize him again, he hurried on, past doors dry-rotted and hanging aslant, past others only shreds of wood clinging to rusted hinges. The floor had been swept recently, but the air still smelled of old dust and mold. Something skittered in the darkness, and he had a knife out before he realized it was just a rat, running from him, no doubt running toward some escape hole it knew.

"Show me the way out," he whispered after it, "and I'll come with you." *Why am I whispering? There's nobody down here to hear me.* It seemed a place for quiet, though. He could feel the whole weight of the Stone over his head, pressing down.

The last door, she had said. That one hung askew, too. He kicked it open, and it fell apart. The room was littered with dim shapes, with crates and barrels and things stacked high against the walls and out into the floor. Dust, too. *The Great Hold! It looks like the basement of an abandoned farmhouse, only worse.* He was surprised that Egwene and Nynaeve had not dusted and tidied while they were down here. Women were always dusting and straightening, even things that did not need it. Footprints crisscrossed the floor, some of them from boots, but no doubt they had had men to shift the heavier items about for them. Nynaeve liked finding ways to make a man work; likely she had deliberately hunted out some fellows enjoying themselves.

What he sought stood out among the jumble. A tall redstone doorframe, looming oddly in the shadows cast by his lamp. When he came closer, it still looked odd. Twisted, somehow. His eye did not want to follow it around; the corners did not join right. The tall hollow rectangle seemed likely to fall over at a breath, but when he gave it an experimental push, it stood steady. He pushed a bit harder, not sure he did not want to heave the thing over, and that side of it scraped through the dust. Goose bumps ran down his arms. There might as well have been a wire fastened to the top, suspending it from the ceiling. He held the lamp up to see. There was no wire. *At least it won't topple while I'm inside. Light, I am going inside, aren't I?*

A clutter of figurines and small things wrapped in rotting cloth occupied the top of a tall, upended barrel near him. He pushed the jumble to one side so he could set the lamp there, and studied the doorway. The *ter'angreal*. If Egwene knew what she was talking about. She probably did; no doubt she had learned all sorts of strange things in the Tower, however much she denied. *She would deny things, wouldn't she now. Learning to be Aes Sedai. She didn't deny this though, now did she?* If he squinted, it just looked like a stone doorframe, dully polished and the duller for dust. Just a plain doorframe. Well, not entirely plain. Three sinuous lines carved deep in the stone ran down each upright from top to bottom. He had seen fancier on farmhouses. He would probably step through and find himself still in this dusty room.

Won't know till I try, will I? Luck! Taking a deep breath—and coughing from the dust—he put his foot through.

He seemed to be stepping through a sheet of brilliant white light, infinitely bright, infinitely thick. For a moment that lasted forever, he was blind; a roaring filled his ears, all the sounds of the world gathered together at once. For just the length of one measureless step.

Stumbling another pace, he stared around in amazement. The *ter'angreal* was still there, but this was certainly not where he had started. The twisted stone doorframe stood in the center of a round hall with a ceiling so high it was lost in shadows, surrounded by strange spiraled yellow columns snaking up into the gloom, like huge vines twining 'round poles that had been taken away. A soft light came from glowing spheres atop coiled stands of some white metal. Not silver; the shine was too dull for that. And no hint of what made the glow; it did not look like flame; the spheres simply shone. The floor tiles spiraled out in white and yellow stripes from the *ter'angreal.* There was a heavy scent in the air, sharp and dry and not particularly pleasant. He almost turned around and went back on the spot.

"A long time."

He jumped, a knife coming into his hand, and peered among the columns for the source of the breathy voice that pronounced those words so harshly.

"A long time, yet the seekers come again for answers. The questioners come once more." A shape moved, back among the columns; a man, Mat thought. "Good. You have brought no lamps, no torches, as the agreement was, and is, and ever will be. You have no iron? No instruments of music?"

The figure stepped out, tall, barefoot, arms and legs and body wound about in layers of yellow cloth, and Mat was suddenly not so sure if it was a man. Or human. It looked human, at first glance, though perhaps too graceful, but it seemed far too thin for its height, with a narrow, elongated face. Its skin, and even its straight black hair, caught the pale light in a way that reminded him of a snake's scales. And those eyes, the pupils just black, vertical slits. No, not human.

"Iron. Instruments of music. You have none?"

Mat wondered what it thought the knife was; it certainly did not seem concerned over it. Well, the blade was good steel, not iron. "No. No iron, and no instruments of— Why—?" He cut off sharply. Three questions, Egwene had said. He was not about to waste one on "iron" or "instruments of music." *Why should he care if I have a dozen musicians in my pocket and a smithy on my back?* "I have come here for true answers. If you are not the one to give them, take me to who can."

The man—it was male at least, Mat decided—smiled slightly. He did not show any teeth. "According to the agreement. Come." He beckoned with one long-fingered hand. "Follow."

Mat made the knife disappear up his sleeve. "Lead, and I will follow." *Just you keep ahead of me and in plain sight. This place makes my skin crawl.*

There was not a straight line to be seen anywhere except for the floor itself, as he trailed the strange man. Even the ceiling was always arched, and the walls bowed out. The halls were continuously curved, the doorways rounded, the windows perfect circles. Tilework made spirals and sinuous lines, and what seemed to be bronze metalwork set in the ceiling at intervals was all complicated scrolls. There were no pictures of anything, no wall hangings or paintings. Only patterns, and always curves.

He saw no one except his silent guide; he could have believed the place empty except for the two of them. From somewhere he had a dim memory of walking halls that had not known a human foot in hundreds of years, and this felt the same. Yet sometimes he caught a flicker of motion out of the corner of his eye. Only, however quickly he turned, there was never anyone there. He pretended to rub his forearms, checking the knives up his coatsleeves for reassurance.

What he saw through those round windows was even worse. Tall wispy trees with only a drooping umbrella of branches at the top, and others like huge fans of lacy leaves, a tangle of growth equal to the heart of any briar-choked thicket, all under a dim, overcast light, though there did not seem to be a cloud in the sky. There were always windows, always along just one side of the curving corridor, but sometimes the side changed, and what surely should have been looking into courtyard or rooms instead gave out into that forest. He never caught as much as a glimpse of any other part of this palace, or whatever it was, through those windows, or any other building, except. . . .

Through one circular window he saw three tall silvery spires, curving in toward each other so their points all aimed at the same spot. They were not visible from the next window, three paces away, but a few minutes later, after he and his guide had rounded enough curves that he had to be looking in another direction, he saw them again. He tried telling himself these were three different spires, but between them and him was one of those fan-shaped trees with a dangling broken branch, a tree that had been in the same spot the first time. After his third sight of the spires and the strange tree with the broken branch, this time ten paces farther on but on the other side of the hallway, he tried to stop looking at what lay outside at all.

The walk seemed interminable.

"When—? Are—?" Mat ground his teeth. Three questions. It was hard to learn anything without asking questions. "I hope you are taking me to those who can answer my questions. Burn my bones, I do. For my sake and yours, the Light know it true."

"Here," the peculiar, yellow-wrapped fellow said, gesturing with one of those thin hands to a rounded doorway twice as large as any Mat had seen before. His strange eyes studied Mat intently. His mouth gaped open, and he inhaled, long and slow. Mat frowned at him, and the stranger gave a writhing hitch of his shoulders. "Here your answers may be found. Enter. Enter and ask."

Mat drew a deep breath of his own, then grimaced and scrubbed at his nose. That sharp, heavy smell was a rank nuisance. He took a hesitant step toward the tall doorway, and looked around for his guide again. The fellow was gone. *Light! I don't know why anything in this place surprises me now. Well, I will be burned if I'll turn back now.* Trying not to think of whether he could find the *ter'angreal* again on his own, he went in.

It was another round room, with spiraling floor tiles in red and white under a domed ceiling. It had no columns, or furnishings of any kind, except for three thick, coiled pedestals around the heart of the floor's spirals. Mat could see no way to reach the top of them except by climbing the twists, yet a man like his guide sat cross-legged atop each, only wrapped in layers of red. Not all men, he decided at a second look; two of those long faces with the odd eyes had a definite feminine cast. They stared at him, intense penetrating stares, and breathed deeply, almost panting. He wondered if he made them nervous in some way. *Not much bloody chance of that. But they're certainly getting under my coat.*

"It has been long," the woman on the right said.

"Very long," the woman on the left added.

The man nodded. "Yet they come again."

All three had the breathy voice of the guide—almost indistinguishable from it, in fact—and the harsh way of pronouncing words. They spoke in unison, and the words might as well have come from one mouth. "Enter and ask, according to the agreement of old."

If Mat had thought his skin crawled before, now he was sure it was writhing. He made himself go closer. Carefully—careful to say nothing that even sounded like a question—he laid the situation before them. The Whitecloaks, certainly in his home village, surely hunting friends of his, maybe hunting him. One of his friends going to face the Whitecloaks, another not. His family, not likely in danger, but with the bloody Children of the bloody Light around. . . . A *ta'veren* pulling at him so he could hardly move. He saw no reason to give names, or mention that Rand was the Dragon Reborn. His first question—and the other two, for that matter—he had worked out before going down to the Great Hold. "Should I go home to help my people?" he asked finally.

Three sets of slitted eyes lifted from him—reluctantly, it seemed—and studied the air above his head. Finally the woman on the left said, "You must go to Rhuidean."

As soon as she spoke their eyes all dropped to him again, and they leaned forward, breathing deeply again, but at that moment a bell tolled, a sonorous brazen sound that rolled through the room. They swayed upright, staring at one another, then at the air over Mat's head again.

"He is another," the woman on the left whispered. "The strain. The strain."

"The savor," the man said. "It has been long."

"There is yet time," the other woman told them. She sounded calm —they all did—but there was a sharpness to her voice when she turned back to Mat. "Ask. Ask."

Mat glared up at them furiously. *Rhuidean? Light!* That was somewhere out in the Waste, the Light and the Aiel knew where. That was about as much as he knew. In the Waste! Anger drove questions about how to get away from Aes Sedai and how to recover the lost parts of his memory right out his head. "Rhuidean!" he barked. "The Light burn my bones to ash if I want to go Rhuidean! And my blood on the ground if I will! Why should I? You are not answering my questions. You are supposed to answer, not hand me riddles!"

"If you do not go to Rhuidean," the woman on the right said, "you will die."

The bell tolled again, louder this time; Mat felt its tremor through his boots. The looks the three shared were plainly anxious. He opened his mouth, but they were only concerned with each other.

"The strain," one of the women said hurriedly. "It is too great."

"The savor of him," the other woman said on her heels. "It has been so very long."

Before she was done the man spoke. "The strain is too great. Too great. Ask. Ask!"

"Burn your soul for a craven heart," Mat growled, "I will that! Why will I die if I do not go to Rhuidean? I very likely will die if I try. It makes no—"

The man cut him off and spoke hurriedly. "You will have sidestepped the thread of fate, left your fate to drift on the winds of time, and you will be killed by those who do not want that fate fulfilled. Now, go. You must go! Quickly!"

The yellow-clad guide was suddenly there at Mat's side, tugging at his sleeve with those too-long hands.

Mat shook him off. "No! I will not go! You have led me from the questions I wanted to ask and given me senseless answers. You will not leave it there. What fate are you talking about? I will have one clear answer out of you, at least!"

A third time the bell sounded mournfully, and the entire room trembled.

"Go!" the man shouted. "You have had your answers. You must go before it is too late!"

Abruptly a dozen of the yellow-clad men were around Mat, seeming to appear out of the air, trying to pull him toward the door. He fought with fists, elbows, knees. "What fate? Burn your hearts, what fate?" It was the room itself that pealed, the walls and floor quivering, nearly taking Mat and his attackers off their feet. "What fate?"

The three were on their feet atop the pedestals, and he could not tell which shrieked which answer.

"To marry the Daughter of the Nine Moons!"

"To die and live again, and live once more a part of what was!"

"To give up half the light of the world to save the world!"

Together they howled like steam escaping under pressure. "Go to Rhuidean, son of battles! Go to Rhuidean, trickster! Go, gambler! Go!"

Mat's assailants snatched him into the air by his arms and legs and ran, holding him over their heads. "Unhand me, you white-livered sons of goats!" he shouted, struggling. "Burn your eyes! The Shadow take your souls, loose me! I will have your guts for a saddle girth!" But writhe and curse as he would, those long fingers gripped like iron.

Twice more the bell tolled, or the palace did. Everything shook as in an earthquake; the walls rang with deafening reverberations, each louder than the last. Mat's captors stumbled on, nearly falling but never stopping their pell-mell race. He did not even see where they were taking him until they suddenly stopped short, heaving him into the air. Then he saw the twisted doorway, the *ter'angreal,* as he flew toward it.

White light blinded him; the roar filled his head till it drove thought away.

He fell heavily onto a dusty floor in dim light and rolled up against the barrel holding his lamp in the Great Hold. The barrel rocked, packets and figurines toppling to the floor in a crash of breaking stone and ivory and porcelain. Bounding to his feet, he threw himself back at the stone doorframe. "Burn you, you can't throw me—!"

He hurtled through—and stumbled against the crates and barrels on the other side. Without a pause, he turned and leaped at it again. With the same result. This time he caught himself on the barrel holding his lamp, which nearly fell onto the already shattered things littering the floor under his boots. He grabbed it in time, burning his hand, and fumbled it back to a steadier perch.

Burn me if I want to be down here in the dark, he thought, sucking his fingers. *Light, the way my luck is running, it probably would have started a fire and I'd have burned to death!*

He glared at the *ter'angreal.* Why was it not working? Maybe the folk on the other side had shut it off somehow. He understood practically nothing of what had happened. That bell, and their panic. You would have thought they were afraid the roof would come down on their heads. Come to think of it, it very nearly had. And Rhuidean, and all the rest of it. The Waste was bad enough, but they said he was fated to marry somebody called the Daughter of the Nine Moons. Marry! And to a noblewoman, by the sound of it. He would sooner marry a pig than a noblewoman. And that business about dying and living again. *Nice of them to add the last bit!* If some black-veiled Aielman killed him on the way to Rhuidean, he would find out how true it was. It was all nonsense, and he did not believe a word of it. Only. . . . The bloody doorway *had* taken him somewhere, and they had only wanted to answer three questions, just the way Egwene had said.

"I won't marry any bloody noblewoman!" he told the *ter'angreal.* "I'll marry when I'm too old to have any fun, that's what! Rhuidean my bloody—!"

A boot appeared, backing out of the twisted stone doorway, followed by the rest of Rand, with that fiery sword in his hands. The blade vanished as he stepped clear, and he heaved a sigh of relief. Even in the dim light, Mat could see he was troubled, though. He gave a start when he saw Mat. "Just poking around, Mat? Or did you go through, too?"

Mat eyed him warily for a moment. At least that sword was gone. He did not seem to be channeling—though how was anybody to tell?—and he did not look particularly like a madman. In fact, he looked very much as Mat remembered. He had to remind himself they were not back home any longer, and Rand was *not* what he remembered. "Oh, I went through, all right. A bunch of bloody liars, if you ask me! What are they? Made me think of snakes."

"Not liars, I think." Rand sounded as if he wished they were. "No, not that. They were afraid of me, right from the first. And when that tolling started. . . . The sword kept them back; they wouldn't even look at it. Shied away. Hid their eyes. Did you get your answers?"

"Nothing that makes sense," Mat muttered. "What about you?"

Suddenly Moiraine appeared from the *ter'angreal,* seeming to step gracefully out of thin air, flowing out. She would be a fine one to dance with if she were not Aes Sedai. Her mouth tightened at the sight of them.

"You! You were both in there. That is why . . . !" She made a vexed hiss. "One of you would have been bad enough, but two *ta'veren* at once—you might have torn the connection entirely and been trapped there. Wretched boys playing with things you do not know the danger of. Perrin! Is Perrin in there, too? Did he share your . . . exploit?"

"The last I saw of Perrin," Mat said, "he was getting ready to go to bed." Maybe Perrin would give him the lie by being the next to step out of the thing, but he might as well deflect the Aes Sedai's anger if he could. No need for Perrin to face it, too. *Maybe he'll make it clear of her, at least, if he gets away before she knows what he's doing. Bloody woman! I'll wager she was noble born.*

That Moraine was angry there was no doubt. The blood had drained out of her cheeks, and her eyes were dark augers boring into Rand. "At least you escaped with your lives. Who told you of this? Which one of them? I will make her wish I had peeled off her hide like a glove."

"A book told me," Rand said calmly. He sat down back on the edge of a crate that creaked alarmingly under his weight and crossed his arms. All very cool; Mat wished he could emulate it. "A pair of books, in fact. *Treasures of the Stone* and *Dealings with the Territory of Mayene.* Surprising what you can dig out of books if you read long enough, isn't it?"

"And you?" She shifted that drilling gaze to Mat. "Did you read it in a book, too? You?"

"I do read sometimes," he said dryly. He would not have been averse to a little hide-peeling for Egwene and Nynaeve after what they had done to make him tell where he had hidden the Amyrlin's letter—tying him up with the Power was bad enough, but the rest!—yet it was more fun to tweak Moiraine's nose. "*Treasures. Dealings.* Lots of things in books." Luckily, she did not insist that he repeat the titles; he had not paid attention once Rand brought up books.

Instead she swung back to Rand. "And your answers?"

"Are mine," Rand replied, then frowned. "It wasn't easy, though. They brought a . . . woman . . . to interpret, but she talked like an old book. I could hardly understand some of the words. I never considered they might speak another language."

"The Old Tongue," Moiraine told him. "They use the Old Tongue— a rather harsh dialect of it—for their dealings with men. And you, Mat? Was your interpreter easily understood?"

He had to work moisture back into his mouth. "The Old Tongue? Is that what it was? They didn't give me one. In fact, I never got to ask any questions. That bell started shaking the walls down, and they hustled me out like I was tracking cow manure on the rugs." She was still staring, her eyes still digging into his head. She knew about the Old Tongue slipping out of him, sometimes. "I . . . almost understood a word here and there, but not to know it. You and Rand got answers. What do they get out of it? The snakes with legs. We aren't going upstairs to find ten years gone, are we, like Bili in the story?"

"Sensations," Moiraine replied with a grimace. "Sensations, emotions, experiences. They rummage through them; you can feel them doing it, making your skin crawl. Perhaps they feed on them in some manner. The Aes Sedai who studied this *ter'angreal* when it was in Mayene wrote of a strong desire to bathe afterward. I certainly intend to."

"But their answers are true?" Rand said as she started to turn away. "You are sure of it? The books implied as much, but can they really give true answers about the future?"

"The answers are true," Moiraine said slowly, "so long as they are in regard to your own future. That much is certain." She watched Rand, and himself, weighing the effect of her words. "As to how, though, there is only speculation. That world is . . . folded . . . in strange ways. I cannot be clearer. It may be that that allows them to read the thread of a human life, read the various ways it may yet be woven into the Pattern. Or perhaps it is a talent of the people. The answers are often obscure, however. If you need help working out what yours mean, I offer my services." Her eyes flickered from one of them to the other, and Mat nearly swore. She did not believe him about no answers. Unless it was simply general Aes Sedai suspicion.

Rand gave her a slow smile. "And will you tell me what you asked, and what they answered?"

For answer, she returned a level, searching look, then started for the door. A small ball of light, as bright as a lantern, was suddenly floating ahead of her, illuminating her way.

Mat knew he should leave it alone, now. Just let her go and hope she forgot he had ever been down here. But a knot of anger still burned inside him. All those ridiculous things they had said. Well, maybe they were true, if Moiraine said so, but he wanted to grab those fellows by the collar, or whatever passed for a collar in those wrappings, and make them explain a few things.

"Why can't you go there twice, Moiraine?" he called after her. "Why not?" He very nearly asked why they worried about iron and musical instruments, too, and bit his tongue. He could not know about those if he had not understood what they were saying.

She paused at the door to the hall, and it was impossible to see if she was looking at the *ter'angreal* or at Rand. "If I knew everything, Matrim, I would not need to ask questions." She peered into the room a moment longer—she *was* staring at Rand—then glided away without another word.

For a time Mat and Rand looked at each other in silence.

"*Did* you find out what you wanted?" Rand asked finally.

"Did you?"

A bright flame leaped into existence, balanced above Rand's palm. Not the smooth glowing sphere of the Aes Sedai, but a rough blaze like a torch. As Rand moved to leave, Mat added another question. "Are you really going to just let the Whitecloaks do whatever they want back home? You know they're heading for Emond's Field. If they are not there already. Yellow eyes, the bloody Dragon Reborn. It's too much, otherwise."

"Perrin will do . . . what he has to do to save Emond's Field," Rand replied in a pained voice. "And I must do what I have to, or more than Emond's Field will fall, and to worse than Whitecloaks."

Mat stood watching the light of that flame fade away down the hall, until he remembered where he was. Then he snatched up his lamp and hurried out. *Rhuidean! Light, what am I going to do?*

CHAPTER 16

Leavetakings

Lying on sweat-soaked sheets, staring at the ceiling, Perrin realized that the darkness was turning to gray. Soon the sun would be edging above the horizon. Morning. A time for new hopes; a time to be up and doing. New hopes. He almost laughed. How long had he been awake? An hour or more, surely, this time. Scratching his curly beard, he winced. His bruised shoulder had stiffened, and he sat up slowly; sweat popped out on his face as he worked the arm. He kept at it methodically, though, suppressing groans and now and again biting back a curse, until he could move the arm freely, if not comfortably.

Such sleep as he had managed had been broken and fitful. When he was awake he had seen Faile's face, her dark eyes accusing him, the hurt he had put there making him cringe inside. When he slept, he dreamed of mounting a gallows, and Faile watching, or worse, trying to stop it, trying to fight Whitecloaks with their lances and swords, and he was screaming while they fitted the noose around his neck, screaming because the Whitecloaks were killing Faile. Sometimes she watched them hang him with a smile of angry satisfaction. Small wonder such dreams wakened him with a jerk. Once he had dreamed of wolves running out of the forest to save both Faile and him—only to be spitted on Whitecloak lances, shot down by their arrows. It had not been a restful night. Washing and dressing as hurriedly as he could, he left the room as if hoping to leave memories of his dreams behind.

Little outward evidence remained of the night's attack, here a sword-slashed tapestry, there a chest with a corner splintered by an axe or a lighter patch on the stone-tiled floor where a bloodstained rug had been removed. The majhere had her liveried army of servants out in force, though many wore bandages, sweeping, mopping, clearing away and replacing. She limped about leaning on a stick, a broad woman with her gray hair pushed up like a round cap by the dressing wound around her head, calling her orders in a firm voice, with the clear intention of removing every sign of the Stone's second violation. She saw Perrin and gave him an infinitesimal curtsy. Even the High Lords did not get much more from her, even when she was well. Despite all the cleaning and scrubbing, under the smell of waxes and polishes and cleaning fluids Perrin could still catch the faint scent of blood, sharply metallic human blood, fetid Trolloc blood, acrid Myrddraal blood with its stink that burned his nostrils. He would be glad to be away from here.

The door to Loial's room was a span across and more than two spans high, with an overlarge door handle in the shape of entwined vines level with Perrin's head. The Stone had a number of rarely used Ogier guest rooms; the Stone of Tear predated even the age of great Ogier stoneworks, but it was a point of prestige to use Ogier stonemasons, at least from time to time. Perrin knocked and at the call of "Come in," in a voice like a slow avalanche, lifted the handle and complied.

The room was on a scale with the door in every dimension, yet Loial, standing in the middle of the leaf-patterned carpet in his shirtsleeves, a long pipe in his teeth, reduced it all to seemingly normal size. The Ogier stood taller than a Trolloc in his wide-toed, thigh-high boots, if not so broad as one. His dark green coat, buttoned to the waist, then flaring to his boot tops like a kilt over baggy trousers, no longer looked odd to Perrin, but one look was enough to tell this was not an ordinary man in an ordinary room. The Ogier's nose was so broad as to seem a snout, and eyebrows like long mustaches dangled beside eyes the size of teacups. Tufted ears poked up through shaggy black hair that hung nearly to his shoulders. When he grinned around his pipestem at the sight of Perrin, it split his face in half.

"Good morning, Perrin," he rumbled, removing the pipe. "You slept well? Not easy, after such a night as that. Myself, I have been up half the night, writing down what happened." He had a pen in his other hand, and ink stains on his sausage-thick fingers.

Books lay everywhere, on Ogier-sized chairs and the huge bed and the table that stood as high as Perrin's chest. That was no surprise, but what was a little startling was the flowers. Flowers of every sort, in every color. Vases of flowers, baskets of them, posies tied with ribbon or even string, great woven banks of flowers standing about like lengths of garden wall. Perrin had certainly never seen the like inside a room. Their scent filled the air. Yet what really caught his eye was the swollen knot on Loial's head, the size of a man's fist, and the heavy limp in Loial's walk. If Loial had been hurt too badly to travel. . . . He felt ashamed at thinking of it that way—the Ogier was a friend—but he had to.

"You were injured, Loial? Moiraine could Heal you. I'm sure she will."

"Oh, I can get around with no trouble. And there were so many who truly needed her help. I would not want to bother her. It certainly is not enough to hamper me in my work." Loial glanced at the table where a large cloth-bound book—large for Perrin, but it would fit in one of the Ogier's coat pockets—lay open beside an uncorked ink bottle. "I hope I wrote it all down correctly. I did not see very much last night until it was done."

"Loial," Faile said, standing up from behind one of the banks of flowers with a book in her hands, "is a hero."

Perrin jumped; the flowers had masked her scent completely. Loial made shushing noises, his ears twitching with embarrassment, and waved his big hands at her, but she went on, her voice cool but her eyes hot on Perrin's face.

"He gathered as many children as he could—and some of their mothers—into a large room, and held the door alone against Trollocs and Myrddraal through the entire fight. These flowers are from the women of the Stone, tokens to honor his steadfast courage, his faithfulness." She made "steadfast" and "faithfulness" crack like whips.

Perrin managed not to flinch, but only just. What he had done was right, but he could not expect her to see it. Even if she knew why, she would not see it. *It was the right thing. It was.* He only wished he felt better about the entire matter. It was hardly fair that he could be right and still feel in the wrong.

"It was nothing." Loial's ears twitched wildly. "It is just that the children could not defend themselves. That's all. Not a hero. No."

"Nonsense." Faile marked her place in the book with a finger and moved closer to the Ogier. She did not come up to his chest. "There is not a woman in the Stone who would not marry you, if you were human, and some would anyway. Loial well named, for your nature is loyalty. Any woman could love that."

The Ogier's ears went stiff with shock, and Perrin grinned. She had obviously been feeding Loial honey and butter all morning in hope the Ogier would agree to take her along no matter what Perrin wanted, but in trying to prick him she had just fed Loial a stone without knowing it. "Have you heard from your mother, Loial?" he asked.

"No." Loial managed to sound relieved and worried at the same time. "But I saw Laefar in the city yesterday. He was as surprised to see me as I to see him; we are not a common sight in Tear. He came from Stedding Shangtai to negotiate repairs on some Ogier stonework in one of the palaces. I have no doubt the first words out of his mouth when he returns to the *stedding* will be 'Loial is in Tear.' "

"That is worrying," Perrin said, and Loial nodded dejectedly.

"Laefar says the Elders have named me a runaway and my mother has promised to have me married and settled. She even has someone chosen. Laefar did not know who. At least, he said he did not. He thinks such things are funny. She could be here in a month's time."

Faile's face was a picture of confusion that almost made Perrin grin again. She thought she knew so much more than he did about the world—well, she did, in truth—but she did not know Loial. Stedding Shangtai was Loial's home, in the Spine of the World, and since he was barely past ninety, he was not old enough to have left on his own. Ogier lived a very long time; by their standards, Loial was no older than Perrin, maybe younger. But Loial had gone anyway, to see the world, and his greatest fear was that his mother would find him and drag back to the *stedding* to marry, never to leave again.

While Faile was trying to figure out what was going on, Perrin stepped into the silence. "I need to go back to the Two Rivers, Loial. Your mother won't find you there."

"Yes. That is true." The Ogier gave an uncomfortable shrug. "But my book. Rand's story. And yours, and Mat's. I have so many notes already, but. . . ." He moved around behind the table, peering down at the open book, the pages filled with his neat script. "I will be the one to write the true story of the Dragon Reborn, Perrin. The only book by someone who traveled with him, who actually saw it unfold. *The Dragon Reborn,* by Loial, son of Arent son of Halan, of Stedding Shangtai." Frowning, he bent over the book, dipping his pen in the ink bottle. "That is not quite right. It was more—"

Perrin put a hand on the page where Loial was going to write.

"You'll write no book if your mother finds you. Not about Rand, at least. And I need you, Loial."

"Need, Perrin? I do not understand."

"There are Whitecloaks in the Two Rivers. Hunting me."

"Hunting you? But why?" Loial looked almost as confused as Faile had. Faile, on the other hand, had donned a complacent smugness that was worrisome. Perrin went on anyway.

"The reasons don't matter. The fact is that they are. They may hurt people, my family, looking for me. Knowing Whitecloaks, they will. I can stop it, if I can get there quickly, but it must be quickly. The Light only knows what they've done already. I need you to take me there, Loial, by the Ways. You told me once there was a Waygate here, and I know there was one at Manetheren. It must still be there, in the mountains above Emond's Field. Nothing can destroy a Waygate, you said. I need you, Loial."

"Well, of course I will help," Loial said. "The Ways." He exhaled noisily, and his ears wilted a bit. "I want to write of adventures, not have them. But I suppose one more time will not hurt. The Light send it so," he finished fervently.

Faile cleared her throat delicately. "Are you not forgetting something, Loial? You promised to take me into the Ways whenever I asked, and before you took anyone else."

"I did promise you a look at a Waygate," Loial said, "and what it is like inside. You can have that when Perrin and I go. You could come with us, I suppose, but the Ways are not traveled lightly, Faile. I would not enter them myself if Perrin did not have need."

"Faile will not be coming," Perrin said firmly. "Just you and me, Loial."

Ignoring him, Faile smiled up at Loial as if he were teasing her. "You promised more than a look, Loial. To take me wherever I wanted, whenever I wanted, and before anyone else. You swore to it."

"I did," Loial protested, "but only because you refused to believe I would show you. You said you would not believe unless I swore. I will do as I promised, but surely you do not want to step ahead of Perrin's need."

"You swore," Faile said calmly. "By your mother, and your mother's mother, and your mother's mother's mother."

"Yes, I did, Faile, but Perrin—"

"You swore, Loial. Do you mean to break your oath?"

The Ogier looked like misery stacked on misery. His shoulders slumped and his ears drooped, the corners of his wide mouth turned down and the ends of his long eyebrows draggled onto his cheeks.

"She tricked you, Loial." Perrin wondered if they could hear his teeth grinding. "She deliberately tricked you."

Red stained Faile's cheeks, but she still had the nerve to say, "Only because I had to, Loial. Only because a fool man thinks he can order my life to suit himself. I'd not have done it, otherwise. You must believe that."

"Doesn't it make any difference that she tricked you?" Perrin demanded, and Loial shook his massive head sadly.

"Ogier *keep* their word," Faile said. "And Loial is going to take me to the Two Rivers. Or to the Waygate at Manetheren, at least. I have a wish to see the Two Rivers."

Loial stood up straight, "But that means I can help Perrin after all. Faile, why did you drag this out? Even Faelar would not think this funny." There was a touch of anger in his voice; it took a good bit to make an Ogier angry.

"If he asks," she said determinedly. "That was part of it, Loial. No one but you and me, unless they asked me. He has to ask me."

"No," Perrin told her while Loial was still opening his mouth. "No, I won't ask. I will ride to Emond's Field first. I'll walk! So you might as well give up this foolishness. Tricking Loial. Trying to force yourself in where . . . where you aren't wanted."

Her calm dropped away in anger. "And by the time you reach there, Loial and I will have done for the Whitecloaks. It will all be over. Ask, you anvil-headed blacksmith. Just ask and you can come with us."

Perrin took hold of himself. There was no way to argue her around to his way of thinking, but he would not ask. She was right—he would need weeks to reach the Two Rivers on his horse; they could be there in two days, perhaps, through the Ways—but he would not ask. *Not after she tricked Loial and tried to bully me!* "Then I'll travel the Ways to Manetheren alone. I'll follow you two. If I stay far enough back not to be part of your party, I won't be breaking Loial's oath. You can't stop me following."

"That is dangerous, Perrin," Loial said worriedly. "The Ways are dark. If you miss a turning, or take the wrong bridge by accident, you could be lost forever. Or until *Machin Shin* catches you. Ask her, Perrin. She said you can come if you do. Ask her."

The Ogier's deep voice trembled speaking the name of *Machin Shin,* and a shiver ran down Perrin's back, too. *Machin Shin.* The Black Wind. Not even Aes Sedai knew whether it was Shadowspawn or something that had grown out of the Ways' corruption. *Machin Shin* was why traveling the Ways meant risking death; that was what Aes Sedai said. The Black Wind ate souls; that Perrin knew for truth. But he kept his voice steady and his face straight. *I'll be burned if I let her think I am weakening.* "I can't, Loial. Or anyway, I won't."

Loial grimaced. "Faile, it will be dangerous for him, trying to follow us. Please relent and let him—" She cut him off sharply.

"No. If he is too stiff-necked to ask, why should I? Why should I even care if he does get lost?" She turned to Perrin. "You can travel close to us. As close as you need to, so long as it's plain you are following. You will trail after me like a puppy until you ask. Why won't you just ask?"

"Stubborn humans," the Ogier muttered. "Hasty and stubborn, even when haste lands you in a hornet nest."

"I would like to leave today, Loial," Perrin said, not looking at Faile.

"Best to go quickly," Loial agreed with a regretful look at the book on the table. "I can tidy my notes on the journey, I suppose. The Light knows what I will miss, being away from Rand."

"Did you hear me, Perrin?" Faile demanded.

"I will get my horse and a few supplies, Loial. We can be on our way by midmorning."

"Burn you, Perrin Aybara, answer me!"

Loial eyed her worriedly. "Perrin, are you certain you could not—"

"No," Perrin interrupted gently. "She is muleheaded, and she likes playing tricks. I won't dance so she can laugh." He ignored the sound coming from deep in Faile's throat, like a cat staring at a strange dog and ready to attack. "I will let you know as soon as I am ready." He started for the door, and she called after him furiously.

" 'When' is my decision, Perrin Aybara. Mine and Loial's. Do you hear me? You had better be ready in two hours, or we'll leave you behind. You can meet us at the Dragonwall Gate stable, if you're coming. Do you hear me?"

He sensed her moving and shut the door behind him just as something thumped into it heavily. A book, he thought. Loial would give her fits about that. Better to hit Loial on the head than harm one of his books.

For a moment he leaned against the door, despairing. All he had done, all he had gone through, making her hate him, and she was going to be there to see him die anyway. The best thing he could say was that she might enjoy it now. *Stubborn, muleheaded woman!*

When he turned to go, one of the Aiel was approaching, a tall man with reddish hair and green eyes who could have been Rand's older cousin, or a young uncle. He knew the man, and liked him, if only because Gaul had never given even a flicker of notice to his yellow eyes. "May you find shade this morning, Perrin. The majhere told me you had come this way, though I think she itched to put a broom in my hands. As hard as a Wise One, that woman."

"May you find shade this morning, Gaul. Women are all hardheaded, if you ask me."

"Perhaps so, if you do not know how to get 'round them. I hear you are journeying to the Two Rivers."

"Light!" Perrin growled before the Aiel could say more. "Does the whole Stone know?" If Moiraine knew—

Gaul shook his head. "Rand al'Thor took me aside and spoke to me, asking me to tell no one. I think he spoke to others, too, but I do not know how many will want to go with you. We have been on this side of the Dragonwall for a long time, and many ache for the Three-fold Land."

"Come with me?" Perrin felt stunned. If he had Aiel with him. . . . There were possibilities he had not dared consider before. "Rand asked you to come with me? To the Two Rivers?"

Gaul shook his head again. "He said only that you were going, and that there were men who might try to kill you. I mean to accompany you, though, if you will have me."

"Will I?" Perrin almost laughed. "I will that. We will be into the Ways in a few hours."

"The Ways?" Gaul's expression did not change, but he blinked.

"Does that make a difference?"

"Death comes for all men, Perrin." It was hardly a comforting answer.

"I cannot believe Rand is that cruel," Egwene said, and Nynaeve added, "At least he did not try to stop you." Seated on Nynaeve's bed, they were finishing the division of the gold Moiraine had provided. Four fat purses apiece to be carried in pockets sewn under Elayne's and Nynaeve's skirts, and another each, not so large as to attract unwanted attention, to carry at the belt. Egwene had taken a lesser amount, there being less use for gold in the Waste.

Elayne frowned at the two neatly tied bundles and the leather script lying beside the door. They held all of her clothes and other things. Cased knife and fork, hairbrush and comb, needles, pins, thread, thimble, scissors. A tinder box and a second knife, smaller than the one at her belt. Soap and bath powder and. . . . It was ridiculous to go over the list again. Egwene's stone ring was snug in her pouch. She was ready to go. There was nothing to hold her back.

"No, he did not." Elayne was proud of how calm and collected she sounded. *He seemed almost relieved! Relieved! And I had to give him that letter, laying my heart open like a stone-blind fool. At least he won't open it until I am gone.* She jumped at the touch of Nynaeve's hand on her shoulder.

"Did you want him to ask you to stay? You know what your answer would have been. You do, don't you?"

Elayne compressed her lips. "Of course I do. But he did not have to look happy about it." She had not meant to say that.

Nynaeve gave her an understanding look. "Men are difficult at the best."

"I still cannot believe he would be so . . . so . . ." Egwene began in an angry mutter. Elayne never learned what she meant to say, for at that moment the door crashed open so hard that it bounced off the wall.

Elayne embraced *saidar* before she had stopped flinching, then felt a moment of embarrassment when the rebounding door slapped hard against Lan's outstretched hand. A moment more, and she decided to hold on to the Source a while longer. The Warder filled the doorway with his broad shoulders, his face a thunderhead; if his blue eyes could really have given off the thunderbolts they threatened, they would have blasted Nynaeve. The glow of *saidar* surrounded Egwene, too, and did not fade.

Lan did not appear to see anyone but Nynaeve. "You let me believe you were returning to Tar Valon," he rasped at her.

"You may have believed it," she said calmly, "but I never said it."

"Never said it? Never said it! You spoke of leaving today, and always linked your leaving with those Darkfriends being sent to Tar Valon. Always! What did you mean me to think?"

"But I never said—"

"Light, woman!" he roared. "Do not bandy words with me!"

Elayne exchanged worried looks with Egwene. This man had an iron self-control, but he was at a breaking point now. Nynaeve was one who often let her emotions rage, yet she faced him coolly, head high and eyes serene, hands still on her green silk skirts.

Lan took hold of himself with an obvious effort. He appeared as stone-faced as ever, as much in control of himself—and Elayne was sure it was all on the surface. "I'd not have known where you were off to if I had not heard that you had ordered a carriage. To take you to a ship bound for Tanchico. I do not know why the Amyrlin allowed you to leave the Tower in the first place, or why Moiraine involved you in questioning Black sisters, but you three are Accepted. Accepted, not Aes Sedai. Tanchico now is no place for anyone except a full Aes Sedai with a Warder to watch her back. I'll not let you go into that!"

"So," Nynaeve said lightly. "You question Moiraine's decisions, and those of the Amyrlin Seat as well. Perhaps I've misunderstood Warders all along. I thought you swore to accept and obey, among other things. Lan, I do understand your concern, and I am grateful—more than grateful—but we all have tasks to perform. We are going; you must resign yourself to the fact."

"Why? For the love of the Light, at least tell me why! Tanchico!"

"If Moiraine has not told you," Nynaeve said gently, "perhaps she has her reasons. We must do our tasks, as you must do yours."

Lan trembled—actually trembled!—and clamped his jaw shut angrily. When he spoke, he was strangely hesitant. "You will need someone to help you in Tanchico. Someone to keep a Taraboner street thief from slipping a knife into your back for your purse. Tanchico was that sort of city before the war began, and everything I've heard says it is worse now. I could. . . . I could protect you, Nynaeve."

Elayne's eyebrows shot up. He could not be suggesting. . . . He just could not be.

Nynaeve gave no sign that he had said anything out of the ordinary. "Your place is with Moiraine."

"Moiraine." Sweat beaded on the Warder's hard face, and he struggled with the words. "I can. . . . I must. . . . Nynaeve, I . . . I. . . ."

"You *will* remain with Moiraine," Nynaeve said sharply, "until she releases you from your bond. You will do as I say." Pulling a carefully folded paper from her pouch, she thrust it into his hands. He frowned, read, then blinked and read again.

Elayne knew what it said.

What the bearer does is done at my order and by my authority. Obey, and keep silent, at my command.

Siuan Sanche
Watcher of the Seals
Flame of Tar Valon
The Amyrlin Seat

The other like it rested in Egwene's pouch, though none of them were sure what good it would do where she was going.

"But this allows you to do anything you please," Lan protested. "You can speak in the Amyrlin's name. Why would she give this to an Accepted?"

"Ask no questions I cannot answer," Nynaeve said, then added with a hint of a grin, "Just count yourself lucky I do not tell you to dance for me."

Elayne suppressed a smile of her own. Egwene made a choking sound of swallowed laughter. It was what Nynaeve had said when the Amyrlin first handed them the letters. *With this I could make a Warder dance.* Neither of them had had any doubt which Warder she had meant.

"Do you not? You dispose of me very neatly. My bond, and my oaths. This letter." Lan had a dangerous gleam in his eye, which Nynaeve seemed not to notice as she took back the letter and replaced it in the pouch on her belt.

"You are very full of yourself, al'Lan Mandragoran. We do as we must, as you will."

"Full of myself, Nynaeve al'Meara? *I* am full of myself?" Lan moved so quickly toward Nynaeve that Elayne very nearly wrapped him in flows of Air before she could think. One moment Nynaeve was standing there, with just time to gape at the tall man sweeping toward her; the next her shoes were dangling a foot off the floor and she was being quite thoroughly kissed. At first she kicked his shins and hammered him with her fists and made sounds of frantic, furious protest, but her kicks slowed and stopped, and then she was holding on to his shoulders and not protesting at all.

Egwene dropped her eyes with embarrassment, but Elayne watched interestedly. Was that how she had looked when Rand. . . . *No! I will not think about him.* She wondered if there was time to write him another letter, taking back everything she had said in the first, letting him know she was not to be trifled with. But did she want to?

After a while Lan set Nynaeve back on her feet. She swayed a bit as she straightened her dress and patted her hair furiously. "You have no right . . ." she began in a breathless voice, then stopped to swallow. "I will not be *manhandled* in that fashion for the whole world to see. I will not!"

"Not the whole world," he replied. "But if they can see, they can hear as well. You have made a place in my heart where I thought there was no room for anything else. You have made flowers grow where I cultivated dust and stones. Remember this, on this journey you insist on making. If you die, I will not survive you long." He gave Nynaeve one of his rare smiles. If it did not exactly soften his face, at least it made it less hard. "And remember also, I am not always so easily commanded, even with letters from the Amyrlin." He made an elegant bow; for a moment Elayne thought he actually meant to kneel and kiss Nynaeve's Great Serpent ring. "As you command," he murmured, "so do I obey." It was difficult to tell whether he meant to be mocking or not.

As soon as the door closed behind him, Nynaeve sank onto the edge of her bed as if letting her knees give way at last. She stared at the door with a pensive frown.

" 'Poke the meekest dog too often,' " Elayne quoted, " 'and he will bite.' Not that Lan is very meek." She got a sharp look and a sniff from Nynaeve.

"He is insufferable," Egwene said. "Sometimes he is. Nynaeve, why did you do that? He was ready to go with you. I know you want nothing more than to break him free of Moiraine. Do not try to deny it."

Nynaeve did not try. Instead she fussed with her dress, and smoothed the coverlet on the bed. "Not like that," she said finally. "I mean him to be mine. All of him. I will not have him remembering a broken oath to Moiraine. I will not have that between us. For him, as well as myself."

"But will it be any different if you bring him to ask Moiraine to release him from his bond?" Egwene asked. "Lan is the kind of man who would see it as much the same thing. All that leaves is to somehow make her let him go of her own accord. How can you manage that?"

"I do not know." Nynaeve firmed her voice. "Yet what must be done, can be done. There is always a way. That is for another time. Work to be done, and we sit here fretting over men. Are you sure you have everything you need for the Waste, Egwene?"

"Aviendha is readying everything," Egwene said. "She still seems unhappy, but she says we can reach Rhuidean in little more than a month, if we are lucky. You will be in Tanchico by then."

"Perhaps sooner," Elayne told her, "if what they say about Sea Folk rakers is true. You will be careful, Egwene? Even with Aviendha for a guide, the Waste cannot be safe."

"I will. You be careful. Both of you. Tanchico is not much safer than the Waste now."

Abruptly they were all hugging one another, repeating cautions to take care, making sure they all remembered the schedule for meeting in *Tel'aran'rhiod*'s Stone.

Elayne wiped tears from her cheeks. "As well Lan left." She laughed tremulously. "He would think we were all being foolish."

"No, he would not," Nynaeve said, pulling up her skirts to settle a purse of gold into its pocket. "He may be a man, but he is not a complete dolt."

There had to be time between here and the carriage to locate paper and pen, Elayne decided. She would find time. Nynaeve had the right of it. Men needed a firm hand. Rand would find he could not get away from her so easily. And he would not find it easy to worm his way back into her good graces.

CHAPTER
17

Deceptions

Favoring his stiff right leg, Thom bowed with a flourish of his gleeman's cloak that set the colorful patches fluttering. His eyes felt grainy, but he made himself speak lightly. "A good morning to you." Straightening, he knuckled his long white mustaches grandly.

The black-and-gold-clad servants looked surprised. The two muscular lads straightened from the gold-studded red lacquer chest, with a shattered lid, that they had been about to lift, and the three women stilled their mops in front of them. The hallway was empty along here except for them, and any excuse to break their labor was good, especially at this hour. They looked as tired as Thom felt, with slumping shoulders and dark circles under their eyes.

"A good morning to you, gleeman," the oldest of the women said. A bit plump and plain-faced, perhaps, she had a nice smile, weary as she was. "Can we help you?"

Thom produced four colored balls from a capacious coatsleeve and began to juggle. "I am just going about trying to raise spirits. A gleeman must do what he can." He would have used more than four, but he was fatigued enough to make even that many an exercise in concentration. How long since he had nearly dropped a fifth ball? Two hours? He stifled a yawn, turned it into a reassuring smile. "A terrible night, and spirits need lifting."

"The Lord Dragon saved us," one of the younger women said. She was pretty and slim, but with a predatory gleam in her dark, shadowed eyes that warned him to temper his smile. Of course, she might be useful if she was both greedy and honest, meaning that she would stay bought once he paid her. It was always good to find another set of hands to place a note, a tongue that would tell him what was heard and say what he wanted where he wanted. *Old fool! You have enough hands and ears, so stop thinking of a fine bosom and remember the look in her eye!* The interesting thing was that she sounded as if she meant what she said, and one of the young fellows nodded agreement to her words.

"Yes," Thom said. "I wonder which High Lord had charge of the docks yesterday?" He nearly fumbled the balls in irritation at himself. Bringing it right out like that. He was too tired; he should be in his bed. He should have been there hours ago.

"The docks are the Defenders' responsibility," the oldest woman told him. "You'd not know that, of course. The High Lords would not concern themselves."

Thom knew it very well. "Is that so? Well, I am not Tairen, of course." He changed the balls from a simple circle to a double loop; it looked more difficult than it was, and the girl with the predatory look clapped her hands. Now that he was into it, he might as well go on. After this, though, he would call it a night. A night? The sun was rising already. "Still, it is a shame no one asked why those barges were at the docks. With their hatches down, hiding all those Trollocs. Not that I am saying anyone knew the Trollocs were there." The double loop wobbled, and he quickly went back to a circle. Light, he was exhausted. "You'd think one of the High Lords would have asked, though."

The two young men frowned thoughtfully at one another, and Thom smiled to himself. Another seed planted, just that easily, if clumsily as well. Another rumor started, whatever they knew for a fact about who had charge of the docks. And rumors spread—a rumor like this would not stop short of the city—so it was another small wedge of suspicion driven between commoners and nobles. Who would the commoners turn to, except the man they knew the nobles hated? The man who had saved the Stone from Shadowspawn. Rand al'Thor. The Lord Dragon.

It was time to leave what he had sown. If the roots had taken hold here, nothing he said now could pull them loose, and he had scattered other seeds this night. But it would not do for anyone to discover he was the one doing the planting. "They fought bravely last night, the High Lords did. Why, I saw. . . ." He trailed off as the women leaped to their mopping and the men grabbed up the chest and hurried away.

"I can find work for gleemen, too," the majhere's voice said behind him. "Idle hands are idle hands."

He turned gracefully, considering his leg, and swept her a deep bow. The top of her head was below his shoulder, but she probably weighed half again what he did. She had a face like an anvil—not improved by the bandage around her temples—an extra chin, and deep-set eyes like chips of black flint. "A good morning to you, gracious lady. A small token of this fresh, new day."

He gestured with a flurry of hands and tucked a golden yellow sunburst blossom, only a little bedraggled for its time up his sleeve, into the gray hair above her bandage. She snatched the flower right out again, of course, and eyed it suspiciously, but that was just as he wanted. He put three limping strides into her moment of hesitation, and when she shouted something after him, he neither listened nor slowed.

Horrible woman, he thought. *If we had turned her loose on the Trollocs, she'd have had them all sweeping and mopping.*

He yawned behind a hand, jaws creaking. He was too old for this. He was tired, and his knee was a knot of pain. Nights with no sleep, battles, plotting. Too old. He should be living quietly on a farm somewhere. With chickens. Farms always had chickens. And sheep. They must not be difficult to look after; shepherds seemed to loll about and play the pipes all the time. He would play the harp, of course, not pipes. Or his flute; weather was not good for the harp. And there would be a town nearby, with an inn where he could amaze the patrons in the common room. He flourished his cloak as he passed two servants. The only point in wearing it in this heat was to let people know he was a gleeman. They perked up at the sight of him, of course, hoping he might pause to entertain for a moment. Most gratifying. Yes, a farm had its virtues. A quiet place. No people to bother him. As long as there was a town close by.

Pushing open the door to his room, he stopped in his tracks. Moiraine straightened as if she had a perfect right to be going through the papers scattered on his table and calmly arranged her skirts as she sat on the stool. Now there was a beautiful woman, with every grace a man could want, including laughing at his quips. *Fool! Old fool! She's Aes Sedai, and you're too tired to think straight.*

"A good morning to you, Moiraine Sedai," he said, hanging his cloak on a peg. He avoided looking at his writing case, still sitting under the table where he had left it. No point in letting her know it was important. Probably no point in checking after she went, for that matter; she could have channeled the lock open and closed again, and he would never be able to tell. Weary as he was, he could not even remember whether he had left anything incriminating in the case. Or anywhere else, for that matter. Everything he could see in the room was right where it belonged. He did not think he could have been foolish enough to leave anything out. Doors in the servants' quarters had no locks or latches. "I would offer you a refreshing drink, but I fear I have nothing but water."

"I am not thirsty," she said in a pleasant, melodious voice. She leaned forward, and the room was small enough for her to place a hand on his right knee. A chill tingle rippled through him. "I wish a good Healer had been near when this happened. It is too late now, I regret."

"A dozen Healers would not have been enough," he told her. "A Halfman did it."

"I know."

What else does she know? he wondered. Turning to pull his lone chair out from behind the table, he bit back an oath. He felt as if he had had a good night's sleep, and the pain was gone from his knee. His limp remained, but the joint was more limber than it had been since he was injured. *The woman didn't even ask if I wanted it. Burn me, what is she after?* He refused to flex the leg. If she would not ask, he would not acknowledge her gift.

"An interesting day, yesterday," she said as he sat down.

"I'd not call Trollocs and Halfmen interesting," he said dryly.

"I did not mean them. Earlier. The High Lord Carleon dead in a hunting accident. His good friend Tedosian apparently mistook him for a boar. Or perhaps a deer."

"I hadn't heard." He kept his voice calm. Even if she had found the note, she could not have traced it to him. Carleon himself would have thought it by his own hand. He did not think she could have, but he reminded himself again that she was Aes Sedai. As if he needed any reminding, with that smooth pretty face across from him, those serene dark eyes watching him full of all his secrets. "The servants' quarters are full of gossip, but I seldom listen."

"Do you not?" she murmured mildly. "Then you will not have heard that Tedosian fell ill not an hour after returning to the Stone, directly after his wife gave him a goblet of wine to wash away the dust of the hunt. It is said he wept when he learned that she means to tend him herself, and feed him with her own hands. No doubt tears of joy at her love. I hear she has vowed not to leave his side until he can rise again. Or until he dies."

She knew. How, he could not say, but she knew. But why was she revealing it to him? "A tragedy," he said, matching her bland tone. "Rand will need all the loyal High Lords he can find, I suppose."

"Carleon and Tedosian were hardly loyal. Even to each other, it seems. They led the faction that want to kill Rand and try to forget he ever lived."

"Do you say so? I pay little attention to such things. The works of the mighty are not for a simple gleeman."

Her smile was just short of laughter, but she spoke as if reading from a page. "Thomdril Merrilin. Called the Gray Fox, once, by some who knew him, or knew of him. Court-bard at the Royal Palace of Andor in Caemlyn. Morgase's lover for a time, after Taringail died. Fortunate for Morgase, Taringail's death. I do not suppose she ever learned he meant her to die and himself to be Andor's first king. But we were speaking of Thom Merrilin, a man who, it was said, could play the Game of Houses in his sleep. It is a shame that such a man calls himself a simple glee-man. But such arrogance to keep the same name."

Thom masked his shock with an effort. How much did she know? Too much if she knew not another word. But she was not the only one with knowledge. "Speaking of names," he said levelly, "it is remarkable how much can be puzzled out from a name. Moiraine Damodred. The Lady Moiraine of House Damodred, in Cairhien. Taringail's youngest half-sister. King Laman's niece. And Aes Sedai, let us not forget. An Aes Sedai aiding the Dragon Reborn since before she could have known that he was more than just another poor fool who could chan-nel. An Aes Sedai with connections high in the White Tower, I would say, else she'd not risk what she has. Someone in the Hall of the Tower? More than one, I'd say; it would have to be. News of that would shake the world. But why should there be trouble? Perhaps it's best to leave an old gleeman tucked away in his hole in the servants' quarters. Just an old gleeman playing his harp and telling his tales. Tales that harm no one."

If he had managed to stagger her even a fraction, she did not show it. "Speculation without facts is always dangerous," she said calmly. "I do not use my House name, by choice. House Damodred had a deservedly unpleasant reputation before Laman cut down *Avendoraldera* and lost the throne and his life for it. Since the Aiel War, it has grown worse, also deservedly."

Would nothing shake the woman? "What do you want of me?" he demanded irritably.

She did not as much as blink. "Elayne and Nynaeve take ship for

Tanchico today. A dangerous city, Tanchico. Your knowledge and skills might keep them alive."

So that was it. She wanted to separate him from Rand, leave the boy naked to her manipulations. "As you say, Tanchico is dangerous now, but then it always was. I wish the young women well, yet I've no wish to stick my head into a vipers' nest. I am too old for that sort of thing. I have been thinking of taking up farming. A quiet life. Safe."

"A quiet life would kill you, I think." Sounding distinctly amused, she busied herself rearranging the folds of her skirt with small, slender hands. He had the impression she was hiding a smile. "Tanchico will not, however. I guarantee that, and by the First Oath, you know it for truth."

He frowned at her despite his best efforts to keep his face straight. She had said it, and she could not lie, yet how could she know? He was sure she could not Foretell; he was certain he had heard her disavow the Talent. But she had said it. *Burn the woman!* "Why should I go to Tanchico?" She could do without titles.

"To protect Elayne? Morgase's daughter?"

"I have not seen Morgase in fifteen years. Elayne was an infant when I left Caemlyn."

She hesitated, but when she spoke her voice was unrelentingly firm. "And your reason for leaving Andor? A nephew named Owyn, I believe. One of those poor fools you spoke of who can channel. The Red sisters were supposed to bring him to Tar Valon, as any such man is, but instead they gentled him on the spot and abandoned him to the . . . mercies of his neighbors."

Thom knocked his chair over standing up, then had to hold on to the table because his knees were shaking. Owyn had not lived long after being gentled, driven from his home by supposed friends who could not bear to let even a man who could no longer channel live among them. Nothing Thom did could stop Owyn not wanting to live, or stop his young wife from following him to the grave inside the month.

"Why . . . ?" He cleared his throat roughly, tried to make his voice less husky. "Why are you telling me this?"

There was sympathy on Moiraine's face. And could it be regret? Surely not. Not from an Aes Sedai. The sympathy had to be false as well. "I would not have done, had you been willing to go simply to help Elayne and Nynaeve."

"Why, burn you! Why?"

"If you go with Elayne and Nynaeve, I will tell you the names of those Red sisters when I see you next, as well as the name of the one who gave them their orders. They did not act on their own. And I *will* see you again. You will survive Tarabon."

He drew an uneven breath. "What good will their names do me?" he asked in a flat voice. "Aes Sedai names, wrapped in all the power of the White Tower."

"A skilled and dangerous player of the Game of Houses might find a use for them," she replied quietly. "They should not have done what they did. They should not have been excused for it."

"Will you leave me, please?"

"I will teach you that not all Aes Sedai are like those Reds, Thom. You must learn that."

"Please?"

He stood leaning on the table until she was gone, unwilling to let her see him sink awkwardly to his knees, see the tears trickling down his weathered face. *Oh, Light, Owyn.* He had buried it all as deeply as he could. *I couldn't get there in time. I was too busy. Too busy with the bloody Game of Houses.* He scrubbed at his face testily. Moiraine could play the Game with the best. Wrenching him around this way, tugging every string he had thought perfectly hidden. Owyn. Elayne. Morgase's daughter. Only fondness remained for Morgase, perhaps a little more than that, but it was hard to walk away from a child you had bounced on your knee. *That girl in Tanchico? That city would eat her alive even without a war. It must be a pit of rabid wolves, now. And Moiraine will give me the names.* All he had to do was leave Rand in Aes Sedai hands. Just as he had left Owyn. She had him like a snake in a cleft stick, damned however he writhed. *Burn the woman!*

Looping the embroidery basket's handle over her arm, Min gathered her skirts with her other hand and strolled out of the dining hall after breakfast in a gliding pace, her back straight. She could have balanced a full goblet of wine on her head without spilling a drop. Partly that was because she could not take a proper stride in her dress, all pale blue silk with a snug bodice and sleeves and a full skirt that would drag its embroidered hem on the ground if she did not hold it up. It was also partly because she was sure she could feel Laras's eyes on her.

A glance back proved her right. The Mistress of the Kitchens, a winecask on legs, was beaming after her approvingly from the dining hall doorway. Who would have thought the woman had been a beauty in her youth, or would have a place in her heart for pretty, flirtatious girls? "Lively," she called them. Who would have suspected she would decide to take "Elmindreda" under her stout wing? It was hardly a comfortable position. Laras kept a protective eye on Min, an eye that seemed to find her anywhere in the Tower grounds. Min smiled back and patted her hair, now a round black cap of curls. *Burn the woman! Doesn't she have something to cook, or some scullion to yell at?*

Laras waved to her, and she waved in return. She could not afford to offend someone who watched her so closely, not when she had no idea how many mistakes she might be making. Laras knew every trick of "lively" women, and expected to teach Min any she did not already know.

One real mistake, Min reflected as she took a seat on a marble bench beneath a tall willow, had been the embroidery. Not from Laras's point of view, but her own. Pulling her embroidery hoop from the basket, she ruefully examined yesterday's work, a number of lopsided yellow ox-eyes and something she had meant to be a pale yellow rosebud, though no one would know unless she told them. With a sigh, she set to picking the stitches out. Leane was right, she supposed; a woman could sit for hours with an embroidery hoop, watching everyone and everything, and nobody thought it strange. It would have helped, though, if she had any skill at all.

At least it was a perfect morning for being out-of-doors. A golden sun had just cleared the horizon in a sky where the few fluffy white clouds seemed arrayed to emphasize the perfection. A light breeze caught the scent of roses and ruffled tall calma bushes with their big red or white blossoms. Soon enough the gravel-covered paths near the tree would be full of people on one errand or another, everyone from Aes Sedai to stablemen. A perfect morning, and a perfect place from which to watch unobserved. Perhaps today she would have a useful viewing.

"Elmindreda?"

Min jumped, and stuck her pricked finger in her mouth. Twisting 'round on the bench, she prepared to assail Gawyn for sneaking up on her, but the words froze in her throat. Galad was with him. Taller than Gawyn, with long legs, he moved with a dancer's grace and a lean, sinewy strength. His hands were long, too, elegant yet strong. And his face. . . . He was, quite simply, the most beautiful man she had ever seen.

"Stop sucking your finger," Gawyn said with a grin. "We know you are a pretty little girl; you do not need to prove it to us."

Blushing, she hastily pulled her hand down, and barely restrained herself from a furious glare that would not have been at all in keeping with Elmindreda. He had needed no threats or commands from the Amyrlin to keep her secret, only her asking, but he did take any opportunity to tease that presented itself.

"It is not right to mock, Gawyn," Galad said. "He did not mean to offend, Mistress Elmindreda. Your pardon, but can it be we have met before? When you frowned at Gawyn so fiercely just then, I almost thought I knew you."

Min dropped her eyes demurely. "Oh, I could never forget meeting *you,* my Lord Galad," she said in her best foolish-girl voice. The simpering tone, and anger at her own slip, sent a tide of heat to her hairline, improving her disguise.

She did not look anything like herself, and the dress and the hair were only a part of it. Leane had acquired creams and powders and an incredible assortment of mysterious scented things in the city and drilled her until she could have used them in her sleep. She had cheekbones, now, and more color in her lips than nature had put there. A dark cream lining her eyelids and a fine powder that emphasized her lashes made her eyes seem larger. Not at all like herself. Some of the novices had told her admiringly how beautiful she was, and even a few Aes Sedai had called her "a very pretty child." She hated it. The dress was quite pretty, she admitted, but she hated the rest of it. Yet there was no point in donning a disguise if she did not keep it up.

"I am sure you would remember," Gawyn said dryly. "I did not mean to interrupt you at your embroidery—swallows, are they? *Yellow* swallows?" Min thrust the hoop back into the basket. "But I wanted to ask you to comment on this." He pushed a small, leather-bound book, old and tattered, into her hands, and suddenly his voice was serious. "Tell my brother this is nonsense. Perhaps he will listen to you."

She examined the book. *The Way of the Light,* by Lothair Mantelar. Opening it, she read at random. "Therefore abjure all pleasure, for goodness is a pure abstract, a perfect crystalline ideal which is obscured by base emotion. Pamper not the flesh. Flesh is weak but spirit is strong; flesh is useless where spirit is strong. Right thought is drowned in sensation, and right action hindered by passions. Take all joy from rightness, and rightness only." It seemed to be dry nonsense.

Min smiled at Gawyn, and even managed a titter. "So many words. I fear I know little of books, my Lord Gawyn. I always mean to read one —I do." She sighed. "But there is so little time. Why, just fixing my hair properly takes hours. Do you think it is pretty?" The outraged startlement on his face nearly made her laugh, but she changed it to a giggle. It was a pleasure to turn the tables on him for a change; she would have to see if she could do it more often. There were possibilities in this disguise she had not considered. This stay in the Tower had turned out to be all boredom and irritation. She deserved *some* amusement.

"Lothair Mantelar," Gawyn said in a tight voice, "founded the Whitecloaks. The Whitecloaks!"

"He was a great man," Galad said firmly. "A philosopher of noble ideals. If the Children of the Light have sometimes been . . . excessive . . . since his day, it does not change that."

"Oh, my. Whitecloaks," Min said breathlessly, and added a little shudder. "They are such rough men, I hear. I cannot imagine a Whitecloak dancing. Do you think there is any chance of a dance here? Aes Sedai do not seem to care for dancing either, and I do so love to dance." The frustration in Gawyn's eyes was delightful.

"I do not think so," Galad said, taking the book from her. "Aes Sedai are too busy with . . . with their own affairs. If I hear of a suitable dance in the city, I will escort you, if you wish it. You need have no fear of being annoyed by those two louts." He smiled at her, unconscious of what he was doing, and she suddenly found herself breathless in truth. Men should not be allowed smiles like that.

It actually took her a moment to remember what two louts he was talking about. The two men who had supposedly asked for Elmindreda's hand in marriage, nearly fighting each other because she could not make up her mind, pressing her to the point of seeking sanctuary in the Tower because she could not stop encouraging them both. Just the entire excuse for her being there. *It's this dress,* she told herself. *I could think straight if I had on my proper clothes.*

"I've noticed the Amyrlin speaks to you every day," Gawyn said suddenly. "Has she mentioned our sister Elayne? Or Egwene al'Vere? Has she said anything of where they are?"

Min wished she could black his eye. He did not know why she was pretending to be someone else, of course, but he had agreed to help her be accepted as Elmindreda, and now he was linking her to women too many in the Tower knew were friends of Min. "Oh, the Amyrlin Seat is such a wonderful woman," she said sweetly, baring her teeth in a smile. "She always asks how I am passing the time, and compliments my dress. I suppose she hopes I'll make a decision soon between Darvan and Goemal, but I just cannot." She widened her eyes, hoping it made her look helpless and confused. "They are both so sweet. Who did you say? Your sister, my Lord Gawyn? The Daughter-Heir herself? I do not think I've ever heard the Amyrlin Seat mention her. What was the other name?" She could hear Gawyn grinding his teeth.

"We should not bother Mistress Elmindreda with that," Galad said. "It is our problem, Gawyn. It is up to us to find the lie and deal with it."

She barely heard him, because suddenly she was staring at a big man with long dark hair curling around slumped shoulders, wandering aimlessly down one of the graveled paths through the trees, under the watchful eyes of an Accepted. She had seen Logain before, a sad-faced, once-hearty man, always with an Accepted for companion. The woman was meant to keep him from killing himself as much as to prevent his escape; despite his size, he truly did not seem up to anything of the latter sort. But she had never before seen a flaring halo around his head, radiant in gold and blue. It was only there for a moment, but that was enough.

Logain had proclaimed himself the Dragon Reborn, had been captured and gentled. Whatever glory he might have had as a false Dragon was far behind him now. All that remained for him was the despair of the gentled, like a man who had been robbed of sight and hearing and taste, wanting to die, waiting for the death that inevitably came to such men in a few years. He glanced at her, perhaps not seeing her; his eyes looked hopelessly inward. So why had he worn a halo that shouted of glory and power to come? This was something she had to tell the Amyrlin.

"Poor fellow," Gawyn muttered. "I cannot help pitying him. Light, it would be a mercy to let him end it. Why do they make him keep on living?"

"He deserves no pity," Galad pronounced. "Have you forgotten what he was, what he did? How many thousands died before he was taken? How many towns were burned? Let him live on as a warning to others."

Gawyn nodded, but reluctantly. "Yet men followed him. Some of those towns were burned after they declared for him."

"I have to go," Min said, getting to her feet, and Galad was instantly all solicitude.

"Forgive us, Mistress Elmindreda. We did not mean to frighten you. Logain cannot harm you. I give you my assurance."

"I. . . . Yes, he's made me feel faint. Do excuse me. I really must go lie down."

Gawyn looked extremely skeptical, but he scooped up her basket before she could touch it. "Let me see you part of the way, at least," he said, his voice oozing false concern. "This basket must be too heavy for you, dizzy as you are. I'd not want you to swoon."

She wanted to snatch the basket and hit him with it, but that was not how Elmindreda would react. "Oh, thank you, my Lord Gawyn. You are so kind. So kind. No, no, my Lord Galad. Do not let me encumber both of you. Do sit down here and read your book. Do say you will. I just could not bear it, otherwise." She even fluttered her eyelashes.

Somehow she managed to ensconce Galad on the marble bench and get away, though with Gawyn right beside her. Her skirts were an irritant; she wanted to pull them up to her knees and run, but Elmindreda would never run, and never expose so much of her legs except when dancing. Laras had lectured her severely on that very point; one time running, and she would nearly destroy the image of Elmindreda completely. And Gawyn . . . !

"Give me that basket, you muscle-brained cretin," she snarled as soon as they were out of Galad's sight, and pulled it away from him before he could comply. "What do you mean by asking me about Elayne and Egwene in front of him? Elmindreda never met them. Elmindreda does not care about them. Elmindreda doesn't want to be mentioned in the same sentence with them! Can't you understand that?"

"No," he said. "Not since you won't explain. But I am sorry." There was hardly enough repentance in his voice to suit her. "It is just that I am worried. Where are they? This news coming upriver about a false Dragon in Tear makes me no easier in my mind. They are out there, somewhere, the Light knows where, and I keep asking myself, what if they are in the middle of the sort of bonfire Logain made out of Ghealdan?"

"What if he isn't a false Dragon?" she asked cautiously.

"You mean because the stories in the streets say he's taken the Stone of Tear? Rumor has a way of magnifying events. I will believe that when I see it, and in any case, it will take more to convince me. Even the Stone could fall. Light, I don't really believe Elayne and Egwene are in Tear, but the not knowing eats at my belly like acid. If she is hurt. . . ."

Min did not know which "she" he meant, and suspected he did not either. In spite of his teasing, her heart went out to him, but there was nothing she could do. "If you could only do as I say and—"

"I know. Trust the Amyrlin. Trust!" He exhaled a long breath. "Do you know Galad has been drinking in the taverns with Whitecloaks? Anyone can cross the bridges if they come in peace, even Children of the bloody Light."

"Galad?" she said incredulously. "In taverns? Drinking?"

"No more than a cup or two, I'm sure. He would not unbend more than that, not for his own nameday." Gawyn frowned as if unsure whether that might be a criticism of Galad. "The point is that he is talking with Whitecloaks. And now this book. According to the inscription, Eamon Valda himself gave it to him. 'In the hope you will find the way.' Valda, Min. The man commanding the Whitecloaks on the other side of the bridges. Not knowing is eating Galad up, too. Listening to Whitecloaks. If anything happens to our sister, or to Egwene . . ." He shook his head. "Do you know where they are, Min? Would you tell me if you did? Why are you hiding?"

"Because I drove two men mad with my beauty and cannot make up my mind," she told him acidly.

He gave a bitter half-laugh, then masked it with a grin. "Well, that at least I can believe." He chuckled, and stroked under her chin with a finger. "You are a very pretty girl, Elmindreda. A pretty, clever little girl."

She doubled a fist and tried to punch him in the eye, but he danced back, and she stumbled over her skirts and nearly fell. "You bloody ox of a thimble-brained man!" she growled.

"Such grace of movement, Elmindreda," he laughed. "Such a dulcet voice, as a nightingale, or a cooing dove of the evening. What man would not grow starry-eyed at the sight of Elmindreda?" The mirth slid away, and he faced her soberly. "If you learn anything, please tell me. Please? I will beg on my knees, Min."

"I will tell you," she said. *If I can. If it's safe for them. Light, but I hate this place. Why can't I just go back to Rand?*

She left Gawyn there and entered the Tower proper by herself, keeping an eye out for Aes Sedai or Accepted who might question why she was above the ground floor and where she was going. The news of Logain was too important to wait until the Amyrlin encountered her, seemingly by accident, some time in the late afternoon as usual. At least, that was what she told herself. Impatience threatened to pop out through her skin.

She only saw a few Aes Sedai, turning a corner ahead of her or entering a room in the distance, which was all to the good. No one simply dropped in on the Amyrlin Seat. The handful of servants she passed, all bustling about their work, did not question her, of course, or even look at her twice except to drop quick curtsies almost without pausing.

Pushing open the door to the Amyrlin's study, she had a simpering tale ready in case anyone was with Leane, but the antechamber was empty. She hurried to the inner door and put her head in. The Amyrlin and the Keeper were seated on either side of Siuan's table, which was littered with small strips of thin paper. Their heads swiveled toward her sharply, a stare like four nails.

"What are you doing here?" the Amyrlin snapped. "You are supposed to be a silly girl claiming sanctuary, not a friend of my childhood. There is to be no contact between us except the most casual, in passing. If necessary, I'll name Laras to watch over you like a nurse over a child. She would enjoy that, I think, but I doubt you would."

Min shivered at the thought. Suddenly Logain did not seem so urgent; it was hardly likely he could achieve any glory in the next few days. He was not really why she had come, though, only an excuse, and she would not turn back now. Closing the door behind her, she stammered out what she had seen and what it meant. She still felt uncomfortable doing so in front of Leane.

Siuan shook her head wearily. "Another thing to worry about. Starvation in Cairhien. A sister missing in Tarabon. Trolloc raids increasing in the Borderlands again. This fool who calls himself the Prophet, stirring up riots in Ghealdan. He's apparently preaching that the Dragon has been Reborn as a Shienaran lord," she said incredulously. "Even the small things are bad. The war in Arad Doman has stopped trade from Saldaea, and the pinch is making unrest in Maradon. Tenobia may even be forced off the throne by it. The only good news I have heard is that the Blight has retreated for some reason. Two miles or more of green beyond the borderstones, without a hint of corruption or pestilence, all the way from Saldaea to Shienar. The first time in memory it has done that. But I suppose good news has to be balanced by bad. When a boat has one leak it is sure to have others. I only wish it was a balance. Leane, have the watch on Logain increased. I can't see what trouble he could cause now, but I do not want to find out." She turned those piercing blue eyes on Min. "Why did you come flapping up here with this like a startled gull? Logain could have waited. The man is hardly likely to find power and glory before sunset."

The near echo of her own thoughts made Min shift uncomfortably. "I know," she said. Leane's eyebrows rose warningly, and she added a hasty, "Mother." The Keeper nodded approvingly.

"That does not tell me why, child," Siuan said.

Min steeled herself. "Mother, nothing I've viewed since the first day has been very important. I certainly have not seen anything that points to the Black Ajah." That name still gave her a chill. "I've told you everything I know about whatever disaster you Aes Sedai are going to face, and the rest of it is just useless." She had to stop and swallow, with that penetrating gaze on her. "Mother, there is no reason I should not go. There's reason I should. Perhaps Rand could make real use of what I can do. If he *has* taken the Stone. . . . Mother, he may need me." *At least I need him, burn me for a fool!*

The Keeper shuddered openly at the mention of Rand's name. Siuan, on the other hand, snorted loudly. "Your viewings have been very useful. It's important to know about Logain. You found the groom who was stealing before suspicion could land on anyone else. And that fire-haired novice who was going to get herself with child . . . ! Sheriam cut that short—the girl won't even think of men until she's finished her training—but we'd not have known until it was too late, without you. No, you cannot go. Sooner or later your viewings will draw me a chart to the Black Ajah, and until they do, they still more than pay their passage."

Min sighed, and not only because the Amyrlin meant to hold on to her. The last time she had seen that redheaded novice, the girl had been sneaking off to a wooded part of the grounds with a muscular guard. They would be married, maybe before the end of summer; Min had known that as soon as she saw them together, though the Tower never let a novice leave until the Tower was ready, even one who could not go any further in her training. There was a farm in that pair's future, and a swarm of children, but it was pointless to tell the Amyrlin that.

"Could you at least let Gawyn and Galad know that Egwene and their sister are all right, Mother?" Asking irked her, and her tone of voice did, too. A child denied a slice of cake begging for a cookie instead. "At least tell them something besides that ridiculous tale about doing penance on a farm."

"I have told you that is none of your concern. Do not make me tell you again."

"They don't believe it any more than I do," Min got out before the Amyrlin's dry smile quieted her. It was not an amused smile.

"So you suggest I change where they are supposed to be? After letting everyone think them on a farm? Do you suppose that might raise a few eyebrows? Everyone but those boys accepts it. And you. Well, Coulin Gaidin will just have to work them that much harder. Sore muscles and enough sweat will take most men's minds off other troubles. Women's minds, too. You ask many more questions, and I'll see what a few days scrubbing pots will do for you. Better to lose your services for two or three days than have you poking your nose where it does not belong."

"You don't even know if they are in trouble, do you? Or Moiraine." It was not Moiraine she meant.

"Girl," Leane said warningly, but Min was not to be stopped now.

"Why haven't we heard? Rumors reached here two days ago. Two days! Why doesn't one of those slips on your desk contain a message from her? Doesn't she have pigeons? I thought you Aes Sedai had people with messenger pigeons everywhere. If there isn't one in Tear, there should be. A man on horseback could have reached Tar Valon before now. Why—?"

The flat crack of Siuan's palm on the table cut her off. "You obey remarkably well," she said wryly. "Child, until we hear something to the contrary, assume the young man is well. Pray that he is." Leane shivered again. "There's a saying in the Maule, child," the Amyrlin went on. " 'Do not trouble trouble till trouble troubles you.' Mark it well, child."

There was a timid knock at the door.

The Amyrlin and the Keeper exchanged glances; then two sets of eyes shifted to Min. Her presence was a problem. There was certainly nowhere to hide; even the balcony was clearly visible from the room in its entirety.

"A reason for you to be here," Siuan muttered, "that doesn't make you any more than the fool girl you're supposed to be. Leane, stand ready at the door." She and the Keeper were on their feet together, Siuan coming around the table while Leane moved to the door. "Take Leane's seat, girl. Move your feet, child; move your feet. Now look sulky. Not angry, sulky! Stick your lower lip out and stare at the floor. I may make you wear ribbons in your hair, huge red bows. That's it. Leane." The Amyrlin put her fists on her hips and raised her voice. "And if you ever walk in on me unannounced again, child, I will."

Leane pulled the door open to reveal a dark novice who flinched at Siuan's continuing tirade, then dropped a deep curtsy. "Messages for the Amyrlin, Aes Sedai," the girl squeaked. "Two pigeons arrived at the loft." She was one of those who had told Min she was beautiful, and she tried to stare past the Keeper with wide eyes.

"This does not concern you, child," Leane said briskly, taking the tiny cylinders of bone out of the girl's hand. "Back to the loft with you." Before the novice finished rising, Leane shut the door, then leaned against it with a sigh. "I have jumped at every unexpected sound since you told me. . . ." Straightening, she came back to the table. "Two more messages, Mother. Shall I . . . ?"

"Yes. Open them," the Amyrlin said. "No doubt Morgase has decided to invade Cairhien after all. Or Trollocs have overrun the Borderlands. It would be of a piece with everything else." Min kept her seat; Siuan had sounded all too realistic with some of those threats.

Leane examined the red wax seal on the end of one of the small cylinders, no larger than her own finger joint, then broke it open with a thumbnail when she was satisfied it had not been tampered with. The rolled paper inside she extracted with a slim ivory pick. "Nearly as bad as Trollocs, Mother," she said almost as soon as she began reading. "Mazrim Taim has escaped."

"Light!" Siuan barked. "How?"

"This only says he was taken away by stealth in the night, Mother. Two sisters are dead."

"The Light illumine their souls. But we've little time to mourn the dead while the likes of Taim are alive and ungentled. Where, Leane?"

"Denhuir, Mother. A village east of the Black Hills on the Maradon Road, above the headwaters of the Antaeo and the Luan."

"It had to be some of his followers. Fools. Why won't they know when they are beaten? Choose out a dozen reliable sisters, Leane. . . ." The Amyrlin grimaced. "Reliable," she muttered. "If I knew who was more reliable than a silverpike, I'd not have the problems I do. Do the best you can, Leane. A dozen sisters. And five hundred of the guards. No, a full thousand."

"Mother," the Keeper said worriedly. "The Whitecloaks—"

"—would not try to cross the bridges if I left them unwatched entirely. They would be afraid of a trap. There is no telling what is going on up there, Leane. I want whoever I send to be ready for anything. And Leane . . . Mazrim Taim is to be gentled as soon as he is taken again."

Leane's eyes opened wide with shock. "The law."

"I know the law as well as you, but I will not risk having him freed again ungentled. I'll not risk another Guaire Amalasan, not on top of everything else."

"Yes, Mother," Leane said faintly.

The Amyrlin picked up the second bone cylinder and snapped it in two with a sharp crack to get the message out. "Good news at last," she breathed, a smile blooming on her face. "Good news. 'The sling has been used. The shepherd holds the sword.' "

"Rand?" Min asked, and Siuan nodded.

"Of course, girl. The Stone has fallen. Rand al'Thor, the shepherd, has *Callandor.* Now I can move. Leane, I want the Hall of the Tower convened this afternoon. No, this morning."

"I don't understand," Min said. "You knew the rumors were about Rand. Why are you calling the Hall now? What can you do that you could not before?"

Siuan laughed like a girl. "What I can do now is tell them right out that I have received word from an Aes Sedai that the Stone of Tear has fallen and a man has drawn *Callandor.* Prophecy fulfilled. Enough of it for my purpose, at least. The Dragon is Reborn. They'll flinch, they'll argue, but none can oppose my pronouncement that the Tower must guide this man. At last I can involve myself with him openly. Openly for the most part."

"Are we doing the right thing, Mother?" Leane said abruptly. "I know. . . . If he has *Callandor,* he must be the Dragon Reborn, but he can channel, Mother. A man who can channel. I only saw him once, but even then there was something strange about him. Something more than being *ta'veren.* Mother, is he so very different from Taim when it comes down to it?"

"The difference is that he *is* the Dragon Reborn, daughter," the Amyrlin said quietly. "Taim is a wolf, and maybe rabid. Rand al'Thor is the wolfhound we will use to defeat the Shadow. Keep his name to yourself, Leane. Best not to reveal too much too soon."

"As you say, Mother," the Keeper said, but she still sounded uneasy.

"Off with you now. I want the Hall assembled in an hour." Siuan thoughtfully watched the taller woman go. "There may be more resistance than I would wish," she said when the door clicked shut.

Min looked at her sharply. "You don't mean. . . ."

"Oh, nothing serious, child. Not as long as they don't know how long I have been involved with the al'Thor boy." She looked at the slip of paper again, then dropped it onto the table. "I could wish Moiraine had told me more."

"Why didn't she say more? And why have we not heard from her before this?"

"More questions with you. That one you must ask Moiraine. She has always gone her own way. Ask Moiraine, child."

Sahra Coventry worked the hoe in desultory fashion, frowning at the tiny sprouts of threadleaf and hensfoot poking up in the rows of cabbages and beets. It was not that Mistress Elward was a harsh taskmistress—she was no more stern than Sahra's mother, and certainly easier than Sheriam—but Sahra had not gone to the White Tower to end up back on a farm hoeing vegetables with the sun barely up. Her white novice dresses were packed away; she wore brown wool her mother might have sewn, the skirt tied up to her knees to keep it out of the dirt. It was all so unfair. She had not done anything.

Wriggling her bare toes in the turned soil, she glared at a stubborn hensfoot and channeled, meaning to burn it out of the ground. Sparks flashed around the leafy sprout, and it wilted. Hurriedly she sliced the thing out of the dirt and her mind. If there was any fairness in the world, Lord Galad would come to the farm while out hunting.

Leaning on the hoe, she lost herself in a daydream of Healing Galad's injuries, received in a fall from his horse—not his fault, of course; he was a wonderful horseman—and him lifting her up in front of him on his saddle, declaring he would be her Warder—she would be Green Ajah, of course—and. . . .

"Sahra Covenry?"

Sahra jumped at the sharp voice, but it was not Mistress Elward. She curtsied as best she could, with her skirts gathered up. "The day's greeting, Aes Sedai. Have you come to take me back to the Tower?"

The Aes Sedai moved closer, not caring that her skirts dragged through the dirt of the vegetable patch. Despite the summer warmth of the morning, she wore a cloak, the hood pulled up to shadow her face. "Just before you left the Tower, you took a woman to the Amyrlin Seat. A woman calling herself Elmindreda."

"Yes, Aes Sedai," Sahra said, a slight question in her voice. She did not like the way the Aes Sedai had said that, as if she had left the Tower for good.

"Tell me everything that you heard or saw, girl, from the moment you took the woman in charge. Everything."

"But I heard nothing, Aes Sedai. The Keeper sent me away as soon as—" Pain racked her, digging her toes into the dirt, arching her back; the spasm lasted only moments, but it seemed eternal. Struggling for breath, she realized her cheek was pressed to the ground, and her still trembling fingers dug into the soil. She did not remember falling. She could see Mistress Elward's laundry basket lying on its side near the stone farmhouse, damp linens spilled out in a heap. Dazed, she thought that that was odd; Moria Elward would never leave her washing lying like that.

"Everything, girl," the Aes Sedai said coldly. She was standing over Sahra now, making no move to help her. She had hurt her; it was not supposed to be that way. "Every person this Elmindreda spoke to, every word she said, every nuance and expression."

"She spoke to Lord Gawyn, Aes Sedai," Sahra sobbed into the earth. "That is all I know, Aes Sedai. All." She began to weep in earnest, sure that was not enough to satisfy this woman. She was right. She did not stop screaming for a long time, and when the Aes Sedai left there was not a sound around the farmhouse except for the chickens, not even breathing.

CHAPTER
18

Into the Ways

B uttoning up his coat, Perrin paused, looking at the axe, still secured on the wall as he had left it since drawing it out of the door. He did not like the idea of carrying the weapon again, but he untied the belt from the peg and buckled it around his waist anyway. The hammer he tied to his already stuffed saddlebags. Draping saddlebags and blanket roll over his shoulder, he gathered a filled quiver and his unstrung longbow from the corner.

The rising sun poured heat and light through the narrow windows. The rumpled bed was the only proof that anyone had stayed here. Already the room had lost the feel of him; it even seemed to smell empty, despite his own scent on the sheets. He never stayed anywhere long enough to make that feel cling past his readiness to leave. Never long enough to put down roots, make it any kind of home. *Well, I'm going home now.*

Turning his back on the already unoccupied room, he went out.

Gaul rose easily from where he had been squatting against the wall beneath a tapestry of men on horseback hunting lions. He bore all of his weapons, with two leather water bottles, and a rolled blanket and a small cookpot were strapped beside the worked-leather bow case on his back. He was alone.

"The others?" Perrin asked, and Gaul shook his head.

"Too long away from the Three-fold Land. I warned you of that, Perrin. These lands of yours are too wet; the air is like breathing water. There are too many people, too close together. They have seen more than they want of strange places."

"I understand," Perrin said, though what he understood was that there would be no rescue after all, no company of Aiel to drive the Whitecloaks out of the Two Rivers. He kept his disappointment inside. It was sharp after thinking he had escaped his fate, but he could not say he had not prepared himself for the alternative. No point in crying when the iron split; you just reforged it. "Did you have any trouble doing what I asked?"

"None. I told one Tairen to take each thing you want to the Dragonwall Gate stable and tell no one of it; they will have seen one another there, but they will think the things are for me, and they will keep silent. The Dragonwall Gate. You would think the Spine of the World was just over the horizon, instead of a hundred leagues or more off." The Aiel hesitated. "The girl and the Ogier make no secret of their preparations, Perrin. She has been trying to find the gleeman, and telling everyone she means to travel the Ways."

Scratching his beard, Perrin breathed heavily, close to a growl. "If she gives me away to Moiraine, I vow she'll not sit down for a week."

"She is very handy with those knives," Gaul said in a neutral tone.

"Not handy enough. Not if she's given me away." Perrin hesitated. No company of Aiel. The gallows still waited. "Gaul, if anything happens to me, if I give you the word, take Faile away. She might not want to go, but take her anyway. See her safely out of the Two Rivers. Will you promise me that?"

"I will do what I can, Perrin. For the blood debt I owe you, I will." Gaul sounded doubtful, but Perrin did not think Faile's knives would be enough to stop him.

They took back passages as much as possible, and narrow stairs meant to carry servants unobtrusively. Perrin thought it too bad the Tairens had not given servants their own corridors, as well. Still, they saw few people even in the broad hallways with their gilded lamp stands and ornate hangings, and no nobles at all.

He commented on the absence, and Gaul said, "Rand al'Thor has called them to the Heart of the Stone."

Perrin only grunted, but he hoped Moiraine had been among those summoned. He wondered whether this was Rand's way of helping him escape her. Whatever the reason, he was glad enough to take advantage of it.

They stepped out of the last cramped stairway onto the ground floor of the Stone, where cavernous hallways as wide as roads led to all the outer gates. There were no wall hangings here. Black iron lamps in iron brackets high on the walls lit the windowless passages, and the floor was paved with broad, rough stones able to stand long wear from horses' shod hooves. Perrin picked his pace up to a trot. The stables lay just in sight ahead down the great tunnel, the wide Dragonwall Gate itself standing open beyond and only a handful of Defenders for guard. Moiraine could not intercept them now, not without the Dark One's own luck.

The stable's open doorway was an arch fifteen paces across. Perrin took one step inside and stopped.

The air was heavy with the smell of straw and hay, underlaid with grain and oats, leather and horse manure. Stalls filled with fine Tairen horses, prized everywhere, lined the walls, with more in rows across the wide floor. Dozens of grooms were at work, currying and combing, mucking out, mending tack. Without pausing, one or another sometimes glanced at where Faile and Loial stood, booted and ready for travel. And beside them, Bain and Chiad, accoutered like Gaul with weapons and blankets, water bottles and cooking pot.

"Are they why you only said you would try?" Perrin asked quietly.

Gaul shrugged. "I will do what I can, but they will take her side. Chiad is Goshien."

"Her clan makes a difference?"

"Her clan and mine have blood feud, Perrin, and I am no spear-sister to her. But perhaps the water oaths will hold her. I will not dance spears with her unless she offers."

Perrin shook his head. A strange people. What were water oaths? What he said, though, was "Why are they with her?"

"Bain says they wish to see more of your lands, but I think it is the argument between you and Faile which fascinates them. They like her, and when they heard of this journey, they decided to go with her instead of you."

"Well, as long as they keep her out of trouble." He was surprised when Gaul threw back his head and laughed. It made him scratch his beard worriedly.

Loial came toward them, long eyebrows sagging anxiously. His coat pockets bulged, as was usual when he was traveling, mainly with the angular shapes of books. At least his limp seemed better. "Faile is becoming impatient, Perrin. I think she might insist on leaving any minute. Please hurry. You could not even find the Waygate without me.

Not that you should try, certainly. You humans make me leap about so I can hardly find my own head. Please hurry."

"I will not leave him," Faile called. "Not even if he is yet too stubborn and foolish to ask a simple favor. Should that be the case, he may still follow me like a lost puppy. I promise to scratch his ears and take care of him." The Aiel women doubled over laughing.

Gaul leaped straight up suddenly, kicking higher, two paces or more above the floor, while twirling one of his spears. "We will follow like stalking ridgecats," he shouted, "like hunting wolves." He landed easily, lightly. Loial stared at him in amazement.

Bain, on the other hand, lazily combed her short, fiery hair with her fingers. "I have a fine wolfskin with my bedding in the hold," she told Chiad in a bored voice. "Wolves are easily taken."

A growl rose in Perrin's throat, pulling both women's eyes to him. For a moment Bain looked on the point of saying something more, but she frowned at his yellow stare and held her peace, not afraid, but suddenly wary.

"This puppy is not well housebroken yet," Faile confided to the Aiel women.

Perrin refused to look at her. Instead he went to the stall that held his dun stallion, as tall as any of the Tairen animals but heavier in shoulder and haunch. Waving away a groom, he bridled Stepper and led him out himself. The grooms had walked the horse, of course, but he had been confined enough to frisk in the quick steps that had made Perrin give him his name. Perrin soothed him with the sure confidence of a man who had shoed many horses. It was no trouble at all putting his high-cantled saddle on and lashing his saddlebags and blanket roll behind.

Gaul watched with no expression. He would not ride a horse unless he had to, and then not a step farther than absolutely necessary. None of the Aiel would. Perrin did not understand why. Pride, perhaps, in their ability to run for long distances. The Aiel made it seem more than that, but he suspected none of them could have explained.

The packhorse had to be readied too, of course, but that was quickly done, since everything Gaul had ordered was waiting in a neat pile. Food and waterskins. Oats and grain for the horses. None of that would be available in the Ways. A few other things, like hobbles, some horse medicines just in case, spare tinderbox and such. Most of the space in the wicker hampers went for leather bottles like those the Aiel used for water, only larger and filled with lamp oil. Once the lanterns, on long poles, were strapped atop the rest, it was done.

Thrusting his unstrung bow under the saddle girth, he swung up into Stepper's saddle with the pack animal's lead in hand. And then had to wait, seething.

Loial was already mounted, on a huge, hairy-fetlocked horse, taller than any other in the stable by hands yet reduced nearly to pony size by the Ogier's long legs hanging down. There had been a time when the Ogier was almost as unwilling a rider as the Aiel, but he was at home on a horse now. It was Faile who took her time, examining her mount almost as if she had never seen the glossy black mare before, though Perrin knew she had put the horse through her paces before buying, soon after they came to the Stone. The horse, Swallow by name, was a fine animal of Tairen breeding, with slender ankles and an arched neck, a prancer with the look of speed and endurance both, though shod too lightly for Perrin's taste. Those shoes would not last. It was all another effort to put him in his place, whatever she thought that was.

When Faile finally mounted, in her narrow divided skirts, she reined closer to Perrin. She rode well, woman and horse moving as one. "Why can you not ask, Perrin?" she said softly. "You tried to keep me away from where I belong, so now you have to ask. Can such a simple thing be so difficult?"

The Stone rang like a monstrous bell, the stable floor leaping, the ceiling quivering on the point of coming down. Stepper leaped, too, screaming, head flailing; it was all Perrin could do to keep his seat. Grooms scrambled off the floor where they had fallen and ran desperately to quiet horses rearing, shrieking, attempting to climb out of their stalls. Loial clung to the neck of his huge mount, but Faile sat Swallow surely as the mare danced and squealed wildly.

Rand. Perrin knew it was him. The pull of *ta'veren* dragged at him, two whirlpools in a stream drawing one another. Coughing in the falling dust, he shook his head as hard as he could, straining not to dismount and run back up into the Stone. "We ride!" he shouted while tremors still shook the fortress. "We ride now, Loial! Now!"

Faile seemed to see no more point to delay; she heeled her mare out of the stable beside Loial's taller horse, their two pack animals pulled along, all galloping before they reached the Dragonwall Gate. The Defenders took one look and scattered, some still on hands and knees; it was their duty to keep people out of the Stone, and they had no orders to keep these in. Not that they would necessarily have been able to think straight enough to do so if they had had orders, not with the tremors just subsiding and the Stone still groaning above them.

Perrin was right behind with his own packhorse, wishing the Ogier's animal could run faster, wishing he could leave Loial's lumbering mount behind and outrun the suction trying to draw him back, that pull of *ta'veren* to *ta'veren*. They galloped together through the streets of Tear, toward the rising sun, barely slowing to avoid carts and carriages. Men in tight coats and women with layered aprons, still shaken by the upheaval, stared at them, dazed, sometimes barely leaping out of the way.

At the walls of the inner city paving stones gave way to dirt, shoes and coats to bare feet and bare chests above baggy breeches held up by broad sashes. The folk here dodged no less assiduously, though, for Perrin would not let Stepper slow until they had galloped past the city's outer wall, past the simple stone houses and shops that clustered outside the city proper, into a countryside of scattered farms and thickets and beyond the pull of *ta'veren*. Only then, breathing almost as hard as his lathered horse, he reined Stepper to a walk.

Loial's ears were stiff with shock. Faile licked her lips and stared from the Ogier to Perrin, white-faced. "What happened? Was that . . . him?"

"I don't know," Perrin lied. *I have to go, Rand. You know that. You looked me in the face when I told you, and said I had to do what I thought I must.*

"Where are Bain and Chiad?" Faile said. "It will take them an hour to catch up now. I wish they would ride. I offered to buy them horses, and they looked offended. Well, we need to walk the horses anyway after that, to let them cool down."

Perrin held back from telling her she did not know as much of Aiel as she thought she did. He could see the city walls behind them, and the Stone rearing above like a mountain. He could even make out the sinuous shape on the banner waving over the fortress, and the displaced birds swirling about; neither of the others could have. It was no difficulty at all to see three people running toward them in long, ground-eating strides, their flowing ease belying the pace. He did not think he could have run that fast, not for long, but the Aiel had to have maintained their speed from the Stone to be this close behind.

"We'll not have to wait that long," he said.

Faile frowned back toward the city. "Is that them? Are you certain?" Abruptly the frown shifted to him for a moment, daring him to answer. Asking him had been too much like admitting he was part of her party, of course. "He is very boastful of his eyesight," she told Loial, "but his memory is not very good. At times I think he would forget to light a candle at night if I did not remind him. I expect he's seen some poor family running from what they think is an earthquake, don't you?"

Loial shifted uncomfortably in his saddle, sighing heavily, and muttered something about humans that Perrin doubted was complimentary. Faile did not notice, of course.

Not too many minutes later, Faile stared at Perrin as the three Aiel drew close enough for her to make out, but she said nothing. In this mood, she was not about to admit he had been right about anything, not if he said the sky was blue. The Aiel were not even breathing hard when they slowed to a halt beside the horses.

"It is too bad it was not a longer run." Bain shared a smile with Chiad, and both gave Gaul a sly look.

"Else we could have run this Stone Dog into the ground," Chiad said as if finishing the other woman's sentence. "That is why Stone Dogs take their vows not to retreat. Stone bones and stone heads make them too heavy to run."

Gaul took no offense, though Perrin noticed he stood where he could keep an eye on Chiad. "Do you know why Maidens are so often used as scouts, Perrin? Because they can run so far. And that comes from being afraid some man might want to marry them. A Maiden will run a hundred miles to avoid that."

"Very wise of them," Faile said tartly. "Do you need to rest?" she asked the Aiel women, and looked surprised when they denied it. She turned to Loial anyway. "Are you ready to go on? Good. Find me this Waygate, Loial. We have stayed here too long. If you let a stray puppy stay close to you, it begins to think you will take care of it, and that will never do."

"Faile," Loial protested, "are you not carrying this too far?"

"I will carry it as far as I must, Loial. The Waygate?"

Ears sagging, Loial puffed out a heavy breath and turned his horse eastward again. Perrin let him and Faile get a dozen paces ahead before he and Gaul followed. He must play by her rules, but he would play them at least as well as she.

The farms, cramped little places with rough stone houses Perrin would not have used to shelter animals, grew more scattered the farther east they rode, and the thickets smaller, until there were neither farms nor thickets, only a rolling, hilly grassland. Grass as far as the eye could see, unbroken except for patches of bush here and there on a hill.

Horses dotted the green slopes, too, in clumps of a dozen or herds of a hundred, the famed Tairen stock. Large or small, each gathering of horses was under the eyes of a shoeless boy or two, mounted bareback. The boys carried long-handled whips that they used to keep the horses together, or turn them, cracking the whips expertly to turn a stray without ever coming close to the animal's hide. They kept their charges clear of the strangers, moving them back if necessary, but they watched the passage of this odd company—two humans and an Ogier mounted, plus three of the fierce Aiel that stories said had taken the Stone—with the bold curiosity of the young.

It was all a pleasing sight to Perrin. He liked horses. Part of the reason he had asked to be apprenticed to Master Luhhan had been the chance to work with horses, not that there were so many as this in Emond's Field, nor so fine.

Not so Loial. The Ogier began muttering to himself, louder the farther they rode across the grassy hills, until at last he burst out in a deep bass rumble. "Gone! All gone, and for what? Grass. Once this was an Ogier grove. We did no great works here, not to compare with Manetheren, or the city you call Caemlyn, but enough that a grove was planted. Trees of every kind, from every land and place. The Great Trees, towering a hundred spans into the sky. All tended devotedly, to remind my people of the *stedding* they had left to build things for men. Men think it is the stonework we prize, but that is a trifling thing, learned during the Long Exile, after the Breaking. It is the trees we love. Men thought Manetheren my people's greatest triumph, but we knew it to be the grove there. Gone, now. Like this. Gone, and it will not come again."

Loial stared at the hills, bare save for grass and horses, with a hard face, his ears drawn back tight to his head. He smelled of . . . fury. Peaceful, most stories called Ogier, almost as pacific as the Traveling People, but some, a few, named them implacable enemies. Perrin had only seen Loial angry once before. Perhaps he had been angry last night, defending those children. Looking at Loial's face, an old saying came back to him. "To anger the Ogier and pull the mountains down on your head." Everyone took its meaning as to try to do something that was impossible. Perrin thought maybe the meaning had changed with the years. Maybe in the beginning, it had been "Anger the Ogier, and you pull the mountains down on your head." Difficult to do, but deadly if accomplished. He did not think he would ever want Loial—gentle, fumbling Loial with his broad nose always in a book—to become angry with him.

It was Loial who took the lead once they reached the site of the vanished Ogier grove, bending their path a little southward. There were no landmarks, but he was sure of his direction, surer with every pace of the horses. Ogier could feel a Waygate, sense it somehow, find it as certainly as a bee could find the hive. When Loial finally dismounted, the grass was little more than knee-high on him. There was only a thick clump of brush to be seen, taller than most, leafy shrubs as tall as the Ogier. He ripped it all away almost regretfully, stacking it to one side. "Perhaps the boys with the horses can use it for firewood when it dries."

And there was the Waygate.

Rearing against the side of the hill, it appeared more a length of gray wall than a gate, and the wall of a palace at that, thickly carved in leaves and vines so finely done that they seemed almost as alive as the bushes had been. Three thousand years at least it had stood there, but not a trace of weathering marred its surface. Those leaves could have rippled with the next breeze.

For a moment they all stared at it silently, until Loial took a deep breath and put his hand on the one leaf that was different from any other on the Waygate. The trefoil leaf of *Avendesora,* the fabled Tree of Life. Until the moment his huge hand touched it, it seemed as much a part of the carving as all the rest, but it came away easily.

Faile gasped loudly, and even the Aiel murmured. The air was full of the smell of unease; there was no saying who it came from. All of them, perhaps.

The stone leaves did seem to stir from an unfelt breeze now; they took a tinge of green, of life. Slowly a split appeared down the middle, and the halves of the Waygate opened out, revealing not the hill behind, but a dull shimmering that faintly reflected their images.

"Once, it is said," Loial murmured, "the Waygates shone like mirrors, and those who walked the Ways walked through the sun and the sky. Gone, now. Like this grove."

Hastily pulling one of the filled pole-lanterns from his packhorse, Perrin got it alight. "It is too hot out here," he said. "A little shade would be good." He booted Stepper toward the Waygate. He thought he heard Faile gasp again.

The dun stallion balked, approaching his own dim reflection, but Perrin heeled him onward. Slowly, he remembered. It should be done slowly. The horse's nose touched its image hesitantly, then merged in as though walking into a mirror. Perrin moved closer to himself, touched. . . . Icy cold slid along his skin, enveloping him hair by hair; time stretched out.

The cold vanished like a pricked bubble, and he was in the midst of endless blackness, the light of his pole-lantern a crushed pool around him. Stepper and the packhorse whickered nervously.

Gaul stepped through calmly and began preparing another lantern. Behind him was what seemed like a sheet of smoked glass. The others were visible out there, Loial getting back on his horse, Faile gathering her reins, all of them creeping, barely moving. Time was different inside the Ways.

"Faile is upset with you," Gaul said once he had his lantern alight. It did not add much illumination. The darkness drank in light, swallowed it. "She seems to think you have broken some sort of agreement. Bain and Chiad. . . . Do not let them get you alone. They mean to teach you a lesson, for Faile's sake, and you will not sit on that animal so easily if they manage what they plan."

"I agreed to nothing, Gaul. I do what she's forced me to do through trickery. We will have to follow Loial as she wants soon enough, but I mean to take the lead for as long as I can." He pointed to a thick white line under Stepper's hooves. Broken and heavily pitted, it led off ahead, vanishing in the blackness only a few feet away. "That leads to the first guidepost. We will need to wait there for Loial to read it and decide which bridge to take, but Faile can follow us that far."

"Bridge," Gaul murmured thoughtfully. "I know that word. There is water in here?"

"No. It isn't exactly that kind of bridge. They look the same, sort of, but. . . . Maybe Loial can explain it."

The Aielman scratched his head. "Do you know what you are doing, Perrin?"

"No," Perrin admitted, "but there's no reason for Faile to know that."

Gaul laughed. "It is fun to be so young, is it not, Perrin?"

Frowning, uncertain whether the man was laughing at him, Perrin heeled Stepper on, drawing the packhorse behind. The lantern light would not be visible at all in here twenty or thirty paces from its edge. He wanted to be completely out of sight before Faile came through. Let her think he had decided to go on without her. If she worried for a few minutes, until she found him at the guidepost, it was the least she deserved.

CHAPTER
19

The Wavedancer

With the golden sun barely over the horizon, the shiny black-lacquered carriage rocked to a halt at the foot of the wharf behind a team of four matched grays, and the lanky dark-haired driver in his black-and-gold striped coat leaped down to open the door. No sigil adorned the door panel, of course; Tairen nobles gave aid to Aes Sedai only under duress, no matter how effusive the smiles, and none wanted their names or houses linked to the Tower.

Elayne got down gratefully without waiting for Nynaeve, straightening her blue linen summer traveling cloak; the streets of the Maule were rutted by carts and wagons, and the carriage's leather springs had not been very good. A breeze slanting across the Erinin actually seemed cool after the heat of the Stone. She had intended to show no effects of the rough ride, but once upright she could not help knuckling the small of her back. *At least last night's rain still holds the dust down,* she thought. She suspected that they had been given a carriage without curtains on purpose.

North and south of her, more docks like wide stone fingers stretched into the river. The air smelled of tar and rope, fish and spices and olive oil, of nameless things rotting in the stagnant water between the piers and peculiar long yellow-green fruits in huge bunches heaped in front of the stone warehouse behind her. Despite the early hour, men wearing leather vests on shirtless shoulders scurried about, toting large bundles on bent backs or pushing handcarts piled with barrels or crates. None spared her more than a passing sullen glance, dark eyes falling quickly, forelock touched grudgingly; most did not raise their heads at all. She was sad to see it.

These Tairen nobles had handled their people badly. Mishandled them was more like it. In Andor she could have expected cheerful smiles and a respectful word of greeting, freely given by straight-backed men who knew their worth as well as hers. It was almost enough to make her regret leaving. She had been raised to lead and one day govern a proud people, and she felt the urge to teach these folk dignity. But that was Rand's job, not hers. *And if he doesn't do it properly, I* will *give him a piece of my mind. A bigger piece.* At least he had begun, by following her advice. And she had to admit he knew how to treat his people. It would be interesting to see what he had done by the time she returned. *If there's a point to coming back.*

A dozen ships were clearly visible from where she stood, and more beyond, but one, moored across the end of the dock she faced, sharp bow upriver, filled her eyes. The Sea Folk raker was easily a hundred paces long, half again as large as the next vessel in sight, with three great towering masts amidships, and one shorter on the raised deck at the stern. She had been on ships before, but never one so big, and never on one going to sea. Just the name of the ship's owners spoke of distant lands and strange ports. The Atha'an Miere. The Sea Folk. Stories meant to be exotic always contained the Sea Folk, unless they were about the Aiel.

Nynaeve climbed out of the carriage behind her, tying a green traveling cloak at her neck and grumbling to herself and to the driver. "Tumbled about like a hen in a windstorm! Thumped like a dusty rug! How did you manage to find every last rut and hole between here and the Stone, goodman? That took true skill. A pity none of it goes into handling horses." He tried to hand her down, his narrow face sullen, but she refused his aid.

Sighing, Elayne doubled the number of silver pennies she was taking from her purse. "Thank you for bringing us safely and swiftly." She smiled as she pressed the coins into his hand. "We told you to go fast, and you did as we asked. The streets are not your fault, and you did an excellent job under poor conditions."

Without looking at the coins, the fellow gave her a deep bow, a grateful look, and a murmured "Thank you, my Lady," as much for the words as the money, she was sure. She had found that a kind word and a little praise were usually received as well as silver was, if not better. Though the silver itself was seldom unappreciated, to be sure.

"The Light send you a safe journey, my Lady," he added. The merest flicker of his eyes toward Nynaeve said that wish was for Elayne alone. Nynaeve had to learn how to make allowances and give consideration; truly she did.

When the driver had handed their bundles and belongings out of the carriage, turned his team and started away, Nynaeve said grudgingly, "I shouldn't have snapped at the man, I suppose. A bird could not make an easy way over those streets. Not in a carriage, at any rate. But after bouncing about all the way here, I feel as if I'd been on horseback a week."

"It isn't his fault you have a sore . . . back," Elayne said, with a smile to take away any sting, as she took up her things.

Nynaeve barked a wry laugh. "I said that, didn't I? You will not expect me to go running after him to apologize, I hope. That handful of silver you gave him should soothe any wounds short of mortal. You really must learn to be more careful with money, Elayne. We do not have the Realm of Andor's resources for our own use. A family could live comfortably for a month on what you hand out to everyone who does the work they've been paid to do for you." Elayne gave her a quietly indignant look—Nynaeve always seemed to think they should live worse than servants unless there was reason not to, instead of the other way around, as made sense—but the older woman did not appear to notice the expression that always put Royal Guardsmen on their toes. Instead, Nynaeve hoisted her bundles and sturdy cloth bags and turned down the dock. "At least this ship will be a smoother ride than that. I do hope smooth. Shall we go aboard?"

As they picked their way down the pier, between working men and stacked barrels and carts full of goods, Elayne said, "Nynaeve, the Sea Folk can be touchy until they know you, or so I was taught. Do you think you might try to be a little . . . ?"

"A little what?"

"Tactful, Nynaeve." Elayne skipped a step as someone spat on the dock in front of her. There was no telling which fellow had done it; when she looked around they all had their heads down and were hard at work. Mishandling by the High Lords or no, she would have said a few quietly sharp words that the culprit would not have soon forgotten if she could have found him. "You might try to be a little tactful for once."

"Of course." Nynaeve started up the raker's rope-railed gangway. "As long as they do not bounce me about."

Elayne's first thought on reaching the deck was that the raker appeared very narrow for its length; she did not know a great deal about ships, in truth, but to her it seemed a huge splinter. *Oh, Light, this thing will toss worse than the carriage, however big it is.* Her second was for the crew. She had heard stories about the Atha'an Miere, but had never seen one before. Even the stories told little, really. A secretive people who kept to themselves, almost as mysterious as the Aiel. Only the lands beyond the Waste could possibly be more strange, and all anyone knew of them was that the Sea Folk brought ivory and silk from there.

These Atha'an Miere were dark, barefoot and bare-chested men, all cleanly shaven, with straight black hair and tattooed hands, moving with the sureness of those who knew their tasks well enough to do them with half a mind but were putting their whole minds to it. There was a rolling grace to their movements, as though, with the ship still, they yet felt the motions of the sea. Most wore gold or silver chains around their necks, and rings in their ears, sometimes two or three in each, and some with polished stones.

There were women among the crew, too, as many as the men, hauling ropes and coiling lines right with the men, with the same tattooed hands, in the same baggy breeches of some dark, oiled cloth, held by colorful narrow sashes and hanging open at the ankle. But the women wore loose colorful blouses, too, all brilliant reds and blues and greens, and they had at least as many chains and earrings as the men. Including, Elayne noticed with a small shock, two or three women with rings in one side of their noses.

The grace of the women outshone even that of the men, and put Elayne in mind of some stories she had heard as a child by listening where she was not supposed to. Women of the Atha'an Miere were, in those tales, the epitome of alluring beauty and temptation, pursued by all men. The women on this ship were no more beautiful than any others, really, but watching them move, she could believe those tales.

Two of the women, on the raised deck at the stern, were obviously not ordinary crew. They were barefoot, too, and their garb of the same cut, but one was clothed entirely in brocaded blue silks, the other in green. The older of the pair, the one in green, wore four small gold rings in each ear and one in the left side of her nose, all worked so they sparkled in the morning sunlight. A fine chain ran from her tiny nose ring to one earring, supporting a row of tiny dangling gold medallions, and one of the chains around her neck held a pierced golden box, like ornate gold lace, that she lifted to sniff from time to time. The other woman, the taller, had only six earrings in total, and fewer medallions. The pierced box she sniffed at was just as finely wrought gold, though. Exotic, indeed. Elayne winced just thinking about the nose rings. And that chain!

Something odd about the sterndeck itself caught her eye, but at first she could not tell what. Then she saw. There was no tiller for the rudder. Some sort of spoked wheel stood behind the women, lashed down so it could not turn, but no tiller. *How do they steer?* The smallest riverboat she had seen had had a tiller. There had been tillers on all the others ships lining the nearby docks. More and more mysterious, these Sea Folk.

"Remember what Moiraine told you," she cautioned as they approached the sterndeck. That had not been much; even Aes Sedai knew little about the Atha'an Miere. Moiraine had imparted the proper phrasings, though; the things that had to be said for good manners. "And remember tact," she added in a firm whisper.

"I will remember," Nynaeve replied sharply. "I can be tactful." Elayne truly hoped she would.

The two Sea Folk women waited for them at the top of the stairs— ladder, Elayne remembered, even when they were stairs. She did not understand why ships had to have different names for common things. A floor was a floor, in a barn or an inn or a palace. Why not on a ship? A cloud of perfume surrounded the two, a slightly musky scent, wafting from the lacy gold boxes. The tattoos on their hands were stars and seabirds surrounded by the curls and whirls of stylized waves.

Nynaeve inclined her head. "I am Nynaeve al'Meara, Aes Sedai of the Green Ajah. I seek the Sailmistress of this vessel, and passage, if it pleases the Light. This is my companion and friend, Elayne Trakand, also Aes Sedai of the Green Ajah. The Light illumine you and your vessel, and send the winds to speed you." That was almost exactly the way Moiraine had instructed them to speak. Not about Aes Sedai of the Green Ajah—Moiraine had seemed resigned to that more than anything else, and amused at their choice of ajah—but the rest.

The older woman, with gray touches in her black hair and fine wrinkles at the corners of her large brown eyes, inclined her head just as formally. Nevertheless, she seemed to be taking them in from head to foot, especially the Great Serpent ring each wore on her right hand. "I am Coine din Jubai Wild Winds, Sailmistress of *Wavedancer.* This is Jorin din Jubai White Wing, my sister of the blood and Windfinder of

Wavedancer. There may be passage available, if it pleases the Light. The Light illumine you, and see you safe to your journey's end."

It was a surprise that the two were sisters. Elayne could see the resemblance, but Jorin looked much younger. She wished the Windfinder were the one they had to deal with; both women had the same reserve, but something about the Windfinder reminded her of Aviendha. It was absurd, of course. These women were no taller than she herself, their coloring could not have been more different from the Aiel woman's, and the only weapon either had in sight was the stout knife tucked in her sash, looking very workmanlike despite carvings and gold-wire inlays on the handle. But Elayne could not help feeling some similarity, between Jorin and Aviendha, anyway.

"Let us talk then, Sailmistress, if it pleases you," Nynaeve said, following Moiraine's formula, "of sailings and ports, and the gift of passage." The Sea Folk did not charge for passage, according to Moiraine; it was a gift, which just coincidentally would be exchanged for a gift of equal value.

Coine glanced away, then, astern toward the Stone and the white banner rippling over it. "We will talk in my cabin, Aes Sedai, if it pleases you." She motioned toward an open hatch behind that strange wheel. "The welcome of my ship to you, and the grace of the Light be upon you until you leave his decks."

Another narrow ladder—staircase—led down into a neat room, larger and taller than Elayne had expected from her experiences on smaller vessels, with windows across the stern and gimbaled lamps on the walls. Almost everything seemed to have been built into the room except for a few lacquered chests of various sizes. The bed was large and low, right under the sternwindows, and a narrow table surrounded by armchairs stood across the middle of the room.

There was very little clutter. Rolled charts lay on the table, a few ivory carvings of strange animals stood on railed shelves, and half a dozen bare-bladed swords of different shapes, some that Elayne had never seen before, rested on hooks on the walls. An oddly worked square brass gong hung from a beam over the bed, while right before the sternwindows, as if in a place of honor, a helmet sat on a featureless wooden head carved for the purpose, a helmet like the head of some monstrous insect, lacquered in red and green, with a narrow white plume to either side, one broken.

The helmet Elayne recognized. "Seanchan," she gasped before thinking. Nynaeve gave her a vexed look, and deservedly; they had agreed it would make more sense, and ring more true, if Nynaeve, as the older, took the lead and did most of the talking.

Coine and Jorin exchanged unreadable glances. "You know of them?" the Sailmistress said. "Of course. One must expect Aes Sedai to know these things. This far east we hear a score of stories, the truest less than half-true."

Elayne knew she should leave it at that, but curiosity tickled her tongue. "How did you come by the helmet? If I may ask."

"*Wavedancer* encountered a Seanchan ship last year," Coine replied. "They wished to take him, but I did not wish to give him up." She shrugged slightly. "I have the helmet to remind me, and the sea took the Seanchan, the Light be merciful to all who sail. I will not go close to a vessel with ribbed sails again."

"You were lucky," Nynaeve said curtly. "The Seanchan hold captive women who can channel, and make them channel as a weapon. If they had had one on that ship, you would be regretting ever having seen it."

Elayne grimaced at her, though it was too late. She could not tell whether Sea Folk women were offended by Nynaeve's tone. The pair kept the same neutral expressions, but Elayne was beginning to realize they did not show very much on their faces, not to strangers, anyway.

"Let us speak of passage," Coine said. "If it pleases the Light, we may call where you wish to go. All things are possible, in the Light. Let us sit."

The chairs around the table did not slide back; they and the table were fastened to the floor—deck. Instead the arms swung out like gates and latched in place once you had sat. The arrangement seemed to bear out Elayne's dire predictions of heaving and pitching. She did very well with it herself, of course, but too much rolling on a riverboat set Nynaeve's stomach jumping. It must be worse on the ocean than on a river, however fierce the wind, and the worse Nynaeve's stomach, the worse her temper. Nynaeve sicking up and in a bad choler at the same time: there were few things more dreadful, in Elayne's experience.

She and Nynaeve were placed together on one side of the table, with the Sailmistress and the Windfinder at the ends. At first it seemed strange, until she realized they would both look at whichever of the two was talking, allowing the other to watch them unobserved. *Do they always deal with passengers this way, or is it because we're Aes Sedai? Well, because they think we are.* It was a caution that everything might not be as simple as they hoped with these people. She hoped Nynaeve was taking notice.

Elayne had not seen any order passed, but a slender young woman with only one ring in each ear appeared, bearing a tray with a square white brass-handled teapot and large handleless cups, not of Sea Folk porcelain as might have been expected, but thick pottery. Less likely to be broken in heavy weather, she decided bleakly. It was the young woman who took her attention, though, and nearly brought a gasp. She was bare to the waist, just like the men above. Elayne hid her shock very well, she thought, but Nynaeve sniffed loudly.

The Sailmistress waited until the girl had poured tea brewed to blackness, then said, "Have we sailed, Dorele, when I did not see? Is there no land in sight?"

The slender woman blushed furiously. "There is land, Sailmistress." It was a miserable whisper.

Coine nodded. "Until there is no land in sight, and has been none for one full day, you will work at cleaning the bilges, where garments are a hindrance. You may leave."

"Yes, Sailmistress," the girl said, even more woefully. She turned away, undoing her red sash dejectedly as she went through the door at the far end of the room.

"Share this tea, if it please you," the Sailmistress said, "that we may talk in peace." She sipped at her own and continued while Elayne and Nynaeve were tasting theirs. "I ask that you forgive any offense, Aes Sedai. This is Dorele's first voyage except between the islands. The young often forget the ways of the shorebound. I will punish her further, if you are affronted."

"There is no need," Elayne said hastily, taking the excuse to set her cup down. The tea was even stronger than it looked, very hot, unsweetened and quite bitter. "Truly, we were not offended. There are different ways among different peoples." *The Light send not too many more as different as that! Light, what if they don't wear any clothes at all once they get out to sea? Light!* "Only a fool takes offense at customs different from her own."

Nynaeve gave her a level look, bland enough for the Aes Sedai they were pretending to be, and took a deep swallow from her cup. All she said was "Please think no more of it." It was not possible to tell if she meant it for Elayne or the Sea Folk women.

"Then we will speak of passage, if it pleases you," Coine said. "To what port do you wish to sail?"

"Tanchico," Nynaeve said, a bit more briskly than she should have. "I know you may not mean to sail there, but we need to go quickly, as quickly as only a raker can, and without stopping, if that is possible. I offer this small gift, for the inconvenience." She took a paper from her belt pouch and unfolded it, pushing it down the table to the Sailmistress.

Moiraine had given that to them, and another like it, letters-of-rights. Each allowed the bearer to draw up to three thousand gold crowns from bankers and moneylenders in various cities, though it was not likely any of those men and women knew it was White Tower money they held. Elayne had goggled at the amount—Nynaeve had gaped openly—but Moiraine said it might be needed to make the Sailmistress forsake her intended ports of call.

Coine touched the letter-of-rights with one finger, read. "A vast sum for the gift of passage," she murmured, "even counting that you ask me to alter my sailing plans. I am more surprised now than before. You know that we very seldom carry Aes Sedai on our ships. Very seldom. Of all who ask passage, only Aes Sedai may be refused, and almost always are, as from the first day of the first sailing. Aes Sedai know this, and so almost never ask." She was looking into her teacup, not at them, but Elayne glanced the other way and caught the Windfinder studying their hands lying on the table. No, their rings.

Moiraine had not said anything about this. She had pointed out the raker as the swiftest ship available and encouraged them to make use of it. Then again, she had given them these letters-of-rights, very likely sufficient to buy a fleet of ships like this one. Well, several ships, at the least. *Because she knew it would take that much to bribe them to carry us?* But why had she kept secrets? A foolish question; Moiraine always kept secrets. But why waste their time?

"Do you mean to refuse us passage?" Nynaeve had abandoned tact for bluntness. "If you do not carry Aes Sedai, why did you bring us down here? Why not tell us up above and be done with it?"

The Sailmistress unlatched one arm of her chair, rose and went to peer out of the sternwindows at the Stone. Her earrings and the medallions across her left cheek glittered in the light of the rising sun. "He can wield the One Power, so I have heard, and he holds the Sword That Cannot Be Touched. The Aiel have come over the Dragonwall to his call; I have seen several in the streets, and it is said they fill the Stone. The Stone of Tear has fallen, and war breaks over the nations of the land. Those who once ruled have returned, and been driven back for the first time. Prophecy is being fulfilled."

Nynaeve looked as confounded as Elayne felt at this change of subject. "The Prophecies of the Dragon?" Elayne said after a moment. "Yes, they are being fulfilled. He is the Dragon Reborn, Sailmistress."

He's a stubborn man who hides his feelings so deeply I cannot find them, that is what he is!

Coine turned. "Not the Prophecies of the Dragon, Aes Sedai. The Jendai Prophecy, the prophecy of the Coramoor. Not the one you wait for and dread; the one we seek, herald of a new Age. At the Breaking of the World our ancestors fled to the safety of the sea while the land heaved and broke as storm waves do. It is said they knew nothing of the ships they took to flee, but the Light was with them, and they survived. They did not see the land again until it was still once more, and by then, much had changed. All—everything—the world—drifted on the water and the wind. It was in the years after that the Jendai Prophecy was first spoken. We must wander the waters until the Coramoor returns, and serve him at his coming.

"We are bound to the sea; the salt water courses in our veins. Most of us set no foot on the land except to await another ship, another sailing. Strong men weep when they must serve ashore. Women ashore go onto a ship to bear their children—into a rowboat if no more is at hand—for we must be born on the water, as we must die on it, and be given to it in death.

"The Prophecy is being fulfilled. He is the Coramoor. Aes Sedai serve him. You are proof of that, that you are here in this city. That is in the Prophecy as well. 'The White Tower shall be broken by his name, and Aes Sedai shall kneel to wash his feet and dry them with their hair.' "

"You will have a long wait if you expect to see me wash any man's feet," Nynaeve said wryly. "What does this have to do with our passage? Will you take us, or not?"

Elayne cringed, but the Sailmistress came back just as directly. "Why do you wish to journey to Tanchico? It is an unpleasant port of call now. I docked there last winter. Shorefolk nearly swarmed my vessel seeking passage out, to anywhere. They did not care, so long as it was away from Tanchico. I cannot believe conditions are any better now."

"Do you always question your passengers so?" Nynaeve said. "I've offered you enough to buy a village. Two villages! If you want more, name your price."

"Not a price," Elayne hissed in her ear. "A gift!"

If Coine was offended, or even had heard, she gave no sign. "Why?"

Nynaeve took a tight grip on her braid, but Elayne laid a hand on her arm. They had planned to keep a few secrets themselves, but surely they had learned enough since sitting down to alter any plan. There was a time for secrecy and a time for truth. "We hunt the Black Ajah,

Sailmistress. We believe some of them are in Tanchico." She met Nynaeve's angry stare calmly. "We must find them, else they may harm . . . the Dragon Reborn. The Coramoor."

"The Light see us safe to docking," the Windfinder breathed. It was the first time she had spoken, and Elayne stared at her in surprise. Jorin was frowning, and not looking at anyone, but she spoke to the Sailmistress. "We can take them, my sister. We must." Coine nodded.

Elayne exchanged looks with Nynaeve and saw her own questions mirrored in the other woman's eyes. Why was it the Windfinder who decided? Why not the Sailmistress? She was the captain, whatever her title. At least they were going to get passage after all. *For how much?* Elayne wondered. *How large a 'gift'?* She wished Nynaeve had not revealed that they had more than was in that one letter-of-rights. *And she accuses me of tossing gold about.*

The door opened and a heavy-shouldered gray-haired man in loose green silk breeches and sash came in, ruffling through a sheaf of papers. Four gold rings decorated each ear, and three heavy gold chains hung at his neck, including one with a perfume box. A long puckered scar down his cheek, and two curved knives tucked in his sash, gave him something of a dangerous air. He was fastening a peculiar wire framework over his ears to hold clear lenses in front of his eyes. The Sea Folk made the best looking glasses and burning lenses and the like, of course, somewhere on their islands, but Elayne had never seen anything like this device. He peered through the lenses at the papers and began talking without looking up.

"Coine, this fool is willing to trade me five hundred snowfox pelts from Kandor for those three small barrels of Two Rivers tabac I got in Ebou Dar. Five hundred! He can have them here by midday." His eyes rose, and he gave a start. "Forgive me, my wife. I did not know you had guests. The Light be with you all."

"By midday, my husband," Coine said, "I will be falling downriver. By nightfall I will be at sea."

He stiffened. "Am I still Cargomaster, wife, or has my place been taken while I did not see?"

"You are Cargomaster, husband, but the trading must stop now and preparations begin for getting under way. We sail for Tanchico."

"Tanchico!" The papers crumpled in his fist, and he brought himself under control with an effort. "Wife—No! Sailmistress, you told me our next port was Mayene, and then eastward to Shara. I have traded with that in mind. Shara, Sailmistress, not Tarabon. What I have in my holds will bring little in Tanchico. Perhaps nothing! May I ask why my trade is to be ruined and *Wavedancer* impoverished?"

Coine hesitated, but when she spoke her voice was still formal. "I am Sailmistress, my husband. *Wavedancer* sails when and where and I say. It must be enough, for now."

"As you say, Sailmistress," he rasped, "so it is." He touched his heart —Elayne thought Coine flinched—and padded out with his back stiff as one of the ship's masts.

"I must make this up to him," Coine murmured softly, staring at the door. "Of course, it is pleasant making up with him. Usually. He saluted me like a deckboy, sister."

"We regret being a cause of trouble, Sailmistress," Elayne said carefully. "And we regret having witnessed this. If we have caused any embarrassment, to anyone, please accept our apologies."

"Embarrassment?" Coine sounded startled. "Aes Sedai, I am Sailmistress. I doubt your presence embarrassed Toram, and I would not apologize to him for that if it did. Trade is his, but I am Sailmistress. I must make up to him—and it will not be easy, since I must keep the reason secret still—because he is right, and I could not think quickly enough to give him a reason beyond what I would give a raw hand. That scar on his face he earned clearing the Seanchan from *Wavedancer*'s decks. He has older scars earned defending my ship, and I have only to put out my hand to have gold placed in it because of his trading. It is the things I cannot tell him I must make up to him, because he deserves to know."

"I do not understand," Nynaeve said. "We would ask you to keep the Black Ajah secret . . ."—she shot a hard look at Elayne, one that promised hard words once they were alone; Elayne intended a few words of her own, about the meaning of tact—"but surely three thousand crowns is reason enough to take us to Tanchico."

"I must keep you secret, Aes Sedai. What you are, and why you travel. Many among my crew consider Aes Sedai bad luck. If they knew they not only carried Aes Sedai, but toward a port where other Aes Sedai may serve the Father of Storms. . . . The grace of the Light shone on us that none was close enough to hear me call you so above. Will it offend if I ask you to keep below as much as possible, and not to wear your rings when on deck?"

For answer, Nynaeve plucked her Great Serpent ring off and dropped it into her pouch. Elayne did the same, a bit more reluctantly; she rather enjoyed having people see her ring. Not quite trusting Nynaeve's remaining store of diplomacy at this point, she spoke up before the other woman could. "Sailmistress, we have offered you a gift of passage, if it pleases you. If it does not, may I ask what would?"

Coine came back to the table to look at the letter-of-rights again, then pushed it back to Nynaeve. "I do this for the Coramoor. I will see you safe ashore where you wish, if it pleases the Light. It shall be done." She touched the fingers of her right hand to her lips. "It is agreed, under the Light."

Jorin made a strangled sound. "My sister, has a Cargomaster ever mutinied against his Sailmistress?"

Coine gave her a flat-eyed stare. "I will put in the gift of passage from my own chest. And if Toram ever hears of it, my sister, I will put you in the bilges with Dorele. For ballast, perhaps."

That the two Sea Folk women had dropped formality was confirmed when the Windfinder laughed aloud. "And then your next port would be in Chachin, my sister, or Caemlyn, for you could not find the water without me."

The Sailmistress addressed Elayne and Nynaeve regretfully. "Properly, Aes Sedai, since you serve the Coramoor, I should honor you as I would Sailmistress and Windfinder of another ship. We should bathe together and drink honeyed wine and tell each other stories to make ourselves laugh and weep. But I must make ready to sail, and—"

Wavedancer rose like his name, leaping, pounding against the dock. Elayne whipped back and forth in her chair, wondering as it continued whether this was really better than being thrown to the deck.

Then, finally, it was over, the leaps slowing, growing smaller. Coine scrambled to her feet and raced for the ladder, Jorin at her heels, already shouting orders to look for damage to the hull.

CHAPTER
20

Winds Rising

E layne struggled to open the latch on an arm of her chair and
darted after them, almost colliding with Nynaeve at the ladder.
The ship still rocked, if not as violently as before. Uncertain
whether they were sinking, she pushed Nynaeve ahead of her, prodding
her to climb faster.

On the deck the crew dashed about, checking the rigging or peering
over the side to inspect the hull, shouting about earthquakes. The same
shouts were rising from the dockmen, too, but Elayne knew better,
despite the tumbled things on the piers and the ships yet pitching at
their moorings.

She stared toward the Stone. The huge fortress was still except for
masses of startled birds swirling about and that pale banner waving,
almost lazily, in an isolated breeze. No sign that anything had ever
touched the mountainous mass. That had been Rand, though. She was
sure of it.

She turned to find Nynaeve looking at her, and for a long moment
their eyes met. "A fine pickling, if he's damaged the ship," Elayne said
finally. "How are we supposed to get to Tanchico if he goes tossing all
the ships about?" *Light, he has to be all right. I can do nothing if he isn't.
He is all right. He is.*

Nynaeve touched her arm reassuringly. "No doubt that second letter of yours touched a nerve. Men always overreact when they let their emotions go; it's the price for holding them in the way they do. He may be the Dragon Reborn, but he must learn, man to woman, that— What are *they* doing here?"

"They" were two men standing amid the bustling Sea Folk on the deck. One was Thom Merrilin, in his gleeman's cloak, with leather-cased harp and flute on his back and a bundle lying at his feet beside a battered wooden box with a lock. The other was a lean handsome Tairen in his middle years, a hard dark man wearing a flat conical straw hat and one of those commoner's coats that fit snugly to the waist, then flared like a short skirt. A notched sword-breaker hung at a belt worn over his coat, and he leaned on a pale staff of nobbly, jointed wood exactly his own height and no thicker than his thumb. A square-tied parcel dangled by a loop from his shoulder. Elayne knew him: his name was Juilin Sandar.

It was obvious the two men were strangers despite standing almost side by side; they held themselves with stiff reticence. Their attentions were directed the same way, though, split between following the Sailmistress's progress toward the sterndeck and peering at Elayne and Nynaeve, plainly uncertain and masking it behind a brisk show of confidence. Thom grinned and stroked his long white mustaches and nodded every time he looked up at the two of them; Sandar made solemn, self-assured bows.

"He is not damaged," Coine said, climbing the ladder. "I can sail within the hour, if it pleases you. Well within, if a Tairen pilot can be found. I will sail without him, if not, though it means never returning to Tear." She followed their gaze to the two men. "They ask passage, the gleeman to Tanchico, and the thief-catcher to wherever you travel. I cannot refuse them, and yet. . . ." Her dark eyes came back to Elayne and Nynaeve. "I will do so, if you ask it." Reluctance to break custom battled in her voice with. . . . Desire to help them? To serve the Coramoor? "The thief-catcher is a good man, even considering that he is shorebound. No offense to you, under the Light. The gleeman I do not know, yet a gleeman can enliven a voyage and lighten tired hours."

"You know Master Sandar?" Nynaeve said.

"Twice he has found those who pilfered from us, and found them quickly. Another shoreman would have taken longer so he might ask more for the work. It is obvious that you know him, as well. Do you wish me to refuse passage?" Her reluctance was still there.

"Let us see why they are here first," Nynaeve said in a flat voice that did not bode well for either man.

"Perhaps I should do the talking," Elayne suggested, gently but firmly. "That way, you can watch to see if they are hiding anything." She did not say that that way Nynaeve's temper would not get the better of her, but the wry smile the other woman gave her said she had heard it anyway.

"Very well, Elayne. I will watch them. Perhaps you might study how I keep calm. You know how you are when you become overwrought."

Elayne had to laugh.

The two men straightened as she and Nynaeve approached. Around them the crew bustled, swarming into the rigging, hauling ropes, lashing some things down and unlashing others, to orders relayed from the Sailmistress. They moved around the four shorepeople with barely a glance.

Elayne frowned at Thom Merrilin thoughtfully. She was sure she had never seen the gleeman before his appearance in the Stone, yet even then she had been struck by something familiar about him. Not that that was likely. Gleemen were village performers, in the main; her mother had certainly never had one at the palace in Caemlyn. The only gleemen Elayne could remember seeing had been in the villages near her mother's country estates, and this white-haired hawk of a man had surely never been there.

She decided to speak to the thief-catcher first. He insisted on that, she remembered; what was a thief-taker elsewhere was a thief-catcher in Tear, and the distinction seemed important to him.

"Master Sandar," she said gravely. "You may not remember us. I am Elayne Trakand, and this is my friend, Nynaeve al'Meara. I understand that you wish to travel to the same destination as we. Might I ask why? The last time we saw you, you had not served us very well."

The man did not blink at the suggestion he might not remember them. His eyes flickered across their hands, noting the absence of rings. Those dark eyes noted everything, and recorded it indelibly. "I do remember, Mistress Trakand, and well. But, if you will forgive me, the *last* time I served you was in the company of Mat Cauthon, when we pulled you both out of the water before the silverpike could get you."

Nynaeve harrumphed, but not loudly. It had been a cell, not the water, and the Black Ajah, not silverpike. Nynaeve in particular did not like being reminded that they had needed help that time. Of course, they would not have been in that cell without Juilin Sandar. No, that was not entirely fair. True, but not completely fair.

"That is all very well," Elayne said briskly, "but you still haven't said why you want to go to Tanchico."

He drew a deep breath and eyed Nynaeve warily. Elayne was not sure that she liked him being more careful of the other woman than of her. "I was rousted out of my house no more than half an hour gone," he said carefully, "by a man you know, I think. A tall, stone-faced man calling himself Lan." Nynaeve's eyebrows rose slightly. "He came on behalf of another man you know. A . . . shepherd, I was told. I was given a great quantity of gold and told to accompany you. Both of you. I was told that if you do not return safely from this journey. . . . Shall we just say it would be better to drown myself than come back? Lan was emphatic, and the . . . shepherd no less so in his message. The Sailmistress tells me I cannot have passage unless you agree. I am not without certain skills that can be useful." The staff whirled in his hands, a whistling blur, and was still. His fingers touched the sword-breaker on his hip, like a short sword but unsharpened, its slots meant to catch a blade.

"Men will find ways to get 'round what you tell them to do," Nynaeve murmured, sounding not unpleased.

Elayne only frowned vexedly. Rand had sent him? He must not have read the second letter before he did. *Burn him! Why does he leap about so? No time to send another letter, and it would probably only confuse him more if I did. And make me look a bigger fool. Burn him!*

"And you, Master Merrilin?" Nynaeve said. "Did the shepherd send a gleeman after us, too? Or the other man? To keep us amused with your juggling and fire-eating, perhaps."

Thom had been scrutinizing Sandar closely, but he shifted his attentions smoothly and made an elegant bow, only spoiling it with a too-elaborate flourish of that patch-covered cloak. "Not the shepherd, Mistress al'Meara. A lady of our mutual acquaintance asked—*asked*—me to accompany you. The lady who found you and the shepherd in Emond's Field."

"Why?" Nynaeve said suspiciously.

"I, too, have useful skills," Thom told her with a glance at the thief-catcher. "Other than juggling, that is. And I have been to Tanchico several times. I know the city well. I can tell you where to find a good inn, and what districts are dangerous in daylight as well as after dark, and who must be bribed so the Civil Watch does not take too close an interest in your doings. They are keen on watching outlanders. I can help you with a good many things."

That familiarity tickled at Elayne's mind again. Before she realized what she was doing, she reached up and tugged at one of his long white mustaches. He gave a start, and she clapped both hands to her mouth, flushing crimson. "Forgive me. I . . . I seemed to remember doing that before. I mean. . . . I *am* sorry." *Light, why did I do that? He must think me an imbecile.*

"I . . . would remember," he said, very stiffly.

She hoped he was not affronted. It was hard to tell from his expression. Men could be offended when they should be amused, and amused when they should be offended. If they were going to be traveling together. . . . That was the first time she realized that she had decided they could come. "Nynaeve?" she said.

The other woman understood the unspoken question, of course. She studied the two men thoroughly, then nodded. "They may come. As long as they agree to do as they are told. I'll not have some wool-brained man going his own way and endangering us."

"As you command, Mistress al'Meara," Sandar said immediately, with a bow, but Thom said, "A gleeman is a free soul, Nynaeve, but I can promise I will not endanger you. Far from it."

"As you are told," Nynaeve said pointedly. "Your word on it, or you will watch this ship sail from the dock."

"The Atha'an Miere do not refuse passage to anyone, Nynaeve."

"Do you think not? Was the thief-taker"—Sandar winced—"the only one told he needed our permission? As you are told, *Master* Merrilin."

Thom tossed his white head like a fractious horse and breathed heavily, but finally he nodded. "My word on it, *Mistress* al'Meara."

"Very well then," Nynaeve said in a bracing voice. "It is settled. You two find the Sailmistress now, and tell her I said to find the pair of you a cubbyhole somewhere if she can, out of our way. Off with you, now. Quickly."

Sandar bowed again and left; Thom quivered visibly before joining him, stiff-backed.

"Are you not being too hard on them?" Elayne said as soon as they were out of earshot. That was not far, with all the hurly-burly on deck. "We do have to travel together, after all. 'Smooth words make smooth companions.' "

"Best to begin as we mean to go on. Elayne, Thom Merrilin knows very well we are not full Aes Sedai." She lowered her voice and glanced around as she said it. None of the crew was even looking at them, except for the Sailmistress, back near the sterndeck where she was listening to the tall gleeman and the thief-catcher. "Men talk—they always do—so Sandar will know it soon enough, as well. They'd present no trouble to Aes Sedai, but two Accepted . . . ? Given half a chance, they would both be doing things they thought for the best no matter what we said. I do not mean to give them even that half-chance."

"Perhaps you are right. Do you think they know why we are going to Tanchico?"

Nynaeve sniffed. "No, or they'd not be so sanguine, I think. And I would rather not tell them until we must." She gave Elayne a meaningful look; there was no need for her to say she would not have told the Sailmistress, either, had it been left to her. "Here is a saying for you. 'Borrow trouble, and you repay tenfold.' "

"You speak as if you don't trust them, Nynaeve." She would have said the other woman was behaving like Moiraine, but Nynaeve would not appreciate the comparison.

"Can we? Juilin Sandar betrayed us once before. Yes, yes, I know no man could have avoided it, but there it is just the same. And Liandrin and the others know his face. We will have to put him in different clothes. Perhaps make him let his hair grow longer. Perhaps a mustache, like that thing infesting the gleeman's face. It might do."

"And Thom Merrilin?" Elayne asked. "I think we can trust him. I don't know why, but I do."

"He admitted being sent by Moiraine," Nynaeve said wearily. "What has he not admitted, though? What did she tell him that he hasn't told us? Is he meant to help us, or something else? Moiraine plays her own game so often, I trust her this much more than I do Liandrin." She held her thumb and forefinger half an inch apart. "She will use us—you and me both—use us up, if it helps Rand. Or rather, if it helps whatever she has planned for Rand. She would leash him for a lapdog if she could."

"Moiraine knows what has to be done, Nynaeve." For once she was reluctant to admit that. What Moiraine knew had to be done might well speed Rand on his way toward Tarmon Gai'don that much faster. On his way toward death, perhaps. Rand balanced against the world. It was silly—foolish and childish—that those scales should tremble so evenly for her. Yet she did not dare make them swing, even in her mind, because she was not sure which way she would send them. "She knows it better than he does," she said, making her voice firm. "Better than we."

"Perhaps." Nynaeve sighed. "But I do not have to like it."

Ropes were cast off at the bow, where triangular sails suddenly broke out, and *Wavedancer* heeled away from the dock. More sails appeared, great white squares and triangles, the sternlines were cast off, and the ship curled out into the river in a great arc through the anchored ships awaiting their turn at the docks, a smooth curve that ended heading south, downriver. The Sea Folk handled their ship as a master horseman would a fine steed. That peculiar spoked wheel worked the rudder, somehow, as one of the bare-chested crewmen turned it. A man, Elayne was relieved to see. Sailmistress and Windfinder stood to one side of the wheel, Coine issuing occasional orders, sometimes after a murmured consultation with her sister. Toram watched for a time, with a face that might have been carved from a deck plank, then stalked below.

There was a Tairen on the sterndeck, a plump, dejected-looking man in a dull yellow coat with puffy gray sleeves, rubbing his hands nervously. He had been hustled aboard just as the gangway was being hauled up, a pilot who was supposed to guide *Wavedancer* downriver; according to Tairen law, no ship could pass through the Fingers of the Dragon without a Tairen pilot aboard. His dejection certainly came from doing nothing, for if he gave any directions, the Sea Folk paid them no heed.

Muttering about seeing what their cabin was like, Nynaeve went downstairs—below—but Elayne was enjoying the breeze across the deck and the feel of starting out. To travel, to see places she had not seen before, was a joy in itself. She had never expected to, not like this. The Daughter-Heir of Andor might make a few state visits, and she would make more once she succeeded to the throne, but they would be bounded about with ceremony and propriety. Not like this at all. Barefoot Sea Folk and a ship headed to sea.

The riverbank slid by quite quickly as the sun climbed, an occasional cluster of huddled stone farmhouses and barns, bleak and lonely, appearing and vanishing behind. No villages, though. Tear would not allow the smallest village on the river between the city and the sea, for even the tiniest might one day become competition for the capital. The High Lords controlled the size of villages and towns throughout the country with a buildings tax that grew heavier the more buildings there were. Elayne was sure they would never have allowed Godan to thrive, on the Bay of Remara, if not for the supposed necessity of a strong presence overlooking Mayene. In a way it was a relief to be leaving such foolish people behind. If only she did not have to leave one foolish man behind as well.

The number of fishing boats, most small and all surrounded by clouds of hopeful gulls and fisher-birds, increased the farther south *Wavedancer* went, especially once the vessel entered the maze of waterways called the Fingers of the Dragon. Often the birds overhead and the long poles that held the nets were all that was visible besides plains of reeds and knifegrass rippling in the breezes, dotted with low islands where odd, twisted trees grew with spidery tangles of roots exposed to the air. Many boats worked right in the reeds, though not with nets. Once Elayne saw some of them close to clear water, men and women dropping hooked lines into the watery growth and pulling up wriggling, dark-striped fish as long as a man's arm.

The Tairen pilot began to pace anxiously once they were in the delta, with the sun overhead, turning up his nose at an offered bowl of thick spicy fish stew and bread. Elayne ate hers hungrily, wiping her pottery bowl with the last scrap of bread, though she shared his unease. Passages broad and narrow ran in every direction. Some ended abruptly, in plain sight, against a wall of reeds. There was no way to tell which of the others might not vanish just as suddenly around the next bend. Coine did not slow *Wavedancer*, regardless, or hesitate at choosing a way. Obviously she knew the channels to take, or the Windfinder did, but the pilot still muttered to himself as if he expected to run aground any moment.

It was late afternoon when the river mouth suddenly appeared ahead, and the endless stretch of the Sea of Storms beyond. The Sea Folk did something with the sails, and the ship shuddered softly to a dead halt. It was only then that Elayne noticed a large rowboat skittering like a many-legged waterbug out from an island where a few forlorn stone buildings stood around the base of a tall narrow tower where men stood small at the top beneath the banner of Tear, three white crescents on a field of red and gold. The pilot took the purse Coine proffered without a word and scrambled down a rope ladder to the boat. As soon as he was aboard, the sails were swung about again, and *Wavedancer* breasted the first rollers of open sea, rising slightly, slicing through. Sea Folk scampered through the rigging, setting more sails, as the ship sped south and west, away from the land.

When the last thin strip of land dropped below the horizon, the Sea Folk women doffed their blouses. All of them, even the Sailmistress and the Windfinder. Elayne did not know where to look. All those women walking about half-dressed and completely unconcerned by the men all around them. Juilin Sandar seemed to be having as hard a time as she was, alternating between staring at the women wide-eyed and staring at his feet until he finally all but ran below. Elayne would not let herself be routed that way. She opted for staring over the side at the sea, instead.

Different customs, she reminded herself. *As long they don't expect me to do the same.* The very thought nearly made her laugh hysterically. Somehow, the Black Ajah was easier to contemplate than that. Different customs. *Light!*

The sky grew purple, with a dull golden sun on the horizon. Scores of dolphins escorted the vessel, rolling and arching alongside, and farther out some sort of sparkling silver-blue fish rose above the surface in schools, gliding on outstretched fins a span across for fifty paces or more before plunging back into the swelling gray-green water. Elayne watched in amazement for a dozen flights before they did not appear again.

But the dolphins, great sleek shapes, were wondrous enough, a guard of honor taking *Wavedancer* back where he belonged. Those she recognized from descriptions in books; it was said if they found you drowning, they would push you to shore. She was not sure she believed it, but it was a pretty story. She followed them along the side of the ship, to the bow, where they frolicked in the bow wave, rolling on their sides to look up at her without losing an inch.

She was almost in the narrowest point of the bow before she realized Thom Merrilin was there before her, smiling down at the dolphins a bit sadly, his cloak catching the wind like the cloud of sails above. He had rid himself of his belongings. He did seem familiar; truly he did. "Are you not happy, Master Merrilin?"

He glanced at her sideways. "Please, call me Thom, my Lady."

"Thom, then. But not my Lady. I am only Mistress Trakand here."

"As you say, Mistress Trakand," he said with a hint of a smile.

"How can you look at these dolphins and be unhappy, Thom?"

"They are free," he murmured, in such a tone that she was not sure he was answering her. "They have no decisions to make, no prices to pay. Not a worry in the world, except finding fish to eat. And sharks, I suppose. And lionfish. And likely a hundred more things I don't know. Perhaps it is not such an enviable life at that."

"Do you envy them?" He did not answer, but that was the wrong question anyway. She needed to make him smile again. No, laugh. For some reason she was sure if she could make him laugh, she would remember where she had seen him before. She chose another topic, one that should be nearer his heart. "Do you mean to compose the epic of Rand, Thom?" Epics were for bards, not gleemen, but there could be no harm in a little flattery. "The epic of the Dragon Reborn. Loial means to write a book, you know."

"Perhaps I will, Mistress Trakand. Perhaps. But neither my composing nor the Ogier's book will make much difference in the long run.

Our stories will not survive, in the long run. When the next Age comes—" He grimaced, and tugged one of his mustaches. "Come to think of it, that may be no more than a year or two off. How is the end of an Age marked? It cannot always be a cataclysm on the order of the Breaking. But then, if the Prophecies are to be believed, this one will be. That is the trouble with prophecy. The original is always in the Old Tongue, and maybe High Chant as well: if you don't know what a thing means beforehand, there's no way to puzzle it out. Does it mean what it says, or is it a flowery way of saying something entirely different?"

"You were talking of your epic," she said, trying to guide him back, but he shook his shaggy white head.

"I was talking of change. My epic, if I compose it—and Loial's book —will be no more than seed, if we are both lucky. Those who know the truth will die, and their grandchildren's grandchildren will remember something different. And *their* grandchildren's grandchildren something else again. Two dozen generations, and you may be the hero of it, not Rand."

"Me?" she laughed.

"Or maybe Mat, or Lan. Or even myself." He grinned at her, warming his weathered face. "Thom Merrilin. Not a gleeman—but what? Who can say? Not eating fire, but breathing it. Hurling it about like an Aes Sedai." He flourished his cloak. "Thom Merrilin, the mysterious hero, toppling mountains and raising up kings." The grin became a rich belly laugh. "Rand al'Thor may be lucky if the next Age remembers his name correctly."

She was right; it was not just a feeling. That face, that mirth-filled laugh; she did remember them. But from where? She had to keep him talking. "Does it always happen that way? I do not think anyone doubts, say, that Artur Hawkwing conquered an empire. The whole world, or near enough."

"Hawkwing, young Mistress? He made an empire, all right, but do you think he did everything the books and stories and epics say he did? The way they say he did it? Killed the hundred best men of an opposing army, one by one? The two armies just stood there while one of the generals—a king—fought a hundred duels?"

"The books say he did."

"There isn't time between sunrise and sunset for one man to fight a hundred duels, girl." She almost stopped him short—*girl?* She was Daughter-Heir of Andor, not *girl*—but he had the bit in his teeth. "And that is only a thousand years back. Go back further, back to the oldest tales I know, from the Age before the Age of Legends. Did Mosk and

Merk really fight with spears of fire, and were they even giants? Was Elsbet really queen of the whole world, and was Anla really her sister? Was Anla truly the Wise Counselor, or was it someone else? As well ask what sort of animal ivory comes from, or what kind of plant grows silk. Unless that comes from an animal, too."

"I do not know about those other questions," Elayne said a bit stiffly; being called girl still rankled, "but you could ask the Sea Folk about ivory and silk."

He laughed again—as she had hoped, though it still did no more than drive home the certainty that she knew him—but instead of calling her foolish, as she half-expected and was prepared for, he said, "Practical and to the point, just like your mother. Both feet on the earth and few flights of fancy."

She lifted her chin a little, made her face cooler. She might be passing herself off as simple Mistress Trakand, but this was something else. He was an amiable old man, and she did want to reason out the puzzle of him, but he was a gleeman after all, and he should not speak of a queen in such familiar tones. Oddly, infuriatingly, he appeared amused. Amused!

"The Atha'an Miere do not know, either," he said. "They see no more of the lands beyond the Aiel Waste than a few miles around the handful of harbors where they are permitted to land. Those places are walled high, and the walls guarded so they cannot even climb up to see what is on the other side. If one of their ships makes landfall anywhere else—or any ship not theirs; only the Sea Folk are allowed to come there—that ship and its crew are never seen again. And that is almost as much as I can tell you after more years of asking than I like to think of. The Atha'an Miere keep their secrets, but I do not believe they know much to keep here. From what I have been able to learn, the Cairhienin were treated the same, when they still had the right to travel the Silk Path across the Waste. Cairhienin traders never saw anything but one walled town, and those who wandered from it vanished."

Elayne found herself studying him much as she had the dolphins. What kind of man was this? Twice now he might have laughed at her— he *had* been amused just then, as much as she hated to admit it—but instead he talked to her as seriously as. . . . Well, as father to daughter. "You might find a few answers on this ship, Thom. They were bound east until we convinced the Sailmistress to take us to Tanchico. To Shara, the Cargomaster said, east of Mayene; that must mean beyond the Waste."

He stared at her for a moment. "Shara, you say? I have never heard any such name before. Is Shara city or nation or both? Perhaps I will learn a little more."

What did I say? she wondered. *I said something to make him think. Light! I told him we convinced Coine to change her plans.* It could not make any difference, but she scolded herself severely. A careless word to this nice old man might do no harm, but the same might kill her in Tanchico, and Nynaeve, too, not to mention the thief-catcher and Thom himself. If he was such a nice old man. "Thom, why did you come with us? Just because Moiraine asked?"

His shoulders shook; she realized he was laughing at himself. "As to that, who can say? Aes Sedai asking favors are not easily resisted. Perhaps it was the prospect of your pleasant company for the voyage. Or perhaps I decided Rand is old enough to look after himself for a while."

He laughed out loud, and she had to laugh with him. The idea of this white-haired old fellow looking after Rand. The feeling that she could trust him came back, stronger than ever, as he looked at her. Not because he could laugh at himself, or not only that. She could not have given a reason beyond the fact that, looking up into those blue eyes, she could not make herself believe this man would ever do anything to harm her.

The urge to pull one of his mustaches again was almost overwhelming, but she schooled her hands to stillness. She was not a child, after all. A child. She opened her mouth—and suddenly everything went out of her head.

"Please excuse me, Thom," she said hurriedly. "I must. . . . Excuse me." She started toward the stern quickly, not waiting for a reply. He probably thought the ship's motion had upset her stomach. *Wavedancer* was pitching more rapidly, moving faster through the great sea swells as the wind freshened.

Two men stood at the wheel on the sterndeck, the muscle of both needed to hold the vessel on course. The Sailmistress was not on deck, but the Windfinder was, standing at the rail beyond the wheelmen, bare to the waist like the men, studying the sky where billowing clouds rolled more fiercely than the ocean. For once it was not Jorin's state of dress—or undress—that bothered Elayne. The glow of a woman embracing *saidar* surrounded her, clearly visible despite the lurid light. That was what she had felt, what had drawn her. A woman channeling.

Elayne stopped short of the sterndeck to study what she was doing. The flows of Air and Water the Windfinder handled were cable-thick, yet her weaving was intricate, almost delicate, and it reached as far as the eye could see across the waters, a web drawn across the sky. The wind rose higher, higher; the wheelmen strained, and *Wavedancer* flew through the sea. The weaving stopped, the glow of *saidar* vanished, and Jorin slumped at the rail, leaning on her hands.

Elayne climbed the ladder quietly, yet the Sea Folk woman spoke in a soft voice without turning her head as soon as she was near enough to hear. "In the middle as I worked, I thought that you were watching me. I could not stop then; there might have been a storm even *Wavedancer* could not survive. The Sea of Storms is well named; it will throw up bad winds enough without my help. I meant not to do this at all, but Coine said we must go quickly. For you, and for the Coramoor." She raised her eyes to peer at the sky. "This wind will hold until morning, if it pleases the Light."

"This is why the Sea Folk do not carry Aes Sedai?" Elayne said, taking a place beside her at the rail. "So the Tower won't learn Windfinders can channel. That is why it was your decision to let us aboard, not your sister's. Jorin, the Tower will not try to stop you. There is no law in the Tower to stop any woman channeling, even if she is not Aes Sedai."

"Your White Tower will interfere. It will try to reach onto our ships, where we are free of the land and landsmen. It will try to tie us to itself, binding us away from the sea." She sighed heavily. "The wave that has passed cannot be called back."

Elayne wished she could tell her it was not so, but the Tower did seek out women and girls who could learn to channel, both to bolster the numbers of Aes Sedai, dwindling now compared to what they once had been, and because of the danger of learning unguided. In truth, a woman who could be taught to touch the True Source usually found herself in the Tower whatever she wanted, at least until she was trained enough not to kill herself or others by accident.

After a moment Jorin went on. "It is not all of us. Only some. We send a few girls to Tar Valon so Aes Sedai will not come looking among us. No ship will carry Aes Sedai whose Windfinder can weave the winds. When you first named yourselves, I thought you must know me, but you did not speak, and you asked passage, and I hoped perhaps you were not Aes Sedai despite your rings. A foolish hope. I could feel the strength of you both. And now the White Tower will know."

"I cannot promise to keep your secret, but I will do what I can." The woman deserved more. "Jorin, I swear by the honor of House Trakand of Andor that I will do my best to keep your secret from any who would harm you or your people, and that if I must reveal it to anyone, I will do all in my ability to protect your people from interference. House Trakand is not without influence, even in the Tower." *And I will make Mother use it, if need be. Somehow.*

"If it pleases the Light," Jorin said fatalistically, "all will be well. All will be well, and all will be well, and all manner of thing will be well, if it pleases the Light."

"There was a *damane* on that Seanchan ship, wasn't there?" The Windfinder gave her a quizzical look. "One of the captive women who can channel."

"You see deeply for one so young. That is why I first thought you might not be Aes Sedai, because you are so young; I have daughters older than you, I think. I did not know she was a captive; that makes me wish we could have saved her. *Wavedancer* outran the Seanchan vessel easily at first—we had heard of the Seanchan and their vessels with ribbed sails, that they demanded strange oaths and punished those who would not give them—but then the—*damane?*—broke two of his masts, and they boarded him with swords. I managed to start fires on the Seanchan vessel—weaving Fire is difficult for me beyond lighting a lamp, but it pleased the Light to make it enough—and Toram led the crew to fight the Seanchan back to their own decks. We cut loose the boarding hooks, and their ship drifted away, burning. They were too occupied with trying to save him to bother us as we limped away. I regretted seeing him burn and sink, then; he was a fine ship, I think, for heavy seas. Now I regret it because we might have saved the woman, the *damane.* Even if she damaged him, perhaps she would not have, free. The Light illumine her soul, and the waters take her peacefully."

Telling the story had saddened her. She needed to be distracted. "Jorin, why do the Atha'an Miere call ships 'he'? Everyone else I've ever met calls them 'she.' I don't suppose it makes any difference, but why?"

"The men will give you a different answer," the Windfinder said, smiling, "speaking of strength and grandness and the like as men will, but this is the truth. A ship is alive, and he is like a man, with a true man's heart." She rubbed the rail fondly, as if stroking something alive, something that could feel her caress. "Treat him well and care for him properly, and he will fight for you against the worst sea. He will fight to keep you alive even after the sea has long since given him his own deathstroke. Neglect him, though, ignore the small warnings he gives of danger, and he will drown you in a flat sea beneath a cloudless sky."

Elayne hoped Rand was not as fickle as that. *Then why does he hop about, glad to see me go one minute and sending Juilin Sandar after me the next?* She told herself to stop thinking about him. He was a long way away. There was nothing to be done about him now.

She glanced over her shoulder toward the bow. Thom was gone. She was sure she had found the key to his puzzle, just before she had felt the Windfinder channeling. Something to do with his smile. It was gone, whatever it was. Well, she meant to find it again before they reached Tanchico, if she had to sit on him. But he would still be there in the morning. "Jorin, how long before we reach Tanchico? I have been told rakers are the fastest ships in the world, but how fast?"

"To Tanchico? To serve the Coramoor, we will not stop at any port between. Perhaps ten days, if I can weave the winds well enough, if it pleases the Light that I find the proper currents. Perhaps as few as seven or eight, with the grace of the Light."

"Ten days?" Elayne gasped. "It cannot be possible." She had seen maps, after all.

The other woman's smile was half pride, half indulgence. "As you yourself said, the fastest ships in the world. The next quickest take half again as long over any stretch, and most more than twice as long. Coasting craft that hug the shore and anchor in the shallows each night . . ." She sniffed contemptuously. ". . . require ten times as much."

"Jorin, would you teach me to do what you were just doing?"

The Windfinder stared, her dark eyes wide and shining in the fading light. "Teach you? But you are Aes Sedai."

"Jorin, I have never woven a flow half as thick as those you were handling. And the scope of it! I am astounded, Jorin."

The Windfinder stared a moment more, no longer in amazement, but as if trying to fix Elayne's face in her mind. Finally she kissed the fingers of her right hand and pressed them to Elayne's lips. "If it pleases the Light, we both shall learn."

CHAPTER
21

Into the Heart

Tairen nobility filled the great vaulted chamber with its huge polished redstone columns, ten feet thick, rising into shadowed heights above golden lamps hanging on golden chains. The High Lords and Ladies were arrayed in a thick hollow circle under the great dome at the chamber's heart with the lesser nobles ranked behind, row on row back into the forest of columns, all in their best velvets and silks and laces, wide sleeves and ruffed collars and peaked hats, all murmuring uneasily so the towering ceiling echoed the sounds of nervous geese. Only the High Lords themselves had ever before been bidden to this place, called the Heart of the Stone, and they had come only four times a year, at the twin demands of law and custom. They came now, all who were not out in the countryside somewhere, at the summons of their new lord, the maker of law and breaker of custom.

The packed crowd gave way before Moiraine as soon as they saw who she was, so she and Egwene moved in a pocket of open space. Lan's absence irritated Moiraine. It was not like the man to vanish when she might need him; his way usually was to watch over her as if she could not fend for herself without a guardian. Had she not been able to feel the bond linking them and known he could not be very far from the Stone, she might have worried.

He fought the strings Nynaeve was tying to him as hard as he had ever fought Trollocs in the Blight, but much as he might deny it, that young woman had bound him as tightly as she herself did, though in other ways. He might as well try tearing steel with his hands as those ties. She was not jealous, exactly, but Lan had been her sword arm, her shield and companion for too many years for her to give him up lightly. *I have done what had to be done, there. She will have him if I die, and not before. Where is the man? What is he doing?*

One red-gowned lace-ruffed woman, a horse-faced Lady of the Land called Leitha, drew her skirts away a bit too assiduously, and Moiraine looked at her. Merely looked, without slowing her step, but the woman shuddered and dropped her eyes. Moiraine nodded to herself. She could accept that these people hated Aes Sedai, but she would not endure open rudeness on top of veiled slights. Besides, the rest shied back another step after seeing Leitha faced down.

"Are you certain he said nothing of what he means to announce?" she asked quietly. In this gabble, no one three paces away could have made out a word. The Tairens kept about that distance now. She did not like being overheard.

"Nothing," Egwene said just as softly. She sounded as irritated as Moiraine felt.

"There have been rumors."

"Rumors? What sort of rumors?"

The girl was not that good at controlling her face and voice; clearly she had not heard the tales of doings in the Two Rivers. Betting that Rand had not, though, might be putting her horse at a ten-foot fence. "You should bring him to confide in you. He needs an attentive ear. It will help him, to talk out his troubles with someone he can trust." Egwene gave her a sidelong glance. She was becoming too sophisticated for such simple methods. Still, Moiraine had spoken unadorned truth—the boy did need someone to listen and by listening lighten his burdens—and it might work.

"He will not confide in anyone, Moiraine. He hides his pains, and hopes he can deal with them before anyone notices." Anger flashed across Egwene's face. "The wool-brained mule!"

Moiraine felt a momentary sympathy. The girl could not be expected to accept Rand's strolling about arm in arm with Elayne, kissing in corners where they thought themselves unseen. And Egwene did not know the half, yet. Commiseration did not last. There was too much of importance to deal with for the girl to be fretting over what she could not have in any case.

Elayne and Nynaeve should be aboard the raker by now, out of the way. Their voyage might eventually tell her if her suspicions about the Windfinders were correct. That was a minor point, though. At worst the pair had enough gold to buy a ship and hire a crew—which might be necessary given the rumors of Tanchico—with enough left for the bribes so often necessary with Taraboner officials. Thom Merrilin's room was empty, and her informants had reported him muttering about Tanchico on his way out of the Stone; he would see they got a good crew and found the right officials. The purported plan with Mazrim Taim was much the more likely of the two, but her messages to the Amyrlin should have taken care of that. The two young women could handle the much less likely eventuality of a mysterious danger hidden in Tanchico, and they were out of her hair and away from Rand. She only regretted that Egwene had refused to go with them. Tar Valon would have been best for all three, but Tanchico would do.

"Speaking of wool-brained, do you mean to continue with this plan to go into the Waste?"

"I do," the girl said firmly. She needed to be back in the Tower, training her strength. *What was Siuan thinking of? She will probably give me one of those sayings about boats and fish, when I can ask her.*

At least Egwene would be out of the way, too, and the Aiel girl would look after her. Perhaps the Wise Ones really could teach her something of Dreaming. That had been the most astounding letter from them, not that she could afford to heed most of it. Egwene's journey into the Waste might be useful in the long run.

The last line of Tairens gave way, making a little hollow, and she and Egwene faced the open area under the vast dome. The nobles' ill ease was most evident here; many studied their feet like sulky children, and others stared at nothing, looking at anything but where they were. Here was where *Callandor* had been kept before Rand took it. Here beneath this dome, untouched by any hand for more than three thousand years, untouchable by any hand but that of the Dragon Reborn. Tairens did not like admitting that the Heart of the Stone existed.

"Poor woman," Egwene murmured.

Moiraine followed the girl's gaze. The High Lady Alteima, already gowned and ruffed and capped in shimmering white as Tairen widows were though her husband still lingered, was perhaps the most composed of all the nobles. She was a slender, lovely woman, made more so by her small sad smile, with large brown eyes and long black hair hanging halfway to her waist. A tall woman, though Moiraine admitted she did tend to judge such things by her own height, and rather too full-bosomed. Cairhienin were not a tall people, and she had been considered short even among them.

"Yes, a poor woman," she said, but she did not mean it for sympathy. It was good to see Egwene had not yet grown sophisticated enough to see beneath the surface all the time. The girl was already far less malleable than she should have been for years yet. She needed to be shaped before she was hardened.

Thom had missed, with Alteima. Or perhaps he had not wanted to see; he seemed to have a strange reluctance to move against women. The High Lady Alteima was far more dangerous than her husband or her lover, both of whom she had manipulated without either knowing it. Perhaps more dangerous than anyone else in Tear, man or woman. She would find others to use soon enough. It was Alteima's style to remain in the background and pull strings. Something would have to be done about her.

Moiraine shifted her gaze along the rows of High Lords and Ladies, until she found Estanda, in brocaded yellow silks with a large ivory lace ruff and a tiny matching cap. A certain sternness marred the beauty of her face, and the occasional glances she gave Alteima were iron hard. Feelings between the two went beyond mere rivalry; had they been men, one would have shed the other's blood in a duel years since. If that antagonism could be sharpened, Alteima would be too busy to make trouble for Rand.

For an instant she regretted sending Thom away. She did not like having to waste her time with these petty affairs. But he had too much influence with Rand; the boy had to depend on her counsel. Hers, and hers alone. The Light knew he was difficult enough without interference. Thom had been settling the boy down to rule Tear when he needed to be moving on to greater things. But that was dealt with for now. The problem of bringing Thom Merrilin to heel could be managed later. Rand was the dilemma now. What did he mean to announce?

"Where is he? He has learned the first art of kings, it seems. Making people wait."

She did not realize she had spoken aloud until Egwene gave her a startled look. She smoothed the irritation from her face immediately. Rand would appear eventually, and she would learn what he meant to do. Learn along with everyone else. She nearly ground her teeth. That blind fool of a boy, running headlong through the night with never a care for cliffs, never thinking he could carry the world over as well as himself. If only she could keep him from rushing back to save his village. He would want to, but he could not afford to do so now. Perhaps he did not know; it could be hoped.

Mat stood across from them, uncombed and slouching with his hands in the pockets of his high-collared green coat. It was half-unbuttoned, as usual, and his boots were scuffed, in sharp contrast to the precise elegance around him. He shifted nervously as he saw her looking at him, then gave one of his rudely defiant grins. At least he was here, under her eye. Mat Cauthon was an exhausting young man to keep track of, avoiding her spies with ease; he never gave any sign that he knew they were there, but her eyes-and-ears reported that he seemed to slide out of sight whenever they got too close.

"I think he sleeps in his coats," Egwene said disapprovingly. "On purpose. I wonder where Perrin is." She went on tiptoes, trying to search over the heads of the assemblage. "I don't see him."

Frowning, Moiraine scanned the crowd, not that she could make out much beyond the front row. Lan could have been back among the columns. She would not strain, though, or jump up on her toes like an anxious child. Lan was due a talking-to he would not soon forget when she laid hands on him. With Nynaeve tugging at him one way and *ta'veren*—Rand, at least—seemingly pulling another, she sometimes wondered how well their bond still held. At least his time with Rand was useful; it gave her another string to the young man.

"Perhaps he is with Faile," Egwene said. "He won't have run away, Moiraine. Perrin has a strong sense of duty."

Almost as strong as a Warder's, Moiraine knew, which was why she did not keep eyes-and-ears on him as she tried to with Mat. "Faile has been trying to talk him into leaving, girl." Quite possibly he was with her; he usually was. "Do not look so surprised. They often talk—and argue—where they can be overheard."

"I am not surprised you know," Egwene said dryly, "only that Faile would try to talk him out of what he knows he has to do."

"Perhaps she does not believe it as he does." Moiraine had not believed it herself, at first, had not seen it. Three *ta'veren*, all the same age, coming out of one village; she must have been blind not to realize they had to be connected. Everything had become much more complicated with that knowledge. Like trying to juggle three of Thom's colored balls one-handed and blindfolded; she had seen Thom do that, but she would not want to try. There was no guide to how they were connected, or what they were supposed to do; the Prophecies never mentioned companions.

"I like her," Egwene said. "She is good for him, just what he needs. And she cares for him deeply."

"I suppose she does." If Faile became too troublesome, Moiraine would have to have a talk with her, about the secrets Faile had been keeping from Perrin. Or have one of her eyes-and-ears do it. That should settle her down.

"You say it as if you don't believe it. They love each other, Moiraine. Can't you see that? Can't you even recognize a human emotion when you see one?"

Moiraine gave her a firm look, one that settled her on her heels in a satisfactory manner. The girl knew so little and thought she knew so much. Moiraine was about to tell her so in withering fashion when startled, even fearful, gasps rose from among the Tairens.

The crowd gave way hurriedly, more than eagerly, those in front ruthlessly forcing those behind farther back, opening a wide passage to the space beneath the dome. Rand strode down that corridor, looking straight ahead, imperious in a red coat embroidered with golden scrolls up his sleeves, cradling *Callandor* in his right arm like a scepter. It was not only he that made the Tairens give way, though. Behind him came perhaps a hundred Aiel, spears and arrow-nocked bows in hand, *shoufa* wrapped around their heads, black veils hiding everything but their eyes. Moiraine thought she recognized Rhuarc at the front, just behind Rand, but only by the way he moved. They were anonymous. Ready for killing. Plainly, whatever he meant to say, Rand intended to quell any resistance before it had a chance to coalesce.

The Aiel halted, but Rand kept on until he stood centered under the dome, then ran his eye around the gathering. He seemed surprised, and perhaps upset, at the sight of Egwene, but he gave Moiraine an infuriating smile, and Mat one that made the pair of them look like boys when Mat returned it. The Tairens were white-faced, not knowing whether to stare at Rand and *Callandor* or the veiled Aiel; either could be death in their midst.

"The High Lord Sunamon," Rand said suddenly, and loudly, making that plump fellow jump, "has guaranteed me a treaty with Mayene, strictly following lines I gave him. He has guaranteed this with his life." He laughed as if he had made a joke, and most of the nobles laughed with him. Not Sunamon, who looked distinctly ill. "If he fails," Rand announced, "he has agreed to be hanged, and he will be obliged." The laughter stopped. Sunamon's face took on a sickly tinge of green. Egwene gave Moiraine a troubled glance; she was gripping her skirt with both hands. Moiraine only waited; he had not brought every noble within ten miles together to tell them of a treaty or threaten a fat fool. She made her hands let go of her own skirts.

Rand turned in a circle, weighing the faces he saw. "Because of this treaty, ships will soon be available to carry Tairen grain west, to find new markets." There were a few appreciative murmurs at that, quickly stifled. "But there is more. The armies of Tear are to march."

A cheer rose, tumultuous shouts ringing from the ceilings. Men capered, even the High Lords, and shook their fists over their heads, and tossed up peaked velvet hats. Women, smiling as rapturously as the men, bestowed kisses on the cheeks of those who would go to war, and delicately sniffed the tiny porcelain bottles of smelling salts no Tairen noblewoman would be without, pretending to be made faint by the news. "Illian shall fall!" someone cried, and hundreds of voices seized it like thunder. "Illian shall fall! Illian shall fall! Illian shall fall!"

Moiraine saw Egwene's lips moving, the words crushed beneath the jubilation. She could read them, though. "No, Rand. Please, no. Please don't." On the far side of Rand, Mat was frowning in disapproving silence. They and she were the only ones not celebrating, aside from the ever-watchful Aiel and Rand himself. Rand's smile was twisted contemptuously, and never touched his eyes. There was fresh sweat on his face. She met his sardonic stare and waited. There would be more, and not, she suspected, to her liking.

Rand raised his left hand. Slowly quiet fell, those in front anxiously shushing those behind. He waited for absolute silence. "The armies will move north, into Cairhien. The High Lord Meilan will command, and under him, the High Lords Gueyam, Aracome, Hearne, Maraconn and Simaan. The armies will be generously financed by the High Lord Torean, the wealthiest of you, who will accompany the armies to see that his money is spent wisely."

Dead silence greeted this pronouncement. No one moved, though plain-faced Torean seemed to be having trouble standing.

Moiraine had to give Rand a mental bow for his choices. Sending those seven out of Tear neatly eviscerated the seven most dangerous plots against him, and none of those men trusted each other enough to scheme among themselves. Thom Merrilin had given him good advice; obviously her spies had missed some of the notes he had had slipped into Rand's pockets. But the rest? It was madness. He could have not have had this for an answer on the other side of that *ter'angreal.* It was not possible, surely.

Meilan obviously agreed with her, if not for the same reasons. He stepped forward hesitantly, a lean hard man but so frightened that the whites of his eyes showed all the way around. "My Lord Dragon. . . ." He stopped, swallowed, and began again in a marginally stronger voice. "My Lord Dragon, intervening in a civil war is stepping into a bog. A dozen factions contend for the Sun Throne, with as many shifting alliances, each one betrayed every day. Besides that, bandits infest Cairhien as fleas on a wild boar. Starving peasants have stripped the land bare. I am reliably informed that they eat bark and leaves. My Lord Dragon, 'a quagmire' barely begins to describe—"

Rand cut him off. "You do not want to extend Tear's sway all the way to Kinslayer's Dagger, Meilan? That is all right. I know who I mean to sit on the Sun Throne. You do not go to conquer, Meilan, but to restore order, and peace. And to feed the hungry. There is more grain in the granaries now than Tear could sell, and the farmers will harvest as much more this year, unless you disobey me. Wagons will carry it north behind the armies, and those *peasants*. . . . Those *peasants* will not have to eat bark any longer, my *Lord* Meilan." The tall High Lord opened his mouth again, and Rand swung *Callandor* down, grounding its crystal point in front of him. "You have a question, Meilan?" Shaking his head, Meilan backed into the crowd as though trying to hide.

"I knew he would not start a war," Egwene said fiercely. "I knew it."

"You think there will be less killing in this?" Moiraine muttered. What was the boy up to? At least he was not running off to save his village while the Forsaken had their way with the rest of the world. "The corpses will be piled as high, girl. You will not know the difference between this and a war."

Attacking Illian and Sammael would have gained him time even if it grew into a stalemate. Time to learn his power, and perhaps to bring down one of his strongest enemies, to cow the rest. What did he gain by this? Peace for the land of her birth, starving Cairhienin fed; she would have applauded another time. It was laudably humane—and utterly senseless, now. Useless bloodshed, rather than confronting an enemy who would destroy him given the slightest opening. Why? Lanfear. What had Lanfear said to him? What had she done? The possibilities chilled Moiraine's heart. Rand would take closer watching than ever now. She would not allow him to turn to the Shadow.

"Ah, yes," Rand said as if just remembering something. "Soldiers don't know much about feeding hungry people, do they? For that, I think a kind, woman's heart is needed. My Lady Alteima, I regret intruding on your grief, but will you undertake to oversee distributing the food? You will have a nation to feed."

And power to gain, Moiraine thought. This was his first slip. Aside

from deciding on Cairhien over Illian, of course. Alteima would certainly return to Tear on an equal footing with Meilan or Gueyam, ready
for more plotting. She would have Rand assassinated before that, if he
was not careful. Perhaps an accident could be arranged in Cairhien.

Alteima swept a graceful curtsy, spreading her full white skirts, only
a touch of her surprise showing. "As my Lord Dragon commands, so
do I obey. It will please me greatly to serve the Lord Dragon."

"I was sure it would," Rand said wryly. "As much as you love your
husband, you'll not want him with you in Cairhien. Conditions will be
hard, for a sick man. I took the liberty of having him moved to the
High Lady Estanda's apartments. She will care for him while you are
away, and send him to meet you in Cairhien when he is well." Estanda
smiled, a tight smile of triumph. Alteima's eyes rolled back in her head,
and she crumpled in a heap.

Moiraine shook her head slightly. He truly was harder than he had
been. More dangerous. Egwene started toward the fallen woman, but
Moiraine put a hand on her arm. "I think she was only overcome by
emotion. I can recognize it, you see. The ladies are tending her." Several of them had clustered around, patting Alteima's wrists and passing
smelling salts under her nose. She coughed and opened her eyes, and
looked ready to faint again when she saw Estanda standing over her.

"Rand just did something very clever, I think," Egwene said in a flat
voice. "And very cruel. He has a right to look ashamed."

Rand did look it at that, grimacing at the floorstones under his boots.
Perhaps he was not as hard as he was trying to be.

"Not undeserved, however," Moiraine observed. The girl showed
promise, picking up on what she did not understand. But she still
needed to learn to control her emotions, to see what had to be done as
well as she saw what she wished could be done. "Let us hope he is
finished with being clever for today."

Very few in the great chamber understood exactly what had happened, only that Alteima's fainting had upset the Lord Dragon. A few
in the back raised shouts of "Cairhien shall fall!" but the cry did not
take hold.

"With you to lead us, my Lord Dragon, we shall conquer the world!"
a lumpy-faced young man shouted, half-supporting Torean. Estean,
Torean's eldest son; the lumpy-faced resemblance was clear, though the
father was still mumbling to himself.

Jerking his head up, Rand appeared startled. Or perhaps angry. "I
will not be with you. I am . . . going away for a time." That certainly
brought silence again. Every eye was on him, but his attentions were all

on *Callandor*. The crowd flinched as he lifted the crystal blade before his face. Sweat rolled down his face, much more sweat than before. "The Stone held *Callandor* before I came. The Stone should hold it again, until I return."

Suddenly the transparent sword blazed in his hands. Whirling it hilt uppermost, he drove it down. Into the stone floor. Bluish lightning arced wildly toward the dome above. The stone rumbled loudly, and the Stone shook, dancing, heaving screaming people from their feet.

Moiraine pushed Egwene off of her while tremors still reverberated through the chamber, and scrambled erect. What *had* he done? And why? Going away? It was the worst of all her nightmares.

The Aiel had already regained their feet. Everyone else lay stunned or huddled on hands and knees. Except for Rand. He was on one knee, both hands holding *Callandor*'s hilt, with the blade driven halfway into the floorstones. The sword was clear crystal again. Sweat glistened on his face. He pried his hands away one finger at a time, held them cupped around the hilt yet not touching it. For a moment Moiraine thought he was going to take hold of it again, but instead he forced himself to his feet. He did have to force himself; she was certain of it.

"Look at this while I am gone." His voice was lighter, more the way it had been when she first found him in his village, but no less sure or firm than it had been moments before. "Look at it, and remember me. Remember I will come back for it. If anyone wants to take my place, all they have to do is pull it out." He waggled a finger at them, grinning almost mischievously. "But remember the price of failure."

Turning on his heel, he marched out of the chamber, the Aiel falling in behind him. Staring at the sword rising out of the floor of the Heart, the Tairens got to their feet more slowly. Most looked ready to run, but too frightened to.

"That man!" Egwene grumbled, dusting off her green linen dress. "Is he mad?" She clapped a hand to her mouth. "Oh, Moiraine, he isn't, is he? Is he? Not yet."

"The Light send he is not," Moiraine muttered. She could not take her eyes from the sword any more than the Tairens could. The Light take the boy. Why could he not have remained the amenable youngling she had found in Emond's Field? She made herself start after Rand. "But I will find out."

Half-running, they caught up quickly in a broad, tapestry-lined hallway. The Aiel, veils hanging loose now but easily raised if needed, moved aside without slowing. They glanced at her, and at Egwene, hard faces unchanging but eyes touched by the wariness Aiel always had around Aes Sedai.

How they could be uneasy at her while calmly following Rand, she did not understand. Learning more than fragments about them was difficult. They answered questions freely—about anything that was of no interest to her. Her informants and her own eavesdropping overheard nothing, and her network of eyes-and-ears would no longer try. Not since one woman had been left bound and gagged, hanging by her ankles from battlements and staring wild-eyed at the four-hundred-foot drop beneath her, and not since the man who had simply disappeared. The man was just gone; the woman, refusing to go higher than the ground floor, had been a constant reminder until Moiraine sent her into the country.

Rand did not slow down any more than the Aiel when she and Egwene fell in on either side of him. His glance was wary, too, but in a different way, and touched with exasperated anger. "I thought you were gone," he said to Egwene. "I thought you went with Elayne and Nynaeve. You should have. Even Tanchico is. . . . Why did you stay?"

"I won't be staying much longer," Egwene said. "I am going to the Waste with Aviendha, to Rhuidean, to study with the Wise Ones."

He missed a step as the girl mentioned the Waste, glancing at her uncertainly, then strode on. He seemed composed now, too much so, a boiling teakettle with the lid strapped down and the spout plugged. "Do you remember swimming in the Waterwood?" he said quietly. "I used to float on my back in a pool and think the hardest thing I'd ever have to do was plow a field, unless maybe it was shearing sheep. Shearing from sunup till bedtime, hardly stopping to eat until the clip was in."

"Spinning," Egwene said. "I hated it worse than scrubbing floors. Twisting the threads makes your fingers so sore."

"Why did you do it?" Moiraine demanded before they could go on with this childhood reminiscing.

He gave her a sidelong look, and a smile mocking enough to belong to Mat. "Could I really have hung her, for trying to kill a man who was plotting to kill me? Would there be more justice in that than in what I did?" The grin slid from his face. "Is there justice in anything I do? Sunamon will hang if he fails. Because I said so. He'll deserve it after the way he's tried to take advantage, with never a care if his own people starved, but he'll not go to the gallows for that. He will hang because I said he would. Because I said it."

Egwene laid a hand on his arm, but Moiraine would not allow him to sidestep. "You know that is not what I mean."

He nodded; this time his smile had a frightening, rictus quality. *"Callandor.* With that in my hands, I can do anything. Anything. I know I can do anything. But now, it's a weight off my shoulders. You don't understand, do you?" She did not, though it nettled her that he saw it. She kept silent, and he went on. "Perhaps it will help if you know it comes from the Prophecies.

"Into the heart he thrusts his sword,
into the heart, to hold their hearts.
Who draws it out shall follow after,
What hand can grasp that fearful blade?

"You see? Straight from the Prophecies."

"You forget one thing," she told him tightly. "You drew *Callandor* in fulfillment of prophecy. The safeguards that held it awaiting you for three thousand years and more are gone. It is the Sword That Cannot Be Touched no longer. I could channel it free myself. Worse, any of the Forsaken could. What if Lanfear returns? She could use *Callandor* no more than I, but she could take it." He did not react to the name. Because he did not fear her—in which case he was a fool—or for another reason? "If Sammael or Rahvin or any male Forsaken puts his hand on *Callandor,* he can wield it as well as you. Think of facing the power you give up so casually. Think of that power in the hands of the Shadow."

"I almost hope they'll try." A threatening light shone in his eyes; they seemed gray storm clouds. "There is a surprise awaiting anyone who tries to channel *Callandor* out of the Stone, Moiraine. Do not think of taking it to the Tower for safekeeping; I could not make the trap pick and choose. The Power is all it needs to spring and reset, ready to trap again. I am not giving *Callandor* up forever. Just until I. . . ." He took a deep breath. *"Callandor* will stay there until I come back for it. By being there, reminding them of who I am and what I am, it makes sure I can come back without an army. A haven of sorts, with the likes of Alteima and Sunamon to welcome me home. If Alteima survives the justice her husband and Estanda will mete out, and Sunamon survives mine. Light, what a wretched tangle."

He could not make it selective, or would not? She was determined not to underrate what he might be capable of. *Callandor* belonged in the Tower, if he would not wield it as he should, in the Tower till he would wield it. "Just until" what? He had been intending to say something other than "until I come back." But what?

"And where are you going? Or do you mean to keep it a mystery?" She was quietly vowing not to let him escape again, to turn him somehow if he meant to go running off to the Two Rivers, when he surprised her.

"Not a mystery, Moiraine. Not from you and Egwene, anyway." He looked at Egwene and said one word. "Rhuidean."

Wide-eyed, the girl appeared as astounded as if she had never heard the name before. For that matter, Moiraine felt scarcely less. There was a murmur among the Aiel, but when she glanced back they were striding along with no expression whatsoever. She wished she could make them leave, but they would not go at her command, and she would not ask Rand to send them away. It would not help her with him to ask favors, especially when he might well refuse.

"You are not an Aiel clan chief, Rand," she said firmly, "and have no need to be one. Your struggle is on this side of the Dragonwall. Unless. . . . Does this come from your answers in the *ter'angreal?* Cairhien, and *Callandor,* and Rhuidean? I told you those answers can be cryptic. You could be misunderstanding them, and that could prove fatal. To more than you."

"You must trust me, Moiraine. As I have so often had to trust you." His face might as well have belonged to an Aiel for all she could read in it.

"I will trust you for now. Just do not wait to seek my guidance until it is too late." *I will not let you go to the Shadow. I have worked too long to allow that. Whatever it takes.*

CHAPTER
22

Out of the Stone

I t was a strange procession Rand led out of the Stone and eastward, with white clouds shading the midday sun and a breath of air stirring across the city. By his order there had been no announcement, no proclamation, but slowly word spread of *something:* citizens stopped whatever they were doing and ran for vantage points. The Aiel were marching through the city, marching out of the city. People who had not seen them come in the night, who had only half-believed they were in the Stone at all, increasingly lined the streets along the route, filled the windows, even climbed onto slate rooftops, straddling roof peaks and upturned corners. Murmurs ran as they counted the Aiel. These few hundred could never have taken the Stone. The Dragon banner still flew above the fortress. There must yet be thousands of Aiel in there. And the Lord Dragon.

Rand rode easily in his shirtsleeves, sure none of the onlookers could take him for anyone out of the ordinary. An outlander, rich enough to ride—and on a superb dappled stallion, best of the Tairen bloodstock— a rich man traveling in the oddest of odd company, but surely just another man for that. Not even the leader of this strange company; that title was surely assigned to Lan or Moiraine despite the fact that they rode some little distance behind him, directly ahead of the Aiel. The soft awed susurration that accompanied his passing certainly rose for the Aiel, not him. These Tairen folk might even take him for a groom, riding his master's horse. Well, no, not that; not out in front as he was. It was a fine day, anyway. Not sweltering, merely warm. No one expected him to mete out justice, or rule a nation. He could simply enjoy riding in anonymity, enjoy the rare breeze. For a time he could forget the feel of his heron-branded palms on the reins. *For a little longer anyway,* he thought. *A little longer.*

"Rand," Egwene said, "do you really think it was right to let the Aiel take all those things?" He looked around as she heeled her gray mare, Mist, up beside him. From somewhere she had gotten a dark green dress with narrow divided skirts, and a green velvet band held her hair at the nape of her neck.

Moiraine and Lan still hung back half a dozen strides, she on her white mare in a full-skirted blue silk riding dress slashed with green, her dark hair caught in a golden net, he astride his great black warhorse, in a color-shifting Warder's cloak that probably brought as many *oohs* and *aahs* as the Aiel. When the breeze stirred the cloak, shades of green and brown and gray rippled across it; when it hung still it somehow seemed to fade into whatever was beyond it, so the eye appeared to be seeing *through* parts of Lan and his mount. It was not comfortable to look at.

Mat was there, too, slumped in his saddle and looking resigned, trying to keep apart from the Warder and Aes Sedai. He had chosen a nondescript brown gelding, an animal he called Pips; it took a good eye to notice the deep chest and strong withers that promised blunt-nosed Pips could likely match Rand's stallion or Lan's for speed and endurance. Mat's decision to come had been a surprise; Rand still did not know why. Friendship, maybe, and then again, maybe not. Mat could be odd in what he did and why.

"Didn't your friend Aviendha explain to you about 'the fifth'?" he asked.

"She mentioned something, but. . . . Rand, you don't think she . . . took . . . things, too?"

Behind Moiraine and Lan, behind Mat, behind Rhuarc at their head, the Aiel walked in long lines to either side of loaded pack mules, rank on rank four abreast. When Aiel took one of the holds of an enemy clan in the Waste, by custom—or maybe law; Rand did not understand it exactly—they carried away one fifth of all it contained, excepting only food. They had seen no reason not to treat the Stone the same. Not that the mules held more than the barest fraction of a fraction of a fifth of the Stone's treasures. Rhuarc said greed had killed more men than steel. The wickerwork pack hampers, topped with rolled carpets and wall hangings, were lightly laden. Ahead lay an eventual hard crossing of the Spine of the World, and then a far harder trek across the Waste. *When do I tell them?* he wondered. *Soon, now; it has to be soon.* Moiraine would doubtless think it daring, a bold stroke; she might even approve. Maybe. She thought she knew his whole plan, now, and made no bones of disapproving that; no doubt she wanted it over and done as soon as possible. But the Aiel. . . . *What if they refuse? Well, if they refuse, they refuse. I have to do it.* As for the fifth. . . . He did not think it would have been possible to stop the Aiel from taking it even had he wanted to, and he had not; they had earned their rewards, and he had no care to help Tairen lords keep what they had wrung from their people over generations.

"I saw her showing Rhuarc a silver bowl," he said aloud. "From the way her sack clinked when she stuffed the bowl in, there was more silver in there. Or maybe gold. Do you disapprove?"

"No." She drew the word out slowly, with a touch of doubt, but then her voice firmed. "I just hadn't thought of her. . . . The Tairens would not have stopped at a fifth if the positions had been reversed. They'd have carted away whatever wasn't part of the stonework, and stolen all the carts to haul it. Just because a people's ways are different doesn't mean they are wrong, Rand. You should know that."

He laughed softly. This was almost like old times, he ready to explain why and how she was wrong, and she snatching his position and tossing his own unvoiced explanation at him. His stallion danced a few steps, catching his mood. He patted the dapple's arched neck. A good day.

"That's a fine horse," she said. "What have you named him?"

"Jeade'en," he said cautiously, losing some of his good spirits. He was a little ashamed of the name, of his reasons for choosing it. One of his favorite books had always been *The Travels of Jain Farstrider,* and that great traveler had named his horse Jeade'en—True Finder, in the Old Tongue—because the animal had always been able to find the way home. It would have been nice to think Jeade'en might carry him home one day. Nice, but not likely, and he did not want anyone suspecting the cause for the name. Boyish fancies had no place in his life now. There was not much room for anything but what he had to do.

"A fine name," she said absently. He knew she had read the book, too, and half-expected her to recognize the name, but she seemed to be mulling over something else, chewing her lower lip pensively.

He was content with silence. The last dregs of the city gave way to country and pitiful scattered farms. Not even a Congar or a Coplin,

Two River folk notorious for laziness among other things, would keep a place as run-down and ramshackle as these rough stone houses, walls slanting as if about to topple over on the chickens scratching in the dirt. Sagging barns leaned against laurels or spicewoods. Roofs of cracked and broken slates all looked as if they leaked. Goats bleated disconsolately in stone pens that might have been thrown together hastily that morning. Barefoot men and women hoed stoop-shouldered in unfenced fields, not looking up even when the large party was passing. Redbeaks and thrushes warbling in the small thickets were not enough to lighten the feel of oppressive gloom.

I have to do something about this. I. . . . No, not now. First things first. I've done what I could for them in a few weeks. I can't do anything more now. He tried not to look at the tumbledown farms. Were the olive groves in the south as bad? The people who worked those did not even own the land; it all belonged to High Lords. *No. The breeze. Nice, the way it cuts the heat. I can enjoy it a bit longer. I have to tell them, soon now.*

"Rand," Egwene said abruptly, "I want to talk to you." Something serious by her expression; those big dark eyes, fixed on him, held a light reminiscent of Nynaeve's when she was about to lecture. "I want to talk about Elayne."

"What about her?" he asked warily. He touched his pouch, where two letters crinkled against a small hard object. If they had not both been in the same elegantly flowing hand, he would not have believed they came from the same woman. And after all that kissing and snuggling. The High Lords were easier to understand than women.

"Why did you let her go in that way?"

Puzzled, he stared at her. "She wanted to go. I'd have had to tie her up to stop her. Besides, she'll be safer in Tanchico than near me—or Mat—if we are going to attract bubbles of evil the way Moiraine says. You would be, too."

"That isn't what I mean at all. Of course she wanted to go. And you had no right to stop her. But why didn't you tell her you wished she would stay?"

"She wanted to go," he repeated, and grew more confused when she rolled her eyes as if he were speaking gibberish. If he had no right to stop Elayne, and she wanted to go, why was he supposed to try to talk her out of it? Especially when she was safer gone.

Moiraine spoke, right behind him. "Are you ready to tell me the next secret? It has been clear you were keeping something from me. At the least I might be able to tell you if you are leading us over a cliff."

Rand sighed. He had not heard her and Lan closing up on him. And Mat as well, although still holding a distance between himself and the Aes Sedai. Mat's face was a study, doubt and reluctance and grim determination all running across it by turns, especially when he glanced at Moiraine. He never looked at her directly, only from the edge of his eye.

"Are you sure you want to come, Mat?" Rand asked.

Mat shrugged and affected a grin, not a very confident one. "Who could pass up a chance to see bloody Rhuidean?" Egwene raised her eyebrows at him. "Oh, pardon my language, *Aes Sedai.* I've heard you say as bad, and for less cause, I'll wager." Egwene stared at him indignantly, but spots of color in her cheeks said he had scored a hit.

"Be glad Mat *is* here," Moiraine said to Rand, her voice cool, and not pleased. "You made a grave error letting Perrin run off, hiding his going from me. The world rests on your shoulders, but they must both support you or you will fall, and the world with you." Mat flinched, and Rand thought he very nearly turned his gelding and rode away on the spot.

"I know my duty," he told her. *And I know my fate,* he thought, but he did not say that aloud; he was not asking sympathy. "One of us had to go back, Moiraine, and Perrin wanted to. You're willing to let anything go to save the world. I. . . . I do what I have to." The Warder nodded, though he said nothing; Lan would not disagree with Moiraine in front of others.

"And the next secret?" she said insistently. She would not give up until she had ferreted it out, and he had no reason to keep it secret any longer. Not this part of it.

"Portal Stones," he said simply. "If we are lucky."

"Oh, Light!" Mat groaned. "Bloody flaming Light! Don't grimace at me, Egwene! Lucky? Isn't once enough, Rand? You almost killed us, remember? No, worse than killed. I would rather ride back to one of those farms and ask for a job slopping pigs the rest of my life."

"You can go your own way if you want, Mat," Rand told him. Moiraine's calm face was a mask over fury, but he ignored the icy stare that tried to still his tongue. Even Lan looked disapproving, for all his hard face did not change very much; the Warder believed in duty before anything else. Rand would do his duty, but his friends. . . . He did not like making people do things; he would not do it to his friends. That much he could avoid, surely. "You've no reason to come to the Waste."

"Oh, yes I do. At least. . . . Oh, burn me! I've one life to give away, don't I? Why not like this?" Mat laughed nervously, and a bit wildly. "Bloody Portal Stones! Light!"

Rand frowned; he was the one they all said was supposed to go mad, but Mat was the one who seemed on the edge of it now.

Egwene blinked at Mat worriedly, but it was Rand she leaned toward. "Rand, Verin Sedai told me a little about Portal Stones. She told me about the . . . journey you took. Do you really mean to do this?"

"It's what I have to do, Egwene." He had to move quickly, and there was no quicker way than Portal Stones. Remnants of an Age older than the Age of Legends; even Aes Sedai of the Age of Legends had not understood them, it seemed. But there was no quicker way. If it worked the way he hoped.

Moiraine had listened to the exchange patiently. Especially to Mat's part of it, though Rand could not see why. Now she said, "Verin also told me of your journey using Portal Stones. That was only a few people and horses, not hundreds, and if you did not almost kill everyone as Mat says, it yet sounded an experience no one would wish to repeat. Nor did it turn out as you expected. It also required a great deal of the Power; almost enough to kill you at least, Verin said. Even if you leave most of the Aiel behind, do you dare risk the attempt?"

"I have to," he said, feeling at his belt pouch, at the small hard shape behind the letters, but she went right on as if he had not spoken.

"Are you even certain there *is* a Portal Stone in the Waste? Verin certainly knows more of them than I, but I have never heard of one. If there is, will it place us any closer to Rhuidean than we are right now?"

"Some six hundred or so years ago," he told her, "a peddler tried to get a look at Rhuidean." Another time it would have been a pleasure to be able to lecture her for a change. Not today. There was too much he did not know. "This fellow apparently didn't see anything of it; he claimed to have seen a golden city up in the clouds, drifting over the mountains."

"There are no cities in the Waste," Lan said, "in the clouds or on the ground. I've fought the Aiel. They have no cities."

Egwene nodded. "Aviendha told me she had never seen a city until she left the Waste."

"Maybe so," Rand said. "But the peddler also saw something sticking out of the side of one of those mountains. A Portal Stone. He described it perfectly. There isn't anything else like a Portal Stone. When I described one to the chief librarian in the Stone . . . ." Without naming what he was after, he did not add. ". . . he recognized it, even if he didn't know what it was, enough to show me four on an old map of Tear—"

"Four?" Moiraine sounded startled. "All in Tear? Portal Stones are not so common as that."

"Four," Rand said definitely. The bony old librarian had been certain, even digging out a tattered yellowed manuscript telling of efforts to move the "unknown artifacts of an earlier Age" to the Great Holding. Every attempt had failed, and the Tairens had finally given up. That was confirmation to Rand; Portal Stones resisted being moved. "One lies not an hour's ride from where we are," he continued. "The Aiel allowed the peddler to leave, since he was a peddler. With one of his mules and as much water as he could carry on his back. Somehow he made it as far as a *stedding* in the Spine of the World, where he met a man named Soran Milo, who was writing a book called *The Killers of the Black Veil*. The librarian brought me a battered copy when I asked for books on the Aiel. Milo apparently based it all on Aiel who came to trade at the *stedding*, and he got almost everything wrong anyway, according to Rhuarc, but a Portal Stone can't be anything but a Portal Stone." He had examined other maps and manuscripts, dozens of them, supposedly studying Tear and its history, learning the land; *no* one could have had a clue what he intended before a few minutes ago.

Moiraine sniffed, and her white mare, Aldieb, frisked a few steps, picking up her irritation. "A supposed story told by a supposed peddler who claimed to have seen a golden city floating in the clouds. Has Rhuarc seen this Portal Stone? He has actually been to Rhiudean. Even if this peddler did go into the Waste, and did see a Portal Stone, it could have been anywhere. A man telling a story usually tries to better what really happened. A city floating in the clouds?"

"How do you know it doesn't?" he said. Rhuarc had been willing to laugh at all the wrong things Milo had written about Aiel, but he had not been very forthcoming about Rhuidean. No, more than that; or less, rather. The Aielman had refused even to comment on the parts of the book supposedly about Rhuidean. Rhuidean, in the lands of the Jenn Aiel, the clan which is not; that was almost the extent of what Rhuarc would say about it. Rhuidean was not to be spoken of.

The Aes Sedai was not best pleased with his flippant remark, but he did not care. She had kept too many secrets herself, made him follow her on blind trust too often. Let it be her turn. She had to learn that he was not a puppet. *I'll take her advice when I think it's right, but I won't dance on Tar Valon's strings again.* He would die on his own terms.

Egwene moved her gray horse closer, riding almost knee-to-knee with him. "Rand, do you really mean to risk our lives on a . . . a chance? Rhuarc did not tell you anything, did he? When I ask Aviendha about Rhuidean, she shuts up tight as a hickory nut." Mat looked sick.

Rand kept his face still, not letting his flash of shame show. He had not meant to frighten his friends. "There is a Portal Stone there," he maintained. He rubbed the hard shape in his pouch again. This had to work.

The librarian's maps had been old, but in a way that was a help. The grasslands they rode now had been forest when those maps were drawn, but few trees remained, far-scattered scraggly copses of white oak and pine and maidenhair, tall solitary trees he did not recognize, with gnarled spindly trunks. He could make out the shape of the land easily, hills shrouded mainly in high grass now.

On the maps two tall bent ridges, one close behind the other, had pointed to the cluster of round hills where the Portal Stone was. If the maps had been well made. If the librarian really had recognized his description, and the green diamond mark actually meant ancient ruins as he claimed. *Why would he lie? I'm getting too suspicious. No, I have to be suspicious. As trusting as a viper, and as cold.* He did not like it, though.

To the north he could just make out hills with no trees at all, speckled with moving shapes that must be horses. The High Lords' herds, grazing across the site of the old Ogier grove. He hoped Perrin and Loial had gotten away safely. *Help them, Perrin,* he thought. *Help them somehow, because I can't.*

The Ogier grove meant the folded ridges must be close, and soon he spotted them a little to the south, like two arrows one inside the other, a few trees along the top making a thin line against the sky. Beyond, low round hills like grass-covered bubbles ran into one another. More hills than on the old map. Too many, for all the patch encompassed less than a square mile. If they did not correspond to the map, which one held the Portal Stone on its side?

"The Aiel have numbers," Lan said quietly, "and sharp eyes."

With a nod of gratitude, Rand reined Jeade'en in, falling back to put the problem before Rhuarc. He only described the Portal Stone, not saying what it was; there would be time enough for that when it was found. He was good at keeping secrets now. Rhuarc probably had no idea what a Portal Stone was, anyway. Few did except for Aes Sedai. He had not known until someone told him.

Striding along beside the dapple stallion, the Aielman frowned slightly—as much as a worried grimace from most other men—then nodded. "We can find this thing." He raised his voice. *"Aethan Dor! Far Aldazar Din! Duadhe Mahdi'in! Far Dareis Mai! Seia Doon! Sha'mad Conde!"*

As he called out, members of the named warrior societies trotted forward, until a good quarter of the Aiel clustered around him and Rand. Red Shields. Brothers of the Eagle. Water Seekers. Maidens of the Spear. Black Eyes. Thunder Walkers.

Rand picked out Egwene's friend, Aviendha, a tall, pretty woman with a haughty unsmiling stare. Maidens had guarded his door, but he did not think he had seen her before the Aiel gathered to leave the Stone. She looked back at him, proud as a green-eyed hawk, then tossed her head and turned her attention to the clan chief.

Well, I wanted to be ordinary again, he thought, a touch ruefully. The Aiel certainly gave him that. They offered even the clan chief only a respectful hearing, without any of the elaborate deference a lord would exact, and obedience that seemed between equals. He could hardly expect more for himself.

Rhuarc gave instructions in few words, and the listening Aiel fanned out ahead into the patch of hills, running easily, some veiling themselves just in case. The rest waited, standing or squatting beside the loaded pack mules.

They represented almost every clan—except the Jenn Aiel, of course; Rand could not get it straight whether the Jenn really existed or not, since the way the Aiel mentioned them, which they seldom did, it could be either way—including some clans that had blood feuds, and others that often fought each other. He had learned that much about them. Not for the first time, he wondered what had held them together so far. Was it just their prophecies of the Stone falling, and the search for He Who Comes With the Dawn?

"More than that," Rhuarc said, and Rand realized he had spoken his thoughts aloud. "Prophecy brought us over the Dragonwall, and the name that is not spoken drew us to the Stone of Tear." The name he meant was "People of the Dragon," a secret name for the Aiel; only clan chiefs and Wise Ones knew or used it, apparently seldom and only with each other. "For the rest? No one may shed the blood of another of the same society, of course, yet mixing Shaarad with Goshien, Taardad and Nakai with Shaido. . . . Even I might have danced the spears with the Shaido, if the Wise Ones had not made everyone who crossed the Dragonwall swear water oath to treat any Aiel as of the same society on this side of the mountains. Even sneaking Shaido. . . ." He shrugged slightly. "You see? It is not easy, even for me."

"These Shaido are enemies of yours?" Rand fumbled the name; in the Stone, the Aiel had gone by societies, not clans.

"We have avoided blood feud," Rhuarc said, "but Taardad and Shaido have never been friendly; the septs sometimes raid each other, steal goats or cattle. But the oaths have held with us all against three blood feuds and a dozen old hatreds between clans or septs. It helps now that we journey toward Rhuidean, even if some will leave us before. None may shed the blood of one traveling to or from Rhuidean." The Aielman looked up at Rand, face completely expressionless. "It may be that soon no one of us will shed another's blood." It was impossible to say whether he found the prospect pleasing.

An ululating cry came from one of the Maidens, standing atop a hill and waving her arms over her head.

"They have found your stone column, it seems," Rhuarc said.

Gathering her reins, Moiraine gave Rand a level look as he rode past her, eagerly heeling Jeade'en to a gallop. Egwene reined her mare near to Mat, leaning from her saddle with a hand on the high pommel of his to engage him in close conversation. She seemed to be trying to make him tell her something, or admit something, and from the vehemence of Mat's gestures, he was either innocent as a babe or lying in his teeth.

Flinging himself out of the saddle, Rand hurriedly climbed up the gentle slope to examine what the Maiden—it was Aviendha—had found half-buried in the ground and obscured by long grass. A weathered gray stone column, at least three spans long and a pace thick. Strange symbols covered every exposed inch, each surrounded by a narrow line of markings he thought were writing. Even if he could have read the language—if it was one—the script—if that was what it was— had long since worn to illegibility. The symbols he could make out a little better. Some of them; many might as well have been the marks of rain and wind.

Pulling grass by the handful so he could see better, he glanced at Aviendha. She had dropped her *shoufa* around her shoulders, baring short reddish hair, and was watching him with a flat, hard expression. "You don't like me," he said. "Why?" There was one symbol he had to find, the only one he knew.

"Like you?" she said. "You may be He Who Comes With the Dawn, a man of destiny. Who can like or dislike such? Besides, you walk free, a wetlander despite your face, yet going to Rhuidean for honor, while I. . . ."

"While you what?" he asked when she stopped. He searched his way slowly upslope. Where was it? Two parallel wavy lines crossed at an angle by an odd squiggle. *Light, if it's buried, it'll take us hours to turn this over.* Abruptly he laughed. Not hours. He could channel and lift the thing out of the ground, or Moiraine could, or Egwene. A Portal Stone might resist being moved, but surely they could move it that much. Channeling would not help him find the wavy lines, though. Only feeling his way along the stone would do that.

Instead of answering, the Aiel woman squatted easily with her short spears across her knees. "You have treated Elayne badly. I would not care, but Elayne is near sister to Egwene, who is my friend. Yet Egwene likes you still, so for her sake I will try."

Still searching the thick column, he shook his head. Elayne again. Sometimes he thought women all belonged to a guild, the way craftsmen in cities did. Put a foot wrong with one, and the next ten you met knew of it, and disapproved.

His fingers stopped, returned to the bit he had just examined. It was weathered almost beyond making out, but he was sure it was the wavy lines. They represented a Portal Stone on Toman Head, not in the Waste, but they located what had been the base of the thing when it stood upright. Symbols at the top represented worlds; those at the bottom, Portal Stones. With a symbol from the top and one from the bottom, he could supposedly travel to a given Portal Stone in a given world. With just one from the bottom, he knew he could reach a Portal Stone in this world. The Portal Stone near Rhuidean, for instance. If he knew the symbol for it. Now was when he needed luck, needed that *ta'veren* tugging at chance to favor him.

A hand reached over his shoulder, and Rhuarc said in a reluctant voice, "These two are used for Rhuidean in old writings. Long ago, even the name was not written." He traced two triangles, each surrounding what appeared to be forked lightnings, one pointing left, one right.

"Do you know what this is?" Rand asked. The Aielman looked away. "Burn me, Rhuarc, I have to know. I know you don't want to talk of it, but you have to tell me. Tell me, Rhuarc. Have you ever seen its like before?"

The other man took a deep breath before answering. "I have seen its like." Each word came as if dragged. "When a man goes to Rhuidean, Wise Ones and clansmen wait on the slopes of Chaendaer near a stone like this." Aviendha stood up and walked away stiffly; Rhuarc glanced after her, frowning. "I know no more of it, Rand al'Thor. May I never know shade if I do."

Rand traced the unreadable script surrounding the triangles. Which one? Only one would take him where he wanted to go. The second might land him on the other side of the world, or the bottom of the ocean.

The rest of the Aiel had gathered at the foot of the hill with their pack mules. Moiraine and the others dismounted and climbed the easy slope, leading their horses. Mat had Jeade'en as well as his own brown gelding, keeping the stallion well away from Lan's Mandarb. The two stallions eyed one another fiercely now that they had no riders.

"You truly don't know what you are doing, do you?" Egwene protested. "Moiraine, stop him. We can ride to Rhuidean. Why are you letting him go on with this? Why don't you say something?"

"What would you suggest I do?" the Aes Sedai said dryly. "I can hardly drag him away by his ear. We may be about to see how useful Dreaming really is."

"Dreaming?" Egwene said sharply. "What does Dreaming have to do with this?"

"Will you two be quiet?" Rand made himself sound patient. "I am trying to decide." Egwene stared at him indignantly; Moiraine showed no emotion at all, but she watched intently.

"Do we have to do it this way?" Mat said. "What do you have against riding?" Rand only looked at him, and he shrugged uncomfortably. "Oh, burn me. If you're trying to decide. . . ." Taking both horses' reins in one hand, he dug a coin from his pocket, a gold Tar Valon mark, and sighed. "It would be the same coin, wouldn't it." He rolled the coin across the backs of his fingers. "I'm . . . lucky sometimes, Rand. Let my luck choose. Head, the one that points to your right; flame, the other. What do you say?"

"This is the most ridiculous," Egwene began, but Moiraine silenced her with a touch on the arm.

Rand nodded. "Why not?" Egwene muttered something; all he caught were "men" and "boys," but it did not sound a compliment.

The coin spun into the air off Mat's thumb, gleaming dully in the sun. At its peak, Mat snatched it back and slapped it down on the back of his other hand, then hesitated. "It's a bloody thing to be trusting to the toss of a coin, Rand."

Rand laid his palm on one of the symbols without looking. "This one," he said. "You chose this one."

Mat peeked at the coin and blinked. "You're right. How did you know?"

"It has to work for me sooner or later." None of them understood—he could see that—but it did not matter. Lifting his hand, he looked at what he and Mat had picked. The triangle pointed left. The sun had slid down from its apex. He had to do this right. A mistake, and they could lose time, not gain it. That had to be the worst outcome. It had to be.

Standing, he dug into his pouch and pulled out the small hard object, a carving of shiny dark green stone that fit easily into his hand, a round-faced round-bodied man sitting cross-legged with a sword across his knees. He rubbed a thumb over the figure's bald head. "Gather everyone close. Everyone. Rhuarc, have them bring those pack animals up here. Everyone has to be as close to me as possible."

"Why?" the Aielman asked.

"We're going to Rhuidean." Rand bounced the carving on his palm and bent to pat the Portal Stone. "To Rhuidean. Right now."

Rhuarc gave him a long flat look, then straightened, already calling to the other Aiel.

Moiraine took a step closer up the grassy slope. "What is that?" she asked curiously.

"An *angreal*," Rand said, turning it in his hand. "One that works for men. I found it in the Great Holding when I was hunting that doorway. It was the sword that made me pick it up, and then I knew. If you are wondering how I mean to channel enough of the Power to take us all—Aiel, pack mules, everybody and everything—this is it."

"Rand," Egwene said anxiously, "I am sure you think you are doing what is best, but are you certain? Are you certain that *angreal* is strong enough? I can't even be sure it *is* one. I believe you if you say it is, but *angreal* vary, Rand. At least, those that women can use do. Some are more potent than others, and size or shape is no guide."

"Of course I'm certain," he lied. There had been no way to test it, not for this purpose, not without letting half of Tear know he was up to something, but he thought it would do. Just. And as small as it was, no one would know it was gone from the Stone unless they decided to inventory the Holding. Not likely, that.

"You leave *Callandor* behind and bring this," Moiraine murmured. "You seem to have considerable knowledge of using Portal Stones. More than I would have thought."

"Verin told me a good bit," he said. Verin had, but it had been Lanfear who first explained them to him. He had known her as Selene, then, but he did not intend explaining that to Moiraine any more than he would tell her of the woman's offer of help. The Aes Sedai had taken the news of Lanfear's appearance too calmly, even for her. And she had that weighing look in her eyes, as if she had him on balance scales in her mind.

"Take a care, Rand al'Thor," she said in that icy, musical voice. "Any *ta'veren* shapes the Pattern to one degree or another, but a *ta'veren* such as you might rip the Age Lace for all of time."

He wished he knew what she was thinking. He wished he knew what *she* was planning.

The Aiel climbed the hill with their pack mules, covering the slope as they crowded close around him and the Portal Stone, crowding in shoulder to shoulder on everyone but Moiraine and Egwene. Those two they left a little space. Rhuarc nodded at him as if saying, It is done, it is in your hands now.

Hefting the shiny green *angreal,* he thought of telling the Aiel to leave the animals, but there was the question of whether they would, and he wanted to arrive with all of them, with all feeling he had done well by them. Goodwill might be in short supply in the Waste. They watched him with imperturbable faces. Some had veiled themselves, though. Mat, nervously rolling that Tar Valon mark across the backs of his fingers over and over, and Egwene, sweat beading on her face, were the only ones who seemed anxious. There was no point in waiting any longer. He had to move faster than anyone thought he could.

He wrapped himself in the Void and reached out for the True Source, that sickly flickering light that was always there, just over his shoulder. The Power filled him, breath of life, wind to uproot oaks, summer wind sweetened with flowers, foul waftings from a midden heap. Floating in emptiness, he fixed the lightning-laced triangle before him and reached through the *angreal,* drew deeply at the raging torrent of *saidin.* He had to carry them all. It had to work. Holding that symbol, he pulled at the One Power, pulled it into him until he was sure he would burst. Pulled more. More.

The world seemed to wink out of existence.

CHAPTER
23

Beyond the Stone

E gwene stumbled, flinging her arms around Mist's neck as the
ground tilted under her feet. All about her, Aiel contended with
braying, sliding pack mules on a steep rocky slope where nothing
grew. Heat remembered from *Tel'aran'rhiod* hammered her. The air
shimmered before her eyes: the ground burned her feet through the
soles of her shoes. Her skin prickled painfully for a moment, then
sweat gushed from every pore. It only dampened her dress, and the
sweat seemed to evaporate immediately.

The struggling mules and tall Aiel nearly hid the surroundings from
her, but she saw a bit in flashes between them. A thick gray stone
column angled out of the ground not three paces from her, scoured by
windblown sand until there was no telling whether it had ever been
twin to the Portal Stone in Tear. Rugged slab-sided mountains that
looked carved by a mad giant's axe broiled beneath a blazing sun in a
cloudless sky. Yet in the center of the long, barren valley far below, a
mass of dense fog hung, billowing like clouds; that scalding sun should
surely have burned it off in moments, but the fog rolled untouched.
And out of that roiling gray stuck the tops of towers, some spired, some
ending abruptly as though the masons still worked.

"He was right," she murmured to herself. "A city in clouds."

Clutching his gelding's bridle, Mat was staring around wide-eyed.

"We made it!" He laughed at her. "We made it, Egwene, and without any. . . . Burn me, we made it!" He tugged open his shirt laces at the neck. "Light, it's hot. Burn me for true!"

Abruptly she realized Rand was on his knees, head down, supporting himself with one hand on the ground. Pulling her mare behind her, she pushed through the milling Aiel to him just as Lan helped him to his feet. Moiraine was already there, studying Rand with apparent calm—and the slight tightness at the corners of her mouth that meant she would like to box his ears.

"I did it," Rand panted, looking around. The Warder was all that was holding him upright; his face was drained and drawn, like a man on his deathbed.

"You came close," Moiraine said coolly. Very coolly. "The *angreal* was not sufficient to the task. You must not do this again. If you take chances, they must be reasoned and for a strong purpose. They must be."

"I don't take chances, Moiraine. Mat's the fellow for chances." Rand forced his right hand open; the *angreal,* the fat little man, had driven the point of its sword into his flesh, right into the branded heron. "Maybe you're right. Maybe I did need one a little stronger. A little bit, maybe. . . ." He gave a huffing laugh. "It worked, Moiraine. That is what's important. I've outrun them all. It worked."

"That is what matters," Lan said, nodding.

Egwene made a vexed *tsk.* Men. One almost killed himself, then tried to make a joke of it, and another told him he had done the right thing. Did they never grow up?

"The fatigue of channeling is not like other tiredness," Moiraine said. "I cannot rid you of it completely, not when you have channeled as much as you did, but I will do what I can. Perhaps what remains will remind you to be more careful in future." She *was* angry; there was a definite hint of satisfaction in her voice.

The glow of *saidar* surrounded the Aes Sedai as she reached up to take Rand's head in her hands. A shuddering gasp burst out of him, and he shivered uncontrollably, then jerked back from her, pulling free of Lan as well.

"Ask, Moiraine," Rand said coldly, stuffing the *angreal* into his belt pouch. "Ask, first. I'm not your pet dog that you can do whatever you want to whenever you want." He scrubbed his hands together to rub away the tiny trickle of blood.

Egwene made that vexed sound again. Childish, and ungrateful to boot. He could stand by himself now, though his eyes still looked weary, and she did not have to see his palm to know the tiny puncture was gone as if it had never been. Purely ungrateful. Surprisingly, Lan did not call him down for speaking to Moiraine in that fashion.

It came to her that the Aiel had gone absolutely still now that they had the mules quieted. They stared outward warily, not toward the valley and the fog-shrouded city that must be Rhuidean, but at two camps, one to either side of them perhaps half a mile away. The two clusters of dozens upon dozens of low, open-sided tents, one twice as large as the other, clung to the mountain slope and very nearly disappeared against it, but the gray-brown Aiel in each camp were clearly visible, short spears and arrow-nocked horn bows in hand, veiling themselves if they were not already. They seemed poised on the balls of their feet, ready to attack.

"The peace of Rhuidean," a woman's voice called from upslope, and Egwene could feel the tension leaving the Aiel surrounding her. Those among the tents began lowering their veils, though they still watched cautiously.

There was a third, much smaller encampment farther up the mountain, she realized, a few of the low tents on a small level patch. Four women were walking down from that camp, sedate and dignified in dark bulky skirts and loose white blouses, with brown or gray shawls around their shoulders despite heat that was beginning to make Egwene feel light-headed, and many necklaces and bracelets of ivory and gold. Two had white hair, one hair the color of the sun, flowing down their backs to the waist and held back from their faces by folded kerchiefs tied around the forehead.

Egwene recognized one of the white-haired women: Amys, the Wise One she had met in *Tel'aran'rhiod.* Again she was struck by the contrast between Amys's sun-darkened features and her snowy hair; the Wise One just did not look old enough. The second white-haired woman had a creased grandmotherly face, and one of the others, with gray-streaked dark hair, seemed almost as old. She was sure all four were Wise Ones, very likely the same who had signed that letter to Moiraine.

The Aiel women stopped ten paces upslope from the gathering around the Portal Stone, and the grandmotherly woman spread her open hands, speaking in an aged yet powerful voice. "The peace of Rhuidean be on you. Who comes to Chaendaer may return to their holds in peace. There shall be no blood on the ground."

With that the Aiel from Tear began to separate, quickly apportioning the pack animals and the contents of the hampers. They were not dividing by societies now; Egwene saw Maidens going with several groups, some of which immediately began making their way around the mountain, avoiding each other and the camps, peace of Rhuidean or no. Others strode toward one or the other large cluster of tents, where finally weapons were being put down.

Not everyone had been sure of the peace of Rhuidean. Lan released the hilt of his still-sheathed sword, although Egwene had not seen him put his hands on it, and Mat hastily slipped a pair of knives back into his sleeves. Rand stood with his thumbs tucked behind his belt, but there was clear relief in his eyes.

Egwene looked for Aviendha, to ask a few questions before she approached Amys. Surely the Aiel woman would be a little more forthcoming about the Wise Ones here, in her own land. She spotted the Maiden, carrying a large clinking jute sack, and two rolled wall hangings over her shoulder, as she started briskly for one of the big encampments.

"You will stay, Aviendha," the Wise One with gray streaks in her hair said loudly. Aviendha stopped in her tracks, not looking at anyone.

Egwene started to go to her, but Moiraine murmured, "Best not to interfere. I doubt she will want sympathy, or see anything else if you offer it."

Egwene nodded in spite of herself. Aviendha did look as if she wanted to be left alone. What did the Wise Ones want with her? Had she broken some rule, some law?

She herself would not have minded some more company. She felt very exposed standing there with no Aiel around her, and all those among the tents watching. The Aiel who had come from the Stone had been courteous even when not exactly friendly; the watchers looked neither. It was a temptation to embrace *saidar*. Only Moiraine, serene and cool as ever despite perspiration on her face, and Lan, as unperturbed as the rocks around them, kept her from it. They would know if there was danger. As long as they accepted the situation, she would. But she did wish those Aiel would stop staring.

Rhuarc climbed the slope with a smile. "I am come back, Amys, though not by the way you expected, I will wager."

"I knew you would be here today, shade of my heart." She reached up to touch his cheek, letting her brown shawl fall down onto her arms. "My sister-wife sends her heart to you."

"That's what you meant about Dreaming," Egwene said softly to Moiraine. Lan was the only other close enough to hear. "That's why you were willing to let Rand try to bring us here by Portal Stone. They knew about it, and told you in that letter. No, that doesn't make sense.

If they had mentioned a Portal Stone, you wouldn't have tried talking him out of it. They knew we'd be here, though."

Moiraine nodded without taking her eyes from the Wise Ones. "They wrote that they would meet us here, on Chaendaer, today. I thought it . . . unlikely . . . until Rand mentioned the Stones. When he was sure—certain beyond my dissuading—that one existed here. . . . Let us just say it suddenly seemed *very* likely we would reach Chaendaer today."

Egwene took a deep breath of hot air. So that was one of the things Dreamers could do. She could not wait to start learning. She wanted to go after Rhuarc and introduce herself to Amys—reintroduce herself— but Rhuarc and Amys were looking into one another's eyes in a way that excluded intruders.

A man had come out from each of the camps, one tall and broad-shouldered, flame-haired and still short of his middle years, the other older and darker, no less tall but more slender. They stopped a few paces to either side of Rhuarc and the Wise Ones. The older, leathery-faced man carried no visible weapon except his heavy-bladed belt knife, but the other carried spears and hide buckler, and held his head high with a fiercely prideful scowl directed at Rhuarc.

Rhuarc ignored him, turning to the older man. "I see you, Heirn. Has one of the sept chiefs decided I am already dead? Who seeks to take my place?"

"I see you, Rhuarc. No one of the Taardad has entered Rhuidean, or seeks to. Amys said she would come meet you here today, and these other Wise Ones traveled with her. I brought these men of the Jindo sept to see they arrived safely."

Rhuarc nodded solemnly. Egwene had the feeling something important had just been said, or hinted at. The Wise Ones did not look at the fiery-haired man, and neither did Rhuarc or Heirn, but from the color rising in the fellow's cheeks, they might as well have been staring at him. She glanced at Moiraine and got a tiny shake of the head; the Aes Sedai did not understand either.

Lan leaned down between them, speaking quietly. "A Wise One can go anywhere safely, into any hold regardless of clan. I think not even blood feud touches a Wise One. This Heirn came to protect Rhuarc from whoever the other camp is, but it would not be honorable to say it." Moiraine lifted one eyebrow a trifle, and he added, "I don't know much of them, but I fought them often before I met you. You have never asked me about them."

"I will remedy that," the Aes Sedai said dryly.

Turning back to the Wise Ones and the three men made Egwene's head swim. Lan pushed an unstoppered leather water bottle into her hands, and she tilted her head back to drink gratefully. The water was lukewarm and smelled of leather, but in the heat it tasted fresh from the spring. She offered the half-empty bottle to Moiraine, who drank sparingly and handed it back. Egwene was glad to gulp down the rest, closing her eyes; water splashed over her head, and she opened them again quickly. Lan was emptying another water bottle over her, and Moiraine's hair already dripped.

"This heat can kill if you are not used to it," the Warder explained as he wet down a pair of plain white linen scarves pulled from his coat. At his instructions, she and Moiraine tied the soaked cloths around their foreheads. Rand and Mat were doing the same. Lan left his own head unprotected to the sun; nothing seemed to faze the man.

The silence between Rhuarc and the Aielmen with him had stretched out, but the clan chief finally turned to the flame-haired man. "Do the Shaido lack a clan chief, then, Couladin?"

"Suladric is dead," the man answered. "Muradin has entered Rhuidean. Should he fail, I will enter."

"You have not asked, Couladin," the grandmotherly Wise One said in that reedy yet strong voice. "Should Muradin fail, ask then. We are four, enough to say yes or no."

"It is my right, Bair," Couladin said angrily. He had the look of a man not used to being balked.

"It is your right to ask," the thin-voiced woman replied. "It is ours to answer. I do not think you will be allowed to enter, whatever happens to Muradin. You are flawed within, Couladin." She shifted her gray shawl, rewrapping it around her angular shoulders in a way that suggested she had said more than she considered necessary.

The flame-haired man's face grew red. "My first-brother will return marked as clan chief, and we will lead the Shaido to great honor! We mean to—!" He snapped his mouth shut, almost quivering.

Egwene thought she would keep an eye on him if he remained anywhere close to her. He reminded her of the Congars and the Coplins back home, full of boasts and trouble. She had certainly never before seen any Aiel display so much raw emotion.

Amys seemed to have dismissed him already. "There is one who came with you, Rhuarc," she said. Egwene expected the woman to speak to her, but Amys's eyes swept straight to Rand. Moiraine was obviously not surprised. Egwene wondered what had been in that letter from these four Wise Ones that the Aes Sedai had not revealed.

Rand looked taken aback for a moment, hesitating, but then he strode up the slope to stand near Rhuarc at eye level to the women. Sweat plastered his white shirt to his body and made darker patches on his breeches. With a twisted white cloth tied around his head, he certainly did not look so grand as he had in the Heart of the Stone. He made an odd bow, left foot advanced, left hand on knee, right hand outstretched palm upward.

"By the right of blood," he said, "I ask leave to enter Rhuidean, for the honor of our ancestors and the memory of what was."

Amys blinked in evident surprise, and Bair murmured, "An ancient form, but the question has been asked. I answer yes."

"I also answer yes, Bair," Amys said. "Seana?"

"This man is no Aiel," Couladin broke in angrily. Egwene suspected he was very nearly always angry. "It is death for him to be on this ground! Why has Rhuarc brought him? Why—?"

"Do you wish to be a Wise One, Couladin?" Bair asked, a frown deepening the creases on her face. "Put on a dress and come to me, and I will see if you can be trained. Until then, be silent when Wise Ones speak!"

"My mother was Aiel," Rand said in a strained voice.

Egwene stared at him. Kari al'Thor had died while Egwene was barely out of her cradle, but if Tam's wife had been Aiel, Egwene would certainly have heard of it. She glanced at Moiraine; the Aes Sedai was watching, smooth-faced, calm. Rand did look a great deal like the Aielmen, with his height and gray-blue eyes and reddish hair, but this was ridiculous.

"Not your mother," Amys said slowly. "Your father." Egwene shook her head. This approached madness. Rand opened his mouth, but Amys did not let him speak. "Seana, how do you say?"

"Yes," the woman with gray-streaked hair said. "Melaine?"

The last of the four, a handsome woman with golden-red hair, no more than ten or fifteen years older than Egwene, hesitated. "It must be done," she said finally, and unwillingly. "I answer yes."

"You have been answered," Amys told Rand. "You may go into Rhuidean, and—" She cut off as Mat scrambled up to copy Rand's bow awkwardly.

"I also ask to enter Rhuidean," he said shakily.

The four Wise Ones stared at him. Rand's head whipped around in surprise. Egwene thought no one could be more shocked than she was, but Couladin proved her wrong. Lifting one of his spears with a snarl, he stabbed at Mat's chest.

332 THE SHADOW RISING

32 THE SHADOW RISING

The glow of *saidar* surrounded Amys and Melaine, and flows of Air lifted the fiery-haired man and flung bim back a dozen paces.

Egwene stared, wide-eyed. They could channel. At least, two of them could. Suddenly Amys's youthfully smooth features beneath that white hair leaped out at her for what they were, something very close to Aes Sedai agelessness. Moiraine was absolutely still. Egwene could almost hear her thoughts buzzing, though. This was plainly as much of a surprise to the Aes Sedai as to herself.

Couladin scrambled to his feet in a crouch. "You accept this outlander as one of us," he rasped, pointing at Rand with the spear he had attempted to use on Mat. "If you say it, then so be it. He is still a soft wetlander, and Rhuidean will kill him." The spear swung to Mat, who was trying to slip a knife back up his sleeve without being noticed. "But he—it is death for him to be here, and sacrilege for him to even *ask* to enter Rhuidean. None but those of the blood may enter. None!"

"Go back to your tents, Couladin," Melaine said coldly. "And you, Heirn. And you, as well, Rhuarc. This is business of Wise Ones, and none of men save those who have asked. Go!" Rhuarc and Heirn nodded and walked away toward the smaller set of tents, talking together. Couladin glared at Rand and Mat, and at the Wise Ones, before jerking around and stalking off toward the larger camp.

The Wise Ones exchanged glances. Troubled glances, Egwene would have said, though they were almost as good as Aes Sedai at keeping their faces blank when they wanted to.

"It is not permitted," Amys said finally. "Young man, you do not know what you have done. Go back with the others." Her eyes brushed across Egwene and Moiraine and Lan, standing alone now with the horses near the wind-scoured Portal Stone. Egwene could not find any recognition for her in that glance.

"I can't." Mat sounded desperate. "I've come this far, but this doesn't count, does it? I have to go to Rhuidean."

"It is not permitted," Melaine said sharply, her long red-gold hair swinging as she shook her head. "You have no Aiel blood in your veins."

Rand had been studying Mat all this time. "He comes with me," he said suddenly. "You gave me permission, and he can come with me whether you say he can or not." He stared back at the Wise Ones, not defiantly, merely determined, set in his mind. Egwene knew him like this; he would not back down whatever they said.

"It is not permitted," Melaine said firmly, addressing her sisters. She pulled her shawl up to cover her head. "The law is clear. No woman may go to Rhuidean more than twice, no man more than once, and none at all save they have the blood of Aiel."

Seana shook her head. "Much is changing, Melaine. The old ways. . . ."

"If he is the one," Bair said, "the Time of Change is upon us. Aes Sedai stand on Chaendaer, and *Aan'allein* with his shifting cloak. Can we hold to the old ways still? Knowing how much is to change?"

"We cannot hold," Amys said. "All stands on the edge of change, now. Melaine?" The golden-haired woman looked at the mountains around them, and the fog-shrouded city below, then sighed and nodded. "It is done," Amys said, turning to Rand and Mat. "You," she began, then paused. "By what name do you call yourself?"

"Rand al'Thor."

"Mat. Mat Cauthon."

Amys nodded. "You, Rand al'Thor, must go into the heart of Rhuidean, to the very center. If you wish to go with him, Mat Cauthon, so be it, but know that most men who enter Rhuidean's heart do not come back, and some return mad. You may carry neither food nor water, in remembrance of our wanderings after the Breaking. You must go to Rhuidean unarmed, save with your hands and your own heart, to honor the Jenn. If you have weapons, place them on the ground before us. They will be here for you when you return. If you return."

Rand unsheathed his belt knife and laid it at Amys's feet, then after a moment added the green stone carving of the round little man. "That is the best I can do," he said.

Mat began with his belt knife and kept right on, pulling knives from his sleeves and under his coat, even one from down the back of his neck, fashioning a pile that seemed to impress even the Aiel women. He made as if to stop, looked at the women, then took two more from each boot top. "I forgot them," he said with a grin and shrug. The Wise Ones' unblinking looks wiped his grin away.

"They are pledged to Rhuidean," Amys said formally, looking over the men's heads, and the other three responded together, "Rhuidean belongs to the dead."

"They may not speak to the living until they return," she intoned, and again the others answered. "The dead do not speak to the living."

"We do not see them, until they stand among the living once more." Amys drew her shawl across her eyes, and one by one the other three did the same. Faces hidden, they spoke in unison. "Begone from among the living, and do not haunt us with memories of what is lost.

Speak not of what the dead see." Silent then, they stood there, holding their shawls up, waiting.

Rand and Mat looked at one another. Egwene wanted to go to them, to speak to them—they wore the fixed too-steady faces of men who did not want anyone to know they were uneasy or afraid—but that might break the ceremony.

Finally Mat barked a laugh. "Well, I suppose the dead can talk to each other, at least. I wonder if this counts for. . . . No matter. Do you suppose it's all right if we ride?"

"I don't think so," Rand said. "I think we have to walk."

"Oh, burn my aching feet. We might as well get on with it then. It'll take half the afternoon just to get there. If we're lucky."

Rand gave Egwene a reassuring smile as they started down the mountain, as if to convince her there was no danger, nothing untoward. Mat's grin was the sort he wore when doing something particularly foolish, like trying to dance on the peak of a roof.

"You aren't going to do anything . . . *crazy* . . . are you?" Mat said. "I mean to come back alive."

"So do I," Rand replied. "So do I."

They passed from hearing, growing smaller and smaller as they descended. When they had dwindled to tiny shapes, barely distinguishable as people, the Wise Ones lowered their shawls.

Straightening her dress, and wishing she were not so sweaty, Egwene climbed the short distance to them leading Mist. "Amys? I am Egwene al'Vere. You said I should—"

Amys cut her off with a raised hand, and looked to where Lan was leading Mandarb and Pips and Jeade'en, behind Moiraine and Aldieb. "This is women's business, now, *Aan'allein.* You must stand aside. Go to the tents. Rhuarc will offer you water and shade."

Lan waited for Moiraine's slight nod before bowing and walking off in the direction Rhuarc had gone. The shifting cloak hanging down his back sometimes gave him the appearance of a disembodied head and arms floating across the ground ahead of the three horses.

"Why do you call him that?" Moiraine asked when he was out of earshot. "One Man. Do you know him?"

"We know of him, Aes Sedai." Amys made the title sound an address between equals. "The last of the Malkieri. The man who will not give up his war against the Shadow though his nation is long destroyed by it. There is much honor in him. I knew from the dream that if you came, it was almost certain *Aan'allein* would as well, but I did not know he obeyed you."

"He is my Warder," Moiraine said simply.

Egwene thought the Aes Sedai was troubled despite her tone, and she knew why. *Almost* certain Lan would come with Moiraine? Lan always followed Moiraine; he would follow her into the Pit of Doom without blinking. Nearly as interesting to Egwene was *"if you came."* Had the Wise Ones known they were coming or not? Perhaps interpreting the Dream was not as straightforward as she hoped. She was about to ask, when Bair spoke.

"Aviendha? Come here."

Aviendha had been squatting disconsolately off to one side, arms wrapped around her knees, staring at the ground. She stood slowly. If Egwene had not known better, she would have thought the other woman was afraid. Aviendha's feet dragged as she climbed to where the Wise Ones stood and set her bag and rolled wall hangings at her feet.

"It is time," Bair said, not ungently. Still, there was no compromise in her pale blue eyes. "You have run with the spears as long as you can. Longer than you should have."

Aviendha flung up her head defiantly. "I am a Maiden of the Spear. I do not want to be a Wise One. I will not be!"

The Wise Ones' faces hardened. Egwene was reminded of the Women's Circle back home confronting a woman who was heading off into some foolishness.

"You have already been treated more gently than it was in my day," Amys said in a voice like stone. "I, too, refused when called. My spear sisters broke my spears before my eyes. They took me to Bair and Coedelin bound hand and foot and wearing only my skin."

"And a pretty little doll tucked under your arm," Bair said dryly, "to remind you how childish you were. As I remember, you ran away nine times in the first month."

Amys nodded grimly. "And was made to blubber like a child for each of them. I only ran away five times the second month. I thought I was as strong and hard as a woman could be. I was not smart, though; it took me half a year to learn you were stronger and harder than I could ever be, Bair. Eventually I learned my duty, my obligation to the people. As you will, Aviendha. Such as you and I, we have that obligation. You are not a child. It is time to put away dolls—and spears—and become the woman you are meant to be."

Abruptly, Egwene knew why she had felt such a kinship with Aviendha from the first, knew why Amys and the others meant her to be a Wise One. Aviendha could channel. Like herself, like Elayne and

Nynaeve—and Moiraine, for that matter—she was one of those rare women who not only could be taught to channel, but who had the ability born in her, so she would touch the True Source eventually whether she knew what she was doing or not. Moiraine's face was still, calm, but Egwene saw confirmation in her eyes. The Aes Sedai had surely known from the first time she came within arm's reach of the Aiel woman. Egwene realized she could feel that same kinship with Amys and Melaine. Not with Bair or Seana, though. Only the first two could channel; she was sure of it. And now she could sense the same in Moiraine. It was the first time she had ever felt that. The Aes Sedai was a distant woman.

Some of the Wise Ones, at least, apparently saw more in Moiraine's face. "You meant to take her to your White Tower," Bair said, "to make her one of you. She is Aiel, Aes Sedai."

"She can be very strong if she is trained properly," Moiraine replied. "As strong as Egwene will be. In the Tower, she can reach that strength."

"We can teach her as well, Aes Sedai." Melaine's voice was smooth enough, but contempt tinged her unwavering green-eyed stare. "Better. I have spoken with Aes Sedai. You coddle women in the Tower. The Three-fold Land is no place for coddling. Aviendha will learn what she can do while you would still have her playing games."

Egwene gave Aviendha a concerned look; the other woman was staring at her feet, defiance gone. If they thought training in the Tower was *coddling*. . . . She had been worked harder and disciplined more strictly as a novice than ever before in her life. She felt a true pang of sympathy for the Aiel woman.

Amys held out her hands, and Aviendha reluctantly laid her spears and buckler in them, flinching when the Wise One threw them aside to clatter on the ground. Slowly Aviendha slid her cased bow from her back and surrendered it, unbuckled the belt holding her quiver and sheathed knife. Amys took each offering and tossed it away like rubbish; Aviendha gave a little jerk each time. A tear trembled at the corner of one blue-green eye.

"Do you have to treat her this way?" Egwene demanded angrily. Amys and the others turned flat stares on her, but she was not about to be intimidated. "You are treating things she cares about as trash."

"She must see them as trash," Seana said. "When she returns—if she returns—she will burn them and scatter the ashes. The metal she will give to a smith to make simple things. Not weapons. Not even a carving knife. Buckles, or pots, or puzzles for children. Things she will give away with her own hands when they are made."

"The Three-fold Land is not soft, Aes Sedai," Bair said. "Soft things die, here."

"The *cadin'sor*, Aviendha." Amys gestured to the discarded weapons. "Your new clothes will await your return."

Mechanically, Aviendha stripped, tossing coat and breeches, soft boots, everything onto the pile. Naked, she stood without wriggling a toe, though Egwene thought her own feet would blister through her shoes. She remembered watching as the clothes she had worn to the White Tower were burned, a severing of ties to an earlier life, but it had not been like this. Not this stark.

When Aviendha started to add the sack and the wall hangings to the pile, Seana took them from her. "These you can have back. If you return. If not, they will go to your family, for remembrance."

Aviendha nodded. She did not seem afraid. Reluctant, angry, even sullen, but not afraid.

"In Rhuidean," Amys said, "you will find three rings, arranged so." She drew three lines in the air, joining together in the middle. "Step through any one. You will see your future laid before you, again and again, in variation. They will not guide you wholly, as is best, for they will fade together as do stories heard long ago, yet you will remember enough to know some things that must be, for you, despised as they may be, and some that must not, cherished hopes that they are. This is the beginning of being called wise. Some women never return from the rings; perhaps they could not face the future. Some who survive the rings do not survive their second trip to Rhuidean, to the heart. You are not giving up a hard and dangerous life for a softer, but for a harder and more dangerous."

A *ter'angreal*. Amys was describing a *ter'angreal*. What kind of place was this Rhuidean? Egwene found herself wanting to go down there herself, to find out. That was foolish. She was not here to take unnecessary risks with *ter'angreal* she knew nothing about.

Melaine cupped Aviendha's chin and turned the younger woman's face to her. "You have the strength," she said with quiet conviction. "A strong mind and a strong heart are your weapons now, but you hold them as surely as you ever held a spear. Remember them, use them, and they will see you through anything."

Egwene was surprised. Of the four, she would have picked the sun-haired woman last to show compassion.

Aviendha nodded, and even managed a smile. "I will beat those men to Rhuidean. They cannot run."

Each Wise One in turn kissed her lightly on each cheek, murmuring, "Come back to us."

Catching Aviendha's hand, Egwene squeezed it and got a squeeze in return. Then the Aiel woman was running down the mountainside in leaps. It seemed she might well catch up to Rand and Mat. Egwene watched her go worriedly. This was something like being raised to Accepted, it seemed, but without any novice training first, without anyone to give small comfort afterward. What would it have been like to be raised Accepted on her first day in the Tower? She thought she might have gone mad. Nynaeve had been raised so, because of her strength; she thought at least some of Nynaeve's distaste for Aes Sedai came from what she had experienced then. *Come back to us,* she thought. *Be steadfast.*

When Aviendha passed out of sight, Egwene sighed and turned back to the Wise Ones. She had her own purpose here, and holding back from it would help no one. "Amys, in *Tel'aran'rhiod* you told me I should come to you to learn. I have."

"Haste," the white-haired woman said. "We have been hasty, because Aviendha struggled so long against her *toh,* because we feared the Shaido might don veils, even here, if we did not send Rand al'Thor into Rhuidean before they could think."

"You believe they'd have tried to kill him?" Egwene said. "But he's the one you sent people over the Dragonwall to find. He Who Comes With the Dawn."

Bair shifted her shawl. "Perhaps he is. We shall see. If he lives."

"He has his mother's eyes," Amys said, "and much of her in his face as well as something of his father, but Couladin could see only his clothes, and his horse. The other Shaido would have as well, and perhaps the Taardad, too. Outlanders are not allowed on this ground, and now there are five of you. No, four; Rand al'Thor is no outlander, wherever he was raised. But we have already allowed one to enter Rhuidean, which is also forbidden. Change comes like an avalanche whether we want it or not."

"It must come," Bair said, not sounding happy. "The Pattern plants us where it will."

"You knew Rand's parents?" Egwene asked cautiously. Whatever they said, she still thought of Tam and Kari al'Thor as Rand's parents.

"That is his story," Amys said, "if he wants to hear it." By the firmness of her mouth, she would not say another word on the subject.

"Come," Bair said. "There is no need for haste, now. Come. We offer you water and shade."

Egwene's knees nearly buckled at the mention of shade. The once-sopping kerchief around her forehead was almost dry; the top of her head felt baked, and the rest of her scarcely less. Moiraine seemed just as grateful to follow the Wise Ones up to one of the small clusters of low, open-sided tents.

A tall man in sandals and hooded white robes took their horses' reins. His Aiel face looked odd in the deep soft cowl, with downcast eyes.

"Give the animals water," Bair said before ducking into the low, unwalled tent, and the man bowed to her back, touching his forehead.

Egwene hesitated over letting the man lead Mist away. He seemed confident, but what would an Aiel know of horses? Still, she did not think he would harm them, and it did look wonderfully darker inside the tent. It was, and delightfully cool compared to outside.

The roof of the tent rose to a peak around a hole, but even under that there was barely room to stand. As if to make up for the drab colors the Aiel wore, large gold-tasseled red cushions lay scattered over brightly colored carpets layered thickly enough to pad the hard ground beneath. Egwene and Moiraine imitated the Wise Ones, sinking to the carpet and leaning on one elbow on a cushion. They were all in a circle, nearly close enough to touch the next woman.

Bair struck a small brass gong, and two young women entered with silver trays, bending gracefully, robed in white, with deep cowls and downturned eyes, like the man who had taken the horses. Kneeling in the middle of the tent, one filled a small silver cup with wine for each of the women reclining on a cushion, and the other poured larger cups of water. Without a word, they backed out bowing, leaving the gleaming trays and pitchers, beaded with condensation.

"Here is water and shade," Bair said, lifting her water, "freely given. Let there be no constraints between us. All here are welcome, as first-sisters are welcome."

"Let there be no constraints," Amys and the other two murmured. After one sip of water, the Aiel women named themselves formally. Bair, of the Haido sept of the Shaarad Aiel. Amys, of the Nine Valleys sept of the Taardad Aiel. Melaine, of the Jhirad sept of the Goshien Aiel. Seana, of the Black Cliff sept of the Nakai Aiel.

Egwene and Moiraine followed the ritual, though Moiraine's mouth tightened when Egwene called herself an Aes Sedai of the Green Ajah.

As if the sharing of water and names had broken down a wall, the mood in the tent changed palpably. Smiles from the Aiel women, a subtle relaxation, and said formalities were done.

Egwene was more grateful for the water than for the wine. It might be cooler in the tent than outside, but just breathing still dried her throat. At Amys's gesture she eagerly poured a second cup.

The people in white had been a surprise. It was foolish, but she realized she had been thinking that except for the Wise Ones Aiel were all like Rhuarc and Aviendha, warriors. Of course they had blacksmiths and weavers and other craftsmen; they must. Why not servants? Only, Aviendha had been disdainful of the servants in the Stone, not letting them do anything for her that she could avoid. These people with their humble demeanor did not act like Aiel at all. She did not recall seeing any white in the two large camps. "Is it only Wise Ones who have servants?" she asked.

Melaine choked on her wine. "Servants?" she gasped. "They are *gai'shain,* not servants." She sounded as if that should explain everything.

Moiraine frowned slightly over her winecup. *"Gai'shain?* How does that translate? 'Those sworn to peace in battle'?"

"They are simply *gai'shain,"* Amys said. She seemed to realize they did not understand. "Forgive me, but do you know of *ji'e'toh?"*

"Honor and obligation," Moiraine replied promptly. "Or perhaps honor and duty."

"Those are the words, yes. But the meaning. We live by *ji'e'toh,* Aes Sedai."

"Do not try to tell them all, Amys," Bair cautioned. "I once spent a month trying to explain *ji'e'toh* to a wetlander, and at the end she had more questions than at the beginning."

Amys nodded. "I will stay to the core. If you wish it explained, Moiraine."

Egwene would as soon have begun talk of Dreaming, and training, but to her irritation, the Aes Sedai said, "Yes, if you will."

With a nod to Moiraine, Amys began. "I will follow the line of *gai'shain* simply. In the dance of spears, the most *ji,* honor, is earned by touching an armed enemy without killing, or harming in any way."

"The most honor because it is so difficult," Seana said, bluish gray eyes crinkling wryly, "and thus so seldom done."

"The smallest honor comes from killing," Amys continued. "A child or a fool can kill. In between is the taking of a captive. I pare it down, you see. There are many degrees. *Gai'shain* are captives taken so, though a warrior who has been touched may sometimes demand to be taken *gai'shain* to reduce his enemy's honor and his own loss."

"Maidens of the Spear and Stone Dogs especially are known for this," Seana put in, bringing a sharp look from Amys.

"Do I tell this, or do you? To continue. Some may not be taken *gai'shain*, of course. A Wise One, a blacksmith, a child, a woman with child or one who has a child under the age of ten. A *gai'shain* has *toh* to his or her captor. For *gai'shain*, this is to serve one year and a day, obeying humbly, touching no weapon, doing no violence."

Egwene was interested in spite of herself. "Don't they try to escape? I certainly would." *I'll never let anyone make me a prisoner again!*

The Wise Ones looked shocked. "It has happened," Seana said stiffly, "but there is no honor in it. A *gai'shain* who ran away would be returned by his or her sept to begin the year and a day anew. The loss of honor is so great that a first-brother or first-sister might go as *gai'shain* as well to discharge the sept's *toh*. More than one, if they feel the loss of *ji* is great."

Moiraine seemed to be taking it all in calmly, sipping her water, but it was all Egwene could do not to shake her head. The Aiel were insane; that was all there was to it. It got worse.

"Some *gai'shain* now make an arrogance of humbleness," Melaine said disapprovingly. "They think they earn honor by it, taking obedience and meekness to the point of mockery. This is a new thing and foolish. It has no part in *ji'e'toh*."

Bair laughed, a startling rich sound compared to her reedy voice. "There have always been fools. When I was a girl, and the Shaarad and the Tomanelle were stealing each other's cattle and goats every night, Chenda, the roofmistress of Mainde Cut, was pushed aside by a young Haido Water Seeker during a raid. She came to Bent Valley and demanded the boy make her *gai'shain;* she would not allow him to gain the honor of having touched her because *she had a carving knife in her hands when he did.* A carving knife! It was a weapon, she claimed, as if she were a Maiden. The boy had no choice but to do as she demanded, for all the laughter when he did. One does not send a roofmistress barefoot back to her hold. Before the year and a day was done, the Haido sept and the Jenda sept exchanged spears, and the boy soon found himself married to Chenda's eldest daughter. With his second-mother still *gai'shain* to him. He tried to give her to his wife as part of his bride gift, and both women claimed he was trying to rob them of honor. He nearly had to take his own wife as *gai'shain*. It came close to raiding between Haido and Jenda again before the *toh* was discharged." The Aiel women almost fell over laughing, Amys and Melaine wiping their eyes.

Egwene understood little of the story—certainly not why it was funny—but she managed a polite laugh.

Moiraine set her water aside for the small silver cup of wine. "I have heard men speak of fighting the Aiel, but I have never heard of this before. Certainly not of an Aiel surrendering because he was touched."

"It is not surrender," Amys said pointedly. "It is *ji'e'toh.*"

"No one would ask to be made *gai'shain* to a wetlander," Melaine said. "Outlanders do not know of *ji'e'toh.*"

The Aiel women exchanged looks. They were uncomfortable. *Why?* Egwene wondered. *Oh.* To the Aiel, not to know *ji'e'toh* must be like not knowing manners, or not being honorable. "There are honorable men and women among us," Egwene said. "Most of us. We know right from wrong."

"Of course you do," Bair murmured in a tone that said that was not the same thing at all.

"You sent a letter to me in Tear," Moiraine said, "before I ever reached there. You said a great many things, some of which have proven true. Including that I would—must—meet you here today; you very nearly commanded me to be here. Yet earlier you said *if* I came. How much of what you wrote did you know to be true?"

Amys sighed and set aside her cup of wine, but it was Bair who spoke. "Much is uncertain, even to a dreamwalker. Amys and Melaine are the best of us, and even they do not see all that is, or all that can be."

"The present is much clearer than the future even in *Tel'aran'rhiod,*" the sun-haired Wise One said. "What *is* happening or beginning is more easily seen than what *will* happen, or *may.* We did not see Egwene or Mat Cauthon at all. It was no more than an even chance that the young man who calls himself Rand al'Thor would come. If he did not, it was certain that he would die, and the Aiel too. Yet he has come, and if he survives Rhuidean, some of the Aiel at least will survive. This we know. If you had not come, he would have died. If *Aan'allein* had not come, you would have died. If you do not go through the rings—" She cut off as if she had bitten her tongue.

Egwene leaned forward intently. Moiraine had to enter Rhuidean? But the Aes Sedai appeared to give no notice, and Seana spoke up quickly to cover Melaine's slip.

"There is no one set path to the future. The Pattern makes the finest lace look coarse woven sacking, or tangled string. In *Tel'aran'rhiod* it is possible to see some ways the future may be woven. No more than that."

Moiraine took a sip of wine. "The Old Tongue is often difficult to translate." Egwene stared at her. The Old Tongue? What about the rings, the *ter'angreal?* But Moiraine went blithely on. *"Tel'aran'rhiod* means the World of Dreams, or perhaps the Unseen World. Neither is really exact; it is more complex than that. *Aan'allein.* One Man, but also The Man Who Is an Entire People, and two or three other ways to translate it as well. And the words we have taken for common use, and never think of their meanings in the Old Tongue. Warders are called 'Gaidin,' which was 'brothers to battle.' Aes Sedai meant 'servant of all.' And 'Aiel.' 'Dedicated,' in the Old Tongue. Stronger than that; it implies an oath written into your bones. I have often wondered what the Aiel are dedicated to." The Wise Ones' faces had gone to iron, but Moiraine continued. "And 'Jenn Aiel.' 'The true dedicated,' but again stronger. Perhaps 'the only true dedicated.' The only true Aiel?" She looked at them questioningly, just as if they did not suddenly have eyes of stone. None of them spoke.

What was Moiraine doing? Egwene did not intend to allow the Aes Sedai to ruin her chances of learning whatever the Wise Ones could teach her. "Amys, could we talk of Dreaming now?"

"Tonight will be time enough," Amys said.

"But—"

"Tonight, Egwene. You may be Aes Sedai, but you must become a pupil again. You cannot even go to sleep when you wish yet, or sleep lightly enough to tell what you see before you wake. When the sun begins to set, I will begin to teach you."

Ducking her head, Egwene peered under the edge of the tent roof. From that deep shade, the light outside glared piercingly through heat shimmers in the air; the sun stood no more than halfway to the mountaintops.

Abruptly Moiraine rose to her knees; reaching behind her, she began undoing her dress. "I presume that I must go as Aviendha did," she said, not as a question.

Bair gave Melaine a hard stare that the younger woman met only for a moment before dropping her eyes. Seana said in a resigned voice, "You should not have been told. It is done, now. Change. One not of the blood has gone to Rhuidean, and now another."

Moiraine paused. "Does that make a difference, that I have been told?"

"Perhaps a great difference," Bair said reluctantly, "perhaps none.

We often guide, but we do not tell. When we saw you go to the rings, each time it was you who brought up going, who demanded the right though you have none of the blood. Now one of us has mentioned it first. Already there are changes from anything we saw. Who can say what they are?"

"And what did you see if I do not go?"

Bair's wrinkled face was expressionless, but sympathy touched her pale blue eyes. "We have told too much already, Moiraine. What a dreamwalker sees is what is likely to happen, not what surely will. Those who move with too much knowledge of the future inevitably find disaster, whether from complacency at what they think must come or in their efforts to change it."

"It is the mercy of the rings that the memories fade," Amys said. "A woman knows some things—a few—that will happen; others she will not recognize until the decision is upon her, if then. Life is uncertainty and struggle, choice and change; one who knew how her life was woven into the Pattern as well as she knew how a thread was laid into a carpet would have the life of an animal. If she did not go mad. Humankind is made for uncertainty, struggle, choice and change."

Moiraine listened with no outward show of impatience, though Egwene suspected it was there; the Aes Sedai was used to lecturing, not being lectured. She was silent while Egwene helped her out of her dress, not speaking until she crouched naked at the edge of the carpets, peering down the mountainside toward the fog-shrouded city in the valley. Then she said, "Do not let Lan follow me. He will try, if he sees me."

"It will be as it will be," Bair replied. Her thin voice sounded cold and final.

After a moment, Moiraine gave a grudging nod and slipped out of the tent into the blazing sunlight. She began to run immediately, barefoot down the scorching slope.

Egwene grimaced. Rand and Mat, Aviendha, now Moiraine, all going into Rhuidean. "Will she . . . survive? If you dreamed of this, you must know."

"There are some places one cannot enter in *Tel'aran'rhiod,*" Seana said. "Rhuidean. Ogier *stedding.* A few others. What happens there is shielded from a dreamwalker's eyes."

That was not an answer—they could have seen whether she came out of Rhuidean—but it was obviously all she was going to get. "Very well. Should I go, too?" She did not relish the thought of experiencing the rings; it would be like being raised to Accepted again. But if everyone else was going. . . .

"Do not be foolish," Amys said vigorously.

"We saw nothing of this for you," Bair added in a milder tone. "We did not see you at all."

"And I would not say yes if you asked," Amys went on. "Four are required for permission, and I would say no. You are here to learn to dreamwalk."

"In that case," Egwene said, settling back on her cushion, "teach me. There must be something you can begin with before tonight."

Melaine frowned at her, but Bair chuckled dryly. "She is as eager and impatient as you were once you decided to learn, Amys."

Amys nodded. "I hope she can keep her eagerness and lose the impatience, for her sake. Hear me, Egwene. Though it will be hard, you must forget that you are Aes Sedai if you are to learn. You must listen, remember, and do as you are told. Above all, you must not enter *Tel'aran'rhiod* again until one of us says you may. Can you accept this?"

It would not be hard to forget she was Aes Sedai when she was not. For the rest, it sounded ominously like becoming a novice again. "I can accept it." She hoped she did not sound doubtful.

"Good," Bair said. "I will now tell you about dreamwalking and *Tel'aran'rhiod,* in a very general way. When I am done, you will repeat back to me what I have said. If you fail to touch all points, you will scrub the pots in place of the *gai'shain* tonight. If your memory is so poor that you cannot repeat what I say after a second hearing. . . . Well, we will discuss that when it happens. Attend.

"Almost anyone can touch *Tel'aran'rhiod,* but few can truly enter it. Of all the Wise Ones, we four alone can dreamwalk, and your Tower has not produced a dreamwalker in nearly five hundred years. It is not a thing of the One Power, though Aes Sedai believe it is. I cannot channel, nor can Seana, yet we dreamwalk as well as Amys or Melaine. Many people brush the World of Dreams in their sleep. Because they only brush against it, they wake with aches or pains where they should have broken bones or mortal hurts. A dreamwalker enters the dream fully, therefore her injuries are real on waking. For one who is fully in the dream, dreamwalker or not, death there is death here. To enter the dream too completely, though, is to lose touch with the flesh; there is no way back, and the flesh dies. It is said that once there were those who could enter the dream in the flesh, and no longer be in this world at all. This was an evil thing, for they did evil; it must never be attempted, even if you believe it possible for you, for each time you will lose some part of what makes you human. You must learn to enter *Tel'aran'rhiod* when you wish, to the degree you wish. You must learn to find what you need to find and read what you see, to enter the dreams of another close by in order to aid healing, to recognize those who are in the dream fully enough to harm you, to. . . ."

Egwene listened intently. It fascinated her, hinting at things she had never suspected were possible, but beyond that she had no intention of ending up scrubbing pots. It did not seem fair, somehow. Whatever Rand and Mat and the others faced in Rhuidean, they were not going to be sent off to scrub pots. *And I agreed to it!* It just was not fair. But then, she doubted they could get any more out of Rhuidean than she would from these women.

CHAPTER
24

Rhuidean

T he smooth pebble in Mat's mouth was not making moisture anymore, and had not been for some time. Spitting it out, he squatted beside Rand and stared at the billowing gray wall maybe thirty paces in front of them. Fog. He hoped at least it was cooler in there than out here. And some water would be appreciated. His lips were cracking. He pulled the scarf from around his head and wiped his face, but there was not much sweat to dampen the cloth. Not much sweat remained in him to come out. A place to sit down. His feet felt like cooked sausages inside his boots; he felt pretty well cooked all over, for that matter. The fog stretched left and right better than a mile and bulked over his head like a towering cliff. A cliff of thick mist in the middle of a barren blistered valley. There had to be water in there.

Why doesn't it burn off? He did not like that part of it. Fooling with the Power had brought him here, and now it seemed he had to fool with it again. *Light, I want free of the Power and Aes Sedai. Burn me, I do!* Anything not to think of stepping into that fog, for just a minute more. "That *was* Egwene's Aiel friend I saw running," he croaked. Running! In this heat. Just thinking of it made his feet hurt worse. "Aviendha. Whatever her name is."

"If you say so," Rand said, studying the fog. He sounded as if he had a mouthful of dust, his face was sunburned, and he wavered unsteadily in his crouch. "But what would she be doing down here? And *naked?*"

Mat let it go. Rand had not seen her—he had hardly taken his eyes off the roiling mist since starting down the mountain—and he did not believe Mat had seen her either. Running like a madwoman and keeping wide of the two of them. Heading for this strange fog, it had seemed to him. Rand appeared no more eager to step into that than he was. He wondered whether he looked as bad as Rand did. Touching his cheek, he winced. He expected he did.

"Are we going to stay out here all night? This valley is pretty deep. It'll be dark down here in another couple of hours. Might be cooler then, but I don't think I would like to meet whatever runs around this place in the night. Lions, probably. I've heard there are lions in the Waste."

"Are you sure you want to do this, Mat? You heard what the Wise Ones said. You can die in there, or go mad. You can make it back to the tents. You left waterbottles and a waterbag on Pips's saddle."

He wished Rand had not reminded him. Best not to think about water. "Burn me, no, I don't want to. I *have* to. What about you? Isn't being the bloody Dragon Reborn enough for you? Do you have to be a flaming Aiel clan chief, too? Why are you here?"

"I have to be, Mat. I have to be." Resignation came through the parch in his voice, but something else, too. A hint of eagerness. The man really was mad; he *wanted* to do this.

"Rand, maybe that's the answer they give everybody. Those snake people, I mean. Go to Rhuidean. Maybe we don't have to be here at all." He did not believe it, but with that fog staring him in the face. . . .

Rand turned his head to look at him, not speaking. Finally he said, "They never mentioned Rhuidean to me, Mat."

"Oh, burn me," he muttered. Somehow or other he meant to find a way back through that twisted doorway in Tear. Absently he pulled the gold Tar Valon mark from his coat pocket, rolled it across the backs of his fingers and thrust it back. Those snaky folk were going to give him a few more answers whether they wanted to or not. Somehow.

Without another word, Rand rose and started toward the fog in an unsteady stride, his eyes fixed straight ahead. Mat hurried after him. *Burn me. Burn me. I do* not *want to do this.*

Rand plunged right into the dense mist, but Mat hesitated a moment before following. It had to be the Power maintaining the fog, after all, with its edge boiling so but never advancing or retreating an inch. The bloody Power, and no bloody choice. That first step was a blessed relief, cool and damp; he opened his mouth to let the mist moisten his tongue. Three steps more and he began to worry. Beyond the tip of his nose was only featureless gray. He could not make out even a shadow that could be Rand.

"Rand?" The sound might as well not have come from his mouth; the murk seemed to swallow it before it reached his own ears. He was not even sure of his direction anymore, and he could always remember his way. Anything might be ahead of him. Or under his feet. He could not see his feet; the fog shrouded him completely below the waist. He picked up his pace regardless. And suddenly stepped out beside Rand into a peculiar shadowless light.

The fog made an enormous hollow dome hiding the sky, its bubbling inner surface glowing in a pale sharp blue. Rhuidean was not nearly so big as Tear or Caemlyn, but the empty streets were broad as any he had ever seen, with wide strips of bare dirt down their centers as if trees had grown there once, and great fountains with statues. Huge buildings flanked the streets, odd flat-sided palaces of marble and crystal and cut glass, ascending hundreds of feet in steps or sheer walls. There was not a small building to be seen, nothing that might have been a simple tavern or an inn or a stable. Only immense palaces, with gleaming columns fifty feet thick climbing a hundred paces in red or white or blue, and grand towers, fluted and spiraled, some piercing the glowing clouds above.

For all its grandeur, the city had never been finished. Many of those tremendous structures ended in the sawteeth of abandoned construction. Colored glass made images in some huge windows: serenely majestic men and women thirty feet tall or more, sunrises and starry night skies; others gaped emptily. Unfinished and long deserted. No water splashed in any fountain. Silence covered the city as completely as the dome of fog. The air was cooler than outside, but just as arid. Dust grated under foot on pale smooth paving stones.

Mat trotted to the nearest fountain anyway, just on the off chance, and leaned on the waist-high white rim. Three unclothed women, twice as tall as he and supporting an odd wide-mouthed fish over their heads, peered down into a wide dusty basin no dryer than his mouth.

"Of course," Rand said behind him. "I should have thought of this before."

Mat looked over his shoulder. "Thought of what?" Rand was staring at the fountain, shaking with silent laughter. "Get hold of yourself,

Rand. You didn't go crazy in the last minute. You should have thought of what?"

A hollow gurgling whipped Mat's eyes back to the fountain. Abruptly water gushed out of the fish's mouth, a stream as thick as his leg. He scrambled into the basin and ran to stand under the downpour, head back and mouth open. Cold sweet water, cold enough to make him shiver, sweeter than wine. It soaked his hair, his coat, his breeches. He drank until he thought he would drown, finally staggering over to lean panting against a woman's stone leg.

Rand was still standing there staring at the fountain, face red and lips cracked, laughing softly. "No water, Mat. They said we couldn't bring water, but they did not say anything about what was already here."

"Rand? Aren't you going to drink?"

Rand gave a start, then stepped into the now ankle-deep basin and splashed across to stand where Mat had been, drinking in the same way, eyes closed and face tilted up to let the water pour over him.

Mat watched worriedly. Not mad, exactly; not yet. But how long would Rand have stood there laughing while thirst turned his throat to stone if he had not spoken? Mat left him there and climbed out of the fountain. Some of the water drenching his clothes had seeped down into his boots. He ignored the squish he made at every step; he was not sure he could get his boots back on if he pulled them off. Besides, it felt good.

Peering at the city, he wondered what he was doing there. Those people had said he would die, otherwise, but was just being in Rhuidean enough? *Do I have to do something? What?*

The empty streets and half-finished palaces, were shadowless in the pale azure light. A prickling grew between his shoulder blades. All those empty windows looking down on him, all those gap-toothed lines of forsaken stonework. Anything could be hiding in there, and in a place like this, anything could be. . . . *Any bloody thing at all.* He wished he still had his boot knives, at least. But those women, those Wise Ones, had stared at him as if they knew he was holding out on them. And they had channeled, one or all of them. It was not wise to step on the wrong side of women who could channel if you could avoid it. *Burn me, if I could get shut of Aes Sedai, I'd never ask for another thing. Well, not for a good long while, anyway. Light, I wonder if anything is hiding in here.*

"The heart has to be that way, Mat." Rand was climbing out of the basin, dripping wet.

"The heart?"

"The Wise Ones said I had to go to the heart. They must mean the center of the city." Rand looked back at the fountain and suddenly the flow dwindled to a trickle, then ceased. "There's an ocean of good water down there. Deep. So deep I nearly didn't find it. If I could bring it up. . . . No need to waste it, though. We can get another good drink when it's time to leave."

Mat shifted his feet uncomfortably. *Fool! Where did you think it came from? Of course he bloody channeled. Did you think it just started flowing again after the Light knows how long?* "Center of the city. Of course. Lead on."

They kept to the middle of the wide street, walking along the edge of the bare strips of dirt, past more dry fountains, some with only the stone basin and a marble base where the statues should have been. Nothing was broken in the city, only . . . incomplete. The palaces loomed to either side like cliffs. There had to be things inside. Furniture, maybe, if it had not rotted. Maybe gold. Knives. Knives would not rust away in this dry air no matter how long they had been there.

There could be a bloody Myrddraal in there for all you know. Light, why did I have to think of that? If only he had thought to bring a quarterstaff with him when he left the Stone. Maybe he could have convinced the Wise Ones it was a walking staff. No use thinking of it, now. A tree would do, if he had a way to cut a good branch and trim it. If, again. He wondered whether whoever built this city had managed to grow any trees. He had worked on his father's farm too long not to know good dirt when he saw it. These long ribbons of exposed soil were poor, no good for growing anything besides weeds, and not many of those. None, now.

After they had walked a mile, the street suddenly ended at a great plaza, perhaps as far across as they had walked and surrounded by those palaces of marble and crystal. Startlingly, a tree stood in the huge square, a good hundred feet tall and spreading its thick, leafy limbs over a hide of dusty white paving stones, near what appeared to be concentric rings of clear, glittering glass columns, thin as needles compared to their height, nearly as much as the tree's. He would have wondered how a tree could grow here, without sunlight, if he had not been too busy staring at the astounding jumble filling the rest of the square.

A clear lane led from each street Mat could see, straight to the columned rings, but in the spaces between, statues stood haphazardly, life-sized down to half that, in stone or crystal or metal, set right down on the pavement. All among them were. . . . He did not know what to call them, at first. A flat silvery ring, ten feet across and thin as a blade. A tapering crystal plinth a pace tall that might have held one of the smaller statues. A shiny black metal spire, narrow as a spear and no longer, yet standing on end as if rooted. Hundreds of things, maybe thousands, in every shape imaginable, every material imaginable, dotting the huge plaza with no more than a dozen feet between any two.

It was the black metal spear, so unnaturally erect, that suddenly told him what they must be. *Ter'angreal.* Some sort of things to do with the Power, anyway. Some of them had to be. That twisted stone doorway in the Stone's Great Holding had resisted falling over, too.

He was ready to turn around and go back right then, but Rand continued on, barely looking at what lined his way. Once Rand paused, staring down at two figurines that hardly seemed to deserve a place with the other things. Two statuettes maybe a foot tall, a man and a woman, each holding a crystal sphere aloft in one hand. He half-bent as if to touch them, but straightened so quickly it could almost have been Mat's imagination.

After a minute, Mat followed, hurrying to catch up. The closer they came to the scintillating rings of columns, the more he tensed. Those things all around them had to do with the Power, and so did the columns. He just knew it. Those impossibly tall thin shafts sparkled in the bluish light, dazzling the eye. *All they said was I had to come here. Well, I'm here. They didn't say anything about the bloody Power.*

Rand stopped so suddenly that Mat went three strides nearer the columned rings before realizing it. Rand was staring at the tree, Mat saw. The tree. Mat found himself moving toward it as if drawn. No tree had those trefoil leaves. No tree but one; a tree of legend.

"*Avendesora,*" Rand said softly. "The Tree of Life. It's here."

Under the spreading branches, Mat leaped to catch one of those leaves; his outstretched fingers fell a good pace short of the lowest. He satisfied himself with walking deeper beneath that leafy roof and leaning back against the thick bole. After a moment he slid down to sit against it. The old stories were true. He felt. . . . Contentment. Peace. Well-being. Even his feet did not bother him much.

Rand sat down cross-legged nearby. "I can believe the stories. Ghoetam, sitting beneath *Avendesora* for forty years to gain wisdom. Right now, I can believe."

Mat let his head fall back against the trunk. "I don't know that I'd trust birds to bring me food, though. You'd have to get up sometime."

But an hour or so would not be bad. Even all day. "It doesn't make sense anyway. What kind of food could birds bring in here? What birds?"

"Maybe Rhuidean wasn't always like this, Mat. Maybe. . . . I don't know. Maybe *Avendesora* was somewhere else, then."

"Somewhere else," Mat murmured. "I would not mind being somewhere else." *It feels . . . good . . . though.*

"Somewhere else?" Rand twisted around to look at the tall thin columns, shining so close. "Duty is heavier than a mountain," he sighed.

That was part of a saying he had picked up in the Borderlands. "Death is lighter than a feather, duty heavier than a mountain." It sounded like pure foolishness to Mat, but Rand was getting up. Mat copied him reluctantly. "What do you think we'll find in there?"

"I think I have to go on alone from here," Rand said slowly.

"What do you mean?" Mat demanded. "I've come this far, haven't I? I am not going to turn tail now." *Wouldn't I just like to, though!*

"It isn't that, Mat. If you go in there, you come out a clan chief, or you die. Or come out mad. I don't believe there's any other choice. Unless maybe the Wise Ones go in there."

Mat hesitated. *To die and live again.* That was what they had said. He had no intention of trying to be an Aiel clan chief, though; the Aiel would probably stick spears through him. "We'll leave it to luck," he said, pulling the Tar Valon mark from his pocket. "Getting to be my lucky coin. Flame, I go in with you; head, I stay out." He flipped the gold coin quickly, before Rand could object.

Somehow he missed grabbing it; the mark careened off his fingertips, clinked to the pavement, bounced twice. . . . And landed on edge.

He glared at Rand accusingly. "Do you do this sort of thing on purpose? Can't you control it?"

"No." The coin fell over, showing an ageless woman's face surrounded by stars. "It looks like you stay out here, Mat."

"Did you just . . . ?" He wished Rand would not channel around him. "Oh, burn me, if you want me to stay out here, I'll stay." Snatching the coin up, he stuffed it back into his pocket. "Listen, you go in, do whatever it is you have to, and get back out. I want to leave this place, and I am not going to stand here forever twiddling my thumbs waiting for you. And you needn't think I'll come in after you, either, so you had best be careful."

"I wouldn't think that of you, Mat," Rand said.

Mat stared at him suspiciously. What was he grinning at? "So long as you understand I won't. Aaah, go on and be a bloody Aiel chief. You have the face for it."

"Don't come in there, Mat. Whatever happens, don't." He waited until Mat nodded before turning away.

Mat stood, watching him walk in among the glittering columns. In the shifting dazzle he seemed to vanish almost immediately. *A trick of the eye,* Mat told himself. That was all it was. *A bloody trick of the eye.*

He started around the array, keeping well back, peering in in an effort to spot Rand again. "You look out what you're bloody doing," he shouted. "You leave me alone in the Waste with Moiraine and the bloody Aiel, and I'll strangle you, Dragon Reborn or no!" After a minute, he added, "I'm not coming in there after you if you get yourself in trouble! You hear me?" There was no answer. *If he's not out of there in an hour. . . .* "He's mad just going in there," he muttered. "Well, I'll not be the one to pull his bacon off the coals. He's the one who can channel. If he's put his head in a hornets' nest, he can bloody channel his way out of it." *I'll give him an hour.* And then he would leave, whether Rand was back or not. Just turn around and leave. Just go. That was what he would do. He would.

The way those thin shafts of glass caught the bluish light, refracting and reflecting, merely looking too hard was enough to give him a headache. He turned away, wandering back the way he had come, uneasily eyeing the *ter'angreal*—or whatever they were—filling the plaza. What was he doing there? Why?

Suddenly he stopped dead, staring at one of those strange objects. A large doorframe of polished redstone, twisted in some way he could not quite catch so his eye seemed to slip trying to follow it around. Slowly he made his way to it, between glittering faceted spires as tall as his head and low golden frames filled with what appeared to be sheets of glass, barely noticing them, never taking his eyes off the doorway.

It was the same. The same polished redstone, the same size, the same eye-wrenching corners. Along each upright ran three lines of triangles, points down. Had the one in Tear had those? He could not remember; he had not been trying to remember all the details last time. It *was* the same; it had to be. Maybe he could not step through the other again, but this one . . . ? Another chance to get at those snake people, make them answer a few more questions.

Squinting against the glitters, he peered back toward the columns. An hour, he had given Rand. In an hour, he could be through this thing and back with time to spare. Maybe it would not even work for him, since he had used its twin. *They* are *the same.* Then again, maybe it would. It just meant rubbing up against the Power one more time.

"Light," he muttered. *"Ter'angreal.* Portal Stones. Rhuidean. What difference can one more time make?"

He stepped through. Through a wall of blinding white light, through a roar so vast it annihilated sound.

Blinking, he looked around and bit back the vilest oath he knew. Wherever this was, it was not where he had gone before.

The twisted doorway stood in the middle of a huge chamber that appeared to be star-shaped, as near as he could make out through a forest of thick columns, each deeply fluted with eight ridges, the sharp edges yellow and glowing softly for light. Glossy black except for the glowing bits, they rose from a dull white floor into murky gloom far overhead where even the yellow stripes faded away. The columns and floor almost looked to be glass, but when he bent to rub a hand across the floor, it felt like stone. Dusty stone. He wiped his hand on his coat. The air had a musty smell, and his own footprints were the only marks in the dust. No one had been here in a very long time.

Disappointed, he turned back to the *ter'angreal.*

"A very long time."

Mat spun back, snatching at his coatsleeve for a knife that was lying back on the mountainside. The man standing among the columns looked nothing at all like the snaky folk. He made Mat regret giving up those last blades to the Wise Ones.

The fellow was tall, taller than an Aiel, and sinewy, but with shoulders too wide for his narrow waist, and skin as white as the finest paper. Pale leather straps studded with silver crisscrossed his arms and bare chest, and a black kilt hung to his knees. His eyes were too big and almost colorless, set deep in a narrow-jawed face. His short-cut, palely reddish hair stood up like a brush, and his ears, lying flat against his head, had a hint of a point at the top. He leaned toward Mat, inhaling, opening his mouth to pull in more air, flashing sharp teeth. The impression he gave was of a fox about to leap on a cornered chicken.

"A very long time," he said, straightening. His voice was rough, almost a growl. "Do you abide by the treaties and agreements? Do you carry iron, or instruments of music, or devices for making light?"

"I have none of those things," Mat replied slowly. This was not the same place, but this fellow asked the same questions. And he behaved the same, with all that smelling. *Rummaging through my bloody experiences, is he? Well, let him. Maybe he'll jog some loose so I can remember them, too.* He wondered if he was speaking the Old Tongue again. It was uncomfortable, not knowing, not being able to tell. "If you can take me to where I can get a few questions answered, lead the way. If not, I will be going, with apologies for bothering you."

"No!" Those big colorless eyes blinked in agitation. "You must not go. Come. I will take you where you may find what you need. Come." He backed away, gesturing with both hands. "Come."

Glancing at the *ter'angreal,* Mat followed. He wished the man had not grinned at him just then. Maybe he meant to be reassuring, but those teeth. . . . Mat decided he would never give up *all* of his knives again, not for Wise Ones or the Amyrlin Seat herself.

The large five-sided doorway looked more like a tunnel mouth, for the corridor beyond was exactly the same size and shape, with those softly glowing yellow strips running along the bends, edging floor and ceiling. It seemed to stretch ahead forever, fading into a murky distance, broken at intervals by more of the great five-sided doorways. The kilted man did not turn to lead until they were both in the hallway, and even then he kept glancing over a wide shoulder as if to make certain Mat was still there. The air was no longer musty; instead it held a faint hint of something unpleasant, something tickling familiarity but not strong enough to recognize.

At the first of the doorways, Mat glanced through in passing, and sighed. Beyond star-shaped black columns, a twisted redstone doorway stood on a dull glassy white floor where dust showed the marks of one set of boots coming from the *ter'angreal,* led toward the corridor by the prints of narrow bare feet. He looked over his shoulder. Instead of ending fifty paces back in another chamber like this, the hallway ran back as far as he could see, a mirror image of what lay ahead. His guide gave him a sharp-toothed smile; the fellow looked hungry.

He knew he should have expected something of the sort after what he had seen on the other side of the doorway in the Stone. Those spires moving from where they should be to where they could not, logically. If spires, why not rooms. *I should have stayed out there waiting for Rand, is what I should have done. I should have done a lot of things.* At least he would have no trouble finding the *ter'angreal* again, if all of the doorways ahead were the same.

He peered into the next and saw black columns, the redstone *ter'angreal,* his footprints and his guide's in the dust. When the narrow-jawed man looked over his shoulder again, Mat gave him a toothy grin. "Never think you have caught a babe in your snare. If you try to cheat me, I will have your hide for a saddlecloth."

The fellow started, pale eyes widening, then shrugged and adjusted the silver-studded straps across his chest; his mocking smile seemed tailored to draw attention to what he was doing. Suddenly Mat found himself wondering where that pale leather came from. Surely not. . . . Oh, Light, I think it is. He managed to stop himself from swallowing, but only just. "Lead, you son of a goat. Your hide is not worth silver studding. Take me where I want to go."

With a snarl, the man hurried on, stiff-backed. Mat did not care if the fellow was offended. He did wish he had just one knife, though. *I'll be burned if I'll let some fox-faced goat-brain make a harness out of* my *hide.*

There was no way of telling how long they walked. The corridor never changed, with its bent walls and its glowing yellow strips. Every doorway showed the identical chamber, *ter'angreal,* footprints and all. The sameness made time slip into formlessness. Mat worried about how long he had been there. Surely longer than the hour he had given himself. His clothes were only damp now; his boots no longer made squishing noises. But he walked, staring at his guide's back, and walked.

Suddenly the corridor ended ahead in another doorway. Mat blinked. He could have sworn that a moment before the hall had stretched on as far as he could see. But he had been watching the sharp-toothed fellow more than what lay ahead. He looked back, and nearly swore. The corridor ran back until the glowing yellow strips seemed to come together in a point. And there was not an opening to be seen anywhere along it.

When he turned, he was alone in front of the big five-sided doorway. *Burn me, I wish they wouldn't do that.* Taking a deep breath, he walked through.

It was another white-floored star-shaped chamber, not so large as the one—or ones—with columns. An eight-pointed star with a glassy black pedestal standing in each point, like a two-span slice out of one of those columns. Glowing yellow strips ran up the sharp edges of room and pedestals. The unpleasant smell was stronger here; he recognized it now. The smell of a wild animal's lair. He hardly noticed it, though, because the chamber was empty except for him.

Turning slowly, he frowned at the pedestals. Surely someone should be up on them, whoever was supposed to answer his questions. He was being cheated. If he could come here, he should be able to get answers.

Suddenly he spun in a circle, searching not the pedestals but the smooth gray walls. The doorway was gone; there was no way out.

Yet before he completed a second turn there was someone standing on each pedestal, people like his guide, but dressed differently. Four were men, the others women, their stiff hair rising in a crest before spilling down their backs. All wore long white skirts that hid their feet. The women had on white blouses that fell below their hips, with high lace necks and pale ruffles at their wrists. The men wore even more straps than the guide, wider and studded with gold. Each harness supported a pair of bare-bladed knives on the wearer's chest. Bronze blades, Mat judged from the color, but he would have given all the gold in his possession for just one of them.

"Speak," one of the women said in that growling voice. "By the ancient treaty, here is agreement made. What is your need? Speak."

Mat hesitated. That was not what the snaky people had said. They were all staring at him like foxes staring at dinner. "Who is the Daughter of the Nine Moons and why do I have to marry her?" He hoped they would count that as one question.

No one answered. None of them spoke. They just continued to stare at him with those big pale eyes.

"You are supposed to answer," he said. Silence. "Burn your bones to ash, answer me! Who is the Daughter of the Nine Moons and why do I have to marry her? How will I die and live again? What does it mean that I have to give up half the light of the world? Those are my three questions. Say something!"

Dead silence. He could hear himself breathing, hear the blood throbbing in his ears.

"I have no intention of marrying. And I have no intention of dying, either, whether I am supposed to live again or not. I walk around with holes in my memory, holes in my life, and you stare at me like idiots. If I had my way, I would want those holes filled, but at least answers to my questions might fill some in my future. You have to answer—!"

"Done," one of the men growled, and Mat blinked.

Done? What was done? What did he mean? "Burn your eyes," he muttered. "Burn your souls! You are as bad as Aes Sedai. Well, I want a way to be free of Aes Sedai and the Power, and I want to be away from you and back to Rhuidean, if you will not answer me. Open up a door, and let me—"

"Done," another man said, and one of the women echoed, "Done."

Mat scanned the walls, then glared, turning to take them all in, standing up there on their pedestals staring down at him. "Done? What is done? I see no door. You lying goat-fathered—"

"Fool," a woman said in a whispered growl, and others repeated it. Fool. Fool. Fool.

"Wise to ask leavetaking, when you set no price, no terms."

"Yet fool not to first agree on price."

"We will set the price."

They spoke so quickly he could not tell which said what.

"What was asked will be given."

"The price will be paid."

"Burn you," he shouted, "what are you talking—"

Utter darkness closed around him. There was something around his throat. He could not breathe. Air. He could not. . . .

CHAPTER
25

The Road to the Spear

Not hesitating at the first row of columns, Rand made himself walk in among them. There could be no turning back now, no looking back. *Light, what is supposed to happen in here? What does it really do?*

Clear as the finest glass, perhaps a foot thick and standing three paces or more apart, the columns were a forest of dazzling light filled with cascading ripples and glares and odd rainbows. The air was cooler here, enough to make him wish he had a coat, but the same gritty dust covered the smooth white stone under his boots. Not a breeze stirred, yet something made each hair on his body shift, even under his shirt.

Ahead and to the right he could just see another man, in the grays and browns of Aiel, stiff and statue-still in the changing lights. That must be Muradin, Couladin's brother. Stiff and still; *something* was happening. Strangely, considering the brilliance, Rand could make out the Aiel's face clearly. Eyes wide and staring, face tight, mouth quivering on the brink of a snarl. Whatever he was seeing, he did not like it. But Muradin had survived that far, at least. If he could do it, Rand could. The man was six or seven paces ahead of him at best. Wondering why he and Mat had not seen Muradin go in, he took another step.

*   *   *

He rode behind a set of eyes, feeling but not controlling a body. The owner of those eyes crouched easily among boulders on a barren mountainside, beneath a sun-blasted sky, peering down at strange half-made stone structures—*No!* Less *than half-made. That's Rhuidean, but without any fog, and only just begun*—peering down contemptuously. He was Mandein, young for a sept chief at forty. Separateness faded; acceptance came. He was Mandein.

"You must agree," Sealdre said, but for the moment he ignored her. The Jenn had made things to draw up water and spill it into great stone basins. He had fought battles over less water than one of those tanks held, with people walking by as though water was of no consequence. A strange forest of glass rose in the center of all their activity, glittering in the sun, and near it the tallest tree he had ever seen, at least three spans high. Their stone structures looked as if each was meant to contain an entire hold, an entire sept, when done. Madness. This Rhuidean could not be defended. Not that anyone would attack the Jenn, of course. Most avoided the Jenn as they avoided the accursed Lost Ones, who wandered searching for the songs they claimed would bring back lost days.

A procession snaked out of Rhuidean toward the mountain, a few dozen Jenn and two palanquins, each carried by eight men. There was enough wood in each of those palanquins for a dozen chief's chairs. He had heard there were still Aes Sedai among the Jenn.

"You must agree to whatever they ask, husband," Sealdre said.

He looked at her then, wanting for a moment to run his hands through her long golden hair, seeing the laughing girl who had laid the bridal wreath at his feet and asked him to marry her. She was serious now, though, intent and worried. "Will the others come?" he asked.

"Some. Most. I have talked to my sisters in the dream, and we have all dreamed the same dream. The chiefs who do not come, and those who do not agree. . . . Their septs will die, Mandein. Within three generations they will be dust, and their holds and cattle belong to other septs. Their names will be lost."

He did not like her talking to the Wise Ones of other septs, even in dreams. But the Wise Ones dreamed true. When they knew, it was true. "Stay here," he told her. "If I do not return, help our sons and daughters to hold the sept together."

She touched his cheek. "I will, shade of my life. But remember. You must agree."

Mandein motioned, and a hundred veiled shapes followed him down the slope, ghosting from boulder to boulder, bows and spears ready, grays and browns blending with the barren land, vanishing even to his eyes. They were all men; he had left all the women of the sept who carried the spear with the men around Sealdre. If anything went wrong and she decided on something senseless to save him, the men would probably follow her in it; the women would see her back to the hold whatever she wanted, to protect the hold and the sept. He hoped they would. Sometimes they could be fiercer than any man, and more foolish.

The procession from Rhuidean had stopped on the cracked clay flat by the time he reached the lower slope. He motioned his men to ground and went on alone, lowering his veil. He was aware of other men moving out from the mountain to his right and left, coming across the baked ground from other directions. How many? Fifty? Maybe a hundred? Some faces he had expected to see were missing. Sealdre was right as usual; some had not listened to their Wise Ones' dream. There were faces he had never seen before, and faces of men he had tried to kill, men who had tried to kill him. At least none were veiled. Killing in front of a Jenn was almost as bad as killing a Jenn. He hoped the others remembered that. Treachery from one, and the veils would be donned; the warriors each chief had brought would come down from the mountains, and this dry clay would be muddied with blood. He half-expected to feel a spear through his ribs any moment.

Even trying to watch a hundred possible sources of death, it was hard not to stare at the Aes Sedai as the bearers lowered their ornately carved chairs to the ground. Women with hair so white it almost seemed transparent. Ageless faces with skin that looked as if the wind might tear it. He had heard the years did not touch Aes Sedai. How old must these two be? What had they seen? Could they remember when his greatfather Comran first found Ogier *stedding* in the Dragonwall and began to trade with them? Or maybe even when Comran's greatfather Rhodric led the Aiel to kill the men in iron shirts who had crossed the Dragonwall? The Aes Sedai turned their eyes on him— sharp blue and dark dark brown, the first dark eyes he had ever seen— and seemed to see inside his skull, inside his thoughts. He knew himself chosen out, and did not know why. With an effort he pulled away from those twin gazes, which knew him better than he knew himself.

A gaunt white-haired man, tall if stooped, came forward from the Jenn flanked by two graying women who might have been sisters, with the same deep-set green eyes and the same way of tilting their heads when they looked at anything. The rest of the Jenn stared uneasily at the earth rather than at the Aiel, but not these three.

"I am Dermon," the man said in a deep strong voice, his blue-eyed scrutiny as steady as any Aiel's. "These are Mordaine and Narisse." He gestured to the women beside him in turn. "We speak for Rhuidean, and the Jenn Aiel."

A stir ran through the men around Mandein. Most of them liked the Jenn claiming to be Aiel no better than he did. "Why have you called us here?" he demanded, though it burned his tongue to admit being summoned.

Instead of answering, Dermon said, "Why do you not carry a sword?" That brought angry mutters.

"It is forbidden," Mandein growled. "Even Jenn should know that." He lifted his spears, touched the knife at his waist, the bow on his back. "These are weapons enough for a warrior." The mutters became approving, including some from men who had sworn to kill him. They still would, given the chance, but they approved of what he had said. And they seemed content to let him talk, with those Aes Sedai watching.

"You do not know why," Mordaine said, and Narisse added, "There is too much you do not know. Yet you must know."

"What do you want?" Mandein demanded.

"You." Dermon ran his eyes across the Aiel, making that one word fit them all. "Whoever would lead among you must come to Rhuidean and learn where we came from, and why you do not carry swords. Who cannot learn, will not live."

"Your Wise Ones have spoken to you," Mordaine said, "or you would not be here. You know the cost to those who refuse."

Charendin pushed his way to the front, alternately glaring at Mandein and the Jenn. Mandein had put that long puckered scar down his face; they had nearly killed each other three times. "Just come to you?" Charendin said. "Whichever of us comes to you will lead the Aiel?"

"No." The word came thin as a whisper, but strong enough to fill every ear. It came from the dark-eyed Aes Sedai sitting in her carved chair with a blanket across her legs as if she felt cold under the broiling sun. "That one will come later," she said. "The stone that never falls will fall to announce his coming. Of the blood, but not raised by the blood, he will come from Rhuidean at dawn, and tie you together with bonds you cannot break. He will take you back, and he will destroy you."

Some of the sept chiefs moved as if to leave, but none took more than a few steps. Each had listened to the Wise One of his sept. *Agree, or we will be destroyed as if we never were. Agree, or we will destroy ourselves.*

"This is some trick," Charendin shouted. Under Aes Sedai stares he lowered his voice, but it held anger yet. "You mean to gain control of the septs. Aiel bend knee to no man or woman." He jerked his head, avoiding the Aes Sedai's eyes. "To no one," he muttered.

"We seek no control," Narisse told them.

"Our days dwindle," Mordaine said. "A day will come when the Jenn are no more, and only you will remain to remember the Aiel. You must remain, or all is for nothing, and lost."

The flatness of her voice, the calm sureness, silenced Charendin, but Mandein had one more question. "Why? If you know your doom, why do this?" He gestured toward the structures rising in the distance.

"It is our purpose," Dermon replied calmly. "For long years we searched for this place, and now we prepare it, if not for the purpose we once thought. We do what we must, and keep faith."

Mandein studied the man's face. There was no fear in it. "You are Aiel," he said, and when some of the other chiefs gasped, he raised his voice. "I will go to the Jenn Aiel."

"You may not come to Rhuidean armed," Dermon said.

Mandein laughed aloud at the temerity of the man. Asking an Aiel to go unarmed. Shedding his weapons, he stepped forward. "Take me to Rhuidean, Aiel. I will match your courage."

Rand blinked in the flickering lights. He had *been* Mandein; he could still feel contempt for the Jenn fading into admiration. Were the Jenn Aiel, or were they not? They had looked the same, tall, with light-colored eyes in sun-darkened faces, dressed in the same clothes except for lacking veils. But there had not been a weapon among them save for simple belt knives, suitable for work. There was no such thing as an Aiel without weapons.

He was farther into the columns than a single step could account for, and closer to Muradin than he had been. The Aiel's fixed stare had become a dire frown.

Gritty dust crunched under Rand's boots as he stepped forward.

His name was Rhodric, and he was nearly twenty. The sun was a golden blister in the sky, but he kept his veil up and his eyes alert. His spears were ready—one in his right hand, three held with his small bullhide buckler—and he was ready. Jeordam was down on the brown grass flat to the south of the hills, where most of the bushes were puny and withered. The old man's hair was white, like that thing called snow the old ones talked of, but his eyes were sharp, and watching the welldiggers haul up filled waterbags would not occupy all of his attention.

Mountains rose to the north and east, the northern range tall and sharp and white-tipped but dwarfed by the eastern monsters. Those looked as if the world was trying to touch the heavens, and perhaps did. Maybe that white was snow? He would not find out. Faced with this, the Jenn must decide to turn east. They had trailed north along that mountainous wall for long months, painfully dragging their wagons behind them, trying to deny the Aiel that followed them. At least there had been water when they crossed a river, even if not much. It had been years since Rhodric had seen a river he could not wade across; most were only cracked dry clay away from the mountains. He hoped the rains would come again, and make things green once more. He remembered when the world was green.

He heard the horses before he saw them, three men riding across the brown hills in long leather shirts sewn all over with metal discs, two with lances. He knew the one on the lead, Garam, son of the chief of the town just out of sight back the way they came and not much older than himself. They were blind, these townsmen. They did not see the Aiel who stirred after they passed, then settled back to near invisibility in the sere land. Rhodric lowered his veil; there would be no killing unless the riders began it. He did not regret it—not exactly—but he could not make himself trust men who lived in houses and towns. There had been too many battles with that kind. The stories said it had always been so.

Garam drew rein, raising his right hand in salute. He was a slight dark-eyed man, like his two followers, but all three looked tough and competent. "Ho, Rhodric. Have your people finished filling their waterskins, yet?"

"I see you, Garam." He kept his voice level and expressionless. It made him uneasy, seeing men on horses, even more so than their carrying swords. The Aiel had pack animals, but there was something unnatural about sitting atop a horse. A man's legs were good enough. "We are close. Does your father withdraw his permission for us to take water on his lands?" No other town had ever given permission before. Water had to be fought for if men were near, just like everything else, and if there was water, then men were near. It would not be easy to take these three by himself. He shifted his feet in readiness to dance, and likely die.

"He does not," Garam said. He had not even noticed Rhodric's shift. "We have a strong spring in the town, and my father says that when you go, we will have the new wells you have dug until we go ourselves. But your grandfather seemed to want to know if the others started to move, and they have." He leaned an elbow on the front of his saddle. "Tell me, Rhodric, are they truly the same people as yourselves?"

"They are the Jenn Aiel; we, the Aiel. We are the same, yet not. I cannot explain it further, Garam." He did not really understand it himself.

"Which way do they move?" Jeordam asked.

Rhodric bowed to his greatfather calmly; he had heard a footfall, the sound of a soft boot, and had known it for an Aiel's. The townsmen had not noticed Jeordam's approach, though, and they jerked their reins in surprise. Only Garam's unflung hand stopped the other two from lowering their lances. Rhodric and his greatfather waited.

"East," Garam said when he had his horse under control again. "Across the Spine of the World." He gestured to the mountains that stabbed the sky.

Rhodric winced, but Jeordam said coolly, "What lies on the other side?"

"The end of the world, for all I know," Garam replied. "I am not sure there is a way across." He hesitated. "The Jenn have Aes Sedai with them. Dozens, I have heard. Does it not make you uneasy traveling close to Aes Sedai? I have heard the world was different once, but they destroyed it."

The Aes Sedai made Rhodric very nervous, though he kept his face blank. They were only four, not dozens, but enough to make him remember stories that the Aiel had failed the Aes Sedai in some way that no one knew. The Aes Sedai must know; they had seldom left the Jenn's wagons in the year since their arrival, but when they did, they looked at the Aiel with sad eyes. Rhodric was not the only one who tried to avoid them.

"We guard the Jenn," Jeordam said. "It is they who travel with Aes Sedai."

Garam nodded as if that made a difference, then leaned forward again, lowering his voice. "My father has an Aes Sedai advisor, though he tries to keep it from the town. She says we must leave these hills and move east. She says the dry rivers will run again, and we will build a great city beside one. She says many things. I hear the Aes Sedai plan to build a city—they have found Ogier to build it for them. Ogier!" He shook his head, pulling himself from legends back to reality. "Do you think they mean to rule the world once more? The Aes Sedai? I think we should kill them before they can destroy us again."

"You must do as you think best." Jeordam's voice gave no hint of his own thoughts. "I must ready my people to cross those mountains."

The dark-haired man straightened in his saddle, plainly disappointed. Rhodric suspected he had wanted Aiel help in killing Aes Sedai. "The Spine of the World," Garam said brusquely. "It has another name. Some call it the Dragonwall."

"A fitting name," Jeordam replied.

Rhodric stared at the towering mountains in the distance. A fitting name for Aiel. Their own secret name, told to no one, was People of the Dragon. He did not know why, only that it was not spoken aloud except when you received your spears. What lay beyond this Dragonwall? At least there would be people to fight. There always were. In the whole world there were only Aiel, Jenn, and enemies. Only that. Aiel, Jenn, and enemies.

Rand drew a deep breath that rasped as if he had not breathed for hours. Eye-splitting rings of light ran up the columns around him. The words still echoed in his mind. Aiel, Jenn, and enemies; that was the world. They had not been in the Waste, certainly. He had seen—lived —a time before the Aiel came to their Three-fold Land.

He was nearer still to Muradin. The Aiel's eyes shifted uneasily, and he seemed to struggle against taking another step.

Rand moved forward.

Squatting easily on the white-cloaked hillside, Jeordam ignored the cold as he watched five people tramp toward him. Three cloaked men, two women in bulky dresses, making hard work of the snow. Winter should have been over long since, according to the old ones, but then they told stories of the seasons changing from what they had always been. They claimed the earth used to shake, too, and mountains rose or sank like the water in a summer pond when you threw a rock in. Jeordam did not believe it. He was eighteen, born in the tents, and this was the only life he had ever known. The snow, the tents, and the duty to protect.

He lowered his veil and stood slowly, leaning on his long spear so as not to frighten the wagon folk, but they stopped abruptly anyway, staring at the spear, at the bow slung across his back and the quiver at his waist. None appeared any older than himself. "You have need of us, Jenn?" he called.

"You name us that to mock us," a tall, sharp-nosed fellow shouted back, "but it is true. We *are* the only true Aiel. You have given up the Way."

"That is a lie!" Jeordam snapped. "I have never held a sword!" He drew a deep breath to calm himself. He had not been put out here to grow angry with Jenn. "If you are lost, your wagons are that way." He pointed southward with his spear.

One woman placed a hand on sharp-nose's arm and spoke quietly. The others nodded, and finally sharp-nose did, too, if reluctantly. She was pretty, with yellow wisps of hair escaping the dark shawl wrapped around her head. Facing Jeordam, she said, "We are not lost." She peered at him suddenly, seeming to see him for the first time, and tightened her shawl around her.

He nodded; he had not thought they were. The Jenn usually managed to avoid anyone from the tents even when they needed help. The few who did not came only in desperation, for the help they could not find elsewhere. "Follow me."

It was a mile across the hills to his father's tents, low shapes partially covered by the last snowfall, clinging to the slopes. His own people watched the new arrivals cautiously, but did not stop what they were doing, whether cooking or tending weapons or tossing snowballs with a child. He was proud of his sept, nearly two hundred people, largest of the ten camps scattered north of the wagons. The Jenn did not seem much impressed, though. It irritated him that there were so many more Jenn than Aiel.

Lewin came out of his tent, a tall, graying man with a hard face; Lewin never smiled, they said, and Jeordam had certainly never seen it. Maybe he had before Jeordam's mother died of a fever, but Jeordam did not believe it.

The yellow-haired woman—her name was Morin—told a story much as Jeordam had expected. The Jenn had traded with a village, a place with a log wall, and then men from the village had come in the night, taking back what had been traded for, taking more. The Jenn always thought they could trust people who lived in houses, always thought the Way would protect them. The dead were listed—fathers, a mother, first-brothers. The captives—first-sisters, a sister-mother, a daughter. That last surprised Jeordam; it was Morin who spoke bitterly of a five-

year-old daughter carried off to be raised by some other woman. Studying her more closely, he mentally added a few years to her age.

"We will bring them back," Lewin promised. He took a bundle of
spears handed to him and thrust them point-down into the ground.
"You may stay with us if you wish, so long as you are willing to defend
yourselves and the rest of us. If you stay, you will never be allowed back
among the wagons." The sharp-nosed fellow turned at that and hurried
back the way they had come. Lewin went on; it was seldom that only
one left at this point. "Those who wish to come with us to this village,
take a spear. But remember, if you take the spear to use against men,
you will have to stay with us." His voice and eyes were stone. "You will
be dead as far the Jenn are concerned."

One of the remaining men hesitated, but each finally pulled a spear
from the ground. So did Morin. Jeordam gaped at her, and even Lewin
blinked.

"You do not have to take a spear just to stay," Lewin told her, "or
for us to bring back your people. Taking the spear means a willingness
to fight, not just to defend yourself. You can put it down; there is no
shame."

"They have my daughter," Morin said.

To Jeordam's shock, Lewin barely paused before nodding. "There is
a first time for all things. For all things. So be it." He began tapping
men on the shoulder, walking through the camps, naming them to visit
this log-walled village. Jeordam was the first tapped; his father had
always chosen him first since the day he was old enough to carry a
spear. He would have had it no other way.

Morin was having problems with the spear, the haft tangling in her
long skirts.

"You do not have to go," Jeordam told her. "No woman ever has
before. We will bring your daughter to you."

"I mean to bring Kirin out of there myself," she said fiercely. "You
will not stop me." A stubborn woman.

"In that case, you must dress like this." He gestured to his own gray-
brown coat and breeches. "You cannot walk cross-country in the night
in a dress." He took the spear away from her before she could react.
"The spear is not easily learned." The two men who had come with
her, awkwardly receiving instruction and nearly falling over their own
feet, were proof of that. He found a hatchet and chopped a pace from
the spear shaft, leaving four feet, counting nearly a foot of steel point.
"Stab with it. No more than that. Just stab. The haft is used for block-

ing, too, but I will find you something to use as a shield in your other hand."

She looked at him strangely. "How old are you?" she asked, even more oddly. He told her, and she only nodded thoughtfully.

After a moment, he said, "Is one of those men your husband?" They were still tripping over their spears.

"My husband mourns Kirin already. He cares more for the trees than his own daughter."

"The trees?"

"The Trees of Life." When he still looked at her blankly, she shook her head. "Three little trees planted in barrels. They care for them almost as well as they do for themselves. When they find a place of safety, they mean to plant them; they say the old days will return, then. They. I said they. Very well. I am not Jenn anymore." She hefted the shortened spear. "This is my husband now." Eyeing him closely, she asked, "If someone stole your child, would you talk of the Way of the Leaf and suffering sent to test us?" He shook his head, and she said, "I thought not. You will make a fine father. Teach me to use this spear."

An odd woman, but pretty. He took the spear back and began to show her, working out what he was doing while he did. With the short haft, it was quick and agile.

Morin was watching him with that strange smile, but the spear had caught him up. "I saw your face in the dream," she said softly, but he did not really hear. With a spear like this, he could be quicker than a man with a sword. In his mind's eye he could see the Aiel defeating all the men with swords. No one would stand against them. No one.

Lights flashed through the glass columns, half-blinding Rand. Muradin was only a pace or two ahead, staring straight in front of him, teeth bared, snarling silently. The columns were taking them back, into the time-lost history of the Aiel. Rand's feet moved of their own accord. Forward. And back in time.

Lewin adjusted the dustveil across his face and peered down into the small camp where the coals of a dying fire still glowed beneath an iron cookpot. The wind brought him a smell of half-burned stew. Mounds of blankets surrounded the coals in the moonlight. There were no horses in sight. He wished he had brought some water, but only the children were allowed water except with meals. He vaguely remembered a time when there had been more water, when the days were not so hot and dusty and the wind had not blown all the time. Night was only a small relief, trading a dull, fiery red sun for cold. He wrapped himself tighter in the cape of wild goatskins he used for a blanket.

His companions scrambled closer, bundled as he was, kicking rocks and muttering until he was sure they would wake the men below. He did not complain; he was no more used to this than they. Dustveils hid their faces, but he could make out who was who. Luca, with his shoulders half again as wide as anyone else's; he liked to play tricks. Gearan, lanky as a stork and the best runner among the wagons. Charlin and Alijha, alike as reflections except for Charlin's habit of tilting his head when he was worried, as he was now; their sister Colline was down in that camp. And Maigran, Lewin's sister.

When the girls' gathering bags were found on ground torn by a struggle, everyone else was ready to mourn and go on as they had done so many times before. Even Lewin's greatfather. If Adan had known what the five of them planned, he would have stopped them. All Adan did now was mutter about keeping faith with the Aes Sedai Lewin had never seen, that and try to keep the Aiel alive. The Aiel as a people, but not any one given Aiel. Not even Maigran.

"They are four," Lewin whispered. "The girls are this side of the fire. I will wake them—quietly—and we will sneak them away while the men sleep." His friends looked at each other, nodded. He supposed they should have made a plan before this, but all they had been able to think of was coming to get the girls, and how to leave the wagons without being seen. He had not been certain they could follow these men, or find them before they reached the village they came from, a collection of rough huts where the Aiel had been driven away with stones and sticks. There would be nothing to be done if the takers got that far.

"What if they do wake?" Gearan asked.

"I will not leave Colline," Charlin snapped, right on top of his brother's quieter "We are taking them back, Gearan."

"We are," Lewin agreed. Luca poked Gearan's ribs, and Gearan nodded.

Making their way down in the darkness was no easy task. Drought-dried twigs snapped under their feet; rocks and pebbles showered down the dry slope ahead of them. The harder Lewin tried to move silently, the more noise he seemed to make. Luca fell into a thornbush that cracked loudly, but managed to extract himself with no more than heavy breathing. Charlin slipped, and slid halfway to the bottom. But nothing moved below.

Short of the camp Lewin paused, exchanging anxious looks with his friends, then tiptoed in. His own breath sounded thunderous in his ears, as loud as the snores coming from one of the four large mounds. He froze as the rough snorts stopped and one of the mounds heaved. It settled, the snoring began again, and Lewin let himself breathe.

Carefully he crouched beside one of the smaller heaps and flipped aside a rough woolen blanket stiff with dirt. Maigran stared up at him, face bruised and swollen, her dress torn to little better than rags. He clapped a hand over her mouth to keep her from crying out, but she only continued to stare blankly, not even blinking.

"I am going to carve you like a pig, boy." One of the larger mounds tumbled aside, and a wild-bearded man in filthy clothes got to his feet, the long knife in his hand glittering dully in the moonlight, picking up the red glow of the coals. He kicked the mounds to either side of him, producing grunts and stirrings. "Just like a pig. Can you squeal, boy, or do you people just run?"

"Run," Lewin said, but his sister only stared dully. Frantic, he seized her shoulders, pulled to try starting her toward where the others were waiting. "Run!" She came out of the blankets stiffly, almost a dead weight. Colline was awake—he could hear her whimpering—but she seemed to be drawing her dirty blankets around her even more tightly, trying to hide in them. Maigran stood there, staring at nothing, seeing nothing.

"Seems you cannot even do that." Grinning, the man was coming around the fire, his knife held low. The others were sitting up in their blankets now, laughing, watching the fun.

Lewin did not know what to do. He could not leave his sister. All he could was die. Maybe that would give Maigran a chance to run. "Run, Maigran! Please run!" She did not move. She did not even seem to hear him. What had they done to her?

The bearded man came closer, taking his time, chuckling, enjoying his slow advance.

"Nooooooooooooooo!" Charlin came hurtling out of the night, throwing his arms around the man with the knife, carrying him to the ground. The other men bounded to their feet. One, his head shaved and shining in the pale light, raised a sword to slash at Charlin.

Lewin was not sure exactly how it happened. Somehow he had the heavy kettle by its iron handle, swinging; it struck the shaved head with a loud crunch. The man collapsed as if his bones had melted. Off balance, Lewin stumbled trying to avoid the fire, and fell beside it, losing the cookpot. A dark man with his hair in braids lifted another sword, ready to skewer him. He scrambled away on his back like a spider, eyes on the sword's sharp point, hands searching frenziedly for something to fend the man off, a stick, anything. His palm fell on rounded wood. He jerked it around, pushed it at the snarling man. The man's dark eyes widened, the sword dropped from his grasp; blood poured from his mouth. Not a stick. A spear.

Lewin's hands sprang away from the haft as soon as he realized what it was. Too late. He crawled backward to avoid the man as he fell, stared at him, trembling. A dead man. A man he had killed. The wind felt very cold.

After a time it came to him to wonder why one of the others had not killed him. He was surprised to see the rest of his friends there around the coals. Gearan and Luca and Alijha, all panting and wild-eyed above their dustveils. Colline still emitted soft sniffling sobs from beneath her blankets, and Maigran still stood staring. Charlin was huddled on his knees, holding himself. And the four men, the villagers. . . . Lewin stared from one motionless bloody shape to another.

"We . . . killed them." Luca's voice shook. "We. . . . Mercy of the Light, be with us now."

Lewin crawled to Charlin and touched his shoulder. "Are you hurt?"

Charlin fell over. Red wetness slicked his hands, gripping the hilt of the knife driven into his belly. "It hurts, Lewin," he whispered. He shuddered once, and the light went out of his eyes.

"What are we going to do?" Gearan asked. "Charlin is dead, and we. . . . Light, what have we done? What do we do?"

"We will take the girls back to the wagons." Lewin could not pull his eyes away from Charlin's glazed stare. "We will do that."

They gathered up everything that was useful, the cookpot and the knives, mainly. Metal things were hard to come by. "We might as well," Alijha said roughly. "They certainly stole it from someone just like us."

When Alijha started to pick up one of the swords, though, Lewin stopped him. "No, Alijha. That is a weapon, made to kill people. It has no other use." Alijha said nothing, only ran his eyes over the four dead bodies, looked at the spears Luca was winding with blankets to carry Charlin's body on. Lewin refused to look at the villagers. "A spear can put food in the pots, Alijha. A sword cannot. It is forbidden by the Way."

Alijha was still silent, but Lewin thought he sneered behind his dustveil. Yet when they finally started away into the night, the swords remained by the dying coals and the dead men.

It was a long walk back through the darkness, carrying the makeshift stretcher bearing Charlin, the wind sometimes gusting to raise choking clouds of dust. Maigran stumbled along, staring straight ahead; she did not know where she was, or who they were. Colline seemed half-terrified, even of her own brother, jumping if anyone touched her. This was not how Lewin had imagined their return. In his mind the girls had been laughing, happy to return to the wagons; they had all been laughing. Not carrying Charlin's corpse. Not hushed by the memory of what they had done.

The lights of the cook fires came into view, and then the wagons, harnesses already spread for men to take their places at sunrise. No one left the shelter of the wagons after dark, so it surprised Lewin to see three shapes come hurrying toward them. Adan's white hair stood out in the night. The other two were Nerrine, Colline's mother, and Saralin, his and Maigran's. Lewin lowered his dustveil with foreboding.

The women rushed to their daughters with comforting arms and soft murmurs. Colline sank into her mother's embrace with a welcoming sigh; Maigran hardly appeared to notice Saralin who looked close to tears at the bruises on her daughter's face.

Adan frowned at the young men, permanent creases of worry deepening in his face. "In the name of the Light, what happened? When we found you were gone, too. . . ." He trailed off when he saw the stretcher holding Charlin. "What happened?" he asked again, as if dreading the answer.

Lewin opened his mouth slowly, but Maigran spoke first.

"They killed them." She was staring at something in the distance, her voice as simple as a child's. "The bad men hurt us. They. . . . Then Lewin came and killed them."

"You must not say things like that, child," Saralin said soothingly. "You—" She stopped, peering into her daughter's eyes, then turned to stare uncertainly at Lewin. "Is it . . . ? Is it true?"

"We had to," Alijha said in a pained voice. "They tried to kill us. They did kill Charlin."

Adan stepped back. "You . . . killed? Killed *men*? What of the Covenant? We harm no one. No one! There is no reason good enough to justify killing another human being. None!"

"They took Maigran, greatfather," Lewin said. "They took Maigran and Colline, and hurt them. They—"

"There is no reason!" Adan roared, shaking with rage. "We must accept what comes. Our sufferings are sent to test our faithfulness. We accept and endure! We do not murder! You have not strayed from the Way, you have abandoned it. You are Da'shain no longer. You are corrupt, and I will not have the Aiel corrupted by you. Leave us, strangers. Killers! You are not welcome in the wagons of the Aiel." He turned his back and strode away as if they no longer existed. Saralin and Nerrine started after him, guiding the girls.

"Mother?" Lewin said, and flinched when she looked back at him with cold eyes. "Mother, please—"

"Who are you that addresses me so? Hide your face from me, stranger. I had a son, once, with a face like that. I do not wish to see it on a killer." And she led Maigran after the others.

"I am still Aiel," Lewin shouted, but they did not look back. He thought he heard Luca crying. The wind rose, picking up dust, and he veiled his face. "I am Aiel!"

Wildly darting lights bored into Rand's eyes. The pain of Lewin's loss still clung to him, and his mind tumbled furiously. Lewin had not carried a weapon. He had not known how to use a weapon. Killing terrified him. It did not make sense.

He was almost abreast of Muradin now, but the man was not aware of him. Muradin's snarl was a rictus; sweat beaded on his face; he quivered as though wanting to run.

Rand's feet took him forward, and back.

CHAPTER
26

The Dedicated

F orward, and back.

Adan lay in the sandy hollow clutching his dead son's weeping children, shielding their eyes against his ragged coat. Tears rolled down his face, too, but silently, as he peered cautiously over the edge. At five and six, Maigran and Lewin deserved the right to cry; Adan was surprised he had any tears left, himself.

Some of the wagons were burning. The dead lay where they had fallen. The horses had already been driven off, except for those still hitched to a few wagons that had been emptied onto the ground. For once he took no notice of the crated things the Aes Sedai had given into Aiel charge, toppled carelessly into the dirt. It was not the first time he had seen that, or dead Aiel, but this time he could not care. The men with the swords and spears and bows, the men who had done the killing, were loading those empty wagons. With women. He watched Rhea, his daughter, shoved up into a wagon box with the others, crowded together like animals by laughing killers. The last of his children. Elwin dead of hunger at ten, Sorelle at twenty of fever her dreams told her was coming, and Jaren, who threw himself off a cliff a year ago, at nineteen, when he found he could channel. Marind, this morning.

He wanted to scream. He wanted to rush out there and stop them from taking his last child. Stop them, somehow. And if he did rush out? They would kill him, and take Rhea anyway. They might well kill the children, too. Some of those bodies sprawled in their own blood were small.

Maigran clutched at him as if she sensed he might leave her, and Lewin stiffened as if he wanted to hold tighter but thought himself too old. Adan smoothed their hair and kept their faces pressed against his chest. He made himself watch, though, until the wagons wheeled away surrounded by whooping riders, after the horses that were already almost out of sight toward the smoking mountains that lined the horizon.

Only then did he stand up, prying the children loose. "Wait here for me," he told them. "Wait until I come back." Clinging to each other, they stared at him with tear-stained white faces, nodded uncertainly.

He walked out to one of the bodies, rolled her over gently. Siedre could have been asleep, her face just the way it appeared beside him when he woke each morning. It always surprised him to notice gray in her red-gold hair; she was his love, his life, and ever young and new to him. He tried not to look at the blood soaking the front of her dress or the gaping wound below her breasts.

"What do you mean to do now, Adan? Tell us that! What?"

He brushed Seidre's hair from her face—she liked to be neat—and stood, turning slowly to confront the knot of angry, frightened men. Sulwin was the leader, a tall man with deep-set eyes. He had let his hair grow, Sulwin had, as if to hide being Aiel. A number of men had. It had made no difference, to these last raiders or those who had come before.

"I mean to bury our dead and go on, Sulwin." His eyes drifted back to Siedre. "What else is there?"

"Go on, Adan? How can we go on? There are no horses. There is almost no water, no food. All we have left are wagons full of things the Aes Sedai will never come for. What are they, Adan? What are they that we should give our lives to haul them across the world, afraid to touch them even. We cannot go on as before!"

"We can!" Adan shouted. "We will! We have legs; we have backs. We will drag the wagons, if need be. We will be faithful to our duty!" He was startled to see his own brandished fist. A fist. His hand trembled as he unclenched it and put it down by his side.

Sulwin stepped back, then held his ground with his companions.

"No, Adan. We are supposed to find a place of safety, and some of us mean to do that. My greatfather used to tell me stories he heard as a boy, stories of when we lived in safety and people came to hear us sing. We mean to find a place where we can be safe, and sing again."

"Sing?" Adan scoffed. "I have heard those old stories, too, that Aiel singing was a wondrous thing, but you know those old songs no more than I do. The songs are gone, and the old days are gone. We will not give up our duty to the Aes Sedai to chase after what is lost forever."

"Some of us will, Adan." The others behind Sulwin nodded. "We mean to find that safe place. And the songs, too. We will!"

A crash whipped Adan's head around. More of Sulwin's cronies were unloading one of the wagons, and a large flat crate had fallen, half breaking open to reveal what looked like a polished doorframe of dark red stone. Other wagons were being emptied, too, and by more than Sulwin's friends. At least a quarter of the people he saw were hard at work clearing wagons of everything but food or water.

"Do not try to stop us," Sulwin cautioned.

Adan made his fist loosen again. "You are not Aiel," he said. "You betray everything. Whatever you are, you are no longer Aiel!"

"We keep the Way of the Leaf as well as you, Adan."

"Go!" Adan shouted. "Go! You are not Aiel! You are lost! Lost! I do not want to look at you! Go!" Sulwin and the others stumbled in their haste to get away from him.

His heart sank lower as he surveyed the wagons, and the dead lying among the litter. So many dead, so many wounded moaning as they were tended. Sulwin and his lost ones were taking some care in their unloading. The men with the swords had broken open crates until they realized there was no gold inside, no food. Food was more precious than gold. Adan studied the stone doorframe, tumbled piles of stone figurines, odd shapes in crystal standing among the potted chora cuttings Sulwin's folk had no use for. Was there a use for any of it? Was this what they were being faithful for? If it was, then so be it. Some could be saved. There was no way to tell what Aes Sedai might consider most important, but some could be saved.

He saw Maigran and Lewin clutching their mother's skirts. He was glad Saralin was alive to look after them; his last son, her husband, the children's father, had died from the very first arrow that morning. Some could be saved. He would save the Aiel, whatever it took.

Kneeling, he gathered Siedre in his arms. "We are still faithful, Aes Sedai," he whispered. "How long must we be faithful?" Putting his head down on his wife's breast, he wept.

*   *   *

Tears stung Rand's eyes; silently, he mouthed, *"Siedre."* The Way of the Leaf? That was no Aiel belief. He could not think clearly; he could hardly think at all. The lights spun faster and faster. Beside him, Muradin's mouth was open in a soundless howl; the Aiel's eyes bulged as if witnessing the death of everything. They stepped forward together.

Jonai stood at the edge of the cliff staring out westward over the sun-sparkled water. A hundred leagues in that direction lay Comelle. Had lain Comelle. Comelle had clung to the mountains overlooking the sea. A hundred leagues west, where the sea now ran. If Alnora were still alive, perhaps it would have been easier to take. Without her dreams, he scarcely knew where to go or what to do. Without her, he hardly cared to live. He felt every gray hair as he turned to trudge back to the wagons, waiting a mile away. Fewer wagons, now, and showing wear. Fewer people, too, a handful of thousands where there had been tens. But too many for the remaining wagons. No one rode now save children too small to walk.

Adan met him at the first wagon, a tall young man, his blue eyes too wary. Jonai always expected to see Willim if he looked around quickly enough. But Willim had been sent away, of course, years ago, when he began to channel no matter how hard he tried to stop. The world had too many men channeling, still; they had to send away boys who showed the signs. They had to. But he wished he had his children back. When had Esole died? So little to be laid in a hastily dug hole, wasted with sickness there was no Aes Sedai to Heal.

"There are Ogier, father," Adan said excitedly. Jonai suspected his son had always thought his stories of the Ogier were just that, stories. "They came from the north."

It was a bedraggled band Adan led him to, no more than fifty in number, hollow-cheeked, sad-eyed, tufted ears drooping. He had become accustomed to his own people's drawn faces and worn, patched clothing, but seeing the same on Ogier shocked him. Yet he had people to care for, and duties to discharge for the Aes Sedai. How long since he had seen an Aes Sedai? Just after Alnora died. Too late for Alnora. The woman had Healed the sick who still lived, taken some of the *sa'angreal,* and gone on her way, laughing bitterly when he asked her where there was a place of safety. Her dress had been patched, and

worn at the hem. He was not sure she had been sane. She claimed one
of the Forsaken was only partly trapped, or maybe not at all; Ishamael
still touched the world, she said. She had to be as mad as the remaining
male Aes Sedai.

He pulled his mind back to the Ogier as they stood, unsteady on
their great legs. His thoughts wandered too much since Alnora's death.
They had bread and bowls in their hands. He was shocked to feel a
prick of anger that someone had shared their meager stock of food.
How many of his people could eat on what fifty Ogier could consume?
No. To share was the way. To give freely. A hundred people? Two
hundred?

"You have chora cuttings," one of the Ogier said. His thick fingers
gently brushed the trefoil leaves of the two potted plants tied to the
side of a wagon.

"Some," Adan said curtly. "They die, but the old folk keep new
cuttings before they do." He had no time for trees. He had a people to
look after. "How bad is it in the north?"

"Bad," an Ogier woman replied. "The Blighted Lands have grown
southward, and there are Myrddraal and Trollocs."

"I thought they were all dead." Not north, then. They could not turn
north. South? The Sea of Jeren lay ten days south. Or did it, any
longer? He was tired. So tired.

"You have come from the east?" another Ogier asked. He wiped his
bowl with a heel of bread and gulped it down. "How is it to the east?"

"Bad," Jonai replied. "Perhaps not so bad for you, though. Ten—no,
twelve days ago, some people took a third of our horses before we
could escape. We had to abandon wagons." That pained him. Wagons
left behind, and what was in them. The things the Aes Sedai had placed
in Aiel charge, abandoned. That it was not the first time only made it
worse. "Almost everyone we meet takes things, whatever they want.
Perhaps they will not be so with Ogier, though."

"Perhaps," an Ogier woman said as if she did not believe it. Jonai
was not certain he did either; there was no safe place. "Do you know
where any of the *stedding* are?"

Jonai stared at her. "No. No, I do not. But surely you can find the
stedding."

"We have run so far, so long," an Ogier back in the huddle said, and
another added in a mournful rumble, "The land has changed so much."

"I think we must find a *stedding* soon or die," the first Ogier woman
said. "I feel a . . . longing . . . in my bones. We must find a *stedding.*
We must."

"I cannot help you," Jonai said sadly. He felt a tightness in his chest. The land changed beyond knowing, changing still so the plain traveled last year might be mountains this. The Blighted Lands growing. Myrddraal and Trollocs still alive. People stealing, people with faces like animals, people who did not recognize Da'shain or know them. He could barely breathe. The Ogier, lost. The Aiel, lost. Everything lost. The tightness broke in pain, and he sank to his knees, doubled over, clutching his chest. A fist held his heart, squeezing.

Adan knelt beside him worriedly. "Father, what is it? What is the matter? What can I do?"

Jonai managed to seize his son's frayed collar and pull his face close. "Take—the people—south." He had to force the words out between spasms that seemed to be ripping his heart out.

"Father, you are the one who—"

"Listen. Listen! Take them—south. Take—the Aiel—to safety. Keep —the Covenant. Guard—what the Aes Sedai—gave us—until they— come for it. The Way—of the Leaf. You must—" He had tried. Solinda Sedai must understand that. He had tried. Alnora.

Alnora. The name faded, the pain in Rand's chest loosened. No sense. It made no sense. How could these people be Aiel?

The columns flashed in blinding pulses. The air stirred, swirling.

Beside him, Muradin's mouth stretched wide in an effort to scream. The Aiel clawed at his veil, clawed at his face, leaving deep bloody scratches.

Forward.

Jonai hurried down the empty streets, trying not to look at shattered buildings and dead chora trees. All dead. At least the last of the long abandoned jo-cars had been hauled away. Aftershocks still troubled the ground beneath his feet. He wore his work clothes, his cadin'sor, of course, though the work he had been given was nothing he had been trained for. He was sixty-three, in the prime of life, not yet old enough for gray hairs, but he felt a tired old man.

No one questioned his entering the Hall of the Servants; there was no one at the great columned entrance to question anyone, or give greeting. Plenty of people darted about inside, arms filled with papers or boxes, eyes anxious, but none so much as looked at him. There was a feel of panic about them, and it grew by increments every time the ground shook. Distressed, he crossed the anteroom and trotted up the broad stairs. Mud stained the silvery white elstone. No one could spare time. Perhaps no one cared.

There was no need to knock at the door he sought. Not one of the great gilded doors to an ingathering hall, but a door plain and unobtrusive. He slipped in quietly, though, and was glad he had. Half a dozen Aes Sedai stood around the long table, arguing, apparently not noticing when the building trembled. They were all women.

He shivered, wondering if men would ever stand in a meeting such as this again. When he saw what was on the table, the shiver became a shudder. A crystal sword—perhaps an object of the Power, perhaps only an ornament; he had no way of telling—held down the Dragon banner of Lews Therin Kinslayer, spread out like a tablecloth and spilling onto the floor. His heart clenched. What was that doing here? Why had it not been destroyed, and memory of the cursed man as well?

"What good is your Foretelling," Oselle was almost shouting, "if you cannot tell us when?" Her long black hair swayed as she shook with anger. "The world rests on this! The future! The Wheel itself!"

Dark-eyed Deindre faced her with a more usual calm. "I am not the Creator. I can only tell you what I Foretell."

"Peace, sisters." Solinda was the calmest of them all, her old-fashioned streith gown only a pale blue mist. The sun-red hair falling to her waist was nearly the color of his own. His greatfather had served her as a young man, but she looked younger than he; she was Aes Sedai. "The time for contention among ourselves is past. Jaric and Haindar will both be here by tomorrow."

"Which means we cannot afford mistakes, Solinda."

"We must know."

"Is there any chance of . . . ?"

Jonai stopped listening. They would see him when they were ready. He was not the only one in the room besides the Aes Sedai. Someshta sat against the wall near the door, a great shape seemingly woven of vines and leaves, his head a little above Jonai's even so. A fissure of withered brown and charred black ran up the Nym's face and furrowed the green grass of his hair, and when he looked at Jonai, his hazelnut eyes seemed troubled.

When Jonai nodded to him, he fingered the rift and frowned. "Do I know you?" he said softly.

"I am your friend," Jonai replied sadly. He had not seen Someshta in years, but he had heard of this. Most of the Nym were dead, he had heard. "You rode me on your shoulders when I was a child. Do you remember nothing of it?"

"Singing," Someshta said. "Was there singing? So much is gone. The Aes Sedai say some will return. You are a Child of the Dragon, are you not?"

Jonai winced. That name had caused trouble, no less for not being true. But how many citizens now believed the Da'shain Aiel had once served the Dragon and no other Aes Sedai?

"Jonai?"

He turned at the sound of Solinda's voice, went to one knee as she approached. The others were still arguing, but more quietly.

"All is in readiness, Jonai?" she said.

"All, Aes Sedai. Solinda Sedai. . . ." He hesitated, took a deep breath. "Solinda Sedai, some of us wish to remain. We can serve, still."

"Do you know what happened to the Aiel at Tzora?" He nodded, and she sighed, reaching out to smooth his short hair as if he were a child. "Of course you do. You Da'shain have more courage than. . . . Ten thousand Aiel linking arms and singing, trying to remind a madman of who they were and who he had been, trying to turn him with their bodies and a song. Jaric Mondoran killed them. He stood there, staring as though at a puzzle, killing them, and they kept closing their lines and singing. I am told he listened to the last Aiel for almost an hour before destroying him. And then Tzora burned, one huge flame consuming stone and metal and flesh. There is a sheet of glass where the second greatest city in the world once stood."

"Many people had time to flee, Aes Sedai. The Da'shain earned them time to flee. We are not afraid."

Her hand tightened painfully in his hair. "The citizens have already fled Paaren Disen, Jonai. Besides, the Da'shain have a part yet to play, if Deindre could only see far enough to say what. In any case, I mean to save something here, and that something is you."

"As you say," he said reluctantly. "We will care for what you have given into our charge until you want them again."

"Of course. The things we gave you." She smiled at him and loosened her grip, smoothing his hair once more before folding her hands. "You will carry the . . . things . . . to safety, Jonai. Keep moving, always moving, until you find a place of safety, where no one can harm you."

"As you say, Aes Sedai."

"What of Coumin, Jonai? Has he calmed?"

He did not know any way but to tell her; he would rather have bitten his tongue out. "My father is hiding somewhere in the city. He tried to talk us into . . . resisting. He would not listen, Aes Sedai. He would not listen. He found an old shocklance somewhere, and. . . ." He could not go on. He expected her to be angry, but her eyes glistened with tears.

"Keep the Covenant, Jonai. If the Da'shain lose everything else, see they keep the Way of the Leaf. Promise me."

"Of course, Aes Sedai," he said, shocked. The Covenant was the Aiel, and the Aiel were the Covenant; to abandon the Way would be to abandon what they were. Coumin was an aberration. He had been strange since he was a boy, it was said, hardly Aiel at all, though no one knew why.

"Go now, Jonai. I want you far from Paaren Disen by tomorrow. And remember—keep moving. Keep the Aiel safe."

He bowed where he knelt, but she was already being drawn back into the argument.

"Can we trust Kodam and his fellows, Solinda?"

"We must, Oselle. They are young and inexperienced, but barely touched by the taint, and. . . . And we have no choice."

"Then we will do what we must. The sword must wait. Someshta, we have a task for the last of the Nym, if you will do it. We have asked too much of you; now we must ask more."

Jonai bowed his way out formally as the Nym rose, his head brushing the ceiling. Already immersed in their plans, they were not looking at him, but he did them this last honor anyway. He did not think he would ever see them again.

He ran from the Hall of the Servants, all the way out of the city to where the great gathering waited. Thousands of wagons in ten lines stretching nearly two leagues, wagons loaded with food and water barrels, wagons loaded with the crated things the Aes Sedai had given into Aiel charge, *angreal* and *sa'angreal* and *ter'angreal,* all the things that had to be kept from the hands of men going mad while they wielded the One Power. Once there would have been other ways to carry them, jo-cars and jumpers, hoverflies and huge sho-wings. Now painfully assembled horses and wagons had to suffice. Among the wagons stood the people, enough to populate a city but perhaps all the Aiel left alive in the world.

A hundred came to meet him, men and women, the representatives demanding word of whether the Aes Sedai had granted leave for some to stay. "No," he told them. Some frowned reluctantly, and he added, "We must obey. We are Da'shain Aiel, and we obey the Aes Sedai."

They dispersed back to their wagons slowly, and he thought he heard Coumin's name mentioned, but he could not let it trouble him. He hurried to his own wagon, at the head of one of the center lines. The horses were all nervous with the ground shaking at intervals.

His sons were already up on the seat—Willim, fifteen, with the reins, and Adan, ten, beside him, both grinning with nervous excitement. Little Esole lay playing with a doll on top of the canvas tied over their possessions—and, more important, their charges from the Aes Sedai. There was no room for any to ride but the young and the very old. A dozen rooted chora cuttings in clay pots sat behind the wagon seat, to be planted when they found a place of safety. A foolish thing to carry, perhaps, but no wagon was without its potted cuttings. Something from a time long gone; symbol of a better time to come. People needed hope, and symbols.

Alnora waited beside the team, glossy black hair tumbling about her shoulders and reminding him of the first time he saw her as a girl. But worry had etched lines around her eyes now.

He managed a smile for her, hiding the worry in his own heart. "All will be well, wife of my heart." She did not answer, and he added, "Have you dreamed?"

"Of no time soon," she murmured. "All will be well, all will be well, and all manner of thing will be well." Smiling tremulously, she touched his cheek. "With you I know it will be so, husband of my heart."

Jonai waved his arms over his head, and the signal rippled down the lines. Slowly the wagons began to move, the Aiel leaving Paaren Disen.

Rand shook his head. Too much. Memories crowding together. The air seemed filled with sheet lightning. The wind swirled gritty dust into dancing whirlwinds. Muradin had clawed deep furrows in his face; he was digging at his eyes now. Forward.

Coumin knelt at the edge of the plowed ground in his working clothes, plain brownish gray coat and breeches and soft laced boots, in a line with others like him that surrounded the field, ten men of the Da'shain Aiel at twice stretched-arms' length and then an Ogier, all the way around. He could see the next field, lined the same way, beyond the soldiers with their shocklances sitting atop armored jo-cars. A hoverfly buzzed overhead in its patrol, a deadly black metal wasp containing two men. He was sixteen, and the women had decided his voice was finally deep enough to join in the seed singing.

The soldiers fascinated him, men and Ogier, the way a colorful poisonous snake might. They *killed*. His father's greatfather, Charn, claimed there had been no soldiers once, but Coumin did not believe it. If there were no soldiers, who would stop the Nightriders and the Trollocs from coming to kill everyone? Of course, Charn claimed there had not been any Myrddraal or Trollocs then, either. No Forsaken, no Shadowwrought. He had many stories he claimed were from a time before soldiers and Nightriders and Trollocs, when he said the Dark Lord of the Grave had been bound away, and no one knew his name, or the word "war." Coumin could not imagine such a world; the war had been old when he was born.

He enjoyed Charn's stories even if he could not make himself believe, but some earned the old man frowns and scoldings. Like when he claimed to have served one of the Forsaken, once. Not just any Forsaken, but Lanfear herself. As well say he had served Ishamael. If Charn had to make up stories, Coumin wished he could say he had served Lews Therin, the great leader himself. Of course, everyone would ask why he was not serving the Dragon now, but that would be better than the way things were. Coumin did not like the way citizens looked at Charn when he said that Lanfear had not always been evil.

A stir at the end of the field told him one of the Nym was approaching. The great form, head and shoulders and chest taller than any Ogier, stepped out onto the seeded ground, and Coumin did not have to see to know he left footprints filled with sprouting things. It was Someshta, surrounded by clouds of butterflies, white and yellow and blue. Excited murmurs rose from the townspeople and the folk whose fields these were, gathered to watch. Each field would have its Nym, now.

Coumin wondered if he could ask Someshta about Charn's stories. He had spoken to him once, and Someshta was old enough to know if Charn was telling the truth; the Nym were older than anyone. Some said the Nym never died, not so long as plants grew. But this was no time to be thinking of questioning a Nym.

The Ogier began it, as was fitting, standing to sing, great bass rumbles like the earth singing. The Aiel rose, men's voices lifting in their own song, even the deepest at a higher pitch than the Ogier's. Yet the songs braided together, and Someshta took those threads and wove them into his dance, gliding across the field in swooping strides, arms wide, butterflies swirling about him, landing on his spread fingertips.

Coumin could hear the seed singing around the other fields, hear the women clapping to urge the men on, their rhythm the heartbeat of new life, but it was a distant knowledge. The song caught him up, and he almost felt that it was himself, not the sounds he made, that Someshta wove into the soil and around the seeds. Seeds no longer, though. Zemais sprouts covered the field, taller wherever the Nym's foot had trod. No blight would touch those plants, nor any insect; seed sung, they would eventually grow twice as high as a man and fill the town's grainbarns. This was what he had been born for, this song and the other seed songs. He did not regret the fact that the Aes Sedai had passed him over at ten, saying he lacked the spark. To have been trained as Aes Sedai would have been wondrous, but surely no more so than this moment.

The song faded slowly, the Aiel guiding its end. Someshta danced a few steps more after the last voices ceased, and it seemed the song still hung faintly in the air for as long as he moved. Then he stopped, and it was done.

Coumin was surprised to see that the townspeople were gone, but he had no time to wonder where they had gone or why. The women were coming, laughing, to congratulate the men. He was one of the men now, not a boy any longer, though the women alternated between kissing him on the lips and reaching up to ruffle his short red hair.

It was then that he saw the soldier, only a few steps away, watching them. He had left his shocklance and fancloth battle cape somewhere, but he still wore his helmet, like some monstrous insect's head, its mandibles hiding his face though his black shockvisor was raised. As if realizing he still stood out, the soldier pulled off the helmet, revealing a dark young man no more than four or five years older than Coumin. The soldier's unblinking brown eyes met his, and Coumin shivered. The face was only four or five years older, but those eyes. . . . The soldier would have been chosen to begin his training at ten, too. Coumin was glad Aiel were spared that choosing.

One of the Ogier, Tomada, came over, tufted ears slanted forward inquisitively. "Do you have news, warman? I saw excitement among the jo-cars while we sang."

The soldier hesitated. "I suppose I can tell you, though it is not confirmed. We have a report that Lews Therin led the Companions on a strike at Shayol Ghul this morning at dawn. Something is disrupting communications, but the report is the Bore has been sealed, with most of the Forsaken on the other side. Maybe all of them."

"Then it is over." Tomada breathed. "Over at last, the Light be praised."

"Yes." The soldier looked around, suddenly seeming lost. "I . . . suppose it is. I suppose. . . ." He peered at his hands, then let them fall to his sides again. He sounded weary. "The local folk could not wait to begin celebrating. If the news is true, it might go on for days. I wonder if . . . ? No, they will not want soldiers joining them. Will you?"

"For tonight, perhaps," Tomada said. "But we have three more towns to visit before our circuit is done."

"Of course. You still have work to do. You have that." The soldier looked around again. "There are still Trollocs. Even if the Forsaken are gone, there are still Trollocs. And Nightriders." Nodding to himself, he started back toward the jo-cars.

Tomada did not appear excited at all, of course, but Coumin felt as stunned as the young soldier. The war was over? What would the world be like without war? Suddenly he had to talk to Charn.

Sounds of merrymaking rolled out to meet him before he reached the town—laughing, singing. The bells in the town-hall tower began ringing exuberantly. Townspeople danced in the streets, men and women and children. Coumin dodged between them, searching. Charn had elected to stay at one of the inns where the Aiel were putting up instead of coming to the singing—even the Aes Sedai could no longer do much for the aches in his aged knees—but surely he would be out for this.

Abruptly something struck Coumin in the mouth and his legs buckled; he was pushing himself to his knees before he realized he was down. A hand put to his mouth came away bloody. He looked up to find an angry-faced townsman standing over him, nursing a fist. "Why did you do that?" he asked.

The townsman spat at him. "The Forsaken are dead. Dead, do you hear? Lanfear will not protect you anymore. We will root out all of you who served the Forsaken while pretending to be on our side, and treat the lot of you as we treated that crazy old man."

A woman was tugging at the man's arm. "Come away, Toma. Come away, and hold your foolish tongue! Do you want the Ogier to come for you?" Suddenly wary, the man let her pull him away into the crowd.

Struggling to his feet, Coumin began to run, heedless of the blood oozing down his chin.

The inn was empty, silent. Not even the innkeeper was there, or the cook, or her helpers. Coumin ran through the building shouting, "Charn? Charn? *Charn?*"

Out back, maybe. Charn liked to sit under the spiceapple trees behind the inn, and tell his stories of the days when he was young.

Coumin ran out the back door, and tripped, falling on his face. It was an empty boot that had caught his toe. One of Charn's red dress boots that he wore all the time, now that he no longer joined in the singing. Something made Coumin look up.

Charn's white-haired body hung from a rope pulled over the ridgepole, one foot bare where he had kicked his boot off, the fingers of one hand caught at his neck where he had tried to pull the rope free.

"Why?" Coumin said. "We are Da'shain. Why?" There was no one to answer. Clutching the boot to his chest, he knelt there, staring up at Charn, as the noise of revelry washed over him.

Rand quivered. The light from the columns was a shimmering blue haze that seemed solid, that seemed to claw the nerves out of his skin. The wind howled, one vast whirlwind sucking inward. Muradin had managed to veil himself; bloody sockets stared blindly above the black veil. The Aiel was chewing, and bloody froth dripped onto his chest. Forward.

Charn made his way down the side of the wide, crowded street beneath the spreading chora trees, their trefoil leaves spreading peace and contentment in the shadows of silvery buildings that touched the sky. A city without choras would seem bleak as wilderness. Jo-cars hummed quietly down the street, and a great white sho-wing darted across the sky, carrying citizens to Comelle or Tzora or somewhere. He seldom used the sho-wings, himself—if he needed to go very far, an Aes Sedai usually Traveled with him—but tonight he would, to M'jinn. Today was his twenty-fifth naming day, and tonight he intended to accept Nalla's latest offer of marriage. He wondered if she would be surprised; he had been putting her off for a year, not wanting to settle down. It would mean changing his service to Zorelle Sedai, whom Nalla served, but Mierin Sedai had already given her blessing.

He rounded a corner and just had time to see a dark, wide-shouldered man with a fashionably narrow beard before the man's shoulder sent him crashing to his back, head bouncing on the walkway so he saw spots. Dazed, he lay there.

"Watch where you are going," the bearded man said irritably, adjusting his sleeveless red coat and flicking the lace at his wrists. His black hair, hanging to his shoulders, was gathered in back. That was the latest fashion, too, as near as anyone who had not sworn to the Covenant would come to imitating Aiel.

The pale-haired woman with him laid a hand on his arm, her dress of shimmery white streith becoming more opaque with her sudden embarrassment. "Jom, look at his hair. He is Aiel, Jom."

Feeling his head to see if it was cracked, Charn's fingers brushed through short-cut, reddish-gold hair. He gave the longer tail at his nape a tug in lieu of shaking his head. A bruise, he thought, but no more.

"So he is." The man's annoyance vanished in consternation. "Forgive me, Da'shain. I am the one who should be watching where he walks. Let me help you up." He was already suiting his words, hoisting Charn to his feet. "Are you all right? Let me call a jumper to take you where you are going."

"I am not hurt, citizen," Charn said mildly. "Truly, it was my fault." It had been, hurrying like that. He could have injured the man. "Did I harm you? Please, forgive me."

The man opened his mouth to protest—citizens always did; they seemed to think Aiel were made of spinglass—but before he could speak, the ground rippled under their feet. The air rippled, too, in spreading waves. The man looked about uncertainly, pulling his stylish fancloth cloak around himself and his lady so their heads seemed to float disembodied. "What is it, Da'shain?"

Others who had seen Charn's hair were gathering around him anxiously asking the same questions, but he ignored them, not even thinking of whether he was being rude. He actually began to push through the crowd, his eyes fixed on the Sharom; the white sphere, a thousand feet in diameter, floated as high above the blue and silver domes of the Collam Daan.

Mierin had said today was the day. She said she had found a new source for the One Power. Female Aes Sedai and male would be able to tap the same source, not separate halves. What men and women could do united would be even greater now that there would be no differences. And today she and Beidomon would tap it for the first time —the last time men and women would work together wielding a different Power. Today.

What seemed a tiny chip of white spun away from the Sharom in a jet of black fire; it descended, deceptively slow, insignificant. Then a hundred gouts spurted everywhere around the huge white sphere. The

Sharom broke apart like an egg and began to drift down, falling, an obsidian inferno. Darkness spread across the sky, swallowing the sun in unnatural night, as if the light of those flames was blackness. People were screaming, screaming everywhere.

With the first spurt of fire, Charn broke into a run toward the Collam Daan, but he knew he was too late. He was sworn to serve Aes Sedai, and he was too late. Tears rolled down his face as he ran.

Blinking to dispel the spots fluttering across his vision, Rand squeezed his head with both hands. The image still drifted through his head, that huge sphere, burning black, falling. *Did I really see the hole being drilled into the Dark One's prison? Did I?* He stood at the edge of the glass columns, staring out at *Avendesora. A chora tree. A city is a wilderness without choras. And now there's only one.* The columns sparkled in the blue glow from the dome of fog above, but once again the light seemed only brilliant reflections. There was no sign of Muradin; he did not think the Aiel had come out of the glass forest. Or ever would.

Suddenly something caught his eye, low in the branches of the Tree of Life. A shape swinging slowly. A man, hanging from a pole laid across two branches by a rope around his neck.

With a wordless roar, he ran for the tree, grabbing at *saidin*, the fiery sword coming into his hands as he leaped, slashing at the rope. He and Mat hit the dusty white paving stones with twin thuds. The pole jarred free and clattered down beside them; not a pole, but an odd black-hafted spear with a short sword blade in place of a spearpoint, slightly curved and single-edged. Rand would not have cared if it was made of gold and *cuendillar* set with sapphires and firedrops.

Letting sword and Power go, he ripped the rope away from Mat's neck and pressed an ear to his friend's chest. Nothing. Desperately, he tore open Mat's coat and shirt, breaking the leather cord that held a silver medallion on Mat's chest. He tossed the medallion aside, listened again. Nothing. No heartbeat. Dead. *No! He'd be all right if I hadn't let him follow me here. I can't let him be dead!*

As hard as he could he pounded his fist against Mat's chest, listened. Nothing. Again he hammered, listened. Yes. There. A faint heartbeat. It was. So faint, so slow. And slowing. But Mat *was* still alive despite the heavy purple welt around his neck. He might yet be kept alive.

Filling his lungs, Rand scrambled around to breathe into Mat's mouth as strongly as he could. Again. Again. Then he leaped astride Mat, seized the waist of his breeches and heaved upward, lifting his hips off the pavement. Up and down, three times, and then back to breathing into his mouth. He could have channeled; he might have been able to do something that way. The memory of that girl in the Stone stopped him. He wanted Mat to live. Live, not be a puppet moved by the Power. Once back in Emond's Field he had seen Master Luhhan revive a boy who had been found floating in the Winespring Water. So he breathed and heaved, breathed and heaved and prayed.

Abruptly Mat jerked, coughed. Rand knelt beside him as he put both hands to his throat and rolled onto his side, sucking air in an agonized rattle.

Mat touched the piece of rope with one hand and shivered. "Those flaming—sons—of goats," he muttered hoarsely. "They tried—to kill me."

"Who did?" Rand asked, looking around warily. Half-finished palaces around the great littered square stared back at him. Surely Rhuidean was empty except for the two of them. Unless Muradin was still alive, somewhere.

"The folk—on the other side—of that—twisted doorway." Swallowing painfully, Mat sat up and took a deep unsteady breath. "There's one here, too, Rand." He still sounded as if his throat had been rasped.

"You could go through it? Did they answer questions?" That could be useful. He desperately needed more answers. A thousand questions, and too few answers.

"No answers," Mat said huskily. "They cheat. And they tried to kill me." He picked up the medallion, a silver foxhead that almost filled his palm, and after a moment stuffed it into his pocket with a grimace. "I got something out of them, at least." Pulling the strange spear to him, he ran his fingers along the black shaft. A line of some strange cursive script ran its length, bracketed by a pair of birds inlaid in metal even darker than the wood. Ravens, Rand thought they were. Another pair were engraved on the blade. With a rough wry laugh, Mat levered himself to his feet, half-leaning on the spear, the sword blade beginning just level with his head. He did not bother to lace up his shirt or button his coat. "I'll keep this, too. Their joke, but I will keep it."

"A joke?"

Mat nodded. "What it says.

'Thus is our treaty written; thus is agreement made.
Thought is the arrow of time; memory never fades.
What was asked is given. The price is paid.'

"A pretty joke, you see. I'll slice them with their own wit if I ever get the chance. I'll give them 'thought and memory.' " He winced, scrubbing a hand through his hair. "Light, but my head hurts. It's spinning, like a thousand bits of dreams, and every one a needle. Do you think Moiraine will do something for it if I ask?"

"I am sure she will," Rand replied slowly. Mat had to be hurting badly if he sought the Aes Sedai's help. He looked at the dark spear shaft again. Most of the script was hidden by Mat's hand, but not all. Whatever it was, he had no idea what it said. How had Mat? Rhuidean's empty windows stared at him mockingly. We hide many secrets still, they seemed to say. More than you know. Worse than you know. "Let's go back now, Mat. I don't care if we have to cross the valley in the night. As you said, it will be cooler. I don't want to stay in here any longer."

"That sounds just fine to me," Mat said, coughing. "As long as we can get another drink of water at that fountain."

Rand kept his pace to Mat's, which was slow at first, hobbling along using the odd spear as a walking staff. He paused once to look at the two figurines of a man and a woman holding crystal spheres, but he left them there. Not yet. Not for a long time yet, if he was lucky.

When they left the square behind, the unfinished palaces rearing along the street had a threatening look, their jagged tops like the walls of great fortresses. Rand embraced *saidin,* though he saw no real threat. But he felt it, as though murderous eyes were boring into his back. Rhuidean lay peaceful and empty, shadowless in the blue glow of its fog roof. The dust in the streets rippled in the wind. . . . The wind. There was no wind.

"Oh, burn me," Mat muttered. "I think we're in trouble, Rand. It's what I get for staying around you. You always get me in trouble."

The ripples came faster, sliding together to make thicker lines, quivering still.

"Can you walk faster?" Rand asked.

"Walk? Blood and ashes, I can run." Slanting the spear across his chest, Mat suited his words with a lurching gallop.

Running alongside, Rand brought his sword back, uncertain of what he could do with it against shivering lines of dust, uncertain that there really was need. It was only dust. *No, it bloody isn't. It's one of those bubbles. The Dark One's evil, drifting along the Pattern, seeking out bloody* ta'veren*. I know it is.*

All around them dust rippled and shivered ever thicker, bunching and gathering. Suddenly, right in front of them, a shape reared up in the basin of a dry fountain, a solid man shape, dark and featureless, with fingers like sharp claws. Silently it leaped at them.

Rand moved instinctively—the Moon Rises Over Water—and the blade of Power sliced through that dark figure. In a twinkling it was only a thick cloud of dust, drifting toward the pavement.

Others replaced it, though, black faceless shapes rushing in from all sides, no two alike, but all with reaching claws. Rand danced the forms among them, blade weaving intricate patterns in the air, leaving floating motes behind. Mat used his spear like a quarterstaff, a spinning blur, but bringing the sword blade into it as if he had always used the weapon. The creatures died—or at least returned to dust—but they were many, and quick. Blood poured down Rand's face, and the old wound in his side burned on the point of splitting open. Red spread across Mat's face, too, and down his chest. Too many, and too quick. *You do not do the tenth part of what you are capable of already.* That was what Lanfear had told him. He laughed as he danced the forms. Learn from one of the Forsaken. He could do that, if not the way she intended. Yes, he could. He channeled, wove strands of the Power, and sent a whirlwind into the middle of each black shape. They exploded in clouds of dust that left him coughing. As far as he could see, dust settled from the air.

Hacking and panting, Mat leaned on his dark-shafted spear. "Did you do that?" he wheezed, wiping blood away from his eyes. "About time. If you knew how, why didn't you bloody do it in the first place?"

Rand started to laugh again—*Because I didn't think of it. Because I didn't know how until I did it*—but it froze in his mouth. Dust drifted out of the air, and as it settled on the ground, it began to ripple. "Run," he said. "We have to get out of here. Run!"

Side by side they sped for the fog, slashing at any lines of dust that seemed to be thickening, kicking at them, anything to keep them from coalescing. Rand sent whirlwinds swirling wildly in every direction. Dispelled dust began shivering back together immediately, even before it reached the ground now. They kept running, into the fog and through, bursting out into dim, sharp-shadowed light.

Side aching, Rand spun, ready to try lightning, or fire, anything. Nothing came through the fog after them. Maybe the mist was a wall to those dark shapes. Maybe it held them in. Maybe. . . . He did not know. He did not really care, so long as the things could not follow.

"Burn me," Mat muttered hoarsely, "we were in there all night. It's nearly sunrise. I didn't think it was that long."

Rand stared at the sky. The sun had not topped the mountains yet; a painfully brilliant nimbus outlined the jagged peaks. Long shadows covered the valley floor. *He will come from Rhuidean at dawn, and tie you together with bonds you cannot break. He will take you back, and he will destroy you.*

"Let's go back up the mountain," he said quietly. "They will be waiting for us." *For me.*

CHAPTER
27

Within the Ways

T he darkness of the Ways compressed the light of Perrin's pole-
lantern to a sharp-edged pool around himself and Gaul. The
creak of his saddle, the gritty click of hooves on stone, seemed
to reach no further than light's rim. There was no smell to the air;
nothing. The Aielman strode along beside Stepper easily, keeping an
eye on the dimly seen lanternglow from Loial's party ahead. Perrin
refused to call it Faile's. The Ways did not seem to bother Gaul, for all
their reputation. Perrin himself could not help listening, as he had for
nearly two days, or what passed for days in this lightless place. His ears
would be first to catch the sound that meant they were all going to die
or worse, the sound of wind rising where no wind ever blew. No wind
but *Machin Shin*, the Black Wind that ate souls. He could not help
thinking that traveling the Ways was slack-witted folly, but when need
called, what was foolish changed.

The faint light ahead stopped, and he drew rein in the middle of
what appeared to be an ancient stone bridge arching through utter
blackness, ancient because of the breaks in the bridge walls, the pits
and shallow ragged craters freckling the roadbed. Very likely it had
stood close to three thousand years, but it seemed ready to fall, now.
Maybe right now.

The packhorse crowded up behind Stepper: the animals whickered to each other and rolled their eyes uneasily at the surrounding dark. Perrin knew how the horses felt. A few more people for company would have lifted some of the endless night's weight. Still, he would not have gone any closer to the lanterns ahead even had he been alone. Not and risk a repeat of what happened back on that first Island, right after entering the Waygate in Tear. He scratched his curly beard irritably. He was not sure what he had expected, but not. . . .

The pole-lantern bobbed as he stepped down from his saddle and led Stepper and the packhorse to the Guiding, a tall slab of white stone covered with cursive silver inlays vaguely reminiscent of vines and leaves, all pitted as if splashed with acid. He could not read it, of course—Loial had to do that; it was Ogier script—and after a moment he walked around it, studying the Island. It was the same as the others he had seen, with a chest-high wall of white stone, simple curves and rounds fitted in an intricate pattern. At intervals bridges pierced the wall, arching out into the darkness, and railless ramps running up or down with no means of support he could see. There were cracks everywhere, ragged pits and shallow craters, as though the stone were rotting. When the horses moved there was a grainy sound of stone flaking away beneath their hooves. Gaul peered into the dark with no visible nervousness, but then, he did not know what might be out there. Perrin did, too well.

When Loial and the others arrived, Faile immediately hopped from her black mare and strode straight to Perrin, eyes intent on his face. He was already regretting making her worry, but she did not look worried at all. He could not have said what her expression was, besides fixed.

"Have you decided to talk to me instead of over my hea—?"

Her full-armed slap made spots dance in front of his eyes. "What did you mean," she practically spat, "charging in here like a wild boar? You have no regard. None!"

He took a slow, deep breath. "I asked you before not to do that." Her dark, tilted eyes widened as if he had said something infuriating. He was rubbing his cheek when her second slap caught him on the other side, nearly unhinging his jaw. The Aiel were watching interestedly, and Loial with his ears drooping.

"I told you not to do that," he growled. Her fist was not very big, but her sudden punch to his shortribs drove most of the air from his lungs, hunching him over sideways, and she drew back her fist again. With a snarl, he seized her by the scruff of her neck and. . . .

Well, it was her own fault. It was. He had asked her not to hit him, told her. Her own fault. He was surprised she had not tried to pull one of her knives, though; she seemed to carry as many as Mat.

She had been furious, of course. Furious with Loial for trying to intervene; she could take care of herself, thank you very much. Furious with Bain and Chiad for *not* intervening; she had been taken aback when they said they did not think she would want them to interfere in a fight she had picked. *When you choose the fight,* Bain had said, *you must take the consequences, win or lose.* But she did not seem even the tiniest bit angry with him any longer. That made him nervous. She had only stared at him, her dark eyes glistening with unshed tears, which made him feel guilty, which in turn made him angry. Why should he be guilty? Was he supposed to stand there and let her hit him to her heart's content? She had mounted Swallow and sat there, very stiff-backed, refusing to sit gingerly, staring at him with an unreadable expression. It made him very nervous. He almost wished she had pulled a knife. Almost.

"They are moving again," Gaul said.

Perrin jerked back to the present. The other light *was* moving. Now it paused. One of them had noticed his light was not following yet. Probably Loial. Faile might not mind if he got lost, and the two Aiel women had twice tried to talk him into walking off a little way with them. He had not needed the slight shake of Gaul's head to refuse. He heeled Stepper forward, leading the packhorse.

The Guiding here was more pocked than most he had seen, but he rode on past it with only a glance. The light of the other lanterns was already starting down one of the gently sloping ramps, and he followed with a sigh. He hated the ramps. Sided only by darkness, it began to curve, down and around, with nothing discernible beyond the squashed light of the lantern swaying above his head. Something told him that a fall over the edge would never end. Stepper and the packhorse kept to the middle without any urging, and even Gaul avoided the brink. Worse, when the ramp ended on another Island, there was no way to escape the conclusion that it lay directly beneath the one they had just left. He was glad to see Gaul glancing upward, glad he was not alone in wondering what held the Islands up and whether it was still sound.

Once more Loial and Faile's lanterns had stopped by the Guiding, so he reined up again, just off the ramp. This time they did not move on, though. After a few moments, Faile's voice called, "Perrin."

He exchanged looks with Gaul, and the Aiel shrugged. She had not spoken to Perrin since he. . . .

"Perrin, come here." Not peremptory, exactly, but not asking, either.

Bain and Chiad were squatting easily beside the Guiding, and Loial and Faile sat their horses close by, pole-lanterns in hand. The Ogier had their packhorses' lead line; his ear tufts twitched as he looked from Faile to Perrin and back again. She, on the other hand, seemed completely absorbed in adjusting her riding gloves, of soft green leather with golden falcons embroidered on their backs. She had changed her dress, too. The new one was cut in the same fashion, with a high neck and narrow divided skirts, but it was a dark green brocaded silk, and somehow it seemed to emphasize her bosom. Perrin had never seen the dress before.

"What do you want?" he asked warily.

She looked up as if surprised to see him, tilted her head thoughtfully, then smiled as though it had just occurred to her. "Oh, yes. I wanted to see if you could be taught to come when I call." Her smile deepened; it had to be because she had heard his teeth grinding. He scrubbed at his nose; there was a faint rank smell here.

Gaul chuckled softly. "As well try to understand the sun, Perrin. It simply is, and it is not to be understood. You cannot live without it, but it exacts a price. So with women."

Bain leaned over to whisper in Chiad's ear, and they both laughed. From the way they looked at Gaul and him, Perrin did not think he would like hearing what the women found so funny.

"It is not that at all," Loial rumbled, ears shifting testily. He gave Faile an accusing look, which did not abash her at all; she smiled at him vaguely and went back to her gloves, snugging each finger all over again. "I am sorry, Perrin. She insisted on being the one to call you. This is why. We are there." He pointed to the base of the Guiding, where a wide pit-broken white line ran off, not to bridge or ramp, but into the darkness. "The Waygate at Manetheren, Perrin."

Perrin nodded, saying nothing. He was not about to suggest they follow the line, not and have Faile call him down for trying to take over. He rubbed his nose again absently; that almost imperceptible scent of rankness was irritating. He was not going to make even the most sensible suggestion. If she wanted to lead, let her. But she sat her saddle, fooling with her gloves, obviously waiting for him to speak so she could make some witty remark. She liked wittiness; he preferred saying what he meant. Irritably, he turned Stepper, meaning to go on without her or Loial. The line led to the Waygate, and he could pick out the *Avendesora* leaf that opened it himself.

Suddenly his ear caught a muffled click of hooves from the darkness, and the fetid smell slammed home in his mind. "Trollocs!" he shouted.

Gaul pivoted smoothly to slide a spear into the black-mailed chest of a wolf-snouted Trolloc dashing into the light with scythelike sword upraised; in the same effortless motion the Aiel pulled his spearpoint free and sidestepped to let the huge shape fall. More came behind it, though, all goatsnouts and boar's tusks, cruel beaks and twisted horns, with curved swords and spiked axes and hooked spears. The horses danced and screamed.

Holding his pole-lantern high—the thought of facing these things in the dark gave him cold sweat—Perrin clawed for a weapon, swung at a face distorted by a sharp-toothed snout. He was surprised to realize he had pulled the hammer free of its lashings on his saddlebags, but if it did not have the axe's sharp edge, ten pounds of steel wielded by a blacksmith's arm still sent the Trolloc staggering back shrieking and clutching a ruined face.

Loial dashed his pole-lantern against a goat-horned head, and the lantern broke; bathed in burning oil, the Trolloc ran howling into the dark. The Ogier flailed about him with the stout pole, a switch in his huge hands, but one that landed with sharp cracks of splintering bone. One of Faile's knives blossomed in an all-too-human eye above a tusked snout. The Aiel danced the spears, having somehow found time to veil themselves. Perrin struck, and struck, and struck. A whirlwind of death that lasted. . . . A minute? Five? It seemed an hour. But suddenly the Trollocs were down, those not already dead kicking in their death throes.

Perrin sucked air into his lungs; his right arm felt as if the weight of the hammer might pull it off. There was a burning sensation on his face, a wetness trickling down his side, another on his leg, where Trolloc steel had gotten through. Each of the Aiel had at least one damp patch darkening their brown-and-gray clothes, and Loial wore a bloody gash down his thigh. Perrin's eyes went right past them, seeking Faile. If she was hurt. . . . She sat atop her black mare, a knife in her hand ready to throw. She had actually managed to pull off her gloves and tuck them neatly behind her belt. He could not see a wound on her. In all the blood smell—human, Ogier, Trolloc—he could not have picked out hers if she were bleeding, but he knew her scent, and she did not have the pained smell of injury. Bright lights hurt Trolloc eyes; they did not adapt quickly. Very likely the only reason they were still alive and the Trollocs dead was that abrupt entry from darkness into light.

That was all the time they had, a moment's respite, long enough to glance around, take breath. With a roar like a hundred pounds of bone falling into a huge meat grinder, a Fade leaped into the light, eyeless stare a stare of death, black sword flickering like lightning. The horses screamed, trying to bolt.

Gaul barely managed to turn that blade with his buckler, losing a slice from the side of it as if the layers of cured bullhide were only paper. He stabbed, eluded a thrust—barely—and stabbed again. Arrows sprouted in the Myrddraal's chest. Bain and Chiad had thrust their spears through the harness holding the cased bows on their backs and were using those curved horn bows. More arrows, pincushioning the Halfman's chest. Gaul's spear, darting, stabbing. One of Faile's knives suddenly stood out in that smooth maggot-white face. The Fade would not fall, would not stop trying to kill. Only the wildest dodging kept its sword from finding flesh.

Perrin bared his teeth in an unconscious snarl. He hated Trollocs as an enemy of his blood, but the Neverborn . . . ? It was worth dying to kill a Neverborn. *To put my teeth in its throat . . . !* Careless of whether he blocked Bain and Chiad's arrows, he guided Stepper closer to the Neverborn's back, forcing the reluctant dun nearer with reins and knees. At the last instant, the creature spun away from Gaul, seemingly ignoring a spearpoint that thrust between its shoulders and came out below its throat, staring up at Perrin with the eyeless gaze that sent fear into every man's soul. Too late. Perrin's hammer fell, shattering head and eyeless gaze alike.

Even down and virtually headless, the Myrddraal still thrashed, lashing aimlessly with its Thakandar-wrought blade. Stepper danced back, whickering nervously, and suddenly Perrin felt as if he had been doused in icy water. That black steel made wounds even Aes Sedai found hard to Heal, and he had ridden in uncaring. *My teeth in its. . . . Light, I have to keep hold of myself. I have to!*

He could still hear smothered sounds from the darkness at the far end of the Island, the clatter of hoofed feet, the scrape of boots, harsh breathing and guttural murmurs. More Trollocs; how many he could not say. A pity they had not been linked to the Myrddraal, yet perhaps they might hesitate to attack without it to drive them. Trollocs were usually cowards in their way, preferring strong odds and easy kills. But even lacking a Myrddraal they could work themselves up to come again eventually.

"The Waygate," he said. "We have to get out before they decide what to do without that." He used the bloody hammer to gesture to the still flailing Fade. Faile reined Swallow around immediately, and he was so surprised, he blurted, "You aren't going to argue?"

"Not when you speak sense," she said briskly. "Not when you speak sense. Loial?"

The Ogier took the lead on his tall, hairy-fetlocked mount. Perrin backed Stepper after Faile and Loial, hammer in hand, the Aiel siding him, all with bows ready now. Shuffling hooves and boots followed in the blackness, and harsh mutters in a language too rough for human tongues. Back and back, with the mutters edging closer, working up courage.

Another sound floated to Perrin, like silk sighing across silk. It sent shivers along his bones. Louder, a distant giant's exhalation, rising, falling, rising higher. "Hurry!" he shouted. "Hurry!"

"I am," Loial barked. "I—That sound! Is it—? The Light illumine our souls, and the Creator's hand shelter us! It's opening. It is opening! I must be last. Out! Out! But not too— No, Faile!"

Perrin risked a glance over his shoulder. Twin gates of apparently living leaves were swinging open, revealing a smoked-glass view of mountainous country. Loial had dismounted to remove the *Avendesora* leaf to unlock the gate, and Faile had their pack animals' leads and his huge mount's reins. With a hasty shout of "Follow me! Quickly!" she booted Swallow's ribs, and the Tairen mare sprang toward the opening.

"After her," Perrin told the Aiel. "Hurry! You cannot fight this." Wisely they hesitated only a heartbeat before peeling back, Gaul seizing the packhorse's lead line. Stepper came abreast of Loial. "Can you lock it shut some way? Block it?" A frantic edge had entered the harsh mutterings; the Trollocs had recognized the sound too, now. *Machin Shin* was coming. Living meant getting out of the Ways.

"Yes," Loial said. "Yes. But go. Go!"

Perrin reined Stepper back quickly toward the Gate, yet before he knew what he was doing he had thrown back his head and howled, defiance and challenge. *Foolish, foolish, foolish!* Still, he kept his eyes on that pitch dark and backed Stepper into the Waygate. An icy ripple slid across him hair by hair, and time stretched out. The jolt of leaving the Ways hit him, as if he had gone from a dead gallop to a stop in one step.

The Aiel were still turning to face the Waygate, spreading out across the slope with arrows nocked, among low bushes and stunted mountain trees, wind-twisted pine and fir and leatherleaf. Faile was just picking herself up from where she had tumbled from Swallow's saddle, the black mare nuzzling her. Galloping out of a Waygate was at least as bad as galloping in; she was lucky she had not broken her neck, and her horse's, too. Loial's tall horse and her packhorses were trembling as though hit between the eyes. Perrin opened his mouth, and she glared at him, daring him to make any comment at all, maybe a sympathetic one least of all. He grimaced wryly and wisely kept silent.

Abruptly Loial came hurtling out of the Waygate, leaping out of a dull silvery mirror with his own reflection growing behind him, and rolled across the ground. Almost on his heels, two Trollocs appeared, ram's horns and snout, eagle's beak and feathered crest, but before they were more than halfway out, the shimmering surface turned dead black, bubbling and bulging, clinging to them.

Voices whispered in Perrin's head, a thousand babbling mad voices clawing at the inside of his skull. *Bitter blood. Blood so bitter. Drink the blood and crack the bone. Crack the bone and suck the marrow. Bitter marrow, sweet the screams. Singing screams. Sing the screams. Tiny souls. Acrid souls. Gobble them down. So sweet the pain.* On and on.

Shrieking, howling, the Trollocs beat at the blackness boiling around them, clawed to pull free as it sucked them deeper, deeper, till only one hairy hand remained, clutching frantically, then only darkness, bulging outward, seeking. Slowly the Waygates appeared, sliding together, squeezing the blackness so it oozed back inside between them. The voices in Perrin's head finally stopped. Loial rushed forward quickly to place not one but two three-lobed leaves among the myriad leaves and vines. The Waygate became stone again, a section of stone wall, carved in intricate detail, standing alone on a sparsely wooded mountainside. Among the myriad leaves and vines was not one, but two *Avendesora* leaves. Loial had replaced the trefoil leaf from inside on the outside.

The Ogier heaved a deep, relieved sigh. "That is the best I can do. It can only be opened from this side now." He gave Perrin a look at once anxious and firm. "I could have locked it forever by not replacing the leaves, but I will not ruin a Waygate, Perrin. We grew the Ways and tended them. Perhaps they can be cleansed someday. I cannot ruin a Waygate."

"It will do," Perrin told him. Had the Trollocs been coming to this Waygate, or had it just been a chance encounter? In either case, it would do.

"Was that—?" Faile began unsteadily, then stopped to swallow. Even the Aiel looked shaken for once.

"Machin Shin," Loial said. "The Black Wind. A creature of the Shadow, or a thing grown of the Ways' own taint—no one knows. I pity the Trollocs. Even them."

Perrin was not sure he did, not even dying like that. He had seen what Trollocs left when they got their hands on humans. Trollocs ate anything, so long as it was meat, and sometimes they liked to keep their meat alive while they butchered. He would not let himself pity Trollocs.

Stepper's hooves crunched on gritty dirt as Perrin turned him to see where they were.

Cloud-capped mountains rose all around; it was the ever-present clouds that gave them their name, the Mountains of Mist. The air was cool at this altitude, even in summer, especially compared to Tear. The late-afternoon sun sat on the western peaks, glinting on streams running down to the river that coursed along the floor of the long valley below. The Manetherendrelle, it was called once it had traveled out of the mountains and much farther west and south, but Perrin had grown up calling the length of it that ran along the south edge of the Two Rivers the White River, an uncrossable stretch of rapids that churned its waters to froth. The Manetherendrelle. Waters of the Mountain Home.

Where bare rock showed in the valley below or on the surrounding slopes, it glittered like glass. Once a city had stood there, covering valley and mountains. Manetheren, city of soaring spires and splashing fountains, capital of a great nation of the same name, perhaps the most beautiful city in the world, according to old Ogier tales. Gone now without a trace, except for the all-but-indestructible Waygate that had stood in the Ogier grove. Burned to barren rock more than two thousand years ago, while the Trolloc Wars still raged, destroyed by the One Power after the death of its last king, Aemon al Caar al Thorin, in his last bloody battle against the Shadow. Aemon's Field, men had named that place, where the village called Emond's Field now stood.

Perrin shivered. That was long ago. Trollocs had come once since, on Winternight more than a year gone, the night before he and Rand and Mat were forced to flee in the darkness with Moiraine. That seemed long ago, too, now. It could not happen again, with the Waygate locked. *It's Whitecloaks I have to worry about, not Trollocs.*

A pair of white-winged hawks wheeled above the far end of the valley. Perrin's eyes barely caught the streak of a rising arrow. One of the hawks cartwheeled and fell, and Perrin frowned. Why would anyone shoot a hawk up here in the mountains? Over a farm, if it was after the chickens or the geese, but up here? Why would anyone even be up here? Two Rivers people avoided the mountains.

The second hawk swooped on snowy wings toward where its mate had fallen, but suddenly it was climbing desperately. A black cloud of ravens burst from the trees, surrounding it in wild melee, and when they settled again, the hawk was gone.

Perrin made himself breathe. He had seen ravens, and other birds, attack a hawk that came too close to their nests before, but he could not make himself believe it that simple this time. The birds had burst up from about where the arrow had risen. Ravens. The Shadow used animals as spies, sometimes. Rats and others that fed on death, usually. Ravens, especially. He had sharp memories of running from sweeping lines of ravens that had hunted him as though they had intelligence.

"What are you staring at?" Faile asked, shading her eyes to peer down the valley. "Were those birds?"

"Just birds," he said. *Maybe they were. I can't frighten everybody until I'm sure. Not while they're still shaky from* Machin Shin.

He was still holding his bloody hammer, he realized, slick with black Myrddraal blood. His fingers found drying blood on his cheek, matting in his short beard. When he climbed down, his side and his leg burned. He found a shirt in his saddlebags to clean the hammer before the Fade's blood etched the metal. In a moment he would find out if there was anything to fear in these mountains. If it was more than men, the wolves would know.

Faile began unbuttoning his coat.

"What are you doing?" he demanded.

"Tending your wounds," she snapped back. "I'll not have you bleeding to death on me. That would be just like you, to die and leave me the work of burying you. You have no consideration. Hold still."

"Thank you," he said quietly, and she looked surprised.

She made him strip off everything but his smallclothes, so she could wash his wounds, rub them with ointment fetched from her saddlebags. He could not see the cut on his face, of course, but it seemed small and shallow, if uncomfortably close to his eye. The slash across his left side was over a hand long, though, straight along a rib, and the hole a spear had made in his right thigh was deep. Faile had to put stitches in that, with needle and thread from her sewing kit. He took it stoically; she was the one who winced at every stitch. She muttered angrily under her breath the whole time she worked, especially while rubbing her dark stinging cream into his cheek, looking almost as if the hurts were hers, and his fault, yet she tied bandages around his ribs and his thigh with a gentle hand. It made a startling contrast, her soft touch and her furious grumbles. Purely confusing.

While he donned a clean shirt and a spare pair of breeches from his saddlebags, Faile stood fingering the slice in the side of his coat. Two inches to the right, and he would not have left that Island. Stamping his feet in his boots, he reached for his coat—and she flung it at him.

"You needn't think I will sew that up for you. I've done all the sewing for you I mean to! Do you hear me, Perrin Aybara?"

"I didn't ask—"

"You needn't think it! That's all!" She stalked away to help the Aiel tend each other and Loial. That was an odd group, the Ogier with his baggy breeches off, Gaul and Chiad eyeing each other like strange cats, Faile spreading her ointment and wrapping bandages and all the while shooting accusing glares at him. What was he supposed to have done now?

Perrin shook his head. Gaul was right, he decided; as well try to understand the sun.

Even knowing what he had to do now, he was reluctant, especially after what had happened in the Ways, with the Fade. Once he had seen a man who had forgotten he was human. The same could happen to him. *Fool. You only have to hold out a few more days. Just till you find the Whitecloaks.* And he had to know. Those ravens.

He sent his mind questing across the valley for the wolves. There were always wolves where men were not, and if they were close, he could talk with them. Wolves avoided men, ignored them as much as possible, but they hated Trollocs for unnatural things, and despised Myrddraal with a hatred too deep to hold. If Shadowspawn were in the Mountains of Mist, the wolves could tell him.

But he found no wolves. None. They should have been there, in this wilderness. He could see deer browsing down in the valley. Perhaps it was just that no wolves were close enough. They could talk over some distance, but even a mile was too far. Maybe it was less in mountains. That could be it.

His gaze swept across the cloud-capped peaks and settled on the valley's far end, where the ravens had come from. Maybe he would find wolves tomorrow. He did not want to think of the alternatives.

CHAPTER
28

To the Tower of Ghenjei

With night so near, they had no choice but to camp there on the mountain near the Waygate. In two camps. Faile insisted on it.

"That is done with," Loial told her in a displeased rumble. "We are out of the Ways, and I have kept my oath. It is finished." Faile put on one of her stubborn expressions, with chin up and fists on hips.

"Leave it alone, Loial," Perrin said. "I'll camp over there a bit." Loial glanced at Faile, who had turned to the two Aiel women as soon as she heard Perrin agree, then shook his huge head and made as if to join Perrin and Gaul. Perrin motioned him back, with a small gesture he hoped none of the women noticed.

He made it a small bit, less than twenty paces. The Waygate might be locked, but there were still the ravens, and whatever they might presage. He wanted to be near if needed. If Faile complained, she could just complain. He was so set to ignore her protests that it irked him when she made none.

Disregarding twinges from his leg and side, he unsaddled Stepper and unloaded the packhorse, hobbled both animals and fitted them with nose bags with a few handfuls of barley and some oats. There was certainly no grazing up here. As to what there was, though. . . . He strung his bow and laid it across his quiver near the fire, slipped the axe free of its belt loop.

Gaul joined him in making a fire, and they had a meal of bread and cheese and dried beef, eaten in silence and washed down with water. The sun slid behind the mountains, silhouetting the peaks and painting the undersides of the clouds red. Shadows blanketed the valley, and the air began to grow crisp.

Dusting crumbs from his hands, Perrin dug his good green wool cloak out of his saddlebags. Perhaps he had grown more accustomed to Tear's heat than he had thought. The women were certainly not eating in silence around their shadow-shrouded fire; he could hear them laughing, and the bits of what they said that he picked up made his ears burn. Women would talk about anything; they had no restraint at all. Loial had moved as far away from them as he could and still be in the light, and was trying to bury himself in a book. They probably did not even realize they were embarrassing the Ogier; they probably thought they were talking quietly enough for Loial not to hear.

Muttering to himself, Perrin sat back down across the fire from Gaul. The Aiel seemed to be taking no notice of the chill. "Do you know any funny stories?"

"Funny stories? I cannot think of one, offhand." Gaul's eyes half-turned to the other fire, and the laughter. "I would if I could. The sun, remember?"

Perrin laughed noisily and made his voice loud enough to carry. "I do. Women!" The hilarity in the other camp faded for a moment before rising again. That should show them. Other people could laugh. Perrin stared glumly into the fire. His wounds ached.

After a moment, Gaul said, "This place begins to look more like the Three-fold Land than most of the wetlands. Too much water, still, and the trees are still too big and too many, but it is not so strange as the places called forests."

The soil was poor here where Manetheren had died in fire, the widely scattered trees all stunted and thick-boled, odd wind-bent shapes, none as much as thirty feet high. Perrin thought it about as desolate a spot as he had ever seen.

"I wish I could see your Three-fold Land someday, Gaul."

"Perhaps you will, when we are done here."

"Perhaps." Not much chance of it, of course. None, really. He could have told the Aielman that, but he did not want to talk of it now, or think of it.

"This is where Manetheren stood? You are of Manetheren's blood?"

"This was Manetheren," Perrin replied. "And I suppose I am." It was hard to believe that the small villages and quiet farms of the Two Rivers held the last of Manetheren's blood, but that was what Moiraine had said. The old blood runs strong in the Two Rivers, she had said. "That was a long time ago, Gaul. We are farmers, shepherds; not a great nation, not great warriors."

Gaul smiled slightly. "If you say it. I have seen you dance the spears, and Rand al'Thor, and the one called Mat. But if you say it."

Perrin shifted uncomfortably. How much had he changed since leaving home? Himself, and Rand, and Mat? Not his eyes, and the wolves, or Rand's channeling; he did not mean that. How much of what was inside remained unchanged? Mat was the only one who still seemed to be just himself, only more so. "You know about Manetheren?"

"We know more of your world than you think. And less than we believed. Long before I crossed the Dragonwall I had read books brought by peddlers. I knew of 'ships' and 'rivers' and 'forests,' or thought I did." Gaul made them sound like words in a strange tongue. "This is how I envisioned a 'forest.' " He gestured at the sparse trees, dwarfed from the height they should have had. "To believe a thing is not to make it true. What of the Nightrunner, and Leafblighter's get? Do you believe it just coincidence they came near this Waygate?"

"No." Perrin sighed. "I saw ravens, down the valley. Maybe that's all they were, but I don't want to take the chance, not after the Trollocs."

Gaul nodded. "They could have been Shadoweyes. If you plan for the worst, all surprises are pleasant."

"I could do with a pleasant surprise." Perrin felt for wolves again, and again found nothing. "I may be able to find out something tonight. Maybe. If anything happens here, you might have to kick me to wake me." That sounded odd, he realized, but Gaul only nodded again. "Gaul, you've never mentioned my eyes, or even given them a second glance. None of the Aiel have." He knew they were glowing golden now, in the firelight.

"The world is changing," Gaul said quietly. "Rhuarc, and Jheran, my own clan chief—the Wise Ones, too—they tried to hide it, but they were uneasy when they sent us across the Dragonwall searching for He Who Comes With the Dawn. I think perhaps the change will not be what we have always believed. I do not know how it will be different, but it will be. The Creator put us in the Three-fold Land to shape us as well as to punish our sin, but for what have we been shaped?" He shook his head suddenly, ruefully. "Colinda, the Wise One of Hot Springs Hold, tells me I think too much for a Stone Dog, and Bair, the eldest Wise One of the Shaarad, threatens to send me to Rhuidean when Jheram dies whether I want to go or not. Beside all of that, Perrin, what does the color of a man's eyes matter?"

"I wish everybody thought that way." The merriment had finally stopped at the other fire. One of the Aiel women—Perrin could not tell which—was taking the first watch, her back to the light, and everyone else had settled down for sleep. It had been a tiring day. Sleep should be easy to find, and the dream he needed. He stretched out beside the fire, pulling his cloak around him. "Remember. Kick me awake, if need be."

Sleep enfolded him while Gaul was still nodding, and the dream came at once.

It was daylight, and he stood alone near the Waygate, which looked like an elegantly carved length of wall, incongruous on the mountainside. Except for that there was no sign any human had ever set foot on that slope. The sky was bright and fine, and a soft breeze up the valley brought him the scent of deer and rabbits, quail and dove, a thousand distinct smells, of water and earth and trees. This was the wolf dream.

For a moment the sense of *being* a wolf rolled over him. He had paws, and. . . . *No!* He ran his hands over himself, relieved to find only his own body, in his own coat and cloak. And the wide belt that normally held his axe, but with the hammer haft thrust through the loop instead.

He frowned at that, and surprisingly, for a moment, the axe flickered there instead, insubstantial and misty. Abruptly it was the hammer again. Licking his lips, he hoped it stayed that way. The axe might be a better weapon, but he preferred the hammer. He could not remember anything like that happening before, something changing, but he knew little of this strange place. If it could be called a place. It was the wolf dream, and odd things happened there, surely as odd as in any ordinary dream.

As though thinking of the oddities triggered one of them, a patch of sky against the mountains darkened suddenly, became a window to somewhere else. Rand stood amid swirling stormwinds, laughing wildly, even madly, arms upraised, and on the winds rode small shapes, gold-and-scarlet, like the strange figure on the Dragon banner; hidden eyes watched Rand, and there was no telling whether he knew it. The odd "window" winked out, only to be replaced by another farther over, where Nynaeve and Elayne stalked cautiously through a demented landscape of twisted, shadowed buildings, hunting some dangerous beast. Perrin could not have said how he knew it was dangerous, but he did. That vanished, and another black blotch spread across the sky. Mat, standing where a road forked ahead of him. He flipped a coin, started down one branch, and suddenly was wearing a wide-brimmed hat and walking with a staff bearing a short sword blade. Another "window," and Egwene and a woman with long white hair were staring at him in surprise while behind them the White Tower crumbled stone by stone. Then they were gone, too.

Perrin drew a deep breath. He had seen the like before, here in the wolf dream, and he thought the sightings were real in some way, or meant something. Whatever they were, the wolves never saw them. Moiraine had suggested that the wolf dream was the same as something called *Tel'aran'rhiod*, and then would say no more. He had overheard Egwene and Elayne speaking of dreams, once, but Egwene already knew too much about him and wolves, perhaps as much as Moiraine. It was not something he could talk about, not even with her.

There was one person he could have talked to. He wished he could find Elyas Machera, the man who had introduced him to the wolves. Elyas had to know about these things. When he thought of the man, it seemed for a moment he heard his own name whispered faintly in the wind, but when he listened, there was only the wind. It was a lonely sound. Here there was only himself.

"Hopper!" he called, and in his mind, *Hopper!* The wolf was dead, and yet not dead, here. The wolf dream was where wolves came when they died, to await being born again. It was more than that, to wolves; they seemed in some way to be aware of the dream even while awake. One was almost as real—maybe as real—as the other, to them. "Hopper!" *Hopper!* But Hopper did not come.

This was all useless. He was there for a reason, and he might as well get on with it. At best, getting down to where he had seen the ravens rise would take hours.

He took a step—the land around him blurred—and his foot came down near a narrow brook beneath stunted hemlock and mountain willow, with cloud-capped peaks towering above. For a moment he stared in amazement. He was at the far end of the valley from the Waygate. In fact, he was at the very spot he had been aiming for, the place where the ravens had come from, and the arrow that killed the first hawk. Such a thing had never happened to him before. Was he learning more of the wolf dream—Hopper had always said he was ignorant—or was it different this time?

He was more cautious with his next step, but it was only a step. There was no evidence of archer or ravens, no track, no feather, no scent. He was not sure what he had expected. There would be no sign unless they had been in the dream, too. But if he could find wolves in the dream, they could help him find their brothers and sisters in the waking world, and those wolves could tell him if there were Shadow-spawn in the mountains. Perhaps if he were higher up they could hear him call.

Fixing his eye on the highest peak bordering the valley, just below the clouds, he stepped. The world blurred, and he was standing on the mountainside, with white billows not five spans overhead. In spite of himself, he laughed. This was fun. From here he could see the entire valley stretched out below.

"Hopper!" No answer.

He leaped to the next mountain, calling, and the next, and the next, eastward, toward the Two Rivers. Hopper did not answer. More troubling, Perrin did not sense any other wolves, either. There were always wolves in the wolf dream. Always.

From peak to peak he sped in blurred motion, calling, seeking. The mountains lay empty beneath him, except for deer and other game. Yet there were occasional signs of men. Ancient signs. Twice great carved figures took nearly an entire mountainside, and in another place strange angular letters two spans high had been incised across a cliff a shade too smooth and sheer. Weathering had worn away the figures' faces, and eyes less sharp than his might have taken the letters themselves for the work of wind and rain. Mountains and cliffs gave way to the Sand Hills, great rolling mounds sparsely covered with tough grass and stubborn bushes, once the shore of a great sea before the Breaking. And suddenly he saw another man, atop a sandy hill.

The fellow was too distant to see clearly, just a tall, dark-haired man, but plainly not a Trolloc or anything of the sort, in a blue coat with a bow on his back, stooping over something on the ground hidden by the low brush. Yet there was something familiar about him.

The wind rose, and Perrin caught his smell faintly. A cold scent, that was the only way to describe it. Cold, and not really human. Suddenly his own bow was in his hand, an arrow nocked, and the weight of a filled quiver tugged at his belt.

The other man looked up, saw Perrin. For a heartbeat he hesitated, then turned and became a streak, slashing away across the hills.

Perrin leaped down to where he had stood, stared at what had occupied the fellow, and without thought pursued, leaving the half-skinned corpse of a wolf behind. A dead wolf in the wolf dream. It was unthink-able. What could kill a wolf here? Something evil.

His prey ran ahead of him in strides that covered miles, never more than barely in sight. Out of the hills and across the tangled Westwood with its wide-scattered farms, over cleared farmland, a quilt of hedged fields and small thickets, and past Watch Hill. It was odd to see the thatched village houses covering the hill with no people in the streets, and farmhouses standing as if abandoned. But he kept his eye on the man fleeing ahead of him. He had become so used to this pursuit that he felt no surprise when one leaping stride put him down on the south bank of the River Taren and the next amid barren hills without trees or grass. North and east he ran, over streams and roads and villages and rivers, intent only on the man ahead. The land grew flat and grassy, broken by scattered thickets, without any sign of man. Then something glittered ahead, sparkling in the sun, a tower of metal. His quarry sped straight for it, and vanished. Two leaps brought Perrin there as well.

Two hundred feet the tower rose, and forty thick, gleaming like bur-nished steel. It might as well have been a solid column of metal. Perrin walked around it twice without seeing any opening, not so much as a crack, not even a mark on that smooth, sheer wall. The smell hung here, though, that cold, inhuman stink. The trail ended here. The man —if man he was—had gone inside somehow. He only had to find the way to follow.

Stop! It was a raw flow of emotion that Perrin's mind put a word to. *Stop!*

He turned as a great gray wolf as tall as his waist, grizzled and scarred, alighted as if he had just leaped down from the sky. He might well have. Hopper had always envied eagles their ability to fly, and here, he could too. Yellow eyes met yellow eyes.

"Why should I stop, Hopper? He killed a wolf."

Men have killed wolves, and wolves men. Why does anger seize your throat like fire this time?

"I don't know," Perrin said slowly. "Maybe because it was here. I didn't know it was possible to kill a wolf here. I thought wolves were safe in the dream."

You chase Slayer, Young Bull. He is here in the flesh, and he can kill.

"In the flesh? You mean not just dreaming? How can he be here in the flesh?"

I do not know. It is a thing dimly remembered from long ago, come again as so much else. Things of the Shadow walk the dream, now. Crea-tures of Heartfang. There is no safety.

"Well, he's inside, now." Perrin studied the featureless metal tower. "If I can find how he got in, I can put an end to him."

Cub foolish, digging in a groundwasps' nest. This place is evil. All know this. And you would chase evil into evil. Slayer can kill.

Perrin paused. There was a sense of finality to the emotions his mind attached the word "kill" to. "Hopper, what happens to a wolf who dies in the dream?"

The wolf was silent for a time. *If we die here, we die forever, Young Bull. I do not know if the same is true for you, but I believe it is.*

"A dangerous place, archer. The Tower of Ghenjei is a bad place for humankind."

Perrin whirled, half-raising his bow before he saw the woman standing a few paces away, her golden hair in a thick braid to her waist, almost the way women wore it in the Two Rivers, but more intricately woven. Her clothes were oddly cut, a short white coat and voluminous trousers of some thin pale yellow material gathered at the ankles above short boots. Her dark cloak seemed to hide something that glinted silver at her side.

She shifted, and the metallic flicker vanished. "You have sharp eyes, archer. I thought that the first time I saw you."

How long had she been watching? It was embarrassing that she had sneaked up without him hearing. At the least Hopper should have warned him. The wolf was lying down in the knee-high grass, muzzle on his forepaws, watching him.

The woman seemed vaguely familiar, though Perrin was certain he would have remembered her had he ever seen her before. Who was she, to be in the wolf dream? Or was it Moiraine's *Tel'aran'rhiod*, too? "Are you Aes Sedai?"

"No, archer." She laughed. "I only came to warn you, despite the prescripts. Once entered, the Tower of Ghenjei is hard enough to leave in the world of men. Here it is all but impossible. You have a bannerman's courage, which some say cannot be told from foolhardiness."

Impossible to leave? The fellow—Slayer—surely had gone in. Why would he do that if he could not leave? "Hopper said it's dangerous, too. The Tower of Ghenjei? What is it?"

Her eyes widened, and she glanced at Hopper, who still lay stretched out on the grass ignoring her and watching Perrin. "You can talk to wolves? Now that is a thing long lost in legend. So that is how you are here. I should have known. The tower? It is a doorway, archer, to the realms of the Aelfinn and the Eelfinn." She said the names as if he should recognize them. When he looked at her blankly, she said, "Did you ever play the game called Snakes and Foxes?"

"All children do. At least, they do in the Two Rivers. But they give it up when they get old enough to realize there's no way to win."

"Except to break the rules," she said. " 'Courage to strengthen, fire to blind, music to daze, iron to bind.' "

"That's a line from the game. I don't understand. What does it have to do with this tower?"

"Those are the ways to win against the snakes and the foxes. The game is a remembrance of old dealings. It does not matter so long as you stay away from the Aelfinn and the Eelfinn. They are not evil the way the Shadow is evil, yet they are so different from humankind they might as well be. They are not to be trusted, archer. Stay clear of the Tower of Ghenjei. Avoid the World of Dreams, if you can. Dark things walk."

"Like the man I was chasing? Slayer."

"A good name for him. This Slayer is not old, archer, but his evil is ancient." She almost appeared to be leaning slightly on something invisible; perhaps that silver thing he had never quite seen. "I seem to be telling you a great deal. I do not understand why I spoke in the first place. Of course. Are you *ta'veren*, archer?"

"Who are you?" She seemed to know a lot about the tower, and the wolf dream. *But she was surprised I could talk to Hopper.* "I've met you before somewhere, I think."

"I have broken too many of the prescripts already, archer."

"Prescripts? What prescripts?" A shadow fell on the ground behind Hopper, and Perrin turned quickly, angry at being caught by surprise again. There was no one there. But he had seen it; the shadow of a man with the hilts of two swords rising above his shoulders. Something about that image teased his memory.

"He is right," the woman said behind him. "I should not be talking to you."

When he turned back, she was gone. As far as he could see were only grassland and scattered thickets. And the gleaming, silvery tower.

He frowned at Hopper, who finally lifted his head from his paws. "It's a wonder you aren't attacked by chipmunks," Perrin muttered. "What did you make of her?"

Her? A she? Hopper stood, looking around. *Where?*

"I was talking to her. Right here. Just now."

You made noises at the wind, Young Bull. There was no she here. None but you and I.

Perrin scratched his beard irritably. She had been there. He had not been talking to himself. "Strange things can happen here," he told himself. "She agreed with you, Hopper. She told me to stay away from this tower."

She is wise. There was an element of doubt in the thought; Hopper still did not believe there had been any "she."

"I've come awfully far afield from what I intended," Perrin muttered. He explained his need to find wolves in the Two Rivers, or the mountains above, explained about the ravens, and the Trollocs in the Ways.

When he was done, Hopper remained silent for a long time, his bushy tail held low and stiff. Finally. . . . *Avoid your old home, Young Bull.* The image Perrin's mind called "home" was of the land marked by a wolfpack. *There are no wolves there now. Those who were and did not flee are dead. Slayer walks the dream there.*

"I have to go home, Hopper. I have to."

Take care, Young Bull. The day of the Last Hunt draws near. We will run together in the Last Hunt.

"We will," Perrin said sadly. It would be nice if he could come here when he died; he was half wolf already, it seemed sometimes. "I have to go now, Hopper."

May you know good hunting, Young Bull, and shes to give you many cubs.

"Goodbye, Hopper."

He opened his eyes to the dim light of dying coals on the mountainside. Gaul was squatting just beyond the edge of the light, watching the night. In the other camp, Faile was up, taking her turn at guard. The moon hung above the mountains, turning the clouds to pearly shadows. Perrin estimated he had been asleep two hours.

"I'll keep guard awhile," he said, tossing off his cloak. Gaul nodded and settled himself on the ground where he was. "Gaul?" The Aiel raised his head. "It may be worse in the Two Rivers than I thought."

"Things often are," Gaul replied quietly. "It is the way of life." The Aielman calmly put his head down for sleep.

Slayer. Who was he? What was he? Shadowspawn at the Waygate, ravens in the Mountains of Mist, and this man called Slayer in the Two Rivers. It could not be coincidence, however much he wished it.

CHAPTER
29

Homecoming

The journey into the Westwood that had taken him perhaps half a dozen strides or so in the wolf dream, out of the mountains and across the Sand Hills, lasted three long days on horses. The Aiel had no trouble keeping up afoot, but then the animals themselves could not manage much speed with the land mostly up and down as it was. Perrin's wounds itched fiercely, healing; Faile's ointment seemed to be working.

It was a quiet journey by and large, broken more often by the bark of a hunting fox or the echoing cry of a hawk than by anyone speaking. At least they saw no more ravens. More than once he thought Faile was about to bring her mare over close to him, about to say something, but each time she restrained herself. He was glad of it; he wanted to talk to her more than anything, but what if he found himself making up with her? He berated himself for wanting to. She had tricked Loial, tricked him. She was going to make everything worse, make it harder. He wished he could kiss her again. He wished she would decide she had had her fill of him and go. Why did she have to be so stubborn?

She and the two Aiel women kept to themselves, Bain and Chiad striding along on either side of Swallow when one or the other was not ranging ahead. Sometimes the three of them murmured softly among themselves, after which they avoided looking at him so pointedly that they might as well have thrown rocks. Loial rode with them at Perrin's request, though the situation obviously upset him no end. Loial's ears twitched as if he wished he had never heard of humans. Gaul seemed to find the entire thing vastly amusing; whenever Perrin looked at him, he wore an inward grin.

For himself, Perrin traveled wrapped in worry, and kept his strung bow across the tall pommel of his saddle. Did this man called Slayer rove the Two Rivers only in the wolf dream, or was he in the waking world, too? Perrin suspected the latter, and that Slayer was the one who had shot the hawk for no reason. It was another complication he could do without, on top of the Children of the Light.

His family lived on a sprawling farm more than half a day beyond Emond's Field, almost to the Waterwood. His father and mother, his sisters, his baby brother. Paetram would be nine now, no doubt objecting more strenuously than ever to being called the baby, Deselle a plump twelve, and Adora sixteen, probably ready to braid her hair. Uncle Eward, his da's brother, and Aunt Magde, stout and looking nearly alike, and their children. Aunt Neain, who visited Uncle Carlin's grave every morning, and their children, and Great-Aunt Ealsin, who had never married, with her sharp nose and sharper eye for discovering what everyone for miles around was up to. Once apprenticed to Master Luhhan, he had seen them only on feastdays; the distance was too great for casual travel, and there had always been work to do. If the Whitecloaks hunted for Aybaras, they were easy to find. They were his responsibility, not this Slayer. He could only do so much. Protect his family, and Faile. That was first. Then came the village, and the wolves, and this Slayer last. One man could not manage everything.

The Westwood grew on stony soil broken by bramble-covered outcrops, a hard, thickly treed land with few farms or paths. He had wandered these heavy woods as a boy, alone or with Rand and Mat, hunting with bow or sling, setting snares for rabbits or simply roaming for the sake of roaming. Bushy-tailed squirrels chittering in the trees, speckled thrushes warbling on branches imitated by black-winged mockers, bluebacked quail bursting up out of the brush in front of the travelers—all spoke to him of home. The very smell of the dirt the horses' hooves turned was a recognition.

He could have headed straight for Emond's Field, but instead he angled more northward through the forest, finally crossing the wide, rough track called the Quarry Road as the sun slanted down toward the treetops. Why "quarry" no one in the Two Rivers knew, and it scarcely looked a road at all, only a weedy stretch that you did not even notice was bare of trees until you saw the overgrown ruts from generations of wagons and carts. Sometimes shards of old pavement worked their way to the surface. Perhaps it had led to a quarry for Manetheren.

The farm Perrin sought lay not far from the road, beyond rows of apple and pear trees where fruit was setting. He smelled the farm before he saw it. The smell of char; not new, yet a full year would not soften that smell.

He reined in at the edge of the trees and sat staring before he made himself ride into what had been the al'Thor farm, the packhorse trailing behind his dun. Only the stone-walled sheep pen still stood, railed gate open and hanging by one hinge. The soot-blackened chimney cast a slanting shadow across the tumbled burned beams of the farmhouse. The barn and the tabac-curing shed were only ashes. Weeds choked the tabac field and the vegetable garden, and the garden had a trampled look; most of what was not sawleaf or feathertop lay broken and brown.

He did not even think of nocking an arrow. The fire was weeks old, the burned wood slicked and dulled by past rains. Chokevine needed nearly a month to grow that tall. It had even enveloped the plow and harrow lying beside the field; rust showed under the pale, narrow leaves.

The Aiel searched carefully, though, spears ready and eyes wary, quartering the ground and poking through the ashes. When Bain clambered out of the ruins of the house, she looked at Perrin and shook her head. At least Tam al'Thor had not died in there.

They know. They know, Rand. You should have come. It was very nearly more than he could do to stop from putting Stepper to a gallop, keeping him there all the way to his family's farm. Trying to, at least; even Stepper would fall dead before he ran that far. Maybe this was Trolloc work. If it was Trollocs, maybe his family was still working their farm, still safe. He drew a deep breath, but the char obliterated any other smell.

Gaul stopped beside him. "Whoever did this is long gone. They killed some of the sheep and scattered the rest. Someone came later to gather the flock and drive it off north. Two men, I think, but the tracks are too old to be sure."

"Is there any clue to who did it?" Gaul shook his head. It could have been Trollocs. Strange, to wish for a thing like that. And foolish. The Whitecloaks knew his name, and they knew Rand's as well, it seemed. *They know my name.* He looked at the ashes of the al'Thor farmhouse, and Stepper moved as the reins trembled in his hands.

Loial had dismounted at the edge of the fruit trees, but his head was still in the branches. Faile rode toward Perrin, studying his face, her mare stepping delicately. "Is this . . . ? Do you know the people who lived here?"

"Rand and his father."

"Oh. I thought it might be. . . ." The relief and sympathy in her voice were enough to finish the sentence. "Does your family live near?"

"No," he said curtly, and she recoiled as if slapped. But she still watched him, waiting. What did he have to do to drive her away? More than he could bring himself to, if he had not managed it already.

The shadows were growing longer, the sun sitting on the treetops. He reined Stepper around, rudely turning his back on her. "Gaul, we will have to camp close by tonight. I want to start early in the morning." He sneaked a glance over his shoulder; Faile was riding back to Loial, sitting stiff in her saddle. "In Emond's Field, they will know. . . ." Where the Whitecloaks were, so he could turn himself in before they hurt his family. If his family was all right. If the farm where he had been born was not already like this. No. He had to be in time to stop that. "They'll know how things are."

"Early, then." Gaul hesitated. "You will not drive her off. That one is almost *Far Dareis Mai,* and if a Maiden loves you, you cannot escape her however hard you run."

"You let me worry about Faile." He softened his voice; it was not Gaul he wanted to be rid of. "Very early. While Faile is still asleep."

Both camps, beneath the apple trees, were quiet that night. Several times one or the other of the Aiel women stood, staring toward the small fire where he and Gaul sat, but an owl hooting and the horses stamping were the only sounds. Perrin could not sleep, and it was still an hour short of first light, with the full moon setting, when he and Gaul slipped away, the Aiel silent in his soft boots and the horses' hooves making little more noise. Bain, or maybe Chiad, watched them go. He could not tell which, but she did not wake Faile, and he was grateful.

The sun had climbed well up by the time they came out of the Westwood a little below the village, amid cart tracks and paths, most bordered by hedges or low rough stone walls. Smoke made feathery gray plumes above farmhouse chimneys, goodwives doing the morning's baking, by the smell. Men dotted the fields of tabac or barley, and boys watched flocks of black-faced sheep in the pastures. Some people took note of their passing, but Perrin kept Stepper at a fast walk and hoped none were close enough to recognize him or wonder at the strangeness of Gaul's clothes, or his spears.

People would be out and about in Emond's Field, too, so he circled around to the east, wide of the village, wide of the hard-packed dirt streets and thatched roofs clustered around the Green, where the Winespring itself gushed from a stone outcrop with enough force to knock a man down and gave birth to the Winespring Water. The damage he remembered from Winternight a year gone, the burned houses and charred roofs, were all rebuilt and repaired. The Trollocs might as well never have come back then. He prayed no one would have to live through that again. The Winespring Inn stood practically at the eastern end of Emond's Field, between the stout wooden Wagon Bridge across the rushing Winespring Water and a huge old stone foundation with a great oak growing up through the middle of it. Tables beneath the thick branches were where folk sat of a fine afternoon and watched the play at bowls. At this hour of the morning, the tables were empty, of course. There were only a few houses farther east. The inn itself was river rock on the first floor, with a whitewashed second story jutting out all the way around and a dozen chimneys rising above a glittering red tile roof, the only tile roof for miles.

Tying Stepper and the packhorse to a hitchpost near the kitchen door, Perrin glanced at the thatch-roofed stable. He could hear men working in there, probably Hu and Tad, mucking out the stalls where Master al'Vere kept the big Dhurran team he rented out for heavy hauling. There were sounds from the other side of the inn, too, the murmur of voices on the Green, geese honking, the rumble of a wagon. What was on the horses, he left; this would be a short stop. He motioned for Gaul to follow and hurried inside, carrying his bow, before either stableman could come out.

The kitchen was empty, both iron stoves and all but one fireplace cold, though the smell of baking still hung in the air. Bread and honey-cakes. The inn seldom had guests except when merchants came down from Baerlon to buy wool or tabac, or a monthly peddler when snow had not made the road impassable, and the village folk who might come for a drink or a meal later in the day would all be hard at work at their own homes now. Someone might be there, though, so Perrin tiptoed along the short hallway leading from the kitchen to the common room and cracked the door to peek inside.

He had seen that square room a thousand times, with its fireplace of river stones stretching half the room's length, the lintel as high as a man's shoulder, Master al'Vere's polished tabac canister and prized clock sitting on the mantel. It all seemed smaller than it had, somehow. The tall-backed chairs in front of the fireplace were where the Village Council met. Brandelwyn al'Vere's books sat on a shelf opposite the fireplace—once, Perrin had been unable to imagine more books in one place than those few dozen mostly worn volumes—and casks of ale and wine lined another wall. Scratch, the inn's yellow cat, sprawled asleep as usual atop one.

Except for Bran al'Vere himself and his wife, Marin, in long white aprons, polishing the inn's silver and pewter at one of the tables, the common room stood empty. Master al'Vere was a wide, round man, with a sparse fringe of gray hair; Mistress al'Vere was slender and motherly, her thick, graying braid pulled over one shoulder. She smelled of baking, and under that of roses. Perrin remembered them as smiling people, but both looked intent now, and the Mayor wore a frown that surely had nothing to do with the silver cup in his hands.

"Master al'Vere?" He pushed open the door and went in. "Mistress al'Vere. It's Perrin."

They sprang to their feet, knocking their chairs over and making Scratch jump. Mistress al'Vere clapped her hands to her mouth; she and her husband gaped as much at him as they did at Gaul. It was enough to make Perrin shift his bow awkwardly from hand to hand. Especially when Bran hurried to one of the front windows—he moved with surprising lightness for a man of his bulk—and twitched the summer curtains aside to peer out, as though for more Aiel outside.

"Perrin?" Mistress al'Vere murmured disbelievingly. "It *is* you. I almost didn't know you, with that beard, and—Your cheek. Were you—? Is Egwene with you?"

Perrin touched the half-healed slash across his cheek self-consciously, wishing he had cleaned up, or at least left the bow and axe in the kitchen. He had not considered how his appearance might frighten them. "No. This has nothing to do with her. She is safe." Safer on her way back to Tar Valon, perhaps, than if still in Tear with Rand, but safe in either case. He supposed he had to give Egwene's mother something more than that bald statement. "Mistress al'Vere, Egwene is studying to be Aes Sedai. Nynaeve, too."

"I know," she said quietly, touching the pocket on her apron. "I have three letters from her in Tar Valon. From what she writes she sent more, and Nynaeve at least one, but only three of Egwene's have reached us. She tells something of her training, which I must say sounds very hard."

"It is what she wants." Three letters? Guilt made him shrug uncomfortably. He had not written a letter to anyone, not since the notes he had left for his family and Master Luhhan the night Moiraine took him away from Emond's Field. Not one.

"So it seems, though not what I had envisioned for her. It isn't something I can tell many people about, now is it? She says she's made friends, anyway, nice girls by the sound of them. Elayne, and Min. Do you know them?"

"We have met. I think you could call them nice girls." How much had Egwene told in those letters? Not much, evidently. Let Mistress al'Vere think what she would; he had no intention of worrying her over things she could do nothing about. What was past, was past. Egwene was safe enough now.

Abruptly realizing that Gaul was just standing there, he made hasty introductions. Bran blinked when Gaul was named Aiel, and frowned at his spears and the black veil hanging down his chest from his *shoufa,* but his wife merely said, "Be welcome to Emond's Field, Master Gaul, and to the Winespring Inn."

"May you always have water and shade, roofmistress," Gaul said formally, bowing to her. "I ask leave to defend your roof and hold."

She barely hesitated before replying as if that were exactly what she was used to hearing. "A gracious offer. But you must allow me to decide when it is needed."

"As you say, roofmistress. Your honor is mine." From under his coat, Gaul produced a gold saltcellar, a small bowl balanced on the back of a cunningly made lion, and extended it to her. "I offer this small guest gift to your roof."

Marin al'Vere made over it as she would have any gift, hardly showing her shock. Perrin doubted there was a piece to equal it in the whole Two Rivers, certainly not in gold. There was little enough gold coin in the Two Rivers, much less gold ornaments. He hoped she never found out it had been looted from the Stone of Tear; at least he would have wagered that it had.

"My boy," Bran said, "perhaps I should be saying 'welcome home,' but why did you return?"

"I heard about the Whitecloaks, sir," Perrin replied simply.

The Mayor and his wife shared somber looks, and Bran said, "Again, why did you return? You cannot stop anything, my boy, or change anything. Best that you go. If you don't have a horse, I will give you one. If you do, climb back in your saddle and ride north. I thought the Whitecloaks were guarding Taren Ferry. . . . Did they give you that decoration on your face?"

"No. It—"

"Then it doesn't matter. If you got past them coming in, you can get past to leave. Their main camp is up at Watch Hill, but their patrols can be anywhere. Do it, my boy."

"Don't wait, Perrin," Mistress al'Vere added quietly but firmly, in that voice that usually ended with people doing as she said. "Not even an hour. I'll make you a bundle to take with you. Some fresh bread and cheese, some ham and roast beef, pickles. You must go, Perrin."

"I cannot. You know they are after me, or you'd not want me to go." And they had not commented on his eyes, even to ask if he was ill. Mistress al'Vere had barely been surprised. They knew. "If I give myself up, I can stop some of it. I can keep my family—" He jumped as the hall door banged open to admit Faile, followed by Bain and Chiad.

Master al'Vere ran a hand over his bald head; even taking in the Aiel women's garb and obviously identifying them with Gaul, he only seemed a little bemused that they were women. Mainly he looked irritated at the intrusion. Scratch sat up to stare suspiciously at all these strangers. Perrin wondered whether the cat considered him one, as well. He wondered how they had found him, too, and where Loial was. Anything to avoid wondering how he was going to manage Faile now.

She gave him little time to ponder, planting herself in front of him with fists on hips. Somehow she managed that trick women had, making herself seem taller through pure quivering outrage. "Give yourself up? Give yourself up! Have you been planning this from the start? You have, haven't you? You utter idiot! Your brain has frozen solid, Perrin Aybara. It was nothing but muscle and hair to begin, but now it isn't even that. If Whitecloaks are hunting you, they will hang you if you surrender to them. Why should they want you?"

"Because I killed Whitecloaks." Looking down at her, he ignored Mistress al'Vere's gasp. "Those the night I met you, and two before that. They know about those two, Faile, and they think I'm a Darkfriend." She would learn that much soon enough. Brought to the point of it, he might have told her why, had they been alone. At least two Whitecloaks, Geofram Bornhald and Jaret Byar, suspected something of his connection with wolves. Not nearly all, but for them the little was enough. A man who ran with wolves had to be a Darkfriend. Maybe one or both was with the Whitecloaks here. "They believe it for true."

"You are no more a Darkfriend than I," she whispered harshly. "The sun could be a Darkfriend first."

"It makes no difference, Faile. I have to do what I have to do."

"You addle-brained lummox! You don't *have* to do any such crackpate thing! You goose-brain! If you try it, I'll hang you myself!"

"Perrin," Mistress al'Vere said quietly, "would you introduce me to this young woman who thinks so highly of you?"

Faile's face went bright red when she realized she had been ignoring Master and Mistress al'Vere, and she began making elaborate curtsies and offered flowery apologies. Bain and Chiad did as Gaul had, asking leave to defend Mistress al'Vere's roof and giving her a small golden bowl worked in leaves and an ornate silver pepper mill bigger than Perrin's two fists, topped by some fanciful creature half horse, half fish.

Bran al'Vere stared and frowned, rubbed his head and muttered to himself. Perrin caught the word "Aiel" more than once in an incredulous tone. The Mayor kept glancing at the windows, too. Not wondering about more Aiel; he had been surprised to learn Gaul was Aiel. Maybe he was worried about Whitecloaks.

Marin al'Vere, on the other hand, took it all in stride, treating Faile and Bain and Chiad the same as any other young women travelers who came to the inn, commiserating with them over how tiring travel was, complimenting Faile on her riding dress—dark blue silk, today—and telling the Aiel women how she admired the color and sheen of their hair. Perrin suspected that Bain and Chiad, at least, did not know quite what to make of her, but in short order, with a sort of calm motherly firmness, she had all three women settled at a table with damp towels to wipe journey dust from hands and faces, sipping tea she poured from a large red-striped pot he remembered well.

It might have been amusing seeing those fierce women—he certainly included Faile—suddenly eager to assure Mistress al'Vere that they were more than comfortable, was there nothing they could do to help, she was doing too much, all of them wide-eyed as children, with a child's chance of resisting her. It would have been amusing if she had not included himself and Gaul, sweeping them just as firmly to the table, insisting on clean hands and clean faces before they got a cup of tea. Gaul wore a small grin the whole time; Aiel had a strange sense of humor.

Surprisingly, she never glanced at his bow or axe, or the Aiel's weapons. People seldom carried even a bow in the Two Rivers, and she always insisted such be set aside before anyone took a place at one of her tables. Always. But she just ignored them now.

Another surprise came when Bran placed a silver cup of apple brandy at Perrin's elbow, not the small tot that men usually drank at the inn, barely enough to cover the last joint of the thumb, but half-full. When he had left he would have been offered cider if not milk, or perhaps well-watered wine, a half-cup with a meal or a full one on a feastday. It was gratifying to be recognized as a grown man, but he only held it. He was used to wine now, but he seldom drank anything stronger.

"Perrin," the Mayor said as he took a chair beside his wife, "no one believes you a Darkfriend. No one with any sense. There is no reason for you to let yourself be hanged."

Faile nodded in fierce agreement, but Perrin ignored her. "I won't be turned aside, Master al'Vere. The Whitecloaks want me, and if they do not get me, they might turn to the next Aybara they can find. Whitecloaks don't need much to decide somebody is guilty. They are not pleasant people."

"We know," Mistress al'Vere said softly.

Her husband stared at his hands on the table. "Perrin, your family is gone."

"Gone? You mean the farm is burned already?" Perrin's fist tightened around the silver cup. "I hoped I was in time. I should have known better, I suppose. Too long before I heard. Maybe I can help my da and Uncle Eward rebuild. Who are they staying with? I want to see them first, at least."

Bran grimaced, and his wife stroked his shoulder comfortingly. But strangely her eyes stayed on Perrin, all sadness and comfort.

"They are dead, my boy," Bran said in a rush.

"Dead? No. They can't be—" Perrin frowned as wetness suddenly slopped over his hand, stared at the crumpled cup as though wondering where it had come from. "I am sorry. I didn't mean to—" He pulled at the flattened silver, trying to force it back out with his fingers. That would not work. Of course not. Very carefully, he put the ruined cup in the middle of the table. "I will replace it. I can—" He wiped his hand on his coat, and suddenly found he was caressing the axe hanging at his belt. Why was everyone looking at him so oddly? "Are you sure?" His voice sounded far away. "Adora and Deselle? Paet? My mother?"

"All of them," Bran told him. "Your aunts and uncles, too, and your cousins. Everybody on the farm. I helped bury them, my boy. On that low hill, the one with the apple trees."

Perrin stuck his thumb in his mouth. Fool thing to do, cutting himself on his own axe. "My mother likes apple blossoms. The Whitecloaks. Why would they—? Burn me, Paet was only nine. The girls. . . ." His voice was very flat. He thought he should have had some emotion in those words. Some emotion.

"It was Trollocs," Mistress al'Vere said quickly. "They have come back, Perrin. Not the way they did when you went away, not attacking the village, but out in the countryside. Most farms without close neighbors have been abandoned. No one goes outside at night, even near to the village. It is the same down to Deven Ride and up to Watch Hill, maybe to Taren Ferry. The Whitecloaks, bad as they are, are our only real protection. They've saved two families that I know, when Trollocs attacked their farms."

"I wished—I hoped—" He could not quite remember what it was he had wished. Something about Trollocs. He did not want to remember. The Whitecloaks protecting the Two Rivers? It was almost enough to make him laugh. "Rand's father. Tam's farm. Was that Trollocs, too?"

Mistress al'Vere opened her mouth, but Bran cut her off. "He deserves the truth, Marin. That was Whitecloaks, Perrin. That, and the Cauthon place."

"Mat's people too. Rand's, and Mat's, and mine." Strange. He sounded as if he were talking about whether it might rain. "Are they dead, too?"

"No, my boy. No, Abell and Tam are hiding in the Westwood somewhere. And Mat's mother and sisters. . . . They're alive, too."

"Hiding?"

"There is no need to go into that," Mistress al'Vere said briskly. "Bran, bring him another cup of brandy. And you drink this one, Perrin." Her husband sat where he was, but she only frowned at him and went on. "I would offer you a bed, but it isn't safe. Some people are like as not to run off hunting for Lord Bornhald if they find out you are here. Eward Congar and Hari Coplin fawn after the Whitecloaks like heel-hounds, eager to please and name names, and Cenn Buie isn't much better. And Wit Congar will carry tales, too, if Daise doesn't stop him. She is the Wisdom, now. Perrin, it is best for to go. Believe me."

Perrin shook his head slowly; it was too much to take in. Daise Congar the Wisdom? The woman was like a bull. Whitecloaks protecting Emond's Field. Hari and Eward and Wit cooperating. Not much more could be expected from Congars or Coplins, but Cenn Buie was on the Village Council. Lord Bornhald. So Geofram Bornhald was there. Faile was watching him, her eyes large and moist. Why should she be on the edge of tears?

"There is more, Brandelwyn al'Vere," Gaul said. "Your face says so."

"There is," Bran agreed. "No, Marin," he added firmly when she gave a small shake of her head. "He deserves the truth. The whole truth." She folded her hands with a sigh; Marin al'Vere very nearly always got her way—except when Bran's face was set, as now, with his eyebrows drawn down hard as a plow.

"What truth?" Perrin asked. His mother liked apple blossoms.

"First off, Padan Fain is with the Whitecloaks," Bran said. "He calls himself Ordeith now, and he won't answer to his own name at all, but it's him, stare down his nose as he will."

"He's a Darkfriend," Perrin said absently. Adora and Deselle always put apple blossoms in their hair in the spring. "Admitted from his own mouth. He brought the Trollocs, on Winternight." Paet liked to climb in the apple trees; he would throw apples at you from the branches if you did not watch him.

"Is he, now," the Mayor said grimly. "Now, that is interesting. He has some authority with the Whitecloaks. The first we heard they were here was after they burned Tam's farm. That was Fain's work; he led the Whitecloaks that did it. Tam feathered four or five of them with arrows before he made it to the woods, and he reached the Cauthon farm in the nick to stop them taking Abell. But they arrested Natti and the girls. And Haral Luhhan, and Alsbet, too. I think Fain might have hung them, except Lord Bornhald wouldn't allow it. Not that he let them go, either. They haven't been harmed, as far as I can discover, but they're being held in the Whitecloak camp up at Watch Hill. For some reason, Fain has a hate for you, and Rand, and Mat. He's offered a hundred pieces of gold for anyone related to the three of you; two hundred for Tam or Abell. And Lord Bornhald seems to have some interest in you, especially. When a Whitecloak patrol comes here, he usually comes, too, and asks questions about you."

"Yes," Perrin said. "Of course. He would." Perrin of the Two Rivers, who ran with wolves. Darkfriend. Fain could have told them the rest. *Fain, with the Children of the Light?* It was a distant thought. Better than thinking about Trollocs, though. He grimaced at his hands, made them be still on the table. "They protect you from the Trollocs."

Marin al'Vere leaned toward him, frowning. "Perrin, we need the Whitecloaks. Yes, they burned Tam's farm, and Abell's, they've arrested people, and they stamp around as if they own everything they see, but Alsbet and Natti and the rest are unharmed, only held, and that can be straightened out somehow. The Dragon's Fang has been scrawled on a few doors, but nobody except the Congars and Coplins pay any mind, and they're likely the ones who did the scrawling. Tam and Abell can stay in hiding until the Whitecloaks go. They have to go sooner or later. But as long as there are Trollocs here, we do need them. Please understand. It isn't that we would not rather have you than them, but we need them and we don't want them to hang you."

"You call this being protected, roofmistress?" Bain said. "If you ask the lion to protect you from wolves, you have only chosen to end in one belly instead of another."

"Can you not protect yourselves?" Chiad added. "I have seen Perrin fight, and Mat Cauthon, and Rand al'Thor. They are the same blood as you."

Bran sighed heavily. "We are farmers, simple people. Lord Luc talks of organizing men to fight the Trollocs, but that means leaving your family unprotected while you go off with him, and no one much likes that idea."

Perrin was confused. Who was Lord Luc? He asked as much, and Mistress al'Vere answered.

"He came about the time the Whitecloaks did. He's a Hunter of the Horn. You know the story, *The Great Hunt of the Horn?* Lord Luc thinks the Horn of Valere is somewhere in the Mountains of Mist above the Two Rivers. But he gave over his hunt because of our problems. Lord Luc is a great gentleman, with the finest manners." Smoothing her hair, she gave an approving smile; Bran looked at her sideways and grunted sourly.

Hunters of the Horn. Trollocs. Whitecloaks. The Two Rivers hardly seemed the same place he had left. "Faile is a Hunter of the Horn, too. Do you know this Lord Luc, Faile?"

"I have had enough," she announced. Perrin frowned as she stood and came around the table to him. Seizing his head, she pulled his face into her midriff. "Your mother is dead," she said quietly. "Your father is dead. Your sisters are dead, and your brother. Your family is dead, and you cannot change it. Certainly not by dying yourself. Let yourself grieve. Don't hold it inside where it can fester."

He took her by the arms, meaning to move her, but for some reason his hands tightened till that grip was the only thing holding him up. It was only then that he realized he was crying, sobbing into her dress like a baby. What must she think of him? He opened his mouth to tell her he was all right, to apologize for breaking down, but what came out was, "I couldn't get here any faster. I couldn't—I—" He gritted his teeth to shut himself off.

"I know," she murmured, stroking his hair for all the world as if he were a child. "I know."

He wanted to stop, but the more she whispered understanding, the more he wept, as though her hands soft on his head were smoothing the tears out of him.

CHAPTER
30

Beyond the Oak

With Faile holding his head beneath her breasts, Perrin lost track of how long he cried. Images of his family flashed in his thoughts, his father smiling as he showed him how to hold a bow, his mother singing while she spun wool, Adora and Deselle teasing him when he shaved the first time, Paet wide-eyed at a gleeman during Sunday long ago. Pictures of graves, cold and lonely in a row. He wept until there were no more tears in him. When he finally pulled back, the two of them were alone except for Scratch, washing himself atop the ale barrel. He was glad the others had not remained to watch him. Faile was bad enough. In a way he was glad she had stayed; he only wished she had not seen or heard.

Taking his hands in hers, Faile sat in the next chair. She was so beautiful, with her slightly tilted eyes, large and dark, and her high cheekbones. He did not know how he was going to be able to make up to her for the way he had treated her these last few days. No doubt she would find a means to make him pay for it.

"Have you given up the notion of surrendering to the Whitecloaks?" she asked. There was no hint in her voice that she had just watched him cry like a baby.

"It seems it wouldn't do any good. They'll be after Rand's father, and Mat's, whatever I do. My family. . . ." He quickly loosened his grip on her hands, but she smiled instead of wincing. "I have to get Master Luhhan and his wife free, if I can. And Mat's mother and sisters; I promised him I would look after them. And do what I can about the Trollocs." Maybe this Lord Luc had some ideas. At least the Waygate was blocked; no more would come through the Ways. He especially wanted to do something about the Trollocs. "I can't manage any of that if I let them hang me."

"I am very glad you see that," she told him dryly. "Any more fool notions about sending me away?"

"No." He braced himself for the storm, but she simply nodded as if the one word were what she expected and all she wanted. A small thing, nothing worth arguing over. She was going to make him pay large.

"We are five, Perrin, six if Loial is willing. And if we can find Tam al'Thor and Abell Cauthon. . . . Are they as good with a bow as you?"

"Better," he said truthfully. "Much better."

She gave him a slight, disbelieving nod. "That will make eight. A beginning. Maybe others will join us. And then there's Lord Luc. He will probably want to take charge, but if he's not a crackbrain, it won't matter. Not everyone who took the Hunter's Oath is sensible, though. I've met some who think they know everything, and are stubborn as mules besides."

"I know." She looked at him sharply, and he managed to keep the smile off his face. "That you've met some like that, I mean. I saw a pair of them once, remember."

"Oh, them. Well, we can hope Lord Luc is not a boasting liar." Her eyes became intent, and her grip tightened on his hands, not uncomfortably, but as though she was trying to add her strength to his. "You will want to visit your family's farm, your home. I will come with you, if you will let me."

"When I can, Faile." Not now, though. Not yet. If he looked at those graves below the apple trees now. . . . It was strange. He had always taken his own strength for granted, and now it turned out that he was not strong at all. Well, he was done with weeping like a babe. It was past time to be doing something. "First things first. Finding Tam and Abell, I suppose."

Master al'Vere put his head into the common room, and came the rest of the way when he saw them sitting apart. "There is an Ogier in the kitchen," he told Perrin with a bemused look. "An Ogier. Drinking tea. The biggest cup looks. . . ." He held two fingers as though gripping a thimble. "Maybe Marin could pretend Aiel walk in here every day, but she nearly fainted when she saw this Loial. I gave her a double tot of brandy, and she tossed it down like water. Nearly coughed herself to death; she doesn't take more than wine, usually. I think she'd have drunk another, if I'd given it to her." He pursed his lips and affected an interest in a nonexistent spot on his long white apron. "Are you all right now, my boy?"

"I'm fine, sir," Perrin said hastily. "Master al'Vere, we cannot remain here much longer. Someone might tell the Whitecloaks you sheltered me."

"Oh, there are not many would do that. Not all the Coplins, and not some of the Congars, even." But he did not suggest they stay.

"Do you know where I can find Master al'Thor and Master Cauthon?"

"In the Westwood somewhere, usually," Bran said slowly. "That's all I know for sure. They move about." Locking his fingers over his broad belly, he tilted his gray-fringed head to one side. "You aren't leaving, are you? Well. I told Marin you would not, but she doesn't believe me. She thinks it best for you to go away—best for you—and like most women she's sure you will see things her way if she talks long enough."

"Why, Master al'Vere," Faile said sweetly, "I for one have always found men to be sensible creatures who only need to be shown the wisest path once to choose it."

The Mayor favored her with an amused smile. "You will be talking Perrin into going then, I take it? Marin's right; that is wisest, if he wants to avoid a noose. The only reason to stay is that sometimes a man can't run. No? Well, no doubt you know best." He ignored her sour look. "Come along, my boy. Let's tell Marin the good news. Set your teeth and hold on to your intentions, because she won't give up trying to shift you."

In the kitchen, Loial and the Aiel were cross-legged on the floor. There was certainly no chair in the inn big enough for the Ogier. He sat with an arm resting on the kitchen table, tall enough sitting to look Marin al'Vere in the eye. Bran had exaggerated the smallness of the cup in Loial's hands, though on second glance Perrin saw it was a white-glazed soup bowl.

Mistress al'Vere was still doing her best to pretend Aiel and Ogier were normal, bustling about with a tray of bread and cheese and pickles, making sure everyone ate, but her eyes did widen each time they landed on Loial, though he tried to put her at ease with compliments for her baking. His tufted ears twitched nervously whenever she looked at him, and she gave a little jump every time they did, then shook her head, the thick graying braid swaying vigorously. Given a few hours, they might send each other to bed with the shakes.

Loial heaved a deep bass sigh of relief at the sight of Perrin and set his cup—bowl—of tea on the table, but the next instant his broad face sagged sadly. "I am sorry to hear your loss, Perrin. I share your grief. Mistress al'Vere . . ." His ears twitched wildly even without looking at her, and she gave another start. ". . . has been telling me you will go, now there's nothing to keep you here. If you wish it, I will sing to the apple trees before we leave."

Bran and Marin exchanged startled looks, and the Mayor actually reamed at his ear with a finger.

"Thank you, Loial. I will appreciate that, when there's time. But I have work to do before I can go." Mistress al'Vere set the tray on the table with a sharp click and stared at him, but he kept on, laying out his plans, such as they were: Find Tam and Abell, and rescue the people the Whitecloaks held. He did not mention Trollocs, though he had vague plans there, too. Perhaps not so vague. He did not mean to leave while there was a Trolloc or Myrddraal alive in the Two Rivers. He fastened his thumbs behind his belt to keep from caressing his axe. "It won't be easy," he finished. "I will appreciate your company, but I will understand if you want to go. This isn't your fight, and you have seen enough trouble through staying close to Emond's Field folk. And you won't write much of your book here."

"Here or there, it is the same fight, I think," Loial replied. "The book can wait. Perhaps I will have a chapter about you."

"I said I would come with you," Gaul put in without being asked. "I did not mean until the journey grew hard. I owe you blood debt."

Bain and Chiad looked questioningly at Faile, and when she nodded, added their decisions to remain, too.

"Stubborn foolish," Mistress al'Vere said, "the lot of you. Very likely you will all end up on gallows, if you live that long. You know that, don't you?" When they only looked at her, she untied her apron and lifted it over her head. "Well, if you are foolish enough to stay, I suppose I had better show you where to hide."

Her husband looked surprised at her sudden surrender, but he recovered quickly. "I thought perhaps the old sickhouse, Marin. No one ever goes there now, and I think it still has most of its roof."

What was still called the new sickhouse, where people were taken to be tended if their illness was contagious, had stood east of the village, beyond Master Thane's mill, since Perrin was a small boy. The old one, in the Westwood, had been all but destroyed in a fierce windstorm back then. Perrin remembered it as half-covered by vines and briars, with birds roosting in what was left of the thatch and a badger's den under the back steps. It would be a good place to hide.

Mistress al'Vere gave Bran a sharp look, as though startled he had thought of it. "That will do, I suppose. For tonight, at least. That is where I will take them."

"No need for you to do it, Marin. I can lead them easy enough, if Perrin doesn't remember the way."

"Sometimes you forget you're the Mayor, Bran. You attract eyes; people wonder where you're going and what you are up to. Why don't you stay here, and if anyone drops by, see they go away thinking everything is just as it should be. There's mutton stew in the kettle, and lentil soup that just needs heating. Now don't mention the sickhouse to anyone, Bran. Best if no one even remembers it exists."

"I am not a fool, Marin," he said stiffly.

"I know you aren't, dear." She patted her husband's cheek, but her fond look tightened as it shifted from Bran to the rest of them. "You do cause trouble," she muttered before handing out instructions.

They were to travel in smaller parties so as not to attract attention. She would cross the village by herself and meet them in the woods on the other side. The Aiel assured her they could find the lightning-split oak she described, and slipped out by the back door. Perrin knew it, a huge tree, a mile beyond the edge of the village, that looked as if it had been cleft down the middle by an axe yet somehow continued to live and even flourish. He was sure he could go straight to the sickhouse itself with no trouble, but Mistress al'Vere insisted everyone meet at the oak.

"You go wandering about by yourself, Perrin, and the Light knows what you might stumble into." She looked up at Loial—standing now, his shaggy hair brushing the ceiling beams—and sighed. "I do wish there was something we could do about your height, Master Loial. I know it is hot, but would you mind wearing your cloak, with the hood up? Even these days most people will soon convince themselves they didn't see what they saw if it isn't what they expect, but if they catch a glimpse of your face. . . . Not that you aren't quite handsome, I'm sure, but you'll never pass for Two Rivers folk."

Loial's smile split his face in two beneath his wide snout of a nose. "The day doesn't seem too warm for a cloak at all, Mistress al'Vere."

Fetching a light, knit shawl with blue fringe, she accompanied Perrin, Faile and Loial out to the stableyard to see them off, and for a moment

it appeared all their efforts at secrecy were doomed. Cenn Buie, looking made from gnarled old roots, was examining the horses with beady
eyes. Especially Loial's tall horse, as big as one of Bran's Dhurrans.
Cenn scratched his head, staring at the great saddle on the big horse.

Those eyes widened when they caught sight of Loial, and Cenn's jaw
flapped. "Tr—Tr—Trolloc!" he managed to get out at last.

"Don't be an old fool, Cenn Buie," Marin said firmly, stepping off to
one side to pull the thatcher's attention with her. Perrin kept his head
down, studying his bow, and did not move. "Would I be standing on my
own back doorstep with a Trolloc?" She gave a contemptuous sniff.
"Master Loial is an Ogier, as you would know if you weren't a cantan-
kerous goose who would rather complain than look at what's under his
nose. Passing through, and with no time to be bothered by the likes of
you. You be on about your business and leave our guests some peace.
You know very well that Corin Ayellin has been after you for months
about the poor work you did on her roof."

Cenn mouthed the word "Ogier," silent and blinking. For a moment
it seemed he might rouse himself in defense of his handiwork, but then
his gaze shifted to Perrin and narrowed. "Him! It's him! They're after
you, you young whelp, rapscallion, running off with Aes Sedai and
becoming a Darkfriend. That was when we had Trollocs before. Now
you're back, and so are they. You going to tell me that's coincidence?
What's wrong with your eyes? You sick? You have some kind of sickness from off you've brought back to kill us all, as if Trollocs are not
enough? The Children of the Light will settle you. See if they don't."

Perrin sensed Faile tensing, and hastily put a hand on her arm when
he realized she was drawing a knife. What did she think she was doing?
Cenn was an irascible old fool, but that was no reason for knives. She
gave an exasperated toss of her head, but at least she left it at that.

"That is enough, Cenn," Marin said sharply. "You keep this to yourself. Or have you started running to the Whitecloaks with tales, like
Hari and his brother Darl? I've my suspicions why the Whitecloaks
came rummaging through Bran's books. They took six off with them,
and lectured Bran under his own roof about blasphemy. Blasphemy, of
all things! Because they didn't agree with what was in a book. You're
lucky I don't make you replace those books for him. They burrowed
through the whole inn like weasels. Hunting for more *blasphemous
writings,* they said, as if anyone would hide a book. Tumbled all the
mattresses from the beds, upset my linen closets. You are lucky I didn't
come haul you back here to put it all to rights again."

Cenn drew in on himself a little more with each sentence, until he looked to be trying to pull his bony shoulders over his head. "I didn't tell them anything, Marin," he protested. "Just because a man mentions—That is, I just happened to say, just in passing—" He shook himself, still avoiding her eye but regaining some of his old manner. "I mean to take this up with the Council, Marin. Him, I mean." He pointed a gnarled finger at Perrin. "We're all in danger as long as he's here. If the Children find out you're sheltering him, they might blame the rest of us. Upset closets won't be in it, then."

"This is Women's Circle business." Marin rewrapped her shawl about her shoulders and moved to stand eye to eye with the thatcher. He was a little taller than she, but her sudden air of grave formality gave her the edge. He spluttered, but she rode right over his attempts to slide a word in. "Circle business, Cenn Buie. If you think it isn't—if you even dare think of calling me a liar—you go flapping your tongue. You breathe a word of Women's Circle business to anyone, including the Village Council . . ."

"The Circle has no right interfering in Council affairs," he shouted.

". . . and see if your wife doesn't have you sleeping in the barn. And eating what your milk cows leave. You think Council takes precedence over Circle? I'll send Daise Congar over to convince you different, if you need convincing."

Cenn flinched, as well he might. If Daise Congar was the Wisdom, she would probably force foul-tasting concoctions down his throat every day for the next year, and Cenn was too scrawny to stop her. Alsbet Luhhan was the only woman in Emond's Field larger than Daise, and Daise had a mean streak and a temper to go with it. Perrin could not imagine her as Wisdom; Nynaeve would probably have a fit when she found out who had replaced her. Nynaeve had always believed she used sweet reason, herself.

"No need to get nasty, Marin," Cenn muttered placatingly. "You want me to keep quiet, I'll keep quiet. But Women's Circle or no, you're risking bringing the Children down on all of us." Marin merely raised her eyebrows, and after a moment he slunk away, grumbling under his breath.

"Well done," Faile said when Cenn disappeared around the corner of the inn. "I think I need to take lessons from you. I am not half so good at handling Perrin as you are with Master al'Vere and that fellow." She smiled at Perrin to show she was joking. At least, he hoped that was what it meant.

"You have to know when to rein them short," the older woman replied absently, "and when there's nothing to do but give them their head. Letting them have their way when it isn't important makes it easier to check them when it is." She was frowning after Cenn, not really paying attention to what she was saying, except maybe when she added, "And some should be tied in the stall and left there."

Perrin leaped in hastily. Faile certainly did not need any advice of this sort. "Will he hold his tongue do you think, Mistress al'Vere?"

Hesitating, she said, "I believe he will. Cenn was born with a sore tooth that's only gotten worse as he ages, but he isn't like Hari Coplin or that lot." Still, she had hesitated.

"We had best be moving," he said. No one argued.

The sun was higher than he had expected, past its midday height already, which meant most people were indoors for their dinner. The few still out, mainly boys minding sheep or cows, were busy eating what they had brought with them wrapped up in a cloth, too absorbed in their food and too far from the cart paths to pay much mind to anyone passing. Still, Loial earned some stares despite the deep hood hiding his face. Even on Stepper Perrin came short of the Ogier's chest on his tall mount. To the people who saw them from a distance they must have looked like an adult with two children, all on ponies, leading packponies. Certainly not a usual sight, but Perrin hoped that was what they thought they saw. Talk would draw notice. He had to avoid that until he got Mistress Luhhan and the others free. If only Cenn kept his peace. He kept the hood of his own cloak up, too. That might also cause talk, but not as much as if anyone saw his beard and realized he was definitely not a child. At least the day was not particularly warm. It almost felt like spring, not summer, after Tear.

He had no trouble finding the split oak, the two halves leaning apart in a wide fork with the inner surface black and hardened like iron, the ground beneath the thick spreading branches clear. Merely crossing the village was much shorter than going around, so Mistress al'Vere was already waiting, shifting her shawl a trifle impatiently. The Aiel were there, too, squatting on the mulch of old oak leaves and squirrel-chewed acorn hulls, Gaul apart from the two women. The Maidens and Gaul watched each other almost as closely as the surrounding woods. Perrin had no doubt they had managed to reach this spot unobserved. He wished he had that ability; he could stalk fairly well in the woods, but the Aiel did not seem to care if it was forest or farmland or city. When they did not want to be seen, they found a way not to be seen.

Mistress al'Vere insisted they go the rest of the way afoot, claiming the way was too overgrown for riding. Perrin did not agree, but he dismounted anyway. No doubt it would not be comfortable leading folk on horseback while on foot. In any case, his head was full of plans. He needed a look at the Whitecloak camp up at Watch Hill before deciding how to rescue Mistress Luhhan and the others. And where were Tam and Abell hiding? Neither Bran nor Mistress al'Vere had said; perhaps they did not know. If Tam and Abell had not brought the prisoners out already, it was not an easy task. He had to do it somehow, though. Then he could turn his attention to Trollocs.

No one from the village had come this way in years, and the path had vanished, yet tall trees kept the undergrowth down to a large extent. The Aiel slipped along silently with everyone else, acceding to Mistress al'Vere's insistence that they all stay together. Loial murmured approvingly at great oaks or particularly tall fir trees and leatherleaf. Occasionally a mocker or redbreast sang in the trees, and once Perrin smelled a fox watching them pass.

Suddenly he caught man scent that had not been there a moment before, heard a faint rustle. The Aiel tensed, crouching with spears ready. Perrin reached to his quiver.

"Be at ease," Mistress al'Vere said urgently, motioning for weapons to be lowered. "Please, be at ease."

Abruptly there were two men standing ahead, one tall and dark and slender to the left, the other short, stocky and graying to the right. Both held bows with arrows nocked, ready to raise and draw, with quivers balancing the swords on their hips. Both wore cloaks that seemed to fade into the surrounding foliage.

"Warders!" Perrin exclaimed. "Why didn't you tell us there are Aes Sedai here, Mistress al'Vere? Master al'Vere never mentioned it either. Why?"

"Because he doesn't know," she said hurriedly. "I did not lie when I said this is Women's Circle business." She turned her attention to the two Warders, neither of whom had relaxed an inch. "Tomas, Ihvon, you know me. Put those bows down. You know I'd not bring anyone here if they meant harm."

"An Ogier," the gray-haired man said, "Aiel, a yellow-eyed man— the one the Whitecloaks seek, of course—and a fierce young woman with a knife." Perrin glanced at Faile; she held a blade ready to throw. He agreed with her this time. These might be Warders, but they showed no sign of lowering their bows yet; their faces might as well have been carved from anvils. The Aiel looked ready to begin dancing the spears without waiting to veil themselves. "A strange group, Mistress al'Vere," the older Warder went on. "We shall see. Ihvon?" The slender man nodded and melted into the undergrowth; Perrin could barely hear the fellow's going. Warders moved like death itself when they wanted to.

"What do you mean, Women's Circle business?" he demanded. "I know Whitecloaks would cause trouble if they knew about Aes Sedai, so you wouldn't want to tell Hari Coplin, but why keep it secret from the Mayor? And us?"

"Because we agreed to," Mistress al'Vere said irritably. The irritation seemed meant in equal parts for Perrin and the Warder still guarding them—there was no other word for it—with maybe a bit left over for the Aes Sedai. "They were at Watch Hill when the Whitecloaks came. No one there knew who they were except the Circle there, who passed them on to us to hide. From everyone, Perrin. It's the best way to keep a secret, if only a few know. Light preserve me, I know two women who have stopped sharing their husbands' beds for fear they might talk in their sleep. We agreed to keep it secret."

"Why did you decide to change that?" the gray-haired Warder asked in a hard voice.

"For what I consider good and sufficient reasons, Tomas." From the way she shifted her shawl, Perrin suspected she was hoping the Circle —and the Aes Sedai—thought so, too. Rumor had it the Circle could be even harder on each other than they were on the rest of the village. "Where better to hide you, Perrin, than with Aes Sedai? Surely you aren't afraid of them, not after leaving here with one. And. . . . You will find out soon enough. You just have to trust me."

"There are Aes Sedai and Aes Sedai," Perrin told her. But those he considered the worst, the Red Ajah, did not bond Warders; the Red Ajah did not like men very much at all. This Tomas had dark unwavering eyes. They might rush him, or better simply leave, but the Warder would surely put an arrow through the first one to do something he did not like, and Perrin was ready to bet the man had more shafts handy for easy nocking. The Aiel seemed to agree; they still looked ready to spring in any direction at any moment, but they looked as if they could stand where they were until the sun froze, too. Perrin patted Faile on the shoulder. "It will be all right," he said.

"Of course it will," she replied, smiling. She had put the knife away. "If Mistress al'Vere says it, I trust her."

Perrin hoped she was right. He did not trust as many people as he once had. Not Aes Sedai. And maybe not even Marin al'Vere. But maybe these Aes Sedai would help him fight Trollocs. He would trust anyone who did that. But how far could he rely on Aes Sedai? They did what they did for their own reasons; the Two Rivers was home, to him, but to them it might be a stone on a stone's board. Faile and Marin al'Vere appeared to be trusting, though, and the Aiel waited. For the moment, it seemed he had little choice.

CHAPTER
31

Assurances

In a few minutes Ihvon returned. "You can go ahead, Mistress al'Vere" was all he said before he and Tomas both vanished into the brush again without so much as the rustle of a leaf.

"They are very good," Gaul muttered, still staring around suspiciously.

"A child could hide in this," Chiad told him, slapping a redberry branch. But she watched the undergrowth as closely as Gaul did.

None of the Aiel appeared eager to go on. Not reluctant, precisely, and certainly not afraid, but definitely not eager. One day Perrin hoped to figure out what it was Aiel did feel toward Aes Sedai. One day. He was not particularly enthusiastic himself, today.

"Let's go meet these Aes Sedai of yours," he told Mistress al'Vere gruffly.

The old sickhouse was even more ramshackle than he remembered, a sprawling single story that leaned drunkenly, half the rooms open to the sky, a forty-foot sourgum tree poking up from one. The forest closed in on every side. A thick net of vines and briars snaked up the walls, covered the remaining thatch with green; he thought they might be all that was holding the building up. The front door was cleared, though. He smelled horses, and a faint aroma of beans and ham, but oddly, no woodsmoke.

Tying their animals to low branches, they followed Mistress al'Vere inside, where vine-shrouded windows admitted only a dim light. The front room was large and bare of furnishings, with dirt in the corners and a few cobwebs that had escaped an obviously hasty cleaning. Four blanket rolls were laid out on the floor, with saddles and saddlebags and neatly tied bundles against the wall, and a small kettle on the stone hearth gave off the cooking smells despite the lack of any fire. A smaller kettle seemed to be water for tea, almost at the boil. Two Aes Sedai awaited them. Marin al'Vere curtsied hastily and launched into an anxious cascade of introductions and explanations.

Perrin leaned his chin against his bow. He recognized the Aes Sedai. Verin Mathwin, plump and square-faced, gray streaking her brown hair despite her smooth-cheeked Aes Sedai agelessness, was Brown Ajah, and like all Browns seemingly lost half the time in the search for knowledge, whether old and lost or new. But sometimes her dark eyes belied that vague dreamy expression, as now, looking past Marin at him sharp as tacks. She was one of two Aes Sedai besides Moiraine he was certain knew about Rand, and he suspected she knew more about himself than she let on. Her eyes took on that slight vagueness again as she listened to Marin, but for an instant they had weighed him on scales, factored him into her own plans. He would have to be very careful around her.

The other, a dark, slender woman in a deep green silk riding dress that contrasted sharply with Verin's plain brown, inkstained at the cuffs, he had never met, and only seen once. Alanna Mosvani was Green Ajah, if he remembered correctly, a beautiful woman with long black hair and penetrating dark eyes. Those eyes sought him, too, while she listened to Marin. Something Egwene had said came back to him. *Some Aes Sedai who shouldn't know about Rand show too much interest in him. Elaida, for instance, and Alanna Mosvani. I don't think I trust either of them.* Perhaps it would be best to be guided by Egwene until he found out differently.

His ears perked up when Marin said, still apprehensive, "You were asking about him, Verin Sedai. Perrin, I mean. All three boys, but Perrin among them. It seemed the easiest way to keep him from getting himself killed was to bring him to you. There just wasn't any time to ask first. Do say you under—"

"It is quite all right, Mistress al'Vere," Verin interrupted in a soothing tone. "You did exactly the correct thing. Perrin is in the right hands, now. Also I will enjoy the chance to learn more about the Aiel, and it is always a pleasure to talk with an Ogier. I will pick your brain, Loial. I have found some fascinating things in Ogier books."

Loial gave her a pleased smile; anything to do with books seemed to please him. Gaul, on the other hand, exchanged guarded looks with Bain and Chiad.

"It is all right as long as you do not do it again," Alanna said firmly. "Unless. . . . You are alone?" she asked Perrin in a voice that required an answer, and right now. "Did the other two return as well?"

"Why are you here?" he demanded right back.

"Perrin!" Mistress al'Vere said sharply. "Mind your manners! You may have picked up some rough ways out in the world, but you can just lose them again now that you are home."

"Do not trouble yourself," Verin told her. "Perrin and I are old friends now. I understand him." Her dark eyes glittered at him for a moment.

"We will take care of him." Alanna's cool words seemed open to interpretation.

Verin smiled and patted Marin's shoulder. "You had better go on back to the village. We don't want anyone wondering why you are walking in the woods."

Mistress al'Vere nodded. Pausing by Perrin, she put a hand on his arm. "You know you have my sympathy," she said gently. "Just remember that getting yourself killed won't help anything. Do what the Aes Sedai tell you." He mumbled something noncommittal, but it seemed to satisfy her.

When Mistress al'Vere had gone, Verin said, "You have our sympathy as well, Perrin. If there was anything we could have done, we would have."

He did not want to think of his family now. "You still haven't answered my question."

"Perrin!" Faile managed to copy Mistress al'Vere's tone almost exactly, but he paid it no mind.

"Why are you here? It seems awfully coincidental. Whitecloaks and Trollocs, and the two of you just happen to be here at the same time."

"Not coincidental at all," Verin replied. "Ah, the tea water is ready." The water subsided from a boil as she began to bustle about, tossing a handful of leaves into the kettle, directing Faile to find metal cups in one of the bundles against the wall. Alanna, with her arms folded beneath her breasts, never took her eyes off Perrin, their heat conflicting with the coolness of her face. "Year by year," Verin continued, "we find fewer and fewer girls who can be taught to channel. Sheriam believes we may have spent the last three thousand years culling the ability out of humankind by gentling every man who can channel we find. The proof of it, she says, is how very few men we do find. Why, even a hundred years ago the records say there were two or three a year, and five hundred years—"

Alanna harrumphed. "What else can we do, Verin? Let them go insane? Follow the Whites' mad plan?"

"I think not," Verin replied calmly. "Even if we could find women willing to bear children by gentled men, there is no guarantee the children would be able to channel, or would be girls. I did suggest that if they wanted to increase the stock, Aes Sedai should be the ones to have the children; themselves, in fact, since they put it forward in the first place. Alviarin was not amused."

"She would not be," Alanna laughed. The sudden flash of delight, breaking her fiery, dark-eyed stare, was startling. "I wish I could have seen her face."

"Her expression was . . . interesting," the Brown sister said musingly. "Calm yourself, Perrin. I will give you the rest of your answer. Tea?"

Trying to wipe the glare from his face, somehow he found himself seated on the floor, his bow beside him and a metal cup full of strong tea in his hand. Everyone sat in a circle in the middle of the room. Alanna took up the explanation of their presence, perhaps to forestall the other Aes Sedai's tendency to ramble.

"Here in the Two Rivers, where I suspect no Aes Sedai had visited in a thousand years, Moiraine found two women who could not only be taught to channel, but who had the ability born in them, and heard of another who had died because she could not teach herself."

"Not to mention three *ta'veren*," Verin murmured into her tea.

"Do you have any idea," Alanna went on, "how many towns and villages we usually must visit to find three girls with the ability inborn? The only wonder is that it took us so long to come hunting more. The old blood is very strong here in the Two Rivers. We were only in Watch Hill a week before the Children appeared, and were very careful not to reveal who we were to any but the Women's Circle there, yet even so we found four girls who can be trained, and one child I think has the ability inborn."

"It was difficult to be sure," Verin added. "She is only twelve. None have anywhere near the potential of Egwene or Nynaeve, but the number is still nothing less than remarkable. There might be another two or three just around Watch Hill. We have had no chance to examine girls here, or farther south. Taren Ferry was a disappointment, I must say. Too much interchange of bloodlines with the outside, I suppose."

Perrin had to admit it made sense. But it did not answer all his questions, or settle all his doubts. He shifted, stretching out his leg. The spear wound in his thigh hurt. "I don't understand why you are hiding here. Whitecloaks arresting innocent people, and here you sit. Trollocs running all over the Two Rivers apparently, and here you sit." Loial muttered under his breath, a muted rumble. Perrin caught "angering Aes Sedai" and "hornet's nest," but he continued to hammer at them. "Why aren't you doing something? You're Aes Sedai! Burn me, why aren't you doing something?"

"Perrin!" Faile hissed before turning an apologetic smile to Verin and Alanna. "Please forgive him. Moiraine Sedai spoiled him. She has an easy manner, I suppose, and she let him get away with things. Please don't be angry with him. He will do better." She shot him a sharp look, indicating she meant that for his ears as much as theirs, or more. He gave her a piece of his glower. She had no right interfering in this.

"An easy manner?" Verin said, blinking. "Moiraine? I never noticed."

Alanna waved Faile to silence. "You certainly do not understand," the Aes Sedai told Perrin in a tight voice. "You do not understand the restrictions under which we labor. The Three Oaths are not merely words. I brought two Warders with me to this place." The Greens were the only Ajah to bond more than a single Warder apiece; a few, he had heard, even had three or four. "The Children caught Owein crossing an open field. I felt every arrow that struck him until he died. I felt him die. Had I been there, I could have defended him, and myself, with the Power. But I cannot use it for revenge. The Oaths do not permit it. The Children are very nearly as vile as men can be, short of Darkfriends, but they are not Darkfriends, and for that reason they are safe from the Power except in self-defense. Stretch that as far as we can, it will only stretch so far."

"As for Trollocs," Verin added, "we have done for a number of them, and two Myrddraal, but there are limits. Halfmen can sense channeling, after a fashion. If we manage to draw a hundred Trollocs down on ourselves, there is very little we can do except run."

Perrin scratched at his beard. He should have expected this, should have known. He had seen Moiraine face Trollocs, and he had some idea of what she could do and what not. He realized he had been thinking of how Rand had killed all the Trollocs in the Stone, only Rand was stronger than either of these Aes Sedai, probably stronger than both together. Well, whether they helped him or not, he still meant to finish every Trolloc in the Two Rivers. After he rescued Mat's family, and the Luhhans. If he thought about it carefully enough, he had to find a way. His thigh ached miserably.

"You are injured." Setting her cup on the floor, Alanna came across to kneel beside him and take his head in her hands. A tingle ran through him. "Yes. I see. You did not do this to yourself shaving, it appears."

"It was the Trollocs, Aes Sedai," Bain said. "When we came out of the Ways in the mountains." Chiad touched her arm, and she stopped.

"I locked the Waygate," Loial added quickly. "No one will use it until it is opened from this side."

"I thought that must be how they were coming," Verin murmured, half to herself. "Moiraine did say they were using the Ways. Sooner or later that is going to present us with a real problem."

Perrin wondered what she thought that was.

"The Ways," Alanna said, still holding his head. "*Ta'veren!* Young heroes!" She made the words sound approving and close to a curse, both together.

"I am not a hero," he told her stolidly. "The Ways were the fastest way to get here. That's all."

The Green sister went on as if he had not spoken. "I will never understand why the Amyrlin Seat let you three go your way. Elaida has been having fits over you three, and she is not the only one, just the most vehement. With the seals weakening and the Last Battle coming, the last thing we need is three *ta'veren* running about loose. I would have tied a string to each of you, even bonded you." He tried to pull back, but she tightened her grip and smiled. "I am not so lost to custom yet as to bond a man against his will. Not quite yet." He was not sure how far from it she was; the smile did not reach her eyes. She fingered the half-healed cut on his cheek. "This has gone too long since it was done. Even Healing will leave a scar now."

"I don't need to be pretty," he muttered—just well enough to do what he had to—and Faile laughed aloud.

"Who told you that?" Faile said. Surprisingly, she shared a smile with Alanna.

Perrin frowned, wondering if they were making fun of him, but before he could say anything, the Healing hit him, like being turned to ice. All he could do was gasp. The few moments before Alanna released him seemed endless.

When he had his breath again, the Green sister had Bain's flame-haired head between her hands, Verin was seeing to Gaul, and Chiad was testing her left arm, swinging it back and forth with a satisfied expression.

Faile took Alanna's place beside Perrin and stroked a finger across his cheek, along the scar beneath his eye. "A beauty mark," she said, smiling slightly.

"A what?"

"Oh, just something Domani women do. It was just an idle comment."

Despite her smile, or maybe because of it, he scowled suspiciously. She *was* making fun of him, only he did not understand how, exactly.

Ihvon slipped into the room, whispered in Alanna's ear, and vanished outside again at her whisper. He hardly made a sound even on the wooden floor. A few moments later the scrape of boots on the steps announced new arrivals.

Perrin sprang to his feet as Tam al'Thor and Abell Cauthon appeared in the doorway, bows in hand, with the rumpled clothes and gray-flecked two-day beards of men who had been sleeping rough. They had been hunting; four rabbits hung at Tam's belt, three at Abell's. It was obvious they were expecting the Aes Sedai, and visitors, too, but they stared in amazement at Loial, more than half again as tall as either of them, with his tufted ears and broad snout of a nose. A flicker of recognition crossed Tam's bluff, lined face at sight of the Aiel.

Tam's gaze only rested thoughtfully on them for a moment, though, before coming to rest on Perrin with a start almost as big as for Loial. He was a sturdy, deep-chested man despite hair that was nearly all gray, the sort it would take an earthquake to knock off his feet and more than that to fluster. "Perrin, lad!" he exclaimed. "Is Rand with you?"

"What about Mat?" Abell added eagerly. He had the look of an older, graying Mat, but with more serious eyes. A man not thickened much by age, with an agile step.

"They are well," Perrin told them. "In Tear." He caught Verin's glance from the corner of his eye; she knew very well what Tear meant for Rand. Alanna hardly seemed to be paying attention at all. "They would have come with me, but we didn't know how bad things are." That was true on both counts, he was sure. "Mat spends his time dicing —and winning—and kissing the girls. Rand. . . . Well, the last I saw of Rand, he was wearing a fancy coat and had a pretty golden-haired girl on his arm."

"That sounds like my Mat," Abell chuckled.

"Maybe it's as well they didn't come," Tam said more slowly, "what with the Trollocs. And the Whitecloaks. . . ." He shrugged. "You know the Trollocs returned?" Perrin nodded. "Was that Aes Sedai right? Moiraine. Were they after you three lads, that Winternight? Did you ever find out why?"

The Brown sister gave Perrin a warning look. Alanna appeared absorbed in rummaging through her saddlebags, but he thought she was listening now. Neither was what made him hesitate, though. There was just no way to come out and tell Tam that his son could channel, that Rand was the Dragon Reborn. How could he tell a man something like that? Instead, he said, "You will have to ask Moiraine. Aes Sedai don't tell you any more than they have to."

"I have noticed," Tam said dryly.

Both Aes Sedai were definitely listening, and making no secret of it now. Alanna arched an icy eyebrow at Tam, and Abell shifted his feet as if he thought Tam was pushing his luck, but it would take more than a stare to upset Tam.

"Can we talk outside?" Perrin asked the two men. "I want a breath of air." He wanted to talk without Aes Sedai eavesdropping and watching, but he could hardly say so.

Tam and Abell were agreeable, and perhaps as eager to escape Verin and Alanna's scrutiny as he, but first there was the matter of the rabbits, all of which they handed over to Alanna.

"We meant to keep two for ourselves," Abell said, "but it seems you have more mouths to feed."

"There is no need for this." The Green sister sounded as though she had said as much often before.

"We like to pay for what we get," Tam told her, sounding the same. "The Aes Sedai were kind enough to do a little Healing for us," he added to Perrin, "and we want to stock up credit in case we need it again."

Perrin nodded. He could understand not wanting to take a gift from Aes Sedai. "An Aes Sedai's gift always has a hook in it," the old saying went. Well, he knew the truth of that. But it did not really matter whether you took the gift or paid for it; Aes Sedai managed to set the hook anyway. Verin was watching him with a tiny smile, as if she knew what he was thinking.

As the three men started out, carrying their bows, Faile rose to follow. Perrin shook his head at her, and amazingly she sat back down. He wondered if she was ill.

After pausing so Tam and Abell could admire Stepper and Swallow, they strolled off a way under the trees. The sun slanted westward, lengthening shadows. The older men made a few jokes about his beard, but they never mentioned his eyes. Strangely, the omission did not bother him. He had more important worries than whether somebody thought his eyes peculiar.

Responding to Abell's query as to whether "that thing" was any good for straining soup, he rubbed his beard and said mildly, "Faile likes it."

"Oh-ho," Tam chuckled. "That's the girl, is it? A spirited look to her, lad. She'll have you lying awake nights trying to tell up from down."

"Only one way to handle that sort," Abell said, nodding. "Let her think she's running things. That way, when it's important, and you say different, by the time she gets over the shock of it, you'll have matters arranged as you want, and it will be too late for her to badger you about changing it."

That seemed to Perrin a great deal like what Mistress al'Vere had told Faile about handling men. He wondered if Abell and Marin had ever compared notes. Not likely. Perhaps it was worth trying with Faile. Only, she seemed to have her own way in any case.

He glanced over his shoulder. The sickhouse was almost hidden by the trees. They had to be safe from the Aes Sedai's ears. He listened carefully, drew a deep breath. A woodpecker drummed somewhere in the distance. There were squirrels in the leafy branches overhead, and a fox had passed this way not long ago with its kill, a rabbit. Aside from the three of them, there was no man scent, nothing to indicate a hidden Warder listening. Perhaps he was being too cautious, but good reasons or no, he could not get past the coincidence of both Aes Sedai being women he had met before, one a woman Egwene did not trust, the other a woman he was not sure he trusted.

"Do you stay here?" he asked. "With Verin and Alanna?"

"Hardly," Abell replied. "How could a man sleep with Aes Sedai under the same roof? What there is of it."

"We thought this would be a good place to hide," Tam said, "but they were here before us. I think those Warders might have killed both of us if Marin and some others of the Women's Circle hadn't been here then, too."

Abell grimaced. "I think it was the Aes Sedai finding out who we were that stopped it. Who our sons were, I mean. They show too much interest in you boys to suit me." He hesitated, fingering his bow. "That Alanna let slip that you're *ta'veren*. All three of you. I've heard Aes Sedai can't lie."

"I haven't seen any signs of it in me," Perrin said wryly. "Or Mat."

Tam glanced at him when he did not mention Rand—he was going to have to learn to lie better, trying to keep his own secrets and everybody else's, too—but what the older man said was, "Maybe you just don't know what to look for. How is it you come to be traveling with an Ogier and three Aiel?"

"The last peddler I saw said there were Aiel this side of the Spine of the World," Abell put in, "but I didn't believe him. Said he'd heard there were Aiel in Murandy, of all places, or maybe Altara. He wasn't too certain of exactly where, but a long way from the Waste."

"None of that has anything to do with ta'veren," Perrin said. "Loial is a friend, and he came to help me. Gaul is a friend, too, I suppose. Bain and Chiad came with Faile, not me. It's all sort of complicated, but it just happened. Nothing to do with ta'veren."

"Well, whatever the reason," Abell said, "the Aes Sedai are interested in you lads. Tam and I traveled all the way to Tar Valon last year, to the White Tower, trying to find out where you were. We could hardly unearth one to admit she knew your names, but it was plain they were hiding something. The Keeper of the Chronicles had us on a boat heading downriver, our pockets stuffed with gold and our heads full of vague assurances, almost before we could make our bows. I don't like the idea the Tower may be using Mat some way."

Perrin wished he could tell Mat's father nothing like that was going on, but he was not sure he was up to that big a lie with a straight face. Moiraine was not watching Mat because she liked his grin; Mat was tangled as deeply with the Tower as he himself, maybe deeper. The three of them were all tied tight, and the Tower held the strings.

A silence descended on them, until at last Tam said quietly, "Lad, about your family. I've sad news."

"I know," Perrin said quickly, and the hush fell again, with each staring at his own boots. Quiet was what was needed. A few moments to pull back from painful emotions and the embarrassment of having them plain on your face.

Wings fluttered, and Perrin looked up to see a large raven alighting in an oak fifty paces away, beady black eyes sharp on the three men. His hand darted for his quiver, but even as he drew fletchings to cheek, two arrows knocked the raven from its perch. Tam and Abell were already nocking anew, eyes scanning the trees and sky for more of the black birds. There was nothing.

Tam's shot had taken the raven in the head, which was no surprise and no accident. Perrin had not lied when he told Faile these two men were better than he with the bow. No one in the Two Rivers could match Tam's shooting.

"Filthy things," Abell muttered, putting a foot on the bird to pull his arrow free. Cleaning the arrow point in the dirt, he returned it to his quiver. "They're everywhere nowadays."

"The Aes Sedai told us about them," Tam said, "spying for the Fades, and we spread the word. The Women's Circle did, too. Nobody paid much mind until they started attacking sheep, though, pecking out eyes, killing some. The clip will be bad enough this year without that. Not that it matters much, I suppose. Between Whitecloaks and Trollocs, I doubt we'll see any merchants after our wool this year."

"Some fool has gone crazy over it," Abell added. "Maybe more than one. We've found all sorts of dead animals. Rabbits, deer, foxes, even a bear. Killed and left to rot. Most not even skinned. It's a man, or men, not Trollocs; I found boot prints. A big man, but too small for a Trolloc. A shame and a waste."

Slayer. Slayer here, and not just in the wolf dream. Slayer and Trollocs. The man in the dream had seemed familiar. Perrin scuffed dirt and leaves over the dead raven with his boot. There would be plenty of time for Trollocs later. A lifetime, if need be. "I promised Mat I'd look after Bode and Eldrin, Master Cauthon. How hard will it be to get them, and the others, free?"

"Hard," Abell sighed, his face sagging. Suddenly he looked his age and more. "Powerful hard. I got close enough to see Natti after they took her, walking outside the tent where they're holding everybody. I could see her—with a couple of hundred Whitecloaks between us. I got a little careless, and one of them put an arrow through me. If Tam hadn't hauled me back here to the Aes Sedai. . . ."

"It's a good-sized camp," Tam said, "right under Watch Hill. Seven or eight hundred men. Patrols, day and night, with the heaviest concentration from Watch Hill down to Emond's Field. If they spread out more, it would make things easier for us, but except for a hundred men or so at Taren Ferry, they've just about given the rest of the Two Rivers over to the Trollocs. It's bad down around Deven Ride, I hear. Another farm burned almost every night. The same between Watch Hill and the River Taren. Bringing Natti and the others out will be hard, and after, we'll have to hope the Aes Sedai will let them stay here. That pair aren't too pleased at anyone knowing where they are."

"Surely someone will hide them," Perrin protested. "You can't tell me everyone's turned their backs on you. They don't really believe you're Darkfriends?" Even as he said it, he was remembering Cenn Buie.

"No, not that," Tam said, "except for a few fools. Plenty of folk will give us a meal, or a night in the barn, sometimes even a bed, but you have to understand they're uneasy about helping people the Whitecloaks are chasing. It's nothing to blame them for. Things are stone hard, and most men are trying to look after their own families the best they can. Asking someone to take in Natti and the girls, Haral and Alsbet. . . . Well, it might be asking too much."

"I thought better of Two Rivers folk than that," Perrin muttered.

Abell managed a weak smile. "Most people feel caught between two millstones, Perrin. They're just hoping they aren't ground to flour between Whitecloaks and Trollocs."

"They should stop hoping and do something." For a moment Perrin felt abashed. He had not been living here; he had no idea what it was like. But he was still right. As long as the people hid behind the Children of the Light, they would have to put up with whatever the Children wanted to do, whether taking books or arresting women and girls. "Tomorrow I'll take a look at this Whitecloak camp. There has to be some way to free them. And once they are, we can turn our attention to Trollocs. A Warder once told me Trollocs call the Aiel Waste 'the Dying Ground.' I mean to make them give that name to the Two Rivers."

"Perrin," Tam began, then stopped, looking troubled.

Perrin knew his eyes caught the light, there in the shadows under the oak. His face felt carved from rock.

Tam sighed. "First we'll see about Natti and the others. Then we can decide what to do about the Trollocs."

"Don't let it eat you inside, boy," Abell said softly. "Hate can grow till it burns everything else out of you."

"Nothing is eating me," Perrin told them in a level voice. "I just mean to do what needs doing." He ran a thumb along the edge of his axe. What needed doing.

Dain Bornhald held himself straight in his saddle as the hundred he had taken on patrol approached Watch Hill. Fewer than a hundred, now. Eleven saddles had cloak-wrapped bodies tied across them, and twenty-three more men nursed wounds. The Trollocs had laid a neat ambush; it might have succeeded against soldiers less well trained, less tough than the Children. What troubled him was that this was his third patrol to be attacked in force. Not a chance encounter, not happening on Trollocs killing and burning, but meeting a planned attack. And only patrols he led personally. The Trollocs tried to avoid the others. The fact presented worrisome questions, and the answers he came up with gave no solutions.

The sun was dropping. A few lights already appeared in the village that covered the hill from top to bottom with thatched roofs. The only tile roof stood at the crest, on the White Boar, the inn. Another evening he might have gone up there for a cup of wine, despite the nervous silence that closed in at the sight of a white cloak with a golden sunburst. He seldom drank, but he sometimes enjoyed being around people outside the Children; after a time they would forget his presence to some extent, and begin to laugh and talk among themselves again. On another evening. Tonight he wanted to be alone to think.

There was activity among the hundred or so colorful wagons gathered less than half a mile from the foot of the hill, men and women in even brighter hues than their wagons, examining horses and harness, loading things that had been lying about the camp for weeks. It seemed the Traveling People meant to live up to their name, probably at first light.

"Farran!" The thick-bodied hundredman heeled his horse closer, and Bornhald nodded toward the Tuatha'an caravan. "Inform the Seeker that if he wishes to move his people, they will move south." His maps said there was no crossing of the Taren except at Taren Ferry, but he had begun learning how old they were as soon as he crossed the river. No one was leaving the Two Rivers to perhaps seal his command into a trap as long as he could stop it. "And Farran? There is no need to use boots or fists, yes? Words will suffice. This Raen has ears."

"By your command, Lord Bornhald." The hundredman sounded only a little disappointed. Touching gauntleted fist to heart, he wheeled away toward the Tuatha'an encampment. He would not like it, but he would obey. Despise the Traveling People as he might, he was a good soldier.

The sight of his own camp brought a moment of pride to Bornhald, the long neat rows of wedge-roofed white tents, the picket lines for the horses precisely arrayed. Even here in this Light-forsaken corner of the world, the Children maintained themselves, never allowing discipline to slack. It was Light-forsaken. The Trollocs proved that. If they burned farms, it only meant some folk here were pure. Some. The rest bowed, and said "yes, my Lord," "as you wish, my Lord," and stubbornly went their own way as soon as his back was turned. Besides which, they were hiding an Aes Sedai. The second day south of the Taren they had killed a Warder; the man's color-shifting cloak had been sufficient proof. Bornhald hated Aes Sedai, meddling with the One Power as if Breaking the World once was not enough. They would do it again if they were not stopped. His momentary good mood faded like spring snow.

His eye sought out the tent where the prisoners were kept, except for a brief exercise period each day, one at a time. None would try running when it meant leaving the others behind. Not that running would get them more that a dozen paces—a guard stood at either end of the tent, and a dozen paces in any direction took in another twenty Children—but he wanted as little trouble as possible. Trouble sparked trouble. If rough treatment was needed with the prisoners, it might raise resentment in the village to a point where something had to be done about it. Byar was a fool. He—and others, Farran especially—wanted to put the prisoners to the question. Bornhald was not a Questioner, and he did not like to use their methods. Nor did he mean to let Farran anywhere near those girls, even if they were Darkfriends, as Ordeith claimed.

Darkfriends or no Darkfriends, he realized more and more that all he really wanted was one Darkfriend. More than the Trollocs, more than Aes Sedai, he wanted Perrin Aybara. He could hardly credit Byar's tales of the man running with wolves, but Byar was clear enough that Aybara had led Bornhald's father into a Darkfriend trap, led Geofram Bornhald to his death on Toman Head at the hands of the Seanchan Darkfriends and their Aes Sedai allies. Perhaps, if neither of the Luhhans talked soon, he might let Byar have his way with the blacksmith. Either the man would crack, or his wife would, watching. One of them would give him the means to find Perrin Aybara.

When he dismounted in front of his tent, Byar was there to meet him, stiff and gaunt as a scarecrow. Bornhald glanced distastefully toward a much smaller collection of tents apart from the rest. The wind was from that direction, and he could smell the other camp. They did not keep their picket lines clean, or themselves. "Ordeith is back, it seems, yes?"

"Yes, my Lord Bornhald." Byar stopped, and Bornhald looked at him questioningly. "They report a skirmish with Trollocs to the south. Two dead. Six wounded, they claim."

"And who are the dead?" Bornhald asked quietly.

"Child Joelin and Child Gomanes, my Lord Bornhald." Byar's hollow-cheeked expression never changed.

Bornhald drew off his steel-backed gauntlets slowly. The two he had sent off to accompany Ordeith, to see what he did on his forays south. Carefully, he did not raise his voice. "My compliments to Master Ordeith, Byar, and—No! No compliments. Tell him, in these words, that I will have his scrawny bones before me now. Tell him, Byar, and bring him if you must arrest him and those filthy wretches who disgrace the Children. Go."

Bornhald held his anger until he was inside his tent, flap lowered, then swept maps and writing case from his camp table with a snarl. Ordeith must think him an imbecile. Twice he had sent men with the fellow, and twice they had been the only deaths in "a skirmish with Trollocs" that left no wounded to show among the rest. Always to the south. The man was obsessed with Emond's Field. Well, he himself might have had his camp there, if not for. . . . No point to it now. He had the Luhhans here. They would give him Perrin Aybara, one way or another. Watch Hill was a much better site if he had to move to Taren Ferry quickly. Military considerations before personal.

For the thousandth time he wondered why the Lord Captain Commander had sent him here. The people seemed no different from those he had seen a hundred other places. Except that only the Taren Ferry folk showed any enthusiasm for rooting out their own Darkfriends. The rest stared with a sullen stubbornness when the Dragon's Fang was scrawled on a door. A village always knew who its own undesirables were; they were always ready to cleanse themselves, with a little encouragement, and any Darkfriends were certain to be swept up with the others the people wanted gone. But not here. The black scrawl of a sharp fang on a door might as well be new whitewash for all of its real effect. And the Trollocs. Had Pedron Niall known the Trollocs would come when he wrote those orders? How could he have? But if not, why had he sent enough of the Children to put down a small rebellion? And why under the Light had the Lord Captain Commander burdened him with a murderous madman?

The tent flap swept aside, and Ordeith swaggered in. His fine gray coat was embroidered with silver, but stained heavily. His scrawny neck was dirty, too, jutting out of his collar and giving him the look of a turtle. "A good evening to you, my Lord Bornhald. A gracious good evening, and splendid." The Lugard accent was heavy today.

"What happened to Child Joelin and Child Gomanes, Ordeith?"

"Such a terrible thing, my Lord. When we came on the Trollocs, Child Gomanes bravely—" Bornhald struck him across the face with his gauntlets. Staggering, the bony man put a hand to his split lip, examined the red on his fingers. The smile on his face no longer mocked. It looked viperish. "Are you forgetting who signed my commission now, lordling? Pedron Niall will be hanging you with your mother's guts if I say a word, after he has the both of you skinned alive."

"That is if you are alive to speak this word, yes?"

Ordeith snarled, crouching like some wild thing, spittle bubbling. Slowly he shook himself, slowly straightened. "We must work together." The Lugarder accent was gone, replaced by a grander, more commanding tone. Bornhald preferred the taunting Lugarder voice to the slightly oily, barely veiled contempt in this one. "The Shadow lies all around us here. Not simply Trollocs and Myrddraal. They are the least of it. Three were spawned here, Darkfriends meant to shake the world, their breeding guided by the Dark One for a thousand years or more. Rand al'Thor. Mat Cauthon. Perrin Aybara. You know their names. In this place, forces are loosed that will harrow the world. Creatures of the Shadow walk the night, tainting men's hearts, corrupting men's dreams. Scourge this land. Scourge it, and they will come. Rand al'Thor. Mat Cauthon. Perrin Aybara." He almost caressed the last name.

Bornhald drew ragged breath. He was not sure how Ordeith had discovered what he wanted here; one day the man had simply revealed his knowledge. "I covered over what you did at the Aybara farm—"

"Scourge them." There was a hint of madness in that grand voice, and sweat on Ordeith's brow. "Flay them, and the three will come."

Bornhald raised his voice. "Covered it over because I had to." There had been no choice. If the truth came out, he would have more than sullen stares to contend with. The last thing he needed was open rebellion on top of Trollocs. "But I will not condone the murder of Children. Do you hear me? What is it you do that you need to hide from the Children?"

"Do you doubt the Shadow will do whatever is needed to stop me?"

"What?"

"Do you doubt it?" Ordeith leaned forward intently. "You saw the Gray Men."

Bornhald hesitated. Fifty of the Children around him, in the middle of Watch Hill, and no one had noticed the pair with their daggers. He had looked right at them and not seen. Until Ordeith killed the pair. The scrawny little fellow had gained considerable standing with the men for that. Later Bornhald had buried the daggers deep. Those blades had looked to be steel, but a touch seared like molten metal. The first earth thrown on them in the pit had hissed and steamed. "You believe they were after you?"

"Oh, yes, my Lord Bornhald. After me. Whatever it takes to stop me. The Shadow itself wants to stop me."

"That still says nothing of murdered—"

"I must do what I do in secret." It was a whisper, almost a hiss. "The Shadow can enter men's minds to find me out, enter men's thoughts and dreams. Would you like to die in a dream? It can happen."

"You are . . . mad."

"Give me a free hand, and I will give you Perrin Aybara. That is what Pedron Niall's orders require. A free hand for me, and I will place Perrin Aybara in yours."

Bornhald was silent for a long time. "I do not want to look at you," he said finally. "Get out."

When Ordeith was gone, Bornhald shivered. What was the Lord Captain Commander up to with this man? But if it put Aybara in his grasp. . . . Tossing his gauntlets down, he began digging through his belongings. Somewhere he had a flask of brandy.

The man who called himself Ordeith, even sometimes thought of himself as Ordeith, slunk through the tents of the Children of the Light, watching the white-cloaked men with a wary eye. Useful tools, ignorant tools, but not to be trusted. Especially not Bornhald; that one might have to be disposed of, if he became too troublesome. Byar would be much more easily handled. But not yet. There were other matters more important. Some of the soldiers nodded respectfully as he passed. He showed them his teeth in what they took for a friendly smile. Tools, and fools.

His eyes skittered hungrily across the tent holding the prisoners. They could wait. For a while yet. A little while longer. They were only tidbits anyway. Bait. He should have restrained himself at the Aybara farm, but Con Aybara had laughed in his face, and Joslyn had called him a filthy-minded little fool for naming her son Darkfriend. Well, they had learned, screaming, burning. In spite of himself he giggled under his breath. Tidbits.

He could feel one of those he hated out there somewhere, south, toward Emond's Field. Which one? It did not matter. Rand al'Thor was the only really important one. He would have known if it was al'Thor. Rumor had not drawn him yet, but it would. Ordeith shivered with desire. It had to be so. More tales must be gotten past Bornhald's guards at Taren Ferry, more reports of the scouring of the Two Rivers, to drift to Rand al'Thor's ears and sear his brain. First al'Thor, then the Tower, for what they had taken from him. He would have all that was his by right.

Everything had been ticking along like a fine clock, even with

Bornhald impeding, until this new one appeared with his Gray Men. Ordeith scrubbed bony fingers through greasy hair. Why could not his dreams at least be his own? He was a puppet no longer, danced about by Myrddraal and Forsaken, by the Dark One himself. He pulled the strings now. They could not stop him, could not kill him.

"Nothing can kill me," he muttered, scowling. "Not me. I have survived since the Trolloc Wars." Well, a part of him had. He laughed shrilly, hearing madness in the cackle, knowing it, not caring.

A young Whitecloak officer frowned at him. This time there was nothing of a smile in Ordeith's bared teeth, and the fuzzy-cheeked lad recoiled. Ordeith hurried on in a slinking shuffle.

Flies buzzed about his own tents, and sullen, suspicious eyes flinched away from his. The white cloaks were soiled here. But the swords were sharp, and obedience instant and unquestioning. Bornhald thought these men were still his. Pedron Niall believed it, too, believed Ordeith his tame creature. Fools.

Twitching aside his tent flap, Ordeith went in to examine his prisoner, stretched out between two pegs thick enough to hold a wagon team. Good steel chain quivered as he checked it, but he had calculated how much was needed, then doubled it. As well he had. One loop less, and those stout steel links would have broken.

With a sigh, he seated himself on the edge of his bed. The lamps were already lit, more than a dozen, leaving no shadow anywhere. The tent was as bright inside as noonday. "Have you thought over my proposal? Accept, and you walk free. Refuse. . . . I know how to hurt your sort. I can make you scream through endless dying. Forever dying, forever screaming."

The chains hummed at a jerk; the stakes driven deep into the ground creaked. "Very well." The Myrddraal's voice was dried snakeskin crumbling. "I accept. Release me."

Ordeith smiled. It thought him a fool. It would learn. They all would. "First, the matter of . . . shall we say, agreements and accord?" As he talked, the Myrddraal began to sweat.

CHAPTER
32

Questions to Be Asked

W e should leave for Watch Hill soon," Verin announced the next morning, with sunrise just pearling the sky outside, "so don't dawdle." Perrin looked up from his cold porridge to meet a steady gaze; the Aes Sedai expected no arguments. After a moment, she added thoughtfully, "Do not think this means I will aid you in any foolishness. You are a tricksome young man. Try none of it with me."

Tam and Abell paused with spoons halfway to their mouths, exchanging surprised looks; clearly they had gone their own way and the Aes Sedai theirs before this. After a moment they resumed eating, although with pensive frowns. They left any objections unvoiced. Tomas, his Warder's cloak already packed away in his saddlebags, gave them—and Perrin—a hard-faced stare anyway, as if he anticipated arguments and meant to stamp them out. Warders did whatever was necessary for an Aes Sedai to do what she wanted.

She intended to meddle, of course—Aes Sedai always did—but having her where he could see her was surely better than leaving her behind his back. Avoiding Aes Sedai entanglements completely was all but impossible when they meant to dabble their fingers in; the only course was to try to use them while they used you, to watch and hope you could jump clear if they decided to stuff you headfirst, like a ferret, down a rabbithole. Sometimes the rabbithole turned out to be a badger's sett, which was hard on the ferret.

"You would be welcome, too," he told Alanna, but she gave him a frosty stare that stopped him in his tracks. She had disdained the porridge, and stood at one of the vine-shrouded windows, peering through the leafy screen.

He could not say whether she was pleased with his plans for a scout. Reading her seemed near to impossible. Aes Sedai were supposed to be cool serenity itself, and she was that, but Alanna tossed off flashes of fiery temper or unpredictable humor when least expected, like heat lightning, crackling then gone. Sometimes she looked at him so that if she had not been Aes Sedai he would have thought she was admiring him. Other times he might as well have been some complicated mechanism she meant to disassemble in order to puzzle out how it worked. Even Verin had the better of that; most of the time she was just plain unreadable. Unnerving, on occasion, but at least he did not have to wonder if she was going to know how to fit his pieces back together.

He wished he could make Faile stay there—that was not the same as leaving her behind, just keeping her safe from Whitecloaks—but she had that stubborn set to her jaw and a dangerous light in her tilted eyes. "I look forward to seeing some of your country. My father raises sheep." Her tone was definite; she was not going to stay unless he tied her up.

For a moment he came close to considering it. But the danger from Whitecloaks should not be that great; he only intended to look, today. "I thought he was a merchant," he said.

"He raises sheep, too." Spots of crimson bloomed in her cheeks: maybe her father was a poor man and not a merchant at all. He did not know why she would pretend, but if that was what she wanted, he would not try to stop her. Embarrassed or not, however, she looked no less stubborn.

He remembered Master Cauthon's method. "I don't know how much you'll see. Some farms may be shearing, I suppose. Probably no different from what your father does. I'll be glad of your company in any case." The startlement on her face when she realized he was not going to argue was almost worth the worry of her coming along. Maybe Abell had something.

Loial was another matter altogether.

"But I want to go," the Ogier protested when told he could not. "I want to help, Perrin."

"You will stand out, Master Loial," Abell said, and Tam added, "We need to avoid attracting any more attention than we must." Loial's ears drooped dejectedly.

Perrin drew him aside, as far from the others as the room would allow. Loial's shaggy hair brushed the roof beams until Perrin motioned him to lean down. Perrin smiled, just jollying him along. He hoped everyone else believed that.

"I want you to keep an eye on Alanna," he said in a near whisper. Loial gave a start, and he caught the Ogier's sleeve, still smiling like a fool. "Grin, Loial. We are not talking about anything important, right?" The Ogier managed an uncertain smile. It would have to do. "Aes Sedai do what they do for their own reasons, Loial." And that might be what you least expected, or not at all what you believed it was. "Who knows what she might take into her head? I've had surprises enough since coming home, and I don't want one of hers added to it. I don't expect you to stop her, only notice anything out of the ordinary."

"Thank you for that," Loial muttered wryly, ears jerking. "Do you not think it best to just let Aes Sedai do what they want?" That was easy for him to say; Aes Sedai could not channel inside an Ogier *stedding*. Perrin just looked at him, and after a moment, the Ogier sighed. "I suppose not. Oh, very well. I can never say being around you is not . . . interesting." Straightening, he rubbed a thick finger under his nose and told the others, "I suppose I would draw eyes at that. Well, it will give me a chance to work on my notes. I have done nothing on my book in days."

Verin and Alanna shared an unreadable look, then turned twin unblinking gazes on Perrin. There was simply no telling what either thought.

The pack animals had to be left behind, of course. Packhorses would surely occasion comment, speaking of long travel; no one in the Two Rivers traveled very far from home in the best of times. Alanna wore a slight, satisfied smile while watching them saddle their mounts, no doubt believing the animals and wicker hampers tied him to the old sickhouse, to her and Verin. She was in for a surprise, if it came to that. He had lived out of a saddlebag often enough since leaving home. For that matter, he had lived out of his belt pouch and coat pockets.

He straightened from tightening Stepper's saddle girth and gave a start. Verin was watching him with a knowing expression, not vague at all, as if she knew what he was thinking and was amused. It was bad enough when Faile did that sort of thing; from an Aes Sedai, it was a hundred times worse. The hammer lashed with his blanket roll and saddlebags seemed to puzzle her, though. He was glad there was something she did not seem to understand. On the other hand, he could have done without her being so intrigued. What could be fascinating to an Aes Sedai about a hammer?

With only the riding animals to prepare, it took no time at all to be ready to go. Verin had a nondescript brown gelding, as plain to the untrained eye as her garb, but its deep chest and strong rump suggested as much endurance as her Warder's ferocious-eyed gray, tall and sleek. Stepper snorted at the other stallion until Perrin patted the dun's neck. The gray was more disciplined—and just as ready to fight, if Tomas let it. The Warder controlled his animal with his knees as much as his reins, the two seeming almost one.

Master Cauthon watched Tomas's horse with interest—war-trained mounts were not much seen in these parts—but Verin's earned an approving nod at first glance. He was as good a judge of horseflesh as there was in the Two Rivers. No doubt he had chosen his and Master al'Thor's rough-coated animals, not so tall as the other horses, but sturdy, with gaits that spoke of good speed and staying power.

The three Aiel glided ahead as the party started north, with long strides that carried them out of sight quickly in the woods, early-morning shadows sharp and long in the brightness of sunrise. Now and then a flash of gray-and-brown was visible through the trees, probably on purpose, to let the others know they were there. Tam and Abell took the lead, bows across the tall pommels of their saddles, with Perrin and Faile behind, and Verin and Tomas bringing up the rear.

Perrin could have done without Verin's eyes on his back. He could feel them between his shoulder blades. He wondered if she knew about the wolves. Not a comfortable thought. Brown sisters supposedly knew things the other Ajahs did not, obscure things, old knowledge. Perhaps she knew how he could avoid losing himself, what was human in him, to the wolves. Short of finding Elyas Machera again, she might be his best chance. All he had to do was trust her. Whatever she knew she would likely use, certainly to help the White Tower, probably to help Rand. The only trouble was that helping Rand might not bring what he wanted now. Everything would have been so much simpler without any Aes Sedai.

Mostly they rode in silence except for the sounds of the forest, squirrels and woodpeckers and occasional birdsong. At one point Faile glanced back. "She will not harm you," she said, her soft tone clashing with the fierce light in her dark eyes.

Perrin blinked. She meant to protect him. Against Aes Sedai. He was never going to understand her, or know what to expect next. She was about as confusing as the Aes Sedai sometimes.

They broke out of the Westwood perhaps four or five miles north of Emond's Field, with the sun standing its own height above the trees to the east. Scattered copses, mainly leatherleaf and pine and oak, lay between them and the nearest hedged fields of barley and oats, tabac and tall grass for hay. Strangely there was no one in sight, no smoke rising from the farmhouse chimneys beyond the fields. Perrin knew the people who lived there, the al'Loras in two of the big houses, the Barsteres in the others. Hardworking folk. If there had been anyone in those houses, they would have been at their labors long since. Gaul waved from the edge of a thicket, then vanished into the trees.

Perrin heeled Stepper up beside Tam and Abell. "Shouldn't we stay under cover as long as we can? Six people on horses won't go unnoticed." They kept their mounts at a steady walk.

"Not many to notice us, lad," Master al'Thor replied, "as long as we stay away from the North Road. Most farms have been abandoned, close by to the woods. Anyway, nobody travels alone these days, not far from their own doorstep. Ten people together wouldn't be noticed twice nowadays, though mostly folk travel by wagon, if at all."

"It'll take us most of daylight to reach Watch Hill as it is," Master Cauthon said, "without trying to cover the distance through the woods. Would be a little faster along the road, but more chance of meeting Whitecloaks, too. More chance somebody might turn us in for the rewards."

Tam nodded. "But we have friends up this way, too. We figure to stop at Jac al'Seen's farm about midday to breathe the horses and stretch our legs. We will make it to Watch Hill while there's still light enough to see."

"There will be enough light," Perrin said absently; there was always light enough for him. He twisted in his saddle to peer back at the farmhouses. Abandoned, but not burned, not ransacked that he could make out. Curtains hung at the windows still. Unbroken windows. Trollocs liked smashing things, and empty houses were an invitation. Weeds stood tall among the barley and oats, but the fields had not been trampled. "Have Trollocs attacked Emond's Field itself?"

"No, they have not," Master Cauthon said in a thankful tone. "They'd have no easy time if they did, mind. People learned to keep a sharp eye out Winternight before last. There's a bow beside every door, and spears and the like. Besides, the Whitecloaks patrol down to

Emond's Field every few days. Much as I hate to admit it, they do keep the Trollocs back."

Perrin shook his head. "Do you have any idea how many Trollocs there are?"

"One's too many," Abell grunted.

"Maybe two hundred," Tam said. "Maybe more. Probably more." Master Cauthon looked surprised. "Think on it, Abell. I don't know how many the Whitecloaks have killed, but the Warders claim they and the Aes Sedai have finished off nearly fifty, and two Fades. It hasn't lessened the number of burnings we hear about. I think it has to be more, but you figure it out for yourself." The other man nodded unhappily.

"Then why haven't they attacked Emond's Field?" Perrin asked. "If two or three hundred came in the night, they could likely burn the whole village and be gone before the Whitecloaks up at Watch Hill even heard about it. Still easier for them to hit Deven Ride. You said the Whitecloaks don't go down that far."

"Luck," Abell muttered, but he sounded troubled. "That's what it is. We've been lucky. What else could it be? What are you getting at, boy?"

"What he's getting at," Faile said, closing up beside them, "is that there must be a reason." Swallow was enough taller than the Two Rivers horses to let her look Tam and Abell in the eye, and she made it a firm look. "I have seen the aftermath of Trolloc raids in Saldaea. They despoil what they do not burn, kill or carry off people and farm animals, whoever and whatever is not protected. Entire villages have disappeared in bad years. They seek wherever is weakest, wherever they can kill the most. My father—" She bit it off, drew a deep breath, and went on. "Perrin has seen what you should have." She flashed him a proud smile. "If the Trollocs have not attacked your villages, they have a reason."

"I have thought of that," Tam said quietly, "but I can't think why. Until we know, luck is as good an answer as any."

"Perhaps," Verin said, joining them, "it is a lure." Tomas still hung back a little, dark eyes searching the country they rode through as relentlessly as any Aiel's. The Warder was watching the sky, too; there was always the chance of a raven. Barely pausing, Verin's gaze brushed across Perrin to the two older men. "News of continued trouble, news of Trollocs, will draw eyes to the Two Rivers. Andor will surely send soldiers, and perhaps other lands as well, for Trollocs this far south. That is if the Children are allowing any news out, of course. I surmise

Queen Morgase's Guards would be little happier to find so many Whitecloaks than they would to find Trollocs."

"War," Abell muttered. "What we have is bad enough, but you are talking war."

"It might be so," Verin said complacently. "It might be." Frowning in a preoccupied manner, she dug a steel-nibbed pen and a small cloth-bound book from her pouch, and opened a little leather case at her belt that held an ink bottle and sandshaker. Wiping the pen absentmindedly on her sleeve, she began jotting in the book despite the awkwardness of writing while riding. She seemed completely oblivious of any unease she might have caused. Perhaps she really was.

Master Cauthon kept murmuring "War," wonderingly, under his breath, and Faile put a comforting hand on Perrin's arm, her eyes sad.

Master al'Thor only grunted; he had been in a war, so Perrin had heard, though not where or how, exactly. Just somewhere outside the Two Rivers, where he had gone as a young man, returning years later with a wife and a child, Rand. Few Two Rivers folk ever left. Perrin doubted if any of them really knew what a war was, except by what they heard from peddlers, or merchants and their guards and wagon drivers. He knew, though. He had seen war, on Toman Head. Abell was right. What they had was bad enough, but it did not come near war.

He held his peace. Maybe Verin was right. And maybe she just wanted to stop them speculating. If Trollocs harrying the Two Rivers were bait for a trap, it had to be a trap for Rand, and the Aes Sedai had to know it. That was one of the problems with Aes Sedai; they could hand you "if"s and "might"s until you were sure they had told you flat out what they had only suggested. Well, if the Trollocs—or whoever sent them, rather; one of the Forsaken, maybe?—thought to trap Rand, they would have to settle for Perrin instead—a simple black-smith instead of the Dragon Reborn—and he did not mean to walk into any traps.

They rode on silently through the morning. In this region farms were scattered, with sometimes a mile or more between. Every last one lay abandoned, fields choked with weeds, barn doors swinging in any er-rant breeze. Only one had been burned, and of that nothing stood except the chimneys, soot-black fingers rising from ashes. The people who had died there—Ayellins, cousins of those who lived in Emond's Field—had been buried near the pear trees beyond the house. Those few who had been found. Abell had to be pressed to talk about it, and Tam would not. They seemed to think it would upset him. He knew what Trollocs ate. Anything that was meat. He stroked his axe absently until Faile took his hand. For some reason she was the one who seemed disturbed. He had thought she knew more of Trollocs than that.

The Aiel managed to stay out of sight even between copses, except when they wanted to be seen. When Tam began angling eastward, Gaul and the two Maidens shifted with them.

As Master Cauthon had predicted, the al'Seen farm came in sight with the sun still shy of its full height. There was not another farm in view, though a few widely separated gray plumes of chimney smoke rose both north and east. Why were they hanging on, isolated like this? If Trollocs came, their only hope was Whitecloaks chancing to be near at the same time.

While the rambling farmhouse was still small in the distance, Tam reined in and waved the Aiel to join them, suggesting they find a place to wait until the rest of them left the farm. "They won't talk about Abell or me," he said, "but you three will set tongues wagging with the best will in the world."

That was putting it mildly, with their odd clothes and their spears, and two of them women. A rabbit apiece dangled beside their quivers, though Perrin could not see how they had found time to hunt while keeping ahead of the horses. They seemed less tired than the horses, for that matter.

"Well enough," Gaul said. "I will find a place to eat my own meal, and watch for your going." He turned and loped away immediately. Bain and Chiad exchanged glances. After a moment Chiad shrugged, and they followed.

"Aren't they together?" Mat's father asked, scratching his head.

"It is a long story," Perrin said. It was better than telling him Chiad and Gaul might decide to kill each other over a feud. He hoped the water oath held. He had to remember to ask Gaul what a water oath was.

The al'Seen farm was just about as big as farms went in the Two Rivers, with three tall barns and five tabac curing sheds. The stone-walled cote, full of black-faced sheep, spread as wide as some pastures, and rail-fenced yards kept white-spotted milk cows separate from black beef cattle. Pigs grunted contentedly in their wallow, chickens wandered everywhere, and there were white geese on a good-sized pond.

The first odd thing Perrin noticed was the boys on the thatched roofs of the house and barns, eight or nine of them, with bows and quivers. They shouted down as soon as they saw the riders, and women hustled children inside before shading their eyes to see who was coming. Men gathered in the farmyard, some with bows, others with pitchforks and bushhooks held like weapons. Too many people. Far too many, even for a farm as big as this. He looked a question at Master al'Thor.

"Jac took in his cousin Wit's people," Tam explained, "because Wit's farm was too close to the Westwood. And Flann Lewin's people after their farm was attacked. Whitecloaks drove the Trollocs off before more than his barns were burned, but Flann decided it was time to go. Jac is a good man."

As they rode into the farmyard, and Tam and Abell were recognized, men and women crowded around with smiles and a babble of welcome while they dismounted. Seeing that, children burst out of the house, followed by the women who had been minding them and others, fresh from the kitchen, wiping hands on aprons. Every generation was represented, from white-haired Astelle al'Seen, bent-backed but using her stick to thump people out of her way more than to walk with, down to a swaddled infant in the arms of a more than stout young woman with a bright smile.

Perrin looked past the stout, smiling woman; then his head whipped back. When he had left the Two Rivers, Laila Dearn had been a slim girl who could dance any three boys into the ground. Only the smile and the eyes were the same. He shivered. There had been a time when he had dreamed of marrying Laila, and she had returned the feeling somewhat. The truth was, she had held on to it longer than he had. Luckily, she was too entranced with her baby and the even wider fellow by her side to pay much attention to him. Perrin recognized the man with her, too. Natley Lewin. So Laila was a Lewin now. Odd. Nat never could dance. Thanking the Light for his escape, Perrin looked around for Faile.

He found her idly flipping Swallow's reins while the mare nuzzled her shoulder. She was too busy smiling admiringly at Wil al'Seen, a cousin from Deven Ride way, to notice her horse, though, and Wil was smiling back. A good-looking boy, Wil. Well, he was a year older than Perrin, but too good-looking not to appear boyish. When Wil came down to Emond's Field for dances, the girls all used to stare at him and sigh. Just the way Faile was now. True, she was not sighing, but her smile was decidedly approving.

Perrin went over and put an arm around her, resting his other hand on his axe. "How are you, Wil?" he asked, smiling for all he was worth. No point in letting Faile think he was jealous. Not that he was.

"Fine, Perrin." Wil's eyes slid away from his and bounced off the axe, a sickly expression oozing over his face. "Just fine." Avoiding looking at Faile again, he hurried off to join the crowd around Verin.

Faile looked up at Perrin, pursing her lips, then took his beard with one hand and gently shook his head. "Perrin, Perrin, Perrin," she murmured softly.

He was not sure what she meant, but he thought it wiser not to ask. She looked as if she did not know herself whether she was angry or—could it possibly be amused? Best not to make her decide.

Wil was not the only one to look askance at his eyes, of course. It seemed that everyone, young or old, male or female, gave a start the first time they met his gaze. Old Mistress al'Seen poked him with her stick, and her dark old eyes widened in surprise when he grunted. Maybe she thought he was not real. Nobody said anything, though.

Soon enough the horses had been led off to one of the barns—Tomas took his gray himself; the animal did not appear to want anyone else to touch the reins—and everybody except the boys on the rooftops had crowded into the house, just about filling it. Adults lined the front room two deep, Lewins and al'Seens interspersed in no particular order or rank, children in their mothers' arms or relegated to peering through the legs of grown-ups packing the doorways to peer in.

Strong tea and high-backed, rush-bottomed chairs were provided for the newcomers, though Verin and Faile got embroidered cushions. There was considerable excitement over Verin, and Tomas, and Faile. Murmurs filled the room like a gabble of geese, and everyone stared at those three as though they wore crowns, or might do tricks any moment. Strangers were always a curiosity in the Two Rivers. Tomas's sword drew especial comment, in near whispers that Perrin heard easily. Swords were not common here, or had not been before the Whitecloaks came. Some thought Tomas was a Whitecloak, others a lord. One boy little more than waist-high mentioned Warders before his elders laughed him down.

As soon as the guests were settled, Jac al'Seen planted himself in front of the wide stone fireplace, a stocky, square-shouldered man with less hair than Master al'Vere, and that just as gray. A clock ticked on the mantel behind his head between two large silver goblets, evidence of his success as a farmer. The babble quieted when he raised a hand, though his cousin Wit, a near twin except for no hair at all, and Flann Lewin, a gnarled, gray-headed beanpole, both shushed their own folk anyway.

"Mistress Mathwin, Lady Faile," Jac said, bowing awkwardly to each. "You are welcome here, for as long as you wish. I have to caution you, though. You know the trouble we have in the countryside. Best for you if you go straightway to Emond's Field, or Watch Hill, and stay there.

They are too big to be troubled. I would advise you to leave the Two Rivers altogether, but I understand the Children of the Light aren't letting anyone cross the Taren. I don't know why, but there it is."

"But there are so many fine stories in the country," Verin said, blinking mildly. "I would miss them all if I remained in a village." Without lying once, she managed to give the impression that she had come to the Two Rivers in search of old stories, the same as Moiraine had done, what seemed so long ago. Her Great Serpent ring lay in her belt pouch, though Perrin doubted that any of these people would know what it meant.

Elisa al'Seen smoothed her white apron and smiled gravely at Verin. Though her hair had less gray than her husband's, she looked older than Verin, her lined face motherly. Very likely she thought she was. "It is an honor to have a real scholar under our roof, yet Jac is right," she said firmly. "You truly are welcome to stay here, but when you leave, you must go immediately to a village. Traveling about isn't safe. The same goes for you, my Lady," she added to Faile. "Trollocs are not something two women should face with only a handful of men for protection."

"I will think on it," Faile said calmly. "I thank you for your consideration." She sipped her tea, as unconcerned as Verin, who had begun writing in her small book again, only looking up to smile at Elisa and murmur, "There are so many stories in the countryside." Faile accepted a butter cookie from a young al'Seen girl, who curtsied and blushed furiously, all the while staring at Faile in wide-eyed admiration.

Perrin grinned to himself. In her green riding silks, they all took Faile for nobly born, and he had to admit she carried it off beautifully. When she wanted to. The girl might not have been so admiring had she seen her in one of her tempers, when her tongue could flay the hide off a wagon driver.

Mistress al'Seen turned to her husband, shaking her head; Faile and Verin were not going to be convinced. Jac looked at Tomas. "Can you convince them?"

"I go where she tells me," Tomas replied. Sitting there with a teacup in his hand, the Warder still seemed on the point of drawing his sword.

Master al'Seen sighed and shifted his attention. "Perrin, most of us have met you one time or another, down to Emond's Field. We know you, after a fashion. At least, we knew you before you ran off last year. We've heard some troubling things, but I suppose Tam and Abell wouldn't be with you if they were true."

Flann's wife, Adine, a plump woman with a self-contented eye, sniffed sharply. "I've heard some things about Tam and Abell, too. And about their boys, running off with Aes Sedai. With Aes Sedai! A dozen of them! You all remember how Emond's Field was burned to the ground. The Light knows what they could have got up to. I heard tell they kidnapped the al'Vere girl." Flann shook his head resignedly and gave Jac an apologetic look.

"If you believe that," Wit said wryly, "you'll believe anything. I talked to Marin al'Vere two weeks ago, and she said her girl went off on her own hook. And there was only one Aes Sedai."

"What are you suggesting, Adine?" Elisa al'Seen put her fists on her hips. "Come out with it." There was more than a hint of "I dare you" in her voice.

"I didn't say I believed it," Adine protested stoutly, "just that I heard it. There are questions to be asked. The Children didn't latch on to those three by pulling names out of a cap."

"If you listen for a change," Elisa said firmly, "you might hear an answer or two." Adine set herself to rearranging her skirts, but though she muttered to herself, she held her tongue otherwise.

"Does anyone else have anything to say?" Jac asked with barely concealed impatience. When no one spoke, he went on. "Perrin, no one here believes you a Darkfriend, any more than we believe Tam or Abell is." He shot Adine a hard look, and Flann put a hand on his wife's shoulder; she kept silent, but her lips writhed with what she did not say. Jac muttered to himself before continuing. "Even so, Perrin, I think we have a right to hear why the Whitecloaks are saying what they are. They accuse you and Mat Cauthon and Rand al'Thor of being Darkfriends. Why?"

Faile opened her mouth angrily, but Perrin waved her to silence. Her obedience surprised him so, he stared at her a moment before speaking. Maybe she *was* ill. "Whitecloaks don't need much, Master al'Seen. If you don't bow and scrape and walk wide of them, you must be a Darkfriend. If you don't say what they want, think what they want, you must be a Darkfriend. I don't know why they think Rand and Mat are." That was the simple truth. If the Whitecloaks knew Rand was the Dragon Reborn, that would be enough for them, but there was no way they could know. Mat confused him entirely. It had to be Fain's work. "Myself, I killed some of them." For a wonder, the gasps that rounded the room did not make him cringe inside, and neither did the thought of what he had done. "They killed a friend of mine and would have killed me. I didn't see my way clear to let them. That's the short of it."

"I can see where you wouldn't," Jac said slowly. Even with Trollocs about, Two Rivers people were not used to killing. Some years ago a woman had murdered her husband because she wanted another man to marry her; that was the last time anybody had died of violence in the Two Rivers that Perrin knew. Until the Trollocs.

"The Children of the Light," Verin said, "are very good at one thing. Making people who have been neighbors all their lives suspicious of each other." All the farm folk looked at her, some nodding after a moment.

"They have a man with them, I hear," Perrin said. "Padan Fain. The peddler."

"I've heard," Jac said. "I hear he calls himself by some other name nowadays."

Perrin nodded. "Ordeith. But Fain or Ordeith, he *is* a Darkfriend. He admitted as much, admitted to bringing the Trollocs on Winternight last year. And he rides with the Whitecloaks."

"That's very easy for you to claim," Adine Lewin said sharply. "You can name anybody Darkfriend."

"So who do you believe?" Tomas said. "Those who came a few weeks ago, arrested people you know, and burned their farms? Or a young man who grew up right here?"

"I am no Darkfriend, Master al'Seen," Perrin said, "but if you want me to go, I will."

"No," Elisa said quickly, shooting her husband a meaningful glance. And Adine a freezing one that made her swallow what she had been about to say. "No. You are welcome to stay here as long as you like." Jac hesitated, then nodded agreement. She came over and looked down at Perrin, resting her hands on his shoulders. "You have our sympathy," she said softly. "Your father was a good man. Your mother was my friend, and a fine woman. I know she'd want you to stay with us, Perrin. The Children seldom come this way, and if they do, the boys on the roof will give us plenty of warning to get you into the attic. You will be safe here."

She meant it. She actually meant it. And when Perrin looked at Master al'Seen, he nodded again. "Thank you," Perrin said, his throat tight. "But I have . . . things to do. Things I have to take care of."

She sighed, patting him gently. "Of course. Just you be sure those things don't get you . . . hurt. Well, at least I can send you off with a full belly."

There were not enough tables in the house to seat everyone for the midday meal, so bowls of lamb stew were handed out with chunks of crusty bread and admonitions not to drip, and everyone ate where they sat or stood. Before they were done eating, a lanky boy with his wrists sticking out of his sleeves and a bow taller than he was came bounding in. Perrin thought he was Win Lewin, but he could not be sure; boys grew fast at that age. "It's Lord Luc," the skinny boy exclaimed excitedly. "Lord Luc is coming."

CHAPTER
33

A New Weave in the Pattern

The lord himself followed almost on the boy's heels, a tall, broad-shouldered man in his middle years, with a hard, angular face and dark reddish hair white-winged at the temples. There was an arrogant cast to his dark blue eyes, and he certainly looked every inch a nobleman, in a finely cut green coat discreetly embroidered in golden scrolls down the sleeves and gauntlets worked in thread-of-gold. Gold-work wrapped his sword scabbard, as well, and banded the tops of his polished boots. Somehow he made the simple act of striding in through the doorway grand. Perrin despised him on sight.

All the al'Seens and Lewins rushed in a mass to greet the lord, men, women and children crowding around him with smiles and bows and curtsies, babbling all over one another about the honor of his presence, the great honor of a visit from a Hunter for the Horn. They seemed most excited about that. A lord under the same roof might be exciting, but one of those sworn to search for the legendary Horn of Valere—that was the stuff of stories. Perrin did not think he had ever seen Two Rivers folk fawn over anybody, but these came close.

This Lord Luc took it as clearly no more than his due, perhaps less. And tiresome to put up with, at that. The farm folk did not seem to see, or maybe they just did not recognize that slightly weary expression, the slightly condescending smile. Maybe they simply thought that was how lords behaved. True enough, a good many did, but it irked Perrin to watch these people—his people—put up with it.

As the hubbub began to diminish, Jac and Elisa presented their other guests—all but Tam and Abell, who had already met him—to Lord Luc of Chiendelna, saying that he was advising them in ways to defend themselves against the Trollocs, that he encouraged them to stand up to the Whitecloaks, stand up for themselves. Approving murmurs of agreement came from the rest of the room. If the Two Rivers had been choosing a king, Lord Luc would have had the al'Seens and Lewins behind him entire. He knew it, too. His apparent bored complacency did not last long, though.

At his first glimpse of Verin's smooth-cheeked face, Luc stiffened slightly, eyes flickering to her hands so quickly many would not have noticed. He very nearly dropped his embroidered gloves. Plump and plainly dressed, she might have been another farm wife, but clearly he knew an Aes Sedai's ageless face, when he saw one. He was not particularly happy to see one here. The corner of his left eye twitched as he listened to Mistress al'Seen name "Mistress Mathwin" "a scholar from outside."

Verin smiled at him as if half-asleep. "A pleasure," she murmured. "House Chiendelna. Where is that? It has a Borderland sound."

"Nothing so grand," Luc replied quickly, giving her a wary, fractional bow. "Murandy, actually. A minor house, but old." He seemed uneasy about taking his eyes from her for the rest of the introductions.

Tomas he barely glanced at. He had to know him for "Mistress Mathwin's" Warder, yet dismissed him out of hand as clearly as if he had shouted it. That was purely strange. However good Luc was with that sword, no one was good enough to dismiss a Warder. Arrogance. The fellow had enough for ten men. He proved it with Faile so far as Perrin was concerned.

The smile Luc offered her was certainly more than self-assured; it was also familiar and decidedly warm. In fact, it was too admiring and too warm by half. He took her hand in both of his to bow over, and peered into her eyes as if trying to see through the back of her head. For an instant Perrin thought she was about to look over at him, but instead she returned the lord's stare with a red-cheeked pretense to coolness and a slight bow of her head.

"I, too, am a Hunter for the Horn, my Lord," she said, sounding a touch breathless. "Do you think to find it here?"

Luc blinked and released her hand. "Perhaps, my Lady. Who can say where the Horn might be?" Faile looked a little surprised—maybe disappointed—at his sudden loss of interest.

Perrin kept his expression neutral. If she wanted to smile at Wil al'Seen and blush at fool lords, she could. She could make an idiot of herself any way she wanted, gawking at every man who came along. So Luc wanted to know where the Horn of Valere was? It was hidden away in the White Tower, that was where. He was tempted to tell the man, just to make him grind his teeth in frustration.

If Luc had been surprised to find out who his other fellows in the al'Seen house were, his reaction to Perrin was peculiar to say the least. He gave a start at the sight of Perrin's face; shock flashed in his eyes. It was all gone in a moment, masked behind lordly haughtiness, except for a wild fluttering at the corner of one eye. The trouble was, it made no sense. It was not his yellow eyes that took Luc aback; he was sure of that. More as if the fellow knew him, somehow, and was surprised to see him here, but he had never met this Luc before in his life. More than that, he would have bet that Luc was afraid of him. No sense at all.

"Lord Luc is the one who suggested the boys go up on the rooftops," Jac said. "No Trolloc will get close without those lads giving warning."

"How much warning," Perrin said dryly. This was an example of the great Lord Luc's advice? "Trollocs see like cats in the dark. They'll be on top of you, kicking in the doors, before your boys raise a shout."

"We do what we can," Flann barked. "Stop trying to frighten us. There are children listening. Lord Luc at least offers helpful suggestions. He was at my place the day before the Trollocs came, seeing I had everybody placed properly. Blood and ashes! If not for him, the Trollocs would have killed us all."

Luc did not seem to hear the praise offered him. He was watching Perrin cautiously while fussing with his gauntlets, tucking them behind the golden wolf's-head buckle of his sword belt. Faile was watching him, too, with a slight frown. He ignored her.

"I thought it was Whitecloaks saved you, Master Lewin. I thought a Whitecloak patrol arrived in the nick of time and drove the Trollocs off."

"Well, they did." Flann scrubbed a hand through his gray hair. "But Lord Luc. . . . If the Whitecloaks hadn't come, we could have. . . . At least he doesn't try to frighten us," he muttered.

"So he doesn't frighten you," Perrin said. "Trollocs frighten me. And the Whitecloaks keep the Trollocs back for you. When they can."

"You want to credit the Whitecloaks?" Luc fixed Perrin with a cold stare, as if pouncing on a weakness. "Who do you think is responsible for the Dragon's Fang scribbled on people's doors? Oh, their hands never hold charcoal, but they are behind it. They stalk into these good people's homes, asking questions and demanding answers as if it were their own roof overhead. I say these people are their own masters, not dogs for the Whitecloaks to call to heel. Let them patrol the country-side—well and good—but meet them at the door and tell them whose land they are on. That is what I say. If you want to be a Whitecloak dog, be so, but do not begrudge these good people their freedom."

Perrin met Luc's eyes stare for stare. "I hold no affection for Whitecloaks. They want to hang me, or hadn't you heard?"

The tall lord blinked as though he had not, or maybe had forgotten in his eagerness to spring. "Exactly what is it you do propose, then?"

Perrin turned his back on the man and went to stand in front of the fireplace. He did not mean to argue with Luc. Let everyone listen. They were certainly all looking at him. He would say what he thought and be done with it. "You have to depend on the Whitecloaks, have to hope they'll keep the Trollocs down, hope they'll come in time if the Trollocs attack. Why? Because every man tries to hang on to his farm, if he can, or to stay as close to it as possible if he can't. You're in a hundred little clusters, like grapes ripe for picking. As long as you are, as long as you have to pray the Whitecloaks can keep the Trollocs from stomping you into wine, you've no choice but to let them ask any questions they want, demand any answers they want. You have to stand by and watch innocent people hauled off. Or does anyone here think Haral and Alsbet Luhhan are Darkfriends? Natti Cauthon? Bodewhin and Eldrin?" Abell's stare around the room dared anyone to hint at a yes, but there was no need. Even Adine Lewin's attention was on Per-rin. Luc frowned at him between studying the reactions of the people crowding the room.

"I know they shouldn't have arrested Natti and Alsbet and all," Wit said, "but that's over." He rubbed a hand across his bald head, and gave Abell a troubled look. "Except for getting them to let everybody go, I mean. They haven't arrested anyone since that I've heard."

"You think that means it's done?" Perrin said. "Do you really think they'll be satisfied with the Cauthons and the Luhhans? With two farms burned? Which of you will be next? Maybe because you said the wrong thing, or just to make an example. It could be Whitecloaks putting a torch to this house instead of Trollocs. Or maybe it'll be the Dragon's Fang scrawled on your door some night. There are always folk who believe that kind of thing." A number of eyes darted to Adine, who shifted her feet and hunched her shoulders. "Even if all it means is having to tug your forelock to every Whitecloak who comes along, do you want to live that way? Your children? You're at the mercy of the Trollocs, the mercy of the Whitecloaks, and the mercy of anybody with a grudge. As long as one has a hold on you, all three do. You're hiding in the cellar, hoping one rabid dog will protect you from another, hoping the rats don't sneak out in the dark and bite you."

Jac exchanged worried looks with Flann and Wit, with the other men in the room, then said slowly, "If you think we're doing wrong, what is it you suggest?"

Perrin was not expecting the question—he had been sure they would get angry—but he went right on telling them what he thought. "Gather your people. Gather your sheep and your cows, your chickens, everything. Gather them up and take them where they might be safe. Go to Emond's Field. Or Watch Hill, since it's closer, though that will put you right under the Whitecloaks' eyes. As long as it's twenty people here and fifty there, you are game for Trolloc taking. If there are hundreds of you together, you have a chance, and one that doesn't depend on bowing your necks for the Whitecloaks." That brought the explosion he expected.

"Abandon my farm completely!" Flann shouted right on top of Wit's "You're mad!" Words poured out on top of one another, from them, and from brothers and cousins.

"Go off to Emond's Field? I'm too far away to do more than check the fields every day right now!"

"The weeds will take everything!"

"I don't know how I'm going to harvest as it is!"

". . . if the rains come . . . !"

". . . trying to rebuild . . . !"

". . . tabac will rot . . . !"

". . . have to leave the clip . . . !"

Perrin's fist smacking the lintel of the fireplace cut them short. "I haven't seen a field trampled or fired, or a house or barn burned, unless there were people there. It's people the Trollocs come for. And if they burn it anyway? A new crop can be planted. Stone and mortar and wood can be rebuilt. Can you rebuild that?" He pointed at Laila's baby, and she clutched the child to her breast, glaring at him as though he had threatened the babe himself. The looks she gave her husband and Flann were frightened, though. An uneasy murmur rose.

"Leave," Jac muttered, shaking his head. "I don't know, Perrin."

"It is your choice, Master al'Seen. The land will still be here when you come back. Trollocs can't carry that off. Think whether the same can be said for your family."

The murmur grew to a buzz. A number of women were confronting their husbands, mostly those with a child or two in tow. None of the men seemed to be arguing.

"An interesting plan," Luc said, studying Perrin. From his face there was no telling whether he approved of it. "I shall watch to see how it turns out. And now, Master al'Seen, I must be on my way. I only stopped to see how you were doing." Jac and Elisa saw him to the door, but the others were too busy with their own discussions to pay much attention. Luc left tight-mouthed. Perrin had the feeling his departures were usually as grand as his arrivals.

Jac came straight from the door to Perrin. "It's a bold plan you have. I will admit I'm not keen on abandoning my farm, but you talk sense. I don't know what the Children will make of it, though. They seem a suspicious lot, to me. They might think we're all plotting something against them if we gather together."

"Let them think it," Perrin said. "A village full of people can take Luc's advice and tell them to be about their business elsewhere. Or do you think it's better to stay vulnerable just to hold the Whitecloaks' goodwill, such as it is?"

"No. No, I see your point. You've convinced me. And everybody else, too, it seems."

It did appear to be true. The murmur of discussion was dying down, but only because everyone looked to be in agreement. Even Adine, who was marshaling her daughters with loud orders for packing immediately. She actually gave Perrin a grudgingly approving nod.

"When do you mean to go?" Perrin asked Jac.

"As soon as I can get everybody ready. We can make Jon Gaelin's place on the North Road before sunset. I'll tell Jon what you say, and everybody down to Emond's Field. Better there than Watch Hill. If we mean to be out from under the Whitecloaks' thumb as well as the Trollocs', best not to sit under their noses." Jac scratched his narrow fringe of hair with one finger. "Perrin, I don't think the Children would actually hurt Natti Cauthon and the girls, or the Luhhans, but it worries me. If they do think we're plotting, who's to say?"

"I mean to get them free as soon as I can, Master al'Seen. And anybody else the Whitecloaks arrest, for that matter."

"A bold plan," Jac repeated. "Well, I had better get people moving if I'm going to have us to Jon's by sundown. Go with the Light, Perrin."

"A very bold plan," Verin said, coming up as Master al'Seen hurried off calling orders for wagons to be hauled out and people to pack what they could carry. She studied Perrin interestedly, head tilted to one side, but no less so than Faile, at her side. Faile looked as though she had never seen him before.

"I don't know why everybody keeps calling it that," he said. "A plan, I mean. That Luc was talking nonsense. Defying Whitecloaks in the door. Boys on the roof to watch for Trollocs. A couple of open gates to disaster. All I did was point it out. They should have been doing this from the start. That man. . . ." He stopped himself from saying Luc irritated him. Not with Faile there. She might misunderstand.

"Of course," Verin said smoothly. "I have not had the opportunity to see it work before this. Or perhaps I have and did not know it."

"What are you talking about? See what work?"

"Perrin, when we arrived these people were ready to hold on here at all costs. You gave them good sense and strong emotion, but do you think the same from me would have shifted them, or from Tam, or Abell? Of any of us, you should know how stubborn Two Rivers people can be. You have altered the course events would have followed in the Two Rivers without you. With a few words spoken in . . . irritation? *Ta'veren* truly do pull other people's lives into their own pattern. Fascinating. I do hope I have an opportunity to observe Rand again."

"Whatever it is," Perrin muttered, "it's to the good. The more people together in one place, the safer."

"Of course. Rand does have the sword, I take it?"

He frowned, but there was no reason not to tell her. She knew about Rand, and she knew what Tear had to mean. "He does."

"Watch yourself with Alanna, Perrin."

"What?" The Aes Sedai's quick changes of topic were beginning to confuse him. Especially when she started telling him to do what he had already thought of, and thought to keep secret from her. "Why?"

Verin's face did not change, but her dark eyes were suddenly bird bright and sharp. "There are many . . . designs in the White Tower. Not all are malignant, by far, but sometimes it is difficult to say until it is too late. And even the most benevolent often allow for a few threads snapped in the weaving, a few reeds broken and discarded in making a basket. A *ta'veren* would make a useful reed in any number of possible plans." Just as suddenly she was looking a little confused by the bustle around her, more at home in a book or her own thoughts than in the real world. "Oh, my. Master al'Seen is not wasting any time, is he? I'll just see if he can spare someone to fetch our horses."

Faile shivered as the Brown sister moved away. "Sometimes Aes Sedai make me . . . uneasy," she murmured.

"Uneasy?" Perrin said. "Most of the time they scare me half to death."

She laughed softly and began playing with a button on his coat, peering at it intently. "Perrin, I . . . have . . . been a fool."

"What do you mean?" She glanced up at him—she was about to twist the button right off—and he hastily added, "You are one of the least foolish people I know." He clamped his teeth shut before he could add "most of the time," and was glad he had when she smiled.

"That is very nice of you to say, but I was." She patted the coat button and began adjusting his coat—which it did not need—and smoothing his lapels—which they did not need. "You were so silly," she said, speaking too fast, "just because that young man looked at me— really, he is much too boyish; not at all like you—that I thought I would make you jealous—just a little—by pretending—just pretending—to be attracted to Lord Luc. I should not have done it. Will you forgive me?"

He tried to sort through the jumbled words. It was good she thought Wil was boyish—if he tried to grow a beard it would probably be strag- gly—but she had not mentioned the way she returned Wil's look. And if she had been pretending to be attracted to Luc, why had she blushed that way? "Of course I forgive you," he said. A dangerous light ap- peared in her eyes. "I mean, there's nothing to forgive." If anything, the light sparkled hotter. What did she want him to say? "Will you forgive me? When I was trying to chase you away, I said things I shouldn't have. Will you forgive me that?"

"You *said* some things that need forgiving?" she said sweetly, and he knew he was in trouble. "I cannot think what, but I will take it into consideration."

Into consideration? She sounded very much the noblewoman there; maybe her father worked for some lord, so she could study the way ladies talked. He had no idea what she meant. Whenever he found out would be too soon, he was certain.

It was a relief to climb back into Stepper's saddle amid the confusion of wagon teams being hitched and people arguing over what they could or could not take and children chasing down chickens and geese and tying their feet for loading. Boys were already driving the cattle east- ward, and others herding the sheep out of the cote.

Faile made no reference to what had been said inside. Indeed, she smiled at him, and compared the keeping of sheep here to in Saldaea, and when one of the girls brought her a bunch of small red flowers, heartsblush, she tried to thread some of them into his beard, laughing at his efforts to stop her. In short, she had him jumping out of his skin. He needed another talk with Master Cauthon.

"Go with the Light," Master al'Seen told him again just as they were ready to ride out, "and look after the boys."

Four of the young men had decided to go with them, on rough-coated horses not nearly as good as those Tam and Abell rode. Perrin was not sure why he was the one who was supposed to look after them. They were all older than he, if not by much. Wil al'Seen was one, with his cousin Ban, one of Jac's sons, who had gotten all the nose in that family, and a pair of the Lewins, Tell and Dannil, who looked so much like Flann that they could have been his sons instead of his nephews. Perrin had tried to talk them out of it, especially when they all made it plain that they wanted to help rescue the Cauthons and the Luhhans from the Whitecloaks. They seemed to think it was a matter of riding into the Children's camp and demanding everybody's return. Casting down our defiance, Tell called it, which nearly made Perrin's hair stand on end. Too many gleeman's tales. Too much listening to fools like Luc. He suspected that Wil had another reason, though he tried to pretend Faile did not exist, but the others were bad enough.

No one else made any objections. Tam and Abell only seemed concerned that they all knew how to use the bows they carried and could stay on a horse, and Verin merely observed, making notes in her little book. Tomas looked amused, and Faile busied herself plaiting a crown from the heartsblush, which turned out to be for Perrin. Sighing, he draped the flowers across the pommel of his saddle. "I will take care of them the best I can, Master al'Seen," he promised.

A mile from the al'Seen farm, he thought he might lose one or two right there, when Gaul and Bain and Chiad suddenly appeared out of a thicket, loping to join them. Lose them to Aiel spears. Wil and his friends took one look at the Aiel and hastily began nocking arrows; without breaking stride the Aiel had spears ready to cast and their faces veiled. It took some minutes to straighten out. Gaul and the two Maidens seemed to think it a huge joke when they understood, laughing uproariously, and that unsettled the Lewins and al'Seens as much as finding out that the three were Aiel, and two of them women. Wil essayed a smile at Bain and Chiad, and they exchanged looks and brief nods. Perrin did not know what was going on there, but he decided to let it alone unless Wil looked to get his throat cut. Time enough to stop it if one of the Aiel women actually took her knife out. Might teach Wil a thing or two about smiling.

He intended that they should push on to Watch Hill as quickly as they could, but a mile or so north of the al'Seen place he saw one of the farms that produced those scattered plumes of chimney smoke. Tam was keeping them far enough away that the people around the farmhouse were only shapes. Except to Perrin's eyes; he could see children in the yard. And Jac al'Seen was the nearest neighbor. Had been, until today. He hesitated, then reined Stepper toward the farm. Not that it was likely to do any good, but he had to try.

"What are you doing?" Tam asked, frowning.

"Giving them the same advice I gave Master al'Seen. It won't take a minute."

Tam nodded, and the others turned with him. Verin was studying Perrin thoughtfully. The Aiel peeled away short of the farm to wait to the north, Gaul running a little apart from the Maidens.

Perrin did not know the Torfinns nor they him, yet to his surprise, once the excitement of strangers was past, the staring at Tomas and Verin and Faile, they listened and began hitching horses to two wagons and a pair of high-wheeled carts before he and the others rode on.

Three more times he stopped when their route took them near to farmhouses, once at a cluster of five close together. It was always the same. The people protested they could not just leave their farms, but each time he left behind a bustle of packing and a gathering of farm animals.

Something else happened, too. He could not stop Wil and his cousin, or the Lewins, from talking with the young men on the farms. Their party grew by thirteen, Torfinns and al'Dais, Ahans and Marwins, armed with bows and riding an ill-matched assortment of ponies and plow horses, all eager to rescue the prisoners from the Whitecloaks.

It was not as smooth as that, of course. Wil and the others from the al'Seen farm thought it unfair that he warned the newcomers about the Aiel, spoiling the fun they hoped to have seeing them jump. They jumped more than enough to suit Perrin, and the way they peered at every bush, much less every stand of trees, made it clear that they thought there must be more Aiel about no matter what he said. At first Wil tried lording it over the Torfinns and the rest on the grounds that he had been the first to join Perrin—one of the first, at least, he admitted when Ban and the Lewins glared at him—while they were latecomers.

Perrin put an end to it by dividing them into two groups of about the same size and putting Dannil and Ban each in charge of one, though there was some grumbling over that, too, in the beginning. The al'Dais thought the leaders should be chosen according to age—Bili al'Dai being the eldest by a year—while others put forward Hu Marwin as the best tracker, and Jaim Torfinn as the best shot, while Kenley Ahan had been to Watch Hill often before the Whitecloaks came and would know his way around the village. They all seemed to think it a lark. Tell's phrase about casting defiance was repeated more than once.

Finally Perrin rounded on them in cold anger, forcing everyone to halt in the grass between two copses. "This is not a game, and it isn't a Bel Tine dance. You do what you're told, or else go back home. I don't know what use you are anyway, and I've no intention of getting killed because you think you know what you are doing. Now line up and shut up. You sound like the Women's Circle meeting in a wardrobe."

They did it, stringing themselves out in two columns behind Ban and Dannil. Wil and Bili wore disgruntled frowns, but they held whatever objections they had. Faile gave Perrin an approving nod, and so did Tomas. Verin watched it all with a smooth, unreadable face, no doubt thinking she was seeing a *ta'veren* at work. Perrin saw no need to tell her he had just tried to think of what a Shienaran he knew, a soldier named Uno, would have said, though no doubt Uno would have put it in harsher words.

Farms began to appear more frequently as they approached Watch Hill, coming in clumps closer together until they ran on continuously the way they did near Emond's Field, a patchwork of hedged or stone-walled fields separated by narrow lanes, footways and wagon paths. Even with their pauses at the four farms, there was still some daylight left, still men working their crops, and boys driving sheep and cattle in from pasture for the night. No one would be leaving their animals out these days.

Tam suggested Perrin cease warning people, and he reluctantly agreed. They would all head for Watch Hill here, alerting the Whitecloaks. Twenty-odd people riding together by the back ways attracted enough eyes, though most people appeared too busy to do more than glance. It would have to be done sooner or later, though, and the sooner the better. So long as people remained in the countryside, needing Whitecloak protection, then the Whitecloaks had a foothold in the Two Rivers they might not want to give up.

Perrin kept a sharp eye out for any sign of Whitecloak patrols, but except for one dust cloud over toward the North Road, heading south, he saw none. After a time Tam suggested they dismount and lead their horses. Afoot there was less chance of being spotted, and the hedges and even the low stone walls shielded them a little.

Tam and Abell knew a thicket that gave a good view of the Whitecloak camp, a tangle of oak and sourgum and leatherleaf that covered three or four hides little more than a mile south and west of Watch Hill over an open stretch of ground. They entered from the south, hurrying. Perrin hoped no one had seen them go in, no one to wonder why they did not come out and comment on it.

"Stay here," he told Wil and the other young men while they were tying their horses to branches. "Keep your bows handy, and be ready to run if you hear a shout. But don't move unless you hear me shout. And if anybody makes any noise, I'll pound his head like an anvil. We're here to look, not pull the Whitecloaks down on us by tramping around like blind bulls." Fingering their bows nervously, they nodded. Perhaps it was beginning to dawn on them just what they were doing. The Children of the Light might not take kindly to finding Two Rivers folk riding about in an armed bunch.

"Were you ever a soldier?" Faile asked quizzically in a low voice. "Some of my father's . . . guards talk that way."

"I'm a blacksmith." Perrin laughed. "I've just heard soldiers talk. It seems to work, though." Even Wil and Bili were peering about uneasily and hardly daring to move.

Creeping from tree to tree, he and Faile followed Tam and Abell to where the Aiel were already crouching near the thicket's north edge. Verin was there, too, and Tomas, of course. The brush made a thin screen of leaves, enough to hide them but no hindrance to observation.

The Whitecloak encampment stretched out at the foot of Watch Hill like a village itself. Hundreds of men, some armored, moved among long, straight rows of white tents, with lines of horses, five deep, staked out to east and west. Animals being unsaddled and curried indicated patrols finishing their day, while a double column of maybe a hundred mounted men, pristine and precise, trailed off toward the Waterwood at a brisk walk, lances all at the same angle. At intervals around the encampment white-cloaked guards marched up and down, lances shouldered like spears, burnished helmets flashing in the sinking sun.

A rumble came to Perrin's ears. Well to the west twenty horsemen appeared, galloping from the direction of Emond's Field, hurrying toward the tents. From the direction he and the others had come. A few minutes slower, and they would have been seen for sure. A horn sounded, and men began moving to the cook fires.

Off to one side lay a much smaller camp, its tents set haphazardly. Some sagged against their guy ropes. Whoever stayed there, most were gone now. Only a few horses flicking their tails against flies along a short picket rope indicated that anyone was there at all. Not Whitecloaks. The Children of the Light were too rigidly tidy for that camp.

Between the thicket and the two sets of tents was an expanse of grass and wildflowers. Very likely the local farmers used to use it for pasture. Not now, however. It was fairly flat ground. Whitecloaks galloping like that patrol could cover it in a minute.

Abell directed Perrin's attention to the large camp. "You see that tent near the middle, with a man standing watch at either end? Can you make it out?" Perrin nodded. The low sun was slanting sharp shadows eastward, but he could see well enough. "That's where Natti and the girls are. And the Luhhans. I've seen them come out and go in. One at a time, and always with a guard, even to the latrines."

"We have tried to sneak in at night three times," Tam said, "but they keep a tight watch over the perimeter of the camp. We barely got away the last time."

It would be like trying to stick your hand into an anthill without being stung. Perrin sat down at the base of a tall leatherleaf with his bow across his knees. "I want to think on this awhile. Master al'Thor, would you settle Wil and that lot down? See none of them takes it into his head to run for home. Like as not they'd ride straight for the North Road, not thinking, and we'd have half a hundred of those Whitecloaks over here to investigate. If any of them thought to bring food, you could see they get something to eat. If we have to run, we may spend the rest of the night in the saddle."

Abruptly he realized he was giving orders, but when he tried to apologize, Tam grinned and said, "Perrin, you took charge back at Jac's place. This isn't the first time I've followed a younger man who could see what had to be done."

"You are doing good, Perrin," Abell said before the two older men slipped back into the trees.

Perplexed, Perrin scratched his beard. He had taken charge? Now that he thought of it, neither Tam nor Abell had really made a decision since leaving the al'Seen farm, only offered suggestions and left it to him. Neither had called him "lad" since then, either.

"Interesting," Verin said. She had her small book out. He wished he could have a chance to read what she had written.

"You going to caution me about being foolish again?" he said.

Instead of answering, she said in a meditative voice, "It will be even more interesting to see what you do next. I cannot say you are shifting the world on its foundations, as Rand al'Thor is, but the Two Rivers is surely moving. I wonder if you have a clue as to where you are moving it."

"I mean to free the Luhhans and the Cauthons," he told her angrily. "That's all!" Except for the Trollocs. He let his head drop back against the bole of the leatherleaf and closed his eyes. "All I'm doing is what I have to do. The Two Rivers will stay right where it always has."

"Of course," Verin said.

He heard her moving away, her and Tomas, slipper and boots alike soft on ground strewn with last year's leaves. He opened his eyes. Faile was staring after the pair, and not best pleased.

"She will not leave you alone," she muttered. The plaited crown of heartsblush he had left on his saddle dangled from her hand.

"Aes Sedai never do," he told her.

She turned on him with a challenging look. "I suppose you mean to try bringing them out tonight?"

It had to be done now. Because he had been passing his warning about, and folks knew who had told them. Maybe the Whitecloaks would not hurt their prisoners. Maybe. He trusted Whitecloak mercy as far as he could throw a horse. He glanced at Gaul, who nodded.

"Tam al'Thor and Abell Cauthon move well for wetlanders, but these Whitecloaks are too stiff to see everything that moves in the dark, I think. I think they expect their enemies to come in numbers, and where they can be seen."

Chiad turned amused gray eyes on the Aielman. "Do you mean to move like wind then, Stone Dog? It will be diverting to see a Stone Dog try to move lightly. When my spear-sister and I have rescued the prisoners, perhaps we will go back for you, if you are too old to find your own way." Bain touched her arm, and she looked at the flame-haired woman in surprise. After a moment, she flushed slightly under her tan. Both women shifted their eyes to Faile, who was still watching Perrin, her head up and her arms crossed now.

He took a long breath. If he told her he did not want her to come, Bain and Chiad almost certainly would not, either. They were still making a point of being with her, not him. Maybe Faile was, too. Perhaps he and Gaul could do it alone, but he could not see how to make her stay if she did not want to. Faile being Faile, she would just as likely sneak after them. "You will stay close to me," he said firmly. "I want to rescue prisoners, not leave another behind."

Laughing, she dropped down beside him, snuggling her shoulder under his arm. "Staying close to you sounds a fine idea." She flipped the crown of red flowers onto his head, and Bain chuckled.

He rolled his eyes up; he could just see the edge of the thing hanging over his forehead. He must look a fool. He left it there, though.

The sun slid down as slowly as a bead in honey. Abell brought some bread and cheese—over half those would-be heroes had not brought anything to eat after all—and they ate and waited. Night came, lit by a moon already high but obscured by scurrying clouds. Perrin waited. Lights vanished in the Whitecloak camp, and in Watch Hill, too, leaving a sprinkling of glowing windows across the otherwise dark mound, and he gathered Tam and Faile and the Aiel around him. Everyone's face was clear, to him. Verin stood close enough to listen. Abell and Tomas were with the other Two Rivers folk, keeping them quiet.

He felt a little odd giving instructions, so kept them simple. Tam was to have everyone ready to ride the moment Perrin returned with the prisoners. The Whitecloaks would be after them as soon as they discovered what was up, so a place to hide was needed. Tam knew one, an empty farmhouse in the edge of the Westwood.

"Try not to kill anybody, if you can manage it," Perrin cautioned the Aiel. "The Whitecloaks will be hot enough at losing their prisoners. They'll set the sun afire if they lose men, too." Gaul and the Maidens nodded as if they looked forward to it. Strange people. They vanished into the night.

"Have a care," Verin told him softly as he slung his bow across his back. "*Ta'veren* does not mean immortal."

"Tomas might be a help, you know."

"Do you think one more would make a difference?" she said musingly. "Besides, I have other uses for him."

Shaking his head, he moved out from the thicket, going to elbows and knees, almost flat to the ground, as soon as he was beyond the brush. Faile imitated him at his side. The grass and wildflowers stood high enough to screen them. He was glad she could not see his face. He was desperately afraid. Not for himself, but if anything happened to her. . . .

Like two more shifting moonshadows they crawled across the open ground, stopping at Perrin's signal about ten paces from where guards paced up and down, cloaks gleaming in the moonlight, a little way out from the first row of tents. Two came face-to-face almost in front of them, stomping to a halt.

"All is well with the night," one announced. "The Light illumine us, and protect us from the Shadow."

"All is well with the night," the other replied. "The Light illumine us, and protect us from the Shadow."

Turning on their heels, they marched away, looking neither left nor right.

Perrin let each take a dozen paces, then touched Faile's shoulder and rose, barely letting himself breathe. He could hardly hear her breathing, either. Almost tiptoeing, they hurried in among the tents, dropping low again as soon as they were past the first. Men snored inside, or muttered in their sleep. Except for that, the camp was silent. The tramp of the guards' boots was plainly audible. The smell of doused cook fires hung in the air, the scents of canvas and horses and men.

Silently he motioned for Faile to follow him. Tent ropes made snares for unwary feet in the darkness. They were clear to him, though, and he wove a path through for them.

He had the location of the prisoners' tent marked in his head, and he started toward it cautiously. Near the center of the camp. A long way there, and a long way back.

The crunch of boots on the ground and a grunt from Faile spun him around just in time to be knocked down by the rush of a big shape in a white cloak, a man as thick as Master Luhhan himself. Iron fingers dug into his throat as the two of them rolled. Perrin seized the man's chin with one hand, forcing his head back, trying to push him off. Prying at the grip on his throat, he pounded at the fellow's ribs with his fist, producing grunts and no other effect he could tell. Blood roared in his ears; his vision narrowed, black creeping in from the sides. He fumbled for his axe, but his fingers felt numb.

Suddenly the man jerked and collapsed atop him. Perrin pushed the limp form off himself and drew in deep lungfuls of sweet night air.

Faile tossed aside a chunk of firewood and rubbed the side of her head. "He did not think I was worth worrying about, beyond knocking down," she whispered.

"A fool," Perrin whispered back. "But a strong one." He was going to have the feel of those fingers at his neck for days. "Are you all right?"

"Of course. I am not a porcelain figurine."

He supposed she was not, at that.

Hastily dragging the unconscious man up against the side of a tent where he hoped no one would find him soon, he stripped off the fellow's white cloak and bound his hands and feet with spare bowstrings. A kerchief found in the fellow's pocket served for a gag. Not very clean, but that was his own fault. Lifting his bow over his head, Perrin settled the cloak around his shoulders. If anyone else saw them, maybe they would mistake him for one of their own. The cloak had a golden knot of rank beneath the flaring sunburst. An officer. Even better.

He walked between the tents openly now, and quickly. Hidden or not, that fellow could be found any moment and the alarm raised. Faile scudded along beside him like his shadow, scanning the camp for signs of life as alertly as he did. Shifting moonshadows obscured the spaces between the tents even for his eyes.

Approaching the prison tent, he slowed, so as not to excite the guards; a white-cloaked man stood at this end, and the gleaming lance point of another rose above the tent's peaked roof.

Suddenly that lance point vanished. There was no sound. It simply fell.

A heartbeat later, two patches of darkness abruptly became veiled Aiel, neither tall enough for Gaul. Before the guard could move, one of them leaped into the air, kicking him in the face. He staggered to his knees, and the other Maiden spun, adding her own kick. The guard dropped bonelessly. Crouching, the Maidens looked around, spears ready, to see if they had roused anyone.

At the sight of Perrin in a white cloak, they nearly went for him, until they saw Faile. One shook her head and whispered to the other, who appeared to laugh silently.

Perrin told himself he should not feel disgruntled, but first Faile saved him from being strangled, and now she saved him from a spear through his liver. For somebody who was supposedly leading a rescue, he was making a fine showing so far.

Tossing the tent flap aside, he put his head into the interior, which was even darker than outside. Master Luhhan lay asleep across the tent's entrance, with the women huddled together toward the back. Perrin put a hand over Haral Luhhan's mouth and, when his eyes popped open, laid a finger across his own lips. "Wake the others," Perrin said in a low voice. "Quietly. We are taking you out of here." Recognition dawned in Master Luhhan's eyes, and he nodded.

Backing out of the tent, Perrin stripped the cloak from the downed guard. The man was still breathing—hoarsely, and bubbling through a thoroughly broken nose—but being manhandled did not wake him. They had to hurry now. Gaul was there, with the cloak from the other guard. The three Aiel watched the other tents cautiously. Faile practically danced with impatience.

When Master Luhhan brought his wife and the other women out, all of them peering about nervously in the moonlight, Perrin hurriedly put one of the cloaks around the blacksmith. It was a poor fit—Haral Luhhan seemed to be made from tree trunks—but it had to do. The other went around Alsbet Luhhan. She was not so large as her husband, but still as big as most men. Her round face looked surprised at first, but then she nodded; pulling the fallen guard's conical helmet from his head, she stuck it on her own, squashing it down atop her thick braid. The two guards they bound and gagged with strips of blanket and laid inside the tent.

Sneaking out again the way they had come in was impossible; Perrin had known that from the start. Even if Master and Mistress Luhhan could have moved quietly enough—which he doubted—Bode and Eldrin were clinging to each other in shocked disbelief at rescue. Only their mother's soft murmurs kept them from breaking into relieved tears already. He had planned for it. Horses were needed, both for a quick burst of speed away from the camp and to carry everyone afterward. There were horses at the picket lines.

The Aiel ghosting ahead, he followed behind with Faile and the Cauthons behind, Haral and Alsbet bringing up the rear. To a casual glance, at least, they looked to be like three Whitecloaks escorting four women.

The picketed horses were guarded, but only on the side away from the tents. After all, why guard them from the men who rode them? It certainly made Perrin's job easier. They simply walked up to the line of horses nearest the tents, each secured by a simple rope hackamore, and untied one apiece, except for the Aiel. The hardest part was getting Mistress Luhhan up barebacked; it took Perrin and Master Luhhan both, and she kept trying to push her skirts down to cover her knees. Natti and her girls scrambled up easily, and Faile, of course. The guards supposedly watching the horses continued their measured rounds, calling to each other about all being well with the night.

"When I give the word," Perrin began, and someone in the camp shouted, then again, more loudly; a horn sounded, and shouting men poured out of the tents. Whether they had found the prisoners gone, or the unconscious man who had attacked him, it made no difference. "Follow me!" Perrin cried, digging his heels into the dark gelding he had chosen. "Ride!"

It was a madcap rush, but he tried to keep an eye on everyone. Master Luhhan was almost as bad a rider as his wife, the pair of them bouncing around, nearly falling as their horses ran. Either Bode or Eldrin was screaming at the top of her lungs, from excitement or terror. Luckily the guards were not expecting trouble from inside the camp. One white-cloaked man peering into the darkness turned just in time to throw himself out of the way of the charging horses with a cry almost as shrill as the Cauthon girl's. More horns bayed behind them, and shouts with the definite sound of orders hammered the night, well before they reached the cover of the thicket. Not that it was much cover now.

Tam had everyone mounted, as Perrin had asked. Or ordered. He swung straight from the gelding to Stepper. Verin and Tomas were the only ones not all but jumping up and down in their saddles; their horses were the only ones not dancing with their riders' nervousness. Abell was trying to hug his wife and daughters all three at the same time, all of them laughing and crying. Master Luhhan was trying to shake every hand he could reach. Everybody except the Aiel, Verin and her Warder seemed to be offering everybody else congratulations, as though it were all done.

"Why, Perrin, it *is* you!" Mistress Luhhan exclaimed. Her round face looked peculiar under the helmet, sitting askew because of her braid. "What is that thing on your face, young man? I am more than grateful to you, but I will not have you at my table looking like a—"

"No time for that," he told her, ignoring the shock on her face. She was not a woman people cut off, but the Whitecloak horns were sounding something besides an alarm now, a short repetitive cry, sharp and insistent. An order of some kind. "Tam, Abell, take Master Luhhan and the women to that hiding place you know. Gaul, you go with them. And Faile." That would add Bain and Chiad. "And Hu and Haim." That should be enough to be safe. "Move quietly. Quiet is better than speed, for a little while anyway. But go now."

Those he named wound off westward with no argument, though Mistress Luhhan, holding her horse's mane with both hands, gave him a very level look. It was the lack of argument from Faile that stunned him, enough that it took him a moment to realize he had called Master al'Thor and Master Cauthon by their first names.

Verin and Tomas had stayed behind, and he eyed her sharply. "Any chance of a little help from you?"

"Not the way you mean, perhaps," she replied calmly, as though the Whitecloak camp were not in turmoil just a mile off. "My reasons are no different today than yesterday. But I think it might rain in . . . oh . . . half an hour. Maybe less. Quite a downpour, I expect."

Half an hour. Perrin grunted and turned to the remaining Two Rivers lads. Practically quivering with the desire to run, they held their bows in white-knuckled grips. He hoped they had all remembered to bring spare bowstrings, at least, since it was going to rain. "We," he told them, "are going to draw the Whitecloaks off so Mistress Cauthon and Mistress Luhhan and the rest can get away safely. We'll take them south along the North Road until we can lose them in the rain. If anyone wants out, he had best ride now." A few hands shifted on their reins, but they all sat their saddles looking at him. "All right, then. Shout like you've gone mad so they'll hear us. Shout until we reach the road."

Bellowing, he wheeled Stepper and galloped for the road. At first he was not really certain they would follow, but their wild howls drowned his roar and the thunder of their hooves. If the Whitecloaks did not hear that, they were deaf.

Not all of them stopped shouting when they reached the hard-packed dirt of the North Road and swung south at a dead run through the night. Some laughed and whooped. Perrin shrugged out of the white cloak and let it fall. The horns sounded again, a little fainter now.

"Perrin," Wil called, leaning forward on the neck of his horse, "what do we do now? What do we do next?"

"We hunt Trollocs!" Perrin shouted over his shoulder. From the way the laughter redoubled, he did not think they believed him. But he could feel Verin's eyes drilling into his back. She knew. Thunder in the night sky echoed the horses' hooves.

CHAPTER
34

He Who Comes With the Dawn

The dawn shadows shortened and paled as Rand and Mat jogged across the barren, still-dark valley floor, leaving fog-shrouded Rhuidean behind. The dry air hinted at heat to come, but the slight breeze actually felt cool to Rand, with no coat. That would not last; full blistering daylight would be on them soon enough. They hurried as best they could in the hope of beating it, but he did not think they would. Their best was not very fast.

Mat trotted in a pained shamble; a dark smear fanned across half his face, and his coat hung open, revealing his unlaced shirt stuck to his chest by more drying blood. Sometimes he gingerly touched the thick weal around his throat, nearly black now, growling under his breath, and he stumbled often, catching himself with the odd, black-hafted spear and clutching at his head. He did not complain, though, which was a bad sign. Mat was a great complainer at small discomforts; if he was silent now, it meant he was in real pain.

The old, half-healed wound in Rand's side felt as though something were boring into it, and the gashes on his face and head burned, yet lumbering along, half-hunched over his aching side, he hardly thought of his own hurts. He was all too conscious of the sun rising behind him, and the Aiel waiting on the bare mountainside ahead. There was water and shade up there, and help for Mat. The rising sun behind, and the Aiel ahead. Dawn and the Aiel.

He Who Comes With the Dawn. That Aes Sedai he had seen, or dreamed he had seen, before Rhuidean—she had spoken as if she had the Foretelling. *He will bind you together. He will take you back, and destroy you.* Words delivered like prophecy. Destroy them. Prophecy said he would Break the World again. The idea horrified him. Perhaps he could escape that part, at least, but war, death and destruction already welled up in his footsteps. Tear was the first place in what seemed a very long time where he had not left chaos behind, men dying and villages burning.

He found himself wishing he could climb on Jeade'en and run as fast as the stallion could carry him. It was not the first time. *But I can't run,* he thought. *I have it to do because there isn't anybody else who can. I do it, or the Dark One wins.* A hard bargain, but the only one there was. *But why would I destroy the Aiel? How?*

That last thought chilled him. It was too much like accepting that he would, that he should. He did not want to harm the Aiel. "Light," he said harshly, "I don't want to destroy anybody." His mouth felt lined with dust again.

Mat glanced at him silently. A wary look.

I am not mad yet, Rand thought grimly.

Upslope the Aiel were stirring in the three camps. The cold fact was, he needed them. That was why he had begun to contemplate this, back when he first discovered that the Dragon Reborn and He Who Comes With the Dawn might well be one and the same. He needed people he could trust, people who followed from something besides fear of him, or greed for power. People who did not mean to use him for their own ends. He had done what was required, and now he would use them. Because he had to. He was not mad yet—he did not think he was—but many would think so before he was done.

Full, glaring sunlight overtook them before they began to scramble up Chaendaer, heat like a club. Rand climbed the uneven slope as fast as he could manage, with its dips and rises and rough outcrops; his throat had forgotten its last drink, and the sun dried his shirt as fast as sweat could moisten it. Mat needed no urging, either. There was water up there. Bair stood in front of the Wise One's low tents, a waterbag in her hands, glistening with condensation. Licking cracked lips, Rand was sure he could see the glisten.

"Where is he? What have you done to him?"

The roar stopped Rand in his tracks. The flame-haired man, Couladin, stood atop a thick thumb of granite jutting out from the mountain. Others of the Shaido clan clustered around its base, all looking at Rand and Mat. Some were veiled.

"Who are you talking about?" Rand called back. His voice croaked with thirst.

Couladin's eyes bulged in outrage. "Muradin, wetlander! He entered two days before you, yet you come out first. He could not fail where you survive! You must have murdered him!"

Rand thought he heard a shout from the Wise One's tents, but before he could even blink, Couladin uncoiled like a snake, casting a spear straight at him. Two more streaked behind it from the Aiel at the base of the granite thumb.

Instinctively Rand snatched for *saidin* and the flame-carved sword. The blade whirled in his hands—Whirlwind on the Mountain; aptly named—slicing a pair of spear shafts in two. Mat's spinning black spear just barely knocked the third aside.

"Proof!" Couladin howled. "They entered Rhuidean armed! It is forbidden! Look at the blood on them! They have murdered Muradin!" Even as he spoke he hurled another spear, and this time it was one of a dozen.

Rand flung himself aside, just conscious of Mat leaping the other way, yet even before they hit the ground the spears came together where Rand had been standing, bouncing off each other. Rolling to his feet, he found the spears all stuck into the stony ground. In a perfect circle surrounding the spot he had jumped from. For a moment even Couladin seemed stunned to stillness.

"Stop!" Bair shouted, running down into the motionless instant. Her long bulky skirt impeded her no more than her age; she bounded down the slope like a girl for all her white hair, and a girl in a fury at that. "The peace of Rhuidean, Couladin!" Her thin voice was an iron rod. "Twice you have tried to break it now. Once more, and you are outlawed! My word on it! You, and anyone else who lifts a hand!" She skidded to a halt in front of Rand, facing the Shaido with the water bag raised as if she meant to bludgeon them with it. "Let who doubts me, raise a weapon! That one will be deprived of shade according to the Agreement of Rhuidean, denied hold or stand or tent. His own sept will hunt him as a wild beast."

Some of the Shaido hastily unveiled their faces—some of them—but Couladin was not dissuaded. "They are armed, Bair! They went armed to Rhuidean! That is—!"

"Silence!" Bair shook a fist at him. "You dare speak of weapons?

You who would break the Peace of Rhuidean, and kill with your face bare to the world? They took no weapon with them; I attest to it." Deliberately she turned her back, but the gaze she swept across Rand and Mat was hardly softer than what she had given Couladin. She grimaced at Mat's strange sword-bladed spear, muttering, "Did you find that in Rhuidean, boy?"

"I was given it, *old woman,*" Mat growled back hoarsely. "I paid for it, and I mean to keep it."

She sniffed. "You both look as if you had rolled in knifegrass. What—? No, you can tell me later." Eyeing Rand's Power-wrought sword, she shivered. "Rid yourself of that. And show them the signs before that fool Couladin tries to whip them up again. With this temper on him, he would take his whole clan into outlawry without blinking. Quickly!"

For a moment he gaped at her. Signs? Then he remembered what Rhuarc had shown him once, the mark of a man who had survived Rhuidean. Letting the sword vanish, he unlaced his left shirt cuff and pushed the sleeve back to his elbow.

Around his forearm wound a shape like that on the Dragon banner, a sinuous golden-maned form scaled in scarlet and gold. He expected it, of course, but it was still a shock. The thing looked like a part of his skin, as though that nonexistent creature itself had settled into him. His arm felt no different, yet the scales sparkled in the sunlight like polished metal; it seemed if he touched that golden mane atop his wrist, he would surely feel each hair.

He thrust his arm into the air as soon as it was bare, high so Couladin and his people could see. Mutters rose among the Shaido, and Couladin snarled wordlessly. The numbers around the granite outcrop were swelling as more Shaido came running from their tents. Rhuarc stood with Heirn and his Jindo a little upslope; they watched the Shaido warily, and Rand with an air of expectation his uplifted arm did not lessen. Lan stood halfway between the two groups, hands resting on his sword hilt, face a thunderhead.

Just as Rand began to realize the Aiel wanted something more, Egwene and the other three Wise Women reached him, scrambling down the mountain. The Aiel women looked out of countenance at having to hurry and every bit as angry as Bair had been. Amys directed her glares at Couladin, while sun-haired Melaine stared blamingly at Rand. Seana just seemed ready to chew rocks. Egwene, with a scarf wrapped around her hair and spread over her shoulders, stared at Mat

and him half in consternation and half as though she had expected
never to see them again.

"Fool man," Bair muttered. "*All* of the signs." Tossing the waterbag
to Mat, she seized Rand's right arm and stripped back his sleeve, exposing a mirror twin of the creature on his left forearm. Her breath
caught, then came out in a long sigh. She seemed balanced on a razor
edge between relief and apprehension. There was no mistaking it; she
had hoped for the second marking, yet it made her afraid. Amys and
the other two Wise Women echoed her sigh almost exactly. It was odd
to see Aiel fearful.

Rand almost laughed. Not that he was amused. "Twice and twice
shall he be marked." That was what the Prophecies of the Dragon said.
A heron branded into each palm, and now these. One of the peculiar
creatures—Dragons, the Prophecy called them—was supposed to be
"for remembrance lost." Rhuidean had certainly supplied that, the lost
history of the Aiel's origins. And the other was for "the price he must
pay." *How soon must I pay it?* he wondered. *And how many have to pay
with me?* Others always had to, even when he tried to pay alone.

Apprehensive or not, Bair did not pause before shoving that arm
above his head, too, and proclaiming loudly, "Behold what has never
been seen before. A *Car'a'carn* has been chosen, a chief of chiefs. Born
of a Maiden, he has come with the dawn from Rhuidean, according to
prophecy, to unite the Aiel! The fulfillment of prophecy has begun!"

The reactions of the other Aiel were nothing like what Rand envisioned. Couladin stared down at him, even more hatefully than before
if that was possible, then leaped from the outcrop and stalked up the
slope to vanish into the Shaido tents. The Shaido themselves began to
disperse, glancing at Rand with unreadable faces before drifting back
to their tents. Heirn and the warriors of the Jindo sept, hardly hesitating, did the same. In moments only Rhuarc remained, his eyes troubled. Lan went over to the clan chief; from his face, the Warder would
just as soon not have seen Rand at all. Rand was not sure what he had
expected, but surely something other than this.

"Burn me!" Mat muttered. He seemed to realize for the first time
that he had the waterbag in his hands. Jerking the plug free, he held
the hide bag high, letting nearly as much splash over his face as into his
mouth. When he finally lowered it, he looked at the markings on
Rand's arms again and shook his head, repeating, "Burn me!" as he
pushed the sloshing bag at him.

Rand stared at the Aiel in consternation, but he was more than glad
to drink. The first gulps hurt his throat, it was so dry.

"What happened to you?" Egwene demanded. "Did Muradin attack you?"

"It is forbidden to speak of what occurs in Rhuidean," Bair said sharply.

"Not Muradin," Rand said. "Where's Moiraine? I expected her to be the first to meet us." He rubbed his face; black flakes of dried blood came off on his hand. "For once, I won't care if she asks before she Heals me."

"Me either," Mat said hoarsely. He swayed, holding himself up with his spear, and pressed the heel of his palm against his forehead. "My brain is spinning."

Egwene grimaced. "She is still in Rhuidean, I suppose. But if you have finally come out, maybe she will, as well. She left right after you. And Aviendha. You've all been gone so long."

"Moiraine went to Rhuidean?" Rand said incredulously. "And Aviendha? Why did—?" Abruptly he registered what else she had said. "What do mean, 'so long'?"

"This is the seventh day," she said. "The seventh day since you all went down into the valley."

The waterbag fell from his hands. Seana snatched it up again before more than a little of its contents, so precious in the Waste, could trickle away down the stony slope. Rand barely noticed. Seven days. Anything could have happened in seven days. *They could be catching up to me, figuring out what I'm planning. I have to move. Fast. I have to keep ahead of them. I haven't come this far to fail.*

They were all staring at him, even Rhuarc and Mat, concern writ large on their faces. And caution. No wonder in that. Who could say what he might do, or how sane he still was? Only Lan did not change his stony scowl.

"I told you that was Aviendha, Rand. Bare as she was born." Mat's voice had a painful rasp to it, and his legs looked none too steady.

"How long before Moiraine comes back?" Rand asked. If she had gone in at the same time, she should return soon.

"If she has not returned by the tenth day," Bair replied, "she will not. No one has ever returned after ten days."

Another three days, maybe. Three more days when he had already lost seven. *Let them come, now. I will not fail!* He barely kept a snarl from his face. "You can channel. One of you can, anyway. I saw how you flung Couladin about. Will you Heal Mat?"

Amys and Melaine exchanged looks he could only call rueful.

"Our paths have gone other ways," Amys said regretfully. "There are

Wise Ones who could do what you ask, after a fashion, but we are not among them."

"What do you mean?" he snapped angrily. "You can channel like Aes Sedai. Why can't you Heal like them? You did not want him to go to Rhuidean in the first place. Do you think you can let him die from it?"

"I'll survive," Mat said, but his eyes were tight with suffering.

Egwene put a hand on Rand's arm. "Not all Aes Sedai can Heal very well," she said in a soothing voice. "The best Healers are all Yellow Ajah. Sheriam, the Mistress of Novices, cannot Heal anything much more serious than a bruise or a small cut. No two women can have exactly the same Talents or skills."

Her tone irritated him. He was not some pettish child to be smoothed down. He frowned at the Wise Ones. Could not or would not, Mat and he would have to wait for Moiraine. If she had not been killed by that bubble of evil, by those dust creatures. It must have dissipated by now; there had been an end to the one in Tear. *They wouldn't have stopped her. She could channel her way through them. She knows what she's doing; she doesn't have to figure it out an inch at a time the way I do.* But then why was she not back? Why had she gone in the first place, and why had he not seen her? Foolish question. A hundred people could have been in Rhuidean without being seen. Too many questions, and no answers until she did return, he suspected. If then.

"There are herbs and ointments," Seana said. "Come out of the sun, and we will tend your injuries."

"Out of the sun," Rand muttered. "Yes." He was being boorish, but he did not care. Why had Moiraine gone into Rhuidean? He did not trust her to stop pushing him in the direction she thought best, and the Dark One take his opinions. If she was in there, could she have affected what he saw? Changed it some way? If she even suspected what he planned. . . .

He started toward the Jindo tents—Couladin's people were not likely to offer him a resting place—but Amys turned him toward the flat farther up where the Wise Ones' tents stood. "They might not be comfortable with you among them just yet," she said. Rhuarc, falling in beside her, nodded agreement.

Melaine glanced at Lan. "This is no business of yours, *Aan'allein*. You and Rhuarc take Matrim and—"

"No," Rand broke in. "I want them with me." Partly it was because he wanted answers from the clan chief, and partly it was sheer stubbornness. These Wise Ones were all set to guide him around on a leash, just like Moiraine. He was not about to put up with it. They looked at one another, then nodded as if acceding to a request. If they thought he would be a good boy because they gave him a sweet, they were mistaken. "I'd have thought you would be with Moiraine," he said to Lan, ignoring the Wise Ones and their nods.

A flash of embarrassment crossed the Warder's face. "The Wise Ones managed to hide her going until nearly sunset," he said stiffly. "Then they . . . convinced me following would serve no purpose. They said even if I did, I could not find her until she was already on her way out, and she would not need me, then. I am no longer certain I should have listened."

"Listened!" Melaine snorted. Her gold and ivory bracelets clattered as she adjusted her shawl irritably. "Trust a man to make himself sound reasonable. You would almost certainly have died, and very likely killed her, too."

"Melaine and I had to hold him down half the night before he would listen," Amys said. Her small smile was a touch amused, a touch wry.

Lan's face might as well have been carved from thunderclouds. Small wonder, if the Wise Ones had used the Power on him. What *was* Moiraine doing in there?

"Rhuarc," Rand said, "how am I supposed to unite the Aiel? They don't even want to look at me." He raised his bare forearms for a moment; the Dragons' scales glittered in the harsh sunlight. "These say I'm He Who Comes With the Dawn, but everybody practically melted away as soon as I showed the things."

"It is one thing to know prophecy will be fulfilled, eventually," the clan chief said slowly, "another to see that fulfillment begun before your eyes. It is said you will make the clans one people again, as long ago, but we have fought one another almost as long as we have fought the rest of the world. And there is more, for some of us."

He will bind you together, and destroy you. Rhuarc must have heard that, too. And the other clan chiefs, and the Wise Ones, if they also had entered that forest of shining glass columns. If Moiraine had not arranged a special vision for him. "Does everyone see the same things inside those columns, Rhuarc?"

"No!" Melaine snapped, eyes like green steel. "Be silent, or send *Aan'allein* and Matrim away. You must go, too, Egwene."

"It is not permitted," Amys said in a just slightly softer voice, "to speak of what occurs within Rhuidean except with those who have been there." A fraction softer, maybe. "Even then, few speak of it, and seldom."

"I mean to change what is permitted and what isn't," Rand told them levelly. "Become used to it." He caught Egwene muttering about him needing his ears boxed, and grinned at her. "Egwene can stay, too, since she asked so nicely." She stuck her tongue out at him, then blushed when she realized what she had done.

"Change," Rhuarc said. "You know he brings change, Amys. It is wondering what change, and how, that makes us like children alone in the dark. Since it must be, let it begin now. No two clan chiefs I have spoken with have seen through the exactly same eyes, Rand, or exactly the same things, until the sharing of water, and the meeting where the Agreement of Rhuidean was made. Whether it is the same for Wise Ones, I do not know, but I suspect it is. I think it is a matter of blood-lines. I believe I saw through the eyes of my ancestors, and you yours."

Amys and the other Wise Ones glowered in grimly sullen silence. Mat and Egwene wore equally confused stares. Lan alone seemed not to be listening at all; his eyes looked inward, no doubt in worry over Moiraine.

Rand felt a little strange himself. Seeing through his ancestors' eyes. He had known for some time that Tam al'Thor was not his real father, that he had been found as a newborn on the slopes of Dragonmount after the last major battle of the Aiel War. A newborn with his dead mother, a Maiden of the Spear. He had claimed Aiel blood in demanding admittance to Rhuidean, but the fact of it was just now being driven home. His ancestors. Aiel.

"Then you saw Rhuidean just begun building, too," he said. "And the two Aes Sedai. You . . . heard what the one of them said." *He will destroy you.*

"I heard." Rhuarc looked resigned, like a man who had learned his leg had to be cut off. "I know."

Rand changed the subject. "What was 'the sharing of water'?"

The clan chief's eyebrows lifted in surprise. "You did not recognize it? But then, I do not see why you should; you have not grown up with the histories. According to the oldest stories, from the day the Break-ing of the World began until the day we first entered the Three-fold Land, only one people did not attack us. One people allowed us water freely when it was needed. It took us long to discover who they were. That is done with, now. The pledge of peace was destroyed; the treekil-lers spat in our faces."

"Cairhien," Rand said. "You're talking about Cairhien, and *Avendoraldera,* and Laman cutting down the Tree."

"Laman is dead for his punishment," Rhuarc said in a flat voice.

"The oathbreakers are done with." He looked at Rand sideways. "Some, such as Couladin, take it for proof we can trust no one who is not Aiel. That is a part of why he hates you. A part of it. He will take your face and blood for lies. Or claim he does."

Rand shook his head. Moiraine sometimes talked of the complexity of Age Lace, the Pattern of an Age, woven by the Wheel of Time from the thread of human lives. If the ancestors of the Cairhienin had not allowed the Aiel to have water three thousand years ago, then Cairhien would never have been given the right to use the Silk Path across the Waste, with a cutting from *Avendesora* for a pledge. No pledge, and King Laman would have had no Tree to cut down; there would have been no Aiel War; and he could not have been born on the side of Dragonmount to be carried off and raised in the Two Rivers. How many more points like that had there been, where a single decision one way or another affected the weave of the Pattern for thousands of years? A thousand times a thousand tiny branching points, a thousand times that many, all twitching the Pattern into a different design. He himself was a walking branching point, and maybe Mat and Perrin, too. What they did or did not do would send ripples ahead through the years, through the Ages.

He looked at Mat, hobbling up the slope with the aid of his spear, head down and eyes squinted in pain. *The Creator could not have been thinking, to set the future on the shoulders of three farmboys. I can't drop it. I have to carry the load, whatever the cost.*

At the Wise Ones' low, wall-less tents, the women ducked inside with murmurs about water and shade. They all but pulled Mat with them; as evidence of how his head and throat hurt, he not only obeyed, he did so silently.

Rand started to follow, but Lan laid a hand on his shoulder. "Did you see her in there?" the Warder asked.

"No, Lan. I'm sorry; I did not. She'll come out safe if anyone can."

Lan grunted and took his hand away. "Watch out for Couladin, Rand. I have seen his kind before. Ambition burns in his belly. He would sacrifice the world to achieve it."

"*Aan'allein* speaks the truth," Rhuarc said. "The Dragons on your arms will not matter if you are dead before the clan chiefs learn of them. I will make sure some of Heirn's Jindo are always near you until we reach Cold Rocks. Even then, Couladin will probably try to make trouble, and the Shaido, at least, will follow him. Perhaps others, too. The Prophecy of Rhuidean said you would be raised by those not of the blood, yet Couladin may not be the only one to see only a wetlander."

"I will try to watch my back," Rand said dryly. In the stories, when somebody fulfilled a prophecy, everyone cried "Behold!" or some such, and that was that except for dealing with the villains. Real life did not seem to work that way.

When they entered the tent, Mat was already seated on a gold-tasseled red cushion with his coat and shirt off. A woman in a cowled white robe had finished washing the blood from his face and was just beginning on his chest. Amys gripped a stone mortar between her knees, blending some ointment with a pestle, while Bair and Seana had their heads together over herbs brewing in a pot of hot water.

Melaine grimaced at Lan and Rhuarc then fixed Rand with cool green eyes. "Strip to the waist," she said curtly. "The cuts on your head do not seem too bad, but let me see what has you hunched over." She struck a small brass gong, and another white-robed woman ducked in at the back of the tent, a steaming silver basin in her hands and cloths over her arm.

Rand took a seat on a cushion, making himself sit up straight. "That's nothing to worry yourself about," he assured her. The second woman in white knelt gracefully by his side and, resisting his efforts to take the damp cloth she wrung out in the basin, began gently washing his face. He wondered who she was. She looked Aiel, but she certainly did not act it. Her gray eyes held a determined meekness.

"It is an old injury," Egwene told the sun-haired Wise One. "Moiraine has never been able to Heal it properly." The look she gave Rand said common courtesy should have made him tell as much. From the glances that passed among the Wise Ones, though, he thought she had said more than enough already. A wound Aes Sedai could not Heal; that was a puzzle to them. Moiraine seemed to know more about him than he knew about himself, and he had a hard time dealing with her. Maybe it would go easier with the Wise Ones if they had to guess about him.

Mat winced as Amys began rubbing her ointment into the slashes on his chest. If it felt anything like it smelled, Rand thought he had cause to wince. Bair shoved a silver cup at Mat. "Drink, *young man*. Timsin root and silverleaf will help your headaches if anything can."

He did not hesitate before gulping it down; a shudder and a twisted face followed. "Tastes like the inside of my boots." But he gave her a seated bow, formal enough for a Tairen except for his being shirtless, and only spoiled a bit by his sudden grin. "I thank you, Wise One. And I won't ask if you added anything just to give it that . . . memorable . . . taste." Bair and Seana's soft laughter might have come because they had or because they had not, but it seemed that as usual Mat had found a way to get on the good of side of the women. Even Melaine gave him a brief smile.

"Rhuarc," Rand said, "if Couladin thinks to make difficulties, I need to jump ahead of him. How do I go about telling the other clan chiefs? About me. About these." He shifted his Dragon-twined arms. The white-robed woman at his side, cleaning the long gash in his hair now, deliberately avoided looking at them.

"There is no set formality," Rhuarc said. "How could there be, for a thing that will happen only once? When there must be a meeting between clan chiefs, there are places where something like the Peace of Rhuidean holds. The closest to Cold Rocks, the closest to Rhuidean, is Alcair Dal. You could show proofs to the clan and sept chiefs there."

"*Al'cair Dal?*" Mat said, giving it a subtly different sound. "The Golden Bowl?"

Rhuarc nodded. "A round canyon, though there is nothing golden about it. There is a ledge at one end, and a man who stands there can be heard by anyone in the canyon without raising his voice."

Rand frowned at the Dragons on his forearms. He was not the only one to have been marked in some way in Rhuidean. Mat no longer spoke a few words of the Old Tongue now and then without knowing what he was saying. He understood, since Rhuidean, though he did not appear to realize it. Egwene was watching Mat. Thoughtfully. She had spent too much time with Aes Sedai.

"Rhuarc, can you send messengers out to the clan chiefs?" he said. "How long will it take to ask them all to Alcair Dal? What will it take to make sure they come?"

"Messengers will take weeks, and more weeks for everyone to gather." Rhuarc's gesture took in all four Wise Ones. "They can speak to every clan chief in his dreams in one night, to every sept chief. And every Wise One, make sure no man takes it for just a dream."

"I appreciate your confidence that we can move mountains, shade of my heart," Amys said wryly, settling herself beside Rand with her ointment, "but that does not make it so. It would take several nights to do what you suggest, with little rest in them."

Rand caught her hand as she started to rub the sharp-smelling mixture on his cheek. "Will you do it?"

"Are you so eager to destroy us?" she demanded, then bit her lip vexedly as the white-cowled woman on Rand's other side started.

Melaine clapped her hands twice. "Leave us," she said sharply, and the women in white bowed their way out with their basins and cloths.

"You goad me like a needleburr next to the skin," Amys told Rand bitterly. "Whatever they are told, those women will talk now of what they should not know." She pulled her hand free, began rubbing in the ointment with perhaps more energy than was necessary. It stung worse than it smelled.

"I do not mean to goad you," Rand said, "but there is no time. The Forsaken are loose, Amys, and if they find out where I am, or what I plan. . . ." The Aiel women did not seem surprised. Had they known already? "Nine still live. Too many, and those that don't want to kill me think they can use me. I have no time. If I knew a way to bring all the clan chiefs here now, and make them accept me, I'd use it."

"What is it you plan?" Amys voice was as stony as her face.

"Will you ask—tell—the chiefs to come to Alcair Dal?"

For a long moment she met his stare. When she finally nodded, it was grudging.

Begrudged or not, some of the tension went out of him. There was no way to win back seven lost days, but perhaps he could avoid losing more. Moiraine, still in Rhuidean with Aviendha, held him here yet, though. He could not simply abandon her.

"You knew my mother," he said. Egwene leaned forward, as intent as he, and Mat shook his head.

Amys's hand paused on his face. "I knew her."

"Tell me about her. Please."

She shifted her attention to the slash above his ear; if a frown could have Healed, he would not have needed her ointment. Finally she said, "Shaiel's story, as I know it, begins when I was still *Far Dareis Mai*, more than a year before I gave up the spear. A number of us had ranged almost to the Dragonwall together. One day we saw a woman, a golden-haired young wetlander, in silks, with packhorses and a fine mare to ride. A man we would have killed, of course, but she had no weapon beyond a simple knife at her belt. Some wanted to run her back to the Dragonwall naked . . ." Egwene blinked; she seemed continually surprised at how hard the Aiel were. Amys continued without pause. ". . . yet she seemed to be searching determinedly for something. Curious, we followed, day by day, without letting her see. Her horses died, her food ran out, her water, but she did not turn back. She stumbled on afoot, until finally she fell and could not rise. We decided to give her water, and ask her story. She was near death, and it was a full day before she could speak."

"Her name was Shaiel?" Rand said when she hesitated. "Where was she from? Why did she come here?"

"Shaiel," Bair said, "was the name she took for herself. She never gave another in the time I knew her. In the Old Tongue it would mean the Woman Who Is Dedicated." Mat nodded agreement, not seeming to realize what he had done; Lan eyed him thoughtfully over a silver cup of water. "There was a bitterness in Shaiel, in the beginning," she finished.

Sitting back on her heels beside Rand, Amys nodded. "She spoke of a child abandoned, a son she loved. A husband she did not love. Where, she would not say. I do not think she ever forgave herself for leaving the child. She would tell little beyond what she had to. It was for us she had been searching, for Maidens of the Spear. An Aes Sedai called Gitara Moroso, who had the Foretelling, had told her that disaster would befall her land and her people, perhaps the world, unless she went to dwell among the Maidens of the Spear, telling no one of her going. She must become a Maiden, and she could not return to her own land until the Maidens had gone to Tar Valon.

She shook her head wonderingly. "You must understand how it sounded, then. The Maidens go to Tar Valon? No Aiel had crossed the Dragonwall since the day we first reached the Three-fold Land. It would be another four years before Laman's crime brought us into the wetlands. And certainly no one not Aiel had ever become a Maiden of the Spear. Some of us thought her mad from the sun. But she had a stubborn will, and somehow we found ourselves agreeing to let her try."

Gitara Moroso. An Aes Sedai with the Foretelling. Somewhere he had heard that name, but where? And he had a brother. A half-brother. Growing up, he had wondered what it would be like to have a brother or a sister. Who, and where? But Amys was going on.

"Almost every girl dreams of becoming a Maiden, and learns at least the rudiments of bow and spear, of fighting with hands and feet. Even so, those who take the final step and wed the spear discover they know nothing. It was harder for Shaiel. The bow she knew well, but she had never run as far as a mile, or lived on what she could find. A ten-year-old girl could beat her, and she did not even know what plants indicate water. Yet she persevered. In a year she had spoken her vows to the spear, a Maiden, adopted into the Chumai sept of the Taardad."

And eventually she had gone to Tar Valon with the Maidens, to die on the slopes of Dragonmount. Half an answer, and leaving new questions. If he could only have seen her face.

"You have something of her in your features," Seana said as though reading his thoughts. She had settled herself cross-legged with a small silver cup of wine. "Less of Janduin."

"Janduin? My father?"

"Yes," Seana said. "He was clan chief of the Taardad, then, the youngest in memory. Yet he had a way to him, a power. People listened to him, and would follow him, even those not of his clan. He ended the blood feud between Taardad and Nakai after two hundred years, and made alliance not only with the Nakai, but the Reyn, and the Reyn were not far short of blood feud. He very nearly ended the feud between Shaarad and Goshien, as well, and might have had Laman not cut down the Tree. Young as he was, it was he who led the Taardad and Nakai, the Reyn and Shaarad, to seek Laman's bloodprice."

Was. So he was dead now, too. Egwene wore sympathy on her face. Rand ignored it; he did not want sympathy. How could he feel loss, for people he had never known? Yet he did. "How did Janduin die?"

The Wise Ones exchanged hesitant glances. At last Amys said, "It was the beginning of the third year of the search for Laman when Shaiel found herself with child. By the laws, she should have returned to the Three-fold Land. A Maiden is forbidden to carry the spear while she carries a child. But Janduin could forbid her nothing; had she asked the moon on a necklace, he would have tried to give it to her. So she stayed, and in the last fight, before Tar Valon, she was lost, and the child was lost. Janduin could not forgive himself for not making her obey the law."

"He gave up his place as clan chief," Bair said. "No one had ever done that before. He was told it could not be done, but he simply walked away. He went north with the young men, to hunt Trollocs and Myrddraal in the Blight. It is a thing wild young men do, and Maidens with less sense than goats. Those who returned said he was killed by a man, though. They said Janduin claimed this man looked like Shaiel, and he would not raise his spear when the man ran him through."

Dead, then. Both dead. He would never lose his love for Tam, never stop thinking of him as father, but he wished he could have seen Janduin and Shaiel, just once.

Egwene tried to comfort him, of course, the way women did. There was no use trying to make her understand that what he had lost was something he had never had. For memories of parents he had Tam al'Thor's quiet laugh, and dimmer remembrance of Kari al'Thor's gentle hands. That was as much as any man could want or need. She seemed disappointed, even a little upset with him, and the Wise Ones appeared to share the feeling to one degree or another, from Bair's openly disapproving frown to Melaine's sniff and ostentatious shifting of her shawl. Women never understood. Rhuarc and Lan and Mat did; they left him alone, as he wanted.

For some reason he did not feel like eating when Melaine had food brought, so he went to lie at the edge of the tent, with one of the cushions under his elbow, where he could watch the slope, and the fog-shrouded city. The sun blasted the valley and the surrounding mountains, burning the shadows. The air that eddied into the tent seemed to come from an open oven.

After a time Mat came over, wearing a clean shirt. He sat beside Rand without speaking, peering into the valley below, the strange spear propped on his knee. Now and again he felt at the cursive script carved into the black haft.

"How is your head?" Rand asked, and Mat jumped.

"It . . . doesn't hurt anymore." He jerked his fingers away from the carving, folded his hands deliberately in his lap. "Not as much, anyway. Whatever that was they mixed up, it did the trick."

He fell silent again, and Rand let him. He did not want to talk, either. He could almost feel time passing, grains of sand in an hourglass dropping one by one, ever so slowly. But everything seemed to tremble, too, the sands ready to explode in a torrent. Foolish. He was just being affected by the shimmering heat haze rising from the mountain's bare rock. The clan chiefs could not reach Alcair Dal one day sooner if Moiraine appeared before him this instant. They were only a part anyway, and maybe the least important part. A little while later he noticed Lan squatting easily atop the same granite outcrop Couladin had used, paying no mind to the sun. The Warder was watching the valley, too. Another man who did not want to talk.

Rand refused a midday meal, too, though Egwene and the Wise Ones took turns trying to make him eat. They seemed to take his refusal calmly enough, but when he suggested returning to Rhuidean to look for Moiraine—and Aviendha, for that matter—Melaine exploded.

"You fool man! No man can go twice to Rhuidean. Even you would not come back alive! Oh, starve if you want to!" She threw half a round loaf of bread at his head. Mat caught it out of the air and calmly began eating.

"Why do you want me to live?" Rand asked her. "You know what that Aes Sedai said in front of Rhuidean. I will destroy you. Why aren't you plotting with Couladin to kill me?" Mat choked, and Egwene planted her fists on her hips, ready to lecture, but Rand kept his attention on Melaine. Instead of answering, she glared at him and left the tent.

It was Bair who spoke. "Everyone thinks they know the Prophecy of Rhuidean, but what they know is what Wise Ones and clan chiefs have told them for generations. Not lies, but not the whole truth. The truth might break the strongest man."

"What is the whole truth?" Rand insisted.

She glanced at Mat, then said, "In this case, the whole truth, the truth known only to Wise Ones and clan chiefs before this, is that you are our doom. Our doom, and our salvation. Without you, no one of our people will live beyond the Last Battle. Perhaps not even until the Last Battle. That is prophecy, and truth. With you. . . . 'He shall spill out the blood of those who call themselves Aiel as water on sand, and he shall break them as dried twigs, yet the remnant of a remnant shall he save, and they shall live.' A hard prophecy, but this has never been a gentle land." She met his gaze without flinching. A hard land, and a hard woman.

He rolled back over and returned to watching the valley. The others left, except for Mat.

In the midafternoon he finally spotted a figure climbing the mountain, scrambling up wearily. Aviendha. Mat had been right; she *was* bare as she was born. And showing some effects of the sun, too, Aiel or not; it was only her hands and face that were sun-darkened, and the rest of her looked decidedly red. He was glad to see her. She disliked him, but only because she thought he had mistreated Elayne. The simplest of motives. Not for prophecy or doom, not for the Dragons on his arms or because he was the Dragon Reborn. For a simple human reason. He almost looked forward to those cool, challenging stares.

When she saw him, she froze, and there was nothing cool in her blue-green eyes. Her gaze made the sun seem cold; he should have been burned to ash on the spot.

"Uh . . . Rand?" Mat said quietly. "I don't think I would turn my back on her if I were you."

A tired sigh escaped him. Of course. If she had been into those glass columns, she knew. Bair, Melaine, the others—they had all had years to grow used to it. For Aviendha, it was a fresh wound with no scab. *No wonder she hates me now.*

The Wise Ones scurried out to meet Aviendha, hurrying her away into another tent. The next time Rand saw her she wore a bulky brown skirt and loose white blouse, with a shawl looped around her arms. She did not look very happy about the clothes. She saw him watching, and the fury on her face—the sheer animal rage—was enough to make him turn away.

Shadows were beginning to stretch to the far mountains by the time Moiraine appeared, falling and staggering back to her feet as she climbed, as sunburned as Aviendha. He was startled to see she had no clothes on either. Women were crazy, that was all.

Lan leaped from the stone outcrop and ran down to her. Scooping her into his arms, he ran back upslope, perhaps faster than he had descended, cursing and shouting for the Wise Ones by turns. Moiraine's head lolled on his shoulder. The Wise Ones came out to take her, Melaine physically barring his way when he tried to follow them into the tent. Lan was left stalking up and down outside, pounding a fist into his hand.

Rand rolled onto his back and stared up at the low tent roof. Three days saved. He should have felt glad Moiraine and Aviendha were back and safe, but his relief was all for days saved. Time was everything. He had to be able to choose his own ground. Maybe he still could.

"What are you going to do now?" Mat asked.

"Something you should like. I am going to break the rules."

"I meant are you going to get something to eat? Me, I'm hungry."

In spite of himself, Rand laughed. Something to eat? He did not care if he ever ate again. Mat stared at him as if he were crazy, and that only made him laugh harder. Not crazy. For the first time *somebody* was going to learn what it meant that he was the Dragon Reborn. He was going to break the rules in a way *no one* expected.

CHAPTER
35

Sharp Lessons

The Heart of the Stone in *Tel'aran'rhiod* was as Egwene remembered it in the real world, huge polished redstone columns rising
to a distant ceiling, and, beneath the great central dome, *Callandor* driven into the pale floorstones. Only people were missing. The
golden lamps were not lit, yet there was a sort of light, somehow dim
and sharp at the same time, that seemed to come from everywhere at
once, or nowhere. It was often like that, indoors in *Tel'aran'rhiod*.

What she did not expect was the woman standing beyond the glittering crystal sword and peering off into the pallid shadows among the
columns. The way she was dressed startled Egwene. Bare feet, and
wide trousers of brocaded yellow silk. Above a darker yellow sash, she
was quite bare except for golden chains hanging around her neck. Tiny
gold rings decorated her ears in sparkling rows, and most startling of
all, another pierced her nose, with a thin, medallion-lined chain running from nose ring to one of the rings in her left ear.

"Elayne?" Egwene gasped, gathering her shawl around her as
though she were the one with no blouse. She had garbed herself as a
Wise One, this time, for no particular reason.

The Daughter-Heir leaped, and when she came down facing Egwene
she was wearing a demure gown of pale green with a high, embroidered
neck and long sleeves that dangled points over her hands. No earrings.

No nose ring. "It is how the Sea Folk women dress at sea," she said hurriedly, with a furious blush. "I wanted to see how it felt, and this seemed the best place. I couldn't do it on the ship, after all."

"How does it feel?" Egwene asked curiously.

"Cold, actually." Elayne looked around at the surrounding columns. "And it makes you feel people are staring at you, even when there's no one there." Abruptly she laughed. "Poor Thom and Juilin. They do not know where to look most of the time. Half the crew are women."

Studying the columns herself, Egwene shrugged uncomfortably. It did feel as if they were being watched. No doubt it was just because they were the only people in the Stone. No one who had access to *Tel'aran'rhiod* could expect to find anyone to watch, here. "Thom? Thom Merrilin? And Juilin Sandar? Are *they* with you?"

"Oh, Egwene, Rand sent them. Rand and Lan. Well, Moiraine sent Thom, actually, but Rand sent Master Sandar. To help us. Nynaeve is quite set up about it, about Lan, though of course she won't let on."

Egwene smothered a small smile. *Nynaeve* was set up? Elayne's face was beaming, and her dress had changed again, to a *much* lower neckline, apparently without her realizing it. The *ter'angreal,* the twisted stone ring, helped the Daughter-Heir reach the World of Dreams as easily as Egwene did, but it did not confer control. That had to be learned. Stray thoughts—such as how she might like to look for Rand —could still alter things for Elayne.

"How is he?" Elayne's voice was a strange blend of forced casualness and apprehension.

"Well," Egwene said. "I think he is." She made it a full report. The Portal Stones, and Rhuidean—as much as she knew from what she had heard; what she had managed to infer from talk of seeing through ancestors' eyes—the strange creature from the Dragon banner marked on Rand's forearms, Bair's revelation that he was the Aiel's doom, the summons of the clan chiefs to Alcair Dal. Amys and the other Wise Ones should be doing that even now; she fervently hoped they were. She even told the strange story of Rand's true parents, in a shorter form. "I don't know, though. He has been acting stranger than ever, since, and Mat hardly less. I don't mean that he's mad, but. . . . He is as hard as Rhuarc or Lan, in some ways at least; maybe harder. He's planning something, I think—something he doesn't mean anybody to know—and he is in a rush to get to it. It is worrying. Sometimes I have the feeling he doesn't see people anymore, only pieces on a stones board."

Elayne did not look worried, or not about that, at any rate. "He is what he is, Egwene. A king, or a general, cannot always afford to see people. When a ruler has to do what is right for a nation, there are times when some will be hurt by what is best for the whole. Rand *is* a king, Egwene, even if without a nation unless you count Tear, and if he won't do anything that will hurt anyone, he will end by hurting everyone."

Egwene sniffed. It might make sense, but she did not have to like it. People were people, and they had to be seen as people. "There is more. Some of the Wise Ones can channel. I don't know how many, but I suspect more than a few, to some degree. From what Amys tells me, they find every last woman who has the spark born in her." No Aiel women died trying to teach themselves to channel while not even knowing what they were trying to do; there was no such thing as a wilder among the Aiel. Men who learned they could channel faced a grimmer fate; they went north, to the Great Blight and maybe beyond, to the Blasted Lands and Shayol Ghul. "Going to kill the Dark One," they called it. None survived long enough to face madness. "Aviendha is one with the spark, it turns out. She'll be very strong, I think. Amys thinks so, too."

"Aviendha," Elayne said wonderingly. "Of course. I should have known. I felt the same kinship for Jorin on first sight that I did for her. And for you, for that matter."

"Jorin?"

Elayne grimaced. "I promised I would keep her secret, and the first chance I get, I let my tongue run wild. Well, I don't suppose you will harm her or her sisters. Jorin is Windfinder on *Wavedancer*, Egwene. She can channel, and so can some of the other Windfinders." She glanced at the columns around them, and her neckline was suddenly back up under her chin. She adjusted a dark lace shawl that had not been there a moment before, covering her hair and shadowing her face. "Egwene, you mustn't tell anyone. Jorin is afraid the Tower will try to force them to become Aes Sedai, or try to control them in some fashion. I promised I would do what I can not to let that happen."

"I won't tell," Egwene said slowly. Wise Ones and Windfinders. Women able to channel among both, and none who had taken the Three Oaths, bound by the Oath Rod. The Oaths were supposed to make people trust Aes Sedai, or at least not fear their power, but Aes Sedai still had to move in secret as often as not. Wise Ones—and Windfinders, she was willing to wager—had honored places in their societies. Without being bound to supposedly make them safe. It was something to think on.

"Nynaeve and I are ahead of schedule, too, Egwene. Jorin has been teaching me to work the weather—you would not believe the size of the flows of Air she can weave!—and between us, we've had *Wavedancer* moving as fast as he ever has, and that is *fast*. We should be in Tanchico in another three days, maybe two, according to Coine. She's the Sailmistress, the captain. Ten days from Tear ot Tanchico, perhaps. That is with stopping to talk with every Atha'an Miere ship we see. Egwene, the Sea Folk think Rand is their Coramoor."

"They do?"

"Coine has some of what happened in Tear wrong—she assumes the Aes Sedai serve Rand now, for one thing; Nynaeve and I thought it best not to put her straight about that—but as soon as she tells another Sailmistress, they're all ready to spread the word and serve Rand. I believe they will do anything he asks of them."

"I wish the Aiel were so accepting," Egwene sighed. "Rhuarc thinks some of them might refuse to acknowledge him, Rhuidean Dragons or no. One fellow, a man called Couladin, I'm sure would kill him in a minute given half a chance."

Elayne took a step forward. "You will see that doesn't happen." It was not a question or a request. There was a sharp light in her blue eyes, and a bared dagger in her hand.

"I will do the best I can. Rhuarc is giving him bodyguards."

Elayne seemed to see the dagger for the first time, and gave a start. The blade vanished. "You must teach me whatever Amys is teaching you, Egwene. It is disconcerting to have things appear and disappear, or suddenly realize I'm wearing different clothes. It just happens."

"I will. When I have time." She had been in *Tel'aran'rhiod* too long already. "Elayne, if I am not here when we are supposed to meet next, don't worry. I will try, but I may not be able to come. Be sure to tell Nynaeve. If I do not come, check every night thereafter. I won't be more than one or two late, I'm sure."

"If you say so," Elayne said doubtfully. "It will surely take weeks to find out if Liandrin and the others are in Tanchico or not. Thom seems to think the city will be very confused." Her eyes went to *Callandor*, driven half its length into the floor. "Why did he do that, do you think?"

"He said it will hold the Tairens to him. As long as they know it's there, they have to know he is coming back. Maybe he knows what he is talking about. I hope so."

"Oh. I thought . . . perhaps he . . . was angry about . . . something."

Egwene frowned at her. This sudden diffidence was not like Elayne at all. "Angry about what?"

"Oh, nothing. It was just a thought. Egwene, I gave him two letters before leaving Tear. Do you know how he took them?"

"No, I don't. Did you say something you think might have angered him?"

"Of course not." Elayne laughed gaily; it sounded forced. Her dress was suddenly dark wool, stout enough for a hard winter. "I would have to be a fool to write things to make him angry." Her hair sprang up in all directions, like a crazed crown. She was not aware of it. "I am trying to make him love me, after all. Just trying to make him love me. Oh, why can't men be simple? Why do they have to cause such difficulties? At least he's away from Berelain." The wool became silk again, cut even lower than before; her hair made shimmers on her shoulders to shame the gown's sheen. She hesitated, nibbling her lower lip. "Egwene? If you find the chance, would you tell him I meant what I said in—Egwene? Egwene!"

Something snatched Egwene. The Heart of the Stone dwindled into blackness as if she were being hauled away by the scruff of her neck.

With a gasp, Egwene started awake, heart pounding, staring up the low roof of the night-darkened tent over her head. Only a little moonlight crept in at the open sides. She lay under her blankets—the Waste was as cold at night as it was hot during the day, and the brazier that exuded the sweetish smell of dried dung burning gave little warmth—beneath her blankets right where she had lain down to sleep. But what had pulled her back?

Abruptly she became aware of Amys, sitting cross-legged beside her, cloaked in shadows. The Wise One's murk-shrouded face seemed as dark and forboding as the night.

"Did you do that, Amys?" she said angrily. "You have no right to just haul me about. I am Aes Sedai of the Green Ajah . . ." The lie came easily to her lips now and you have no right—"

Amys cut her off with a grim voice. "Beyond the Dragonwall, in the White Tower, you are Aes Sedai. Here, you are an ignorant pupil, a fool child crawling through a den of vipers."

"I know I said I would not go to *Tel'aran'rhiod* without you," Egwene said, trying to sound reasonable, "but—"

Something seized her ankles, hauled her feet into the air; blankets tumbled away, her shift dropped to bunch in her armpits. Upside down, she hung with her face level with that of Amys. Furious, she opened herself to *saidar*—and found herself blocked.

"You wanted to go off alone," Amys hissed softly. "You were warned, but you had to go." Her eyes seemed to glow in the dark, brighter and brighter. "Never a care for what might be waiting. There are things in dreams to shatter the bravest heart." Around eyes like blue coals, her face melted, stretched. Scales sprouted where skin had been; her jaws thrust out, lined with sharp teeth. "Things to *eat* the bravest heart," she growled.

Screaming, Egwene battered vainly at the shield holding her from the True Source. She tried to beat at that horrible face, at the thing that could not be Amys, but something gripped her wrists, stretched her taut and quivering in midair. All she could do was shriek as those jaws closed around her face.

Screaming, Egwene sat up, clutching at her blankets. With an effort she managed to snap her mouth shut, but she could do nothing about the shudders that racked her. She was in the tent—or was she? There was Amys, cross-legged in the shadows, glowing with *saidar*—or was it she? Desperately, she opened herself to the Source, and nearly howled when she found the barrier again. Tossing the blankets aside, she scrambled across the layered rugs on hands and knees, scattered her neatly folded clothes with both hands. She had a belt knife. Where was it? Where? There!

"Sit down," Amys said acerbically, "before I dose you for vapors and fidgets. You will not like the taste."

Egwene twisted around on her knees, the short knife held in both hands; they would have trembled if not clutched together around the hilt. "Is it really you this time?"

"I am myself, now and also then. Sharp lessons are the best lessons. Do you mean to stab me?"

Hesitating, Egwene sheathed the knife. "You have no right to—"

"I have every right! You gave me your word. I did not know Aes Sedai could lie. If I am to teach you, I must know you will do as I say. I will not watch a pupil of mine cut her own throat!" Amys sighed; the glow around her vanished, and so did the barrier between Egwene and *saidar*. "I cannot shield you any longer. You are far stronger than I. In the One Power, you are. You very nearly battered down my shield. But if you cannot keep your word, I do not know that I want to instruct you."

"I will keep my word, Amys. I promise I will. But I have to meet with my friends, in *Tel'aran'rhiod*. I promised them, too. Amys, they might need my help, my advice." Amys's face was not easy to make out in the darkness, but Egwene did not see any softening. "Please, Amys. You've taught me so much already. I think I could find them wherever they are, now. Please, don't stop when there is so much yet for me to learn. Whatever you want me to do, I will."

"Braid your hair," Amys said in a flat tone.

"My hair?" Egwene said uncertainly. It would certainly be no inconvenience, but why? She wore it loose now, falling below her shoulders, yet it was not that long ago that she had almost burst with pride on the day the Women's Circle back home had said she was old enough to put her hair in a braid like the one Nynaeve still wore. In the Two Rivers, a braid said you were old enough to be considered a woman.

"One over each ear." Amys's voice was still like a flat rock. "If you have no ribbon to twine in the braids, I will give you some. That is how little girls wear their hair among us. Girls too young to be held to their word. When you prove to me that you can keep yours, you can stop wearing it so. But if you lie to me again, I will make you cut your skirts off short, like little girls' dresses, and find you a doll to carry. When you decide to behave as a woman, you will be treated as a woman. Agree to it, or I will teach you no more."

"I will agree if you will accompany me when I must meet—"

"Agree, *Aes Sedai!* I do not bargain with children, or those who cannot keep their word. You will do as I say, accept what I choose to give, and no more. Or else go off and get yourself killed on your own. I —will—not—aid it!"

Egwene was glad of the dark; it hid her scowl. She *had* given her word, but this was all so unfair. No one was trying to hedge Rand around with silly rules. Well, perhaps he *was* different. She was not sure she wanted to trade Amys's edicts for Couladin's desiring to put a spear through her, in any case. Mat would certainly not put up with other people's rules. Yet *ta'veren* or not, Mat had nothing to learn; all he had to do was be. Very likely he would refuse to learn anything given the chance, unless it had to do with gambling or raising fool. She wanted to learn. Sometimes it seemed an unending thirst; however much she absorbed, she could not quench it. That still did not make it fair. *Only the way things are,* she thought ruefully.

"I agree," she said. "I will do as you say, accept what you give, and no more."

"Good." After a long pause, as if waiting to see whether Egwene wanted to say more—she wisely held her tongue—Amys added, "I mean to be hard on you, Egwene, but not without purpose. That you think I have taught you much already only shows how little you knew to begin. You have a strong talent for the dream; very likely you will outstrip any of us by far, one day. But if you do not learn what I can teach you—what we four can all teach you—you will never develop that talent fully. It is most likely you will not live long enough to do so."

"I will try, Amys." She thought she managed a good approximation of meekness. Why did the woman not say what she wanted to hear? If Egwene could not go to *Tel'aran'rhiod* alone, then Amys had to come, too, when she next met Elayne. Or it might be Nynaeve, next time.

"Good. Do you have anything else to say?"

"No, Amys."

The pause was longer this time; Egwene waited as patiently as she could, hands folded on her knees.

"So you can hold your demands inside when you wish," Amys said at last, "even if it does make you twitch like a goat with the itch. Do I mistake the cause? I can give you an ointment. No? Very well. I will accompany you when you must meet your friends."

"Thank you," Egwene said primly. A goat with an itch indeed!

"In case you did not listen when I first told you, learning will be neither easy nor short. You think you have worked these last days. Prepare to give real time and effort now."

"Amys, I will learn as much as you can teach me, and I will work as hard as you want, but between Rand and the Darkfriends. . . . Time to learn may turn out to be a luxury, and my purse empty."

"I know," Amys said wearily. "He troubles us already. Come. You have wasted enough time with your childishness. There is women's business to be discussed. Come. The others are waiting."

For the first time Egwene realized Nynaeve's blankets were empty. She reached for her dress, but Amys said, "That will not be needed. We only go a short way. Throw a blanket around your shoulders and come. I have done a great deal of work for Rand al'Thor already, and I must do more when we are finished."

Shrugging a blanket around her doubtfully, Egwene followed the older woman into the night. It was *cold*. Skin turning to tight goose bumps, she hopped from bare foot to bare foot over stony ground that seemed little short of ice. After the heat of day, the night seemed as frigid as the heart of a Two Rivers winter. Her breath turned to thin mist in front of her mouth, absorbed immediately by the air. Cold or not, the air was still dry.

At the rear of the Wise Ones' camp stood a small tent she had not seen before, low like the others, but staked tightly down all around. To her surprise, Amys began stripping off her clothes, and motioned her to do the same. Clenching her teeth to keep them from chattering, she followed Amys's example slowly. When the Aiel woman had shed down to her skin, she stood there just as if the night were not freezing, taking deep breaths and flailing herself with her arms before finally ducking inside. Egwene darted after her with alacrity.

Damp heat hit her like a stick between the eyes. Sweat popped out of every pore.

Moiraine was already there, and the other Wise Ones, and Aviendha, all bare-skinned and sweating, sitting around a large iron kettle full to the brim with sooty stones. Kettle and stones alike radiated heat. The Aes Sedai looked mostly recovered from her ordeal, though there was a tightness around her eyes that had not been there before.

As Egwene was gingerly finding a place to sit—no layered rugs here; only rocky ground—Aviendha scooped a handful of water from a smaller kettle at her side and tossed it into the larger one. The water hissed to steam, leaving not even a damp spot on the stones. Aviendha had a sour look on her face. Egwene knew how she felt. Novices in the Tower were also given chores; she was not sure if she had hated scrubbing floors more than pots or the other way around. This task did not look nearly so onerous.

"We must discuss what to do about Rand al'Thor," Bair said when Amys was seated, too.

"Do about him?" Egwene said, alarmed. "He has the signs. He is the one you have been looking for."

"He is the one," Melaine said grimly, brushing long strands of red-gold hair from her damp face. "We must try to see that as many of our people as possible survive his coming."

"Just as importantly," Seana said, "we must assure that he survives to fulfill the rest of the prophecy." Melaine glared at her, and Seana added in a patient tone, "Else none of us will survive."

"Rhuarc said he would set some of the Jindo for bodyguards," Egwene said slowly. "Has he changed his mind?"

Amys shook her head. "He has not. Rand al'Thor sleeps in the Jindo tents, with a hundred men awake to see he wakes as well. But men often see things differently than we. Rhuarc will follow him, perhaps oppose him in decisions he thinks are wrong, but he will not try to guide him."

"Do you think he needs guiding?" Moiraine arched an eyebrow at that, but Egwene ignored it. "He has done what he had to without guidance so far."

"Rand al'Thor does not know our ways," Amys replied. "There are a hundred mistakes he could make to turn a chief or clan against him, to make them see a wetlander instead of He Who Comes With the Dawn. My husband is a good man and a fine chief, but he is no peacetalker, trained to guide angry men to ground their spears. We must have someone close to Rand al'Thor who can whisper in his ear when he seems ready to step wrongly." She motioned Aviendha to throw more water on the hot rocks; the younger woman complied with a sullen grace.

"And we must watch him," Melaine put in sharply. "We must have some idea of what he means to do before he does it. The fulfillment of the Prophecy of Rhuidean has begun—it cannot be halted short of its end, one way or another—but I mean to see that as many of our people survive as is possible. How that can be managed depends on what Rand al'Thor intends."

Bair leaned toward Egwene. She seemed to be all bone and sinew. "You have known him from childhood. Will he confide in you?"

"I doubt it," Egwene told her. "He does not trust as he used to." She avoided looking at Moiraine.

"Would she tell us if he did confide?" Melaine demanded. "I raise no anger here, but Egwene and Moiraine are Aes Sedai. What they seek may not be what we seek."

"We served Aes Sedai once," Bair said simply. "We failed them then. Perhaps we are meant to serve again." Melaine flushed with obvious embarrassment.

Moiraine gave no sign that she saw, or that she had heard the woman's earlier words, for that matter. Except for that tightness around her eyes she looked as calm as ice. "I will help as I can," she said coolly, "but I have little influence with Rand. For the present, he weaves the Pattern to his own design."

"Then we must watch him closely and hope." Bair sighed. "Aviendha, you will meet Rand al'Thor when he wakes each day and do not leave him until he goes to his blankets at night. You will stay as close to him as the hair on his head. Your training must come as we can manage, I fear; it will be a burden on you, doing both things, but it cannot be avoided. If you talk to him—and especially listen—you should have no trouble remaining near him. Few men will send away a pretty young woman who listens to them. Perhaps he will let something slip."

Aviendha grew stiffer by the word. When Bair finished, she spat, "I will not!" Dead silence fell, and every eye swung to her, but she stared back defiantly.

"Will not?" Bair said softly. "Will not." She seemed to be tasting words strange in her mouth.

"Aviendha," Egwene said gently, "no one is asking you to betray Elayne, only to talk to him." If anything, the former Maiden of the Spear looked even more eager to find herself a weapon.

"Is this the discipline Maidens learn now?" Amys said sharply. "If it is, you will find we teach a harder. If there is some reason you cannot stay near to Rand al'Thor, speak it." Aviendha's defiance wilted a trifle, and she mumbled inaudibly. Amys's voice took on a knife edge. "I said, speak it!"

"I do not like him!" Aviendha burst out. "I hate him! Hate him!" Had Egwene not known better, she would have thought her close to tears. The words shocked her, though; surely Aviendha could not mean it.

"We are not asking you to love him, or take him to your bed," Seana said acidly. "We are *telling* you to *listen* to the man, and you will obey!"

"Childishness!" Amys snorted. "What kind of young women is the world producing now? Do *none* of you grow up?"

Bair and Melaine were even sharper, with the older woman threatening to tie Aviendha on Rand's horse in place of his saddle—she sounded as if she meant it precisely—and Melaine suggesting that instead of sleep Aviendha should perhaps spend the night digging holes and filling them in to clear her head. The threats were not intended to coerce her, Egwene realized; these women expected and intended to be obeyed. Any useless labor Aviendha earned herself would be for being stubborn. That stubbornness seemed to be shrinking, with four sets of Wise Ones' eyes boring at her—she settled into more of a defensive crouch, on her knees—but she was holding on.

Egwene leaned over to put a hand on Aviendha's shoulder. "You've told me we are near-sisters, and I think we are. Will you do it for me? Think of it as looking after him for Elayne. You like her, too, I know. You can tell him she says she meant what she said in her letters. He will like hearing that."

Aviendha's face spasmed. "I will do it," she said, slumping. "I will watch him for Elayne. For Elayne."

Amys shook herself. "Foolishness. You will watch him because we told you to, girl. If you think you have another reason, you will find you are painfully mistaken. More water. The steam is fading."

Aviendha hurled another handful onto the rocks as though hurling a spear. Egwene was glad to see her spirit returning, but she thought she would caution her when they were alone. Spirit was all very well, but there were some women—these four Wise Ones, for example, and Siuan Sanche—with whom it was common sense to keep a check on your spirit. You could shout at the Women's Circle all day, and you still ended up doing what they wanted anyway, wishing you had kept your mouth shut.

"Now that that is settled," Bair said, "let us enjoy the steam in silence while we can. There is much for some of us yet to do tonight, and for nights to come, if we are to bring a gathering to Alcair Dal for Rand al'Thor."

"Men always find ways to make work for women," Amys said. "Why should Rand al'Thor be different?"

Quiet settled over the tent except for the hiss when Aviendha tossed more water on the hot rocks. The Wise Ones sat with hands on knees, breathing deeply. It was really quite pleasant, even relaxing, the damp heat, the slick, cleansing feel of sweat on the skin. Egwene thought it was worth missing a little sleep.

Moiraine did not look relaxed, though. She stared at the steaming kettle as if seeing something else, far off.

"Was it bad?" Egwene said softly so as not to disturb the Wise Ones. "Rhuidean, I mean?" Aviendha looked up quickly, but said nothing.

"The memories fade," Moiraine said, just as quietly. She did not look away from her distant vision, and her voice was almost chill enough to take away the heat in the air. "Most are already gone. Some, I knew already. Others. . . . The Wheel weaves as the Wheel wills, and we are only the thread of the Pattern. I have given my life to finding the Dragon Reborn, finding Rand, and seeing him ready to face the Last Battle. I will see that done, whatever it requires. Nothing and no one can be more important than that."

Shivering despite her sweat, Egwene closed her eyes. The Aes Sedai did not want comforting. She was a lump of ice, not a woman. Egwene settled herself to trying to recapture that pleasant feeling. She suspected such would be few and far between in the days to come.

CHAPTER
36

Misdirections

The Aiel broke camp early and were away from Rhuidean while the not-yet-risen sun still sharply silhouetted the far mountains. In three parties they wound around Chaendaer, down onto rough flats broken by hills and tall stone spires and flat-topped buttes, gray and brown and every hue between, some streaked with long swirls in shades of red and ocher. Occasionally a great natural arch loomed as they moved north and west, or strange, huge slabs of rock balanced improbably, forever on the brink of falling. Every way Rand looked, jagged mountains reared in the distance. All the wreckage of the Breaking of the World seemed gathered here in the place called the Aiel Waste. Where the hard ground was not cracked clay, yellow or brown or something between, it was stony and stark, and everywhere split by dry gulleys and hollows. The scattered vegetation was sparse and low, thorny bushes and leafless things with spines; the few blossoms, white or red or yellow, were startling in their isolation. Occasionally stretches of tough grass covered the ground, and rarely, there was a stunted tree also likely to have thorns or spines. Compared to Chaendaer and the valley of Rhuidean, it almost looked lush. The air was so clear, the land so barren, it seemed Rand could see for miles and miles.

That air was no less dry, though, the heat no less relentless, with the sun a lump of molten gold high in a cloudless sky. Rand had wrapped a *shoufa* around his head in an effort to keep the sun off, and drank from the waterbag on Jeade'en's saddle frequently. Oddly, wearing his coat seemed to help; he did not sweat any less, but his shirt stayed damp beneath the red wool, cooling him somewhat. Mat used a strip of cloth to tie a large white kerchief atop his head, like some odd cap that hung down the back of his neck, and he kept shading his eyes against the glare. He carried the raven-marked sword-spear like a lance, the butt tucked into his stirrup.

Four hundred or so Jindo comprised their party; Rand and Mat rode at the front alongside Rhuarc and Heirn. The Aiel walked, of course, their tents and some of the booty from Tear on packmules and horses. A number of the Jindo Maidens fanned ahead as scouts, and Stone Dogs trailed behind as a rear guard, with the main column hedged by watchful eyes, ready spears, and bows with arrows nocked. Supposedly the Peace of Rhuidean extended until those who had gone to Chaendaer returned to their own holds, but as Rhuarc explained to Rand, mistakes had been known to happen, and apologies and blood-price did not bring the dead out of their graves. Rhuarc seemed to think a mistake especially likely this time, certainly in part because of the Shaido party.

The lands of the Shaido clan lay beyond those of the Jindo's Taar-dad, in the same direction from Chaendaer, and they paralleled the Jindo some quarter of a mile distant. According to Rhuarc, Couladin should have waited another day for his brother to return. That Rand had seen Muradin after he had plucked out his own eyes made no difference; ten days was the time allotted. To leave sooner was to aban-don whoever had entered Rhuidean. Yet Couladin had set the Shaido to folding their tents as soon as he saw the Jindo pack animals being loaded. The Shaido moved along now with their own scouts and rear guard, seemingly ignoring the Jindo, but the space between never wid-ened much beyond three hundred paces. It was usual to have witnesses from perhaps half a dozen of the larger septs when a man sought the marking of a clan chief, and Couladin's people outnumbered the Jindo by at least two to one. Rand suspected that the third party, halfway between Shaido and Taardad, was the reason the interval did not nar-row suddenly and violently.

The Wise Ones walked just like all the other Aiel, including those strange, white-robed men and women Rhuarc called *gai'shain,* who led their packhorses. Not servants, exactly, but Rand was unsure he really understood Rhuarc's explanation about honor and obligation and captives; Heirn had been even more confusing, as though making an effort to explain why water was wet. Moiraine, Egwene and Lan rode with the Wise Ones, or at least the two women did. The Warder had his warhorse a little off on the side of the Shaido, watching them as closely as he did the rugged landscape. Sometimes Moiraine or Egwene or both got down to walk awhile, talking with the Wise Ones. Rand would have given his last penny to hear what they said. They looked in his direction often, quick glances that he was doubtless not supposed to notice. For some reason, Egwene was wearing her hair in two braids, plaited with lengths of red ribbon, like a bride's. He did not know why. He had commented on them before leaving Chaendaer—just mentioned them—and she nearly took his head off.

"Elayne is the woman for you."

He looked down at Aviendha in confusion. The challenging look was back in her blue-green eyes, but still layered atop stark dislike. She had been waiting outside the tent when he awoke that morning, and had not strayed more than three paces from him since. Clearly the Wise Ones had set her to spy, and clearly he was not supposed to realize it. She was pretty, and he was assumed to be fool enough not to see beyond that. No doubt that was the real reason she wore skirts now, and carried no weapon beyond a small beltknife. Women seemed to think men were simple-minded. Come to think of it, none of the other Aiel had commented at her change of clothing, but even Rhuarc avoided looking at her for too long. Probably they knew why she was there, or had some inkling of the Wise Ones' plan, and did not want to speak of it.

Rhuidean. He still did not know why she had gone; Rhuarc muttered about "women's business," plainly reluctant to discuss it around her. Considering the way she clung to Rand's side, that meant not discussing it at all. The clan chief was certainly listening now, and Heirn, and every Jindo in earshot. It was hard to tell with Aiel, sometimes, but he thought they looked amused. Mat was whistling softly, ostentatiously looking at anything but the two of them. Even so, this was the first time all day she had spoken to him.

"What do you mean?" he asked.

Her bulky skirts did not hinder her, walking along beside Jeade'en. No, not walking. Stalking. If she were a cat, she would be lashing her tail. "Elayne is a wetlander, your own kind." She tossed her head arrogantly. The short tail that Aiel warriors wore at the nape of the neck was missing. The folded scarf around her temples nearly enveloped her hair. "Exactly the woman for you. Is she not beautiful? Her back is straight, her limbs supple and strong, her lips like plump loveapples. Her hair is spun gold, her eyes blue sapphires. Her skin is smoother than the finest silk, her bosom fine and well-rounded. Her hips are—"

He cut her off frantically, his cheeks heating. "I know she's pretty. What are you doing?"

"I am describing her." Aviendha frowned up at him. "Have you seen her in her bath? There is no need for me to describe her if you have seen—"

"I have *not* seen!" He wished he did not sound strangled. Rhuarc and the others *were* listening, faces too blank for anything but amusement. Mat rolled his eyes with an open, roguish grin.

The woman only shrugged and rearranged her shawl. "She should have arranged it. But I have seen her, and I will act as *her* near sister." The emphasis seemed to say *his* "near sister" might have done the same; Aiel customs were strange, but this was mad! "Her hips—"

"Stop that!"

She gave him a sideways glare. "She is the woman for you. Elayne has laid her heart at your feet for a bridal wreath. Do you think there was anyone in the Stone of Tear who does not know?"

"I do not want to talk about Elayne," he told her firmly. Certainly not if she meant to go on as she had begun. The thought made his face go hot again. The woman did not seem to care *what* she said, or who heard!

"You do well to blush, putting her aside when she has bared her heart to you." Aviendha's voice was hard and contemptuous. "Two letters she wrote, baring all as if she had stripped herself beneath your mother's roof. You entice her into corners for kisses, then reject her. She meant every word of those letters, Rand al'Thor! Egwene told me so. She meant every word. What do you mean toward her, wetlander?"

Rand scrubbed a hand through his hair, and had to rearrange his *shoufa.* Elayne meant every word? In both letters? That was flat impossible. One contradicted the other nearly point for point! Suddenly he gave a start. *Egwene* had told her? About Elayne's letters? Did women discuss these things among themselves? Did they plan out between them how best to confuse a man?

He found himself missing Min. Min had never made him look a fool. Well, not more than once or twice. And she had never insulted him. Well, she had called him "sheepherder" a few times. But he felt comfortable around her, warm, in a strange way. She never made him feel a complete idiot, like Elayne, and Aviendha.

His silence seemed to irritate the Aiel woman more, if such was possible. Muttering to herself, striding along as though she wanted to trample something, she adjusted and readjusted her shawl half a dozen times. Finally her grumbling faded away. Instead, she began staring at him. Like a vulture. He could not see how she did not trip and fall on her face.

"Why are you looking at me like that?" he demanded.

"I am listening, Rand al'Thor, since you wish me to be silent." She smiled around gritted teeth. "Do you not enjoy having me listen to you?"

He glanced beyond her at Mat, who shook his head. There was just no understanding women. Rand tried to set himself to considering what lay ahead, but it was difficult with the woman's eyes on him. Pretty eyes, if they had not been full of spite, but he did wish she would look at something else.

Shading his eyes against the sun's glare, Mat did his best to avoid looking at Rand and the Aiel woman striding along between their horses. He could not understand why Rand put up with her. Aviendha was pretty enough, to be sure—more than just pretty, especially now she wore a semblance of proper clothes—but with a viper for a tongue and a temper to make Nynaeve look meek. He was just glad Rand was stuck with her and not him.

He pulled the kerchief from his head and wiped the sweat off of his face, then tied it back. The heat and the eternal sun in his eyes were beginning to get to him. Was there no such thing as shade in this whole land? Sweat stung his wounds. He had refused Healing the night before, when Moiraine wakened him after he had finally gotten to sleep. A few cuts were a small price to avoid having the Power used on you, and the Wise Ones' filthy-tasting tea had settled his headache. Well, after a fashion, anyway. What else ailed him, he did not think Moiraine could do anything about, and he had no intention of telling her until he understood it himself. If then. He did not even want to think of it.

Moiraine and the Wise Ones were watching him. Watching Rand actually, he supposed, but it felt the same. Surprisingly, the sun-haired one, Melaine, had climbed up on Aldieb behind the Aes Sedai, riding awkwardly and holding Moiraine around the waist as they talked. He had not known Aiel would ride at all. A very pretty woman, Melaine, with those fiery green eyes. Except, of course, that she could channel. A man would have to be an utter fool to tangle himself with one of those. Shifting in Pips's saddle, he reminded himself that it did not matter to him what Aiel did.

I've been to Rhuidean. I've done what those snake folk said I had to. And what did he have to show for it? *This bloody spear, a silver medallion, and. . . . I could go now. If I have any sense, I will.*

He could go. Try to find his own way out of the Waste—before he died of thirst or sunstroke. He could if Rand was not still pulling at him, holding him. The easiest manner of finding out was just to try leaving. Looking at the bleak landscape, he grimaced. A wind picked up—it felt as if it blew across an overheated cookstove—and small whirlwinds spun funnels of yellow dust across the cracked ground. Heat-haze made the distant mountains shimmer. Maybe it was best to stay around a while longer.

One of the Maidens who had been scouting ahead came trotting back and fell in beside Rhuarc, speaking for his ear alone. She flashed Mat a grin when she was done, and he busied himself picking a sharp burr out of Pips's mane. He remembered her all too well, a red-haired woman named Dorindha, about Egwene's age. Dorindha was one of those who had talked him into trying Maidens' Kiss. She had collected the first forfeit. It was not that he did not want to meet her eyes, certainly not that he could not; keeping your horse free of burrs and the like was important.

"Peddlers," Rhuarc announced when Dorindha sprinted off the way she had come. "Peddlers' wagons, heading in this direction." He did not sound pleased.

Mat brightened considerably, though. A peddler might be just the thing. If the fellow knew the way in, he knew the way out. He wondered if Rand suspected what he was thinking; the man had gone as blank-faced as any of the Aiel.

The Aiel picked up their pace a little—Couladin's people imitated the Jindo and the Wise Ones' party with hardly a hestitation; their own scouts had probably brought word, too—a quick enough step that the horses had to maintain a brisk walk. The sun did not bother the Aiel at all, not even the *gai'shain* in their white robes. They flowed over the broken ground.

Less than two miles brought the wagons in sight, a dozen and a half of them, strung out in a line. All showed the wear of hard travel, with spare wheels lashed everywhere. Despite a coat of yellow dust, the first two looked like white-painted boxes on wheels, or little houses, complete with wooden steps at the back and a metal stove-chimney sticking through the roof. The last three, drawn by twenty-mule hitches, appeared no more than huge barrels, also white, doubtless full of water. Those in between could have done for peddlers' wagons in the Two Rivers, with high stout-spoked wheels and clanking clusters of pots and things in big net bags tied all along the tall round canvas covers.

The wagondrivers drew rein as soon as they spotted the Aiel, waiting for the columns to come to them. A heavy man in a pale gray coat and dark, wide-brimmed hat climbed down from the back of the lead wagon and stood watching, now and then taking off his flat-crowned hat to wipe his forehead with a large white handkerchief. If he was nervous, looking at maybe fifteen hundred Aiel sweeping toward him, Mat could not blame him. The strange thing was the expressions on the Aiel nearest Mat. Rhuarc, trotting ahead of Rand's horse, looked grim, and Heirn wore a face that could break rocks.

"I don't understand," Mat said. "You look like you're going to kill somebody." That would certainly put paid to his hopes. "I thought there were three kinds of people you Aiel let come out here in the Waste; peddlers, gleemen, and the Traveling People."

"Peddlers and gleemen are welcome," Heirn replied curtly. If this was a welcome, Mat did not want to see Aiel being unwelcoming.

"What about the Traveling People?" he asked curiously. When Heirn kept silent, he added, "Tinkers? The Tuatha'an?" The sept chief's face grew even harder before he turned his eyes back to the wagons. Aviendha shot Mat a look as if he were a fool.

Rand drew Jeade'en close to Pips. "I'd not mention Tinkers to the Aiel if I were you," he said in a low voice. "They are . . . a touchy subject."

"If you say so." Why would *Tinkers* be a touchy subject? "Looks to me like they're being touchy enough about this peddler. Peddler! I can remember merchants who came to Emond's Field with fewer wagons."

"He came into the Waste," Rand chuckled. Jeade'en tossed his head and danced a few steps. "I wonder if he will leave it again?" Rand's twisted grin did not reach his eyes. Sometimes Mat almost wished Rand would decide whether he was mad or not and get it over with. Almost.

Three hundred paces short of the wagons, Rhuarc signaled a halt, and he and Heirn went on alone. At least, that seemed to have been his intention, but Rand heeled his dapple stallion after them, and the inevitable bodyguard of a hundred Jindo followed. And Aviendha, of course, keeping close as though tied to Rand's horse. Mat rode right with them. If Rhuarc sent this fellow packing, he did not mean to miss his chance to go along.

Couladin came trotting out from the Shaido. Alone. Perhaps he meant to do as Rhuarc and Heirn had intended, but Mat suspected the man was pointing out that he went alone where Rand needed a hundred guards. At first it seemed Moiraine was coming, too, but words passed between the Wise Ones and her, and they all stayed where they were. Watching, though. The Aes Sedai dismounted, playing with something small that sparkled, and Egwene and the Wise Ones clustered around her.

Despite his face mopping, the big, gray-coated fellow did not appear uneasy up close, although he jumped when Maidens suddenly rose out of the ground, encircling his wagons. The wagon drivers, hard-faced men with more than enough scars and broken noses to go around, looked ready to crawl under their seats; they were tough alley dogs compared to Aiel wolves. The peddler recovered right away. He was not fat for all his size; that heaviness was muscle. Rand and Mat on their horses earned his curious glances, but he singled out Rhuarc at once. His hooked beak of a nose and dark, tilted eyes gave his square swarthy face a predatory look not lessened when he put on a wide smile and swept his broad-brimmed hat off in a bow. "I am Hadnan Kadere," he said, "peddler. I seek Cold Rocks Hold, good sirs, but I will trade with one and all. I have many fine—"

Rhuarc cut him off like an icy knife. "You head well away from Cold Rocks, or any hold. How is it you have come this far from the Dragonwall without acquiring a guide?"

"I do not really know, good sir." Kadere did not lose his smile, but the corners of his mouth tightened a trifle. "I have traveled openly. This is my first visit to the Threefold Land so far south. I thought perhaps here there are no guides." Couladin snorted loudly, twirled one of his spears lazily. Kadere hunched his shoulders as if he felt steel sliding into his thick body already.

"There are always guides," Rhuarc said coldly. "You have luck to have come so far without one. Luck that you are not dead, or walking back to the Dragonwall in your skin." Kadere flashed an uneasy, toothy smile, and the clan chief went on. "Luck to meet us. Had you continued this way another day or two, you would have reached Rhuidean."

The peddler's face went gray. "I have heard. . . ." He stopped to swallow. "I did not know, good sirs. You must believe, I would not do such a thing deliberately. Nor by accident," he added hastily. "The Light illumine my words for truth, good sirs, I would not!"

"That is well," Rhuarc told him. "The penalties are severe. You may travel with me to Cold Rocks. It would not do for you to become lost again. The Three-fold Land can be a dangerous place for those who do not know it."

Couladin's head came up defiantly. "Why not with me?" he said in a sharp voice. "The Shaido are the more numerous here, Rhuarc. By custom, he travels with me."

"Have you become a clan chief when I did not see?" The fire-haired Shaido flushed, but Rhuarc showed no hint of satisfaction, only went on in that level voice. "The peddler seeks Cold Rocks. He will journey with me. The Shaido with you may trade with him as we travel. The Taardad are not so starved for peddlers that we try to keep them to ourselves."

Couladin's face went even darker, yet he moderated his tone, even if it did creak with the effort. "I will camp near Cold Rocks, Rhuarc. He Who Comes With the Dawn concerns *all* Aiel, not only the Taardad. The Shaido will have their proper place. The Shaido, too, will follow He Who Comes With the Dawn." He had not, Mat realized, acknowledged that that was Rand. Peering at the wagons, Rand did not seem to be listening.

Rhuarc was silent a moment. "The Shaido will be welcome guests in the lands of the Taardad, if they come to follow He Who Comes With the Dawn." And that could be taken two ways, as well.

Kadere had been mopping his face all this time, likely seeing himself in the middle of a battle between Aiel. He punctuated Rhuarc's invitation with a heavy sigh of relief. "Thank you, good sirs. Thank you." Probably for not killing him. "Perhaps you would care to see what my wagons have to offer? Some special thing you might like?"

"Later," Rhuarc said. "We will stop at Imre Stand for the night, and you may show your wares then." Couladin was already striding away, having heard the name of Imre Stand, whatever that was. Kadere started to put his hat back on.

"A hat," Mat said, reining Pips closer to the peddler. If he had to remain in the Waste a bit longer, at least he could keep that bloody sun out of his eyes. "I'll give a gold mark for a hat like that."

"Done!" called a woman's huskily melodious voice.

Mat looked around, and gave a start. The only woman in sight beside Aviendha and the Maidens was walking up from the second wagon, but she certainly did not match that voice, one of the loveliest he had ever heard. Rand frowned at her and shook his head, and he had cause. A foot shorter than Kadere, she must have weighed as much or more. Rolls of fat nearly hid her dark eyes, disguising whether they were tilted or not, but her nose was a hatchet that dwarfed the peddler's. In a dress of pale-cream silk stretched tight around her bulk, with a white lace shawl held above her head on elaborate ivory combs thrust into long, coarse black hair, she moved with incongruous lightness, almost like one of the Maidens.

"A good offer," she said in those musical tones. "I am Keille Shaogi, peddler." She snatched the hat away from Kadere and thrust it up at Mat. "Stout, good sir, and nearly new. You will need its like to survive the Three-fold Land. Here, a man can die . . ." Fat fingers made a whip-crack. ". . . like so." Her sudden laugh had the same throaty, caressing quality as her voice. "Or a woman. A gold mark, you said." When he hesitated, her half-buried eyes glittered raven black. "I seldom offer any man a bargain twice."

A peculiar woman to say the least. Kadere made no protest beyond the slightest grimace. If Keille was his partner, there was no doubt who was the senior. And if the hat kept Mat's head from broiling, it really was worth the price so far as he was concerned. She bit the Tairen mark he handed her before releasing the hat. For a wonder, it fit. And if it was no cooler under that wide brim, at least it was blessedly shady. The kerchief went into his coat pocket.

"Anything for the rest of you?" The stout woman ran her eye over the Aiel, murmuring, "What a pretty child" to Aviendha with a baring of teeth that might have been a smile. To Rand, she said sweetly, "And you, good sir?" That voice coming out of that face was truly jarring, especially when it took on this honeyed tone. "Something to shelter you from this desperate land?" Turning Jeade'en so he could peer at the wagon drivers, Rand only shook his head. With that *shoufa* around his face, he really did look like an Aiel.

"Tonight, Keille," Kadere said. "We open trade tonight, at a place called Imre Stand."

"Do we, now." For a long moment she peered at the Shaido column, and at the Wise Ones' party for a longer. Abruptly she turned for her own wagon, saying over her shoulder to the other peddler, "Then why are you keeping these good sirs standing here? Move, Kadere. Move." Rand stared after her, shaking his head again.

There was a gleeman back by her wagon. Mat blinked, thinking the heat had gotten to him, but the fellow did not vanish, a dark-haired man in his middle years wearing a patch-covered cloak. He watched the gathering apprehensively until Keille shoved him up the wagon's step ahead of her. Kadere looked at her white wagon with less expression than one of the Aiel before stalking off to his own. Truly an odd lot.

"Did you see the gleeman?" Mat asked Rand, who nodded vaguely, eyeing the line of wagons as if he had never seen a wagon before. Rhuarc and Heirn were already on their way back to the rest of the Jindo. The hundred surrounding Rand waited patiently, dividing their gaze between him and anything that might hide even a mouse. The drivers began gathering their reins, but Rand did not move. "Strange people these peddlers, wouldn't you say, Rand? But I suppose you have to be strange to come to the Waste. Look at us." That brought a grimace from Aviendha, but Rand seemed not to have heard. Mat wanted him to say something. Anything. This silence was unnerving. "Would you have thought escorting a peddler would be such an honor Rhuarc and Couladin would argue over it? Do you understand any of this *ji'e'toh?*"

"You *are* a fool," Aviendha muttered. "It had nothing to do with *ji'e'toh.* Couladin tries to behave as a clan chief. Rhuarc cannot allow that until—unless—he has gone to Rhuidean. The Shaido would steal bones from a dog—they would steal the bones *and* the dog—yet even they deserve a true chief. And because of Rand al'Thor we must allow a thousand of them to pitch their tents in our lands."

"His eyes," Rand said without looking away from the wagons. "A dangerous man."

Mat frowned at him. "Whose eyes? Couladin's?"

"Kadere's eyes. All that sweating, going white in the face. Yet his eyes never changed. You always have to watch the eyes. Not what he seems."

"Sure, Rand." Mat shifted in his saddle, half lifted his reins as if to ride on. Maybe silence had not been so bad. "You have to watch the eyes."

Rand changed his study to the tops of the nearest spires and buttes, twisting his head this way and that. "Time is the risk," he murmured. "Time sets snares. I have to avoid theirs while setting mine."

There was nothing up there that Mat could make out beyond an occasional scattering of brush and now and then a stunted tree. Aviendha frowned at the heights, then at Rand, adjusting her shawl. "Snares?" Mat said. *Light, let him give me an answer that isn't crazy.* "Who's setting snares?"

For a moment Rand looked at him as if he did not understand the question. The peddlers' wagons were starting off with an escort of Maidens loping alongside, turning to follow the Jindo as they trotted past, mirrored by the Shaido. More Maidens sped ahead to scout. Only the Aiel around Rand stood still, though the Wise Ones' party dawdled and watched, and from Egwene's gestures, Mat thought she wanted to come check on them.

"You can't see it, or feel it," Rand said finally. Leaning a little toward Mat, he whispered loudly, as though pretending. "We ride with evil now, Mat. Watch yourself." He wore that twisted grin again, as he watched the wagons lumber by.

"You think this Kadere is *evil?*"

"A dangerous man, Mat—the eyes always give it away—yet who can say? But what cause have I to worry, with Moiraine and the Wise Ones watching out for me? And we mustn't forget Lanfear. Has any man ever been under so many watchful eyes?" Abruptly Rand straightened in his saddle. "It has begun," he said quietly. "Wish that I have your luck, Mat. It has begun, and there is no turning back, now, however the blade falls." Nodding to himself, he started his dapple after Rhuarc, Aviendha trotting alongside, the hundred Jindo following.

Mat was glad enough to follow too. Better than being left there, certainly. The sun burned high in a stark blue sky. There was a lot of traveling yet to be done before sunset. It had begun? What did he mean, it had begun? It had begun in Rhuidean; or better, in Emond's Field on Winternight a year gone. "Riding with evil" and "no turning back"? And Lanfear? Rand was walking the razor's edge, now. No doubt about it. There had to be a way out of the Waste before it was too late. From time to time Mat studied the peddlers' wagons. Before it was too late. If it was not already.

CHAPTER
37

Imre Stand

The sun still stood more than its own height above the jagged western horizon when Rhuarc said that Imre Stand, where he intended to stay for the night, lay only a mile or so ahead.

"Why are we stopping already?" Rand asked. "There are hours more daylight left."

It was Aviendha, walking along on the other side of Jeade'en from the clan chief, who answered, in the scornful tone he had come to expect. "There is water at Imre Stand. It is best to camp near water when the chance presents itself."

"And the peddlers' wagons cannot go much farther," Rhuarc added. "When the shadows lengthen, they must stop or begin breaking wheels and mules' legs. I do not want to leave them behind. I cannot spare anyone to watch over them, and Couladin can."

Rand twisted in his saddle. Flanked now by Jindo *Duadhe Mahdi'in*, Water Seekers, the wagons were making heavy going a few hundred paces off to the side, lurching along, raising a tall plume of yellow dust. Most gullies were too deep or too steep-walled, forcing the drivers to go around, so the train twisted like a drunken snake. Loud curses floated from the wavering line, most blaming the mules for it all. Kadere and Keille were still inside their white-painted wagons.

"No," Rand said, "you don't want to do that." He laughed softly in spite of himself.

Mat was looking at him oddly from under the broad brim of his new hat. He smiled in what he hoped was a reassuring way, but Mat's expression did not change. *He's going to have to take care of himself,* Rand thought. *Too much is riding on this.*

Speaking of taking care, he became aware of Aviendha studying him, her shawl wrapped around her head much like a *shoufa.* He straightened himself again. Moiraine might have told her off to nurse him, but he had the impression the woman was waiting to see him fall. Doubtless she would find that funny, Aiel humor being what it was. He would have liked to think she simply resented being stuffed into a dress and set to watch him, but the glitter in her eyes seemed too personal for that.

For once Moiraine and the Wise Ones were *not* watching him. Halfway between the Jindo and the Shaido, Moiraine and Egwene were walking with Amys and the others, all six women looking at something in the Aes Sedai's hands. It caught the light of the falling sun, sparkling like a gem; they certainly seemed as intent as any girl on a pretty. Lan rode back among the *gai'shain* and packhorses, as though they had sent him away.

The scene made Rand uneasy. He was used to being the center of attention for that lot. What had they found more interesting? Surely nothing he could be happy about, not with Moiraine, likely not with Amys or the others. They all had their plans for him. Egwene was the only one of them he really trusted. *Light, I hope I can still trust her.* The only one he could really trust was himself. *When the boar breaks cover, there's only you and your spear.* His laugh was a touch bitter this time.

"You find the Three-fold Land amusing, Rand al'Thor?" Aviendha's smile was the merest flash of white teeth. "Laugh while you can, wetlander. When this land begins to break you, it will be a fitting punishment for your treatment of Elayne."

Why would the woman not let up? "You didn't show any respect for the Dragon Reborn," he snapped, "but you could try finding a little for the *Car'a'carn.*"

Rhuarc chuckled. "A clan chief is not a wetlander king, Rand, nor is the *Car'a'carn.* There is respect—though women generally show as little as they can get away with—but anyone can speak to a chief." Even so, he sent a frown in the direction of the woman on the other side of Rand's horse. "Some do push the bounds of honor."

Aviendha must have known that last was meant for her ears; her face went stony. But she strode along without saying another word, fists clenched at her sides.

A pair of the scouting Maidens appeared, coming back at a dead run. They were plainly not together; one headed straight for the Shaido, the other for the Jindo. Rand recognized her, a yellow-haired woman named Adelin, handsome but hard-faced, with a scar making a fine white line across her sun-dark cheek. She was one of those who had been in the Stone, though older than most of the Maidens there, perhaps ten years more than he. The quick look she gave Aviendha before falling in beside Rhuarc, an equal blend of curiosity and sympathy, made Rand bristle. If Aviendha had agreed to do the Wise Ones' spying, she certainly did not deserve sympathy. His company was not so onerous as that. Him, Adelin ignored altogether.

"There is trouble at Imre Stand," she told Rhuarc, her speech quick and clipped. "There is no one to be seen. We have kept hidden and not gone close."

"Good," Rhuarc replied. "Inform the Wise Ones." Unconsciously hefting his spears, he dropped back to the main body of Jindo. Aviendha muttered to herself, plucking at her skirts, obviously wanting to join him.

"I think they already know," Mat said as Adelin sped toward the Wise Ones' party.

From the agitation among the women around Moiraine, Rand thought he was right. They all appeared to be talking at once. Egwene was shading her eyes, staring at either Adelin or him, her other hand to her mouth. How they knew had to be a question for later.

"What kind of trouble might it be?" he asked Aviendha. Still muttering to herself, she did not answer. "Aviendha? What kind of trouble?" Nothing. "Burn you, woman, you can answer a simple question! What kind of trouble?"

She flushed, but her reply came in a level tone. "It is most likely to be a raid, for goats or sheep; either could be herded at Imre for pasture, but most likely goats, because of the water. Probably it was the Chareen, the White Mountain sept or the Jarra. They are closest. Or it might be a sept from the Goshien. The Tomanelle are too far, I think."

"Will there be fighting?" He reached out for *saidin;* the sweet rush of the Power flooded him. The rancid taint oozed through him, and fresh sweat burst from every pore. "Aviendha?"

"No. Adelin would have said if the raiders were still there. The herd and the *gai'shain* are miles gone by now. We cannot recover the herd because we must accompany you."

He wondered why she did not mention recovering the captives, the *gai'shain*, but he did not wonder long. The effort of staying upright while holding on to *saidin*, of not folding up and being swept away, left little room for thought.

Rhuarc and the Jindo swept ahead at a run, already veiling their faces, and Rand followed more slowly. Aviendha shot him impatient frowns, but he kept Jeade'en to a brisk walk. He would not go galloping into someone else's trap. At least Mat was in no hurry; he hesitated, looking at the peddlers' wagons, before cantering Pips up. Rand never glanced at the wagons.

The Shaido fell behind, slowing until the Wise Ones began to move again. Of course. This was Tardaad land. Couladin would not care if someone raided here. Rand hoped the clan chiefs could be gathered at Alcair Dal quickly. How could he unite a people who seemed to fight each other all the time? The least of his worries, now.

When Imre Stand finally came in sight, it was something of a surprise. A few widely scattered clumps of long-haired white goats browsed on patches of tough grass and even the leaves of thorny bushes. At first he did not see the crude stone building set against the base of a tall butte; the rough stonework blended in perfectly, and several thornbushes had taken root on the dirt-covered roof. Not very big, it had arrowslits for windows and only one door that he could see. After a moment he spotted another building, no larger, tucked onto a ledge some twenty paces higher. A deep crevice ran up to the ledge and beyond from behind the stone house at the base; there was no other evident way to reach the ledge.

Rhuarc, standing openly four hundred or so paces from the butte with his veil lowered, was the only Jindo in sight. That did not mean the others were not there, of course. Rand reined in beside him and dismounted. The clan chief continued to study the stone buildings.

"The goats," Aviendha said, sounding troubled. "Raiders would not have left any goats behind. Most are gone, but it almost looks as if the herd has just been allowed to wander."

"For days," Rhuarc agreed, not taking his eyes from the buildings, "or more would remain. Why does no one come out? They should be able to see my face, and know me." He started forward, and made no objection when Rand joined him leading Jeade'en. Aviendha had one hand on her belt knife, and Mat, riding behind, carried that black-hafted spear as if he expected to need it.

The door was rough wood, pieced together from short, narrow planks. Some of the stout bracing was broken, hacked by axes. Rhuarc hesitated a moment before pushing it open. He hardly glanced inside before turning to run his eyes over the surrounding country.

Rand put his head in. There was no one there. The interior, light streaming in bars through the arrowslits, was all one room and plainly not a dwelling, just a place for herdsmen to shelter, and defend themselves if attacked. There were no furnishings, no tables or chairs. A raised open hearth stood beneath a sooty smoke hole in the roof. The wide crevice at the back had steps chiseled into the gray rock. The place had been ransacked. Bedding, blankets, pots, all lay scattered across the stone floor amid slashed cushions and pillows. Some liquid had been splashed over everything, the walls, even the ceiling, and had dried black.

When he realized what it was, he jerked back, the Power-wrought sword coming into his hands before he even thought. Blood. So much blood. There had been slaughter done here, as savage as anything he could imagine. Nothing moved out there except the goats.

Aviendha backed out as fast as she went in. "Who?" she demanded incredulously, her large blue-green eyes filled with outrage. "Who would do this? Where are the dead?"

"Trollocs," Mat muttered. "It looks like Trolloc work to me."

She snorted contemptuously. "Trollocs do not come into the Three-fold Land, wetlander. No more than a few miles below the Blight, at least, and then seldom. I have heard they call the Three-fold Land the Dying Ground. We hunt Trollocs, wetlander; they do not hunt us."

Nothing moved. Rand let the sword go, pushed *saidin* away. It was hard. The sweetness of the Power was nearly enough to overcome the feel of filth from the taint, the sheer exhilaration almost enough to make him not care. Mat was right whatever Aviendha said, but this was old, the Trollocs gone. Trollocs in the Waste, at a place he had come to. He was not fool enough to think it coincidence. *But if they think I am, maybe they'll grow careless.*

Rhuarc signaled the Jindo to come in—they seemed to rise out of the ground—and some time later the others appeared, the Shaido and the peddlers' wagons and the Wise Ones' party. Word spread quickly of what had been found, and among the Aiel, tension became palpable. They moved as if they expected momentary attack, perhaps from each other. Scouts fanned out in every direction. Unharnessing their mules, the wagon drivers looked around jerkily, and seemed ready to dive under their wagons at the first shout.

For a time all was a stirred hive of ants. Rhuarc made sure the peddlers lined their wagons up on the edge of the Jindo camp. Cou-

ladin glowered, since it meant any Shaido who wanted to trade had to
go to the Jindo, but he did not argue. Perhaps even he could see that
might lead to dancing the spears, now. The Shaido tents went up a
scant quarter-mile away, with the Wise Ones, as usual, in between. The
Wise Ones examined the inside of the building, and Moiraine and Lan
did, as well, but if they reached any conclusions, they told no one.

The water at Imre Stand turned out to be a tiny spring at the back of
the crevice, feeding a deep, roughly round pool—what Rhuarc called a
tank—less than two paces across. Enough for herdsmen, enough for
the Jindo to fill some of their waterskins. No Shaido went near; in
Taardad land, the Jindo had first claim on water. It seemed the goats
got their moisture purely from the thick leaves of the thorny bushes.
Rhuarc assured Rand there would be much more water at the next
night's stop.

Kadere produced a surprise while the wagon drivers were unhitching
their teams and fetching buckets from the waterwagons. When he came
out of his wagon, a dark-haired young woman accompanied him, in a
red silk gown and red velvet slippers more suited to a palace than to
the Waste. A filmy red scarf wound almost like *shoufa* and veil provided no protection from the sun, and certainly did nothing to hide a
palely beautiful heart-shaped face. Clinging to the peddler's thick arm,
she swayed enticingly as he took her to see the blood-splashed room;
Moiraine and the others had gone off to where the *gai'shain* were
erecting the Wise Ones' camp. When the pair came back out, the
young woman shuddered delicately. Rand was sure it was pretense, just
as he was sure she had asked to view that butcher's workroom. Her
show of revulsion lasted all of two seconds, and then she was peering
about interestedly at the Aiel.

It appeared that Rand himself was one of the sights she wanted to
see. Kadere seemed ready to take her back to the wagon, but she
guided him to Rand instead, the alluring smile on her full lips plain
behind her diaphanous veil. "Hadnan has been telling me of you," she
said in a smoky voice. She might have been hanging on the peddler, but
her dark eyes traced Rand boldly. "You are the one the Aiel talk of. He
Who Comes With the Dawn." Keille and the gleeman came out of the
second wagon and stood together at a distance, watching.

"It seems I am," he said.

"Strange." Her smile became wickedly mischievous. "I thought you
would be handsomer." Patting Kadere on the cheek, she sighed. "This
dreadful heat is so wearing. Do not be too long."

Kadere did not speak until she had climbed the steps back inside.

His hat had been replaced by a long white scarf tied atop his head, the ends hanging down his neck. "You must forgive Isendre, good sir. She is . . . too forward, sometimes." His voice was mollifying, but his eyes belonged on a bird of prey. He hesitated, then went on. "I have heard other things. I have heard that you took *Callandor* out of the Heart of the Stone."

The man's eyes never changed. If he knew about *Callandor*, he knew Rand was the Dragon Reborn, knew he could wield the One Power. And his eyes never changed. A dangerous man. "I have heard it said," Rand told him, "that you should believe nothing you hear, and only half of what you see."

"A wise rule," Kadere said after a moment. "Yet to achieve greatly, a man must believe something. Belief and knowledge pave the road to greatness. Knowledge is perhaps the most valuable of all. We all seek the coin of knowledge. Your pardon, good sir. Isendre is not a patient woman. Perhaps we will have another opportunity to talk."

Before the man had taken three steps, Aviendha said in a low, hard voice, "You belong to Elayne, Rand al'Thor. Do you stare so at every woman who comes in front of your eyes, or only those who go half-naked? If I strip off my clothes, will you stare so at me? You belong to Elayne!"

He had forgotten she was there. "I don't *belong* to anyone, Aviendha. Elayne? She cannot seem to make up her mind what she thinks."

"Elayne laid her heart bare to you, Rand al'Thor. If she did not show you in the Stone of Tear, did her two letters not tell you what she feels? You are hers, and no other's."

Rand threw up his hands and stalked away from her. At least, he tried. She followed on his heels, a disapproving shadow in the sun's glare.

Swords. The Aiel might have forgotten why they did not carry swords, but they had kept the contempt for them. Swords might make her leave him alone. Seeking out Lan in the Wise Ones' camp, he asked the Warder to watch him work the forms. Bair was the only one of the four in view, and a scowl surely deepened the creases on her face. Egwene was not to be seen either. Moiraine wore calm like a mask, dark eyes cool; he could not say whether she approved.

He was not out to offend the Aiel, so he set up with Lan between the Wise Ones' tents and the Jindo's. He used one of the practice swords Lan carried in his baggage, a bundle of loosely tied lathes in place of a blade. The weight and balance were right, though, and he could forget himself in the dancelike flow from form to form, the practice sword alive in his hands, a part of him. Usually it was that way. Today the sun was a furnace in the sky baking out moisture and strength. Aviendha squatted off to one side, hugging her knees to her chest and staring at him.

Finally, panting, he let his arms drop.

"You lost concentration," Lan told him. "You must hold on to that even when your muscles turn to water. Lose it, and that is the day you die. And it will probably be a farmboy who has his hands on a sword for the first time who does it." His smile was sudden, odd on that stony face.

"Yes. Well, I'm not a farmboy any longer, am I?" They had gained an audience, if at a distance. Aiel lined the edge of both the Shaido and Jindo camps. Keille's cream-wrapped bulk stood out among the Jindo, the gleeman beside her in his cloak of colored patches. Which one did he choose? He did not want them to see him watching them. "How do Aiel fight, Lan?"

"Hard," the Warder said dryly. "They never lose concentration. Look here." With his sword he drew on the hard, cracked clay, a circle and arrows. "Aiel change tactics according to circumstances, but here is one they favor. They move in a column, divided into quarters. When they meet an enemy, the first quarter rushes in to pin them. The second and third sweep wide to either side, hitting the flanks and rear. The last quarter waits in reserve, often not even watching the battle, except for their leader. When a weakness opens—a hole, anything—the reserve strikes there. Finish!" His sword stabbed into a circle already pierced with arrows.

"How do you beat that?" Rand asked.

"With difficulty. When you make first contact—you'll not spot Aiel before they strike unless you are lucky—immediately send out horsemen to break up, or at least delay, their flanking attacks. If you keep most of your strength back and defeat the holding attack, then you can wheel on the others in turn and defeat them, too."

"Why do you want to learn how to fight Aiel?" Aviendha burst out. "Are you not He Who Comes With the Dawn, meant to bind us together and return us all to old glories? Besides, if you want to know how to fight Aiel, ask Aiel, not a wetlander. His way will not work."

"It has worked well enough with Bordermen from time to time." Rhuarc's soft boots made very little sound on the hard ground. He had a waterskin under his arm. "Allowances are always made when someone suffers a disappointment, Aviendha, but there is a limit to sulking.

You gave up the spear for your obligation to the people and the blood. One day no doubt you will be making a clan chief do what you want instead of what he wants, but if instead you are Wise One to the smallest hold of the smallest sept of the Taardad, the obligation remains, and it cannot be met by tantrums."

A Wise One. Rand felt a fool. Of course that was why she had gone to Rhuidean. But he would never have thought Aviendha would choose to give up the spear. It certainly explained why she had been chosen to spy on him, though. Suddenly he found himself wondering if she could channel. It seemed Min had been the only woman in his life since that Winternight who could not.

Rhuarc tossed him the sloshing waterskin. The lukewarm water slid down his throat like chilled wine. He tried not to splash any over his face, not to waste it, but it was hard.

"I thought you might like to learn the spear," Rhuarc said when Rand finally lowered the half-empty skin. For the first time Rand realized the clan chief was carrying only two spears, and a pair of bucklers. Not practice spears if there were any such, a foot of sharp steel tipped each.

Steel or wood, his muscles cried out for rest. His legs wanted him to sit down, and his head wanted to lie down. Keille and the gleeman were gone, but Aiel were still watching from both camps. They had seen him practicing with a despised sword, if a wooden one. They were his people. He did not know them, but they were his, in more senses than one. Aviendha was still watching him, too, glowering as though blaming him for Rhuarc having set her down. Not that she had anything to do with his decision, of course. The Jindo and Shaido were watching; that was it.

"That mountain can grow awfully heavy sometimes," he sighed, taking a spear and buckler from Rhuarc. "When do you find a chance to put it down awhile?"

"When you die," Lan said simply.

Forcing his legs to move—and trying to ignore Aviendha—Rand squared off with Rhuarc. He did not mean to die just yet. No, not for a long time yet.

Leaning against a tall wheel in the shade of one of the peddlers' wagons, Mat glanced at the line of Jindo watching Rand. All he could see now was their backs. The man was a pure fool, leaping about in this heat. Any sensible man would find a bit of protection from the sun, something to drink. Shifting his seat in the shade, he peered into the mug of ale he had bought from one of the drivers and grimaced. Ale just did not taste right when it was as warm as soup. At least it was wet. The only other thing he had bought, aside from the hat, was a short-stemmed pipe with a silver-worked bowl, snuggled now in his coat pocket with his tabac pouch. Trading was not on his mind. Unless it was for passage out of the Waste, a commodity the peddlers' wagons did not seem to be offering at the moment.

They were doing a steady business, if not for ale. The Aiel did not mind the temperature, but they seemed to think it too weak. Most were Jindo, but there was a steady stream of Shaido from the other camp. Couladin and Kadere had their heads together for a long time, though they came to no agreement, since Couladin left empty-handed. Kadere must not have liked losing the trade; he stared after Couladin with those hawk's eyes, and a Jindo who wanted his attention had to speak three times before he was heard.

The Aiel did not show much in the way of coin, but the peddlers and their people were quick to accept silver bowls or gold figurines or fine wall hangings looted from Tear, and Aiel pouches produced raw nuggets of gold and silver that made Mat sit up. But an Aiel who lost at dice might well reach for his spears. He wondered where the mines were. Where one man could find gold, another could. It was probably a lot of work, though, mining gold. Taking a long drink of warm ale, he settled back against the wagon wheel.

What sold and what did not, and at what price, was interesting. The Aiel were no simple fools to hand over a gold saltcellar, say, for a bolt of cloth. They knew the value of things and bargained hard, though they had their own wants. Books went immediately; not everyone wanted them, but those who did took every last one the wagons held. Laces and velvets vanished as soon as they were brought out, for astonishing quantities of silver and gold, and ribbons for not much less, but the finest silks just lay there. Silk was cheaper in trade to the east, he overheard a Shaido tell Kadere. A heavy-set, broken-nosed driver tried to talk a Jindo Maiden into a carved ivory bracelet. She pulled one wider, thicker and more ornate from her pouch and offered to wrestle him for the pair. He hesitated before refusing, which showed Mat he was even dumber than he looked. Needles and pins were snapped up, but the pots, and most of the knives, earned sneers; Aiel smiths did better work. Everything changed hands, from vials of perfumes and bath salts to kegs of brandy. Wine and brandy fetched good prices. He was startled to hear Heirn ask for Two Rivers tabac. The peddlers had none.

One driver kept trying to interest the Aiel in a heavy, gold-worked crossbow with no success. The crossbow caught Mat's eye, all those inlaid gold lions with what seemed to be rubies for eyes. Small, but still rubies. Of course, a good Two Rivers longbow could shoot six arrows while a crossbowman was still cranking back the bowstring for his second shot. A longer range for a crossbow that size, though, by a hundred paces. With two men doing nothing but keeping a crossbow with bolt in place in the hands of each crossbowman, and stout pikemen to hold the cavalry off. . . .

Wincing, Mat let his head fall back against the spokes. It had happened again. He had to get out of the Waste, away from Moiraine, away from any Aes Sedai. Maybe back home for a while. Maybe he could get there in time to help with this Whitecloak trouble. *Small chance of that, unless I use the bloody Ways, or another bloody Portal Stone.* That would not solve his problems anyway. For one thing, there were no answers in Emond's Field to what those snaky folk had meant about marrying the Daughter of the Nine Moons, or dying and living again. Or Rhuidean.

Through his coat he rubbed the silver foxhead medallion, hung around his neck again. The pupil of the fox's eye was a tiny circle split by a sinuous line, one side polished bright, the other shaded in some way. The ancient symbol of Aes Sedai, before the Breaking. The black-hafted spear, sword-blade point marked with two ravens, he took from where it was leaning beside him and laid it across his knees. More Aes Sedai work. Rhuidean had provided no answers, only more questions, and. . . .

Before Rhuidean his memory had been full of holes. Casting back in his mind then, he would be able to remember walking up to a door in the morning and leaving in the evening, but nothing between. Now there was something in between, filling all those holes. Waking dreams, or something very like. It was as if he could remember dances and battles and streets and cities, none of which he had ever really seen, none of which he was sure had ever existed, like a hundred pieces of memory from a hundred different men. Better to think of them as dreams, maybe—a little better—yet he was as sure in them as in any of his own remembrances. Battles numbered the most, and sometimes they crept up on him in a way, as with the crossbow. He would find himself looking at a piece of ground and planning how to set an ambush there, or defend against one, or how to set an army for battle. It was madness.

Without looking, he traced the flowing script carved into the black spear shaft. He could read it as easily as any book now, though it had taken him the whole trip back to Chaendaer to realize it. Rand had not said anything, but he suspected he had given himself away, there in Rhuidean. He knew the Old Tongue now, sifted whole out of those dreams. *Light, what did they do to me?*

"*Sa souvraya niende misain ye,*" he said aloud. "I am lost in my own mind."

"A scholar, for this day and Age."

Mat looked up to find the gleeman looking at him with dark, deep-set eyes. The fellow was taller than most, somewhere in his middle years and likely attractive to women, but with an oddly apprehensive way of holding his head cocked as if trying to look at you sideways.

"Just something I heard once," Mat said. He had to be more careful. If Moiraine decided to pack him off to the White Tower for study, they would never let him out of there again. "You hear scraps of things and remember them. I know a few phrases." That should cover any slips he was stupid enough to make.

"I am Jasin Natael. A gleeman." Natael did not flourish his cloak the way Thom would; he could have been saying he was a carpenter or a wheelwright. "Do you mind if I join you?" Mat nodded to the ground next to him, and the gleeman folded his legs, tucking his cloak under to sit on. He seemed fascinated by the Jindo and Shaido milling around the wagons, most still carrying their spears and bucklers. "Aiel," he murmured. "Not what I would have expected. I can still hardly credit it."

"I've been with them for weeks now," Mat said, "and I don't know that I believe them myself. Odd people. If any of the Maidens ask you to play Maidens' Kiss, my advice is to refuse. Politely."

Natael frowned at him questioningly. "You lead an intriguing life, it seems."

"What do you mean?" Mat asked cautiously.

"Surely you do not think it is a secret? Not many men travel in company with . . . an Aes Sedai. The woman Moiraine Damodred. And then there is Rand al'Thor. The Dragon Reborn. He Who Comes With the Dawn. Who can say how many prophecies he is supposed to fulfill? An unusual traveling companion, certainly."

The Aiel had talked, of course. Anyone would. Still, it was a little unsettling to have a stranger calmly talk about Rand this way. "He suits well enough for now. If he interests you, talk to him. Myself, I'd just as soon not be reminded."

"Perhaps I will. Later, perhaps. Let us talk of you. I understand you went into Rhuidean, where none save Aiel have gone in three thousand years. You got that there?" He reached for the spear on Mat's knees, but let his hand fall when Mat drew it away slightly. "Very well. Tell me what you saw."

"Why?"

"I am a gleeman, Matrim." Natael had his head cocked to one side in that uneasy manner, but his voice held irritation at having to explain. He lifted a corner of his cloak with its colorful patches as though for proof. "You have seen what none have, save a handful of Aiel. What stories can I make with the sights your eyes have seen? I will even make you the hero, if you wish."

Mat snorted. "I don't want to be any bloody hero."

Yet there was no reason to keep silent. Amys and that lot could chatter about not speaking of Rhuidean, but he was no Aiel. Besides, it might pay to have somebody with the peddlers who had a little good-will toward him, somebody who could put in a word when it was needed.

He told the story from reaching the wall of fog to coming out, leaving out selected bits. He had no intention of telling anyone else about that twisted-doorway *ter'angreal,* and he would rather forget the dust gathering into creatures that tried to kill him. That strange city of huge palaces was surely enough, and *Avendesora.*

The Tree of Life Natael passed over quickly, but he took Mat through the rest again and again, asking more and more detail, from exactly what it felt like walking through that fog and how long it took to the color of the shadowless light inside, to descriptions of every last thing Mat could remember seeing in the great square in the heart of the city. Those Mat gave reluctantly; a slip, and he would find himself talking about *ter'angreal,* and who knew where that might lead? Even so he drained the last of the warm ale, and still talked until his throat was dry. It sounded rather dull the way he told it, as though he had just walked in and waited while Rand went off, then walked out again, but Natael seemed intent on digging out every last scrap. He did remind Mat of Thom then; sometimes Thom concentrated on you as though he meant to wring you dry.

"Is this what you are meant to be doing?"

Mat jumped in spite of himself at the sound of Keille's voice, hard under its mellifluous tones. The woman put him on edge, and now she looked ready to rip his heart out, and the gleeman's as well.

Natael scrambled to his feet. "This young man has just been telling me the most fascinating things about Rhuidean. You will not believe it."

"We are not here for Rhuidean." The words came out as sharp as her hatchet of a nose. At least she was only glaring at Natael now.

"I tell you—"

"You tell me nothing."

"Do not try to silence me!"

Ignoring Mat, they moved off down the wagons, arguing in low voices, gesticulating fiercely. Keille seemed to have been browbeaten into a grim silence by the time they disappeared into her wagon.

Mat shivered. He could not imagine sharing living quarters with that woman. It would be like sharing with a bear with a sore tooth. Isendre, now. . . . That face, those lips, that swaying walk. If he could get her away from Kadere, maybe she would find a young hero—the dust creatures could be ten feet tall, for her; he would give her every detail he could remember or invent—a handsome young hero more to her liking than a stuffy old peddler. It was worth thinking about.

The sun slid below the horizon, and small fires of thorny branches made pools of yellow light among the tents. The smells of cooking filled the camp; goat, roasting with dried peppers. Cold filled the camp, too, the cold of night in the Waste. It was as if the sun had taken all the heat with it. Mat had never expected he would wish for a stout cloak when he packed to leave the Stone. Maybe the peddlers had one. Maybe Natael would dice for his.

He ate at Rhuarc's fire with Heirn and Rand. And Aviendha, of course. The peddlers were there, and Natael close by Keille, and Isendre all but wrapped around Kadere. It might be harder separating Isendre from the hook-nosed man than he had hoped—or easier. Twined around the fellow or not, she had smoky eyes for Rand and no one else. You would have thought she already had his ears clipped, a sheep marked for its owner's flock. Neither Rand nor Kadere seemed to notice; the peddler hardly took his eyes off Rand. Aviendha noticed, and glared at Rand. At least the fire gave off some warmth.

When the roast goat was finished—and some sort of flecked yellow mush that was spicier than it looked—Rhuarc and Heirn filled short-stemmed pipes, and the clan chief asked Natael for a song.

The gleeman blinked. "Why, of course. Of course. Let me bring a harp." His cloak billowed on the dry, cold breeze as he vanished toward Keille's wagon.

The fellow certainly was different from Thom Merrilin. Thom hardly got out of bed without flute or harp or both. Mat thumbed his silver-worked pipe full of tabac, and was puffing contentedly by the time Natael returned and struck a pose suitable for a king. That was like Thom. With a strummed cord, the gleeman began.

"Soft, the winds, like springtime's fingers.
Soft, the rains, like heaven's tears.
Soft, the years roll by in gladness,
never hinting storms to come,
never hinting whirlwinds' ravage,
rain of steel and battle thunder,
war to tear the heart asunder."

It was "Midean's Ford." An old song; of Manetheren, oddly enough, and war before the Trolloc Wars. Natael did a fair job of it; nothing like Thom's sonorous recitals, of course, but the rolling words drew a crowd of Aiel thick around the edge of the fire's light. Villainous Aedomon led the Saferi down on unsuspecting Manetheren, pillaging and burning, driving all before them until King Buiryn gathered Manetheren's strength, and the men of Manetheren met the Saferi at Midean's Ford, holding, though heavily outnumbered, through three days of unrelenting battle, while the river ran red and vultures blacked the sky. On the third day, numbers dwindling, hope fading, Buiryn and his men fought their way across the ford in a desperate sortie, driving deep into Aedomon's horde, seeking to turn the enemy back by killing Aedomon himself. But forces too great to overpower swept in around them, trapping them, driving them ever in on themselves. Surrounding their king and the Red Eagle banner, they fought on, refusing surrender even when their doom became clear.

Natael sang how their courage touched even Aedomon's heart, and how at last he allowed the remnant to go free, turning his army back to Safer in honor of them.

"Back across the blood-red water,
marching back with heads held high.
No surrender, arm or sword,
no surrender, heart or soul.

Honor be theirs, ever after,
honor all the Age shall know."

He plucked the final chord, and the Aiel whistled their approval, drumming spears on their hide bucklers, some raising ululating cries. It had not been that way, of course. Mat could remember—*Light, I don't want to!* But it came anyway—he remembered counseling Buiryn not to accept the offer, being told in return that the smallest chance was better than none. Aedomon, glossy black beard hanging below the steel mesh that veiled his face, drew his spearmen back, waited until they were strung out and nearly to the ford before the hidden archers rose and the cavalry charged in. As for turning back to Safer. . . . Mat did not think so. His last memory at the ford was trying to keep his feet, waist-deep in the river with three arrows in him, but there was something later, a fragment. Seeing Aedomon, gray-bearded now, go down in a sharp fight in a forest, toppling from his rearing horse, the spear in his back put there by an unarmored, beardless boy. This was worse than the holes had been.

"You did not like the song?" Natael said.

It took Mat a moment to realize the man was speaking to Rand, not him. Rand rubbed his hands together, peering into the small fire, before answering. "I'm not certain how wise it is, depending on an enemy's generosity. What do you think, Kadere?"

The peddler hesitated, glancing at the woman clinging to his arm. "I do not think of such things," he said at last. "I think of profits, not battles." Keille laughed coarsely. At least, until she saw Isendre's smile, condescending to a woman who could make three of her; then her dark eyes glittered dangerously behind those rolls of fat.

Suddenly warning cries rose in the dark beyond the tents. Aiel snatched veils across their faces, and a moment later Trollocs poured in out of the night, snouted faces and horned heads, towering over the humans, howling and swinging scythe-curved swords, stabbing with hooked spears and barbed tridents, hacking with spiked axes. Myrddraal flowed with them, like deadly eyeless snakes. A heartbeat it took, but the Aiel fought as if they had had an hour's warning, meeting the charge with their own flickering spears.

Mat was vaguely aware of Rand with that fiery sword suddenly in hand, but then he was sucked into the maelstrom himself, wielding his spear as spear and quarterstaff both, slash and thrust, haft whirling. For once he was glad of those dream memories; the way of this weapon seemed familiar, and he needed every scrap of skill he could find. It was all chaotic madness.

Trollocs rose up in front of him and went down to his spear, or an Aiel spear, or spun away into the confusion of shouts and howls and clanging steel. Myrddraal faced him, black blades meeting his raven-marked steel with flashes of blue light like sheet lightning, faced him and were gone in the tumult. Twice a short spear streaking by his head took Trollocs about to run him through the back. He thrust the short-sword blade into a Myrddraal's chest and knew he was going to die when it did not fall, but grinned with those bloodless lips, eyeless stare shivering fear into his bones, and drew back its black sword. An instant later the Halfman jerked as Aiel arrows pincushioned it, jerked for the moment Mat needed to leap back from the thing as it fell still trying to stab at him, stab at anything.

A dozen times the spear's iron-hard black haft barely deflected a Trolloc thrust. It was Aes Sedai work, and he was glad of it. The silver foxhead on his chest seemed to pulse with cold as if to remind him that it, too, bore the mark of Aes Sedai. Right then, he did not care; if it took Aes Sedai work to keep him alive, he was ready to follow Moiraine like a puppy.

He could not have said if it went on for minutes or hours, but suddenly there was not a Myrddraal or Trolloc still standing in sight, though cries and howls from the darkness spoke of pursuit. Dead and dying littered the ground, Aiel and Shadowspawn, the Halfmen still thrashing. Groans filled the air with pain. Suddenly he realized his muscles felt like water, and his lungs were afire. Panting, he slid down to his knees, leaning on his spear. Flames made bonfires of three of the peddlers' canvas-topped wagons, one with a driver pinned to the side by a Trolloc spear, and some of the tents were burning. Shouts from the direction of the Shaido camp, and glows too large for campfires, said they had been attacked, too.

Fiery sword still in hand, Rand came to where Mat knelt. "Are you all right?" Aviendha shadowed him. Somewhere she had found a spear and buckler, had tucked up a corner of her shawl to veil her face. Even in skirts she looked deadly.

"Oh, I am fine," Mat muttered, struggling to his feet. "Nothing like a little dance with Trollocs to ready you for sleep. Right, Aviendha?" Uncovering her face, she gave him a tight smile. The woman had probably *enjoyed* it. He was sweat all over; he thought it might freeze on him.

Moiraine and Egwene had appeared with two of the Wise Ones,

Amys and Bair, circulating among the wounded. The convulsion of Healing followed the Aes Sedai, though sometimes she merely shook her head and moved on.

Rhuarc strode up with a grim face.

"Bad news?" Rand said quietly.

The clan chief grunted. "Aside from Trollocs here where they should not be, not by two hundred leagues or more? Perhaps. Some fifty Trollocs attacked the Wise Ones' camp. Enough to overwhelm it, had it not been for Moiraine Sedai and luck. However, it seems the Shaido were hit by fewer than struck us, though since they are the larger camp the reverse should have been true. I might almost think they were attacked only to keep them from coming to our aid. Not that that would be certain, with Shaido, but Trollocs and Nightrunners might not know that."

"And if they knew an Aes Sedai was with the Wise Ones," Rand said, "that attack could have been meant to keep her away, too. I bring enemies with me, Rhuarc. Remember that. Wherever I am, my enemies are never far."

Isendre poked her head out of the lead wagon. A moment later Kadere climbed down past her, and she ducked back inside, shutting the white-painted door behind him. He stood looking around at the carnage, the light of his burning wagons painting rippling shadows across his face. The group around Mat held his attention most. The wagons seemed to interest him not at all. Natael got down from Keille's wagon, too, speaking up the stairs to her still inside, his eyes on Mat and the others.

"Fools," Mat muttered, half to himself. "Hiding inside the wagons, as if that would make any difference to a Trolloc. They could all have roasted alive, easy as not."

"They are still alive," Rand said, and Mat realized he had seen them, too. "That is always important, Mat, who stays alive. It's like dice. You can't win if you can't play, and you can't play if you are dead. Who can say what game the peddlers play." He laughed quietly, and the fiery sword vanished from his hands.

"I am going to get some sleep," Mat said, already turning away. "Wake me if the Trollocs show up again. Or better, let them kill me in my blankets. I am too tired to wake up again." Rand was definitely going over the edge. Maybe tonight would convince Keille and Kadere to turn back. If they did, he intended to be with them.

*   *   *

Rand let Moiraine look at him, muttering to herself, though he had taken no wound. With so many who had, she could not spare the strength to wash away his fatigue with the One Power.

"This was aimed at you," she told him, surrounded by the moans of the injured. The Trollocs were being dragged away into the night, by packhorses and the peddlers' mules. The Aiel apparently intended to leave the Myrddraal where they lay until they stopped moving, to make sure they were really dead. The wind gusted up, like ice with no moisture in it.

"Was it?" he said. Her eyes glittered in the firelight before she turned back to the wounded.

Egwene came to him, too, but only to say in a low, fierce whisper, "Whatever you are doing to upset her, stop it!" The glance she shot past him at Aviendha left no doubt who she meant, and she went off to help Bair and Amys before he could say he had done nothing. She looked ridiculous with those two braids twined with ribbons. The Aiel seemed to think so, too; some of them grinned at her back.

Stumbling, shivering, he sought his tent. He had never been this tired before. The sword had almost not come. He hoped that was the tiredness. Sometimes there was nothing there when he reached for the Source, and sometimes the Power would not do what he wanted, but almost from the first the sword had come practically without thought. Now of all times. . . . It had to be the tiredness.

Aviendha insisted on following him as far as the tent, and when he woke the next morning she was sitting outside crosslegged, though without the spear and buckler. Spy or not, he was glad to see her. At least he knew who and what she was, and what she felt for him.

CHAPTER
38

Hidden Faces

The Garden of Silver Breezes was not a garden at all but a huge wineshop, much too large to be called a shop really, atop a hill centered on the Calpene, the westernmost of Tanchico's three peninsulas below the Great Circle. A part of the name, at least, came from the breezes that wafted in where polished green-streaked marble columns and balustrades replaced one wall except on the topmost floor. Golden oiled-silk curtains could be lowered in case of rain. The hill fell away sharply on that side, and the tables along the balustrades gave a clear view, across white domes and spires, of the great harbor, crowded with more ships than ever. Tanchico needed everything, desperately, and there was gold to be made—until the gold and time ran out.

With its gilded lamps and ceilings inlaid with brass fretwork polished to a golden gleam, its serving women and men chosen for grace and beauty and discretion, the Garden of the Silver Breezes had been the most expensive wineshop in the city even before the troubles. Now it was outrageous. But those who dealt in huge sums still came, those who dealt in power and influence, or thought they did. In some ways there was less to deal in than before; in others, more.

Low walls surrounded each table, making islands dotted across the green and golden floor tiles. Each wall, pierced with lacy carving so no

eavesdropper could listen unseen, stood just high enough to hide who met whom from the casual glances of passersby. Even so, patrons usually went masked, especially of late, and some had a bodyguard beside their table, also masked to avoid recognition if the patron was prudent. And tongueless, rumor said, for the most prudent. No guard was visibly armed; the proprietress of the Garden of Silver Breezes, a sleek woman of indeterminate age named Selindrin, allowed no weapons past the street now. Her rule was not broken, at least openly.

From her usual table against the balustrade, Egeanin watched the ships in the harbor, especially those under sail. They made her want to be back on a deck giving orders. She had never expected duty to bring her to this.

Unconsciously she adjusted the velvet mask that hid the upper half of her face; she felt ridiculous wearing the thing, but it was necessary to blend in to some extent. The mask—blue to match her high-necked silk gown—the gown itself, and her dark hair, grown down to her shoulders now, were as far as she could make herself go. Passing for a Taraboner was unnecessary—Tanchico bulged with refugees, a good many of them foreigners swept up in the troubles—and it was beyond her in any case. These people were animals; they had no discipline, no order.

Regretfully, she turned from the harbor to her table companion, a narrow-faced fellow with a weasel's greedy smile. Floran Gelb's frayed collar did not belong in the Garden of Silver Breezes, and he continually wiped his hands on his coat. She always met them here, the greasy little men she was forced to deal with. It was a reward for them, and a means of keeping them off balance.

"What do you have for me, Master Gelb?"

Wiping his hands again, he lifted a coarse jute bag onto the table and watched her anxiously. She held the bag down beside her before opening it. A silvery metal a'dam lay inside, a collar and bracelet connected by a leash cunningly worked and joined. She closed the bag and set it on the floor. This made three that Gelb had recovered, more than anyone else.

"Very good, Master Gelb." A small purse went across the table the other way; Gelb made it disappear under his coat as if it held the Empress's crown instead of a handful of silver. "And do you have anything else?"

"Those women. The ones you want me to look for?" She had grown used to the quick speech of these people, but she wished he would not lick his lips that way. It did not make him any harder to understand, but it was unsightly.

She very nearly told him she was not interested anymore. But this was a part of why she was in Tanchico, after all; maybe the whole reason, now. "What of them?" That she could even think of shirking her duty made her speak more harshly than she had intended, and Gelb flinched.

"I . . . I think I've found another one."

"You are sure? There have been . . . mistakes."

Mistakes was a gentle way to put it. Near a dozen women who came only vaguely near the descriptions had been nuisances she could ignore once she had seen them. But that noblewoman, a refugee from estates burned out by the war. Gelb had kidnapped the woman off the street, thinking to earn more for delivering her than for telling where she was. In his defense, the Lady Leilwin closely matched one of the women Egeanin sought, but she had told him they would not speak with any accent he recognized, certainly not a Taraboner accent. Egeanin had not wanted to kill the woman, yet even in Tanchico someone might have listened to her story. Leilwin had gone bound and gagged onto one of the courier boats in the dead of night; she was young and pretty, and someone would find a better use for her than slitting her throat. But Egeanin was not in Tanchico to find serving girls for the Blood.

"No mistakes, Mistress Elidar," he said hastily, flashing that smile full of teeth. "Not this time. But . . . I need a little gold. To be sure. To get close enough. Four or five crowns?"

"I pay for results," Egeanin told him firmly. "After your . . . mistakes, you are lucky that I pay you at all."

Gelb licked his lips nervously. "You said. . . . Back in the beginning, you said you'd have a few coins for those as could do *special* sorts of work." A muscle in his cheek twitched; his eyes darted as if someone might be listening at the lace-carved wall around three sides of the table, and his voice dropped to a hoarse whisper. "Stirring up trouble, as it were? I heard a rumor—from a fellow who's bodyservant to Lord Brys—about the Assembly, and choosing the new Panarch. I think maybe it's true. The man was drunk, and when he realized what he had said, he nearly fouled himself. Even if it isn't, it would still rip Tanchico wide open."

"Do you really believe there is any need to buy trouble in this city?" Tanchico was a rotting bellfruit ready to fall in the first wind. The whole of this wretched land was. For a moment she was tempted to buy his "rumor." She was supposed to be a trader in whatever goods or information came along, and she had even sold some. But dealing with Gelb sickened her. And her own doubts frightened her. "That will be all,

Master Gelb. You know how to make contact with me if you find another of these." She touched the rough-woven sack.

Instead of rising, he sat staring, trying to see through her mask. "Where are you from, Mistress Elidar? The way you talk, all slurred out and soft-like—begging your pardon; no offense meant—I can't place you."

"That will be all, Gelb." Maybe it was the quarterdeck voice, or maybe the mask failed to hide her cold stare, but Gelb bounced to his feet, ducking bows and stammering apologies while he fumbled open the door in the lacework wall.

She sat there after he was gone, giving him time to leave the Garden of Silver Breezes. Someone would follow him outside, to make certain he did not wait to shadow her. All this skulking and hiding disgusted her; she almost wished something would destroy her disguise and give her an honest face-to-face fight.

A new ship was sweeping into the harbor below, a Sea Folk raker with its towering masts and clouds of sail. She had examined a captured raker, but she would have given almost anything to take one out, though she expected a Sea Folk crew would be necessary to wring the most from the vessel. The Atha'an Miere were stubborn about taking the oaths; it would not be as good if she had to buy a crew. Buy an entire crew! The amount of gold that came in by the courier boats for her to fling about was going to her head.

Taking up the jute bag, she started to rise, then sat back down hurriedly at the sight of a wide, thick-shouldered man leaving another table. Dark hair, long to his shoulders, and a beard that left his upper lip bare framed Bayle Domon's round face. He was not masked, of course; he ran a dozen coasting vessels in and out of Tanchico and apparently did not care who knew his whereabouts. Masked. She was not thinking straight. He would not recognize her in a mask. Still, she waited until he was gone before leaving her table. The man might have to be dealt with yet, if he became a danger.

Selindrin took the gold she proffered with a sleek smile and murmured wishes for Egeanin's continued patronage. Dark hair in dozens of narrow braids, the proprietress of the Garden of Silver Breezes wore clinging white silk, nearly thin enough for a serving girl, and one of those transparent veils that always made Egeanin want to ask Taraboners what dances they could perform. Shea dancers wore almost identical veils and little more. Still, Egeanin thought as she started toward the street, the woman had a sharp mind, else she could not maneuver through the shoals of Tanchico, catering to every faction while earning the enmity of none.

A reminder of that was the tall, white-cloaked man, gray at the temples but hard-faced and hard-eyed, who passed Egeanin and was greeted by Selindrin. Jaichim Carridin's cloak bore a golden sunburst on the breast, with four golden knots below and a crimson shepherd's crook behind. An Inquisitor of the Hand of the Light, a high officer in the Children of the Light. The very concept of the Children outraged Egeanin, a military body answerable only to itself. But Carridin and his few hundred soldiers had power of a sort in Tanchico, where any kind of authority seemed to be lacking most of the time. The Civil Watch no longer patrolled the streets, and the army—as much as was still loyal to the King—was too busy holding the fortresses around the city. Egeanin noted that Selindrin did not even glance at the sword on Carridin's hip. He definitely had power.

As soon as she stepped into the street her bearers came running with her chair from the cluster waiting for their patrons, and her bodyguards closed in around her with their spears. They were a mismatched lot, some in steel caps, three wearing leather shirts sewn with steel scales; rough-faced men, possibly deserters from the army, but aware that continued full bellies and silver to spend depended on her continued safety. Even the bearers carried stout knives, and cudgels stuck out of their sashes. No one who looked as though they had money dared appear out-of-doors unguarded. In any case, had she cared to risk it, it would only draw attention to her.

The guards forced a way through the crowds with no trouble. The throngs eddied and swirled in the narrow streets that wound through the city's hills, creating clear pockets around sedan chairs surrounded by bodyguards. There were very few carriages to be seen. Horses were becoming an extravagance.

Worn was the only fit description for the milling masses, worn and frenzied. Worn faces, worn clothes, and too-bright, frenzied eyes, desperate, hoping when they knew there was no hope. Many had surrendered, crouching against walls, huddled in doorways, clutching wives, husbands, children, not simply worn but ragged and blank-faced. Sometimes they roused enough to cry out to some passerby for a coin, a crust, anything.

Egeanin kept her eyes straight ahead, of necessity trusting the bodyguards to detect any danger. Meeting a beggar's eyes meant twenty of them jamming themselves hopefully around her chair. Tossing a coin meant a hundred crowding in, clamoring and weeping. She was already using part of the money the courier boats brought to support a soup kitchen, just as if she were one of the Blood. She shuddered to think what discovery of that overstepping of her place would mean. As well put on a brocaded robe and shave her head.

All of this could be put aright once Tanchico fell, with everyone fed, everyone put in their proper place. And she could abandon dresses and things she had no experience or taste for, return to her ship. Tarabon, at least, and perhaps Arad Doman as well, were ready to crumble at a touch, like charred silk. Why was the High Lady Suroth holding back? Why?

Jaichim Carridin lounged in his chair, cloak spread over the carved arms, studying the Taraboner noblemen who occupied the private room's other chairs. They sat stiffly in their gold-embroidered coats, mouths tight below masks fancifully worked to resemble hawks' faces, and lions' and leopards'. He had more to worry him than they, but he managed a calm demeanor. It was two months since he had received word of a cousin found skinned alive in his own bedchamber, three since his youngest sister, Dealda, being carried off from her bridal feast by a Myrddraal. The family steward wrote disbelievingly, frantic with all the tragedy befalling House Carridin. Two months. He hoped Dealda had died quickly. It was said women did not cling to sanity long in Myrddraal hands. Two whole months. Anyone else but Jaichim Carridin would have been sweating blood.

Each man held a golden goblet of wine, but there were no servants present. Selindrin had served them before removing herself with an assurance that they would not be disturbed. There was, in fact, no one else on this, the highest floor of the Garden of Silver Breezes. Two men who had come with the nobles—members of the King's Life Guard, unless Carridin missed his guess—stood at the foot of the stairs to guarantee continued privacy.

Carridin sipped his wine. None of the Taraboners had touched theirs. "So," he said lightly, "King Andric wishes the Children of the Light to aid in restoring order in the city. We do not often let ourselves become involved in the internal affairs of nations." Not openly. "Certainly I cannot remember such a request. I do not know what the Lord Captain Commander will say." Pedron Niall would say to do what was needed and make sure the Taraboners knew that they owed a debt to the Children, make sure they paid it in full.

"There is no time for you to request instructions from Amador," a man in a black-spotted leopard mask said urgently. None had offered names, but Carridin did not need them.

"What we ask is necessary," another snapped, his thick mustache below a hawk mask giving him the look of a peculiar owl. "You must understand that we would not make this request unless it were necessary in the extreme. We must have unity, not more division, yes? There are many divisive elements, even within Tanchico. They must be suppressed if there is to be even the hope of imposing peace on the countryside."

"The death of the Panarch has made matters most difficult," the first fellow added.

Carridin raised an eyebrow questioningly. "Have you discovered yet who killed her?"

His own supposition was that Andric himself had had the deed done, in the belief that the Panarch favored one of the rebel claimants to the throne. The King may have been right, but he had discovered after calling what he could of the Assembly of Lords—a good many were with one or another of the rebel groups out in the country—that they were remarkably stubborn about ratifying his choice. Even had the Lady Amathera not been currently sharing Andric's bed, election of King and Panarch was the only real power the Assembly had, and they did not seem to want to give it up. The difficulties over the Lady Amathera were not supposed to be known. Even the Assembly realized that that news might set off riots.

"One of the Dragonsworn madmen assuredly," the owl-looking man said, giving his mustache a fierce tug. "No true Taraboner would harm the Panarch, yes?" He almost sounded as if he believed it.

"Of course," Carridin said smoothly. He took another sip of wine. "If I am to secure the Panarch's Palace for the ascension of the Lady Amathera, I must hear from the King himself. Otherwise, it might appear the Children of the Light were reaching for power in Tarabon, when all we seek is, as you say, an end to division, and peace under the Light."

An older, square-jawed leopard, white streaking his dark yellow hair, spoke up in cold tones. "I have heard that Pedron Niall seeks unity against the Dragonsworn. Unity under himself, is it not?"

"The Lord Captain Commander seeks no dominion," Carridin replied just as icily. "The Children serve the Light, as do all men of good will."

"There can be no question," the first leopard put in, "of Tarabon being subject in any way to Amador. No question!" Angry agreement rumbled from nearly every chair.

"Of course not," Carridin said as though the thought had never crossed his mind. "If you wish my aid, I will give it—under the conditions I have stated. If you do not, there is always work for the Children. Service to the Light never ends, for the Shadow waits everywhere."

"You will have sureties signed and sealed by the King," a graying, lion-masked man said, the first words he had spoken. He was, of course, Andric himself, though Carridin was not supposed to know. The King could not meet with an Inquisitor of the Hand of the Light without causing talk any more than he could visit a wineshop, even the Garden of Silver Breezes.

Carridin nodded. "When they are in my hand, I will secure the Panarch's Palace, and the Children will suppress any . . . divisive elements . . . who attempt to interfere with the investiture. Under the Light, I swear it." Tension drained out of the Taraboners visibly; they upended their goblets as if trying to replace it with wine, even Andric.

So far as the people of Tarabon were concerned, the Children would have the blame for the inevitable killings, not the King, or the army of Tarabon. Once Amathera was invested with the Crown and Staff of the Tree, a few more of the Assembly might well join the rebels, but if the rest admitted they had not elected her the news would set Tanchico afire. As for any tales that came from those who fled—why, rebels would spread any sort of treasonous lie. And the King and Panarch of Tarabon would both dangle on strings Carridin could hand to Pedron Niall to do with as he pleased.

Not such a grand prize as it would have been when the King of Tarabon controlled more than a few hundred square miles around Tanchico, yet it might be grand again. With the aid of the Children—a legion or two would be needed at least; not just the five hundred men Carridin had—the Dragonsworn might yet be crushed, the various rebels defeated, even the war with Arad Doman successfully prosecuted. If either country still realized it was fighting the other. Arad Doman was in worse condition than Tarabon, so Carridin heard.

In truth, he hardly cared if Tarabon fell under the Children's sway, or Tanchico, or any of it. There were motions to go through, things to do that he had always done, but it was difficult to think of anything except when his own throat would be cut. Perhaps he would long to have his throat cut. Two whole months since the last report.

He did not stay to drink with the Taraboners, but made his goodbyes, as shortly as he could. If they took offense, they needed him too much to show it. Selindrin saw him come down, and a stableboy was trotting his horse up to the front door when he reached the street. Tossing the boy a copper, he spurred the black gelding to a quick canter. The ragged folk in the twisty streets got out of his way, which was to the good; he was not sure he would notice if he trampled one of them. Not that it would be any loss. The city was full of beggars; he could hardly breathe without the stench of old, sour sweat and dirt. Tamrin ought to sweep them up and sweep them out; let the rebels in the country contend with them.

It was the country that held his mind, but not the rebels. They could be dealt with easily enough, after word began to spread that this one or that was a Darkfriend. And once he managed to turn a few of them over to the Hand of the Light, they would stand up before everyone and confess to worshipping the Dark One, eating children, anything and everything they were told. The rebels could not last long after that; the pretenders still in the field would wake to find themselves alone. But the Dragonsworn, the men and women who had actually declared for the Dragon Reborn, would not fall away for a charge of being Darkfriends. Most people already considered them so, swearing to follow a man who could channel.

It was the man they had sworn to follow who was the problem, the man whose name they did not even know. Rand al'Thor. Where was he? A hundred bands of Dragonsworn out there, at least two large enough to be called armies, fighting the King's army—such of it as still held allegiance to Andric—fighting the rebels—who were busy fighting each other as often as Andric or the Dragonsworn—yet Carridin had no clue to which band sheltered Rand al'Thor. He could be on Amoth Plain or in Arad Doman, where the situation was the same. If he was, Jaichim Carridin was a dead man in all likelihood.

At the palace on the Verana he had commandeered for the Children's headquarters, he tossed his reins to one of the white-cloaked guards and stalked inside without returning their salutes. The owner of this ornate mass of pale domes and lacy spires and shaded gardens had put forward a claim to the Throne of the Light, and no one complained at the occupation. Least of all the owner; what was left of his head still adorned a spike above the Traitors' Steps, on the Maseta.

For once Carridin barely glanced at fine Tarabon carpets, or furnishings worked with gold and ivory, or fountained courts where splashing water made a cool sound. Broad hallways with golden lamps and high ceilings covered in delicate gold-work scrolls interested him not at all. This palace could match the finest in Amadicia, if not the largest, yet foremost in his mind right then was the strong brandy in the room he had taken for a study.

He was halfway across a priceless carpet, all patterned blue and scarlet and gold, eyes fixed on the carved cabinet that held a silver flask of double-distilled brandy, when suddenly he realized he was not alone. A woman in a clinging, pale-red gown stood near the tall, narrow windows overlooking one of the tree-shaded gardens, her honey-colored hair in braids that brushed her shoulders. A misty scrap of veil did nothing to hide her face. Young and pretty, with a rosebud mouth and large brown eyes, she was no servant, not dressed like that.

"Who are you?" he demanded irritably. "How did you get in here? Leave at once, or I'll have you tossed into the street."

"Threats, Bors? You should be more welcoming to a guest, yes?"

That name jolted him to his heels. Before he thought, he had his sword out, lunging for her throat.

Something seized him—the air turned to crawling jelly—something forced him to his knees, encased him from the neck down. It tightened around his wrist until bones grated; his hand popped open, and his sword fell. The Power. She was using the One Power on him. A Tar Valon witch. And if she knew that name. . . .

"Do you remember," she said, coming closer, "a meeting where Ba'alzamon himself appeared, and showed us the faces of Matrim Cauthon, and Perrin Aybara, and Rand al'Thor?" She practically spat the names, especially the last; her eyes could have drilled holes in steel. "You see? I know who you are, yes? You pledged your soul to the Great Lord of the Dark, Bors." Her sudden laugh was a tinkling of bells.

Sweat popped out on his face. Not just a despised Tar Valon witch. Black Ajah. She was Black Ajah. He had thought it would be a Myrddraal that came for him. He had thought there was time yet. More time. Not yet. "I have tried to kill him," he babbled. "Rand al'Thor. I have tried! But I cannot find him. I cannot! I was told my family would be killed if I failed, one by one. I was promised I would be last! I have cousins, yet. Nephews. Nieces. I have another sister! You must give me more time!"

She stood there, watching him with those sharp brown eyes, smiling with that plump little mouth, listening to him spew out where Vanora could be found, where her bedchamber lay, how she liked to ride alone in the forest beyond Carmera. Perhaps if he shouted some of the guards would come. Perhaps they could kill her. He opened his mouth wider—and that thick invisible jelly oozed in, forcing his jaws apart until they creaked in his ears. Nostrils flaring, he sucked air in frantically. He could still breathe, but he could not scream. All that came out were muffled groans, like a woman wailing behind walls. He wanted to scream.

"You are very amusing," the honey-haired woman said finally. "Jaichim. That is a good name for a dog, I think. Would you like to be my dog, Jaichim? If you are a very good dog, I may allow you to watch Rand al'Thor die one day, yes?"

It took a moment for what she was saying to sink in. If he was to see Rand al'Thor die, she was not. . . . She was not going to kill him, skin him alive, do the things his mind had conjured that would make flaying a release. Tears rolled down his face. Sobs of relief shook him, as much as he could shake, trapped as he was. That trap abruptly vanished, and he collapsed on hands and knees, still weeping. He could not stop.

The woman knelt beside him and tangled a hand in his hair, pulled his head up. "Now you will listen to me, yes? The death of Rand al'Thor is for the future, and you will see it only if you are a good dog. You are going to move your Whitecloaks to the Panarch's Palace."

"H-how do y-you know that?"

She shook his head from side to side, not gently. "A good dog does not question his mistress. I throw the stick; you fetch the stick. I say kill; you kill. Yes? Yes." Her smile was just a flash of teeth. "There will be difficulty in taking the Palace? The Panarch's Legion is there, a thousand men, sleeping in the hallways, the exhibition rooms, the courtyards. You do not have so many of your Whitecloaks."

"They. . . ." He had to stop and swallow. "They will make no trouble. They will believe Amathera has been chosen by the Assembly. It is the Assembly that—"

"Do not bore me, Jaichim. I do not care if you kill the entire Assembly so long as you hold the Panarch's Palace. When will you move?"

"It . . . it will take three or four days for Andric to deliver sureties."

"Three or four days," she murmured half to herself. "Very well. A little longer delay should cause no harm." He was wondering what delay she meant when she cut away the little ground remaining under his feet. "You will keep control of the Palace, and you will send the Panarch's fine soldiers away."

"That is impossible," he gasped, and she jerked his head back so hard he did not know if his neck would break or his scalp tear loose first. He did not dare resist. A thousand invisible needles pricked him, on his face, his chest, his back, arms, legs, everywhere. Invisible, but he was sure no less real for that.

"Impossible, Jaichim?" she said softly. "Impossible is a word I do not like to hear."

The needles twisted deeper; he groaned, but he had to explain. What she wanted *was* impossible. He panted with haste. "Once Amathera is invested as Panarch, she will control the Legion. If I try to hold the Palace, she will turn them on me, and Andric will help her. There is no way I can hold against the Panarch's Legion, and against whatever Andric can strip from the Ring forts."

She studied him so long he began to sweat. He did not dare to flinch, hardly even to blink; those thousand biting little stabs did not allow it.

"The Panarch will be dealt with," she said finally. The needles vanished, and she stood.

Carridin stood, too, trying to steady himself. Perhaps some bargain could be reached; the woman seemed willing to listen to reason now. His legs quivered with shock, but he made his voice as firm as he could. "Even if you can influence Amathera—"

She cut him off. "I told you not to question, Jaichim. A good dog obeys his mistress, yes? I promise you, if you do not you will beg me to find a Myrddraal to play with you. Do you understand me?"

"I understand," he said leadenly. She continued to stare, and after a moment he did understand. "I will do as you say . . . mistress." Her brief, approving smile made him flush. She moved toward the door, turning her back on him as if he really were a dog, and a toothless one. "What . . . ? What is your name?"

Her smile was sweet this time, and mocking. "Yes. A dog should know his mistress's name. I am called Liandrin. But that name must never touch a dog's lips. Should it, I will be most displeased with you."

When the door closed behind her, he staggered to a high-backed chair inlaid with ivory and fell into it. The brandy he left where it was; the way his stomach was twisting, it would make him vomit. What interest could she possibly have in the Panarch's Palace? A dangerous line of questioning, perhaps, but even if they served the same master he could not feel anything but revulsion for a Tar Valon witch.

She did not know as much as she thought. With the King's sureties in hand, he could keep Tamrin and the army away from his throat with the threat of revelation, and Amathera, too. They could still rouse the mob, though. And the Lord Captain Commander might be more than disapproving of the entire affair, might believe he was reaching for personal power. Carridin dropped his head in his hands, envisioning

568 THE SHADOW RISING

Niall signing his death warrant. His own men would arrest him, and hang him. If he could arrange the death of the witch. . . . But she had promised to protect him from the Myrddraal. He wanted to weep again. She was not even here, yet she had him trapped as tightly as ever, steel jaws clamped on both legs and a noose snug around his neck.

There had to be a way out, but every way he looked there was only another trap.

Liandrin ghosted through the halls, easily avoiding servants and Whitecloaks. When she stepped out of a small back door into a narrow alley behind the palace, the tall young guard there stared at her with a blend of relief and unease. Her little trick of opening someone to her suggestions—just a whip-crack trickle of the Power—had not been needed with Carridin, but it had easily convinced this fool that she should be allowed in. Smiling, she motioned him to bend closer. The lanky lout grinned as if expecting a kiss, a grin that froze as her narrow blade went through his eye.

She leaped nimbly back as he fell, a boneless sack of flesh. He would not speak of her even by accident now. Not so much as a spot of blood stained her hand. She wished she had Chesmal's skill at killing with the Power, or even Rianna's lesser talent. Strange that the ability to kill with the Power, to stop a heart or boil blood in the veins, should be so closely linked to Healing. She herself could not Heal much more than scrapes or bruises; not that she had any interest in it.

Her sedan chair, red-lacquered and inlaid with ivory and gold, was waiting at the end of the alley, and with it her bodyguards, a dozen big men with faces like starving wolves. Once in the streets, they cleared a path through the crowds with ease, spears clubbing any not quick enough to move aside. They were all dedicated to the Great Lord of the Dark, of course, and if they did not know exactly who she was, they knew that other men had disappeared, men who failed to serve properly.

The house she and the others had taken, two sprawling stories of flat-roofed stone and white plaster on a hillside at the base of the Verana, Tanchico's easternmost peninsula, belonged to a merchant who had also sworn his oaths to the Great Lord. Liandrin would have preferred a palace—one day perhaps she would have the King's Palace on the Maseta; she had grown up staring enviously at the Lords' palaces, but why should she settle for one of them?—yet despite her preferences, it made sense to stay hidden awhile yet. There was no way the fools in Tar Valon could suspect they were in Tarabon, but the Tower was surely still hunting them, and Siuan Sanche's pets could be sniffing anywhere.

Gates gave onto a small courtyard, windowless except on the upper floor. Leaving the guards and bearers there, she hurried inside. The merchant had furnished a few servants; all sworn to the Great Lord, he assured them, but barely enough to provide for eleven women who rarely stirred outside. One, a sturdily handsome, dark-braided woman called Gyldin, was sweeping the entry hall's red and white tiles when Liandrin entered.

"Where are the others?" she demanded.

"In the front withdrawing room." Gyldin gestured to the double-arched doors to the right as though Liandrin might not know where that was.

Liandrin's mouth tightened. The woman did not curtsy; she used no titles of respect. True, she did not know who Liandrin really was, but Gyldin certainly knew she was high enough to give orders and be obeyed, to send that fat merchant bowing and scraping and bundling his family off to some hovel. "You are supposed to be cleaning, yes? Not standing about? Well, clean! There is dust everywhere. If I find a speck of the dust this evening, you cow you, I will have you beaten!" She clamped her teeth shut. She had copied the manner in which nobles and the wealthy spoke for so long that sometimes she forgot her father had sold fruit from a barrow, yet in one moment of anger the speech of a commoner rolled off her tongue. Too much stress. Too much waiting. With a last, snapped, "Work!" she pushed into the withdrawing room and slammed the door behind her.

The others were not *all* there, which irritated her even more, but enough. Round-faced Eldrith Jhondar seated at a lapis-inlaid table beneath a hanging on one white-plastered wall, was making careful notes from a tattered manuscript; sometimes she absently cleaned the nib of her pen on the sleeve of her dark wool dress. Marillin Gemalphin sat beside one of the narrow windows, blue eyes dreamily staring out at the tiny fountain tinkling in a little courtyard, idly scratching the ears of a scrawny yellow cat and apparently unaware of the hairs it shed all over her green silk dress. She and Eldrith were both Browns, but if Marillin ever found out that Eldrith was the reason the stray cats she brought in continually disappeared, there would be trouble.

They had been Browns. Sometimes it was difficult to remember they no longer were, or that she herself was no longer a Red. So much of what had marked them clearly as members of their old Ajahs remained even now that they were openly pledged to the Black. Take the two former Greens. Coppery-skinned, swan-necked Jeaine Caide wore the thinnest, most clinging silk dresses she could find—white, today—and laughed that the gowns would have to do, since there was nothing available in Tarabon to catch a man's eye. Jeaine was from Arad Doman; Domani women were infamous for their scandalous clothes. Asne Zeramene, with her dark, tilted eyes and bold nose, looked almost demure in pale gray, plainly cut and high-necked, but Liandrin had heard her regret leaving her Warders behind more than once. And as for Rianna Andomeran. . . . Black hair with a stark white streak above her left ear framed a face with the cold, arrogant certainty only a White could assume.

"It is done," Liandrin announced. "Jaichim Carridin will move his Whitecloaks to the Panarch's Palace and hold it for us. He does not yet know we will have guests . . . of course." There were a few grimaces; changing Ajahs had certainly not altered anyone's feelings toward men who hated women who could channel. "There is an interesting thing. He believed I was there to kill him. For failing to kill Rand al'Thor."

"That makes no sense," Asne said, frowning. "We are to bind him, control him, not kill him." She laughed suddenly, soft and low, and leaned back in her chair. "If there is a way to control him, I would not mind binding him to me. He is a good-looking young man, from the little I saw." Liandrin sniffed; she had no liking for men at all.

Rianna shook her head worriedly. "It makes troubling sense. Our orders from the Tower were clear, yet it is also clear that Carridin has others. I can only postulate dissension among the Forsaken."

"The Forsaken," Jeaine muttered, folding her arms tightly; thin white silk molded her breasts even more revealingly. "What good are promises that we will rule the world when the Great Lord returns if we are crushed between warring Forsaken first? Does anyone believe we could stand against any of them?"

"Balefire." Asne looked around, dark tilted eyes challenging. "Balefire will destroy even one of the Forsaken. And we have the means to produce it." One of the *ter'angreal* they had removed from the Tower, a fluted black rod a pace long, had that use. None of them knew why they had been ordered to take it, not even Liandrin herself. Too many of the *ter'angreal* were like that, taken because they had been told to, with no reasons given, but some orders had to be obeyed. Liandrin wished they had been able to secure even one *angreal.*

Jeaine gave a sharp sniff. "If any of us could control it. Or have you forgotten that the one test we dared nearly killed me? And burned a hole through both sides of the ship before I could stop it? Fine good it would have done us to drown before reaching Tanchico."

"What need have we of balefire?" Liandrin said. "If we can control the Dragon Reborn, let the Forsaken think how they will deal with us." Suddenly she became aware of another presence in the room. The woman Gyldin, wiping down a carved, low-backed chair in one corner. "What are you doing here, woman?"

"Cleaning." The dark-braided woman straightened unconcernedly. "You told me to clean."

Liandrin almost struck out with the Power. Almost. But Gyldin certainly did not know they were Aes Sedai. How much had the woman heard? Nothing of importance. "You will go to the cook," she said in a cold fury, "and tell him he is to strap you. Very hard! And you are to have nothing to eat until the dust it is all gone." Again. The woman had made her speak like a commoner again.

Marillin stood, nuzzling the yellow cat's nose with hers, and handed the creature to Gyldin. "See that he gets a dish of cream when the cook is done with you. And some of that nice lamb. Cut it small for him; he doesn't have many teeth left, poor thing." Gyldin looked at her, not blinking, and she added, "Is there something you don't understand?"

"I understand." Gyldin's mouth was tight. Perhaps she did finally understand; she was a servant, not their equal.

Liandrin waited a moment after she left, the cat cradled in her arms, then snatched open one of the doors. The entry hall was empty. Gyldin was not eavesdropping. She did not trust the woman. But then, she could not think of anyone she did trust.

"We must be concerned with what concerns us," she said tightly, closing the door. "Eldrith, have you found a new clue in those pages? Eldrith?"

The plump woman gave a start, then stared around at them, blinking. It was the first time she had raised her head from the battered yellow manuscript; she seemed surprised to see Liandrin. "What? Clue? Oh. No. It is difficult enough getting into the King's Library; if I extracted so much as a page, the librarians would know it immediately. But if I disposed of them, I would never find anything. That place is a maze. No, I found this in a bookseller's near the King's Palace. It is an interesting treatise on—"

Embracing *saidar*, Liandrin sent the pages showering across the floor. "Unless they are a treatise on the controlling of Rand al'Thor, let them be burned! What have you learned about what we seek?"

Eldrith blinked at the scattered papers. "Well, it is in the Panarch's Palace."

"You learned that two days ago."

"And it must be a *ter'angreal*. To control someone who can channel must require the Power, and since it is a specialized use that means a *ter'angreal*. We will find it in the exhibition room, or perhaps among the Panarch's collection."

"Something new, Eldrith." With an effort Liandrin made her voice less shrill. "Have you found anything that is new? Anything?"

The round-faced woman blinked uncertainly. "Actually. . . . No."

"It does not matter," Marillin said. "In a few days, once they have invested their precious Panarch, we can begin searching, and if we must inspect every candlestick, we will find it. We are on the brink, Liandrin. We will put Rand al'Thor on a leash and teach him to sit up and roll over."

"Oh, yes," Eldrith said, smiling happily. "On a leash."

Liandrin hoped it was so. She was tired of waiting, tired of hiding. Let the world know her. Let people bend knee as had been promised when she first forswore old oaths for new.

Egeanin knew she was not alone as soon as she stepped into her small house by the kitchen door, but she dropped her mask and the jute bag carelessly on the table and walked over to where a bucket of water stood beside the brick fireplace. As she bent to take the copper ladle, her right hand darted into a low hollow where two bricks had been removed behind the bucket; she spun erect, a small crossbow in her hand. No more than a foot long, it had little power or range, but she always kept it drawn, and the dark stain tipping the sharp steel bolt would kill in a heartbeat.

If the man leaning casually in the corner saw the crossbow, he gave no outward sign. He was pale-haired and blue-eyed, in his middle years, and good-looking if too slender for her taste. Clearly he had watched her cross the narrow yard through the iron-grilled window beside him. "Do you think that I threaten you?" he said after a moment.

She recognized the familiar accents of home, but she did not lower the crossbow. "Who are you?"

For answer he dipped two fingers carefully into his belt pouch— apparently he could see after all—and brought out something small and flat. She motioned him to lay it on the table and back up again.

Only after he was back in the corner did she move close enough to pick up what he had set there. Never taking her eyes or the crossbow away from him, she lifted it up where she could see. A small ivory plaque bordered in gold, engraved with a raven and a tower. The raven's eyes were black sapphires. A raven, symbol of the Imperial family; the Tower of Ravens, symbol of Imperial justice.

"Normally this would be enough," she told him, "but we are far from Seanchan, in a land where the bizzare is almost commonplace. What other proof can you offer?"

Smiling with silent amusement, he removed his coat, unlaced his shirt and stripped it off. On either shoulder was the tattoo of raven and tower.

Most Seekers for Truth bore the ravens as well as the tower, but not even someone who dared steal a Seeker's plaque would have himself marked so. To wear the ravens was to be the property of the Imperial family. There was an old story of a fool young lord and lady who had themselves tattooed while drunk, some three hundred years gone. When the then Empress learned of it, she had them brought to the Court of the Nine Moons and set to scrubbing floors. This fellow might be one of their descendants. The mark of the raven was forever.

"My apologies, Seeker," she said, setting the crossbow down. "Why are you here?" She did not ask a name; any he gave might or might not be his.

He left her holding the plaque while he re-dressed himself in a leisurely manner. A subtle reminder. She was a captain and he property, but he was also a Seeker, and under the law he could have her put to the question on his own authority. By law he had the right to send her out to buy the rope to bind her while he put her to the question right here, and he would expect her to return with it. Flight from a Seeker was a crime. Refusal to cooperate with a Seeker was a crime. She had never in her life considered any criminal act, no more than she had considered treason against the Crystal Throne. But if he asked the wrong questions, demanded the wrong answers. . . . The crossbow was still close to her hand, and Cantorin was far away. Wild thoughts. Dangerous thoughts.

"I serve the High Lady Suroth and the *Corenne*, for the Empress," he said. "I am checking on the progress of the agents the High Lady has placed in these lands."

Checking? What had to be checked, and by a Seeker? "I have heard nothing of this from the courier boats." His smile deepened, and she flushed. Of course the crews would not speak of a Seeker. Yet he answered while lacing up his shirt.

"The courier boats are not to be risked with my trips. I have taken passage on the vessels of a local smuggler, a man called Bayle Domon. His craft stop everywhere in Tarabon and Arad Doman and between."

"I have heard of him," she said calmly. "All goes well?"

"It does now. I am glad that you, at least, understood your instructions properly. Among the others, only the Seekers did. It is regrettable that there are not more Seekers with the *Hailene.*" Settling his coat on his shoulders, he plucked the Seeker's plaque from her hand. "There has been some embarrassment over the return of *sul'dam* deserters. Such desertions must not become common knowledge. Much better that they simply vanish."

Only because she had a little time to think was she able to keep her face smooth. *Sul'dam* had been left behind in the debacle at Falme, she had been told. Possibly some had deserted. Her instruction, delivered by the High Lady Suroth herself, had been to return any who could be found, whether they wanted to return or not, and if that was not possible, dispose of them. The last had seemed only a final alternative. Until now.

"I regret that these lands do not know kaf," he said, taking a seat at the table. "Even in Cantorin, only the Blood still have kaf. Or it was so when I left. Perhaps supply ships have arrived from Seanchan since. Tea must do. Fix me tea."

She very nearly knocked him out of his chair. The man was property. And a Seeker. She brewed tea. And served it to him, standing beside his chair with the pot to keep his cup full. She was surprised he did not ask her to don a veil and dance on the table.

She was permitted to sit at last, after fetching pen and ink and paper, but only to sketch maps of Tanchico and its defenses, to draw every other city and town she knew the least thing about. She listed the various forces in the field, as much as she knew of their strength and loyalties, what she had deduced of their dispositions.

When she was done, he stuffed it all in his pocket, told her to send the contents of the jute sack by the next courier boat, and left with one of those amused smiles, saying he might check on her progress again in a few weeks.

She sat there for a long time after he was gone. Every map she had drawn, every list she had made, duplicated papers sent out by courier boats long since. Having her do it all again while he watched might have been a punishment for forcing him to show his tattoos. Deathwatch Guards flaunted their ravens; Seekers rarely did. It might have been that. At least he had not gone down to the basement before she arrived. Or had he? Had he just been waiting for her to speak?

The stout iron lock hung seemingly undisturbed on the door in the hall just beyond the kitchen, but it was said Seekers knew how to open locks without keys. Taking the key from her belt pouch, she unfastened the lock and went down the narrow steps.

One lamp on a shelf lit the dirt-floored basement. Just four brick walls, cleared of everything that might help an escape. A faint smell of the slop pail hung in the air. On the side opposite the lamp, a woman in a dirty dress sat despondently on a few rough woolen blankets. Her head lifted at the sound of Egeanin's steps, dark eyes fearful and pleading. She had been the first *sul'dam* Egeanin had found. The first, the only. Egeanin had all but stopped looking, after she found Bethamin. And Bethamin had been in this basement since, while courier boats came and went.

"Did anyone come down here?" Egeanin said.

"No. I heard footsteps overhead, but. . . . No." Bethamin stretched out her hands. "Please, Egeanin. This is all a mistake. You have known me for ten years. Take this thing off of me."

A silver collar encircled her neck, attached by a thick silver leash to a bracelet of the same metal that hung on a peg a few feet above her head. It had been almost an accident, putting it on her, simply a means of securing her for a few moments. And then she had managed to knock Egeanin down, trying a dashing for freedom.

"If you bring it to me, I will," Egeanin said angrily. She was angry with many things, not with Bethamin. "Bring the *a'dam* over here, and I will remove it."

Bethamin shivered, let her hands fall. "It is a mistake," she whispered. "A horrible mistake." But she made no move toward the bracelet. Her first attempted flight had left her writhing on the floor upstairs, wracked by nausea, and had left Egeanin stunned.

Sul'dam controlled *damane,* women who could channel, by means of *a'dam.* It was *damane* who could channel, not *sul'dam.* But an *a'dam* could only control a woman who could channel. No other woman, and not a man—young men with that ability were executed, of course— only a woman who could channel. A woman who had that ability and was collared could not move more than a few steps without her bracelet on the wrist of a *sul'dam* to complete the link.

Egeanin felt very tired climbing the stairs and locking the door again. She wanted some tea herself, but the little the Seeker had left was cold, and she did not feel like brewing more. Instead she sat down and pulled the *a'dam* out of the jute bag. To her it was only finely jointed silver; she could not use it, and it could not harm her unless somebody hit her with it.

Even linking herself with an *a'dam* that far, denying its ability to control her, was enough to send a shiver down her spine. Women who could channel were dangerous animals rather than people. It had been they who Broke the World. They must be controlled, or they would turn everyone into their property. That was what she had been taught, what had been taught in Seanchan for a thousand years. Strange that that seemed not to have happened here. No. That was a dangerous, foolish line of thought.

Tucking the *a'dam* back into the bag, she cleaned the tea things to settle her mind. She liked tidiness, and there was a small satisfaction in making the kitchen so. Before she realized it she was brewing a pot of tea for herself. She did not want to think about Bethamin, and that was dangerously foolish too. Settling herself back at the table, she stirred honey into a cup of tea as black as she could make it. Not kaf, but it would do.

Despite her denials, despite her pleas, Bethamin could channel. Could other *sul'dam?* Was that why the High Lady Suroth wanted those left behind at Falme killed? It was unthinkable. It was impossible. The yearly testings all across Seanchan found every girl who had the spark of channeling in her: each was struck from the rolls of citizens, struck from family records, taken away to become collared *damane*. The same testings found the girls who could learn to wear the bracelet of the *sul'dam*. No woman escaped being tested each year until she was old enough that she would have begun channeling if the spark was there. How could even one girl be taken for *sul'dam* when she was *damane?* Yet there Bethamin was in the basement, held by an *a'dam* as by an anchor.

One thing was certain. The possibilities here were potentially deadly. This involved the Blood, and Seekers. Maybe even the Crystal Throne. Would the High Lady Suroth dare keep knowledge of this sort from the Empress? A mere ship captain could die screaming for a misplaced frown in that company, or find herself property for a whim. She had to know more if she hoped to avoid the Death of Ten Thousand Tears. To begin with, that meant spreading more money to Gelb and other ferrety skulkers like him, finding more *sul'dam* and seeing if *a'dam* held them. Beyond that. . . . Beyond that she was sailing uncharted reefs with no linesman in the bow.

Touching the crossbow, still lying there with its lethal bolt, she realized that something else was certain. She was not going to let the Seekers kill her. Not just to help the High Lady Suroth keep a secret. Perhaps not for any reason. It was a thought shiveringly close to treason, but it would not go away.

CHAPTER
39

A Cup of Wine

Wh   hen Elayne came on deck with her things neatly bundled,
                the setting sun seemed to be just touching the water out
                beyond the mouth of Tanchico's harbor, and the final thick
hawsers were being tied to snug *Wavedancer* to a ship-lined dock, only
one of many along this westernmost peninsula of the city. Some of the
crew were furling the last sails. Beyond the long wharves the city rose
on hills, shining white, domed and spired, with polished weather vanes
glittering. Perhaps a mile north she could make out high, round walls;
the Great Circle, if she remembered correctly.

Slinging her bundle on the same shoulder as her leather script, she
went to join Nynaeve by the gangplank, with Coine and Jorin. It
seemed almost odd to see the sisters fully dressed again, in bright
brocaded silk blouses that matched their wide trousers. Earrings and
even nose rings she had become used to, and the fine gold chain across
each woman's dark cheek hardly made her wince at all now.

Thom and Juilin stood apart with their own bundles, looking a touch
sullen. Nynaeve had been right. They had tried to second-guess, starting when the real purpose of this journey, or some of it, was revealed to
them two days ago. Neither seemed to think two young women were
competent—*competent!*—to seek the Black Ajah. A threat by Nynaeve
to have them transferred to another Sea Folk ship, headed the other

way, had nipped that in the bud. At least it had once Toram and a
dozen crewmen gathered ready to shove them into a boat to be rowed
across. Elayne gave them a searching look. Sullenness meant rebellion;
they were going to have more trouble from these two.

"Where will you go now, Coine?" Nynaeve was asking as Elayne
reached them.

"To Dantora, and the Aile Jafar," the Sailmistress replied, "and then
on to Cantorin and the Aile Somera, spreading news of the Coramoor,
if it pleases the Light. But I must allow Toram to trade here, or he will
burst."

Her husband was down on the docks now, without his strange wire-
framed lens, bare-chested and be-ringed, talking earnestly with men in
baggy white trousers and coats embroidered with scrollwork on the
shoulders. Each Tanchican wore a dark, cylindrical cap, and a transparent veil across his face. The veils looked ridiculous, especially on the
men with thick mustaches.

"The Light send you a safe voyage," Nynaeve said, shifting her bundles on her back. "If we discover any danger here that might threaten
you before you sail, we will send word." Coine and her sister looked
remarkably calm. Knowledge of the Black Ajah hardly fazed them; it
was the Coramoor, Rand, who was important.

Jorin kissed her fingertips and pressed them to Elayne's lips. "The
Light willing, we shall meet again."

"The Light willing," Elayne responded, duplicating the Windfinder's
gesture. It still felt odd, but it was an honor, too, used only between
close family members or lovers. She was going to miss the Sea Folk
woman. She had learned a great deal, and taught a little, as well. Jorin
could certainly weave Fire much better now.

When they reached the foot of the gangplank, Nynaeve heaved a
sigh of relief. An oily potion Jorin produced had settled her stomach
after two days at sea, but all the same she had been tight-eyed and
tight-mouthed until Tanchico came in sight.

The two men bracketed them immediately, without any instructions,
Juilin taking the lead with his bundle on his back and his pale, thumb-
thick staff held in both hands, dark eyes alert. Thom brought up the
rear, somehow managing a dangerous look despite his white hair and
his limp and his gleeman's cloak.

Nynaeve pursed her lips for a moment but said nothing, which
Elayne thought wise. Before they had gone fifty paces down the long
stone dock she had seen as many slitty-eyed, hungry-faced men studying them, and Tanchicans and others shifting crates and bales and sacks

on the dock. She suspected any of them would have been willing to cut her throat in the hope that a silk dress meant money in her purse. They did not frighten her; she could handle any two or three of them, she was sure. But she and Nynaeve had their Great Serpent rings in their pouches, and it would be useless to pretend no connection with the White Tower if she channeled in front of a hundred men. Best if Juilin and Thom looked as fierce as they could. She would not have minded having ten more just like them.

Suddenly there was a roar from the deck of one of the smaller ships. "You! It do be you!" A wide, round-faced man in a green silk coat leaped onto the dock, ignoring Juilin's raised staff to stare at her and Nynaeve. A beard with no mustache marked him as an Illianer, and so did his accent. He seemed vaguely familiar.

"Master Domon?" Nynaeve said after a moment, giving her braid a sharp tug. "Bayle Domon?"

He nodded. "Aye. I did never think to see you again. I . . . did wait as long as I could in Falme, but the time did come when I must sail or watch my ship burn."

Elayne knew him now. He had agreed to carry them out of Falme, but chaos had seized that city before they could reach his vessel. That coat said he had done well since.

"A pleasure to see you again," Nynaeve said coolly, "but if you will excuse us, we must find rooms in the city."

"That will be hard. Tanchico do burst its caulking. I do know a place where my word may bring something, though. I could no remain longer in Falme, but I do feel I owe you some debt." Domon paused, frowning with sudden unease. "Your being here. Will the same happen here as in Falme, then?"

"No, Master Domon," Elayne said when Nynaeve hesitated. "Of course not. And we will be glad to accept your help."

She half-expected some protest out of Nynaeve, yet the older woman only nodded thoughtfully and made introductions among the men. Thom's cloak made Domon's eyebrows rise, but Juilin's Tairen garb brought a frown that was returned in kind. Neither man said anything, though; perhaps they could keep the animosity between Tear and Illian out of Tanchico. If they could not, she would have to speak firmly with them.

Domon talked of what had happened with him since Falme as he accompanied them down the dock, and he had indeed done well. "A dozen good coasting ships the Panarch's taxmen do know about," he laughed, "and four deepwater they do no."

He could hardly have acquired so many honestly in so short a time. It shocked her to hear him speak so openly on a dock full of men.

"Aye, I do smuggle, and make such profits as I did never believe. A tenth the amount of the excise in the customs men's pockets do turn their eyes and seal their mouths."

Two Tanchicans in those veils and round hats strolled past, hands clasped behind their backs. Each wore a heavy brass key dangling from a thick chain about his neck; it had the look of a mark of office. They nodded to Domon in a familiar way. Thom looked amused, but Juilin glared at Domon and the two Tanchicans equally. As a thief-catcher he had a proper dislike of those who flouted the law.

"I do no believe it will last much longer though," Domon said when the Tanchicans had passed. "Things do be even worse in Arad Doman than here, and it do be bad enough here. Perhaps the Lord Dragon does no Break the World yet, but he did break Arad Doman and Tarabon."

Elayne wanted to say something sharp to him, but they had reached the foot of the dock, and she watched in silence while he hired sedan chairs and bearers, and a dozen men with stout staves and hard faces. Guards with swords and spears stood at the end of the dock, with the look of hired men, not soldiers. From across the wide street along the row of docks, hundreds of defeated, sunken faces stared at the guards. Sometimes eyes flickered toward the ships, but mainly they fixed on the men holding them back from those ships. Remembering what Coine had said about people here mobbing her vessel, desperate to buy passage anywhere away from Tanchico, Elayne shivered. When these hungry eyes looked at the ships, need burned in them. Elayne sat rigidly in her chair as it jounced through the crowds behind prodding staves, and tried not to look at anything. She did not want to see those faces. Where was their king? Why was he not taking care of them?

A sign above the gate of the white-plastered inn Domon took them to, below the Great Circle, proclaimed the Three Plum Court. The only court Elayne saw was the high-walled courtyard paved with flagstones in front of the inn, which was three square stories with no windows near the ground and the upper windows grilled with fanciful ironwork. Inside, men and women crowded the common room, most in Tanchican clothes, and the buzz of voices nearly drowned out the tune of a hammered dulcimer.

Nynaeve gasped at her first sight of the innkeeper, a pretty woman not much older than herself with brown eyes and pale honey braids, her veil not hiding a plump rosebud of a mouth. Elayne gave a start, too, but it was not Liandrin. The woman—her name was Rendra—obviously knew Domon well. With welcoming smiles for Elayne and Nynaeve, and making much over Thom being a gleeman, she gave them her last two rooms at what Elayne suspected might be less than the going rate. Elayne made sure she and Nynaeve got the one with the larger bed; she had shared a bed with Nynaeve before, and the woman was free with her elbows.

Rendra also provided supper in a private room, laid out by two veiled young serving men. Elayne found herself staring at a plate of a roast lamb with spiced apple jelly and some sort of long yellowish beans prepared with pinenuts. She could not touch it. All those hungry faces. Domon ate readily enough, him and his smuggling and his gold. Thom and Juilin showed no reticence either.

"Rendra," Nynaeve said quietly, "does anyone here help the poor? I can lay my hands on a good bit of gold if it would help."

"You could donate to Bayle's kitchen," the innkeeper replied, giving Domon a smile. "The man avoids all of the taxes, yet he taxes himself. For each crown he gives as the bribe, he gives two for the soup and the bread for the poor. He has even talked me into giving, and *I* pay my taxes."

"It do be less than the taxes," Domon muttered, hunching his shoulders defensively. "I do make a very healthy profit, Fortune prick me if I do no."

"It is good that you like to help people, Master Domon," Nynaeve said when Rendra and the servants had gone. Thom and Juilin both got up to see they really had gone. With a half-bow, Thom let Juilin open the door; the hall outside was empty. Nynaeve went right on. "We may need your help, too."

The Illianer's knife and fork paused in cutting a piece of lamb. "How?" he asked suspiciously.

"I do not know exactly, Master Domon. You have ships. You must have men. We may need ears and eyes. Some of the Black Ajah may very well be in Tanchico, and we must find them if they are." Nynaeve lifted a forkful of beans to her mouth as if she had said nothing out of the ordinary. She seemed to be telling everyone about the Black Ajah of late.

Domon gaped at her, then stared incredulously at Thom and Juilin as they settled back in their chairs. When they nodded, he pushed his plate aside and put his head down on his arms. He very nearly earned himself a thump from Nynaeve, if the way her mouth tightened was any indication, and Elayne would not have blamed her. Why should he need them to confirm her word?

Finally Domon roused himself. "It do be going to happen again. Falme all over. Maybe it do be time for me to pack up and go. If I do take the ships I have back to Illian, I will be a wealthy man there, too."

"I doubt you'd find Illian congenial," Nynaeve told him in a firm voice. "I understand that Sammael rules there now, if not openly. You might not enjoy your wealth under one of the Forsaken." Domon's eyes nearly came out of his head, but she went right on. "There are no safe places any longer. You can run like a rabbit, but you cannot hide. Is it not better to do what you can to fight back like a man?"

Nynaeve was being too hard; she always had to bully people. Elayne smiled and leaned over to put a hand on Domon's arm. "We do not mean to browbeat you, Master Domon, but we truly may need your help. I know you for a brave man, else you would not have waited for us as long as you did at Falme. We will be most grateful."

"You do this very well," Domon muttered. "One with an ox driver's stick, the other with a queen's honey. Oh, very well. I will help as I can. But I will no promise to remain for another Falme."

Thom and Juilin set in to question him closely about Tanchico as they ate. At least, Juilin did in a roundabout manner, suggesting questions to Thom about what districts thieves and cutpurses and burglars frequented, what wineshops they used, and who bought their stolen goods. The thief-catcher maintained that such people often knew more of what was going on in a city than the authorities did. He did not seem to want to talk to the Illianer directly, and Domon snorted every time he answered one of the Tairen's questions put by Thom. He did not answer *until* they were put by Thom. Thom's own questions made no sense, at least not coming from a gleeman. He asked of nobles and factions, of who was allied to whom and who opposed, of who had what stated aims, and what their actions brought about, and whether the results were different from what they supposedly wanted. Not the kind of questions she expected from him at all, even after all their conversations on *Wavedancer*. He had been willing enough to talk with her—he even seemed to enjoy it—but somehow every time she thought she might dig out something about his past, that was just when he managed to put her back up and send her stalking away. Domon answered Thom with more alacrity than he did Juilin. In either case, though, he seemed to know Tanchico very well, both its lords and officials and its dark underbelly; as he talked, it often sounded as if there were little difference.

Once the two men had wrung the smuggler dry, Nynaeve summoned Rendra to bring pen and ink and paper, and wrote out a list describing each of the Black sisters. Holding the sheets gingerly in one big hand, Domon frowned at them uneasily, as though they were the women themselves, but he promised to have such of his men as were in port keep their eyes open. When Nynaeve reminded him that they all should take extreme care, he laughed the way he would had she told him not to run himself through with a sword.

Juilin left on Domon's heels, twirling his pale staff and saying night was the best time to find thieves and people who lived off thieves. Nynaeve announced she was retiring to her room—her room—to lie down awhile. She looked a bit unsteady, and suddenly Elayne realized why. Nynaeve had become used to *Wavedancer*'s heaving; now she was having trouble with the ground *not* heaving. The woman's stomach was not a pleasant traveling companion.

She herself followed Thom down to the common room, where he had promised Rendra he would perform. For a wonder she found a bench at an empty table, and cool looks sufficed to ward off the men who suddenly seemed to want to sit there. Rendra brought her a silver cup of wine, and she sipped as she listened to Thom play his harp, singing love songs like "The First Rose of Summer" and "The Wind That Shakes the Willow," and funny songs like "Only One Boot" and "The Old Gray Goose." His listeners were appreciative, slapping the tables for applause. After a while Elayne slapped hers, too. She had not drunk more than half her wine, but a handsome young serving man smiled at her and filled it up. It was all strangely exciting. In her whole life she had not been in an inn's common room half a dozen times, and never to sip wine and be entertained like one of the common people.

Flourishing his cloak to set the multihued patches fluttering, Thom told stories—"Mara and the Three Foolish Kings," and several tales about Anla, the Wise Counselor—and recited a long stretch of *The Great Hunt of the Horn,* reciting it so that horses seemed to prance and trumpets blare in the common room, and men and women fought and loved and died. On into the night he sang and recited, only pausing now and then to wet his throat with a sip of wine as the patrons eagerly clamored for more. The woman who had been playing the dulcimer sat in a corner with her instrument on her knees and a sour expression on her face. People often tossed coins to Thom—he had enlisted a small boy to gather them up—and it was unlikely they had produced as much for her music.

It all seemed to suit Thom, the harp, and especially the recital. Well, he was a gleeman, but it seemed more than that. Elayne could have sworn she had heard him recite *The Great Hunt* before, but in High Chant, not Plain. How could that be? He was just a simple old gleeman.

Finally, in the deep hours of the night, Thom bowed with a last sweeping flourish of his cloak and headed for the stairs amid great slapping of tables. Elayne slapped hers as vigorously as anyone.

Rising to follow, she slipped and sat back down hard, frowning at her silver winecup. It was full. Surely she had drunk a little. She felt dizzy for some reason. Yes. That sweet young man with those melting brown eyes had refilled her cup—how many times? Not that it mattered. She never drank more than one cup of wine. Never. It was being off *Wavedancer* and back on dry land. She was reacting like Nynaeve. That was all.

Getting carefully to her feet—and refusing the sweet young man's most solicitous offer of help—she managed to climb the stairs despite the way they swayed. Not stopping at the second floor, where her and Nynaeve's room was, she went up to the third and knocked on Thom's door. He opened it slowly, peering out suspiciously. He seemed to have a knife in his hand, and then it was gone. Strange. She seized one of his long white mustaches.

"I remember," she said. Her tongue did not seem to be working properly; the words sounded . . . fuzzy. "I was sitting on your knee, and I pulled your mustache . . ." She gave it a yank to demonstrate, and he winced. ". . . and my mother leaned over your shoulder and laughed at me."

"I think it best you go to your room," he said, trying to pry her hand free. "I think you need some sleep."

She refused to let go. In fact, she seemed to have pushed him back into his room. By his mustache. "My mother sat on your knee, too. I saw it. I remember."

"Sleep is the thing, Elayne. You will feel better in the morning." He managed to get her hand loose and tried ushering her to the door, but she slipped around him. The bed had no posts. If she had a bedpost to hold on to, perhaps the room would stop tilting back and forth.

"I want to know why Mother sat on your knee." He stepped back, and she realized she was reaching for his mustache again. "You're a gleeman. My mother would not sit on a gleeman's knee."

"Go to bed, child."

"I am *not* a child!" She stamped her foot angrily, and almost fell.

The floor was lower than it looked. "Not a child. You will tell me. Now!"

Thom sighed and shook his head. At last he said stiffly, "I was not always a gleeman. I was a bard, once. A Court-bard. In Caemlyn, as it happens. For Queen Morgase. You were a child. You are just remembering things wrong, that's all."

"You were her lover, weren't you?" The flinch of his eyes was enough. "You were! I always knew about Gareth Bryne. At least, I figured it out. But I always hoped she would marry him. Gareth Bryne, and you, and this Lord Gaebril Mat said she looks calf-eyes at now, and. . . . How many more? How many? What makes her any different from Berelain, tripping every man who catches her eye into her bed. She is no different—" Her vision shivered, and her head rang. It took her a moment to realize he had slapped her. *Slapped* her! She drew herself up, wishing he would not sway. "How dare you? I am Daughter-Heir of Andor, and I will not be—"

"You are a little girl with a skinful of wine throwing a temper tantrum," he snapped. "And if I ever hear you say anything like that about Morgase again, drunk or sober, I'll put you over my knee however you channel! Morgase is a fine woman, as good as any there is!"

"Is she?" Her voice quavered, and she realized she was crying. "Then why did she—? Why—?" Somehow she had her face buried against his coat, and he was smoothing her hair.

"Because it is lonely being a queen," he said softly. "Because most men attracted to a queen see power, not a woman. I saw a woman, and she knew it. I suppose Bryne saw the same in her, and this Gaebril, too. You have to understand, child. Everyone wants someone in their life, someone who cares for them, someone they can care for. Even a queen."

"Why did you go away?" she mumbled into his chest. "You made me laugh. I remember that. You made her laugh, too. And you rode me on your shoulder."

"A long story." He sighed painfully. "I will tell you another time. If you ask. With luck, you'll forget this by morning. It's time for you to go to bed, Elayne."

He guided her to the door, and she took the opportunity to tug at his mustache again. "Like that," she said with satisfaction. "I used to pull it just like that."

"Yes, you did. Can you make it downstairs by yourself?"

"Of course I can." She gave him her haughtiest stare, but he looked readier than ever to follow her into the hall. To prove there was no need, she walked—carefully—as far as the head of the stairs. He was still frowning at her worriedly from the doorway when she started down.

Luckily she did not stumble until she was out of his sight, but she did walk right by her door and had to come back. Something must have been wrong with that apple jelly; she knew she should not have eaten so much of it. Lini always said. . . . She could not remember what it was Lini said, but something about eating too many sweets.

There were two lamps burning in the room, one on the small round table by the bed and the other on the white-plastered mantel above the brick fireplace. Nynaeve lay stretched out on the bed atop the coverlet, fully dressed. With her elbows stuck out, Elayne noted.

She said the first thing that came into her head. "Rand must think I'm crazy, Thom is a bard, and Berelain isn't my mother after all." Nynaeve gave her the oddest look. "I am a little dizzy for some reason. A nice boy with sweet brown eyes offered to help me upstairs."

"I will wager he did," Nynaeve said, biting off each word. Rising, she came to put an arm around Elayne's shoulders. "Come over here a moment. There's something I think you should see." It appeared to be a bucket of extra water by the washstand. "Here. We'll both kneel down so you can look."

Elayne did, but there was nothing in the bucket but her own reflection in the water. She wondered why she was grinning that way. Then Nynaeve's hand went to the back of her neck, and her head was in the water.

Flailing her hands, she tried to straighten up, but Nynaeve's arm was like an iron bar. You were supposed to hold your breath under water. Elayne knew you were. She just could not remember how. All she could do was flail and gurgle and choke.

Nynaeve hauled her up, water streaming down her face, and she filled her lungs. "How dare—you," she gasped. "I am—the Daughter-Heir of—" She managed to get out one wail before her head went back in with a splash. Seizing the bucket with both hands and pushing did no good. Drumming her feet on the floor did no good. She was going to drown. Nynaeve was going to drown her.

After an Age she was back out in the air again. Sodden strands of hair hung all across her face. "I think," she said in the steadiest voice she could find, "that I am going to sick up."

Nynaeve got the big white-glazed basin down from the washstand just in time, and held Elayne's head while she brought up everything she had ever eaten in her life. A year later—well, hours anyway; it seemed that long—Nynaeve was washing her face and wiping her mouth, bathing her hands and wrists. There was nothing solicitous in her voice, though.

"How could you do this? Whatever possessed you? I might expect a fool man to drink until he can't stand, but you! And tonight."

"I only had one cup," Elayne muttered. Even with that young man refilling it, she could not have had more than two. Surely not.

"A cup the size of a pitcher." Nynaeve sniffed, helping her to her feet. Hauling her, really. "Can you stay awake? I am going to look for Egwene, and I still don't trust myself to get out of *Tel'aran'rhiod* without someone to wake me."

Elayne blinked at her. They had looked for Egwene, unsuccessfully, every night since she had disappeared so abruptly out of that meeting in the Heart of the Stone. "Stay awake? Nynaeve, it is my turn to look, and better it's me. You know you cannot channel unless you are angry, and. . . ." She realized the other woman was surrounded by the glow of *saidar*. And had been for some time, she thought. Her own head felt stuffed full of wool; thought had to burrow through. She could barely sense the True Source. "Maybe you had better go. I will stay awake."

Nynaeve frowned at her, but finally nodded. Elayne tried to help undress her, but her fingers did not seem to work very well when it came to those little buttons. Grumping under her breath, Nynaeve managed on her own. In only her shift, she threaded the twisted stone ring onto the leather cord she wore hanging around her neck, alongside a man's ring, heavy and golden. That was Lan's ring; Nynaeve always wore it between her breasts.

Elayne pulled a low wooden stool over beside the bed while Nynaeve stretched out again. She did feel rather sleepy, but she would not fall asleep sitting on that. The problem seemed to be not falling on the floor. "I will judge an hour and wake you."

Nynaeve nodded, then closed her eyes, both hands clutched around the two rings. After a time her breathing deepened.

The Heart of the Stone was quite empty. Peering into the dimness among the great columns, Nynaeve had circled *Callandor,* sparkling out of the floorstones, completely before she realized she was still in her shift, the leather cord dangling about her neck with the two rings. She frowned, and after a moment she was wearing a Two Rivers dress of good brown wool, and stout shoes. Elayne and Egwene both seemed to find this sort of thing easy, but it was not easy for her. There had been embarrassing moments in earlier visits to *Tel'aran'rhiod,* mostly after stray thoughts of Lan, but changing her garb deliberately took concentration. Just that—remembering—and her dress was silk, and as transparent as Rendra's veil. Berelain would have blushed. So did Nynaeve, thinking of Lan seeing her in it. It took an effort to bring the brown wool back.

Worse, her anger had faded—that fool girl; did she not realize what happened when you drank too much wine? Had she never been alone in a common room before? Well, possibly she had not—and the True Source might as well not exist so far as she was concerned. Perhaps it would not matter. Uneasy, she stared into the forest of huge redstone columns, turning in one spot. What had made Egwene leave here abruptly?

The Stone was silent, with a hollow emptiness. She could hear the blood rushing in her own ears. Yet the skin between her shoulder blades prickled as if someone were watching her.

"Egwene?" Her shout echoed in the silence among the columns. "Egwene?" Nothing.

Rubbing her hands on her skirt, she found she was holding a gnarled stick with a thick knob on the end. A fat lot of good that would do. But she tightened her grip on it. A sword might be more use—for an instant the stick flickered, half a sword—but she did not know how to use a sword. She laughed to herself ruefully. A cudgel was as good as a sword here; both practically useless. Channeling was the only real defense, that and running. Which left her only one choice at the moment.

She wanted to run now, with that feel of eyes on her, but she would not give up so quickly. Only what was she to do? Egwene was not here. She was somewhere in the Waste. Rhuidean, Elayne said. Wherever that was.

Between one step and the next she was suddenly on a mountainside, with a harsh sun rising over more jagged mountains beyond the valley below, baking the dry air. The Waste. She was in the Waste. For a moment the sun startled her, but the Waste was far enough east for sunrise there to still be night in Tanchico. In *Tel'aran'rhiod* it made no difference anyway. Sunlight or darkness there seemed to bear no relation to what was in the real world as far as she could determine.

Long, pale shadows still covered almost half the valley, but strangely a mass of fog billowed down there, not seeming to grow less for the sun beating on it. Great towers rose out of the fog, some appearing unfinished. A city. In the Waste?

Squinting, she could make out a person down in the valley, too. A man, though all she could see at this distance was someone who seemed to be wearing breeches and a bright blue coat. Certainly not an Aiel. He was walking along the edge of the fog, every now and again stopping to poke at it. She could not be sure, but she thought his hand stopped short each time. Maybe it was not fog at all.

"You must get away from here," a woman's voice said urgently. "If that one sees you, you are dead, or worse."

Nynaeve jumped, spinning with her club raised, nearly losing her footing on the slope.

The woman standing a little above her wore a short white coat and voluminous, pale yellow trousers gathered above short boots. Her cloak billowed on an arid gust of wind. It was her long golden hair, intricately braided, and the silver bow in her hands that made a name pop incredulously into Nynaeve's mouth.

"Birgitte?" Birgitte, hero of a hundred tales, and her silver bow with which she never missed. Birgitte, one of the dead heroes the Horn of Valere would call back from the grave to fight in the Last Battle. "It's impossible. Who are you?"

"There is no time, woman. You must go before he sees." In one smooth motion she pulled a silver arrow from the quiver at her waist, nocked it and drew fletching to ear. The silver arrowhead pointed straight at Nynaeve's heart. "Go!"

Nynaeve fled.

She was not sure how, but she was standing on the Green in Emond's Field, looking at the Winespring Inn with its chimneys and red tile roof. Thatched roofs surrounded the Green, where the Winespring gushed out of a stone outcrop. The sun stood high here, though the Two Rivers lay far west of the Waste. Yet despite a cloudless sky, a deep shadow lay across the village.

She had only a moment to wonder how they were doing without her. A flicker of movement caught her eye, a flash of silver and a woman ducking behind the corner of Ailys Candwin's neat house beyond the Winespring Water. Birgitte.

Nynaeve did not hesitate. She ran for one of the footbridges across the narrow rushing stream. Her shoes pounded on the wooden planks. "Come back here," she shouted. "You come back here and answer me! Who was that? You come back here, or I'll hero you! I'll thump you so you think you've had an adventure!"

Rounding the corner of Ailys's house, she really only half-expected to see Birgitte. What she did not expect at all was a man in a dark coat trotting toward her less than a hundred paces down the hard-packed dirt street. Her breath caught. Lan. No, but he had the same shape to his face, the same eyes. Halting, he raised his bow and shot. At her. Screaming, she threw herself aside, trying to claw her way awake.

Elayne jumped to her feet, toppling the stool over backward, as Nynaeve screamed and sat up on the bed, eyes wide.

"What happened, Nynaeve? What happened?"

Nynaeve shuddered. "He looked like Lan. He looked like Lan, and he tried to kill me." She put a trembling hand to her left arm, where a shallow slash oozed blood a few inches below her shoulder. "If I hadn't jumped, it would have gone through my heart."

Seating herself on the edge of the bed, Elayne examined the cut. "It is not bad. I'll wash and bandage it for you." She wished she knew how to Heal; trying without knowing might well make it worse. But it really was little more than a long nick. Not to mention that her head still seemed full of jelly. Quivering jelly. "It was not Lan. Calm yourself. Whoever it was, it was not Lan."

"I know that," Nynaeve said acidly. She recounted what had happened in much the same angry voice. The man who had shot at her in Emond's Field, and the man in the Waste; she was not sure they were one and the same. Birgitte herself was incredible enough.

"Are you certain?" Elayne asked. "Birgitte?"

Nynaeve sighed. "The only thing I am certain of is that I did not find Egwene. And that I am not going back there tonight." She pounded a fist on her thigh. "Where is she? What happened to her? If she met that fellow with the bow. . . . Oh, Light!"

Elayne had to think a minute; she wanted to sleep so badly, and her thoughts kept shimmering. "She said she might not be there when we are supposed to meet again. Maybe that is why she left so hurriedly. Whyever she can't. . . . I mean. . . ." It did not seem to make a great deal of sense, but she could not get it out properly.

"I hope so," Nynaeve said wearily. Looking at Elayne, she added, "We had better get you to bed. You look ready to fall over."

Elayne was grateful to be helped out of her clothes. She did remember to bandage Nynaeve's arm, but the bed looked so inviting she could hardly think of anything else. In the morning perhaps the room would have stopped its slow spin around the bed. Sleep came as soon as her head touched the pillow.

In the morning she wished she were dead.

With sunlight barely in the sky, the common room was empty except for Elayne. Head in her hands, she stared at a cup Nynaeve had set on the table before going off to find the innkeeper. Every time she breathed, she could smell it; her nose tried to clench. Her head felt. . . . It was not possible to describe how her head felt. Had someone offered to cut it off, she might have thanked him.

"Are you all right?"

She jerked at the sound of Thom's voice and barely stifled a whimper. "I am quite all right, thank you." Talking made her head throb. He fiddled with one of his mustaches uncertainly. "Your stories were wonderful last night, Thom. What I remember of them." Somehow she managed a small, self-deprecating laugh. "I am afraid I don't remember very much of anything except sitting there listening. I seem to have eaten some bad apple jelly." She was not about to admit to drinking all that wine; she still had no idea how much. Or to making a fool of herself in his room. Above all, not that. He seemed to believe her, from the relieved way he took a chair.

Nynaeve appeared, handing her a damp cloth as she sat down. She also pushed the cup with its horrible brew closer. Elayne pressed the cloth to her forehead gratefully.

"Have either of you seen Master Sandar this morning?" the older woman asked.

"He did not sleep in our room," Thom replied. "Which I should be grateful for, considering the size of the bed."

As though the words had summoned him, Juilin came in through the front door, his face weary and his snug-fitting coat rumpled. There was a bruise beneath his left eye, and the short black hair that normally lay flat on his head looked rough-combed with his fingers, but he smiled as he joined them. "The thieves in this city are as numerous as minnows in reeds, and they will talk if you buy a cup of something. I have talked with two men who claim to have seen a woman with a white streak in her hair above the left ear. I think I believe one of them."

"So they are here," Elayne said, but Nynaeve shook her head.

"Perhaps. More than one woman can have a white streak in her hair."

"He could not say how old she was," Juilin said, hiding a yawn behind his hand. "No age at all, he claimed. He joked that maybe she was Aes Sedai."

"You go too fast," Nynaeve told him in a tight voice. "You do us no good if you bring them down on us."

Juilin flushed darkly. "I am careful. I have no wish for Liandrin to put her hands on me again. I do not ask questions; I talk. Sometimes of women I used to know. Two men bit on that white streak, and neither ever knew it was more than a scrap of idle talk over cheap ale. Tonight maybe another will swim into my net, only this time maybe it will be a fragile woman from Cairhien with very big blue eyes." That would be Temaile Kinderode. "Bit by bit, I will narrow where they have been seen, until I know where they are. I will find them for you."

"Or I will." Thom sounded as if he thought that much more likely. "Rather than thieves, would they not be meddling with nobles and politics? Some lord in this city will begin doing what he usually does not, and he will draw me to them."

The two men eyed one another. In another moment Elayne expected one of them to offer to wrestle. Men. First Juilin and Domon, now Juilin and Thom. Very likely Thom and Domon would get in a fistfight to complete it. Men. That was the only comment she could think of.

"Perhaps Elayne and I will succeed without either of you," Nynaeve said dryly. "We will begin looking ourselves, today." Her eyes barely shifted toward Elayne. "At least, I will. Elayne may need a little more rest to recover from . . . the voyage."

Setting the cloth down carefully, Elayne used both hands to pick up the cup in front of her. The thick, gray-green liquid tasted worse than it smelled. Shuddering, she made herself keep swallowing. When it hit her stomach, for an instant she felt like a cloak flapping in a high wind. "Two pairs of eyes can see better than one," she told Nynaeve, setting the empty cup back down with a clink.

"A hundred pairs can see even better," Juilin said hastily, "and if that Illianer eel truly sends his people out, we will have at least that many, what with the thieves and cutpurses."

"I—we—will find these women for you if they can be found," Thom said. "There is no need for you to stir from the inn. This city has a dangerous feel even if Liandrin is not here."

"Besides which," Juilin added, "if they are here, they know the two of you. They know your faces. Much better if you stay here at the inn, out of sight."

Elayne stared at them in amazement. A moment gone they had been trying to stare each other down, and now they were shoulder to shoulder. Nynaeve had been right about them causing trouble. Well, the Daughter-Heir of Andor was not about to hide behind Master Juilin Sandar and Master Thom Merrilin. She opened her mouth to tell them so, but Nynaeve spoke first.

"You are right," she said calmly. Elayne stared at her incredulously; Thom and Juilin looked surprised, and at the same time disgustingly satisfied. "They do know us," Nynaeve went on. "I took care of that this morning, I think. Ah, here is Mistress Rendra with our breakfast."

Thom and Juilin exchanged disconcerted frowns, but they could say nothing with the innkeeper smiling at them all through her veil.

"About what I asked you?" Nynaeve said to her as the woman placed a bowl of honeyed porridge in front of her.

"Ah, yes. It will be no problem to find the clothes to fit both of you. And the hair—you have such lovely hair; so long—it will be the work of no time to put it up." She fingered her own deep golden braids.

Thom's and Juilin's faces made Elayne smile. They might have been ready for arguments; they had no defense against being ignored. Her head was actually feeling a little better; Nynaeve's vile mixture seemed to be working. As Nynaeve and Rendra discussed costs and cut and fabric—Rendra wanted to duplicate her clinging dress, pale green today; Nynaeve was opposed, but seemed to be wavering—Elayne took a spoon of porridge to wash the taste from her mouth. It reminded her that she was hungry.

There was one problem none of them had mentioned yet, one that Thom and Juilin did not know. If the Black Ajah was in Tanchico, then so was whatever it was that endangered Rand. Something able to bind him with his own Power. Finding Liandrin and the others was not enough. They had to find that, too. Suddenly her newfound appetite was completely gone.

CHAPTER
40

Hunter of Trollocs

R emnants of the early-morning rain still dripped from the leaves
of the apple trees, and a purple finch hopped along a limb
where fruit was forming that would not be harvested this year.
The sun was well up, but hidden behind thick gray clouds. Seated cross-
legged on the ground, Perrin unconsciously tested his bowstring; the
tightly wrapped, waxed cords had a tendency to go slack in wet
weather. The storm Verin had called up to hide them from pursuit the
night of the rescue had surprised even her with its ferocity, and beating
rains had come three more times in the six days since. He believed it
was six days. He had not really thought since that night, only drifted as
events took him, reacting to what presented itself. The flat of his axe
blade dug into his side, but he hardly noticed.

Low, grassy mounds marked generations of Aybaras buried here.
The oldest among the carved wooden headpieces, cracked and barely
legible, bore dates nearly three hundred years old, over graves indistinguishable from undisturbed ground. It was the mounds smoothed by
rains but barely covered by grass that stabbed him. Generations of
Aybaras buried here, but surely never fourteen at one time. Aunt
Neain over by Uncle Carlin's older grave, with their two children beside her. Great Aunt Ealsin in the row with Uncle Eward and Aunt
Magde and their three children, the long row with his mother and his

father. Adora and Deselle and little Paet. A long row of mounds with bare, wet earth still showing through the grass. He counted the arrows remaining in his quiver by touch. Seventeen. Too many had been damaged, worth recovering only for the steel arrowheads. No time to make his own; he would have to see the fletcher in Emond's Field soon. Buel Dawtry made good arrows, even better than Tam.

A faint rustle behind his back made him sniff the air, "What is it, Dannil?" he said without looking around.

There was a catch of breath, a moment of startled surprise, before Dannil Lewin said, "The Lady is here, Perrin." None of them had gotten used to him knowing who was who before he saw them, or in the dark, but he no longer really cared what they found strange.

He frowned over his shoulder. Dannil looked leaner than he had; farmers could only feed so many at once, and food had been feast or famine as the hunting went. Mostly famine. "The Lady?"

"The Lady Faile. And Lord Luc, too. They came from Emond's Field."

Perrin rose smoothly, taking long strides that made Dannil hurry to keep up. He managed not to look at the house. The charred timbers and sooty chimneys that had been the house where he grew up. He did scan the trees for his lookouts, those nearest the farm. Close to the Waterwood as it was, the land held plenty of tall oak and hemlock, and good-sized ash and bay. Thick foliage hid the lads well—drab farm clothes made for good hiding—so even he had difficulty picking them out. He would have to talk with those farther out; they were supposed to see that no one came close without a warning. Even Faile and this Luc.

The camp, in a large thicket where he had once pretended to be in a far wilderness, was a rough place among the undergrowth, with blankets strung between trees to make shelters, and more scattered on the ground between the small cook fires. The branches dripped here, too. Most of the nearly fifty men in the camp, all young, were unshaven, either in imitation of Perrin or because it was unpleasant shaving in cold water. They were good hunters—he had sent home any who were not—but unaccustomed to more than a night or two outdoors at a time. And not used to what he had them doing, either.

Right then they were standing around gaping at Faile and Luc, and only four or five had longbow in hand. The rest of the bows lay with the bedding, and the quivers, too, more often than not. Luc stood idly flipping the reins of a tall black stallion, the very pose of indolent, red-coated arrogance, cold blue eyes ignoring the men around him. The man's smell stood out among the others, cold and separate, too, almost as if he had nothing in common with the men around him, not even humanity.

Faile came hurrying to meet Perrin with a smile, her narrow divided skirts making a soft *whisk-whisk* as gray silk brushed silk. She smelled faintly of sweet herbal soap, and of herself. "Master Luhhan said we might find you here."

He meant to demand what she was doing there, but found himself putting his arms around her and saying into her hair, "It's good to see you. I have missed you."

She pushed back enough to look up at him. "You look tired."

He ignored that; he had no time to be tired. "You got everyone safely to Emond's Field?"

"They are at the Winespring Inn." She grinned suddenly. "Master al'Vere found an old halberd and says if the Whitecloaks want them, they will have to go through him. Everyone's in the village now, Perrin. Verin and Alanna, the Warders. Pretending to be someone else, of course. And Loial. He certainly created a sensation. Even more than Bain and Chiad." The grin faded into a frown. "He asked me to deliver a message to you. Alanna vanished twice without a word, once alone. Loial said Ihvon seemed surprised to find her gone. He said I wasn't to let anyone else know." She studied his face. "What does it mean, Perrin?"

"Nothing, maybe. Just that I can't be sure I can trust her. Verin warned me against her, but can I trust Verin? You say Bain and Chiad are in Emond's Field? I suppose that means he knows about them." He jerked his head toward Luc. A few of the men had approached him, asking diffident questions, and he was answering with a condescending smile.

"They came with us," she said slowly. "They are scouting around your camp now. I do not think they have a very high opinion of your sentries. Perrin, why don't you want Luc to know about the Aiel?"

"I've talked to a number of people who were burned out." Luc was too far to overhear, but he held his voice low. "Counting Flann Lewin's place, Luc was at five on the day they were attacked, or the day before."

"Perrin, the man's an arrogant fool in some ways—I hear he's hinted at a claim to one of the Borderland thrones, for all he told us he's from Murandy—but you cannot really believe he is a Darkfriend. He gave some very good advice in Emond's Field. When I said everyone was there, I meant everyone." She shook her dark head wonderingly.

"Hundreds and hundreds of people have come in from north and south, from every direction, with their cattle and their sheep, all talking of Perrin Goldeneyes's warnings. Your little village is preparing to defend itself if need be, and Luc has been everywhere the last days."

"Perrin who?" he gasped, wincing. Trying to change the subject, he said, "From the south? But this is as far south as I've gone. I haven't talked to a farmer more than a mile below the Winespring Water."

Faile tugged at his beard with a laugh. "News spreads, my fine general. I think half of them expect you to form them into an army and chase the Trollocs all the way back to the Great Blight. There will be stories about you in the Two Rivers for the next thousand years. Perrin Goldeneyes, hunter of Trollocs."

"Light!" he muttered.

Hunter of Trollocs. There had been little so far to justify that. Two days after freeing Mistress Luhhan and the others, the day after Verin and Tomas rode on their own way, they had come on the still-smoking ruins of a farmhouse, he and the fifteen Two Rivers lads with him then. After burying what they found in the ashes, it was easy enough to follow the Trollocs, between Gaul's tracking and his own nose. The sharp fetid stink of the Trollocs had not had time to fade away, not to him. Some of the lads had grown hesitant when they realized he meant what he had said about hunting Trollocs. If they had had to go very far, he suspected most would have drifted away when no one was looking, but the trail led to a thicket no more than three miles off. The Trollocs had not bothered with sentries—they had no Myrddraal with them to overawe their laziness—and the Two Rivers men knew how to stalk silently. Thirty-two Trollocs died, many in their filthy blankets, pierced through with arrows before they could raise a howl, much less sword or axe. Dannil and Ban and the others had been ready to celebrate a great triumph—until they found what was in the Trollocs' big iron cookpot sitting in the ashes of the fire. Most dashed away to throw up, and more than one wept openly. Perrin dug the grave himself. Only one: there was no way to tell what had belonged to whom. Cold as he felt inside, he was not sure he could have stood it himself if there had been.

Late the next day no one hesitated when he picked up another fetid trail, though a few mutters wondered what he was following, until Gaul found the tracks of hooves and boots too big for men. Another thicket, close to the Waterwood, held forty-one Trollocs and a Fade, with sentries set, though most snored at their posts. It would have made no difference had they all been awake. Gaul killed those that were, sliding through the trees like a shadow, and the Two Rivers men were nearly thirty themselves by then. Besides, those who had not seen the cookpot had heard of it; they shouted as they shot, with a satisfaction not much less savage than the guttural Trolloc howls. The black-garbed Myrddraal had been last to die, a porcupine quilled with arrows. No one cared to recover a shaft from that, even after it finally stopped thrashing.

That evening the second rain came, hours of drenching downpour with a sky full of roiling black clouds and stabbing lightning. Perrin had not smelled Trolloc scent since, and the ground had been washed clean of tracks. Most of their time had been spent avoiding Whitecloak patrols, which everyone said were more numerous than in the past. The farmers Perrin had spoken to said the patrols seemed more interested in finding their prisoners again and those who had broken them free than in looking for Trollocs.

Quite a few of the men had gathered around Luc now. He was tall enough for his red-gold hair to show above their darker heads. He seemed to be talking, and they listening. And nodding.

"Let's see what he has to say," Perrin said grimly.

The Two Rivers men gave way before Faile and him with only a little prodding. They were all intent on the red-coated lord, who was indeed holding forth.

". . . so the village is quite secure, now. Plenty of people gathered together to defend it. I must say I enjoy sleeping under a roof when I can. Mistress al'Vere, at the inn, provides a tasty meal. Her bread is among the best I have ever eaten. There truly is nothing like fresh-baked bread and fresh-churned butter, and putting your feet up of an evening with a fine mug of wine, or some of Master al'Vere's good brown ale."

"Lord Luc was saying we should go to Emond's Field, Perrin," Kenley Ahan said, scrubbing his reddened nose with the back of a grimy hand. He was not the only one who had been unable to wash as often as he would like, and not the only one coming down with a cold, either.

Luc smiled at Perrin much the way he would have at a dog he expected to see do a trick. "The village *is* quite secure, but there is always a need for more strong backs."

"We are hunting Trollocs," Perrin said coolly. "Not everyone has left their farms yet, and every band we find and kill means farms not burned and more people with a chance to reach safety."

Wil al'Seen barked a laugh. He was not so pretty with a red puffy nose and a spotty, six-day growth of beard. "We've not *smelled* a Trolloc in days. Be reasonable, Perrin. Maybe we've killed them all already." There were mutters of agreement.

"I do not mean to spread dissension." Luc spread his hands guilelessly. "No doubt you have had many great successes beside those we have heard of. Hundreds of Trollocs killed, I expect. You may well have chased them all away. I can tell you, Emond's Field is ready to give you all a hero's welcome. The same must be true at Watch Hill for those who live up that way. Any Deven Riders?" Wil nodded, and Luc clapped him on the shoulder with a hollow good fellowship. "A hero's welcome, without a doubt."

"Anyone who wants to go home, can," Perrin said in a level voice. Faile directed a warning frown at him; this was no way to be a general. But he did not want anyone with him who did not want to be there. He did not want to be a general, for that matter. "Myself, I don't think the job is done yet, but it is your choice."

No one took him up, though Wil at least looked ready to, but twenty more stared at the ground and scuffed their boots in last year's leaves.

"Well," Luc said casually, "if you have no Trollocs left to chase, perhaps it is time to turn your attentions to the Whitecloaks. They are not happy at you Two Rivers folk deciding to defend yourselves. And I understand they meant to hang the lot of you in particular, as outlaws, for stealing their prisoners."

Anxious frowns passed between a good many of the Two Rivers lads.

It was then that Gaul came pushing through the crowd, followed close by Bain and Chiad. Not that the Aiel had to push, of course; the men cleared aside as soon as they realized who it was. Luc frowned at Gaul thoughtfully, perhaps disapprovingly; the Aielman stared back stony-faced. Wil and Dannil and the others brightened at sight of the Aiel; most still believed hundreds more were hiding somewhere in the thickets and forests. They never questioned why all those Aiel stayed hidden, and Perrin certainly never brought it up. If believing in a few hundred Aiel reinforcements helped them keep their courage, well and good.

"What did you find?" Perrin asked. Gaul had been gone since the day before; he could move as fast as a man on horseback, faster in woods, and he could see more.

"Trollocs," Gaul replied as though reporting the presence of sheep, "moving up through this well-named Waterwood to the south. They number no more than thirty, and I believe they mean to make camp on the edge of the forest and strike tonight. There are men still holding to the soil to the south." He gave a sudden, wolfish grin. "They did not see me. They will have no warning."

Chiad leaned closer to Bain. "He moves well enough, for a Stone Dog," she whispered loudly enough to be heard twenty feet off. "He makes little more noise than a lame bull."

"Well, Wil?" Perrin said. "Do you want to go to Emond's Field? You can shave, and maybe find a girl to kiss while these Trollocs have supper tonight."

Wil flushed a dark red. "I will be wherever you are tonight, Aybara," he said in a hard voice.

"Nobody means to go home if there are Trollocs still about, Perrin," Kenley added.

Perrin looked around at the others, meeting only agreeing nods. "What of you, Luc? We would be pleased to have a lord and Hunter for the Horn with us. You could show us how it is done."

Luc smiled fractionally, a gash on stone that never came close to those cold blue eyes. "I regret the defenses of Emond's Field still need me. I must see to protecting your people, should the Trollocs come there in greater numbers than thirty. Or the Children of the Light. My Lady Faile?" He held out a hand to assist her in mounting, but she shook her head.

"I will remain with Perrin, Lord Luc."

"A pity," he murmured, shrugging as if to say there was no accounting for women's taste. Tugging on his wolf-embroidered gauntlets, he swung into the black stallion's saddle smoothly. "Good luck to you, Master Goldeneyes. I do hope you all have good luck." With a half-bow to Faile, he whirled his tall horse showily and spurred him to a gallop that forced some of the men to leap out of his way.

Faile frowned at Perrin in a manner that suggested a lecture on rudeness when they were alone. He listened to Luc's horse until he could hear it no more, then turned to Gaul. "Can we get ahead of the Trollocs? Be waiting somewhere before they reach wherever they mean to stop?"

"The distances are right if we start now," Gaul said. "They are moving in a straight line, and not hurrying. There is a Nightrunner with them. It will be easier surprising them in their blankets than facing them awake." He meant that the Two Rivers men might do better; there was no fear smell on him.

There was certainly fear smell on some of the others, yet no one suggested that a confrontation with Trollocs up and alert, and a Myrddraal to boot, might not be the best plan. They broke camp as soon as he gave the order, dousing the fires and scattering the ashes, gathering their few pots and mounting their ill-assorted horses and ponies. With the sentries in—Perrin reminded himself to have that word with them —they numbered nearly seventy. Surely enough to ambush thirty Trollocs. Ban al'Seen and Dannil each still led half—it seemed the way to keep arguments down—with Bili al'Dai and Kenley and others each heading ten or so. Wil, too; he was not too bad a fellow usually, when he could keep his mind off the girls.

Faile rode Swallow close beside Stepper as they started south with the Aiel running ahead. "You truly do not trust him at all," she said. "You think he is a Darkfriend."

"I trust you and my bow and my axe," he told her. Her face looked sad and pleased at the same time, but it was the simple truth.

For two hours Gaul led them south before turning into the Waterwood, a tangle of towering oak and pine and leatherleaf, bushy bay trees and cone-shaped redoil trees, tall round-topped ash and sweetberry and black willow, with thickets of vine-woven brush below. A thousand squirrels chittered on the branches, and thrushes and finches and redwings darted everywhere. Perrin smelled deer and rabbits, too, and foxes. Tiny streams abounded, and rush-bordered pools and ponds dotted the forest, often shaded but sometimes open, from less than ten paces across to a few almost fifty. The ground seemed sodden after all the rain it had received, squelching under the horses' hooves.

Between a large, willow-ringed pond and a narrow rivulet a pace wide, perhaps two miles into the wood, Gaul halted. Here the Trollocs would come if they continued as they had been. The three Aiel melted into the trees to make sure of that, and bring back warning of their approach.

Leaving Faile and a dozen men to watch the horses, Perrin spread the others out in a narrow curve, a cup into which the Trollocs should march. After making certain each man was well hidden and knew what he was to do, he placed himself at the bottom of the cup, beside an oak with a trunk thicker than he was tall.

Easing his axe in its belt loop, he nocked an arrow and waited. A light breeze blew in his face, swelling and falling. He should be able to smell the Trollocs long before they came in sight. They should be coming right at him. Touching the axe again, he waited. Minutes passed. An hour. More. How long before the Shadowspawn appeared? Much longer in this damp and bowstrings would need to be changed.

The birds vanished a moment before the squirrels went silent. Perrin drew a deep breath, and frowned. Nothing. On that breeze he should surely be able to smell Trollocs as soon as the animals sensed them.

A vagrant gust brought him the putrid stink, like centuries-old sweat and rot. Whirling, he shouted, "They're behind us! Rally to me! Two Rivers to me!" Behind. The horses. "Faile!"

Screams and shouts erupted from every side, howls and savage cries. A ram-horned Trolloc leaped into the open twenty paces away, raising a long curved bow. Perrin drew fletchings to ear and fired in one smooth motion, reaching for another shaft as soon as his arrow cleared bow. His broadhead point took the Trolloc between its eyes; it bellowed once as it fell. And its arrow, the size of a small spear, took Perrin in the side like a hammerblow.

Gasping with shock, he hunched over, dropping bow and fresh arrow alike. Pain spread out in sheets from the black-fletched shaft; it quivered when he drew breath, and every quiver shot out new pain.

Two more Trollocs leaped over their dead companion, wolf snout and goat horns, black-mailed shapes half again as tall as Perrin and twice as broad. Baying, they rushed at him, curved swords upraised.

Forcing himself upright, he gritted his teeth and snapped the thumb-thick arrow off short, pulled his axe free and rushed to meet them. Howling, he realized dimly. Howling with rage that filmed his eyes red. They towered over him, their armor all spikes at elbows and shoulders, but he swung his axe in a frenzy, as if trying to cut down a tree with every blow. For Adora. For Deselle. "My mother!" he screamed. "Burn you! My mother!"

Abruptly he realized he was hacking at bloody shapes on the ground. Growling, he made himself stop, shaking with the effort as much as with the pain in his side. There was less shouting now. Fewer screams. Was anyone left but him? "Rally to me! Two Rivers to me!"

"Two Rivers!" someone shouted frantically, off through the damp woods, and then another, "Two Rivers!"

Two. Only two. "Faile!" he cried. "Oh, Light, Faile!"

A flicker of black flowing through the trees announced a Myrddraal before he could see it clearly, snakelike black armor down its chest, inky cloak hanging undisturbed by its running. As it came closer, it slowed to a sinuous, assured walk; it knew he was hurt, knew him for easy meat. Its pale-faced, eyeless stare stabbed him with fear. "Faile?" it said mockingly. Its voice made the name sound like burned leather crumbling. "Your Faile—was delicious."

Roaring, Perrin hurled himself at it. A black-bladed sword turned his first stroke. And his second. His third. The thing's slug-white face became fixed with concentration, but it moved like a viper, like lightning. For the moment he had it on the defensive. For the moment. Blood trickled down his side; his side burned like a forge-fire. He could not keep this up. And when his strength failed, that sword would find his heart.

His foot slipped in the mud churned up beneath his boots, the Fade's blade drew back—and a blurring sword half-severed the eyeless head, so it fell over on one shoulder in a fountain of black blood. Stabbing blindly, the Myrddraal staggered forward, stumbling, refusing to die completely, still instinctively trying to kill.

Perrin scrambled out of its path, but his attention was all for the man coolly wiping his blade with a fistful of leaves. Ihvon's color-shifting cloak hung down his back. "Alanna sent me to find you. I almost didn't, the way you have been moving, but seventy horses do leave tracks." The dark, slender Warder seemed as composed as if he were lighting his pipe before a fireplace. "The Trollocs were not linked to that . . ." He indicated the Myrddraal with his sword; it had fallen, but still stabbed randomly. ". . . more's the pity, but if you can gather your people together, they might not be willing to try you without one of the Faceless to goad them. I would estimate about a hundred, to begin. A few less, now. You have bloodied them some." He began a calm survey of the shadows beneath the trees, only the blade in his hand indicating anything out of the ordinary.

For a bare moment Perrin gaped. Alanna wanted him? She had sent Ihvon? Just in time to save his life. Shaking himself, he raised his voice again. "Two Rivers to me! For the love of the Light, rally to me! Here! Rally! Here!"

This time he kept it up until familiar faces appeared, stumbling through the trees. Blood-streaked faces, often as not. Shocked, staring faces. Some men half-supported others, and some had lost their bows. The Aiel were among them, apparently unhurt except that Gaul limped slightly.

"They did not come as we expected" was all the Aielman said. The night was colder than we expected. There was more rain than we expected. That was how he said it.

Faile seemed to materialize with the horses. With half the horses, including Stepper and Swallow, and nine of the twelve men he had left with her. A scrape marred one cheek, but she was alive. He tried to hug her, but she pushed his arms away, muttering angrily over the broken-off arrow even while she gently pulled his coat away from the thick shaft in an effort to examine where it had gone in.

Perrin studied the men around him. They had stopped coming now, yet there were faces missing. Kenley Ahan. Bili al'Dai. Teven Marwin. He made himself name the missing, made himself count them. Twenty-seven. Twenty-seven not there. "Did you bring all the wounded?" he asked dully. "Is anybody left out there?" Faile's hand trembled on his side; her expression as she frowned at his wound was a blend of worry and fury. She had a right to be angry. He should never have gotten her into this.

"Only the dead," Ban al'Seen said in a voice as leaden as his face.

Wil looked to be frowning at something just out of sight. "I saw Kenley," he said. "His head was in the crook of an oak, but the rest of him was down at the foot. I saw him. His cold won't bother him now." He sneezed, and looked startled.

Perrin sighed heavily, and wished he had not; pain shooting up his side clenched his teeth. Faile, a green-and-gold silk scarf wadded in her hand, was trying to pull his shirt out of his breeches. He pushed her hands away despite her scowl; there was no time for tending wounds now. "Wounded on the horses," he said when he could speak. "Ihvon, will they attack us?" The forest seemed too still. "Ihvon?" The Warder appeared, leading a dark gray gelding with a fierce eye. Perrin repeated his question.

"Perhaps. Perhaps not. On their own, Trollocs kill whomever is easiest. Without a Halfman, they would probably rather find a farm than someone who might put arrows in them. Make sure everyone who can stand upright carries a bow with an arrow nocked even if they cannot draw it. They may decide the price is too high for the fun."

Perrin shivered. If the Trollocs did attack, they would have as much fun as a dance at Sunday. Ihvon and the Aiel were the only ones really ready to fight back. And Faile; her dark eyes shone with fury. He had to get her to safety.

The Warder did not offer his own horse for the wounded, which made sense. The animal was not likely to let anyone else on its back, and a war-trained horse with its master in the saddle would be a formidable weapon if the Trollocs came again. Perrin tried to put Faile up on Swallow, but she stopped him. "The wounded, you said," she told him softly. "Remember?"

To his disgust, she insisted he ride Stepper. He expected the others to protest, after he had brought them to disaster, but no one did. There were just enough horses for those who could not walk, and those unable to walk far—grudingly he admitted that he was one of the latter—so he ended up in his saddle. Half the other riders had to cling to theirs. He sat upright, gritting his teeth to do it.

Those who walked or stumbled, and some who rode, clutched their bows as if they meant salvation. Perrin carried one, too, and so did Faile, though he doubted she could even draw a Two Rivers longbow. It was appearance that counted now; illusion that might see them safe. Like Ihvon, alert as a coiled whip, the three Aiel looked unchanged as they glided ahead, spears stuck through the harness of the bow cases on their backs, horn bows in hand and ready. The rest, including himself, were a ragbag remnant, nothing like the band he had led here, so confident and full of his own pride. Yet illusion worked as well as reality. For the first mile through the tangle vagrant breezes brought him Trolloc stink, the scent of Trollocs shadowing, stalking. Then the stench slowly faded and vanished as the Trollocs fell behind, deluded by a mirage.

Faile walked beside Stepper, one hand on Perrin's leg as though she meant to hold him up. Now and then she looked up at him, smiling encouragingly, but with worry creasing her forehead. He smiled back as best he could, trying to make her think he was all right. Twenty-seven. He could not stop the names from running through his head. Colly Garren and Jared Aydaer, Dael al'Taron and Ren Chandin. Twenty-seven Two Rivers folk he had killed with his stupidity. Twenty-seven.

They took the most direct route back out of the Waterwood, breaking clear sometime in the afternoon. It was hard to tell exactly how late with the sky still blanketed in gray and everything blandly shadowed. High-grass pasture dotted with trees stretched in front of them, and some scattered sheep, and a few farmhouses in the distance. No smoke rose from any of the chimneys; if there was anyone in those houses, something hot would have been cooking in the fireplace. The nearest rising smoke plume looked five miles off at least.

"We should find a farm for the night," Ihvon said. "Some place under cover in case it rains again. A fire. Food." He looked at the Two Rivers men and added, "Water and bandages."

Perrin only nodded. The Warder was better than he at knowing the right thing to do. Old Bili Congar with his head full of ale was probably better. He just let Stepper follow Ihvon's gray.

Before they had gone much beyond a mile, a faint thread of music caught Perrin's ear, fiddles and flutes playing merry tunes. At first he thought he was dreaming, but then the others heard, too, exchanging incredulous looks, then relieved grins. Music meant people, and happy people by the sound, someone celebrating. That anyone might have something to celebrate was enough to pick their feet up somewhat.

CHAPTER
41

Among the Tuatha'an

A gathering of wagons came in sight, a little off to the south, like small houses on wheels, tall wooden boxes painted and lacquered in violent shades of red and blue and green and yellow, all standing in a large, rough circle around a few broad-limbed oak trees. The music came from there. Perrin had heard there were Tinkers, Traveling People, in the Two Rivers, but he had not seen them until now. Hobbled horses cropped the long grass nearby.

"I will sleep elsewhere," Gaul said stiffly when he saw Perrin meant to go to the wagons, and loped away without another word.

Bain and Chiad spoke softly yet urgently to Faile. Perrin caught enough to know they were trying to convince her to spend the night with them in some snug thicket and not with "the Lost Ones." They sounded appalled at the idea of speaking to the Tinkers, much less eating or sleeping with them. Faile's hand tightened on his leg as she refused, quietly, firmly. The two Maidens frowned at each other, blue eyes meeting gray with a deep measure of concern, but before the Traveling People's wagons came much closer, they trotted away after Gaul. They seemed to have recovered some of their spirits, though. Perrin heard Chiad suggesting they induce Gaul to play some game called Maidens' Kiss. They were both laughing as they passed out of his earshot.

Men and women were working in the camp, sewing, mending harness, cooking, washing clothes and children, levering a wagon up to replace a wheel. Other children ran playing, or danced to the tunes of half a dozen men playing fiddle or flute. From oldest to youngest, the Tinkers wore clothes even more colorful than their wagons, in eye-wrenching combinations that had to have been chosen blindly. No sane man would have worn anything near those hues, and not many women.

As the ragtag party approached the wagons, silence fell, people stopping where they were to watch with worried expressions, women clutching infants and children running to hide behind adults, peering around a leg or hiding their faces in skirts. A wiry man, gray-haired and short, stepped forward and bowed gravely, both hands pressed to his chest. He wore a bright blue, high-collared coat and baggy trousers of a green that almost seemed to glow tucked into kneeboots. "You are welcome to our fires. Do you know the song?"

For a moment, trying not to hunch around the arrow in him, Perrin could only stare. He knew this man, the Mahdi, or Seeker, of this band. *What chance?* he wondered. *Of all the Tinkers in the world, what chance it should be folk I know?* Coincidences made him uneasy; when the Pattern produced coincidence, the Wheel seemed to be forcing events. *I'm beginning to sound like a bloody Aes Sedai.* He could not manage the bow, but he remembered the ritual. "Your welcome warms my spirit, Raen, as your fires warm the flesh, but I do not know the song." Faile and Ihvon gave him startled looks, but no more than did the Two Rivers men. Judging by the mutters he heard from Ban and Tell and others, he had just given them something else to talk about.

"Then we seek still," the wiry man intoned. "As it was, so shall it be, if we but remember, seek, and find." Grimacing, he surveyed the bloody faces confronting him, his eyes flinching away from the weapons. The Traveling People would not touch anything they considered a weapon. "You are welcome to our fires. There will be hot water, and bandages and poultices. You know my name," he added, looking at Perrin searchingly. "Of course. Your eyes."

Raen's wife had come to his side as he spoke, a plump woman, gray-haired but smooth-cheeked, a head taller than her husband. Her red blouse and bright yellow skirt and green-fringed shawl jarred the eye, but she had a motherly manner. "Perrin Aybara!" she said. "I thought I knew your face. Is Elyas with you?"

Perrin shook his head. "I have not seen him in a long time, Ila."

"He leads a life of violence," Raen said sadly. "As you do. A violent life is stained even if long."

"Do not try to bring him to the Way of the Leaf standing here, Raen," Ila said briskly, but not unkindly. "He is hurt. They all are."

"What am I thinking of?" Raen muttered. Raising his voice, he called, "Come, people. Come and help. They are hurt. Come and help."

Men and women gathered quickly, murmuring their sympathy as they helped injured men down from their horses, guiding men toward their wagons, carrying them when necessary. Wil and a few of the others looked concerned over being separated, but Perrin was not. Violence was the farthest thing from the Tuatha'an. They would not raise a hand against anyone, even to defend their own lives.

Perrin found he had to accept Ihvon's assistance to dismount. Climbing down sent jolts of pain radiating out from his side. "Raen," he said, a touch breathless, "you shouldn't be out here. We fought Trollocs not five miles from this spot. Take your people to Emond's Field. They will be safe there."

Raen hesitated—and seemed surprised at it—before shaking his head. "Even if I wished to, the people would not want it, Perrin. We try not to camp very close to even the smallest village, and not only because the villagers may falsely accuse us of stealing whatever they have lost or of trying to convince their children to find the Way. Where men have built ten houses together, there is the potential for violence. Since the Breaking the Tuatha'an have known this. Safety lies in our wagons, and in always moving, always seeking the song." A plaintive expression came over his face. "Everywhere we hear news of violence, Perrin. Not just here in your Two Rivers. There is a feel in the world of change, of destruction. Surely we must find the song soon. Else I do not believe it will ever be."

"You will find the song," Perrin said quietly. Maybe they abhorred violence too much for a *ta'veren* to overcome; maybe even a *ta'veren* could not fight the Way of the Leaf. It had seemed attractive to him once, too. "I truly hope that you will."

"What will be, will be," Raen said. "All things die in their time. Perhaps even the song." Ila put a comforting arm around her husband, though her eyes were as troubled as his.

"Come," she said, trying to hide her ill ease, "we must get you inside. Men will talk if their coats are afire." To Faile, she said, "You are quite beautiful, child. Perhaps you should beware of Perrin. I never see him but in the company of beautiful girls." Faile gave Perrin a flat, considering look, then tried to gloss it over quickly.

He made it as far as Raen's wagon—yellow trimmed in red, with red and yellow spokes in tall, red-rimmed wheels, and red and yellow trunks lashed to the outside, standing beside a cook fire in the middle of the camp—but when he put his foot on the first of the wooden steps at the back, his knees gave way. Ihvon and Raen more than half-carried him inside, followed hurriedly by Faile and Ila, and laid him on the bed built into the front of the wagon, with just room to get by to the sliding door leading to the driver's seat.

It truly was like a little house, even to pale pink curtains at the two small windows on either side. He lay there staring at the ceiling. Here, too, the Tinkers used of their colors; the ceiling was lacquered sky blue, the high cabinets green and yellow. Faile unfastened his belt and took away his axe and quiver while Ila rummaged in one of the cabinets. Perrin could not seem to rouse any interest in what they were doing.

"Anyone can be surprised," Ihvon said. "Learn from it, but do not take it too much to heart. Not even Artur Hawkwing won every battle."

"Artur Hawkwing." Perrin tried to laugh, but it turned into a groan. "Yes," he managed. "I am certainly not Artur Hawkwing, am I?"

Ila frowned at the Warder—or at his sword, rather; she seemed to find that even worse than Perrin's axe—and came to the bed with a wad of folded bandages. Once she had pulled Perrin's shirt away from the arrow stub, she winced. "I do not think I am competent to remove this. It is bedded deep."

"Barbed," Ihvon said in a conversational tone. "Trollocs do not use bows very often, but when they do the arrows are barbed."

"Out," the plump woman said firmly, rounding on him. "And you as well, Raen. Tending the sick is no business of men. Why don't you go see if Moshea has that wheel on his wagon yet."

"A good idea," Raen said. "We may want to move tomorrow. There has been hard traveling this last year," he confided to Perrin. "All the way to Cairhien, then back again to Ghealdan, then up into Andor. Tomorrow, I think."

When the red door shut behind him and Ihvon, Ila turned to Faile worriedly. "If it is barbed, I do not think I can remove it at all. I will try if I must, but if there is anyone nearby who knows more of such things."

"There is someone in Emond's Field," Faile assured her. "But is it safe to leave it in him until tomorrow?"

"Safer than me cutting, perhaps. I can mix something for him to drink for the pain, and blend a poultice against infection."

Glaring at the two women, Perrin said, "Hello? Do you remember me? I am right here. Stop trying to talk over my head."

They looked at him for a moment.

"Keep him still," Ila told Faile. "It is all right to let him talk, but do not allow him to move about. He may injure himself more."

"I will see to it," Faile replied.

Perrin gritted his teeth and did his best to help in getting his coat and shirt off, but they had to do most of the work. He felt as weak as the worst wrought iron, ready to bend to any pressure. Four inches of thumb-thick arrow stuck out almost atop his last rib, rising from a puckered gash thick with dried blood. They pushed his head down on a pillow, for some reason not wanting him to look at it. Faile washed the wound while Ila prepared her salve with a stone mortar and pestle— plain smooth gray stone, the first things he had seen in the Tinker camp that were not brightly colored. They mounded the salve around the arrow and wrapped him with bandages to hold it.

"Raen and I will sleep beneath the wagon tonight," the Tuatha'an woman said at last, wiping her hands. Frowning at the arrow stub sticking up from his bandages, she shook her head. "Once I thought he might eventually find the Way of the Leaf. He was a gentle boy, I think."

"The Way of the Leaf is not for everyone," Faile said gently, but Ila shook her head again.

"It is for everyone," she replied just as gently, and a touch sadly, "if they only knew it."

She left then, and Faile sat on the edge of the bed blotting his face with a folded cloth. He seemed to be sweating a great deal for some reason.

"I blundered," he said after a time. "No, that is too soft. I don't know the right word."

"You did not blunder," she said firmly. "You did what seemed fitting at the time. It *was* fitting; I cannot imagine how they got behind us. Gaul is not one to make a mistake about where his enemies are. Ihvon was right, Perrin. Anyone can find circumstances that have changed when he did not know. You held everyone together. You brought us out."

He shook his head hard and made his side hurt worse. "Ihvon brought us out. What I did was get twenty-seven men killed," he said bitterly, trying to sit up to face her. "Some of them were my friends, Faile. And I got them killed."

Faile threw her weight on his shoulders to push him back down. It was a measure of his weakness, how easily she held him. "There will be time enough for that in the morning," she said firmly, peering down into his face, "when we have to put you back on your horse. Ihvon did *not* bring us out; I do not think he cared particularly if anyone but you and he did get out. Those men would have scattered in every direction if not for you, and then we'd all have been hunted down. They would not have held together for Ihvon, a stranger. As for your friends—" Sighing, she sat back down again. "Perrin, my father says a general can take care of the living or weep for the dead, but he cannot do both."

"I am not a general, Faile. I am a fool of a blacksmith who thought he could use other people to help him get justice, or maybe revenge. I still want it, but I don't want to use anyone else for it any longer."

"Do you think the Trollocs will go away because you decide your motives are not pure enough?" The heat in her voice made him raise his head, but she pushed it back to the pillow almost roughly. "Are they any less vile? Do you need a purer reason to fight them than what they are? Another thing my father says. The worst sin a general can commit, worse than blundering, worse than losing, worse than anything, is to desert the men who depend on him."

A tap came at the door, and a slender, handsome young Tinker in a red-and-green striped coat put his head in. He flashed a smile at Faile, all white teeth and oozing charm, before looking at Perrin. "Grandfather said it was you. I thought this was where Egwene said she came from." He frowned suddenly, disapprovingly. "Your eyes. I see you have followed Elyas after all, to run with the wolves. I was sure you would never find the Way of the Leaf."

Perrin knew him; Aram, Raen and Ila's grandson. He did not like him; he smiled like Wil. "Go away, Aram. I am tired."

"Is Egwene with you?"

"Egwene's Aes Sedai now, Aram," he growled, "and she would rip your heart out with the One Power if you asked her to dance. Go away!"

Aram blinked, and hastily shut the door. With himself outside.

Perrin let his head fall back. "He smiles too much," he muttered. "I cannot abide a man who smiles too much." Faile made a choking noise, and he looked at her suspiciously. She was biting her underlip.

"I have something in my throat," she said in a strangled voice, getting up hastily. She hurried to the wide shelf below the foot of the bed where Ila had prepared her poultice and stood with her back to him, pouring water from a green-and-red pitcher into a blue-and-yellow mug. "Would you like something to drink, too? Ila left this powder, for the pain. It will help you sleep."

"I don't want any powder," he said. "Faile, who is your father?"

Her back went very stiff. After a moment she turned with the mug in both hands and an unreadable look in her tilted eyes. Another minute passed before she said, "My father is Davram of House Bashere, Lord of Bashere, Tyr and Sidona, Guardian of the Blightborder, Defender of the Heartland, Marshal-General to Queen Tenobia of Saldaea. And her uncle."

"Light! What was all that about him being a wood merchant, or a fur dealer? I seem to remember him dealing in ice peppers once, too."

"It was not a lie," she said sharply, then in a weaker voice, "Just not . . . the whole truth. My father's estates do produce lumber and fine woods, and ice peppers, and furs, and more besides. And his stewards sell them for him, so he does trade in them. In a way."

"Why couldn't you just tell me? Hiding things. Lying. You're a lady!" He frowned at her accusingly. He had not expected this. A small merchant for a father, a former soldier, maybe, but not this. "Light, what are you doing running around as a Hunter of the Horn? Don't tell me the Lord of Bashere and all that just sent you off to find adventure."

Still holding the cup, she came back to sit beside him. For some reason she seemed very intent on his face. "My two older brothers died, Perrin, one fighting Trollocs, the other in a fall from his horse hunting. That made me the eldest, and it meant I had to study account books and trading. While my younger brothers learned to be soldiers, while they were being readied for adventures, I had to learn how to manage the estates! It is the eldest's duty. Duty! It is dull, dry and boring. Buried in paper and clerks.

"When Father took Maedin with him to the Blightborder—he's two years younger than I—that was more than I could stand. Girls are not taught the sword, or war, in Saldaea, but father had named an old soldier from his first command as my footman, and Eran was always more than happy to teach me to use knives and fight with my hands. I think it amused him. In any case, when Father took Maedin with him, the news had arrived calling the Great Hunt of the Horn, so I . . . left. I wrote mother a letter explaining, and I . . . left. And I reached Illian in time to take the oath of a Hunter. . . ." Picking up the cloth, she patted at the sweat on his face again. "You really should sleep if you can."

"I suppose you are the Lady Bashere or some such?" he said. "How did you ever come to like a common blacksmith?"

"The word is 'love,' Perrin Aybara." The firmness of her voice was at sharp odds with the gentle way that the cloth moved on his face. "And you are not such a common blacksmith, I think." The cloth paused.

"Perrin, what did that fellow mean about running with wolves? Raen mentioned this Elyas, too."

For a moment he was frozen, unbreathing. Yet he had just berated her for keeping secrets from him. It was what he got for being hasty and angry. Swing a hammer in haste, and you usually hit your own thumb. He exhaled slowly, and told her. How he had met Elyas Machera and learned he could talk to wolves. How his eyes had changed color, grown sharper, and his hearing and his sense of smell, like a wolf's. About the wolf dream. About what would happen to him, if he ever lost his hold on humanity. "It's so easy. Sometimes, especially in the dream, I forget I'm a man, not a wolf. If one of these times I don't remember quickly enough, if I lose hold, I'll *be* a wolf. In my head, at least. A sort of half-wrong image of a wolf. There won't be anything of *me* left." He stopped, waiting for her to flinch, to move away.

"If your ears are really that sharp," she said calmly, "I will have to watch what I say close to you."

He caught her hand to stop her patting. "Did you hear anything I said? What will your father and mother think, Faile? A half-wolf black-smith. You're a lady! Light!"

"I heard every word. Father will approve. He has always said our family blood is growing too soft; not like it was in the old days. I know he thinks I am terribly soft." She gave him a smile fierce enough for any wolf. "Of course, mother always wanted me to marry a king who splits Trollocs in two with one stroke of his sword. I suppose your axe will suffice, but could you tell her you are the king of the wolves? I don't think anyone will come forward to dispute your claim to that throne. In truth, the splitting of Trollocs will probably do for mother, but I truly think she would like the other."

"Light!" he said hoarsely. She sounded almost serious. No, she did sound serious. If she was even *half* serious, he was not sure the Trollocs might not be better than meeting her parents.

"Here," she said, holding the mug of water to his lips. "You sound as though your throat is dry."

Swallowing, he spluttered at the bitter taste. She had stirred in Ila's powder! He tried to stop, but she filled his mouth, and it was a matter of swallow or choke. By the time he could push the mug away, she had emptied half of it into him. Why did medicine always taste so vile? He suspected women did it on purpose. He would have bet that whatever they took for themselves did not taste that way. "I told you I did not want any of that. Gaaah!"

"Did you? I must not have heard. But whether you did or not, you need sleep." She stroked his curly hair. "Sleep, my Perrin."

He tried to tell her he had indeed told her so, and she had heard it, but the words seemed to tangle around his tongue. His eyes wanted to slide shut. In fact, he could not keep them open. The last thing he heard was her soft murmurs.

"Sleep, my wolf king. Sleep."

CHAPTER
42

A Missing Leaf

P errin stood near the Tuatha'an wagons under bright sunlight, alone, and there was no arrow in his side, no pain. Among the wagons firewood was stacked ready to be lit beneath iron cookpots hanging from tripods, and clothes hung from washlines; there were no people or horses. He wore neither coat nor shirt, but a blacksmith's long leather vest that left his arms bare. It could have been any dream, perhaps, except that he was aware it was a dream. And he knew the feel of the wolf dream, the reality and solidity of it, from the long grass around his boots to the breeze out of the west that ruffled his curly hair, to the scattered ash and hemlock. The Tinkers' gaudy wagons did not seem real, though; they had an air of insubstantiality, a feel that they might shimmer and be gone any moment. They never remained long in one place, Tinkers. No soil held them.

Wondering how much the land held him, he rested a hand on his axe —and looked down in surprise. The heavy blacksmith's hammer hung in the loop on his belt, not the axe. He frowned; once he would have chosen that way, had even thought he had, but surely no more. The axe. He had chosen the axe. Hammerhead suddenly became half-moon blade and thick spike, flickered back to stout cylinder of cold steel, fluttered between. Finally it stopped, as his axe, and he exhaled slowly. That had never happened before. Here, he could change things as he wanted with ease, things about himself at least. "And I want the axe," he said firmly. "The axe."

Looking around, he could just see a farmhouse to the south, and deer browsing the barley field, surrounded by a rough stone wall. There was no feel of wolves, and he did not call Hopper. The wolf might or might not come, or even hear, but Slayer could well be out there somewhere. A bristling quiver abruptly tugged at his belt opposite the axe, and he had a stout longbow in his hand with a broadhead arrow nocked. A long leather bracer covered his left forearm. Nothing moved except those deer.

"Not likely I'll wake soon," he muttered to himself. Whatever that stuff was that Faile had fed him, it had taken him right off; he remembered it as clearly as if he had watched over her shoulder. "Fed it to me like I was a babe," he growled. *Women!*

He took one of those long strides—the land blurred around him—and stepped into the farmyard. Two or three chickens scattered, running as if they had already gone feral. The rock-walled sheepfold stood empty, and both thatch-roofed barns were barred shut. Despite curtains still at the windows, the two-story farmhouse had the look of emptiness. If this was a true reflection of the waking world—and the wolf dream usually was, in an odd way—the people here had been gone for days. Faile was right; his warning had spread beyond the places he had gone.

"Faile," he murmured wonderingly. Daughter of a lord. No, not just a lord. Three times a lord, a general, and uncle to a queen. "Light, that makes her a queen's cousin!" And she loved a simple blacksmith. Women were wondrous strange.

Seeking to see how far the word had spread, he zigzagged more than halfway to Deven Ride, a mile or more at a stride, doubling back and crisscrossing his own path. Most farms he saw had that same emptiness; less than one in five showed signs of habitation, doors open and windows up, wash hung out on a line, dolls or hoops or carved wooden horses lying around a doorstep. The toys especially made his stomach clench. Even if they had not believed his warning, surely there were enough burned farms about to tell them the same, tumbled heaps of charred timbers, soot-black chimneys like stark, dead fingers.

Bending to replace a doll with a smiling glass face and a flower-embroidered dress—some woman had loved her daughter to do all that tiny needlework—he blinked. The same doll still sat on the fieldstone steps where he had picked it up. As he reached out, the one in his hand faded and vanished.

Flashes of black in the sky cut short his amazement. Ravens, twenty or thirty together, winging toward the Westwood. Toward the Mountains of Mist, where he had first seen Slayer. He watched coldly while the ravens dwindled to black specks and disappeared. Then he set off after them.

Long, racing strides carried him five miles each, the land a blur except in the moment between one step and the next, into the thick-treed, rocky Westwood, across the scrub-covered Sand Hills, into the cloud-capped mountains, where fir and pine and leatherleaf forested valleys and slopes, to the very valley where he had first seen the man Hopper called Slayer, to the mountainside where he had returned from Tear.

The Waygate stood there, closed, the *Avendesora* leaf seemingly just one among a myriad of intricately carved leaves and vines. Scattered trees, wizened and wind-sculpted, dotted the sparse soil among the glazed stone where Manetheren had been burned away. Sunlight sparkled on the waters of the Manetherendrelle below. A faint wind up the valley brought him the scent of deer, rabbits, foxes. Nothing moved that he could see.

On the point of leaving, he stopped. The *Avendesora* leaf. *One leaf.* Loial had locked the Waygate by placing both leaves on this side. He turned, and his hackles rose. The Waygate stood open, twin masses of living greenery stirring in the breeze, exposing that dull silvery surface; his reflection shimmered in it. *How?* he wondered. *Loial locked the bloody thing.*

Unaware of crossing the distance, suddenly he was right at the Waygate. There was no trefoil leaf among the verdant tangle on the inside of the two gates. Strange to think that at that moment, in the waking world, someone—or something—was passing through where he stood. Touching the dull surface, he grunted. It might as well have been a mirror; his hand slid across it as across the smoothest glass.

From the corner of his eye he caught the *Avendesora* leaf suddenly in its place on the inside, and leaped back just as the Waygate began swinging shut. Someone—or something—had come out, or gone in. *Out. It has to be out.* He wanted to doubt that it was more Trollocs, and Fades, coming into the Two Rivers. The gates merged, became stone carvings again.

A sense of being watched was all the warning he had. He jumped—a half-seen image of black streaking through where his chest had been; an arrow—jumped in one of those world-blurring stretches, landed on a far slope and jumped again, out of the valley of Manetheren into a stand of towering fir, and again. Running, he thought furiously, picturing the valley in his mind, and that brief glimpse of the arrow. It had come from *that* direction, at *that* angle when it reached him, so it had to have come from. . . .

A final bound took him back onto a slope above Manetheren's grave, crouching among meager, wind-slanted pines with bow ready to draw. Below him, among the stunted trees and boulders, the arrow had been fired. Slayer had to be down there somewhere. He had to be down. . . .

Without thinking, Perrin leaped away, the mountains a smear of gray and brown and green.

"Almost," he growled. Almost, he had duplicated his mistake in the Waterwood, thinking again an enemy would move to suit him, wait where he wanted.

This time he ran as hard as he could, only three flashing strides to the edge of the Sand Hills, hoping he had not been seen. This time he circled wide, coming back higher on that same mountainside, up where the air felt thin and cold and the few trees were thick-trunked bushes fifty paces or more apart, up above where a man might set himself to watch for another who meant to sneak up on the place that arrow had fired.

And there his quarry was, a hundred paces below, dark-haired and dark-coated, a tall man crouched beside a table-sized granite outcrop, his own half-drawn bow in hand, studying the slope farther down with eager patience. This was the first time Perrin had gotten a good look at him; a hundred paces was little distance for his eyes. This Slayer's high-collared coat had a Borderland cut, and his face looked enough like Lan's to be the Warder's brother's. Only Lan had no brothers—no living kin at all, that Perrin knew—and if he had had any, they would not have been here. A Borderlander, though. Maybe Shienaran, though his hair was long, not shaved to a topknot, and was held back by a braided leather cord just like Lan's. He could not be Malkieri; Lan was the last living Malkieri.

Wherever he came from, Perrin felt no compunction at all in drawing his bow, broadhead point aimed at Slayer's back. The man had tried to kill him from ambush. A downhill shot could be tricky.

Perhaps he had taken too long, or perhaps the fellow felt his cold gaze, but suddenly Slayer became a blur, streaking away east.

With a curse, Perrin pursued, three strides to the Sand Hills, another into the Westwood. Among the oaks and leatherleaf and underbrush, Slayer seemed to vanish.

Halting, Perrin listened. Silence. The squirrels and birds had gone still. He inhaled deeply. A small herd of deer had passed that way not long since. And a faint tinge of something, human but too cold for a man, too emotionless, a scent that tickled his mind with familiarity. Slayer was somewhere close. The air lay as still as the forest; no stir of breeze to tell him which way that scent came.

"A neat trick, Goldeneyes, locking the Waygate."

Perrin tensed, ears straining. No telling from where in this dense growth that voice had come. Not so much as a leaf rustled.

"If you knew how many of the Shadowwrought died trying to get out of the Ways there, it would lift your heart. *Machin Shin* feasted at that gate, Goldeneyes. But not a good enough trick. You saw: the gate is open now."

There, off to the right. Perrin slipped through the trees as silently as he had when he had hunted here.

"It was only a few hundred to begin, Goldeneyes. Just enough to keep those fool Whitecloaks off balance and see that the renegade died." Slayer's voice became angry. "The Shadow consume me if that man does not have more luck than the White Tower." Abruptly he chuckled. "But you, Goldeneyes. Your presence was a surprise. There are those who want your head on a pike. Your precious Two Rivers will be harrowed from end to end, now, to root you out. What do you say to that, Goldeneyes?"

Perrin froze close beside the gnarled trunk of a great oak. Why was the man talking so much? Why was he talking at all? *He's drawing me right to him.*

Putting his back against the oak's thick bole, he studied the forest. No movement. Slayer *wanted* him to come nearer. No doubt into an ambush. And he wanted to find the man and rip his throat out. Yet it could easily be himself who died, and if that happened, no one would know the Waygate was open, and Trollocs coming by hundreds, maybe even thousands. He would not play Slayer's game.

With a mirthless smile he stepped out of the wolf dream, telling himself to wake, and . . .

. . . Faile twined her arms around his neck and nipped his beard with small white teeth, while Tinkers' fiddles sang some wild, heated tune around the campfires. *Ila's powder. I can't wake up!* Awareness that it was a dream faded. Laughing, he scooped Faile up in his arms and carried her into the shadows, where the grass was soft.

*   *   *

Waking was a slow process wrapped around the dull pain filling his side. Daylight streamed in at the small windows. Bright light. Morning. He tried to sit up, and fell back with a groan.

Faile sprang up from a low stool; her dark eyes looked as if she had not slept. "Lie still," she said. "You did enough thrashing in your sleep. I have not kept you from rolling over and driving that thing the rest of the way through you just to watch you do it now you're awake." Ihvon stood leaning against the doorframe like a dark blade.

"Help me up," Perrin said. Talking hurt, but so did breathing, and he had to talk. "I have to get to the mountains. To the Waygate."

She put a hand to his forehead, frowning. "No fever," she murmured. Then, more strongly, "You are going to Emond's Field, where one of the Aes Sedai can Heal you. You are *not* going to kill yourself trying to ride into the mountains with an arrow in you. Do you hear me? If I hear one more word about mountains or Waygates, I will have Ila mix something that will put you back to sleep, and you will travel on a litter. I'm not certain you should not anyway."

"The Trollocs, Faile! The Waygate is open again! I have to stop them!"

The woman did not even hesitate before shaking her head. "You can do nothing about it, the state you are in. It is Emond's Field for you."

"But—!"

"But me no buts, Perrin Aybara. Not another word on it."

He ground his teeth. The worst was that she was right. If he could not rise from a bed alone, how could he stay in the saddle as far as Manetheren? "Emond's Field," he said graciously, but she still sniffed and muttered something about "pigheaded." What did she want? *I was bloody gracious, burn her for stubborn!*

"So there will be more Trollocs," Ihvon said musingly. He did not ask how Perrin knew. Then he shook his head as if dismissing Trollocs. "I will tell the others you are awake." He slipped out, closing the door behind him.

"Am I the only one who sees the danger?" Perrin muttered.

"I see an arrow in you," Faile said firmly.

The reminder gave him a twinge; he just stifled a groan. And she gave a satisfied nod. Satisfied!

He wanted to be up and on the way immediately; the sooner he was Healed, the sooner he could see to closing the Waygate again, permanently this time. Faile insisted on feeding him breakfast, a broth thick with mashed vegetables suitable for a toothless infant, one spoon at a time, with pauses to wipe his chin. She would not let him feed himself, and whenever he protested or asked her to go faster, she shoved the words back into his mouth with a spoonful of pap. She would not even let him wash his own face. By the time she got around to brushing his hair and combing his beard, he had settled on dignified silence.

"You are pretty when you sulk," she said. And pinched his nose!

Ila, in green blouse and blue skirt this morning, climbed into the wagon with his coat and shirt, both cleaned and mended. To his irritation, he had to let the two women help him don them. He had to let them help him *sit up* to don them, the coat unbuttoned and the shirt not tucked in, but bunched around the arrow stub.

"Thank you, Ila," he said, fingering the neat darns. "This is fine needlework."

"It is," she agreed. "Faile has a deft touch with a needle."

Faile colored, and he grinned, thinking of how fiercely she had told him she would never mend his clothes. A glint in her eye held his tongue. Sometimes silence was the wiser course. "Thank you, Faile," he said gravely instead. She blushed even redder.

Once they had him on his feet he reached the door easily enough, but he had to let the two women half-support him to climb down the wooden steps. At least the horses were saddled, and all the Two Rivers lads gathered, bows slung on their backs. With clean faces and clothes, and only a few bandages out where they showed.

A night with the Tuatha'an had obviously been good for their spirits, too, even those who still looked as though they could not walk a hundred paces. The haggardness that had been in their eyes yesterday was only a shadow now. Wil had each arm around a pretty, big-eyed Tinker girl, of course, and Ban Lewin, with his nose and a bandage around his head making his dark hair stand up in a brush, held hands with another, smiling shyly. Most of the others held bowls of thick vegetable stew and spoons, shoveling away.

"This is good, Perrin," Dannil said, giving up his empty bowl to a Tinker woman. She gestured as if to ask the beanpole fellow whether he wanted more, and he shook his head, but said, "I don't think I could ever get enough of it, do you?"

"I had my fill," Perrin told him sourly. Mashed vegetables and broth.

"The Tinker girls danced last night," Dannil's cousin Tell said, wide-eyed. "All the unmarried women, and some of the married! You should have seen it, Perrin."

"I've seen Tinker women dance before, Tell."

Apparently he had not kept his voice clear of what he had felt watching them, for Faile said dryly, "You've seen the tiganza, have you?

Someday, if you are good, I may dance the sa'sara for you, and show you what a dance really is." Ila gasped in recognition of the name, and Faile went even redder than she had inside.

Perrin pursed his lips. If this sa'sara set the heart pounding any harder than the Tinker women's swaying, hip-rolling dance—the tiganza, was it?—he definitely would like to see Faile dance it. He carefully did not look at her.

Raen came, in the same bright green coat but trousers redder than any red Perrin had ever seen before. The combination made his head ache. "Twice you have visited our fires, Perrin, and for the second time you go without a farewell feast. You must come again soon so we can make up for it."

Pushing away from Faile and Ila—he could stand by himself, at least —he put a hand on the wiry man's shoulder. "Come with us, Raen. No one in Emond's Field will harm you. At worst it's safer than out here with the Trollocs."

Raen hesitated, then shook himself, muttering, "I do not know how you can even make me consider such things." Turning, he spoke loudly. "People, Perrin has asked us to come with him to his village, where we will be safe from Trollocs. Who wishes to go?" Shocked faces stared back at him. Some women gathered their children close, and the children hid in their skirts, as if the very idea frightened them. "You see, Perrin?" Raen said. "For us, safety lies in moving, not in villages. I assure you, we do not spend two nights in one place, and we will travel all day before stopping again."

"That may not be enough, Raen."

The Mahdi shrugged. "Your concern warms me, but we will be safe, if the Light wills it."

"The Way of the Leaf is not only to do no violence," Ila said gently, "but to accept what comes. The leaf falls in its proper time, uncomplaining. The Light will keep us safe for our time."

Perrin wanted to argue with them, but behind all the warmth and compassion on their faces lay a stony firmness. He thought he would get Bain and Chiad to don dresses and give up their spears—or Gaul to!—before he made these people budge an inch.

Raen shook Perrin's hand, and with that the Tinker women began hugging the Two Rivers lads, and Ihvon, too, and the Tinker men began shaking hands, all laughing and saying goodbyes and wishing everyone a safe journey, hoping they would come again. Almost all the men did. Aram stood off to one side, frowning to himself, hands thrust into his coat pockets. The last time Perrin met him he had seemed to have a sour streak, odd for a Tinker.

The men did not content themselves with shaking Faile's hand, but hugged her. Perrin kept his face smooth when some of the younger men became overly enthusiastic, only grinding his teeth a little; he managed to smile. No woman much younger than Ila hugged him. Somehow, even while Faile was letting some skinny, gaudy-coated Tinker fold his arms around her and try to squeeze her flat, she stood guard on him like a mastiff. Women without gray in their hair took one look at her face and chose someone else. Meanwhile Wil appeared to be kissing every woman in the camp. So was Ban, and his nose. Even Ihvon was enjoying himself, for that matter. It would serve Faile right if one of those fellows cracked a rib for her.

Finally the Tinkers moved back, except for Raen and Ila, opening a space around the Two Rivers folk. The wiry, gray-haired man bowed formally, hands to chest. "You came in peace. Depart now in peace. Always will our fires welcome you. The Way of the Leaf is peace."

"Peace be on you always," Perrin replied, "and on all the People." *Light, let it be so.* "I will find the song, or another will find the song, but the song will be sung, this year or in a year to come." He wondered if there ever had been a song, or if the Tuatha'an had begun their endless journey seeking something else. Elyas had told him they did not know what song, only that they would know it when they found it. *Let them find safety, at least. At least that.* "As it once was, so shall it be again, world without end."

"World without end," the Tuatha'an responded in a solemn murmur. "World and time without end."

A few final hugs and handshakes were handed 'round while Ihvon and Faile were helping Perrin up on Stepper. A few last kisses collected by Wil. And Ban. Ban! *And* his nose! Others, the badly wounded, were half-lifted onto their horses, with Tinkers waving as if to old neighbors off on a long journey.

Raen came to shake Perrin's hand. "Will you not reconsider?" Perrin asked. "I remember hearing you say once there was wickedness loose in the world. It's worse now, Raen, and here."

"Peace be on you, Perrin," Raen replied, smiling.

"And on you," he said sadly.

The Aiel did not appear until they were a mile north of the Tinker camp, Bain and Chiad looking to Faile before trotting ahead to their usual place. Perrin was not sure what they thought might have happened to her among Tuatha'an.

Gaul moved in beside Stepper, striding easily. The party was not moving very fast, with nearly half the men walking. He glanced at Ihvon measuringly, as usual, before turning to Perrin. "Your injury is well?"

His injury hurt like fury; every step his horse took jolted that arrowhead. "I feel fine," he said, not gritting his teeth. "Maybe we'll have a dance in Emond's Field tonight. And you? Did you pass a good night playing Maidens' Kiss?" Gaul stumbled and nearly fell on his face. "What is the matter?"

"Who did you hear suggest this game?" the Aielman said quietly, staring straight ahead.

"Chiad. Why?"

"Chiad," Gaul muttered. "The woman is Goshien. Goshien! I should take her back to Hot Springs as *gai'shain.*" The words sounded angry, but not his odd tone. "Chiad."

"Will you tell me what is the matter?"

"A Myrddraal has less cunning than a woman," Gaul said in a flat voice, "and a Trolloc fights with more honor." After a moment he added, in a fierce undertone, "And a goat has more sense." Quickening his pace, he ran forward to join the two Maidens. He did not speak to them, as far as Perrin could make out, only slowed to walk alongside.

"Did you understand any of that?" Perrin asked Ihvon. The Warder shook his head.

Faile sniffed. "If he thinks to make trouble for them, they will hang him by his heels from a branch to cool off."

"Did you understand it?" Perrin asked her. She walked along, neither looking at him nor answering, which he took to mean she did not. "I think I might have to find Raen's camp again. It has been a long time since I saw the tiganza. It was . . . interesting."

She muttered something under her breath, but he caught it: "You could do with hanging by the heels yourself!"

He smiled down at the top of her head. "But I won't have to. You promised to dance this sa'sara for me." Her face went crimson. "Is it anything close to the tiganza? I mean, there is no point, otherwise."

"You muscle-brained oaf!" she snapped, glaring up at him. "Men have thrown their hearts and fortunes at the feet of women who danced the sa'sara. If mother suspected I knew it—" Her teeth clicked shut as though she had said too much, and her head whipped back to face forward; scarlet mortification covered her from her dark hair down to the neck of her dress.

"Then there isn't any reason for you to dance it," he said quietly. "My heart and fortune, such as they are, already lie at your feet."

Faile missed a step, then laughed softly and pressed her cheek against his booted calf. "You are too clever for me," she murmured. "One day I will dance it for you, and boil the blood in your veins."

"You already do that," he said, and she laughed again. Pushing her arm behind his stirrup, she hugged his leg to her as she walked.

After a while even the thought of Faile dancing—he extrapolated from the Tinker dance; it must be something to top that—could not compete with the pain in his side. Every stride Stepper took was agony. He held himself upright. It seemed to hurt a fraction less that way. Besides, he did not want to spoil the lift the Tuatha'an had given everyone's spirits. The other men were sitting up straight in their saddles, too, even those who had been hunched over and clinging the day before. And Ban and Dannil and the others walked with heads up. He would not be the first to slump.

Wil began to whistle "Coming Home from Tarwin's Gap," and three or four more took it up. After a time, Ban began to sing in a clear, deep voice.

> "My home is waiting there for me,
> and the girl I left behind.
> Of all the treasure that waits for me,
> that's what I want to find.
> Her eyes so merry, and her smile so sweet,
> her hugs so warm, and her ankle neat,
> her kisses hot, now there's a treat.
> If there's a treasure greater, it lies not in my mind."

More joined in on the second verse, until everyone sang, even Ihvon. And Faile. Not Perrin, of course; he had been told often enough that he sounded like a stepped-on frog, singing. Some even fell into step with the music.

> "Oh, I have seen stark Tarwin's Gap,
> and the Trollocs' raving horde.
> I have stood 'fore the Halfman's charge,
> and walked on death's cold borde.
> But a winsome lass, she waits for me,
> for a dance, and a kiss 'neath the apple tree. . . ."

Perrin shook his head. A day before they had been ready to run and hide. Today they sang, about a battle so long ago that it had left no memory but this song in the Two Rivers. Perhaps they were becoming soldiers. They would have to, unless he managed to close that Waygate.

Farms began to appear more often, closer together, until they traveled along hard-packed dirt between fields bordered by hedges or low, rough stone walls. Abandoned farms. No one here clung to the land.

They came to the Old Road, which ran north from the White River, the Manetherendrelle, through Deven Ride to Emond's Field, and at last began to see sheep in the pastures, great clumps like a dozen men's flocks gathered together, with ten shepherds where there once would have been one, and half of them grown men. Bow-armed shepherds watched them pass, singing at the tops of their lungs, not knowing quite what to make of it.

Perrin did not know what to make of his first view of Emond's Field, and neither did the other Two Rivers men, from the way their singing faltered and died.

The trees, fences and hedges closest to the village were simply gone, cleared away. The westernmost houses of Emond's Field had once stood among the trees on the edge of the Westwood. The oaks and leatherleaf between the houses remained, but now the forest's brim stood five hundred paces away, a long bowshot, and axes rang loud as men pushed it back farther. Row on row of waist-high stakes, driven into the ground at an angle, surrounded the village a little out from the houses and presented a continuous hedge of sharpened points, except where the road ran in. At intervals behind the stakes men stood like sentries, some wearing bits of old armor or leather shirts sewn with rusty steel discs, a few in dented old steel caps, with boar spears, or halberds rooted out of attics, or bush hooks fitted to long poles. Other men, and boys, were up on some of the thatched roofs with bows; they stood when they saw Perrin and the others coming, and shouted to people below.

Beside the road behind the stakes stood a contraption of wood and thick, twisted rope, with a nearby pile of stones bigger than a man's head. Ihvon noticed Perrin frowning at it as they came closer. "Catapult," the Warder said. "Six, so far. Your carpenters knew what to do once Tomas and I showed them. The stakes will hold off charging Trollocs or Whitecloaks, either one." He might have been discussing the prospects for more rain.

"I told you your village was preparing to defend itself." Faile sounded fiercely proud, as though it were her village. "A hard people, for such a soft land. They could almost be Saldaean. Moiraine always said Manetheren's blood runs strong here still."

Perrin could only shake his head.

The hard-packed dirt streets were nearly crowded enough for a city, the gaps between houses filled with carts and wagons, and through open doors and unshuttered windows he could see more people. The crowd parted before Ihvon and the Aiel, and rustling whispers accompanied them along the street.

"It's Perrin Goldeneyes."

"Perrin Goldeneyes."

"Perrin Goldeneyes."

He wished they would not do that. These people knew him, some of them. What did they think they were doing? There was horse-faced Neysa Ayellin, who had paddled his ten-year-old backside that time Mat talked him into stealing one of her gooseberry pies. And there was pink-cheeked, big-eyed Cilia Cole, the first girl he had ever kissed and still pleasingly plump, and Pel Aydaer, with his pipe and his bald head, who had taught Perrin how to catch trout with his hands, and Daise Congar herself, a tall, wide woman who made Alsbet Luhhan seem soft, with her husband Wit, a scrawny man overshadowed as always by his wife. And they were all staring at him, and whispering to the people from off, who might not know who he was. When old Cenn Buie lifted a little boy up on his shoulder, pointing at Perrin and talking enthusiastically to the boy, Perrin groaned. They had all gone mad.

Townsfolk trailed after Perrin and the others, around them, in a parade that rode a swell of murmurs. Chickens scurried every which way under people's feet. Bawling calves and pigs squealing in pens behind the houses competed with the noise of the humans. Sheep crowded the Green, and black-and-white milkcows cropped the grass in company with flocks of geese, gray and white.

And in the middle of the Green rose a tall pole, the red-bordered white banner at its peak rippling lazily, displaying a red wolf's head. He looked at Faile, but she shook her head, as surprised as he.

"A symbol."

Perrin had not heard Verin approach, though now he caught hushed whispers of "Aes Sedai" floating around her. Ihvon did not look surprised. People stared at her with awe-filled eyes.

"People need symbols," Verin went on, resting a hand on Stepper's shoulder. "When Alanna told a few of the villagers how much Trollocs fear wolves, everyone seemed to think this banner a grand idea. Don't you, Perrin?" Was there a dryness in her voice then? Her dark eyes looked up at him, birdlike. A bird watching a worm?

"I wonder what Queen Morgase will think of that," Faile said. "This is part of Andor. Queens seldom like strange banners being raised in their realms."

"That's nothing but lines on a map," Perrin told her. It was good to be still; the throbbing from the arrowhead seemed to have abated somewhat. "I did not even know we were supposed to be part of Andor until I went to Caemlyn. I doubt many people here do."

"Rulers have a tendency to believe maps, Perrin." There was no doubt of the dryness in Faile's tone. "When I was a child, there were parts of Saldaea that had not seen a taxman in five generations. Once father could turn his attention from the Blight for a time, Tenobia made sure they knew who their queen was."

"This is the Two Rivers," he said, grinning, "not Saldaea." They did sound very fierce, up there in Saldaea. As he turned back to Verin, the grin became a frown. "I thought you were . . . hiding . . . who you are." He could not say which was more disturbing; Aes Sedai there in secret, or Aes Sedai in the open.

The Aes Sedai's hand hovered an inch from the broken-off arrow jutting from his side. Something tingled around the wound. "Oh, this is not good," she murmured. "Caught in the rib, and some infection in spite of that poultice. This needs Alanna, I think." She blinked and pulled her hand back; the tingle went, too. "What? Hiding? Oh. With what has been stirred up here now, we could hardly remain hidden. I suppose we could have . . . gone away. You wouldn't want that, would you?" There was that sharp, considering, birdlike stare again.

He hesitated, and finally sighed. "I suppose not."

"Oh, that is good to hear," she said with a smile.

"Why did you really come here, Verin?"

She did not seem to hear him. Or did not want to. "Now we need to see to that thing in you. And these other lads need to be looked after, too. Alanna and I will see to the worst, but. . . ."

The men with him were as stunned by what they had found here as he was. Ban scratched his head at the banner, and a few just stared around in amazement. Most looked at Verin, though, wide-eyed and uneasy; they had surely heard the whispers of "Aes Sedai." Perrin was not escaping those looks entirely himself, he realized, talking to an Aes Sedai as though she were just any village woman.

Verin considered them right back, then suddenly, without seeming to look, reached behind her to snatch a girl of about ten or twelve out of the onlookers. The girl, her long dark hair caught up with blue ribbons, went rigid with shock. "You know Daise Congar, girl?" Verin said. "Well, you find her and tell her there are injured men who need a Wisdom's herbs. And tell her to jump. You tell her I'll have no patience with her airs. Do you have that? Off with you."

Perrin did not recognize the girl, but evidently she did know Daise, because she flinched at the message. But Verin was an Aes Sedai. After a moment of weighing—Daise Congar against an Aes Sedai—the girl scampered away into the crowd.

"And Alanna will take care of you," Verin said, peering up at him again.

He wished she did not sound as though there might be two meanings to that.

CHAPTER
43

Care for the Living

Taking Stepper's bridle, Verin led him to the Winespring Inn herself, the crowd melting back to let her through, then falling in after. Dannil and Ban and the others trailed along on horse and afoot, kin mingling with them now. Astounded as they were by the changes in Emond's Field, the lads still showed their pride by striding even if they limped, or sitting up straighter in the saddle; they had faced Trollocs and come home. But women ran their hands over sons and nephews and grandsons, often biting back tears, and their low moans made a soft, pained murmur. Tight-eyed men tried to hide their worries behind proud smiles, clapping shoulders and exclaiming over newly begun beards, yet frequently their hugs just happened to turn into a shoulder to lean on. Sweethearts rushed in with kisses and loud cries, equal parts happiness and commiseration, and little brothers and sisters, uncertain, alternated between fits of weeping and clinging in wide-eyed wonder to a brother everyone seemed to be taking for a hero.

It was the other voices Perrin wished he could not hear.

"Where is Kenley?" Mistress Ahan was a handsome woman, with streaks of white in her nearly black braid, but she wore a fear-filled frown as she scanned faces and saw eyes flinch from hers. "Where's my Kenley?"

"Bili!" old Hu al'Dai called uncertainly. "Has anyone seen Bili al'Dai?"

". . . Hu . . . !"

". . . Jared . . . !"

". . . Tim . . . !"

". . . Colly . . . !"

In front of the inn, Perrin fell out of the saddle in his need to escape those names, not even seeing whose hands caught him. "Get me inside!" he grated. "Inside!"

". . . Teven . . . !"

". . . Haral . . . !"

". . . Had . . . !"

The door cut off the heart-lost wails, and the cries of Dael al'Taron's mother for someone to tell her where her son was.

In a Trolloc cookpot, Perrin thought as he was lowered into a chair in the common room. *In a Trolloc's belly, where I put him, Mistress al'Taron. Where I put him.* Faile had his head in her hands, peering into his face worriedly. *Care for the living,* he thought. *I'll weep for the dead later. Later.*

"I am all right," he told her. "I just got a little light-headed dismounting. I've never been a good rider." She did not seem to believe him.

"Can't you do something?" she demanded of Verin.

The Aes Sedai calmly shook her head. "I think better not, child. A pity neither of us is Yellow, but Alanna is still a much better Healer than I. My Talents lie in other directions. Ihvon will bring her. Wait with patience, child."

The common room had been turned into an armory of sorts. Except in front of the fireplace, the walls were a solid mass of propped spears of every description, with the occasional halberd or bill mixed in, and some polearms with oddly shaped blades, many pitted and discolored where old rust had been scoured away. Even more surprisingly, a barrel near the foot of the stairs held swords all jumbled together, most without scabbards and no two alike. Every attic within five miles must have been turned out for relics dust-covered for generations. Perrin would not have suspected there were five swords in the whole Two Rivers. Before the Whitecloaks and Trollocs came, anyway.

Gaul took a place off to one side, near the stairs that led up to the inn's rooms and the al'Veres' living quarters, watching Perrin but plainly aware of Verin and every move she made. On the other side of the room, watching Faile and all else, the two Maidens cradled their spears in the crook of an elbow and took a hipshot stance that seemed at once casual and yet balanced on the toes. The three young fellows who had carried Perrin in shifted their feet by the door, staring at him and the Aes Sedai and the Aiel with equally wide eyes. That was all.

"The others," Perrin said. "They need—"

"They will be taken care of," Verin interrupted smoothly, seating herself at another table. "They will want to be with their families. Much better to have loved ones close."

Perrin felt a stab of pain—the graves below the apple trees flashed in his mind—but he pushed it down. *Take care of the living,* he reminded himself harshly. The Aes Sedai brought out her pen and ink and began making notes in that small book in a precise hand. He wondered whether she cared how many Two Rivers folk died, so long as he lived, to be used in the White Tower's plans for Rand.

Faile squeezed his hand, but it was to the Aes Sedai that she spoke. "Should we not take him up to a bed?"

"Not yet," Perrin told her irritably. Verin looked up and opened her mouth, and he repeated in a firmer voice, "Not yet." The Aes Sedai shrugged and went back to her note-taking. "Does anyone know where Loial is?"

"The Ogier?" one of the three by the door said. Dav Ayellin was stockier than Mat, but he had that same twinkle in his dark eyes. He had the same rumpled, uncombed look about him as Mat, too. In the old days, what little mischief Mat did not get up to, Dav did, though Mat usually led the way. "He's out with the men clearing back the Westwood. You'd think we were cutting down his brother every time we cut a tree, but he clears three to anybody else's one with that monstrous axe he had Master Luhhan make. If you want him, I saw Jaim Thane running to tell them you had come in. I'll bet they all come to get a look at you." Peering at the broken-off arrow, he winced and rubbed his own side in sympathy. "Does it hurt much?"

"It hurts enough," Perrin said curtly. *Coming to get a look at him. What am I, a gleeman?* "What about Luc? I don't want to see him, but is he here?"

"I'm afraid not." The second man, Elam Dowtry, rubbed his long nose. Incongruous with his farmer's wool coat and his cowlick, he wore a sword at his belt; the hilt had been freshly wrapped in rawhide and the leather scabbard flaked and peeling. "Lord Luc is off hunting the Horn of Valere, I think. Or maybe Trollocs."

Dav and Elam were Perrin's friends, or had been, companions in hunting and fishing, both his age near enough, but their thrilled grins

THE SHADOW RISING

made them seem younger. Either Mat or Rand could have passed for five years older at least. Maybe he could, too.

"I hope he comes back soon," Elam went on. "He has been showing me how to use a sword. Did you know he's a Hunter for the Horn? And a king, if he had his rights. Of Andor, I hear."

"Andor has queens," Perrin muttered absently, meeting Faile's gaze, "not kings."

"So he is not here," she said. Gaul shifted slightly; he looked ready to go hunting for Luc, his eyes blue ice. It would not have surprised Perrin to see Bain and Chiad veil themselves on the spot.

"No," Verin said vaguely, manifestly more intent on her notes than what she was saying. "Not that he hasn't been a help sometimes, but he does have a way of causing trouble when he is here. Yesterday, before anyone knew what he was doing, he led a delegation out to meet a Whitecloak patrol and told them Emond's Field was closed to them. He apparently told them not to come within ten miles. I cannot approve of Whitecloaks, but I do not suppose they took that very well. Not wise to antagonize them more than is strictly necessary." Frowning at what she had written, she rubbed her nose, seemingly unaware of leaving a smudge of ink.

Perrin did not much care how the Whitecloaks took anything. "Yesterday," he breathed. If Luc had come back to the village yesterday, it was not likely he could have had anything to do with Trollocs being where they were not expected. The more Perrin thought about how that ambush turned around, the more he thought the Trollocs must have been expecting them. And the more he wanted to blame Luc. "Wanting won't make a stone cheese," he muttered. "But he still smells like cheese to me."

Dav and the other two looked at each other doubtfully. Perrin supposed he must not seem to be making much sense.

"It was a bunch of Coplins, mainly," the third fellow said in a startlingly deep voice. "Darl and Hari and Dag and Ewal. And Wit Congar. Daise gave him a fit over it."

"I heard they all liked the Whitecloaks." Perrin thought the bass-voiced fellow seemed familiar. He was younger than Elam and Dav by two or three years yet an inch taller, lean-faced but with wide shoulders.

"They did." The fellow laughed. "You know them. They drift naturally toward anything that makes trouble for somebody else. Since Lord Luc has been talking, they're all for marching up to Watch Hill and telling the Whitecloaks to get out of the Two Rivers. Anyway, they're for somebody else marching up there. I think they mean to be well back in the pack."

If that face had been pudgy, and half a foot or more nearer the ground. . . . "Ewin Finngar!" Perrin exclaimed. It could not be; Ewin was a stout, squeaky little nuisance who tried to crowd in whenever the older fellows got together. This lad would be as big as he was, or bigger, by the time he stopped growing. "Is that you?"

Ewin nodded with a broad grin. "We've been hearing all about you, Perrin," he said in that surprising bass, "fighting Trollocs, and having all kinds of adventures out in the world, so they say. I can still call you Perrin, can't I?"

"Light, yes!" Perrin barked. He was more than tired of this Golden-eyes business.

"I wish I'd gone with you last year." Dav rubbed his hands together eagerly. "Coming home with Aes Sedai, and Warders, and an Ogier." He made them sound like trophies. "All I ever do is herd cows and milk cows, herd cows and milk cows. That and hoe, and chop wood. You've had all the luck."

"What was it like?" Elam put in breathlessly. "Alanna Sedai said you've been all the way to the Great Blight, and I hear you've seen Caemlyn, and Tear. What's a city like? Are they really ten times as big as Emond's Field? Did you see a palace? Are there Darkfriends in the cities? Is the Blight really full of Trollocs and Fades and Warders?"

"Did a Trolloc give you that scar?" Voice like a bull or not, Ewin managed a sort of squeaky excitement. "I wish I had a scar. Did you see a queen? Or a king? I think I'd rather see a queen, but a king would be grand. What is the White Tower like? Is it as big as a palace?"

Faile smiled, amused, but Perrin blinked at the onslaught. Had they forgotten the Trollocs on Winternight, forgotten the Trollocs in the countryside right then? Elam clutched his sword hilt as if he wanted to be off for the Blight on the instant, and Dav was up on his toes, eyes gleaming, and Ewin looked ready to grab Perrin's collar. Adventure? They were idiots. Yet there were hard times coming, harder than the Two Rivers had seen so far, he was afraid. It could not hurt if they had a little while longer before they learned the truth.

His side hurt, but he tried to answer. They seemed disappointed he had never seen the White Tower, or a king or a queen. He thought Berelain might suffice for a queen, but with Faile there he was not about to mention her. Some other things he shied away from; Falme, and the Eye of the World, the Forsaken, *Callandor*. Dangerous subjects, those, leading inevitably to the Dragon Reborn. He could tell them a little of Caemlyn, though, and Tear, of the Borderlands and the Blight. It was odd what they accepted and what not. The corrupted landscape of the Blight, seeming to rot while you looked at it, they ate up, and top-knotted Shienaran soldiers, and Ogier *stedding* where Aes Sedai could not wield the Power and Fades were reluctant to enter. But the size of the Stone of Tear, or the immensity of cities. . . .

About his own supposed adventures, he said, "Mainly I've just tried to keep from having my head split open. That's what adventures are, that and finding a place to sleep for the night, and something to eat. You go hungry a lot having adventures, and sleep cold or wet or both."

They did not like that very much, or appear to believe it any more than they believed that the Stone was as big as a small mountain. He reminded himself that he had known as little of the world before he left the Two Rivers. It did not help much. He had never been this wide-eyed. Had he? The common room seemed to be hot. He would have taken his coat off, but moving seemed too much effort.

"What about Rand and Mat?" Ewin demanded. "If it's all being hungry and getting rained on, why didn't they come home, too?"

Tam and Abell had come in, Tam with a sword belted on over his coat and both men with bows—oddly, the sword looked right on Tam, farm coat or no—so he told it much as he had before, Mat gambling and carousing in taverns and chasing girls, and Rand in his fine coat with a pretty, yellow-haired girl on his arm. He made Elayne a lady, expecting they would never believe the Daughter-Heir of Andor, and was proved right when they expressed incredulity. Still, it all seemed satisfactory, the kind of thing they wanted to hear, and disbelief faded a bit when Elam pointed out that Faile was a lady and seemed to be dancing attendance on Perrin pretty sharp. That made Perrin grin; he wondered what they would say if he told them she was cousin to a queen.

Faile no longer appeared to be amused for some reason. She turned on them with a stare to match Elayne's haughtiest, stiff-backed and frosty-faced. "You have badgered him enough. He is wounded. Off with you, now."

For a wonder, they bowed clumsily—Dav made an awkward leg, looking a complete fool—and murmured hasty apologies—to her, not him!—and turned to go. Their departure was delayed by the arrival of Loial, stooping through the doorway with his shaggy hair brushing the transom. They stared at the Ogier almost as if seeing him for the first time—then glanced at Faile and hurried on their way. That cold, lady's stare of hers did work.

When Loial straightened, his head came just short of the ceiling. His capacious coat pockets bore the usual squared bulges of books, but he carried a huge axe. Its haft stood as tall as he did, and its head, shaped like a wood-axe, was at least as big as Perrin's battle-axe. "You are hurt," he boomed as soon as his eyes fell on Perrin. "They told me you had returned, but they did not say you were hurt, or I would have come faster."

The axe gave Perrin a start. Among Ogier, "putting a long handle on your axe" meant being hasty, or angry—Ogier seemed to see the two as much the same thing for some reason. Loial did look angry, tufted ears drawing back, frowning so his dangling eyebrows hung down on his broad cheeks. At having to cut trees, no doubt. Perrin wanted to get him alone and find out if he had seen anything more concerning Alanna's doings. Or Verin's. He rubbed his face and was surprised to find it dry; he felt as if he should be sweating.

"He is also stubborn," Faile said, turning on Perrin with the same commanding look she had used on Dav and Elam and Ewin. "You should be in a bed. Where is Alanna, Verin? If she is to Heal him, where is she?"

"She will come." The Aes Sedai did not look up. She was back into her little book again, frowning thoughtfully, pen poised.

"He should still be in a bed!"

"I will have time for that later," Perrin said firmly. He smiled at her to soften it, but all that did was make her look worried and mutter "stubborn" under her breath. He could not ask Loial about the Aes Sedai in front of Verin, but there was something else at least as important. "Loial, the Waygate is unlocked, and Trollocs coming through. How can that be?"

The Ogier's brows sank even deeper, and his ears wilted. "My fault, Perrin," he rumbled mournfully. "I put both *Avendesora* leaves on the outside. That locked the Waygate on the inside, but from the outside, anyone could still open it. The Ways have been dark for long generations, yet we grew them. I could not bring myself to destroy the Gate. I am sorry, Perrin. It is all my fault."

"I did not believe a Waygate *could* be destroyed," Faile said.

"I did not mean destroy, exactly." Loial leaned on his long-handled axe. "A Waygate was destroyed once, less than five hundred years after the Breaking, according to Damelle, daughter of Ala daughter of Soferra, because the Gate was near a *stedding* that had fallen to the Blight. There are two or three Gates lost in the Blight as it is. But she wrote that it was very difficult, and required thirteen Aes Sedai working together with a *sa'angreal.* Another attempt she wrote of, by only nine, during the Trolloc Wars, damaged the Gate in such a way that the Aes Sedai were pulled into—" He cut off, ears wriggling with embarrassment, and knuckled his wide nose. Everyone was staring at him, even Verin and the Aiel. "I do let myself be carried away, sometimes. The Waygate. Yes. I cannot destroy it, but if I remove both *Avendesora* leaves completely, they will die." He grimaced at the thought. "The only means of opening the Gate again will be for the Elders to bring the Talisman of Growing. Though I suppose an Aes Sedai could cut a hole in it." This time he shuddered. Damaging a Waygate must have seemed like tearing up a book to him. A moment later, he was grim-faced once more. "I will go now."

"No!" Perrin said sharply. The arrowhead seemed to throb, but it did not really hurt anymore. He was talking too much; his throat was dry. "There are Trollocs up there, Loial. They can fit an Ogier into a cook-pot as well as a human."

"But, Perrin, I—"

"No, Loial. How are you going to write your book if you go off and get yourself killed?"

Loial's ears twitched. "It is my responsibility, Perrin."

"The responsibility is mine," Perrin said gently. "You told me what you were doing with the Waygate, and I didn't suggest anything different. Besides, the way you jump every time your mother is mentioned, I don't want her coming after me. I will go, as soon as Alanna Heals this arrow out of me." He wiped his forehead, then frowned at his hand. Still no sweat. "Can I have a drink of water?"

Faile was there in an instant, her cool fingers where his hand had been. "He is burning up! Verin, we cannot wait for Alanna. You must—!"

"I am here," the dark Aes Sedai announced, appearing from the door at the back of the common room, Marin al'Vere and Alsbet Luhhan at her heels, and Ihvon right behind them. Perrin felt the tingle of the Power before Alanna's hand replaced Faile's, and she added in a cool, serene voice, "Carry him into the kitchen. The table there is large enough to lay him out. Quickly. There is not much time."

Perrin's head spun, and abruptly he realized Loial had leaned his axe beside the door and picked him up, cradling him in his arms. "The Waygate is mine, Loial." *Light, I'm thirsty.* "My responsibility."

The arrowhead truly did not seem to hurt as much as it had, but he ached all over. Loial was carrying him somewhere, bending through doorways. There was Mistress Luhhan, biting her lip, eyes squinched as if about to cry. He wondered why. She never cried. Mistress al'Vere looked worried, too.

"Mistress Luhhan," he murmured, "mother says I can come be apprenticed to Master Luhhan." No. That was a long time ago. That was. . . . What was? He could not seem to remember.

He was lying on something hard, listening to Alanna speak. ". . . barbs are caught on bone as well as flesh, and the arrowhead has twisted. I must realign it with the first wound and pull it out. If the shock does not kill him, I can then Heal the damage I have done as well as the rest. There is no other way. He is near the brink now." Nothing to do with him.

Faile smiled down at him tremulously, her face upside down. Had he really once thought her mouth was too wide? It was just right. He wanted to touch her cheek, but Mistress al'Vere and Mistress Luhhan were holding his wrists for some reason, leaning with all their weight. Someone was lying across his legs, too, and Loial's big hands swallowed his shoulders, pressing them flat to the table. Table. Yes. The kitchen table.

"Bite down, my heart," Faile said from far away. "It will hurt."

He wanted to ask her what would hurt, but she was pressing a leather-wrapped stick into his mouth. He smelled the leather and the spicewood and her. Would she come hunting with him, running across the endless grassy plains after endless herds of deer? Icy cold shivered through him; vaguely he recognized the feel of the One Power. And then there was pain. He heard the stick snap between his teeth before blackness covered everything.

CHAPTER
44

The Breaking Storm

P errin opened his eyes slowly, staring up at the plain white plastered ceiling. It took a moment to realize he was in a four-
posted bed, lying on a feather mattress with a blanket over him
and a goose-down pillow under his head. A myriad of scents danced in
his nose; the feathers and the wool of the blanket, a goose roasting,
bread and honeycakes baking. One of the Winespring Inn's rooms.
With unmistakable bright morning light streaming in at the white-
curtained windows. Morning. He fumbled at his side. Unbroken skin
met his fingers, but he felt weaker than at any time since being shot. A
small enough price, though, and a fair enough exchange. His throat felt
parched, too.

When he moved, Faile leaped up from a chair beside the small stone
fireplace, tossing aside a red blanket and stretching. She had changed
to a darker narrow-skirted riding dress, and wrinkles in the gray silk
said she had slept in that chair. "Alanna said you needed sleep," she
said. He reached toward the white pitcher on the small table beside the
bed, and she hurriedly poured a cup of water and held it for him to
drink. "You need to stay right here for another two or three days, until
you have your strength back."

The words sounded normal, except for an undercurrent he barely
caught, a tightness at the corners of her eyes. "What is wrong?"

She replaced the cup carefully on the bedside table and smoothed her dress. "Nothing is wrong." The taut underlying tone was even clearer.

"Faile, don't lie to me."

"I do not lie!" she snapped. "I will have some breakfast brought up to you, and you're lucky I do that, calling me—"

"Faile." He said her name as sternly as he could, and she hesitated, her most arrogant, chin-up glare changing to forehead-creasing worry and back again. He met her gaze straight on; she was not going to get away with any fine lady's haughty tricks with him.

At last, she sighed. "I suppose you have a right to know. But you are still staying in that bed until Alanna and I say you can get up. Loial and Gaul are gone."

"Gone?" He blinked in confusion. "What do you mean gone? They *left?*"

"In a way. The sentries saw them go, this morning at first light, trotting off into the Westwood together. None of them thought anything of it; certainly none tried to stop them, an Ogier and an Aiel. I heard of it less than an hour ago. They were talking about trees, Perrin. About how the Ogier sing to trees."

"Trees?" Perrin growled. "It's that bloody Waygate! Burn me, I told him not to. . . . They'll get themselves killed before they reach it!"

Throwing off the blanket, he swung his legs over the side of the bed, wobbling to his feet. He had nothing on, he realized, not even his smallclothes. But if they expected to keep him caged under a blanket, they were sadly mistaken. He could see everything folded neatly on the tall-backed chair by the door, with his boots beside it and his axe hanging by its belt from a peg on the wall. Stumbling to his clothes, he began dressing as quickly as he could.

"What are you doing?" Faile demanded. "You put yourself back in that bed!" One fist on her hip, she pointed commandingly, as if her finger could transport him there.

"They can't have gotten that far," he told her. "Not afoot. Gaul won't ride, and Loial always did claim he trusted his own feet more than any horse. I can catch them up on Stepper by midday latest." Pulling his shirt over his head, he left it hanging loose over his breeches and sat down—dropped, actually—to draw on his boots.

"You are mad, Perrin Aybara! What chance you can even find them in that forest?"

"I am not so bad at tracking, myself. I can find them." He smiled at her, but she was not having any.

"You can get yourself killed, you hairy fool! Look at you. You can hardly stand. You would fall out of the saddle before you had gone a mile!"

Hiding the effort involved, he stood and stamped his feet to settle them in his boots. Stepper would do all the work; he only needed to hold on. "Nonsense. I'm strong as a horse. Stop trying to bully me." Shrugging into his coat, he snatched up his axe and belt. Faile caught his arm as he opened the door, and was pulled along, vainly trying to haul him back.

"Sometimes you have the brains of a horse," she panted. "Less! Perrin, you must listen to me. You must—"

The room lay only a few steps along the narrow hallway from the stairs leading down to the empty common room, and it was the stairs that betrayed him. When his knee bent to lower him that first step, it kept right on bending; he toppled forward, vainly trying to catch the banister, pulling a yelling Faile with him. Rolling over and over, they thumped down the stairs to come up with a final thud against the barrel at the bottom, Faile lying stretched full-length atop him. The barrel teetered and spun, rattling the swords inside, before settling with a final clank.

It took a moment for Perrin to gather enough breath to speak. "Are you all right?" he said anxiously. She was sprawled limply on his chest. He shook her gently. "Faile, are you—?"

Slowly she raised her head and brushed a few short strands of dark hair from her face, then stared at him intently. "Are *you* all right? Because if you are, I may very well do something violent to you."

Perrin snorted; she was probably hurt less than he. Gingerly, he felt at where the arrow had been, but that was in no worse shape than the rest of him. Of course, the rest of him seemed bruised from head to toe. "Get off of me, Faile. I need to fetch Stepper."

Instead, she seized his collar with both hands and leaned very close, until their noses almost touched. "Listen to me, Perrin," she said urgently. "You—can—not—do—everything. If Loial and Gaul have gone to lock the Waygate, you must let them. Your place is here. Even if you were strong enough—and you are not! Do you hear me? You are not strong enough!—but even if you were, you must not go after them. You cannot do everything!"

"Why, whatever are you two doing?" Marin al'Vere said. Wiping her hands on her long white apron, she came from the back door of the common room. Her eyebrows looked to be trying to climb into her hair. "I expected Trollocs after all that racket, but not this." She sounded half scandalized, and half amused.

What they looked like, Perrin realized, with Faile lying on him that way, their heads close together, was a couple playing kissing games. On the floor of the common room.

Faile's cheeks reddened and she got up very quickly, dusting her dress. "He is as stubborn as a Trolloc, Mistress al'Vere. I told him he was too weak to rise. He must go back to his bed immediately. He has to learn he cannot do everything himself, especially when he cannot even walk down a flight of steps."

"Oh, my dear," Mistress al'Vere said, shaking her head, "that is quite the wrong way." Leaning close to the younger woman, she whispered softly, but Perrin heard every word. "He was an easy little boy to manage most of the time, if you handled him properly, but when you tried to push him, he was as muley as any in the Two Rivers. Men don't really change that much, only grow taller. If you go telling him what he *must* and *musn't* do, he will surely lay his ears back and dig his heels in. Let me show you." Marin turned a beaming smile on him, ignoring his glare. "Perrin, don't you think one of my good goose-feather mattresses is better than that floor? I'll bring you some of my kidney pie just as soon as we have you tucked in. You must be hungry, after no supper last night. Here. Why don't you let me help you up?"

Pushing their hands away, he stood on his own. Well, with the aid of the wall. He thought he might have sprained half the muscles in his body. Muley? He had never been muley in his life. "Mistress Luhhan, would you have Hu or Tad saddle Stepper?"

"When you're better," she said, trying to turn him toward the stairs. "Don't you think you could do with just a little more rest?" Faile took his other arm.

"Trollocs!" The cry from outside came muffled through the walls, echoed by a dozen voices. "Trollocs! Trollocs!"

"That needn't concern you today," Mistress al'Vere said, firm and soothing at the same time. It made him want to grit his teeth. "The Aes Sedai will handle things nicely. In a day or two we'll have you back on your feet. You will see."

"My horse," he said, trying to pull free. They had good holds on his coatsleeves; all he accomplished was swinging them back and forth. "For the love of the Light, will you stop tugging at me and let me get my horse? Let go of me."

Looking at his face, Faile sighed and released his arm. "Mistress al'Vere, will you have his horse saddled and brought around?"

"But my dear, he really needs—"

"If you please, Mistress al'Vere," Faile said firmly. "And my horse, too." The two women looked at each other as if he did not exist. At last Mistress al'Vere nodded.

Perrin frowned at her back as she hurried across the common room and vanished toward the kitchen, and the stable. What had Faile said different from what he had? Turning his attention to her, he said, "Why did you change your mind?"

Tucking his shirt in for him, she muttered under her breath. Doubtless he was not supposed to hear well enough to understand. "I musn't say must, must I? When he is too stubborn to see straight, I must lead him with honey and smiles, must I?" She shot him a glare that surely had no honey in it, then abruptly changed to a smile so sweet he very nearly backed away. "My dear heart," she almost cooed, pulling his coat straight, "whatever is happening out there, I do hope you will stay in your saddle, and as far from Trollocs as you can. You really are not up to facing a Trolloc just yet, are you? Maybe tomorrow. Please remember you are a general, a leader, and every bit as much a symbol to your people as that banner out there. If you are up where people can see you, it will lift everyone's heart. And it is much easier to see what needs doing and give orders if you aren't in the fighting yourself." Picking his belt off the floor, she buckled it around his waist, settling the axe carefully on his hip. She also batted her eyes at him! "Please say you will do that. Please?"

She was right. He would not last two minutes against a Trolloc. More like two seconds against a Fade. And much as he hated to admit it, he would not last two miles in the saddle chasing after Loial and Gaul. *Fool Ogier. You're a writer, not a hero.* "All right," he said. A mischievous impulse seized him. The way she and Mistress Luhhan had been talking over his head, and batting her eyes as if he were a fool. "I can't refuse you anything when you smile so prettily."

"I *am* glad." Still smiling, she brushed at his coat, picking lint he could not see. "Because if you don't, and you manage to survive, I'll do to you what you did to me that first day in the Ways. I don't think you are strong enough yet to stop me." That smile beamed up into his face, all springtime and sweetness. "Do you understand me?"

He chuckled in spite of himself. "Sounds as if I had better let them kill me." She did not seem to think that was funny.

Hu and Tad, the lanky stablemen, led Stepper and Swallow around soon after they stepped outside. Everyone else seemed to be gathered at the far end of the village, beyond the Green, with its sheep and cows and geese, and that crimson-and-white wolfhead banner rippling on the morning breeze. As soon as he and Faile were up on their horses, the stablemen took off running that way, too, without a word.

Whatever was going on, it was clearly not an attack. He could see women and children in the crowd, and the shouts of "Trolloc" had died down to a murmur like an echo of the geese. He rode slowly, not wanting to waver in his saddle; Faile kept Swallow close, watching him. If she could change her mind once for no reason, she could again, and he did not want any arguments about whether he should be there.

The babbling crowd did appear to contain everyone in Emond's Field, villagers and farmers alike, all jammed shoulder to shoulder, but they made way for him and Faile when they saw who he was. His name entered the murmurs, usually tagged with Goldeneyes. He picked up the word "Trollocs," too, but in tones more wondering than frightened. From Stepper's back he had a good view over their heads.

The knotted mass of people stretched all the way beyond the last houses to the hedge of sharpened stakes. The edge of the forest, nearly six hundred paces off across a field of stumps nearly level with the ground, was quiet and empty of men with axes. Those men made a sweaty, bare-chested ring in the crowd surrounding Alanna and Verin and two men. Jon Thane, the miller, was wiping a smear of blood from his ribs, lantern jaw on his chest so he could stare at what his hands were doing. Alanna straightened from the other man, a grizzle-haired fellow Perrin did not know, who leaped to his feet and danced a step as if not quite believing he could. He and the miller both looked at the Aes Sedai with awe.

The tangle around the Aes Sedai was too tight for anyone to shift aside for Stepper and Swallow, but there were smaller clear pockets around Ihvon and Tomas, off to either side on their warhorses. Folk did not want to come too near those fierce-eyed animals, both looking as though they only wanted an opportunity to bite or trample.

Perrin managed to reach Tomas without too much trouble. "What happened?"

"A Trolloc. Only one." Despite the graying Warder's conversational tone, his dark eyes did not rest on Perrin and Faile, but kept an almost equal watch on Verin and on the treeline. "They usually are not very smart, alone. Sly, but not smart. The timbering party drove it away before it did more than draw some blood."

From out of the trees the two Aiel women appeared, running, heads *shoufa*-wrapped and veiled so he could not tell which was which. They slowed to snake between the sharp-pointed stakes, then slipped deftly through the crowd, people moving out of their way as much as possible in that press. By the time they reached Faile, they had unveiled, and she leaned down to listen.

"Perhaps five hundred Trollocs," Bain told her, "probably no more than a mile or two behind us." Her voice was level, but her dark blue eyes sparkled with eagerness. So did Chiad's gray.

"As I expected," Tomas said calmly. "That one likely wandered off from the larger body hoping to find a meal. The rest will be coming soon, I think." The Maidens nodded.

Perrin gestured in consternation at the jam of people. "They shouldn't be out here, then. Why haven't you cleared them away?"

It was Ihvon, bringing his gray into the gathering, who answered. "Your people do not seem to want to listen to outsiders, not when they can watch Aes Sedai. I would suggest you see what you can do."

Perrin was sure they could have imposed some sort of order had they really tried. Verin and Alanna surely could have. *So why did they wait and leave it to me, if they expected Trollocs?* It would have been easy to put it down to *ta'veren*—easy, and foolish. Ihvon and Tomas were not going to let Trollocs kill them—or Verin, or Alanna—while waiting for a *ta'veren* to tell them what to do. The Aes Sedai were maneuvering him, risking everyone, maybe even themselves. But to what possible end? He met Faile's eyes, and she nodded slightly, as if she knew what he was thinking.

He had no time to try figuring it out now. Scanning the crowd, he spotted Bran al'Vere, putting his head together with Tam al'Thor and Abell Cauthon. The Mayor had a long spear on his shoulder and a dented old round steel cap on his head. A leather jerkin sewn all over with steel discs strained around his bulk.

All three men looked up when Perrin pushed Stepper through the crowd to them. "Bain says Trollocs are heading this way, and the Warders think we may be attacked soon." He had to shout because of the incessant drone of voices. Some of the nearer folk heard and fell silent; quiet spread on ripples of "Trolloc" and "attack."

Bran blinked. "Yes. It had to come, didn't it? Yes, well, we know what to do." He should have looked comic, with his jerkin ready to pop its seams and his steel cap wobbling when he nodded, but he only looked determined. Raising his voice, he announced, "Perrin says the Trollocs will be here soon. You all know your places. Hurry, now. Hurry."

The crowd stirred and flowed, women herding children back toward

the houses, men milling every which way. Confusion seemed to grow
more rather than less.

"I'll see to getting the shepherds in," Abell told Perrin, and dove into
the throng.

Cenn Buie pushed past in the moil, using a halberd to herd sour-
faced Hari Coplin and Hari's brother Darl and old Bili Congar, who
staggered as if already full of ale this morning, which he probably was.
Of the three, Bili carried his spear most as if he meant to use it. Cenn
touched his forehead to Perrin in a sort of salute. A number of the men
did. It made him uncomfortable. Dannil and the other lads were one
thing, but these men were half again his age and more.

"You are doing fine," Faile said.

"I wish I knew what Verin and Alanna were up to," he muttered.
"And I don't mean right now." Two of the catapults the Warders had
had built stood at this end of the village, squarish things taller than a
man, all heavy timbers and thick, twisted ropes. From their horses,
Ihvon and Tomas were overseeing the stout wooden beams being
winched down. The two Aes Sedai were more interested in the big
fieldstones, fifteen or twenty pounds each, being loaded in cups on the
end of those arms.

"They mean you to be a leader," Faile replied quietly. "It is what you
were born for, I think."

Perrin snorted. He had been born to be a blacksmith. "I'd be a lot
more comfortable if I knew why they wanted it." The Aes Sedai were
looking at him, Verin with head tilted, birdlike, Alanna with a franker
stare and a small smile. Did they both want the same thing, and for the
same reason? That was one of the troubles with Aes Sedai. There were
always more questions than answers.

Order asserted itself with surprising quickness. Along this west end
of the village a hundred men knelt on one knee right behind the bristle
of stakes, uneasily fingering spears or halberds or some polearm made
from a bush hook or scythe. Here and there one wore a helmet or some
bit of armor. To their rear, twice as many formed two lines holding
good Two Rivers longbows, each with a pair of quivers at his belt.
Young boys came running from the houses with bundles of more arrows that the men drove point-down in the ground in front of their
feet. Tam seemed to be in charge, dressing the ranks and speaking a
few words to each man, but Bran marched along with him, offering his
own encouragement. Perrin could not see that they needed him at all.

To his surprise, Dannil and Ban and all the other lads who had
ridden with him came trotting out of the village to surround him and

Faile, all with their bows. They looked odd, in a way. The Aes Sedai had apparently Healed the more seriously injured, leaving those less hurt for Daise's poultices and ointments, so fellows who had been barely clinging to a saddle yesterday walked along spritely now, while Dannil and Tell and others still limped or wore bandages. If he was surprised to see them, he was disgusted by what they brought. Leof Torfinn, the dressing wrapped around his head making a pale cap above his deep-set eyes, had his bow slung on his back and carried a tall staff with a smaller version of the red-bordered banner with its wolfhead.

"I think one of the Aes Sedai had it made," Leof said when Perrin asked where it came from. "Milli Ayellin brought it to Wil's da, but Wil didn't want to carry it." Wil al'Seen hunched his shoulders a bit.

"I wouldn't want to carry it, either," Perrin said dryly. They all laughed as if he had made a joke, even Wil, after a minute.

The hedge of stakes looked fierce enough, but on the other hand, it seemed a pitiful thing to keep Trollocs out. Maybe it would, but he did not want Faile there if they made it through. When he looked at her, though, she had that look in her eyes again as if she knew what he was thinking. And did not like it. If he tried to send her back, she would argue and balk, refusing to see sense. Weak as he felt right then, she probably had a better chance of leading him back to the inn than he her. The way she was sitting her saddle so ferociously, *she* likely intended to defend *him,* if the Trollocs broke through. He would just have to keep a close eye on her; that was all there was to it.

Suddenly she smiled, and he scratched his beard. Maybe she *could* read his mind.

Time passed, the sun inching up, the day's warmth building. Now and then a woman called from the houses to ask what was happening. Here and there men sat down, but Tam or Bran was on them before they had their legs folded, chivying them back into line. No more than a mile or two, Bain had said. She and Chiad were sitting near the stakes, playing some game that apparently involved flipping a knife into the foot of ground between them. Surely if the Trollocs were coming, they would have come by now. He was beginning to find it hard to sit up straight. Conscious of Faile's watchful eyes, he kept his back stiff.

A horn blared, brazen and shrill.

"Trollocs!" half a dozen voices shouted, and bestial, black-mailed shapes flooded out of the Westwood, howling as they ran across the stumpy ground, waving scythe-curved swords and spiked axes, spears and tridents. Three Myrddraal rode behind them on black horses, darting back and forth as though driving the Trolloc charge before them. Their dead black cloaks hung motionless no matter how their mounts dashed or whirled. The horn sounded continuously in sharp, urging cries.

Twenty arrows leaped out as soon as the first Trolloc appeared, the strongest shot falling nearly a hundred paces short.

"Hold, you lack-witted sheep-brains!" Tam shouted. Bran jumped and gave him a startled look, no less incredulous than those coming from Tam's friends and neighbors; some muttered about not standing still for that kind of talk, Trollocs or no Trollocs. Tam rode right over their protests, though. "You hold till I give the word, the way I showed you!" Then, as if hundreds of shrieking Trollocs were not galloping toward him, Tam turned calmly to Perrin. "At three hundred paces?"

Perrin nodded quickly. The man was asking him? Three hundred paces. How quickly could a Trolloc cover three hundred paces? He eased his axe in its loop. That horn wailed and wailed. The spearmen crouched behind the stakes as if forcing themselves not to edge back. The Aiel had veiled their faces.

Onward the screaming tide came, all horned heads and faces with snouts or beaks, each half again as tall as a man, each shrieking for blood. Five hundred paces. Four hundred. Some were stretching out in front. They ran as fast as horses. Had the Aiel been right? Could there be only five hundred? It looked like thousands.

"Ready!" Tam called, and two hundred bows were raised. The young men with Perrin hurridly formed up in front of him in imitation of their elders, ranking themselves with that fool banner.

Three hundred paces. Perrin could see those misshapen faces, contorted with rage and frenzy, as clearly as if they were right on top of him.

"Loose!" Tam shouted. Bowstrings slapped like one huge whip-crack. With twin crashes of beam against leather-padded beam, the catapults fired.

Broadhead arrows rained down into the Trollocs. Monstrous shapes fell, but some rose and staggered on, harried by the Fades. That horn wove into their guttural bellowing, sounding forward for the kill. The catapults' stones fell among them—and exploded in fire and shards, ripping open holes in the mass. Perrin was not the only one to jump; so that was what the Aes Sedai had been doing with the catapults. He wondered wildly what would happen if they dropped one of those stones loading it into the cup.

Another flight of arrows leaped out, and another, another, and again and again, and more stones from the catapults, if at a slower pace. Fiery explosions tore at the Trollocs. Broadhead points hailed down on them. And they came on, shrieking, howling, falling and dying, but always running forward. They were close now, close enough that the bowmen spread out, no longer firing in flights but choosing their targets. Men screamed their own rage, screamed in the face of death as they shot.

And then there were no more Trollocs standing. Only one Fade, bristling with arrows yet still staggering blindly. The shrill shrieks of a Myrddraal's thrashing horse competed with the moaning bellows of downed and dying Trollocs. The horn had fallen silent at last. Here and there across the stump-filled field, a Trolloc heaved and fell back. Under it all, Perrin could hear men panting as if they had run ten miles. His own heart seemed to be pounding out of his chest.

Suddenly someone raised a loud huzzah, and with that men began capering and shouting euphorically, waving bows or whatever they had over their heads, tossing caps in the air. Women rushed out from the houses, laughing and cheering, and children, all celebrating and dancing with the men. Some came running to grab Perrin's hand and shake it.

"You've led us to a great victory, my boy." Bran laughed up at him. He had his steel cap perched on the back of his head. "I suppose I shouldn't call you that, now. A great victory, Perrin."

"I didn't do anything," he protested. "I just sat on my horse. You did it." Bran listened no more than any of the others. Embarrassed, Perrin sat up straight, pretending to survey the field, and after a while they left him alone.

Tam had not joined in the celebrating; he stood close behind the stakes, studying the Trollocs. The Warders were not laughing, either. Black-mailed shapes littered the field among the low stumps. There could be five hundred of them. Maybe less. Some, a few, might have made it back to the trees. None lay closer than fifty paces from the pointed hedge. Perrin found the other two Fades, writhing on the ground. That accounted for all three. They would admit they were dead eventually.

The Two Rivers folk raised a thunderous cheer, for him. "Perrin Goldeneyes! Huzzah! Huzzah! Huzzah!"

"They had to know," he muttered. Faile looked at him questioningly. "The Halfmen had to know this wouldn't work. Look out there. Even I can see it, now; they must have from the start. If this was all they had, why did they try? And if there are more Trollocs out there, why didn't they all come? Twice as many, and we'd have had to fight them at the stakes. Twice that, and they might have broken through to the village."

"You've a good natural eye," Tomas said, reining in beside them. "This was a test. To see if you would break at the sight of a charge, perhaps to see how quickly you could react, or how your defenses are organized, or maybe something I've not thought of, but still a test. Now they see." He pointed to the sky, where a lone raven winged over the field. A natural raven would have lighted to feast among the dead. The bird completed a last circle and peeled off toward the forest. "The next attack will not come right away. I saw two or three Trollocs reach the forest, so word of this will spread. The Halfmen will have to make them remember they're more afraid of Myrddraal than of dying. That attack will come, however, and it will certainly be stronger than this. How strong depends on how many the Faceless have brought through the Ways."

Perrin grimaced. "Light! What if there are ten thousand of them?"

"Not likely," Verin said, walking up to pat Tomas's mount on the neck. The warhorse allowed her touch as meekly as a pony. "At least, not yet. Not even a Forsaken could move a large party through the Ways safely, I think. One man alone risks death or madness between the closest Waygates, but . . . say . . . a thousand men, or a thousand Trollocs, would very likely draw *Machin Shin* within minutes, a monstrous wasp to a bowl of honey. It is much more probable that they travel no more than ten or twenty together, fifty at most, and the groups spaced out. Of course, the questions remain of how many groups they are bringing, and how much time they allow to elapse between. And they would lose some anyway. It might be that Shadow-spawn attract *Machin Shin* less than humankind, but. . . . Hmmn. Fascinating thought. I wonder. . . ." Patting Tomas on the leg much in the manner she had patted his horse, she turned away, already lost in study. The Warder heeled his horse after her.

"If you ride even one step near the Westwood," Faile said calmly, "I will haul you back to the inn by your ear and stuff you into that bed myself."

"I wasn't thinking of it," Perrin lied, turning Stepper so his back was to the woods. One man and an Ogier might escape notice, make it to the mountains safely. They might. The Waygate had to be locked per-manently if Emond's Field was to have any chance. "You talked me out of it, remember?" Another man might find them, knowing they were there. Three sets of eyes could keep sharper watch than two, especially when one set was his, and he was certainly not doing anything here. His clothes stuffed with straw and set on Stepper could do as much.

Suddenly, above the shouting and carrying on around him, he heard sharper shouts, a clamor from the south, near the Old Road.

"He said they wouldn't come again soon!" he growled, and dug his heels into Stepper's flanks.

CHAPTER
45

The Tinker's Sword

Galloping through the village with Faile at his heels, Perrin found the men on the south side in a cluster, peering out over the cleared fields and muttering, some with bows half-drawn. Two wagons blocked the gap the Old Road made in the sharp stakes. The nearest low stone fence still standing, bordering a field of tabac, lay five hundred paces off, with nothing between taller than barley stubble; the ground short of it sprouted arrows like weeds. Smoke curled up in the far distance, a dozen or more thick black plumes, some wide enough to be fields burning.

Cenn Buie was there, and Hari and Darl Coplin. Bili Congar had an arm around the shoulders of his cousin Wit, Daise's bony husband, who looked as if he wished Bili would not breathe on him. None smelled of fear, only excitement. And Bili of ale. At least ten men at once tried to tell him what had happened; some were louder than others.

"The Trollocs tried us here, as well," Hari Coplin shouted, "but we showed them, didn't we?" There were murmurs of agreement, but just as many or more eyed each other doubtfully and shifted their feet.

"We've some heroes here, too," Darl said in a loud, rough voice. "Your lot up at the wood aren't the only ones." A bigger man than his brother, he had that same weasel-narrow Coplin face, the same tight mouth as if he had just bitten a green persimmon. When he thought

Perrin was not looking, he shot him a spiteful look. It did not necessarily mean he really wished he had been up facing the Westwood; Darl and Hari and most of their relatives usually found a way to see themselves being cheated, whatever the situation.

"This calls for a drink!" old Bili announced, then scowled in disappointment when no one echoed him.

A head lifted above the distant wall and hurriedly ducked back down, but not before Perrin saw a brilliant yellow coat. "Not Trollocs," he growled disgustedly. "Tinkers! You were shooting at Tuatha'an. Get those wagons out of the way." Standing in his stirrups, he cupped hands to his mouth. "You can come on!" he shouted. "It is all right! No one will hurt you! I said move those wagons," he snapped at the men standing around staring at him. Taking Tinkers for Trollocs! "And go fetch your arrows; you'll have real need for them sooner or later." Slowly some moved to obey, and he shouted again, "No one will harm you! It is all right! Come on!" The wagons rolled to either side with the creak of axles that needed grease.

A few brightly garbed Tuatha'an climbed over the fence, then a few more, and started toward the village in a hesitant, footsore half-run, seeming almost as afraid of what lay ahead as whatever lay behind. They huddled together at the sight of men dashing out from the village, balancing on the edge of turning back even when the Two Rivers folk trotted by, looking at them curiously, to begin pulling arrows out of the dirt. Yet they did stumble on.

Perrin's insides turned to ice. Twenty men and women, perhaps, some carrying small children, and a handful of older children running, too, their dazzling colors all torn and stained with dirt. And some with blood, he saw as they came closer. That was all. Out of how many in the caravan? There was Raen, at least, shuffling as though half-dazed and being guided by Ila, one side of her face a dark, swollen bruise. At least they had survived.

Short of the opening, the Tuatha'an stopped, staring uncertainly at the sharp stakes and the mass of armed men. Some of the children clutched their elders and hid their faces. They smelled of fear, of terror. Faile jumped down and ran to them, but though Ila hugged her, she did not take another step nearer. The older woman seemed to be drawing comfort from the younger.

"We won't hurt you," Perrin said. *I should have made them come. The Light burn me, I should have made them!* "You are welcome to our fires."

"Tinkers." Hari's mouth twisted scornfully. "What do we want with a bunch of thieving Tinkers? Take everything that isn't nailed down."

Darl opened his mouth, to support Hari no doubt, but before he could speak someone in the crowd shouted, "So do you, Hari! And you'll take the nails, too!" Sparse laughter snapped Darl's jaws shut. Not many laughed, though, and those that did eyed the bedraggled Tuatha'an and looked down in discomfort.

"Hari is right!" Daise Congar called, bulling through, pushing men out of her path. "Tinkers steal, and not just things! They steal children!" Shoving her way to Cenn Buie, she shook a finger as thick as Cenn's thumb under his nose. He backed away as much as he could in the press; she overtopped him by a head and outweighed him by half. "You are supposed to be on the Village Council, but if you don't want to listen to the Wisdom, I'll bring the Women's Circle into this, and we will take care of it." Some of the men nodded, muttering.

Cenn scratched his thinning hair, eyeing the Wisdom sideways. "Aaah . . . well . . . Perrin," he said slowly in that scratchy voice, "the Tinkers do have a reputation, you know, and—" He cut off, jumping back as Perrin whirled Stepper to face the Two Rivers folk.

A good many scattered before the dun, but Perrin did not care. "We'll not turn anyone away," he said in a tight voice. "No one! Or do you mean to send children off for the Trollocs?" One of the Tuatha'an children began to cry, a sharp wailing, and he wished he had not said that, but Cenn's face went red as a beet, and even Daise looked abashed.

"Of course we'll take them in," the thatcher said gruffly. He rounded on Daise, all puffed up like a banty rooster ready to fight a mastiff. "And if you want to bring the Women's Circle into it, the Village Council will sit the whole lot of you down sharp! You see if we don't!"

"You always were an old fool, Cenn Buie," Daise snorted. "Do you think we'd let you send children back out there for Trollocs?" Cenn's jaw worked furiously, but before he could get a word out Daise put a hand on his narrow chest and thrust him aside. Donning a smile, she strode out to the Tuatha'an and put a comforting arm around Ila. "You just come along with me, and I'll see you all get hot baths and somewhere to rest. Every house is crowded, but we'll find places for everyone. Come."

Marin al'Vere came hurrying through the crowd, and Alsbet Luhhan, Natti Cauthon and Neysa Ayellin and more women, taking up children or putting arms around Tuatha'an women, urging them along, scolding the Two Rivers men to make way. Not that anybody was balking, now; it just took a little time for so many to jostle back and open a path.

Faile gave Perrin an admiring look, but he shook his head. This was not *ta'veren* work; Two Rivers people might need the right way pointed out to them sometimes, but they could see it when it was. Even Hari Coplin, watching the Tinkers brought in, did not look as sour as he had. Well, not quite as sour. There was no use expecting miracles.

Shambling by, Raen looked up at Perrin dully. "The Way of the Leaf *is* the right way. All things die in their appointed time, and. . . ." He trailed off as if he could not remember what he had been going to say.

"They came last night," Ila said, mumbling because of her swollen face. Her eyes were almost as glazed as her husband's. "The dogs might have helped us escape, but the Children killed all the dogs, and. . . . There was nothing we could do." Behind her, Aram shivered in his yellow-striped coat, staring at all the armed men. Most of the Tinker children were crying now.

Perrin frowned at the smoke rising to the south. Twisting in his saddle, he could make out more to the north and east. Even if most of those represented houses already abandoned, the Trollocs had had a busy night. How many would it take to fire that many farms, even running between and taking no more time than needed to toss a torch into an empty house or unwatched field? Maybe as many as they had killed today. What did that say about Trolloc numbers already in the Two Rivers? It did not seem possible one band had done it all, burning all those houses and destroying the Traveling People's caravan, too.

Eyes falling on the Tuatha'an being led away, he felt a stab of embarrassment. They had seen kith and kin killed last night, and here he was coldly considering numbers. He could hear some of the Two Rivers men muttering, trying to decide which smoke represented whose farm. To all of these people those fires meant real losses, lives to be rebuilt if they could, not just numbers. He was useless here. Now, while Faile was caught up in helping see to the Tinkers, was the time for him to be off after Loial and Gaul.

Master Luhhan, in his blacksmith's vest and long leather apron, caught Stepper's bridle. "Perrin, you have to help me. The Warders want me to make parts for more of those catapults, but I've twenty men clamoring for me to repair bits of armor their grandfathers' fool grandfathers bought from some fool merchants' guards."

"I would like to give you a hand," Perrin said, "but I have something else that needs doing. I'd likely be rusty, anyway. I haven't had much work at a forge the last year."

"Light, I didn't mean that. Not for you to work a hammer." The blacksmith sounded shocked. "Every time I send one of those goose-brains off with a bee in his ear, he's back ten minutes later with a new argument. I cannot get any work done. They'll listen to you."

Perrin doubted it, not if they would not listen to Master Luhhan. Aside from being on the Village Council, Haral Luhhan was big enough to pick up nearly any man in the Two Rivers and toss him out bodily if need be. But he went along to the makeshift forge Master Luhhan had set up beneath a hastily built, open-sided shed near the Green. Six men clustered around the anvils salvaged from the smithy the Whitecloaks had burned, and another idly pumping the big leather bellows until the blacksmith chased him away from the long handles with a shout. To Perrin's surprise they did listen when he told them to go, with no speech to bend them 'round a ta'veren's will, just a plain statement that Master Luhhan was busy. Surely the blacksmith could have done as much himself, but he shook Perrin's hand and thanked him profusely before setting to work.

Bending down from Stepper's saddle, Perrin caught one of the men by the shoulder, a bald-headed farmer named Get Eldin, and asked him to stay and warn off anyone else who tried to bother Master Luhhan. Get must have been three times his age, but the leathery, wrinkle-faced man just nodded and took up a station near where Haral had his hammer ringing on hot iron. Now he could be off, before Faile turned up.

Before he could as much as turn Stepper, Bran appeared, spear on his shoulder and steel cap under one stout arm. "Perrin, there has to be a faster way to bring the shepherds and herdsmen in if we're attacked again. Even sending the fastest runners in the village, Abell couldn't get half of them back here before those Trollocs came out of the wood."

That was easy to solve, a matter of remembering an old bugle, tarnished nearly black, that Cenn Buie had hanging on his wall, and settling on a signal of three long blasts that the farthest shepherd could hear. It did bring up signals for other things, of course, such as sending everyone to their places if an attack was expected. Which led to how to know when an attack was expected. Bain and Chiad and the Warders turned out to be more than amenable to scouting, but four were hardly enough, so good woodsmen and trackers had to be found, and provided with horses so they could reach Emond's Field ahead of any Trollocs they spotted.

After that, Buel Dowtry had to be settled down. The white-haired old fletcher, with a nose nearly as sharp as a broadhead point, knew very well that most farmers usually made their own arrows, but he was adamantly opposed to anyone helping him here in the village, as if he could keep every quiver filled by himself. Perrin was not sure how he smoothed Buel's ruffled temper, but somehow he left the man happily teaching a knot of boys to tie and glue goose-feather fletchings.

Edward Candwin, the stout cooper, had a different problem. With so many folk needing water, he had more buckets and barrels to make than he could hoop in weeks, alone. It did not take long to find him hands he trusted to chamfer staves at least, but more people came with questions and problems they seemed to think only Perrin had the answers for, from where to burn the bodies of the dead Trollocs to whether it was safe to return to their farms to save what they could. That last he answered with a firm no whenever it was asked—and it was asked more often than any other, by men and women frowning at the smoke rising in the countryside—but most of the time he simply inquired what the questioner thought was a good solution and told him to do that. It was seldom he really had to come up with an answer; people knew what to do, they just had this fool notion they had to ask him.

Dannil and Ban and the others found him and insisted on riding about at his heels with that banner, as if the big one over the Green was not bad enough, until he sent them off to guard the men who had gone back to felling trees along the Westwood. It seemed that Tam had told them some tale about something called the Companions, in Illian, soldiers who rode with the general of an Illianer army and were thrown in wherever the battle was hottest. Tam, of all people! At least they took the banner with them. Perrin felt a right fool with that thing trailing after him.

In the middle of the morning, Luc rode in, all golden-haired arrogance, nodding slightly to acknowledge a few cheers, though why anyone wanted to cheer him seemed a mystery. He brought a trophy that he pulled out of a leather bag and had set on a spear at the edge of the Green for everyone to gawk at. A Myrddraal's eyeless head. The fellow was modest enough, in a condescending sort of way, but he did let slip that he had killed the Fade when he ran into a band of Trollocs. An admiring train took him around to see the scene of the battle here— they were calling it that—where horses were dragging Trollocs off to great pyres already sending up pillars of oily black smoke. Luc was properly admiring in turn, making only one or two criticisms of how Perrin had disposed his men; that was how the Two Rivers folk told it, with Perrin lining everybody up and giving orders he certainly never had.

To Perrin, Luc gave a patronizing smile of approval. "You did very well, my boy. You were lucky, of course, but there is such a thing as the luck of the beginner, is there not."

When he went off to his room in the Winespring Inn, Perrin had the head taken down and buried. Not a thing people should be staring at, especially the children.

The questions continued as the day wore on, until he suddenly realized the sun stood straight overhead, he had had nothing to eat, and his stomach was talking to him in no uncertain terms. "Mistress al'Caar," he said wearily to the long-faced woman at his stirrup, "I suppose the children can play anywhere, so long as somebody watches to make sure they don't go beyond the last houses. Light, woman, you know that. You certainly know children better than I do! If you don't, how have you managed to raise four of your own?" Her youngest was six years older than he was!

Nela al'Caar frowned and tossed her head, gray-streaked braid swinging. For a moment he thought she was going to snap his nose off, talking that way to her. He almost wished she would, for a change from everybody wanting to know what he thought should be done. "Of course I know children," she said. "I just want to make sure it's done the way you want. That's what we'll do, then."

Sighing, he only waited for her to turn away before reining Stepper around toward the Winespring Inn. Two or three voices called to him, but he refused to listen. What he wanted done. What was wrong with these people? Two Rivers folk did not follow this way. Certainly not Emond's Fielders. They wanted a say in everything. Arguments in front of the Village Council, arguments among the Council, had to come to blows before they occasioned comment. And if the Women's Circle thought they kept their own affairs more circumspect, there was not a man who did not know the meaning of tight-jawed women stalking about with their braids all but bristling like angry cats' tails.

What I want? he thought angrily. *What I want is something to eat, someplace where no one is jabbering in my ear.* Stepping down in front of the inn, he staggered, and thought he could add a bed to that short list. Only midday, with Stepper doing all the work, and he already felt bone-weary. Maybe Faile had been right after all. Maybe going after Loial and Gaul really was a bad idea.

When he walked into the common room, Mistress al'Vere took one look at him and all but pushed him into a chair with a motherly smile.

"You can just give over handing out orders for a while," she told him firmly. "Emond's Field can very well survive an hour by itself while you put some food inside you." She bustled away before he could say Emond's Field could very well survive by itself without him at all.

The room was almost empty. Natti Cauthon sat at one table, rolling bandages and adding them to the pile in front of her, but she also managed to keep an eye on her daughters, across the room, though both were old enough to be wearing their hair in a braid. The reason was plain enough. Bode and Eldrin sat on either side of Aram, coaxing the Tinker to eat. Feeding him, actually, and wiping his chin, too. From the way they were grinning at the fellow, Perrin was surprised Natti was not at the table with them, braids or no. The fellow was good-looking, he supposed; maybe handsomer than Wil al'Seen. Bode and Eldrin certainly seemed to think so. For his part, Aram smiled back occasionally—they were plumply pretty girls; he would have to be blind not to see it, and Perrin did not think Aram was ever blind to a pretty girl—but he hardly swallowed without running a wide-eyed gaze over the spears and polearms against the walls. For a Tuatha'an, it had to be a horrible sight.

"Mistress al'Vere said you had finally gotten tired of your saddle," Faile said, popping in through the door to the kitchen. Startlingly, she wore a long white apron like Marin's; her sleeves were pushed up above her elbows, and she had flour on her hands. As if just realizing it, she whipped the apron off, wiping her hands hastily, and laid it across the back of a chair. "I have never baked anything before," she said, shoving her sleeves down as she joined him. "It is rather fun kneading dough. I might like to do it again someday."

"If you don't bake," he said, "where are we going to get bread? I don't intend to spend my whole life traveling, buying meals or eating what I can snare or fetch with bow or sling."

She smiled as if he had said something very pleasing, though he could not for the life of him see what. "The cook will bake, of course. One of her helpers, really, I suppose, but the cook will oversee it."

"The cook," he mumbled, shaking his head. "Or one of her helpers. Of course. Why didn't I think of that?"

"What is the matter, Perrin? You look worried. I don't think the defenses could be any sounder without a fortress wall."

"It isn't that. Faile, this Perrin Goldeneyes business is getting out of hand. I do not know who they think I am, but they keep asking me what to do, asking if it's all right, when they already know what has to be done, when they could figure it out with two minutes' thought."

For a long moment she studied his face, those dark, tilted eyes thoughtful, then said, "How many years has it been since the Queen of Andor ruled here in fact?"

"The Queen of Andor? I don't really know. A hundred years, maybe. Two hundred. What does that have to do with anything?"

"These people do not remember how to deal with a queen—or a king. They are trying to puzzle it out. You must be patient with them."

"A king?" he said weakly. He let his head drop down onto his arms on the table. "Oh, Light!"

Laughing softly, Faile ruffled his hair. "Well, perhaps not that. I doubt very much that Morgase would approve. A leader, at least. But she would very definitely approve a man who brought lands back to her that her throne has not controlled in a hundred years or more. She would surely make that man a lord. Perrin of House Aybara, Lord of the Two Rivers. It has a good sound."

"We do not need any lords in the Two Rivers," he growled at the oak tabletop. "Or kings, or queens. We are free men!"

"Free men can have a need to follow someone, too," she said gently. "Most men want to believe in something larger than themselves, something wider than their own fields. That is why there are nations, Perrin, and peoples. Even Raen and Ila see themselves as part of something more than their own caravan. They have lost their wagons and most of their family and friends, but other Tuatha'an still seek the song, and they will again, too, because they belong to more than a few wagons."

"Who owns these?" Aram asked suddenly.

Perrin raised his head. The young Tinker was on his feet, staring uneasily at the spears lining the walls. "They belong to anybody who wants one, Aram. Nobody is going to hurt you with any of them, believe me." He was not sure if Aram did believe, not the way he began walking slowly around the room with his hands stuffed into his pockets, eyeing spears and halberds sideways.

Perrin was more than grateful to dig in when Marin brought him a plate of sliced roast goose, with turnips and peas and good crusty bread. At least, he would have dug in, if Faile had not tucked a flower-embroidered napkin under his chin and snatched the knife and fork out of his hands. She seemed to find it amusing to feed him the way Bode and Eldrin had been feeding Aram. The Cauthon girls giggled at him, and Natti and Marin wore little smiles, too. Perrin did not see what was so funny. He was willing to indulge Faile, though, even if he could have fed himself more easily. She kept making him stretch his neck to take what she had on the fork.

Aram's slow wandering took him around the room three times before he stopped at the foot of the stairs, staring at the barrel of ill-assorted swords. Then he reached out and pulled a sword from the cluster, hefting it awkwardly. The leather-wrapped hilt was long enough for both of his hands. "Can I use this one?" he asked.

Perrin nearly choked.

Alanna appeared at the head of the stairs, with Ila; the Tuatha'an woman looked weary, but the bruise was gone from her face. ". . . best thing is sleep," the Aes Sedai was saying. "It is shock to his mind that troubles him most, and I cannot Heal that."

Ila's eyes fell on her grandson, on what he held, and she screamed as if that blade had gone into her flesh. "No, Aram! Nooooo!" She almost fell in her haste to get down the stairs and flung herself on Aram, trying to pull his hands from the sword. "No, Aram," she panted breathlessly. "You must not. Put it down. The Way of the Leaf. You must not! The Way of the Leaf! Please, Aram! Please!"

Aram danced with her, fending her off clumsily, trying to hold the sword away from her. "Why not?" he shouted angrily. "They killed Mother! I saw them! I might have saved her, if I had had a sword. I could have saved her!"

The words sliced at Perrin's chest. A Tinker with a sword seemed an unnatural thing, almost enough to make his hackles stand, but those words. . . . His mother. "Leave him alone," he said, more roughly than he intended. "Any man has a right to defend himself, to defend his. . . . He has a right."

Aram pushed the sword toward Perrin. "Will you teach me how to use it?"

"I don't know how," Perrin told him. "You can find someone, though."

Tears rolled down Ila's contorted face. "The Trollocs took my daughter," she sobbed, her entire body shaking, "and all my grandchildren but one, and now you take him. He is Lost, because of you, Perrin Aybara. You have become a wolf in your heart, and now you will make him one, too." Turning, she stumbled back up the steps, still racked with sobs.

"I could have saved her!" Aram called after her. "Grandmother! I could have saved her!" She never looked back, and when she vanished around the corner, he slumped against the banister, weeping. "I could have saved her, grandmother. I could have. . . ."

Perrin realized Bode was crying, too, with her face in her hands, and the other women were frowning at him as though he had done something wrong. No, not all of them. Alanna studied him from the head of the stairs with that unreadable Aes Sedai calm, and Faile's face was nearly as blank.

Wiping his mouth, he tossed the napkin on the table and got up. There was still time to tell Aram to put the sword back, to go ask Ila's pardon. Time to tell him . . . what? That maybe next time he would not be there to watch his loved ones die? That maybe he could just come back to find their graves?

He put a hand on Aram's shoulder, and the man flinched, hunching around the sword as if expecting him to take it. The Tinker's scent carried a wash of emotions, fear and hate and bone-deep sadness. Lost, Ila had called him. His eyes looked lost. "Wash your face, Aram. Then go find Tam al'Thor. Say I ask him to teach you the sword."

Slowly the other man raised his face. "Thank you," he stammered, scrubbing at the tears on his cheeks with his sleeve. "Thank you. I will never forget this. Never. I swear it." Suddenly he hoisted the sword to kiss the straight blade; the hilt had a brass wolfhead for a pommel. "I swear. Is that not how it is done?"

"I suppose it is," Perrin said sadly, wondering why he should feel sad. The Way of the Leaf was a fine belief, like a dream of peace, but like the dream it could not last where there was violence. He did not know of a place without that. A dream for some other man, some other time. Some other Age perhaps. "Go on, Aram. You have a lot to learn, and there may not be much time." Still bubbling thanks, the Tinker did not wait to wash his tears away, but ran straight out of the inn, carrying the sword upright before him in both hands.

Conscious of Eldrin's scowl and Marin's fists on her hips and Natti's frown, not to mention Bode's weeping, Perrin walked back to his chair. Alanna had gone from her place at the top of the stairs. Faile watched him pick up his knife and fork. "You disapprove?" he said quietly. "A man has a right to defend himself, Faile. Even Aram. No one can make him follow the Way of the Leaf if he doesn't want to."

"I do not like to see you in pain," she said very softly.

His knife paused in cutting a piece of goose. Pain? That dream was not for him. "I am just tired," he told her, and smiled. He did not think she believed him.

Before he had time to take a second mouthful, Bran stuck his head in at the front door. He wore his round steel cap again. "Riders coming from the north, Perrin. A lot of riders. I think it must be the Whitecloaks."

Faile darted away as Perrin rose, and by the time he was outside on

Stepper, with the Mayor muttering to himself about what he meant to say to the Whitecloaks, she came riding her black mare around the side of the inn. More people were running north than stayed at their tasks. Perrin was in no particular hurry. The Children of the Light might well be there to arrest him. They probably were. He did not mean to go along in chains, but he was not anxious to ask people to fight Whitecloaks for him. He followed behind Bran, joining the stream of men and women and children crossing the Wagon Bridge across the Winespring Water, Stepper's and Swallow's hooves clattering on the thick planks. A few tall willows grew here along the water. The bridge was where the North Road began, then ran to Watch Hill and beyond. Some of the distant smoke plumes had thinned to wisps as fires burned themselves out.

Where the road left the village, he found a pair of wagons blocking the road and men gathered behind pointed, slanting stakes with their bows and spears and such, smelling of excitement, murmuring to each other and all jammed together to watch what was coming down the road: a long double column of white-cloaked horsemen trailing a cloud of dust, conical helmets and burnished plate-and-mail shining in the afternoon sun, steel-tipped lances all at the same angle. At their head rode a youngish man, stiff-backed and stern-faced, who looked vaguely familiar to Perrin. With the arrival of the Mayor, the murmurs hushed expectantly. Or maybe it was Perrin's arrival that quieted them.

Two hundred paces or so from the stakes, the stern-faced man raised a hand, and the column halted with sharp orders echoing down the files. He came on with just half a dozen Whitecloaks for company, running his eyes over the wagons and sharp stakes and the men behind. His manner would have named him a man of importance even without the knots of rank beneath the flaring sunburst on his cloak.

Luc had appeared from somewhere, resplendent on his shiny black stallion in rich red wool and golden embroidery. Perhaps it was natural enough that the Whitecloak officer chose to address himself to Luc, though his dark eyes continued to probe. "I am Dain Bornhald," he announced, reining in, "Captain of the Children of the Light. You have done this for us? I have heard that Emond's Field is closed to the Children, yes? Truly a village of the Shadow if it is closed to the Children of the Light."

Dain Bornhald, not Geofram. A son, perhaps. Not that it made any difference. Perrin supposed one would try to arrest him as soon as another. Sure enough, Bornhald's gaze swept past him, then jerked back. A convulsion seemed to seize the man; one gauntleted hand darted to his sword, his lips peeled back in a silent snarl, and for a moment Perrin was sure the man was about to charge, fling his horse onto the spiky barrier, to reach him. The man looked as if he bore Perrin a personal hatred. Up close, that hard face had a touch of slackness to it, a shine in those eyes that Perrin was used to seeing in Bili Congar's. He thought he could smell brandy fumes.

The hollow-cheeked man beside Bornhald was more than familiar. Perrin would never forget those deep-set eyes, like dark burning coals. Tall and gaunt and hard as an anvil, Jaret Byar truly did look at him with hate. Whether or not Bornhald was a zealot, Byar surely was.

Luc apparently had the sense not to try usurping Bran's place—indeed, he appeared intent on examining the white-cloaked column as the dust settled, revealing more Children stretching up the road—to Perrin's disgust, though Bran looked to him—to the blacksmith's apprentice—waited for his nod before answering. He was the *Mayor!* Bornhald and Byar plainly took note of the silent exchange.

"Emond's Field is not precisely closed to you," Bran said, standing up straight with his spear propped out to one side. "We have decided to defend ourselves, and have this very morning. If you want to see our work, look there." He pointed toward the smoke rising from the Trollocs' pyres. A sickly-sweet smell of burning flesh drifted in the air, but no one except Perrin seemed to notice.

"You have killed a few Trollocs?" Bornhald said contemptuously. "Your luck and skill amaze me."

"More than a few!" somebody called out of the Two Rivers crowd. "Hundreds!"

"We had a battle!" another voice cried, and dozens more shouted angrily on top of one another.

"We fought them and won!"

"Where were you?"

"We can defend ourselves without any Whitecloaks!"

"The Two Rivers!"

"The Two Rivers and Perrin Goldeneyes!"

"Goldeneyes!"

"Goldeneyes!"

Leof, who should have been over guarding the woodsmen, started waving that crimson wolfhead banner.

Bornhald's hot-eyed hate took them all in, but Byar danced his bay gelding forward with a snarl. "Do you farmers think you know battle?" he roared. "Last night one of your villages was all but wiped out by Trollocs! Wait until they come at you in numbers, and you will wish your mother had never kissed your father!" He fell silent at a weary gesture from Bornhald, a fierce-trained dog obeying his master, but his words had quieted the Two Rivers people.

"Which village?" Bran's voice was dignified and troubled both. "We all know people in Watch Hill, and Deven Ride."

"Watch Hill has not been troubled," Bornhald replied, "and I know nothing of Deven Ride. This morning a rider brought me word that Taren Ferry hardly exists any longer. If you have friends there, many people did escape across the river. Across the river." His face tightened momentarily. "I myself lost nearly fifty good soldiers."

The news produced a few queasy murmurs; no one liked to hear that sort of thing, but on the other hand, no one here knew anyone in Taren Ferry. Likely none of them had ever been that far.

Luc pushed his horse forward, the stallion snapping at Stepper. Perrin reined his own mount tightly before the two began fighting, but Luc appeared not to notice or care. "Taren Ferry?" he said in a flat voice. "Trollocs attacked Taren Ferry last night?"

Bornhald shrugged. "I said it, did I not? It seems that the Trollocs have at last decided to raid the villages. How providential that you here were warned in time to prepare these fine defenses." His stare ran over the pointed hedge and the men behind it before settling on Perrin.

"Was the man called Ordeith at Taren Ferry last night?" Luc asked.

Perrin stared at him. He had not known Luc even knew of Padan Fain, or the name he used now. But people did talk, especially when someone they knew as a peddler came back with authority among Whitecloaks.

Bornhald's reaction was as strange as the question. His eyes glittered a hate as strong as he had shown for Perrin, but his face went pale, and he scrubbed at slack lips with the back of his hand as though he had forgotten he wore steel-backed gauntlets. "You know Ordeith?" he said, leaning toward Luc in his saddle.

It was Luc's turn to shrug casually. "I have seen him here and there since coming to the Two Rivers. A disreputable-looking man, and those who follow him no less. The sort who might have been careless enough to allow a Trolloc attack to succeed. Was he there? If so, one can hope he died for his folly. If not, one hopes you have him here with you, close under your eye."

"I do not know where he is," Bornhald snapped. "Or care! I did not come here to talk of Ordeith!" His horse pranced nervously as Bornhald flung out a hand, pointing at Perrin. "I arrest you as a Darkfriend. You will be taken to Amador, and there tried under the Dome of Truth."

Byar stared at his Captain in disbelief. Behind the barrier separating the Whitecloaks from the Two Rivers men, angry mutters rose, spears and bills were hefted, bows raised. The farther Whitecloaks began spreading out in a gleaming line under shouted orders from a fellow as big in his armor as Master Luhhan, sliding lances into holders along their saddles, unlimbering short horsebows. At that range they could do little more than cover the escape of Bornhald and the men with him, if they did indeed manage an escape, but Bornhald appeared oblivious of any danger, and of anything at all save Perrin.

"There will be no arrests," Bran said sharply. "We have decided that. No more arrests without proof of some crime, and proof *we* believe. You'll never show me anything to convince me Perrin is a Darkfriend, so you might as well put your hand down."

"He betrayed my father to his death at Falme," Bornhald shouted. Rage shook him. "Betrayed him to Darkfriends and Tar Valon witches who murdered a thousand of the Children with the One Power!" Byar nodded vigorously.

Some of the Two Rivers folk shifted uncertainly; word had spread of what Verin and Alanna had done that morning, and the deeds had grown in spreading. Whatever they thought about Perrin, a hundred tales of Aes Sedai, almost all wrong, made for easy belief in Aes Sedai destroying a thousand Whitecloaks. And if they believed that, they might come to believe the rest.

"I betrayed no one," Perrin said in a loud voice, so everyone could hear. "If your father died at Falme, those who killed him are called the Seanchan. I don't know whether they are Darkfriends, but I do know they use the One Power in battle."

"Liar!" Spittle flew from Bornhald's lips. "The Seanchan are a tale concocted by the White Tower to hide their foul lies! You are a Darkfriend!"

Bran shook his head wonderingly, pushing his steel cap over to one side so he could scratch his fringe of gray hair. "I don't know anything about these—Seanchan?—about these Seanchan. What I do know is that Perrin is no Darkfriend, and you are not arresting anybody."

The situation was growing more dangerous by the minute, Perrin realized. Byar saw it and tugged at Bornhald's arm, whispering to him, but the Whitecloak captain would not, or perhaps could not, back away now that he had Perrin in front of his eyes. Bran and the Two Rivers men had their heels planted, too; they might not be willing to let the

Whitecloaks take him even if he confessed to everything Bornhald claimed. Unless someone tossed some water fast, everything was going to explode like a fistful of dry straw tossed on a forge-fire.

He hated having to think quickly. Loial had the right of it. Hasty thinking led to people being hurt. But he thought he saw a way here. "Are you willing to hold off my arrest, Bornhald? Until the Trollocs are done with? I won't be going anywhere before then."

"Why should I hold off?" The man was blind with hate. If he went on, a good many men were going to die, including him most likely, and he could not see. There was no use pointing it out.

"Haven't you noticed all the farms burning this morning?" Perrin said instead. He made a sweeping gesture that took in all the dwindling plumes of smoke. "Look around. You said it yourself. The Trollocs aren't content with raiding a farm or two each night anymore. They're up to raiding villages. If you try to make it back to Watch Hill, you may not get there. You were lucky to come this far. But if you stay here, in Emond's Field . . ." Bran rounded on him, and other men shouted loud noes; Faile rode close and seized his arm, but he ignored all of them. ". . . you will know where I am, and your soldiers will be welcome to help our defenses."

"Are you sure about this, Perrin?" Bran said, grabbing Stepper's stirrup, while from the other side Faile said urgently. "No, Perrin! It is too great a risk. You must not—I mean . . . please don't—Oh, the Light burn me to bloody ash! You *must* not do this!"

"I won't have men fighting men if I can stop it," he told them firmly. "We are not going to do the Trollocs' work for them."

Faile practically flung his arm away. Scowling at Bornhald, she produced a sharpening stone from her pouch and a knife from somewhere, and began honing the blade with a silk-soft *whisk-whisk*.

"Hari Coplin won't know what to think, now," Bran said wryly. Straightening his round helmet, he turned back to the Whitecloaks and planted his spear butt. "You have heard his terms. Now hear mine. If you come into Emond's Field, you arrest no one without the say-so of the Village Council, which you will not get, so you arrest no one. You don't go into anybody's house unless you are asked. You make no trouble, and you share in the defense where and when you're asked. And I don't want to so much as *smell* a Dragon's Fang! Will you agree? If not, you can ride back as you came." Byar stared at the round man as if a sheep had reared up on its hind legs and offered to wrestle.

Bornhald never took his eyes off Perrin. "Done," he said at last. "Until the Trolloc threat is gone, done!" Wrenching his horse around, he galloped back toward the line of his men, snowy cloak billowing behind him.

As the Mayor ordered the wagons rolled aside, Perrin realized that Luc was looking at him. The fellow sat slumped easily in his saddle, a languorous hand on his sword hilt, blue eyes amused.

"I thought you would object," Perrin said, "the way I hear you've been talking people up against the Whitecloaks."

Luc spread his hands smoothly. "If these people want Whitecloaks among them, let them have Whitecloaks. But you should be careful, young Goldeneyes. I know something of taking an enemy into your bosom. His blade goes in quicker when he is close." With a laugh, he pushed his stallion off through the crowd, back into the village.

"He is right," Faile said, still stropping her knife on the stone. "Perhaps this Bornhald will keep his word not to arrest you, but what is to stop one of his men from putting a blade in your back? You should not have done this."

"I had to," he told her. "Better than doing the Trollocs' work."

The Whitecloaks were beginning to ride in, Bornhald and Byar at their head. Those two glared at him with unabated hatred, and the others, riding by in pairs. . . . Cold hard eyes in cold, hard faces swung to regard him as they passed. They did not hate, but they saw a Darkfriend when they saw him. And Byar, at least, was capable of anything.

He had had to do it, but he thought maybe it would not be such a bad idea to let Dannil and Ban and the others follow him around the way they wanted to. He was not going to be able to sleep easy without somebody guarding his door. Guards. Like some fool lord. At least Faile would be happy. If only he could make them lose that banner somewhere.

CHAPTER
46

Veils

The crowds were thick in the confined winding streets of the Calpene near the Great Circle; the smoke of countless cook fires rising above the high white walls gave the reason. Sour smells of smoke and cooking and long unwashed sweat hung heavy in the humid morning air with the crying of children and the vague murmurs that always clung to large masses of people, together enough to muffle the shrill caws of the gulls sailing overhead. The shops in this area had long since locked the iron grilles over their doors for good.

Disgusted, Egeanin threaded her way through the throng afoot. It was dreadful that order had broken down enough for penniless refugees to take over the circles, sleeping among the stone benches. It was as bad as their rulers letting them starve. Her heart should have been gladdened—this dispirited rabble could never resist the *Corenne,* and then proper order would be restored—but she hated looking at it.

Most of the ragged people around her seemed too apathetic to wonder at a woman in their midst in a clean, well-tended blue riding dress, silk if plainly cut. Men and women in once fine garb, soiled and wrinkled now, speckled the crowd, so perhaps she did not stand out enough for contrast. The few who seemed to wonder whether her clothes meant coins in her purse were dissuaded by the competent way she carried her stout staff, as tall as she was. Guards and chair and bearers had had to be left behind today. Floran Gelb would surely have realized he was being followed by that array. At least this dress with its divided skirts gave her a little freedom of movement.

Keeping the weasely little man in sight was easy even in this mass of people, despite having to dodge oxcarts or the occasional wagon, hauled by sweating bare-chested men more often than animals. Gelb and seven or eight companions, burly rough-faced men all, shoved through in a knot, an eddy of curses following them. Those fellows angered her. Gelb meant to try kidnapping again. He had found three women since she sent him the gold he had asked for, none more than casually resembling any on her list, and had whined over every one she rejected. She should never have paid him for that first woman he snatched off the street. Greed and the memory of gold had apparently washed out the hide-flaying tongue-lashing she had given him along with the purse.

Shouts from behind pulled her head around and tightened her hands on the staff. A small space had opened up, as it always did around trouble. A bellowing man in a torn, once-fine yellow coat was on his knees in the street, clutching his right arm where it bent the wrong way. Huddling over him protectively, a weeping woman in a tattered green gown was crying at a veiled fellow already melting into the crowd. "He only asked for a coin! He only asked!" The crowd swirled in around them again.

Grimacing, Egeanin turned back. And stopped with an oath that drew a few startled glances. Gelb and his fellows had vanished. Pushing her way to a small stone fountain where water gushed from the mouth of a bronze fish on the side of a flat-roofed wineshop, she roughly displaced two of the women filling pots and leaped up onto the coping, ignoring their indignant curses. From there she could see over the heads of the crowd. Cramped streets ran off in every direction, twisting around the hills. Bends and white-plastered buildings cut her view to less than a hundred paces at best, but Gelb could not have gone farther than that in those few moments.

Abruptly she found him, hiding in a deep doorway thirty paces on, but up on his toes to peer down the street. The others were easy enough to locate then, leaning against buildings to either side of the street, trying not to be noticed. They were not the only ones lining the walls, but where the rest huddled dispiritedly, their scared, broken-nosed faces held expectation.

So it was to be here, their abduction. Certainly no one would interfere, any more than people had when that fellow's arm was broken. But who? If Gelb had finally found someone on the list, she could go away and wait for him to sell her the woman, wait her chance to see if an *a'dam* truly could hold other *sul'dam* besides Bethamin. However, she did not mean to face again the choice between slitting some unfortunate woman's throat and sending her off to be sold.

There were plenty of women climbing up the street toward Gelb, most in those transparent veils, their hair braided. Without a second glance Egeanin ruled out two in sedan chairs, with bodyguards marching alongside; Gelb's street toughs would not tangle with near their own number, nor face swords with their fists. Whoever they were after would have no more than two or three men for company if that, and none armed. That seemed to include all the other women in her view, whether in rags or drab country dresses or the more clinging styles Taraboner women favored.

Suddenly two of those women, talking together as they rounded a far bend, seized Egeanin's eye. With their hair in slender braids and transparent veils across their faces, they appeared to be Taraboners, but they were out of place here. Those thin, scandalously draped dresses, one green, the other blue, were silk, not linen or finespun wool. Women clothed like that rode in sedan chairs; they did not walk, especially not here. And they did not carry barrel staves on their shoulders like clubs.

Dismissing the one with red-gold hair, she studied the other. Her dark braids were unusually long, nearly to her waist. At this distance, the woman looked very much like a *sul'dam* named Surine. Not Surine, though. This woman would have come no higher than Surine's chin.

Muttering under her breath, Egeanin jumped down and began pushing through the jostling mass between her and Gelb. With luck she could reach him in time to call him off. The fool. The greedy, weasel-brained fool!

"We should have hired chairs, Nynaeve," Elayne said again, wondering for the hundredth time how Taraboner women talked without catching the veils in their mouths. Spitting it out, she added, "We are going to have to use these things."

A weedy-faced fellow stopped drifting toward them through the crowd when Nynaeve hefted her barrel stave threateningly. "That is what they are for." Her glare might have encouraged the man's loss of interest. She fumbled at the dark braids hanging over her shoulders and made a disgusted sound; Elayne did not know when she would become used to not having that one thick braid to tug. "And feet are for walking. How could we look or ask questions being carried around like pigs to sale? I would feel a complete fool in one of those idiot chairs. In any case, I'd rather trust to my own wits than men I do not know."

Elayne was sure Bayle Domon could have provided trustworthy men. The Sea Folk certainly would have; she wished *Wavedancer* had not sailed, but the Sailmistress and her sister had been eager to spread word of the Coramoor to Dantora and Cantorin. Twenty bodyguards would have suited her very well.

She sensed as much as felt something brushing the purse at her belt; clutching at the purse with one hand, she spun around, raising her own stave. The throng flowing by spread a little around her, people barely glancing her way as they elbowed one another, but there was no sign of the would-be cutpurse. At least she could still feel the coins inside. She had taken to wearing her Great Serpent ring and the twisted stone *ter'angreal* on a cord around her neck in imitation of Nynaeve after the first time she had nearly lost a purse. In their five days in Tanchico she *had* lost three. Twenty guards would be just about right. And a carriage. With curtains at the windows.

Resuming the slow climb up the street beside Nynaeve, she said, "Then we should not be wearing these dresses. I can remember a time when you stuffed me into a farmgirl's dress."

"They make a good disguise," Nynaeve replied curtly. "We blend in."

Elayne gave a small sniff. As if plainer dresses would not have blended even better. Nynaeve would not admit she had come to enjoy wearing silks and pretty dresses. Elayne simply wished she had not taken it so far. True, everyone took them for Taraboners—until they spoke, at least—but even with a lace-trimmed neck right up under her chin, this close-draped green silk at least *felt* more revealing than any-thing she had ever worn before. Certainly anything she had ever worn in public. Nynaeve, on the other hand, strode along the cramped street as if no one was looking at them at all. Well, maybe no one was—not because of how their dresses fit, anyway—but it surely seemed they were.

Their shifts would have been almost as decent. Cheeks heating, she tried to stop thinking of how the silk molded itself to her. *Stop that! It is perfectly decent. It is!*

"Didn't this Amys tell you anything that might help us?"

"I told you what she said." Elayne sighed. Nynaeve had kept her up until the small hours talking about the Aiel Wise One who had been

with Egwene in *Tel'aran'rhiod* last night, and then started in again before they sat down to breakfast. Egwene, with her hair in two braids for
some reason and shooting sullen frowns at the Wise One, had said
almost nothing beyond that Rand was well and Aviendha was looking
after him. White-haired Amys had done all the talking, a stern lecture
on the dangers of the World of Dreams that had nearly made Elayne
feel as if she were ten again, and Lini, her old nurse, had caught her
sneaking out of bed to steal candies, followed by cautions about concentration and controlling what she thought if she must enter
Tel'aran'rhiod. How could you control what you thought? "I truly did
think Perrin was with Rand and Mat." That had been the biggest surprise, after Amys's appearance. Egwene apparently had thought he was
with Nynaeve and her.

"He and that girl have probably gone somewhere he can be a blacksmith in peace," Nynaeve said, but Elayne shook her head.

"I do not think so." She had strong suspicions about Faile, and if
they were even half right, Faile would not settle for being a blacksmith's wife. She spat out the veil once more. Idiotic thing.

"Well, wherever he is," Nynaeve said, fumbling with her braids
again, "I hope he is safe and well, but he is not here, and he cannot
help us. Did you even *ask* Amys if she knew any way to use
Tel'aran'rhiod to—?"

A bulky, balding man in a worn brown coat shoved through the
crowd and tried to throw thick arms around her. She whipped the
barrel stave from her shoulder and gave him a crack across his broad
face that sent him staggering back, clutching a nose that had surely
been broken for at least the second time.

Elayne was still gathering breath for a startled scream when a second
man, just as big and with a thick mustache, pushed her aside to reach
for Nynaeve. She forgot about being afraid. Her jaw tightened furiously, and just as his hands touched the other woman, she brought her
own stave down on top of his head with every bit of strength she could
muster. The fellow's legs folded, and he toppled on his face in a most
satisfactory fashion.

The crowd scattered back, no one wanting to be caught up in someone else's trouble. Certainly no one offered to help. And they needed
it, Elayne realized. The man Nynaeve had hit was still on his feet,
mouth twisted in a snarl, licking away the blood than ran down from his
nose, flexing thick hands as if he wanted to squeeze a throat. Worse, he
was not alone. Seven more men were fanning out with him to cut off
any escape, all but one as large as he, with scarred faces and hands that

looked as if they had been hammered on stone for years. A scrawny, narrow-cheeked fellow, grinning like a nervous fox, kept panting, "Don't let her get away. She's gold, I tell you. Gold!"

They knew who she was. This was no try for a purse; they meant to dispose of Nynaeve and abduct the Daughter-Heir of Andor. She felt Nynaeve embracing *saidar*—if this had not made her angry enough to channel, nothing ever would—and opened herself to the True Source as well. The One Power rushed into her, a sweet flood filling her from toes to hair. A few woven flows of Air from either of them could deal with these ruffians.

But she did not channel, and neither did Nynaeve. Together they could drub these fellows as their mothers should have. Yet they did not dare, unless there was no other choice.

If one of the Black Ajah was close enough to see, they had already betrayed themselves with the glow of *saidar*. Channeling enough for those few flows of Air could betray them to a Black sister on another street a hundred paces or more away, depending on her strength and sensitivity. That was most of what they themselves had been doing the last five days, walking through the city trying to sense a woman channeling, hoping the feeling would draw them to Liandrin and the others.

The crowd itself had to be considered, too. A few people still went by to either side, brushing tight against the walls. The rest milled about, beginning to find other ways to go. Only a handful acknowledged the two women in danger with as much as shamefully averted eyes. But if they saw big men flung about by nothing visible . . . ?

Aes Sedai and the One Power itself were not in particularly good odor in Tanchico at the moment, not with old rumors from Falme still floating about and newer tales claiming that the White Tower supported the Dragonsworn in the countryside. Those people might run if they saw the Power wielded. Or they might turn into a mob. Even if she and Nynaeve managed to avoid being torn limb from limb where they stood—which she was not certain they could—there was no way to cover it up after. The Black Ajah would hear of Aes Sedai in Tanchico before the sun set.

Setting herself back-to-back with Nynaeve, Elayne gripped her stave tightly. She felt like laughing hysterically. If Nynaeve even mentioned going out alone again—*walking*—she would see who liked having her head dunked in a bucket of water. At least none of these louts looked eager to be the first to have his head cracked like the fellow lying still on the paving stones.

"Go on," the narrow-faced man urged, waving his hands forward.

"Go on! It's only two women!" He made no move to rush in himself, though. "Go on, I say. We just need the one. She's gold, I tell you."

Suddenly there was a loud *thunk,* and one of the ruffians staggered to his knees, clutching groggily at a split scalp, and a dark-haired, stern-faced woman in a blue riding dress flung herself past him, twisted sharply to backhand another fellow in the mouth with her fist, knocked his legs out from under him with a staff, then kicked him in the head as he fell.

That there was help at all was startling, much less the source, but Elayne was of no mind to pick and choose. Nynaeve left her back with a wordless roar, and she dashed out shouting, "Forward the White Lion!" to belabor the nearest lout as hard and fast as she could. Flinging his arms up to defend himself, he looked shocked out of his wits. "Forward the White Lion!" she shouted again, the battle cry of Andor, and he turned tail and ran.

Laughing in spite of herself, she whirled about seeking another to drub. Only two had not yet fled or fallen. That first broken-nosed fellow turned to run, and Nynaeve gave him a final full-armed thwack across the backside. The stern-faced woman somehow tangled the other's arm and shoulder with her staff, pulling him close and up on his toes at the same time; he would have overtopped her by a head flat-footed and he weighed twice what she did, but she coolly slammed the heel of her free hand up into his chin three times in rapid succession. His eyes rolled up in his head, but as he sagged, Elayne saw the narrow-faced man picking himself up off the street; his nose dripped blood and his eyes looked half-glazed, yet he pulled a knife from his belt and lunged at the woman's back.

Without thinking, Elayne channeled. A fist of Air hurled the man and his knife into a backflip. The stern-faced woman spun, but he was already scrambling away on all fours until he could get his feet under him and burrow into the crowd farther up the street. People had stopped to watch the odd battle, though none had raised a hand to help except the dark-haired woman. She herself was staring from Elayne to Nynaeve uncertainly. Elayne wondered whether she had noticed the scrawny fellow being knocked down apparently by nothing.

"I give you my thanks," Nynaeve said a touch breathlessly as she approached the woman, straightening her veil. "I think we should leave here. I know the Civil Watch doesn't come out in the streets much, but I'd not like to explain this if they do happen by. Our inn is not far. Will you join us? A cup of tea is the least we can offer someone who actually lifts a hand to help someone in this Light-forsaken city. My name is Nynaeve al'Meara, and this is Elayne Trakand."

The woman hesitated visibly. She *had* noticed. "I. . . . I would . . . like that. Yes. I would." She had a slurred way of speaking, difficult to understand, but somehow vaguely familiar. She was quite a lovely woman, really, seeming even fairer than she was because of her dark hair, worn almost to the shoulder. A bit too hard to be called a beauty. Her blue eyes had a strong look, as if she were used to giving orders. A merchant, perhaps, in that dress. "I am called Egeanin."

Egeanin showed no hesitation in leaving with them down the nearest side street. The crowds were already gathering around the fallen men. Elayne expected those fellows would wake to find themselves stripped of anything of value, even clothes and boots. She wished she knew how they had discovered her identity, but there was no way to bring one along to find out. They were *definitely* going to have bodyguards from now on, no matter what Nynaeve said.

Egeanin might not have been hesitant, but she was uneasy. Elayne could see it in her eyes as they wove through the crowd. "You saw, didn't you?" she asked. The woman missed a step, all the confirmation Elayne needed, and she added hurriedly, "We won't harm you. Certainly not after you came to our rescue." Again she had to spit out her veil. Nynaeve did not seem to have that problem. "You needn't frown at me, Nynaeve. She saw what I did."

"I know that," Nynaeve said dryly. "And it was the right thing to do. But we are not snug in your mother's palace tucked away from prying ears." Her gesture took in the people around them. Between Egeanin's staff and their staves, most were giving them a wide berth. To Egeanin she said, "The larger part of any rumors you may have heard are not true. Few of them are. You need not be afraid of us, but you can understand there are matters we do not care to speak of here."

"Afraid of you?" Egeanin looked startled. "I had not thought I should be. I will keep silent until you wish to speak." She was as good as her word; they walked on in silence through the murmurs of the crowd all the way back down the peninsula to the Three Plum Court. All this walking was making Elayne's feet ache.

A handful of men and women sat in the common room despite the early hour, nursing their wine or ale. The woman with her hammered dulcimer was being accompanied by a thin man playing a flute that sounded as reedy as he was. Juilin sat at a table near the door, smoking a short-stemmed pipe. He had not returned from his nightly foray when they left. Elayne was glad to see that for once he did not have a new bruise or cut; what he called the underside of Tanchico seemed even rougher than the face the city presented to the world. His one concession to Tanchican dress had been to replace his flat straw hat with one of those dark conical felt caps, which he wore perched on the back of his head.

"I have found them," he said, popping up from his bench and snatching off his cap, before he saw they were not alone. He gave Egeanin a hooded look and a small bow; she returned it with an inclination of her head and a look just as guarded.

"You've found them?" Nynaeve exclaimed. "Are you sure? Speak, man. Have you swallowed your tongue?" And her with her warnings about talking in front of other people.

"I should have said I found where they were." He did not look at Egeanin again, but he chose his words carefully. "The woman with the white stripe in her hair led me to a house where she was staying with a number of other women, though few were ever seen outside. The locals thought they were rich escapees from the countryside. Little remains now save a few scraps of food in the pantry—even the servants are gone—but from one thing and another I would say they left late yesterday or early last night. I doubt they have any fear of the night in Tanchico."

Nynaeve had a fistful of her narrow braids in a white-knuckled grip. "You went inside?" she said in a very level voice. Elayne thought she was an inch from raising the stave dangling at her side.

Juilin seemed to think so, too. Eyeing the stave, he said, "You know very well I take no risks with them. An empty house has a look about it, a feel, no matter how big. You cannot chase thieves as long as I have without learning to see as they do."

"And if you had triggered a trap?" Nynaeve almost hissed the words. "Does your grand talent for *feeling* things extend to traps?" Juilin's dark face went a little gray; he wet his lips as if to explain or defend himself, but she cut him off. "We will talk of this later, *Master* Sandar." Her eyes shifted slightly toward Egeanin; finally she had remembered there were other ears there to hear. "Tell Rendra we will take tea in the Falling Blossoms Room."

"Chamber of Falling Blossoms," Elayne corrected softly, and Nynaeve shot her a look. Juilin's news had left the older woman in a bad humor.

He bowed deeply with his hands spread. "As you command, Mistress al'Meara, so I obey from the heart," he said wryly, then stuck his dark cap back on top of his head and stalked off, his back eloquently indignant. It must be uncomfortable to find yourself taking orders from someone with whom you had once tried to flirt.

"Fool man!" Nynaeve growled. "We should have left both of them on the dock in Tear."

"He is your servant?" Egeanin said slowly.

"Yes," Nynaeve snapped, just as Elayne said, "No."

They looked at each other, Nynaeve still frowning.

"Perhaps he is, in a way," Elayne sighed, right on top of Nynaeve's muttered, "I suppose he is not, at that."

"I . . . see," Egeanin said.

Rendra came bustling between the tables with a smile on her rose-bud lips behind her veil. Elayne wished she did not look so much like Liandrin. "Ah. You are so pretty this morning. Your dresses, they are magnificent. Beautiful." As if the honey-haired woman had not had as much to do with choosing the fabric and cut as they. Her own was red enough for a Tinker and definitely not suitable for public. "But you have been foolish again, yes? That is why the fine Juilin, he wears the large scowl. You should not worry him so." A twinkle in her big brown eyes said Juilin had found someone for his flirting. "Come. You will take your tea in the cool and the privacy, and if you must go out again, you will allow me to provide the bearers and the guards, yes? The pretty Elayne would not have lost so many purses if you were properly guarded. But we will not talk of such things now. Your tea, it is nearly prepared. Come." It had to be a learned skill, that was how Elayne saw it; you must have to learn how to talk without eating your veil.

The Chamber of Falling Blossoms, located down a short corridor off the common room, was a small, windowless room with a low table and carved chairs with red seat cushions. Nynaeve and Elayne took their meals there—with Thom or Juilin or both, when Nynaeve was not in a taking at them. The plastered brick walls, painted with a veritable grove of plum trees and a namesake shower of flowers, were thick enough to preclude any eavesdropping. Elayne practically tore her veil off and tossed the filmy scrap on the table before sitting; even Taraboner women did not try to eat or drink wearing the things. Nynaeve merely unfastened hers from her hair on one side.

Rendra kept up her chatter while they were being served, her topics bouncing from a new seamstress who could sew them dresses in the newest style from the thinnest imaginable silk—she suggested Egeanin try the woman, getting a level look for reply; it did not faze her even a trifle—to why they should listen to Juilin since the city was just too dangerous for a woman to go out alone now even in daylight, to a

scented soap that would put the finest sheen on their hair. Elayne
sometimes wondered how the woman ran such a successful inn when
she seemed to think of nothing but her hair and her clothes. That she
did was obvious; it was the how that puzzled Elayne. Of course, she did
wear pretty clothes; just not entirely *suitable*. The servant who brought
the tea and blue porcelain cups and tiny cakes on a tray was the slender, dark-eyed young man who had kept filling Elayne's winecup on
that very embarrassing night. And had tried again more than once,
though she had privately vowed never again to drink more than a single
cup. A handsome man, but she gave him her coolest stare, so that he
hurried from the room gladly.

Egeanin watched quietly until Rendra left, too. "You are not what I
expected," she said then, balancing her cup on her fingertips in an odd
way. "The innkeeper babbles of frivolities as if you were her sisters and
as foolish as she, and you allow it. The dark man—he is a servant of
sorts, I think—mocks you. That serving boy stares with open hunger in
his eyes, and you allow it. You are . . . Aes Sedai, are you not?"
Without waiting for an answer, she shifted her sharp blue eyes to
Elayne. "And you are of the. . . . You are nobly born. Nynaeve spoke
of your mother's palace."

"Such things do not count for very much in the White Tower,"
Elayne told her ruefully, hastily brushing cake crumbs from her chin. It
was very spicy cake; almost sharp. "If a queen went there to learn, she
would have to scrub floors like any other novice and jump when she
was told."

Egeanin nodded slowly. "So that is how you rule. By ruling the rulers. Do . . . many . . . queens go to be trained so?"

"None that I know of." Elayne laughed. "Though it is our tradition
in Andor for the Daughter-Heir to go. A good many noblewomen go,
really, though they usually do not want it known and most leave having
failed to even sense the True Source. It was only an example."

"You are also of the . . . a noble?" Egeanin asked, and Nynaeve
snorted.

"My mother was a farmwife, and my father herded sheep and
farmed tabac. Few where I come from can make do without wool and
tabac both to sell. What of your parents, Egeanin?"

"My father was a soldier, my mother the . . . an officer on a ship."
For a moment she sipped her unsweetened tea, studying them. "You
are searching for someone," she said at last. "For these women the
dark man spoke of. I do some small trade in information, among other

things. I have sources who tell me things. Perhaps I can help. I would not charge, except to ask you to tell me more of Aes Sedai."

"You have helped too much already," Elayne said hastily, remembering Nynaeve telling almost everything to Bayle Domon. "I *am* grateful, but we could not accept more." Letting this woman know about the Black Ajah and letting her become involved without knowing were equally out of the question. "Truly we could not."

Caught with her mouth half-open, Nynaeve glared at her. "I was about to say the same," she said in a flat voice, then went on more brightly. "Our gratitude certainly extends to answering questions, Egeanin. As much as we can." She surely meant there were a good many questions for which they had no answers, but Egeanin took it differently.

"Of course. I will not pry into the secret affairs of your White Tower."

"You seem very interested in Aes Sedai," Elayne said. "I cannot sense the ability in you, but perhaps you can learn to channel."

Egeanin almost dropped her porcelain cup. "It . . . can be *learned?* I did not. . . . No. No, I do not want to . . . to learn."

Her agitation made Elayne sad. Even among people not fearful of Aes Sedai, too many still feared anything to do with the One Power. "What *do* you want to know, Egeanin?"

Before the woman could speak, a rap at the door was followed by Thom, in the rich brown cloak he had taken to wearing when he went out. It certainly attracted less notice than the gleeman's patch-covered garment. In fact, it made him appear quite dignified, with that mane of white hair, though he should brush it more. Imagining him younger, Elayne thought she could see what had first attracted her mother. That did not absolve him of leaving, of course. She smoothed her face before he could see her frown.

"I was told you were not alone," he said, giving Egeanin a guarded look almost identical to Juilin's; men were always suspicious of anyone they did not know. "But I thought you might like to hear that the Children of the Light surrounded the Panarch's Palace this morning. The streets are beginning to buzz over it. It seems the Lady Amathera is to be invested as Panarch tomorrow."

"Thom," Nynaeve said wearily, "unless this Amathera is really Liandrin, I do not care if she becomes Panarch, King, and Wisdom of the whole Two Rivers all rolled together."

"The interesting thing," Thom said, limping to the table, "is that rumor says the Assembly refused to choose Amathera. Refused. So why is she being invested? Things this odd are worth noting, Nynaeve."

As he started to lower himself into a chair, she said quietly, "We are having a private conversation, Thom. I am sure you will find the common room more congenial." She took a sip of tea, eyeing him over the cup in clear expectation of his departure.

Flushing, he levered himself back up without ever having actually sat, but he did not leave immediately. "Whether the Assembly has changed its mind or not, this will likely cause riots. The streets still believe Amathera has been rejected. If you must insist on going out, you cannot go alone." He was looking at Nynaeve, but Elayne had the impression that he almost put a hand on her shoulder. "Bayle Domon is mired in that little room down near the docks, tying up his affairs in case he has to run, but he has agreed to provide fifty picked men, tough fellows used to a brawl and handy with knife or sword."

Nynaeve opened her mouth, but Elayne cut her off. "We are grateful, Thom, to you and Master Domon both. Please tell him we accept his kind and generous offer." Meeting Nynaeve's flat stare, she added meaningfully, "I would not want to be kidnapped on the streets in broad daylight."

"No," Thom said. "We would not want that." Elayne thought she heard a half-said "child" at the end of that, and this time he did touch her shoulder, a swift brush of fingers. "Actually," he went on, "the men are already waiting in the street outside. I am trying to find a carriage; those chairs are too vulnerable." He seemed to know he had gone too far, bringing Domon's men before they agreed, not to mention this talk of a carriage without a hint of asking first, but he faced them like an old wolf at bay, bushy eyebrows drawn down. "I would . . . regret . . . personally, if anything happened to you. The carriage will be here as soon as I can find a team. If there is one to be found."

Eyes wide, Nynaeve was obviously teetering on the edge of whether or not to give him an upbraiding he would never forget, and Elayne would not have minded adding a gentler admonishment. Somewhat gentler; child, indeed!

He took advantage of their hesitation to sweep a bow that would have graced any palace and departed while he had the chance.

Egeanin had set down her cup and was staring at them in consternation. Elayne supposed they had not given a very good appearance of being Aes Sedai, letting Thom bully them. "I must go," the woman said, rising and taking her staff from against the wall.

"But you have not asked your questions," Elayne protested. "We owe you answers to them, at the very least."

"Another time," Egeanin said after a moment. "If it is permitted, I will come another time. I need to learn about you. You are not what I expected." They assured her she could come any time they were there and tried to convince her to stay long enough to finish her tea and cakes, but she was adamant that she had to leave now.

Turning from seeing the woman to the door, Nynaeve put her fists on her hips. "Kidnap you? If you have forgotten, Elayne, it was me those men tried to grab!"

"To take you out of the way so they could seize me," Elayne said. "If you have forgotten, I *am* the Daughter-Heir of Andor. My mother would have made them wealthy to have me back."

"Perhaps," Nynaeve muttered doubtfully. "Well, at least they were nothing to do with Liandrin. That lot wouldn't send a pack of louts to try stuffing us in a sack. Why do men always do things without asking? Does growing hair on their chests sap their brains?"

The sudden change did not confuse Elayne. "We do not have to worry about finding bodyguards, at any rate. You do agree they are necessary, even if Thom did overstep himself?"

"I suppose so." Nynaeve had a remarkable dislike for admitting she was wrong. Thinking those men had been after *her,* for instance. "Elayne, do you realize we still have nothing except an empty house? If Juilin—or Thom—slips and lets himself be found out. . . . We must find the Black sisters without them suspecting, or we will never have a chance of following them to whatever this thing is that's dangerous to Rand."

"I know," Elayne said patiently. "We *have* discussed it."

The older woman frowned at nothing. "We still have not a glimmer as to what it is, or where."

"I know."

"Even if we could bag Liandrin and the rest right this minute, we cannot leave it floating about out there, waiting for someone else to find."

"I know that, Nynaeve." Reminding herself to be patient, Elayne softened her tone. "We will find them. They must make some sort of slip, and between Thom's rumors, and Juilin's thieves, and Bayle Domon's sailors, we will learn of it."

Nynaeve's frown became thoughtful. "Did you notice Egeanin's eyes when Thom mentioned Domon?"

"No. Do you think she knows him? Why would she not say so?"

"I do not know," Nynaeve said vexedly. "Her face did not change, but her eyes. . . . She was startled. She knows him. I wonder what—" Someone tapped softly on the door. "Is everyone in Tanchico going to march in on us?" she growled, jerking it open.

Rendra gave a start at the look on Nynaeve's face, but her ever-present smile returned immediately. "Forgive me for disturbing you, but there is the woman below who asks for you. Not by name, but she describes you as you stand. She says that she believes she knows you. She is. . . ." That rosebud mouth tightened in a slight grimace. "I forgot to ask her name. This morning I am the witless goat. She is a well-dressed woman, not yet to her middle years. Not of Tarabon." She gave a little shiver. "A stern woman, I think. When first she saw me, she looked at me as my older sister did when we were children and she was thinking of tying my braids to the bush."

"Or have they found us first?" Nynaeve said softly.

Elayne embraced the True Source before she thought of it, and felt a shudder of relief that she could, that she had not been shielded un-aware. If the woman below was Black Ajah. . . . But if she was, why announce herself? Even so, she wished the glow of *saidar* surrounded Nynaeve, too. If only the woman could channel without anger.

"Send her in," Nynaeve said, and Elayne realized she was very much aware of her lack, and afraid. As Rendra turned to go, Elayne began weaving flows of Air, thick as cables and ready to bind, flows of Spirit to shield another from the Source. If this woman so much as resembled one on their list, if she tried to channel a spark. . . .

The woman who stepped into the Chamber of Falling Blossoms, in a shimmering black silk gown of unfamiliar cut, was no one Elayne had ever seen before, and surely not on the list of the women who had gone with Liandrin. Dark hair spilling loose to her shoulders framed a stur-dily handsome face with large, dark eyes and smooth cheeks, but not with Aes Sedai agelessness. Smiling, she closed the door behind her. "Forgive me, but I thought you were—" The glow of *saidar* surrounded her, and she. . . .

Elayne released the True Source. There was something very com-manding in those dark eyes, in the halo around her, the pale radiance of the One Power. She was the most regal woman Elayne had ever seen. Elayne found herself hurriedly curtsying, flushing that she had considered. . . . What had she considered? So hard to think.

The woman studied them for a moment, then gave a satisfied nod and swept to the table, taking the carved chair at its head. "Come here where I can see you both more closely," she said in a peremptory voice. "Come. Yes. That's it."

Elayne realized she was standing beside the table, looking down at the dark-eyed, glowing woman. She did hope that was all right. On the other side of the table Nynaeve had a tangle of her long, thin braids gripped in her fist, but she stared at the visitor with a foolishly rapt expression. It made Elayne want to giggle.

"About what I have come to expect," the woman said. "Little more than girls, and obviously not close to half-trained. Strong, though; strong enough to be more than troublesome. Especially you." She fixed Nynaeve with her eyes. "You might become something one day. But you've blocked yourself, haven't you? We would have had that out of you though you howled for it."

Nynaeve still had that tight hold on her braids, but her face went from a pleased, girlish smile at praise to shamed lip-trembling. "I am sorry I blocked myself," she almost whimpered. "I'm afraid of it . . . all that power . . . the One Power . . . how can I—?"

"Be silent unless I ask a question," the woman said firmly. "And do not start crying. You are joyful at seeing me, ecstatic. All you want is to please me and answer my questions truthfully."

Nynaeve nodded vigorously, smiling even more rapturously than before. Elayne realized that she was, too. She was sure she could answer the questions first. Anything to please this woman.

"Now. Are you alone? Are there any other *Aes Sedai* with you?"

"No," Elayne said quickly in answer to the first question, and just as fast, to the second, "There are no Aes Sedai with us." Perhaps she should tell that they were not really Aes Sedai either. But she had not been asked that. Nynaeve glared at her, knuckles white on her braids, furious at being beaten to the answer.

"Why are you in this city?" the woman said.

"We are hunting Black sisters," Nynaeve burst out, shooting Elayne a triumphant look.

The handsome woman laughed. "So that is why I have not felt you channel before today. Wise of you to keep low when it is eleven to two. I have always followed that policy myself. Let other fools leap about in full view. They can be brought low by a spider hiding in the cracks, a spider they never see until it is too late. Tell me all you have discovered about these Black sisters, all you know of them."

Elayne spilled out everything, battling with Nynaeve to be first. It was not very much. Their descriptions, the *ter'angreal* they had stolen, the murders in the Tower and the fear of more Black sisters still there, aiding one of the Forsaken in Tear before the Stone fell, their flight here seeking something dangerous to Rand. "They were all staying in a house together," Elayne finished up, panting, "but they left last night."

"It seems you came very close," the woman said slowly. "Very close. *Ter'angreal.* Turn out your purses on the table, your pouches." They did, and she fingered quickly through coins and sewing kits and handkerchiefs and the like. "Do you have any *ter'angreal* in your rooms? *Angreal* or *sa'angreal?*"

Elayne was conscious of the twisted stone ring hanging between her breasts, but that was not the question. "No," she said. They had none of those things in their room.

Pushing everything away, the woman leaned back, speaking half to herself. "Rand al'Thor. So that is his name now." Her face crumpled in a momentary grimace. "An arrogant man who stank of piety and goodness. Is he still the same? No, do not bother to answer that. An idle question. So Be'lal is dead. The other sounds like Ishamael, to me. All his pride at being only half-caught, whatever the price—there was less human left in him than any of us when I saw him again; I think he half-believed he was the Great Lord of the Dark—all his three thousand years of machinations, and it comes to an untaught boy hunting him down. My way is best. Softly, softly, in the shadows. Something to control a man who can channel. Yes, it would have to be that." Her eyes turned sharp, studying them in turn. "Now. What to do with you."

Elayne waited patiently. Nynaeve wore a silly smile, her lips parted expectantly; it looked especially foolish with the way she was gripping her braids.

"You are too strong to waste; you may be useful one day. I would love to see Rahvin's eyes the day he meets you unblocked," she told Nynaeve. "I would put you off this hunt of yours, if I could. A pity compulsion is so limited. Still, with the little you have learned, you are too far behind to catch up now. I suppose I must collect you later and see to your . . . retraining." She stood, and suddenly Elayne's entire body tingled. Her brain seemed to shiver; she was conscious of nothing but the woman's voice, roaring in her ears from a great distance. "You will pick up your things from the table, and when you have replaced them where they belong, you will remember nothing of what happened here except that I came thinking you were friends I knew from the country. I was mistaken, I had a cup of tea, and I left."

Elayne blinked and wondered why she was tying her purse back beside her belt pouch. Nynaeve was frowning at her own hands, adjusting her pouch.

"A nice woman," Elayne said, rubbing her forehead. She had a head-ache coming on. "Did she give her name? I don't remember."

"Nice?" Nynaeve's hand came up and gave a sharp tug to her braids; she stared as if it had moved of its own accord. "I . . . do not think she did."

"What were we talking of when she came in?" Egeanin had just gone. What had it been?

"I remember what I was about to say." Nynaeve's voice firmed. "We must find the Black sisters without them suspecting, or we will never have a chance of following them to whatever this thing is that's danger-ous to Rand."

"I know," Elayne said patiently. Had she said that already? Of course not. "We *have* discussed it."

At the arched gates leading from the inn's small courtyard, Egeanin paused, studying the hard-faced men who lounged, barefoot and often bare-chested, among the idlers on this side of the narrow street. They looked as if they could use the curved boarding swords hanging at their belts or thrust through their sashes, but none of those faces looked familiar. If any of them had been on Bayle Domon's ship when she took him and it to Falme, she did not remember. If any had been, it was to be hoped none connected a woman in a riding dress to the woman in armor who had captured their vessel.

Suddenly she realized her palms were damp. Aes Sedai. Women who could wield the Power, and not decently leashed. She had sat at the same table with them, talked with them. They were not at all what she had expected; she could not dig that thought out of her head. They could channel, therefore they were dangerous to proper order, there-fore they must be safely leashed—and yet. . . . Not at all what she had been taught. It could be *learned.* Learned! As long as she could avoid Bayle Domon—he would surely recognize her—she should be able to return. She had to learn more. More than ever, she had to.

Wishing she had a hooded cloak, she took a firm grip on her staff and started up the street, threading her way into the passing throng. None of the sailors looked at her twice, and she watched them to be sure.

She did not see the pale-haired man in filthy Tanchican garb huddled against the front of a white-plastered wineshop on the other side of the street. His eyes, blue above a dingy veil and a thick mustache held in place with glue, followed her before sliding back to the Three Plum

Court. Standing, he crossed the street, ignoring the disgusting way people brushed against him. Egeanin had nearly spotted him when he had
forgotten himself enough to break that fool's arm. One of the Blood, as
such things were reckoned in these lands, reduced to begging and without enough honor to open his veins. Disgusting. Perhaps he could learn
more of what she was up to, in this inn, once they realized he had more
coin than his clothes suggested.

CHAPTER
47

The Truth of a Viewing

The papers scattered on Siuan Sanche's desk held little real inter-est for her, but she persevered. Others handled the day-to-day routine of the White Tower, of course, to leave the Amyrlin Seat free for important decisions, but her habit had always been to check one or two things at random each day, with no notice beforehand, and she would not break it now. She would not let herself be distracted by worries. Everything was sailing along according to plan. Shifting her striped stole, she dipped her pen carefully in the ink and ticked off another corrected total.

Today she was examining lists of kitchen purchases, and the mason's report on an addition to the library. The sheer number of petty pecula-tions people thought they could slip by always amazed her. So did the number that escaped notice by the women who oversaw these matters. For instance, Laras seemed to think watching accounts was beneath her since her title had been changed officially from simple chief cook to Mistress of the Kitchens. Danelle, on the other hand, the young Brown sister who was supposed to be watching Master Jovarin, the mason, was most likely letting herself be distracted by the books the fellow kept finding for her. That was the only way to explain her failure to question the number of workmen Jovarin claimed to have hired, with the first shipments of stone from Kandor just arriving at Northharbor. He could rebuild the entire library with that many men. Danelle was simply too dreamy, even for a Brown. Perhaps a little time on a farm working penance would wake her. Laras would be more difficult to discipline; she was not Aes Sedai, so her authority with undercooks and scullions and potboys could be swamped all too easily. But perhaps she, too, could be sent for a "rest" in the country. That would. . . .

With a snort of disgust Siuan threw her pen down, grimacing at the blot it made on a page of neatly totaled columns. "Wasting my time deciding whether to send Laras out to pull weeds," she muttered. "The woman is too fat to bend over far enough!"

It was not Laras's weight that had her temper jumping, and she knew it; the woman was no heavier now than she had always been, or so it seemed, and it never interfered with her running the kitchens. There was no news. That was what had her flapping like a fisher-bird whose catch had been stolen. One message from Moiraine that the al'Thor boy had *Callandor,* then nothing in the weeks since, although rumors in the streets were already beginning to get his name right. Still nothing.

Lifting the hinged lid of the ornately carved blackwood box where she kept her most secret papers, she rummaged inside. A small warding woven around the box ensured no hand but hers could safely open it.

The first paper she pulled out was a report that the novice who had seen Min's arrival had vanished from the farm she had been sent to, and the woman who owned the farm, too. Hardly unheard of for a novice to run away, but the farmer leaving too was troublesome. Sahra would have to be found, certainly—she had not progressed far enough in her training to be let loose—but there was no real reason to keep the report in the box. It mentioned neither Min's name nor the reason the girl had been sent to hoe cabbages, but she put it back anyway. These were days to take care that might seem unreasonable at another time.

A description of a gathering in Ghealdan to listen to this man who called himself the Prophet of the Lord Dragon. Masema, it seemed his name was. Odd. That was a Shienaran name. Nearly ten thousand people had come to listen to him speak from a hillside, proclaiming the return of the Dragon, a speech followed by a battle with soldiers trying to disperse them. Aside from the fact that the soldiers apparently got the worst of it, the interesting thing was that this Masema knew Rand al'Thor's name. That definitely went back into the box.

A report that nothing had yet been found of Mazrim Taim. No reason for that to be in there. Another on worsening conditions in Arad Doman and Tarabon. Ships vanishing along the Aryth Ocean coast. Rumors of Tairen incursions into Cairhien. She was getting into the habit of putting everything in this box; none of that needed to be kept secret. Two sisters had vanished in Illian, and another in Caemlyn. She shivered, wondering where the Forsaken were. Too many of her agents had gone silent. There were lionfish out there, and she was swimming in darkness. There it was. The silk-thin slip of paper crackled as she unrolled it.

The sling has been used. The shepherd holds the sword.

The Hall of the Tower had voted as she had expected, unanimously and with no need for arm-twisting, much less invoking on her authority. If a man had drawn *Callandor,* he must be the Dragon Reborn, and that man had to be guided by the White Tower. Three Sitters for three different Ajahs had proposed holding all plans close in the Hall before she even suggested it; the surprise had been that one was Elaida, but then the Reds would surely want the tightest hawsers possible kept on a man who could channel. The sole problem had been to stop a delegation from being sent to Tear to take him in hand, and that had not really been difficult, not when she was able to say that her news came from an Aes Sedai who had already managed to put herself close to the man.

But what was he doing now? Why had Moiraine not sent further word? Impatience hung so thick in the Hall now that she almost expected the air to sparkle. She kept a tight hold on her anger. *Burn the woman! Why hasn't she sent word?*

The door crashed open, and she straightened furiously as more than a dozen women strode into her study, led by Elaida. All wore their shawls, most red-fringed, but cool-faced Alviarin, a White, was at Elaida's side, and Joline Maza, a slender Green, and plump Shemerin of the Yellow came close behind with Danelle, her big blue eyes not dreamy at all. In fact, Siuan saw at least one woman from every Ajah except the Blue. Some looked nervous, but most wore grim determination, and Elaida's dark eyes held stern confidence, even triumph.

"What is the meaning of this?" Siuan snapped, slapping the black-wood box shut with a sharp crack. She bounced to her feet and strode around the desk. First Moiraine and now this! "If this is about *Tairen* matters, Elaida, you know better than to bring others into it. And you know better than to walk in here as if this were your mother's kitchen! Make your apologies and leave before I make you wish you were an ignorant novice again!"

Her cold rage should have sent them scurrying, but though a few shifted uneasily, none made a move toward the door. Little Danelle actually smirked at her. And Elaida calmly reached out and pulled the striped stole from Siuan's shoulders. "You will not need this any longer," she said. "You were never fit for it, Siuan."

Shock turned Siuan's tongue to stone. This was madness. This was impossible. In a rage she reached for *saidar*—and suffered her second shock. A barrier lay between her and the True Source, like a wall of thick glass. She stared at Elaida in disbelief.

As if to mock her, the radiance of *saidar* sprang up around Elaida. She stood helpless as the Red sister wove flows of Air around her from shoulders to waist, crushing her arms to her side. She could barely breathe. "You must be mad!" she rasped. "All of you! I'll have your hides for this! Release me!" No one answered; they almost seemed to ignore her.

Alviarin ruffled through the papers on the table, quickly yet unhurriedly. Joline and Danelle and others began tilting up the books on the reading stands, shaking them to see if anything fell out from between the pages. The White sister gave a small hiss of vexation at not finding what she sought on the table, then flipped open the lid of the blackwood box. Instantly the box flared in a ball of flame.

Alviarin leaped back with a cry, shaking a hand where blisters were already forming. "Warded," she muttered, as close to open anger as a White ever came. "So small that I never felt it until too late." Nothing remained of the box and its contents but a heap of gray ash atop a square charred into the tabletop.

Elaida's face showed no disappointment. "I promise you, Siuan, that you will tell me every word that burned, who it was meant for, and to what purpose."

"You must be taken by the Dragon!" Siuan snapped. "I will have your hide for this, Elaida. All of your hides! You will be lucky if the Hall of the Tower doesn't vote to still all of you!"

Elaida's tiny smile did not touch her eyes. "The Hall convened not an hour ago—enough Sitters to meet our laws—and by unanimous vote, as required, you are no longer Amyrlin. It is done, and we are here to see it enforced."

Siuan's stomach turned to ice, and a small voice in the back of her head shrieked, *What do they know? Light, how much do they know? Fool! Blind, fool woman!* She kept her face smooth, though. This was not the first hard corner she had ever been in. A fifteen-year-old girl with nothing but her bait knife, hauled into an alley by four hard-eyed louts with their bellies full of cheap wine—that had been harder to escape than this. So she told herself.

"Enough to meet the laws?" she sneered. "A bare minimum, heavy with your friends and those you can influence or bully." That Elaida had been able to convince even a relatively small number of Sitters was enough to dry her throat, but she would not let it show. "When the full Hall meets, with all the Sitters, you'll learn your mistake. Too late! There has never been a rebellion inside the Tower; a thousand years from now they'll be using your fate to teach novices what happens to rebels." Tendrils of doubt crept onto some of those faces; it seemed Elaida did not have as tight a grip on her conspirators as she thought. "It's time to stop trying to hack a hole in the hull, and start bailing. Even you can still mitigate your offense, Elaida."

Elaida waited with chill calm until she was done. Then her full-armed slap exploded across Siuan's face; she staggered, silver-black flecks dancing in her vision.

"You are finished," Elaida said. "Did you think I—we—would allow you to destroy the Tower? Bring her!"

Siuan stumbled as two of the Reds pushed her forward. Barely keeping her feet, she glared at them, but went as they directed. Who did she need to get word to? Whatever charges had been brought, she could counter them, given time. Even charges involving Rand; they could not fasten more than rumors to her, and she had played the Great Game too long to be beaten by rumors. Unless they had Min; Min could clothe rumors in truth. She ground her teeth. *Burn my soul, I'll use this lot for fish bait!*

In the antechamber, she stumbled again, but not from pushing, this time. She had half-hoped that Leane had been away from her post, but the Keeper stood as Siuan did, arms stiffly at her sides, mouth working soundlessly, furiously, around a gag of Air. She had certainly sensed Leane being bound and never realized it; in the Tower, there was always the feel of women channeling.

Yet it was not the sight of Leane that made her miss her step, but the tall, slender gray-haired man stretched on the floor with a knife rising from his back. Alric had been her Warder for close to twenty years, never complaining when her path kept them in the Tower, never muttering when being the Amyrlin's Warder sent him hundreds of leagues from her, a thing none of the Gaidin liked.

She cleared her throat, but her voice was still husky when she spoke. "I'll have your hide salted and stretched in the sun for this, Elaida. I swear it!"

"Consider your own hide, Siuan," Elaida said, moving closer to stare her in the eyes. "There is more to this than has been revealed so far. I know it. And you are going to tell me every last scrap of it. Every—last —scrap." The sudden quiet in her voice was more frightening than all her hard stares had been. "I promise it, Siuan. Take her below!"

Clutching bolts of blue silk, Min strolled in through the North Gate near midday, her simper all ready for the guards with the Flame of Tar Valon on their chests, the girlish swirl of her green skirts that Elmindreda would give. She had actually begun before she realized there were no guards. The heavy iron-strapped door of the star-shaped guardhouse stood open; the guardhouse itself looked empty. It was impossible. No gate to the Tower grounds was ever unguarded. Halfway to the huge bone-white shaft of the Tower itself, a plume of smoke was rising above the trees. It seemed to be near the quarters for the young men who studied under the Warders. Maybe the fire had pulled the guards away.

Still feeling a little uneasy, she started down the unpaved path through the wooded part of the grounds, shifting the bolts of silk. She did not really want another dress, but how could she refuse when Laras pressed a purse of silver into her hands and told her to use it for this silk the stout woman had seen; she claimed it was just the color to set off "Elmindreda's" complexion. Whether or not she wanted her complexion set off was less important than keeping Laras's goodwill.

A rattle of swords reached her ears through the trees. The Warders must have their students practicing harder than usual.

It was all very irritating. Laras and her beauty hints, Gawyn and his jokes, Galad paying her compliments and never realizing what his face and smile did to a woman's pulse. Was this how Rand wanted her? Would he actually *see* her, if she wore dresses and simpered at him like a brainless chit?

He has no right to expect it, she thought furiously. It was all his fault. She would not be there now, wearing a fool dress and smiling like an idiot, if not for him. *I wear coat and breeches, and that is that! Maybe I'll wear a dress once in a while—maybe!—but not to make some man look at me! I wager he's staring at some Tairen woman with half her bosom exposed right this minute. I can wear a dress like that. Let's see what he thinks when he sees me in this blue silk. I'll have a neckline down to—* What was she thinking? The man had robbed her of her wits! The

Amyrlin Seat was keeping her here, useless, and Rand al'Thor was addling her brain! *Burn him! Burn him for doing this to me!*

The clash of swords came again from the distance, and she stopped as a horde of young men burst out of the trees ahead of her carrying spears and bared blades, Gawyn at their head. She recognized others from among those who had come to study with the Warders. Shouts rose somewhere else in the grounds, a roar of angry men.

"Gawyn! What is happening?"

He whirled at the sound of her voice. Worry and fear filled his blue eyes, and his face was a mask of determination not to give in to them. "Min. What are you doing—? Get out of the grounds, Min. It is dangerous." A handful of the young men ran on, but most waited impatiently for him. It seemed to her that most of the Warders' students were there.

"Tell me what's happening, Gawyn!"

"The Amyrlin was deposed this morning. Leave, Min!"

The bolts of silk fell from her hands. "Deposed? It can't be! How? Why? In the name of the Light, why?"

"Gawyn!" one of the young men called, and others took it up, brandishing their weapons. "Gawyn! The White Boar! Gawyn!"

"I have no time," he told her urgently. "There's fighting everywhere. They say Hammar is trying to break Siuan Sanche free. I have to go to the Tower, Min. Leave! Please!"

He turned and set out at a run toward the Tower. The others followed, bristling with upraised weapons, some still shouting, "Gawyn! The White Boar! Gawyn! Forward the Younglings!"

Min stared after them. "You did not say what side you are on, Gawyn," she whispered.

The sounds of fighting were louder, clearer now that she was paying attention, and the shouts and yells, the clash of steel on steel, seemed to come from every direction. The clamor made her skin crawl and her knees shake; this could not be happening, not here. Gawyn was right. It would be much the safer thing, much the smarter, to leave the Tower grounds immediately. Only there was no telling when or if she would be allowed back, and she could not think of much good she could do outside.

"What good can I do inside?" she asked herself fiercely.

But she did not turn back toward the gate. Leaving the silk where it lay, she hurried into the trees, looking for a place to hide. She did not think anyone would spit "Elmindreda" like a goose—shivering, she wished she had not thought of it that way—but there was no use in taking foolish chances. Sooner or later the fighting had to die down, and by that time she needed to decide what to do next.

In the pitch blackness of the cell, Siuan opened her eyes, stirred, winced, and was still. Was it morning yet outside? The questioning had gone on for a long time. She tried to forget pain in the luxury of knowing she was still breathing. The rough stone beneath her scraped her welts and bruises, though, those on her back. Sweat stung all of them—she felt a solid mass of pain from knees to shoulders—and made her shiver in the cold air, besides. *They could have left me my shift, at least.* The air smelled of old dust and dried mold, of age. One of the deep cells. No one had been confined down here since Artur Hawkwing's time. Not since Bonwhin.

She grimaced into the dark; there was no forgetting. Clamping her teeth, she pushed up to a sitting position on the stone floor and felt around her for a wall to lean against. The stone blocks of the wall were cool against her back. *Small things,* she told herself. *Think of small things. Heat. Cold. I wonder when they'll bring me some water. If they will.*

She could not help feeling for her Great Serpent ring. It was no longer on her finger. Not that she expected it; she thought she remembered when they had ripped it off. Things had grown hazy after a time. Thankfully, blessedly hazy. But she remembered telling them everything, eventually. Almost everything. The triumph of holding back a scrap here, a bit there. In between howling answers, eager to answer if only they would stop, even for a little while, if only. . . . She wrapped her arms around herself to stop her shudders; it did not work very well. *I will remain calm. I am not dead. I must remember that above everything else. I am not dead.*

"Mother?" Leane's unsteady voice came out of the darkness. "Are you awake, Mother?"

"I'm awake," Siuan sighed. She had hoped they had released Leane, put her out of the city. Guilt stabbed her at feeling a bit of comfort from the presence of the other woman sharing her cell. "I am sorry I got you into this, daugh—" No. She had no right to call her that, now. "I am sorry, Leane."

There was a long moment of silence. "Are you . . . all right, Mother?"

"Siuan, Leane. Just Siuan." Despite herself she tried to embrace *saidar.* There was nothing there. Not for her. Only the emptiness inside. Never again. A lifetime of purpose, and now she was rudderless, adrift on a sea far darker than this cell. She scrubbed a tear from her cheek, angry at letting it fall. "I am not the Amyrlin Seat anymore, Leane." Some of the anger crept into her voice. "I suppose Elaida will be raised in my place. If she hasn't been already. I swear, one day I will feed that woman to the silverpike!"

Leane's only answer was a long, despairing breath.

The grate of a key in the rusty iron lock brought Siuan's head up; no one had thought to oil the works before throwing Leane and her in, and the corroded parts did not want to turn. Grimly she forced herself to her feet. "Up, Leane. Get up." After a moment she heard the other woman complying, and muttering to herself between soft moans.

In a slightly louder voice, Leane said, "What good will it do?"

"At least they won't find us huddling on the floor and weeping." She tried to make her voice firm. "We can fight, Leane. As long as we are alive, we can fight." *Oh, Light, they stilled me! They* stilled *me!*

Forcing her mind to blankness, she clenched her fists, and tried to dig her toes into the uneven stone floor. She wished the noise in her throat did not sound so much like a whimper.

Min set her bundles on the floor and tossed back her cloak so she could use both hands on the key. Twice as long as her hand, it was as rusty as the lock, just like the other keys on the big iron ring. The air was cold and damp, as though summer did not reach this far down.

"Hurry, child," Laras muttered, holding the lantern for Min, peering both ways down the otherwise dark stone hall. It was hard to believe that the woman, with all her chins, had ever been a beauty, but Min surely thought her beautiful now.

Fighting the key, she shook her head. She had encountered Laras while sneaking back to her room for the plain gray riding dress she now wore, and for a few other things. Actually, she had found the massive woman looking for *her*, in a tizzy of worry about "Elmindreda," exclaiming over how lucky Min was to be safe and proposing to all but lock her in her room until the trouble was past to keep her so. She was still not sure how Laras had wormed her intentions out of her, and she still could not get over her shock when the woman reluctantly announced she would help. *A venturesome lass after her own heart indeed. Well, I hope she can—how did she put it?—keep me out of the pickling kettle.* The bloody key would *not* turn; she threw all of her weight into trying to twist it.

In truth, she was grateful to Laras in more ways than one. It was doubtful she could have readied everything by herself, or even found some of it, surely not this quickly. Besides which. . . . Besides which, when she ran into Laras, she had already begun telling herself she was a fool even to think of doing this, that she should be on a horse and off for Tear while she had the chance, before someone decided to add her head to those decorating the front of the Tower. Running away, she suspected, would have been the sort of thing she would never have been able to forget. That alone had made her grateful enough not to object in the slightest when Laras added some pretty dresses to what she herself had already packed. The rouges and powders could always be "lost" somewhere. *Why won't this bloody key turn? Maybe Laras can—*

The key shifted suddenly, twisted with a snap so loud that Min feared something had broken. But when she pushed at the rough wooden door, it opened. Snatching up the bundles, she stepped into the bare stone cell—and stopped in confusion.

The lantern light revealed two women clad only in dark bruises and red welts, shielding their eyes from the sudden light, but for a moment Min was not sure they were the right two. One was tall and coppery-skinned, the other shorter, sturdier, more fair. The faces looked right—almost right—and untouched by whatever had been done to them, so she should have been certain. But the agelessness that marked Aes Sedai seemed to have melted away; she would have had no hesitation at all in thinking these women were just six or seven years older than herself at most, and not Aes Sedai at all. Her face heated with embarrassment at the thought. She saw no images, no auras, around either; there were always images and auras around Aes Sedai. *Stop that,* she told herself.

"Where—?" one of the two began wonderingly, then paused to clear her throat. "How did you get those keys?" It was Siuan Sanche's voice.

"It is her." Laras sounded disbelieving. She poked Min with a thick finger. "Hurry, child! I am too old and slow to be having adventures."

Min gave her a startled look; the woman had *insisted* on coming; she would not be left out, she had said. Min wanted to ask Siuan why the pair of them suddenly looked so much younger, but there was no time for frivolous questions. *I'm too bloody used to being Elmindreda!*

Thrusting one of her bundles at each of the naked women, she spoke rapidly. "Clothes. Dress as quickly as you can. I don't know how much time we have. I let the guard think I'd trade a few kisses for a chance to repay you for a grudge, and while he was distracted, Laras came up behind him and cracked him over the head with a rolling pin. I do not know how long he'll sleep." She leaned back through the door to peer worriedly down the hall toward the guardroom. "We had best hurry."

Siuan had already undone her bundle and begun to put on the clothes it contained. Except for a linen shift, they were all plain woolens in shades of brown, suitable for farm women come to the White Tower to consult the Aes Sedai, though the skirts divided for riding were a little unusual. Laras had done most of the needlework; Min had mostly just stuck herself. Leane was also covering her nakedness, but she seemed more interested in the short-bladed knife hanging from her belt than in the clothes themselves.

Three plainly dressed women had a chance, at least, of leaving the Tower without attracting notice. A number of petitioners and people seeking help had been caught inside the Tower by the fighting; three more creeping out of hiding should be hustled into the street at worst. So long as they were not recognized. The other women's faces might help, too. No one was likely to take a pair of young—young-seeming, at least—women for the Amyrlin Seat and the Keeper of the Chronicles. Former Amyrlin and former Keeper, she reminded herself.

"Only one guard?" Siuan said, wincing as she tugged on thick stockings. "Strange. They'd guard a cutpurse better than that." Eyeing Laras, she pushed her feet into the sturdy shoes. "It is good to see some do not believe the charges against me. Whatever they are."

The stout woman frowned and lowered her chins, giving herself a fourth. "I am loyal to the Tower," she said sternly. "Such matters are not for me. I am only a cook. This foolish girl has had me remembering too much of being a foolish girl myself. I think— Seeing you— It is time for me to remember I am not a willowy girl any longer." She pushed the lantern into Min's hands.

Min caught her stout arm as she turned to go. "Laras, you won't give us away? Not now, after all you have done."

The woman's wide face split in a smile, half-reminiscent, half-rueful. "Oh, Elmindreda, you do remind me of me when I was your age. Foolish doings, and near to getting myself hanged, sometimes. I will not betray you, child, but I must live here. When Second is rung, I will send a girl with wine for the guard. If he has not wakened or been discovered by then, that will give you more than an hour." Turning to the other two women, she suddenly wore the hard scowl Min had seen directed at undercooks and the like. "You use that hour well, hear! They mean to stick you in the scullery, I understand, so they can haul you out for examples. I'd not care one way or the other—such matters are for Aes Sedai, not cooks; one Amyrlin is the same as another, to me—but if you get this child caught, you can expect me to be striping your hides from sunup to sundown whenever you're not head-down in greasy pots or cleaning slop jars! You will wish they had cut off your heads before I am done. And don't think they'll believe I helped. Everyone knows I keep to my kitchens. You mark me, and jump!" The smile popped back onto her face, and she pinched Min's cheek. "You hurry them along, child. Oh, I am going to miss dressing you. Such a pretty child." With a last vigorous pinch, she waddled out of the cell at a near trot.

Min rubbed her cheek irritably; she hated it when Laras did that. The woman was as strong as a horse. Near to *hanging?* What kind of "lively girl" had Laras been?

Gingerly pulling her dress over her head, Leane sniffed loudly. "To think she could speak to you in that manner, Mother!" Her face popped out at the top, scowling. "I am surprised she helped at all if she feels that way."

"But she did help," Min told her. "Remember that. And I think she'll keep her word not to give us away. I am sure of it." Leane sniffed again.

Siuan swung her cloak around her shoulders. "It makes a difference, Leane, that I have no more claim to that title. It makes a difference when tomorrow you and I might be two of her scullery girls." Leane clasped her hands to keep them from shaking and would not look at her. Siuan went on calmly, if in a dry tone. "I also suspect Laras will keep her word about . . . other things . . . so even if you don't care whether Elaida hangs us up like a pair of netted sharks for the world to see, I suggest you move yourself. Myself, I hated greasy pots when I was a girl, and I don't doubt I still would."

Leane sullenly began doing up the laces of the country dress.

Siuan turned her attention to Min. "You may not be so eager to help us when I tell you we've both been . . . stilled." Her voice did not shake, but it was stiff with the effort of saying the word, and her eyes looked pained, and lost. It was a shock to realize her calm was all on the surface. "Any one of the Accepted could tie the pair of us into a running sheepsfoot, Min. Most of the novices could."

"I know," Min said, careful to keep her tone clear of the smallest hint of sympathy. Sympathy now might break what self-control the other women had left, and she needed them in control of themselves. "It was announced at every square in the city, and posted wherever they could nail up a notice. But you are still alive." Leane gave a bitter laugh, which she ignored. "We had best go. That guard might wake, or somebody check on him."

"Lead, Min," Siuan said. "We are in your hands." After a moment Leane gave a short nod and hurriedly donned her cloak.

In the guardroom at the end of the dark hall, the lone guard lay stretched out, facedown on the dusty floor. The helmet that would have saved him a sore head sat on the rough plank table beside the single lantern that provided the room's light. He seemed to be breathing all right. Min did not spare him more than a glance, though she hoped he was not badly hurt; he had not tried to press the advantage of her offer.

She hurried Siuan and Leane through the far door, all thick planks and wide iron straps, up the narrow, stone stairs. They had to keep moving. Passing for petitioners would not save them from questioning if they were seen coming from the cells.

They saw no more guards, nor anyone else, as they climbed out of the bowels of the Tower, but Min still found herself holding her breath until they reached the small door that let into the Tower proper. Cracking it just enough to poke her head through, she peeked both ways down the corridor.

Gilded lamp stands stood against frieze-banded walls of white marble. To the right two women moved swiftly out of sight without looking back. The sureness of their steps marked them Aes Sedai even if she could not see their faces; in the Tower, even a queen walked hesitantly. In the other direction half a dozen men stalked away, just as clearly Warders, with their wolfish grace and cloaks that faded into the surroundings.

She waited until the Warders were gone, too, before slipping through the doorway. "It's clear. Come on. Keep your hoods up and your heads down. Act a little frightened." For her part, it was no pretense. From the silent way the two women followed her, she did not think they needed to pretend either.

The halls of the Tower were seldom full, yet now they seemed empty. Occasionally someone appeared for a moment ahead of them, or down a side corridor, but whether Aes Sedai or Warder or servant, all were hurrying, too intent on their own affairs to notice anyone else. The Tower was silent, too.

Then they passed a crossing hallway where dark blotches of dried blood flecked the pale green floor tiles. Two larger patches stretched off in long smears, as if bodies had been dragged away.

Siuan stopped, staring. "What has happened?" she demanded. "Tell me, Min!" Leane gripped the hilt of her belt knife and peered around as if expecting an attack.

"Fighting," Min said reluctantly. She had hoped the two women would be out of the Tower grounds, even out of the city, before learning of this. She herded them around the dark stains, prodded them on when they tried to look back. "It began yesterday, right after you were taken, and did not stop until maybe two hours ago. Not completely."

"You mean the Gaidin?" Leane exclaimed. "Warders, fighting *each other?*"

"Warders, the guardsmen, everyone. It started when some men who came claiming to be masons—two or three hundred of them—tried to seize the Tower itself right after your arrest was announced."

Siuan scowled. "Danelle! I should have realized there was more to it than not paying attention." Her face twisted more, until Min thought she might begin crying. "Artur Hawkwing could not do it, but we did it ourselves." Edge of tears or not, her voice was fierce. "The Light help us, we have broken the Tower." Her long sigh seemed to empty her of breath, and anger, too. "I suppose," she said sadly after a moment, "I should be glad that some of the Tower supported me, but I almost wish they had not." Min tried to keep her face expressionless, but those sharp blue eyes seemed to interpret every flicker of an eyelash. "Or did they support me, Min?"

"Some did." She had no intention of telling her how few, not yet. But she had to prevent Siuan thinking she still had partisans inside the Tower. "Elaida didn't wait to find out if the Blue Ajah would stand for you or not. There isn't a Blue sister still in the Tower, not alive, I know that."

"Sheriam?" Leane asked anxiously. "Anaiya?"

"I don't know. There are not many Greens left, either. Not in the Tower. The other Ajahs split, one way and another. Most of the Reds are still here. As far as I know, everybody who opposed Elaida has either fled or else they are dead. Siuan. . . ." It seemed odd, calling her that—Leane muttered angrily under her breath—but calling her Mother would only be a mockery now. "Siuan, the charges posted against you claim you and Leane arranged Mazrim Taim's escape. Logain got away during the fighting, and they've blamed that on you, too. They don't quite name you Darkfriends—I suppose that would be too close to Black Ajah—but they do not miss by much. I think everyone is meant to understand, though."

"They won't even admit the truth," Siuan said softly, "that they mean to do exactly what they pulled me down for."

"Darkfriends?" Leane murmured in bewilderment. "They named us . . . ?"

"Why would they not?" Siuan breathed. "What would they not dare, when they dared so much?"

They hunched their shoulders in their cloaks and let Min lead them as she would. She just wished their faces did not look so hopeless.

As they drew nearer an outside door, she began to breathe more easily. She had horses hidden in a wooded part of the grounds, not far from one of the western gates. There was still the question of how easy it would be to actually ride out, but once they reached the horses she would feel the next thing to free. Surely the gate guards would not stop three women leaving. She kept telling herself that.

The door she sought appeared ahead—a small, plain-paneled door, letting onto a path not much used, just opposite where this hall met the broad corridor that ran all the way around the Tower—and Elaida's face caught her eye, sweeping down the outer corridor toward her.

Min's knees thudded onto the floor tiles, and she huddled, head down and face hidden by her hood, heart trying to pound through her ribs. *A petitioner, that's all I am. Just a simple woman, with nothing to do with what's happened. Oh, Light, please!* She raised her head just enough to peek under the edge of her hood, half-expecting to see a gloating Elaida staring down at her.

Elaida swept by without a glance in Min's direction, the broad, striped stole of the Amyrlin Seat around her shoulders. Alviarin followed, wearing the stole of the Keeper of the Chronicles, white for her Ajah. A dozen or more Aes Sedai passed at Alviarin's heels, mostly Reds, though Min saw two yellow-fringed shawls, a green one and a brown. Six Warders flanked the procession, hands on hilts and eyes wary. Those eyes swept across the three kneeling women and dismissed them.

They were all three kneeling, Min realized, and realized, too, that she had almost expected Siuan and Leane to launch themselves at Elaida's throat. Both women had lifted their heads just enough to watch the procession make its way on down the corridor.

"Very few women have been stilled," Siuan said, as if to herself, "and none have survived long, but it is said that one way to survive is to find something you want as much as you wanted to channel." That lost look was gone from her eyes. "At first I thought I wanted to gut Elaida and hang her in the sun to dry. Now I know I want nothing—nothing!—so much as the day I can tell that leech of a woman that she'll live a long life showing others what happens to anyone who claims I am a Dark-friend!"

"And Alviarin," Leane said in a tight voice. "And Alviarin!"

"I was afraid they'd sense me," Siuan went on, "but there is nothing for them to sense, now. An advantage to having been . . . stilled, it seems." Leane jerked her head angrily, and Siuan said, "We must use whatever advantages we can find. And be glad for them." The last sounded as if she were trying to convince herself.

The final Warder disappeared around the distant curve, and Min swallowed the lump in her throat. "We can talk of advantages later," she croaked, and stopped to swallow again. "Let us just go to the horses. That *has* to have been the worst."

Indeed, as they hurried out of the Tower into the noonday sun, it seemed the worst must have passed. A column of smoke rising toward a cloudless sky in the east of the Tower grounds was the only sign of old trouble. Groups of men moved in the distance, but none gave a second glance to the three women as they scurried past the library, which was built like towering waves frozen in stone. A footpath led deeper into the grounds and westward, into a wood of oaks and evergreens that could have stood far from any city. Min's steps lightened when she found the three saddled horses still tied where she and Laras had left them, in a small clearing surrounded by leatherleaf and paperbark.

Siuan went immediately to a stout, shaggy mare two hands shorter than the others. "A suitable mount for my present circumstances. And she looks more placid than the other two; I was never a good rider." She stroked the mare's nose, and the mare nuzzled into her palm. "What is her name, Min? Do you know?"

"Bela. She belongs to—"

"Her horse." Gawyn stepped from behind a wide-trunked paperbark, one hand on the long hilt of his sword. The blood streaking his face made exactly the pattern Min had seen in her viewing, her first day back in Tar Valon. "I knew you must be up to something, Min, when I saw her horse." His red-gold hair was matted with blood, his blue eyes half-dazed, but he walked toward them smoothly, a tall man with a catlike grace. A cat stalking mice.

"Gawyn," Min began, "we—"

His sword was out of its scabbard, flicking back Siuan's hood, sharp edge laid against the side of her throat, all faster than Min could follow. Siuan's breath caught audibly, and she was still, looking up at him, outwardly as serene as though she yet wore the stole.

"Don't, Gawyn!" Min gasped. "You must not!" She took a step

toward him, but he flung up his free hand without looking at her, and she stopped. He was as tight as coiled steel, ready to burst out in any direction. She noticed Leane had shifted her cloak to hide one hand and prayed the woman was not fool enough to draw her belt knife.

Gawyn studied Siuan's face, then slowly nodded. "It is you. I was not sure, but it is. This . . . disguise cannot—" He did not appear to move, but a sudden widening of Siuan's eyes spoke of a keen edge pressing harder. "Where are my sister and Egwene? What have you done with them?" Most frightening to Min, with that blood-masked face and half-glazed eyes, with his body tensed almost to quivering and his hand upflung as if he had forgotten it, he never raised his voice or put any emotion into it. He only sounded tired, more tired than she had ever heard anyone sound in her life.

Siuan's voice was nearly as neutral. "The last I heard from them, they were safe and well. I cannot say where they are, now. Would you rather they were here, in the middle of this feeding frenzy?"

"No Aes Sedai word games," he said softly. "Tell me where they were, straight out, so I know you speak the truth."

"Illian," Siuan said without hesitation. "In the city itself. They are studying with an Aes Sedai named Mara Tomanes. They should still be there."

"Not Tear," he murmured. For a moment he appeared to think that over. Abruptly, he said, "They say you are a Darkfriend. Black Ajah, that would be, would it not?"

"If you really believe that," Siuan said calmly, "then strike off my head."

Min almost screamed as his knuckles whitened on his sword hilt. Slowly she reached out and rested her fingers against his outstretched wrist, careful not to make him think she meant to do anything more than touch. It was like resting her fingers on rock. "Gawyn, you know me. You can't think I would help the Black Ajah." His eyes never wavered from Siuan's face, never blinked. "Gawyn, Elayne supports her and everything she's done. Your own sister, Gawyn." His flesh was still stone. "Egwene believes in her, too, Gawyn." His wrist trembled under her fingers. "I swear it, Gawyn. Egwene believes."

His eyes flickered to her, then back to Siuan. "Why shouldn't I drag you back by the scruff of your neck? Give me a reason."

Siuan met his stare with a good deal more calm than Min felt. "You could do it, and I suppose my struggles wouldn't give you much more trouble than a kitten's. Yesterday, I was one of the most powerful women in the world. Perhaps the most powerful. Kings and queens would come if I summoned them, even if they hated the Tower and all it stood for. Today, I'm afraid that I may have nothing to eat tonight, and that I'll have to sleep under a bush. In the space of one day I've been reduced from the most powerful woman in the world to one hoping to find a farm where I might earn my keep in the fields. Whatever you think I have done, isn't that a fitting punishment?"

"Perhaps," he said after a moment. Min took a deep breath of relief as he resheathed his sword in a flowing motion. "But that is not why I will let you go. Elaida might take your head yet, and I cannot allow that. I want what you know to be there, if I need it."

"Gawyn," Min said, "come with us." A Warder-trained swordsman might be useful in the days to come. "That way, you'd have her ready to hand to answer your questions." Siuan's gaze flickered to her, not really leaving Gawyn's face and not exactly indignant; she pressed on anyway. "Gawyn, Egwene and Elayne believe in her. Can't you believe, too?"

"Do not ask more than I can give," he said quietly. "I will take you to the nearest gate. You would never get out without me. That's all I can do, Min, and it is more than I should. Your arrest has been ordered; did you know that?" His eyes swung back to Siuan. "If anything happens to them," he said in that expressionless voice, "to Egwene or my sister, I will find you, wherever you hide, and I will make sure the same happens to you." Abruptly he stalked a dozen paces away and stood with his arms folded, head down as if he could not bear to look at them any longer.

Siuan half-raised a hand to her throat; a tiny line of red on the fair skin marked where his blade had rested. "I've been too long with the Power," she said, a trifle unsteadily. "I had forgotten what it is like to face someone who can pick you up and snap you like a thread." She peered at Leane then, as if seeing her for the first time, and touched her own face as though unsure what it looked like. "From what I have read it is supposed to take longer to fade, but perhaps Elaida's rough treatment had something to do with it. A disguise, he called it, and it may serve for one." She clambered awkwardly onto Bela's back, handling the reins as if the shaggy mare were a spirited stallion. "Another advantage, it seems, to being. . . . I have to learn to say it without flinching. I have been stilled." She said the words slowly and deliberately, then nodded. "There. If Leane is any guide, I've lost a good fifteen years, maybe more. I've known women who would pay any price for that. A third advantage." She glanced at Gawyn. He still had his back turned, but she lowered her voice anyway. "Along with a certain loosening of the tongue, shall we say? I had not thought of Mara in years. A friend of my girlhood."

"Will you age like the rest of us, now?" Min asked as she climbed into her saddle. Better than commenting on the lie. Better just to remember that she *could* lie now. Leane mounted the third mare with smooth skill and walked her in a circle, testing her step; she had surely been on a horse before.

Siuan shook her head. "I really don't know. No stilled woman has ever lived long enough to find out. I intend to."

"Do you mean to go," Gawyn asked harshly, "or sit there talking?" Without waiting for an answer, he strode off through the trees.

They heeled their mares after him, Siuan pulling her hood well forward to hide her face. Disguise or no, it seemed she was taking no chances. Leane was already shrouded as deeply in hers as she could be. After a moment, Min imitated them. Elaida wanted *her* arrested? That had to mean that she knew "Elmindreda" was Min. How long had the woman known? How long had Min been walking around thinking herself hidden while Elaida watched and smirked at her for a fool? It was a shivery thought.

As they caught up to Gawyn at a graveled path, twenty or more young men appeared, striding toward them, some perhaps a few years older than he, others little more than boys. Min suspected some of those last did not have to shave yet, at least not regularly. All carried swords at their belts or on their backs, though, and three or four had breastplates. More than one sported a bloody bandage, and most wore clothes spotted with blood. Each had the same unblinking stare as Gawyn. At the sight of him they stopped, clapping right fists to chests. Without slowing, Gawyn acknowledged the salute with a nod, and the young men fell in behind the women's horses.

"The students?" Siuan murmured. "They also took part in the fighting?"

Min nodded, keeping her face expressionless. "They call themselves the Younglings."

"A fitting name." Siuan sighed.

"Some are no more than children," Leane muttered.

Min was not about to tell them that Warders from the Blue and Green Ajahs had planned to free them before they were stilled, and might have succeeded if Gawyn had not roused the students, "children" too, and led them into the Tower to stop it. The fighting had been among the deadliest, student against teacher and no mercy, no quarter.

The tall, bronze-studded Alindrelle Gates stood open, but guarded heavily. Some guards wore the Flame of Tar Valon on their chests; others had workmen's coats, and mismatched breastplates and helmets. Guardsmen, and fellows who had come disguised as masons. Both sorts looked hard and resourceful, used to their weapons, but they kept apart, eyeing each other distrustfully. A grizzled officer stood out from the Tower guardsmen with his arms folded and watched Gawyn and the others approach.

"Writing materials!" Gawyn snapped. "Quickly!"

"Well, you must be these Younglings I've heard of," the grizzled man said. "A fine bunch of bloody young cockerels, but I've had orders to let no one leave the Tower grounds. Signed by the Amyrlin Seat herself. Who do you think you are to countermand that?"

Gawyn raised his head slowly. "I am Gawyn Trakand of Andor," he said softly. "And I mean to see these women leave, or you dead." The other Younglings moved up behind him, spreading out to face the guards with hands on swords, unblinking, perhaps not caring that they were outnumbered.

The grizzled man shifted uneasily, and one of the others muttered, "He's the one they say killed Hammar and Coulin."

After a moment, the officer jerked his head toward the guardhouse, and one of the guardsmen ran inside, returning with a lapdesk, a small red stick of sealing wax burning in a brass holder at one corner. Gawyn let the man hold the desk while he scribbled furiously.

"This will let you past the bridge guards," he said, letting a pool of red wax drip beneath his signature. He pressed his signet ring into it firmly.

"You killed Coulin?" Siuan said in a cold tone fitting her former office. "And Hammar?"

Min's heart sank. *Be quiet, Siuan! Remember who you are now, and be quiet!*

Gawyn spun to face the three women, his eyes like blue fire. "Yes," he grated. "They were my friends, and I respected them, but they sided with . . . with Siuan Sanche, and I had to—" Abruptly he shoved the paper he had sealed into Min's hand. "Go! Go, before I change my mind!" He slapped her mare, then darted to slap the other two as Min's horse leaped through the open gates. "Go!"

Min let her horse cross the great plaza surrounding the Tower grounds at a quick trot, Siuan and Leane right behind her. The plaza was empty, and so were the streets beyond. The ring of their horses' hooves on the paving stones echoed hollowly. Whoever had not already fled the city was hiding.

She studied Gawyn's paper as they rode. The blob of red wax bore the imprint of a charging boar. "This just says we have permission to leave. We could use it to board a ship as well as at the bridges." It seemed smart to be going a way no one knew, not even Gawyn. She did not really think he would change his mind, but he was brittle, ready to shatter at the wrong blow.

"That might be a good idea," Leane said. "I always thought Galad was the more dangerous of those two, but I am no longer sure. Hammar, and Coulin. . . ." She shivered. "A ship would take us farther, faster than these horses can."

Siuan shook her head. "Most of the Aes Sedai who fled will have crossed the bridges, for sure. That is the quickest way out of the city if someone might be chasing you, quicker than waiting while a ship's crew casts off. I must stay close to Tar Valon if I'm to gather them in."

"They won't follow you," Leane said in a monotone freighted with meaning. "You have no right to the stole any longer. Not even to the shawl or the ring."

"I may no longer wear the stole," Siuan replied just as flatly, "but I still know how to ready a crew for a storm. And since I cannot wear the stole, I must see they choose the right woman in my place. I'll not let Elaida get away with calling herself the Amyrlin. It has to be someone strong in the Power, someone who sees things the right way."

"Then you mean to go on aiding this . . . this *Dragon!*" Leane snapped.

"What else would you have me do? Curl up and die?"

Leane shuddered as if she had been struck in the face, and they rode in silence for a time. All of those fabulous buildings around them, like wind-sculpted cliffs and waves and great flights of birds, loomed frighteningly with no people in the streets save themselves, and one lone fellow who came darting around a corner up ahead, scuttling from doorway to doorway as if scouting their way for them. He did not lessen the emptiness, only emphasized it.

"What else can we do?" Leane said eventually. She rode slumped in her saddle now like a sack of grain. "I feel so . . . empty. Empty."

"Find something to fill it up," Siuan told her firmly. "Anything. Cook for the hungry, tend the sick, find a husband and raise a houseful of children. Me, I mean to see Elaida does not get away with this. I could almost forgive her, if she truly believed I had endangered the Tower. Almost, I could. Almost. But she has been filled with envy since the day

I was raised Amyrlin instead of her. That drives her as much as any-thing else, and for that I mean to pull her down. That is what fills me, Leane. That, and the fact that Rand al'Thor must not fall into her hands."

"Perhaps that will be enough." The coppery-skinned woman sounded doubtful, but she straightened. The contrast between her ob-vious experience and Siuan's precarious seat on the shorter mare made her look as if she must be the leader. "But how can we even begin? We have three horses, the clothes on our backs, and whatever Min has in her purse. Hardly enough to challenge the Tower."

"I am glad you did not decide on a husband and home. We will find other—" Siuan grimaced. "We will find Aes Sedai who fled, find what we need. We may have more than you think, Leane. Min, what does that pass Gawyn gave us say? Does it mention three women? What? Quickly, girl."

Min glared at her back. Siuan had been peering at the darting man ahead, a large, dark-haired fellow, dressed well but plainly in somber browns. The woman sounded as if she were still Amyrlin. *Well, I wanted her to find her backbone, didn't I?*

Siuan turned to stare at her with those sharp blue eyes; somehow they seemed no less intimidating than before. " 'The bearers are autho-rized to depart Tar Valon on my authority,' " Min quoted hastily from memory. " 'Who impedes them will answer to me.' Signed—"

"I know his name," Siuan snapped. "Follow me." She heeled Bela's flanks, nearly losing her seat when the shaggy mare lumbered to a slow gallop. She hung on, though, bouncing awkwardly and drumming her heels for more speed.

Min exchanged one startled look with Leane, and they were both galloping after her. The man looked back at the sound of running hooves and began to run himself, but Siuan cut Bela in front of him; he bounced off the mare with a grunt. Min reached them just in time to hear Siuan say, "I did not think to meet you here, Logain."

Min gaped. It *was* him. Those despairing eyes and that once hand-some face framed by dark hair curling to his broad shoulders were unmistakable. Just who they needed to find. A man the Tower wanted very likely as much as Siuan.

Logain slumped to his knees as though his fatigued legs would not hold him any longer. "I cannot harm anyone now," he said tiredly, staring at the paving stones beneath Bela's hooves. "I just wanted to get away, to die somewhere in peace. If you only knew what it was like to have lost. . . ." Leane sawed her reins angrily as he trailed off; he began again without noticing. "The bridges are all guarded. They will let no one across. They did not know me, but they would not let me cross. I have tried them all." Abruptly he laughed, wearily, but as if it were very funny indeed. "I have tried them all."

"I think," Min said carefully, "we should be going. He probably wants to avoid those *who must be looking for him.*" Siuan shot her a look that almost made her rein her horse back, all icy eyes and hard chin. It would not have been dreadful if the woman had retained a little of the uncertainty she displayed previously.

Raising his head, the big man looked from one of them to the next, a slow frown forming. "You are not Aes Sedai. Who are you? What do you want of me?"

"I am the woman who can take you out of Tar Valon," Siuan told him. "And perhaps give you a chance to strike back at the Red Ajah. You would like a chance to get back at those who captured you, wouldn't you?"

A shudder passed through him. "What must I do?" he said slowly.

"Follow me," she replied. "Follow me, and remember that I am the only one in the entire world who will give you your chance of revenge."

From his knees he studied them with his head tilted, examining each face, then pushed himself to his feet, his eyes fixed on Siuan. "I am your man," he said simply.

Leane's face looked as incredulous as Min felt. What use under the Light could Siuan possibly have for a man of doubtful sanity who had once falsely proclaimed himself the Dragon Reborn? At the least he might turn on them to steal one of their horses! Eyeing the height of him, the breadth of his shoulders, Min thought they had better keep their belt knives handy. Suddenly, for a moment, that flaring halo of gold and blue shone about his head, speaking of glory to come as surely as it had the first time she had seen it. She shivered. Viewings. Images.

She glanced over her shoulder toward the Tower, the thick white shaft dominating the city, whole and straight, yet broken as surely as if it lay in ruins. For a moment she let herself think of the images she had glimpsed, just for a moment, flickering around Gawyn's head. Gawyn kneeling at Egwene's feet with his head bowed, and Gawyn breaking Egwene's neck, first one then the other, as if either could be the future.

The things she saw were very rarely as clear in meaning as those two, and she had never before seen that fluttering back and forth, as though not even the viewing could tell which would be the true future. Worse, she had a feeling near to certainty that it was what she had done this day that had turned Gawyn toward those two possibilities.

Despite the sun, she shivered again. *What's done is done.* She glanced at the two Aes Sedai—former Aes Sedai—both now studying Logain as though he were a trained hound, ferocious, possibly dangerous, but useful. Siuan and Leane turned their horses toward the river, Logain striding between. Min followed more slowly. *Light, I hope it was worth it.*

CHAPTER
48

An Offer Refused

"I s that the kind of woman you like?" Aviendha said contemptuously.

Rand looked down at her, striding along at Jeade'en's stirrup in her heavy skirts, brown shawl doubled over her head. Big blue-green eyes flashed up at him from beneath her wide headscarf as if she wished she still had the spear the Wise Ones had scolded her for taking up during the Trolloc attack.

Sometimes it made him uncomfortable, her walking while he rode, but he had tried walking with her, and his feet were grateful for a horse. Occasionally—*very* occasionally—he had managed to get her to ride behind his saddle, by complaining that he was getting a crick in his neck talking to her. Riding a horse did not exactly violate custom, it turned out, yet contempt for not using your own legs to carry you kept her afoot most of the time. One laugh from any of the Aiel, especially a Maiden, even one looking the other way, was enough to have her off Jeade'en in a flash.

"She is soft, Rand al'Thor. Weak."

He glanced back over at the boxlike white wagon leading the peddlers' train in a crooked, lurching snake across the dusty, broken landscape, escorted by Jindo Maidens again today. Isendre was up with Kadere and the driver, seated on the heavyset peddler's lap, her chin

on his shoulder while he held a small, blue silk parasol to shade her—
and himself, too—from the harsh sun. Even in a white coat, Kadere
continually mopped his dark face with a large handkerchief, more affected by the heat than she, in her sleek, clinging gown that matched
the parasol. Rand was not close enough to be sure, but he thought her
dark eyes were on him above the misty scarf wrapped about her face
and head. She usually seemed to be watching him. Kadere did not
appear to mind.

"I do not think Isendre is soft," he said quietly, adjusting the *shoufa*
around his head; it did keep the broiling sun off after a fashion. He had
resisted donning any more Aiel garb, no matter how much more suited
to the climate than his red wool coat. Whatever his blood, whatever the
marks on his forearms, he was not Aiel, and he would not pretend.
Whatever he had to do, he could hang on to that scrap of decency.
"No, I would not say that."

On the driver's seat of the second wagon, fat Keille and the gleeman,
Natael, were arguing again. Natael had the reins, though he did not
drive as well as the man who usually did the job. Sometimes they
looked at Rand, too, quick glances before diving back into their quar-
rel. But then, everyone did. The long column of Jindo on the other side
of him, the Wise Ones beyond them, with Moiraine and Egwene and
Lan. Among the more distant, thicker line of Shaido he thought heads
turned toward him, too. It did not surprise him now any more than it
ever had. He was He Who Comes With the Dawn. Everyone wanted to
know what he would do. They would find out soon enough.

"Soft," Aviendha grunted. "Elayne is not soft. You belong to Elayne;
you should not be caressing eyes with this milk-skinned wench." She
shook her head fiercely, muttering half to herself. "Our ways shock her.
She could not accept them. Why should I care if she can? I want no
part of this! It *cannot* be! If I could, I would take you *gai'shain* and give
you to Elayne!"

"Why should Isendre accept Aiel ways?"

The wide-eyed look she gave him was so startled he almost laughed.
Immediately she scowled as if he had done something infuriating. Aiel
women were surely no easier to understand than any others.

"You are certainly not soft, Aviendha." She should take it for a
compliment; the woman was as rough as a honing stone sometimes.
"Explain to me about the roofmistress again. If Rhuarc is clan chief of
the Taardad and chief of Cold Rocks Hold, how is it that the hold
belongs to his wife and not him?"

She glowered at him a moment longer, lips working as she muttered under her breath, before answering. "Because she is *roofmistress,* you stone-headed wetlander. A man cannot own a roof any more than he can own land! Sometimes you wetlanders sound like savages."

"But if Lian is roofmistress of Cold Rocks because she is Rhuarc's wife—"

"That is different! Will you never understand? A child understands!" Taking a deep breath, she adjusted the shawl around her face. She was a pretty woman, except for looking at him most of the time as if he had committed some crime against her. What it might be, he did not know. White-haired Bair, leathery-faced and as reluctant to speak of Rhuidean as ever, had finally, unwillingly told him that Aviendha had *not* visited the glass columns: she would not do that until she was ready to become a Wise One. So why did she hate him? It was a mystery he would have liked an answer to.

"I will attack it from another direction," she grumbled at him. "When a woman is to marry, if she does not already own a roof, her family builds one for her. On her wedding day her new husband carries her away from her family across his shoulder, with his brothers holding off her sisters, but at the door he puts her down and asks her permission to enter. The roof is *hers.* She can. . . ."

These lectures had been the most pleasant thing in the eleven days and nights since the Trolloc attack. Not that she had been willing to talk at first, beyond one more tirade on his supposed ill-treatment of Elayne and later another embarrassing lecture meant to convince him Elayne was the perfect woman. Not until he mentioned to Egwene in passing that if Aviendha would not even speak to him, he wished she would at least stop staring at him. Within the hour a white-robed *gai'shain* man came for Aviendha.

Whatever the Wise Ones had to say to her, she returned in a quivering fury to demand—demand!—that he let her teach him about Aiel ways and customs. No doubt in hope he would reveal something of his plans by the questions he asked. After the viperish subtleties of Tear, the openness of the Wise Ones' spying was refreshing. Still, it was doubtless wise to learn what he could, and talking with Aviendha could actually be enjoyable, especially on those occasions when she seemed to forget she despised him for whatever reason. Of course, whenever she realized they had begun to talk like two people instead of captor and captive, she did have a tendency to throw one of her white-hot outbursts, as though he had lured her into a trap.

Yet even with that their conversations were pleasurable, certainly by comparison with the rest of the journey. He was even beginning to find her tantrums amusing, though he was wise enough not to let her know. If she saw a man she hated, at least she was too wrapped up in that to see He Who Comes With the Dawn, or the Dragon Reborn. Just Rand al'Thor. At any rate, she knew what she thought of him. Not like Elayne, with one letter that made his ears grow hot and another written the same day that made him wonder if he had grown fangs and horns like a Trolloc.

Min was just about the only woman he had ever met who had not tangled his wits into a ball. But she was off in the Tower—safe there, at least—and that was one place he meant to avoid. Sometimes he thought life would be simpler if he could just forget women altogether. Now Aviendha had started creeping into his dreams, as if Min and Elayne were not bad enough. Women tied his emotions in knots, and he had to be clearheaded now. Clearheaded and cold.

He realized he was looking at Isendre again. She wriggled slender fingers at him past Kadere's ear; he was sure those full lips curved into a smile. *Oh, yes. Dangerous. I have to be cold and hard as steel. Sharp steel.*

Eleven days and nights into the twelfth, and nothing else had changed. Days and nights of odd rock formations and flat-topped stone spires and buttes thrusting up from a broken, blistered land criss-crossed by mountains seemingly stuck in at random. Days of baking sun and searing winds, nights of bone-shaking cold. Whatever grew seemed to have thorns or spines, or else a touch itched like fury. Some Aviendha said were poisonous; that list seemed longer than the one of those edible. The only water was in hidden springs and tanks, though she pointed out plants that meant a deep hole would fill with slow seepage, enough to keep one or two men alive, and others that could be chewed for a sour, watery pulp.

One night lions killed two of the Shaido packhorses, roaring in the darkness as they were driven from their prey to vanish into the gullies. A wagon driver disturbed a small brown snake as they were making camp the fourth evening. A two-step, Aviendha called it later, and it proved its name. The fellow screamed and tried to run for the wagons despite seeing Moiraine hurrying toward him; he fell on his face at his second stride, dead before the Aes Sedai could dismount from her white mare. Aviendha listed venomous snakes, spiders and lizards. Poisonous lizards! Once she found one for him, two feet long and thick, with yellow stripes running down its bronze scales. Casually pinning it under a soft-booted foot, she drove her knife into the thing's wide head, then held it up where he could see the clear, oily fluid oozing over sharp bony ridges in its mouth. A *gara,* she explained, could bite through a boot; it could also kill a bull. Others were worse, of course. The *gara* was slow, and not really dangerous unless you were stupid enough to step on it. When she flung the huge lizard off of her blade, the yellow and bronze faded right into the cracked clay. Oh, yes. Just do not be stupid enough to step on it.

Moiraine divided her time between the Wise Ones and Rand, usually attempting, in that Aes Sedai way, to bully him into revealing his plans. "The Wheel weaves as the Wheel wills," she had told him just that morning, voice coolly calm, ageless face serene, but dark eyes hot as she stared at him over Aviendha's head, "but a fool can strangle himself in the Pattern. Have a care you do not weave a noose for your neck." She had acquired a pale cloak, almost *gai'shain* white, that shimmered in the sun, and beneath the wide hood she wore a damp, snowy scarf folded around her forehead.

"I make no nooses for my neck." He laughed, and she wheeled Aldieb so quickly the mare nearly knocked Aviendha down, galloping back to the Wise Ones' party, cloak streaming behind her.

"It is stupid to anger Aes Sedai," Aviendha muttered, rubbing her shoulder. "I did not think you were a stupid man."

"We will just have to see whether I am or not," he told her, not feeling like laughing anymore. Stupid? There were some risks you had to take. "We will just have to see."

Egwene rarely left the Wise Ones, walking with them as often as she rode Mist, sometimes taking one of them up behind her on the gray mare for a time. He had finally figured out that she was passing for full Aes Sedai again. Amys and Bair, Seana and Melaine, seemed to accept it as readily as the Tairens had, though not at all in the same way. At times one or another of them argued with her so loudly he could almost make out what they were shouting more than a hundred paces away. It was almost the manner they used with Aviendha, though her they seemed to bully rather than argue with, but then, sometimes they held what appeared to be rather heated discussions with Moiraine, too. Especially sun-haired Melaine.

The tenth morning Egwene had finally stopped wearing her hair in those two braids, though it was the oddest thing. The Wise Ones talked to her for the longest time, off by themselves, while the *gai'shain* were folding their tents and Rand was saddling Jeade'en. Had he not known her better, he might have thought Egwene's head-down stance was an attempt at meekness, but that word could only be applied to her in comparison with Nynaeve. And maybe Moiraine. Suddenly Egwene clapped her hands, laughing and hugging each of the Wise Ones in turn before hurriedly unraveling the plaits.

When he asked Aviendha what was going on—she had been sitting outside his tent when he woke—she muttered sourly, "They have decided she has grown—" Cutting off abruptly, she gave him a level look, folding her arms, and went on in a cool voice. "It is Wise Ones' business, Rand al'Thor. Ask them, if you wish, but be prepared to hear that it is no concern of yours."

Egwene had grown what? Her hair? It made no sense. Aviendha would not say another word on the matter; instead she scraped a bit of grayish lichen from a rock and began describing how to poultice a wound with it. The woman was learning a Wise One's ways too quickly to suit him. The Wise Ones themselves paid him little apparent attention; of course, they did not need to, with Aviendha perched on his shoulder in a manner of speaking.

The rest of the Aiel, the Jindo at any rate, became a bit less standoffish each day, perhaps a little less uneasy about what He Who Comes With the Dawn meant for them, but Aviendha was the only one who spoke to him at any length. Each evening Lan came to practice the sword, and Rhuarc to teach him the spears and the Aiel's odd way of fighting with both hands and feet. The Warder knew something of that, and joined the practice sessions. Most others avoided Rand, especially the wagondrivers, who had learned he was the Dragon Reborn, a man who could channel; when he caught one of those rough-faced men looking at him, the fellow might as well have been staring at the Dark One. Not Kadere, though, or the gleeman.

Almost every morning as they started out, the peddler rode over on one of the mules from the wagons the Trollocs had burned, his face seeming even darker for the long white scarf tied about his head and hanging down his neck. With Rand he was all diffidence, but his cold, unchanging eyes made his hooked nose look an eagle's beak in truth.

"My Lord Dragon," he had begun the morning after the attack, then wiped sweat from his face with his ever-present handkerchief and shifted uncomfortably on the battered old saddle he had found somewhere for the mule. "If I may call you that?"

The charred wreckage of the three wagons was dwindling in the distance to the south, and with them the graves of two of Kadere's men and a good many more Aiel. The Trollocs had been dragged from the camps and left for the scavengers, yipping, big-eared creatures—Rand did not know whether they were large foxes or small dogs; they looked like bits of each—and vultures with red-tipped wings, some still circling in the sky as if fearful of landing in the melee among their fellows.

"Call me as you will," Rand told him.

"My Lord Dragon. I have been thinking of what you said yesterday." Kadere looked around as if he feared being overheard, though Aviendha was with the Wise Ones, and his own train of wagons, fifty paces or more away, held the nearest ears. He dropped his voice near a whisper anyway, and wiped his face nervously. His eyes never altered, though. "What you said about knowledge being valuable, paving the way to greatness. It is true."

Rand looked at him for a long moment, not blinking, keeping his face blank. "You said that, not I," he said finally.

"Well, perhaps I did. But it is true, is it not, my Lord Dragon?" Rand nodded, and the peddler went on, still whispering, eyes still shifting for eavesdroppers. "Yet there can be danger in knowledge. In giving more than receiving. A man who sells knowledge must have not only his price, but safeguards. Assurances and sureties against . . . repercussions. Would you not agree?"

"Do you have knowledge you want to . . . sell, Kadere?"

The heavyset man frowned at his train. Keille had dropped down to walk awhile despite the growing heat, her bulk sheathed in white and a white lace shawl on the ivory combs in her coarse dark hair. Every so often she glanced at the two men riding together, her expression unreadable at this distance. It still seemed odd, someone so large moving so lightly. Isendre had climbed out onto the driver's seat of the first wagon and was watching more openly, hanging on to lean around the corner of the white-painted wagon as it swayed and lurched.

"That woman may be the death of me yet," Kadere muttered. "Perhaps we can talk again later, my Lord Dragon, if it please you." Booting the mule hard, he trotted to the lead wagon and swung himself onto the driver's seat with surprising nimbleness, tying the mule's reins to an iron ring at the corner of the big wagonbox. He and Isendre disappeared inside and did not emerge again until they stopped for the night.

He returned the next day, and other days when he saw that Rand was alone, always hinting at knowledge he might sell for the proper price, if the proper safeguards were set. Once he went so far as to say that anything—murder, treason, anything at all—could be forgiven in return for knowledge, and seemed increasingly nervous when Rand would not agree with him. Whatever he wanted to sell, he apparently wanted Rand's blanket protection for every misdeed he might ever have done.

"I don't know that I want to buy knowledge," Rand told him more than once. "There's always the question of price, isn't there? Some prices I might not want to pay."

Natael drew Rand aside that first evening, after the fires were lit and cooking smells began to drift among the low tents. The gleeman seemed almost as nervous as Kadere. "I have thought a good deal about you," he said, peering at Rand sideways, head tilted to one side. "You should have a grand epic to tell your tale. The Dragon Reborn. He Who Comes With the Dawn. Man of who knows how many prophecies, in this Age and others." He drew his cloak around him, the colorful patches fluttering in the breeze. Twilight was short in the Waste; night and cold came on quickly and together. "How do you feel about your prophesied destiny? I must know, if I am to compose this epic."

"Feel?" Rand looked around the camp, at the Jindo moving among the tents. How many of them would be dead before he was done? "Tired. I feel tired."

"Hardly a heroic emotion," Natael murmured. "But to be expected, given your destiny. The world riding on your shoulders, most people willing to kill you given the chance, the rest fools who think to use you, ride you to power and glory."

"Which are you, Natael?"

"I? I am a simple gleeman." The man lifted an edge of his patch-covered cloak as if for proof. "I would not take your place for all the world, not with the fate that accompanies it. Death or madness, or both. 'His blood on the rocks of Shayol Ghul. . . .' That is what *The Karaethon Cycle,* the Prophecies of the Dragon, says, is it not? That you must die to save fools who will heave a sigh of relief at your death. No, I would not accept that for all your power and more."

"Rand," Egwene said, stepping out of the deepening darkness with her pale cloak wrapped around her, the hood well up, "we have come to see how you have held up after your Healing, and a day in that heat." Moiraine was with her, face shrouded in the deep cowl of her white cloak, and Bair and Amys, Melaine and Seana, heads swathed in dark shawls, all watching him, calm and cold as the night. Even Egwene. She did not have the Aes Sedai agelessness yet, but she had Aes Sedai eyes.

He did not notice Aviendha at first, trailing behind the others. For a moment he thought he saw compassion on her face, but if it was there, it vanished as soon as she saw him looking. Imagination. He *was* tired.

"Another time," Natael said, speaking to Rand but looking at the women in that peculiar sidelong manner. "We will talk another time." With the slightest of bows he strode away.

"Does the future chafe you, Rand?" Moiraine said quietly when the gleeman was gone. "Prophecies speak in flowery, hidden language. They do not always mean what they seem to say."

"The Wheel weaves as the Wheel wills," he told her. "I will do what I must. Remember that, Moiraine. I will do what I must." She seemed satisfied; with Aes Sedai, it was hard to tell. She would not be satisfied when she learned everything.

Natael returned the next evening, and the next, and the next, always talking about the epic he would compose, but he displayed a morbid streak, digging for how Rand meant to face madness and death. His tale was meant to be a tragedy, it appeared. Rand certainly had no desire to root his fears out into the open; what was in his heart and head could remain buried there. Finally the gleeman seemed to tire of hearing him say "I will do what I must," and stopped coming. It seemed that he did not want to compose his epic unless it could be full of pained emotion. The man looked frustrated when he stalked off for the last time, cloak fluttering furiously behind him.

The fellow was odd, but going by Thom Merrilin, so were all gleemen. Natael certainly demonstrated other gleeman's traits. For instance, he certainly had a fine opinion of himself. Rand did not care whether the man called him by titles, but Natael addressed Rhuarc, and Moiraine, the few times he was around her, as if he was plainly their equal. That was Thom to perfection. And he gave up performing for the Jindo at all, beginning to spend most of every night at the Shaido camp. There were more of the Shaido, he explained to Rhuarc as if it were the most obvious thing in the world. A larger audience. None of the Jindo liked it, but there was nothing even Rhuarc could do. In the Three-fold Land, a gleeman was allowed anything short of murder without being called down for it.

Aviendha spent her nights among the Wise Ones, and sometimes walked with them for an hour or so during the day, all of them gathered around her, even Moiraine and Egwene. At first Rand thought they must be advising her on how to handle him, how to pull what they wanted to know out of his head. Then one day, with the sun molten overhead, a ball of fire as big as a horse suddenly burst into being ahead of the Wise Ones' party and went spinning and tumbling away, blazing a furrow across the sere land, until it finally dwindled and winked out.

Some of the wagon drivers pulled their startled, snorting teams to a halt and stood to watch, calling to each other in a blend of fear, confusion and coarse curses. Murmurs rippled through the Jindo, and they stared, as did the Shaido, but the two columns of Aiel kept moving with barely a pause. It was among the Wise Ones that real excitement was evident. The four of them clustered around Aviendha, all apparently talking at once, with considerable arm-waving. Moiraine and Egwene, leading their horses, tried to get in a word; even without hearing, Rand knew that Amys told them in no uncertain terms, shaking a furiously admonishing finger, to stay out of it.

Staring at the blackened gouge stretching arrow-straight for half a mile, Rand sat back down in his saddle. Teaching Aviendha to channel. Of course. That was what they were doing. He scrubbed sweat from his forehead with the back of his hand; the sun had nothing to do with it. When that fireball leaped out into existence, he had instinctively reached for the True Source. It had been like trying to dip water with a torn sieve. All his clawing at *saidin* might as well have been clawing at air. One day that could happen when he needed the Power desperately. He had to learn, too, and he had no teacher. He had to learn not just because the Power would kill him before he had to worry about going mad if he did not; he had to learn because he had to use it. Learn to use it; use it to learn. He began laughing so hard that some of the Jindo looked at him uneasily.

He would have enjoyed Mat's company any time during those eleven days and nights, but Mat never came near for more than a minute or two, the broad brim of his flat-crowned hat pulled down to shade his eyes, the black-hafted spear lying across the pommel of Pips's saddle, with its odd raven-marked, Power-wrought point, like a short, curving sword blade.

"If your face darkens from the sun any more, you *will* turn into an Aielman," he might say, laughing or, "Do you mean to spend the rest of your life here? There's a whole world the other side of the Dragonwall. Wine? Women? You remember these things?"

But Mat looked plainly uneasy, and he was even more reluctant than the Wise Ones to speak of Rhuidean, or what had happened to them there. His hand tightened on that black haft at the very mention of the fog-domed city, and he claimed not to remember anything of his journey through the *ter'angreal*—then proceeded to contradict himself by saying, "You stay out of that thing, Rand. It isn't like the one in the Stone at all. They cheat. Burn me, I wish I'd never seen it!"

The one time Rand mentioned the Old Tongue, he snapped, "Burn you, I don't know anything about the bloody Old Tongue!" and galloped straight back to the peddlers' wagons.

That was where Mat spent most of his time, dicing with the drivers—until they realized he won a very great deal more often than he lost, no matter whose dice he used—engaging Kadere or Natael in long talks at every opportunity, pursuing Isendre. It was clear what was on his mind from the first time he grinned at her and straightened his hat, the morning after the Trolloc attack. He spoke to her nearly every evening for as long as he could, and pricked himself so badly plucking white blossoms from a spiky-thorned bush that he could barely handle his reins for two days, though he refused to allow Moiraine to Heal him. Isendre did not precisely encourage him, but her slow, sultry smile was hardly calculated to drive him away, either. Kadere saw—and said not a word, though sometimes his eyes followed Mat like a vulture's. Others did comment.

Late one afternoon as the mules were being unhitched and the tents going up, and Rand was unsaddling Jeade'en, Mat was standing with Isendre in the meager shade of one of the canvas-topped wagons. Standing very close. Shaking his head, Rand watched as he wiped the dapple down. The sun burned low on the horizon, and tall spires stretched long shadows across the camp.

Isendre fiddled with her diaphanous scarf as if idly thinking of removing it, smiling, full lips half pouting, ready for a kiss. Encouraged, Mat grinned confidently and moved closer still. She dropped her hand, and slowly shook her head, but that inviting smile never faded. Neither of them heard Keille approach, so light on her feet despite her size.

"Is that what you want, good sir? Her?" The pair jumped apart at the sound of her mellifluous voice, and she laughed just as musically, just as oddly out of that face. "A bargain for you, Matrim Cauthon. A Tar Valon mark, and she is yours. A chit like that cannot be worth more than two, so it is a clear bargain."

Mat grimaced, looking as though he wished he were anywhere else but there.

Isendre, however, turned slowly to face Keille, a mountain cat facing a bear. "You go too far, old woman," she said softly, eyes hard above the veiling scarf. "I will put up with your tongue no longer. Have a care. Or perhaps you would like to remain here in the Waste."

Keille smiled broadly, yet mirth never touched the obsidian eyes glittering behind her fat cheeks. "Would *you?*"

Nodding decisively, Isendre said, "A Tar Valon mark." Her voice was iron. "I will see you have a Tar Valon mark when we leave you. I only wish I could see you trying to drink it." Turning her back, she strode to the lead wagon, not swaying seductively at all, and vanished inside.

Keille watched, round face unreadable, until the white door closed, then suddenly rounded on Mat, who was on the point of slipping away. "Few men have ever refused an offer from me once, much less twice. You should have a care I do not take it in mind to do something about it." Laughing, she reached up and pinched his cheek with thick fingers, hard enough to make him wince, then turned in Rand's direction. "Tell him, my Lord Dragon. I have a feeling you know something of the dangers of scorning a woman. That Aiel girl who follows you about, glaring. I hear you belong to another. Perhaps she feels scorned."

"I doubt it, Mistress," he said dryly. "Aviendha would plant a knife in my ribs if she believed I had thought of her that way."

The immense woman laughed uproariously. Mat flinched as she reached for him again, but all she did was pat the cheek she had pinched before. "You see, good sir? Scorn a woman's offer, and perhaps she thinks nothing of it, but perhaps"—she made a skewering motion—"the knife. A lesson any man can learn. Eh, my Lord Dragon?" Wheezing with laughter, she hurried off to check on the men tending the mules.

Rubbing his cheek, Mat muttered, "They're *all* crazy," before he, too, left. He did not abandon his pursuit of Isendre, though.

So it went, for eleven days and into the twelfth, across a barren, hard-baked land. Twice they saw other stands, small, rough stone buildings much like Imre Stand, sited for easy defense against the sheer side of spire or butte. One had three hundred sheep or more, and men who were as startled to learn of Rand as they were of Trollocs in the Threefold Land. The other was empty; not raided, only not in use. Several times Rand spotted goats, or sheep, or pale, long-horned cattle in the distance. Aviendha said the herds belonged to nearby sept holds, but he saw no people, surely no structure that deserved the name hold.

The twelfth day, with the thick columns of Jindo and Shaido flanking the Wise Ones' party, and the peddlers' wagons lurching along with Keille and Natael arguing, and Isendre eyeing Rand from Kadere's lap.

". . . and that is how it is," Aviendha said, nodding to herself. "Surely you must understand about a roofmistress, now."

"Not really," Rand admitted. He realized that for some time he had just been listening to the sound of her voice, not to the words. "I'm sure it works just fine, though."

She growled at him. "When you marry," she said in a tight voice, "with the Dragons on your arms proving your blood, will you follow that blood, or will you demand to own everything but the dress your wife stands in, like some wetland savage?"

"That's not at all the way it is," he protested, "and any woman where I come from would brain a man who thought it was. Anyway, don't you think that ought to be settled between me and whoever I *do* decide to marry?" If anything, she scowled harder than before.

To his relief, Rhuarc came trotting back from the head of the Jindo. "We are there," the Aielman announced with a smile. "Cold Rocks Hold."

CHAPTER
49

Cold Rocks Hold

F rowning, Rand looked around. A mile ahead stood a tight cluster of tall, sheer-sided buttes, or perhaps one huge butte broken by fissures. To his left the land ran off in patches of tough grass and leafless spiny plants, scattered thorny bushes and low trees, across arid hills and jagged gullies, past huge, rough stone columns to jagged mountains in the distance. To the right the land was the same, except the cracked yellowish clay lay flatter, the mountains closer. It could have been any piece of the Waste he had seen since leaving Chaendaer.

"Where?" he said.

Rhuarc glanced at Aviendha, who was looking at Rand as though he had lost his wits. "Come. Let your own eyes show you Cold Rocks." Dropping his *shoufa* to his shoulders, the clan chief turned and loped bareheaded toward the fissured rock wall ahead.

The Shaido had already halted, milling about and beginning to set up their tents. Heirn and the Jindo fell in behind Rhuarc at a trot with their pack mules, uncovering their heads and shouting wordlessly, and the Maidens escorting the peddlers cried for the drivers to hasten their teams and follow the Jindo. One of the Wise Ones lifted her skirts to her knees and ran to join Rhuarc—Rand thought it was Amys, from the pale hair; surely Bair could not move that nimbly—but the rest of the Wise Ones' party maintained its original pace. For a moment

Moiraine looked as if she would break away, toward Rand, then hesitated, arguing with one of the other Wise Ones, hair still hidden by her shawl. Finally the Aes Sedai reined her white mare back beside Egwene's gray and Lan's black stallion, just ahead of the white-robed *gai'shain* who were tugging the pack animals along. They were heading the same way as Rhuarc and the others, though.

Rand leaned down to offer a hand to Aviendha. When she shook her head, he said, "If they are going to be making all that noise, I won't be able to hear you down there. What if I make a wool-headed mistake because I can't hear what you say?"

Muttering under her breath, she glanced at the Maidens around the peddlers' wagons, then sighed and clasped his arm. He hoisted her up, ignoring her indignant squawk, and swung her onto Jeade'en behind the saddle. Whenever she tried to mount by herself, she came close to pulling him out of the saddle. He gave her a moment to settle her heavy skirts, though at best they bared her legs well above her soft, knee-high boots, then heeled the dapple to a canter. It was the first time Aviendha had ridden faster than a walk; she flung her arms around his waist and hung on.

"If you make me look the fool before my sisters, wetlander," she snarled warningly against his back.

"Why would they think you a fool? I've seen Bair and Amys and the others ride behind Moiraine or Egwene sometimes to talk."

After a moment, she said, "You accept changes more easily than I, Rand al'Thor." He was not sure what to make of that.

When he brought Jeade'en up with Rhuarc and Heirn and Amys, a little ahead of the still shouting Jindo, he was surprised to see Couladin running easily alongside, flame-colored hair bare. Aviendha tugged Rand's own *shoufa* down to his shoulders. "You must enter a hold with your face clear to be seen. I told you that. And make noise. We have been seen long since, and they will know who we are, but it is customary, to show you are not trying to take the hold by surprise."

He nodded, but held his tongue. Neither Rhuarc nor any of the three with him were making a sound, and neither was Aviendha. Besides, the Jindo made enough clamor to be heard for miles.

Couladin's head swung toward him. Contempt flashed across that sun-dark face, and something else. Hate and disdain Rand had come to expect, but amusement? What did Couladin find amusing?

"Fool Shaido," Aviendha muttered at his back. Maybe she was right; maybe the amusement was for her riding. But Rand did not think so.

Mat galloped up trailing a cloud of yellowish brown dust, hat pulled low and spear resting upright on his stirrup iron like a lance. "What is this place, Rand?" he asked loudly, to be heard over the shouts. "All those women would say was 'Move faster. Move faster.' " Rand told him, and he frowned at the towering rock face of the butte. "You could hold that thing for years, I suppose, with supplies, but it isn't a patch on the Stone, or the Tora Harad."

"The Tora what?" Rand said.

Mat rolled his shoulders before answering. "Just something I heard of, once." He stood in his stirrups to peer back over the heads of the Jindo toward the peddlers' train. "At least they're still with us. I wonder how long before they finish trading and go."

"Not before Alcair Dal. Rhuarc says there's a sort of fair whenever clan chiefs meet, even if it's only two or three. With all twelve coming, I don't think Kadere and Keille will want to miss it."

Mat did not look pleased at the news.

Rhuarc led the way straight to the widest fissure in the sheer stone wall, ten or twelve paces across at the broadest, and shadowed by the height of its sheer sides as it wove deeper and deeper, dark and even cool beneath a ribbon of sky. It felt odd to be in so much shade. The Aiels' wordless shouts swelled, magnified between the gray-brown walls; when they suddenly ceased, the silence, broken only by the clatter of mules' hooves and the creak of wagon wheels far behind, seemed very loud.

They rounded another curve, and the fissure opened abruptly into a wide canyon, long and almost straight. From every side, shrill ululating cries broke from hundreds of women's mouths. A thick crowd lined the way, women in bulky skirts, shawls wrapped about their heads, and men wearing grayish brown coats and breeches, the *cadin'sor,* and Maidens of the Spear, too, waving their arms in welcome, beating on pots or whatever could make a noise.

Rand gaped, and not just for the pandemonium. The canyon walls were green, in narrow terraces climbing halfway up both sides. Not all were really terraces, he realized. Small, flat-roofed houses of gray stone or yellow clay seemed to be stacked practically atop one another, in clusters with paths winding between, and every roof a garden of beans and squashes, peppers and melons and plants he did not know. Chickens ran loose, redder than those he knew, and some strange sort of fowl, larger and speckled gray. Children, most garbed like their elders, and white-robed *gai'shain* moved among the rows with big clay pitchers, apparently watering individual plants. The Aiel did not have cities, he had always been told, but this was certainly a fair-sized town at least, if as odd a one as he had ever seen. The din was too great for him to ask any of the questions that popped into his head—such as, what were those round fruits, too red and shiny for apples, growing on low, pale-leaved bushes, or those straight, broad-leafed stalks lined with long, fat, yellow-tasseled sprouts? He had been too long a farmer not to wonder.

Rhuarc and Heirn slowed, and so did Couladin, but only to a quick walk, thrusting their spears through the bow-case harnesses on their backs. Amys ran on ahead, laughing like a girl, while the men continued their steady advance along the crowd-lined canyon floor, the cries of the hold's women vibrating in the air and nearly overshadowing the clanging of pots. Rand followed, as Aviendha had told him to. Mat looked as if he wanted to turn around and ride right back out again.

At the far end of the canyon, the wall leaned inward, making a deep, dark pocket. The sun never reached to the back of it, so Aviendha had said, and the rocks there, always cool, gave the hold its name. In front of the shadows, Amys stood with another woman atop a wide gray boulder, its top smoothed for a platform.

The second woman, slender in her bulky skirts, scarf-bound yellow hair spilling below her waist and touched with white from her temples, appeared older than Amys though certainly more than handsome, with a few fine wrinkles at the corners of her gray eyes. She was dressed the same as Amys, a plain brown shawl over her shoulders, her necklaces and bracelets of gold and carved ivory no finer or richer, but this was Lian, the roofmistress of Cold Rocks Hold.

The wavering, high-pitched cries dwindled away to nothing as Rhuarc halted before the boulder, a step closer than Heirn and Couladin. "I ask leave enter your hold, roofmistress," he announced in a loud, carrying tone.

"You have my leave, clan chief," the yellow-haired replied formally, and just as loudly. Smiling, she added in a much warmer voice, "Shade of my heart, you will always have my leave."

"I give thanks, roofmistress of my heart." That did not sound particularly formal, either.

Heirn stepped forward. "Roofmistress, I ask leave to come beneath your roof."

"You have my leave, Heirn," Lian told the stocky man. "Beneath my roof, there is water and shade for you. The Jindo sept is always welcome here."

"I give thanks, roofmistress." Heirn clapped Rhuarc on the shoulder and left to rejoin his people; Aiel ceremony was short, it seemed, and to the point.

Swaggering, Couladin joined Rhuarc. "I ask leave to enter your hold, roofmistress."

Lian blinked, frowning at him. A murmur rose behind Rand, an astonished buzz from hundreds of throats. A sudden feel of danger hung in the air. Mat certainly felt it, too, fingering his spear and half-turning to see what the mass of Aiel was doing.

"What is the matter?" Rand asked quietly over his shoulder. "Why doesn't she say something?"

"He asked as if he were a clan chief," Aviendha whispered disbelievingly. "The man *is* a fool. He must be mad! If she refuses him, it will mean trouble with the Shaido, and she may, for such an insult. Not blood feud—he is not their clan chief, however swollen his head—but trouble." Between one breath and the next her voice sharpened. "You did not listen, did you? You did not listen! She could have refused permission even to Rhuarc, and he would have had to leave. It would break the clan, but it is in her power. She can refuse even He Who Comes With the Dawn, Rand al'Thor. Women are not powerless among us, not like your wetlander women who must be queens or nobles or else dance for a man if they wish to eat!"

He shook his head slightly. Every time he was on the point of berating himself for how little he had learned about the Aiel, Aviendha reminded him how little she knew about anyone not Aiel. "Someday I would like to introduce you to the Women's Circle in Emond's Field. It will be . . . interesting . . . to hear you explain to them how powerless they are." He felt her shifting against his back, trying to get a good look at his face, and carefully kept his expression smooth. "Maybe they'll explain a few things to you, too."

"You have my leave," Lian began—Couladin smiled, swelling up where he stood—"to step beneath my roof. Water and shade will be found for you." Soft gasps from hundreds of mouths made quite a loud sound.

The fire-haired man quivered as if struck, face red with rage. He did not seem to know what to do. He took a challenging step forward, staring up at Lian and Amys, clutching his own forearms as though to keep his hands from his spears, then whirled and strode back toward the gathering, glaring this way and that, daring anyone to speak. Finally he stopped not far from where he had begun, staring at Rand. Coals could not have been hotter than his blue eyes.

"As one friendless and alone," Aviendha whispered. "She has welcomed him as a beggar. The gravest insult to him, and none to the Shaido." Suddenly she fisted Rand so hard in the ribs that he grunted.

"Move, wetlander. You hold such honor as I have left in your hands; all will know I have taught you! Move!"

Swinging a leg over, he slid from Jeade'en's back and strode up beside Rhuarc. *I am not Aiel,* he thought. *I do not understand them, and I cannot let myself come to like them too much. I cannot.*

None of the other men had done so, but he bowed to Lian; that was how he had been brought up. "Roofmistress, I ask leave to come beneath your roof." He heard Aviendha's breath catch. He had been supposed to say the other thing, what Rhuarc had. The clan chief's eyes narrowed worriedly, watching his wife, and Couladin's flushed face twisted in a scornful smile. The soft murmurs from the crowd sounded puzzled.

The roofmistress stared at Rand even harder than she had at Couladin, taking him in from hair to boots and back again, the *shoufa* lying on the shoulders of a red coat that would surely never be worn by an Aiel. She looked questioningly at Amys, who nodded.

"Such modesty," Lian said slowly, "is becoming in a man. Men seldom know where to find it." Spreading her dark skirts, she curtsied, awkwardly—it was not a thing Aiel women did—but still a curtsy, in return for his bow. "The *Car'a'carn* has leave to enter my hold. For the chief of chiefs, there is ever water and shade at Cold Rocks."

Another great ululation rose from the women in the crowd, but whether for him or for the ceremony, Rand did not know. Couladin paused to stare implacable hatred at him, then stalked off, brushing roughly past Aviendha as she slid ungracefully from the dapple stallion. He melded quickly into the dispersing crowd.

Mat slowed in the act of dismounting to stare after the man. "Watch your back with that one, Rand," he said quietly. "I mean it."

"Everybody tells me that," Rand said. The peddlers were already setting up to trade in the center of the canyon, and at the entrance, Moiraine and the rest of the Wise Ones' company were arriving to a few shouts and the drumming of pots, but nothing like the cries that had welcomed Rhuarc. "He isn't who I have to worry about." His dangers were not Aiel. *Moiraine to one side and Lanfear to the other. How could I have more danger than that?* It was nearly enough to make him laugh.

Amys and Lian had climbed down, and to Rand's surprise, Rhuarc put an arm around each of them. They were both tall, as most Aiel women seemed to be, but neither came higher than the clan chief's shoulder. "You have met my wife Amys," he said to Rand. "Now you must meet my wife Lian."

Rand realized his mouth was hanging open and closed it quickly. After Aviendha had told him the roofmistress of Cold Rocks was Rhuarc's wife and named Lian, he was sure he had misunderstood back at Chaendaer, all that "shade of my heart" between the man and Amys. He had had other things on his mind then anyway. But this. . . .

"*Both* of them?" Mat spluttered. "Light! Two! Oh, burn me! He's the luckiest man in the world or the biggest fool since creation!"

"I had thought," Rhuarc said, frowning, "that Aviendha was teaching you our customs. She leaves out much, it appears."

Leaning to look around her husband—*their* husband—Lian raised an eyebrow at Amys, who said dryly, "She seemed ideal to tell him what he needs to know. Something to keep her from trying to run back to the Maidens whenever our backs were turned, too. Now it seems I must have a long talk with her in a quiet place. No doubt she has been teaching him Maiden handtalk, or how to milk a *gara.*"

Flushing slightly, Aviendha tossed her head irritably; her dark reddish hair had grown over her ears, long enough to sway in a fringe below her head scarf. "There were more important matters to speak of than marriages. Anyway, the man does not listen."

"She has been a good teacher," Rand put in quickly. "I have learned a great deal about your customs, and the Three-fold Land, from her." Handtalk? "Any mistakes I make are mine, not hers." How did you milk a venomous two-foot lizard? Why? "She has been a good teacher, and I'd like to keep her as such, if that is all right." *Why in the Light did I say that?* The woman could be pleasant enough sometimes, when she forgot herself, anyway; the rest of the time she was a burr under his coat. Yet at least he knew who the Wise Ones had set to watch him as long as she was there.

Amys studied him, those clear blue eyes as sharp as an Aes Sedai's. But then, she could channel; her face merely looked younger than it should, not ageless, but maybe she was as much Aes Sedai as an Aes Sedai. "That sounds a fine arrangement to me," she said. Aviendha opened her mouth, all bristling indignation—and closed it again, sullenly, when the Wise One shifted that stare to her. Perhaps the woman had thought her time with him was done, now they had reached Cold Rocks.

"You must be tired after your journey," Lian said to Rand, her gray eyes motherly, "and hungry as well. Come." Her warm smile included Mat, who was hanging back and beginning to look to the peddlers' wagons. "Come beneath my roof."

Fetching his saddlebags, Rand left Jeade'en to the care of a *gai'shain* woman, who took Pips as well. Mat gave the wagons a final stare before tossing his saddlebags over his shoulder and following.

Lian's roof, her house, sat on the highest level on the west side, with the steep canyon wall rising a good hundred paces above. Dwelling of the clan chief and roofmistress or no, from the outside it appeared to be a modest rectangle of large yellow-clay bricks with narrow, glassless windows covered by plain white curtains, a vegetable garden on its flat roof and another in front on a small terrace separated from the house by a narrow path paved with flat gray stones. Big enough for two rooms, maybe. Except perhaps for the square bronze gong hanging beside the door, it looked much like the other structures Rand could see, and from that vantage point the entire length of the valley was laid out below him. A small, simple house. Inside, it was something else.

The brick part was one large room, floored with reddish brown tiles, but it was only part. Carved into the stone behind were more rooms, high-ceilinged and surprisingly cool, with wide, arched doorways and silver lamps giving off a scent that hinted of green places. Rand saw only one chair, tall-backed and lacquered red and gold, with a look of not much use; the chief's chair, Aviendha called it. There was little more wood to be seen, beyond a few polished or lacquered boxes and chests, and low reading stands holding open books; the reader would need to lie on the floor. Intricately woven carpets covered the floors, and bright rugs in layers; he recognized some patterns from Tear and Cairhien and Andor, even Illian and Tarabon, while other designs were unfamiliar, broad jagged stripes and no two colors alike, or linked hollow squares in grays and browns and blacks. In sharp contrast to the harsh sameness outside this valley, there was vivid color everywhere, wall hangings he was sure had come from the other side of the Spine of the World—perhaps in the same way wall hangings had left the Stone of Tear—and cushions of all sizes and hues, often tasseled or fringed or both in silk of red or gold. Here and there, in niches carved into the walls, stood a thin porcelain vase or a silver bowl or an ivory carving, often of some strange animal or other. So these were the "caves" the Tairens spoke of. It could have had the garishness of Tear—or the Tinkers—but instead it seemed dignified, formal and informal at the same time.

With a small grin for Aviendha to show her he *had* listened, Rand pulled a guest gift for Lian from his saddlebags, a finely worked golden lion. It had been looted from Tear and bought from a Jindo Water Seeker, but if he was ruler of Tear, maybe it was like stealing from himself. After a moment of hesitation, Mat produced a gift, too, a

Tairen necklace of silver flowers, no doubt from the same source origi-
nally, and no doubt intended for Isendre.

"Exquisite," Lian smiled, holding up the lion. "I have always had a
taste for Tairen craftwork. Rhuarc brought me two pieces many years
ago." In a voice suitable for a goodwife reminiscing over some particularly fine sugarberries, she said to her husband, "You took them from
the tent of a High Lord just before Laman was beheaded, did you not?
A pity you did not reach Andor. I have always wanted a piece of
Andoran silver. This necklace is beautiful, too, Mat Cauthon."

Listening to her heap praise on both gifts, Rand masked his shock.
For all her skirts and motherly eyes, she was as Aiel as any Maiden of
the Spear.

By the time Lian finished, Moiraine and the other Wise Ones arrived
with Lan and Egwene. The Warder's sword drew a single disapproving
glance, but the roofmistress welcomed him warmly after Bair called
him *Aan'allein.* Yet that was nothing to her greeting for Egwene and
Moiraine.

"You honor my roof, Aes Sedai." The roofmistress's tone made it
sound an understatement; she came very close to bowing to them. "It is
said that we served Aes Sedai before the Breaking of the World and
failed them, and for that failure were sent here to the Three-fold Land.
Your presence says that perhaps our sin was not beyond forgiving." Of
course. She had not been to Rhuidean; apparently the prohibition
against speaking of what happened in Rhuidean with anyone who had
not been there applied even between husband and wife. And between
sister-wives, or whatever the relationship was between Amys and Lian.

Moiraine tried to give Lian a guest gift, too, tiny crystal-and-silver
flasks of scent all the way from Arad Doman, but Lian spread her
hands. "Your very presence is guest gift beyond value, Aes Sedai. To
accept more would dishonor my roof, and me. I could not bear the
shame." She sounded entirely serious, and troubled that Moiraine
might press the scent on her. It was an indication of the relative importance of the *Car'a'carn* and an Aes Sedai.

"As you wish," Moiraine said, returning the flasks to her belt pouch.
She was icily serene in blue silk, her pale cloak thrown back. "Your
Three-fold Land will surely see more Aes Sedai. We have never had
reason to come, before."

Amys did not look best pleased over that at all, and flame-haired
Melaine stared at Moiraine like a green-eyed cat wondering if she
should do something about a large dog that had wandered into her

barnyard. Bair and Seana exchanged troubled glances, but nothing like the two who could channel.

A flurry of *gai'shain*—men and women alike graceful in cowled white robes, their downcast eyes seeming so strangely submissive in Aiel faces—took Moiraine and Egwene's cloaks, brought damp towels for hands and faces, and tiny silver cups of water to be drunk formally, and finally a meal, served with silver bowls and trays fit for a palace yet eaten from pottery with a blue-striped glaze. Everyone ate lying on the floor, where white tiles had been set into the stone for a table, heads together, cushions under their chests, radiating out like spokes in a wheel while *gai'shain* slipped between to place dishes.

Mat struggled, shifting this way and that on his cushions, but Lan lounged as if he had always eaten that way, and Moiraine and Egwene looked almost as comfortable. No doubt they had had practice in the Wise Ones' tents. Rand found it awkward, yet the food itself was peculiar enough to take most of his attention.

A dark, spicy stew of goat with chopped peppers was unfamiliar but hardly strange, and peas were peas anywhere, or squash. The same could not be said of the crumbly, coarse yellow bread, or long, bright red beans mixed in with the green, or a dish of bright yellow kernels and bits of pulpy red that Aviendha called *zemai* and *t'mat*, or a sweet, bulbous fruit with a tough greenish skin she said came from one of those leafless, spiny plants, called *kardon*. It was all tasty, though.

He might have enjoyed the meal more if she had not lectured him on everything. Not sister-wives. That was left to Amys and Lian, lying on either side of Rhuarc and smiling at each other almost as much as at their husband. If they had both married him so as not to break up their friendship, it was plain they both loved him. Rand could not see Elayne and Min agreeing to such an arrangement; he wondered why he had even thought of it. The sun must have cooked his brains.

But if Aviendha left that one explanation to others, she explained *every*thing else in tooth-grinding detail. Maybe she thought him an idiot for not knowing about sister-wives. Turned on her right side to face him, she smiled almost sweetly as she told him the spoon could be used for eating the stew or the *zemai* and *t'mat*, but her eyes shone with a light that said it was the Wise Ones being there that kept her from hurling a bowl of something at his head.

"I do not know what I've done to you," he said quietly. He was very conscious of Melaine on his other side, seeming engrossed in her own low conversation with Seana. Bair put in a word now and then, but he thought she was bending an ear his way, too. "But if you hate being my

teacher so much, you do not have to be. It just popped out. I'm sure
Rhuarc or the Wise Ones will find someone else." The Wise Ones
certainly would, if he rid himself of this spy.

"You have done nothing to me . . ." She bared teeth at him; if it
was meant to be a smile, it fell considerably short. ". . . and you never
will. You may lie however is most comfortable for eating, and talk to
those around you. Except for those of us who must instruct instead of
sharing the meal, of course. It is considered polite to talk with those on
both sides." From behind her, Mat looked at Rand and rolled his eyes,
clearly relieved to be spared that. "Unless you are forced to face one in
particular, as to teach him. Take food with your right hand—unless you
must lean on that elbow—and. . . ."

It was torture, and she seemed to enjoy it. The Aiel seemed to set
great store by the giving of gifts. Maybe if he gave her a gift. . . .

". . . all talk for a time when the meal is done, unless one of us
must teach instead, and. . . ."

A bribe. It did not seem fair to have to bribe someone who was
spying on him, but if she meant to go on even half like this, it would be
worth it for a little peace.

When the meal was cleared away by *gai'shain,* and silver cups of dark
wine brought, Bair fixed Aviendha with a grim eye across the white
tiles, and she subsided sulkily. Egwene knelt up to reach over Mat and
pat her, but it did not appear to help. At least she was quiet. Egwene
gave him a tight look; either she knew what he was thinking or she
considered Aviendha's sulks his fault.

Rhuarc dug out his short-stemmed pipe and tabac pouch, thumbing
the bowl full then passing the leather pouch to Mat, who had produced
his own silver-mounted pipe. "Some have taken news of you to heart,
Rand al'Thor, and quickly it seems. Lian tells me word has come that
Jheran, who is clan chief of the Shaarad Aiel, and Bael, of the Goshien,
have already reached Alcair Dal. Erim, of the Chareen, is on his way."
He allowed a slender young *gai'shain* woman to light his pipe with a
burning twig. From the way she moved, with a different sort of grace
than the other white-robed men and women, Rand suspected she had
been a Maiden of the Spear not too long ago. He wondered how long
she had to continue in her year and a day of service, meek and humble.

Mat grinned at the woman as she knelt to light his pipe; the green-
eyed stare she gave him from the depths of her cowl was not meek at
all, and wiped the grin right off his face. Irritably, he rolled onto his
belly, a thin blue streamer rising from his pipe. It was too bad he did
not see the satisfaction on her face, or see it wiped away in a blush by

one glance from Amys; the green-eyed young woman scurried away looking shamed beyond belief. And Aviendha, who so hated having had to give up the spear, who still saw herself as spear-sister to a Maiden of whatever clan . . . ? She frowned at the departing *gai'shain* as Mistress al'Vere would have glared at someone who had spit on the floor. A strange people. Egwene was the only one Rand saw with any sympathy in her eyes at all.

"The Goshien and the Shaarad," he muttered at his wine. Rhuarc had told him each clan chief would bring a few warriors to the Golden Bowl, for honor, and each sept chief, as well. Added together, it meant perhaps a thousand from each clan. Twelve clans. Twelve thousand men and Maidens, eventually, all tied up in their strange honor and ready to dance the spears if a cat sneezed. Maybe more, because of the fair. He looked up. "They have a feud, don't they?" Rhuarc and Lan both nodded. "I know you said that something like the Peace of Rhuidean holds at Alcair Dal, Rhuarc, but I saw how far that Peace held Couladin and the Shaido. Maybe I had better go right away. If the Goshien and the Shaarad start fighting. . . . A thing like that could spread. I want *all* the Aiel behind me, Rhuarc."

"The Goshien are not Shaido," Melaine said sharply, shaking her red-gold mane like a lioness.

"Nor are the Shaarad." Bain's reedy voice was thinner than that of the younger woman, but no less definite. "Jheran and Bael may try to kill one another before they return to their holds, but not at Alcair Dal."

"None of which answers Rand al'Thor's question," Rhuarc said. "If you go to Alcair Dal before all of the chiefs arrive, those who have not come yet will lose honor. It is not a good way to announce that you are *Car'a'carn,* dishonoring men you will call to follow you. The Nakai have farthest to come. A month, and all will be at Alcair Dal."

"Less," Seana said with a brisk shake of her head. "I have walked Alsera's dreams twice, and she says Bruan means to run all the way from Shiagi Hold. Less than a month."

"A month before you leave, to be sure," Rhuarc told Rand. "Then three days to Alcair Dal. Perhaps four. All will be there then."

A month. He rubbed his chin. Too long. Too long, and no choice. In stories, things always happened as the hero planned, seemingly when he wanted them to happen. In real life it rarely occurred that way, even for a *ta'veren* with prophecy supposedly working for him. In real life it was scratch and hope, and luck if you found more than half a loaf where you needed a whole. Yet a part of his plan was following the path he had hoped for. The most dangerous part.

Moiraine, stretched out between Lan and Amys, sipped her wine lazily, eyes lidded as if sleepy. He did not believe it. She saw everything, heard everything. But he had nothing to say now that she should not hear. "How many will resist, Rhuarc? Or oppose me? You have hinted, but you've never said for sure."

"I cannot be sure in it," the clan chief replied around his pipestem. "When you show the Dragons, they will know you. There is no way to imitate the Dragons of Rhuidean." Had Moiraine's eyes flickered? "You are the one prophesied. I will support you, and Bruan certainly, and Dhearic, of the Reyn Aiel. The others . . . ? Sevanna, Suladric's wife, will bring the Shaido since the clan has no chief. She is young to be roofmistress of a hold, doubtless displeased she will have only one roof and not an entire hold when someone is chosen to replace Suladric. And Sevanna is as wily and untrustworthy as any Shaido ever born. But even if she makes no trouble, you know that Couladin will; he acts the clan chief, and some Shaido may follow him without his entering Rhuidean. Shaido are fools enough for that. Han, of the Tomanelle, may move in any direction. He is a prickly man, hard to know and difficult to deal with, and—"

He cut off as Lian murmured softly, "Is there any other kind?" Rand did not think the clan chief had been meant to hear. Amys hid a smile behind her hand; her sister-wife buried her face innocently in her winecup.

"As I was saying," Rhuarc said, frowning resignedly from one of his wives to the other, "it is not a thing I can be sure of. Most will follow you. Perhaps all. Perhaps even the Shaido. We have waited three thousand years for the man who bears two Dragons. When you show your arms, none will doubt you are the one sent to unite us." And break them; but he did not mention that. "The question is how they will decide to react." He tapped his teeth with his pipestem for a moment. "You will not change your mind and don the *cadin'sor?*"

"And show them what, Rhuarc? A pretend Aiel? As well dress Mat for Aiel." Mat choked on his pipe. "I will not pretend. I am what I am; they must take me as I am." Rand raised his fists, coatsleeves falling enough to uncover the golden-maned heads on the backs of his wrists. "These prove me. If they aren't enough, then nothing is."

"Where do you mean to 'lead the spears to war once more'?" Moiraine asked suddenly, and Mat choked again, snatching the pipe out of his mouth and staring at her. Her dark eyes were not lidded any longer.

Rand's fists tightened convulsively, till his knuckles cracked. Trying to be clever with her was dangerous; he should have learned that long since. She remembered every word that she heard, filed it away, sorted and examined until she knew just what it meant.

He got to his feet slowly. They were all watching him. Egwene frowned even more worriedly than Mat, but the Aiel just watched. Talk of war did not upset them. Rhuarc looked—ready. And Moiraine's face was all frozen calm.

"If you will excuse me," he said, "I am going to walk around awhile."

Aviendha rose to her knees, and Egwene stood, but neither followed him.

CHAPTER
50

Traps

Outside, on the stone-paved path between the yellow brick house and the terraced vegetable garden, Rand stood staring down the canyon, not seeing much beyond afternoon shadows creeping across the canyon floor. If only he could trust Moiraine not to hand him to the Tower on a leash; he had no doubt she could do it, without using the Power once, if he gave her an inch. The woman could manipulate a bull through a mousehole without ever letting it know. He could use her. *Light, I'm as bad as she is. Use the Aiel. Use Moiraine. If only I could trust her.*

He headed toward the mouth of the canyon, slanting down whenever he found a footpath leading that way. They were all narrow, paved with small stones, some of the steeper carved in steps. Hammers ringing in several smithies echoed faintly. Not all of the buildings were houses. Through one open door he saw several women working looms, and another showed a silversmith putting up her small hammers and gouges, a third a man at a potter's wheel, his hands in the clay and the brick kilns hot behind him. Men and boys, except the youngest, all wore the *cadin'sor,* the coat and breeches in grays and browns, but there were often subtle differences between warriors and craftsmen, a smaller belt knife or none at all, perhaps a *shoufa* with no black veil attached. Yet watching a blacksmith heft a spear he had just given a foot-long point, Rand had no doubt the man could use the weapon as readily as make it.

The paths were not crowded, but there were plenty of people about. Children laughed, running and playing, the smaller girls almost as likely to be carrying pretend spears as dolls. *Gai'shain* carried tall clay jars of water on their heads, or weeded in the gardens, often under the direction of a child of ten or twelve. Men and women going about the tasks of their lives, not really that different from the things they might have done in Emond's Field, whether sweeping in front of a door or mending a wall. The children hardly gave him a glance, for all his red coat and thick-soled boots, and the *gai'shain* were so self-effacing it was difficult to say whether they noticed him or not. But craftsmen or fighters, men or women, the adults looked at him with an air of speculation, an edge of uncertain anticipation.

Very young boys ran barefoot in robes much like those of the *gai'shain*, but in the grayish-brown of the *cadin'sor*, not white. The youngest girls darted about on bare feet, too, in short dresses that sometimes failed to cover their knees. One thing about the girls caught his eye; up to perhaps twelve or so, they wore their hair in two braids, one over each ear, plaited with brightly colored ribbons. Just the way Egwene had worn hers. It had to be coincidence. Likely the reason she had stopped was that one of the Aiel women had told her that was how young Aiel girls wore their hair. A foolish thing to be thinking about anyway. Right now he had one woman to deal with. Aviendha.

On the canyon floor, the peddlers were doing a brisk trade with the Aiel crowding around the canvas-topped wagons. At least the drivers were, and Keille, a blue lace shawl on her ivory combs today, was bargaining hard in a loud voice. Kadere sat on an upturned barrel in the shade of his white wagon in a cream-colored coat, mopping his face, making no effort to sell anything. He eyed Rand and made as if to rise before sinking back. Isendre was nowhere to be seen, but to Rand's surprise, Natael was, his patch-covered cloak attracting a flock of following children, and some adults. Apparently the attraction of a new and larger audience had pulled him away from the Shaido. Or maybe Keille just did not want him out of her sight. Engrossed in her trading as she was, she found time to frown at the gleeman often.

Rand avoided the wagons. Questions asked of Aiel told him where the Jindo had gone, each to the roof of his or her society here at Cold Rocks. The Roof of the Maidens lay halfway up the still brightly lit east wall of the canyon, a garden-topped rectangle of grayish stone doubtless larger inside than it looked. Not that he saw the inside. A pair of

Maidens squatting beside the door with spears and bucklers refused him entrance, amused and scandalized that a man wanted to enter, but one agreed to carry his request in.

A few minutes later the Jindo and Nine Valleys Maidens who had gone to the Stone came out. And all the other Maidens of Nine Valleys sept in Cold Rocks, too, crowding the path to either side and climbing up on the roof among the rows of vegetables to watch, grinning as if they expected entertainment. *Gai'shain,* male as well as female, followed to serve them small cups of dark-brewed tea; whatever rule kept men outside the Roof of the Maidens apparently did not apply to *gai'shain.*

After he had examined several offerings, Adelin, the yellow-haired Jindo woman with the thin scar on her cheek, produced a wide bracelet of ivory heavily carved with roses. He thought it should suit Aviendha; whoever made it had carefully shown thorns among the blossoms.

Adelin was tall even for an Aiel woman, only a hand too short to look him in the eyes. When she heard why he wanted it—almost why; he just said it was a present for Aviendha's teachings, not a sop to soothe the woman's temper so he could stand to be near her—Adelin looked around at the other Maidens. They had all stopped grinning, their faces expressionless. "I will take no price for this, Rand al'Thor," she said, putting the bracelet in his hand.

"Is this wrong?" he asked. How would Aiel see it? "I don't want to dishonor Aviendha in any way."

"It will not dishonor her." She beckoned a *gai'shain* woman carrying pottery cups and pitcher on a silver tray. Pouring two cups, she handed one to him. "Remember honor," she said, sipping from his cup.

Aviendha had never mentioned anything like this. Uncertain, he took a sip of bitter tea and repeated, "Remember honor." It seemed the safest thing to say. To his surprise, she kissed him lightly on each cheek.

An older Maiden, gray-haired but still hard-faced, appeared in front of him. "Remember honor," she said, and sipped.

He had to repeat the ritual with every Maiden there, finally just touching the cup to his lips. Aiel ceremonies might be short and to the point, but when you had to repeat one with seventy-odd women, even sips could fill you up. Shadows were climbing the east side of the canyon by the time he escaped.

He found Aviendha near Lian's house, vigorously beating a blue-striped carpet hung on a line, more piled beside her in a heap of colors. Brushing sweat-damp strands of hair from her forehead, she stared at him expressionlessly when he handed her the bracelet and told her it was a gift in return for her teaching.

"I have given bracelets and necklaces to friends who did not carry the spear, Rand al'Thor, but I have never worn one." Her voice was perfectly flat. "Such things rattle and make noise to give you away when you must be silent. They catch when you must move quickly."

"But you can wear it now that you are going to be a Wise One."

"Yes." She turned the ivory circle over as if unsure what to do with it, then abruptly thrust her hand through it and held her wrist up to stare at it. She could have been looking at a manacle.

"If you do not like it. . . . Aviendha, Adelin said it would not touch your honor. She even seemed to approve." He mentioned the tea-sipping ceremony, and she squeezed her eyes shut and shuddered. "What is wrong?"

"They think you are trying to attract my interest." He would not have believed her voice could be so flat. Her eyes held no emotion at all. "They have approved of you, as if I still carried the spear."

"Light! Simple enough to set them straight. I don't—" He cut off as her eyes blazed up.

"No! You accepted their approval, and now you would reject it? That *would* dishonor me! Do you think you are the first man to try to catch my eye? They must think as they think, now. It means nothing." Grimacing, she gripped the woven carpetbeater with both hands. "Go away." With a glance at the bracelet, she added, "You truly know nothing, do you? You know nothing. It is not your fault." She seemed to be repeating something she had been told, or trying to convince herself. "I am sorry if I ruined your meal, Rand al'Thor. Please go. Amys says I must clean all of these rugs and carpets no matter how long it takes. It will take all night, if you stand here talking." Turning her back to him, she thwacked the striped carpet violently, the ivory bracelet jumping on her wrist.

He did not know whether the apology sprang from his gift or an order from Amys—he suspected the latter—yet she actually sounded as if she meant it. She was certainly not pleased—judging by the sharp grunt of effort that accompanied every full-armed swing of the beater —but she had not looked hateful once. Upset, appalled, even furious, but not hateful. That was better than nothing. She might become civil eventually.

As he stepped into the brown-tiled entry chamber of Lian's house, the Wise Ones were talking together, all four with shawls draped loosely over their elbows. They fell silent at his appearance.

"I will have you shown to your sleeping room," Amys said. "The others have seen theirs."

"Thank you." He glanced back at the door, frowning slightly. "Amys, did you tell Aviendha to apologize to me for dinner?"

"No. Did she?" Her blue eyes looked thoughtful for a moment; he thought Bair almost smiled. "I would not have ordered her to, Rand al'Thor. A forced apology is no apology."

"The girl was told only to dust carpets until she had sweated out some of her temper," Bair said. "Anything more came from her."

"And not in hopes of escaping her labors," Seana added. "She must learn to control her anger. A Wise One must be in control of her emotions, not they in control of her." With a slight smile, she glanced sideways at Melaine. The sun-haired woman compressed her lips and sniffed.

They were trying to convince him Aviendha was going to be wonderful company from now on. Did they really think he was blind? "You must know that I know. About her. That you set her to spy on me."

"You do not know as much as you think," Amys said, for all the world like an Aes Sedai with hidden meanings she did not intend to let him see.

Melaine shifted her shawl, eyeing him up and down in a considering manner. He knew a little about Aes Sedai; if she were Aes Sedai, she would be Green Ajah. "I admit," she said, "that at first we thought you would not see beyond a pretty young woman, and you are handsome enough that she should have found your company more amusing than ours. We did not reckon with her tongue. Or other things."

"Then why are you so eager for her to stay with me?" There was more heat in his voice than he wanted. "You can't think I will reveal anything to her now that I don't want you to know."

"Why do you allow her to remain?" Amys asked calmly. "If you refused to accept her, how could we force her on you?"

"At least this way I know who the spy is." Having Aviendha under his eye had to be better than wondering which of the Aiel were watching him. Without her, he would probably suspect that every casual comment from Rhuarc was an attempt to pry. Of course, there was no way to say it was not. Rhuarc was married to one of these women. Suddenly he was glad he had not confided more in the clan chief. And sad that he had thought of it. Why had he ever believed the Aiel would be simpler than Tairen High Lords? "I'm satisfied to leave her right where she is."

"Then we are all satisfied," Bair said.

He eyed the leathery-faced woman leerily. There had been a note of something in her voice, as if she knew more than he did. "She will not find out what you want."

"What we want?" Melaine snapped; her long hair swung as she tossed her head. "The prophecy says 'a remnant of a remnant shall be saved.' What we want, Rand al'Thor, *Car'a'carn*, is to save as many of our people as we can. Whatever your blood, and your face, you have no feeling for us. I will make you know our blood for yours if I have to lay the—"

"I think," Amys cut her off smoothly, "that he would like to see his sleeping room now. He looks tired." She clapped her hands sharply, and a willowy *gai'shain* woman appeared. "Show this man to the room that has been prepared for him. Bring him whatever he needs."

Leaving him standing there, the Wise Ones headed for the door, Bair and Seana looking daggers at Melaine, like members of the Women's Circle eyeing someone they meant to call to account sharply. Melaine ignored them; as the door closed behind them she was muttering something that sounded like "talk sense into that fool girl."

What girl? Aviendha? She was already doing what they wanted. Egwene maybe? He knew she was studying something with the Wise Ones. And what was Melaine willing to "lay" in order to make him "know their blood for his"? How could laying something make him decide he was Aiel? *Lay a trap, maybe? Fool! She wouldn't say right out she means to lay a trap. What sorts of things do you lay? Hens lay eggs,* he thought, laughing softly. He was tired. Too tired for questions now, after twelve days in the saddle and part of a thirteenth, all of them oven-hot and dry; he did not want to think of how he would feel if he had walked that distance at the same pace. Aviendha must have steel legs. He wanted a bed.

The *gai'shain* was pretty, despite a thin scar slanting just above one pale blue eye into hair so light as to look almost silver. Another Maiden; only not for the moment. "If it pleases you to follow me?" she murmured, lowering her eyes.

The sleeping room was not a bedchamber, of course. Unsurprisingly, the "bed" consisted of a thick pallet unfolded atop layered, brightly colored rugs. The *gai'shain*—her name was Chion—looked shocked when he asked for wash water, but he was tired of sweat baths. He was willing to bet Moiraine and Egwene had not had to sit in a tent full of steam to get clean. Chion brought the water, though, hot in a large brown pitcher meant for watering the garden, and a big white bowl for a washbasin. He chased her out when she offered to wash him. Strange people, all of them!

The room was windowless, lit by silver lamps hanging from brackets on the walls, but he knew it could not yet be full dark outside when he finished washing. He did not care. Only two blankets lay on the pallet, neither particularly thick. No doubt a sign of Aiel hardiness. Remembering the cold nights in the tents, he dressed again except for his coat and boots before blowing out the lamps and crawling beneath the blankets in pitch darkness.

Tired as he was, he could not stop tossing and thinking. What did Melaine mean to lay? Why did the Wise Ones not care that he knew Aviendha was their spy? Aviendha. A pretty woman, if surlier than a mule with four stone-bruised hooves. His breathing slowed, his thoughts became misty. A month. Too long. No choice. Honor. Isendre smiling. Kadere watching. Trap. Lay a trap. Whose trap? Which trap? Traps. If only he could trust Moiraine. Perrin. Home. Perrin was probably swimming in. . . .

Eyes closed, Rand stroked through the water. Nicely cool. And so wet. It seemed that he had never before realized how good *wet* felt. Lifting his head, he looked around at the willows lining one end of the pond, the big oak at the other, stretching thick, shading limbs over the water. The Waterwood. It was good to be home. He had the feeling he had been away; where was not exactly clear, but not important, either. Up to Watch Hill. Yes. He had never been farther than that. Cool and wet. And alone.

Suddenly two bodies hurtled through the air, knees clutched to chest, landing with great splashes that blinded him. Shaking the water out of his eyes, he found Elayne and Min smiling at him from either side, just their heads showing above the pale green surface. Two strokes would take him to either woman. Away from the other. He could not love both of them. Love? Why had that popped into his head?

"You do not know who you love."

He spun about in a swirl of water. Aviendha stood on the bank, in *cadin'sor* rather than skirt and blouse. Not glaring, though, just looking. "Come into the water," he said. "I'll teach you how to swim."

Musical laughter pulled his head around to the opposite bank. The woman who stood there, palely naked, was the most beautiful he had ever seen, with big, dark eyes that made his head whirl. He thought he knew her.

"Should I allow you to be unfaithful to me, even in your dreams?" she said. Somehow he was aware without looking that Elayne and Min and Aviendha were not there anymore. This was beginning to feel very odd.

For a long moment she considered him, completely unconscious of her nudity. Slowly she posed on toetips, arms swept back, then dove cleanly into the pond. When her head popped above the surface, her shining black hair was not wet. That seemed surprising, for a moment. Then she had reached him—had she swum, or was she just *there?*—tangling arms and legs around him. The water was cool, her flesh hot.

"You cannot escape me," she murmured. Those dark eyes seemed far deeper than the pond. "I will make you enjoy this so you never forget, asleep or awake."

Asleep or . . . ? Everything shifted, blurred. She wrapped herself around him tighter, and the blur went away. Everything was as it had been. Rushes filled one end of the pond; leatherleaf and pine grew almost to the water's edge at the other.

"I know you," he said slowly. He thought he must, or why would he be letting her do this? "But I don't. . . . This is not right." He tried to pull her loose, but as fast as he pried an arm away, she had it back again.

"I ought to mark you." There was a fierce edge in her voice. "First that milk-hearted Ilyena, and now. . . . How many women do you hold in your thoughts?" Suddenly her small white teeth burrowed at his neck.

Bellowing, he hurled her away and slapped a hand to his neck. She had broken the skin; he was bleeding.

"Is this how you amuse yourself when I wonder where you have gone?" a man's voice said contemptuously. "Why should I hold to anything when you risk our plan this way?"

Abruptly the woman was on the bank, clothed in white, narrow waist belted in wide woven silver, silver stars and crescents in her midnight hair. The land rose slightly behind her to an ash grove on a mound. He did not remember seeing ash before. She was facing—a blur. A thick, gray, man-sized fuzzing of the air. This was all . . . wrong, somehow.

"Risk," she sneered. "You fear risk as much as Moghedien, don't you? You would creep about like the Spider herself. Had I not hauled you out of your hole, you'd still be hiding, and waiting to snatch a few scraps."

"If you cannot control your . . . appetites," the blur said in the man's voice, "why should I associate with you at all? If I must take risks, I want a greater reward than pulling strings on a puppet."

"What do you mean?" she said dangerously.

The blur shimmered; somehow Rand knew it for hesitation, uncertainty over having said too much. And then suddenly the blur was gone. The woman looked at him, still neck-deep in the pond; her mouth tightened with irritation, and she vanished.

He started awake and lay still, peering up into blackness. A dream. But an ordinary dream, or something else? Fumbling a hand from under the blankets, he felt the side of his neck, felt the tooth marks and the thin trickle of blood. Whatever kind of dream, she had been in it. Lanfear. He had not dreamed *her*. And that other; a man. A cold smile crept onto his face. *Traps all around. Traps for unwary feet. Have to watch where I step, now.* So many traps. Everybody was laying them.

Laughing softly, he twisted around to go back to sleep—and froze, holding his breath. He was not alone in the room. *Lanfear.*

Frantically he reached for the True Source. For an instant he feared fear itself might defeat him. Then he floated in the cold calm of the Void, filled with a raging river of the Power. He sprang to his feet, lashing out. The lamps burst alight.

Aviendha sat cross-legged by the door, mouth hanging open and green eyes bulging by turns at the lamps and the bonds, invisible to her, that wrapped her completely. Not even her head could move; he had expected someone standing, and the weave extended well above her. He released the flows of Air immediately.

She scrambled to her feet, nearly losing her shawl in her haste. "I. . . . I do not believe I will ever become used to. . . ." She gestured at the lamps. "From a man."

"You have seen me wield the Power before." Anger oozed across the surface of the Void surrounding him. Sneaking into his room in the dark. Frightening him half to death. She was lucky he had not hurt her, killed her by accident. "You had best grow used to it. I am He Who Comes With the Dawn whether you want to admit it or not."

"That is not part—"

"Why are you here?" he demanded coldly.

"The Wise Ones are taking turns watching over you from outside. They meant to continue watching from. . . ." She trailed off, her face reddening.

"From where?" She only stared at him, her face growing more and more crimson. "Aviendha, from wh—?" Dreamwalkers. Why had it never occurred to him? "From inside my dreams," he said harshly. "How long have they been spying inside my head?"

She let out a long, heavy breath. "I was not supposed to let you know. If Bair finds out—Seana said it was too dangerous tonight. I do not understand it: I cannot enter the dream without one of them to help me. Something dangerous tonight is all I know. That is why they are taking turns at the door to this roof. They are all worried."

"You still haven't answered my question."

"I do not know why I am here," she muttered. "If you need protection. . . ." She glanced at her short belt knife, touched the hilt. The ivory bracelet seemed to irritate her; she folded her arms so it was tucked into her armpit. "I could not protect you very well with a knife this small, and Bair says if I pick up a spear again without someone actually attacking me, she will have my hide for a waterskin. I do not know why I should give up sleep to protect you at all. Because of you, I was beating rugs until less than a hour ago. By moonlight!"

"That wasn't the question. How long—?" He cut off suddenly. There was a feel in the air, a sense of wrongness. Of evil. It could be imagination, residue from his dream. It could be.

Aviendha gasped as the flame-red sword appeared in his hands, its slightly curved blade marked with the heron. Lanfear had accused him of using only the tenth part of what he was capable of, yet most of that tenth came by guess and fumbling. He did not *know* even the tenth part of what he could do. But he knew the sword.

"Stay behind me." He was just aware of her unsheathing her belt knife as he padded from the room in his stocking feet, soundless on the carpets. Oddly, the air was no cooler than when he had lain down. Perhaps those stone walls held what heat there was, for the farther out he went, the colder it grew.

Even the *gai'shain* must have sought their pallets by now. The halls and chambers stood silent and empty, most dimly illuminated by the scattered lamps still burning. Here where extinguished lamps meant pitch dark at noon, some lamps were always left lit. The feeling was still vague, but it would not go away. Evil.

He stopped suddenly, in the wide archway leading to the brown-tiled entry chamber. One silver lamp at each end of the room gave a pale light. In the middle of the floor a tall man stood with his head bowed over the woman wrapped in his black-cloaked arms, her head flung back and her white cowl fallen while he nuzzled at her throat. Chion's eyes were nearly closed, and she wore an ecstatic smile. A flush of embarrassment slid across the surface of the Void. Then the man raised his head.

Black eyes regarded Rand, too big in a pale, gaunt-cheeked face; a puckered, red-lipped mouth opened in a parody of a smile, showing sharp teeth. Chion crumpled to the floor as the cloak unfolded, spread into wide, batlike wings. The Draghkar stepped over her, white, white hands reaching for Rand, the long, slender fingers tipped with claws. Claws and teeth were not the danger, though. It was the Draghkar's kiss that killed, and worse.

Its crooning, hypnotic song clung tight around the Void. Those dark, leathery wings moved to enfold him as he stepped forward. One moment of startlement flashed in the huge black eyes before the Power-made sword clove the Draghkar's skull to the bridge of its nose.

A steel blade would have bound, but the blade woven of fire pulled free easily as the creature fell. For a moment, deep in the heart of the Void, Rand examined the thing at his feet. That song. Had he not been shielded from emotion by emptiness, kept dispassionate and distant, that song would have snared his mind. The Draghkar surely believed it had when he came to it so willingly.

Aviendha ran past him to half-kneel beside Chion and feel the *gai'shain*'s throat. "Dead," she said, thumbing the woman's eyelids the rest of the way shut. "Perhaps better for it. Draghkar eat the soul before they consume life. A Draghkar! Here!" She glared at him from her crouch. "Trollocs at Imre Stand, and now a Draghkar here. You bring ill times to the Three-fold—" With a cry, she threw herself flat across Chion as he leveled the sword.

A bar of solid fire shot over her from his blade to strike the chest of the Draghkar just filling the outer doorway. Bursting into flame, the Shadowspawn staggered back screaming, stumbling across the path, beating wings that dripped fire.

"Rouse everyone," Rand said calmly. Had Chion fought? How far had her honor held her? It would have made no difference. Draghkar died more easily than Myrddraal, but they were more dangerous in their own way. "If you know how to sound the alarm, do it."

"The gong by the door—"

"I will do it. Wake them. There may be more than two."

Nodding, she dashed back the way they had come, shouting, "Up spears! Wake and up spears!"

Rand stepped outside warily, sword ready, the Power filling him, thrilling him. Sickening him. He wanted to laugh, to vomit. The night was freezing, but he was barely aware of the cold.

The burning Draghkar was sprawled in the terrace garden, stinking of burning meat, adding the light of its low fire to the moon. A little way down the path Seana lay, long graying hair spread in a fan, staring at the sky with wide, unblinking eyes. Her belt knife lay beside her, but she had had no chance against a Draghkar.

Even as Rand snatched the leather-padded mallet hanging beside the square bronze gong, pandemonium erupted from the canyon mouth, human shouts and Trolloc howls, the clash of steel, screams. He sounded the gong hard, a sonorous toll that echoed down the canyon; almost immediately another gong sounded, then more, and from dozens of mouths the cry, "Up spears!"

Confused yells rose around the peddlers' wagons below. Rectangles of light appeared, doors flung open on the two boxlike wagons, gleaming white in the moonlight. Someone was shouting angrily down there —a woman; he could not tell who.

Wings beat in the air above him. Snarling, Rand raised the fiery sword; the One Power burned in him, and fire roared from the blade. The stooping Draghkar exploded in a rain of burning chunks that fell into the darkness below.

"Here," Rhuarc said. The clan chief's eyes were hard above his black veil; fully dressed, he carried buckler and spears. Mat stood behind him, coatless and bareheaded, shirt half tucked in, blinking uncertainly and gripping his black-hafted spear with both hands.

Rand took the *shoufa* from Rhuarc, then let it drop. A bat-winged shape wheeled across the moon, then swooped low on the far side of the canyon, vanishing in the shadows. "They hunt for me. Let them see my face." The Power surged in him; the sword in his hand flared till it seemed a small sun illumined him. "They can't find me if they do not know where I am." Laughing, because they could not see the joke, he ran down toward the sound of battle.

Pulling his spear free of a boar-snouted Trolloc's chest, Mat crouched, eyes searching the moonlit darkness near the canyon mouth for another. *Burn Rand!* None of the shapes he saw moving were big enough to be a Trolloc. *Always dumping me into these bloody things!* Low moans came from the wounded. A shadowy form he thought was Moiraine knelt beside a downed Aiel. Those balls of fire she tossed about were impressive, almost as much as that sword of Rand's, spurting bars of flame. The thing still shone so a circle of light surrounded the man. *I should have stayed in my blankets is what I should have done. It's bloody cold, and this is nothing to do with me!* More Aiel were beginning to appear, women in skirts come to help with the injured. Some of those women carried spears; they might not do the fighting normally, but once the battle had reached into the hold they had not stood by and watched.

A Maiden stopped beside him, unveiling. He could not make out her face, all moonshadows. "You dance your spear well, gambler. Strange days when Trollocs come to Cold Rocks." She glanced at the shadowy shape he thought was Moiraine. "They might have forced a way in without the Aes Sedai."

"There weren't enough for that," he said without thinking. "They were meant to pull attention here." *So those Draghkar would have a free hand to reach Rand?*

"I think you are right," she said slowly. "Are you a battle leader among the wetlanders?"

He wished he had kept his mouth shut. "I read a book once," he muttered, turning away. *Bloody pieces of other men's bloody memories.* Maybe the peddlers would be ready to leave after this.

When he stopped by the wagons, though, neither Keille nor Kadere was anywhere to be seen. The drivers were all clumped together, hastily passing around jars of something that smelled like the good brandy they had been selling, muttering and as agitated as if the Trollocs had actually come within smelling distance of them. Isendre stood at the top of the steps to Kadere's wagon, frowning at nothing. Even with her brows furrowed she was beautiful behind that misty scarf. He was glad that at least his memories of women were his own.

"The Trollocs are done," he told her, leaning on his spear so she would be sure to notice it. *No point risking having my skull split without getting a little good out of it.* No effort at all was needed to sound tired. "A hard fight, but you're safe, now."

She stared down at him, face expressionless, eyes glittering in the moonlight like dark, polished stone. Without a word she turned and went inside, slamming the door. Hard.

Mat expelled a long, disgusted breath and stalked away from the wagons. What did it take to impress the woman? Bed was what he wanted. Back in his blankets, and let Rand deal with Trollocs and bloody Draghkar. The man seemed to *enjoy* it. Laughing like that.

Rand was coming up the canyon now, the glow of that sword like lamplight around him in the night. Aviendha appeared, running to meet him with her skirts pulled up above her knees, then stopped. Letting her skirts fall, she smoothed them and fell in beside Rand, lifting her shawl around her head. He seemed not to see her, and her face was blank as stone. They deserved each other.

"Rand," a hurrying shadow called with Moiraine's voice, nearly as melodious as Keille's, but a cool music. Rand turned, waiting, and she slowed before she could be seen clearly, entering the light regally enough for any palace. "Matters grow more dangerous, Rand. The attack at Imre Stand could have been aimed at the Aiel—not likely, yet it could have been—but tonight the Draghkar were surely aimed at you."

"I know." Just like that. As calm as she and even colder.

Moiraine's lips compressed, and her hands were too still on her skirts; she was not best pleased. "Prophecy is most dangerous when you try to make it happen. Did you not learn that in Tear? The Pattern weaves itself around you, but when you try to weave it, even you cannot hold it. Force the Pattern too tight, and pressure builds. It can explode wildly in every direction. Who can say how long before it settles to focus on you again, or what will happen before it does?"

"As clear as most of your explanations," Rand said dryly. "What do you want, Moiraine? It is late, and I am tired."

"I want you to confide in me. Do you think you have already learned all there is to know, little more than a year out of your village?"

"No, I haven't learned everything yet." Now he sounded amused; sometimes Mat was not sure he was still as sane as he looked. "You want me to confide in you, Moiraine? All right. Your Three Oaths won't let you lie. Say plainly that whatever I tell you, you won't try to stop me, won't hinder me in any way. Say you won't try to use me for the Tower's ends. Say it plain and straight so I know it's true."

"I will do nothing to hinder you fulfilling your destiny. I have devoted my life to that. But I will not promise to watch while you lay your head on a chopping block."

"Not good enough, Moiraine. Not good enough. But if I could confide in you, I'd still not do it here. The night has ears." There were people moving all around in the darkness, but none close enough to hear. "Even dreams have ears." Aviendha tugged her shawl forward to shadow her face; even an Aiel could feel the cold, apparently.

Rhuarc stepped into the light, black veil hanging loose. "The Trollocs were only a diversion for the Draghkar, Rand al'Thor. Too few to be else. Draghkar meant for you, I think. Leafblighter does not want you to live."

"The danger grows," Moiraine said quietly.

The clan chief glanced at her before going on. "Moiraine Sedai is right. Since the Draghkar failed, I fear we can expect the Soulless next; what you call Gray Men. I want to put spears around you at all times. For some reason, the Maidens have volunteered for this task."

The cold *was* getting to Aviendha. Shoulders hunched, she had her hands shoved into her armpits as far as they would go.

"If they wish it," Rand said. He sounded a touch uncomfortable under all that ice. Mat did not blame him; he would not have put himself in the Maidens' hands again for all the silk on Sea Folk ships.

"They will watch better than anyone else," Rhuarc said, "having asked for the task. I do not mean to leave it to them alone, however. I will have everyone on guard. I believe it will be the Soulless next time, but that does not mean it cannot be something else. Ten thousand Trollocs instead of a few hundred."

"What about the Shaido?" Mat wished he had not cracked his teeth when they all looked at him. Maybe they had not even realized he was there until then. Still, he might as well say it. "I know you don't like them, but if you think there's really any chance of a bigger attack, wouldn't it be better to have them in here than outside?"

Rhuarc grunted; from him, that equaled a curse from most men. "I would not bring near a thousand Shaido inside Cold Rocks if Grass-burner were coming. I could not in any case. Couladin and the Shaido folded their tents at nightfall. We are well rid of them. I sent runners to make sure they leave Taardad land without taking a few goats or sheep with them."

That sword vanished from Rand's hand, the abrupt absence of its light like blindness. Mat squeezed his eyes shut to help them adapt, but when he opened them again, the moonlight still seemed dark.

"Which way did they go?" Rand asked.

"North," Rhuarc told him. "No doubt Couladin means to meet Sevanna on her way to Alcair Dal, to influence her against you. He may succeed. The only reason she laid her bridal wreath at Suladric's feet instead of his was that she meant to wed a clan chief. But I told you to expect trouble from her. Sevanna delights in causing trouble. It should not matter. If the Shaido will not follow you, they are small loss."

"I mean to go to Alcair Dal," Rand said firmly. "Now. I will apologize to any chief who feels dishonored by coming late, but I'll not let Couladin be there any longer before me than I can manage. He won't stop at turning Sevanna against me, Rhuarc. I cannot afford to hand him a month for it."

After a moment, Rhuarc said, "Perhaps you are right. You bring change, Rand al'Thor. At sunrise, then. I will choose out ten Red Shields for my honor, and the Maidens will provide yours."

"I mean to be leaving when first light hits the sky, Rhuarc. With every hand that can carry a spear or draw a bow."

"Custom—"

"There are no customs to cover me, Rhuarc." You could have cracked rocks with Rand's voice, or put a skim of ice on wine. "I have to make new customs." He laughed roughly. Aviendha looked shocked, and even Rhuarc blinked, taken aback. Only Moiraine was unaffected, with those considering eyes. "Someone had best let the peddlers know," Rand continued. "They won't want to miss the fair, but if they don't stop those fellows drinking they will be too drunk to handle reins. What of you, Mat? Are you coming?"

He certainly did not intend to let the peddlers get away from him, not his way out of the Waste. "Oh, I am right behind you, Rand." The worst of it was, it felt right saying that. *Bloody* ta'veren *tugging at me!* How had Perrin pulled free? *Light, I wish I was with him right now.* "I guess I am."

Shouldering his spear, he strode off up the canyon. There was still time to get a little sleep at least. Behind him he could hear Rand chuckling.

CHAPTER
51

Revelations in Tanchico

E layne fumbled with the two slim red-lacquered sticks, trying to
set them properly in her fingers. *Sursa,* she reminded herself.
Not sticks; sursa. A fool way to eat, whatever they're called.
On the other side of the table in the Chamber of Falling Blossoms,
Egeanin frowned at her own sursa, one upright in each hand as if they
really were sticks. Nynaeve held hers nestled in her hand the way Rendra had showed them, but so far she had managed to lift one sliver of
meat and a few sliced peppers as far as her mouth; her eyes were tight
with determination. A great many small white bowls covered the table,
each filled with slices and tiny slivers of meat and vegetables, some in
sauces dark or pale. Elayne thought it might take the rest of the day to
finish this meal. She gave the honey-haired innkeeper a grateful smile
when the woman leaned over her shoulder to position the sursa properly.

"Your land is at war with Arad Doman," Egeanin said, sounding
almost angry. "Why do you serve the dishes of your enemy?"

Rendra shrugged, making a moue behind her veil; she wore the
palest possible red today, and beads of the same color woven into her
narrow braids made soft clicks when she moved her head. "It is the
fashion, now. Four days ago the Garden of Silver Breezes began it, and
now almost every patron asks for the Domani food. I think maybe it is

that if we cannot conquer the Domani, at least we can conquer their food. Maybe in Bandar Eban they eat the lamb with the honey sauce and the glazed apples, yes? In four days more, perhaps it is something else. The fashion, it changes quickly now, and if someone whips up the mob against this. . . ." She shrugged again.

"Do you think there will be *more* riots?" Elayne asked. "Over what sort of food inns are serving?"

"The streets, they are restive," Rendra said, spreading her hands fatalistically. "Who can say what will spark them again? The uproar the day before yesterday, it came from a rumor Maracru had declared for the Dragon Reborn, or maybe fallen to the Dragonsworn, or the rebels perhaps—how seems to have made little difference—but does the mob turn on the people from Maracru? No. They rampage through the streets, pulling people from the carriages, and then burn the Grand Hall of the Assembly. Perhaps the word comes that the army, it has won a battle—or lost one—and the mob rises against those who serve Domani food. Or maybe it burns warehouses on the Calpene docks. Who can say?"

"No proper order," Egeanin muttered, thrusting the sursa firmly between the fingers of her right hand. From the expression on her face, they might have been daggers she was going to use to stab what was in the bowls. A bit of meat dropped out of Nynaeve's sursa short of her lips; growling, she snatched it from her lap, dabbing at the cream-colored silk with her napkin.

"Aah, order." Rendra laughed. "I remember order. Maybe it will come again one day, yes? Some thought the Panarch Amathera would put the Civil Watch back at their duties, but were I she, with the memory of the mob brawling outside my investiture. . . . The Children of the Light, they killed very many of the rioters. Perhaps this means there will not be another riot, but perhaps it means the next riot, it will be twice so big, or ten times. I think that I, too, would keep the Watch and the Children close around me. But this is no talk to disturb the meal." Examining the table, she nodded to herself in approval, the beads in her thin plaits clicking. As she turned toward the door, she paused with a small smile. "It is the fashion to eat the Domani food with the sursa, and of course one does what is the fashion. But . . . there are none here to see save yourselves, yes? Should you perhaps wish the spoons and the forks, they are under the napkin." She indicated the tray on the end of the table. "Enjoy."

Nynaeve and Egeanin waited until the door closed behind the inn-keeper, then grinned at each other and reached for the tray with decidedly unseemly haste. Elayne still managed to get her spoon and fork first; neither of the others had ever had to eat in the few minutes between a novice's chores and lessons.

"It is tasty enough," Egeanin said after her first mouthful, "when you can put any on your tongue." Nynaeve laughed with her.

In the seven days since meeting the dark-haired woman with her sharp blue eyes and slow drawl, they had both come to like her. She was a refreshing change from Rendra's chatter about hair and clothes and complexions, or stares in the street from people who looked as if they would slit a throat for a copper. This was her fourth visit since that first meeting, and Elayne had enjoyed every one. Egeanin had a directness and an air of independence she admired. The woman might be only a small trader in whatever came her way, but she could challenge Gareth Bryne for saying what she meant and bowing to no one.

Still, Elayne wished the visits had not been so frequent. Or rather that she and Nynaeve had not been at the Three Plum Court so often for Egeanin to find. Almost constant riots since Amathera's investiture made moving about the city all but impossible, however, despite their coterie of Domon's tough sailors. Even Nynaeve had admitted as much after they had had to flee a shower of fist-sized stones. Thom still promised to find them a carriage and team, but she was not too certain how hard he was looking. He and Juilin both seemed insufferably pleased that she and Nynaeve were mired inside the inn. *They come back bruised or bleeding and don't want us to even stub a toe,* she thought wryly. Why did men always think it was right to keep you safer than they kept themselves? Why did they think their injuries mattered less than yours?

From the taste of the meat, she suspected Thom should look in the kitchens here if he wanted to find horses. The thought of eating horse made her stomach queasy. She chose a bowl containing only vegetables, bits of dark mushroom, red peppers and some sort of feathery green sprouts in a pale, tangy sauce.

"What shall we discuss today?" Nynaeve asked Egeanin. "You have asked almost every question I can think of." Nearly every one they knew how to answer at any rate. "If you want to learn any more about Aes Sedai, you'll have to go to the Tower as a novice."

Egeanin flinched unconsciously, as she did at any words linking the Power to her. For a moment she stirred the contents of one of the small bowls, frowning at it. "You have not made any real effort," she said slowly, "to keep secret from me that you are looking for someone.

Women. If it does not intrude on your secrets, I would ask—" She cut off at a knock on the door.

Bayle Domon strode in without waiting, grim satisfaction warring with uneasiness on his round face. "I have found them," he began, then gave a start at the sight of Egeanin. "You!"

Shockingly, Egeanin knocked over her chair leaping up, and threw a fist at Domon's thick middle almost too fast to see. Somehow Domon caught her wrist in a big hand, twisted—there was a flurried instant where they seemed to be trying to hook each other's ankle with a foot; Egeanin attempted to strike him in the throat—then somehow, she was facedown on the floor, Domon's boot on her shoulder and her arm levered up hard against his knee. Despite that she snatched her belt knife free.

Elayne wove flows of Air around the pair before she even knew she had embraced *saidar,* freezing them where they were. "What is the meaning of this?" she demanded in her best icy tone.

"How dare you, Master Domon?" Nynaeve's voice was equally cold. "Unhand her!" More warmly, worriedly, she added, "Egeanin, why did you try to hit him? I told you to release her, Domon!"

"He cannot, Nynaeve." Elayne did wish the other woman could at least see flows clearly without being angry. *She* did *try to hit him first.* "Egeanin, why?"

The dark-haired woman lay there with eyes shut and mouth tight; her knuckles stood out bloodless from her grip on the knife hilt.

Domon glared from Elayne to Nynaeve, his odd Illianer beard nearly bristling. His head was all that Elayne had left free to move. "The woman do be Seanchan!" he growled.

Elayne exchanged startled looks with Nynaeve. Egeanin? Seanchan? It was impossible. It must be impossible.

"Are you certain?" Nynaeve asked slowly, quietly. She sounded as stunned as Elayne felt.

"I will never forget her face," Domon replied firmly. "A ship captain. It did be she who did take me to Falme, me and my ship, captives to the Seanchan."

Egeanin made no effort to deny it, only lay there gripping her knife. Seanchan. *But I like her!*

Carefully, Elayne shifted the weave of flows until Egeanin's knife hand lay uncovered to the wrist. "Let go of it, Egeanin," she said, kneeling beside the woman. "Please." After a moment, Egeanin's hand fell open. Elayne picked up the knife and backed away, loosing the flows completely. "Let her up, Master Domon."

"She be Seanchan, Mistress," he protested, "and hard as iron spikes."

"Let her up."

Muttering under his breath, he released Egeanin's wrist, moving away from her quickly as if he expected she might come at him again. The dark-haired woman—the *Seanchan* woman—merely stood, though. She worked the shoulder he had wrenched, eyeing him thoughtfully, glanced at the door, then raised her head and waited with every outward appearance of calm. It was hard not to keep on admiring her.

"Seanchan," Nynaeve growled. She clutched a fistful of her long braids, then gave her hand an odd stare and let go, but her brows were still furrowed and her eyes hard. "Seanchan! Worming your way into our friendship. I thought you had all gone back where you came from. Why are you here, Egeanin? Was our meeting really an accident? Why did you seek us out? Did you mean to lure us somewhere your filthy *sul'dam* could lock their leashes around our throats?" Egeanin's blue eyes widened fractionally. "Oh, yes," Nynaeve told her sharply. "We know about you Seanchan and your *sul'dam* and *damane*. We know more than you. You chain women who channel, but those you use to control them can channel too, Egeanin. For every woman who can channel that you've leashed like an animal, you walk by another ten or twenty every day without realizing it."

"I know," Egeanin said simply, and Nynaeve's mouth fell open.

Elayne thought her own eyes were going to pop out of her head. "You know?" She took a breath and went on in something less like an incredulous squeal. "Egeanin, I think you are lying. I've not met many Seanchan before, and never for more than a few minutes, but I know someone who has. Seanchan don't even hate women who channel. They think they are animals. You'd not take it so easily if you knew, or even believed."

"Women who can wear the bracelet are women who can learn to channel," Egeanin said. "I did not know it *could* be learned—I was taught a woman either could or could not—but when you told me that girls must be guided if they are not born with it, I reasoned it out. May I sit down?" So cool.

Elayne nodded, and Domon set Egeanin's chair upright, standing behind it while she sat. Looking over her shoulder at him, the dark-haired woman said, "You were not so . . . difficult . . . an opponent the last time we met."

"You did have twenty armored soldiers on my deck then, and a *damane* ready to break my ship apart with the Power. Just because I can hook a shark from a boat, I do no offer to wrestle it in the water." Surprisingly, he grinned at her, rubbing his side where she must have gotten in a blow Elayne had not seen. "You are no so easy an opponent yourself as I did think you would be without your armor and sword."

The woman's world had to have been turned upside down by her own reasoning, but she was taking it matter-of-factly. Elayne could not imagine what would spin her own world topsy-turvy that way, but she hoped that if she ever found out she could face it with Egeanin's calm reserve. *I have to stop liking her. She is Seanchan. They'd have collared me for a pet if they could. Light, how do you stop liking someone?*

Nynaeve appeared to be having no such difficulty. Planting her fists on the table, she leaned toward Egeanin so fiercely her braids dangled among the small bowls. "Why are you here in Tanchico? I thought you had all fled after Falme. And why have you tried to wriggle your way into our trust like some egg-eating snake? If you think you can collar us, think again!"

"That was never my intention," Egeanin said stiffly. "All I ever wanted from you was to learn about Aes Sedai. I. . . ." For the first time she seemed hesitant, unsure of herself. Compressing her lips, she looked from Nynaeve to Elayne and shook her head. "You are not as I was taught. The Light be upon me, I . . . like you."

"You like us." Nynaeve made it sound a crime. "That answers none of my questions."

Egeanin hesitated again, then held her head up, defying them to do their worst. "*Sul'dam* were left behind at Falme. Some deserted after the disaster. A few of us were sent to bring them back. I only found one, but I discovered that an *a'dam* would hold her." Seeing Nynaeve's fists tighten, she quickly added, "I let her go last night. I will pay dearly if that is ever discovered, but after talking with you, I could not. . . ." Grimacing, she shook her head. "That is why I stayed with you after Elayne revealed herself. I knew Bethamin was a *sul'dam*. To discover the *a'dam* held her, that she could. . . . I had to know, to understand, about women who could channel." She took a deep breath. "What do you mean to do with me?" Her hands, folded on the table, did not tremble.

Nynaeve opened her mouth angrily, and closed it again slowly. Elayne knew her difficulty. Nynaeve might hate Egeanin now, but what *were* they to do with her? It was not clear she had committed any crime in Tanchico, and in any event the Civil Watch seemed interested in nothing beyond saving its own collective skin. She was Seanchan, she had used *sul'dam* and *damane,* but on the other hand, she claimed to have let this Bethamin go free. For what crime could they punish her? Asking questions they had answered freely? Making them like her?

"I'd like to stripe your hide till you glow like a sunset," Nynaeve growled. Abruptly her head swung toward Domon. "You found them? You said you found them. Where?" He shifted his feet, shooting a meaning look at the back of Egeanin's head, eyebrows rising in a question.

"I do not believe she is a Darkfriend," Elayne said when Nynaeve hesitated.

"I certainly am not!" Egeanin's stare was fierce-eyed and offended.

Folding her arms as if to keep from tugging her braids, Nynaeve glared at the woman, then shifted an accusatory frown to Domon, as though this entire mess were his fault. "There isn't anywhere to lock her," she said finally, "and Rendra would surely demand reasons. Go ahead, Master Domon."

He gave a last, doubtful look at Egeanin. "At the Panarch's Palace, one of my men did see two of the women on your list. The one with the cats, and the Saldaean woman."

"Are you certain?" Nynaeve said. "At the Panarch's Palace? I wish you had seen for yourself. More women than Marillin Gemalphin like cats. And Asne Zeramene is not the only woman from Saldaea, even in Tanchico."

"A narrow-faced blue-eyed woman with a wide nose feeding a dozen cats in this city where people do eat cats? In the company of another with that Saldaean nose and tilted eyes? That is no so common a pair, Mistress al'Meara."

"It is not," she agreed. "But the Panarch's Palace? Master Domon, in case you have forgotten, five hundred Whitecloaks guard that place, commanded by an Inquisitor of the Hand of the Light! Jaichim Carridin and his officers at least must know Aes Sedai on sight. Would they remain if they saw the Panarch sheltering Aes Sedai?" He opened his mouth, but Nynaeve's point was telling, and nothing came out.

"Master Domon," Elayne said, "what was one of your men doing at the Panarch's Palace?"

He tugged at his beard in an embarrassed way, and rubbed his bare upper lip with a wide finger. "You see, the Panarch Amathera do be known to like ice peppers, the white kind that be very hot, and whether or no she be amenable to gifts herself, the customs men will know who did give her one and be more amenable themselves."

"Gifts?" Elayne said in her best reproving voice. "You were more honest on the docks, and called them bribes." Surprisingly, Egeanin had twisted around in her chair to give him a disapproving look, too.

"Fortune prick me," he muttered, "you did no ask me to give up my trade. And I would no if you did, no if you did bring my aged mother to ask. A man do have a right to his trade." Egeanin snorted and righted herself.

"His bribes are not our problem, Elayne." Nynaeve sounded exasperated. "I don't care if he bribes the entire city and smuggles—" A rap at the door cut her off. With a cautioning look at the others, she snapped "You sit quiet" to Egeanin, and raised her voice. "Come."

Juilin stuck his head into the room with that silly cylindrical cap on, frowning as usual at Domon. The gash on his dark cheek, the blood already dried, was not unusual either; the streets were rougher now by daylight than they had been by dark in the beginning. "May I speak to you alone, Mistress al'Meara?" he said when he saw Egeanin sitting at the table.

"Oh, come in," Nynaeve told him sharply. "After what she's heard already, it won't matter if she hears a little more. Have you found them in the Panarch's Palace, too?"

In the act of shutting the door, he shot an unreadable, tight-mouthed glance at Domon. The smuggler smiled, showing too many teeth. For a moment it seemed they might come to blows.

"So the Illianer is ahead of me," Juilin muttered ruefully. Ignoring Domon, he addressed Nynaeve. "I told you the woman with the white stripe would lead me to them. That is a very distinctive thing. And I saw the Domani woman there, too. From a distance—I am not fool enough to wade into a school of silverpike—but I cannot believe there is another Domani woman besides Jeaine Caide in all of Tarabon."

"You mean they *are* in the Panarch's Palace?" Nynaeve exclaimed.

Juilin's face did not change, but his dark eyes widened slightly, flickered toward Domon. "So he had no proof," he murmured in a satisfied tone.

"I did have proof," Domon avoided looking at the Tairen. "If you did no accept it before this fisherman did come, Mistress al'Meara, it be no fault of mine."

Juilin drew himself up, but Elayne cut in before the thief-catcher could speak. "You both found them, and you both brought proof. Very likely neither would have been sufficient without the other. Now we know where they are because of you both." If anything, they looked more disgruntled than before. Men could be absolutely silly at times.

"The Panarch's Palace." Nynaeve jerked a fistful of braids, then flung the long plaits over her shoulder with a toss of her head. "What they are after must be there. But if they have it, why are they still in Tanchico? The palace is huge. Maybe they haven't found it yet. Not that that helps if we are out here while they are inside!"

Thom, as usual, entered without knocking, taking in everyone at one glance. "Mistress Egeanin," he murmured, with an elegant bow his limp did nothing to diminish. "Nynaeve, if I could speak with you alone, I have important news."

The fresh bruise on his leathery cheek made Elayne even angrier than the new tear in his good brown cloak. The man was too old to be braving the streets of Tanchico. Or any rough streets, for that matter. It was time she arranged a pension for him, and somewhere safe and comfortable to live. No more gleeman wanderings from village to village for him. She would see to it.

Nynaeve gave Thom a sharp look. "I've no time for that now. The Black sisters are in the Panarch's Palace, and for all I know, Amathera is helping them search it from cellar to attic."

"I found out less than an hour ago," he said disbelievingly. "How did you . . . ?" He looked at Domon and Juilin, both still glowering like boys who had each wanted the whole cake.

It was obvious that he dismissed either as Nynaeve's source of information. Elayne felt like grinning. He did so pride himself on knowing all the undercurrents, all the hidden doings. "The Tower has its ways, Thom," she told him, cool and mysterious. "It is best not to inquire too closely into the methods of Aes Sedai." He frowned, bushy white eyebrows drawing down uncertainly. Most satisfactory. She became aware of Juilin and Domon frowning at her, too, and suddenly it was all she could do not to blush. If they talked, she *would* look a fool. They would, eventually; men did. Best to bury it quickly and hope. "Thom, have you heard anything that might indicate whether Amathera is a Darkfriend?"

"Nothing." He tugged one long mustache irritably. "Apparently she has not seen Andric since donning the Crown of the Tree. Maybe the troubles in the streets make travel between the King's Palace and the Panarch's too dangerous. Maybe she has simply realized that her power equals his now, and is no longer as compliant as before. Nothing to say what her allegiances are." With a glance at the dark-haired woman in the chair, he added, "I am grateful for the aid Mistress Egeanin gave you with those robbers, but to now I have thought she was a casually met friend. May I ask who she is to be brought into this? I seem to recall you threatening to tie a knot in any careless tongues, Nynaeve."

"She's Seanchan," Nynaeve told him. "Close your mouth before you swallow a moth, Thom, and sit down. We can eat while we try to figure out what to do."

"In front of her?" Thom said. "Seanchan?" He had heard some of the story of Falme from Elayne—some of it—and he had certainly heard the rumors here; he studied Egeanin as if wondering where she hid her horns. Juilin seemed to be strangling, if his bulging eyes were any indication; he must have heard the Tanchican rumors, too.

"Do you suggest I ask Rendra to lock her in a storeroom?" Nynaeve asked calmly. "That *would* cause comment, wouldn't it? I'm fairly certain three big, hairy men can protect Elayne and me if she pulls a Seanchan army out of her pouch. Sit, Thom, or else eat standing up, but stop staring. All of you, sit. I mean to eat before it grows cold."

They did, Thom looking as ill-contented as Juilin and Domon. Sometimes Nynaeve's bullying manner did seem to work. Perhaps Rand *would* respond to occasional bullying.

Putting Rand out of her mind, she decided it was time to add something of worth. "I cannot see how the Black sisters can be in the Panarch's Palace without Amathera's knowledge," she said, pulling her chair under her. "As I see it, that makes for three possibilities. One, Amathera is a Darkfriend. Two, she thinks they are Aes Sedai. And three, she is their prisoner." For some reason, Thom's approving nod made her feel warm inside. Silly. Even if he did know the Game of Houses, he was just a foolish bard who had thrown it all away to become a gleeman. "In any case, she will help them look for what they seek, but it seems to me that if she thinks they are Aes Sedai, we might be able to gain her help with the truth. And if she is a prisoner, we could gain it by freeing her. Even Liandrin and her companions could not hold on to the palace if the Panarch ordered it cleared, and that would give *us* a free hand to search."

"The problem is discovering whether she is ally, dupe or captive," Thom said, gesturing with his pair of sursa. He knew how to use the things perfectly!

Juilin shook his head. "The real problem is to reach her, whatever her situation. Jaichim Carridin has five hundred Whitecloaks around the palace like fisher-birds around the docks. The Panarch's Legion has nearly twice that, and the Civil Watch almost as many. Few of the ring forts are held half so well."

"We are not going to fight them," Nynaeve said dryly. "Stop thinking with the hair on your chest. This is a time for wits, not muscle. As I see it. . . ."

The discussion went on through the meal, continuing after the last small bowl was emptied. Egeanin even offered a few cogent comments after a while spent silently, not eating and not seeming to listen. She had a sharp mind, and Thom readily accepted any of her suggestions he agreed with, though he stubbornly rejected out of hand those he did not, just the way he treated everyone else. Even Domon, rather surprisingly, supported Egeanin when Nynaeve wanted her to keep quiet. "She do make sense, Mistress al'Meara. Only a fool do reject sense, wherever it do come from."

Unfortunately, knowing where the Black sisters were did little good without knowing whether or not Amathera was with them; that, or what they were after. In the end, almost two hours of discussion came to not much more than that and a few suggestions as to how to find out about Amathera. All of which, it seemed, were to be used by the men with their spiderweb of contacts crisscrossing Tanchico.

None of the fool men wanted to leave them alone with one of the Seanchan—until Nynaeve became angry enough to wrap them all three in flows of Air while they dithered before the door. "Do you not think," she said icily, surrounded by the glow of *saidar*, "that one of us might be able to do the same to her if she says boo?" She would not release any of them until they all nodded their heads, the only bits they could move.

"You keep a taut crew," Egeanin said as soon as the door closed behind them.

"Be quiet, Seanchan!" Nynaeve folded her arms tightly; she seemed to have given up trying to pull at those braids when she was angry. "Sit down, and—be—quiet!"

It was frustrating waiting there, staring at the plum trees and falling blossoms painted on the windowless walls, pacing the floor or watching Nynaeve pace, while Thom and Juilin and Domon were out actually doing something. Yet it was worse when each man came back at intervals, to report another trail faded away to nothing, another thread snapped, hear what the others had learned, and hurry out again.

The first time Thom returned—with a second purple bruise, on the other cheek—Elayne said, "Wouldn't you do better here, Thom, where you could hear whatever Juilin and Master Domon report? You could evaluate much better than Nynaeve or I."

He shook his foolish shaggy white head while Nynaeve sniffed loudly enough to be heard in the hallway. "I've a lead to a house on the Verana, where Amathera supposedly went sneaking some nights before she was raised Panarch." And he was gone before she could say another word.

When he next returned—limping distinctly more, reporting that the house was the home of Amathera's old nurse—Elayne spoke in her firmest voice. "Thom, I want you to sit down. You will stay here. I will not have you getting yourself hurt."

"Hurt?" he said. "Child, I never felt better in my life. Tell Juilin and Bayle there is supposedly a woman named Cerindra somewhere in this city who claims to know all sorts of dark secrets about Amathera." And off he hobbled, cloak swirling behind him. He had another tear in that, too. Stubborn, stubborn, foolish old man.

Once a clamor penetrated the thick walls, brutal shouts and cries from the street. Rendra bustled into the room just when Elayne had decided to go down and see for herself what it was. "Some little trouble outside. Do not disturb yourself. Bayle Domon's men, they keep it away from us, yes. I did not want you to worry."

"A riot here?" Nynaeve said sharply. The immediate neighborhood of the inn had been one of the few calm areas in the city.

"Not to worry," Rendra said soothingly. "Perhaps they want food. I will tell them where Bayle Domon's soup kitchen is, and they will go away."

The noise did die down after a while, and Rendra sent up some wine. Not until the serving man was leaving, with a sulky look on his face, did Elayne realize it was the young man with the beautiful brown eyes. The man had begun reacting to her coldest stares as if they were smiles. Did the fool think she had time to notice him now?

Waiting and pacing, pacing and waiting. Cerindra turned out to be a tirewoman dismissed for theft; not at all grateful for not being imprisoned, she would make any accusation against Amathera that was suggested to her. A fellow who claimed to have proof that Amathera was Aes Sedai and Black Ajah also claimed that the same documents proved King Andric the Dragon Reborn. The group of women whom Amathera used to meet in secret were friends Andric despised, and the shocking discovery that she financed several smuggling craft led nowhere. Almost every noble but the King himself had a finger in smuggling. Every trail ended that way. The worst Thom could discover was that Amathera had convinced two handsome young lords that each was the true love of her life and Andric only a means to an end. On the other hand, she had given audiences in the Panarch's Palace to various lords, both alone and in company with various women recognizable as

Liandrin and others on the list, and reportedly asked and accepted their advice for her decisions. Ally, or captive?

When Juilin came back, a good three hours after sunset, spinning a thumb-thick staff of ridged wood and muttering about some pale-haired fellow who had tried to rob him, Thom and Domon were already slumped disconsolately at the table with Egeanin.

"This will be Falme again," Domon growled at the air. The stout cudgel he had acquired somewhere lay in front of him, and he wore a short sword at his belt now. "Aes Sedai. The Black Ajah. Meddling with the Panarch. If we do no find something tomorrow, I do mean to take myself out of Tanchico. The next day for certain, if my own sister do ask me to stay!"

"Tomorrow," Thom said wearily, elbows on the table and chin on fists. "I am too tired to think straight any longer. I found myself listening to a laundryman from the Panarch's Palace who claims he has heard Amathera singing bawdy songs, the sort you hear in the roughest taverns on the docks. I actually listened to him."

"For me," Juilin said, reversing a chair to straddle it, "I mean to look on tonight. I found a roofman who says the woman he keeps company with was another of Amathera's tirewomen. According to him, Amathera discharged all of her tirewomen without warning the same evening she was invested Panarch. He will take me to talk with her after he finishes some business of his own at a merchant's house."

Nynaeve moved to the end of the table, fists on hips. "You will not be going anywhere tonight, Juilin. The three of you will be taking turns guarding our door." The men protested volubly, of course, all together.

"I do have my own trade to keep up, and if I must spend my days asking questions for you. . . ."

"Mistress al'Meara, this woman is the first person I have found who's actually seen Amathera since she was raised. . . ."

"Nynaeve, I'll hardly be able to *find* a rumor tomorrow, much less trace it, if I spend the night playing at. . ."

She let them argue themselves out. When they began to trail off, obviously thinking her convinced, she said, "Since we have nowhere else to keep the Seanchan woman, she will have to sleep with us. Elayne, will you ask Rendra to have a pallet made up? On the floor will do nicely." Egeanin glanced at her, but said nothing.

The men were neatly boxed; either they refused flatly, and openly broke their word to do as Nynaeve said, or else argued on, sounding as if they were whining. They glowered and spluttered—and acquiesced.

Rendra was clearly surprised they requested only a pallet, but accepted the tale that Egeanin feared to risk the streets at night. She did look miffed when Thom seated himself in the hall beside their door. "Those fellows, they did not get inside however hard they tried. I told you the soup kitchen would take them away, yes? Guests at the Three Plum Court have no need for the bodyguards on their rooms."

"I am sure not," Elayne told her, gently trying to push her out with the door. "It's just that Thom and the others do worry so. You know how men are." Thom shot her a hawkish stare beneath those thick white eyebrows, but Rendra sniffed, agreeing that she did indeed know, and let Elayne shut the door.

Nynaeve immediately turned to Egeanin, who was spreading her pallet on the far side of the bed. "Take off your clothes, Seanchan. I want to be sure you don't have another knife hidden away."

Egeanin calmly stood and undressed down to her linen shift. Nynaeve searched through her dress thoroughly, then insisted on searching Egeanin as well, and none too gently. Finding nothing did not seem to soothe her.

"Hands behind your back, Seanchan. Elayne, bind her."

"Nynaeve, I don't think she—"

"Bind her with the Power, Elayne," Nynaeve said roughly, "or I'll cut strips from her dress and bind her hands and heels. You remember how she handled those fellows in the street. Probably her own hirelings. She could probably kill us in our sleep with her bare hands."

"Really, Nynaeve, with Thom outside—"

"She's Seanchan! Seanchan, Elayne!" She sounded as if she hated the dark-haired woman for a personal wrong, which made no sense. Egwene had been in their hands, but not Nynaeve. The set of her jaw said she meant to have her way, with the Power or with ropes if she could find them.

Egeanin had already placed her wrists together in the small of her back, compliant if not meek. Elayne wove a flow of Air around them and tied it off; at least it would be more comfortable than bindings cut out of her dress. Egeanin flexed her arms slightly, testing the bonds she could not see, and shivered. She could as easily have broken steel chains. Shrugging, she laid herself down awkwardly on the pallet and turned her back to them.

Nynaeve began undoing her own dress. "Let me have the ring, Elayne."

"Are you sure, Nynaeve?" She looked at Egeanin in a significant manner. The woman seemed to be paying no attention to them.

"She'll not go running to betray us tonight." Pausing to pull the dress over her head, Nynaeve sat on the edge of the bed in her thin silk Taraboner shift to roll down her stockings. "Tonight is the agreed night. Egwene will expect one of us, and it is my turn. She will be worried if neither of us appears."

Elayne fished the leather cord around her neck out of the bosom of her dress. The stone ring, all flecks and stripes in blue and brown and red, lay snuggled against the golden serpent eating its own tail. Unknotting the string long enough to hand the *ter'angreal* to Nynaeve, she retied and replaced it. Nynaeve strung the stone *ter'angreal* with her own Great Serpent ring and Lan's heavy gold ring, let them hang between her breasts.

"Give me an hour after you are certain I'm asleep," she said, stretching out atop the blue coverlet. "It should take no longer than that. And keep an eye on her."

"What can she do bound, Nynaeve?" Elayne hesitated before adding, "I don't think she would try to harm us if she were loose."

"Don't you dare!" Nynaeve raised her head to glare at Egeanin's back, then lay back on the pillows again. "An hour, Elayne." Closing her eyes, she wriggled to make herself more comfortable. "That should be more than enough," she murmured.

Hiding a yawn behind her hand, Elayne brought the low stool to the foot of the bed, where she could watch Nynaeve, and Egeanin, too, though that hardly seemed necessary. The woman lay huddled on her pallet with her knees up, hands securely fastened. It had been a strangely tiring day considering that they had never left the inn. Nynaeve was already muttering softly in her sleep. With her elbows jutting out.

Egeanin lifted her head and looked over her shoulder. "She hates me, I think."

"Go to sleep." Elayne stifled another yawn.

"You do not."

"Don't be too sure of yourself," she said firmly. "You are taking this very calmly. How can you be so calm?"

"Calm?" The other woman's hands moved involuntarily, twisting at her Air-woven bonds. "I am so terrified I could weep." She did not sound it. Yet it sounded the simple truth.

"We won't harm you, Egeanin." Whatever Nynaeve wanted, she would see to that. "Go to sleep." After a moment Egeanin's head lowered.

An hour. It was right not to worry Egwene needlessly, but she wished that hour could be spent on their problem instead of wandering uselessly in *Tel'aran'rhiod.* If they could not find out whether Amathera was prisoner or captive. . . . *Set that aside; I won't puzzle it out here.* Once they did find out, how could they get inside the palace with all those soldiers about, and the Civil Watch, not to mention Liandrin and the others?

Nynaeve had started snoring softly, a habit she denied even more heatedly than she did flinging her elbows about. Egeanin appeared to be taking the long, slow breaths of deep sleep. Yawning into the back of her hand, Elayne shifted on the hard wooden seat and began planning how to sneak into the Panarch's Palace.

CHAPTER
52

Need

For a moment Nynaeve stood in the Heart of the Stone not seeing it, not thinking of *Tel'aran'rhiod* at all. Egeanin was Seanchan. One of those vile people who had put a collar on Egwene's neck and tried to put one on hers. Knowing it still made her feel hollow. Seanchan, and she had snaked her way into Nynaeve's affections. True friends had seemed so few and far between since leaving Emond's Field. To find a new one, then lose her in this way. . . .

"I hate her for that worst of all," she growled, folding her arms tightly. "She made me like her, and I cannot stop, and I hate her for it!" Said aloud, it made no sense at all. "I do not have to make sense." She laughed quietly, with a rueful shake of her head. "I am supposed to be Aes Sedai." But not to be wool-gathering like a fool girl.

Callandor sparkled, the crystal sword rising out of the floorstones beneath the great dome, and the massive redstone columns ran off in shadowed rows through that odd, dim light that came from everywhere. Easy to remember the feel of being watched, to imagine it again. If it had been imagination before. If it was now. Anything might be hiding back in there. A good stout stick appeared in her hands as she peered among the columns. Where was Egwene? Just like the girl to keep her waiting. All that murkiness. For all she knew, something could be about to jump out at—

"That is an odd dress, Nynaeve."

Just stifling a yelp, she spun around heavily, rattling metallically, heart thumping in her throat. Egwene stood on the other side of *Callandor* with two women in bulky skirts and dark shawls over white blouses, snowy hair held by folded scarves falling to their waists. Nynaeve swallowed, hoping none of them noticed, tried to make herself breathe normally again. Sneaking up on her that way!

One of the Aiel women she knew from Elayne's description; Amys's face was much too young for such hair, but apparently it had been almost silver even as a child. The other, thin and bony, had pale blue eyes in a leathery, wrinkled face. That must be Bair. The tougher of the two, in Nynaeve's opinion now that she saw them, not that this Amys looked very—Odd dress? *I rattled?*

Staring down at herself, she gasped. Her dress looked vaguely like a Two Rivers garment; if Two Rivers women wore dresses fashioned from steel mail, with pieces of plate armor like those she had seen in Shienar. How did men run about and jump into saddles in these things? It dragged at her shoulders as if it weighed a hundred pounds. The good stick was metal now, and spiked at the end like a shiny steel sandburr. Without touching her head she knew she had on some sort of helmet. Blushing furiously, she concentrated, changed it all to good Two Rivers woolens and a walking staff. It felt good to have her hair back in one proper braid, hanging over her shoulder.

"Uncontrolled thoughts are troublesome when you walk the dream," Bair said in a thin, strong voice. "You must learn to control them if you mean to continue."

"I can control my thoughts very well, thank you," Nynaeve said crisply. "I—" Bair's voice was not all that was thin. The Two Wise Ones seemed . . . misty, almost, and Egwene, in a pale blue riding dress, was very nearly transparent. "What's the matter with you? Why do you look that way?"

"You try entering *Tel'aran'rhiod* while half-asleep in a saddle," Egwene said dryly. She seemed to flicker. "It is morning in the Threefold Land, and we are on the move. I had to talk Amys into letting me come at all, but I was afraid you would be worried."

"It is a difficult enough task without the horse," Amys said, "sleeping shallowly when you wish to be awake. Egwene has not learned it entirely yet."

"I will," Egwene said with an irritated determination. She was always too hasty and stubborn in her desire to learn; if these Wise Ones did not hold on to the scruff of her neck she would very likely jump into all sorts of trouble.

Nynaeve stopped worrying about Egwene and trouble as the younger woman began to speak of Trollocs and Draghkar attacking Cold Rocks Hold. Seana, a Wise One dreamwalker, among the dead. Rand hurrying the Taardad Aiel toward this Alcair Dal, apparently in violation of all custom, sending out runners to bring more septs. The boy was confiding his intentions to no one, the Aiel were jumpy, and Moiraine was ready to bite the heads off nails. Moiraine's frustration would have been some relief—she had hoped he could escape that woman's influence somehow—if Egwene had not frowned so worriedly.

"I don't know whether it is madness or design," Egwene finished. "I could almost bear it either way if I knew. Nynaeve, I'll admit it isn't prophecy, or Tarmon Gai'don, that makes me anxious right now. Maybe it is foolish, but I promised Elayne to look after him, and I do not know how."

Nynaeve walked around the crystal sword to put an arm around her. At least she felt solid, even if she did look a reflection in a foggy mirror. Rand's sanity. There was nothing she could do about that, no comfort she could offer. Egwene was the one there to see him. "The best you can do for Elayne is to tell him to read what she wrote. She worries about it sometimes; she won't talk, but I think she's afraid she said more than she should have. If he believes she is totally besotted, he's more likely to feel the same, which will not hurt her in the least. At least we have some good news in Tanchico. Some." When she explained, though, it barely seemed to justify "some."

"So you still don't know what it is they're after," Egwene said after she finished, "but even if you did, they are on top of it and still might find it first."

"Not if I can help it." Nynaeve fixed the two Wise Ones with a firm, level look. From what Elayne said of Amys's reluctance to give anything but warnings, she would need firmness to deal with them. The pair was so hazy a strong puff might blow them away like fog. "Elayne thinks you know all sorts of tricks with dreams. Is there any way I could get into Amathera's dreams to see if she is a Darkfriend?"

"Foolish girl." Bair's long hair swung as she shook her head. "If Aes Sedai, a foolish girl still. To step into another's dream is very dangerous unless she knows you and expects you. It is *her* dream, not as here. There, this Amathera will control all. Even you."

She had been sure that was the way. It was irritating to learn differently. And "foolish girl"?

"I am not a girl," she snapped. She wanted to yank her braid, but clenched a fist at her side instead; for some reason, pulling at her hair felt strangely uncomfortable of late. "I was Wisdom of Emond's Field before I . . . became Aes Sedai . . ." She hardly stumbled over the lie at all now. "and I told women as old as you when to sit down and be quiet. If you know how to help me, say so instead of giving me *foolish maunderings* about what is dangerous. I know danger when I see it."

Abruptly she realized her single braid had split in two, one over each ear, red ribbons woven through to make tassels on the ends. Her skirt was so short it showed her knees, she wore a loose white blouse like the Wise Ones, and her shoes and stockings were gone. Where had *this* come from? She had surely never thought of wearing anything like it. Egwene put a hasty hand over her mouth. Was she aghast? Surely not smiling.

"Uncontrolled thoughts," Amys said, "can be very troublesome indeed, Nynaeve Sedai, until you learn." Despite her bland tone, her lips quirked in barely masked amusement.

Nynaeve kept her face smooth with an effort. They could not have had anything to do with it. *They can't have!* She struggled to change back, and it *was* a struggle, as though something held her as she was. Her cheeks grew hotter and hotter. Suddenly, just at the point when she was ready to break down and ask advice, or even help, her clothes and hair were as they had been. She wriggled her toes gratefully in good stout shoes. It *had* just been some odd, stray thought. In any case, she was not about to voice any suspicions; they looked far too amused as it was, even Egwene. *I am not here for some fool contest. I just won't dignify them.*

"If I cannot enter her dream, can I bring her into the World of Dreams? I need some way to talk to her."

"We would not teach you that if we knew how," Amys said, hitching her shawl angrily. "It is an evil thing you ask, Nynaeve Sedai."

"She would be as helpless here as you in her dream." Bair's thin voice sounded like an iron rod. "It has been handed down among dreamwalkers since the first that no one must ever be *brought* into the dream. It is said that that was the way of the Shadow in the last days of the Age of Legends."

Nynaeve shifted her feet under those hard stares; realizing she had an arm around Egwene, she held still. She was not about to let Egwene think they had made her uneasy. Not that they had. If she thought of being hauled before the Women's Circle before she was chosen Wisdom, it was nothing at all to do with the Wise Ones. Firmness was what was. . . . They stared at her. Hazy or not, these women could duel Siuan Sanche stare for stare. Especially Bair. Not that they intimidated her, but she could see the point of being reasonable. "Elayne and I need help. The Black Ajah is sitting on top of something that can harm Rand. If they find it before we do, they may be able to control him. We need to find it first. If there is anything you can do to help, anything you can tell me. . . . Anything at all."

"Aes Sedai," Amys said, "you can make a request for help sound a demand." Nynaeve's mouth tightened—demand? She had all but begged. Demand, indeed!—but the Aiel woman did not seem to notice. Or chose to ignore it. "Yet a danger to Rand al'Thor. . . . We cannot allow the Shadow to have that. There is a way."

"Dangerous." Bair shook her head vigorously. "This young woman knows less than Egwene did when she came to us. It is too dangerous for her."

"Then maybe I could—" Egwene began, and the two cut her off as one.

"You are going to complete your training; you are too eager to go beyond what you know," Bair said sharply at the same time Amys said, not the slightest bit softer, "You are not there in Tanchico, you do not know the place, and you cannot have Nynaeve's need. She is the hunter."

Under those iron eyes, Egwene subsided sulkily, and the two Wise Ones looked at each other. Finally Bair shrugged and lifted her shawl up around her face; clearly she washed her hands of the entire matter.

"It is dangerous," Amys said. They made it sound as if breathing was dangerous in *Tel'aran'rhiod.*

"I—!" Nynaeve cut off as Amys's eyes actually grew harder; she would not have thought it possible. Keeping a firm image of her clothes as they were—of course they had had nothing to do with that; it simply seemed wise to make sure her dress remained as it was—she changed what she had been going to say. "I will be careful."

"It is not possible," Amys told her flatly, "but I do not know another way. Need is the key. When there are too many people for the hold, the sept must divide, and the need is for water at the new hold. If no location with water is known, one of us may be called to find one. The key then is the need for a proper valley or canyon, not too far from the first, with water. Concentrating on that need will bring you near to what you want. Concentrating on the need again will bring you closer. Each step brings you nearer, until at last you are not only in the valley, but standing beside where water is to be found. It may be harder for you, because you do not know exactly what you are seeking, though the depth of need may make up for it. And you know already in a rough fashion where it lies, in this palace.

"The danger is this, and you must be aware of it." The Wise One leaned toward her intently, driving her words home with a tone as sharp as her gaze. "Each step is made blind, with eyes closed. You cannot know where you will be when you open your eyes. And finding the water does no good if you are standing in a den of vipers. The fangs of a mountain king kill as quickly in the dream as waking. I think these women Egwene speaks of will kill more quickly than the snake."

"I did that," Egwene exclaimed. Nynaeve felt her jump as the Aiel women's eyes went to her. "Before I met you," she said hastily. "Before we went to Tear."

Need. Nynaeve felt warmer toward the Aiel women now that one of them had given her something she could use. "You must keep a close eye on Egwene," she told them, hugging the younger woman to show she meant it fondly. "You are right, Bair. She will try to do more than she knows how. She has always been that way." For some reason Bair arched a white eyebrow at *her.*

"I do not find her so," Amys said in a dry voice. "She is a biddable student, now. Is that not so, Egwene?"

Egwene's mouth set in a stubborn line. These Wise Ones did not know her well if they believed a Two Rivers woman would call herself biddable. On the other hand, she did not say anything. That was unexpected. As hard a lot as Aes Sedai, it appeared, these Aiel women.

Her hour was slipping away, and impatience bubbled to try this method now; if Elayne woke her, it might take hours to get back to sleep. "In seven days," she said, "one of us will meet you here again."

Egwene nodded. "In seven days, Rand will have shown himself to the clan chiefs as He Who Comes With the Dawn, and the Aiel will all be behind him." The Wise Ones' eyes shifted slightly, and Amys adjusted her shawl; Egwene did not see it. "The Light knows what he means to do then."

"In seven days," Nynaeve said, "Elayne and I will have taken whatever Liandrin is hunting away from the lot of them." Or else, very likely, the Black Ajah would have it. So the Wise Ones were not more certain the Aiel would follow Rand than Egwene was of his plans. No certainty anywhere. But no point in burdening Egwene with more doubts, either. "When one of us sees you next, we'll have laid them by the heels and stuffed them all in sacks to cart to the Tower for trial."

"Try to be careful, Nynaeve. I know you don't know how to, but try anyway. Tell Elayne I said so, too. She isn't as . . . bold . . . as you are, but she can come close." Amys and Bair each laid a hand on Egwene's shoulder, and they were gone.

Try to be careful? Fool girl. She was always careful. What had Egwene been about to say rather than bold? Nynaeve folded her arms tightly in lieu of pulling her braid. Maybe better she did not know.

She realized she had not told Egwene about Egeanin. Perhaps best not to stir up Egwene's memories of her captivity. Nynaeve could remember all too well the other woman's nightmares for weeks after she was freed, waking up screaming that she would not be chained. Much the best to let it lie. It was not as if Egwene need ever meet the Seanchan woman. *Burn that woman! Burn Egeanin to ash! Burn her!*

"This is not using my time wisely," she said aloud. The words echoed through the tall columns. With the other women gone, they looked even more foreboding than before, more a hiding place for unseen watchers and things that jumped out at you. Time to be away.

First, though, she changed her hair to a tassel of long narrow braids, her dress to clinging folds of dark green silk. A transparent veil covered her mouth and nose, fluttering slightly when she breathed. With a grimace she added beads of green jade woven into the thin plaits. Should any of the Black sisters be using their stolen *ter'angreal* to enter the World of Dreams and see her in the Panarch's Palace, they would think her only a Taraboner woman who had dreamed herself there in more ordinary fashion. Some knew her by sight, though. Lifting a handful of bead-strung braids, she smiled. Pale honey. She had not realized that was possible. *I wonder what I look like. Could they still know me?*

Suddenly a tall stand-mirror stood beside *Callandor*. In the glass, her big brown eyes widened in shock, her rosebud of a mouth fell open. She had Rendra's face! Her features flickered back and forth, eyes and hair flashing darker then lighter; straining, she settled them as the innkeeper's. No one would know her now. And Egwene thought she did not know how to be careful.

Closing her eyes, she concentrated on Tanchico, on the Panarch's Palace, on need. Something dangerous to Rand, to the Dragon Reborn, need. . . . Around her, *Tel'aran'rhiod* shifted; she *felt* it, a sliding lurch, and opened her eyes eagerly to see what she had found.

It was a bedchamber, as big as any six at the Three Plum Court, the white plaster walls worked in painted friezes, golden lamps hanging from the ceiling by gilded chains. The tall posts of the bed spread carved limbs and leaves in a canopy above the mattresses. A woman well short of her middle years stood stiffly with her back to one of the posts at the foot of the bed; she was really quite lovely, in that pouty-mouthed way that Nynaeve herself had adopted. Atop her dark braids sat a crown of golden trefoil leaves among rubies and pearls with a moonstone larger than a goose egg, and around her neck hung a broad stole, dangling to her knees and embroidered along its length with trees. Aside from crown and stole she wore only a glistening coat of sweat.

Her tremulous eyes were fixed on the woman lying at her ease on a low couch. The second woman's back was to Nynaeve, as misty as Egwene had been earlier. She was short and slight, dark hair flowing loose to her shoulders, wide-skirted gown of pale yellow silk definitely not Taraboner. Nynaeve did not have to see her face to know it had large blue eyes and a foxlike shape, or see the bonds of Air holding the woman against the bedpost to know she was looking at Temaile Kinder-ode.

". . . learn so much when you use your dreams instead of wasting sleep," Temaile was saying with a Cairhienin accent, laughing. "Are you not enjoying yourself? What shall I teach you next? I know. 'I Have Loved a Thousand Sailor Men.' " She waggled an admonishing finger. "Be sure you learn all the words properly, Amathera. You know I would not want to—What are you gaping at?"

Abruptly Nynaeve realized the woman against the bedpost—Amathera? The Panarch?—was staring straight at her. Temaile shifted lazily as though to turn her head.

Nynaeve clamped her eyes shut. Need.

Shift.

Letting herself sag against the narrow column, Nynaeve gulped air as if she had run twenty miles, not even wondering where she was. Her heart pounded like a wild drum. Speak of landing in a vipers' den. Temaile Kinderode. The Black sister Amico had said enjoyed causing pain, enjoyed it enough to have made one of the Black Ajah comment. And her not able to channel a spark. She could have ended up decorating a bedpost beside Amathera. *Light!* She shivered, seeing it. *Calm yourself, woman! You are out of there, and even if Temaile saw you, she saw a honey-haired woman who vanished, just a Taraboner who dreamed herself into* Tel'aran'rhiod *for a moment.* Surely Temaile could not have been aware of her long enough to sense she could channel; even when she could not do it, the ability was there to be felt by one who shared it. Only a moment. Not long enough, with luck.

At least she knew Amathera's situation now. The woman was certainly no ally of Temaile. This method of searching had already repaid use. But not enough, not yet. Controlling her breathing as best she could, she looked around.

Rows of the thin white columns ran the length and breadth of a huge chamber nearly as wide as it was long, with smooth polished white floorstones below and gilded bosses on the ceiling high above. A thick rope of white silk ran all the way around the room on waist-high posts of dark polished wood, except where it would have blocked the doorways with double-pointed arches. Stands and open cabinets lined the walls, and the bones of peculiar beasts, with more display cases out in the floor, also roped off. The main exhibition hall of the palace, from Egwene's description. What she sought must be in this very chamber. Her next step would not be as blind as the first; there were certainly no vipers, no Temailes, here.

A handsome woman suddenly appeared beside a glass case with four carved legs out in the middle of the floor. She was no Taraboner, with her dark hair falling in waves to her shoulders, yet that was not what made Nynaeve gape. The woman's dress seemed to be mist, sometimes silvery and opaque, sometimes gray and so thin as to show her limbs and body clearly. From wherever she had dreamed herself here, she assuredly had a vivid imagination to conceive that! Even the scandalous Domani dresses she had heard of surely could not equal this.

The woman smiled at the glass case, then continued on up the hall, stopping on the far side to study something Nynaeve could not make out, something dark atop a white stone stand.

Frowning, Nynaeve released her grip on a fistful of honey-colored braids. The woman would disappear at any moment; few dreamed themselves into Tel'aran'rhiod for long. Of course, it did not matter if the woman saw her; she was certainly no one on their list of Black sisters. And yet she seemed somehow. . . . Nynaeve realized she had taken hold of a handful of braids again. The woman. . . . Of its own accord her hand pulled—hard—and she stared at it in amazement; her knuckles were white, her hand quivering. It was almost as if thinking of that woman. . . . Arm shaking, her hand tried to yank her hair out of her scalp. *Why under the Light?*

The mist-clad woman still stood in front of the distant white pedestal. Trembling spread from Nynaeve's arm into her shoulder. She had certainly never seen the woman before. And yet. . . . She tried to open her fingers; they only clamped down harder. Surely she never had. Shivering from head to toe, she hugged herself with the one arm she had free. Surely. . . . Her teeth wanted to chatter. The woman seemed. . . . She wanted to weep. The woman. . . .

Images burst into her head, exploding; she slumped against the column beside her as if they had physical force; her eyes bulged. She saw it again. The Chamber of Falling Blossoms, and that sturdily handsome woman surrounded by the glow of *saidar*. Herself and Elayne, babbling like children, fighting to be first to answer, pouring out everything they knew. How much had they told? It was difficult to bring out details, but she dimly remembered keeping some things back. Not because she wanted to; she would have told the woman anything, done anything she asked. Her face heated with shame, and anger. If she had managed to hide any scraps, it was only because she had been so—*eager!*—to answer the last question asked that she passed over earlier.

It makes no sense, a small voice said in the back of her head. *If she's a Black sister I don't know about, why did she not hand us over to Liandrin? She could have. We'd have gone with her like lambs.*

Cold rage would not let her listen. A Black sister had made her dance like a puppet and then told her to forget. Ordered her to forget. And she had! Well, now the woman would find out what it was like to face her ready and forewarned!

Before she could reach for the True Source, Birgitte was suddenly beside the next column in that short white coat and wide yellow trousers gathered at the ankle. Birgitte, or some woman dreaming she was Birgitte, with golden hair in an elaborate braid. A warning finger pressed against her lips, she pointed at Nynaeve, then urgently toward one of the double-arched doorways behind them. Bright blue eyes compelling, she vanished.

Nynaeve shook her head. Whoever the woman was, she had no time. Opening herself to *saidar,* she turned, filled to overflowing with the One Power and righteous wrath. The woman clothed in mist was gone. Gone! Because that golden-haired fool had distracted her! Perhaps that one was still about, waiting for her. Wrapped in the Power, she strode through the doorway the woman had indicated.

The golden-haired woman was waiting in a brightly carpeted hallway where unlit golden lamps gave off the scent of perfumed oil. She held a silver bow now, and a quiver of silver arrows hung at her waist.

"Who are you?" Nynaeve demanded furiously. She would give the woman a chance to explain herself. And then teach her a lesson she would not soon forget! "Are you the same fool who shot at me in the Waste, claiming she was Birgitte? I was about to teach a member of the Black Ajah manners when you let her get away!"

"I am Birgitte," the woman said, leaning on her bow. "At least, that is the name you would know. And the lesson might have been yours, here as surely as in the Three-fold Land. I remember the lives I have lived as if they were books well-read, the longer gone dimmer than the nearer, but I remember well when I fought at Lews Therin's side. I will never forget Moghedien's face, any more than I will forget the face of Asmodean, the man you almost disturbed at Rhuidean."

Asmodean? Moghedien? That woman was one of the Forsaken? A Forsaken in Tanchico. And one at Rhuidean, in the Waste! Egwene would certainly have said something if she knew. No way to warn her, not for seven days. Anger—and *saidar*—surged in her. "What are you doing here? I know that you all vanished after the Horn of Valere called you, but you are. . . ." She trailed off, a trifle flustered at what she had been about to say, but the other woman calmly finished for her.

"Dead? Those of us who are bound to the Wheel are not dead as others are dead. Where better for us to wait until the Wheel weaves us out in new lives than in the World of Dreams?" Birgitte laughed suddenly. "I begin to talk as if I were a philosopher. In almost every life I can remember I was born a simple girl who took up the bow. I am an archer, no more."

"You're the heroine of a hundred tales," Nynaeve said. "And I saw what your arrows did at Falme. Seanchan channeling did not touch you. Birgitte, we face near a dozen of the Black Ajah. And one of the Forsaken as well, it seems. We could use your help."

The other woman grimaced, embarrassed and regretful. "I cannot, Nynaeve. I cannot touch the world of flesh unless the Horn calls me again. Or else the Wheel weaves me out. If it did this moment, you would find only an infant mewling at her mother's breast. As for Falme, the Horn had called us; we were not there as you were, in the flesh. That is why the Power could not touch us. Here, *all* is part of the dream, and the One Power could destroy me as easily as you. More easily. I told you; I am an archer, a sometime soldier, no more." Her complex golden braid swung as she shook her head. "I do not know why I am explaining. I should not even be talking to you."

"Why not? You've spoken to me before. And Egwene thought she saw you. That was you, wasn't it?" Nynaeve frowned. "How do you know my name? Do you just *know* things?"

"I know what I see and hear. I have watched you, and listened, whenever I could find you. You and the other two women, and the young man with his wolves. According to the precepts, we may speak to none who know they are in *Tel'aran'rhiod*. And yet, evil walks the dream as well as the world of flesh; you who fight it attract me. Even knowing I can do almost nothing, I find myself wanting to help you. But

I cannot. It violates the precepts, precepts which have held me for so many turns of the Wheel that in my oldest, faintest memories I know I had already lived a hundred times, or a thousand. Speaking to you violates precepts as strong as law."

"It does," said a harsh, male voice.

Nynaeve jumped and almost lashed out with the Power. The man was dark and strongly muscled, with the long hilts of two swords thrusting above his shoulders as he strode the few paces from where he had appeared to Birgitte. With what she had heard from Birgitte, the swords were enough to name him as Gaidal Cain, but where fair, golden-haired Birgitte was as beautiful as in the stories, he was definitely not. In fact, he was perhaps as ugly a man as Nynaeve had ever seen, his face wide and flat, his heavy nose too big, and his mouth a gash, far too broad. Birgitte smiled at him, though; her touch on his cheek held more than fondness. It was a surprise to see he was the shorter. Stocky and muscled as he was, powerful in his movements, he gave the impression of being taller than he was.

"We have almost always been linked," Birgitte told Nynaeve without taking her eyes from Cain's. "He is usually born well before me—so I know my time approaches again when I cannot find him—and I usually hate him at first sight in the flesh. But we nearly always end lovers or wed. A simple story, but I think we have spun it out in a thousand variations."

Cain ignored Nynaeve as though she did not exist. "The precepts exist for a reason, Birgitte. Nothing but strife and trouble has ever come from breaking them." His voice was indeed harsh, Nynaeve realized. Not at all like that of the man in the stories.

"Perhaps I cannot sit by while evil fights," Birgitte said quietly. "Or perhaps I simply hunger for the flesh again. It has been long since we were born last. The Shadow rises again, Gaidal. It rises here. We must fight it. That is the reason we were bound to the Wheel."

"When the Horn calls us, we will fight. When the Wheel weaves us, we will fight. Not until then!" He glowered at her. "Have you forgotten what Moghedien promised you when we followed Lews Therin? I saw her, Birgitte. She will know you here."

Birgitte turned to Nynaeve. "I will aid you as I can, but do not expect too much. *Tel'aran'rhiod* is the whole of my world, and I can do less here than you."

Nynaeve blinked; the dark, heavy man had not moved that she had seen, but he suddenly stood two paces away, drawing a honing stone along one of his swords with a soft, silky rasp. Plainly, as far as he was concerned, Birgitte was speaking to the air.

"What can you tell of Moghedien, Birgitte? I must know what I can, to face her."

Leaning on her bow, Birgitte frowned thoughtfully. "Facing Moghedien is difficult, and not only because she is Forsaken. She hides and takes no risks. She attacks only where she sees weakness, and moves only in shadows. If she fears defeat, she will run; she is not one to fight to the last, even when doing so has the chance of victory. A chance is not enough for Moghedien. But do not take her lightly. She is a serpent coiled in high grass, waiting her own moment to strike, with less compassion than the snake. Especially here do not take her lightly. Lanfear always claimed *Tel'aran'rhiod* for her own, but Moghedien could do things here far beyond Lanfear, though she has not Lanfear's strength in the world of flesh. I think she would not take the risk of confronting Lanfear."

Nynaeve shivered, fear warring with the anger that let her contain the Power. Moghedien. Lanfear. This woman spoke so casually of the Forsaken. "Birgitte, what did Moghedien promise you?"

"She knew what I was, even though I did not. How, I do not know." Birgitte glanced at Cain; he appeared absorbed in his sword, but she lowered her voice anyway. "She promised to make me weep alone for as long as the Wheel turns. She said it as a fact that simply had not happened yet."

"And yet you are willing to help."

"As I can, Nynaeve. Remember that I told you not to expect too much." Once more she looked at the man sharpening his sword. "We will meet again, Nynaeve. If you are careful, and survive." Hefting her silver bow, she went to put an arm around Cain's shoulders and murmur in his ear. Whatever she said, Cain was laughing as they vanished.

Nynaeve shook her head. Careful. Everybody was telling her to be careful. A legendary hero who said she would help, only there was not much she could do. And one of the Forsaken in Tanchico.

The thought of Moghedien, of what the woman had done to her, strengthened her anger until the One Power pulsed in her like the sun. Abruptly she was back in the great hall where she had been standing before, almost hoping the woman had returned. But the hall was empty of life except for herself. Fury and the Power roared through her till she thought her skin would crisp and blacken. Moghedien, or any of the Black sisters, could sense her far more easily holding the Power than without, but she held it anyway. She almost wanted them to find her, so she could strike at them. Temaile was very likely still in *Tel'aran'rhiod.* If she went back up to that bedchamber, she could settle Temaile once and for all. She could settle Temaile—and warn the rest. It was enough to make her growl.

What had Moghedien been smiling at? Striding out to the case, a wide glass box atop a carved table, she peered in. Six mismatched figurines stood in a circle beneath the glass. A foot-tall nude woman balanced on the toes of one foot, dancing, all flowing lines, and a shepherd less than half as large, playing the pipes with his crook on his shoulder and a sheep at his feet, were as similar as any two. She had no doubt what had attracted the Forsaken's smile, though.

In the center of the circle a red-lacquered wooden stand held a disc as big as a man's hand, divided into halves by a sinuous line, one side gleaming whiter than snow, the other blacker than pitch. It was made of *cuendillar,* she knew; she had seen its like, and only seven had ever been made. One of the seals on the Dark One's prison; a focus for one of the locks that held him away from the world in Shayol Ghul. This was perhaps as important a discovery as whatever it was that threatened Rand. This had to be gotten away from the Black Ajah.

Suddenly she became aware of her reflection. The top of the case was the finest glass, without bubbles, and gave an image as clear as a mirror, if fainter. Dark green folds of silk draped her body so they showed every curve of breast and hip and thigh. Long honey braids full of jade beads framed a face with big brown eyes and a pouting mouth. The glow of *saidar* did not show, of course. Disguised so she did not even know herself, she walked about carrying a painted sign that screamed Aes Sedai.

"I *can* be careful," she muttered. Yet she held on a moment longer. The Power filling her was like life bubbling along her limbs, all the pleasures she had ever known seeping through her flesh. In the end, feeling foolish took enough edge from her anger to allow her to let go. Or maybe it dulled her anger to where she could no longer hold on.

Whatever the reason, it did not help her search. What she was after had to be somewhere in this huge hall among all these displays. Pulling her eyes away from what looked like the bones of a toothy lizard ten paces long, she closed them. Need. Danger to the Dragon Reborn, to Rand. Need.

Shift.

She was standing inside the white silk rope along the walls, the edge of a white stone pedestal touching her dress. What lay on top did not look very dangerous at first glance—a necklace and two bracelets of jointed black metal—but she could come no closer to anything than this. *Not without sitting on it,* she thought wryly.

She stretched her hand out to touch it—*Pain. Sorrow. Suffering*—and jerked it back, gasping, the raw emotions still echoing in her head. Even her faint doubts vanished. This was what the Black Ajah was hunting. And if it still sat on this pedestal in *Tel'aran'rhiod,* it sat there in the waking world, too. She had beaten them. This white stone pedestal.

Whirling around, she stared toward the glass case that held the *cuendillar* seal, located the place she had been standing where she first saw Moghedien. The woman had been looking at this pedestal, at the bracelets and collar. Moghedien had to know. But. . . .

Everything around her spun and blurred, fading.

"Wake up, Nynaeve," Elayne muttered, suppressing a yawn as she shook the sleeping woman's shoulders. "It has to be an hour by now. I want some sleep, too. Wake up, or I'll see how you like your head in a bucket of water."

Nynaeve's eyes popped open, staring up at her. "If she knows what it is, why hasn't she given it to them? If they know who *she* is, why does she have to look at it in *Tel'aran'rhiod?* Is she hiding from them, too?"

"What are you talking about?"

Braids tossing about as she wriggled up to sit with her back against the head of the bed, Nynaeve jerked her silk shift down. "I will tell you what I am talking about."

Elayne's mouth fell open as she unfolded the tale of what her meeting with Egwene had become. Searching with need. Moghedien. Birgitte and Gaidal Cain. The black metal necklace and bracelets. Asmodean in the Waste. One of the seals on the Dark One's prison in the Panarch's Palace. Elayne sank down weakly onto the side of the mattress long before Nynaeve came to Temaile and the Panarch, thrown in almost as an afterthought. And changing her appearance, masquerading as Rendra. If Nynaeve's face had not been grimly serious, Elayne could have thought it one of Thom's wilder stories.

Egeanin, sitting up cross-legged in her linen shift, hands on knees, looked close to disbelieving. Elayne hoped Nynaeve did not start a row because she had loosed the woman's wrists.

Moghedien. That was the most horrifying part. One of the Forsaken in Tanchico. One of the Forsaken weaving the Power around the two of them, making them tell her everything. Elayne could not remember a bit of it. The thought was enough to press both her hands to a suddenly queasy stomach. "I don't know whether Moghedien"—*Light, could she really have just walked in and made us . . . ?*—"is hiding from Liandrin and the others, Nynaeve. It sounds like what Birgitte"—*Light, Birgitte giving her advice!*—"said of her."

"Whatever Moghedien is up to," Nynaeve said in a tight voice, "I mean to pick a bone clean with her." She slumped back against the flower-carved headboard. "In any case, we have to get the seal away from them as well as this necklace and bracelets."

Elayne shook her head. "How can jewelry be dangerous to Rand? Are you sure? Are they a *ter'angreal* of some sort? What did they look like exactly?"

"They looked like a necklace and bracelets," Nynaeve snapped in exasperation. "Two jointed bracelets made of some black metal, and a wide necklace like a black collar. . . ." Her eyes darted to Egeanin, but no faster than Elayne's.

Unperturbed, the dark-haired woman knelt up to sit on her heels. "I have never heard of an *a'dam* made for a man, or any like the one you describe. No one tries to control a man who can channel."

"That is exactly what this is for," Elayne said slowly. *Oh, Light, I suppose I was hoping it didn't exist.* At least Nynaeve had found it first; at least they had a chance to stop it being used against Rand.

Nynaeve's eyes narrowed as she took in Egeanin's free hands, but she did not mention them. "Moghedien must be the only one who knows. It makes no sense, otherwise. If we can find a way into the palace, we can take the seal and the . . . whatever it is. And if we can bring Amathera out as well, Liandrin and her cronies will find the Panarch's Legion and the Civil Watch, and maybe the Whitecloaks, closing in. They'll not all be able to channel their way out of that! The problem is getting inside undetected."

"I have had a few thoughts on that," Elayne told her, "but I fear the men are going to give us difficulties over it."

"You leave them to me," Nynaeve snorted. "I—" A thumping clatter rose in the hall, a man shouted; as quickly as it began, silence fell once more. Thom was on watch out there.

Elayne darted to pull open the door, embracing *saidar* as she rushed out, but Nynaeve scrambled off the bed right behind her. Egeanin as well.

Thom was just picking himself up off the floor, a hand to his head. Juilin with his staff and Bayle Domon with his cudgel stood over a man with pale yellow hair lying facedown on the floor, unconscious.

Elayne hurried to Thom, trying gently to help him up. He gave her a grateful smile, but stubbornly pushed her hands away. "I am quite all right, child." All right? A knot was rising on his temple! "The fellow was walking down the hall, when suddenly he kicked me in the head. After my purse, I suppose." Just like that. Kicked in the head, and he was all right.

"He would have had it, too," Juilin said, "if I had not come to see if Thom wanted a relief."

"Did *I* not decide," Domon muttered. Their hostility seemed less focused for a change.

It took Elayne only a moment to realize why. Nynaeve and Egeanin were in the hall in their shifts. Juilin was eyeing them both in an approving manner that would have caused trouble if Rendra had seen it, though he was at least trying not to be obvious. Domon made no effort at all to hide his frank appraisal of Egeanin, crossing his arms and pursing his lips in disgusting fashion while looking her up and down.

The situation dawned on the other women quickly, but their reactions were quite different. Nynaeve, in her thin white silk, gave the thief-catcher a flat stare and strode stiffly into the room, poking a somewhat flushed face back around the side of the doorframe. Egeanin, whose linen shift was considerably longer and thicker than Nynaeve's—Egeanin, who had been cool serenity while being made prisoner, who fought like a Warder—Egeanin went wide-eyed and crimson-faced, gasping in horror. Elayne stared, amazed, as the Seanchan woman gave a mortified shriek and *leaped* back inside.

Doors flung open and down the hall heads popped out; they vanished instantly, to the bang of slamming doors, at the sight of a man stretched out on the floor and others standing over him. Heavy dragging noises suggested people blocking themselves in with beds or wardrobes.

Long moments later, Egeanin finally peeked out opposite Nynaeve, still scarlet to her hair. Elayne really did not understand. The woman was in her shift, true, but it covered her very nearly as well as Elayne's Taraboner dress did. Still, Juilin and Domon had no right to ogle. She fixed the pair with a stare that should have set them to rights immediately.

Unfortunately, Domon was too busy chuckling and rubbing his upper lip to notice. At least Juilin saw, even if he did sigh heavily the way men did when they considered themselves put upon unfairly. Avoiding her eyes, he bent to heave the pale-haired fellow onto his back. A handsome enough man, slender.

"I know this fellow," Juilin exclaimed. "This is the man who tried to rob me. Or so I thought," he added more slowly. "I do not believe in coincidence. Not unless the Dragon Reborn is in the city."

Elayne exchanged frowns with Nynaeve. Surely the stranger was not in the employ of Liandrin; the Black Ajah would not use men to sneak about the halls any more. . . . Any more than they would have hired street toughs. Elayne moved her gaze to Egeanin questioningly. Nynaeve's was more demanding.

"He is Seanchan," Egeanin said after a moment.

"A rescue attempt?" Nynaeve murmured dryly, but the other woman shook her head.

"I do not doubt he was looking for me, but not for rescue, I think. If he knows—or even suspects—that I let Bethamin go free, he would be wanting to . . . talk with me." Elayne suspected it was rather more than talk, confirmed when Egeanin added, "It might be best if you slit his throat. He may try to make trouble for you, too, if he thinks you are my friends, or if he discovers you are Aes Sedai." The big Illianer smuggler gave her a shocked look, and Juilin's jaw dropped almost to his chest. Thom, on the other hand, nodded in a disturbingly thoughtful fashion.

"We are not here to slit Seanchan throats," Nynaeve said as though that might change later. "Bayle, Juilin, put him out in the alley behind the inn. By the time he wakes, he'll be lucky to have his smallclothes. Thom, find Rendra and tell her we want strong tea in the Chamber of Falling Blossoms. And ask if she has any willowbark or acem; I will make you something for your head." The three men stared at her. "Well, move!" she snapped. "We have plans to make!" She barely gave Elayne time to get back inside before closing the door with a bang and beginning to pull her dress over her head. Egeanin scrambled into hers as though the men were still looking at her.

"The better way is to ignore them, Egeanin," Elayne said. It was odd to be advising someone older than Nynaeve, but however competent the Seanchan woman was in other ways, she clearly knew little about men. "It only encourages them, otherwise. I do not know why," she admitted, "but it does. You were quite decently covered. Really."

Egeanin's head pushed out at the top of her dress. "Decent? I am not a serving girl. I am no shea dancer!" Her scowl became a perplexed frown. "He is rather good-looking, though. I had not thought of him so before."

Wondering what a shea dancer was, Elayne went to help her with her buttons. "Rendra will have something to say to you if you allow Juilin to flirt with you."

The dark-haired woman gave her a startled look over her shoulder. "The thief-catcher? It was Bayle Domon I meant. A properly set-up man. But a smuggler," she sighed regretfully. "A lawbreaker."

Elayne supposed there was no accounting for tastes—Nynaeve certainly loved Lan, and he was much too stone-faced and intimidating— but Bayle Domon? The man was half as wide as he was tall, as thick as an Ogier!

"You chatter like Rendra, Elayne," Nynaeve snapped. She was struggling to do up her dress, both hands behind her. "If you have finished blathering about men, perhaps you won't mind skipping over the new seamstress you've no doubt found? We must make plans. If we wait until we're with the men, they will try to take it over, and I am in no mood to waste time putting them in their place. Have you finished with her yet? I could use some help myself."

Quickly fastening Egeanin's last small button, Elayne went coolly to Nynaeve. She did *not* talk about men and dresses. Not *nearly* as much as Rendra. Holding her braids out of the way, Nynaeve gave her a frown when she tugged sharply at the other woman's dress to do up the buttons. The close-spaced triple row up the back was necessary, not simply ornament. Nynaeve *would* let Rendra talk her into the most fashionably tight bodices. And then say *other* people spent all their time thinking about clothes. *She* certainly thought of other things. "I have been thinking how we can move inside the palace unnoticed, Nynaeve. We can be all but invisible."

As she talked, Nynaeve's frowns smoothed out. Nynaeve herself had conceived a way to enter the palace. When Egeanin made a few suggestions, Nynaeve's mouth tightened, but the notions were sensible, and even Nynaeve could not reject them out of hand. By the time they were ready to go down to the Chamber of Falling Blossoms, they had a plan agreed upon, and no intention of letting the men change a whit of it. Moghedien, the Black Ajah, whoever were running things in the Panarch's Palace, were going to lose their prizes before they knew what had happened.

CHAPTER
53

The Price of a Departure

O nly three candles and two lamps lit the common room of the
Winespring Inn, since candles and oil both were in short supply. The spears and other weapons were gone from the walls;
the barrel that had held old swords was empty. The lamps stood on two
of the tables pushed together in front of the tall stone fireplace, where
Marin al'Vere and Daise Congar and others of the Women's Circle
were going over lists of the scanty food remaining in Emond's Field.
Perrin tried not to listen.

At another table Faile's honing stone made a soft, steady *whisk-whisk*
as she sharpened one of her knives. A bow lay in front of her, and a
bristling quiver hung at her belt. She had turned out to be a fairly good
shot, but he hoped she never discovered that it was a boy's bow; she
could not draw a man's Two Rivers longbow, though she refused to
admit it.

Shifting his axe so it would not dig into his side, he tried to put his
mind back on what he was discussing with the men around the table
with him. Not that all of them were keeping their own attention where
it should be.

"They have lamps," Cenn muttered, "and we make do with tallow."
The gnarled old man glared at the pair of candles in brass candlesticks.

"Give over, Cenn," Tam said wearily, pulling pipe and tabac pouch from behind his sword belt. "For once, give over."

"If we had to read or write," Abell said, his voice less patient than the words, "we'd have lamps." A bandage was wound around his temples.

As if to remind the thatcher that he was Mayor, Bran adjusted the silver medallion hanging on his wide chest, showing a pair of scales. "Keep your mind to the business at hand, Cenn. I'll have none of your wasting Perrin's time."

"I just think we should have lamps," Cenn complained. "Perrin would tell me if I was wasting his time."

Perrin sighed; the night tried to drag his eyelids down. He wished it were someone else's turn to represent the Village Council, Haral Luhhan or Jon Thane or Samel Crawe, or anybody but Cenn with his carping. But then, sometimes he wished one of these men would turn to him and say, *"This is business for the Mayor and the Council, young fellow. You go on back to the forge. We'll let you know what to do."* Instead they worried about wasting his time, deferred to him. Time. How many attacks had there been in the seven days since the first? He was not sure any longer.

The bandage on Abell's head irritated Perrin. The Aes Sedai only Healed the most serious wounds now; if a man could manage without, they let him. It was not that there were many badly wounded yet, but as Verin pointed out wryly, even an Aes Sedai only had so much strength; apparently their trick with the catapult stones took as much as Healing. For once he did not want to be reminded of limits to Aes Sedai strength. Not many badly wounded. Yet.

"How are the arrows holding out?" he asked. That was what he was supposed to be thinking about.

"Well enough," Tam said, puffing his pipe alight from one of the candles. "We still recover most of what we shoot, in daylight at least. They drag a lot of their dead away at night—fodder for the cookpots, I suppose—and we lose those." The other men were digging out their pipes, too, from pouches and coat pockets, Cenn muttering that he seemed to have forgotten his pouch. Grumbling, Bran passed his across, his bald pate gleaming in the candlelight.

Perrin rubbed at his forehead. What had he meant to ask next? The stakes. There was fighting at the stakes in most attacks now, especially at night. How many times had the Trollocs nearly broken through? Three? Four? "Does everyone have a spear or some sort of polearm now? What's left to make more?" Silence answered him, and he lowered his hand. The other men were staring at him.

"You asked that yesterday," Abell said gently. "And Haral told you then there isn't a scythe or pitchfork left in the village that hasn't been made into a weapon. We've more than we have hands for, in truth."

"Yes. Of course. It just slipped my mind." A snatch of conversation from the Women's Circle caught his ear.

". . . mustn't let the men know," Marin was saying softly, as if repeating a caution voiced before.

"Of course not," Daise snorted, but not much louder. "If the fools find out the women are on half rations, they'll insist on eating the same, and we can't. . . ."

Perrin closed his eyes, tried to close his ears. Of course. The men did the fighting. The men had to keep their strength up. Simple. At least none of the women had had to fight yet. Except the two Aiel women, of course, and Faile, but she was smart enough to stay back when it came to pushing spears among the stakes. That was the reason he had found the bow for her. She had the heart of a leopard, and more courage than any two men.

"I think it is time you went to bed, Perrin," Bran suggested. "You cannot go on like this, sleeping an hour here and an hour there."

Scrubbing his beard vigorously, Perrin tried to look alert. "I'll sleep later." When it was over. "Are the men getting enough sleep? I've seen some sitting up when they should be—"

The front door banged open to admit skinny Dannil Lewin out of the night, bow in hand and all in a lather. He wore one of the swords from the barrel on his hip; Tam had been giving classes when he had the time, and sometimes one of the Warders did as well.

Before Dannil could open his mouth, Daise snapped, "Were you raised in a barn, Dannil Lewin?"

"You can certainly treat my door a little more gently." Marin divided her meaning look between the lanky man and Daise, a reminder that it *was* her door.

Dannil ducked his head, clearing his throat. "Pardon, Mistress al'Vere," he said hastily. "Pardon, Wisdom. Sorry to burst in, but I've a message for Perrin." He hurried to the table of men as if afraid the women would stop him again. "The Whitecloaks brought in a man who wants to talk to you, Perrin. He won't talk to anybody else. He's hurt bad, Perrin. They only brought him to the edge of the village. I don't think he could make it as far as the inn."

Perrin pushed himself to his feet. "I'm coming." Not another attack, at any rate. They were worst at night.

Faile snatched up her bow and joined him before he reached the door. And Aram stood up, hesitating, from the shadows on the foot of the stairs. Sometimes Perrin forgot the man was there, he kept so still. He looked odd with that sword strapped on his back atop his grimy, yellow-striped Tinker coat, his eyes so bright, hardly ever seeming to blink, and his face without expression. Neither Raen or Ila had spoken to their grandson since the day he picked up that sword. Nor to Perrin, either.

"If you're coming, come," he said gruffly, and Aram fell in at his heels. The man followed him like a hound whenever he was not pestering Tam or Ihvon or Tomas to teach him that sword. It was as if he had replaced his family and people with Perrin. Perrin would have done without the responsibility if he could, but there it was.

Moonlight shone down on thatched roofs. Few houses had a light in more than one window. Stillness clung to the village. Some thirty of the Companions stood guard outside the inn with their bows, as many wearing swords as could find them; everyone had adopted that name, and Perrin found himself using it, too, to his private disgust. The reason for guards on the inn, or wherever Perrin was, lay on the Green, no longer so crowded with sheep and cows. Campfires crowded above the Winespring, beyond where that fool wolfhead banner hung limp now, bright pools in the darkness surrounded by pale cloaks gleaming with the moon.

No one had wanted Whitecloaks in their homes, already crowded, and Bornhald did not want his soldiers split up in any case. The man seemed to think the village would turn on him and his men any moment; if they followed Perrin, they must be Darkfriends. Even Perrin's eyes could not make out faces around the fires, but he thought he could feel Bornhald's stare, waiting, hating.

Dannil readied ten Companions to escort Perrin, all young men who should have been laughing and carousing with him, all with bows ready to see him safe. Aram did not join them as Dannil led the way down the dark, dirt street; it was Perrin he was with and no one else. Faile kept hard by Perrin's side, dark eyes shining in the moonlight, scanning the surroundings as though *she* were his whole protection.

Where the Old Road entered Emond's Field the blocking wagons had been drawn aside to admit the Whitecloak patrol, twenty snowy-cloaked men with lances who sat their horses in burnished armor, no less impatient than their stamping mounts. They stood out in the night for any eye, and most Trollocs could see as well in darkness as Perrin, but the Whitecloaks insisted on their patrols. Sometimes their scouting had brought warnings, and maybe their harrassment kept the Trollocs a little off balance. It would have been good, though, if he had known what they were doing before it was done.

A cluster of villagers and farmers wearing bits of old armor and a few rusty helmets stood clustered around a man in a farmer's coat lying in the roadway. They gave way for Faile and him, and he went to one knee beside the man.

The odor of blood was strong; sweat glistened on the man's moon-shadowed face. A thumb-thick Trolloc arrow like a small spear was stuck through his chest. "Perrin—Goldeneyes," he muttered hoarsely, laboring for breath. "Must—get through—to Perrin—Goldeneyes."

"Has someone sent for one of the Aes Sedai?" Perrin demanded, lifting the man as gently as he could, cradling his head. He did not listen for the answer; he did not think this man would last till an Aes Sedai came. "I am Perrin."

"Goldeneyes? I—cannot see—very well." His wide, wild stare was right at Perrin's face; if he could see at all, the fellow must see his eyes shining golden in the dark.

"I am Perrin Goldeneyes," he said reluctantly.

The man seized his collar, pulling his face close with surprising strength. "We are—coming. Sent to—tell you. We are co—" His head fell back, eyes staring at nothing now.

"The Light be with his soul," Faile murmured, slinging her bow across her back.

After a moment Perrin pried the man's fingers loose. "Does anyone know him?" The Two Rivers men exchanged glances, shook their heads. Perrin looked up at the mounted Whitecloaks. "Did he say anything else while you were bringing him in? Where did you find him?"

Jaret Byar stared down at him, gaunt-faced and hollow-eyed, an image of death. The other Whitecloaks looked away, but Byar always made himself meet Perrin's yellow eyes, especially at night, when they glowed. Byar growled under his breath—Perrin heard "Shadowspawn!" —and booted his horse in the ribs. The patrol galloped into the village, as eager to be away from Perrin as from Trollocs. Aram stared after them, expressionless, one hand over his shoulder to finger his sword hilt.

"They said they found him three or four miles south." Dannil hesitated, then added, "They say the Trollocs are all scattered out in little bunches, Perrin. Maybe they're finally giving up."

Perrin laid the stranger back down. *We are coming.* "Keep a close watch. Maybe some family who tried to hold on to their farm is finally coming in." He did not believe anyone could have survived out there this long, but it might be so. "Don't shoot anybody by mistake." He staggered to his feet, and Faile put a hand on his arm.

"It is time you were in bed, Perrin. You have to sleep sometime."

He only looked at her. He should have made her stay in Tear. Somehow, he should have made her. If he had only thought well enough he could have.

One of the runners, a curly-haired boy about chest-high, slipped through the Two Rivers men to tug at Perrin's sleeve. Perrin did not know him; there were many families in from the countryside. "There's something moving in the Westwood, Lord Perrin. They sent me to tell you."

"Don't call me that," Perrin told him sharply. If he did not stop the children, the Companions were going to start using it, too. "Go tell them I will be there." The boy darted away.

"You belong in your bed," Faile said firmly. "Tomas can handle any attack very well."

"It isn't an attack, or the boy would have said so, and somebody would be sounding Cenn's bugle."

She hung on to his arm, trying to pull him toward the inn, and so she was dragged along when he started the opposite way. After a few futile minutes she gave up and pretended she had been merely holding his arm all along. But she muttered to herself. She still seemed to think that if she spoke softly enough he could not hear. She began with "foolish," "mule-headed," and "muscle-brained"; after that it escalated. It was quite a little procession, her muttering at him, Aram heeling him, Dannil and the ten Companions surrounding him like a guard of honor. If he had not been so tired, he would have felt a proper fool.

There were guards spaced in small clusters all along the sharp stake fence to watch the night, each with a boy for a runner. At the west end of the village the men on guard were all gathered up against the inside of the broad barrier, fingering spears and bows as they peered toward the Westwood. Even with the moonlight, the trees had to be blackness in their eyes.

Tomas's cloak seemed to make parts of him vanish in the night. Bain and Chiad were with him; for some reason the two Maidens had spent every night at this end of Emond's Field since Loial and Gaul left. "I'd not have bothered you," the Warder said to Perrin, "but there only seems to be one out there, and I thought you might be able to. . . ."

Perrin nodded. Everyone knew about his vision, especially in darkness. The Two Rivers people seemed to think it something special, something that marked him out an idiot hero. What the Warders thought, or the Aes Sedai, he had no idea. He was too tired to care tonight. Seven days, and how many attacks?

The edge of the Westwood lay five hundred paces away. Even to his eyes the trees ran together in shadows. Something moved. Something big enough to be a Trolloc. A big shape carrying. . . . The burden lifted an arm. A human. A tall shadow carrying a human.

"We will not shoot!" he shouted. He wanted to laugh; in fact, he realized he was laughing. "Come on! Come on, Loial!"

The dim shape lumbered forward faster than a man could run, resolving into the Ogier, speeding toward the village, carrying Gaul.

Two Rivers men shouted encouragement as if it were a race. "Run, Ogier! Run! Run!" Perhaps it was a race; more than one assault had come out of those woods.

Short of the stakes Loial slowed with a lurch; there was barely room for his thick legs to edge through the barrier sideways. Once on the village side, he let the Aielman down and sank to the ground, leaning back against the hedge, panting, tufted ears drooping wearily. Gaul limped on one leg until he could sit, too, with Bain and Chiad both fussing over his left thigh, where his breeches were ripped and black with dry blood. He only had two spears left, and his quiver gaped emptily. Loial's axe was gone, too.

"You fool Ogier," Perrin laughed fondly. "Going off like that. I ought to let Daise Congar switch you for a runaway. At least you're alive. At least you're back." His voice sank at that. Alive. And back in Emond's Field.

"We did it, Perrin," Loial panted, a tired drumlike boom. "Four days ago. We closed the Waygate. It will take the Elders or an Aes Sedai to open it again."

"He carried me most of the way from the mountains," Gaul said. "A Nightrunner and perhaps fifty Trollocs chased us the first three days, but Loial outran them." He was trying to push the Maidens away without much success.

"Lie still, Shaarad," Chiad snapped, "or I will say I have touched you armed and allow you to choose how your honor stands." Faile gave a delighted laugh. Perrin did not understand, but the remark reduced the imperturbable Aielman to splutters. He let the Maidens tend his leg.

"Are you all right, Loial?" Perrin asked. "Are you hurt?"

The Ogier pulled himself up with an obvious effort, swaying for a moment like a tree about to fall. His ears still hung limp. "No, I am not hurt, Perrin. Only tired. Do not worry yourself about me. A long time out of the *stedding*. Visits are not enough." He shook his head as if his thoughts had wandered. His wide hand engulfed Perrin's shoulder. "I will be fine after a little sleep." He lowered his voice. For an Ogier, he did; it was still a huge bumblebee rumble. "It is very bad out there, Perrin. We followed the last bands down, for the most part. We locked the gate, but I think there must be several thousand Trollocs in the Two Rivers already, and maybe as many as fifty Myrddraal."

"Not so," Luc announced loudly. He had galloped up along the edge of the houses from the direction of the North Road. He reined his rearing black stallion to a flashy halt, forehooves pawing. "You are no doubt fine at singing to trees, Ogier, but fighting Trollocs is something different. I estimate less than a thousand now. A formidable force to be sure, but nothing these stout defenses and brave men cannot hold at bay. Another trophy for you, Lord Perrin Goldeneyes." Laughing, he tossed a bulging cloth bag at Perrin. The bottom gleamed darkly wet in the moonlight.

Perrin caught it out of the air and hurled it well over the stakes despite its weight. Four or five Trolloc heads, no doubt, and perhaps a Myrddraal. The man brought in his trophies every night, still seeming to expect them to be put up for everyone to admire. A bunch of the Coplins and Congars had given him a feast the night he came in with a pair of Fades' heads.

"Do I also know nothing of fighting?" Gaul demanded, struggling to his feet. "*I* say there are several thousand."

Luc's teeth showed white in a smile. "How many days have you spent in the Blight, Aiel? I have spent many." Perhaps it was more snarl than smile. "Many. Believe what you wish, Goldeneyes. The endless days will bring what they bring, as they always have." He pulled the stallion up on its hind legs again to whirl about, and galloped in among the houses and the trees that had once been the rim of the Westwood. The Two Rivers men shifted uneasily, peering after him or out into the night.

"He is wrong," Loial said. "Gaul and I saw what we saw." His face sagged wearily, broad mouth turned down and long eyebrows drooping on his cheeks. No wonder, if he had carried Gaul for three or four days.

"You have done a lot, Loial," Perrin said, "you and Gaul both. A great thing. I am afraid your bedroom has half a dozen Tinkers in it now, but Mistress al'Vere will make you up a pallet. It is time for you to get some of that sleep you want."

"And time for you as well, Perrin Aybara." Scudding clouds made moonshadows play across Faile's bold nose and high cheekbones. She was so beautiful. But her voice was firm enough for a wagon bed. "If you do not go now, I will have Loial carry you. You can hardly stand."

Gaul was having trouble walking with his wounded leg. Bain supported him from one side. He tried to stop Chiad from taking the other, but she murmured something that sounded like *"gai'shain"* in a threatening way, and Bain laughed, and the Aielman allowed them both to help him, growling furiously to himself. Whatever the Maidens were going on about, it did have Gaul in a taking.

Tomas clapped Perrin on the shoulder. "Go, man. Everyone needs to sleep." He himself sounded good for three more days without it.

Perrin nodded.

He let Faile guide him back to the Winespring Inn with Loial and the Aiel following, and Aram, and Dannil and the ten Companions encircling him. He was not sure when the others fell away, but somehow he and Faile were alone in his room on the second floor of the inn.

"Whole families are making do with no more space than this," he muttered. A candle burned on the stone mantel over the small fireplace. Others did without, but Marin lit one here as soon as it turned dark so he would not have to be bothered. "I can sleep outside with Dannil and Ban and the others."

"Do not be an idiot," Faile said, making it sound affectionate. "If Alanna and Verin each has her own room, you should, too."

He realized she had his coat off and was untying the laces of his shirt. "I am not too tired to undress myself." He pushed her gently outside.

"You take everything off," she ordered. "Everything, do you hear? You cannot sleep properly fully dressed, the way you seem to think."

"I will," he promised. When he had the door closed, he did tug off his boots before blowing out the candle and lying down. Marin would not like dirty boots on her coverlet.

Thousands, Gaul and Loial said. Yet how much could the two of them have seen, hiding on the way into the mountains, fleeing on the way back? Maybe one thousand at most, Luc claimed, but Perrin could not make himself trust the man for all the trophies he brought in. Scattered, according to the Whitecloaks. How close could they have come, armor and cloaks shining in the darkness like lanterns?

There was a way to see for himself, perhaps. He had avoided the wolf dream since his last visit; the desire to hunt down this Slayer rose up whenever he thought of going back, and his responsibilities lay here in Emond's Field. But now, perhaps. . . . Sleep rolled in while he was still considering.

He stood on the Green bathed by an afternoon sun low in the sky, a few white clouds drifting. There were no sheep or cattle around the tall pole where a breeze ruffled the red wolfhead banner, though a bluefly buzzed past his face. No people among the thatched houses. Small piles of dry wood atop ashes marked the Whitecloaks' fires; he had rarely seen anything burning in the wolf dream, only what was ready to burn or already charred. No ravens in the sky.

As he scanned for the birds, a patch of sky darkened, became a window to somewhere else. Egwene stood among a crowd of women, fear in her eyes; slowly the women knelt around her. Nynaeve was one of them, and he believed he saw Elayne's red-gold hair. That window faded and was replaced. Mat stood naked and bound, snarling; an odd spear with a black shaft had been thrust across his back behind his elbows, and a silver medallion, a foxhead, hung on his chest. Mat vanished, and it was Rand. Perrin thought it was Rand. He wore rags and a rough cloak, and a bandage covered his eyes. The third window disappeared; the sky was only sky, empty except for the clouds.

Perrin shivered. These wolf-dream visions never seemed to have any real connection to anything he knew. Maybe here, where things could change so easily, worry over his friends became something he could see. Whatever they were, he was wasting time fretting at them.

He was not surprised to find he wore a blacksmith's long leather vest and no shirt, but when he put a hand to his belt, he found the hammer, not his axe. Frowning, he concentrated on the long half-moon blade and thick spike. That was what he needed now. That was what he was now. The hammer changed slowly, as if resisting, but when the axe finally hung in the thick loop, it kept shining dangerously. Why did it fight him so? He knew what he wanted. A filled quiver appeared on his other hip, a longbow in his hand, a leather bracer on his left forearm.

Three land-blurring strides took him where the nearest Trolloc camps supposedly lay, three miles from the village. The last step landed him among nearly a dozen tall heaps of wood laid on old ashes amid trampled-down barley, the logs mixed with broken chairs and table legs and even a farmhouse door. Great black iron cauldrons stood ready to be hung over the laid cook fires. Empty cauldrons, of course, though he knew what would be cut up into them, what would be spitted on the thick iron rods stretched over some of the fires. How many Trollocs would these fires serve? There were no tents, and the blankets scattered about, filthy and stinking of old acrid Trolloc sweat, were no real guide; many Trollocs slept like animals, uncovered on the ground, even hollowing out a hole to lie in.

In smaller steps that covered no more than a hundred paces each, the land seeming only to haze, he circled Emond's Field, from farm to farm, pasture to barley field to rows of tabac, through scattered copses of trees, along cart tracks and footpaths, finding more and more clusters of waiting Trolloc fires as he slowly spiraled outward. Too many. Hundreds of fires. That had to mean several thousand Trollocs. Five thousand or ten or twice that—it would make little difference to Emond's Field if they all came at once.

Farther south the signs of Trollocs vanished. Signs of their immediate presence, at least. Few farmhouses or barns stood unburned. Scattered fields of charred stubble remained where barley or tabac had been torched; others had great swathes trampled through the crops. No reason for it but the joy of destruction; the people had been long gone when most of it was done. Once he lighted in the midst of large patches of ash, some charred wagon wheels still showing hints of bright color here and there. The site of the Tuatha'an caravan's destruction pained him even more than the farmhouses. The Way of the Leaf should have a chance. Somewhere. Not here. Not letting himself look, he leaped south a mile or more.

Eventually he came to Deven Ride, rows of thatch-roofed houses surrounding a green and a pond fed by a spring walled 'round with stone, the spillover splashing from cuts long since worn deeper than they had been made. The inn at the head of the green, the Goose and Pipe, was roofed with thatch, too, yet a little larger than the Winespring Inn, though Deven Ride surely had even fewer visitors than Emond's Field. The village was certainly no bigger. Wagons and carts drawn close by every house spoke of farmers who had fled here with their families. Other wagons blocked the streets and the spaces between the houses all the way around the edge of the village. The precautions were not enough to have halted even one of the assaults made on Emond's Field the last seven days.

In three circuits around the village Perrin found only half a dozen Trolloc camps. Enough to keep people in. Pen them until Emond's Field was dealt with. Then the Trollocs could fall on Deven Ride at the

Fades' leisure. Perhaps he could find a way to get word to these villagers. If they fled south, they might find some way across the White River. Even trying to cross the trackless Forest of Shadows below the river was better than waiting to die.

The golden sun had not moved an inch. Time was different, here.

Running north as hard as he could, even Emond's Field passed by in a blur. Watch Hill on its round prominence was bordered as Deven Ride had been with wagons and carts between the houses. A banner waved lazily in the breeze, on a tall pole in front of the White Boar on the hill's crest. A red eagle flying across a field of blue. The Red Eagle had been the symbol of Manetheren. Perhaps Alanna or Verin had told ancient stories while they were in Watch Hill.

Here, too, he found only a few Trolloc camps, enough to pen the villagers. There was an easier way out from here than trying to cross the White, with its endless stretch of rapids.

On northward he ran, to Taren Ferry, on the bank of the Tarendrelle, which he had grown up calling the River Taren. Tall, narrow houses built on high stone foundations to escape the Taren's yearly flooding when the snows melted in the Mountains of Mist. Nearly half those foundations supported only piles of ash and charred beams in that unchanging afternoon light. There were no wagons here, no signs of any defense. And no Trolloc camps that he could find. Perhaps no people remained here.

At the water's edge stood a stout wooden dock, a heavy rope drooping as it arced across the swift-flowing river. The rope ran through iron rings on a flat-decked barge snugged against the dock. The ferry was still there, still usable.

A jump took him across the river, where wheel ruts scarred the bank and household objects lay about. Chairs and stand-mirrors, chests, even a few tables and a polished wardrobe with birds carved on the doors, all the things panicked people had tried to save, then abandoned to run faster. They would be spreading the word of what had happened here, what was happening in the Two Rivers. Some could have reached Baerlon by now, a hundred miles or more north, and surely the farms and villages between Baerlon and the river. Word spreading. In another month it might reach Caemlyn, and Queen Morgase with her Queen's Guards and her power to raise armies. A month with luck. And as much to return, once Morgase believed. Too late for Emond's Field. Maybe too late for the whole Two Rivers.

Still, it hardly made sense that the Trollocs had let anyone escape. Or the Myrddraal at any rate; Trollocs did not seem to think much beyond the moment. He would have thought destroying the ferry would have been the Fades' first task. How could they be sure there were not enough soldiers at Baerlon to come down on them?

He bent to pick up a doll with a painted wooden face, and an arrow streaked through where his chest had been.

Springing out of his crouch he leaped up the bank, a blur streaking a hundred paces into the woods to crouch below a tall leatherleaf. Brush and flood-toppled trees woven with creepers covered the forest floor around him.

Slayer. Perrin had an arrow nocked, and wondered if he had drawn it from his quiver or simply thought it there. Slayer.

On the point of leaping away again, he paused. Slayer would know roughly where he was. Perrin had followed the man's blurring form easily enough; that elongated streak was clear if you were standing still. Twice now he had played the other's game and nearly lost. Let Slayer play his this time. He waited.

Ravens swooped above the treetops, searching and calling. No movement to give him away; not a twitch. Only his eyes moved, studying the forest around him. A vagrant puff of air brought him a cold smell, human yet not, and he smiled. No sound save the ravens, though; this Slayer stalked well. But he was not used to being hunted. What else did Slayer forget beside smells? He surely would not expect Perrin to remain where he had landed. Animals ran from the hunter; even wolves ran.

A hint of movement, and for an instant a face appeared above a fallen pine some fifty paces away. The slanting light illuminated it clearly. Dark hair and blue eyes, a face all hard planes and angles, so reminiscent of Lan's face. Except that in that brief glimpse Slayer licked his lips twice; his forehead was creased, and his eyes darted as they searched. Lan would not have let his worry show if he stood alone against a thousand Trollocs. Just an instant, and the face was gone again. The ravens darted and swirled above as if they shared Slayer's anxiety, fearing to come below the treetops.

Perrin waited and watched, motionless. Silence. Only the cold smell to say he was not alone with the ravens overhead.

Slayer's face appeared again, peering around a thick-boled oak off to his left. Thirty paces. Oaks killed most of what grew close to them; only a few mushrooms and weedy things sprouted from the leafy mulch beneath its limbs. Slowly the man emerged into the open, boots making no sound.

In one motion Perrin drew and fired. The ravens screamed warning, and Slayer spun to take the broadhead shaft in his chest, but not through the heart. The man howled, clutching the arrow with both hands; black feathers rained down as the ravens beat their wings in a frenzy. And Slayer faded, him and his cry together, growing misty, transparent, vanishing. The ravens' shrieks vanished as if severed with a knife; the arrow that had transfixed the man dropped to the ground. The ravens were gone, too.

With a second shaft half-drawn, Perrin exhaled slowly, let off his tension on the bowstring. *Was that how you died here? Simply fading away, gone forever?*

"At least I finished him," he muttered. And let himself be diverted in the process. Slayer was no part of why he had come to the wolf dream. At least the wolves were safe now. The wolves—and maybe a few others.

He stepped out of the dream . . .

. . . and woke staring at the ceiling, his shirt clinging sweatily. The moon gave a little light through the windows. There were fiddles playing somewhere in the village, a wild Tinker tune. They would not fight, but they had found a way to help, by keeping spirits up.

Slowly Perrin sat up, pulling on his boots in the pale-lit dark. How to do what he had to do? It would be difficult. He had to be cunning. Only, he was not sure he had ever been cunning in his life. Standing, he stamped his feet to settle them in.

Sudden shouts outside and a fading clatter of hooves made him stride to the nearest window and throw up the sash. The Companions were milling about below. "What's going on down there?"

Thirty faces turned up to him, and Ban al'Seen yelled, "It was Lord Luc, Lord Perrin. He nearly rode down Wil and Tell. I don't think he even saw them. He was all hunched over in his saddle like he was hurt, and spurring that stallion for all he was worth, Lord Perrin."

Perrin tugged at his beard. Luc had certainly not been wounded earlier. Luc . . . and Slayer? It was impossible. Dark-haired Slayer looked like Lan's brother or cousin; if Luc, with his red-gold hair, resembled anyone, maybe it was Rand a little. The two men could not have been more dissimilar. And yet. . . . That cold smell. They did not smell the same, but both had an icy, hardly human scent. His ears picked up the sound of wagons being hauled out of the way down at the Old Road, shouts for haste. Even if Ban and the Companions ran, they would not catch the man now. Hooves galloped south hard.

"Ban," he called, "if Luc shows up again, he's to be put under guard and kept there." He paused long enough to add, "And don't call me that!" before hauling the sash down with a bang.

Luc and Slayer; Slayer and Luc. How could they be the same? It *was* impossible. But then, less than two years gone he had not really believed in Trollocs or Fades. Time enough to worry about it if he ever laid hands on the man again. Now there was Watch Hill and Deven Ride and. . . . Some could be saved. Not everyone in the Two Rivers had to die.

On his way to the common room, he paused at the top of the stairs. Aram stood up from the bottom step, watching him, waiting to follow where he led. Gaul lay stretched out on a pallet near the fireplace with a bandage thick around his left thigh, apparently asleep. Faile and the Two Maidens sat cross-legged on the floor near him, talking softly. A much larger pallet lay on the far side of the room, but Loial sat on a bench with his legs stretched out so they would fit under one of the tables, nearly doubled over so he could scribble furiously with a pen by the light of a candle. No doubt he was recording what had happened on the journey to close the Waygate. And if Perrin knew Loial at all, the Ogier would have Gaul doing it all, whether he had or not. Loial did not seem to think anything he himself did was brave, or worth writing down. Except for them, the common room was empty. He could still hear those fiddles playing. He thought he recognized the tune. Not a Tinker song, now. "My Love Is a Wild Rose."

Faile looked up at Perrin's first step down, rising gracefully to meet him. Aram took his seat again when Perrin made no move toward the door.

"Your shirt is wet," Faile said accusingly. "You slept in it, didn't you? And your boots, I shouldn't wonder. It has not been an hour since I left you. You march yourself back upstairs before you fall down."

"Did you see Luc leave?" he said. Her mouth tightened, but sometimes ignoring her was the only way. She managed to win too often when he argued with her.

"He came running through here a few minutes ago and dashed out through the kitchen," she said finally. Those were the words; her tone said she was not finished with him and bed.

"Did he seem to be . . . injured?"

"Yes," she said slowly. "He staggered, and he was clutching something to his chest under his coat. A bandage, maybe. Mistress Congar is in the kitchen, but from what I heard he all but ran over her. How did you know?"

"I dreamed it." Her tilted eyes took on a dangerous light. She must not be thinking. She knew about the wolf dream; did she expect him to explain where Bain and Chiad could hear, not to mention Aram and Loial? Well, maybe not Loial; he was so absorbed in his notes he would not have noticed a flock of sheep herded into the common room. "Gaul?"

"Mistress Congar gave him something to make him sleep, and a poultice for his leg. When the Aes Sedai wake in the morning, one of them will Heal him, if they think it serious enough."

"Come sit down, Faile. I want you to do something for me." She eyed him suspiciously, but let him lead her to a chair. When they were seated, he leaned across the table, trying to make his voice serious, but not urgent. On no account urgent. "I want you to take a message to Caemlyn for me. On the way, you can let Watch Hill know how things are here. Actually, it might be best if they crossed the Taren until it's all done." That had sounded properly casual; just a bit thrown in on the spur of the moment. "I want you to ask Queen Morgase to send us some of the Queen's Guards. I know it's a dangerous thing I'm asking, but Bain and Chiad can get you to Taren Ferry safely, and the ferry is still there." Chiad stood up, staring at him anxiously. Why was she anxious?

"You will not have to leave him," Faile told her. After a moment the Aiel woman nodded and resumed her seat beside Gaul. Chiad and Gaul? They were blood enemies. Nothing was making sense tonight.

"It is a long way to Caemlyn," Faile went on quietly. Her eyes very intent on his, but her face could have been wood for all the expression it had. "Weeks to ride there, plus however long it might take to reach and convince Morgase, then more weeks to return with the Queen's Guards."

"We can hold out that long easily," he told her. *Burn me if I can't lie as well as Mat!* "Luc was right. There can't be more than a thousand Trollocs still out there. The *dream?*" She nodded. At last she understood. "We can hold out here for a very long time, but in the meanwhile they'll be burning crops and doing the Light knows what. We'll need the Queen's Guards to rid ourselves of them completely. You are the logical one to go. You know how to talk to a queen, being a queen's cousin and all. Faile, I know what I'm asking is dangerous . . ." Not as dangerous as staying. ". . . But once you reach the ferry, you'll be on your way."

He did not hear Loial approach until the Ogier laid his book of notes down in front of Faile. "I could not help overhearing, Faile. If you are going to Caemlyn, would you carry this? To keep it safe until I can come for it." Squaring the volume up almost tenderly, he added, "They print many very fine books in Caemlyn. Forgive me for interrupting, Perrin." But his teacup eyes were on her, not him. "Faile suits you. You should fly free, like a falcon." Patting Perrin on the shoulder, he murmured in a deep rumble, "She should fly free," then made his way to his pallet and lay down facing the wall.

"He is very tired," Perrin said, attempting to make it seem just a comment. The fool Ogier could ruin everything! "If you leave tonight, you can be at Watch Hill by daybreak. You'll have to swing to the east; the Trollocs are fewer there. This is very important to me . . . to Emond's Field, I mean. Will you do it?"

She stared at him silently for so long he wondered if she meant to answer. Her eyes seemed to glisten. Then she got up and sat down on his lap, stroking his beard. "This needs trimming. I like it on you, but I do not want it down to your chest."

He came close to gaping. She often changed the subject on him, but usually when she was losing an argument. "Faile, please. I need you to carry this message to Caemlyn."

Her hand tightened in his beard, and her head swung as if she were arguing with herself inside her head. "I will go," she said at last, "but I want a price. You always make me do things the hard way. In Saldaea, I would not have to be the one who asked. My price is. . . . A wedding. I want to marry you," she finished up in a rush.

"And I you." He smiled. "We can say the betrothal vows in front of the Women's Circle tonight, but I'm afraid the wedding has to wait a year. When you come back from Caemlyn—" She very nearly yanked a handful of beard out of his chin.

"I will have you for husband tonight," she said in fierce, low tones, "or I will not go until I do!"

"If there was any way, I would," he protested. "Daise Congar would crack my head if I wanted to go against custom. For the love of the Light, Faile, just carry the message, and I'll wed you the very first day I can." He would. If that day ever came.

Suddenly she was very intent on his beard, smoothing it and not meeting his eyes. She started speaking slowly but picked up speed like a runaway horse. "I . . . just happened to mention . . . in passing . . . I just *mentioned* to Mistress al'Vere how we had been traveling together—I don't know how it came up—and she said—and Mistress Congar agreed with her—not that I talked to everybody!—she said that we probably—certainly—could be considered betrothed already under your customs, and the year is just to make sure you really do get on well together—which we do, as anyone can see—and here I am being as forward as some Domani hussy or one of those Tairen galls—if you ever even *think* of Berelain—oh, Light, I'm babbling, and you won't even—"

He cut her off by kissing her as thoroughly as he knew how.

"Will you marry me?" he said breathlessly when he was done. "Tonight?" He must have done ever better with the kiss than he thought; he had to repeat himself six times, with her giggling against his throat and demanding he say it again, before she seemed to understand.

Which was how he found himself not half an hour later kneeling opposite her in the common room, in front of Daise Congar and Marin al'Vere, Alsbet Luhhan and Neysa Ayellin and all the Women's Circle. Loial had been roused to stand for him with Aram, and Bain and Chiad stood for Faile. There were no flowers to put in her hair or his, but Bain, guided by Marin, tucked a long red wedding ribbon around his neck, and Loial threaded another through Faile's dark hair, his thick fingers surprisingly deft and gentle. Perrin's hands trembled as he cupped hers.

"I, Perrin Aybara, do pledge you my love, Faile Bashere, for as long as I live." *For as long as I live and after.* "What I possess in this world I give to you." *A horse, an axe, a bow. A hammer. Not much to gift a bride. I give you life, my love. It's all I have.* "I will keep and hold you, succor and tend you, protect and shelter you, for all the days of my life." *I can't keep you; the only way I can protect you is to send you away.* "I am yours, always and forever." By the time he finished, his hands were shaking visibly.

Faile moved her hands to hold his. "I, Zarine Bashere . . ." That was a surprise; she hated that name. ". . . do pledge you my love, Perrin Aybara. . . ." Her hands never trembled at all.

CHAPTER
54

Into the Palace

Seated on the tail end of the high-wheeled cart trundling up a twisty Tanchican street behind four sweating men, Elayne scowled through the grimy veil that covered her from eyes to chin, kicking her bare feet irritably. Every lurch over the paving stones jarred her to the top of her skull; the more she braced herself by holding on to the rough wooden planks of the cart bed, the worse it was. It did not seem to bother Nynaeve much; she jounced about like Elayne, but, frowning slightly and eyes looking inward, she appeared hardly aware of it. And Egeanin, crowded against Nynaeve on the other side, veiled and with her dark hair in braids to her shoulders, rode each jolt easily, arms folded. Finally Elayne emulated the Seanchan woman; she could not avoid swaying into Nynaeve, but the ride no longer felt as if her lower teeth were going to be driven through the upper.

She would have walked gladly, even barefoot, but Bayle Domon had said it would not look right; people might wonder why women were not riding when there was plenty of room, and the last thing they wanted was anyone thinking about them twice. Of course he was not being bounced about like a sack of turnips; he was walking, at the head of the cart with ten of the twenty sailors he had brought along for escort.

More would seem suspicious, he claimed. She suspected he would not have had so many if not for her and the other two women.

The cloudless sky still stretched gray overhead, though first light had crept on before they set out; the streets were still largely empty, and silent except for the rumble of the cart and the creak of its axle. When the sun topped the horizon people would begin to venture out, but now the few she saw were knots of men in baggy trousers and dark cylindrical caps, scuttling along with the furtive air of having been up to no good while dark had held. The old piece of canvas tossed over the cart's load was carefully arranged so anyone could see it covered only three large baskets, yet even so one or another of those small clusters would pause like a pack of dogs, veiled faces all coming up together, eyes swiveling to follow the cart. Apparently twenty men with boarding swords and cudgels were too many to face, because all eventually hurried on.

The wheels dropped into a large hole where paving stones had been pried up in one of the riots; the cart fell away beneath her. She almost bit her tongue as she and the cart bed met again with a hard smack. Egeanin and her casual arm-folding! Grabbing the edge of the cart bed, she frowned at the Seanchan woman. And found her tight-lipped and holding on with both hands also.

"Not quite the same as standing on deck after all," Egeanin said with a shrug.

Nynaeve grimaced slightly and tried to edge away from the Seanchan woman, though how she might manage it without climbing into Elayne's lap was difficult to see. "I am going to speak to Master Bayle Domon," she muttered meaningfully, just as if the cart had not been her suggestion in the first place. Another lurch clicked her teeth shut.

They all three wore drab brown wool, thin-woven but coarse and not very clean, poor farm women's dresses like shapeless sacks compared with the clinging silks of Rendra's taste. Refugees from the countryside earning a meal as they could; that was what they were supposed to be. Egeanin's relief at her first sight of the dresses had been quite evident, and almost as strange as her presence on the cart. Elayne would not have thought the latter conceivable.

There had been quite a lot of discussion—that was what the men called it—in the Chamber of Falling Blossoms, but she and Nynaeve had countered most of their fool objections and ignored the rest. The two of them had to enter the Panarch's Palace, and as soon as possible. That was when Domon had raised another objection, one not as silly as the rest.

"You can no go into the palace alone," the bearded smuggler muttered, staring at his fists on the table. "You say you will no channel unless you must, no to warn these Black Aes Sedai." Neither of them had seen any need to mention one of the Forsaken. "Then you must have muscle to swing a club if the need do arise, and eyes to watch your backs will no be amiss either. I am known there, to the servants. I did take gifts to the old Panarch too. I will go with you." Shaking his head, he growled, "You do make me stretch my neck on the headsman's block because I did leave you at Falme. Fortune prick me if you do no! Well, it do be done now; you can no object to *this!* I will go in with you."

"You are a fool, Illianer," Juilin said contemptuously before she or Nynaeve could open their mouths. "You think the Taraboners will allow you to wander about the palace as you wish? A scruffy smuggler from Illian? I know the ways of servants, how to duck my head and make some empty-headed noble think. . . ." He cleared his throat hastily, and hurried on without looking at Nyaneve—or at her! "I should be the one to go with them."

Thom laughed at the other two men. "Do you think *either* of you could pass for a Taraboner? I can; these will do in a pinch." He knuckled his long mustaches. "Besides, you cannot run around the Panarch's Palace carrying cudgel or staff. A more . . . subtle . . . method of protection is needed." He flourished a hand, and a knife suddenly appeared, spinning through his fingers to vanish just as quickly; up his sleeve, Elayne believed.

"You all know what you have to do," Nynaeve snapped, "and you cannot do it trying to watch over us like a pair of geese for market!" Taking a deep breath, she went on, in a milder tone. "If there was a way one of you could come along, I'd appreciate the extra eyes if nothing else, but it cannot be. We have to go alone, it seems, and that is all there is to it."

"I can accompany you," Egeanin announced suddenly from where Nynaeve had made her stand in the corner of the room. Everybody turned to look at her; she frowned back as though not quite certain herself. "These women are Darkfriends. They should be brought to justice."

Elayne was simply startled at the offer, but Nynaeve, the corners of her mouth going white, looked ready to drub the woman for it. "You think we would trust you, Seanchan?" she said coldly. "Before we leave, you'll be locked securely in a storeroom however much talk it—"

"I give oath by my hope of a higher name," Egeanin broke in, putting her hands over her heart, one atop the other, "that I will not betray you in any way, that I will obey you and guard your backs until you are safely out of the Panarch's Palace." Then she bowed three times, deeply and formally. Elayne had no idea what "hope of a higher name" meant, but the Seanchan woman certainly made it sound binding.

"She can do it," Domon said with slow reluctance. He eyed Egeanin and shook his head. "Fortune prick me if there be more than two or three of my men I would wager on, coin for coin, against her."

Nynaeve frowned at her hand gripping half a dozen of her long braids, then quite deliberately gave them a yank.

"Nynaeve," Elayne told her firmly, "you yourself said you would like another pair of eyes, and I definitely would. Besides which, if we are to do this without channeling, I would not mind having someone along who can handle a nosy guard if need be. I am not up to thumping men with my fists, and neither are you. You remember how she can fight."

Nynaeve glared at Egeanin, frowned at Elayne, and then stared at the men as if they had plotted this behind her back. At last, though, she nodded.

"Good," Elayne said. "Master Domon, that means three sets of dresses, not two. Now, the three of you had best be off. We want to be on our way by daybreak."

The cart jerking to a halt brought Elayne out of her reverie.

Dismounted Whitecloaks were questioning Domon. Here the street ran into a square behind the Panarch's Palace, a much smaller square than the one in front. Beyond, the palace stood in piles of white marble, slender towers banded with lacy stonework, snowy domes capped with gold and topped by golden spires or weather vanes. The streets to either side were much wider than most in Tanchico, and straighter.

The slow *clop-clop* of a horse's hooves on the square's broad paving stones announced another rider, a tall man in burnished helmet, armor gleaming beneath his white cloak with its golden sunburst and crimson shepherd's crook. Elayne put her head down; the four knots of rank under the flaring sun told her this was Jaichim Carridin. The man had never seen her, but if he thought she was staring he might wonder why. The hooves passed on along the square without pausing.

Egeanin had her face right down, too, but Nynaeve frowned openly after the Inquisitor. "That man is very worried about something," she murmured. "I hope he's not heard—"

"The Panarch is dead!" a man's voice shouted from somewhere across the square. "They've killed her!"

There was no telling who had shouted, or where. The streets Elayne could see were blocked by Whitecloaks on horses.

Looking back down the street the cart had just climbed, she wished the guards would question Domon more quickly. People were gathering down at the first bend, milling about and peering up toward the square. It seemed Thom and Juilin had made a good job of seeding their rumors during the night. Now if only things did not erupt while they sat out here in the middle of it. If a riot started now. . . . The only thing that kept her hands from shaking was her double grip on the cart bed. *Light, a mob out here and the Black Ajah inside, maybe Moghedien. . . . I'm so frightened my mouth is dry.* Nynaeve and Egeanin were watching the crowd growing down the street, too, and not even blinking, much less trembling. *I will not be a coward. I will not!*

The cart rumbled forward, and she heaved a sigh of relief. It took her a moment to realize she had heard twin echoes from the other two women.

Before gates not much wider than the cart Domon was questioned again, by men in pointed helmets, their breastplates embossed with a tree painted gold. Soldiers of the Panarch's Legion. The questions were shorter this time; Elayne thought she saw a small purse change hands, and then they were inside, rumbling across the rough-paved yard outside the kitchens. Except for Domon, the sailors remained out with the soldiers.

Elayne hopped down as soon as the cart halted, working her bare feet on the paving; the uneven stones were *hard.* It was difficult to believe the thin sole of a slipper could make so much difference. Egeanin scrambled up into the cart to pass the baskets out, Nynaeve taking the first on her back, one hand twisted behind her underneath, the other over her shoulder to grip the rim. Long white peppers, a little wizened by their journey all the way from Saldaea, filled the baskets nearly to the top.

As Elayne was taking hers, Domon came to the end of the cart and pretended to inspect the ice peppers. "The Whitecloaks and the Panarch's Legion do be close to blows, it do appear," he murmured, fingering peppers. "That lieutenant did say the Legion could protect the Panarch themselves if most of the Legion had not been sent to the ring forts. Jaichim Carridin do have access to the Panarch, but no the Lord Captain of the Legion. And they are no pleased that all the guards inside do be Civil Watch. A suspicious man might say someone do want the Panarch's guards to watch each other more than anything else."

"That is good to know," Nynaeve murmured without looking at him. "I've always said you can learn useful things listening to men's gossip." Domon grunted sourly. "I will take you inside; then I must go back to my men to make sure they do not get caught up in the mob." Every sailor from every ship Domon had in port was out in the streets around the palace.

Hefting her own basket on her back, Elayne followed the other two women behind him, keeping her head down and wincing at every step until she was on the reddish-brown tiles of the kitchen. The smells of spices and cooking meat and sauces filled the room.

"Ice peppers for the Panarch," Domon announced. "A gift from Bayle Domon, a good shipowner of this city."

"More of the ice peppers?" a stout, dark-braided woman in a white apron and the ever-present veil said, barely looking up from a silver tray where she was arranging an ornately folded white napkin among dishes of thin, golden Sea Folk porcelain. There were a dozen or more aproned women in the kitchen, as well as a pair of boys turning dripping roasts on spits in two of the six fireplaces, but clearly she was the chief cook. "Well, the Panarch, she seems to have enjoyed the last. Into the storeroom there." She gestured vaguely toward one of the doors on the far side of the room. "I have no time to bother with you now."

Elayne kept her eyes on the floor as she trailed after Nynaeve and Egeanin, sweating, and not for the heat of the iron stoves and fireplaces. A skinny woman in green silk not of Tarabon cut stood beside one of the wide tables, scratching the ears of a scrawny gray cat as it lapped cream from a porcelain dish. The cat named her, as well as her narrow face and wide nose. Marillin Gemalphin, once of the Brown Ajah, now of the Black. If she looked up from that cat, if she really became aware of them, there would be no need for channeling for her to know that two of them could; this close the woman would be able to sense the ability itself.

Sweat dripped from the end of Elayne's nose by the time she pushed the storeroom door shut behind her with a hip. "Did you see her?" she demanded in a low voice, letting her basket half-fall to the floor. Fretwork carved through the plastered wall just under the ceiling let in dim light from the kitchen. Rows of tall shelves filled the floor of the large room, laden with sacks and net bags of vegetables and large jars of spice. Barrels and casks stood everywhere, and a dozen dressed lambs and twice as many geese hung on hooks. According to the sketchy floorplan Domon and Thom had drawn between them, this was the smallest storeroom for food in the palace. "This is disgusting," she said. "I know Rendra keeps a full kitchen, but at least she buys what she needs as she can. These people have been feasting while—"

"Hold your concern until you can do something about it," Nynaeve told her in a sharp whisper. She had upended her basket on the floor and was stripping off her rough farm woman's dress. Egeanin was already down to her shift. "I did see her. If you want her to come in here to see what the noise is about, keep talking."

Elayne sniffed, but let it pass. She had not been making that much noise. Pulling off her own dress, she dumped the peppers out of her basket, and what had been hidden under them as well. Among other things, a dress of white belted in green, fine-spun wool embroidered above the left breast with a green tree of spreading branches atop the outline of a trefoil leaf. Her grimy veil was replaced by a clean one, of linen scraped nearly as sheer as silk. White slippers with padded soles were welcome on feet bruised by that walk from cart to kitchen.

The Seanchan woman had been the first out of her old clothes, but she was the last into her white garment, muttering all the while about "indecent" and "serving girl," which made no sense. The dresses *were* servants' dresses; the whole point was that servants could go anywhere and a palace had too many for anyone to notice three more. And as for indecent. . . . Elayne could remember being a touch hesitant about wearing the Tarabon style in public, but she had become used to it soon enough, and even this thin wool could not cling as silk did. Egeanin seemed to have very strict ideas of modesty.

Eventually, though, the woman had done up her last lace, and the farm clothes had been stuffed into the baskets and covered with ice peppers.

Marillin Gemalphin was gone from the kitchen, though the raggedy-eared gray cat still lapped cream on the table. Elayne and the other two started for the door that led deeper into the palace.

One of the undercooks was frowning at the cat, fist on her ample hips. "I would like to strangle this cat," she muttered, pale brown braids swinging as she shook her head angrily. "It eats the cream, and because I put the drop of cream on the berries for my breakfast, I have the bread and water for my meals!"

"Count yourself lucky you are not out in the street, or swinging from the gallows." The chief cook did not sound sympathetic. "If a lady says you have stolen, then you have stolen, even if it is the cream for her cats, yes? You, there!"

Elayne and her companions froze at the shout.

The dark-braided woman shook a long wooden spoon at them. "You come into my kitchen and stroll about as in the garden, you lazy sows you? You have come for the breakfast of the Lady Ispan, yes? If you do not have it there when she wakes, you will learn how to jump. Well?" She gestured at the silver tray she had been laboring over before, covered now with a snowy linen cloth.

There was no way to speak; if any one of them opened her mouth, her first words would show her no Taraboner. Thinking quickly, Elayne bobbed a servant's curtsy and picked up the tray; a servant carrying something was going about her work and not likely to be stopped or told to do something else. Lady Ispan? Not an uncommon name in Tarabon, but there was an Ispan on the list of Black sisters.

"So you mock me, do you, you little cow you?" the stout woman roared, and started around the table waving her thick wooden spoon threateningly.

There was nothing to do without giving herself away; nothing but stay and be hit, or run. Elayne darted out of the kitchen with the tray, Nynaeve and Egeanin at her heels. The cook's shouts followed them, but not the cook, thankfully. An image of the three of them running through the palace pursued by the stout woman made Elayne want to giggle hysterically. *Mock her?* She was sure that had been exactly the same curtsy servants had given her thousands of times.

More storerooms lined the narrow hallway leading away from the kitchen, and tall cupboards for brooms and mops, buckets and soaps, linens for tables, and all sorts of assorted things. Nynaeve found a fat feather duster in one. Egeanin took an armful of folded towels from another, and a stout stone pestle out of a mortar in a third. She hid the pestle under the towels.

"A cudgel is sometimes handy," she said when Elayne raised an eyebrow. "Especially when no one expects you to have it."

Nynaeve sniffed but said nothing. She had hardly acknowledged Egeanin at all since agreeing to her presence.

Deeper in the palace the hallways broadened and heightened, the white walls carved with friezes and the ceilings set with gleaming arabesques of gold. Long, bright carpets ran along white-tiled floors. Ornate golden lamps on gilded stands gave light and the scent of perfumed oil. Sometimes the corridor opened into courtyards rounded by walks with slim, fluted columns, overlooked by balconies screened by filigreed stonework. Large fountains burbled; fish red and white and golden swam beneath lily pads with huge white flowers. Not at all like the city outside.

Occasionally they saw other servants, men and women in white, tree and leaf embroidered on one shoulder, hurrying about their tasks, or men in the gray coats and steel caps of the Civil Watch carrying staffs or cudgels. No one spoke to them or even looked twice, not at three serving women obviously at their work.

At last they came to the narrow servants' stairs marked on their sketchy map.

"Remember," Nynaeve said quietly, "if there are guards on her door, leave. If she is not alone, leave. She is far from the most important reason we are here." She took a deep breath, making herself look at Egeanin. "If you let anything happen to her—"

A trumpet sounded faintly from outside. A moment later a gong rang inside, and shouted orders drifted down the hall. Men in steel caps appeared for a moment down the hallway, running.

"Maybe we will not have to worry about guards on her door," Elayne said. The riot had begun in the streets. Rumors spread by Thom and Juilin to gather the crowd. Domon's sailors to egg them on. She regretted the necessity, but the disturbance would pull most of the guards out of the palace, maybe all with luck. Those people out there did not know it, but they fought in a battle to save their city from the Black Ajah and the world from the Shadow. "Egeanin should go with you, Nynaeve. Your part *is* the most important. If one of us needs someone to watch her back, it is you."

"I've no need for a Seanchan!" Shouldering her duster like a pike, Nynaeve strode off down the hall. She really did not move like a servant. Not with that militant stride.

"Should we not be about our own task?" Egeanin said. "The riot will not hold attention completely for long."

Elayne nodded. Nynaeve had passed out of sight around a corner.

The stairs were narrow and hidden in the wall, to keep servants as unseen as possible. The corridors on the second floor were much as those on the first, except that double-pointed arches were almost as likely to give onto a stone-latticed balcony as onto a room. There seemed to be far fewer servants as they made their way to the west side of the palace, and none more than glanced at them. Wonderfully, the hallway outside the Panarch's apartments was empty. No guards in front of the wide, tree-carved doors set in a double-peaked frame. Not that she had meant to retreat had there been guards, no matter what she had told Nynaeve, but it did make things simpler.

A moment later she was not so sure. She could feel someone channeling in those rooms. Not strong flows, but definitely the Power being

woven, or maybe a weave maintained. Few women knew the trick of
tying a weave.

"What is the matter?" Egeanin asked.

Elayne realized she had stopped. "One of the Black sisters is in
there." One, or more? Only one channeling, certainly. She pressed
close to the doors. A woman was *singing* in there. She put her ear to the
carved wood, heard raucous words, muffled yet clearly understandable.

> *"My breasts are round, and my hips are too.*
> *I can flatten a whole ship's crew."*

Startled, she jerked back, porcelain dishes sliding on the tray under
the cloth. Had she somehow come to the wrong room? No, she had
memorized the sketch. Besides, in the entire palace the only doors
carved with the tree led to the Panarch's apartments.

"Then we must leave her," Egeanin said. "You can do nothing without warning the others of your presence."

"Perhaps I can. If they feel me channel, they will think it is whoever
is in there." Frowning, she bit her lower lip. How many were there?
She could do at least three or four things at once with the Power,
something only Egwene and Nynaeve could match. She ran down a list
of Andoran queens who had shown courage in the face of great danger,
until she realized it was a list of all the queens of Andor. *I will be queen
one day; I can be as brave as they.* Readying herself, she said, "Throw
open the doors, Egeanin, then drop down so I can see everything." The
Seanchan woman hesitated. "Throw open the doors." Elayne's own
voice surprised her. She had not tried to *make* it anything, but it was
quiet, calm, commanding. And Egeanin nodded, almost a bow, and
immediately flung open both doors.

> *"My thighs are strong are strong as anchor chain.*
> *My kiss can burst—"*

The dark-braided singer, standing wrapped in flows of Air to her
neck and a soiled, wrinkled Taraboner gown of red silk, cut off short as
the doors banged back. A frail-appearing woman, lounging in pale blue
of a high-necked Cairhienin cut on a long padded bench, ceased nodding her head to the song and leaped to her feet, outrage replacing the
grin on her fox-shaped face.

The glow of *saidar* already surrounded Temaile, but she did not have
a chance. Appalled at what she saw, Elayne embraced the True Source

and lashed out hard with flows of Air, webbing her from shoulders to ankles, wove a shield of Spirit and slammed it between the woman and the Source. The glow around Temaile vanished, and she went flying across the bench as if she had been struck by a galloping horse, eyes rolling up into her head, to land unconscious on her back three paces away on the green-and-gold carpet. The dark-braided woman gave a start as the flows around her winked out of existence, felt at herself in wondering disbelief as she stared from Temaile to Elayne and Egeanin.

Tying off the weave holding Temaile, Elayne hurried into the room, eyes searching for others of the Black Ajah. Behind her, Egeanin closed the doors after them. There did not seem to be anyone else. "Was she alone?" she demanded of the woman in red. The Panarch, by Nynaeve's description. Nynaeve *had* mentioned *some*thing about a song.

"You are not . . . with them?" Amathera said hesitantly, dark eyes taking in their dresses. "You are Aes Sedai also?" She seemed willing to doubt that despite the evidence of Temaile. "But not with them?"

"Was she alone?" Elayne snapped, and Amathera gave a little jump.

"Yes. Alone. Yes, she. . . ." The Panarch grimaced. "The others made me sit on my throne and speak the words they put into my mouth. It amused them to make me sometimes give justice, and sometimes pronouncements of horrible injustice, rulings that will cause strife for generations if I cannot put them aright. But her!" That full-lipped little mouth opened in a snarl. "Her they set to watch over me. She hurts me for no reason except to make me weep. She made me eat an entire trayful of white ice peppers and would not let me drink a drop until I begged on my knees while she laughed! In my dreams she hoists me to the top of the Tower of Morning by my ankles and lets me fall. A dream, but it seems real, and each time she lets me fall scream-ing a little nearer the ground. And she laughs! She makes me learn lewd dances, and filthy songs, and laughs when she tells me that before they leave she will make me sing and dance to entertain the—" With a shriek like a pouncing cat she threw herself across the bench onto the bound woman, slapping wildly, pummeling with her fists.

Egeanin, arms folded in front of the doors, seemed ready to let it go on, but Elayne wove flows of Air around Amathera's waist. To her surprise she was able to lift her off the already senseless woman and set her on her feet. Perhaps learning how to handle those heavy weavings from Jorin had increased her strength.

Amathera kicked at Temaile, turning her glare on Elayne and Ege-anin when her slippered feet missed. "I am the Panarch of Tarabon, and I mean to dispense justice to this woman!" That rosebud mouth had a very sulky look. Had the woman no sense of herself, of her position? She was equal to the king, a ruler!

"And I am the Aes Sedai who has come to rescue you," Elayne said coolly. Realizing she still held the tray, she set it on the floor hurriedly. The woman seemed to be having enough trouble seeing beyond the white servants' dresses without that. Temaile's face was quite red; she would wake to bruises. No doubt fewer than she deserved. Elayne wished there was a way to take Temaile with them. A way to bring even one to justice in the Tower. "We have come—at considerable risk!—to take you out of here. Then you can reach the Lord Captain of the Panarch's Legion, and Andric and his army, and you can chase these women out. Perhaps we will be lucky enough to take some of them for trial. But first we must get you away from them."

"I do not need Andric," Amathera muttered. Elayne would have sworn she almost said "now." "There are soldiers of my Legion around the palace. I know this. I have been allowed to speak to none of them, but once they see me, and hear my voice, they will do what must be done, yes? You Aes Sedai cannot use the One Power to harm. . . ." She trailed off, scowling at the unconscious Temaile. "You cannot use it as a weapon, at least, yes? I know this."

Elayne surprised herself by weaving tiny flows of Air, one to each of Amathera's braids. The braids lifted straight up into the air, and the pouty-mouth fool had no choice but to follow them up on tiptoe. Elayne walked her that way, on tiptoe, until the woman stood right in front of her, dark eyes wide and indignant.

"You will listen to me, Panarch Amathera of Tarabon," she said in icy tones. "If you try to walk out to your soldiers, Temaile's cronies may very well tie you up in a bundle and hand you back to her. Worse, they will learn that my friends and I are here, and that I will not allow. We are going to *creep* out of here, and if you will not agree to that, I'll bind and gag you and leave you beside Temaile for her friends to find." There *had* to be some way to take Temaile, too. "Do you understand me?"

Amathera nodded slightly, held up as she was. Egeanin made an approving sound.

Elayne loosed the flows; the woman's heels dropped to the carpet. "Now let's see if we can find you something to wear that is suitable for sneaking." Amathera nodded again, but her mouth was set at its sulkiest. Elayne hoped Nynaeve was having an easier time of it.

* * *

Nynaeve entered the great exhibition hall with its multitude of thin columns, feather duster already moving. This collection must always need dusting, and surely no one would look twice at a woman doing what was needed. She looked around, eyes drawn to wired-together bones that looked like a long-legged horse with a neck that pushed its skull up twenty feet. The vast chamber stretched emptily in all directions.

But someone could come in at any moment; servants who actually had been sent to clean, or Liandrin and all of her fellows come to search. Still holding the duster prominently, just in case, she hurried down to the white stone pedestal that had held the dull black collar and bracelets. She did not realize she had been holding her breath until she exhaled on seeing the things still there. The glass-sided table holding the *cuendillar* seal lay another fifty paces on, but this came first.

Climbing over the wrist-thick white silk rope, she touched the wide, jointed collar. *Suffering. Agony. Woe.* They rolled through her; she wanted to weep. What kind of thing could absorb all that pain? Pulling her hand back, she glared at the black metal. Meant to control a man who could channel. Liandrin and her Black sisters meant to use it to control Rand, turn him to the Shadow, force him to serve the Dark One. Someone from her village, controlled and used by Aes Sedai! Black Ajah, but Aes Sedai as surely as Moiraine with her scheming! *Egeanin, making me like a filthy Seanchan!*

The sudden incongruity of the last thought hit her; abruptly she realized she was deliberately making herself angry, angry enough to channel. She embraced the Source; the Power filled her. And a serving woman with the tree-and-leaf on her shoulder entered the columned hall.

Quivering with the urge to channel, Nynaeve waited, even lifting the duster, running the feathers over the collar and bracelets. The serving woman started down the pale floorstones; she would go in a moment, and Nynaeve could. . . . What? Slip the things into her belt pouch and take them, but. . . .

The serving woman would go? *Why did I think she'll leave instead of staying to work?* She glanced sideways up the room at the woman coming toward her. Of course. No broom or mop, no feather duster, not even a rag. *Whatever she's here for, it cannot take lo—*

Suddenly she saw the woman's face clearly. Sturdily handsome, framed by dark braids, smiling in an almost friendly fashion but not really paying her any mind. Certainly not threatening in any way. Not quite the same face, but she knew it.

Before thought she struck out, weaving a hammer-hard flow of Air to smash that face. In an instant the glow of *saidar* surrounded the other woman, her features changed—somehow more regal now, prouder, Moghedien's face remembered; and startled as well, surprised that she had not approached unsuspected—and Nynaeve's flow was sliced razor clean. She staggered under the whiplash recoil, like a physical blow, and the Forsaken struck with a complex weave of Spirit streaked by Water and Air. Nynaeve had no idea what it was meant to do; frantically she tried to cut it as she had seen the other woman do, with a keen-edged weave of Spirit. For a heartbeat she felt love, devotion, worship for the magnificent woman who would deign to allow her to. . . .

The intricate weave parted, and Moghedien missed a step. A tinge remained in Nynaeve's mind, like a fresh memory of wanting to obey, to grovel and please, what had happened at their first meeting all over again; it heated her rage. The knife-sharp shield that Egwene had used to still Amico Nagoyin sprang into being, more weapon than shield, lashed at Moghedien—and was blocked, woven Spirit straining against woven Spirit, just short of severing Moghedien from the Source forever. Again the Forsaken's counterblow came, slashing like an axe, intended to cut Nynaeve off in the same way. Forever. Desperately Nynaeve blocked it.

Suddenly she realized that under her anger she was terrified. Holding off the other woman's attempt to still her while trying to do the same to her took everything she had. The Power boiled in her till she thought she must burst; her knees quivered with the effort of standing. And all went into those two things; she could not spare enough to light a candle. Moghedien's axe of Spirit waxed and waned in sharpness, but that would not matter if the woman managed to drive it home; Nynaeve could not see any real difference in outcome between being stilled by the woman and merely—*merely!*—being shielded and at her mercy. The thing brushed against the flow of Power from the Source into her, like a knife hovering over a chicken's stretched neck. The image was all too apt; she wished she had not thought of it. In the back of her mind a tiny voice gibbered at her. *Oh, Light, don't let her. Don't let her! Light, please, not that!*

For a moment she considered letting go her own attempt to cut Moghedien off—for one thing, she had to keep forcing it back to a razor edge; the woven flows did not want to hold the keenness—letting go and using that strength to force Moghedien's attack further back, maybe sever it. But if she tried, the other woman would not need to defend; she could add that strength to her own attack. And she was one of the Forsaken. Not just a Black sister. A woman who had been Aes Sedai in the Age of Legends, when Aes Sedai had been able to do things undreamed of now. If Moghedien threw her whole strength at her. . . .

A man who came in then, or any woman unable to channel, would have seen only two women facing each other across the white silk rope from a distance of less than ten feet. Two women staring at one another in a vast hall full of strange things. They would have seen nothing to say it was a duel. No leaping about and hacking with swords as men would do, nothing smashed or broken. Just two women standing there. But a duel all the same, and maybe to the death. Against one of the Forsaken.

"All my careful planning ruined," Moghedien said abruptly in a tight, angry voice, white-knuckled hands gripping her skirts. "At the very least I shall have to go to untold effort to put everything back as it was. It may not be possible. Oh, I do mean to make you pay for that, Nynaeve al'Meara. This has been such a cozy hiding place, and those blind women have a number of very useful items in their possession even if they do not—" She shook her head, lips peeling back to bare her teeth in a snarl. "I think I will take you with me this time. I know. I shall keep you for a live mounting block. You will be brought out to kneel on all fours so I can step from your back to my saddle. Or perhaps I shall give you to Rahvin. He always repays favors. He does have a pretty little queen to amuse him now, but pretty women were always Rahvin's weakness. He likes to have two or three or four at once dancing attendance on him. How will you like that? To spend the rest of your life competing for Rahvin's favors. You will want to, once he has his hands on you; he has his little tricks. Yes, I do believe Rahvin shall have you."

Anger welled up in Nynaeve. Sweat streamed down her face, and her legs shook as if they might give way, but anger gave her strength. Furious, she managed to push her weapon of Spirit a hair closer to severing Moghedien from the Source before the woman halted it again.

"So you discovered that little gem behind you," Moghedien said in a moment of precarious balance. Surprisingly, her voice was almost conversational. "I wonder how you did that. It does not matter. Did you come to take it away? Perhaps to destroy it? You cannot destroy it. That is not metal, but a form of *cuendillar*. Even balefire cannot destroy *cuendillar.* And if you mean to use it, it does have . . . drawbacks, shall we say? Put the collar on a man who channels, and a woman wearing the bracelets can make him do whatever she wishes, true, but it will not stop him going mad, and there is a flow the other way, too. Eventually he will begin to be able to control you, too, so you end with a struggle at every hour. Not very palatable when he is going mad. Of course, you can pass the bracelets around, so no one has too much exposure, but that does mean trusting someone else with him. Men are always so good at violence; they make wonderful weapons. Or two women can each wear one bracelet, if you have someone you trust enough; that slows the seepage considerably, I understand, but it also lessens your control, even if you work in perfect unison. Eventually, you will find yourselves in a struggle for control with him, each of you needing him to remove your bracelet as surely as he needs you to remove the collar." She tilted her head, lifted a quizzical eyebrow. "You are following this, I trust? Controlling Lews Therin—Rand al'Thor as he is called now—would be most useful, but is it worth the price? You can see why I have left the collar and bracelets where they are."

Trembling to contain the Power, to hold her woven flows, Nynaeve frowned. Why was the woman telling her all of this? Did she think it did not matter because she was going to win? Why her sudden change from rage to talk? There was sweat on Moghedien's face, too. Quite a lot of sweat, beading on her broad forehead, running down her cheeks.

Suddenly everything changed in Nynaeve's mind. Moghedien's was not a voice tight with anger; it was a voice tight with strain. Moghedien was not suddenly going to hurl all of her strength at her; she already was. The woman was putting out as much effort as she. She was facing one of the Forsaken, and far from being plucked like a goose for supper, she had not lost a feather. She was meeting one of the Forsaken, strength for strength! Moghedien was trying to distract her, to gain an opening before her own strength gave out! If only she could do the same. Before her strength went.

"Do you wonder how I know all this? The collar and bracelets were made after I was. . . . Well, we will not talk of that. Once I was free, the first thing I did was seek information about those last days. Last years, really. There are a good many fragments here and there that make no sense to anyone who does not have some idea to begin with. The Age of Legends. Such a quaint name you have given my time. Yet even your wildest tales no more than hint at the half. I had lived over two hundred years when the Bore was opened, and I was still young, for an Aes Sedai. Your 'legends' are but pale imitations of what we could do. Why. . . ."

Nynaeve stopped listening. A way to distract the woman. Even if she could think of something to say, Moghedien would be on her guard against the method she herself was using. She could not spare effort for as much as a thread-thin weave, any more than. . . . Any more than Moghedien could. A woman from the Age of Legends, a woman long used to wielding the One Power. Perhaps used to doing almost everything with the Power before she was imprisoned. In hiding since being freed, how used to doing things without the Power had she become?

Nynaeve let her legs sag. Dropping the feather duster, she caught hold of the pedestal to support herself. There was very little fakery needed.

Moghedien smiled and took a step nearer. ". . . travel to other worlds, even worlds in the sky. Do you know that the stars are. . . ." So sure, that smile. So triumphant.

Nynaeve seized the collar, ignoring the joltingly pained emotions that spilled into her, and hurled it, all in one motion.

The Forsaken had only begun to gape when the wide black circlet struck her between the eyes. Not a hard blow, certainly not enough to stun, but not expected, either. Moghedien's control over her woven flows faltered, just slightly, only for an instant. Yet for that instant the balance between them shifted. The shield of Spirit slid between Moghedien and the Source; the halo surrounding her winked out.

The woman's eyes bulged. Nynaeve expected her to leap for her throat; that was what she would have done. Instead, Moghedien jerked her skirts to her knees and ran.

With no need to defend herself, it took only a little effort for Nynaeve to weave Air around the fleeing woman. The Forsaken froze in midstride.

Hurriedly Nynaeve tied her weaving. She had done it. *I faced one of the Forsaken and beat her,* she thought incredulously. Looking at the woman held from the neck down by air with the consistency of stone, even seeing her leaning forward on one foot, it was hard to believe. Examining what she had done, she saw it had not been as complete a victory as she had wanted. The shield had blurred its sharp edge before it slid home. Moghedien was captured and shielded, but not stilled.

Trying not to totter, she walked around in front of the other woman. Moghedien still looked queenly, but a very frightened queen, licking her lips, eyes darting wildly. "If . . . if you f-free me, we can c-come to s-some arrangement. There is m-much I can t-teach you—"

Ruthlessly Nynaeve cut her off, weaving a gag of Air that held the woman's jaws gaping. "A live mounting block. Wasn't that what you said? I think that is a very good idea. I like to ride." She smiled at the woman, whose eyes looked to be coming out of her head.

Mounting block indeed! Once Moghedien had been put on trial in the Tower and stilled—there could be no doubt of the sentence for one of the Forsaken—she would surely be put to some useful work in kitchens or gardens or stables, except when she was brought out to show that even the Forsaken could not escape justice, and treated no differently from any other servant, beyond being watched. But let her think Nynaeve was as cruel as she. Let her think it until she was actually put on. . . .

Nynaeve's mouth twisted. Moghedien was not going to be put on trial. Not now, anyway. Not unless she could figure out some way to get her out of the Panarch's Palace. The woman seemed to believe the grimace portended something ill for her; tears leaked from her eyes, and her mouth worked, trying to force words past the gag.

Disgusted with herself, Nynaeve walked unsteadily back to where the black collar lay, stuffing it quickly into her belt pouch before the stark emotions in it could do more than touch her. The bracelets followed, with the same feelings of suffering and sorrow. *I was ready to torture her by letting her think I would! She deserves it surely, but that is not me. Or is it? Am I no better than Egeanin?*

She jerked around, furious that she could even consider such a question, and stalked past Moghedien to the glass-walled table. There had to be some way to bring the woman to justice.

There were seven figurines in the case. Seven, and no seal.

For a moment she could only stare. One of the figures, an odd animal shaped roughly like a pig but with a large round snout and feet as wide as its thick legs, stood where the seal had, in the center of the table. Suddenly her eyes narrowed. It was not really there; the thing was woven from Air and Fire, in flows so minute they made cobwebs seem cables. Even concentrating, she could barely see them. She doubted if Liandrin or any of the other Black sisters could have. A tiny, slicing flick of the Power, and the fat animal vanished, in its place the black-and-white seal on its red-lacquered stand. Moghedien, the hider, had hidden it in plain sight. Fire melted a hole in the glass, and the seal went into her pouch, too. It bulged now, and pulled her belt down.

Frowning at the woman poised on the toe of one slipper, she tried to think of some means of taking her as well. But Moghedien would not fit in her pouch, and she rather thought that even if she could pick the other woman up, the sight might raise a few eyebrows. Still, as she made her way to the nearest arched doorway, she could not help looking back every other step. If only there was some way. Pausing for one last, regretful look from the doorway, she turned to go.

This door opened onto a courtyard with a fountain full of lilypads. On the other side of the fountain, a slim, coppery-skinned woman in a pale cream Taraboner dress that would have made Rendra blush was just raising a fluted black rod a pace in length. Nynaeve recognized Jeaine Caide. More, she recognized the rod.

Desperately she flung herself to one side, so hard that she slid along the smooth white floorstones until one of the thin columns stopped her with a jar. A leg-thick bar of white shot through where she had been standing, as if the air had turned to molten metal, slicing all the way across the exhibition hall; where it struck, pieces simply vanished out of columns, priceless artifacts ceased to exist. Hurling flows of Fire behind her blindly, hoping to strike something, anything, in the courtyard, Nynaeve scrambled away across the hall on hands and knees. Little more than waist-high, the bar sawed sideways, carving a swathe through both walls; between, cases and cabinets and wired skeletons collapsed and crashed. Severed columns quivered; some fell, but what dropped into that terrible sword did not survive to smash displays and pedestals to the floor. The glass-walled table fell before the molten shaft vanished, leaving a purplish bar that seemed burned into Nynaeve's vision; the *cuendillar* figures were all that dropped out of that molten white shaft, bouncing on the floor.

The figurines did not break, of course. It seemed Moghedien was right; not even balefire could destroy *cuendillar*. That black rod was one of the stolen *ter'angreal*. Nynaeve could remember the warning appended to their list in a firm hand. *Produces balefire. Dangerous and almost impossible to control.*

Moghedien seemed to be trying to scream through her invisible gag, head whipping back and forth in a frenzy as she fought her bonds of Air, but Nynaeve spared her no more than a glance. As soon as the balefire disappeared, she raised herself up enough to peer back across the hall, through the rent sawed along the chamber wall. Beside the fountain, Jeaine Caide was swaying, one hand to her head, the black rod almost falling from the other. But before Nynaeve could strike at her, she had clutched the fluted rod again; balefire burst from its end, destroying everything in its path through the chamber.

Dropping almost to her belly, Nynaeve crawled the other way as fast as she could, amid the crash and clatter of falling columns and masonry. Panting, she pulled herself into a corridor slashed through both walls. There was no telling how far the balefire had sliced; all the way out of the palace, perhaps. Twisting about on a carpet littered with bits of stone, she peeked cautiously around the side of the doorframe.

The balefire had gone again. Silence held in the ruined exhibition hall, except when a weakened piece of stonework gave way and smashed to the rubble-strewn floor. There was no sign of Jeaine Caide, though enough of the far wall had fallen to show the fountained court-yard clearly. She was not about to risk going to see if the *ter'angreal* had killed the woman in using it. Her breath came raggedly, and her arms and legs trembled enough that she was glad to lie there a moment. Channeling took energy the same as any other work; the more you did, the more energy. And the wearier you were, the less you could channel. She was not entirely certain she herself was up to facing even a weakened Jeaine Caide right then.

Such a fool she had been. Battling Moghedien with the Power, and never thinking that channeling that strong would have every Black sister in the palace jumping out of her skin. She was lucky the Domani woman had not arrived with her *ter'angreal* while she was still absorbed with the Forsaken. They very likely both would have died before they knew she was there.

Suddenly she stared in disbelief. Moghedien was gone! The balefire had not come nearer than ten feet from where she had stood, but she was not there any longer. It was impossible. She had been shielded.

"How do I know what's impossible?" Nynaeve muttered. "It was impossible for me to beat one of the Forsaken, but I did it."

Still no sign of Jeaine Caide.

Pushing herself to her feet, she hurried for the appointed meeting place. If only Egwene had not run into any trouble, they might make it out of here safely after all.

CHAPTER
55

Into the Deep

Servants boiled along the halls as Nynaeve ran, shouting frantic questions. They might not be able to sense channeling, but they had certainly felt the palace being torn half apart. She threaded her way through, just one more serving woman in a panic as far as they were concerned.

Saidar faded from her as she sped down corridors and across courtyards. Holding on to anger was difficult when she was increasingly uneasy for Elayne. If the Black sisters had found her. . . . Who knew what they had beside the balefire *ter'angreal?* The list they had been given certainly did not give a use for everything.

Once she saw Liandrin, with her pale honey braids, and Riana, with that white streak in her black hair, hurrying down a flight of broad marble stairs; she could not see the glow of *saidar* around them, but from the way servants cried out and leaped from their path, they were whipping a way clear for themselves with the Power. It made her glad she had not tried to cling to the Source herself; they would have picked her out of the throng in an instant by the glow, and until she had some rest, she was not up to facing either of them, much less both. She had what she had come for. They had to wait.

The crowd thinned and disappeared by the time she reached the narrow hall on the west side of the palace that was the meeting place.

The others were waiting for her beside a small, bronze-studded door fastened with a large iron lock. Including Amathera, standing very straight, wearing a light linen cloak with the hood up. The Panarch's white dress might pass for serving-woman garb if you did not look closely enough to see it was silk, and the veil that did not hide her face was certainly servant's linen. The sound of shouts came muffled through the door. Apparently the riot was still going on. Now if only the men were doing the rest of their part.

Ignoring Egeanin, Nynaeve threw her arms around Elayne in a quick hug. "I was so worried. Did you have any trouble?"

"Not a bit," Elayne replied. Egeanin shifted slightly, and the younger woman gave her a meaningful look, then added, "Amathera did cause a little problem, but we sorted it out."

Nynaeve frowned. "Trouble? Why would she give trouble? Why would you give trouble?" That last was for the Panarch, who held her head high, refusing to look at anyone. Elayne seemed as reluctant.

It was the Seanchan woman who answered. "She tried to sneak off to rouse her soldiers to harry the Darkfriends out. After she had been warned." Nynaeve refused to look at her.

"Do not scowl so, Nynaeve," Elayne said. "I chased her down quickly, and we had a little talk. I think she is in perfect agreement with me now."

The Panarch's cheek twitched. "I am in agreement, Aes Sedai," she said hastily. "I will do exactly as you say, and I will provide papers that should make even the rebels let you pass unhindered. There is no need for more . . . talking."

Elayne nodded as if all of that made sense, motioning for the women to be quiet. Whereupon the Panarch obediently closed her mouth. A trifle sullenly, but perhaps that was just the shape of her mouth. Clearly there had been some very odd goings on, and Nynaeve intended to find the bottom of them. Later. The narrow hallway was still empty in both directions, but panicked shouts still echoed from deeper in the palace. The mob rumbled beyond the small door.

"But what of you?" Elayne went on with a frown. "You were supposed to be here half an hour ago. Did you cause all of this? I felt two women channeling enough of the Power to shake the palace down, and then a bit later someone did try to shake it down. I thought it must be you. I had to restrain Egeanin from going to find you."

Egeanin? Nynaeve hesitated, then made herself touch the Seanchan woman's shoulder. "Thank you." Egeanin looked as though she did not quite understand herself what she had done, but she gave a quick nod.

"Moghedien found me, and because I was worrying about how to bring her out for trial, Jeaine Caide nearly took my head off with balefire." Elayne gave a small squeak, and she hurried to reassure her. "It didn't really come close to me."

"You *captured* Moghedien? You captured one of the *Forsaken?*"

"Yes, but she got away." There. She had admitted everything. Conscious of all their eyes on her, she shifted uncomfortably. She did not like being in the wrong. She especially did not like being in the wrong when it was she who had pointed out that it was wrong in the first place. "Elayne, I know what I said about being careful, but once I had her in my hands, it seemed all I could think of was bringing her to trial." Taking a deep breath, Nynaeve made her voice apologetic. She hated doing that. Where were those fool men? "I endangered everything because I didn't keep my mind on what we were about, but please don't scold me."

"I won't," Elayne said firmly. "So long as you remember to be careful in the future." Egeanin cleared her throat. "Oh, yes," Elayne added hastily. The waiting seemed to be getting to her; there were spots of color in her cheeks. "Did you find the collar, and the seal?"

"I have them." She patted her pouch. The shouting outside seemed to be getting louder. And the shouts echoing down the halls were, too. Liandrin must be turning the palace upside down to find out what had happened. "What is keeping those men?"

"My Legion," Amathera began. Elayne looked at her, and she snapped her mouth shut. Whatever talk they had had must have been something. The Panarch was pouting like a girl afraid of being sent to bed without supper.

Nynaeve glanced at Egeanin. The Seanchan woman was watching the door intently. She had wanted to come after her. *Why won't she let me hate her? Am I so different from her?*

Suddenly the door swung open. Juilin pulled two thin bent metal rods out of the lock and straightened from a crouch. Blood ran down the side of his face. "Hurry. We must be away from here before it gets out of hand."

Staring past him wide-eyed, Nynaeve wondered what he considered out of hand. Bayle Domon's sailors, at least three hundred of them, formed a semicircle two deep about the door, Domon himself waving a cudgel, shouting to encourage them. He had to shout for the roar that filled the wide street. Men jostled and struggled and shouted in a seething mass, barely held back by the sailors' clubs and staffs. Not that they were really interested in the sailors. Scattered through the crowd, clumps of mounted Whitecloaks swung their swords at men crowding them with pitchforks and barrel staves and bare hands. Showers of stones fell around them, sometimes banging off a helmet, but silently in the uproar. A lone Whitecloak's horse suddenly screamed and reared, and toppled over backward; it scrambled to its feet quickly, minus its rider. Other riderless animals dotted the mass of men. Was this what they had set off just to cover themselves? She tried reminding herself why—put her hand on her pouch to feel the *cuendillar* seal, the collar and bracelets—but it was hard. Men were dying out there, surely.

"Will you women move?" Thom called, waving for them to come out. He had a bleeding gash over one bushy eyebrow, perhaps from a stone, and his brown cloak would not even do for the ragbag now. "If the Panarch's Legion ever stops running, this could grow messy."

Amathera made a startled sound, just before Elayne pushed her firmly out. Nynaeve and Egeanin followed, and as soon as all four women were out, the sailors folded in around them in a tight ring that began struggling away from the palace. It was all Nynaeve could do to keep her feet, jostled by the men who were trying to protect her. Once Egeanin slipped and nearly fell. Nynaeve caught her arm, helped her back up, and got a grateful grin. *We are not so different,* she thought. *Not the same, but not all that different.* She did not have to make herself smile encouragingly at the Seanchan woman.

The milling mass lasted several streets away from the palace, but once they broke clear the narrow twisting ways were almost empty. Those who were not actually involved in the riot seemed wise enough to stay clear of it. The sailors spread out a little, giving the women more room. Any straggler who looked in their direction got hard stares, though. The streets of Tanchico were still the streets of Tanchico. Somehow that surprised Nynaeve. It seemed that she had been weeks inside the palace. Surely the city should be different.

When the babble began to fade behind them, Thom managed a quite elegant bow to Amathera as he limped along. "An honor, Panarch," he said. "If I may be of any service, you have only to speak."

Shockingly, Amathera glanced at Elayne, grimaced slightly, and said, "You mistake me, good sir. I am only a poor refugee from the country-side, rescued by these good women."

Thom exchanged startled looks with Juilin and Domon, but when he opened his mouth, Elayne said, "Could we get on to the inn, Thom? This is hardly the place for conversation."

When they reached the Three Plum Court, it was scarcely less sur-prising to hear Elayne introduce the Panarch to Rendra as Thera, a refugee with no money who needed a pallet, and maybe some work to earn her meals. The innkeeper shrugged resignedly, but as she led "Thera" away to the kitchens she was already telling the woman what lovely hair she had and how pretty she would look in the right dress.

Nynaeve waited until the rest of them were in the Chamber of Falling Blossoms with the door closed before saying, "*Thera?* And she went along! Elayne, Rendra will have the woman serving at table in the common room!"

Elayne did not seem surprised. "Yes, very likely." Sinking into a chair with a sigh, she kicked off her slippers and began massaging her feet vigorously. "It was not difficult to convince Amathera she should stay in hiding for a few days. It really isn't that far from 'The Panarch is dead' to 'Death to the Panarch.' I think seeing the riot helped, too. She doesn't want to depend on Andric to put her back on her throne; she wants her own soldiers to do it, even if it means hiding until she can get in touch with the Lord Captain of the Legion. I believe Andric is in for a surprise with her. It is too bad he doesn't surprise *her.* She deserves it." Domon and Juilin exchanged glances, shook their heads uncomprehendingly. Egeanin nodded to herself as if she, at least, understood, and approved.

"But why?" Nynaeve demanded. "You may have been upset because she sneaked off on her own, but this? How did she manage that anyway, with two of you watching her?" Egeanin's eyes flickered toward Elayne, so quickly Nynaeve was not sure she had really seen it.

Elayne bent to rub the sole of one foot. It must have hurt; there was red in her cheeks. "Nynaeve, the woman has no idea what the lives of the common people are like." As if she did! "She does seem to have a true concern for justice—I think she does—yet it did not bother her at all that there was enough food in the palace for a year. I mentioned the soup kitchens, and she did not know what I was talking about! A few days working for her supper will do her good." Stretching her legs under the table, she worked her bare toes. "Oh, that does feel good. Not that she'll have many, I suppose. Not if she is to rally the Panarch's Legion to pry Liandrin and the others out of the palace. A pity, but there it is."

"Well, she has to," Nynaeve told her firmly. It was good to sit down, though she could not understand the girl's concern with her feet. They had hardly walked at all today. "And the sooner the better. We need the Panarch, and not in Rendra's kitchen." She did not think there was any need to worry about Moghedien. That woman had had every opportunity to come into the open, after she had freed herself. That still puzzled her; she must have been careless in tying off the shield. But if Moghedien had been unwilling to face her then, when she must have known Nynaeve was nearly exhausted, she could not think the woman would come after them. Not for something she seemed to think was not worth very much. The same did not apply to Liandrin, however. If Liandrin figured out half of what had happened, she *would* be hunting them.

"The justice of the Daughter-Heir," Thom murmured, "may yet supersede the justice of the Panarch. There were men streaming in through that door as we left, and I think some had already got in the front. I saw smoke coming out of several windows. By tonight, little more than a fire-gutted ruin will remain. No need for soldiers to chase the Black Ajah, and thus 'Thera' can have her few days to learn the lesson you want to teach. You will make a fine queen one day, Elayne of Andor."

Elayne's pleased smile faded as she looked at him. Rising to pad around the table, she rummaged in his coat pockets for a kerchief and began dabbing blood from his forehead despite his protests. "Hold still," she told him, sounding for all the world like a mother tending an unruly child.

"Could we at least see what we risked our necks for?" he said when it became clear Elayne was going to do exactly as she wished.

Opening her belt pouch, Nynaeve laid the contents out on the table, the black-and-white disc that helped hold the Dark One's prison shut, the collar and bracelets that sent ripples of sorrow through her before she could lay them down. Everyone gathered close to stare.

Domon fingered the seal. "I did own a thing like this once."

Nynaeve doubted it. Only seven had been made. Three were broken now, *cuendillar* or no. Another was in Moiraine's hands. Four surviving. How well could four keep that prison at Shayol Ghul locked? A shivery thought.

Egeanin touched the collar, pushed the bracelets away from the collar. If she felt the emotions trapped in them, she did not show it. Perhaps that sensitivity came only with the ability to channel. "It is not an *a'dam*," the Seanchan woman said. "That is made of a silvery metal, and all of one piece."

Nynaeve wished she had not mentioned *a'dam*. *But she never wore the bracelet of one. And she did let that poor woman she told us about go. Poor woman. She—this Bethamin—was the one who controlled women with an* a'dam. Egeanin had showed more mercy than Nynaeve would have. "It is as least as much like an *a'dam* as you and I are alike,

Egeanin." The woman looked startled, but after a moment she nodded. Not so different. Two women, each doing the best she could.

"Do you mean to keep on pursuing Liandrin?" Juilin seated himself, arms folded on the table, studying the things there. "Whether or not she is chased out of Tanchico, she is still out there. And the others. But these seem too important to leave lying about. I am only a thief-catcher, but I would say these must be taken to the White Tower for safekeeping."

"No!" Nynaeve was startled at her own vehemence. So were the others, by the way they stared at her. Slowly she picked up the seal and replaced it in her pouch. "This goes to the Tower. But that. . . ." She did not want to touch the black things again. If those were in the Tower, Aes Sedai might decide to use them just as the Black Ajah had intended to. To control Rand. Would Moiraine? Siuan Sanche? She would not take the chance. "That is too dangerous to risk it ever falling back into the hands of Darkfriends. Elayne, can you destroy them? Melt them. I don't care if they burn through the table. Just destroy them!"

"I see what you mean," Elayne said with a grimace. Nynaeve doubted she did—Elayne believed in the Tower wholeheartedly—but she believed in Rand, too.

Nynaeve could not see the glow of *saidar,* of course, but the intent way the girl stared at the vile objects told her she was channeling. The bracelets and necklace lay there. Elayne frowned; her stare became more intent. Abruptly she shook her head. Her hand poised hesitantly for a moment, close to one of the bracelets, before picking it up. And dropped it again, with a gasp. "It feels. . . . It's full of. . . ." Drawing a deep breath, she said, "I did what you asked, Nynaeve. A hammer would be burning a puddle for the Fire I wove into it, but it isn't even warm."

So Moghedien had not lied. Doubtless she had thought there was no need, that she would surely win. *How* did *the woman get loose?* But what to do with the things? She was not going to let them fall into *anyone's* hands.

"Master Domon, do you know a very deep part of the sea?"

"I do, Mistress al'Meara," he said slowly.

Gingerly, trying not to feel the emotions, Nynaeve shoved the collar and bracelets across the table to him. "Then drop these into it, where no one can ever fish them out again."

After a moment, he nodded. "I will." He stuffed them into his coat pocket hurriedly, clearly disliking to touch something that must have to do with the Power. "In the deepest part of the sea I do know, near the Aile Somera."

Egeanin was frowning at the floor, no doubt thinking about the Illianer leaving. Nynaeve had not forgotten the woman calling him "a properly set-up man." She herself felt like laughing. It was all but done. As soon as Domon could sail, the hateful collar and bracelets would be gone forever. They could leave for Tar Valon. And then. . . . Then back to Tear, or wherever al'Lan Mandragoran was. Facing Moghedien, realizing how close she had been to being killed or worse, only made her urgency to deal with him greater. A man she had to share with a woman she hated, but if Egeanin could look fondly on a man she once took prisoner—and Domon was certainly eyeing her with interest—and if Elayne could love a man who would go mad, then she could puzzle out some way to enjoy what she could have of Lan.

"Shall we go downstairs and see how 'Thera' is taking to being a servant?" she suggested. Soon for Tar Valon. Soon.

CHAPTER
56

Goldeneyes

The common room of the Winespring Inn was silent but for the scratch of Perrin's pen. Silent, and empty but for him and Aram. Late-morning light made small pools beneath the windows. No cooking smells came from the kitchen; there were no fires lit anywhere in the village, and even coals banked in ashes had been doused. No point in giving the gift of fire easy to hand. The Tinker—he sometimes wondered whether it was proper to think of Aram that way any longer, but a man could not stop being what he was, sword or no—stood against the wall by the front door, watching Perrin. What did the man expect? What did he want? Dipping his pen in the small stone ink jar, Perrin set aside the third sheet of paper and began a fourth.

Pushing through the door, bow in hand, Ban al'Seen rubbed an uneasy finger up and down his big nose. "The Aiel are back," he said quietly, but his feet moved as if he could not make them be still. "Trollocs coming, from north and south. Thousands of them, Lord Perrin."

"Don't call me that," Perrin said absently, frowning at the page. He had no way with words. He certainly did not know how to say things in the fancy way women liked. All he could was write what he felt. Dipping the pen again, he added a few lines.

I will not ask your forgiveness for what I did. I do not know if you could give it, but I will not ask. You are more precious to me than life. Never think I have abandoned you. When the sun shines on you, it is my smile. When you hear the breeze stir through the apple blossoms, it is my whisper that I love you. My love is yours forever.

Perrin

For a moment he studied what he had written. It did not say enough, but it would have to do. He did not have the right words any more than he had time.

Carefully blotting the damp ink with sand, he folded the pages together. He very nearly wrote "Faile Bashere" on the outside before making it "Faile Aybara." He realized he did not even know if a wife took her husband's name in Saldaea; there were places where they did not. Well, she had married him in the Two Rivers; she would have to put up with Two Rivers customs.

He placed the letter in the middle of the mantel over the fireplace— perhaps it would reach her eventually—and adjusted the wide red marriage ribbon behind his collar so it hung down his lapels properly. He was supposed to wear it for seven days, an announcement to everyone who saw him that he was newly wed. "I will try," he told the letter softly. Faile had tried to tie one in his beard; he wished he had let her.

"Pardon, Lord Perrin?" Ban said, still shifting his feet anxiously. "I didn't hear." Aram was chewing his lip, his eyes wide and frightened.

"Time to see to the day's work," Perrin said. Perhaps the letter would reach her. Somehow. He took his bow from the table and slung it on his back. Axe and quiver already hung at his belt. "And don't call me that!"

In front of the inn, the Companions were gathered on their horses, Wil al'Seen with that fool wolfhead banner, the long staff resting on his stirrup iron. How long since Wil had refused to carry the thing? The survivors of those who had joined him the first day jealously guarded the right, now. Wil, with his bow on his back and a sword at his hip, looked proud as an idiot.

As Ban scrambled into his saddle, Perrin heard him say, "The man is as cool as a winter pond. Like ice. Maybe it won't be so bad today." He barely paid attention. The women were gathered on the Green.

They made a circle five or six deep around the tall pole where the larger red wolfhead flapped out in a breeze. Five or six deep, shoulder to shoulder, with polearms made from scythes and pitchforks, and wood-axes, and even stout kitchen knives and cleavers.

Throat tight, he mounted Stepper and rode toward them. The children were a tight mass inside the circle of women. All the children in Emond's Field.

Riding slowly along the ranks, he felt the women's eyes following him, and the children's. Fear scent, and worry; the children showed it on their too-pale faces, but all smelled of it. He reined in where Marin al'Vere and Daise Congar and the rest of the Women's Circle stood together. Alsbet Luhhan had one of her husband's hammers on her shoulder, and her Whitecloak helmet acquired the night of her rescue sat slightly crooked because of her thick braid. Neysa Ayellin held a long-bladed carving knife firm in her hand, and had two more stuck behind her belt.

"We have planned this out," Daise said, looking up at him as if she expected an argument and did not intend to allow it. She held a pitchfork, fastened to a pole nearly three feet taller than she, upright in front of her. "If the Trollocs break through anywhere, you men are going to be busy, so we will take the children out. The older ones know what to do, and they've all played hide-and-seek in the woods. Just to keep them safe until they can come out."

The older ones. Boys and girls of thirteen and fourteen had toddlers strapped on their backs, and held smaller children by the hand. Girls older than that stood in the ranks with the women; Bode Cauthon had a wood-axe gripped in both hands, her sister Eldrin a boar spear with a broad point. Boys older were out with the men, or up on the thatched rooftops with their bows. The Tinkers were in with the children. Perrin glanced down at Aram, standing by his stirrup. They would not fight, but each adult had two babes fastened on his or her back and another cradled in the crook of an elbow. Raen and Ila, each with an arm around the other, would not look at him. Just to keep them safe until they could come out.

"I'm sorry." He had to stop and clear his throat. He had not meant it to come to this. Think as hard as he could, nothing else came that he could have done. Even giving himself to the Trollocs would not have stopped them killing and burning. The end would have been the same. "It was not fair, what I did with Faile, but I had to. Please understand that. I had to."

"Don't be silly, Perrin," Alsbet said, voice emphatic but round face smiling warmly. "I can never abide it when you're silly. Do you think we would expect you to do any different?"

A heavy cleaver in one hand, Marin reached up to pat his knee with the other. "Any man worth cooking a meal for would have done the same."

"Thank you." Light, but he sounded hoarse. In a minute he would be snuffling like a girl. But for some reason he could not smooth his voice. They must think him an idiot. "Thank you. I shouldn't have fooled you, but she'd not have gone if she suspected."

"Oh, Perrin." Marin laughed. She actually laughed, with all they faced, and smelling of fear as she did; he wished he had half her courage. "We knew what you were up to before you ever put her on her horse, and I am not sure she didn't as well. Women do find themselves doing what they don't want just to please you men. Now you go on and do what you have to. This is Women's Circle business," she added firmly.

Somehow he managed to smile back at her. "Yes, mistress," he said, knuckling his forehead. "Beg pardon. I know enough to keep my nose out of that." The women around her laughed in soft amusement as he turned Stepper away.

Ban and Tell were riding right behind him, he realized, with the rest of the Companions strung out after Wil and the banner. He motioned the pair to come up beside him. "If things go badly today," he said when they were on either side of him, "the Companions are to come back here and help the women."

"But—"

He cut Tell's protest short. "You do what I say! If it goes wrong, you get the women and children out! You hear me?" They nodded; reluctantly, but they did it.

"What about you?" Ban asked quietly.

Perrin ignored him. "Aram, you stick with the Companions."

Striding along between Stepper and Tell's shaggy horse, the Tinker did not even look up. "I go where you go." He said it simply, but his tone left no room for argument; he was going to do as he wanted whatever Perrin said. Perrin wondered if real lords ever had problems like this.

At the west end of the Green, the Whitecloaks were all mounted, cloaks with the golden sunburst bright, helmets and armor gleaming, lance points shining, a long column of fours that stretched back between the nearest houses. They must have spent half the night polishing. Dain Bornhald and Jaret Byar swung their horses to face Perrin. Bornhald sat straight in his saddle, but he smelled of apple brandy.

Byar's gaunt face twisted with an even deeper rage than usual as he stared at Perrin.

"I thought you would be at your places by now," Perrin said.

Bornhald frowned at his horse's mane, not answering. After a moment, Byar spat, "We are leaving here, Shadowspawn." An angry mutter rose from the Companions, but the hollow-eyed man ignored them as he did Aram's reaching over his shoulder to his sword hilt. "We will cut our way back to Watch Hill through your friends and rejoin the rest of our men."

Leaving. Over four hundred soldiers, leaving. Whitecloaks, but mounted soldiers, not farmers, soldiers who had agreed—Bornhald had agreed!—to support the Two Rivers men wherever the fighting was hottest. If Emond's Field was to have any chance at all, he had to hang on to these men. Stepper tossed his head and snorted as if catching his rider's mood. "Do you still believe I'm a Darkfriend, Bornhald? How many attacks have you seen so far? Those Trollocs have tried to kill me as much as anybody else."

Bornhald raised his head slowly, eyes haunted and at the same time half-glazed. Hands in steel-backed gauntlets flexed on his reins unconsciously. "Do you think I do not know by now that these defenses were prepared without you? It was none of your doing, yes? I will not keep my men here to watch you feed your own villagers to the Trollocs. Will you dance atop a pile of their bodies when it is done, Shadowspawn? Not ours! I mean to live long enough to see you brought to justice!"

Perrin patted Stepper's neck to quiet the stallion. He had to keep these men. "You want me? Very well. When it's over, when the Trollocs are done, I'll not resist if you try to arrest me."

"No!" Ban and Tell shouted together, and growls built behind them from the others. Aram peered up at Perrin, stricken.

"An empty promise," Bornhald sneered. "You mean everyone to die here save yourself!"

"You'll never know if you run away, will you?" Perrin made his voice hard and contemptuous. "I will keep my promise, but if you run, you might never find me again. Run, if you want! Run, and try to forget what happens here! All your talk of protecting people from Trollocs. How many died at Trolloc hands after you came? My family wasn't the first, and certainly not the last. Run! Or stay, if you can remember you're men. If you need to find the courage, look at the women, Bornhald. Any one of them is braver than the whole lot of you Whitecloaks!"

Bornhald shook as though every word were a blow; Perrin thought the man might fall out of his saddle. Swaying upright, Bornhald stared at him. "We will remain," he said hoarsely.

"But, my Lord Bornhald," Byar protested.

"Clean!" Bornhald roared at him. "If we must die here, we will die clean!" He wrenched his head back to Perrin, spittle on his lips. "We will remain. But at the last I will see you dead, Shadowspawn! For *my* family, for *my* father, I—will—see—you—*dead!*" Sawing his horse around roughly, he cantered back to his white-cloaked column. Byar bared his teeth in a wordless snarl at Perrin before following.

"You do not mean to keep that promise?" Aram said anxiously. "You cannot."

"I have to check everyone," Perrin said. Small chance he would live long enough to keep it. "There isn't much time." He booted Stepper in the flanks and the horse leaped forward, toward the west end of the village.

Behind the sharp stakes facing the Westwood, men crouched with their spears and halberds and polearms fashioned by Haral Luhhan, who was there in his blacksmith's vest with a scythe blade on the end of an eight-foot shaft. Behind them stood the men with bows in ranks broken by four catapults, Abell Cauthon walking along slowly to speak to each man.

Perrin reined in beside Abell. "Word is they're coming from north and south," he said quietly, "but keep a sharp eye."

"We'll watch. And I'm ready to send half my men wherever they are needed. They'll not find Two Rivers folk easy meat." Abell's grin was reminiscent of his son's.

To Perrin's embarrassment, the men raised a ragged cheer as he rode by, with the Companions and the banner at his heels: "Goldeneyes! Goldeneyes!" and now and then a "Lord Perrin!" He knew he should have stamped harder on that in the beginning.

To the south, Tam had charge, more grim-faced than Abell and striding almost like a Warder, hand resting on his sword hilt. That wolfish, deadly grace looked strange on the blocky, gray-haired farmer. Yet his words to Perrin were not so different from Abell's. "We Two Rivers folk are a tougher lot than most know," he said quietly. "Don't you worry we will not do ourselves proud today."

Alanna was at one of the six catapults here, fussing over a large stone being lifted into the cup on the end of the thick arm. Ihvon sat his horse near her in his Warder's color-changing cloak, slender as a steel blade and alert as a hawk; there was no doubt he had chosen his ground—wherever Alanna was—and his fight—to bring her out alive whatever. He barely looked at Perrin. But the Aes Sedai paused, hands hovering over the stone, eyes following him as he passed. He could all but feel her weighing and measuring and judging. Those cheers followed him, too.

Where the hedge of stakes ran beyond the few houses east of the Winespring Inn, Jon Thane and Samel Crawe had charge between them. Perrin told them what he had Abell, and once again got much the same reply. Jon, in a mail shirt with holes rusted through in several places, had seen the smoke of his mill burning, and Samel, with his horse face and long nose, was sure he had seen the smoke of his farm. Neither expected an easy day, but both wore stony determination like cloaks.

It was to the north that Perrin had decided to make his fight. Fingering the ribbon hanging down one lapel, he peered in the direction of Watch Hill, the direction Faile had gone, and wondered why he had chosen the northside. *Fly free, Faile. Fly free, my heart.* He supposed it was good a place to die as any.

Bran supposedly was in charge here, in his steel cap and disc-sewn metal jerkin, but he stopped checking the men along the hedge to give Perrin as much of a bow as his girth would allow. Gaul and Chiad stood ready, heads wrapped in *shoufa* and faces hidden to the eyes behind black veils. Side by side, Perrin noted; whatever had passed between them, it seemed to outweigh their clans' blood feud. Loial had a pair of woodaxes, dwarfed in his huge hands; his tufted ears thrust forward fiercely, and his wide face was grim.

Do you think I would run away? he had said when Perrin suggested he could slip off into the night after Faile. His ears had dropped with weariness and hurt. *I came with you, Perrin, and I will stay until you go.* And then he had laughed suddenly, a deep booming sound that almost rattled the dishes. *Perhaps someone will even tell a story of me, one day. We do not go in for such things, but there could be an Ogier hero, I suppose. A joke, Perrin. I made a joke. Laugh. Come, we will tell each other jokes, and laugh, and think of Faile flying free.*

"It is no joke, Loial," Perrin murmured as he rode along the lines of men, trying not to listen to their cheers. "You are a hero whether you want to be or not." The Ogier gave him a tight, wide-mouthed grin before setting his eyes back on the cleared ground beyond the hedge. White-striped sticks marked hundred-pace intervals out to five hundred; beyond that lay quilted fields, tabac and barley, most trampled in earlier attacks, and hedges and low stone fences, and copses of leatherleaf, pine and oak.

So many faces Perrin knew in those waiting ranks of men. Stout Eward Candwin and lantern-jawed Paet al'Caar with spears. White-haired Buel Dowtry, the fletcher, stood with the bowmen, of course. There was stocky, gray-haired Jac al'Seen and his bald cousin Wit, and gnarled Flann Lewin, a lanky beanpole like all of his male kin. Jaim Torfinn and Hu Marwin, among the first to ride after him; they had felt too uncomfortable to join the Companions, as if missing the ambush in the Waterwood had opened some gap between them and the others. Elam Dowtry, and Dav Ayellin, and Ewin Finngar. Hari Coplin and his brother Darl, and old Bili Congar. Berin Thane, the miller's brother, and fat Athan Dearn, and Kevrim al'Azar, whose grandsons had grown sons, and Tuck Padwhin, the carpenter, and. . . .

Making himself stop counting them, Perrin rode to where Verin stood beside one of the catapults under the watchful eye of Tomas on his gray. The plump, brown-clad Aes Sedai studied Aram a moment before turning her birdlike gaze up to Perrin, one eyebrow raised as if to question why he was bothering her.

"I am a little surprised to see you and Alanna still here," he told her. "Hunting girls who can learn to channel can't be worth getting killed. Or keeping a string tied to a *ta'veren,* either."

"Is that what we are doing?" Folding her hands at her waist, she tilted her head to one side thoughtfully. "No," she said at last, "I do not think we could go quite yet. You are a very interesting study, as much as Rand, in your own way. And young Mat. Could I only split myself into three, I would latch one onto each of you and follow you every moment of the day and night even if I had to marry you."

"I already have a wife." It felt odd, saying that. Odd, and good. He had a wife, and she was safe.

She shattered his moment of reverie. "Yes, you do. But you do not know what marrying Zarine Bashere means, do you?" She reached up to turn his axe in its loop on his belt, studying it. "When are you going to give this up for the hammer?"

Staring at the Aes Sedai, he reined Stepper back a pace, pulling the axe out of her hands, before he knew it. What marrying Faile *meant?* Give up the axe? What did she mean? What did she know?

"ISAM!" The guttural roar rose like thunder, and Trollocs appeared, each half again as tall as a man and twice as wide, trotting into the fields to beyond bowshot, a hulking, black-mailed mass, deep and stretching the length of the village. Thousands of them packed to-gether, huge faces distorted by beaks and snouts, heads with horns or feathered crests, spikes at elbows and shoulders, scythe-curved swords

and spiked axes, hooked spears and barbed tridents, a seemingly endless sea of cruel weapons. Behind them, Myrddraal galloped up and
down on midnight horses, raven-black cloaks hanging undisturbed as
they whirled their mounts.

"ISAM!"

"Interesting," Verin murmured.

Perrin would not have thought that was the word. This was the first
time the Trollocs had shouted anything understandable. Not that he
had any idea what it meant.

Smoothing his marriage ribbon, he forced himself to ride calmly to
the center of the Two Rivers line. The Companions formed behind
him, the breeze lifting the banner with its red wolfhead. Aram had his
sword out in both hands. "Be ready!" Perrin called. His voice was
steady; he could not believe it.

"ISAM!" And the black tide rolled forward, howling wordlessly.

Faile was safe. Nothing else mattered. He would not let himself see
the faces of the men stretched out to either side of him. He heard the
same howls drifting from the south. Both sides at once. They had never
tried that before. Faile was safe. "At four hundred paces . . . !" All
along the ranks, bows rose together. Closer the howling mass came,
long thick legs eating ground. Closer. "Loose!"

The snap of bowstrings was lost in the Trolloc roar, but a goose-
fletched hail streaked the sky as it arced out, plunged down into the
black-mailed horde. Stones from the catapults erupted in fiery balls
and sharp splinters in those seething ranks. Trollocs fell. Perrin saw
them go down, trampled beneath boots and hooves. Even some Myrddraal fell. Yet the tidal wave rushed on, closing holes and gaps, apparently undiminished.

There was no need to order another volley. A second followed the
first as quickly as men could nock arrows, a second rain of broadhead
points rising before the first dropped, the third following behind, the
fourth, the fifth. Fire exploded among the Trollocs as fast as the catapult arms could be winched down, Verin galloping from catapult to
catapult to lean down from her saddle. And the huge bellowing forms
came on, crying in no language Perrin understood, but crying for blood,
human blood and flesh. Men crouching behind the stakes readied
themselves, hefting their weapons.

Perrin felt cold inside. He could see the ground behind the Trolloc
charge already littered with their dead and dying, yet it hardly seemed
they were fewer. Stepper pranced nervously, but he could not hear the
dun's whicker for the rolling howls of Trollocs. The axe came into his

hand smoothly, long half-moon blade and thick spike catching the sun-light. Not midday yet. *My heart is yours forever, Faile.* This time, he did not think the stakes would . . .

Not even slowing, the front rank of Trollocs ran onto the sharp stakes, faces contorted by snouts or beaks twisting with pained shrieks, howling as they were impaled, driven down by more huge shapes scrambling up over their backs, some of those falling among the stakes, replaced by more, always more. One last volley of arrows drove home at point-blank range, and then it was the spears and halberds and home-made polearms, thrusting and stabbing at towering forms in black mail, sometimes falling while the bowmen shot as best they could at the inhuman faces above their friends' heads, boys shooting down from the rooftops as well, madness and death and earsplitting roars and screams and howls. Slowly, inexorably, the Two Rivers line bulged inward at a dozen places. If it broke, anywhere. . . .

"Fall back!" Perrin bellowed. A boar-snouted Trolloc, already bleed-ing, forced its way through the ranks of men, shrieking and striking with its thick, curved sword. Perrin's axe split its head to the snout. Stepper was trying to rear, screaming silently in the din. "Fall back!" Darl Coplin went down, clutching a thigh transfixed by a wrist-thick spear; old Bili Congar tried to drag him backward while awkwardly wielding a boar spear; Hari Coplin swung his halberd in defense of his brother, mouth wide in a seemingly soundless shout. "Fall back be-tween the houses!"

He was not sure whether others heard and passed the order, or the mountainous weight of Trollocs simply pressed in, but slowly, one grudging step at a time, the humans moved back. Loial swung his bloodied axes like mallets, wide mouth snarling. Beside the Ogier, Bran thrust his spear grimly; he had lost his steel cap, and blood ran in his fringe of gray hair. From his stallion Tomas carved a space around Verin; hair in wild disarray, she had lost her horse; balls of fire streaked from her hands, and every Trolloc struck exploded in flames as if soaked in oil. Not enough to hold. The Two Rivers men edged back, jostling around Stepper. Gaul and Chiad fought back-to-back; she had only one spear left, and he slashed and stabbed with his heavy knife. Back. To west and east men had curved out from the defenses there to keep the Trollocs from flanking them, pouring arrows in. Not enough. Back.

Suddenly a huge ram-horned shape was trying to pull Perrin out of the saddle, trying to climb up after him. Thrashing, Stepper went down under the combined weight. Leg pinned and pained near to breaking,

Perrin struggled to bring his axe around, to fight hands bigger than an Ogier's away from his throat. The Trolloc screamed as Aram's sword sliced into its neck. Even as it collapsed atop Perrin, spraying blood, the Tinker spun smoothly to run another Trolloc through the middle.

Grunting with pain, Perrin kicked his way clear, aided by Stepper scrambling to his feet, but there was no time to think of remounting. He barely rolled aside as a black horse's hooves stamped where his head had been. Pale, eyeless face snarling, the Fade leaned from its saddle as he tried to rise, dead-black sword slashing, brushing his hair as he dropped. Ruthlessly he swung his axe, chopping one of the horse's legs out from under it. Horse and rider toppled together; as they fell, he buried his axe where the Halfman's eyes should have been.

He wrenched the blade free in time to see Daise Congar's pitchfork tines take a goat-snouted Trolloc in the throat. It seized the long shaft with one hand, stabbing a barbed spear at her with the other, but Marin al'Vere calmly hamstrung it with one blow of her cleaver; the leg gave way, and she just as coolly severed the Trolloc's spine at the base of its neck. Another Trolloc lifted Bode Cauthon into the air by her braid; mouth wide in a terrified scream, she sank her wood-axe into its mailed shoulder just as her sister, Eldrin, thrust her boar spear through its chest and gray-braided Neysa Ayellin drove a thick butchering knife in as well.

All up and down the line, as far as Perrin could see, the women were there. Their numbers were the only reason the line still held, almost driven back against the houses. Women among the men, shoulder to shoulder; some no more than girls, but then, some of those "men" had never shaved yet. Some never would. Where were the Whitecloaks? *The children!* If the women were here, there was no one to get the children out. *Where are the bloody Whitecloaks?* If they came now, at least they might buy another few minutes. A few minutes to get the children away.

A boy, the same dark-haired runner who had come for him the night before, seized his arm as he turned to search for the Companions. The Companions had to try to cut a way out for the children. He would send them, and do what he could here. "Lord Perrin!" the boy shouted at him through the deafening din. "Lord Perrin!"

Perrin tried to shake him off, then snatched him up kicking under one arm; he belonged with the other children. Split up, in tight ranks stretching from house to house, Ban and Tell and the other Companions were shooting from their saddles, over the heads of the men and women. Wil had driven the banner's staff into the ground so he could work his bow, too. Somehow, Tell had managed to catch up Stepper; the dun's reins were tied to Tell's saddle. The boy could go on Stepper's back.

"Lord Perrin! Please listen! Master al'Thor says somebody's attacking the Trollocs! Lord Perrin!"

Perrin was halfway to Tell, hobbling on his bruised leg, when it penetrated. He stuffed the axe haft through his belt to hoist the boy up in front of his face by the shoulders. "Attacking them? Who?"

"I don't know, Lord Perrin. Master al'Vere said to tell you he thought he heard somebody shouting 'Deven Ride.' "

Aram grabbed Perrin's arm, wordlessly pointing with his bloody sword. Perrin turned in time to see a hail of arrows plunge into the Trollocs. From the north. Another flight was already rising toward the top of its arc.

"Go back to the other children," he said, setting the boy down. He had to be up where he could see. "Go! You did well, boy!" he added as he ran awkwardly for Stepper. The little fellow scampered back into the village grinning. Every step sent a jolt of pain up Perrin's leg; maybe the thing *was* broken. He had no time to worry about that.

Seizing the reins Tell tossed him, he hauled himself up into his saddle. And wondered if he was seeing what he wanted to see instead of what was really there.

Beneath a red-eagle banner at the edge of where the fields had been stood long rows of men in farmer's clothes, shooting their bows methodically. And beside the banner, Faile sat Swallow's saddle, Bain at her stirrup. It had to be Bain behind that black veil, and he could see Faile's face clearly. She looked excited, fearful, terrified and exuberant. She looked beautiful.

Myrddraal were trying to turn some of the Trollocs around, trying to lead a charge against the Watch Hill men, but it was useless. Even Trollocs who did turn went down before they covered fifty strides. A Fade and its horse fell, not to arrows, but to panicked Trolloc hands and spears. It was the Trollocs moving back now, then running in a frenzy, fleeing shots from both sides once the Emond's Field men had room to lift bows, too, Trollocs falling, Myrddraal going down. It was a slaughter, but Perrin hardly saw. Faile.

The same boy appeared at his stirrup. "Lord Perrin!" he shouted. To be heard above cheering now, men and women shouting for joy and relief as the last Trollocs who had not made it out of bow range fell. Not many had, Perrin believed, but he was barely able to think. Faile. The boy tugged at his breeches' leg. "Lord Perrin! Master al'Vere said to tell you the Trollocs are breaking! And they *are* shouting 'Deven Ride'! The men, I mean. I heard them!"

Perrin bent to ruffle the boy's curly hair. "What's your name, lad?"

"Jaim Aybara, Lord Perrin. I'm your cousin, I think. Sort of, anyway."

Perrin squeezed his eyes shut for a moment to keep the tears in. Even when he opened them his hand still trembled on the lad's head. "Well, Cousin Jaim, you tell your children about today. You tell your grandchildren, your grandchildren's children."

"I'm not going to have any," Jaim said stoutly. "Girls are horrible. They laugh at you, and they don't like to do anything worth doing, and you never understand what they're saying."

"I think one day you'll find out they're the opposite of horrible. Some of it won't change, but that will." Faile.

Jaim looked doubtful, but then he brightened, a wide grin spreading across his face. "Wait till I tell Had Lord Perrin called me cousin!" And he darted away to tell Had, who would have children, too, and all the other boys who would, one day. The sun stood straight overhead. An hour, maybe. It had all taken no more than an hour. It felt like a lifetime.

Stepper moved forward, and he realized he must have dug his heels in. Cheering people made way for the dun, and he hardly heard them. There were great gaps where Trollocs had broken down the stakes with sheer weight of numbers. He rode through one over a mound of dead Trollocs and never noticed. Dead Trollocs bristling with arrows carpeted the open ground, and here and there a pincushioned Fade flailed and thrashed. He saw none of it. He had eyes for only one thing. Faile.

She started out from the Watch Hill men, pausing to stop Bain from following, and rode to meet him. She rode so gracefully, as if the black mare were part of her, slimly erect, guiding Swallow more with her knees than the reins held so casually in one hand. The red marriage ribbon still twined through her hair, the ends dangling past her shoulders. He must find her flowers.

For a moment those tilted eyes studied him, her mouth. . . . Surely she could not be uncertain, but she smelled it. "I said I would go," she said finally, holding her head high. Swallow danced sideways, neck arched, and Faile mastered the mare without seeming to notice. "I did not say how far. You cannot say I did."

He could not say anything. She was so beautiful. He just wanted to look at her, to see her, beautiful, alive, with him. Her scent was clean sweat with just the slightest hint of herbal soap. He was not sure whether he wanted to laugh or cry. Maybe both. He wanted to pull all the smell of her into his lungs.

Frowning, she went on. "They were ready, Perrin. Truly, they were. I barely had to say anything to convince them to come. The Trollocs had hardly bothered them at all, but they could see the smoke. We traveled hard, Bain and I, and reached Watch Hill well before first light, and we started back as soon as the sun rose." Her frown became a wide smile, eager and proud. Such a beautiful smile. Her dark eyes sparkled. "They followed me, Perrin. They followed me! Even Tenobia has never led men in battle. She wanted to once, when I was eight, but father had a talk with her alone in her chambers, and when he rode off to the Blight she stayed behind." With a rueful grin, she added, "I think you and he use the same methods sometimes. Tenobia exiled him, but she was only sixteen, and the Council of Lords managed to change her mind after a few weeks. She will be blue with envy when I tell her." Again she paused, this time drawing a deep breath and planting a fist on her hip. "Aren't you going to say anything?" she demanded impatiently. "Are you just going to sit there like a hairy lump? I did not say I would leave the Two Rivers. You said that, not I. You've no right to be angry because I did not do what I never promised! And you trying to send me away because you thought you were going to die! I came back to—"

"I love you." It was all he could say, but strangely it seemed to be enough. No sooner were the words out of his mouth than she reined Swallow close enough to throw an arm around him and press her face against his chest; she seemed to be trying to squeeze him in two. He stroked her dark hair gently, just feeling the silkiness of it, just feeling her.

"I was so afraid I would be too late," she said into his coat. "The Watch Hill men marched as fast as they could, but when we arrived, and I saw the Trollocs fighting right in among the houses, so many of them, as if the village were being buried in an avalanche, and I couldn't see you. . . ." She drew a shivering breath and let it out slowly. When she spoke again, her voice was calmer. Just. "Did the men from Deven Ride come?"

He gave a start, and his hand stopped stroking. "Yes, they did. How did you know? Did you arrange that, too?" She began shaking; it took him a moment to know she was laughing.

"No, my heart, though I would have if I could. When that man came with his message—'We are coming'—I thought—hoped—that that was what it meant." Pulling her face back a little, she looked up at him seriously. "I could not tell you, Perrin. I could not raise your hopes when I only suspected. It would have been too cruel if. . . . Don't be angry with me, Perrin."

Laughing, he lifted her out of her saddle and set her sideways in front of his; she laughed her protests, and stretched across the high pommel to put both arms around him. "I will never, ever be angry with you, I sw—" She cut him off with a hand over his mouth.

"Mother says the worst thing father ever did to her was vow never to be angry with her. It took her a year to force him to take it back, and she says he was hardly fit to live with long before then from holding in. You *will* be angry with me, Perrin, and I with you. If you want to make me another wedding vow, vow you will not hide it when you are. I cannot deal with what you will not let me see, my husband. My husband," she repeated in a satisfied tone, snuggling against him. "I do like the sound of that."

He noticed she did not say she would always let him know when *she* was angry; on past experience, he would have to discover it the hard way at least half the time. And she made no promises not to keep secrets from him again, either. Right then, it did not matter so long as she was with him. "I will let you know when I'm angry, my wife," he promised. She gave him a slanted look, as if she was not sure how to take that. *You won't ever come to understand them, Cousin Jaim, but you won't care.*

Abruptly he became aware of the dead Trollocs all around him, like a black field full of feathered weeds, the thrashing Myrddraal still refusing to die finally. Slowly he turned Stepper. A slaughter yard and a shambles of Shadowspawn stretching for hundreds of paces in every direction. Crows hopped across the ground already, and vultures soared overhead in a huge milling cloud. No ravens, though. And the same to the south, according to Jaim; he could see the vultures wheeling beyond the village for proof. Not enough to repay for Deselle or Adora or little Paet or. . . . Not enough; it would never be enough. Nothing could ever repay for them. He hugged Faile; hard enough to make her grunt, but when he tried to ease up, she put her hands on his arms, gripping just as hard to keep them where they were. She was enough.

People were streaming out of Emond's Field, Bran limping and using his spear for a staff, Marin smiling with an arm around him, Daise being hugged by her husband, Wit, and Gaul and Chiad hand in hand with their veils down. Loial's ears drooped wearily, and Tam had blood on his face, and Flann Lewin was standing only with the help of his wife, Adine; there was blood on nearly everyone, and hasty bandages. But they came out in a widening throng, Elam and Dav, Ewin and Aram, Eward Candwin and Buel Dowtry, Hu and Tad the stablemen from the Winespring Inn, Ban and Tell and the Companions riding with that banner still. This time he did not see the missing faces, only those who were still there. Verin and Alanna on their horses, with Tomas and Ihvon riding close behind. Old Bili Congar waving a jug that surely held ale, or better yet brandy, and Cenn Buie as gnarled as ever if bruised, and Jac al'Seen with an arm around his wife, and his sons and daughters around him with their wives and husbands. Raen and Ila, still with the babes on their backs. More. Faces he did not know at all; men who must be from Deven Ride and the farms down there. Boys and girls running among them, laughing.

They fanned out to either side, forming a great hollow circle with the Watch Hill men, Faile and him at its center. Everyone avoided the dying Fades, but it was as if they did not see the Shadowspawn lying everywhere, only the pair on Stepper. Silently they watched, until Perrin began to feel nervous. *Why doesn't somebody say something? Why are they staring like that?*

The Whitecloaks appeared, riding slowly out of the village in their long gleaming column of fours, Dain Bornhald at their head with Jaret Byar. Every white cloak shone as though freshly laundered; every lance slanted at precisely the same angle. Sullen mutters rose, but people moved aside to let them enter the circle.

Bornhald raised a gauntleted hand, halting the column in a jingle of bridles and creak of saddles, when he faced Perrin. "It is done, Shadowspawn." Byar's mouth quivered on the brink of a snarl, but Bornhald's face never changed, his voice never rose. "The Trollocs are done here. As we agreed, I arrest you now for Darkfriend and murderer."

"No!" Faile twisted around to stare up at Perrin, eyes angry. "What does he mean, as you *agreed?*"

Her words were nearly drowned by the roar from every side. "No! No!" and "You will not take him!" and "Goldeneyes!"

Keeping his gaze on Bornhald, Perrin lifted a hand, and silence descended slowly. When all was quiet, he said, "I said I would not resist, if you aided." Surprising, how calm his voice was; inside he seethed with a slow, cold anger. "If you *aided*, Whitecloak. Where were you?" The man did not answer.

Daise Congar stepped out from the encircling throng with Wit, who clung to her as if he never intended to let go of her again. For that matter, her stout arm was wrapped around Wit's shoulders in much the same fashion. They made an odd picture as she planted her pitchfork-polearm firmly, her the taller by a head and holding her considerably smaller husband as though she meant to protect him. "They were on the Green," she announced loudly, "all lined up and sitting their horses pretty as girls ready for a dance at Sunday. They never stirred. It was that that made us come . . ." A fierce murmur of agreement rippled from the women. ". . . when we saw you were about to be overrun, and they just sat there like bumps on a log!"

Bornhald did not take his eyes from Perrin for an instant; he did not even blink. "Did you think I would trust you?" he sneered. "Your plan only failed because these others arrived—yes?—and you can claim no part in that." Faile shifted; without looking away from the man, Perrin laid a finger across her lips just as she opened her mouth. She bit him —hard—but she did not say anything. Bornhald's voice finally began to rise. "I will see you hang, Shadowspawn. I will see you hang, whatever it takes! I will see you dead if the world burns!" The last came as a shout. Byar's sword slid a hand of bare steel from its scabbard; a massive Whitecloak behind him—Farran, Perrin thought his name was—drew his completely, with a pleased smile rather than Byar's toothy snarl.

They froze as quivers rattled to arrows being drawn, and bows came up all around the circle, fletchings drawn to ear, every broadhead shaft pointed at a Whitecloak. Up and down the thick column, high-cantled saddles creaked as men shifted uneasily. Bornhald showed no sign of fear, and he did not smell of it, either; his scent was all hate. He ran almost fevered eyes over the Two Rivers folk encircling his men and returned them to Perrin just as hot and hate-filled.

Perrin motioned downward, and tension was let off bowstrings reluctantly, bows lowered slowly. "You would not help." His voice was cold iron, anvil-hard. "Since you came to the Two Rivers, the help you've given has been almost accidental. You never really cared if people were burned out, killed, so long as you could find somebody to call Darkfriend." Bornhald shivered, though his eyes still burned. "It is time for you to go. Not just from Emond's Field. It is time for you to gather up your Whitecloaks and leave the Two Rivers. Now, Bornhald. You are going now."

"I *will* see you hang one day," Bornhald said softly. He jerked his hand for the column to follow and booted his horse forward as if he meant to ride Perrin over.

Perrin moved Stepper aside; he wanted these men gone, not more killing. Let the man have a final gesture of defiance.

Bornhald never turned his head, but hollow-cheeked Byar stared silent hate at Perrin, and Farran seemed to look at him with regret for some reason. The others kept their eyes front as they passed in a jingle of tack and the clop of hooves. Silently the circle opened to let them out, heading north.

A knot of ten or twelve men approached Perrin on foot, some in mismatched bits and pieces of old armor, all grinning anxiously, as the last of the Whitecloaks went by. He did not recognize any of them. A wide-nosed, leathery-faced fellow seemed to be their leader, his white hair bare but a rusty mail shirt covering him to the knees, though the collar of a farmer's coat poked up around his neck. He bowed awkwardly over his bow. "Jerinvar Barstere, my Lord Perrin. Jer, they call me." He spoke hurriedly, as if afraid of being interrupted. "Pardon for bothering you. Some of us will see the Whitecloaks along, if that's all right with you. A good many want to get on home, even if we can't get there before dark. There's as many Whitecloaks again in Watch Hill, but they would not come. Had orders to hold fast, they said. Bunch of fools, if you ask me, and we're more than tired of having them around, poking their noses into people's houses and trying to make you accuse your neighbor of something. We'll see them off, if that's all right with you." He gave Faile an abashed look, ducking his broad chin, but the flow of words did not slow. "Pardon, my Lady Faile. Didn't mean to bother you and your lord. Just wanted to let him know we're with him. A fine woman you have there, my Lord. A fine woman. No offense meant, my Lady. Well, we've daylight still, and talk shears no sheep. Pardon for bothering you, my Lord Perrin. Pardon, my Lady Faile." He bowed again, imitated by the others, and they hurried away with him herding them, muttering at them, "No time for us to be bothering the lord and his lady. There's work to do yet."

"Who was that?" Perrin said, a trifle stunned by the torrent; Daise and Cenn together could not talk that much. "Do you know him, Faile? From Watch Hill?"

"Master Barstere is the Mayor of Watch Hill, and the others are the Village Council. The Watch Hill Women's Circle will be sending a delegation down under their Wisdom once they're certain it is safe. To see if 'this Lord Perrin' is right for the Two Rivers, they say, but they all wanted me to show them how to curtsy to you, and the Wisdom, Edelle Gaelin, is bringing you some of her dried-apple tarts."

"Oh, burn me!" he breathed. It was spreading. He knew he should have stamped it down hard in the beginning. "Don't call me that!" he shouted after the departing men. "I'm a blacksmith! Do you hear me? A blacksmith!" Jer Barstere turned to wave at him and nod before hurrying the others on.

Chortling, Faile tugged at his beard. "You are a sweet fool, my Lord Blacksmith. It is too late to turn back now." Suddenly her smile became truly wicked. "Husband, is there any possibility you might be alone with your wife any time soon? Marriage seems to have made me as bold as a Domani gall! I know you must be tired, but—" She cut off with a small shriek and clung to his coat as he booted Stepper to a gallop toward the Winespring Inn. For once the cheers that followed did not bother him at all.

"Goldeneyes! Lord Perrin! Goldeneyes!"

From the thick branch of a leafy oak on the edge of the Westwood, Ordeith stared at Emond's Field, a mile to the south. It was impossible. *Scourge them. Flay them.* Everything had been going according to plan. Even Isam had played into his hands. *Why did the fool stop bringing Trollocs? He should have brought in enough to turn the Two Rivers black with them!* Spittle dripped from his lips, but he did not notice, any more than he realized that his hand was fumbling at his belt. *Harry them till their hearts burst! Harrow them into the ground screaming!* All planned to pull Rand al'Thor to him, and it came to this! The Two Rivers had not even been scratched. A few farms burned did not count, nor a few farmers butchered alive for Trolloc cookpots. *I want the Two Rivers to* burn, *burn so the fire lives in men's memories for a thousand years!*

He studied the banner waving over the village, and the one not that far below him. A scarlet wolfhead on scarlet-bordered white, and a red eagle. Red for the blood the Two Rivers must shed to make Rand al'Thor howl. Manetheren. *That's meant to be Manetheren's banner.* Someone had told them of Manetheren, had they? What did these fools know of the glories of Manetheren? *Manetheren. Yes.* There was more than one way to scourge them. He laughed so hard he nearly fell out of the oak before he realized that he was not holding on with both hands, that one gripped his belt where a dagger should have hung. The laugh twisted into a snarl as he stared at that hand. The White Tower held what had been stolen from him. What was his by right as old as the Trolloc Wars.

He let himself drop to the ground, and scrambled onto his horse before looking at his companions. His hounds. The thirty or so

Whitecloaks remaining no longer wore their white cloaks, of course. Rust spotted their dull plate-and-mail, and Bornhald would never have recognized those sullen, suspicious faces, dirty and unshaven. The humans watched Ordeith, distrustful yet afraid, not even glancing at the Myrddraal in their midst, its slug-pale, eyeless face as bleakly wooden as theirs. The Halfman feared Isam would find it; Isam had not at all been pleased when that raid on Taren Ferry let so many escape to carry away word of what was happening in the Two Rivers. Ordeith giggled at the thought of Isam discomforted. The man was a problem for another time, if he still lived.

"We ride for Tar Valon," he snapped. Hard riding, to beat Bornhald to the ferry. Manetheren's banner, raised again in the Two Rivers after all these centuries. How the Red Eagle had harried him, so long ago. "But Caemlyn first!" *Scourge them and flay them!* Let the Two Rivers pay first, and then Rand al'Thor, and then. . . .

Laughing, he galloped north through the forest, not looking back to see if the others followed. They would. They had nowhere else to go now.

CHAPTER
57

A Breaking in the Three-fold Land

The molten afternoon sun broiled the Waste, flinging shadows across the mountains to the north, just ahead now. The dry hills passed beneath Jeade'en's hooves, high and low like swells in an ocean of cracked clay, miles rolling away behind. The mountains had held Rand's eyes since they first came in sight the day before, not snowcapped, not so tall as the Mountains of Mist, much less the Spine of the World, but jagged slabs of brown and gray stone, streaked in some places with yellow or red or bands of glittering flecks, tumbled about so that a man might think to try the Dragonwall afoot first. Sighing, he settled in his saddle and adjusted the *shoufa* he wore with his red coat. In those mountains lay Alcair Dal. Soon there would be an ending of sorts, or a beginning. Maybe both. Soon, perhaps.

Yellow-haired Adelin strode easily ahead of the dapple stallion, and nine more sun-dark *Far Dareis Mai* made a wide ring around him, all with bucklers and spears in hand, cased bows on their backs, black veils dangling on their chests ready to be lifted. Rand's honor guard. The Aiel did not call it that, yet the Maidens came to Alcair Dal for Rand's honor. So many differences, and he did not know what half really were even when he saw them.

For instance, Aviendha's behavior toward the Maidens, and theirs to her. Most of the time, as now, she walked beside his horse with her arms folded in the shawl around her shoulders; green eyes intent beneath her dark head scarf on the mountains ahead, she seldom spoke with the Maidens beyond a word or two, but that was not the oddity. Her arms folded; that was the heart of it. The Maidens knew she wore the ivory bracelet, yet seemed to pretend not to see it; she would not take it off, yet hid her wrist whenever she thought one of them might be looking.

You have no society, Adelin had told him when he suggested some other than the Maidens of the Spear might provide his escort. Each chief, whether of clan or sept, would be accompanied by men from the society he had belonged to before becoming chief. *You have no society, but your mother was a Maiden.* The yellow-haired woman and the other nine had not looked at Aviendha, a few steps away in the entry hall to Lian's roof; they had *not* looked intently. *For countless years Maidens who would not give up the spear have given their babes for the Wise Ones to hand to other women, none knowing where the child went or even whether boy or girl. Now a Maiden's son has come back to us, and we know him. We will go to Alcair Dal for your honor, son of Shaiel, a Maiden of the Chumai Taardad.* Her face was so set—all of their faces were, including Aviendha's—that he thought they might offer to dance the spears if he refused.

When he accepted, they made him go through that ritual of "Remember honor" again, this time with some drink called *oosquai,* made from *zemai,* drinking to the bottom of a small silver cup with each of them. Ten Maidens; ten little cups. The stuff looked like faintly brown-tinged water, tasted almost like it—and was stronger than double-distilled brandy. He had not been able to walk straight, after and they had got him to bed, laughing at him, no matter how he protested, as much as he could with all of them tickling him so he could barely breathe for laughing himself. All but Aviendha. Not that she went away; she stayed and watched the whole thing with a face as blank as stone. When Adelin and the others finally tucked him into his blankets and left, Aviendha sat down beside the door, spreading her dark, heavy skirts, watching him stonily until he fell asleep. At his waking, she was still there, still watching. And refusing to talk about Maidens or *oosquai* or any of it; as far as she was concerned, it seemed not to have happened. Whether the Maidens would have been as reticent, he did not know; how could you possibly look ten women in the face and ask why they had gotten you drunk and made a game of taking your clothes off and putting you to bed?

So many differences, so few that made much sense that he could see, and no telling which might trip him up and ruin all his plans. Yet he could not afford to wait. He glanced over his shoulder. What was done, was done. *And who can say what's yet to come?*

Well behind, the Taardad followed him. Not just the Nine Valley Taardad and the Jindo, but the Miadi and the Four Stones, the Chumai and the Bloody Water and more, broad columns surrounding the peddlers' lurching wagons and the Wise Ones' party, reaching back two miles through the shimmering heat haze, ringed by scouts and outrunners. Every day more had come in response to the runners Rhuarc had sent that first day, a hundred men and Maidens here, three hundred there, five hundred, according to the size of each sept and what each hold needed to keep for safety.

In the distance to the south and west, another band was approaching at a run, trailing dust for their pace; perhaps they belonged to some other clan on its way to Alcair Dal, but he thought not. Only two-thirds of the septs represented yet, but he estimated there were well over fifteen thousand Taardad Aiel strung out behind him. An army on the march, and still growing. Nearly an entire clan coming to a meeting of chiefs, in violation of all custom.

Suddenly Jeade'en topped a rise, and there in a long, wide hollow below was the fair gathered for the meeting, and on the hills beyond, the camps of the clan and sept chiefs who had already arrived.

Spread among two or three hundred of the low, wall-less tents, all widely spaced, were pavilions of the same grayish brown material that were tall enough to stand beneath, with goods displayed on blankets in the shade, brightly glazed pottery and even brighter rugs, jewelry in silver or gold. Aiel crafts mainly, but there would be things from beyond the Waste as well, including perhaps silk and ivory from far to the east. No one seemed to be trading; the few men and women in sight sat in one or another of the pavilions, usually alone.

Of the five camps scattered on heights around the fair, four looked just as empty, only a few dozen men or Maidens stirring amid tents set up for as many as a thousand. The fifth camp sprawled over twice as much ground as any of the others, with hundreds of people visible, and likely as many more inside the tents.

Rhuarc trotted up the hill behind Rand with his ten *Aethan Dor,* Red Shields, followed by Heirn with ten *Tain Shari,* True Bloods, and forty-odd more sept chiefs with their escorts for honor, all with spears and bucklers, bows and quivers. It made a formidable force, more than had taken the Stone of Tear. Some of the Aiel in the camps and among the pavilions were peering at the hilltop. Not at the Aiel gathered there,

Rand suspected. At him; a man on a horse. A thing seen very seldom in the Three-fold Land. He would show them more before he was done.

Rhuarc's gaze settled on the largest camp, where more Aiel in *cadin'sor* were boiling out of the tents, all to stare in their direction. "Shaido, unless I mistake myself," he said quietly. "Couladin. You are not the only one to break custom, Rand al'Thor."

"Perhaps as well I did." Rand dragged the *shoufa* from around his head and stuffed it into his coat pocket atop the *angreal,* the carving of a round-faced man with a sword across his knees. The sun began baking his bare head to show him how much protection the cloth had been. "If we had come according to custom. . . ." The Shaido were loping toward the mountains, leaving behind apparently empty tents. And causing some little stir in the other camps, and the fair; the Aiel gave over staring at a man on a horse to peer after the Shaido. "Could you have forced a way into Alcair Dal against two-to-one odds or better, Rhuarc?"

"Not before nightfall," the clan chief replied slowly, "not even against Shaido dogrobbers. This is more than violation of custom! Even Shaido should have more honor than this!"

Angry mutters of agreement rose from the other Taardad on the hilltop. Except the Maidens; for some reason they had gathered around Aviendha off to one side, talking seriously among themselves. Rhuarc spoke a few quiet words to one of his Red Shields, a green-eyed fellow who looked as if his face had been used to pound fence posts, and the man turned downhill, running swiftly back toward the approaching Taardad.

"Did you expect this?" Rhuarc asked Rand as soon as the Red Shield left. "Is that why you summoned the entire clan?"

"Not this exactly, Rhuarc." The Shaido began forming lines before a narrow gap into the mountains; they were veiling themselves. "But there was no other reason for Couladin to leave in the night except that he was eager to be somewhere, and where would he better like to be than here, causing me trouble? Are the others already in Alcair Dal? Why?"

"The opportunity presented by chiefs meeting is not to be missed, Rand al'Thor. There will be discussions of boundary disputes, grazing rights, a dozen things. Water. If two Aiel from different clans meet, they discuss water. Three from three clans, and they discuss water and grazing."

"And four?" Rand asked. Five clans represented already, and the Taardad made six.

Rhuarc hesitated a moment, hefting one of his short spears unconsciously. "Four will dance the spears. But it should not be so here."

The Taardad parted to let the Wise Ones through, shawls over their heads, with Moiraine and Lan and Egwene riding behind. Egwene and the Aes Sedai wore those white cloths around their temples, in damp imitation of the Aiel women's head scarves. Mat rode up, too, off by himself, black-hafted spear across his pommel. His wide-brimmed hat shadowed his face as he studied what lay ahead.

The Warder nodded to himself when he saw the Shaido. "That could be messy," he said softly. His black stallion rolled an eye at Rand's dapple; only that, and Lan was intent on the Aiel ranks before the gap, yet he patted Mandarb's neck soothingly. "But not now, I think."

"Not now," Rhuarc agreed.

"If only you would . . . *allow* me to go in with you." Except for that one slight hitch, Moiraine's voice was as serene as ever; cool calm painted her ageless features, but her dark eyes looked at Rand as if her gaze alone could force him to relent.

Amys's long pale hair, hanging below her shawl, swung as she shook her head firmly. "It is not his decision, Aes Sedai. This is the business of chiefs, men's business. If we let you go into Alcair Dal now, the next time Wise Ones meet, or roofmistresses, some clan chief will want to put his nose in. They think we meddle in their affairs, and often try to meddle in ours." She gave Rhuarc a quick smile meant to convey that she did not include him; her husband's lack of expression told Rand he thought otherwise.

Melaine gripped her shawl under her chin, precisely staring at Rand. If she did not agree with Moiraine, at least she mistrusted what he would do. He had hardly slept since leaving Cold Rocks; if they had peered into his dreams, they had seen only nightmares.

"Be careful, Rand al'Thor," Bair said as if she had read his thoughts. "A tired man makes mistakes. You cannot afford mistakes today." She pulled her shawl down around her thin shoulders, and her thin voice took on an almost angry note. *"We* cannot afford for you to make mistakes. The Aiel cannot afford it."

The coming of more riders to the hilltop had drawn eyes back to them. Among the pavilions several hundred Aiel, men in *cadin'sor* and long-haired women in skirts and blouses and shawls, made a watchful crowd. Its attention shifted when Kadere's dusty white wagon appeared behind its team of mules off to the right, with the heavy, cream-coated peddler on the driver's seat, and Isendre all in white silk holding a matching parasol. Keille's wagon followed, with Natael handling the reins at her side, and the canvas-topped wagons, and finally the three big waterwagons like huge barrels on wheels with their long mule teams. They looked at Rand as the wagons rumbled past in a squeal of ungreased axles, Kadere and Isendre, Natael in his gleeman's patch-covered cloak, Keille's great bulk encased in snowy white, a white lace shawl on her ivory combs. Rand patted Jeade'en's arched neck. Men and women began spilling out of the fair below to meet the approaching wagons. The Shaido were waiting. Soon, now.

Egwene moved her gray mare close to Jeade'en; the dapple stallion tried to nuzzle Mist and got nipped for his trouble. "You've not given me any chance to speak to you since Cold Rocks, Rand." He said nothing; she was Aes Sedai now, and not just because she called herself one. He wondered if she had spied on his dreams, too. Her face looked tight, her dark eyes tired. "Do not keep to yourself, Rand. You do not fight alone. Others do battle for you, too."

Frowning, he tried not to look at her. His first thought was of Emond's Field and Perrin, but he did not see how she could know where Perrin had gone. "What do you mean?" he said finally.

"I fight for you," Moiraine said before Egwene could open her mouth, "as does Egwene." A look flashed between the two women. "People fight for you who do not know it, any more than you know them. You do not realize what it means that you force the form of the Age Lace, do you? The ripples of your actions, the ripples of your very existence, spread across the Pattern to change the weave of life-threads of which you will never be aware. The battle is far from yours alone. Yet you stand in the heart of this web in the Pattern. Should you fail, and fall, all fails and falls. Since I cannot go with you into Alcair Dal, let Lan accompany you. One more pair of eyes to watch your back." The Warder turned slightly in his saddle, frowning at her; with the Shaido veiled for killing, he would not be eager to leave her alone.

Rand did not think he was supposed to have seen that look pass from Moiraine to Egwene. So they had a secret to keep from him. Egwene *did* have Aes Sedai eyes, dark and unreadable. Aviendha and the Maidens had come back to him. "Let Lan stay with you, Moiraine. *Far Dareis Mai* carries my honor."

Moiraine's mouth tightened at the corners, but apparently that was exactly the right thing to say so far as the Maidens were concerned. Adelin and the others donned wide grins.

Below, Aiel were crowding around wagon drivers as they began unhitching the mules. Not everyone was paying attention to the Aiel. Keille and Isendre stared at one another from beside their wagons,

Natael speaking urgently to one woman, Kadere to the other, until they finally stopped their duel of eyes. The two women had been like that for some time. Had they been men, Rand would have expected it to come to blows long since.

"Be on your guard, Egwene," Rand said. "All of you, be on your guard."

"Even the Shaido will not bother Aes Sedai," Amys told him, "any more than they will bother Bair or Melaine or myself. Some things are beyond even Shaido."

"Just be on your guard!" He had not meant to be that sharp. Even Rhuarc stared at him. They did not understand, and he dared not tell them. Not yet. Who would spring their trap first? He had to risk them as well as himself.

"What about me, Rand?" Mat said suddenly, rolling a gold coin across the fingers of one hand as though unaware of it. "You have any objections to my going with you?"

"Do you want to? I thought you'd stay with the peddlers."

Mat frowned at the wagons below, looked to the Shaido lined before the mountain gap. "I don't think it will be so easy to get out of here if you get yourself killed. Burn me if you don't stick me in the rendering kettle one way or. . . *Dovienya*," he muttered—Rand had heard him say that before; Lan said it meant "luck" in the Old Tongue—and flipped the gold coin into the air. When he tried to snatch it back, it bounced off his fingertips and fell to the ground. Somehow, improbably, the coin landed on edge, rolling downhill, bounding across cracks in the baked clay, glittering in the sunlight, all the way down to the wagons, where it finally fell over. "Burn me, Rand," he growled, "I wish you wouldn't do that!"

Isendre picked up the coin and stood fingering it, peering up at the hilltop. The others stared, too; Kadere, and Keille, and Natael.

"You can come," Rand said. "Rhuarc, isn't it about time?"

The clan chief glanced over his shoulder. "Yes. Just about. . . ." Behind him, pipes began playing a slow dancing tune. ". . . now."

Singing rose to the pipes. Aiel boys stopped singing when they reached manhood, except for certain occasions. Only in battle songs and laments for the dead did an Aielman sing once he had taken up the spear. There were surely Maidens' voices in that chanted harmony of parts, but deep male voices swallowed them.

> *"Wash the spears—while the sun climbs high.*
> *Wash the spears—while the sun falls low."*

Half a mile to right and left Taardad appeared, running in time to their song in two wide columns, spears ready, faces veiled, seemingly endless columns rolling toward the mountains.

> *"Wash the spears—Who fears to die?*
> *Wash the spears—No one I know!"*

In the clan camps and in the fair, Aiel stared in amazement; something in the way they held themselves told Rand they were silent. Some of the wagon drivers stood as if stunned; others let their mules run loose and dove under their wagons. And Keille and Isendre, Kadere and Natael, watched Rand.

> *"Wash the spears—while life holds true.*
> *Wash the spears—until life ends.*
> *Wash the spears. . . ."*

"Shall we go?" He did not wait for Rhuarc's nod to heel Jeade'en to a walk down the hill, Adelin and the other Maidens falling in around him. Mat hesitated a moment before booting Pips to follow, but Rhuarc and the Taardad sept chiefs, each with his ten, stepped off with the dapple. Once, halfway to the fair tents, Rand looked back to the hilltop. Moiraine and Egwene sitting their horses with Lan. Aviendha standing with the three Wise Ones. All watching him. He had almost forgotten what it was like not to have people watching him.

As he rode abreast of the fair, a delegation came out, ten or a dozen women in skirts and blouses and much gold and silver and ivory, as many men in the grays and browns of the *cadin'sor* but unarmed save for a belt knife, and that usually smaller than the heavy-bladed weapon Rhuarc wore. Still, they took a position that forced Rand and the others to halt, and appeared to ignore the veiled Taardad streaming by to east and west.

> *"Wash the spears—Life is a dream.*
> *Wash the spears—All dreams must end."*

"I did not expect this of you, Rhuarc," a heavyset, gray-haired man said. He was not fat—Rand had not seen a fat Aiel—his heaviness was muscle. "Even from the Shaido it was a surprise, but you!"

"Times change, Mandhuin," the clan chief replied. "How long have the Shaido been here?"

"They arrived just at sunrise. Why they traveled in the night, who can say?" Mandhuin frowned slightly at Rand, tilted his head toward Mat. "Strange times indeed, Rhuarc."

"Who is here besides the Shaido?" Rhuarc asked.

"We Goshien arrived first. Then the Shaarad." The heavy man grimaced over his blood enemies' name, without stopping his study of the two wetlanders. "The Chareen and the Tomanelle came later. And last the Shaido, as I said. Sevanna convinced the chiefs to go in only a short time ago. Bael saw no reason to meet today, nor did some of the others."

A broad-faced woman in her middle years, with hair yellower than Adelin's, put fists on her hips in a rattle of ivory and gold bracelets. She wore as many, and as many necklaces, as Amys and her sister-wife combined. "We hear He Who Comes With the Dawn has come out of Rhuidean, Rhuarc." She was frowning at Rand and Mat. The entire delegation was. "We hear that the *Car'a'carn* will be announced today. Before all of the clans arrive."

"Then someone spoke you a prophecy," Rand said. He touched the dapple's flanks with his heels; the delegation moved out of his way.

"Dovienya," Mat murmured. *"Mia dovienya nesodhin soende."* Whatever it meant, it sounded a fervent wish.

The Taardad columns had come up on either side of the Shaido and turned to face them across a few hundred paces, still veiled, still singing. They made no move that could be considered threatening, really, only stood there, fifteen or twenty times the Shaido numbers, and sang, voices thundering in chanting harmony.

> *"Wash the spears—till shade is gone.*
> *Wash the spears—till water turns dry.*
> *Wash the spears—How long from home?*
> *Wash the spears—Until I die!"*

Riding closer to the black-veiled Shaido, Rand saw Rhuarc lift a hand to his own veil. "No, Rhuarc. We are not here to fight them." He meant that he hoped it would not come to that, but the Aielman took it differently.

"You are right, Rand al'Thor. No honor to the Shaido." Leaving his veil hanging, Rhuarc raised his voice. "No honor to the Shaido!"

Rand did not turn his head to look, but he had the feeling black veils were being lowered behind him.

"Oh, blood and ashes!" Mat muttered. "Blood and bloody ashes!"

"Wash the spears—till the sun grows cold.
Wash the spears—till water runs free.
Wash the spears. . . ."

The lines of Shaido shifted uneasily. Whatever Couladin or Sevanna had told them, they could count. To dance the spears with Rhuarc and those with him was one thing, even if it went against all custom; to face enough Taardad to sweep them away like an avalanche was something else. Slowly they parted, moving back to let Rand ride through, stepping back to make a wide path.

Rand heaved a sigh of relief. Adelin and the other Maidens, at least, walked looking straight ahead, as though the Shaido did not exist.

"Wash the spears—while I breathe.
Wash the spears—my steel is bright.
Wash the spears. . . ."

The chant faded to a murmur behind them as they passed into the wide, steep-walled gorge, deep and shadowed as it wound into the mountains. For minutes the loudest sounds were the clatter of hooves on stone, the whisper of soft Aiel boots. Abruptly the passage gave way to Alcair Dal.

Rand could see why the canyon had been called a bowl, though there was nothing golden about it. Almost perfectly round, its gray wall sloped all the way around except at the far end, where it curled inward like a breaking wave. Clusters of Aiel dotted the slopes, heads and faces bare, many more clusters than there were clans. The Taardad who had come with the sept chiefs peeled away toward one or another of those. According to Rhuarc, grouping by society rather than clan was an aid to keeping peace. Only his Red Shields and the Maidens continued on with Rand and the Taardad chiefs.

The sept chiefs of the other clans all sat by clan, cross-legged before a deep ledge beneath the curling overhang. Six small knots, one of Maidens, stood between the sept chiefs and the ledge. Supposedly these were the Aiel who had come for the honor of clan chiefs. Six, although only five clans were represented. Sevanna would have the Maidens—though Aviendha had been quick to point out that Sevanna had never been *Far Dareis Mai*—but the extra. . . . Eleven men in that, not ten. Even seeing only the back of a flame-haired head, Rand was sure it was Couladin.

On the ledge itself stood a golden-haired woman in as much jewelry as the woman back at the fair tents, gray shawl draped over her arms—Sevanna, of course—and four clan chiefs, none armed save for his long belt knife, and one the tallest man Rand had ever seen. Bael of the Goshien Aiel, by the descriptions Rhuarc had given; the fellow had to be at least a hand taller than Rhuarc or himself. Sevanna was speaking, and some trick of the canyon's shape carried her words clearly throughout.

". . . allow him to speak!" Her voice was tight and angry. Head high and back straight she tried to dominate the ledge by force of will. "I demand it as my right! Until a new chief is chosen, I stand for Suladric and the Shaido. I demand my rights!"

"You stand for Suladric until a new chief is chosen, roofmistress." The white-haired man who spoke in irascible tones was Han, clan chief of the Tomanelle. With a face like dark, wrinkled leather, he would have been taller than average in the Two Rivers; for an Aiel, he was short, if stocky. "I have no doubt you know the rights of a roofmistress well, but perhaps not so well those of a clan chief. Only one who has entered Rhuidean may speak here—and you, who stand in Suladric's place"—Han did not sound happy about that, but then he sounded as if he was seldom happy—"but the dreamwalkers have told our Wise Ones Couladin was refused the right to enter Rhuidean."

Couladin shouted something, plainly furious yet indistinct—apparently the canyon's trick only worked from the ledge—but Erim, of the Chareen, his own bright red hair nearly half-white, cut him off sharply. "Have you no respect for custom and law, Shaido? Have you no honor? Stand silent here."

A few eyes on the slopes turned to see who the newcomers were. A ripple of nudges brought more around at the sight of two outlanders on horseback at the head of the sept chiefs, and one of the riders followed close by Maidens. How many Aiel peered down at him, Rand wondered. Three thousand? Four? More? None made a sound.

"We have gathered here to hear a great announcement," Bael said, "when all the clans have come." His dark reddish hair was graying, too; there were no young men among clan chiefs. His great height and deep voice drew eyes to him. "When all the clans have come. If all Sevanna wishes to speak of now is letting Couladin speak, I will go back to my tents and wait."

Jheran, of the Shaarad, blood enemy of Bael's Goshien, was a slender man, gray streaked heavily through his light brown hair. Slender, as a steel blade is slender, he spoke to no one of the chiefs in particular. "I say we do not return to our tents. Since Sevanna has brought us in,

let us discuss what is only somewhat less important than the announcement we await. Water. I wish to discuss the water at Chain Ridge
Stand." Bael turned toward him threateningly.

"Fools!" Sevanna snapped. "I will have done with waiting! I—"

It was then that those on the ledge became aware of the new arrivals.
In utter silence they watched them approach, the clan chiefs frowning,
Sevanna scowling. She was a pretty woman, well short of her middle
years—and younger-looking for standing among men well the other
side of theirs—but with a greedy mouth. The clan chiefs were dignified,
even Han in a sour-mouthed fashion; her pale green eyes had a calculating look. Unlike any Aiel woman Rand had ever seen, she wore her
loose white blouse undone low enough to show considerable tanned
cleavage, framed by her many necklaces. He could have known the
men for clan chiefs by their manner; if Sevanna was a roofmistress, she
was surely nothing like Lian.

Rhuarc strode straight to the ledge, gave his spears and buckler, his
bow and quiver, to his Red Shields, and climbed up. Rand handed his
reins to Mat—who muttered, "Luck with us!" as he eyed the surrounding Aiel; Adelin nodded encouragingly to Rand—and stepped straight
from his saddle to the ledge. A startled murmur rolled around the
canyon.

"What do you do, Rhuarc," Han demanded, scowling, "bringing this
wetlander here? If you will not kill him, at least send him down from
standing like a chief."

"This man, Rand al'Thor, has come to speak to the chiefs of the
clans. Did not the dreamwalkers tell you that he would come with
me?" Rhuarc's words brought a louder murmur from the listeners.

"Melaine told me many things, Rhuarc," Bael said slowly, frowning
at Rand. "That He Who Comes With the Dawn had come out of
Rhuidean. You cannot mean that this man. . . ." He trailed off in
disbelief.

"If this wetlander can speak," Sevanna said quickly, "so may Couladin." She lifted a smooth hand, and Couladin scrambled onto the
ledge, face an angry red.

Han rounded on him. "Stand down, Couladin! It is bad enough that
Rhuarc violates custom without you doing it as well!"

"It is time to be done with worn-out customs!" the fiery-haired
Shaido shouted, stripping off his gray-and-brown coat. There was no
need for shouting—his words echoed across the canyon—but he did
not lower his voice. "I am He Who Comes With the Dawn!" Shoving
shirtsleeves above his elbows, he thrust his fists into the air. Around

each forearm wound a serpentine creature scaled in crimson and gold, glittering metallically feet each tipped with five golden claws, golden-maned heads resting on the backs of his wrists. Two perfect Dragons. "I am the *Car'a'carn!*" The roar that came back was like thunder, Aiel leaping to their feet and shouting joyously. The sept chiefs were on their feet, too, the Taardad clustered worriedly, the others shouting as loudly as anyone.

The clan chiefs looked stunned, even Rhuarc. Adelin and her nine Maidens hefted their spears as if they expected to use them any moment. Eyeing the gap leading out, Mat pulled his hat low and guided the two horses close to the ledge, motioning surreptitiously for Rand to get back into his saddle.

Sevanna smiled smugly, adjusting her shawl, as Couladin strode to the front of the ledge with his arms high. "I bring change!" he shouted. "According to the prophecy, I bring new days! We will cross the Dragonwall again, and take back what was ours! The wetlanders are soft, but rich! You remember the wealth brought back when last we went into the wetlands! This time, we will take it all! This time . . . !"

Rand let the man's tirade wash over him. Of things possible, he had never suspected this. *How?* The word kept sliding through his head, yet he could not believe how composed he was. Slowly he took off his coat, hesitating a moment before fishing the *angreal* from his pocket; sticking it into the waistband of his breeches, he dropped the coat and walked to the front of the ledge, calmly undoing the laces of his sleeves. They slid down as he raised his arms above his head.

It took a moment for the assembled Aiel to notice the Dragons wrapped around his arms, too, shining in the sunlight. Their hush came by increments, but it was total. Sevanna's mouth dropped open; she had not known of this. Obviously Couladin had not thought Rand would follow so quickly, had not told her another bore the markings, too. *How?* The man must have believed he would have time; once he had established himself, Rand could be dismissed as a fraud. *Light, how?* If the roofmistress of Comarda Hold was stunned now, so were the clan chiefs, save only Rhuarc. Two men marked as prophecy said only one could be.

Couladin ranted on, waving his arms to make sure all saw. ". . . will not stop with the lands of the oathbreakers! We will take all the lands to the Aryth Ocean! The wetlanders cannot stand against—" Suddenly he became aware of the silence where eager cries had been. He knew what had caused it. Without turning to look at Rand, he shouted, "Wetlander! Look at his clothes! A wetlander!"

"A wetlander," Rand agreed. He did not raise his voice, but the canyon carried it to everyone. The Shaido looked startled for a moment, then grinned triumphantly—until Rand went on. "What does the Prophecy of Rhuidean say? 'Born of the blood.' My mother was Shaiel, a Maiden of the Chumai Taardad." *Who was she really? Where did she come from?* "My father was Janduin, of the Iron Mountain sept, clan chief of the Taardad." *My father is Tam al'Thor. He found me, raised me, loved me. I wish I could have known you, Janduin, but Tam is my father.* " 'Born of the blood, but raised by those not of the blood.' Where did the Wise Ones send to look for me? Into the holds of the Three-fold Land? They sent across the Dragonwall, where I was raised. According to the prophecy."

Bael and the other three nodded slowly, but reluctantly; there was still the matter of Couladin also bearing the Dragons, and doubtless they would rather have one of their own. Sevanna's face had firmed; no matter who bore the real markings, there was no doubt whom she supported.

Couladin's confidence never wavered; he sneered openly at Rand, the first time he had even looked at him. "How long since the Prophecy of Rhuidean was first spoken?" He still seemed to think he had to shout. "Who can say how much the words have changed? My mother was *Far Dareis Mai* before she gave up the spear. How much has the rest changed? Or been changed! It is said we once served the Aes Sedai. I say they mean to bind us to them once more! This wetlander was chosen because he resembles us! He is none of our blood! He came with Aes Sedai leading him on a leash! And the Wise Ones greeted them as they would first-sisters! You have all heard of Wise Ones who can do things beyond belief. The dreamwalkers used the One Power to keep me from this wetlander! They used the One Power, as Aes Sedai are said to do! The Aes Sedai have brought this wetlander here to bind us with fakery! And the dreamwalkers help them!"

"This is madness!" Rhuarc strode up beside Rand, staring out at the still silent gathering. "Couladin never went to Rhuidean. I heard the Wise Ones refuse him. Rand al'Thor did go. I saw him leave Chaendaer, and I saw him return, marked as you see."

"And why did they refuse me?" Couladin snarled. "Because the Aes Sedai told them to! Rhuarc does not tell you that one of the Aes Sedai went down from Chaendaer with this wetlander! That is how he returned with the Dragons! By Aes Sedai witchery! My brother Muradin died below Chaendaer, murdered by this wetlander and the Aes Sedai Moiraine, and the Wise Ones, doing Aes Sedai bidding, let them walk free! When night came, I went to Rhuidean. I did not reveal myself until now because this is the proper place for the *Car'a'carn* to show himself! I *am* the *Car'a'carn!*"

Lies, touched with just enough flecks of truth. The man was all victorious confidence, sure he had an answer for anything.

"You say you went to Rhuidean without the permission of the Wise Ones?" Han demanded, frowning. Towering Bael looked just as disapproving with his arms folded, Erim and Jheran only slightly less so. The clan chiefs, at least, still wavered. Sevanna gripped her belt knife, glaring at Han as if she would like to drive it into his back.

Couladin had his answer, though. "Yes, without it! He Who Comes With the Dawn brings change! So says the prophecy! Useless ways must change, and I will change them! Did I not arrive here with the dawn?"

The clan chiefs stood balanced on the edge, and so did all the watching Aiel, all on their feet now, staring silently, waiting in their thousands. If Rand could not convince them, he likely would not leave Alcair Dal alive. Mat motioned again to Jeade'en's saddle. Rand did not even bother to shake his head. There was a consideration beyond getting out alive; he needed these people, needed their loyalty. He *had* to have people who followed him because they believed, not to use him, or for what he could give them. He had to.

"Rhuidean," he said. The word seemed to fill the canyon. "You claim you went to Rhuidean, Couladin. What did you see there?"

"All know Rhuidean is not to be spoken of," Couladin shot back.

"We can go apart," Erim said, "and speak in private so you can tell us—" The Shaido cut him off, face flushed angrily.

"I will speak of it with no one. Rhuidean is a holy place, and what I saw was holy. *I* am holy!" He raised his Dragon marked arms again. "These make me holy!"

"I walked among glass columns beside *Avendesora.*" Rand spoke quietly, but the words carried everywhere. "I saw the history of the Aiel through my ancestors' eyes. What did you see, Couladin? I am not afraid to speak. Are you?" The Shaido quivered with rage, face nearly the color of his fiery hair.

Uncertain looks passed between Bael and Erim, Jheran and Han. "We must go apart for this," Han muttered.

Couladin did not seem to realize he had lost his advantage with the four, but Sevanna did. "Rhuarc has told him these things," she spat. "One of Rhuarc's wives is a dreamwalker, one of those who aids the Aes Sedai! Rhuarc has told him!"

"Rhuarc would not," Han snapped at her. "He is clan chief, and a man of honor. Do not speak of what you do not know, Sevanna!"

"I am not afraid!" Couladin shouted. "No man can call me afraid! I, too, saw with my ancestors' eyes! I saw our coming to the Three-fold Land! I saw our glory! The glory I will bring back to us!"

"I saw the Age of Legends," Rand announced, "and the beginning of the Aiel journey to the Three-fold Land." Rhuarc caught his arm, but he shook the clan chief off. This moment had been fated since the Aiel gathered before Rhuidean the first time. "I saw the Aiel when they were called the Da'shain Aiel, and followed the Way of the Leaf."

"No!" The shout rose from out in the canyon and spread in a roar. "No! No!" From thousands of throats. Spearpoints shaken in the air caught the sunlight. Even some of the Taardad sept chiefs were shouting. Adelin stared up at Rand, stricken. Mat shouted something at Rand, lost in the thunder, waving urgently for him to take his saddle.

"Liar!" The canyon's shape carried Couladin's bellow, wrath mixed with triumph, over the shouts of the gathering. Shaking her head frantically, Sevanna reached for him. She must at least have suspected now that he was the fake, yet if she could keep him quiet they might yet pull it off. As Rand hoped, Couladin pushed her away. The man knew Rand had been to Rhuidean—he could not possibly believe half of his own story—but neither could he believe this. "He proves himself a fraud from his own mouth! We have always been warriors! Always! To the beginning of time!"

The roar swelled, spears shaking, but Bael and Erim, Jheran and Han stood in stony silence. They knew now. Unaware of their looks, Couladin waved his Dragon-wreathed arms to the assembled Aiel, exulting in the adulation.

"Why?" Rhuarc said softly beside Rand. "Did you not understand why we do not speak of Rhuidean? To face that we were once so different from everything we believe, that we were the same as the despised Lost Ones you call Tuatha'an. Rhuidean kills those who cannot face it. Not more than one man in three lives who goes to Rhuidean. And now you have spoken for all to hear. It cannot be stopped here, Rand al'Thor. It will spread. How many will be strong enough to bear it?"

He will take you back, and he will destroy you. "I bring change," Rand said sadly. "Not peace, but turmoil." *Destruction follows on my heels everywhere. Will there ever be anywhere I do not tear apart?* "What will be, will be, Rhuarc. I can't change it."

"What will be, will be," the Aielman murmured after a moment.

Couladin still strode up and down, shouting to the Aiel of glory and conquest, unaware of the clan chiefs staring at his back. Sevanna did not look at Couladin at all; her pale green eyes were intent on the clan chiefs, lips pulled back in a grimace, breasts heaving with anxious breaths. She had to know what their silent stares meant.

"Rand al'Thor," Bael said loudly, the name slicing through Couladin's shouts, cutting off the roar of the crowd like a blade. He stopped to clear his throat, head swinging as though seeking a way out of this. Couladin turned, folding his arms confidently, no doubt expecting a sentence of death for the wetlander. The very tall clan chief took a deep breath. "Rand al'Thor is the *Car'a'carn*. Rand al'Thor is He Who Comes With the Dawn." Couladin's eyes widened in incredulous fury.

"Rand al'Thor is He Who Comes With the Dawn," leathery-faced Han announced, just as reluctantly.

"Rand al'Thor is He Who Comes With the Dawn." That from Jheran, grimly, and from Erim, "Rand al'Thor is He Who Comes With the Dawn."

"Rand al'Thor," Rhuarc said, "is He Who Comes With the Dawn." In a voice too soft to carry even from the ledge, he added, "And the Light have mercy on us."

For a long, stretched moment the silence lasted. Then Couladin leaped snarling from the ledge, snatching a spear from one of his *Seia Doon*, hurling it straight at Rand. Yet as he moved down, Adelin leaped up; his spearpoint stabbed through the layered bullhide of her outstretched buckler, swinging her around.

Pandemonium exploded through the canyon, men shouting and shoving. The other Jindo Maidens jumped up beside Adelin, forming a screen in front of Rand. Sevanna had climbed down to shout urgently at Couladin, hanging on his arm as he tried to lead his Shaido Black Eyes against the Maidens between him and Rand. Heirn and a dozen more Taardad sept chiefs joined Adelin, spears ready, but others were shouting loudly. Mat scrambled up, gripping his black-hafted spear with its raven-marked sword point, roaring what had to be curses in the Old Tongue. Rhuarc and the other clan chiefs raised their voices, vainly trying to restore order. The canyon boiled like a cauldron. Rand saw veils lifted. A spear flashed, stabbing. Another. He had to stop this.

He reached out for *saidin,* and it flooded into him until he thought he would burst if he did not burn first; the filth of the taint spreading through him seemed to curdle his bones. Thought floated outside the Void; cold thought. Water. Here where water was so scarce, the Aiel always talked of water. Even in this dry air there was some water. He channeled, not really knowing what he did, reached out blindly.

Sharp lightning crackled above Alcair Dal, and the wind rushed in from every direction, howling across the lip of the canyon to drown the Aiel's shouts. Wind, bringing minute traces of water, more and more, until something happened no man had ever seen there. A mist of rain began to fall. The wind above shrieked and swirled. Wild lightnings streaked the sky. And the rain grew heavier and heavier, to a driving downpour, sweeping over the ledge, plastering his hair to his head and his shirt to his back, blanking out everything fifty paces away.

Abruptly the rain stopped hitting him; an invisible dome expanded around him, pushing Mat and the Taardad away. Through the water pouring down its side he could dimly see Adelin pounding at it, trying to force her way through to him.

"You utter fool, playing games with these other fools! Wasting all my planning and effort!"

Water dripped down his face as he turned to face Lanfear. Her silver-belted white dress was perfectly dry, the black waves of her hair untouched by a single raindrop among the silver stars and crescents. Those large black eyes stared at him furiously; anger twisted her beautiful face.

"I didn't expect you to reveal yourself yet," he said quietly. The Power still filled him; he rode the buffeting torrents, holding on with a desperation he kept out of his voice. It was not necessary to pull in more, only to let it come till it seemed his bones would crisp to ash. He did not know if she could shield him while *saidin* actually roared through him, but he let it fill him against the possibility. "I know you are not alone. Where is he?"

Lanfear's beautiful mouth tightened. "I knew he would give himself away, coming into your dream. I could have managed matters if his panic—"

"I knew from the start," he broke in. "I expected it from the day I left the Stone of Tear. Out here, where anyone could see I was fixed on Rhuidean and the Aiel. Do you think I did not expect some of you to come after me? But the trap is *mine*, Lanfear, not yours. Where is he?" The last came as a cold shout. Emotion skittered uncontrollably around the Void that surrounded him inside, the emptiness that was not empty, the emptiness filled with the Power.

"If you knew," she snapped back, "why did you chase him away with your talk of fulfilling your destiny, of doing *what has to be done?*" Scorn weighted the words like stones. "I brought Asmodean to teach you, but he was always one to leap to another plan if the first proved difficult. Now he thinks he has found something better for himself in Rhuidean. And he is off to take it while you stand here. Couladin, the Draghkar, all to hold your attention while he made sure. All my plans for nothing because you must be stubborn! Do you have any idea what effort it will take to convince him again? It must be him. Demandred or Rahvin or Sammael would kill you before teaching you to lift a hand unless they have you bound like a dog at heel!"

Rhuidean. Yes. Of course. Rhuidean. How many weeks to the south? Yet he had done something once. If he could remember how. . . .

"And you let him go? After all your talk of aiding me?"

"Not openly, I said. What could he find in Rhuidean worth my coming into the open? When you agree to stand with me will be time enough. Remember what I told you, Lews Therin." Her voice took on a seductive note; those full lips curved, those dark eyes tried to swallow him like bottomless pools. "Two great *sa'angreal*. With those, together, we can challenge—" This time she stopped on her own. He had remembered.

With the Power he *folded* reality, *bent* a small patch of what was. A door opened beneath the dome in front of him. That was the only way to describe it. An opening into darkness, into somewhere else.

"You do remember a few things, it seems." She eyed the doorway, shifted that suddenly suspicious gaze to him. "Why are you so anxious? What is in Rhuidean?"

"Asmodean," he said grimly. For a moment he hesitated. He could not see beyond the rain-drenched dome. What was happening out there? And Lanfear. If only he could remember how he had shielded Egwene and Elayne. *If only I could make myself kill a woman who's only frowning at me. She is one of the Forsaken!* It was no more possible now than it had been in the Stone.

Stepping through the door, he left her on the ledge and closed it behind him. No doubt she knew how to make one of her own, but the making of it would slow her down.

CHAPTER 58

The Traps of Rhuidean

Darkness surrounded him once the door vanished, blackness stretching in all directions, yet he could see. There was no sensation of heat or cold, even wet as he was; no sensation at all. Only existence. Plain gray stone steps rose in front of him, each step hanging unsupported, arching out until they dwindled from sight. He had seen these before, or their like; somehow he knew they would take him where he had to go. He ran up the impossible stairs, and as his boot left each one behind with its damp footprint, it faded away, vanished. Only steps ahead waited, only those taking him where he had to go. That was as it had been before, too.

Did I make *these with the Power, or do they exist some other way?*

With the thought, the gray stone under his foot began to fade, and all the others ahead shimmered. Desperately he concentrated on them, gray stone and real. Real! The shimmering stopped. They were not so plain now, but polished, the edges carved in a fancy border he thought he recalled seeing somewhere before.

Not caring where—not sure he dared think too long on it—he ran as hard as he could, taking the steps three at a time through the endless dark. They would take him where he wanted to go, but how long would it take? How much head start did Asmodean have? Did the Forsaken know a faster way to travel? That was the trouble. The Forsaken had all the knowledge; all he had was desperation.

Looking ahead, he winced. The steps had accommodated themselves to his long stride, with wide spaces between requiring those leaps now, across black as deep as. . . . As what? A fall here might never end. He forced himself to ignore the gaps, to keep running. The old, half-healed wound in his side began to throb, a vague awareness. But if he was aware of it at all, wrapped inside *saidin*, the wound was close to breaking open. *Ignore it.* The thought floated across the Void inside him. He did not dare lose this race, not if it killed him. Would these steps never stop climbing? How far had he come?

Suddenly he saw a figure in the distance ahead and off to his left, a man it seemed, in a red coat and red boots, standing on a glistening silvery platform that slid through the darkness. Rand needed no closer look to be sure it was Asmodean. The Forsaken was not running like a half-spent country boy; he was riding that whatever-it-was.

Rand stopped dead on one of the stone steps. He had no idea what that platform was, shining like polished metal, but. . . . The steps ahead of him vanished. The piece of stone beneath his boots began to glide forward, faster and faster. There was no wind in his face to tell him he was moving, nothing in that vast black to mark motion at all—except that he was beginning to catch up to Asmodean. He did not know if he was doing this with the Power; it just seemed to happen. The step wobbled, and he made himself stop wondering. *I don't know enough yet.*

The dark-haired man stood at his ease, one hand on a hip, pensively fingering his chin. A spill of white lace dripped from his neck; more half-hid his hands. His high-collared red coat seemed shinier than silk satin, and was oddly cut, with tails hanging almost to his knees. What seemed to be black threads, like fine steel wires, ran off from the man, disappearing into the surrounding dark. Those Rand had surely seen before.

Asmodean turned his head, and Rand gaped. The Forsaken could change their faces—or at least make you see a different face; he had seen Lanfear do it—but these were the features of Jasin Natael, the gleeman. He had been sure it would be Kadere, with his predatory eyes that never changed.

Asmodean saw him at the same moment and gave a start. The Forsaken's silver perch darted forward—and suddenly a huge sheet of fire, like a thin slice from a monstrous flame, swept back toward Rand, a mile high and a mile wide.

He channeled at it desperately; just as it was about to strike him, it suddenly burst into shards, hurtling away from him, winking out. Yet even as the fiery curtain vanished it revealed another rushing at him. He shattered that, exposing another, splintered the third to reveal a fourth. Asmodean was getting away, Rand was sure of it. He could not see the Forsaken at all for the flames. Anger slid across the surface of the Void, and he channeled.

A wave of fire enveloped the crimson curtain sweeping toward him and rolled on, carrying it away, not a thin slice, but wild, billowing gouts as if whipped by stormwinds. He quivered with the Power roaring through him; anger at Asmodean clawed at the surface of the Void.

A hole appeared in the erupting surface. No, not a hole exactly. Asmodean and his shining platform stood in the middle of it, but as the flaming wave washed forward it slid together again. The Forsaken had built some sort of shield around himself.

Rand made himself ignore the distant anger outside the Void. It was only in cold calm that he could touch *saidin;* acknowledging anger would shatter the Void. The billows of fire ceased to exist as he stopped channeling. He had to catch the man, not kill him.

The stone step slid through the blackness even faster. Asmodean drew closer.

Abruptly the Forsaken's platform stopped. A bright hole appeared in front of him, and he jumped through; the silvery thing vanished, and the door began to close.

Rand lashed out wildly with the Power. He had to hold it open; once it closed, he would have no idea where Asmodean had fled. The shrinking stopped. A square of harsh sunlight, big enough to step through. He had to hold it open, reach it before Asmodean could go too far. . . .

Even as he thought about stopping, the step halted dead. It halted, but he hurtled forward, flying through the doorway. Something tugged his boot, and then he was tumbling head over heels across hard ground, to land finally in a breathless heap.

Fighting to fill his lungs, he pushed himself to his feet, not daring to let himself be helpless a moment. The One Power still filled him with life and vileness; his bruises felt as distant as his struggle for breath, as far off as the yellow dust that covered his damp clothes, covered him. Yet at the same time he was aware of every stir of furnace air, every grain of dust, every minute crack in the hard-baked clay. Already the sun was baking away the moisture, sucking it from his shirt and breeches. He was in the Waste, in the valley below Chaendaer, not fifty steps from fog-shrouded Rhuidean. The doorway was gone.

He took a step toward the wall of mist and stopped, lifting his left foot. His bootheel was sliced cleanly though. The tug he had felt; the doorway closing. He was dimly aware of shivering in spite of the heat. He had not known it was that dangerous. The Forsaken had all the knowledge. Asmodean would not escape him.

Grimly he adjusted his clothes, tucking the carved little man and his sword firmly in place, ran to the fog and in. Gray blindness enveloped him. The Power filling him did nothing to make him see better here. Running blind.

Abruptly he threw himself down, rolling the last stride out of the fog onto gritty paving stones. Lying there, he stared up at three bright ribbons, silver-blue in the strange light of Rhuidean, stretching to left and right, floating in the air. When he stood, they were at the level of his waist, chest and neck, and so thin that they vanished edge-on. He could see how they had been made and hung, even if he did not understand it. Hard as steel, sharp enough to make a razor seem a feather. Had he run into those, they would have sliced through him. A tiny surge of the Power, and the silver ribbons fell in dust. Cold anger, outside the Void; inside, cold purpose, and the One Power.

The bluish glow of the fog dome cast its shadowless light on the half-finished, slab-sided palaces of marble and crystal and cut glass, the cloud-piercing towers, fluted and spiraled. And down the broad street ahead of him ran Asmodean, past dry fountains, toward the great plaza at the heart of the city.

Rand channeled—it seemed oddly difficult; he pulled at *saidin,* wrenched at it until it raged into him—he channeled, and thick bolts of jagged lightning shot from the dome-clouds. Not at Asmodean. Just ahead of the Forsaken, gleaming pillars of red and white, fifty feet thick and a hundred paces high, centuries old, exploded and toppled across the street in rubble and clouds of dust.

From huge windows of colored glass, images of majestically serene men and women seemed to look at Rand in reproof. "I have to stop him," he told them; his voice seemed to echo in his own ears.

Asmodean paused, starting back from the collapsing masonry. The dust drifting toward him never touched his shiny red coat; it parted around him, leaving clear air.

Fire bloomed around Rand, enveloped him as the air *became* flame —and vanished before he was even aware of how he did it. His clothes were dry and hot; his hair felt singed, and baked dust fell at every step as he ran. Asmodean was scrambling over the broken stone blocking the street; more lightning flashed, raising gouts of shattered paving stone ahead of him, ripping open crystal palace walls to rain ruin before him.

The Forsaken did not slow, and as he vanished, lightning flashed from the glowing clouds toward Rand, stabbing blindly but meant to kill. Running, Rand wove a shield around himself. Shards of stone bounded from it as he dodged crackling blue bolts, leaped over the holes they tore in the pavement. The air itself sparkled; the hair of his arms lifted with it, the hair on his head stirred.

There was something woven into the barrier of shattered columns. He hardened the shield around himself. Great tumbled chunks of red and white stone exploded as he reached to climb, a burst of pure light and flying stone. Safe inside his bubble, he ran through, only vaguely aware of the rumble of collapsing buildings. He had to stop Asmodean. Straining—and it took strain—he threw lightning ahead, balls of fire ripping up out of the ground, anything to slow the red-coated man. He was catching up. He entered the plaza only a dozen paces behind. Trying to increase his speed, he redoubled his efforts at slowing Asmodean, and fleeing, Asmodean fought to kill him.

The *ter'angreal* and other precious things the Aiel had given their lives to bring here were hurled into the air by lightning, tossed wildly by spinning whirlwinds of fire, constructs of silver and crystal shattering, strange metal shapes toppling as the ground shivered and broke open in wide rents.

Searching wildly, Asmodean ran. And flung himself at what might seem the least significant thing in all that litter. A carved white stone figurine perhaps a foot long, lying on its back, a man holding a crystal sphere in one upraised hand. Asmodean closed his hands on it with an exultant cry.

A heartbeat later, Rand's hands grasped it, too. For the barest instant he stared into the Forsaken's face; he looked no different than he had as a gleeman, except for a wild desperation in his dark eyes, a somewhat handsome man in his middle years—nothing at all to say he was one of the Forsaken. The barest instant, and they both reached through the figure, through the *ter'angreal,* for one of the two most powerful *sa'angreal* ever made.

Vaguely Rand was aware of a great, half-buried statue in far-off Cairhien, of the huge crystal sphere in its hand, glowing like the sun, pulsing with the One Power. And the Power in him surged up like all the seas of the world in storm. With this surely he could do anything;

surely he could even have Healed that dead child. The taint swelled as much, curling 'round every particle of him, seeping into every crevice, into his soul. He wanted to howl; he wanted to explode. Yet he only held half what that *sa'angreal* could deliver; the other half filled Asmodean.

Back and forth they struggled, tripping over scattered and broken *ter'angreal*, falling, neither daring to let go of the figure with even one finger for fear the other would pull it away. Yet as they rolled over and over, banging now against a redstone doorframe that somehow still stood, now against a fallen crystal statue lying on its side unbroken, a nude woman clasping a child to her breast, as they fought for possession of the *ter'angreal*, the battle was fought on another level, too.

Hammers of Power large enough to level mountains struck at Rand, and blades that could have pierced the earth's heart; unseen pincers tried to tear his mind from his body, ripped at his very soul. Every scrap of Power he could draw went to hurl those attacks away. Any one could destroy him as if he had never been; he was sure of it. Where they went he could not be sure. The ground bounded beneath them, shaking them as they struggled, flinging them about in a writhing tangle of straining muscle. Dimly he was aware of vast rumbles, of a thousand whining hums like some strange music. The glass columns, quivering, vibrating. He could not worry about them.

All those nights without sleep were catching up to him, the running he had done on top of it. He was tired, and if he could even know it inside the Void, then he was near exhaustion. Tossed by the quaking earth, he realized he was no longer trying to pull the *ter'angreal* from Asmodean, only to hold on. Soon his strength would go. Even if he managed to retain his grip on the stone figure, he would have to let go of *saidin* or be swept away by the rush of it, destroyed as surely as Asmodean would do it. He could not pull another thread through the *ter'angreal;* he and Asmodean were equally balanced, each with half of what the great *sa'angreal* in Cairhien could draw. Asmodean panted in his face, snarling; sweat dripped from the Forsaken's forehead, ran down his cheeks. The man was tired, too. But as tired as he?

The flailing earth heaved Rand on top for an instant, and just as quickly spun Asmodean up, but in that brief moment Rand felt something pressed between them. The carving of the fat little man with the sword, still tucked into his waistband. An insignificant thing next to the immense Power they drew upon. A cup of water compared to a vast river, to an ocean. He did not even know if he could use it while linked to the great *sa'angreal*. And if he could? Asmodean's teeth bared. Not a grimace, but a weary rictus of a smile; the man thought he was winning. Perhaps he was. Rand's fingers trembled, weakening around the *ter'angreal;* it was all he could do to hold on to *saidin,* even linked as he was to the huge *sa'angreal.*

He had not seen those strange things like black steel wires around Asmodean since leaving the dark place, but he could visualize them even in the Void, place them in his mind around the Forsaken. Tam had taught him the Void as an aid to archery, to be one with the bow, the arrow, the target. He made himself one with those imagined black wires. He barely saw Asmodean frown. The man must be wondering why his face had grown calm; there was always calm in the moment before the arrow was loosed. He reached through the small *angreal* in his waistband, and more of the Power flowed into him. He did not waste time on exulting; it was such a small flow beside what he already contained, and this was his final blow. This would use his final strength. He formed it like a sword of Power, a sword of Light, and struck; one with the sword, one with the imagined wires.

Asmodean's eyes went wide, and he screamed, a howl from the depths of horror; like a struck gong the Forsaken quivered. For an instant there seemed to be two of him, shivering away from each other; then they slid back together. He fell over on his back, arms flung out in his now dirty, tattered red coat, chest heaving; staring up at nothing, his dark eyes looked lost.

As he collapsed, Rand lost his hold on *saidin,* and the Power left him. He had barely enough strength to clutch the *ter'angreal* to his chest and roll away from Asmodean. Pushing himself to his knees felt like climbing a mountain; he huddled around the figure of the man with his crystal sphere.

The earth had stopped moving. The glass columns still stood—he was grateful for that; destroying them would have been like obliterating the history of the Aiel—and though trefoil leaves littered the pavement beneath *Avendesora,* only one branch on the great tree hung broken. But the rest of Rhuidean. . . .

The plaza looked as if everything had been picked up and flung about by a mad giant. Half the great palaces and towers were only heaps of rubble, some spilling into the square; huge toppled columns marred others, and fallen walls, and empty gaps where huge windows of colored glass had been. A rift ran the whole way across the city, a split in the earth fifty feet wide. The destruction did not end there. The dome of fog that had hidden Rhuidean for so many centuries was dissipating; the underside no longer glowed, and harsh sunlight poured through great new gaps. Beyond, Chaendaer's peak looked different, lower, and on the other side of the valley some of the mountains were definitely lower. Where one mountain had stood, a fan of stone and dirt stretched across the north end of the valley.

I destroy. Always I destroy! Light, will it ever end?

Asmodean rolled onto his belly, pushed to hands and knees. His eyes found Rand, and the *ter'angreal,* and he made as if to crawl toward them.

Rand could not have channeled a spark, but he had learned how to fight before his first nightmare of channeling. He lifted a fist. "Don't even think about it." The Forsaken stopped, swaying wearily. His face sagged, yet despair and desire warred across it; hate and fear glittered in his eyes.

"I do like to see men fight, but you two cannot even stand." Lanfear moved into Rand's view, surveying the devastation. "You have made a thorough job of it. Can you feel the traces? This place was shielded in some way. You did not leave enough for me to say how." Dark eyes suddenly bright, she knelt in front of Rand, peering at what he held. "So that is what he was after. I thought they were all destroyed. Only half remains of the single one I have seen; a fine trap for some unwary Aes Sedai." She put out a hand, and he clutched the *ter'angreal* tighter. Her smile did not touch her eyes. "Keep it, certainly. To me it is no more than a figurine." Rising, she dusted her white skirts though they did not need it. When she realized he was watching her, she stopped searching the rubble-strewn plaza with her eyes, made her smile brighter. "What you used was one of the two *sa'angreal* I told you of. Did you feel the *immensity* of it? I have wondered what it must be like." She seemed unaware of the hunger in her voice. "With those, together, we can displace the Great Lord of the Dark himself. We can, Lews Therin! Together."

"Help me!" Asmodean crawled toward her unsteadily, his upraised face painted in dread. "You don't know what he has done. You must help me. I would not have come here if not for you."

"What has he done?" she sniffed. "Beaten you like a dog, and not half so well as you deserve. You were never meant for greatness, Asmodean, only to follow those who are great."

Somehow Rand managed to stand, still holding the stone-and-crystal figure to his chest. He would not continue on his knees in her presence. "You *Chosen*"—he knew taunting her was dangerous, but he could not stop himself—"gave your souls to the Dark One. You let him attach himself to you." How many times had he replayed his battle with

Ba'alzamon? How many times before he began to suspect what those black wires were? "I cut him off from the Dark One, Lanfear. I cut him off!"

Her eyes widened in shock, staring from him to Asmodean. The man had begun to weep. "I did not think that was possible. Why? Do you think to bring *him* to the Light? You've changed nothing about him."

"He is still the same man who gave himself to the Shadow in the first place," Rand agreed. "You told me how little you *Chosen* trust one another. How long could he keep it secret? How many of you would believe he didn't do it himself somehow? I am glad you thought it impossible; maybe the rest of you will as well. You gave me the whole idea, Lanfear. A man to teach me how to control the Power. But I won't be taught by a man linked to the Dark One. Now I don't have to be. He may be the same man, but he doesn't have much choice, does he? He can stay and teach me, hope I win, help me win, or he can hope the rest of you don't take the excuse to turn on him. Which do you think he'll choose?"

Asmodean stared wild-eyed at Rand from his crouch, then thrust out a pleading hand toward Lanfear. "They will believe you! You can tell them! I would not be here except for you! You must tell them! I am faithful to the Great Lord of the Dark!"

Lanfear stared at Rand, too. For the first time ever that he had seen, she looked uncertain. "How much *do* you remember, Lews Therin? How much is you, and how much the shepherd? This is the sort of plan you might have devised when we—" Drawing a deep breath, she turned her head to Asmodean. "Yes, they will believe me. When I tell them you went over to Lews Therin. Everyone knows you will leap wherever you think your best chance lies. There." She nodded to herself in satisfaction. "Another little present for you, Lews Therin. That shield will allow a trickle through, enough for him to teach. It will dissipate with time, but he'll not be able to challenge you for months, and by that time he *will* have no choice but to remain with you. He was never very good at breaking through a shield; you must be willing to accept pain, and he never could."

"NOOOOOO!" Asmodean crawled toward her. "You cannot do this to me! Please, Mierin! Please!"

"My name is *Lanfear!*" Rage twisted her face to ugliness, and the man lifted into the air, spread-eagled; his clothes pressed to him and the flesh of his face distorted, spread out like butter under a rock.

Rand could not let her kill the man, but he was too tired to touch the True Source unaided; he could barely sense it, a dim glow just out of sight. For an instant his hands tightened on the stone man with the crystal sphere. If he reached through to the huge *sa'angreal* in Cairhien again now, that much of the Power might destroy him. Instead, he reached through the carving in his waistband; with the *angreal,* it was a feeble flow, a hair-thin trickle compared to the other, but he was too weary to pull more. He hurled it all between the two Forsaken, hoping to distract her if nothing else.

A bar of white-hot fire ten feet tall streaked between the pair in a blur surrounded by arcing blue lightning, searing a pace-deep groove across the square, a smooth-sided gash glowing with melted earth and stone; the fiery shaft struck a green-streaked palace wall and exploded, the roar buried in the rumble of collapsing marble. On one side of the melted slash Asmodean dropped to the pavement in a shuddering heap, blood trickling from nose and ears; on the other, Lanfear staggered back as if struck, then rounded on Rand. He swayed with the effort of what he had done, and lost *saidin* once more.

For a moment rage engorged her face as deeply as it had for Asmodean. For a moment Rand stood on the brink of death. Then fury vanished with startling abruptness, buried behind a seductive smile. "No, I mustn't kill him. Not after we have gone to so much effort." Moving closer, she reached up to stroke the side of his neck, where her bite from the dream was just healing; he had not let Moiraine know of it. "You still bear my mark. Shall I make it permanent?"

"Did you harm anyone at Alcair Dal, or in the camps?"

Her face never stopped smiling, but her caress changed, fingers suddenly poised as if to rip out his throat. "Such as who? I thought you had realized you did not love that little farmgirl. Or is it the Aiel jade?" A viper. A deadly viper who loved him—*The Light help me!*—and he did not know how to stop her if she decided to bite, whether him or someone else.

"I don't want anyone hurt. I need them yet. I can use them." It was painful saying that, painful for the amount of truth in it. But keeping Lanfear's fangs out of Egwene and Moiraine, away from Aviendha and anyone else close to him, that was worth a little pain.

Throwing back her beautiful head, she laughed like chiming bells. "I can remember when you were too softhearted to use anyone. Devious in battle, hard as stone and arrogant as the mountains, but open and softhearted as a girl! No, I did not harm any of your precious Aes Sedai, or your precious Aiel. I do not kill without cause, Lews Therin. I do not even hurt without cause." He was careful not to look at Asmodean; white-faced, drawing jagged breaths, the man had pushed up on one hand, using the other to wipe blood from his mouth and chin.

Turning slowly, Lanfear surveyed the great square. "You have destroyed this city as well as any army could have." But it was not the ruined palaces she stared at, though she pretended; it was the broken square with its jumbled litter of *ter'angreal* and who knew what else. The corners of her mouth were tight when she turned back to Rand; her dark eyes held a spark of suppressed anger. "Use his teachings well, Lews Therin. The others are still out there, Sammael with his envy of you, Demandred with his hate, Rahvin with his thirst for power. They will be more eager to bring you down, not less, if—when—they discover you hold that."

Her gaze flickered to the foot-tall figure in his hands, and for an instant he thought she was considering taking it from him. Not to keep the others from his back, but because with it he might be too powerful for her to handle. Right then he was not certain he could stop her if she used nothing but her hands. One instant she was weighing whether to leave the *ter'angreal* in his possession, the next measuring his tiredness. However much she talked of loving him, she would want to be far from him when he regained enough strength to use the thing. Briefly she scanned the plaza again, lips pursed; then abruptly a door opened beside her, not a door to blackness, but into what seemed a palace chamber, all carved white marble and white silk hangings.

"Which one were you?" he said as she stepped toward it, and she paused, looking over a shoulder at him with an almost coy smile.

"Do you think I could stand to be fat, ugly Keille?" She ran hands down her rounded slimness for emphasis. "Isendre, now. Slim, beautiful Isendre. I thought if you suspected, you would suspect her. My pride is strong enough to support a little fat, when it must." The smile became a baring of teeth. "Isendre thought she was dealing with simple Friends of the Dark. I would not be surprised if right now she is frantically trying to explain to some angry Aiel women why a large quantity of their gold necklaces and bracelets are in the bottom of her chest. She actually did steal some of them herself."

"I thought you said you didn't harm anyone!"

"Now your soft heart shows. I can show a tender, woman's heart when I choose. You'll not be able to save her being welted, I think—she deserves that for the least of the looks she gave me—but if you return quickly, you can prevent them sending her off with one waterskin to walk out of this blighted land. They are quite hard on thieves, it seems, these Aiel." She gave an amused laugh, shaking her head in wonder.

"So different from what they were. You could slap a Da'shain's face, and all he did was ask what he had done. Slap again, and he asked if he had offended. He would not change if you continued all day." Giving Asmodean a contemptuous sidelong look, she added, "Learn well and quickly, Lews Therin. I mean us to rule together, not to watch Sammael kill you or Graendal add you to her collection of handsome young men. Learn well and quickly." She stepped into the chamber of white marble and silk, and the doorway seemed to turn sideways, narrowed, vanished.

Rand drew the first deep breath he had taken since her appearance. Mierin. A name remembered from the glass columns. The woman who had found the Dark One's prison in the Age of Legends, who had bored into it. Had she known what it was? How had she escaped that fiery doom he had seen? Had she given herself to the Dark One even then?

Asmodean was struggling to his feet, unsteady and nearly falling again. He no longer bled, but blood still traced thin lines from his ears down the sides of his neck, made a smear across his mouth and chin. His filthy red coat was torn, his white lace ripped and snagged. "It was my link to the Great Lord that allowed me to touch *saidin* without going mad," he said hoarsely. "All you have done is make me as vulnerable as you. You might as well let me go. I am not a very good teacher. She only chose me because—" His lips writhed, trying to pull the words back.

"Because there isn't anyone else," Rand finished for him and turned away.

On tottering legs Rand crossed the broad square, picking his way through the litter. He and Asmodean had been flung halfway around the forest of glass columns from *Avendesora*. Crystal plinths lay against fallen statues of men and women, some broken in chunks, some not even chipped. A great flat ring of silvery metal had been flipped up on chairs of metal and stone, strange shapes in metal and crystal and glass, all mixed in a heap with shattered bits, a black metal shaft like a spear standing upright, improbably balanced on the pile. The entire plaza was like that.

Out from the great tree, a little searching among the jumble found what he sought. Kicking aside pieces of what seemed to be spiraled glass tubes, he shoved a plain-carved chair of red crystal aside and picked up a foot-tall figurine, a robed woman with a serene face, worked in white stone, holding up a clear sphere in one hand. Unbroken. As useless to him, or to any man, as its male twin was to Lanfear.

He considered breaking it. One swing of his arm could shatter that crystal globe on the paving stones, surely.

"She was looking for that." He had not realized Asmodean had followed him. Wavering, the man scrubbed at his bloody mouth. "She will rip your heart out to put her hands on it."

"Or yours, for keeping it secret from her. She *loves* me." *Light help me. Like being loved by a rabid wolf!* After a moment he put the female statue in the crook of his arm with the male. *There might be a use for it. And I don't want to destroy anything else.*

Yet as he looked around, he saw something besides destruction. The fog was almost gone from the ruined city; only a few wispy sheets remained to drift among the buildings still standing beneath the sinking sun. The valley floor tilted sharply to the south now, and water spilled out of the great rent across the city, the gash that went all the way down to where that deep hidden ocean of water lay. Already the lower end of the valley was filling. A lake. It might reach nearly to the city eventually, a lake maybe three miles long in a land where a pool ten feet across drew people. People would come to this valley to live. He could almost see the surrounding mountains already terraced with crops growing green. They would tend *Avendesora,* the last chora tree. Perhaps they would even rebuild Rhuidean. The Waste would have a city. Perhaps he would even live to see it.

With the *angreal,* the round little man with his sword, he was able to open a doorway to blackness. Asmodean stepped through with him reluctantly, sneering faintly when a single carved stone step appeared, just wide enough for the two of them. Still the same man who had given himself to the Dark One. His calculating, sideways glances were reminder enough of that, if Rand needed any.

They only spoke twice as the step soared through the darkness.

Once Rand said, "I cannot call you Asmodean."

The man shivered. "My name was Joar Addam Nesossin," he said at last. He sounded as if he had stripped himself bare, or lost something.

"I can't use that either. Who knows what scrap holds that name somewhere? The idea is to keep someone from killing you for a Forsaken." And to keep anyone from knowing he had a Forsaken for teacher. "You will have to go on being Jasin Natael, I think. Gleeman to the Dragon Reborn. Excuse enough for keeping you close." Natael grimaced, but said nothing.

A little later, Rand said, "The first thing you'll show me is how to guard my dreams." The man only nodded, sullenly. He would cause problems, but they could not be as large as the problems of ignorance.

The step slowed, stopped, and Rand *folded* again. The doorway opened on the ledge in Alcair Dal.

The rain had stopped, though the evening-shadowed floor of the canyon was still sodden, churned to mud by Aiel feet. Fewer Aiel than before, perhaps as many as a fourth fewer. But not fighting. Staring at the ledge, where Moiraine and Egwene, Aviendha and the Wise Ones had joined the clan chiefs, who stood talking with Lan. Mat was squatting a little distance from them, hat brim pulled down and black-hafted spear propped on his shoulder, Adelin and her Maidens standing around him. They gaped as Rand stepped out of the doorway, stared more when Natael followed in his tattered shiny red coat and white lace. Mat jumped to his feet with a grin, and Aviendha half-raised a hand toward him. The Aiel in the canyon watched silently.

Before anyone could speak, Rand said, "Adelin, would you send someone out to the fair and tell them to stop beating Isendre? She is not as big a thief as they think." The yellow-haired woman looked startled, but immediately spoke to one of the Maidens, who dashed off.

"How did you know about that?" Egwene exclaimed, at the same time Moiraine demanded, "Where have you been? How?" Her wide dark eyes darted from him to Natael, her Aes Sedai calm nowhere in evidence. And the Wise Ones . . . ? Sun-haired Melaine looked ready to drag answers out of him with her bare hands. Bair scowled as though she meant to switch them out. Amys shifted her shawl and ran fingers through her pale hair, unable to decide whether she was worried or relieved.

Adelin handed him his coat, still damp. He wrapped it around the two stone figures. Moiraine was considering those, too. He did not know if she even suspected what they were, but he intended to hide them as best he could from anyone. If he could not trust himself with *Callandor*'s power, how much less with the great *sa'angreal*? Not until he had learned more of how to control it, and himself.

"What happened here?" he asked, and the Aes Sedai's mouth tightened at being ignored. Egwene did not look much more pleased.

"The Shaido have gone, behind Sevanna and Couladin," Rhuarc said. "All who remain acknowledge you as *Car'a'carn.*"

"The Shaido were not the only ones who fled." Han's leathery face twisted sourly. "Some of my Tomanelle went as well. And Goshien, and Shaarad, and Chareen." Jheran and Erim nodded almost as dourly as Han.

"Not with the Shaido," tall Bael rumbled, "but they went. They will spread what happened here, what you revealed. That was ill done. I saw men throw away their spears and run!"

He will bind you together, and destroy you.

"No Taardad left," Rhuarc put in, not pridefully but as a simple statement of fact. "We are ready to go where you lead."

Where he led. He was not done with the Shaido, with Couladin, or Sevanna. Scanning the Aiel around the canyon he could see shaken faces, for all they had chosen to stay. What must those who had run be like? Yet the Aiel were only a means to an end. He had to remember that. *I have to be even harder than they.*

Jeade'en waited beside the ledge with Mat's gelding. Motioning Natael to stay close, Rand climbed into the saddle, coat-wrapped bundle secure under his arm. Mouth twisted, the once Foresaken came to stand by his left stirrup. Adelin and her remaining Maidens leaped down to form around them, and surprisingly, Aviendha climbed down to take her usual place on his right. Mat jumped to Pips's saddle in one bound.

Rand looked back up at the people on the ledge, all of them watching, waiting. "It will be a long road back." Bael turned his face away. "Long, and bloody." The Aiel faces did not change. Egwene half stretched out a hand toward him, eyes pained, but he ignored her. "When the rest of the clan chiefs come, it begins."

"It began long ago," Rhuarc said quietly. "The question is where and how it ends."

For that, Rand had no answer. Turning the dapple, he rode slowly across the canyon, surrounded by his peculiar retinue. Aiel parted in front of him, staring, waiting. The night's cold was already coming on.

And when the blood was sprinkled on ground where nothing could grow, the Children of the Dragon did spring up, the People of the Dragon, armed to dance with death. And he did call them forth from the wasted lands, and they did shake the world with battle.

—from *The Wheel of Time* by Sulamein so Bhagad
Chief Historian at the Court of the Sun, the Fourth Age

The End
of the Fourth Book of
The Wheel of Time

GLOSSARY

A Note on Dates in This Glossary. The Toman Calendar (devised by Toma dur Ahmid) was adopted approximately two centuries after the death of the last male Aes Sedai, recording years After the Breaking of the World (AB). So many records were destroyed in the Trolloc Wars that at their end there was argument about the exact year under the old system. A new calendar, proposed by Tiam of Gazar, celebrated freedom from the Trolloc threat and recorded each year as a Free Year (FY). The Gazaran calendar gained wide acceptance within twenty years after the Wars' end. Artur Hawkwing attempted to establish a new calendar based on the founding of his empire (FF, From the Founding), but only historians now refer to it. After the death and destruction of the War of the Hundred Years, a third calendar was devised by Uren din Jubai Soaring Gull, a scholar of the Sea Folk, and promulgated by the Panarch Farede of Tarabon. The Farede Calendar, dating from the arbitrarily decided end of the War of the Hundred Years and recording years of the New Era (NE), is currently in use.

Accepted, the: Young women in training to be Aes Sedai who have reached a certain level of power and passed certain tests. It normally takes five to ten years to be raised from novice to the Accepted. Accepted are somewhat less confined by rules than novices, and are allowed to choose their own areas of study, within limits. Accepted wear a Great Serpent ring, but only on the third finger of the left hand. When an Accepted is raised Aes Sedai, she chooses her Ajah, gains the right to wear the shawl, and may wear the ring on any finger or not at all if circumstances warrant. *See also* Aes Sedai.

a'dam (AYE-dam): A Seanchan device for controlling a woman who can channel, consisting of a collar and bracelet linked by a leash, all of silvery metal. It has no effect on a woman who cannot channel. *See also* damane; Seanchan; *sul'dam.*

Adelin (AD-ehl-ihn): A woman of the Jindo sept of the Taardad Aiel. A Maiden of the Spear who came to the Stone of Tear.

Aes Sedai (EYEZ seh-DEYE): Wielders of the One Power. Since the Time of Madness, all surviving Aes Sedai are women. Widely distrusted and feared, even hated. Blamed by many for the Breaking of the World, and thought to meddle in the affairs of nations. At the same time, few rulers are without an Aes Sedai advisor, even in lands where such a connection must be kept secret. After some years of channeling the One Power, Aes Sedai take on an ageless quality, so that one old enough to be a grandmother may show no signs of age except perhaps a few gray hairs. *See also* Ajah; Amyrlin Seat; Time of Madness.

Age Lace: Alternative name for the Pattern. *See* Pattern of an Age.

Age of Legends: Age ended by the War of the Shadow and the Breaking of the World. A time when Aes Sedai performed wonders now only dreamed of. *See also* Wheel of Time; Breaking of the World; War of the Shadow.

Aiel (eye-EEL): The people of the Aiel Waste. Fierce and hardy. Veil their faces before they kill, giving rise to the saying "acting like a black-veiled Aiel" to describe someone being violent. Deadly warriors with weapons or with bare hands, they will not touch a sword. Their pipers play them into battle with the music of dances. Aiel call battle "the dance," and "the dance of spears." *See also* Aiel warrior societies; Aiel Waste.

Aiel War, the: (976–78 NE) When King Laman (LAY-mahn) of Cairhien cut down *Avendoraldera,* four clans of the Aiel crossed the Spine of the World. They looted and burned the capital city of Cairhien as well as many other cities and towns, and the conflict extended into Andor and Tear. By the conventional view, the Aiel were finally defeated at the Battle of the Shining Walls, before Tar Valon; in fact, Laman was killed in that battle, and having done what they came for, the Aiel recrossed the Spine. *See also Avendoraldera;* Cairhien.

Aiel warrior societies: Aiel warriors are all members of one of the warrior societies, such as the Stone Dogs *(Shae'en M'taal),* the Red Shields *(Aethan Dor),* the Water Seekers *(Duahde Mahdi'in)* or the Maidens of the Spear *(Far Dareis Mai).* Each has its own customs, and sometimes specific duties. For example, Red Shields act as police. Stone Dogs are often used as rear guards during retreats, while Maidens are often scouts. Aiel clans frequently raid and battle, but members of the same society will not fight each other even if their clans do so. Thus there are always lines of contact between the clans even during open warfare. *See also* Aiel; Aiel Waste; *Far Dareis Mai.*

Aiel Waste: Harsh, rugged and all-but-waterless land east of the Spine of the World. Called the Three-fold Land by the Aiel. Few outsiders enter; the Aiel consider themselves at war with all other peoples and do not welcome strangers. Only peddlers, gleemen, and the Tuatha'an are allowed safe entry, although Aiel avoid all contact with the Tuatha'an, whom they call "the Lost Ones." No maps of the Waste itself are known to exist.

Aile Jafar (EYEL jah-FAHR): A group of Sea Folk islands approximately due west of Tarabon.

Aile Somera (EYEL soh-MEER-ah): A group of Sea Folk islands approximately due west of Toman Head.

Ajah (AH-jah): Societies among the Aes Sedai, seven in number and designated by colors: Blue, Red, White, Green, Brown, Yellow and Gray. All Aes Sedai except the Amyrlin Seat belong to one. Each follows a specific philosophy of the use of the One Power and the purposes of the Aes Sedai. The Red Ajah bends its energies to finding men who can channel, and to gentling them. The Brown forsakes involvement with the mundane world and dedicates itself to seeking knowledge, while the White, largely eschewing both the world and the value of worldly knowledge, devotes itself to questions of philosophy and truth. The Green Ajah (called the Battle Ajah during the Trolloc Wars) holds itself ready for Tarmon Gai'don, the Yellow concentrates on the study of Healing, and Blue sisters involve themselves with causes and justice. The Gray are mediators, seeking harmony and consensus. Rumors of a Black Ajah, dedicated to serving the Dark One, are officially denied.

Alanna Mosvani (ah-LAN-nah mos-VANH-nie): An Aes Sedai of the Green Ajah.

al'Meara, Nynaeve (al-MEER-ah, NIGH-neev): A woman once the

Wisdom of Emond's Field, in the Two Rivers district of Andor (AN-door). Now one of the Accepted.

al'Thor, Rand (al-THOR, RAND): A young man from Emond's Field who is *ta'veren*. Once a shepherd. Now proclaimed as the Dragon Reborn.

al'Thor, Tam (al-THOR, TAM): A farmer and shepherd in the Two Rivers. As a young man, he left to become a soldier, returning with a wife (Kari, now deceased) and a child (Rand).

Alteima (ahl-TEEM-ah): A High Lady of Tear, ambitious and concerned for her husband's health.

al'Vere, Egwene (eh-GWAIN): A young woman from Emond's Field. Now one of the Accepted.

Alviarin (ahl-vee-AH-rihn): An Aes Sedai of the White Ajah.

Amyrlin Seat (AHM-ehr-lin SEAT): (1) Leader of the Aes Sedai. Elected for life by the Hall of the Tower, which consists of three representatives (called Sitters, as in "a Sitter for the Green") from each Ajah. The Amyrlin Seat has, theoretically, supreme authority among the Aes Sedai, and ranks as the equal of a king or queen. A slightly less formal usage is "the Amyrlin." (2) The throne on which the leader of the Aes Sedai sits.

Amys (ah-MEESE): Wise One of Cold Rocks Hold, and a dreamwalker. An Aiel of the Nine Valleys sept of the Taardad Aiel. Wife of Rhuarc, sister-wife to Lian (lee-AHN), who is roofmistress of Cold Rocks Hold, and sister-mother to Aviendha.

angreal **(anh-gree-AHL):** Remnants of the Age of Legends that allow anyone capable of channeling to handle a greater amount of the Power than would be safe or even possible unaided. Some were made for use by women, others by men. Rumors of *angreal* usable by both men and women have never been confirmed. Their making is no longer known. Few remain in existence. *See also* channel; *sa'angreal; ter'angreal.*

Arad Doman (AH-rad do-MAHN): Nation on the Aryth Ocean. Presently wracked by civil war and simultaneously by wars against those who have declared for the Dragon Reborn and against Tarabon. Most Domani merchants are women, and according to the saying, to "let a man trade with a Domani" is to do something extremely foolish. Domani women are famous—or infamous—for their beauty, seductiveness, and scandalous clothes.

Aram (AH-rahm): A handsome young man of the Tuatha'an.

Artur Hawkwing: Legendary king, Artur Paendrag Tanreall (AHR-tuhr PAY-ehn-DRAG tahn-REE-ahl). Ruled FY 943–94. United all lands west of the Spine of the World, as well as some beyond the Aiel Waste. Sent armies across the Aryth Ocean (FY 992), but contact with these was lost at his death, which set off the War of the Hundred Years. His sign was a golden hawk in flight. *See also* War of the Hundred Years.

Atha'an Miere (ah-thah-AHN mee-EHR): *See* Sea Folk.

Avendesora (AH-vehn-deh-SO-rah): In the Old Tongue, "the Tree of Life." Mentioned in many stories and legends, which give various locations.

Avendoraldera (AH-ven-doh-ral-DEH-rah): Tree grown in the city of Cairhien from a sapling of *Avendesora,* a gift from the Aiel in 566 NE, although no record shows any connection between the Aiel and *Avendesora. See also* Aiel War.

Aviendha (ah-vee-EHN-dah): A woman of the Bitter Water sept of the Taardad Aiel.

Aybara, Perrin (ay-BAHR-ah, PEHR-rihn): A young man from Emond's Field, formerly a blacksmith's apprentice. He is *ta'veren. See also ta'veren.*

Ba'alzamon (bah-AHL-zah-mon): In the Trolloc tongue, "Heart of the Dark." Believed by most, erroneously, to be the Trolloc name for the Dark One. *See also* Dark One; Trollocs.

Bain (BAYN): A woman of the Black Rock sept of the Shaarad Aiel. A Maiden of the Spear.

Bair (BAYR): A Wise One of the Haido sept of the Shaarad Aiel. A dreamwalker.

Berelain sur Paendrag (BEH-reh-lain suhr PAY-ehn-DRAG): First of Mayene, Blessed of the Light, Defender of the Waves, High Seat of House Paeron (pay-eh-ROHN). A beautiful and willful young woman, and a skillful ruler. She will have what she wants, whatever it takes, and she always keeps her word. *See* Mayene.

Birgitte (ber-GEET-teh): Hero of legend and story, renowned for her beauty almost as much as for her bravery and skill at archery. Carried a silver bow and silver arrows with which she never missed. One of the heroes called back when the Horn of Valere is sounded. Always linked with the hero-swordsman, Gaidal Cain. *See also* Cain, Gaidal; Horn of Valere.

Blight, the: *See* Great Blight, the.

Borderlands, the: The nations bordering the Great Blight: Saldaea, Arafel, Kandor, and Shienar.

Bornhald, Dain (BOHRN-hahld, DAY-ihn): A Captain of the Children of the Light.

Breaking of the World, the: During the Time of Madness, male Aes Sedai who had gone insane, able to wield the One Power to a degree now unknown, changed the face of the earth. They leveled mountain ranges and raised new mountains, lifted dry land where seas had been and made the ocean cover once dry land. Many parts of the world were completely depopulated, the survivors scattered like dust on the wind. This destruction is remembered in stories, legends, and history as the Breaking of the World. *See also* Time of Madness; Hundred Companions, the.

Byar, Jaret (BY-ahr, JAH-ret): An officer of the Children of the Light.

cadin'sor **(KAH-dihn-sohr):** Garb of Aiel warriors; coat and breeches in browns and grays that fade into rock or shadow, along with soft, laced knee-high boots. In the Old Tongue, "working clothes."

Caemlyn (KAYM-lihn): The capital city of Andor.

Cain, Gaidal (KAIN, GAY-dahl): hero-swordsman of legend and story, always linked to Birgitte and said to be as handsome as she was beautiful. Said to be invincible when his feet were on his native soil. One of the heroes called back when the Horn of Valere is sounded. *See also* Birgitte; Horn of Valere.

Cairhien (KEYE-ree-EHN): Both a nation along the Spine of the World and the capital city of that nation. The city was burned and looted during the Aiel War, as were many other towns and villages. The abandonment of farmland near the Spine of the World after the war made necessary the importation of grain. The assassination of King Galldrian (998NE) resulted in war for succession to the Sun Throne, causing the disruption of grain shipments and famine. The banner of Cairhien is a many-rayed golden sun rising on a field of sky blue.

Callandor (CAH-lahn-DOOR): The Sword That Is Not a Sword, the Sword That Cannot Be Touched. Crystal sword once held in the Stone of Tear. A powerful male *sa'angreal.* Its removal from the chamber called the Heart of the Stone was, along with the fall of the Stone, a major sign of the Dragon's Rebirth and the approach of Tarmon Gai'don. *See also* Dragon Reborn, the; *sa'angreal;* Stone of Tear, the.

Carridin, Jaichim (CAHR-ih-dihn, JAY-kim): An Inquisitor of the Hand of the Light, a high officer of the Children of the Light.

Cauthon, Abell (CAW-thon, AY-bell): A farmer in the Two Rivers. Father of Mat Cauthon. Wife: Natti (NAT-tee). Daughters: Eldrin (EHL-drihn), and Bodewhin (BOHD-wihn), called Bode.

Cauthon, Mat: A young man from Emond's Field in the Two Rivers who is *ta'veren*. Full name: Matrim (MAT-trim) Cauthon.

Chaendaer (CHAY-ehn-DARE): A mountain in the Aiel Waste, above the valley of Rhuidean. *See also:* Aiel Waste, the; Rhuidean.

channel (verb): To control the flow of the One Power. *See also* One Power.

Chiad (CHEE-ahd): A woman of the Stones River sept of the Goshien Aiel, who have blood feud with the Shaarad. A Maiden of the Spear.

Children of the Light: Society of strict ascetic beliefs, owing allegience to no nation and dedicated to the defeat of the Dark One and the destruction of all Darkfriends. Founded during the War of the Hundred Years by Lothair Mantelar (LOH-thayr MAHN-tee-LAHR) to proselytize against an increase in Darkfriends, they evolved during the war into a completely military organization. Extremely rigid in their beliefs, and certain that only they know the truth and the right. Consider Aes Sedai and any who support them to be Darkfriends. Known disparagingly as Whitecloaks. Their sign is a golden sunburst on a field of white. *See also* Questioners.

Chronicles, Keeper of the: Second in authority to the Amyrlin Seat among Aes Sedai, she also acts as secretary to the Amyrlin. Chosen for life by the Hall of the Tower, usually from the same Ajah as the Amyrlin. A slightly less formal usage is "the Keeper." *See also* Amyrlin Seat; Ajah.

Congar, Daise (COHN-gahr, DAYS): A woman of the Two Rivers, now Wisdom of Emond's Field. Husband: Wit.

Couladin (COO-lah-dihn): An ambitious man of the Domai sept of the Shaido Aiel. His warrior society is *Seia Doon,* the Black Eyes.

cuendillar **(CWAIN-deh-yar):** An indestructible substance created during the Age of Legends. Any force used in an attempt to break it is absorbed, making *cuendillar* stronger. Also called heartstone.

damane **(dah-MAH-nee):** In the Old Tongue, literally: "leashed one." Seanchan term for women who can channel and who are, as they see it, properly controlled by use of *a'dam*. All across Seanchan, young women are tested each year until the age when the inborn ability to channel would have manifested itself. Just as with young men found able to channel (who are executed), *damane* are written out of family records and removed from the rolls of citizens, in effect ceasing to exist as people. Women who can channel but who have not yet been made *damane* are called *marath'damane*, literally, "those who must be leashed." *See also a'dam;* Seanchan; *sul'dam.*

Damodred, Lord Galadedrid (DAHM-oh-drehd, gah-LAHD-eh-drihd): Half-brother to Elayne and Gawyn, sharing the same father, Taringail (TAH-rihn-gail) Damodred. His sign is a winged silver sword, point down.

Darkfriends: Those who follow the Dark One and believe they will gain great power and rewards, and even immortality, when he is freed from his prison.

Dark One: Most common name, used in every land, for Shai'tan (SHAY-ih-TAN). The source of evil, antithesis of the Creator. Imprisoned by the Creator in Shayol Ghul at the moment of Creation. An attempt to free him brought about the War of the Shadow, the tainting of *saidin,* the Breaking of the World, and the end of the Age of Legends.

Dark One, naming the: Saying the true name of the Dark One (Shai'tan) draws his attention, inevitably bringing ill fortune at best, disaster at worst. For that reason, many euphemisms are used, among them the Dark One, Father of Lies, Sightblinder, Lord of the Grave, Shepherd of the Night, Heartsbane, Soulsbane, Heartfang, Old Grim, Grassburner, and Leafblighter. Darkfriends call him the Great Lord of the Dark. Someone who seems to be inviting ill fortune is often said to be "naming the Dark One."

Daughter-Heir: Title of the heir to the throne of Andor. The eldest daughter of the Queen succeeds her mother on the throne. Without a surviving daughter, the throne goes to the nearest female blood relation of the Queen.

Daughter of the Night: *See* Lanfear.

din Jubai Wild Winds, Coine (dihn joo-BUY: coh-EEN): A woman of the Atha'an Miere, the Sea Folk. Sailmistress of the raker *Wavedancer.* Sister of Jorin.

din Jubai White Wing, Jorin (joh-RIHN): A woman of the Atha'an Miere, the Sea Folk. Windfinder of the raker *Wavedancer.* Sister of Coine.

Domon, Bayle (DOH-mon, BAIL): Sea-captain born in Illian, once a captive of the Seanchan, now a successful smuggler into and between war-torn Tarabon and Arad Doman. A sometime collector of antiquities, and a man who pays his debts.

Dragon, false: Name given to various men who have claimed to be the

Dragon Reborn. Some began wars that involved many nations. Over the centuries most were men unable to channel, but a few could do so. All, however, either disappeared or were captured or killed without fulfilling any of the Prophecies of the Dragon. Among those who could channel, the most powerful were Raolin Darksbane (335–36 AB), Yurian Stonebow (circa 1300–1308 AB), Davian (FY 351), Guaire Amalasan (FY 939–43), and Logain (997 NE). *See also* Dragon Reborn; War of the Second Dragon.

Dragon, Prophecies of the: Generally little known and seldom spoken of, the Prophecies, given in *The Karaethon Cycle* (ka-REE-ah-thon), foretell that the Dark One will be freed again to touch the world, and that Lews Therin Telamon, the Dragon, Breaker of the World, will be reborn to fight Tarmon Gai'don, the Last Battle against the Shadow. He will, say the Prophecies, save the world—and Break it again. *See also* Dragon, the.

Dragon, the: Name by which Lews Therin Telamon was known during the War of the Shadow, some three thousand or more years ago. In the madness that overtook all male Aes Sedai, Lews Therin killed everyone who carried any of his blood, as well as everyone he loved, thus earning the name Kinslayer. *See also* Hundred Companions, the: Dragon Reborn; Dragon, Prophecies of the.

Dragon Reborn: According to the Prophecies of the Dragon, the man who is the Rebirth of Lews Therin Kinslayer. *See also* Dragon, the; Dragon, false; Dragon, Prophecies of the.

Dreadlords: Men and women able to channel, who went over to the Shadow during the Trolloc Wars, acting as generals over armies of Trollocs and Darkfriends. Occasionally confused with the Forsaken by the less well educated.

Dreamer: *See* Talents.

dreamwalker: Aiel name for a woman able to enter *Tel'aran'rhiod*.

Egeanin (egg-ee-AHN-ihn): A Seanchan ship's captain on detached duty.

Elaida (eh-LY-da): An Aes Sedai of the Red Ajah. Formerly advisor to Queen Morgase of Andor. She sometimes has the Foretelling.

Elayne (ee-LAIN) of House Trakand (trah-KAND): Queen Morgase's daughter, the Daughter-Heir to the Throne of Andor. Now one of the Accepted. Her sign is a golden lily.

Estanda (eh-STAHN-dah): A High Lady of Tear who believes in extracting what is owed slowly but in full.

Faile (fah-EEL): In the Old Tongue, means "falcon." Name assumed by Zarine Bashere (zah-REEN bah-SHEER), a young woman from Saldaea.

***Far Dareis Mai* (FAHR DAH-rize MY):** Literally "Maidens of the Spear." An Aiel warrior society which, unlike any other, admits women and only women. A Maiden may not marry and remain in the society, nor may she fight while carrying a child. Any child born to a Maiden is given to another woman to raise, in such a way that no one knows the child's mother. ("You may belong to no man, nor may any man belong to you, nor any child. The spear is your lover, your child, and your life.") *See also* Aiel; Aiel warrior societies.

Five Powers, the: There are threads to the One Power, named according to the sorts of things that can be done using them—Earth, Air (sometimes called Wind), Fire, Water, and Spirit, which are called the Five Powers. A wielder of the Power will have a greater strength with one, or possibly two, of these, and lesser with the others. In the Age of Legends, Spirit was found equally in men and in women, but great ability with Earth and/or Fire occurred much more often among men, with Water and/or Air among women. Despite exceptions, it was so often so that Earth and Fire came to be regarded as male Powers, Air and Water as female.

Flame of Tar Valon: Symbol of Tar Valon, the Amyrlin Seat, and the Aes Sedai. A stylized representation of a flame; a white teardrop, point upwards.

Forsaken, the: Name given to thirteen of the most powerful Aes Sedai of the Age of Legends, thus among the most powerful ever known, who went over to the Dark One during the War of the Shadow in return for the promise of immortality. According to both legend and fragmentary records, they were imprisoned along with the Dark One when his prison was resealed. The names given to them are still used to frighten children. They were: Aginor (AGH-ih-nohr), Asmodean (ahs-MOH-dee-an), Balthamel (BAAL-thah-mell), Be'lal (BEH-lahl), Demandred (DEE-man-drehd), Graendal (GREHN-dahl), Ishamael (ih-SHAH-may-EHL), Lanfear (LAN-feer), Mesaana (meh-SAH-nah), Moghedien (moh-GHEH-dee-ehn), Rahvin (RAAV-ihn), Sammael (SAHM-may-EHL), and Semirhage (SEH-mih-RHAHG).

Gaidin (GYE-deen): Literally, "Brother to Battles." A title used by Aes Sedai for the Warders. *See also* Warder.

Galad (gah-LAHD): *See* Damodred; Lord Galadedrid.

Game of Houses, the: Name given the scheming, plots, and manipulations for advantage by noble Houses. Great value is given to subtlety, to aiming at one thing while seeming to aim at another, and to achieving ends with the least visible effort. Also known as the Great Game, and sometimes by its name in the Old Tongue: *Daes Dae'mar* (DAH-ess day-MAR).

Gaul (GAHWL): A man of the Imran sept of the Shaarad Aiel, who have blood feud with the Goshien. A Stone Dog.

Gawyn (GAH-wihn) of House Trakand (trah-KAND): Queen Morgase's son, and Elayne's brother, who will be First Prince of the Sword when Elayne ascends to the throne. His sign is a white boar.

Gelb, Floran (GEHLB, FLOHR-an): A former sailor with reasons to avoid Bayle Domon.

gentling: The act, performed by Aes Sedai, of shutting off a male who can channel from the One Power. Necessary because any man who channels will go insane from the taint on *saidin* and almost certainly do horrible things with the Power in his madness. One who has been gentled can still sense the True Source, but cannot touch it. Whatever madness has come before gentling is arrested but not cured, and if it is done soon enough death can be averted. *See also* One Power, the; stilling.

gleeman: A traveling storyteller, musician, juggler, tumbler, and all-around entertainer. Known by trademark cloaks of many-colored patches, gleemen perform mainly in the villages and smaller towns.

Gray Man: One who has voluntarily surrendered his or her soul in order to become an assassin serving the Shadow. Gray Men are so ordinary in appearance that the eye can slide right past without noticing them. The vast majority of Gray Men are indeed men, but a small number are women. Also called the Soulless.

Great Blight, the: A region in the far north, entirely corrupted by the Dark One. A haunt of Trollocs, Myrddraal, and other creatures of the Shadow.

Great Hunt of the Horn, The: A cycle of stories concerning the legendary search for the Horn of Valere, in the years between the end of the Trolloc Wars and the beginning of the War of the Hundred Years. If told in its entirety, the cycle would take many days. *See also* Horn of Valere.

Great Lord of the Dark: The name by which Darkfriends refer to the Dark One, claiming that to speak his true name would be blasphemous.

Great Serpent: A symbol for time and eternity, ancient before the Age of Legends began, consisting of a serpent eating its own tail. A ring in the shape of the Great Serpent is awarded to women who have been raised to the Accepted among the Aes Sedai.

hide: A unit of area for measuring land, equal to 100 paces by 100 paces.

High Lords of Tear: Acting as a council, the High Lords are historically the rulers of the nation of Tear, which has neither king nor queen. Their numbers are not fixed, and have varied from as many as twenty to as few as six. Not to be confused with the Lords of the Land, who are lesser Tairen lords.

Horn of Valere (vah-LEER): Legendary object of the Great Hunt of the Horn. Supposedly can call back dead heroes from the grave to fight against the Shadow. A new Hunt of the Horn has been called, and oaths have been administered to the Hunters in Illian.

Hundred Companions, the: One hundred male Aes Sedai, among the most powerful of the Age of Legends, who, led by Lews Therin Telamon, launched the final stroke that ended the War of the Shadow by sealing the Dark One back into his prison. The Dark One's counterstroke tainted *saidin;* the Hundred Companions went mad and began the Breaking of the World. *See also* Time of Madness; Breaking of the World; True Source; One Power.

Illian (IHL-lee-an): A great port on the Sea of Storms, capital city of the nation of the same name.

Isendre (ih-SEHN-dreh): A beautiful and mysterious woman traveling in the Aiel Waste.

Kadere, Hadnan (kah-DEER, HAHD-nahn): A peddler traveling the Aiel Waste. A man with knowledge to sell, if he can find the right price.

kaf (KAAF): A Seanchan drink, brewed black and drunk steaming hot, sometimes sweetened but often not. A stimulating beverage.

Keille Shaogi: *See* Shaogi, Keille.

Lan (LAN); al'Lan Mandragoran (AHL-LAN man-DRAG-or-an): A Warder, bonded to Moiraine. Uncrowned King of Malkier, Dai Shan (Battle Lord), and the last surviving Malkieri lord. *See also* Warder; Moiraine; Malkier.

Lanfear (LAN-fear): In the Old Tongue: "Daughter of the Night." One of the Forsaken, perhaps the most powerful next to Ishamael. Unlike the others, she chose this name herself. Said to have loved Lews Therin Telamon, and to have hated his wife, Ilyena. *See also* Forsaken; Dragon, the.

Laras (LAH-rahs): Mistress of the Kitchens in the White Tower, the center of Aes Sedai power, in Tar Valon. A woman of surprising knowledge and shocking past.

league: *See* Length, units of.

Leane (lee-AHN-eh): An Aes Sedai of the Blue Ajah. Keeper of the Chronicles. *See also* Ajah; Chronicles, Keeper of the.

Length, units of: 10 inches = 1 foot; 3 feet = 1 pace; 2 paces = 1 span; 1000 spans = 1 mile; 4 miles = 1 league.

Lews Therin Telamon; Lews Therin Kinslayer: *See* Dragon, the.

Liandrin (lee-AHN-drihn): An Aes Sedai formerly of the Red Ajah, from Tarabon. Now known to be of the Black Ajah.

Lini (LIHN-nee): Childhood nurse to the Lady Elayne, and before her to Elayne's mother, Morgase.

Logain (loh-GAIN): A man who once claimed to be the Dragon Reborn, now gentled and imprisoned in the White Tower in Tar Valon.

Loial (LOY-ahl) son of Arent (AH-rehnt) son of Halan (HAY-lahn): An Ogier from Stedding Shangtai. Would-be author of a book about the Dragon Reborn.

Luhhan, Haral (LOOH-hahn, HAH-rahl): Blacksmith of the Two Rivers, and member of the Village Council of Emond's Field. His wife Alsbet (AHLS-beht) is a member of the Women's Circle.

Malkier (mahl-KEER): A nation, once one of the Borderlands, now consumed by the Blight. The sign of Malkier was a golden crane in flight.

Manetheren (mahn-EHTH-ehr-ehn): One of the Ten Nations that made the Second Covenant. Also the capital city of that nation. Both city and nation were utterly destroyed in the Trolloc Wars. *See also* Trolloc Wars.

Mayene (may-EHN): City-state on the Sea of Storms, hemmed in and historically oppressed by Tear. Derives its wealth and its independence from knowledge of where to find the oilfish shoals, which rival in economic importance the olive groves of Tear, Illian, and Tarabon. Oilfish and olives provide nearly all lamp oil. The ruler of Mayene is styled "the First"; Firsts claim to be descendants of Artur Hawkwing. The banner of Mayene is a golden hawk in flight on a field of blue.

Melaine (meh-LAYN): A Wise One of the Jhirad sept of Goshien Aiel. A dreamwalker.

Merrilin, Thom (MER-rih-lihn, TOM): A not-so-simple gleeman.

mile: *See* Length, units of.

Min (MIN): A young woman with the ability to read things about people in the auras and images she sometimes sees surrounding them.

Moiraine (mwah-RAIN): An Aes Sedai of the Blue Ajah. Born in House Damodred, though not in line of succession to the throne, and raised in the Royal Palace in Cairhien.

Morgase (moor-GAYZ): By the Grace of the Light, Queen of Andor, Defender of the Realm, Protector of the People, High Seat of House Trakand. Her sign is three golden keys. The sign of House Trakand is a silver keystone.

Myrddraal (MUHRD-draal): Creatures of the Dark One, commanders of the Trollocs. Twisted offspring of Trollocs in which the human stock used to create the Trollocs has resurfaced, but tainted by the evil that made the Trollocs. They have no eyes, but can see like eagles in light or dark. They have certain powers stemming from the Dark One, including the ability to cause paralyzing fear with a look, and to vanish wherever there are shadows. Among known weaknesses is that they are reluctant to cross running water. In different lands they are known by many names, among them Halfman, the Eyeless, Shadowman, Lurk, Fetch, and Fade.

Natael, Jasin (nah-TAYL, JAY-sihn): A gleeman traveling the Aiel Waste.

Niall, Pedron (NEYE-awl, PAY-drohn): Lord Captain Commander of the Children of the Light. *See also* Children of the Light.

Oaths, Three: The oaths taken by an Accepted on being raised to Aes Sedai. Spoken while holding the Oath Rod, a *ter'angreal* that makes oaths binding. They are: (1) To speak no word that is not true. (2) To make no weapon with which one man may kill another. (3) Never to use the One Power as a weapon except against Shadowspawn, or in the last extreme of defense of her own life, or that of her Warder or another Aes Sedai. The second oath was the first adopted, in reaction to the War of the Shadow. The first oath, while held to the letter, is often circumvented by careful speaking. It is believed that the last two are inviolable.

Ogier (OH-gehr): (1) A non-human race, characterized by great height (ten feet is average for adult males), broad, almost snout-like noses, and long, tufted ears. They live in areas called *stedding*. Their separation from these *stedding* after the Breaking of the World (a time called the Exile by Ogier) resulted in what is called the Longing; an Ogier who is too long out of the *stedding* sickens and dies. They rarely leave their *stedding* and typically have little contact with humankind. Knowledge of them among humans is sparse, and many believe Ogier to be only legends. Although thought to be a pacific people and extremely slow to anger, some old stories say they fought alongside humans in the Trolloc Wars, and call them implacable enemies. By and large, they are extremely fond of knowledge, and their books and stories often contain information lost to humans. A typical Ogier life-span is at least three to four times that of a human. (2) Any individual of that non-human race. *See also* Breaking of the World; *stedding;* Treesinger.

Old Tongue: The language spoken during the Age of Legends. It is generally expected that nobles and the educated will have learned to speak it, but most know only a few words. Translation is often difficult, as it is a language capable of many subtly different meanings.

One Power, the: The power drawn from the True Source. The vast majority of people are completely unable to learn to channel the One Power. A very small number can be taught to channel, and an even tinier number have the ability inborn. These few have no need to be taught; they will channel whether they want to or not, often without even realizing what they are doing. This inborn ability usually manifests itself in late adolescence or early adulthood. If control is not taught, or self-learned (extremely difficult, with a success rate of only one in four), death is certain. Since the Time of Madness, no man has been able to channel the Power without eventually going completely, horribly mad, and then, even if he has learned some control, dying from a wasting sickness that causes the sufferer to rot alive, a sickness caused, as is the madness, by the Dark One's taint on *saidin. See also* Aes Sedai; channel; Five Powers; Time of Madness; True Source.

Ordeith (OHR-deeth): In the Old Tongue, "Wormwood." Name taken by a man who advises Pedron Niall.

Pattern of an Age: The Wheel of Time weaves the threads of human lives into the Pattern of an Age, often called simply the Pattern, which forms the substance of reality for that Age. *See also* ta'veren.

Questioners, the: An order within the Children of the Light. Avowed purposes are to discover the truth in disputations and uncover Darkfriends. In the search for truth and the Light, their normal method of inquiry is torture; their normal manner that they know the truth already and must only make their victim confess to it. Refer to themselves as the Hand of the Light, the Hand that digs out truth, and at times act as if they were entirely separate from the Children and the Council of the Anointed, which commands the Children. The head of the Questioners is the High Inquisitor, who sits on the Council of the Anointed. Their sign is a blood-red shepherd's crook.

Rendra (REHN-drah): A woman of Tarabon. Innkeeper of the Three Plums Court, in Tanchico.

Rhuarc (RHOURK): An Aiel, clan chief of the Taardad Aiel.

Rhuidean (RHUY-dee-ahn): A place in the Aiel Waste to which must go any man wanting to be a clan chief and any woman wanting to be a Wise One. Men may enter only once, women twice. Only one man in three survives his journey to Rhuidean. The survival rate for women is considerably higher for both visits. Its location is a secret closely guarded by the Aiel. The prescribed penalty for a non-Aiel entering the valley of Rhuidean is death, though some who are favored (such as peddlers or gleemen) might simply be stripped naked, given waterskins, and allowed to attempt to walk out of the Waste.

sa'angreal **(SAH-ahn-GREE-ahl):** Remnants of the Age of Legends that allow channeling much more of the One Power than would otherwise be possible or safe. A *sa'angreal* is similar to, but more powerful than, an *angreal.* The amount of the Power that can be wielded with a *sa'angreal* compares to the amount that can be handled with an *angreal* as the Power wielded with the aid of an *angreal* does to the amount that can be handled unaided. The making of them is no longer known. As with *angreal,* there are male and female *sa'angreal.* Only a handful remain, far fewer even than *angreal.*

sa'sara (sah-SAHR-rah): An indecent Saldaean dance, outlawed by a number of Saldaean queens, but to no avail. Saldaean history records three wars, two rebellions, and countless unions and/or feuds between noble houses, as well as innumerable duels, sparked by women dancing the sa'sara. One rebellion was supposedly quelled when a defeated queen danced it for the victorious general; he married her and restored her throne. This tale is not found in any official history and has been denied by every queen of Saldaea.

saidar **(sah-ih-DAHR);** *saidin* **(sah-ih-DEEN):** *See* True Source.

Sandar, Juilin (sahn-DAHR, JUY-lihn): A thief-catcher from Tear.

Sea Folk: More properly, the Atha'an Miere, the People of the Sea. A secretive people. Inhabitants of islands in the Aryth (AH-rihth) Ocean and the Sea of Storms, they spend little time ashore, living most of their lives on their ships. Most seaborne trade is carried by Sea Folk ships.

Seana (see-AHN-ah): A Wise One of the Black Cliffs sept of the Nakai Aiel. A dreamwalker.

Seanchan (SHAWN-CHAN): (1) Descendants of the armies Artur Hawkwing sent across the Aryth Ocean, who conquered the lands there. They believe that any woman who can channel must be controlled for the safety of everyone else, and any man who can channel must be killed for the same reason. (2) The land from which the Seanchan come.

Seekers for Truth: A police/spy organization of the Seanchan Imperial Throne. Although most are property of the Imperial family, they have wide powers. Even one of the Blood (a Seanchan noble) can be arrested for failure to answer any question put by a Seeker, or for failure to cooperate fully with a Seeker, this last defined by the Seekers themselves, subject only to review by the Empress.

Servants, Hall of the: In the Age of Legends, the great meeting hall of the Aes Sedai.

Sevanna (seh-VAHN-nah): A woman of the Domai sept of the Shaido Aiel. Widow of Suladric (soo-LAH-dric), who was clan chief of the Shaido, and thus roofmistress of Comarda Hold until a new clan chief is chosen.

Shaogi, Keille (shah-OH-ghe, KEYEL-lee): A peddler traveling the Aiel Waste. A woman with plans even larger than she is.

Shayol Ghul (SHAY-ol GHOOL): A mountain in the Blasted Lands, the site of the Dark One's prison.

Siuan Sanche (SWAHN SAHN-chay): Daughter of a Tairen fisherman, she was, according to Tairen law, put on a ship to Tar Valon before the second sunset after discovery that she had the potential to channel. Formerly of the Blue Ajah.

Soulless: *See* Gray Man.

span: *See* Length, units of.

Spine of the World, the: A towering mountain range, with few passes, which separates the Aiel Waste from the lands to the west.

stedding **(STEHD-ding):** An Ogier (OH-geer) homeland. Many *stedding* have been abandoned since the Breaking of the World. They are shielded in some way, no longer understood, so that within them no Aes Sedai can channel the One Power, nor even sense the True

Source. Attempts to wield the One Power from outside a *stedding* have no effect inside the *stedding* boundary. No Trolloc will enter a *stedding* unless driven, and even Myrddraal will do so only at the greatest need and with the greatest reluctance. Even Darkfriends, if truly dedicated, feel uncomfortable within a *stedding*.

stilling: The act, performed by Aes Sedai, of shutting off a woman who can channel from the One Power. A woman who has been stilled can sense the True Source, but cannot touch it. So seldom has it been done that novices are required to learn the names and crimes of all women who have suffered it. Officially, stilling is the result of trial and sentence for a crime. When it happens accidentally, it is called being burned out. In practice, the term stilling is often used for both.

Stone of Tear: A great fortress in the city of Tear, said to have been made by use of the One Power soon after the Breaking of the World. Attacked and besieged unsuccessfully countless times, it fell in a single night to the Dragon Reborn and a few hundred Aiel, thus fulfilling two parts of the Prophecies of the Dragon. The Stone contains a collection of *an'greal* and *ter'angreal* rivaling that of the White Tower, a collection gathered, some say, in an attempt to diminish the glare of possessing *Callandor*.

sul'dam **(SOOL-dam):** Literally, "leash holder." Seanchan term for a woman with the ability to control, by means of an *a'dam,* a woman who can channel. Young women in Seanchan are tested for this ability at the same time as the testing for *damane* and to the same age. A fairly honored position among the Seanchan. Many more *sul'dam* are found than *damane. See also a'dam; damane;* Seanchan.

sursa **(SUHR-sah):** Thin, paired sticks used as eating implements in Arad Doman in place of forks. Some say the difficulty of eating with *sursa* is the source of Domani merchants' fabled perseverance; others claim it is the source of the equally fabled Domani temper.

Talents: Abilities in the use of the One Power in specific areas. The best known of these is Healing. Some, such as Traveling, the ability to shift from one place to another without crossing the intervening space, have been lost. Others, such as Foretelling (the ability to foretell future events, but in a general way), are now found rarely. Another Talent long thought lost is Dreaming, which involves, among other things, interpreting the Dreamer's dreams to foretell future events in more specific fashion than Foretelling does. Some Dreamers had the ability to enter *Tel'aran'rhiod,* the World of Dreams, and (it is said) even other people's dreams. The last known Dreamer was

Corianin Nedeal (coh-ree-AHN-ihn neh-dee-AHL), who died in 526 NE, but there is now another, known to but a few.

ta'maral'ailen (tah-MAHR-ahl-EYE-lehn): In the Old Tongue, "Web of Destiny." A great change in the Pattern of an Age, centered around one or more people who are *ta'veren*. *See also* Pattern of an Age; *ta'veren*.

Tarabon (TAH-rah-BON): Nation on the Aryth Ocean. Capital city: Tanchico (tan-CHEE-coh). Once a great trading nation, a source of rugs, dyes and fireworks produced by the Guild of Illuminators, among other things. Now wracked by civil war, as well as by simultaneous wars against Arad Doman and people sworn to the Dragon Reborn.

Tarmon Gai'don (TAHR-mohn GAY-dohn): The Last Battle. *See also* Dragon, Prophecies of the; Horn of Valere.

ta'veren (tah-VEER-ehn): A person around whom the Wheel of Time weaves all surrounding life-threads, perhaps ALL life-threads, to form a Web of Destiny. *See also* Pattern of an Age.

Tear (TEER): A nation on the Sea of Storms. Also the capital city of that nation, a great seaport. The banner of Tear is three white crescent moons slanting across a field half red, half gold. *See also* Stone of Tear.

Telamon, Lews Therin (TEHL-ah-mon, LOOZ THEH-rihn): *See* Dragon, the.

Tel'aran'rhiod (tel-AYE-rahn-rhee-ODD): In the Old Tongue, "the Unseen World," or "the World of Dreams." A world glimpsed in dreams which was believed by the ancients to permeate and surround all other possible worlds. Unlike other dreams, what happens to living things in the World of Dreams is real; a wound taken there will still be there on awakening, and one who dies there does not wake at all.

ter'angreal (TEER-ahn-GREE-ahl): Remnants of the Age of Legends that use the One Power. Unlike *angreal* and *sa'angreal*, each *ter'angreal* was made to do a particular thing. Some *ter'angreal* are used by Aes Sedai, but the original purposes of many are unknown. Some require channeling, while others may be used by anyone. Some will kill or destroy the ability to channel of any woman who uses them. *See also* angreal; sa'angreal.

Time of Madness: The years after the Dark One's counterstroke tainted the male half of the True Source, when male Aes Sedai went mad and Broke the World. The exact duration of this period is unknown, but it is believed to have lasted nearly one hundred years. It ended completely only with the death of the last male Aes Sedai. *See also* Hundred Companions; True Source; One Power.

Torean (toh-ree-AHN): A High Lord of Tear. A man who desires what neither his vast fortune nor his face will gain him.

Traveling People: *See* Tuatha'an.

Trollocs (TRAHL-lohks): Creatures of the Dark One, created during the War of the Shadow. Huge of stature, they are a twisted blend of animal and human stock. Divided into tribe-like bands, among them the Dha'vol, the Ko'bal, and the Dhai'mon. Vicious by nature, they kill for the pure pleasure of killing. Deceitful in the extreme, they cannot be trusted unless coerced by fear.

Trolloc Wars: A series of wars, beginning about 1000 AB and lasting more than three hundred years, during which Trolloc armies ravaged the world. Eventually the Trollocs were driven back into the Great Blight, but some nations ceased to exist, and others that survived were almost depopulated. All records of the time are fragmentary.

True Source: The driving force of the universe, which turns the Wheel of Time. Divided into a male half (*saidin*) and a female half (*saidar*), which work at the same time with and against each other. Only a man can draw on *saidin*, only a woman on *saidar*. Since the beginning of the Time of Madness, *saidin* has been tainted by the Dark One's touch. *See also* One Power.

Tuatha'an (too-AH-thah-AHN): A wandering folk, also known as the Tinkers and as the Traveling People, who live in brightly painted wagons and follow a totally pacifist philosophy called the Way of the Leaf. They are among the few who can cross the Aiel Waste unmolested, for the Aiel strictly avoid all contact with them.

Verin Mathwin (VEHR-ihn MAH-thwihn): An Aes Sedai of the Brown Ajah.

Warder: A warrior bonded to an Aes Sedai. The bonding is a thing of the One Power: by it he gains such gifts as quick healing, the ability to go long periods without food, water, or rest, and the ability to sense the taint of the Dark One at a distance. So long as a Warder lives, the Aes Sedai to whom he is bonded knows he is alive however far away he is, and when he dies she will know the moment and manner of his death. The bonding does not tell her how far he is, though, nor in what direction. While most Ajahs believe an Aes Sedai may have one Warder bonded to her at a time, the Red Ajah refuses to bond any Warders at all, while the Green Ajah believe an

Aes Sedai may bond as many as she wishes. Ethically the Warder must accede to the bonding voluntarily, but it has been known to be done against the Warder's will. What the Aes Sedai gain from the bonding is a closely held secret. *See also* Aes Sedai.

War of Power: *See* War of the Shadow.

War of the Hundred Years (FY 994–FY 1117): A series of overlapping wars among constantly shifting alliances, precipitated by the death of Artur Hawkwing and the resulting struggle for his empire. The War of the Hundred Years depopulated large parts of the lands between the Aryth Ocean and the Aiel Waste, from the Sea of Storms to the Great Blight. So great was the destruction that only fragmentary records of the time remain. The empire of Artur Hawkwing was pulled apart, and the nations of the present day were formed. *See also* Hawkwing, Artur.

War of the Second Dragon (FY 939–43): War fought against the false Dragon Guaire Amalasan. During this war a young king named Artur Tanreall Paendrag, later known as Artur Hawkwing, rose to overwhelming prominence.

War of the Shadow: Also known as the War of Power. Began shortly after the attempt to free the Dark One, and soon involved the whole world. In a world where even the memory of war had been forgotten, every facet of war was rediscovered, often twisted by the Dark One's touch on the world, and the One Power was used as a weapon. The war was ended by the resealing of the Dark One into his prison. *See also* Hundred Companions, the; Dragon, the.

Weight, units of: 10 ounces = 1 pound; 10 pounds = 1 stone; 10 stone = 1 hundredweight; 10 hundredweight = 1 ton.

Wheel of Time, the: Time is a wheel with seven spokes, each spoke an Age. As the Wheel turns, Ages come and go, each leaving memories that fade to legend, then to myth, and are forgotten by the time that Age comes again. The Pattern of an Age is slightly different each time an Age comes, and each time it is subject to greater change.

Whitecloaks: *See* Children of the Light.

wilder: A woman who has learned to channel the One Power on her own, surviving the crisis as only one in four does. Such women usually build barriers against knowing what it is they are doing, but if these can be broken down, wilders are among the most powerful of channelers. The term is often used in derogatory fashion.

Wisdom: In villages, a woman chosen by the Women's Circle for her knowledge of such things as healing and foretelling the weather, as well as common good sense. Generally considered the equal of the

Mayor, and in some villages his superior. She is chosen for life, and it is very rare for a Wisdom to be removed from office before her death. Depending on the land, she may instead have another title, such as Guide, Healer, Wise Woman, or Seeker.

Wise One: Among the Aiel, Wise Ones are women chosen by other Wise Ones and trained in healing, herbs and other things, much like Wisdoms. Usually there is a single Wise One to each clan or sept hold. Some Wise Ones are said to have wondrous healing abilities, and to do things that seem miraculous. They have great authority and responsibility, as well as great influence with sept and clan chiefs, though these men often accuse them of meddling.

About the Author

Robert Jordan was born in 1948 in Charleston, South Carolina, where he now lives with his wife, Harriet, in a house built in 1797. He taught himself to read when he was four with the incidental aid of a twelve-year-older brother, and was tackling Mark Twain and Jules Verne by five. He is a graduate of The Citadel, the Military College of South Carolina, with a degree in physics. He served two tours in Vietnam with the U.S. army; among his decorations are the Distinguished Flying Cross, the Bronze Star with "V," and two Vietnamese Crosses of Gallantry. A history buff, he has also written dance and theater criticism. He enjoys the outdoor sports of hunting, fishing, and sailing, and the indoor sports of poker, chess, pool, and pipe collecting. He has been writing since 1977 and intends to continue until they nail shut his coffin.